P9-CJM-653

W. E. B. GRIFFIN

THREE COMPLETE NOVELS

ALSO BY W. E. B. GRIFFIN

HONOR BOUND

HONOR BOUND

BLOOD AND HONOR

SECRET HONOR

BROTHERHOOD OF WAR

BOOK I. THE LIEUTENANTS

BOOK II. THE CAPTAINS

BOOK III. THE MAJORS

BOOK IV. THE COLONELS

BOOK V. THE BERETS

BOOK VI. THE GENERALS

BOOK VII. THE NEW BREED

BOOK VIII. THE AVIATORS

BOOK IX. SPECIAL OPS

THE CORPS

BOOK I. SEMPER FI

BOOK II. CALL TO ARMS

BOOK III. COUNTERATTACK

BOOK IV. BATTLEGROUND

BOOK V. LINE OF FIRE

BOOK VI. CLOSE COMBAT

BOOK VII. BEHIND THE LINES

BOOK VIII. IN DANGER'S PATH

BADGE OF HONOR

BOOK I. MEN IN BLUE

BOOK II. SPECIAL OPERATIONS

BOOK III. THE VICTIM

BOOK IV. THE WITNESS

BOOK V. THE ASSASSIN

BOOK VI. THE MURDERERS

BOOK VII. THE INVESTIGATORS

MEN AT WAR

BOOK I. THE LAST HEROES

BOOK II. THE SECRET WARRIORS

BOOK III. THE SOLDIER SPIES

BOOK IV. THE FIGHTING AGENTS

W. E. B. GRIFFIN

THREE COMPLETE NOVELS

Brotherhood of War

The Lieutenants

The Captains

The Majors

G. P. PUTNAM'S SONS
NEW YORK

This is a work of fiction. Names, characters, places, and incidents either are the product of the author's imagination or are used fictitiously, and any resemblance to actual persons, living or dead, business establishments, events, or locales is entirely coincidental.

G. P. Putnam's Sons
Publishers Since 1838
a member of
Penguin Putnam Inc.
375 Hudson Street
New York, NY 10014

Library of Congress Cataloging-in-Publication Data
Griffin, W.E.B.
[Selections. 2001]
Three complete novels : brotherhood of war / W.E.B. Griffin.
p. cm.
Contents: The lieutenants—The captains—The majors.
ISBN 0-399-14730-6
1. World War, 1939–1945—Fiction. 2. War stories, American. I. Title.
PS3557.R489137 A6 2001 00-053328
813'.54—dc21

Printed in the United States of America

3 5 7 9 10 8 6 4 2

Book design by Jennifer Ann Daddio

For Uncle Charley and The Bull.
RIP October 1979.

And for Donn.
Who would have ever believed four *stars?*

CONTENTS

The Lieutenants

I

On 14 February 1943, strong German armored units sallied forth from passes in south-central Tunisia on the front of the II U.S. Corps, commanded by Major General Lloyd R. Fredendall, in an attempt to turn the flank of the British First Army (Lt. Gen. Kenneth A. N. Anderson) and capture the base of operations that the Allies had set up around Tebessa. In a series of sharp armored actions, the Germans defeated the Allies and forced a withdrawal by American troops all the way back through Kasserine Pass and the valley beyond.

AMERICAN MILITARY HISTORY *1607–1953*
DEPARTMENT OF THE ARMY, JULY 1956

[ONE]
Near Sidi-Bou-Zid, Tunisia
17 February 1943

Two tanks, American, which showed signs of hard use, moved slowly down a path. The terrain was undulating desert. Not sand dunes, but arid, gritty soil, with crumbling, fist-sized rocks and sparse vegetation. The dips in the land were just deep enough to conceal a tank. The high spots did not provide for much visibility. You could see for a mile, perhaps more, but a tank could be concealed in a dip a hundred yards away.

Major Robert Bellmon, riding in the open turret of the lead M4A2 "Sherman" tank, his tanned body outside the hatch, was a tall and rangy young man who had graduated from the United States Military Academy at West Point in 1939. He wore the Academy ring, a simple gold wedding band, and an issue Hamilton watch. The issue band had rotted, and had been replaced by a band stitched from the tail of a khaki shirt by the battalion tailor.

Bellmon wore a khaki shirt, a cotton tanker's jacket with a zipper front and knit cuffs and collar, wool olive-drab trousers, and a pair of nonregulation tanker's boots, which looked like a combination of dress low quarters, field shoes, and combat boots; their uppers reached ten inches up his calves. He also wore an old style tanker's helmet, which was like a football helmet to which earphones had been riveted. A Colt Model 1911A1 pistol was suspended half under his arm in a shoulder holster, and a pair of Zeiss binoculars, inherited from his father, hung around his neck.

Although he had stopped the tank and carefully searched the desert three minutes before, and only thirty seconds before had ordered Sergeant Pete Fortin, the driver, to get moving, he did not see the Afrika Korps Panzerkampfwagen IV until the muzzle blast of its 75 mm turret cannon caught his eye. A half-second later the tungsten-steel projectile slammed into the hull of his M4A2.

The Sherman shuddered. There was an awesome roar, followed immediately by the horrible screeching sound of tearing metal, lasting no more than a second. The M4A2 turned to the right, halfway off the track it had been following, and stopped dead. It had moved no more than eight feet after being struck.

The impact of the armor-piercing shell threw Bellmon against the edge of the commander's hatch, catching him in the rib cage. It bruised him severely, knocking the breath out of him, and almost throwing him out of the commander's turret.

He heard a groan, which sounded somewhat surprised, from inside the tank, but couldn't tell who it was. When he looked down, dense black smoke had already begun to fill the tank's interior. Without really thinking about what he was doing, acting in pure animal reflex, he hoisted himself out of the turret. There was a wave of pain.

He just had time to curse himself for getting out of the turret—his duty clearly was to have gone into the hull to help the others—when an intensely hot spurt of flame erupted upward from the turret. He knew what had caused it. Pieces of metal from the projectile, and pieces torn from the hull itself, had ripped into the brass cases of the 75 mm cannon ammunition, slicing them open and spilling their powder. Then the powder had caught fire. When unconfined powder burns, it does not explode. The explosion came a moment later, as intact shell cases and gasoline fumes detonated.

Bellmon felt himself flying through the air. He landed on his back upon the rocky ground, his shoulders striking the ground first, throwing him into a backward somersault, and knocking what was left of the wind in his lungs out of him. When he came to rest, he was conscious, but was incapable of movement.

He was dimly aware of a second shot from a tank cannon, a sharp cracking noise, followed immediately by a heavier thump. Despite the pain in his ribs, he tried to get control of himself. He forced himself to take a deep breath, and then another. And another.

Finally he was able to roll onto his side to see what had happened to the second M4A2, the other tank which had come out with him "to locate and assist the 705th Field Artillery Battalion." It was immobile. There was no one in the turret, and oily smoke oozed out around the fuel tanks and the turret ring. No one had gotten out of that one.

He heard the sound of a tank engine. He let himself fall slowly onto his face. He would play dead, though it was a slim chance at best. The crew of the German tank would more than likely give him a burst with the 7.93 mm machine gun. Prisoners were a nuisance in fast-moving tank warfare.

He closed his eyes, and tried to breathe very slowly. His only hope was to make them think that he had been killed when his tank blew up. If he tried to surrender, all he would do would be to give them a better target.

The PzKwIV ground to a halt near him. It was now the standard German medium tank, an efficient killing machine, into which had been incorporated all the lessons the German Panzertruppen had learned in France and Russia and here in Africa. Bellmon would have been willing to admit, privately, that it was a better tank than the Sherman.

He knew the German tank commander was watching him. Then he heard the crunch of footsteps on the gritty soil.

"Was ist er?"

"Ein Offizier, Herr Leutnant. Mit einem gelben Blatt."

"Ein Major?" the first voice said. "Is he dead?"

"No," the self-confident voice above him said, matter-of-factly. "He's breathing. Playing dead."

Good God, is my pretense that transparent?

There was the sound of more booted feet on the gritty soil.

"Please do not make it necessary for me to kill you, Herr Major," the first voice said.

A hand grabbed his shoulder, and rolled him onto his back. Bellmon opened his eyes and found himself looking into the muzzle of a .45 Colt automatic. It was in the hands of a young, blond, good-looking lieutenant of the Afrika Korps. He wore the black tunic of the Panzertruppen above standard gray Wehrmacht trousers. He smiled at Bellmon. Then he reached down with his free hand and took Bellmon's .45 from his shoulder holster.

"You may sit up, please, Major," he said. His English was British accented. "Are you injured?"

Bellmon sat up. The lieutenant handed Bellmon's .45 to the soldier with him. Another nice-looking, clean-cut, blond-headed boy, Bellmon thought.

"Will you also give me, please, the holster?" the lieutenant asked. Bellmon pulled it over his head and held it out. The soldier held his Schmeisser 9 mm machine-pistol between his knees, took Bellmon's shoulder holster, and put it over his head.

"Make sure that isn't loaded," the lieutenant cautioned. The soldier took the magazine from the butt of the .45, saw that it was full, emptied it, and then put it back in the pistol, and then slipped the pistol into the holster.

"The Colt is a very fine pistol, Major," the lieutenant said.

Bellmon didn't reply.

"Help the major to his feet," the lieutenant said.

"Are you going to see to my men?" Bellmon asked, getting painfully to his feet unaided.

The lieutenant actually looked unhappy as he made a sad gesture toward the two American tanks. They were both burning steadily. There was the smell of burned flesh. Bellmon willed back a spasm of nausea. He would not, he vowed, show weakness before his captors.

The soldier took his arm and led him to the PzKwIV.

"Please to get inside, Herr Major," the lieutenant said.

Bellmon climbed over the bogies, the wheels around which the track of the tank moved, and by which it was supported. A two-piece hatch in the side of the turret was open. The sweat-soaked face of an older man—probably the platoon sergeant,

Bellmon judged, because there was something about him that told him he wasn't an officer—looked out at him. Bellmon lowered his head and started to crawl into the turret.

"Nein," the face said to him. *"Fuss vorwärts."*

Bellmon pulled his head back out, turned around, and backed into the turret hatch.

Inside the hull, which was more cramped than the hull of an M4A2, he was motioned to sit down on the floor. One of the crewmen (the driver, probably, he thought) came up with a length of field telephone wire. He looped it around Bellmon's ankles, and then around his wrists, and tied his wrists to his ankles.

Then he climbed out of sight. In a moment, there was the clash of gears, and the PzKwIV turned on one track, then went back in the direction from which it had come, to the east, toward the German lines.

I am alive, Bellmon told himself. Bruised, a little groggy, but not really injured. This is where I am supposed to think that I will live to fight another day.

He became aware that tears were blurring his vision and running down his cheeks. Was it shock? Was he weeping for Sergeant Pete Fortin and all the others? Or because the worst thing that could happen to an officer, capture, had happened to him? Did it matter? He lowered his head on his knees so that his captors would not see him crying.

[TWO]
Hq, 393rd Tank Destroyer Battalion (Reinforced)
Youks-Les-Bains, Algeria
24 February 1943

The command post was built against the side of a stony hill, facing away from the front lines and the German artillery. At the crest of the hill, four half-tracks, two mounting 75 mm antitank cannon and two mounting multiple .50 caliber machine guns in powered turrets, were dug in facing the front.

On the ground, on the friendly side of the hill, two more half-tracks with multiple .50s faced the opposite direction. A half-moon of barbed wire with sandbagged machine-gun emplacements guarded the command post dugouts. The dugouts were holes in the side of the hill, with timber supporting sandbag roofs.

Two jeeps, traveling well above the posted 25 mph speed limit, approached the 393rd CP from the rear. Each held three men, and an air-cooled Browning .50 caliber machine gun on a pillar. The front jeep had nonstandard accouterments: the seats were thickly padded leather, instead of the normal thin canvas pad; a hand bar had been welded to the top of the windshield; and a combination flashing red light and siren of the type usually found on a police car was mounted on the right fender. It had been painted olive-drab, but the paint, here and there, had flecked off the chrome. An eight-by-twelve-inch sheet of tin, painted red and with a single silver star in the middle, was placed above the front and rear bumpers. Communications radios were bolted to the fender wells in the back seat, and their antennae whipped in the air. Spring clips had been bolted to the dashboard. Each held a Thompson .45 ACP caliber submachine gun.

The driver of the lead jeep was a master sergeant in his thirties, a pug-nosed, squat, muscular man with huge hands. He wore a tanker's jacket and a Colt .45 automatic in a shoulder holster. Beside him sat a firm-jawed, silver-haired, almost handsome man in his fifties, wearing an Army Air Corps pilot's horsehide jacket, with a silver star on each epaulet. A yellow silk scarf, neatly knotted, was around his neck. He also carried a .45 in a shoulder holster. The man in the back seat was young, clean-cut, and dressed like the general, the only difference being the silver bars of a first lieutenant on the epaulets of his pilot's horsehide jacket.

The second jeep contained three enlisted men, a technical sergeant and two staff sergeants, armed with both Garand M1 rifles and Colt pistols carried in holsters suspended from web belts around their waists. Their helmets had "MP" painted on their sides.

As they approached the gate to the command post of the 393rd Tank Destroyer Battalion (Reinforced), the master sergeant driving the lead jeep saw that the road was barred by a weighted telephone pole suspended horizontally across the road. He reached down and flipped the siren switch. The siren growled, just long enough to signal the soldier at the gate to raise the telephone pole.

He did not do so. The two jeeps skidded to a stop.

The master sergeant at the wheel of the lead jeep started to rise in his seat. The general, with a little wave of his left hand, signaled him to sit back down.

"It's all right, Tommy," he said.

This wasn't garrison, and the guard was not ceremonial. The German advance had been stopped a thousand yards away.

The guard was a very large, six-foot-tall, very black PFC, carrying a Garand rifle slung over his shoulder. He stood at the weighted end of the pole, examined the passengers in the jeep carefully, and then, satisfied, stood erect, grasped the leather sling of his M1 with his left hand, saluted crisply with his right, and then pushed the weighted end of the pole down. The barrier end lifted. The guard then waved them through. He stood at attention until both jeeps had passed, and then he quickly cranked the EE-8 field telephone at his feet.

"General officer headed for the CP," he said. "Porky Waterford."

By the time the two jeeps had reached the bunker with the American flag and the battalion guidon before it, a very tall, flat-nosed Negro lieutenant colonel whose brown skin was somewhat darker than his boots had stepped outside the bunker. He was dressed in olive-drab shirt and trousers, with a yellow piece of parachute silk wrapped around his neck as a foulard. He carried a World War I Colt New Service .45 ACP revolver in an old-fashioned cavalry-style holster (one with a swivel, so the holster would hang straight down even when mounted).

The guard at the door to the CP carried a Thompson .45 caliber submachine gun. He saluted the moment the jeep stopped, and the brigadier general in the front seat jumped out.

The lieutenant colonel, whose features and dark skin made him look very much like an Arab, took three steps away from the door, came to attention, and saluted.

"Lieutenant Colonel Parker, sir, commanding," he said.

The brigadier general returned the salute, and then put out his hand.

"How are you, Colonel?" he asked. The handshake was momentary, pro forma.

"Very well, thank you, General," Lt. Col. Philip Sheridan Parker III said. "Will the general come into the CP?"

"Thank you," Brigadier General Peterson K. Waterford said.

Colonel Parker waved him ahead into the CP. Someone called "Attention."

"Rest, gentlemen," General Waterford said, immediately.

The command post was crowded, but neat and orderly. One wall was covered with large maps and charts, overlaid with celluloid. There was a field switchboard, communications radios, folding tables equipped with portable typewriters. A large, open, enameled coffee pot simmered on an alcohol stove. There were perhaps twenty men, officers and enlisted, all black, in the room.

"Would the general care to examine our situation?" Colonel Parker said, gesturing toward the situation map.

"Actually, Colonel," General Waterford said, "I took the chance that you would have a minute or two for me on a personal matter."

"Perhaps the general would care to come to my quarters?" Lieutenant Colonel Parker offered.

"That's very kind of you, Colonel," General Waterford said.

"Captain," Parker said to a stout, round-faced captain, "would you brief the general's aide?"

The captain came to attention. "Yes, sir."

Colonel Parker pushed aside a piece of tarpaulin that served as the door to his quarters, an eight-by-eight-foot chamber hacked out of the hill. Inside were a GI cot, a GI folding table, two GI folding chairs, a GI desk, and two footlockers.

"Will the general have a seat?" Colonel Parker inquired. When Waterford had sat down, Parker knelt and opened one of the footlockers and took out two bottles, one of scotch and one of bourbon. He looked at General Waterford, who indicated the scotch by pointing his finger. He poured scotch into one cheese glass, and bourbon into the other. He handed the general the scotch, then tapped it with his glass of bourbon.

"Mud in your eye, Porky," he said.

"Health and long life, Phil," the general replied. They drank their whiskey neat, all of it. Parker asked with raised eyebrows if Waterford wanted another, and Waterford declined with a shake of his head.

"I'm really sorry about Bob Bellmon, Porky," Colonel Parker said. "I was going to get my thoughts together, and then ask if you thought I should write Marjorie."

"What are your thoughts?" Waterford asked.

"I'll tell you what I know," Parker said. "We were withdrawing. That's a week ago today. About three miles from Sidi-Bou-Zid, we came across two shot-up M4s.

I had a moment or two, so I went and looked. The bumper markings identified them as belonging to 73rd Medium Tank. Numbers two and fourteen."

"Tony Wilson took the time to tell me what he knew," Waterford said. "Bob went out in number two. He was trying to link up with the 705th Field. Two lousy tanks was all that Tony could spare. Tony said Bob convinced him that they had to try with what they had. Neither of them knew, of course, but the 705th had already been rolled over."

Lt. Col. Philip Sheridan Parker III felt sorry for Lieutenant Colonel Anthony Wilson, who commanded the 73rd Medium Tank Battalion. Losing men was always bad. Having to explain how they were lost in person to a man who was simultaneously the father-in-law, a general officer, and an old friend must have been very rough indeed.

"Both tanks had been struck with something big," Parker said. "I'd say a high velocity tungsten-cored round from the Mark IV Panzer. Both had burned. One of them had exploded."

"Which one?" Waterford asked.

"I'm sorry, I don't remember which one," Parker said.

"That's all right," Waterford said. "Did you get a body count?"

"They burned and blew up, Porky," Colonel Parker said. "And I didn't have much time. We were under intermittent fire."

"But?"

"I hate to say this, because it might give hope where there is none," Colonel Parker said. "But I have a feeling that one man may have gotten out. And that he was carried off as a prisoner. There were Mark IV tracks, and footsteps. But they may just have been looking over the hulks."

Waterford sat with his shoulders bent, examining his hands.

"Yes, of course," Waterford said, after a long silence.

Parker poured an inch and a half of scotch in the cheese glass and handed it to Waterford. Waterford took it and tossed it down.

"I'm sorry, Porky," Parker said, gently, "but that's all I have."

"When we go back," General Waterford said, retaining control of his voice with a visible effort, "the Graves Registration people will probably be able to tell us something. They're really quite good at this sort of thing."

"If Bobby didn't make it, Porky," Colonel Parker said, "he went out quick."

"He went out too young. Bobby was . . . *is* . . . twenty-five," Waterford said. "God, I hate to write Barbara."

"That's what I've been doing," Parker said. "Writing the next of kin."

"You came out of it better than most," Waterford said. "We got the shit kicked out of us, Phil."

"I lost seven officers and sixty-three troopers," Parker said.

"Equipment?"

"I put all the old 37 mm stuff out in front. I lost seventeen tracks. Nine from mechanical failure. I blew them."

"I repeat, you came out of it a lot better than most," Waterford said.

"Are they going to relieve Lloyd Fredendall? That's the rumor."

"Probably," Waterford replied. "He lost the battle."

"Who's going to get the Corps?" Parker asked.

"I hope Seward. That'd put me in line for the division. But I suppose Georgie Patton will get it. Eisenhower still calls him 'Sir,' when he's not careful."

"I hope you get it, Porky," Parker said.

"No, you don't, you bastard. You're just saying that. You're jealous."

"Of course I'm jealous. But if you get the division, maybe you'll take us with you."

"If I get the division, Phil, you can bank on it. You've got some fine troops."

"I think so," Parker said. "None of mine ran."

General Waterford stood up. "I wish I could say the same thing," he said. "You know what the history books are going to say: 'In their first major armor engagement of World War II, at Kasserine Pass, Tunisia, the Americans got the shit kicked out of them. Many of them ran.' "

"They call that blooding, Porky," Phil Parker said.

General Waterford stood up, put his arm around Parker's shoulder, and hugged him.

"Thank you for your time, Phil," he said.

"I'm sorry I wasn't of more help," Parker said.

"I didn't ask, Phil," Waterford said. "Where's Phil?"

"A sophomore at Norwich. He'll be in the class of '45."

"Maybe we can wind it up by then," Waterford said.

"God, I hope so."

[**THREE**]
Carmel, California
28 February 1943

Barbara Waterford Bellmon, a lanky, auburn-haired, freckle-faced brunette of twenty-four, stood by her locker in the ladies' locker room of the Pebble Beach Country Club and held out her hand for her winnings. She had gone around in 82, four over ladies' par, and they had been playing for a dollar a stroke. She had just won thirty-three dollars, and it was important to her that she be paid.

As the losers searched in their coin purses and wallets for the money, Barbara thought again that she really didn't like women. Women, she thought, were really lousy losers; they paid up reluctantly. She knew that the other members of her foursome would have preferred not to pay up at all, to let the settling-up slide until it was forgotten. It wasn't the money. These women were all well-to-do. It was some quirk of the female character.

"All I've got is a fifty," Susan Forbes said, examining the contents of her wallet, but not offering the fifty dollar bill. Susan was a long-legged blond, who looked considerably younger than her thirty-three years. Barbara took a twenty and a ten from her wallet and held it out.

"Oh, here's a twenty," Susan said.

As if you didn't know, Barbara thought, and snatched it from Susan's hand. Surprise, surprise.

"Thank you very much," Barbara said, sweetly. "Next?"

"The least you could do is buy us lunch," Patricia Stewart said, as she passed over a crisp ten dollar bill. Pat, whom Barbara thought of privately as the archetypical Tweedy Lady, was, at thirty-six, the oldest of the golfers. Barbara handed her a dollar change.

"I have a date," she said.

"Sounds exciting," Susan said. "Anyone we know?"

"He's tall, dark, handsome, and a Catholic priest," Barbara said.

"Shame on you," Susan said.

Standing on one leg, Barbara took off her golf shoes, put them into her locker, and then stuffed her golf socks into her purse. Finally, she slipped her bare feet into a pair of loafers.

They went through what Barbara considered the ludicrous routine of making smacking noises with their lips in the general vicinity of each others' cheeks. Then Barbara walked out the ladies' locker room, back onto the course rather than into the clubhouse itself, and went around the building to the parking lot.

She got behind the wheel of her mother's car, a 1937 Ford convertible sedan. After performing the elaborate but necessary ritual it required to get going (pump the gas pedal twice, then hold it down while the starter cranked, release it instantly when it coughed, while simultaneously praying), she backed out of the parking slot and drove home.

Home was Casa Mañana, her parents' home, a rambling Spanish-style building with red-tiled roofs set on ten acres overlooking the Pacific. There were three flagpoles set in a brick-lined patch of grass in front of the house. An American flag, just barely moving in the wind, hung from the taller center pole. The two smaller poles were bare.

Casa Mañana, roughly translated, meant the "house for tomorrow." For three generations, it had been the home to which the Waterfords planned to retire, and where their women waited when the men had gone off to war. It was at Casa Mañana that the family gathered, when possible, at Christmas, and it was a family tradition that the babies were christened according to the rites of the Episcopal Church of St. Matthew's in Carmel, no matter where in the world they were born. It was home to people whose profession saw them spending a good part of their lives in foreign countries or in remote military posts.

There was enough money to keep it open, staffed, ready for occupancy, when there was no member of the family closer than a thousand miles. Over the years, the Waterfords and the Bellmons had slowly and wisely invested their money, so there was now enough to live "comfortably" if unostentatiously.

Just inside the door, on shelves, were two red flags neatly folded into triangles.

One of them bore a single silver star, and the other two silver stars. The single-starred flag belonged to the present owner of the house, her father, Brigadier General Peterson K. Waterford, who had inherited the house from his father, Major General Alfred B. Waterford. The two-starred flag had belonged to Bob's father, Major General Robert F. Bellmon, Sr. They'd buried Bob's father from Casa Mañana, taking the remains to the military cemetery at the Presidio of San Francisco. When they'd hauled his flag down from the pole for the last time, they had folded it up and put it beside General Waterford's flag, where it would be ready when it was needed again. Porky Waterford was almost sure to make major general soon, and then he could fly it as his own. Or it could just stay there until Bob, twenty years from now, was himself entitled to the red flag of a general officer.

The flags were well made; they'd last that long. General Waterford's flag had belonged to his father.

With long and almost masculine strides, Barbara walked through the house, in search of her mother. It must be noon, Barbara realized. Mother and the kids were having their noontime cocktail. Marjorie Waterford never took a drink until noon, and she rarely made it to twelve fifteen without one. She called it a cocktail, but it was invariably bourbon and water, one ice cube. The kids got ginger ale with a maraschino cherry.

"How did you do?" Barbara's mother inquired, asking with her eyes if Barbara wanted a drink.

"No, I don't think so, thank you," Barbara said. "I don't want to smell of it. When I come back." She smiled with self-satisfaction at her mother. "I went around in 82 and took them for thirty-three bucks."

"Good for you," her mother said. "Father Bob called. He asked if he could bring somebody with him."

"Did he say who?"

"No. He said he had two. He didn't give any names. I think he would have, if it was someone we know."

"Yes," Barbara replied, as if distracted.

"I had Consuela do a pork loin," Mrs. Waterford said. "I thought that and over-brown potatoes, and a salad."

"That will be very nice," Barbara said. "I don't know how he stands it, doing that, day after day after day."

"That's what priests are for," her mother said. "And he's probably used to it by now."

"I'd better get changed," Barbara said.

When she came out of the shower and was drying herself, she heard the kids' voices in her bedroom. She wondered if Bobby just wanted to be with Mommy or if Bobby was already developing a curiosity about females. He was hardly old enough for that, but on the other hand, he was Bob's son. She remembered the first time Bob had talked her into taking her clothes off. At Fort Riley. She remembered that very clearly. She was seven, so Bob must have been eight. A naked little girl and a naked little boy, staring at each other with frank curiosity. He had a thing, and she didn't.

The next time he had seen her without her pants she had been twenty and he had been a twenty-one-year-old second lieutenant. It had been in a room in the Carlyle Hotel in New York City on the first night of their honeymoon.

"Jesus Christ," Bob had said. "It grew a beard."

The bastard. So had his. And she'd told him so.

Barbara stuck her head through the bathroom door.

"Scram, Bobby," she said.

"Why?"

"Because boys aren't supposed to be around when ladies aren't wearing clothes," Barbara said. "Go wait for Chaplain McGrory."

"Is he coming *again?*"

"Yes, he is," Barbara said. "Now beat it."

When he had finally made a reluctant retreat, Barbara came out of the bathroom naked and got dressed. Eleanor, a year younger than her brother, sat in the middle of the bed and watched her get dressed, first a bra and pants and a half-slip and a garter belt and stockings (no girdle, not even after two kids), and then making up her face and doing her hair. Finally she put on a gray suit, and last, her jewelry: her wedding ring and her engagement ring, and the miniature of Bob's West Point class ring.

She always had a question in her mind about wearing the engagement ring on occasions like this. It was a four-carat, emerald-cut diamond. Worth a bundle. It had been Bob's mother's. When, to absolutely no one's surprise, she had come back from the Spring Hop at the Point and announced that she and Bob were going to be married the day after he graduated, General Bellmon had given Bob the ring to give to her. She hadn't even had to have it resized.

It had never been a problem with the enlisted wives, who either didn't notice it, or thought it was costume jewelry, or thought that all officers' wives had diamonds like that. But it had gotten looks from some of the officers' wives on whom she had made "notification calls" with Father Bob.

The army sent a chaplain, and an officer of equal or senior rank, and, if one was available (as Barbara inarguably was), a regular officer's wife to offer what help and comfort she could.

She had received some jealous looks, a jealousy born of the fact that she was an officer's wife whose husband was still alive, who wasn't being visited by a notification team. That entirely understandable jealousy, however, sometimes changed into material jealousy. She couldn't be blamed for bearing condolences, for being the visitor instead of the visited. But she could be resented for being rich, for being part of the aristocracy within the army: those with private means, those who waited for the men to come home in a fifteen-room, servant-filled house on ten acres overlooking the Pacific instead of a tiny rented apartment, those with four-carat, emerald-cut engagement rings worth a major's annual pay and allowances.

But she always ended up wearing it. It was a symbol. It had been on the third finger of an officer's lady's left hand for half a century, and one day, Bobby's lady would wear it.

Barbara stood on one foot again and slipped her feet into brown pumps. They were too tight. Her feet always seemed to swell after she played eighteen holes.

Then she gestured toward the door and followed as Eleanor toddled out of her bedroom and down the tiled corridor to the living room, a large and airy room full of books and souvenirs and General Waterford's collection of silver cups from polo fields and equestrian competition all over the world.

The Reverend Robert T. McGrory, S.J., Colonel, Chaplain's Corps, United States Army, got to his feet when he saw her walk in the room. Some chaplains looked like what they really were, clergymen in a uniform that was actually the antithesis of their calling. "Father Bob" was tall, red-haired, ruddy-faced, and built like a football player. His uniforms were impeccably tailored, and he wore them with every bit as much flair as General Waterford wore his; more, Barbara had often thought, than Bob did.

Every time she saw Father Bob, she remembered reading that the Jesuits had acquired a great deal of power by making themselves available to the nobility in Europe, and wondered if that was what Mac had really been up to all these years.

Normally, she called him "Bob." She was Episcopal, after all; and Bob had been in her life, on and off, as long as she could remember. Calling him "Father" seemed a little forced.

But today, he had brass with him. A bird colonel she didn't recognize.

"Hello, Father," Barbara said. "Handsome as ever, I see."

"Barbara, this is Colonel Destin," Mac said, putting his arm around her shoulders, and then stooping over to pick up Eleanor.

"How do you do, Colonel?" Barbara said, giving him her hand.

"Mrs. Bellmon," the colonel replied.

"Someone senior this time?" Barbara asked.

"I'm afraid so," Colonel Destin said.

I don't like the way that sounds, Barbara thought. Father McGrory put his arm around her shoulders again.

"Mrs. Bellmon," Colonel Destin said. "I have the unfortunate duty to inform you that your husband, Lieutenant Colonel Robert F. Bellmon, is missing in action and presumed to be dead after action near Sidi-Bou-Zid, Tunisia, as of 17 February."

"Oh, *shit*," Barbara Bellmon said. Without being aware that she was doing it, she balled her hands into fists and then smashed them together.

"It's only presumed, Barbara," Father Bob said.

"Save it, *Chaplain*," Barbara said, nastily. She took Eleanor from him, and held her as she walked to the window looking down on the Pacific. The child cuddled up close and didn't struggle to be put down. Finally, Barbara set the child on her feet. Then she sat down on the windowsill and looked at the two officers.

"Who's the other one?" she asked. Destin didn't understand what she was asking.

"A warrant officer named Sanchez," Father Bob said. "We got word that he died in a prison camp in the Philippines."

"Would you like a cup of coffee, or something to eat, before we go see her?" Barbara asked.

Father McGrory took a long time to reply.

"Are you sure you want to, Barbara?" he asked, finally.

"What else should I do?" she replied. "Sit around here and have hysterics?"

Fighting back the tears, she walked across the living room and down the corridor to the front door and outside. She looked up at the flag, and went to the pole and lowered it to half-mast. Then she looked up at it. She leaned her forehead against the flagpole, and fought back the urge to weep.

"What the hell am I doing?" she asked aloud, pushing herself erect. "I'll believe he's dead when I see his casket, and not before." Then she ran the flag all the way back up the pole again.

She wept a little later that day, with Mrs. Sanchez, but that was for Mrs. Sanchez, not for Bob or herself. She didn't weep again, not that evening at dinner, looking at her mother's face, nor that night, when she went to bed, nor the next morning when she woke up early and lay in bed and told herself that the way the army worked, the odds were that Bob really had bought the farm, and the only reason they hadn't come out and said so was because they hadn't found his body. And that meant that this was the first day of her life that she could remember that Bob wasn't going to be around.

She wept ten days later when they called from the Western Union office and said they had a telegram for her, and did she want them to read it to her. She knew what it would be, and she didn't want to hear it read over the phone, so she said she would be in the village and would pick it up herself. After she wept, she got dressed and drove the old Ford convertible into the village and picked up the yellow envelope in the Western Union office and carried it out to the car to read it.

WAR DEPARTMENT
WASHINGTON DC

MRS. BARBARA BELLMON
CASA MAÑANA
CARMEL, CALIFORNIA

A LIST FURNISHED BY THE GERMAN AUTHORITIES VIA THE INTERNATIONAL RED CROSS STATES THAT LT COL ROBERT F. BELLMON, 0-348808, IS A PRISONER OF WAR. NO CONFIRMATION IS AVAILABLE, NOR IS ANY OTHER INFORMATION OF ANY KIND AVAILABLE AT THIS TIME. YOU WILL BE PROMPTLY NOTIFIED IN THE EVENT ANY INFORMATION DOES BECOME AVAILABLE.

INFORMATION REGARDING PRISONERS OF WAR GENERALLY IS AVAILABLE FROM THE PERSONNEL OFFICER OF ANY MILITARY CAMP POST OR

STATION. FOR YOUR INFORMATION, THE CLOSEST MILITARY INSTALLATION TO YOUR HOME IS: HUNTER-LIGGETT MILITARY RESERVATION, CALIFORNIA.

YOU MIGHT ALSO WISH TO MAKE CONTACT WITH THE PENINSULA INTERSERVICE OFFICERS LADIES ASSOCIATION, PO BOX 34, CARMEL, CALIFORNIA. THIS UNOFFICIAL GROUP OFFERS ADVICE AND SOME FINANCIAL ASSISTANCE IF REQUIRED.

EDWARD F. WITZELL
MAJOR GENERAL
THE ADJUTANT GENERAL

When she learned Bob was alive, then she let it out, right there in the car, and then she went home and told her mother that it would be all over Carmel that she'd been on a crying jag, right downtown.

[FOUR]
Bizerte, Tunisia
9 March 1943

The POW enclosure had its prisoners under canvas, much of it American, captured during the German offensive. The enlisted men were separated from the officers, and the company grade officers were separated from the field grade.

The squad tent in which Major Robert Bellmon was housed also held a lieutenant colonel of the Quartermaster Corps, who had been captured while looking for a place to put his ration and clothing dump, and an artillery major who had been captured while serving as a forward observer.

They had been treated well, so far, and fed with captured American rations. The camp was surrounded by coiled barbed wire, called concertina, and wooden guard towers in which machine guns had been mounted. There was no possibility of escape for the moment.

A Wehrmacht captain, accompanied by a sergeant, walked up to Bellmon's tent and called his name.

"Yes?" Bellmon replied. He looked up from the GI cot on which he sat, but did not rise.

"Come with me, please, Herr Major," the captain, a middle-aged man wearing glasses, said in thickly accented English. He gestured with his hand.

Bellmon walked out of the tent. The QM light bird and the artillery major looked at him quizzically. Bellmon shook his shoulders. He had no more idea of what was going on than they did.

The German sergeant took up a position behind him, and Bellmon followed the captain across the compound and through a gate. It had been cold the night before, but now, just before noon, the sun had come out, and it was actually warmer outside than it had been in the tent.

He was led to the prison compound office, a sunlit corner of a single-story building within the outer ring of barbed wire of the prison enclosure, and separated from the prisoner area by a double ring of barbed wire.

"The major wishes to see you," the captain said, pushing open a door and motioning Bellmon through it.

Bellmon was faced with a question of protocol. The code of military courtesy provides that salutes be exchanged between junior and senior officers, even when one is a prisoner of the other. For the life of him, he could not recall what was expected of him, in his prisoner status, when reporting to a German major. In the American army, he would not have saluted another major. He decided that if it was good enough for the U.S. Army, it was good enough for where he was now.

He marched up to the desk, and stood at attention, but did not salute. If he were British, Bellmon thought, he could have stamped his foot as a sort of signal that he was now present as ordered.

The major behind the desk was an older version of the lieutenant who had stuck the captured .45 in his face the day he was captured. A good-looking, fair-skinned blond German, very military in appearance, very self-confident. The German officer looked up at Bellmon, smiled, and touched his hand to his eyebrow in a very sloppy salute. There was nothing to do but return it. The German smiled at him.

"Major Robert Bellmon," Bellmon said. "0-348808. 17 August 1917." Name, rank, serial number, and date of birth, as required by the Geneva Convention.

"Yes, I know, Herr Oberstleutnant," the German major said. "Won't you please sit down?" He indicated a folding chair. Bellmon recognized it as American. So was the bottle of bourbon on the major's desk.

"I have some pleasant news for you," the German major said. "Herr Oberstleutnant."

"My rank is major," Bellmon said.

"That's my pleasant news, Herr Oberstleutnant," the major said, and he slid a mimeographed sheet across the desk to Bellmon. It could easily be a forgery, but it looked perfectly authentic. It was a paragraph extracted from a general order of Western Task Force, and it announced the promotion of Major Robert F. Bellmon, Armor (1st Lt, RA), to the grade of Lieutenant Colonel, Army of the United States, effective 16 February 1943—the day before he was captured.

"And I have these for you, as well," the major said. He opened a drawer in the desk and took from it a small sheet of cardboard, to which two silver oak leaves were pinned. The name of the manufacturer was printed on the face of the card. The insignia were American.

"Thank you," Bellmon said. "May I have this as well?" he asked, indicating the promotion orders.

"Certainly," the major said. As Bellmon folded them up and put them in the breast pocket of his newly issued olive-drab shirt, the major poured whiskey into two glasses. He handed one to Bellmon. Another problem of protocol, Bellmon thought.

Is accepting a glass of captured whiskey from an enemy who has just presented me with a light bird's leaf and the orders to go with it considered *trafficking with the enemy?*

"I don't normally drink at this hour," Bellmon said.

"A promotion is a special occasion," the German said. "No matter what the hour or the circumstances."

Bellmon picked up the glass and drank from it.

"Congratulations, Herr Oberstleutnant," the major said, raising his glass.

"Danke schön, Herr Major," Bellmon said. His German was fluent.

"You will be given an extra POW postcard," the major said. "I've sent for one. I'm sure General Waterford will be pleased to learn that you know of your promotion."

"Bellmon," Bellmon said. "Lieutenant Colonel. 0-348808. 17 August 1917." He said it with a smile, but it reminded the major that he was not going to discuss anything that could possibly be of use to the enemy.

"While this is technically an interrogation, Herr Oberstleutnant," the major said, tolerantly, "I really am not trying to cleverly get you to reveal military secrets."

"I'm sure you're not," Bellmon said, pleasantly sarcastic.

"No, I'm serious," the major said. "We know most of the things about you that we try to find out. You're an academy graduate, seventeenth in your class, of 1939. Your father was Major General Bellmon. You are married to Brigadier General Peterson K. Waterford's daughter Barbara."

Bellmon just looked at him and smiled. The major took a copy of the U.S. Army Registry and laid it on the table. Bellmon smiled wider.

"And we know where General Waterford is," the major said.

"I'm sure you do." Bellmon suddenly thought that if he was seeking information, he would have said where General Waterford was to get confirmation, or simply to check his reaction.

"And I really think, Herr Oberstleutnant," the major went on. "That I know more of the present order of battle than you do. You were captured during the fluid phase of the battle, and couldn't possibly know how things stand now."

"Even if I were not bound by regulation and the Geneva Convention," Bellmon said, "and could talk freely, I rather doubt there is anything of value I could tell you."

"Probably not," the major said. "Front-line soldiers either know very little of interest to their interrogators, or have entirely the wrong idea of what's really going on."

What he's trying to do, Bellmon decided, is lull me into making some kind of slip. But what he says is true. I don't know any more about the order of battle of the II U.S. Corps than a cook in a rifle company.

"But just between us, Colonel," the major went on. "What do you think of we Germans, now that we have met on the field of battle?"

Bellmon didn't reply.

"Certainly someone who speaks German as well as you do can't believe we're savages?"

Damn it, why did I speak German.

"Not all of you, certainly," he said, in English.

"Some of us, you will doubtless be surprised to learn, are civilized to the point where we scrupulously obey the Geneva Convention," the major said. "And adhere rigidly to the standard of conduct expected of officers."

"I'm very glad to hear that," Bellmon said.

"Rank has its privileges," the major said, "even in confinement. You will be flown to Italy, and possibly all the way to Germany. Majors and below are sent by ship."

"I see," Bellmon said, with a sinking feeling in his stomach. He had had a desperate hope that the Americans would counterattack, and that he would be freed.

"We make a real effort to insure that once senior professional officers are out of the war, they stay out of the war," the major said. "You can conscript soldiers. Staff officers and battalion commanders cannot be trained in six months."

"I have to agree with your reasoning," Bellmon said.

A sergeant knocked, was told to enter, and laid a POW postcard on the major's desk. The major took a fountain pen from his tunic and handed it to Bellmon. There was space for name, rank, serial number, and a twenty-word message, one blank line provided for each word.

Bellmon filled it in, addressed it to Barbara Bellmon in Carmel, California, had a moment's painful mental image of the house there, and then wrote his message: "Alive, well, uninjured. Kiss the children. I love you. Bob."

He wondered when he would see them again. He capped the fountain pen and handed it and the card to the major.

"Thank you," he said.

"My pleasure, Herr Oberstleutnant," the major said. He put out his hand. "Good luck, and may we meet again under different circumstances."

Bellmon took his hand. He told himself that if the circumstances were reversed, he hoped that he would behave as the major had behaved toward him: correct, and compassionate. He realized he had been dismissed. Thirty minutes later, he realized that he had given the enemy information. He had confirmed that he was indeed Porky Waterford's son-in-law. He should not have gone even that far. He didn't know how they could use that information, how valuable it was to them, but he knew he should not have handed it to them on a platter the way he had.

[FIVE]
Friedberg, Hesse
12 April 1943

The bunker had been excavated under the castle at Friedberg, which stands at the crest of the ring of low mountains ringing the resort of Bad Nauheim, thirty-five miles north of Frankfurt am Main, in Hesse. The excavation had been conducted with the secrecy and the disregard of costs associated with anything that had Adolph Hitler's personal attention.

The bunker itself was beneath at least twenty feet of granite, and where there had been an insufficient layer of granite, reinforced concrete had been poured to provide the required protection. Siemens had installed an enormous communications switchboard, which provided nearly instantaneous telephone, radio-telephone, and teletype communication with Berlin and the various major commands in the East, West, the Balkans, and North Africa.

A battalion of the Leibstandarte Adolph Hitler, augmented by a reserve regiment of Pomeranian infantry and a regiment of Luftwaffe antiaircraft artillery, provided security.

Camouflage netting, placed twenty feet off the ground in the thick groves of pine which surrounded Schloss Friedberg, concealed the fleet of cars and trucks necessary to support a major headquarters. It was changed to reflect the coloring of the seasons. The Führer's train, when he was present, was protected from either view or assault by a concrete revetment, long enough to contain both his train and one other.

The bunker itself was an underground office building, four stories deep; access was by stairs for the workers and a private elevator for the senior officers. The Führer today was in Rastenburg, in East Prussia, so there was an acrid cloud of cigarette smoke throughout the bunker. When the Führer was in the bunker, smoking was forbidden.

The lieutenant colonel of the Feldgendarmerie, a portly, balding middle-aged officer, delivered his report to the generalmajor with assurance. He had been a policeman all his life, and thus trained to present facts—separate from conclusions and theory—to his superiors.

The Generalmajor, who was assistant to the chief of the Politico-military Affairs Division, asked several questions, all intelligent ones, and carefully examined the physical evidence which the Oberstleutnant of the Feldgendarmerie had brought in two bulging briefcases from Smolensk.

There were buttons from Polish Army uniforms; regimental crests; insignia of rank; identification papers; labels from uniforms bearing addresses of tailors in Warsaw; and a half-inch-thick sheath of photographs of bodies, open graves, and close-ups of entrance and exit wounds in skulls.

"There is no question in your mind, I gather, Herr Oberstleutnant, of what happened here?"

"There is no question at all."

The unspoken question was whether the SS could possibly have been involved. Both of them knew that the SS was entirely capable of an atrocity like this one. The unspoken question continued unspoken.

"If you will be good enough to wait for me, Herr Oberstleutnant," the Generalmajor said, "Perhaps we can arrange to route you via Dresden on your way back."

"I am at the Herr Generalmajor's pleasure," the portly policeman in uniform said.

The Generalmajor walked out of his concrete office, down a flight of stairs, and presented himself to a Generaloberst in his slightly larger office.

"I have the full report, Herr General," he said. "Together with some insignia taken from the bodies—"

The colonel Generaloberst stopped him, with a wave of his hand, from opening his briefcase.

"Has intelligence come up with the name of someone who can handle this matter?"

"Von Greiffenberg," the Generalmajor said. "For the moment, he's the only one readily available. He's on convalescent leave."

"And is he physically able to undertake the journey?"

"Yes, sir."

"His wife is a member of the Russian nobility," the colonel general said. "It will be suggested that he would believe the communists to be capable of anything."

"He was at Samur with General Waterford. It is considered important that Lieutenant Colonel Bellmon voluntarily inspect the site."

The Generaloberst shrugged. "What do you need from me?" he asked.

"Travel documents, and authority to take the American from the stalag."

"And if he won't give his parole?" the colonel general asked. But even as he asked it, he pushed a button which summoned a badly scarred Oberstleutnant, who stood at the door at attention. "The general will tell you what he must have," the Generaloberst said. "See that he has it, please."

He dropped his eyes to the documents on his desk, and then raised them.

"Let me know what happens, will you?" he asked, politely.

The Generalmajor clicked his heels, walked out of the office, and picked up the telephone on the Oberstleutnant's desk.

"Would you get me, on this number, Colonel von Greiffenberg at his home in Marburg, please?" he said, and then hung up and told the Oberstleutnant what he was going to need in the way of transportation, money, documentation, and supplies.

While the necessary arrangements were being made, the telephone rang. The operator reported that the Colonel Graf von Greiffenberg was not available, but that he had Frau Grafin on the line.

"My dear Frederika," the Generalmajor said, in Russian, which caused the badly scarred Oberstleutnant to raise his eyebrows. "Would you be so good as to tell the Graf that I would be very grateful to be received by him at half past two?"

The Mercedes was crowded. There were four flat-sided cans of gasoline in the trunk, filling it, and two more on the floor-board in the back seat. The fumes filled the car, whose canvas roof was up, and this made smoking impossible. There was salami and a half dozen tins of butter, captured from the English, and four cartons of American cigarettes. The Generalmajor's aide-de-camp rode in the back with the groceries under his feet and the cigarettes, wrapped in gray paper, on his lap. The Generalmajor rode in front beside the driver.

They drove north from Freidberg on the road through Bad Nauheim which took them past the rear of the Kurhotels that faced the large municipal park. In the old days, a *Kur* had meant bathing in the waters of Bad Nauheim and taking a salt-free diet. Now the *Kur* was for convalescent wounded. The roofs of the Kurhotels, small

Victorian-era structures, were now painted with the Red Cross, and the streets and the park were full of soldiers, some ambulatory patients, some pushed in wheelchairs.

They entered upon the autobahn at Bad Nauheim, and drove fifteen miles until they turned off onto another country road—sometimes cobblestone, sometimes macadam. This took them through Giessen. From Giessen, they followed the Lahn River to Marburg an der Lahn and drove to the center of town.

Marburg, one of the ancient university towns, was built up around the old castle which rose from the top of the rocky upcropping in the center of town. They were stopped by a Feldgendarmerie roadblock, and for a moment the Generalmajor wondered if he should have taken the Feldgendarmerie Oberstleutnant with him. Embarrassing questions could be asked about the petrol and the food. He immediately decided he had made the right decision. The less the Feldgendarmerie knew about what he was doing with the information they had provided, the better. The Feldgendarmerie was entirely too cozy with the SS and the Gestapo. Tomorrow or the next day he would turn over what he had found to the Sicherheitsdienst, as a matter probably falling under their responsibility; but he would not let them know what the army was doing on its own about the situation.

They drove past Schloss Greiffenberg, which was several hundred meters off the road. Its steep roofs were also painted with the Red Cross. The Schloss was serving as a neuropsychiatric rehabilitation center.

Three miles beyond the Schloss, they turned off the highway onto a fairly wide dirt road that cut through a pine forest. A mile down the road they came to a cottage. There was a bicycle chained to a steel fence in the stone wall around the cottage, and the tiny garage next to it was open, revealing a tiny two-seater Fiat inside.

"This is the place," the Generalmajor said, when it seemed the driver was about to pass it up. The driver braked the car sharply.

"Help the lieutenant with the packages, and then put the gasoline out of sight in the garage," he said. "Hoarding" of gasoline was a serious offense, even for a man like Greiffenberg.

"Jawohl, Herr Generalmajor."

Colonel Graf von Greiffenberg came out from the cottage. He was a tall gaunt man with wavy silver hair, who wore a shabby tweed jacket, plus fours from some prewar golf-course locker, and a faded cotton plaid shirt.

"The Generalmajor will forgive me," he said. "I was walking in the woods, and just this moment got home." Peter-Paul von Greiffenberg was not at all pleased with the Generalmajor's visit. He believed that it had nothing whatever to do with a discussion of any future command. He suspected that it had something to do with airing dirty linen, and he was not at all interested in that.

"I believe, Colonel," the Generalmajor said, "that convalescent officers are encouraged to play golf and other sports, which will hasten their return to full physical capacity."

"I have been poaching," the Graf said, "not golfing." The remark was a hair's breadth away from insolence.

"Any luck?" the Generalmajor asked with a smile.

"Yesterday and today," the Graf said, wondering what it was that had made him try to provoke a lifelong friend. Possibly, he thought, because he finds me dressed like a peasant and living in a forester's cottage.

"A boar yesterday," von Greiffenberg said, now smiling. "For our lunch today. And a rehbuck today. For tomorrow." The Graf's eyes fell on the sergeant, who was busy taking fuel cans from the trunk. "The Generalmajor is more than kind. I especially appreciate the petrol."

"I have no idea what you're talking about, Colonel," the Generalmajor said. "Certainly you are aware of the regulations prohibiting the diversion of petrol to nonmilitary channels."

A tall woman and a thin girl of about fifteen were now in the doorway of the cottage. The woman had been born a duchess in what was once Petrograd. She had married a count. She carried herself like an aristocrat, the Generalmajor decided, but no one would have mistaken her for a duchess. Her clothing was worn and faded, and she wore neither makeup nor jewelry except for a thin wedding band. The girl, who curtsied as the Generalmajor approached, looked more like a forester's daughter than the product of the union of two ancient and noble families.

"You are soon going to be quite as lovely as your mother," the Generalmajor said. He bowed and kissed the woman's hand. "Elizabeth, you are as lovely as ever."

"Welcome, Herr Generalmajor, to our forester's cabin," the woman said. She spoke in Russian. "Ilse and I have been gardening. Carrots and cabbage. No roses."

"Better times will come," the Generalmajor said. "We must believe that, mustn't we?"

"As we devoutly believe in the final victory," she said, with exquisite sarcasm. The Generalmajor thought that Greiffenberg was wise to keep his wife here in the country. She was unable to conceal that she held the Nazis in nearly as much scorn as she held the communists of her homeland.

"I must, I'm afraid, Frederika, pass up the great pleasure of your company at lunch," the Generalmajor said. "I must speak privately with Peter-Paul."

"Have you a command for him?" Frederika, Grafin von Greiffenberg asked.

"Not quite yet," the Generalmajor said. "The hospital has not seen fit to declare him fit for field service. But I need him to do an errand for me."

"Ilse," the Grafin said to the young girl. "Would you please remove two place settings from the table? And then you and I will take a walk in the woods."

"I am grateful for your understanding," the Generalmajor said.

"I am grateful that you are not sending my husband back to Russia," the Grafin replied, somewhat icily. "Perhaps there will be time for a glass of wine together?"

"Of course," the Generalmajor said.

When the wine had been drunk, and the loin of roast boar put onto the table, and the Grafin and her daughter had left, the Generalmajor decided that he would eat his lunch in peace before opening the briefcase and talking business. What was in the briefcase would ruin anyone's lunch.

[SIX]
Near Szczecin (Stettin), Poland
15 April 1943

There were still patches of unmelted snow here and there on the ground, and it was cold in the rear seat of the Feisler Storche, but the sun was shining brightly, and it was evident that spring would soon bring green to the brown land.

Colonel Graf von Greiffenberg was in pain. His shattered knee hurt from the vibration of the four-hour flight in the small airplane. They had refueled in Leipzig after taking off from the Luftwaffe's fighter plane airstrip in Marburg an der Lahn. Because he had been badly frostbitten in Russia, his toes, fingers, ears, and nose ached—in spite of his woolen socks and gloves and the woolen muffler wrapped around his head. From time to time shivers of pain swept through his body as if his fingers were broken.

He had waited all the previous day for the two Storches to show up. There had been some problem getting two of them at once. When they did finally shown up in Marburg just before dark, he had decided to wait until the following morning to leave. It was a question of his getting where he was going without problems. It would have been foolhardy to make the flight at night, although the pilots, two boys who looked as if they should still be in a Gymnasium someplace, were disappointed at his decision.

Their orders, marked SECRET, directed them to pick up the colonel in two airplanes, and fly him and anyone else he so designated anywhere he desired within lands controlled by the German state. Since they thought that what they were up to was quite different from the facts, they were eager to get at it.

They had taken off from the fighter base at Marburg, which was a one runway affair, built right down the center of what once had been a 160 hectare cornfield. This had been von Greiffenberg land, "rented" to the Luftwaffe for "the duration." Their destination in northern Poland was another fighter strip laid down on what, too, had once been a field owned by a landed member of the aristocracy.

As they approached the field, the colonel saw the stalag next to it. It contained a barracks, and to judge by the line of one-story stables off to one side, a cavalry barracks. There didn't seem to be an artillery park, so it must have been a cavalry barracks. It had once housed, perhaps, some of the Poles who had been sent out to challenge Panzerkampfwagen IIs and IIIs with sabers and glistening lances.

It was now a prisoner-of-war camp, Stalag XVII-B, surrounded by barbed wire, guardhouses, and probably, von Greiffenberg thought, a minefield. They had captured vast quantities of Russian and English mines early in the war, and there had been a period of madness when any flat surface which even remotely could pose a threat to the security of the German Army had been mined.

The pilot of the Storche was unable to establish radio contact with the field, so they flew over it once, to let them know they had arrived, and then landed. A bored junior Luftwaffe officer swaggered out to the Storche, then saw the colonel's insignia on von Greiffenberg's greatcoat, and snapped to attention.

The colonel, once a car had been arranged for him, gave the senior of the two boy pilots their ultimate destination and told him to prepare the most careful possible flight plan—with alternate landing fields and refueling sites. The second passenger must not be endangered in any way, von Greiffenberg told him.

He showed the major commanding the fighter strip enough of his orders to impress him with the fact that he was traveling with the highest priority under the authority of the Oberkommando of the Wehrmacht. And then he went out to the POW compound, taking a strange pleasure in seeing that he was right. It had been a cavalry barracks.

God, what a bloody shame, those horses! Some of the finest in Europe! Slaughtered senselessly.

The stalag commander was an elderly lieutenant colonel of infantry; his uniform carried wound stripes from World War I. A decent chap, von Greiffenberg decided on the spot, given this duty because he was too old for any other.

"How may I be of service to the Herr Oberst Graf?"

Von Greiffenberg produced his orders.

"I wish to confer with Lieutenant Colonel Robert Bellmon," von Greiffenberg announced. "I may take him off your hands for a few days."

That roused the commandant's curiosity, but he was a soldier of the old school. He would ask no questions. If he was to have an explanation beyond the official orders, it would be given to him.

"I'll send for him. And may I offer the Herr Oberst Graf a brandy and something to eat while he is waiting?"

"Yes, please," von Greiffenberg said. "And bring enough to serve Colonel Bellmon, too, if you would be so kind."

While he was waiting, von Greiffenberg left the food untouched—a plate of cold cuts, bread, and what looked like real butter; but he helped himself twice to the French brandy, wondering idly where the commandant had gotten it. The early days of the war, when there had been a good deal of French wine and perfume available to the services, were long over.

Lieutenant Colonel Robert Bellmon marched in, wearing a faded tanker's jacket and woolen olive-drab pants. He stopped before the desk and saluted.

"Lieutenant Colonel Bellmon reporting to the Herr Oberst as directed, sir." His German was fluent. He was a fine-looking officer, von Greiffenberg thought.

"I'm comfortable in English, Colonel," Colonel Graf von Greiffenberg said. "But please don't take that as a reflection upon your German. It's quite good."

"I have been working on it rather hard, Herr Oberst," Bellmon continued in German. "There isn't much else to do here."

"I daresay not," Von Greiffenberg said, in English. He unfastened the lower right-hand pocket of his tunic and took from it an envelope and handed it to Bellmon without explanation.

Bellmon opened the small envelope and took a picture from it. It was of the Colonel Graf von Greiffenberg as a young cavalry officer. He held a child, a girl most likely, of about eighteen months in his arms, beaming down at her with pure delight.

Bellmon looked at it, then at von Greiffenberg, and then started to hand it back.

"You don't recognize the lady, Colonel Bellmon?" von Greiffenberg asked. "I rather hoped you would."

Bellmon looked at the picture again without recognition, and shook his head. "Sorry," he said. "Never saw her before."

"You are married to the lady, Colonel," von Greiffenberg said. "That is Barbara Dianne Waterford Bellmon at age sixteen months."

Bellmon looked again. Now there was no question about it. The baby had Barbara's eyes. He looked at von Greiffenberg for an explanation.

"It was taken at Samur, the French cavalry school," von Greiffenberg said, "by, I recall, your mother-in-law. Your father-in-law was at the time—as he did frequently—cooking beefsteaks over an open fire. The usual result was meat charred on the outside, raw inside, and generally inedible. This never discouraged him in the least."

Bellmon had to smile, although in the back of his mind there was a feeling that he had best be very careful dealing with this man.

"I am sorry, Colonel," Bellmon said. "But I don't recall my father-in-law ever mentioning your name."

"We last exchanged Christmas greetings in 1940," the colonel said. "After that, obviously, it was awkward."

"What is it you want of me, Colonel?" Bellmon asked.

"I had hoped to find that you were the sort of officer who does not hate his enemy," von Greiffenberg said. "Who is aware that there are some events which transcend the war immediately at hand. And I hoped that you would believe that despite our present situation, I regard Porky Waterford as a dear friend and colleague, and I dare to presume he feels the same way about me."

"I regret the war, of course," Bellmon said. "But I must in honesty tell you that I believe the government which you serve is morally reprehensible."

Von Greiffenberg neither reacted to that nor seemed even to hear it.

"Colonel, it has come to the attention of the High Command that the Soviets, in the Katyn Forest, near Smolensk, executed approximately five thousand Polish officers and cadets, who were their prisoners, and buried them in a mass, unmarked grave."

Bellmon didn't reply. It sounded like something from a propaganda movie. But Colonel von Greiffenberg was real. And unless he had lost all powers of judgment, he knew von Greiffenberg was dead earnest, not at all the sort of man who would be capable of invoking an old friendship for some propaganda gimmick. Bellmon looked at von Greiffenberg and waited for him to continue.

The colonel opened his briefcases and placed thirty or more large photographs on the desk and then, next to them, he laid out corroded and rotting insignia, identification papers, tailor's labels, the evidence that had been turned over to him in the forester's cottage outside Marburg.

"Identification of the remains is underway," von Greiffenberg said. "So far we have positively identified the remains of two general officers, sixty-one colonels, large numbers of other grades, and more than 150 officer cadets. Each was shot in the back of the head with a .32 caliber pistol. And each had his hands bound behind him at the time."

"Forgive me, Colonel," Bellmon said, trying very hard to keep his voice under control, "but how do I know this atrocity took place under the Russians?"

"At the site, at this moment, are fourteen forensic scientists, all from neutral countries. They are prepared to give their professional judgment as to how long the prisoners have been dead. Even given the widest latitude so far as the date of death is concerned, there is absolutely no possibility that German forces could have been involved. During the time of the atrocity, Soviet forces, and Soviet forces alone, held the area."

"Doubtless, you will make these facts known, via the International Red Cross, and other agencies."

"And doubtless, our accusations will be rejected as anti-Soviet propaganda," von Greiffenberg said.

"And that's where I come in?" Bellmon asked.

"I rather doubt that even you, Colonel Bellmon, would be believed outside the military establishment," von Greiffenberg said. "Our thinking is this. The honor of the German officer corps is involved. We want a member of the American officer corps, the son of a general, the son-in-law of a general, a man likely himself to become a general officer, to see this outrage with his own eyes. To spare him, if you like, from having to decide from secondhand information whether or not this is anti-Soviet propaganda."

"To what end?" Bellmon asked.

"That should be obvious," von Greiffenberg said. "What I would like from you, Colonel, what I beg of you, is your parole for whatever time it takes us to fly to Katyn, which is near Smolensk. There you will confer with the neutral physicians and scientists on the scene and then return here."

"If you're going to win the war, what difference does it make?" Bellmon asked.

Von Greiffenberg paused a long moment before replying.

"When we win the war, Colonel, I shall take great pleasure in bringing the barbarians who did this terrible thing to justice."

"But there is the possibility, which you must consider by now, that the war is lost," Bellmon said. "Is that it?"

"As a loyal officer, of course, I believe in the final victory," von Greiffenberg said.

"You understand, of course," Bellmon said, "that I could not make any statements of any kind so long as I'm a prisoner."

"Naturally not," von Greiffenberg said. "However, it is our routine practice to exchange the severely wounded and the dying, and routine practice to assign several officer prisoners to accompany the wounded and dying."

"If I go along, you're offering to have me exchanged?" He wondered if he was being bribed.

"It would be in our interests to do so," von Greiffenberg said. "And in yours. Should you become convinced this was a Soviet atrocity, as I believe you will by the evidence, you will then be in great danger should the fortunes of war see you come into Soviet hands."

"I'm sure you have considered the possibility that I would accept the offer to be exchanged, and then accuse your side," Bellmon said.

"The evidence is irrefutable," von Greiffenberg said. "And furthermore, Colonel Bellmon, I believe you to be an officer and a gentleman."

I am being soft-soaped, Bellmon thought. But then, he thought, what possible harm could it do?

"Very well," Bellmon said. "I will give you my parole. When do we leave?"

"Immediately."

[SEVEN]
Stalag XVII-B, Stettin
11 October 1944

There had been Christmas packages from the Red Cross. By some fluke in the distribution system, they had arrived in Stettin, in northwest Poland, a week after they had come into German hands in Sweden. The commandant had agreed to issue them immediately. The important thing was that for a few days there would be powdered coffee (*real* coffee) and chocolate and gloves and handkerchiefs and paperback copies of Ernest Hemingway novels. There was no sense in putting the packages into a warehouse for issue on Christmas Day. Christmas Day here would be 25 December 1944, no different at all from 24 December and 26 December, just one more day in a former cavalry barracks in northwest Poland.

Bellmon had made the decision that he would drink his powdered coffee full strength, black. He would not drink it all at once, but save it for when he really wanted a cup of coffee, and then have a real cup of coffee, strong and black. He would not try to stretch it, to make it last longer. He would have as many cups of strong coffee as there were in the tin, whenever he wanted one, and then he would do without.

He had never felt quite so alone, quite so fearful for his sanity.

Eighteen months had passed since his trip to the Katyn forest. During that time there had been thirty-one letters from Barbara, single sheets of paper which folded to make a self-contained envelope. Some of these had arrived out of sequence, and none had arrived on any sort of predictable schedule. He had once gone five months without any letters at all.

He kept the letters in a Dutch Masters cigar box on the table beside his bed. The cigars had come without explanation six months before, half a box for each officer. Before the cigars had come, he had kept Barbara's letters wrapped up in a sweater.

Bellmon was executive officer of the prisoner staff. The senior prisoner was an infantry full colonel who had never served in the infantry. He was a professor of art history at the University of Wisconsin who had been commissioned as a military government officer, and who had been captured in Italy. He was not a soldier, although he wanted to behave like one, and he vacillated between relief that he had a professional soldier on whom to rely for decisions, and resentment toward Bellmon, based on the fact that Bellmon's competence pointed out his own incompetence.

Bellmon had not told the colonel about Katyn, and he had not told him about the package he kept hidden within the thin cotton mattress on his bed. The package, according to a letter from Colonel Count Peter-Paul von Greiffenberg, contained twenty-four eight-by-ten-inch photographs of the horrors of Katyn. Others showed Bellmon at the site with the neutral forensic experts. It also contained identification papers, letters, and insignia taken from the corpses. It was sealed with a wax seal of the Oberkommando of the Wehrmacht, and beneath a sheet of acetate was a letter on OKW stationery, signed by Generaloberst Hasso von Manteuffel, stating that the package was in the possession of Lieutenant Colonel Robert Bellmon, United States Army, by direction of the OKW, and that it was neither to be examined, nor taken from him, by any member of the German military or security forces for any reason. The letter bore the seals of both the OKW and the SS. Bellmon could not read the signature of the SS official.

He was clearly being used by the Germans. And he had been tempted, more than once, to throw the package into the small cast-iron stove, to remove any suggestion at all that he was offering aid and comfort to the enemy.

But there was no question in his mind that the Soviet secret police, with the full support of the Red Army, had in fact taken 5,000 captured Polish officers—among them at least 250 cadets, some of whom were no older than fourteen—tied their hands behind their back, forced them to lie in open trenches, and then shot each of them in the back of the neck with a small caliber pistol.

There was no question in his mind, either, after seeing this atrocity with his own eyes, that at Katyn he had become one with Colonel von Greiffenberg and other Germans like him, and that now the Russian ally had become his enemy. Sure, war by its very nature was obscene, and there were atrocities on battlefields. He'd heard about those all his life, and he'd seen some in North Africa. Indeed, he had expected to be shot, instead of taken prisoner, when they got his tank.

But that was the battlefield. What the Russians had done was barbaric beyond understanding. They had decided to subdue the Poles for the future by wiping out their leaders, young and old, even their chaplains. Bellmon had identified with the dead Poles. Many of them wore cavalry boots. They were cavalry officers, captured probably as he had been, without real fault of their own. Because they had been taught to expect it, they would have expected the treatment required by the Geneva Convention. Instead, they had been slaughtered like cattle.

At first, he had told himself that when he was exchanged, as Colonel von Greiffenberg said he would be, he would wait thirty days to regain control of his emotions and of his ability to think clearly and objectively, before he turned the package over to the proper authorities.

But then it had become apparent that he was not to be exchanged. He didn't understand why, and there were fifty possibilities. But he had come to accept that he was not going to be exchanged, that there would not be thirty days' liberation leave to spend with Barbara in Carmel, at least not until the war was over. He had no idea what had kept him from being exchanged as von Greiffenberg had promised; but he sensed, somehow, that it had nothing to do with the German officer.

As executive officer of the prisoner staff he was ex-officio chairman of the escape committee. The escape committee was brave, enthusiastic, imaginative, and in Bellmon's professional judgment, incredibly stupid. There was no way that they could get out of Poland, much less out of German-occupied Europe. There was no underground here who could help them, as there was supposed to be in France. That was the primary reason the Stalag had been established in Poland. The Germans were not fools.

Of course, he questioned that judgment, too, wondering if he had lost his courage, or if he was subconsciously identifying with the German enemy because of what he had seen at Katyn, because von Greiffenberg had gone to the cavalry school at Samur with Porky Waterford and cradled Barbara in his arms.

He had imagined he'd get some sort of pressure from the Germans, at least a subtle pointing out that the Germans and the Americans were the same kind of people, functioning under a Christian ethic; that it was really absurd that they should be fighting each other, rather than the common, godless Soviet enemy; that Hitler, had after all, gone out of his way not to get into a war with the Americans.

But there had been nothing at all like that. The only propaganda to which he had been subjected was the magazines and newspapers in the Stalag library. And that was to be expected. There was nothing more reprehensible about providing captured American officers copies of the German Army magazine *Signal* than there was in providing captured German officers copies of *Yank*.

In September, the British and French officers who had been in the stalag with them had been transferred elsewhere. Stalag XVII-B was now entirely American.

That had posed certain administrative and logistic problems. Without Bellmon having paid much attention to it, captured British and French enlisted men had been the logistic backbone of the stalag. They were the cooks, the orderlies, the latrine cleaners, the laundry workers, the bedmakers.

When the British and French officers left, so did their enlisted men, and that left the kitchen and the laundry without people to operate them. There was a cook, a phlegmatic Bavarian, and a laundry supervisor, but no labor force.

Bellmon had crossed with the senior prisoner over that.

"What we'll have to do," the senior prisoner said, "is simply take turns. On a roster. Make it fair."

Bellmon was furious but kept his temper. If the colonel did not realize that they were not boy scouts out roughing it in the woods, he would have to teach him.

"We are officers," Bellmon said. "In many cases field-grade officers. We will not work in laundries. Commissioned officers of the United States will not be kitchen helpers. Commissioned officers will not clean latrines."

"Oh, for God's sake, Bob, we're prisoners."

"We're officers," Bellmon said. "You, Colonel, as a reservist, as much as me."

"Since you bring that up, Bob," the colonel said, without much conviction, "I *am* the senior officer. I could order you to do what has to be done."

"And I would obey your order. And the day we get out of here, I would bring you up on charges of conduct unbecoming an officer and a gentleman," Bellmon said.

"Who the hell would ever know if your precious officer's dignity was relaxed?" the senior prisoner demanded. When he said that, Bellmon had sensed he had won. The colonel was more afraid of him than of the Germans.

"The enemy," Bellmon said, gently. "That's the point, Colonel."

The commandant said that he had requested a contingent of enlisted prisoners to take over the housekeeping duties, but he had no idea when, or even if, they would be sent.

No officer details were sent to the kitchen, and none to the laundry. Two German soldiers were sent to the kitchen to help the cook. Officers carried their mess plates to the mess, ate, washed their plates and cutlery, and left with them. Officers washed their own underwear, and if they wanted clean outer garments, washed and pressed them themselves.

Bellmon spent long hours with a cast-iron clothes press, keeping his trousers, shirts, and tunic neat. He tested the principle of inspiring by example. It had a thirty percent effectiveness factor, he found. One officer in three followed his example and tried to look as much like an officer as he could. Two out of three let themselves go.

Bellmon stopped talking to the unpressed and unshaven, or even acknowledging them with a nod of his head. When they sought him out, mostly for his skill as an interpreter, or for his opinion on the legality of a move they planned in connection with an escape attempt, he refused to deal with them.

"Can I have a moment of your time, Colonel?"

"You need a shave, Lieutenant. And your uniform is foul."

They came back, shaven, in slightly more presentable uniforms. He told them what they wanted to know. He shamed the senior prisoner, who not only resumed shaving daily, but began a British-style mustache.

The slovenly percentage dropped to fifty percent and then below. Some of the shaven and self-laundered began to mock him with crisp salutes whenever they met him. He returned the salutes as crisply, with motions right off the parade ground at the Point. The mockery in the salutes gave way to casual touching of the hand to the eyebrow. But they were still salutes. Not to everybody from everybody, but from all the company grade to all the field grade, and from everybody to the senior prisoner and Bellmon.

He was in command. What good it would do, specifically, he didn't know. But he believed, devoutly, that the prisoner complement of Stalag XVII-B was a military formation, and a military formation must have discipline. Without discipline, a body of men becomes rabble. Rabble dies, either on the battlefield or in a POW camp.

Six weeks after the French and British left, a convoy of canvas-topped Hanomag trucks came through the heavy wooden gates of the compound and discharged four truckloads of American enlisted prisoners, twenty-two to a truck.

Bellmon heard the sound of the trucks and looked out his window and watched the troops get off. Some showed signs of long imprisonment (how he could tell, he didn't know, but he knew), and others had apparently only recently been captured. They were all dispirited. They sat in groups immediately to the side of the trucks that had brought them, and waited for whatever was going to happen to them. Many of them looked as if they really didn't care.

Bellmon buttoned his tunic, straightened his tie in the mirror he had carefully made by polishing a sheet of steel with ashes, and went out into the courtyard.

At first none of the prisoners reacted to his presence beyond looking at him expectantly. Bellmon put his hands on his hips and let his eyes fall on them, one at a time, looking carefully and without expression. He had looked at perhaps thirty of the prisoners that way when one of them suddenly got to his feet and walked over to him.

"Sergeant MacMillan, sir," he said.

MacMillan wore the stripes of a technical sergeant sewn to the gabardine tunic issued to paratroops. Bellmon could see where the insignia of the 82nd Airborne had been cut from it. The Germans regarded that insignia as a special souvenir, much as Americans were delighted to get their hands on the death's-head insignia of the SS.

MacMillan was a young man, stocky and muscular, a typical parachutist. Irish, Bellmon thought. Or maybe Scotch. But he sensed something about this noncom. Somehow he knew that this sergeant was a regular.

"Is that the way you were taught to report to an officer, Sergeant?" Bellmon asked, quietly. Sergeant MacMillan looked at him for a moment, then popped to attention. He threw his hand to his forehead, held it.

"Technical Sergeant MacMillan reports to the colonel with party of eighty-seven, sir," he said.

Bellmon returned the salute.

"Fall the men in, Sergeant," he said.

Macmillan did a precise about-face movement.

"All right," he bellowed. "Fall in!"

There was some stirring, and one or two men got to their feet, but there was no movement toward Sergeant MacMillan, no suggestion that they intended to obey this order.

MacMillan didn't move for a full minute. Then, very deliberately, he walked to the man sitting nearest to him on the ground. He bent over him, picked him up by his shirt front, and punched him in the mouth. The soldier, a buck sergeant, fell on his rear end and put his hand to his bleeding mouth.

None of the others moved at all, but one man spit.

"Get up," T/Sgt MacMillan said, softly, and pointed with his left hand, finger extended, to the spot where he wanted the man to stand. The buck sergeant backed away from MacMillan like a crab, but then got to his feet and walked to where MacMillan had indicated, and more or less came to attention.

"Anybody else?" MacMillan asked, looking at the faces of the others. No one moved or said a word. "Fall in on him," MacMillan said. "Three ranks."

Slowly, resentfully, the others formed on him. When they were all in place, standing at a position that charitably could be called attention, MacMillan did another snappy about-face and saluted again.

"Sir," he said, "the detachment is formed."

"Very good, Sergeant," Bellmon ordered. "Prepare the detachment for inspection."

MacMillan did another about-face movement, and gave the commands. "Dress, right, *dress!* Open ranks, *march!"*

Bellmon marched to the left-hand corner of the formation. MacMillan marched to join him. Bellmon went down the ranks, pausing to look at each man, giving each man a chance to look at him. Then he marched out in front again.

"Stand at ease," he ordered. "My name is Bellmon. I am the executive officer. The first thing we are going to do is feed you, show you where you will be quartered, and see that you have a shower. We have to fend for ourselves here. Sergeant MacMillan will appoint mess hall, shower point, and delousing details of six men under a noncom each." He looked at MacMillan, who was standing at parade rest in front of the formation. "First Sergeant," Bellmon called. "Front and center."

MacMillan walked up and saluted still again. Bellmon told him where the kitchen and the shower were.

"When you get things running, come to my quarters," he said.

MacMillan nodded.

Bellmon raised his voice.

"First Sergeant, take the detachment," he said, and then did an about-face and marched back to his barracks building.

A group of officers had been watching from inside.

"Colonel, can I ask a question?" one of the captains said. Bellmon nodded. "What would you have done if they had just kept on sitting there?"

Bellmon felt anger sweep through him. It must have shown on his face, for the captain quickly said, "Sir, the question wasn't supposed to sound flip."

"That's a regular army sergeant out there, Captain," Bellmon said. "He would have been unable to leave them sitting there. An officer had called for them to fall in, and they would have fallen in, or somebody, maybe the sergeant, would have been dead."

He wondered how he knew, why he was so sure, that Technical Sergeant MacMillan, who was hardly more than a boy, was regular army.

When MacMillan came to his room, he gave him a cup of the real coffee.

"How long has the colonel been a prisoner, sir?"

"Since North Africa," Bellmon said. "Kasserine Pass."

"They got me about three weeks ago," MacMillan said. "Just before the goddamn war is about over."

"We hadn't heard the 82nd was engaged," Bellmon said. When MacMillan looked surprised that he had known his division, Bellmon explained he had seen where the patches had been cut off.

"Operation fucking Market-Garden," MacMillan said. "We tried to grab the Rhine bridges. Biggest fuck-up in the war. We got the shit kicked out of us."

"That's normally when they catch prisoners," Bellmon said. "Kasserine was a big fuck-up, too."

"How'd the colonel get caught, if you don't mind my asking?"

"I was in a tank. A PzKwIV got us. I got blown off."

"We went across this fucking river," MacMillan said. "Little fucking English boats. No fucking oars. Collapsible sides. They mortared the shit out of us in the water. And then when we got to the other side, there was no fucking ammo. No fucking ammo. How the fuck do they expect you to fight without ammo?"

"So what happened?"

"So we took it off the dead, and shot that, and when that was over . . . what the fuck was I supposed to do? Do a John Wayne? Charge with a fucking carbine bayonet in my hand?"

"What did you do?" Bellmon asked.

"I got out of my fucking hole and put my hands up, that's what I did."

"I tried to play dead," Bellmon said, aware this was the first time he had ever told the story. "But they saw me breathing, rolled me over, and stuck a .45 up my nose."

"So what happens to us now, Colonel?" MacMillan asked.

"We wait for the war to end," Bellmon said.

"We was nine days on the train, plus half a day on the truck," MacMillan said. "We're a long way from our lines. How far are we from the Russians?"

"I just don't know," Bellmon said.

"There's no sense in trying to get out of this fucking place now," Macmillan said. "There's no way we can get back on our own, goddamn it."

"MacMillan," Bellmon said, "there is an active, enthusiastic escape committee here."

MacMillan looked at him.

"If they ever reach the point where they're going to try it, I will order them not to," Bellmon said. "But in the meantime, I don't think you should let your opinion of the situation be known."

"Keep 'em busy, huh, Colonel?"

"If I had some whitewash, I'd have them painting rocks, Sergeant," Bellmon said. He laughed. He realized it was the first time in a very long time that he had laughed.

MacMillan grunted understandingly. They were smiling at each other now, two hometown people who had found each other in an alien land.

"Are there any more regulars here, Colonel? Or is it you and me?"

"Just you and me, MacMillan," Bellmon said.

"Ah, what the fuck, Colonel," MacMillan said. "If it wasn't for the war, you'd still probably be a first john, and I'd still be a corporal."

II

[ONE]

United States Military Academy
West Point, New York
22 December 1944

Cadet Corporal Sanford T. Felter, of the class of 1946, sat at attention on the edge of a straight-backed, rather ornately carved wooden chair in the outer office of the Commandant of the Corps of Cadets. His rigid back was three inches from the rear of the chair, and he held his plumed shako in a white-gloved hand. He had been summoned from the dismissal formation following the formal parade immediately preceding the Christmas holidays.

He was small and slight, rather pasty-faced in complexion, and his face showed signs of the acne which had nearly cost him his competitive appointment to the Academy.

He was staring straight ahead at a portrait of a senior officer he had never heard of, but who apparently had done something sufficiently meritorious to have his portrait hung in the outer office of the commandant. He was going over in his mind what would likely happen inside the commandant's office, and what his responses should be. He was uneasy, but determined.

"If Felter is out there," a metallic voice came over the intercom, "send him in."

"You may go in," the commandant's secretary said.

Felter stood up. He put his shako squarely on his head, and picked up his M1 Garand rifle. As long as he had been at the Point, he had never before reported under arms to an officer indoors. He wasn't sure if he should march in with the piece at right shoulder arms, and then come to present arms, or whether he should march in with the piece at trail arms, come to attention, and render the rifle salute.

He decided, right then, to do it at trail arms.

He knocked at the door, waited for the command to enter, and then marched in, coming to a stop eighteen inches from the huge, polished mahogany desk. He came to attention, lowered the butt of the Garand onto the carpet, and rendered the first movement of the rifle salute. He moved his right hand across his body, fingers extended and stiff, so the fingertips of his right hand contacted the stacking swivel of the M1 he held in his left hand.

"Sir, Cadet Corporal Felter, Sanford T., reporting to the Commandant of Cadets as ordered, Sir," he said.

The major general behind the desk, who was the Commandant of Cadets, returned the salute. He was an athletic man in his late forties, who wore his gray hair in a closely cropped crew cut. He was the sort of man one *knew* had played football in college, and now spent as much time as he could spare on the golf course.

Felter completed the salute, snapping his right hand quickly back across his body to his side. He stared six inches above the commandant's head, at the knees of a portrait of General Philip H. Sheridan.

"Stand at ease, Felter," the commandant said. Felter moved the muzzle of the Garand four inches forward, moved his left foot six inches to the side, and put his left hand in the small of his back. The position was that of parade rest, but this was the commandant's office and the commandant, and he was a cadet corporal, and parade rest seemed to be the position to assume. In at ease it was permissible to look around. Cadet Corporal Felter lowered his eyes and met those of the commandant.

"I have your resignation, Felter," the general said. "You want to tell me about it?"

"Sir, I believe it speaks for itself," Felter said, without hesitation.

"Oh, no, it doesn't," the general said. "I want to know what curious line of thinking is responsible for it."

"Sir, I believe the war will be over before I would graduate," Felter said.

"And do you have some notion that you will be able to cover yourself with glory?" The general had pushed himself back in his chair, tilting it.

"No, sir."

"But you would like to get in, personally, on the fall of the Thousand Year Reich, is that it? You have a personal involvement?"

"If the general is making reference to my Jewish faith, no, sir."

"Then what the hell is it?" the general snapped, impatiently.

"Sir, I have decided that what I would learn in the active army during the last stages of the war would be more valuable in my military career than what I would learn here, as a cadet."

"Has it occurred to you, Felter, that your idea has been considered, and discarded, by a number of your superiors? It is their considered judgment, with which I fully agree, that the best place for a cadet at this time is at the Academy."

"Yes, sir."

"But you don't agree?" Now there was sarcasm in his tone.

"No, sir."

"You know what's going to happen to you, don't you? You're going to be sent to an infantry replacement training center, run through basic training, and put into the pipeline. Three months from now, maybe less, you'll be a rifleman in a line company."

Cadet Corporal Felter did not reply.

"I asked you if you knew what this resignation means to you, Felter," the general said, coldly. "Please pay me the courtesy of a reply."

"Sir, I very much dislike having to dispute you, sir," Felter said, forcing himself to meet the general's eyes.

"Goddamn you, you arrogant little pup, dispute me!" the general said.

"Sir," Felter said. "According to regulations, when a cadet who has completed two or more years at the Academy enters the ranks, he will be given constructive credit for basic training, sir, and will be eligible for further assignment."

"I presume you're sure of that," the general said. "I confess I didn't know that. But all that means is that they will hand you an M1 and a bayonet that much sooner. Goddamn it, Son, the army has invested two years in you. We don't want you killed off as a goddamned private."

"Sir, I have reason to believe that I qualify for one or two procurement programs."

"What kind of procurement programs?"

"There is a critical shortage of interpreters in German and Polish and Russian. There is a critical shortage of POW interrogators with fluency in the same languages. I'm not sure I meet the criteria for a POW interrogator, but I am sure that I am qualified as an interpreter. If the shortage still exists when I go in the ranks, I think it is reasonable to presume that I would be assigned such duties."

"And if they hand you a rifle and tell you go stick the bayonet in somebody?"

"That is the worst possible projection, sir," Felter said. "But even in that event, I believe that service as an infantry rifleman would be of more value to me in my future career than spending the next year as a cadet and missing active service, sir."

"You keep talking about your career, Felter. You are resigning your appointment. How is that going to affect your career?"

"I intend to apply for readmission to the Academy following the war, sir, under the regulations providing for the admission of regular army enlisted men."

"And what makes you so sure that they'd let you back in?"

"I don't feel that active service would be a bar to readmission, sir," Felter said.

"There used to be an offense, Felter, called silent insolence. That remark came pretty close to it."

"I beg the general's pardon. No insolence was intended."

"This whole goddamned resignation is insolent!" the Commandant of Cadets snapped.

"It is not so intended, sir."

"OK, Felter. I'm calling your bluff. I will give you precisely sixty seconds to reconsider your resignation. You may consult your watch."

Felter raised his wrist, watched as the sweep second hand completed a circle from seventeen seconds past the minute. Then he put his hand back to his side.

"Corporal, I now give you an opportunity to withdraw your resignation," the commandant said, formally, but not unkindly.

"Thank you, sir, but no, sir," Felter said.

"Report to your battalion tactical officer," the general said. "Tell him that your resignation is being processed, and that you will remain assigned to your company pending further action. You will not, repeat not, go on Christmas leave."

"Yes, sir."

"You are dismissed, Mister Felter," the general said.

Cadet Corporal Sanford T. Felter rendered the rifle salute, did an about-face, and marched out of the Commandant of Cadets' office. His stomach hurt, and he was afraid that he was going to be sick to his stomach.

The Commandant of Cadets put Cadet Corporal Felter's personal and academic records together in a neat stack, and then he asked his secretary to ask the General's secretary if the General could give him a couple of minutes. "The General" was the Commandant, the United States Military Academy at West Point, and the Commandant of Cadets immediate and only superior at the Point. He was a lieutenant general. The Commandant of Cadets was aware that there was something actually ludicrous in a situation where a twenty-year-old cadet corporal had backed a major general into a corner, where he had to go ask a lieutenant general what to do.

When the Commandant of Cadets' secretary called back a minute later to say that the General was free to see him, he picked up Felter's records and walked down the portrait-lined corridor of the building to the office of the Commandant, the United States Military Academy.

"Would you like coffee, Charley, or something a little stronger?" the Commandant asked, when he had waved him into his large, rather elegantly furnished office. The Commandant was a tall, thin, very erect man whose uniform hung loosely over his shoulders. He was known to the Corps of Cadets behind his back as either the Hawk or the Vulture.

"Strong, please, sir," the Commandant of Cadets said. "I guess the little sonofabitch got to me. There aren't many people I can't stare down."

"And you were probably thinking, Charley, 'If I can't go, why the hell should you get to go?' "

"Christ, I suppose so," the Commandant of Cadets said. " 'What did you do in the war, Daddy? Why, I wiped noses and changed diapers at the Academy, that's what Daddy did.' "

The Commandant chuckled. He handed him a scotch and water.

"Thank you, sir," he said.

"Plus, of course," the Commandant said, "he's right."

"You really think so?"

"So do you," the Commandant of West Point said. "You don't, you can't, learn about war sitting in a classroom."

"Christ, the whole class of '46 will try this, once it gets out."

"Not necessarily," the Commandant said.

"I think they will," the Commandant of Cadets said. "Hell, I would."

"They're not eligible for direct commissions," the Commandant said. "Felter is."

"He didn't say anything about a direct commission," the Commandant of Cadets said, visibly surprised. "That's the first I heard about that."

"He probably figured that would really make you blow your top. But the fact is, he is eligible for a direct commission as a linguist-interrogator. Two years of college, and fluency in one, or preferably more languages on the short list. He speaks Russian, Polish, and German."

"If he gets a direct commission, he could never come back here," the Commandant of Cadets said.

"I disagree with you there. We're already starting to pick up bright young reserve officers to run them through here. If he's right, he could come back."

"Right about what, sir?"

"That the war will shortly be over," the Commandant said. "He may be wrong. This may be a lot longer war than we think it will be. We're getting the shit kicked out of us in the Bulge, Charley."

"Yeah, while you and I sit here drinking scotch whiskey, and watching that little Jew manipulate the system."

"If I thought he was manipulating it for his personal benefit, I would personally see to it that he wound up in a line company," the Commandant of West Point said. "But what I think we have here, Charley, is a perfectly bona fide case of devotion to duty."

"What do you want me to do, General? Discharge him from the Corps of Cadets and turn him over to his draft board?"

"No," the Commandant said. "What I want you to do, Charley, is to change the training schedule."

"Sir?"

"I want the reveille formation on 2 January 1945 to be in full dress. I want the band there, not just the drums and the bugles. I want the color guard. I want Felter there in pinks and greens. *You*, in your pinks and greens and all your decorations, will hold the Bible while I, wearing mine, swear him in. I want an adjutant, an officer not a cadet, to read his orders in a very loud voice. 'Second Lieutenant Whateverhisnameis Felter will immediately proceed to the Overseas Replacement Depot, Camp Kilmer, New Jersey, for priority air-shipment to'—a division in the field. Have him sent somewhere flashy, maybe the 82nd Airborne, or the Big Red One, or one of the armored divisions. You follow me, Charley?"

"Yes, Sir," the Commandant of Cadets said. "I see what you're doing."

"I want the flags flying, and the band playing 'Army Blue,' " the Commandant of the United States Military Academy said. "When the the Corps of Cadets marches by, at eyes right, I want every goddamned eye to be wet with emotion and green with envy. If I thought I could get away with it, I'd have the bugler sound the charge."

[TWO]

First Lieutenant Wallace T. Rogers, Infantry (USMA '43) was Cadet Corporal Sanford T. Felter's tactical officer. A tactical officer is mixture of disciplinarian, mother hen, and observer of the cadets committed to his charge. He was having as much trouble with the resignation of Corporal Felter as was the Commandant of Cadets.

Lieutenant Rogers had volunteered for the airborne, and upon graduation had been sent to the Parachute School at Fort Benning, Georgia; and upon graduation from there, he'd been sent to the Airborne Center at Fort Bragg, North Carolina, where, on his very first jump as a platoon commander, he had been blown off the drop zone and into a stand of pine trees. He'd suffered a compound fracture of his left leg, just above the ankle.

On his release from the Fort Bragg Army Hospital to limited duty, he had been assigned to the United States Military Academy at West Point as a tactical officer.

His classmates, his friends, were in combat, commanding troops around the world, and here he was baby-sitting the cadets. And now Felter was trying to pull this resignation business.

Lieutenant Rogers, moreover, was aware that he did not like Cadet Corporal Sanford T. Felter. He was even willing to admit that there just might be an element of anti-Semitism in his dislike, but he really believed that it wasn't anti-Semitism but a personality clash based on chemistry. He just didn't like Felter's type.

Rogers was tall, Felter was short. Rogers was muscular, Felter was skinny. Rogers had had to really crack the books, Felter seemed to have a mind like a camera. He saw or heard something once, and thereafter could effortlessly call it forth from his memory. Rogers was gregarious, Felter was a loner. Rogers was a team player, Felter, as this resignation business proved, was completely immune to peer group pressure.

Wallace T. Rogers, aware of his personal feelings toward Cadet Corporal Sanford T. Felter, leaned over backward to make sure that not only did he treat Felter exactly as he treated the other cadets, but that Felter would never suspect that Rogers considered him to be a wise-ass Jewboy who had no business being in the Corps, or in the regular army.

When the word from the Commandant of Cadets had made its way down the chain of command to the company, instead of sending the charge of quarters to fetch Felter, Lt. Rogers told the CQ he was going to see Felter in his room.

Felter's door was open, and Felter was in the process of buttoning himself into his greatcoat. He sensed the presence of Lieutenant Rogers, turned, and snapped to attention.

"Rest," Rogers said, immediately, and smiled. "I seem to have caught you as you were leaving."

"Sir, I was going to the telephone."

"Then I'm glad I caught you, Felter," Rogers said, smiling. "I just got the word from the Commandant of Cadets. You are authorized Christmas leave."

"Yes, sir," Felter said. "Thank you, sir. Sir, may I ask if there is some reason they changed their minds?"

"They didn't say, Felter. I can guess . . ."

"Please do, sir."

"Well, I don't imagine with everything shut down for the holidays, that very much can be done about your resignation. And the commandant probably realized there was no reason you shouldn't be granted leave."

"Yes, sir," Felter said. "That seems logical. Thank you, sir."

Felter decided that what it really was was that the Commandant of Cadets was giving him another chance to think it over, that after his leave he would be given another chance to withdraw his resignation.

"You're going to have to hustle to make the 4:48, Felter," Lieutenant Rogers said.

"Yes, sir."

"Get your gear, and I'll run you to the station in my car."

"Thank you very much, sir."

There was no time for Felter to call home and tell them he would be late. He called home from Grand Central. His mother answered the telephone and told him that Sharon and his father had gone to Pennsylvania Station in Newark to meet him, and hadn't come back yet. He told his mother that he had missed the first train and would be home in about an hour.

On the train ride down the Hudson River to New York, he had considered again what, if anything, he should tell his parents, and more importantly, Sharon, of his intended resignation. He decided again to tell them nothing about it until he knew for sure what would happen. There was no point in going through the explosion that would follow his announcement until he had to. He had no intention of debating the issue with them.

Felter took the Hudson tubes from Manhattan to Newark attracting curious stares in his long, gray, brass-buttoned greatcoat and brimmed cap with the brim precisely one inch over his eyebrows; and again there were stares on the bus from the station to the Weequahic section of Newark. There weren't that many West Point cadets anywhere, and there was only one in the Weequahic section of Newark.

Nice, upwardly mobile young Jewish boys from Weequahic tried to get in Yale and Harvard, not the United States Military Academy. Although some had rushed to the recruiting stations after Pearl Harbor, and there were as many blue-starred flags hanging from windows to announce a son or a father in the service in Weequahic as there were anywhere else, Sandy Felter was aware that he was probably the only individual in Weequahic who did not plan to take off his uniform as soon as the war was over.

When she saw him get off the bus, Sharon came out of the Old Warsaw Bakery, on Aldine Street, and let him hug her. The greatcoat was so bulky that he really couldn't feel any of her except the warmth of her back under his hands.

Inside the bakery over the cash register, there was a picture of him as a plebe in a small frame with two little American flags crossed over it. It rather embarrassed him. He knew the only reason his parents were happy that he was at West Point was because it kept him out of what his father called the trenches. His father had been a Polish conscript in World War I.

When he saw Sharon, and smelled her, and tasted her, he wondered if he had done the right thing. If he stayed, he would live. The war was going to be over. He and Sharon could be married the day he graduated, and then he would have the four years of his obligated service to convince her that being a regular army officer was just as good and just as prestigious a way of life as a lawyer's or a doctor's or some other professional's. Right now, Sharon, her parents, and his thought he was still behaving like a child.

He had, he realized, made the right decision about not telling them about resigning. It would have ruined Christmas. They were Jews, Polish and Russian Jews on Sandy Felter's side, and Czech and German Jews on Sharon's, but they celebrated

Christmas anyway. Not in a religious sense of course, but with a Christmas tree and the exchange of presents and all sorts of Christmas baked goods from the old country. There was even a roast goose for Christmas dinner.

He couldn't ruin that.

On Christmas Day after dinner, when both he and Sharon were feeling the wine they'd had with the goose, Sharon's mother caught them kissing on the back stairs. He didn't know how long she had watched them before she made her presence known, but she hadn't seemed all that angry—even though Felter knew that Sharon's mother had taken great pains to make sure they weren't alone in circumstances "where something could happen." They even had to take Sharon's brother with them to the damned movies.

Whenever he could get Sharon alone for a moment to kiss her, he considered again that if he stayed at the Point, in eighteen months he could marry Sharon, and they wouldn't have to take her little brother with them anymore. He didn't believe that Sharon had the same thing happen to her that happened to him (his nuts ached), but he suspected, *knew* somehow, that she wanted to make love with him as much as he wanted to do it with her.

If he went off to the war, he was not only going to break his mother's and his father's heart, but he was liable to get killed, and then he would have died without ever having done it with Sharon.

On 28 December 1944, the field-grade duty officer at West Point telephoned the residence of Thaddeus Felter (formerly Taddeus Felztczy) in Newark, N.J., asked to speak to Cadet Corporal Felter, and told him, after he came on the line, that his leave had been cancelled and that he was to report back to the Academy as soon as possible.

Cadet Corporal Felter was not given a second chance to reconsider his resignation as he'd expected. He was ordered to turn in his cadet uniforms and equipment. He was then outfitted in an insignia-less olive-drab uniform, the "Ike" jacket and trousers now authorized for wear by both officers and enlisted men, and assigned a room in the Hotel Thayer.

He spent December 30 and 31 filling out forms and being fitted for uniforms. He ate a solitary dinner in the Hotel Thayer dining room on New Year's Eve. He called his parents and Sharon, separately, two calls, and wished them a Happy New Year, and told them that no, nothing was wrong.

At 0445 on 2 January 1945, Lieutenant Wallace T. Rogers came to the Hotel Thayer, his arms loaded with uniforms from the officers' sales store and a canvas Valv-pak with FELTER S.T. 2ND LT 0-3478003 already stencilled on its sides. He watched as Felter put on a green tunic and pink trousers and a gabardine trench coat, nodded his approval, and then delivered him to the quarters of the Commandant of Cadets, who fed him breakfast.

At 0615 on the plain, with a light snow falling, Sanford T. Felter raised his right hand and repeated after the Commandant of the United States Military Academy that he would protect and defend the Constitution of the United States from enemies, foreign and domestic, that he would obey all orders of the officers appointed over him, and that he would faithfully discharge the duties of the office he was about to enter. The Commandant of the United States Military Academy ('18), the Commandant of Cadets ('20), First Lieutenant Wallace T. Roger ('43), and the cadet colonel of the Corps of Cadets ('45) shook his hand.

A bull-voiced lieutenant colonel ('28), the sheet of paper flapping in his hands, bellowed, "Attention to Orders," and then went on.

"Second Lieutenant Sanford T. Felter, Infantry, Army of the United States, 0–3478003, having reported upon active duty will proceed immediately to the Overseas Replacement Depot, Camp Kilmer, New Jersey, for further shipment by military air transport, Priority AAA1, to Headquarters, 40th Armored Division, in the field, European Theater of Operations."

He about-faced and saluted the Commandant of West Point and the Commandant of Cadets.

"March past!" the Commandant of West Point ordered.

The cadet colonel and Second Lieutenant Felter marched up onto the low reviewing stand after the adjutant. The band played "The Washington Post March," and the Corps of Cadets marched past the reviewing stand. When the color guard reached the reviewing stand, the band segued to "Army Blue."

"Eyes right!" the first battalion commander called out.

Four bandsmen struck four bass drums. *Boom.*

Everyone knew the lyrics.

"We Say Farewell to Kay-det Gray." *Boom.* "And Don the Army Blue." *Boom.*

The Commandant of West Point looked out the corner of his eye, as he held the hand salute, at the Commandant of Cadets, and Second Lieutenant Felter, and the cadet colonel.

"We Say Farewell to Kay-det Gray." *Boom.* "And Don the Army Blue." *Boom.*

The Commandant of West Point's eyes were misty.

The band segued to "Dixie!"

That sonofabitch, the Commandant of West Point thought. The Commandant of Cadets was a goddamned Rebel, and he was always slipping the word to the bandmaster to play "Dixie." He'd have a word with him.

And then he had second thoughts.

This wasn't the first time the band had played "Dixie" on the plain when a cadet resigned his appointment to go off to a war. The band had played "Dixie" at the last parade for the cadets who had resigned their appointments so they could fight for the Confederacy.

The Corps of Cadets, forming a Long Gray Line, marched off the plain to the strains of "Dixie" to return to the barracks and change uniforms and go, three-quarters of an hour late, to class. Second Lieutenant Sanford T. Felter walked off the reviewing stand and got into the Commandant of Cadets' Ford staff car and was driven to the railroad station.

Lieutenant Wallace T. Rogers saw him onto the train.

"Good luck, Lieutenant," he replied.

"Thank you, sir," Lieutenant Felter replied.

He was home just before three and his father wept and his mother shrieked and wailed as he thought they would.

Sharon told him just after supper, when they were left alone for an hour, that she had made up her mind that she wanted him to do it to her, but that her time of the month had come early and she was sorry that they couldn't.

He reported to the Overseas Replacement Depot at Camp Kilmer at fifteen minutes before midnight, and two days later the Transportation Corps people took him and eight other people by bus to Newark Airport and put him on a C-54 just about full of crates marked FOR MEDICAL OFFICER ETO WHOLE BLOOD RUSH.

[THREE]
Stalag XVII-B
Near Stettin, Poland
3 March 1945

The regulation stated only that a photograph of the Führer would be "prominently displayed." It did not say that there had to be one in every room, or specifically that one be hung on the wall of the commanding officer, although the Führer's stern visage had frowned down from the walls of every commanding officer's office that Colonel Graf Peter-Paul von Greiffenberg could call to mind.

Nevertheless, he would be in this office for the indefinite future, and he simply did not want Adolf Hitler, the Bavarian corporal, staring over his shoulder in an obscene parody of paintings of Christ or photographs of the Pope inspiring the faithful.

He walked to the wall and unhooked the framed photograph. The photo had been hanging there for some time, and the outline of the frame was clearly visible. He could, he thought, hang a swastika large enough to conceal the frame's outline. Anything would be better than the Bavarian corporal.

There was a knock on the open door, and he turned to look at his adjutant, Karl-Heinz von und zu Badner.

"Der Amerikaner Oberstleutnant Bellmon ist hier, Herr Oberst Graf," the lieutenant said. Badner, a tall, erect Prussian with sunken eyes, had left his left arm in Russia, and his tunic sleeve was folded double and pinned up.

"Ask him to come in," Colonel Graf von Greiffenberg said. "I wish to see him alone."

"Jawohl, Herr Oberst Graf," the lieutenant said, and nodded with his head for Bellmon to enter. He closed the door behind him.

"How are you, Colonel?" von Greiffenberg said. "It's good to see you again."

"Very well, thank you, Colonel," Bellmon said. "May I offer the hope that that isn't serious?" There was just the slightest nod of his head toward the colonel's left leg, which, obviously bandaged (and perhaps in a cast), stretched the material of his trouser leg.

"It is recovering well, thank you," von Greiffenberg said. "Some muscle damage. A piece of shrapnel. Enough to keep me from field duty, I'm afraid. It has been decided that I am fit enough to command this stalag."

"I see."

"I regret that I was unable to arrange your repatriation," he continued. He wondered if Bellmon would react to that, if Bellmon blamed him for still being here, when von Greiffenberg had as much as promised that he would be exchanged.

"So do I," Bellmon said, with a smile.

"It could not be arranged," von Greiffenberg said. "I made inquiries."

"I understand, Colonel," Bellmon said, and then he gave into the temptation: "I cry a lot, but I understand."

The remark surprised von Greiffenberg. It was not the sort of jesting remark a professional German officer would make.

"You have the material I sent you?" the colonel asked, formally. He did not expect Bellmon to have it. The risk was too great, and disposing of the Katyn Forest massacre evidence would have been simply a matter of throwing it in a fire.

"Yes, of course," Bellmon said, as if surprised by the question.

So he was an officer, an officer who kept his word even when it was difficult to do so, even at the possible risk of his life. Von Greiffenberg decided to reply in kind.

"I was wounded in the Ardenne Forest," he said. "I was in command of a Panzer regiment. The plan was to capture Liege and Antwerp, primarily to sever your supply lines, and, it was hoped, to avail ourselves of your petrol and rations."

"I see."

"The plan, as I saw it, was audacious," the colonel went on. "It had a fair chance of success." He watched Bellmon's face for his reaction. It was not customary for officers to discuss military operations with their prisoners.

"But apparently, it did not," Bellmon said.

"It was necessary for us to alter the plan, and reestablish our lines," the colonel said, either quoting or paraphrasing the official explanation for the failure.

"I see," Bellmon said again.

"What the plan failed to take into consideration was the capability of your logistic trains, and the limitations of ours. We were, regrettably, unable to maintain the force of the assault as long as necessary. On the other hand, your service of supply was equal to the demands put upon it. I understand that General Patton was able to disengage a six division force, move it one hundred fifty kilometers, and mount a successful counterattack on a six division front, within a total of six days."

That was not the official version of a defeat and Bellmon knew it. He took another chance.

"Do you know General Patton, Colonel?" he asked.

"I played polo with him—against him—in Madrid, sometime in the thirties," von Greiffenberg said. "He was at Samur two years before I was there. I believe he and your father-in-law are quite close, aren't they?"

"No, as a matter of fact, they're not," Bellmon said. "My father-in-law never forgave Patton for going back to the infantry after the first war."

"I wondered why Porky wasn't with Patton's Third Army, but with Simpson's Ninth," von Greiffenberg said. "You've answered that question."

"I think that's just the way the chips fell, Colonel," Bellmon said. "I don't think personalities were involved."

It was the first he had known where Major General Waterford was.

Von Greiffenberg shrugged his shoulders and went on.

"Our attack rather seriously drew down our reserves of forces and supplies," von Greiffenberg said. "A critical part of the plan was to capture Bastogne, a road and rail center. Much of our artillery was expended in an attempt to reduce your forces there. They held out much longer than it was thought they could, and they were ultimately relieved by elements of the 1st Armored Division."

"Bastogne did not fall?"

"After considering the fluidity of the situation," Colonel von Greiffenberg said, a light but unmistakable tone of bitter mockery in his voice, "the Führer decided that the capture of Bastogne was no longer necessary to the plans for final victory."

"And how are the Russians doing?" Bellmon asked.

"It has been necessary to adjust our lines across the Soviet Union and Poland." He paused for a moment, then resumed. "I understand it is the Soviet intention to take over this area within sixty days, although I am sure the Führer has plans that will thwart that intention."

"If the readjustment of your lines in this area is subject to revision," Bellmon asked, "are there any plans to insure the safety of the prisoners of war?"

"My primary duty as commandant of this stalag," von Greiffenberg said, "is to insure the safety of the prisoners. Generaloberst von Heteen felt it necessary to remind me of that when informing me of my posting. While I have every faith that the Führer will be able to stop the Soviet forces, I have, of course, made contingency plans for the evacuation of this stalag and its prisoners to the west."

"How long do you think it will take?" Bellmon suddenly asked.

Von Greiffenberg looked at him for a moment.

"You are not very delicate, Colonel, are you?" he asked.

"I beg your pardon, sir," Bellmon said.

"Sixty days," von Greiffenberg said. It was out in the open now. Bellmon obviously knew how the war was going. There was no real reason for him to be "delicate" either. "There is talk of a last-ditch defense in the Alps, but I think that is whistling in the dark."

Bellmon pursed his lips, and then nodded, as if what he had just been told confirmed what he already believed. But he said nothing.

"If it should come to pass that you should fall into Soviet control," von Greiffenberg said, "it would be very dangerous for you to be found with the Katyn material."

"Yes," Bellmon said, "I've thought of that."

"I release you from your word, Colonel Bellmon, to deliver them to your appropriate superiors," von Greiffenberg said.

"I'll hang on to them," Bellmon said, flatly.

"Colonel, I'll spell it out for you. If the Russians find that material in your possession, you will die."

"Perhaps," Bellmon said, gently mocking von Greiffenberg's vaguely Biblical phraseology, " 'it will come to pass' that I will be freed by American forces."

"That is very unlikely, I'm afraid," von Greiffenberg said.

"It is often darkest just before the dawn," Bellmon said.

"So the Führer has been saying," von Greiffenberg said dryly.

Bellmon looked at him. Their eyes locked. The American and the German smiled at each other.

[FOUR]
April Fool's Day, 1945

The commanding officer of Stalag XVII-B, Oberst Graf Peter-Paul von Greiffenberg sent Oberleutnant Karl-Heinz von und zu Badner to fetch Lt. Col. Robert F. Bellmon five minutes after he received the movement order. He spent three of the five minutes in thought, one in prayer on his knees, and one pouring himself and drinking a very stiff brandy.

The middle-aged sergeant major and the more than middle-aged corporal on duty in the office rose to their feet and came to attention as the two officers entered the outer room of the commandant's office. The corporal always jumped to his feet and stood at attention when an officer of either army entered the office. Colonel Count von Greiffenberg was a stickler for correct military behavior: corporals demonstrate respect to rank no matter what the army. The sergeant major was normally preoccupied when Wehrmacht officers below the grade of major or American officers of any grade had business in the office. But he rose and stood at attention for Colonel Bellmon.

"Guten Abend, Oberfeldwebel," Colonel Bellmon said, in fluent German, acknowledging the sergeant major's gesture with a crisp salute.

"Guten Abend, Herr Oberstleutnant," the sergeant major said. "The Oberst Graf will see you now." He pushed open the door to Oberst Graf von Greiffenberg's office.

"Herr Graf," he said. *"Herr Oberstleutnant Bellmon."*

Bellmon removed his overseas cap with the silver Lieutenant Colonel's leaf pinned to its front, and which he had worn in the manner of armored soldiers, cocked to the left. Holding it in his left hand, he saluted again.

"Come in, please, Colonel," the commandant of Stalag XVII-B said in English. And then, over Colonel Bellmon's shoulder: *"Du auch, Karl."* The intimate *"Du"* was magnified by his use of the Oberleutnant's Christian name. *"Und schliess die Türe, bitte."*

Wordlessly, Colonel Count von Greiffenberg handed Colonel Bellmon and Oberleutnant von und zu Badner Stubberweg cognac snifters. He picked up his own glass, raised it to his companions, and then drank it down.

"I am in receipt, Colonel," the count began, "of movement orders which affect your officers." He spoke in English as if reciting from memory. "There have been certain temporary adjustments of the line, which make it necessary, in order to maintain the safety of our prisoners, to move them."

"I see," Bellmon said.

"Perhaps you might wish to examine the map," Colonel Graf von Greiffenberg said. He gestured—an elegant movement—toward his desk. Both Colonel Bellmon and Oberleutnant Stubberweg tried, and did not manage, to conceal their surprise at this offer. It is the duty of prisoners of war to make an attempt to escape. The most essential equipment in an attempt to escape is a map. Maps are therefore guarded with great care by the captors.

"If you are in any way uncomfortable, Oberleutnant von und zu Badner," von Greiffenberg said, "you may withdraw."

Oberleutnant von und zu Badner did not hesitate. He came to attention.

"With the Oberst Graf's kind permission, the Oberleutnant will remain in the hope that he might be of some small service."

"Thank you, Karl," von Greiffenberg said.

"It is my privilege, Herr Oberst Graf," von und zu Badner said.

"Very well," Colonel Graf von Greiffenberg said, pointing with a long, well-manicured finger to a point on the map. "We are here, Colonel Bellmon. Specifically, five kilometers from the center of Stettin."

Colonel Bellmon nodded, but said nothing.

"The temporary situation which requires adjustment in our lines," the count went on, in a dry, faintly mocking voice, as if he were once again addressing a class at the Kriegsschule, "involves certain pressures from this area." His thin finger pointed toward the direction of Warsaw. "Consequently, I have been ordered to effect a movement, which I am assured will be temporary, to the west, in this direction." His finger moved west and came to rest on the map near Berlin.

Bellmon leaned over the map, found the scale, and measured the distance with his fingers.

"At the moment, Colonel Bellmon, no transport is available for your officers," von Greiffenberg went on. "It will therefore be necessary for your officers to proceed by foot."

"I trust, Colonel, that arrangements have been made to feed my officers," Bellmon said.

"I am assured, Colonel," the count said, "that supplies and vehicles will be provided at approximately this point in our route," the count said, pointing with his finger.

"Peter," Colonel Bellmon said, suddenly deciding to take the risk, "we're not going to make the rendezvous point with the trucks, much less the Berlin area. Why don't we just stand pat and let the Russians roll over us?"

Von Greiffenberg involuntarily looked at Oberleutnant von and zu Badner to see his reaction to Bellmon's addressing him by his first name. He knew that the young officer was very much aware that he and Bellmon were more than prisoner and captor.

But their public relationship had been correct. He didn't know how Badner would react when the prisoner suggested treason as the only logical thing to do, and he did nothing about it.

Karl-Heinz von und zu Badner said nothing, and it was impossible to tell from his face what he was thinking.

"My duty, as I see it, Robert," the colonel said, "is quite clear. In addition to seeing that you remain in custody, it is to protect you."

"Should our positions be reversed, Peter," Bellmon said, "should the fortunes of war see you in my custody, I would feel precisely the same way."

"Yes, I know you would," the count said. "But I have Katyn Forest in my mind."

"The Russians would get to you over my dead body," Bellmon said.

"Yes, they would," the count said. "I have reminded you of that very real possibility before." Now Badner looked confused. "Colonel Bellmon is rendering the German officer corps a very real service, Badner. I will explain that to you later."

"That is quite unnecessary, Herr Oberst Graf," the young officer said.

"You're in command, Colonel," Bellmon said.

"Yes," the count said. "For the moment. Perhaps you noticed, Colonel, that the message made no reference to your enlisted men."

"Yes, I did."

"Perhaps the thinking is that it is better to let the Russians have the enlisted men if that is the price for keeping the officers," the count said. "But in any event, I'm afraid your men are going to have to fend for themselves. Without instructions, I cannot move your enlisted men."

Bellmon looked at him for a long moment, trying to read his meaning.

"It has come to my attention, Colonel, that there is a good bit of neutral power shipping at Odessa," the count said. Bellmon immediately looked at the map. Odessa was on the Black Sea. He folded his three center fingers, put his thumb on Poznan, and stretched his little finger toward Odessa. The span was too great. He rolled his hand over, so that the palm was up, and laid his fingers flat on the map. Then, against the scale, he repeated the movement.

"That's more than 1,700 kilometers," he said.

"I understand," the count went on, "that an effort is being made to protect certain artworks and other treasures from the ravages of war by shipping them from the country in neutral ships."

"Oh?" Bellmon asked. He was obviously confused.

"Colonel, what the colonel means," Oberleutnant von und zu Badner said, "is that the SS, the regular SS, not the Waffen SS, is shipping their loot out of the country on neutral ships."

"Oh," Bellmon said again. He still didn't quite understand, but he didn't want to wait for an explanation.

"I understand, further, that the personnel situation is such that many such shipments are being shipped by truck without military escort," the count went on. "And I also understand that escaped prisoners of war are being summarily shot by the SS and some units of the Feldgendarmerie."

"I understand," Colonel Bellmon said.

"I further have reliably been given to understand that the Russians are often unable to make the distinction between Germans and escaped prisoners of war, and that when there is some question, they are prone to err on the side of their security."

"As they resolved the Katyn question," Bellmon said.

"So I have been led to believe," the count said. "And now, Colonel, if you will excuse us, Oberleutnant von und zu Badner and I have to see what we can do about rations for tomorrow."

Colonel Count von Greiffenberg made one of his graceful gestures, ordering the young officer to precede him out of the room. At the door, before he closed it, he said, "The Oberfeldwebel will see you back to your quarters, Robert. Please inform your officers we will march at first light."

Colonel Bellmon immediately picked up the map and started to fold it. Beneath the map was a Colt .32 caliber automatic pistol and a spare clip. The pistol was finely engraved. It was obviously Greiffenberg's personal weapon. He thought a moment, then jammed the pistol in his waistband. He put the spare clip in his sock.

Then he saw that the lower right drawer of Greiffenberg's desk was open, and he saw the dull gleaming metal. He pulled the drawer open. There was a Schmeisser 9 mm machine pistol in there, disassembled. He looked at it a long moment before reaching for it. He unfastened his belt and trousers. He slipped the machine pistol in one pants leg, and the three magazines in the other. He closed his fly, fastened his belt, flexed his knees. His trousers were tucked into the tops of his tanker boots, held in place by extra-long bootlaces.

It wasn't the most secure arrangement in the world, but it would have to do.

He took his overseas cap from beneath the epaulet of his Ike jacket and put it on his head. Then he opened the door to the outer office. The Oberfeldwebel came to attention.

"The Herr Oberstleutnant is finished?" the Oberfeldwebel asked, politely. "In which case, I will escort the Herr Oberstleutnant to his quarters."

"I think that I would like to see Wachtmeister MacMillan before I turn in," Bellmon said.

"Whatever the Herr Oberstleutnant wishes," the Oberfeldwebel said.

When they reached the enlisted men's quarters, the German noncom saluted crisply and left him. Bellmon then rapped once on MacMillan's door and walked in without waiting for a reply. MacMillan jumped to his feet.

"Rest, Mac," Bellmon said. MacMillan, he saw, was freshly shaven and neatly cropped. His boots were even shined.

"How goes it, Mac?" Colonel Bellmon asked.

"What did old Von want?" MacMillan asked.

"We're being moved, on foot, at first light," Bellmon said.

"Shit! I was practicing to kiss my first Russian," MacMillan said.

"The enlisted men aren't going," Bellmon said.

"We're not?"

"You can take your chances, Mac," Bellmon said. "You can sit here and wait to get rolled over by the Red Army."

"Or?"

"I'll tell it the way I got it from von Greiffenberg," Bellmon said. When he had finished, MacMillan looked very carefully at him.

"You trust him, Colonel, don't you?"

"He's a regular, Mac, like we are," Colonel Bellmon said.

"What do you think we should do?"

"If you are caught by the SS or the Feldgendarmerie, you're liable to be shot. Under those circumstances, Sergeant, you have no obligation to attempt to escape."

"Just my fucking luck. Five combat jumps, and I'm going to get shot two weeks before the war is over."

"If you like, I'll insist that you be taken with us."

"Into Germany? No, thank you."

"I've got a map for you," Bellmon said. "If you want it."

"Von?" MacMillan said, taking and unfolding it. "That the route these loot trucks are taking?"

"Yeah. I'm not sure how current it is. As current, and as accurate, I'm sure, as von Greiffenberg can make it."

Bellmon took the Colt pistol and laid it on MacMillan's bed.

"Not, as I understand it, that anyone is paying a whole lot of attention to it, but possession of a firearm by an escaped POW is sufficient grounds under the Geneva Convention to use weaponry in his apprehension."

MacMillan looked at the pistol.

"Maybe you better keep that, Colonel," he said. He hoisted the front of his Ike jacket. Bellmon saw the angled butt of a Luger.

"How long have you had that?"

"Fritz gave me two of them," he said. "Two of them and two Schmeissers. A dozen clips. About thirty minutes ago. When he told me that Von had your marching orders, and they didn't include us."

"So what are you going to do, Mac?" Bellmon asked.

"I've got one guy who speaks German, and others who speak German *and* Polish," MacMillan said. "I've got two German uniforms, one of them a captain's."

"That'll get you shot as a spy," Bellmon said.

"If we can grab one of those trucks and put some distance between here and us, we might be able to make it."

"Who are you taking with you? How many?"

"There will be twenty-two of us. The rest want to wait for the Russians."

"Do they know what they're getting into?"

"I think so," MacMillan said. "If they don't, they'll damned sure find out soon enough after we're on our way."

They looked at each other. Bellmon sensed that this was the time he should have something to say to MacMillan. He could think of only one thing.

"Good luck, Mac," Colonel Bellmon said.

"Same to you, Colonel," MacMillan said. He grabbed Bellmon's hand and shook it.

"This is the second time since I've been a soldier I don't really know what to do," the colonel said.

It was a confession of inadequacy and MacMillan saw this. He was embarrassed for Lt. Col. Robert F. Bellmon.

"Yeah, you do," he said. "You gotta take care of those reservists. If you're worried about me, don't be. I've had enough of this POW shit. I don't want to get stood up against a wall without a fight."

"Thank you, Mac," Bellmon said, emotionally.

"Fuck it, Colonel," MacMillan replied, his own voice breaking. "Have the bugler sound the charge."

[**FIVE**]

At 0500 hours the next morning, the 240 officer prisoners of Stalag XVII-B formed ranks in the courtyard of what, long before, had been a Polish cavalry barracks. It was cold and damp, and many of them coughed rackingly and spit up phlegm. They were sullen, resentful, and disheartened.

Colonel Graf Peter-Paul von Greiffenberg appeared. Oberleutnant Karl-Heinz von und zu Badner called "Attention." Colonel von Greiffenberg stepped in front of the formation, and formally announced that a readjustment of German lines made necessary the removal of Stalag XVII-B to the west. He expressed regret that motor transport was not presently available.

"Colonel Bellmon," he concluded, "will you have your officers follow me, please?"

Bellmon saluted.

Von Greiffenberg walked to one end of the formation.

"Company!" Bellmon barked. " 'Ten-hut! Uh-right-*face!* Forward, harch! Route step, harch!"

The prisoner complement, under armed guard, shuffled, rather than marched after the prison commandant. They went out the gate, and then turned toward Stettin.

Technical Sergeant Rudy MacMillan watched them move out. He waited until the last guard had had time to come from his watchtower. He waited ten minutes more to be sure. Then he formed his ranks where the officers had stood. A coal miner from Pennsylvania, dressed in the uniform of a Wehrmacht captain, and a steelworker from Gary, Indiana, in the uniform of a corporal, both carrying Schmeisser machine pistols slung from their shoulders, marched the twenty men in American uniforms, MacMillan second back in the left rank, onto the highway, and off in the other direction.

They marched for about forty-five minutes before the right circumstances presented themselves. A Hanomag truck, its body enclosed in canvas tarpaulin, its front fender bearing the double lightning bolt runes of the SS, came down the cobblestone road.

"Take a left, Vrizinsky," MacMillan called out. The double column of men drifted across the road. The Hanomag truck squealed to a halt. The driver opened the door and shouted an obscenity. The SS Hauptsturmführer on the passenger side stood on the running board.

MacMillan, holding the Luger in both hands, and squatting halfway to give himself stability, shot him in the forehead. PFC Vrizinsky couldn't get his Schmeisser to fire. Private Loczowcza dropped his Schmeisser in his excitement. MacMillan jumped onto the running board and shot the driver twice in the back with his Luger.

The bodies were dragged off the road and stripped, while Private Loczowcza opened the Hanomag hood and pretended to work on it. The truck was full of wooden crates. As soon as MacMillan could change into the SS captain's uniform, which required that he search for and find a stream to wash the blood and brain matter out of the uniform cap, he supervised the off-loading of enough crates so there would be room for the men lying two deep on their sides, inside the truck, within a cavern of crates.

Outside of Wroclaw, four hours later, they came across a similar truck. Its crew was changing a flat tire by the side of the road. MacMillan had hoped to wait until the tire was changed before taking any action, but the SS Sturmscharführer in charge persisted in trying to engage the captain in conversation, and it became necessary to shoot him and the driver and to finish changing the tire themselves.

In twenty-four hours they were in L'vov, in the Ukraine. They picked up fuel and a few rations there and kept driving. The papers of the trucks were in order, and they passed through all but one Feldgendarmerie roadblock without incident. Near Podolskiy, Moldavia, an overzealous Unterfeldwebel of the Feldgendarmerie paid for his professional intuition that there was something wrong with this two-truck SS convoy with two 9 mm slugs in the back of his head.

Eight hours after that, they rolled into Odessa. There were seven ships tied to a pier. It was necessary for MacMillan to walk down the pier to look at the port of call painted on the stern of the MV *José Harrez*. He did not recognize the flag of Argentina. When it said "Buenos Aires" on the stern, he decided that he had drawn and filled an inside straight. The MV *José Harrez* was loading cargo, and her booms would handle the trucks.

With Private Loczowcza marching behind him, he took the salute of the Service Corps Feldwebel guarding the gangplank and marched up the gangplank to the ship. An officer directed him to the captain's cabin.

The captain's name was Kramer. He looked like a German. He spoke German.

"Do you speak English?" MacMillan asked.

"Yes, Herr Hauptsturmführer," the captain said. "I speak English." If he was surprised to be addressed by a German officer in English, he didn't show it.

"There will shortly be two trucks on the dock," MacMillan said. "I want you to pick them up and put them in your hold."

The captain replied in German. MacMillan had no idea what he said.

"He said why should he do that, Mac," Loczowcza translated.

"Because I will shoot you right where you sit if you don't," MacMillan said. He unholstered the Luger, but held it at his side.

"Under those circumstances, I don't have much choice, do I?" the captain replied. He wasn't flustered.

"None," MacMillan said.

"If the German authorities learn that I am loading, or have loaded the trucks, would I be in danger?"

"From me, Captain," MacMillan said.

"I suppose you have considered that this, in effect, is an act of piracy, punishable under international law? Wherever we dock next?"

"If the Germans catch us now, we're all dead, right here," MacMillan replied.

"I was about to say British," the captain said. "But you're American, aren't you?"

"Yes," MacMillan said. "I'm an American."

"And to the victor go the spoils?"

"Spoils? You mean loot? You're welcome to whatever is on the trucks."

"Go get your trucks," the captain said.

The *José Harrez* sailed at four the next morning. It was to proceed via the Suez Canal for Dar es Salaam, Capetown, and Buenos Aires. The trucks were unloaded during the day and dropped over the side after nightfall. The SS and Wehrmacht uniforms went over the side when a launch flying the flag of the Royal Navy came out to the *Harrez* off Port Said.

Neither MacMillan nor the captain ever mentioned the contents of the crates, even though MacMillan knew they had been opened, and even though he and the captain had become rather friendly during the seven-day voyage from Odessa.

As the launch pulled alongside the *Harrez*, Captain Kramer handed MacMillan an envelope.

"It's all I can spare from the ship's funds without questions being asked," he said.

"Thank you," MacMillan said. It was obviously money, but he didn't count it. He just jammed it in his trousers pocket. His attention was on the crew of the launch. They were in whites. Short white pants, white knee socks, starched white shirts, with officer's shoulder boards on the shirts.

MacMillan, wearing a woolen olive-drab shirt, OD pants, and combat boots, saluted the moment the Limey officer stepped onto the deck of the *Harrez*.

"Sir, Technical Sergeant R. J. MacMillan, United States. Army, reporting with a party of twenty-two," MacMillan said.

"I beg your pardon?" the Limey said. He did not return the salute.

[SIX]
Cairo, Egypt
21 April 1945

The military attaché at the U.S. Embassy, Cairo, was an Air Corps full bird, an old one. He returned MacMillan's salute casually and handed him a message form. MacMillan was still wearing the tunic in which he had been captured.

"I don't know what to think of this, MacMillan," he said. "But nobody seems to know about you." The colonel was an old soldier. He knew an old soldier when he saw one. There was a SNAFU someplace, but that didn't help matters.

```
WAR DEPT WASH DC
20 APR 1945

US EMBASSY CAIRO EGYPT
FOR MILATTACHE

REF YOUR TWX 49765 9APR45:
(1) WITH EXCEPTION MACMILLAN, PERSONNEL LISTED SUBJECT TWX
    AUTHORIZED PRIORITY SHIPMENT VIA MILITARY AIR TO ZONE OF
    INTERIOR. ALL PROVISIONS LIBERATED PRISONERS OF WAR
    APPLY. NOTIFY WAR DEPT DEPUTY CHIEF OF STAFF PERSONNEL BY
    PRIORITY RADIO HOUR AND DATE OF DEPARTURE AND ETA ZI
    RECEIVING STATION.
(2) NO RECORD EXISTS OF POW TECHNICAL SERGEANT MACMILLAN,
    RUDOLPH GEORGE ASN 12 279 656. PENDING SEARCH OF OTHER
    FILES AND INVESTIGATION BY COUNTERINTELLIGENCE CORPS
    PERSONNEL, YOU ARE DIRECTED TO DETAIN MACMILLAN.
    POSSIBILITY EXISTS HE IS GERMAN DESERTER.

                                     FOR THE CHIEF OF STAFF
                                        EDWARD W. WATERSON
                                     THE ADJUTANT GENERAL
```

"I'll be a sonofabitch," MacMillan said.

"I'll tell you what I'm going to do, Sergeant," the military attaché said. "Five minutes after your plane leaves."

"What's that, sir?" MacMillan asked. He was not unduly upset. He was an old soldier; he was used to fuck-ups. He was pissed, but not disturbed. He didn't think he was about to be shot by the U.S. Army as a German spy.

The military attaché handed him a message form.

```
FROM MILATTACHE USEMB CAIRO

FOR WAR DEPARTMENT WASHDC
ATTN DEPUTY CHIEF OF STAFF PERSONNEL

REFERENCE YOUR TWX 10APR45 RE TWENTY-THREE LIBERATED POWS.
REGRET INFORM YOU ALL PERSONNEL MY BASIC TWX DEPART CAIRO BY
MILAIR PRIORITY A1A 0700 HOURS 21APR45 FOR ZONE OF INTERIOR.
DESTINATION FORT DEVENS MASS. ETA 1800 22 APR45.

                                              BRUCE C. BLEVITT
                                             COLONEL, AIR CORPS
                                              MILITARY ATTACHE
```

"Thank you, Colonel," MacMillan said.

"If you're a German spy, Sergeant, I'm Hermann Göring," the colonel said.

Two agents of the Counterintelligence Corps met the C-54 which had come from Cairo, via Casablanca and the Azores, to Logan Field in Boston. They were both Jewish. They rather conspicuously carried snub-nosed .38 caliber Colt revolvers in small holsters attached to their trouser belts.

They came on the plane before any passengers were allowed to debark.

"Which one of you is Tech Sergeant Macmillan?" one of them asked.

"I am," MacMillan called.

They came to where he was sitting. One of them got in the aisle ahead of MacMillan; the other positioned himself so that MacMillan would be between them in the aisle.

"If you'll come with us, please, Technical Sergeant MacMillan," the one in front said.

"Jesus, Mac," Loczowcza said, "he's got a worse accent than Fritz the Feldwebel."

"You will kindly keep to your own business," the CIC agent said. "This does not concern you."

MacMillan got out of his seat and started to walk down the aisle.

"Achtung!" the CIC agent behind MacMillan suddenly shouted. MacMillan turned around very slowly, at first confused, and then realized that the CIC agent was trying to "catch" him obeying a command in German, and thus "proving" he was a German spy.

"Achtung! yourself, Humphrey Bogart!" he said, laughing, not angry.

The CIC agent, flustered, angry, suddenly drew his revolver.

"Put the cuffs on him!" he ordered.

"Jewboy," Loczowcza said, firmly, not a shout, "you better put that thing away before Sergeant Mac makes you eat it. Or before I personally stick it up your ass."

The CIC agent spun to face Loczowcza. Loczowcza found himself facing a pistol. He slapped the CIC agent's hand, knocking the pistol out of the way; and the revolver fired. The sound inside the aircraft's enclosed fuselage was loud enough to be painful.

"Oh, shit!" someone shouted, almost a scream. "I've been shot!"

Loczowcza leaped from his seat and knocked the CIC agent down, and then pinned him to the aisle floor.

The other CIC agent, standing in the middle of the aisle, held his pistol in both hands and aimed it at first one and then another of the passengers, many of whom were getting to their feet.

"At ease!" MacMillan's voice boomed. "At *goddamn* ease, goddamnit!"

There was silence.

"Let him up, Polack," MacMillan ordered. Loczowcza backed away from the downed CIC agent.

"Everything's going to be all right," MacMillan said. "Just everybody take it easy." He turned to the CIC agent wielding the pistol. He put his hands out to be handcuffed.

[SEVEN]
Fort Devens, Massachusetts
22 April 1945

The general's aide-de-camp, a young first lieutenant in pinks and greens, opened the door to the general's office and nodded at MacMillan.

"The general will see you now, MacMillan," he said.

MacMillan, attired in brand-new ODs, their packing creases still visible, with brand-new low quarters on his feet and his Ike jacket sleeves bare of insignia, marched into the general's office. He stopped three feet from the general's desk.

"Sir," he snapped, as his hand rose in salute, "Technical Sergeant MacMillan reporting to the commanding general as ordered."

"Stand at ease," the major general, a plump, ruddy-faced man in his early fifties, said, returning the salute. That was a reflex, a conditioned response, as automatic as was MacMillan's instant crisp shifting of position from attention to parade rest. No matter what a general says to you, you don't slouch. When a general gives you "at ease" you go to "parade rest."

The commanding general of Fort Devens, Mass., looked at MacMillan as if he didn't know where to begin.

"Welcome home, MacMillan," the general said, finally. "I don't suppose anyone has said that to you here, have they?"

"Thank you, sir. No, sir, they haven't."

"If the incredibly stupid behavior of those two clowns from CIC didn't want to make you weep, if it wasn't for the trooper with the .38 slug in his leg, this whole mess could be funny," the general said.

"Sir, may the sergeant ask how Private Latier is?" MacMillan said.

"Very well. I checked on him right after I sent for you. I thought you'd want to know."

"Thank you, sir."

"Well, we've finally got this mess straightened out," the general said. MacMillan, still peering into space six inches over the general's head, stiff as a board, said nothing.

"You don't seem surprised," the general said.

"Sir, the sergeant knew that it would be straightened out in good time."

"You're not curious what happened?"

"Sir, it doesn't matter."

"If you're going to be an officer, MacMillan—" the general said, with a smile. "Correction: Now that you *are* an officer, you're going to have to learn the difference between 'at ease' and 'parade rest.' "

MacMillan's hands, which had been crossed in the small of his back, palms open, fingers stiff and together, fell awkwardly to his side. He made an effort to stand less at attention. His eyes looked at the general, and then snapped back to where they had been directed, six inches over the general's head.

"Ed," the general said to his aide-de-camp, "would you ask the sergeant to get Lieutenant MacMillan and myself a cup of coffee? And under the circumstances, I think that perhaps we might like to have a little character in the coffee. Sit down, Lieutenant MacMillan. On the couch."

MacMillan, half afraid this was some kind of incredibly detailed nightmare, walked stiffly to the general's couch, and sat down. A tech sergeant, crisply uniformed, obviously the general's sergeant, who just as obviously had been standing ready with the tray with the coffee pitcher and the cups and saucers and the Old Bartlesville 100-Proof Sour Mash Kentucky Bourbon, bent over the coffee table in front of the couch, lowered the tray, and winked at MacMillan.

"Perhaps the lieutenant," the tech sergeant said, "would like his character straight-up." He handed MacMillan a shot glass. Mac tossed it down. He felt the liquor burn his throat. This was no dream.

"As well as I have been able to piece this thing together, MacMillan," the general said, walking to the couch and sitting down beside MacMillan, "on 20 September 1944, acting on the recommendation of your battalion commander, the commanding general of the 82nd Airborne Division directly commissioned you as a second lieutenant."

"I don't remember anything about that, General," MacMillan said. "Colonel Vandervoort said I was in command, but I don't remember nothing about a commission."

"Obviously, you misunderstood your colonel," the general said. "When were you captured?"

"On the twenty-first," MacMillan said. He looked at the general with embarrassment, even shame in his eyes. "We were on the far side of the canal. We were supporting the 504th. We were out of bazooka ammo. We had one clip for the BAR. We were down to four guys, and two of them was bad wounded. General, there was more krauts than we had ammo!" He looked very close to tears.

The general snapped his fingers, then gestured "bring me" with his fingers. His aide-de-camp went to his desk, picked up a sheet of paper, and handed it to the general. The general put his glasses on. He began to read:

"Second Lieutenant Rudolph George MacMillan, 0-589866, then commanding reconnaissance platoon, 508th Parachute Infantry Regiment, 82nd Airborne Division, then engaged against German forces in the area known as Groesbeek Heights, near Nijmegen, the Netherlands, suffered the loss of eighty percent of his command while leading them to effect a join-up with the 504th Parachute Infantry Regiment.

"Despite his own wounds, Lieutenant MacMillan personally took over operation of a rocket launcher, and ignoring a murderous hail of small arms, mortar, and artillery fire, personally destroyed five German tanks. His action prevented the enemy from forcing a breech in the ranks of the 504th Parachute Infantry Regiment, and consequently saved many American lives.

"Again ignoring his wounds, and without regard to his personal safety, Lieutenant MacMillan then personally carried two of his men through a murderous hail of enemy fire to medical facilities, during which activity he was again wounded. In order to make an attempt to save the lives of other members of his platoon, he returned a third time to his forward position.

"After expending his last rounds of rifle ammunition, and after having been wounded a fifth time, Lieutenant MacMillan was last seen advancing toward the enemy with a Thompson submachine gun, which he was firing with one hand."

"That's bullshit," MacMillan said. Tears were running down his cheeks. The tech sergeant touched his shoulder and when MacMillan looked up, the tech sergeant handed him another shot glass. MacMillan tossed it down, shuddered, and suddenly leaned forward and held his face in his hands.

"Why is it bullshit?" the general asked, softly.

"Well, I wasn't *wounded*, for one thing," MacMillan said. "Not really shot, or bad hurt. Just some scratches when I got knocked down by concussion, and fell down. You know what I mean. And that last part, about 'advancing toward the enemy with a Thompson.' Shit! What I did when we ran out of ammo was lie in that fucking hole until the krauts came and rolled over us and then I put my hands up over my head."

"I thought that paragraph was a bit colorful," the general said, dryly. He picked up the paper and resumed reading.

"Lieutenant MacMillan's actions were above and beyond the call of duty. His heroism, valor, and leadership characteristics are in the finest traditions of the United States Army and reflect great credit upon him and the military service. Entered the military service from Pennsylvania."

"Sir, can I ask, what is that you're reading, anyway?" MacMillan asked.

"This is what the military aide to the President of the United States is going to read aloud when the President hangs the Medal of Honor around your neck, Lieutenant MacMillan."

MacMillan looked at him in utter disbelief.

"There was some doubt as to whether you had survived the action," the general went on. "So award of the medal was held in abeyance until we should get some positive information about you. Or get you back. The records of Technical Sergeant MacMillan were closed. The records of Lieutenant MacMillan were flagged, so that if you should show up in one piece, we could roll out the red carpet for you. That's why there was no record of you when the military attaché sent his TWX."

MacMillan had two stiff drinks in him. He was relaxing somewhat.

"Well," he said. "Second Lieutenant MacMillan. What do you know about that?"

"First Lieutenant," the general corrected him. "Automatic promotion after six months."

"What happens now?" MacMillan asked.

"Well, either Tuesday or Wednesday, we'll fly you to Washington. We'll have your wife meet you there, of course. And on Thursday, you'll go to the White House. There are six people in the ceremony, as I understand it."

"What happens today?" MacMillan asked. He added, "Sir?" It was obvious that the announcement had, indeed, got to him. He had forgotten his military courtesy.

"It's Friday afternoon, I'm afraid," the general said. "There's not much that can be done. Get you moved into a BOQ, of course. Run you by the officer's sales store to be fitted for pinks and greens. They expect you at the hospital at 0730 tomorrow morning. Complete physical. Relax, MacMillan. For the next week or so, people will be doing things for you. And after Washington, you're entitled to a thirty-day liberation leave . . . not charged as leave, by the way. They've taken over the Greenbrier Hotel for that. Ever heard of the Greenbrier?"

"No, sir, I haven't," MacMillan said. "When do I get to see my wife?"

"I'm sure Second Army is already working on that. We'll have her on hand when you get off the plane in Washington. Don't you worry about that."

"I want to see her as soon as I can," MacMillan said. "Tonight."

"I'm afraid that's quite out of the question, Lieutenant MacMillan," the general said, and Mac recognized the tone of voice. There would be no argument.

"Yes, sir," he said.

The general looked at his watch.

"Well, MacMillan," he said. "If you want to get yourself fitted, you're going to have to run along."

MacMillan stood up and popped to attention. "Yes, sir," he said. "Thank you, sir."

The general put out his hand. "It's been an honor to meet you, Lieutenant," he said. "Oh, there's one more thing I think I should tell you. I'm putting you in for the DSC for your escape."

MacMillan didn't say anything.

"And I'm sure, Lieutenant, that nothing more will be heard about the little administrative SNAFU, will there?" the general said. "It was just one of those things, wasn't it?"

"Yes, sir," MacMillan said. "That's all it was."

The general's aide-de-camp took MacMillan in the general's Ford staff car to the officer's sales store, where he was measured for uniforms. The enlisted man's uniform he was wearing was, at the aide-de-camp's insistence, pressed on the spot. It occurred to MacMillan that he could probably get out of turning the ODs in, and he would then be ahead one uniform.

There was a small problem about insignia. It could be cleared up in the morning, the aide-de-camp said, or by Monday at the latest. But for the time being, MacMillan would have to do without the embroidered insignia of the 82nd Airborne Division; without his Expert Combat Infantry Badge; without his parachutists wings; without, in fact, everything except the silver bars of a lieutenant and the crossed rifles of infantry.

"It'll be enough, Mac," the aide-de-camp said, "to get you into the officer's club to eat. And first thing in the morning, we'll turn you over to a team from PIO, who'll take care of everything while you're being briefed for the White House affair, and the press conference."

The aide-de-camp got him settled into the bachelor officer's quarters, and then left him, after pointing out the officer's mess, across the parade field.

There was a telephone in the BOQ and Mac got on it, and after several telephone calls learned that the guys, "except the one got hisself shot" had already been processed and were gone on liberation leave. A nurse in the hospital told him that the man who was shot on the C-54 could not be called to the telephone; his family had just arrived to greet him.

First Lieutenant Rudy G. MacMillan saw a small sign on the wall behind the telephone: OFF-POST TAXI 4550.

The dumb bastards, he thought, were convinced that he would be a good boy and stay sober and on the post because they hadn't paid him. He had the money, nearly a thousand dollars, that the captain of the MV *José Harrez* had given him at Port Said. He had seen no reason to share it with the others. For one thing, he knew they would be paid the moment they got to the States. For another, if it hadn't been for him, they would still be in Poland someplace.

He put his finger in the telephone and dialed a four, two fives, and a zero.

[EIGHT]
Boston
22 April 1945

"Please deposit $2.35, sir."

Nine quarters bonged and a dime binged into the slots. He heard the number start to ring. On the third ring, somebody picked it up.

"Hello?"

His eyes watered and his throat tightened so much it hurt.

"Long distance is calling Mrs. Roxanne MacMillan."

"This is Mrs. MacMillan."

"Go ahead, sir."

Nine quarters and a dime dropped into Massachusetts Bell's coin box with a crash.

"Roah," MacMillan said. Goddamnit, he couldn't talk.

"Hello?"

"Roxy?"

"Hello?"

"Roxy, this is Mac."

"Mac?" There was disbelief in her voice.

"Honey, how are you?"

"Oh, Mac! Oh, shit, I thought you were dead! Oh, *Mac!*"

"Why did you think I was dead?"

"The army's been calling up here and at work, and they're supposed to call about now and come over. Mac, I thought they were going to tell me you were dead!"

"I'm all right, honey," Mac said. "I'm all right."

"Honey, where are you?"

"In a railroad station in Boston."

"What are you doing there? When can you come home?"

"Can you borrow your brother's car? Can you come to New York?"

"Yeah, I'm sure I can. Tommy's home. He'll drive me."

"I don't want him to drive you. I want you to come by yourself."

"Where in New York, Mac?"

Christ, he hadn't thought about that.

"Where should I come, Mac?"

"You remember that hotel where we stayed when I was at Camp Kilmer? The Dixie?"

"Yeah, sure."

"I'll meet you there, Roxy," Mac said.

"What about the people from the army?"

"Take off right now, honey, before they get there."

"Mac, are you in some kind of trouble?"

"Just come, will you, Roxy, for Christ's sake?"

[NINE]
New York City
24 April 1945

The desk clerk of the Dixie Hotel told the soldier that he was sorry, but they were all full up.

The soldier reached in the chest pocket of his Ike jacket and came out with a folded wad of money. He peeled off a twenty dollar bill, and then another.

"Like I said," the soldier said. "I'd like a double room, with a double bed, for two nights." He held the two twenty dollar bills up in front of him.

"Well, I . . ."

"You better take it," the soldier said. "That's all I'm going to put up."

"I think we just may have a cancellation, sir," the desk clerk said, and snatched the forty dollars.

While the soldier signed the registry card, the desk clerk looked around for the woman. He saw no one.

He examined the card, more than a little surprised that Lieutenant and Mrs. Smith had not just registered. The card read "1/Lt and Mrs. R. G. MacMillan, Mauch Chuck, Penna."

"Where's the bar?" Lieutenant MacMillan asked.

"Right across the lobby, sir. Your luggage, sir?"

"No luggage," MacMillan said.

"Then I'll have to have payment in advance, sir," the desk clerk said.

The soldier produced the wad of money again and paid for two days in advance. Then he walked across the lobby and went into the cocktail lounge.

An hour later, he reappeared at the desk and asked for his key. His face was liquor flushed, and there was a woman hanging tightly on his arm. She was a redhead, and her breasts overfilled the dress, straining the buttons.

"You got my key, Mac?" the soldier asked.

"Yes, sir. Eleven-seventeen. I'll get you a bellman."

"I don't need no bellman, just give me the goddamn key."

"Yes, sir."

The desk clerk watched them get on the elevator. As soon as they turned around, before the operator could close the door, the soldier dropped his hand to the redhead's buttock and gave it a little squeeze.

"Behave yourself, for Christ's sake," the redhead said.

And then the elevator door closed and took Lieutenant and Mrs. MacMillan to their floor.

[TEN]
Washington, D.C.
28 April 1945

"I understand, Lieutenant," the gray-haired man in the glasses said to him, "unofficially, of course, that there was some doubt that you were going to find the time to come here today."

First Lieutenant MacMillan, his wife Roxanne hanging tightly on to his arm, could not form a reply.

"One of the things I learned when I was a battery commander, Lieutenant, was, that there was AWOL, and then there was *AWOL*. Are they giving you any trouble?"

"They were pretty mad, sir," Lieutenant MacMillan said.

"If they give you any real trouble, you let me know," the man in the glasses said. He lifted the medal suspended around MacMillan's neck on a starred blue ribbon. "That ought to be worth a weekend pass, anyhow. If they give you any real trouble, tell them the Commander in Chief told you that."

[ONE]
Kilometer 835, Frankfurt–Kassel Autobahn
Near Bad Nauheim, Germany
6 April 1945

A BMW sidecar motorcycle bounced up the median of the autobahn. It was driven by a huge black American T/4, an MP brassard on his arm. A three-by-six-foot American flag was just barely flapping from an antenna rigged as a flagpole, and a small passenger was hanging onto the lip of the sidecar cockpit.

Endless ranks of gray-uniformed prisoners marched listlessly down the median in the opposite direction. There were four tightly packed columns of American vehicles on the autobahn itself, on both sides of the median. On the left, moving northward in what were customarily the southbound lanes, was a slow-moving armored column and a second slightly faster-moving line of General Motors six-by-six trucks. The north-bound lanes were jammed with a stopped double column of trucks.

The BMW motorcycle came to a bridge over a deep gorge. Its center span was blown and lay in a pile of crumbled concrete and steel two hundred feet below. The combat engineers had laid a one-lane Bailey Bridge over the gap, and a trio of military policemen directed traffic over it. Six tanks were waved across with impatient gestures, then six of the trucks from the columns on the left. The columns on the right were going to have to wait, and they had the message. Their drivers were sitting on the hoods of the GMCs. The line of prisoners wended its way down the far bank of the gorge and then up the near side.

The BMW with the sidecar had a siren, and the passenger shouted for the motorcycle driver to sound it as they approached the MPs. One of the MPs heard it, looked, stepped in front of it, and raised his hand. The passenger of the motorcycle waved his hand violently, imperiously, motioning the MP aside.

The MP swore, but he saw the MP brassard on the driver, and he thought he saw the glint of officer's insignia on the collar points of the passenger. He looked to his left. There was a fifteen-foot gap between two of the M4A3 tanks about to enter on the bridge. What the fuck, if they got run over, they could be quickly pushed out of the way. Without signaling the tank to stop or slow, he waved the motorcycle into the moving line.

First with a roar of the engine to pull ahead of the tank, then the squeal of brakes to keep from running under the tank ahead of it, the motorcycle pulled into line, and then bounced over the Bailey Bridge, somewhat cockeyed: the wheels of the motorcycle rode in the tread of the bridge, and the wheel of the sidecar was on the planks of the Bailey, six inches lower than the road.

When they reached the far side of the Bailey, they were going too fast, and the motorcycle lurched dangerously as it bounced off the Bailey and onto the undamaged portion of the bridge.

Five hundred yards off the bridge, a cluster of vehicles was parked in a field to the left. There were six military police jeeps, each with sirens and flashing lights mounted in their fenders and in their rear a machine gun on a pedestal. There were four half-tracks, each with a four-barreled multiple .50 on a turret in the bed. There were three M4A3 tanks, and half a dozen GMCs with van bodies, plus another GMC guarded by two MPs. Three flags were stuck into the ground beside its rear-opening door. One was the national colors, the second was the two-starred red flag of a major general, and the third carried an enlargement of the shoulder insignia of the 40th Armored Division, a triangular patch, yellow, blue, and red, with the number forty at the top.

As the BMW motorcycle turned out of the moving tank column with its flag catching the breeze, Major General Peterson J. Waterford came out of the van. He stopped at the top of the folding stairs and put a tanker's helmet on his head. The 40th Divisional insignia was on each side of the helmet, and there were two stars on the front. The general wore a fur-collared aviator's jacket (stars on the epaulets, the zipper fastened only at the web waistband) a shade 31 (pink) shirt, shade 31 riding breeches, with dark suede inner knees, and glistening riding boots. A shoulder holster held a .45 Colt automatic, and there was a yellow scarf at his throat.

The general smiled. "Jesus, Charley," he said. "Get a load of that, will you?"

He had seen the BMW with the large black T/4 and the flapping American flag whose passenger was doing his damndest to hang on as the sidecar bounced him around.

The motorcycle slid to a halt, and that damned near sent the passenger flying out on his ass. The general was barely able to restrain himself from laughing out loud. The passenger stood up in the sidecar and saluted. That sight was too much. The passenger was about five feet five or six, and the helmet and the goggles nearly covered his head. He looked, the general thought, like a mushroom. The general chuckled loudly, almost a laugh, as he returned the salute. Fat Charley, his G-3, laughed out loud.

"General Waterford, sir," the saluting mushroom said, and scrambled out of the sidecar, bending over it to pick up a Schmeisser machine pistol, and then trotting up to the van steps. The mushroom saluted again. General Waterford saw that it was a little Jew, and that the little Jew had a second lieutenant's bar pinned to his collar.

"Lieutenant, where the hell did you get that motorcycle?" General Waterford demanded, with a broad smile.

"Sir, Lieutenant S. T. Felter requests permission to speak to the general, sir."

"Speak," Major General Peterson K. Waterford said, amused.

"Sir, I think we should speak in private," Lieutenant Felter said. "It's a personal matter."

"A personal matter?" General Waterford was no longer amused.

"A personal matter involving the general, sir," Felter said.

Waterford looked at him without expression for ten seconds. Then he turned around and stepped back inside the van, signaling for the lieutenant to follow him. Fat Charley, the G-3, stepped to one side to let the lieutenant pass.

The interior of the van had been fitted out as a mobile command post. There were desks and a half dozen telephones. On two of the walls were large maps covered with celluloid on which troop dispositions and the flow of forces had been marked with colored grease pencils.

"All right, Lieutenant," General Waterford said. "Who are you, and what do you want?"

The lieutenant took off the helmet, and pushed the goggles down over his chin, so they dangled from their strap around his neck. He rubbed the bridge of his nose, and then came almost to attention.

"Sir, I am Lieutenant S. T. Felter, attached to the POW interrogation branch of the 40th MP Company."

"And?"

"General, I believe I have located Lieutenant Colonel Bellmon."

"Which Bellmon would that be?" General Waterford asked, making an effort—and succeeding—to keep his voice under control.

"Lieutenant Colonel Robert F. Bellmon, sir. Your son-in-law."

"You're sure, Lieutenant?" Waterford asked. Fat Charley stepped into the van. "He says he's located Bob," Waterford said.

"How reliable is your information, Lieutenant?" Fat Charley asked.

"I would rate it as ninety percent reliable," Felter said. "I have three separate prisoner interrogations to base it on. One of the prisoners taken near Hoescht was a captain who was formerly assigned to Stalag XVII-B."

"I heard he was in Stalag XVII-B," Waterford said. "That's not news."

"The officer prisoners of Stalag XVII-B are being evacuated, on foot, from near Stettin," Lieutenant Felter said. "May I use the map, sir?"

"Go ahead," the general said. Felter went to a map of Germany mounted on the wall of the van, pointing out where Stalag XVII-B had been located near Stettin. Then he pointed out the route reported to be, and most likely to be, the one it would take if moving westward on foot.

Both the general and Fat Charley followed the map with interest.

"Have you any report on Colonel Bellmon's physical condition?" General Waterford asked.

"Yes, sir. He is in good physical condition. I understand he is the *de facto* senior prisoner."

"As opposed to *de jure?"* Waterford asked, half sarcastically. "Where did you go to school, Lieutenant?"

"Yes, sir. As opposed to *de jure.* I understand the senior prisoner is a full colonel suffering from depression."

Cocky little bastard, General Waterford thought. He wondered where he had come from. CCNY Jew, the general guessed. Then Harvard Law.

"I asked where you went to school," General Waterford said.

"I was at the Academy for two and a half years, sir," Felter said.

"West Point?" the general asked, incredulously.

"Yes, sir. I resigned."

"Well, then, Lieutenant," General Waterford said, "you will understand my position. While I am very grateful to you for bringing me this information, you will understand why I cannot act upon it. Why I must let things happen as they will. I cannot, as much as I would like to, send a column to free them."

"Yes, sir."

"Oh, for Christ's sake, Porky," Fat Charley said. "Why not? We have the assets!"

"I rather doubt that Colonel Bellmon would want me to," General Waterford said. "It would clearly be special privilege."

"It would be freeing prisoners. Bob's not the only one."

"The subject is not open for discussion, Colonel," Waterford said. He looked at Felter, then walked to the door of the van. As he reached it, he turned around.

"Charley," he said, "get the lieutenant's name, and write a letter of commendation to be put in his file. That was good detective work, Lieutenant, and you demonstrated a tact in presenting your information that becomes you. Thank you very much, and please keep me posted."

Then he walked down the steps of the van.

Fat Charley picked up a sheet of paper and a pencil and bent over the built-in map table.

"Name, rank, and serial number, Lieutenant," he said.

Felter gave it to him.

Then Fat Charley made up his mind.

He took a second sheet of lined notepaper and wrote on it. He gave it to Felter. Felter read it.

Phil: Porky says he will not order a relief column because it would be special privilege. Charley.

"Two point three miles beyond the bridge," Fat Charley said, "the one we fixed with a Bailey?"

"Yes, sir. I came that way."

"You will find the 393rd Tank Destroyer Regiment. I want you to tell the commanding officer, Colonel Parker, precisely what you told General Waterford."

"Yes, sir," Felter said. "Sir, if Colonel Parker is going to lead a rescue operation, I would very much like to go along."

"I have no idea, Lieutenant," Fat Charley said, "what Colonel Parker may do."

"Yes, sir."

"What I am going to do, Lieutenant, is telephone your commanding officer and tell him that I have pressed you into temporary duty here for a few days. General Waterford is a busy man, and I see no reason to bother him with any of this. Do you understand?"

"Yes, sir." Felter pulled the goggles back up over his chin and adjusted them. He picked up his helmet.

"Lieutenant, may I make a suggestion?"

"Yes, sir," Lieutenant Felter replied. "Of course."

"If you put a couple of handkerchiefs, or socks, or something, between the top of the straps and the inside of the helmet liner, it will keep your helmet from riding so low on your head."

"Really?" Second Lieutenant Felter said. He took two handkerchiefs from his field jacket pocket and jammed them into the helmet.

"There," Fat Charley said when Felter had put it on. "Now you'll be able to see."

"I never wore it much," Felter confessed. "But I heard the general was very firm about helmets."

"On your way, Felter," Fat Charley said, smiling. He touched Felter's shoulder in a gesture of affection as Felter walked past him. "Good luck."

[TWO]
Kilometer 829, Frankfurt–Kassel Autobahn
Near Bad Nauheim, Germany
6 April 1945

The officers and the first grade noncoms (the regimental sergeant major, the battalion sergeants major, the first sergeants, and the other six-stripers, the S-3 and S-2 operations sergeants, the regimental motor sergeant and band sergeant) gathered in a half-circle around Colonel Philip Sheridan Parker III, commanding the 393rd Tank Destroyer Regiment.

Colonel Parker, in a zippered tanker's jacket, tanker's boots, and with his Colt New Service Model 1917 revolver hanging from a pistol belt around his waist, stood on the curved brick entryway to a mansion the 393rd had taken over as a command post three days before.

Built into the walls of the mansion, which looked more French than German, were flag holders. The American flag hung loosely from one, and the 393rd's flag, a representation of a tiger eating a tank, and which the colonel personally thought was more Walt Disney than military, hung from the other.

They didn't look like the Long Gray Line, in that some of them were fat, and some of them were short, and some of them were fat and short, and all of them were colored. But neither, Colonel Parker thought, as he often did when he looked at them, did they look like a Transportation Corps port battalion.

They looked like what they were, combat soldiers, who had proved themselves under fire, and knew they were good. Colonel Philip Sheridan Parker thought, all things considered, that his men were just as good as the Buffalo Soldiers, the 9th United States Cavalry (Colored) which had charged up Kettle Hill under Colonel Theodore Roosevelt and Master Sergeant Philip Sheridan Parker, Sr.

"Ten-hut!" his adjutant said, softly.

"Rest!" Parker said.

His noncoms and officers stood at a loose but respectful parade rest.

This was not, Colonel Parker thought again, the Fow-Fowty-Fow Double Clutchin', Motha-Fuckin' QM Truck. These were soldiers.

"Gentlemen," he said, "I think it is pretty clear that this campaign is about over. It is equally clear to me that we are at the moment about as useful to current operations as teats on a boar hog."

There were chuckles.

"It is my judgment that we have been committed to action for the last time. We may, and probably will, move again, but I think we have had our last action against tanks. The Germans seem to have run out of tanks, or at least out of any fuel to run the ones they have left.

"On the other hand, they are dug in here and there, and apparently haven't gotten the word the ball game is all over but the shouting. What I am attempting to do is paint the situation as one where we can, with our heads held high for doing our duty as well as anyone, just sit still and wait for the capitulation.

"It has, however, come to my attention that about 250 captured American officers are being marched on foot from western Poland into Germany. It is my intention to lead a column to liberate them. I have not, repeat *not,* been ordered to do so. I am proceeding under my general authority to engage targets of opportunity wherever and whenever encountered. I intend to engage whatever targets I happen to find in eastern Germany with two dozen tracks, ten jeeps, and thirty six-by-sixes, which will carry what supplies we need and whatever American prisoners we are fortunate enough to encounter.

"I will not ask for volunteers. However, those of you who would prefer to make the intelligent, rational, honorable decision to remain here until the war is over may return now to whatever you were doing before I called this officer and non-com call. Atten-hut. Dis-missed."

Not a man moved.

Colonel Parker waited until he was sure the lump in his throat had gone down sufficiently so that it would not interfere with his speaking voice.

"All of you obviously can't go," he said. "Officers may plead their cases to the exec, who is not going, and enlisted men to the sergeant major, who is. We obviously can't have a force made up entirely of officers and master sergeants. For one thing, it has been my experience that, as a general rule of thumb, such people make lousy track crewmen."

There was again the polite, respectful chuckling.

"I will not, repeat *not*, listen to appeals of the decisions made by the exec and the sergeant major," Colonel Parker said. "We move out in thirty minutes."

Lieutenant Sanford K. Felter was denied by Colonel Parker himself the honor of leading Task Force Parker into eastern Germany in the sidecar of his liberated BMW motorcycle. Parker felt the motorcycle was a good idea, and so was the flag flapping from its jury-rigged antenna (in fact, he ordered every American flag but one in the regiment carried along in the tracks, unfurled); but Lieutenant Felter was too valuable an asset for the operation to risk having him blown away while riding in the van in a motorcycle. Lieutenant Felter spoke Russian, and that was going to be necessary.

Lieutenant Felter rode in the third vehicle of the column, the first track, behind the motorcycle and a jeep, standing up in the rear, holding on to the mount of the multiple .50.

There was a military vehicle in the convoy that Sanford Felter had never seen before. It was constructed of aluminum and cloth and had an eighty-five horsepower engine. It was a Piper Cub. The 393rd's self-propelled 105 mm howitzer battery was considered to be separate artillery and thus entitled to its own artillery spotter, although the normal distribution of artillery spotters was one per battalion, three batteries of artillery.

Colonel Parker elected to employ the aircraft for column control. As they made their way through badly bombed Giessen and then wholly untouched Marburg an der Lahn, it flew ahead of the convoy reporting where the road was blocked by American units waiting to advance, and where secondary roads, often unpaved, would give them passage.

Beyond Marburg an der Lahn, at Colbe, the column turned dead east. Forty miles down that road, once they were in enemy-held territory, the Piper Cub began to report actual, or possible, or likely German emplacements and alternate routes to bypass them without a fight. The Cub, for which there were two pilots, landed at the head of the advancing column, swapped pilots, refueled, and was airborne again before the last of the tracks and trucks had rolled past it. The pilot now on the ground rode in Colonel Parker's track and pointed out on the map what he had seen from the air.

Task Force Parker averaged 16.5 miles per hour over the ground from the point of departure to the point of link-up with forces of the Union of Soviet Socialist Republics near Zwenkau, in Saxony.

This over-the-road movement time was calculated excluding the seven hours the first night Task Force Parker halted (forming its vehicles in a circle with the gas and food trucks inside, very much like a wagon train in the Wild West) and the six hours it stopped the second night on the crest of the hill overlooking Zwenkau. The convoy spent eight hours in movement the first day and fourteen the second, twenty-two hours of movement covering 363 miles on the road, about one half that distance as the crow flies.

At first light on the morning of the third day, a line of Red Army infantry skirmishers appeared, moving toward them from Zwenkau. Colonel Parker ordered one of the tracks, flying unfurled American flags, to make itself visible. It was immediately brought under heavy machine gun and small arms fire and withdrew with two of its crew wounded, but not critically.

Colonel Parker denied permission to return fire, and instead asked for two volunteers, one to drive the BMW motorcycle and the second to hold erect in the sidecar a white flag of truce. He denied Lieutenant Felter's offer of his services. Sooner or later, they were going to have to talk to the Russians, and he was the only one who spoke Russian.

The MP whose motorcycle it was insisted on driving the machine, and Lieutenant Booker T. Washington Fernwall, who had been associate professor of Romance Languages at Mississippi State Normal and Agricultural College for Colored, and who spoke French and German but not Russian, rode in the sidecar.

Watching through binoculars, Colonel Parker and Lieutenant Felter saw short, squat, gray-clad troops rise from the ground and intercept the motorcycle. And then Lieutenant Fernwall and the MP T/4 were seen being marched down the road into Zwenkau.

When they did not reappear in thirty minutes, Colonel Parker summoned Major L. J. Conzalve, who was functioning as a replacement for his bitterly disappointed executive officer who had been left with the regiment outside Bad Nauheim. He informed the major that he was going into Zwenkau in his track and that if he did not reappear or otherwise communicate in sixty minutes, the major was to move into Zwenkau with the remaining tracks, returning fire if fired upon.

Colonel Parker then ordered the multiple .50 mounts on the half-tracks to be pointed to the rear, so as to visually demonstrate a nonbelligerent attitude. Next he ordered his driver to move out. As they approached the stone fence which was obviously the outer ring of the Russian line, he motioned Felter to stand beside him in the front seat.

At that moment, a half dozen Soviet soldiers, in battle-soiled quilted cotton jackets, rough wool pants, and canvas and rubber shoes, stepped out in front of them, their submachine guns held menacingly.

One soldier stood in the middle of the road, blocking their passage.

They were, Colonel Parker realized with surprise, Orientals of some sort. And then he identified them: Mongols. He had heard that the Russians were using Mongols as their assault troops.

"Do not the soldiers of the Soviet Union salute a colonel of the United States Army?" Felter snapped in Russian. There was no reply and no salute.

"Get that man out of the road, or we'll drive over him," Felter went on. Then he told the driver to drive on. As soon as the gears clashed, and the engine revved, the Mongolian soldier stepped out of the way.

They rolled, past stone farm buildings into Zwenkau and came to the center of town, a wide marketplace with a flowing water pipe. An ancient church stood on the far side of the square. Lieutenant Fernwall and the motorcycle driver were standing by the motorcyle. There were three Russians with them, troops that somehow both Felter and Parker recognized to be company-grade officers. One of them walked up to the track and saluted.

"This is Colonel Parker, of the United States Army 393rd Tank Destroyer Regiment," Felter said. "Send for your commanding officer."

"I am the commanding officer," one of the Mongolian officers said.

"We do not deal with captains," Felter said.

"He spoke a little German," Lieutenant Fernwall said. "I think he sent for somebody."

"Ask him where the Americans are," Colonel Parker said to Felter.

"I don't think we'd better ask," Felter said. "I think we had better give them the idea we know where they are."

"All right," Parker said. "I've got to take a leak. Come with me."

He opened the door of the track and climbed down.

"Inform your superiors that the colonel is here," Felter said to the Russian officer. Then he followed Colonel Parker across the cobblestones to what had apparently been a tavern, a gasthaus. Parker, with intentional arrogance, pushed the door open. Half a dozen women, in torn clothing, cowered in a corner of what had been the dining room. There were two naked women lying on the floor, dead, one from a bullet wound in the face, the other slashed across the stomach.

"There is a 'Herren' sign," Felter said, "if you want the men's room."

Parker followed the nod of Felter's head. There was a urinal trough in the men's room, but there were feces in it and in piles on the floor already attracting hordes of flies.

"Savages! Savages!" Parker said. He relieved himself in the urinal. He looked at Felter. "Are you all right? You're not going to pass out?"

"No, sir."

When Colonel Parker had zipped his trousers, he marched back out of the gasthaus, looking at neither the bodies nor the women cowering against the wall. A jeep was now drawn up with its bumper against the bumper of the track, and a Caucasian officer standing beside it. His uniform was of much finer material than the uniforms of the Mongolians. He was not, Parker sensed, a combat officer.

"What is he?" Parker asked. "Do you know the insignia?"

"Major of military government," Felter said. "Either military government or service of supply."

The major saluted, and walked toward Parker and Felter.

"Good morning, Colonel," he said, in heavily accented English. "You seem to be lost."

"Good morning, Major," Felter replied, in Russian. "May I present Colonel Parker of the 393rd Tank Destroyer Regiment?"

"You speak Russian very well, Lieutenant," the major said, in Russian, looking at him with interest. "Are you perhaps Russian?"

"I am an American," Felter said. The major shook hands almost absent-mindedly with Colonel Parker.

"But then you must have Russian parents," he said. He switched to English. "I was saying, Colonel, that you seem to have lost your way."

"We are not lost," Parker said. "Quite the contrary. We have come for the American prisoners."

"What American prisoners?" the Russian major asked, innocently.

"The prisoners of Stalag XVII-B," Parker said.

"I'm afraid I have no idea what you're talking about," the major said.

"I'm very sorry to hear that," Parker said. "I had hoped you would be able to help us find our countrymen. Now we'll just have to look for them."

"This is the front line, Colonel," the Russian major said, coldly. "It would be dangerous for you to move around very much here."

"Yes, it probably will be," Parker said. "But one has one's orders, and one does what one can to carry them out."

"As I say, I know of no prisoners—" the major said.

Parker interrupted him, calling up to the driver of the track. "Have Major Conzalve send a half dozen tracks down here, Sergeant."

"Colonel," the major said, in English, "I must insist that you withdraw."

"What did he say, Lieutenant?" Parker asked politely.

"I said," the Russian said, "I must insist that you not send—"

"Major," Felter said, in Russian. "Why don't you say what you want in Russian, and then I will translate for you."

"I said," the Russian said, now blustering, the Russian words coming out in a torrent, "that you must withdraw. This area is occupied by the Soviet Army."

"I don't quite understand what you mean," Parker said. "Withdraw? Withdraw where?"

The sound of half-track engines could now be heard.

"Please tell your colonel that I insist he withdraw his forces to American lines," the Russian said, furiously.

"Colonel," Felter repeated. "The major insists that you withdraw to American lines."

"Ask him what he means by that," Parker replied.

Felter repeated the question in Russian.

The major glowered at both of them, but said nothing. The sounds of half-track engines and the clanking of their tracks were now loud in the early morning quiet. The Americans were coming. The only way they could be stopped was by firing at them. The Russian major was not prepared to do that.

"Ask him where the prisoners are, Felter," Colonel Parker said, coldly, looking directly at the Russian major.

The first of the tracks became visible down the narrow street leading to the marketplace. There was a very large black officer standing up beside the driver, and its four .50 caliber Brownings were manned and pointing forward. Ten feet behind it came a second track, and ten feet behind that a third. When the tracks reached the marketplace, they formed a line, six abreast, and then sat with their engines idling.

"Ask the major, Felter," Colonel Parker said, "if he will lead us to the prisoners, or if he wants us to go find them ourselves."

"A protest will be made," the Russian major said.

"Tell the major what he can do with his protest, Felter," Colonel Parker said.

[THREE]
Zwenkau, Russian-occupied Germany
8 April 1945

The two hundred and thirty-eight American officers, formerly interned in Stalag XVII-B, were in the huge and ancient timbered barn of a farm two miles east of Zwenkau. A detachment of soldiers assigned to the Military Government and Civil Affairs Division of the Red Army had laid a single roll of concertina barbed wire in a circle twenty yards from the barn. They had made clear the purpose of the barbed wire by firing a jeep-mounted machine gun into the ground ahead of a party of American officers who wished to pass the barbed wire while serving as burial detail.

The first German to die had been Oberleutnant Karl-Heinz von und zu Badner. One of the Russians who had overtaken the column of prisoners had knocked Colonel Graf Peter-Paul von Greiffenberg to the ground with the butt of his machine pistol. When Badner had tried to protect the fallen colonel from being kicked in the mouth, he had been summarily executed.

Thirty minutes later, just after the Americans were shoved into the barn, the rest of the Germans had been lined up against the stone walls of the building and machine-gunned. The Russians then denied the Americans permission to bury the bodies anywhere but in the barnyard under the manure. Then, as if to show there were no personal hard feelings, the Russians had pushed through the open barn gates a dozen German women, making their intentions clear with wide grins and the international hand language for copulation.

The females, ranging in age from thirteen to sixty-four, had already been raped repeatedly before being turned over to the Americans for their pleasure.

Lt. Col. Robert F. Bellmon had had to tackle and wrestle to the ground a previously quiet and mild-mannered Signal Corps major who had quite seriously announced his intention to take the Barisnikov submachine gun away from the Russian commander and blow his fucking head off with it.

If they were to break out of here violently, Bellmon thought, that wasn't the way to do it. The possibility that they should take some action was a very real one. He had Katyn in mind, and that, he believed, presented two duties to him. As the actual commander, he had a very deep responsibility to make sure that his officers did not wind up in a ditch with their hands bound and a .32 caliber bullet in the base of their skulls.

He also had the responsibility to get the documents of the Katyn massacre to the proper American authorities. That was a double responsibility; first, a general one as an officer, and second, a personal one to Colonel Graf Peter-Paul von Greiffenberg, who had been murdered here in Saxony.

He forced himself to think calmly, to think the problem through. They had been captured by front-line assault troops. If they were going to be shot down, chances were the front-line troops would have done it, and done it already. Front-line troops of any army were more prone to commit summary executions than the service of supply troops who followed them into an area. When the supply troops moved up here, the chances of the American prisoners being massacred would diminish. It was, of course, possible that they would still be eliminated. The Poles at Katyn had been murdered by rear area troops, but it would take an order to get service troops to do something like that; and with the war about to end, Bellmon thought that an officer would be less likely to take that responsibility.

What was most likely to happen would be that vehicles would arrive and transport them to the Russian rear. If there was a movement order, Bellmon was determined to resist it, although at the moment he had no clear idea how he could.

He had Greiffenberg's Colt .32 automatic. He had been stripped of the Schmeisser.

One little pistol against a hundred armed Russians was almost the same thing as being completely unarmed. A wild thought, holding the pistol to the head of the Russian commander, came to his mind. It was not a sound plan, but it was all that he had.

And his command was in bad shape, physically and mentally exhausted. More than a dozen of his officers were nearly catatonic. They were lice-infested, dirty, hungry, and weak. Many were bootless.

He had sent one of the lieutenants up the inside wall of the barn, to the peak of the roof, where an opening gave a partial view of the rest of the farm, but not of the road leading to it, nor of the barnyard itself.

"I hear tanks, Colonel!" the lieutenant called down softly.

Bellmon had a quick mental picture of a half-circle of T-34's turning their machine guns on his officers. He dismissed it, thinking first that the tanks were on their way to the front, and if they weren't, they were vehicles entirely suitable to accompany a force of two hundred and thirty-eight men being marched to the rear.

He heard the roar of engines now himself, and the clank of tracks. The vehicles were in the barnyard now, apparently forming up in front of the fifteen-foot-tall doors.

Then the engines were killed. There was the crack of backfires, the screech of steel treads on cobblestones. Then the sound of muffled voices. He had a moment's wild suspicion, born of desperation, that he heard English. He forced that from his mind, desperately searching for a plan of action.

And then there was the sound of a trumpet, faint but unmistakable, through the heavy wooden doors. He didn't believe what he heard, because he was afraid that he had finally gone off the deep end and was hallucinating.

But in the last seconds before the ass-end of a half-track came crashing through the heavy wooden doors, he couldn't dismiss what he heard as impossible. Some sonofabitch out there *really* was playing "When the Saints Go Marching In."

The knocking down of the barn doors with the track had set up a huge cloud of dust, which billowed outward into the yard. A man staggered out through it, his arms at his sides, and looked at the tracks. His uniform was in tatters, and he was skeleton thin. But there was an overseas cap on his head, cocked to the left in the tradition of armor.

Colonel Philip S. Parker VI pressed the button on his microphone.

"Bring up the trucks," he ordered. "We've found them."

A half dozen others staggered out after him, blinking in the sunlight, shielding their eyes.

The trumpet player, a fat, very black staff sergeant with tears running down his cheeks, put his horn to his lips and played again, not quite able to do what he was trying to do, play what the army called a "spirited air." It came out more like a dirge, but it was still "When the Saints Go Marching In."

The emaciated officer looked in the direction of that track, and half smiled, making a gesture with his hand. Then he saw the commanding officer of the detachment of soldiers from the Red Army, and advanced on him, his arms spread and bent, his fingers extended, violence obviously on his mind.

Two of the men who had followed him out of the barn started after him. One of them broke into a run.

One of the Russian soldiers fired a burst with his Barisnikov machine pistol onto the cobblestones before him. The officer stopped. A half-second later, the multiple .50 caliber machine guns on one of the tracks fired a second's burst. Forty .50 caliber bullets, eight of them tracers, slammed into the cobblestones in front of the Russians. One of the Russians, not the commanding officer, slumped to the ground, the top of his head and the back of his helmet blown away by a ricocheting projectile.

By then, Lieutenant Felter was out of his half-track, across the cobblestones, and standing in front of the officer with violence on his mind.

"Colonel," Felter said. "For God's sake!"

Bellmon looked at him, as if surprised to see him.

There was the sound of starters grinding and the whine of electric motors as the multiple .50 mounts turned to bear on the Russians.

"Goddamn you, Jamison!" Colonel Parker shouted at the gunner who had let fly with the burst.

Another track, racing, came around the corner of the barn, followed by a six-by-six, a T/4 at the .50 caliber in the ring turret over the cab.

Colonel Parker jumped out of the track and signaled where he wanted the line of trucks to go, and then he went over to where Bellmon and Felter stood facing each other.

"If there are any radios in that Russian jeep," he ordered Felter, "smash them." Then he turned to Bellmon.

"Bobby," he said, very gently. "We've got to load your people and haul ass," he said.

Bellmon looked at him without recognition for a moment.

"It's Colonel Parker, isn't it?" he asked.

Parker, obviously having a hard time keeping his emotions under control, nodded. "Bobby," he repeated, "we've got to load your people right now."

"Yes," Bellmon said, dreamily, then seemed to regain some control as he said: "Yes, of course, sir." He turned and staggered back toward the door of the barn.

"Disarm them," Parker said, indicating the Russians. "Throw their weapons down a well. Lock them up in the farmhouse. Tie them up with commo wire." Parker ran back to his half-track, climbed in, and picked up the ground-to-air radio.

"We've had a little trouble down here," he said, calmly. "We're going to run back through Zwenkau. Check to see if they've tried to block the road."

The L-4 which had been circling overhead banked steeply, and flew low over the farmyard, as if the pilot was curious and wanted to see what was going on, and then flew off toward Zwenkau.

[FOUR]
57th U.S. Army Field Hospital
Giessen, Germany
11 April 1945

Carrying a bottle of Pinch Bottle Haig under his arm, Major General Peterson K. Waterford walked into a private third floor room in the neat, modern, airy hospital, which had been built for the Wehrmacht for the care of gastrointestinal illness.

"Can you handle this?" he asked, extending the bottle to the pale man with shrunken eyes, who sat on the edge of a hospital bed wearing a purple U.S. Army Medical Corps bathrobe and white cotton pajamas.

Lt. Col. Robert F. Bellmon nodded his head. General Waterford put out his hand, to shake that of Colonel Bellmon, and then suddenly changed his mind. His arm went up and around Bellmon's shoulders, and still clutching the bottle in his fist, he hugged Bellmon to him.

"I'm sorry," he said, when they had broken apart, "that I couldn't get here sooner."

"I understand."

"You are suffering from exhaustion and malnutrition," General Waterford said. "That's all."

"This is the neuropsychiatric ward," Bellmon said. "I'm surprised there isn't a sign."

"You have never been in the N-P ward," Waterford said. "The surgeon is an old friend of mine."

"I'm not really crazy, you know," Bellmon said. "Skinny, certainly, and my teeth seem to be falling out. And in a rage. But not crazy."

Waterford didn't reply. He walked to the bedside table and spilled some of the scotch into a water glass, then picked up the glass and handed it to Bellmon. "Drink that, Bob," he said.

Bellmon took the glass, and a mouthful, and swirled it around his mouth before swallowing it.

"First in a long time, huh?" General Waterford asked.

"No, actually, it's not," Bellmon said. "Philip Sheridan Parker III, in the sacred tradition of the cavalry, had a bottle in his saddlebags, when he sounded the charge and rode to the rescue."

"I have to tell you this, Bob," Waterford said. "If I had known what Phil Parker was planning to do, I would have stopped him."

"What the hell's the matter with you?" Bellmon exploded. "Don't hand me any of that noble, no special privileges bullshit. I wasn't the only officer there; and if Parker hadn't shown up when and where he did, two hundred and thirty-eight officers, including me, would now be pushing up daisies or on our way to a Siberian prison camp."

"I don't intend to debate the matter with you," Waterford said, coldly. "I just wanted you to know my position in the matter."

Bellmon looked at his father-in-law with ice in his eyes, apparently on the edge of saying something. He said nothing. Then he drank the rest of the scotch in the glass and helped himself to more.

"What happens to me now?" he asked.

"I've got you a uniform. You'll put it on. And then you'll be driven to Frankfurt. You'll be home in thirty-six hours."

"Thank you very much for the special privilege, sir," Bellmon said, sarcastically. "But if it's all right with you, I'll just stay here and press charges."

"You didn't hear me, Bob," General Waterford said. "You will be driven to Frankfurt, and you will be flown home. If you are not in a mental condition to be able to obey a lawful order when you receive one, you will be sent home in a padded cell on a hospital ship."

"You're ordering me home?" Bellmon asked.

"You'd damned well better be grateful for special privilege. George Patton is ordering you home. Eisenhower and all of his staff want you locked in the booby hatch."

"Do you understand the nature of the charges I'm bringing?" Bellmon asked.

"The counterintelligence officer you spoke to is another old friend of mine. He came to me before he passed the story upstairs."

"He wanted me to give him the photographs," Bellmon said, "and the other evidence."

"I think you'd better give them to me," Waterford said.

"Over my dead body," Bellmon said. "This is not going to be whitewashed."

"I want whatever you have, Bob," Waterford said. "I'm asking for them as nicely as I intend to."

"You can have them taken from me, I suppose," Bellmon replied. "But you'll have to use force. And that will force Barbara to choose between us."

"Just what the hell do you think you can do with that stuff? For God's sake, those allegations have already been considered and dismissed as enemy propaganda."

"They're not 'allegations,' " Bellmon said, furiously. "Goddamnit. I was there."

"You were a prisoner, subject to enormous psychological pressure."

"I was taken to Katyn by Peter-Paul von Greiffenberg," Bellmon said. "Did your CIC friend tell you that, too?"

"No," Waterford said. He was visibly surprised to hear that. "He did not."

"And did he tell you that the ranking officer of the group of Germans who had made themselves my prisoners, who our Russian allies stood against the wall at Zwenkau, shot, then made us bury under a pile of cow shit, was your old friend, Colonel Count Peter-Paul von Greiffenberg?"

"Good God!" Waterford said.

"I'm not crazy, Dad," Bellmon said. "Two hundred and thirty-eight officers saw what those bastards did."

"The Germans' hands aren't clean, Bob," Waterford said.

"What's that got to do with it?"

"One of my regiments ran over a place where the Germans took the Russians and Polish, and for that matter, their own Jews. They gassed them, Bob, by the tens of thousands, maybe even by the millions. Then, after they shaved off their hair and pulled their teeth for the gold, they burned them in ovens."

Bellmon looked at him.

"I can't believe you'd tell me something like that if it wasn't true," he said.

"It's true. I went and saw it myself," Waterford said.

"Then I suppose, under the rules of land warfare, we are going to have to try the Germans responsible for that, and hang them. As I intend to have the Russians responsible for Katyn and Zwenkau tried and hung."

"You can forget Zwenkau," Waterford said.

"Forget it?"

"It was a regrettable misunderstanding, with error on both sides," Waterford said.

"Because one Russian got himself blown away with a ricochet?"

Waterford nodded.

"Prisoners were taken from me," Bellmon said. "And shot down in cold blood."

"The Russian story is that they liberated you from the Germans, who were killed in the engagement."

"My officers will tell you different."

"The senior prisoner is mad," Waterford said. "Certifiably mad. He is going home in a padded cell on a hospital ship."

"I had assumed command," Bellmon said. Waterford shook his head 'no'.

"Just for the hell of it, Dad," Bellmon said, sarcastically, "let me tell you about the little girl the Russians gave us. Pretty little thing. About thirteen, I would say. They had raped her, and then when they got tired of that, before they gave her to us, they stuck a bayonet up her anus. She died in the half-track on the way back. Because we couldn't stand the smell, we buried her by the side of the road. Her mother was so afraid of the Russians she begged us not to leave her. She wouldn't even get out of the half-track long enough to watch us bury her daughter."

"Oh, for Christ's sake, this is getting us nowhere," General Waterford said, impatiently. "Don't you think I've heard these stories before?"

"If you have, they don't seem to bother you very much," Bellmon said.

"I'll lay it out for you, Bob, and hope you can understand what I'm saying. You can continue making noise about this. You have my word it will get you nowhere. No matter what you say the Russians have done, the Germans have done worse. If you continue to make noise here, you will be sent home for psychiatric care. That would be the end of your career, and you know it."

"If this is how I am supposed to behave as an officer, I'm not sure I want a career."

"You can go home now and keep your mouth shut, bide your time, and decide in a year or so if you want to make a stink then. Get it through your head you cannot make a stink now. No one will listen. It would be an exercise in futility."

"Shit!" Bellmon said, and walked to the window of his hospital room. The sun was shining, and the trees just starting to turn green. But Bellmon smelled burned wood and stagnant water, perhaps even a faint odor of rotting human flesh in the air. He looked at the glass of whiskey in his hand, raised it to his lips, and drank it down. Then he walked back to the bedside table and poured more scotch in his glass.

"So what's your advice?" he asked, turning to face his father-in-law.

"I think you should go home, get your weight and your strength back, be with Barbara and the kids, and take time to make up your mind."

"My mind is made up!"

"Decide whether you can be of greater service to your country as a general officer when that time comes, or as a shrill, forcefully retired officer who went mad in a POW camp," General Waterford said.

"You're saying that no one will believe me?"

"I didn't say that," Waterford said. "I believe you. Patton believes you. That's why he's sticking his neck out for you. I'm saying that if you expect anything to be done, you're wrong."

"What did Colonel Parker do? I presume he got a speech like this."

"Patton pinned a Silver Star on him and then he got him out of theater before the chair-warmers around Ike could relieve him of his command. You owe Phil Parker, Bob. That operation he mounted to go get you cost him his star."

"What the hell kind of a war is this?"

"A shitty kind of a war," General Waterford said. "Do you know of any other kind?"

[**FIVE**]

Mrs. Robert F. Bellmon, her mother, Mrs. Peterson K. Waterford, and the Bellmon children were on hand at Andrews Army Air Corps Base near Washington, D.C., when Lt. Col. Robert F. Bellmon was returned from the European Theater of Operations by military aircraft.

The first thing Barbara Bellmon thought when she saw her husband walk stiffly down the portable stairway rolled up against the Military Air transport Command C-54 was that he was an old man.

All the returned prisoners were reunited with their families in a hangar which had been cleared of aircraft and support equipment on a semipermanent basis for that purpose.

The aide-de-camp to the commanding general of Andrews Army Air Corps Base waited until Lt. Col. Bellmon had a moment to embrace his wife, his children, and his mother-in-law; and then he went to him and gently touched his arm. When he had his attention, he quietly told Bellmon there was a car waiting for him outside the hangar, that it would not be necessary for him to ride with the others on the bus to the Walter Reed U.S. Army Medical Center. The commanding general of Andrews and Major General Peterson K. Waterford had been classmates at the Academy.

Lt. Col. Bellmon's children had no idea who he was.

Barbara Bellmon was sure that Bob would blow his cork when he found out that he would be required to undergo, for seventy-two hours a comprehensive physical and psychiatric examination before he could go on leave. But he said nothing at all about it, just nodded his head; and she wondered if there was perhaps something wrong with him mentally.

She had already been briefed by an army psychiatrist, who told her that she should prepare herself for significant psychological changes in her husband's behavior. Imprisonment was, he said, a psychological trauma.

On the morning of his fourth day home, he called her where she was staying at the Wardman Park Hotel.

"Have you got any money?" he asked.

"I don't know what you mean?"

"If I don't stick around here to get paid, I can leave now," he said.

"Come," she said. "Come right now."

Mrs. Waterford took the kids to the Smithsonian Institution, and said that she would probably buy them supper somewhere.

When he tried to make love to her, he couldn't.

"The psychiatrist warned me this was liable to happen," he said. "I'm sorry."

"Don't be silly, Bob," she said. "We have the rest of our lives to catch up."

It didn't seem to bother him, she saw with enormous relief. He immediately changed the subject.

He rolled away from her on the bed and handed her his copy of his physical examination. It had been determined, she read, that he was of sound mind and body, though showing signs of malnutrition. He had been warned to seek dental attention, since prolonged malnutrition made the gums shrink, loosening teeth and causing other oral-dental problems.

The very phrase "prolonged malnutrition" filled Barbara with pity.

"I'm on a thirty days' returned prisoner-of-war leave," Bob told her. "And we have reservations at the Greenbrier Hotel, at government expense. Do you want to go?"

"Do you?" Barbara asked.

"I don't know," he said listlessly.

"What would you like to do?" Barbara pursued.

"I'd like to buy a car," he said. "And take a long, slow drive to Carmel."

"OK," she said. "When do you want to look for a car?"

"How about now?" he asked.

Barbara got out of bed and started to get dressed.

Mrs. Waterford returned to Carmel with the children by train. Lt. Col. Bob Bellmon bought a 1941 Buick convertible sedan and started out with Barbara on a slow, cross-country drive. One of their stops was at Manhattan, Kansas, outside Fort Riley, where Colonel Bellmon presented his respects to recently retired Colonel Philip S. Parker III.

Later Mrs. Parker confided to Barbara that so long as they had been married, she had never seen her husband quite as drunk as he got with Bob Bellmon. The two women tried to determine what it was that had so gotten to their husbands. They each took what solace they could from learning that neither husband had chosen to confide in his wife.

Barbara Bellmon was tempted to inquire of Mrs. Parker if her husband was impotent, too. But the words would not come. Officers' ladies did not discuss that sort of thing among themselves.

It took them thirteen days to reach Carmel. Once there, Bob spent long hours working on the Buick, completely rebuilding the straight-eight engine and lining the brakes, all by himself in the garage. He took long walks, alone, very early in the morning along the Pacific Ocean, and ritually drank himself into a sullen stupor by five in the afternoon.

Barbara Bellmon concluded that it was a vicious circle. He drank because he was impotent; and because he was hung over and/or drunk, he couldn't get it up. After doing everything but appear in pasties and a G-string, she sensed somehow that the thing to do was wait.

He asked for, and was granted, a thirty-day extension of his leave. His orders, to the Airborne Board at Fort Bragg, N.C., came in the mail on the tenth day of the extension.

"You getting a little bored, honey?" he asked. "You want to report in early and see about getting someplace decent to live?"

"I think that would be a good idea," Barbara said.

Right after lunch on the day before they left Carmel, he began a frenzied search through his footlockers, which had been stored at Fort Knox during the war, then shipped to Carmel after his return. He took from them what he thought they would need in the first weeks at Bragg before their household goods arrived.

Mrs. Waterford had arranged a small cocktail party for old friends for five that afternoon. Barbara, afraid that he would be drunk when the party started, and afraid to say anything that would make it inevitable, nevertheless went to their bedroom; and under pretense of getting dressed for the party and helping him pack, she gave him company.

At a quarter to five, when Barbara was looking through already packed suitcases for a slip, she heard the lid of a footlocker slam and turned to look at him.

He was smiling.

"Finished?" she asked.

"Finished," he said. "Everything I won't need is in the one we'll take with us. And everything I will need is in the other one, which will arrive in time for Christmas, 1948."

"You'd better get dressed, then," she said, and bent over the suitcase again.

"That's exactly the opposite of what I have in mind," he said.

She didn't quite get his meaning until he had walked up behind her, pressed his erection against her rear end, and slipped his hand under the elastic of her panties.

She straightened, and pressed her head backward against his; and very slowly, very carefully, very much afraid that when she touched it, it would go down, she moved her hand to his crotch.

Then she turned around without taking her hand off him, pulled him toward the bed, and lay down on it. She pushed her panties out of the way and guided him into her.

The Bellmon kids had a ball on the drive to Fort Bragg from Carmel. They were left much to themselves. They even had their own room in the motels at night. About the only thing wrong with the trip was the embarrassment their parents caused them by constantly holding hands and smooching and not acting their age.

[SIX]
Camp 263
Near Kyrtym'ya, Russian Soviet Federated Republic
21 June 1945

The German prisoners were ordered from the trains immediately on arrival. A detail was picked from them to load coal into the tender of the locomotive. Since there were no shovels, the loading was accomplished by a chain of prisoners between the coal pile and the tender. Each prisoner carried an eight- or ten-inch lump of coal and passed it along until it reached the tender. The locomotive was then detached from the string of cars and reattached to the other end. The train immediately left the siding. Since there was a shortage in Russia of both train cars and locomotives, the ones they had were kept moving as much as possible.

Bread and sausage were distributed among the prisoners. They had not eaten much in the past three weeks, and they fought over the food.

Portable barricades—sawhorses laced with barbed wire—were emplaced by prisoner laborers around the siding. Guard posts and a deadline were also established. More elaborate security measures were not required, for Kyrtym'ya was an island in the swamps, completely water-filled in the spring from melting snow. There was no place else for the prisoners to go, even if they had the strength.

The prisoners were kept where they had gotten down from the boxcars for four days, while the administrative processing was completed.

The records of some of the prisoners, and all of the SS, were immediately separated. These would be immediately put to work draining the swamp.

The records were also searched for prisoners whose skills were needed to administer the camp. Prisoners who spoke Russian were in great demand, and so were carpenters, foresters, tailors, and supply clerks. There was a surplus of food service personnel.

Some of the NKVD records were flagged. These prisoners had either actual or professed socialist and/or Russian sympathies; and after a period of time, it was contemplated that they might be of some use. These were to be assigned duties which would give them a greater chance—by no means a sure chance—of surviving a winter or two in the swamp.

Other prisoners' records were flagged in a manner indicating that they were to be kept alive. The phrase used was that "the physical condition and status of reeducation of this prisoner will be reported monthly." The NKVD expected to hear that the prisoner in question was not only alive, but that his reeducation was progressing satisfactorily.

One of the prisoners whose records were so flagged was identified on the NKVD records as Greiffenberg, Peter P. von (formerly Colonel), 88-234-017.

Number 88-234-017 was assigned to work as a clerk in the office of the logging master. It was inside work, and that was important in the winter in the swamp.

IV

[ONE]
Fort Bragg, North Carolina
9 July 1945

There were twelve multicolored ribbons above the breast pocket of Lt. Colonel Paul Hanrahan's tunic, and above them was pinned the CIB, the Expert Combat Infantry insignia: a silver flintlock rifle on a blue background circled by an open silver wreath, and above that, parachutist's wings with two stars signifying two jumps into combat.

There were no ribbons above Lieutenant Rudolph G. MacMillan's breast pocket, just his CIB and his jump wings with five stars.

MacMillan walked into Hanrahan's office and saluted. There was a pleased smile on his face.

"How the hell are you, you kiltless Scotchman?" Hanrahan said, returning the salute casually, and then coming around his desk to warmly shake MacMillan's hand.

"Permit the lieutenant to say," MacMillan said, grinning broadly, "that the colonel, so help me God, even looks like a colonel."

"With one exception, Mac," Hanrahan said, waving him into an upholstered chair, "you don't look so bad yourself."

"What's the exception?"

"There's an order around here, Mac," Colonel Hanrahan said, "that officers are supposed to wear their ribbons."

MacMillan shrugged, unrepentant.

"You want some coffee, Mac?" Hanrahan asked.

"Please," MacMillan said. "What's this all about, anyway?"

In 1940, Hanrahan had been a second john, and MacMillan had been a corporal. They had made their first jump together, when the entire airborne force of the United States Army had been the 1st Battalion (Airborne) (Provisional) (Test) of the 82nd Infantry Division. They had been paratroopers together before anyone knew if the idea would work, and long before the 82nd Infantry Division had become the 82nd Airborne.

They had last seen one another in 1942, when First Lieutenant Paul Hanrahan had suddenly vanished from the 508th Parachute Infantry Regiment in 1942. Nobody knew for sure where he had gone, but rumor had it that he was on some hush-hush operation in Greece with something called the OSS.

"You are about to be counseled about your career by a senior officer of suitable rank and experience," Colonel Hanrahan said. "So pay attention." He handed MacMillan a china cup full of steaming black coffee.

"Thanks," MacMillan said. "Can you get me away from those goddamned historians? I'm losing my marbles."

"The day after one war is over, we start training for the next one," Hanrahan said. "The historians have a place in that. The presumption is that somebody who lives through a war must have been doing something right. So they will write down the Saga of Mac MacMillan, and force unsuspecting people to read it. You'll be immortal, Mac."

"Bullshit, is what it is," MacMillan said.

"Shame on you!" Hanrahan said, laughing.

"The division is coming home," MacMillan said. "Can you get me a company?"

"I could, but I won't," the colonel said, looking directly at MacMillan.

"Why not?"

"Can I talk straight, Mac, and not have you quoting me all around the division?"

"Sure," Mac said.

"If we were going to war, you'd have a company," the colonel said. "But we're going to have peace, Mac, and that's a whole new ball game. They don't want company commanders, even with the Medal, who quit school in the tenth grade." He looked at MacMillan to get his reaction. MacMillan didn't seem very surprised.

"The war is over, soldiers and dogs keep off the grass?" he replied.

"Don't feel crapped upon," Hanrahan said. "They don't want twenty-six-year-old light birds, either."

"They gonna bust you back?"

"They're trying hard," Hanrahan said. "I want to show you something, Mac." He motioned Mac to the desk, where he had MacMillan's service record open before him, and pointed to a line on one of its pages.

```
18Apr45 Returned US Mil Control, US Embassy Cairo Egypt
20Apr45 Transit Cairo Egypt via Mil Air Ft Devens, Mass
22Apr45 VOP 4 days lv
26Apr45 Transit Hq War Dept
29Apr45 Hq Ft Bragg Dy w/US Army Historical Section
```

"What the hell is VOP?" Mac asked. He could translate without thinking all other abbreviations, but VOP was new to him.

"I had to ask to find out," the colonel said. "It stands for Verbal Order of the President."

"That's funny," Mac said. "He told me when I was there, that when he was a battery commander, he found out there 'was AWOL and then there was *AWOL*.' "

"It's not funny, Mac," the colonel said. "That VOP is going to follow you around the army from now on. Forever, until you turn in the suit."

"What's wrong with it?"

"The bottom line is that you went AWOL," the colonel said.

"Not according to that, I didn't. I went VOP," Mac said, smiling, pronouncing it as a word, not as individual letters.

"You went AWOL and were pardoned by the President. *You went AWOL!* And every time somebody asks what the hell is 'VOP,' that story will be told. And what they are going to remember, because they will want to remember it, is that you went AWOL. That gives them a hook, Mac. And you better get used to the fact that the hook is going to be out for you from now on."

"What the hell are you talking about? I'm a goddamn hero. Didn't you read that bullshit citation?"

"Don't mock it. You *are* a hero. And that's your problem."

"I don't have idea fucking one what you're talking about," MacMillan said.

"Then pay attention. One officer in twenty gets into combat. Of the officers who do get into combat, maybe one in ten gets any kind of a medal, and one in what—ten thousand? fifty thousand?—gets *the* Medal."

"So?"

"So there's a hell of a lot more of them, Mac, then there is of you. Call it jealousy. 'How come that dumb sonofabitch, and not me?' "

"So they're jealous, so what?"

"So they will stick whatever they can—your lousy education, for example—up your ass whenever they can."

MacMillan didn't like what he had heard, but he trusted the colonel; they went back a long way. He decided he was getting the straight poop.

"What about me getting out and re-upping as a master sergeant?"

"No sense giving anything away," Hanrahan said.

"You just as much as told me I don't have what it takes to be a good company commander," Mac said. "I may not be. But I *know*, goddamnit, that I'd be a good first sergeant."

"I didn't say that you wouldn't be a good company commander, Mac," Hanrahan said. "You're not listening to me."

"Then what the hell *are* you saying?"

"You're a brand-new first lieutenant," Hanrahan said. "So you can forget about getting promoted for a long time. Five years, maybe six. Maybe longer."

"I don't find anything wrong with being a first lieutenant," MacMillan said. "But I thought you were just saying they'd try to take it away from me."

"What you have to do is pass the time doing something where you can't get in trouble, where there won't be too much competition for your job."

"That brings us right back to me commanding a company. Goddamn, airborne is what I know. Airborne is *all* I know."

Hanrahan was losing his patience. No getting around it, MacMillan was none too bright.

"Airborne is dead. It just doesn't know enough to fall over," Hanrahan said, patiently. "But for Christ's sake, Mac, don't quote me on that."

"That's a hell of a thing to say," MacMillan said. He was truly shocked. It was as if the colonel had accused Jim Gavin of cowardice.

"For Christ's sake, think. You were at Sicily. Look what our own navy did to us, by mistake. How many planeloads got shot down before they got near the goddamned drop zone? You made Normandy. Look how they tore us up in Normandy. And you jumped across the Rhine. That was a disaster, and you know it was."

MacMillan was looking at him, Hanrahan thought, like a hurt little boy.

"For Christ's sake, Mac," Hanrahan said, "you were there. You were bagged there. And you don't understand what a colossal waste of assets and people that was?"

"I never expected to hear something like that from you, of all people," MacMillan said. "Jesus Christ, you and me started airborne!"

"I'm a soldier, Mac. Not an airborne soldier, not any kind of special soldier. I'm a soldier. My duty is to see things as they are, not how I'd like them to be."

"And you think airborne is finished? You *really* think that?"

"It's a very inefficient way of getting troops on the ground. And it will grow more inefficient every passing day. And it wastes a lot of talent."

"What's that supposed to mean?" Mac demanded. They were no longer colonel and lieutenant, or even lieutenant and corporal. They were friends and professionals. They were, in fact, comrades in arms.

"You've heard that an airborne corporal is just as good, just as highly trained, just as efficient a leader, as a leg lieutenant?"

"And I believe it," MacMillan said, firmly. "For Christ's sake, if I had volunteered six months later, they wouldn't have taken me. I didn't have a high enough Army General Classification Test score."

"That's my point. They had almost as high qualifications for jump school as they did for OCS."

"Your goddamn right they did," MacMillan said, righteously.

"Then apply some logic. Extend the argument," Hanrahan said. "If a man is good enough to be a lieutenant, we should be using him as a lieutenant, not an assistant squad leader. If we're going to spend people, which is the name of the game, Mac, keep the price high. Every airborne sergeant we spent, dead before he hit the ground, probably could have kept twenty legs alive if he had been a leg sergeant."

"Jesus!" MacMillan said.

He walked to the window and looked out. Hanrahan saw that he was disturbed and was pleased. To get his point across, he was going to have to really shake MacMillan up.

MacMillan finally turned from the window and leaned against the sill, supporting himself on his hands.

"You're trying to tell me the whole airborne idea was wrong?"

"There were two mistakes in War II, Mac," Hanrahan said, gently. "Airborne and bombers."

"Somebody did something right. We won," Mac said, sarcastically.

"The navy did what it was supposed to do," the colonel said. "And so did the artillery. But the ones who really came through, on both sides, were the tankers."

Mac just looked at him.

"You ever wonder why we didn't jump across the Rhine near Cologne? You *know* why we didn't jump on Berlin?" Hanrahan pursued.

"You tell me, Red," Mac said. "I'm just a dumb paratrooper who apparently doesn't know his ass from a hole in the ground."

"Because when the tanks crossed the Rhine, they brought their support with them, and they brought firepower with them. Not some lousy 105 howitzers with fifty rounds a gun. The big stuff and all the ammo they needed for them. And we didn't jump on Berlin because the 2nd Armored was already across the Elbe."

"The Russians took Berlin."

"Correction. Three mistakes in War II. Ike giving Berlin to the Russians. 2nd Armored could have taken it. Eisenhower ordered them to hold in place."

"He did?" MacMillan had apparently never heard that before. "What for?"

"Political considerations," Hanrahan said, watching his tongue very carefully. He thought it was entirely possible that MacMillan had never considered why World War II was fought. The more he thought about that, the more sure he was he was right. MacMillan had fought in World War II, fought superbly, risked his ass a hundred times, simply because he was a soldier and somebody had issued an order.

"I didn't know that," Mac said. The colonel said nothing. "What are you telling me I should do, Red? Go to armor? I'm infantry. *Airborne infantry.*"

"No, you shouldn't go to armor. First of all, they wouldn't take you. And if they did, they'd eat you up worse than airborne would."

"They'd eat me up? I'm airborne. But the way you talk, *you* don't think of yourself as airborne," Mac said.

"I haven't been airborne since I left the 508th Parachute Infantry," Hanrahan said.

"I notice you're wearing two combat jump stars on your wings," MacMillan replied.

"I went into Greece twice," Hanrahan said. "Once out of a B-25, the other time out of a B-24. A combat jump is defined as a jump into enemy-held territory."

"I never thought about that," MacMillan said. "You know what I think of when I think of a combat jump? A whole regiment, a whole division."

"I've known you long enough to say this," Hanrahan said. "Without you thinking I'm just making an excuse for leaving the 508."

"Say what?" Macmillan asked.

"Mac, we jumped in four guys, five guys at a time. Sometimes just one guy. But we did more damage to the enemy than a battalion of parachutists, maybe a regiment. Maybe even, goddamnit, a division."

"You and three, four other guys?" Mac asked, in disbelief.

"We had more Germans chasing us around Greece than you would believe. And every German that was chasing us wasn't fighting someplace else. That's the name of the game, neutralizing the enemy's forces, Mac, not 'Geronimo,' not 'Blood on the Risers.' "

MacMillan was made uncomfortable by the discussion. He realized that he really thought, at first, that jumping all by yourself out an Air Corps bomber wasn't really a combat jump. But then he carried that further. At least when the regiment had jumped, he hadn't been alone. Hanrahan's jumping had been more dangerous than even his own jumping in as a pathfinder had been, and the pathfinders had gone in a couple of hours before the rest of the division had jumped. Hanrahan, MacMillan realized, with something close to awe, had jumped into Greece *knowing* that there would be no regiment jumping after him.

"So what are you going to do, in this peacetime army we're about to have?" he asked.

"I'm going back to Greece," Hanrahan said.

"Why do you want to do that?" MacMillan replied, surprised. "I didn't even know we had any troops there."

"Because I like being a lieutenant colonel, for one reason, and they tell me that if I'm in Greece, I can keep it, at least for a while. I hope I can keep it long enough to keep it, period."

"What are you going to do in Greece?" MacMillan asked.

"Train the Greeks to do their own fighting," Hanrahan said. "We send in an experienced company-grade officer and a couple of really good noncoms, make them advisors to a company, or even a battalion. That's where it's going to be, Mac: for the price of three or four people, you get a company."

"Special people, huh? Regular soldiers, who really know what they are doing?"

"Special people, but stop smiling; you can't go."

"Why the hell not?"

"Because you're a *hero*, MacMillan. I keep trying to tell you what that means. It would be embarrassing for the army if we lost a Medal of Honor winner on some Greek hill in a war we aren't even admitting we're fighting."

"Fuck the medal, I'll give it back."

"Don't be an ass, Mac," Hanrahan said. "That medal is your guarantee of a pension at twenty years as a major, maybe even a light bird."

"I don't want to sound like damned fool, but I don't want to spend the next fifteen years as somebody's dog robber," MacMillan said. "I'm a soldier."

"For the next couple of years, until things simmer down and get reasonably back to normal, all you have to do is keep your ass out of the line of fire."

"Like doing what, for example?"

"Army aviation," Hanrahan said.

"You've got to be kidding," MacMillan said. "Army aviation, shit!"

Hanrahan lost his temper. His voice was icy and contemptuous when he replied, "Engage your brain, Mac, before opening your mouth."

MacMillan colored and glared at him. Hanrahan did not back down.

"OK," MacMillan said, after a long pause. "I'm listening. Tell me about Army aviation."

"Those little airplanes, and helicopters, too, are going to be around the army from now on. And it's going to get bigger, not smaller and smaller. The Air Corps is going to go after bigger and bigger bombers, and the army is going to have to fend for itself with light airplanes."

"What's that got to do with me?"

"It's a very good place for you to be," Hanrahan said. "There aren't very many aviators around who know their ass from a hole in the ground about the army. And don't underestimate your medal. You can be a very big fish in a small pond."

"You know, I don't believe any of this conversation," MacMillan said.

"I'm not finished," the colonel said. "I've got you a space at Riley."

"The Ground General School? Doing what?"

"For a fourteen-week course, after which you will be an army liaison pilot," the colonel said.

"You've got to be kidding," MacMillan said. "All those guys are is commissioned jeep drivers."

"Some of them are, and some of them are just as good soldiers as you are," Hanrahan said, coldly. Then he lightened his voice. "They get flight pay, which is the same dough as jump pay. What have you got to lose?"

"I'm supposed to spend the next ten, fifteen years flying one of those little airplanes? An aerial jeep driver?"

"By then, you'll be a captain. With a little bit of luck, a major." He looked at MacMillan. "Airborne is dead, Mac. You either go to army aviation or you spend your time as a talking dummy for the PIO guys, giving speeches to the VFW. Believe me."

MacMillan looked at Hanrahan for a full minute before he finally said anything. *"Army aviation?"* he asked, incredulous.

Hanrahan nodded his head.

"Oh, goddamn," MacMillan said. "Wait till Roxy hears about this."
"Happy landings, Mac," Hanrahan said.

[TWO]
Sandhofen, Germany
16 February 1946

It was Major General Peterson K. Waterford's custom to receive newly assigned junior officers in his office at Headquarters, United States Constabulary. The headquarters was established in a Kaserne designed, it was rumored, by Albert Speer himself, and intended to provide the officer cadets of the SS with far more luxurious accommodations than those provided to officer cadets of the army, navy, and air force.

The office now occupied by General Waterford was the most impressive he had ever occupied. His red, two-starred major general's flag and the cavalry yellow flag of the Constabulary were crossed against the wall behind a desk. (The insignia of the Constabulary, sewn into the middle of the flag, was a "C" pierced by a lightning bolt, giving the irreverent cause to refer to the United States Constabulary, the police force of the United States Army of Occupation, as "the Circle C Cab Company.") The desk itself was twelve feet long and six feet wide. It was forty-four feet from the forward edge of the desk to the door to the office.

General Waterford lined newly arrived officers up before his enormous desk, and gave them a thirty-minute pep talk and "Welcome to the U.S. Constabulary" handshake, before sending them down for duty to the regiments and battalions and companies and platoons.

Twenty or thirty company-grade officers every week or so were gathered in the general's outer office by Lieutenant Davis, his junior aide-de-camp. They were given a cup of coffee, while the aide briefed them on what was expected of them when they passed through the door onto which was fastened a gleaming brass nameplate that read: MAJOR GENERAL PETERSON K. WATERFORD, COMMANDING GENERAL.

The aide-de-camp explained that the reception was designed to make them feel part of the outfit, to give them an understanding of the great privilege it was for them to be in the Constab, and under the command of Major General Peterson K. Waterford himself.

Lieutenant Davis briefed groups of junior officers so often that he hardly paid any attention to individual officers at all. The only reason that First Lieutenant MacMillan had caught First Lieutenant Davis's eye at all was because of what MacMillan wore on the tunic of his pinks and greens when he reported at the prescribed time to be received by the general. Everybody else in the room was wearing the ribbons representing the decorations they had been awarded. The general desired that every officer and trooper of the United States Constabulary wear his authorized ribbons. The general's desire was made known in the mimeographed Memo to Newly Assigned Officers furnished each newcomer.

Lieutenant MacMillan was not wearing any ribbons at all when he showed up in

General Waterford's outer office. He did, however, have three metal qualification devices pinned to his tunic. On top was the Expert Combat Infantry Badge. Below the CIB was a set of paratrooper's wings, with five stars signifying jumps in combat, and below them he wore a set of aviator's wings.

General Waterford said nothing about MacMillan's defiance vis-à-vis the wearing of authorized ribbons, but when all the hands had been shaken, and the newcomers had been dismissed and were leaving his office, Major General Waterford said: "Lieutenant MacMillan, will you please stay a moment after these gentlemen have gone?"

It was Lieutenant Davis's firm belief that Lieutenant MacMillan's first step in the Constab had been into a bucket of shit. He was going to have his ass eaten out, in General Waterford's legendary manner, for not having worn his ribbons.

And it had started out that way, too.

"Lieutenant MacMillan," the general said. "I am somewhat surprised to see that you are not wearing your ribbons."

MacMillan came to attention but said nothing.

Oh, you poor bastard, Lieutenant Davis thought.

"If I had your decorations, Lieutenant MacMillan, I would wear them proudly," the general said. MacMillan responded to that with a slightly raised quizzical eyebrow.

"Oh, yes, Lieutenant MacMillan," the general said. "I know all about your decorations, and how you came by them. It has also been brought to my attention that under stress, you are prone to use foul and obscene language to senior officers."

"Sir?" MacMillan asked.

" 'Fuck it, Colonel,' " the general said. " 'Have the bugler sound the charge.' "

MacMillan looked really confused now. The general allowed him to sweat for a full sixty seconds before walking up to him with his hand extended. "Bobby Bellmon's my son-in-law, Mac. Welcome aboard."

"Thank you, sir," MacMillan said.

"Take a good look at this officer, Davis," the general had said. "There are very few men who get so much as a Bronze Star without getting their ass shot up. MacMillan has never been so much as scratched. But if he were wearing all his ribbons, the way he's supposed to, he would be wearing that little blue one with the white stars."

"Yes, sir," Lieutenant Davis said.

"I don't know what the hell I'm going to do with you, Mac," the general said. "Bobby wrote and asked me to take care of you, and you know I'll do that. And I'll be damned if I'll have a Medal of Honor winner doing nothing more than flying a puddle jumper."

"Sir," MacMillan said, "if the Lieutenant may be permitted to make a suggestion?"

Waterford gestured with his hand, "come on."

"How about a company of armored infantry, sir?"

Waterford shook his head. "Bobby said you'd ask for one," he said. "But I don't think so."

"Yes, sir," MacMillan said.

"What did you do before, Mac? Before you started jumping out of airplanes?"

"I was a dog robber, sir."

"A dog robber? For whom?"

"Colonel Neal, in the old 18th Infantry."

The general looked thoughtful for a minute. Then he said, "Why not? That's a good idea."

"Sir?" MacMillan said.

"For the time being," General Waterford said, "you can be my *flying* aide-de-camp. I'll be losing my senior aide before long, anyway. You can be my aide *and* fly me around. How does that sound?"

"Whatever the General decides, sir."

"It's settled then," Waterford said. "Davis, see to his orders, and then see that he's settled down in quarters, will you?" He shook MacMillan's hand again. "In a couple of days, when you're settled, Mrs. Waterford and I would like to have you and Mrs. MacMillan for dinner. Just family, Mac. Bobby feels that way about you, and I'm sure we will."

Some time later, a friend in the office of the chief of staff told Davis that Waterford had written a letter to the War Department, urging the special promotion of Lieutenant MacMillan to captain, stating that in his present assignment he had "demonstrated an ability to perform in a staff capacity very nearly as well as his record indicates he can perform in ground combat."

MacMillan's "ability to perform in a staff capacity," Lieutenant Davis somewhat bitterly thought, was not quite what it sounded like on paper. MacMillan was an ace scrounger. If the Class Six (wine, beer, and spirits) weekly ration for the division included one case of really good scotch and really good bourbon, it appeared in the general's mess and in his quarters. When Mrs. Waterford gave a buffet dinner for senior officers and their ladies, it contained roast wild boar and venison, even if that meant a squad of soldiers had to be sent out into the Tanaus Mountains with orders not to return until they had boar and deer in the back of their weapons carriers. MacMillan turned up a Hungarian bootmaker in a displaced persons' camp and put him to work turning out handmade tanker's boots for the senior officers and shoes for their wives. He even found a deserted railway car once owned by some Nazi bigwig, and put fifteen people to work turning it into a private "rolling command post" for General Waterford. Waterford was permitted to roll into Berlin to visit an old classmate with all the splendor of Reichsmarschall Göring. He rolled around Hesse in a Horche that had once belonged to Rommel. MacMillan found it, and arranged for it to be put into like-new order.

There was nothing whatever Davis could do but nurse his ill feelings in private. Among other things, Mrs. Waterford's golf partner and crony was Mrs. Roxanne MacMillan. MacMillan had moved in, and he was squeezed out. He didn't like it, but there was nothing whatever he could do about it.

The only one who had been able to resist him at all was Major Robert Robbins, the division aviation officer. Robbins was that rara avis, a West Pointer who was also an army aviator. And he knew how to play the game. By constantly reminding the general that a general should have a field-grade officer to fly him about, rather than a lowly lieutenant, and by subtly reminding the general that Lieutenant MacMillan was fresh from flight school, where he had been flying since 1941, he had remained the general's personal pilot.

[THREE]
The Frankfurt am Main–Chemnitz Autobahn
Near Bad Hersfeld, Germany
10 May 1946

The highway winds its way through pine forests and fields, its two double lanes often so far apart that one cannot be seen from the other. When there is no traffic, as there was none today, there is a pleasant feeling of being suspended in time and space.

The car was a Chevrolet, a brand new one, dark blue, which had been shipped as parts from the States and assembled at a General Motors truck factory in Belgium. It bore the license plates carried on personal automobiles of soldiers of the Army of Occupation, and a smaller plate identifying its owner as an enlisted man.

The driver was a hulking, square-faced man in his late forties, his hair so closely cropped that a six-inch scar on his scalp was clearly visible. There were four rows of ribbons above his breast pocket, and an Expert Combat Infantry Badge. On his sleeves there were the chevrons—three up and three down, individual stripes of felt sewn on a woolen background—of a master sergeant. On one sleeve were nine diagonal felt stripes, each signifying three years of service, and on the other were six-inch-long golden stripes, each signifying six months of overseas service during World War II.

Beside him on the front seat was a slight, gray-haired woman of about his age. She was wearing a skirt and a blouse and an unbuttoned sweater. Her only jewelry was a well-worn golden wedding band and a wristwatch. From time to time, she took a cigarette from her purse. Whenever she did, without taking his eyes from the road, the master sergeant produced a Ronson lighter and held it out for her.

The back seat of the four-door sedan was jammed full of wooden boxes and paper bags. The ends of cigarette cartons, soap powder boxes, and other grocery items could be seen, as could bloodstained packages of meat.

All of a sudden, when they came around a curve on the highway, two soldiers stepped into the road and signaled for the car to pull over. They wore varnished helmet liners with Constabulary insignia painted on their sides and leather Sam Brown belts; and they were armed with .45 Colt pistols.

"Oh, goddamnit!" the master sergeant said, when he realized they had been bagged by a Constabulary speed trap. Then, glancing in embarrassment at the woman beside him, he said, "Sorry."

"It's all right, Tom," the woman said.

He braked the Chevrolet and pulled to the shoulder of the road.

One of the two Constabulary troopers walked to the car. The master sergeant rolled down the window.

"Got you good, Sergeant," the Constabulary trooper said. "Sixty-eight miles per hour." The speed limit was fifty miles per hour and strictly enforced.

"Now what?" the master sergeant asked.

"Pull it over there, and report to the lieutenant," the Constabulary trooper said, pointing to a nearly hidden dirt road. Twenty yards up it three jeeps and a three-quarter-ton weapons carrier were parked, and a canvas fly had been erected over a field desk.

The master sergeant nodded, rolled up the window, and started up the road.

"I'm sorry about this."

"It couldn't be helped," the woman replied.

"What do you think I should do?" he asked.

"Pay the two dollars," she said, and laughed.

He stopped the car, pulled on the parking brake, then took his overseas cap from the seat, put it on his head, and got out of the car. As he walked to the fly-shielded field desk, he tugged the hem of his Ike jacket down over his trousers.

The lieutenant, the woman noticed, took his sweet time in making himself available to receive the sergeant; but he finally walked behind the desk, sat down on a folding chair, and permitted the sergeant to salute and report as ordered.

She saw him handing over his driver's license and the vehicle registration. Then the lieutenant swaggered over to the car.

"You German, lady?" he asked.

"No," the woman said. "I'm American."

"What have you got in the back?" the lieutenant demanded, and then, without waiting for a reply, jerked open the back door.

"Jesus Christ," he said. Look at this. What were you planning to do, open a store?"

"Hey, lieutenant!" the master sergeant called.

"What did you say? What did you say, Sergeant? Did I hear you say 'Hey' to me?"

"Excuse me, sir," the master sergeant said. "No disrespect intended."

"You just stand where you are, come to attention, and stay there until ordered otherwise, clear?"

The master sergeant looked at the woman. She made a slight gesture to him, warning him to keep his temper. The master sergeant came to attention.

"Just what do you think you're doing, Lieutenant?" the woman asked.

"What I think I'm doing, lady, is stopping your little black market operation."

"I wasn't aware that it was illegal to have commissary goods in a personal automobile," she said, reasonably.

"Who you trying to kid, lady?" the lieutenant said. "You got enough goddamned goodies in there to start a store."

"They're intended as a gift," she said.

"And pigs have wings," he said. He called to the troopers standing under the fly, and pointed out two of them. "You guys start unloading this car," he ordered. "I want a complete inventory."

"You are charging us with blackmarketing?" the woman asked.

"That's right," he said.

"Arresting us?"

"You got it," he said.

"May I make a telephone call?" she asked."

"No, you can't make a telephone call," he said. "You and your husband are under arrest. Understand?"

"I understand that when you're arrested, you are permitted a telephone call," she said. "I'm politely asking you to make that call."

He looked at her for a long moment before he replied. "Who you want to call?"

"Does it matter?"

"OK," he said. "Come on." He walked ahead of her to the table, on which sat a field telephone. She saw that the Constab corporal, a pleasant-faced young kid, was embarrassed by the lieutenant's behavior. "Get the switchboard for her," the lieutenant ordered. The kid cranked the field phone.

"Ma'am," he said, "this is the 14th Constab switchboard."

"You know how to work a field phone?" the lieutenant said. "You got to push the butterfly switch to talk."

"Thank you," she said. She took the handset and depressed the butterfly switch. "Patch me through to Jailer Six Six," she said.

The lieutenant looked at her with interest. Jailer Six was the Constabulary's provost marshal. Jailer Six Six, he decided, was probably the provost marshal sergeant. This guy had six stripes; it was therefore logical to conclude that he was an old buddy of the provost marshal sergeant. The Old Soldier Network. Well, she was wasting her time.

"Oh, Charley," she said to the telephone, "I'm so glad I caught you in."

Charley, whoever Charley was, said something the lieutenant couldn't hear. Then the woman went on: "Charley, Tom and I just got ourselves arrested. No, I'm not kidding. About ten miles out of Bad Hersfeld. Speeding, and I'm afraid we're guilty of that. But also for black-marketing, and I plead absolutely innocent to that charge."

"Yes, there's an officer here," she said. She handed the telephone to the lieutenant.

"Lieutenant Corte," he said, sharply.

"Lieutenant," the voice at the other end of the line said, "the correct manner of answering a military telephone, unless you know that the caller is junior to you, is to append the term 'sir' after your name."

Christ, she knows some officer.

"Yes, sir," he said. "I beg your pardon, sir."

"Let me get this straight, Lieutenant. I have been given to understand that you have arrested Master Sergeant Thomas T. Dawson and charged him with speeding?"

"Yes, sir. Sixty-eight miles per hour in a fifty-mile-per-hour zone."

"Are you aware, Lieutenant, that Master Sergeant Dawson is the sergeant major of the Constabulary?"

"No, sir, I was not. But with all respect, sir, the sergeant was speeding and admits as much."

"You've also charged him with black-marketing, is that correct?"

"Yes, sir. Him and his wife. Their car is loaded down with enough commissary and PX stuff to start a store."

"His wife, did you say?"

"Yes, sir. The lady who called you."

"The lady who called me, Lieutenant," the voice said, "is not Mrs. Dawson. She is Mrs. Marjorie Waterford. Mrs. Peterson K. Waterford."

Lieutenant Corte's face went white, but he said nothing.

"Lieutenant, on my authority as provost marshal of the Constabulary, you may permit Master Sergeant Dawson and Mrs. Waterford to proceed on their own recognizance," the provost marshal said. "You will forward, by the most expeditious means, the report of this incident to Constabulary headquarters, marked for my personal attention. Do you understand all that?"

"Yes, sir."

"Then please let me speak to Mrs. Waterford again, Lieutenant," the provost marshal said.

Lieutenant Corte heard: "Oh, I didn't mind so much for myself, Charley, but what he did to Tom was inexcusable. I've never seen an officer talk to a senior noncom the way this one did to Tom as long as I've been around the service."

When she hung up, she turned to face Lieutenant Corte.

"I presume we are free to go, Lieutenant?"

"Yes, ma'am," Corte said. "Mrs. Waterford, if I had any idea you were the general's wife . . ."

"You miss the point, Lieutenant," Marjorie Waterford said. "A gentleman would have been just as courteous to a sergeant's wife as he would be to a general's lady."

"Ma'am?"

"You may legally be an officer," she said. "But I fear that you are not a gentleman, Lieutenant." She waited for a reply. There was none. "Good afternoon, Lieutenant," she said. She turned and thanked the corporal who had cranked the field phone for her, and then she went and got back in the car.

When they were on the autobahn again, Master Sergeant Dawson took his eyes from the road a moment and looked at her.

"You gonna tell the boss about that jerk, Miss Marjorie?"

"I've been thinking about that, Tom," she said. "And I don't think so. Fear of the unknown is worse than having the ax fall. I think it will be better to just let him think about it."

He chuckled. "Maybe you're right," he said. "But that wasn't right, what he did."

"I think he'll think twice before he acts like that again," she said.

"That he will," the master sergeant said, chuckling.

They drove into Bad Hersfeld, close to the dividing line between the American and Russian zones of occupation, and finally stopped in front of a four-story, walk-up apartment building.

With their arms loaded with bags and boxes, they climbed four flights of stairs and knocked at the glass window of a door.

A tall, gaunt, gray-haired man in a worn, patched sweater opened it.

"Hello, Gunther," Mrs Waterford said. "You remember Sergeant Dawson, of course?"

"Nice to see the general again, Sir," Master Sergeant Dawson said.

"Marjorie, your generosity shames me," the general said.

"Don't be silly," Mrs. Waterford said. "There's more in the car. Would you help Sergeant Dawson fetch it while I say hello to Greta?"

"Of course," he said. He raised his voice. "Greta, it's Marjorie Waterford, again."

Frau Generalmajor Gunther von Hamm looked no more elegant than her husband. Her clothing was worn and patched. Her face was gray, and her eyes sunken.

"Oh, Marjorie," she said. "You constantly embarrass us. We can make out."

"I know you can," Marjorie Waterford said, kissing her cheek. "Give what you can't use to someone who can." She reached into the bag she was carrying and came out with a bottle of scotch whiskey. "I don't know about you, but I desperately need a little of this."

It took Generalmajor Gunther von Hamm, who had been at Samur with Major General Peterson K. Waterford, and Master Sergeant Dawson three trips to unload all the groceries and conveniences from Dawson's car.

"Have one of these, Tom," Mrs. Waterford said, when they had finished. "You look like you can use it."

"Not now, Miss Marjorie, thank you just the same," he said.

"Have one, Tom," she said, smiling, but firmly.

"Yes, ma'am," he said. Marjorie Waterford understood that Tom Dawson was uneasy drinking with general officers and their ladies, but she was afraid that Gunther von Hamm would think he was refusing to drink with a former enemy. He wasn't, but Gunther was very sensitive, and having to accept the food and cigarettes and soap that she had brought was enough of a blow to his pride without being snubbed by an enlisted man.

Marjorie told them that Porky was starting up a polo team, and that seemed to please Gunther, for it brought memories of happier days. But the von Hamms' news for the Waterfords was not at all pleasant.

"Elizabeth von Greiffenberg killed herself ten days ago," Greta von Hamm said.

"Oh, no!" Marjorie Waterford said.

"We just found out yesterday," Gunther von Hamm said. "Poison."

"That's terrible," Marjorie said. She felt especially bad because Elizabeth von Greiffenberg's husband, Colonel Count Peter-Paul von Greiffenberg, had been commandant of the POW camp in which her son-in-law had been held. He had been killed right at the end of the war, shot down in cold blood by the Russians.

"She was not stable," Gunther said.

"I feel personally responsible," Marjorie said. "I should have done something to help her."

"What could you do, more than you have done?" Greta said, kindly.

"Something," Marjorie said.

"She wouldn't see you," Greta said. "She told me to leave her alone when I was there. She . . . she . . ."

"Was not stable," Gunther von Hamm filled in for her.

"What about the girl?" Marjorie asked.

Greta von Hamm shook her head.

"No one knows where she is," she said. "What everyone is afraid of is that she went to East Germany, where there are relatives."

"Oh, my God," Marjorie Waterford said. "The poor thing. How old is she? Sixteen?"

"Seventeen," Greta said.

"Excuse me, Miss Marjorie," Master Sergeant Dawson said. "We've got to get going."

"Yes," Marjorie Waterford said. "We do. It's a long ride, and we don't want to get arrested for speeding, again, do we, Tom?"

[FOUR]
Mannheim, Germany
11 May 1946

There were four Stinson L-5s lined up on the Eighth Constabulary Squadron's airstrip. They had the legend US ARMY and a serial number painted on the tail. The star-and-bars which identified all U.S. military aircraft was painted on the side of the fuselage. Immediately below the rear passenger seat was the "Circle C" insignia of the U.S. Constabulary.

A Horche sedan, which it was alleged had belonged personally to Field Marshal Rommel himself, pulled onto the airstrip behind a pair of MPs on Harley Davidson motorcycles with red lights flashing and sirens wailing. The open convertible was trailed by two jeeps each equipped with a machine gun and manned by three soldiers in chrome-plated helmets.

The convoy pulled up beside the nearest L-5. The driver of the Horche jumped out and opened the rear door.

Major General Peterson K. Waterford, attired in a highly varnished helmet liner with glistening stars forward and Constabulary insignia on the sides, stood up, clutching his riding crop. He acknowledged the salutes of the personnel in the area by touching his riding crop to the brim of his helmet liner. Then he descended from the Horche and marched toward the closest Stinson L-5. Major Robert Robbins saluted for the second time.

"Good morning, General," he said.

"Morning," the general said, touching his helmet liner with his riding crop. He climbed into the rear seat of the aircraft. Major Robbins took a red plate on which two silver stars had been mounted and slipped it into a holder on the fuselage, then climbed into the front seat.

Everything was in readiness. The plane had been gone over from propeller to tail wheel. Robbins threw on the master switch, primed the engine, and pushed the starter switch down. The starter motor groaned, and ground. The propeller went unevenly through several rotations, once sending a puff of blue smoke from the exhaust past the cockpit. The starter motor groaned and ground again. The propeller jerked spasmodically through its arc. The engine refused to start.

"Tell me, Major," General Peterson K. Waterford asked, icily, "do you suppose that Captain MacMillan remembered to wind up his aircraft?"

"Yes, sir. I'm sure, sir, that the backup aircraft is operational."

"Good, good," General Waterford said, with transparently artificial joviality.

"I'm very embarrassed about this, General," Major Robbins said.

"Nonsense," the General said. "We all break our rubber bands from time to time, don't we, Robbins?"

"Captain MacMillan's aircraft is right next to us, General. But I don't see how we'll be able to take Captain MacMillan with us, sir."

"I do, Major," the general said. "We'll let Captain MacMillan drive, while you stay here and get another rubber band for this one."

General Waterford climbed out of the plane, snatched his two-starred plate from the fuselage, and strode purposefully to the adjacent L-5. He handed it to MacMillan, who stood by the aircraft. He looked him up and down.

"Does your airplane work, Mac?"

"Yes, sir, I believe it will," Captain MacMillan said.

"And have you been briefed on our destination?" the general asked.

"Yes, sir."

"Then I suggest we proceed," the general said. He climbed into the back seat and strapped himself in again.

Major Robert Robbins came to the airplane and started to get into the pilot's seat.

"I told you that I was going to go with Captain MacMillan," the general said.

"Sir, may I respectfully point out to the general that Captain MacMillan is a recent graduate of flight school?"

"I have it in reliable authority that whatever else Captain MacMillan may be, Major, he is not a fool."

"Yes, sir."

"If he believes himself to be safe flying this thing, I will accede to his judgment," the general said. "What are we waiting for now, MacMillan?"

MacMillan got in the pilot's seat.

He pushed the starter button and the engine coughed and caught immediately. The major stood just beyond the wing tip, nearly at attention, looking uncomfortable, waiting for MacMillan to taxi away. The general folded down the upper portion of the window-door and beckoned to him. The major, holding one hand on his hat to keep the prop wash from blowing it away, went to the window.

"I've never believed that *'L'audace, l'audace, toujours l'audace'* crap, Robbins," he said. "The boy scouts have got it right. *Be prepared*, Robbins. Goddamn it, Robbins, remember that! *Be prepared!*"

He closed the window. MacMillan looked over his shoulder at his passenger.

The general made a "wind it up" signal with his index finger. MacMillan taxied onto the runway, checked the magnetos, pushed the throttle forward. The little airplane slowly gathered speed. MacMillan edged the stick forward, so that the tail wheel lifted off. When he reached flying speed, he inched back on the stick. The little L-5 began to fly.

He made a circling turn, still climbing.

"To hell with that," the general's voice came over the intercom. "Fly up the autobahn."

MacMillan nodded his head to show he had heard the order. "And don't get too high," the general said.

MacMillan nodded again. He leveled off at about seven hundred feet.

"What did you do to Robbins's airplane, Mac?" the general inquired. "Nothing, I trust, that he can blame you for."

"I didn't do a thing to it, General," MacMillan said.

"Bullshit," General Waterford said. "That was too good to be an innocent happenstance."

"He did look a mite embarrassed, didn't he, General?" MacMillan said.

The general chuckled.

"I wouldn't be surprised, when they examine the engine," MacMillan said, "if they find that somebody forgot to tighten the spark plugs."

"You sneaky bastard you. But what if it had gotten up in the air, and then the engine had stopped? With me in it?"

"I double-checked it myself, General," MacMillan said.

"You're damned near as devious as I am," the general said, and then changed the subject: "Everything laid on at Nauheim, Mac?"

"Yes, sir. I was up there this morning. Everything's greased."

The autobahn, a four lane superhighway, was now below their left wheel. They reached Rhine-Main in a matter of minutes; then, on their right, the rubble of Frankfurt am Main appeared, and then disappeared. Thirty miles further along, MacMillan banked again to the right.

"I led the most powerful tactical force ever assembled up that goddamned highway," the general said in his earphones. "I was in the van of Combat Command A, and they were in the van of the division, and the division was in the van of the whole goddamned Ninth United States Army."

MacMillan nodded his head once again.

"The only thing I forgot was a brilliant and unforgettable remark for posterity," the general said. "You're one up on me there, MacMillan. I don't think I'll ever forgive you for that."

"Yes, sir," MacMillan said.

"Every time Bobby Bellmon tells the story of leaving you in the POW camp, I think about that. 'Fuck it, Colonel. Have the bugler sound the charge.' Great line, Mac. I would have had to clean it up, of course—you can't say 'fuck it' in history books—but I should have thought of something like that."

"There it is, sir," MacMillan said, gesturing to the right front.

They were over the municipal park in Bad Nauheim. There were a pair of goalposts set in a flat area, and a line of army trucks parked to the left of the field. MacMillan came in low and slow, and touched down. He slowed and taxied back up the field. A herd of horses grazed on the grass.

He braked to a stop at the head of the line of the army trucks.

A young lieutenant trotted up to the little Stinson. He wore golden ropes through his epaulets, and the two-starred shield of a major general's aide-de-camp on his lapels.

He saluted, and opened the L-5's door.

"I trust the general had a pleasant flight," he said.

"Once I got into an airplane they remembered to wind up, I did," the general said.

"Anything go wrong, Davis?" MacMillan asked.

"Everything is laid out, MacMillan," the aide-de-camp replied, coldly. There was no love lost between Captain MacMillan and Lieutenant Davis. Davis was painfully aware that before MacMillan had shown up, he was in line to become General Waterford's senior aide-de-camp. He had naturally expected to be named senior aide after doing his time as junior aide, and he had been cheated out of it. He was still the junior aide, doing dog robbers' tasks.

Like most general officers, General Waterford used his aides-de-camps in dual roles. The junior aides saw to the general's personal comfort and attended to his social duties. The senior aide attended the general officially. The idea was that being close to the commanding general in all sorts of situations would give him insight into the problems and functioning of a high command which would be useful in his own career. Davis had dog-robbed without complaint, biding his time until he would become senior aide. But MacMillan had been named senior aide, and Davis still did the dirty work.

"Well, Davis," the general said. "Where are my polo players?"

"Right this way, General," MacMillan replied for Davis. "I think the general will be reasonably pleased with what I've come up with."

"I better be, Mac," the general said. "I better be."

With MacMillan and Davis just behind, General Peterson K. Waterford, slapping his riding boot with his crop at every third step, marched across the field. A line of a dozen men came to attention at his approach. They were wearing GI riding breeches, except for one middle-aged man who wore officer pink riding breeches.

They came to attention without command. "Good to see you, Charley," the general said to the middle-aged officer at the end of the line. "Fat and all. Well, we'll get that off you in no time."

"Nice to see you again, General," the middle-aged officer said.

"Let's get that straight right now," the general said, raising his voice so that everybody could clearly hear him. "We are here to play polo, not fight a war. You are ordered to forget that you are playing with a man who can, with a snap of his fingers, ruin your military careers. There will be no rank on the field. You will consider yourselves sportsmen first and soldiers second. I will address you by your Christian names, and you will call me—" he paused—"sir."

He got the laughter he expected, and turned to the next man in the rank.

"Frank Dailey, sir," he said.

"You played much polo, Frank?" the general asked. "You rated?"

"One goal, sir," Frank Dailey said.

He went down the line, going through essentially the same questioning. He came to the end of the line, to a tall, muscular, rather handsome young man.

"Craig Lowell, sir," the young man said.

"No offense, Craig, but you don't look old enough to have played much polo. I don't suppose you're rated, are you, Son?"

"Three goals, sir," Craig Lowell said.

"Where did you play, Craig?" the general asked, gently.

"West Palm, sir, Ramapo, Houston, Los Angeles."

"You know Bryce Taylor?"

"Yes, sir, I do," Craig Lowell replied.

"And how is he, these days?" the general asked, idly.

"Rather poorly, sir, I'm afraid," Lowell said. "I think he may even be dead. My grandfather wrote he'd spoken to Mrs. Taylor . . ."

"You come with me and keep me company, Craig," the general said. "While I get out of my shirt."

The general winked at MacMillan. Goddamn, he had at least a three-goal rated player. With Fat Charley, who was rated at two before the war, and that ugly man halfway down the line, he just might be able to field a team that could take the frogs. A three-goal player was more than he had hoped for. The general was rated at seven.

The general bounded up the folding metal stairs of a van. The inside was plush, ornate. The general had crossed Europe in this vehicle. His rolling home and command post. There was coffee steaming in a pot, a jug with ice water, a plate of sandwiches covered with a towel.

"Help yourself, Craig," he said. "And tell me the bad news about Bryce."

The general pulled off the leather jacket, and the pink uniform shirt beneath it, and a sleeveless silk undershirt under that. He pulled on a GI T-shirt, which had been neatly lettered, front and back, with the numeral 1.

Craig Lowell told him what he had learned from his grandfather about the terminal illness of Bryce Taylor.

"What did you say your grandfather's name was?" General Waterford asked.

"Geoffrey Craig, sir."

"Oh," Waterford said. "You're a Craig."

"My mother's name is Craig," Lowell said.

"That's right, you're a Lowell. The Cabots speak only to the Lowells, and the Lowells speak only to God. Boston, right?"

"No, sir," Lowell said. "New York."

"But you have the Harvard accent," the general said.

"I went to Harvard, sir."

"Yes," the general said, pleased with himself. "Of course you did." Then he turned to look at MacMillan.

"I want you to find out about my old friend Bryce Taylor, Mac," the general said. "(A) If he's dead. If he is dead, write a nice letter of condolence. Get the address from Craig here. (B) If he's still alive, find out where and in what condition, and what I can do."

"Yes, sir," MacMillan said.

"Where do you usually play, Craig?" the general asked, unzipping his fly, tucking the T-shirt in, and grunting as he fastened the tight trouser band against his middle.

"Three, sir."

"OK, we'll try it that way. Go tell the others to mark their shirts. But you'll play number three against me. Tell Fat Charley he's number one with you. We need to get some of that high-living fat off him."

"Yes, sir," Craig Lowell said. He walked back out of the van and crossed the field. A sergeant had led four ponies up to the van. They weren't much, in Lowell's judgment, as a string. But they were the best available, and they had been reserved for the general. What were left over for the others to play were worse.

They played two "fool-around chukkers," as the general put it, and then they played a game, six chukkers. Blues, led by the general, won 7–4.

The general accepted a large glass of heavily sweetened iced-coffee, and drank it quickly. He was in a very good mood.

"Gentlemen," he said, "MacMillan has arranged accommodations for us in one of the Bad Nauheim Kurhotels. The Germans, among other odd notions, apparently believed that the foul water in this bucolic Dorf had medicinal qualities. "What we are going to do now is load into the staff cars, go have a bath, and get something to drink. Mac has imported the water to mix with the whiskey."

The general and Fat Charley got into a Ford staff car. MacMillan rode in front with the driver. The others, with one exception, got into other staff cars. The procession started off.

"Stop the goddamned car!" the general shouted. The driver slammed on the brakes. The cars behind almost ran into his car. "Where the *hell* is he going?" the general demanded rhetorically. He rolled down the window.

"Craig, goddamnit, where are you going?" he shouted.

"To walk the horses, sir," Craig Lowell replied.

"Goddamnit, we have enlisted men to do that."

"General," MacMillan said, "I didn't have time, the way the general sort of rushed out there on the field, to . . ."

"What are you telling me, Mac?" the general asked, slowly.

"Sir, that's Private Lowell."

The general waved at Private Craig Lowell, rolled up the window, and gestured for the driver to move on.

"Mac, goddamnit, you shouldn't have done that to me. I embarrassed that boy."

"No excuse, sir," MacMillan said.

"Goddamn it, I told you to round me up every polo player in the division, and in division support troops," the general said.

"Yes, sir. That's exactly what the general said."

"What the hell is a three-goal polo player doing in the goddamned ranks?" the general asked. "And he's a gentleman, too, Mac, goddamnit. He's a Lowell *and* a Craig. You heard what he said. For Christ's sake! What the hell is he doing as a goddamned private?"

"He's on the division golf team, General," Mac replied, taking the question literally.

"The golf team! The *golf team!*"

"Yes, sir," Mac said. "He's a jock."

"I didn't think you'd go rooting around in the goddamned Form 20s, for God's sake. Sometimes, Mac, you're just too *goddamned* efficient a dog robber."

"May I have the general's permission to explain, Sir?"

"You can try, Mac. Right now my first thought is to send you back there to help him shovel the horseshit," the general said.

"With the general's permission, sir, it happened this way. When the general laid this requirement on me, I was faced with the problem of not knowing very much about polo."

"Or about much else, either," the general said.

"I asked around if anyone happened to know anything about polo. Lowell did, and he helped me out. He really knows a good deal about the game, General."

"I saw that," the general said. "If Fat Charley had been able to get his ass out of dead low gear, the Reds would have won. He set you up half a dozen times, Charley, and you blew it."

"I'm a little out of shape, sir," Fat Charley said.

"That's the understatement of the week. Go on, Mac."

"General, I brought Private Lowell along just to be prepared," MacMillan said. "All the other players are officers."

"Mac," the general said. "(A) In six weeks and two days, my polo team is going to play the team of the Deuxième Division Mécanique of the French Army, under General Quillier. (B) Because the French do not socialize with enlisted men, my team will be made up solely of officers. (C) My team will win. (D) My team cannot win without that Lowell boy as my number three."

"I believe I take the General's meaning, sir," Lieutenant MacMillan said.

[FIVE]
Bad Nauheim, Germany
12 May 1946

After Private Craig W. Lowell, working with the German stableboys, had walked the horses, he got in his privately owned black jeep and drove across town to the Constabulary golf course, where he was billeted in an attic room over the pro shop.

He fantasized about being stopped by one of the Constabulary MPs, or better yet, by one of the more chickenshit young officers of the Constabulary.

"Trooper," he would be challenged. The Constabulary was playing cavalry, and soldiers were "troopers" not soldiers. "Trooper, where the hell did you get so dirty?"

"Actually," he could then reply, "I've been playing polo with General Waterford. And the provost marshal."

He was not stopped. He parked the jeep behind the pro shop and climbed the narrow stairs to his tiny room. The only thing that could really be said for his special billet was that it was away from the barracks. He was left alone. If they wanted him, they had to send for him, and that was generally too much trouble, so some other "trooper" would be grabbed and given an unpleasant task to perform.

He pulled off his boots, and then stripped out of the sweat-soaked breeches, shirt, and underwear. The general had run their asses off. If the others were as tired as he was, he thought with a certain satisfaction, the officers and gentlemen with whom he had played must really be dragging their asses. All of them except the general, he thought. The general was the only one who had not looked to be on the edge of exhaustion when the jeep horn signaled the end of the last chukker.

Lowell had been as surprised to find that General Waterford was a first-rate polo player as the general had been surprised to learn that Craig was a private.

Naked, Lowell bent over and examined his inner legs. He was tall and well muscled, not like a football player, but with something of the same suggestion of great strength and endurance. He was chapped, slightly, or that was heat rash. Nothing serious.

He wrapped a towel around his middle and went down the stairs to the men's locker room and took a shower. He took his razor with him, and shaved under the streaming hot water. His beard was as light as his hair, but for some reason, more than eight hours' growth stood out on his skin as much as if it had been jet black. The Constab was big on clean-shaven troopers.

Lowell was mildly concerned about what would happen now that Major General Peterson K. Waterford had learned of his enlisted status. But he was more curious than worried. For one thing, he certainly hadn't tried to pass himself off as anything but a private. Lieutenant MacMillan knew he was a private. If the general decided to send lightning bolts of rage, his target would be MacMillan. Privates were invisible to generals.

In any event Lowell thought it unlikely that MacMillan would be struck by a lightning bolt and toppled. Craig Lowell had realized—while eavesdropping on the conversations of majors and colonels at the nineteenth hole of the Bad Nauheim golf course—that they had erred in their assessment of Lt. MacMillan. It was generally believed that MacMillan was the jester in the court of King Waterford. A pleasant fool who had somehow won the Medal. MacMillan's third-person manner of speaking to the general and other very senior officers was probably close to the official division joke.

But it was Private Craig Lowell's assessment of MacMillan that if he wasn't the *éminence gris* behind the throne, then he was at least a Knight Companion of the Bath. Not a simple dog robber and not a jester. Lowell had nothing really concrete on which to base this opinion, except for a combination of small things. There was a certain look in the general's eye, a certain shading of his behavior, when, for some reason, MacMillan was not at his side, and a certain relaxation when he showed up.

Lowell also had gotten to know Mrs. Waterford. She was a tall, thin, gray-haired woman, not at all the counterpart of her flamboyant husband. When she called the golf club, she asked when it would be convenient for her to play. The two other generals' wives, Mrs. Deputy Commanding General, and Mrs. Chief of Staff, as well as the senior colonels' wives, Mesdames G-1, G-2, G-3, and G-4, even Mrs. Division Surgeon, called to announce when they intended to play.

Mrs. Waterford asked when she could play, and she generally played very early in the morning, and invariably with Mrs. Rudolph G. (Roxy) MacMillan, a red-headed, buxom woman with a hearty belly laugh. There were seven children between them. Mrs. Waterford was twice a grandmother.

The first time Lowell had met Mrs. Waterford, she had understandably come to the conclusion that he was German. She had overheard him talking to the caddies in German. The only thing lower on the social scale than a private was a kraut.

"Good morning," Mrs. Waterford had said, graciously, in rather badly accented German in the belief he was a kraut. "Isn't it a lovely morning?"

"A beautiful morning, Frau General," Lowell had replied, and then switched to English. "I'm Private Lowell, the caddy master."

"And you're also the best golfer in the division, according to Lieutenant MacMillan," she replied, without missing a stroke. "Do you think you could play with us? We could kill two birds with one stone. God knows, we need golf instruction. Mrs. MacMillan and I are ashamed to play with anybody but each other. And we both need practice in conversational German."

"Oh, do we need you!" Mrs. MacMillan said. She put out her hand. "I'm Roxy MacMillan."

By the time they had finished the first round, Lowell decided he liked both of them very much. Mrs. Waterford was a lady who reminded him of his late grandmother, and Mrs. MacMillan was—he thought of the old-fashioned phrase his grandmother had used to describe nice people who were rather simple—"a diamond in the rough."

The role of golf in the army had surprised Lowell when he had first come to Bad Nauheim and the U.S. Constabulary. He had always thought golf to be the sport of the middle and upper classes, not at all the sort of thing sergeants (who were the yeomen in the military social hierarchy) would do. But apparently, before the war, everybody in the army over the grade of corporal had been out there swatting balls. He finally realized that it was because the government paid for the upkeep of the courses, and that in order to justify the expense, and thus their own playing, the brass had had to encourage the yeomen to get out there and knock the ball around.

Lieutenant MacMillan, whom Lowell at first had also pegged as one of the yeomen, played every Wednesday afternoon, usually with the Constabulary finance officer, Major Emmons. They were joined infrequently by the general, but normally it was just MacMillan and Major Emmons. They played nine holes, and then spent a couple of hours at the nineteenth hole, eating hamburgers and drinking beer.

Several weeks after Lowell had begun to play with Mrs. Waterford and Mrs. MacMillan on a more or less regular basis, MacMillan had come up to Lowell when Lowell had been leaning against the wall of the caddy house and pro shop, devoutly hoping not to be pressed into service as a golf instructor. When MacMillan walked up to him, he handed Lowell a dollar in script.

"Get us a couple of beers and meet me in the locker room," he said. He spoke pleasantly enough, but it was a command, not an invitation.

When Lowell brought the beer into the locker room MacMillan was coming out of the shower, a towel wrapped around his middle. MacMillan turned his back, dropped the towel, and pulled on a pair of jockey shorts.

"I understand you've been giving my wife golf lessons," he said, his back still to Lowell.

"Yes, sir," Lowell replied.

"And German lessons," MacMillan pursued, as he turned around.

"Yes, sir."

"Where did you learn to speak German?" MacMillan asked. He did not like Lowell's type. He was generally suspicious of handsome young men, and this handsome young man was also charming, had a hoity-toity manner of speaking, and was a draftee to boot.

"A lady who took care of me when I was a kid was German," Craig replied.

"What do you want out of the army, Lowell?" Mac asked.

"I don't quite understand you, sir."

"Military government is always looking for people who speak German," he said. "You could make buck sergeant in six months, probably staff before your time is over."

"Well, if I have a choice, sir, I'd rather stay right here."

"That's right, you don't need the money, do you?" MacMillan said.

"No, sir, I don't." Lowell wondered how MacMillan had found out about that; but he was not surprised that he had.

"My wife thinks you're a very nice young man," MacMillan said. "If you change your mind, let me know."

"Thank you, sir."

"I was a jock myself before the war," MacMillan offered. "I was Hawaiian Department light-heavyweight champ." He opened the beer bottle, drained it, and finished dressing. Lowell couldn't think of anything to say.

"I don't think you're a nice young man," MacMillan said to him, finally. "I think you're a goddamn feather merchant." When he saw that this had sort of stunned Lowell, he went on. "A word of advice, feather merchant: Don't try to take advantage of being the general's lady's golf pro and instructor in kraut."

Lowell flushed, but said nothing.

"I know, of course, that that had never entered your mind, Private Lowell," MacMillan said. Then he walked out of the locker room.

A month after that, MacMillan sought him out again.

"I've got a question for you, feather merchant," he said. "What do you know about polo?"

"What would you like to know?"

"What would I like to know, *sir,"* MacMillan corrected him.

"Yes, sir," Lowell said. He had just noticed that MacMillan's lieutenant's bar had been replaced with the railroad tracks of a captain. "I wasn't trying to be disrespectful."

"I don't suppose you were," MacMillan said, after looking at him for a moment. "But I'll tell you something, Lowell. That's the way you come across. As if you think everybody in the army is a horse's ass."

"I don't mean to do that," Lowell said, sincerely.

"But you do think that we're a bunch of horse's asses, don't you?"

"I don't think *you* are," Lowell replied, without thinking. MacMillan's eyes tightened, and his eyebrows went up. Lowell remembered only a moment later to add, "Captain."

"I'm flattered," MacMillan said, sarcastically. But it was evident to Lowell that the sarcasm was pro forma. MacMillan had recognized the truth when he heard it, and he was flattered.

"Speaking of horse's asses," MacMillan said, "tell me about polo."

"What would you like to know?"

"Everything. All I know is that you play it riding on horses."

"Sir, it would help if I knew why you want to know."

"The general has decided to play polo," MacMillan said. "What the hell is a seven-goal player?"

"One hell of a polo player," Lowell said. "Sir."

"The general is a seven-goal polo player," MacMillan said. "What does it mean?"

"It's a handicap," Lowell explained. He explained the handicap system and the game of polo. MacMillan asked several questions, but Lowell never had to explain something twice.

"Between now and 0600 tomorrow morning, Lowell, I want you to make up a list of all the equipment we're going to need to field a polo team. Everything, from boots to horseshoes. I've found horses in Austria. There's a warehouse full of equipment at Fort Riley, and I've got an old buddy there who'll ship us what we need. But I'll need to know what. Decide exactly what you'll need. And then triple the quantities."

"Sir, I'm charge of quarters tonight."

"No, you're not. As of an hour ago, you're working for me. I've already fixed it with headquarters company. The general wants a polo team, Lowell, and you and I are going to see that he gets one."

Two days after that, Craig Lowell found himself a passenger in one of the Constabulary's Stinson L-5s, flown by the Constabulary aviation officer himself, Major Robert Robbins. Robbins flew him to the Alps near Salzburg, Austria, where military government held nearly five hundred horses captured from the Germans. There had originally been thousands, but the draft animals had been quickly released to the German and Austrian economies to till the land.

The horses still held were obviously not livestock but thoroughbred animals. They were kept as valuable property, which the Germans had presumably obtained illegally and which the authorities intended to return to their rightful owners.

A week after that, a ten-truck convoy of open flatbed trailers appeared at the horse farm and loaded the seventy animals Craig Lowell had chosen for the trip back to Germany. There wasn't a polo pony among them. But there were some fine saddle horses (a German groom told Craig they had come from Hungary in the last days of the war) which could, with work, be trained for polo.

It was a five-day trip to Bad Nauheim. The horses survived the journey. The German grooms had had a good deal of experience in moving animals under worse conditions. When they arrived in Bad Nauheim, Captain MacMillan had everything waiting, from stables and food to a polo field in the municipal park and accommodations for the grooms. In the stables were two dozen wooden crates shipped from Fort Riley, Kansas, by air. Each crate was stenciled: PRIORITY AIR SHIPMENT. VETERINARY SUPPLIES. PERISHABLE. DO NOT DELAY.

The crates were full of saddles, horseshoes, tack, polo mallets, riding breeches, everything Craig Lowell had asked for and more. The day after the horses arrived, players began to arrive from all over the Constabulary. And two days after that, Private Craig Lowell met Major General Peterson K. Waterford and informed him that their mutual acquaintance, Bryce Taylor, was ill of terminal cancer.

[SIX]

The problem of how to get Pvt. Lowell onto the polo field as a commissioned officer remained. MacMillan went through his service record. Lowell had been thrown out of college. College graduates, under certain circumstances, could be directly commissioned. MacMillan toyed with the idea of making certain "corrections" to Lowell's service record but decided against it; he was only nineteen years old, and there was no way he could correct that, too. Two "corrections" of that magnitude would be too noticeable.

Next, MacMillan went and had a talk with Major William C. Emmons, the Constab's finance officer. They were friends in the sense that they both had been stationed at Fort Riley before the war. MacMillan could not honestly remember ever having seen Specialist Six Emmons at Riley, but they had talked, and they remembered other people together. Sergeant MacMillan had had little to do with the pencil-pushers in the old days, and the pencil-pushers had had little to do with the troops. On Pearl Harbor Day, Major Emmons had been a Specialist Six, a PFC with three three-year hash marks, drawing the same pay as a first sergeant (Pay Grade Six) because of his specialist's skill in the intricacies of army finance. A month later, he had been directly commissioned as a first lieutenant of the Finance Corps, and had spent the entire war in the Prudential Insurance Company Building in Newark, N.J., in command of an army of civilian clerks who made up and mailed out allotment checks and insurance checks to dependents and the deceased's next of kin. He had ultimately risen to major doing that.

Major Emmons not only knew the army game and understood MacMillan's problem, but offered a solution to it. It was understood between them that MacMillan owed Emmons a Big One. There was no swap, no tit for tat, just an understanding between them that when Major Emmons wanted something, Captain MacMillan, senior aide to the commanding general, would make a genuine effort to see that he got it.

Pvt. Craig Lowell, who was either playing polo or training the polo ponies from sunup to sundown, had no idea that the wheels of army administration were grinding in his behalf.

HEADQUARTERS
UNITED STATES CONSTABULARY
APO 109 NEW YORK NY

SPECIAL ORDERS 19 May 1946
NUMBER 134

EXTRACT

****

35. PVT LOWELL, Craig W. US32667099 MOS 7745 Hq &Hq Co U.S. Constab APO 109 relvd, trfd in gr WP Svc Co Hq U.S. Constab APO 109 for dy with U.S. Constab Finance Office. No tvl involved. PCS. AUTH: Ltr, Hq U.S. Constab, 7 Jan 46, Subj: "Critical Shortage Enl Finance Personnel."

****

BY COMMAND OF
MAJOR GENERAL WATERFORD
Charles A. Webster
Colonel, AGC
Adjutant General

HEADQUARTERS
OFFICE OF THE FINANCE OFFICER
UNITED STATES CONSTABULARY
APO 109 US FORCES

19 May 1946

SUBJECT: Critical Shortage of Commissioned Finance Officers
THRU: Commanding General
U.S. Constabulary
APO 109, US Forces
TO: Commanding General
US Forces, European Theater
APO 757, US Forces

1. Reference is made to Letter, Subject as Above, Hq USFET, dated 3 April 1946.

2. The Finance Section, this Hq, is three (3) officers, MOS 1444 (Fiscal Accounting Officer) below authorized Table of Organization and Equipment strength, and has been advised that no replacement officers will be assigned from the Zone of the Interior for a minimum of six (6) months.

3. The Finance Section, this Hq, had been authorized to directly commission two (2) suitably qualified enlisted men as 2ND LT. FIN C USAR, to fill this critical shortage of personnel.

4. Reference Para 2 above: Request authority to directly commission one (1) additional qualified enlisted man as 2 LT FIN C USAR for a total of three (3).

William C. Emmons
Major, Finance Corps
Division Finance Officer

1st Ind

HQ U.S. CONSTAB APO 109 19 MAY 46

TO: COMMANDING GENERAL USFET APO 757 US FORCES

1. The Commanding General United States Constabulary is personally aware of the critical shortage of qualified

commissioned financial officers, and of the serious threat this shortage poses to the operational status of this division.

2. The Commanding General strongly recommends approval.

BY COMMAND OF
MAJOR GENERAL WATERFORD
Charles A. Webster
Colonel, AGC
Adjutant General

2nd Ind

HQ USFET APO 757 22 MAY 1946

TO: COMMANDING GENERAL U.S. CONSTABULARY APO 109

Authority granted herewith to directly commission as 2nd Lt, Finance Corps, U.S. Army Reserve, one (1) additional highly qualified enlisted man.

BY COMMAND OF GENERAL CLAY
Edward K. MacNeel
Colonel, AGC
Adjutant General

3rd Ind

HQ US CONSTAB APO 109 23 MAY 1946

TO: FINANCE OFFICER, US CONSTAB
For compliance.

BY COMMAND OF
MAJOR GENERAL WATERFORD
Charles A. Webster
Colonel, AGC
Adjutant General

HEADQUARTERS
UNITED STATES CONSTABULARY
APO 109 NEW YORK NY

SPECIAL ORDERS 24 May 1946
NUMBER 137

EXTRACT

****

16. PVT LOWELL, CRAIG W. US32667099 Svc Co U.S. Constabulary, APO 109, is relvd prs asgmt and HON DISCH the mil service UP AR 615-365 (Convenience of the Govt) for purp of accept comm as officer. EM auth transp at govt expense from New York NY to home of record (Broadlawns, Glencove, LI NY) PCS. S-99-999-999.

17. 2ND LT LOWELL, CRAIG W. FinC, 0-495302, having reported on active duty Svc Co U.S. Constabulary is asgd dy with Service Company, Finance Section. Off auth transport at Govt Expense from home of record (Broadlawns, Glencove, LI NY) to New York NY. PCS. S-99-999-999.

18. 2ND LT LOWELL, CRAIG W. FinC, 0-495302, Finance Sec Hq U.S. Constab, is detailed to Armor Branch for pd of one yr for dy w/troops. (Auth: Letter, Hq War Dept, Subj: "Asgmt of newly comm off of tech services to combat arms for dy w/trps.) No tvl included.

19. 2ND LT LOWELL, CRAIG W. 0-495302 FinC (Det/ARM) Finance Sec Hq U.S. Constab, trfd in gr WP Hq Sq 17th Armd Cav Squadron APO 117 for dy w/troops. In Compl with Msg, Hq U.S. Constab, Subj: "Asgmt of Armor/Armored Cav Off to Provisional Horse Platoon." Off is further placed on TDY, WP Hq 40th Horse Platoon (Prov) for dy. TDN. TCS. S-99-999-999.

****

BY COMMAND OF
MAJOR GENERAL WATERFORD
Charles A. Webster
Colonel, AGC
Adjutant General

[SEVEN]
40th Horse Platoon (Prov)
U.S. Constabulary
Bad Nauheim, Germany

Private Craig W. Lowell drove up to the stables of the 40th Horse Platoon in his black, privately owned jeep and blew the horn. In a moment, the left of the huge matching doors, large enough to pass the jeep, was opened by one of the German grooms, and Lowell drove through it.

After Lowell had passed through the door, the groom closed it again and walked to where Lowell had stopped next to the stairwell leading to the second floor of the stables. He then helped Private Lowell unload what he had beneath a scrap of tent canvas in the back seat.

There was a Zenith Transoceanic portable radio still in its carton. There were two jumbo-sized boxes of Rinso; a half dozen bars of Ivory soap; three cartons of Camel cigarettes; two boxes of Dutch Masters cigars; a case of Coca-Cola; a case of Schlitz beer, in cans; a carton of Hershey chocolate bars (plain) and a carton of Hershey chocolate bars (with almonds); and six large cans of Nescafé instant coffee.

Private Lowell had been shopping at the PX.

"Put the radio, the beer, and the cigars in my room," Private Lowell directed the groom, in German. "You know what to do with the rest of it."

"Jawohl, Herr Rittmeister," the groom said. Literally translated, "Rittmeister" meant "Riding Master." It had also been a rank in the German cavalry, corresponding to captain, as well as a rank in the minor German nobility. All the grooms had taken to referring to him as the "Herr Rittmeister" and Lowell thought it rather amusing.

Before he went to his apartment, he inspected both wings of the stable, all the horses in their stalls, the tack room, and the dressing room where the polo players kept their riding equipment. He had had a little trouble at the very beginning with the grooms, but that had quickly passed when they learned that not only did the young soldier speak fluent German, but he knew horses. Lowell found nothing to complain about in the condition of the animals, the cleanliness of the stables or the saddle-soaping of the tack and saddles, and he saw that the open lockers in the dressing room each contained two complete, freshly laundered and pressed riding costumes.

Then he went up the stairs to his apartment. He had known about the rooms over the stables from the very beginning and had immediately concluded that they offered much nicer accommodations than his tiny room over the pro shop at the golf course.

The morning after the first time he had played polo with General Waterford, he had made his move.

"Captain," he had said to MacMillan. "There's a place I can sleep over the stables. Could I move over there?"

"Where are you sleeping now?"

"Over the pro shop."

"Go ahead."

All the grooms were supposed to be equal. They were hired by the army as laborers for a minimum wage, given one hot meal a day, and provided with died-black army fatigues as work clothes. One of them, Ludwig, was more equal than the others, sort of a straw boss.

Ludwig arranged for the furnishing of the two rooms and bath over the stables. Overnight, a bed (as opposed to a GI steel cot) appeared. As did two upholstered chairs, a desk, a table, an insulated box full of ice, two floor lamps, a desk lamp, a lamp that clipped onto the headboard of the bed, and a carpet for the floor. The next night, there was an extension telephone sitting on a small table between one of the upholstered armchairs and the bed. Private Lowell could now take calls without having to rush downstairs to the telephone in the stable office.

When he got to his room, he saw that his laundry had been delivered, and that his other OD uniform was crisply pressed and hanging in the wardrobe. His riding costume was hanging beside it, and his boots, freshly polished, were at the foot of the bed. He took off his Ike jacket, pulled his necktie down, took a cold beer from the ice-filled insulated box, and then unpacked the Zenith Transoceanic portable radio.

He read the instruction book that came with it, opened the back, installed the large, heavy storage battery that had come as an accessory, and turned it on. He tuned in AFN-Frankfurt, the American radio station, and picked up Burns and Allen. With his feet on an upholstered footstool, a can of beer in his hands, and half listening to George's running battle with Gracie, he began to study the Transoceanic's operating instructions.

There was a knock at the door.

"Who's that?" he called, in German.

"Captain MacMillan."

"Come in," Lowell said. Shit. The last person Lowell expected to see at the door of his apartment was Captain Rudolph G. MacMillan. He had thought it was one of the grooms, who made predictable trips to his room to report on the condition of the horses in the certain knowledge they would be offered both a beer and a package of cigarettes.

Lowell had come to the conclusion that he was the only member of the Army of Occupation who was buying cigarettes on the black market. Every other mother's son was selling not only their ration, but having them shipped from the States to sell as well.

Lowell had considered writing his mother and telling her to send him a case of cigarettes. He did not. His mother would not understand. He would either get a carton of cigarettes, or, more likely, a cigarette case, suitably monogrammed. It wasn't worth the effort. He could afford to buy three cartons a week here and dispense them judiciously among the German grooms, in exchange for having his dirty clothing washed and pressed and his boots polished, and for having the assurance that the animals and tack were in impeccable condition when they were led to the field for the officers to ride. This was a better job than being caddy master. He intended to do what he could to keep it.

MacMillan made no secret of his dislike for him, and it was entirely possible that when he saw the apartment, he would order Lowell to move back into the barracks with the other peasants.

MacMillan came into the room and looked around.

"Very nice," he said.

"Thank you, sir," Lowell said.

"You got another one of those beers?" MacMillan asked.

"Yes, sir," Lowell said. "Of course."

MacMillan walked around the apartment, opening the door to the bathroom, and then the door to the wardrobe.

"Very nice," he repeated. "Even an icebox. Like I said, Lowell, you're a survivor."

He was caught now. There was nothing to do but take a chance.

"My company commander thinks I'm sleeping on straw in a sleeping bag," he said, handing MacMillan a can of Schlitz, then a metal church key, and finally a glass.

"Very classy," MacMillan said. "Crystal, isn't it?"

"Yes, it is. Bohemian, about 1880, according to the markings. I looked it up in the library."

"You're interested in crystal?" MacMillan asked. His concern was evident. An interest in crystal was tantamount to a public announcement of homosexuality. MacMillan didn't think that was likely, but now that he thought about it, it wasn't beyond possibility either. Shit.

"Not really. When I was offered this by one of the grooms, he told me it was quite good. I was checking up on him more than anything else. The beer tastes the same."

MacMillan chuckled. Lowell thought that it was entirely possible that MacMillan was going to permit him to continue living in comfort.

"You got hot plans for tonight?" MacMillan asked.

"I was going to lie here and listen to my radio," Lowell said, nodding toward the new Transoceanic. "I just bought it."

"How would you like to come to my house for supper?" MacMillan said. When Lowell was obviously reluctant to reply, MacMillan went on. "Come on, Roxy's been wanting to have you over."

"That's very kind of you, Captain," Lowell said. "And I appreciate it, but . . ."

"What the hell's the matter with you?" MacMillan snapped.

"Look, I mean it. I do appreciate what you're doing. Take care of the lonely troops. I really appreciate it. But I'm sure that as seldom as you get to spend a night at home, Mrs. MacMillan would really rather spend it alone with you, instead of entertaining one of your troops."

MacMillan didn't say anything.

"Honest, Captain. I'm used to being alone, and I like it. And I really appreciate the thought."

"Take a shave," MacMillan ordered. "I'll wait. That a fresh uniform?"

"Yes, sir," Lowell said.

"Wear it," Captain MacMillan ordered.

[EIGHT]

Captain and Mrs. Rudolph G. MacMillan had been assigned a fourteen-room villa on the slope of the Tanaus Mountains looking down on the resort town itself. Lowell thought that it looked very much like the house his cousin Porter Lowell had built in East Hampton. He wondered where the Germans who owned it were now living.

He parked his jeep beside MacMillan's Buick and followed him up the brick stairs to the door. A German maid opened the door, but Roxy, in a white blouse, unbuttoned blue sweater, and pleated skirt, came rushing out of the living room.

She grabbed Lowell's arm, planted a kiss on his cheek, and said, "Congratulations, I'm so happy for you!"

He had no idea what that was all about, and he was aware that MacMillan had signaled his wife to shut up.

"Ooops," Roxy said. "Me and my big mouth. What do you drink, Craig? We got it all."

"I'll have a beer if you have one," Craig said.

"Good, that'll go with the steaks," Roxy said. She looked at her husband. "Oh, for Christ's sake, Mac, why don't you tell him?"

"Yes, indeed, please, Captain, sir, tell me," Craig said.

"Get us a beer, Roxy, and bring it out on the porch," MacMillan said.

The "porch" was actually a veranda, a thirty-by-eighty-foot area paved in red flagstone, along the edges of which a two-and-a-half-foot tall, foot-thick brick wall had been laid. Bad Nauheim was spread out below them. Craig could see the six-story white brick and glass headquarters building, the only modern building in town. And the municipal park, and the polo field, and even, he thought, the red tile roof of his stable.

"It's beautiful," he said.

Roxy came onto the veranda and handed him a beer.

"It's a long way from the chicken coop, I'll say that," she said. She banged the neck of her beer bottle against his. "Mud in your eye, kid."

"The chicken coop?" Lowell asked, smiling.

"Our first home," Roxy said. "Mac and I got married in Manhattan. That's Manhattan, *Kansas.* Outside Riley. We lived with my folks, at first, and then Mac went airborne, and we went to Benning. Some redneck farmer had decided he could make more money gouging GIs than he could raising eggs, so he hosed out his chicken coop and turned it into three apartments. Plywood walls, and a two-holer fifty yards away. He charged us fifty bucks a month and Mac was drawing a hundred and fifty-two eighty, including jump pay. And we were glad to get it."

"Well, *this* is lovely," Lowell said, sincerely, gesturing around the patio and up at the house itself.

"It's supposed to be field grade," Roxy said. "But Mac pulled a couple of favors in."

Lowell didn't know what to say, so he just smiled.

"Have you told him? For Christ's sake, tell him, so we can start the party."

"Jesus, Roxy, you can really screw things up," Mac said.

"You want me to tell him? OK, I'll tell him," Roxy said.

"I'll tell him," MacMillan said. "I'll tell him." Lowell looked at him expectantly.

"Have you ever thought of becoming an officer?" MacMillan said.

"Not for long," Lowell said. "They wanted me to go to OCS in Basic . . ."

"You should have," Roxy said.

"I really don't mean to be rude, Mrs. MacMillan," Lowell said, "but I was in the army about three days when I realized that I didn't belong in the army."

"That's only because all you've seen of the army is the crap," Roxy said. "It's a good life, you'll see." He wondered what the hell she meant by that. But she was a good woman, and he would have been incapable of saying anything to hurt her feelings, even if he hadn't been afraid of her husband.

He smiled at her. "You have fifteen months and eleven days to convince me," he said.

"Tomorrow morning at 0800," MacMillan announced in a flat voice, "you're going to be sworn in as a second lieutenant."

"I beg your pardon?" Lowell asked.

"You heard what I said," MacMillan said. He was smiling at Lowell's discomfiture.

"I heard what you said, Captain," Lowell said. "But I can't believe it."

"Believe it. You got it from me. You can believe it," MacMillan said.

"Now we can party," Roxy MacMillan said, and kissed him again, wetly, on the cheek.

"Now just a moment," Lowell said. "I don't think I want to be an officer."

"What the hell kind of talk is that?" Roxy said. "What's the matter with you?"

"Let me spell it out for you, Lowell," MacMillan said. "The general wants to beat the frogs in a polo game. Now I don't know why that's important to him, and I don't care. I'll tell you this, though: it's more than wanting to beat them at a game on horses."

"I was an enlisted wife," Roxy said. "I know what it's like. And it's a hell of a lot better on officers' row."

"Roxy, for Christ's sake, will you shut up?" Rudy MacMillan said.

She gave him a dirty look.

"The general thinks the only way he can beat the frogs is if you're playing polo," MacMillan said to Lowell. "And frog officers don't play polo with enlisted men. The general says you will play. You with me so far?"

Lowell nodded, but said nothing.

"So tomorrow you get sworn in as a second lieutenant," MacMillan said. "You don't know enough about the army, about soldiering, to make a pimple on a good corporal's ass, much less a good officer. I know that, and you know that, but that's not the point. The point is that you *will be* an officer and a gentleman, and you will get on your horse and play polo. You got that?"

"And what happens at the end of polo season?" Lowell asked.

"The general's sure to get another star, and pretty soon. That means going back to the States. You keep your nose clean, and I give you my word we'll take that gold bar off you as quick as we put it on."

"And I go back to being a private?"

"You get out," MacMillan said, his voice hard. "I will see to it that your application for relief from active duty for hardship reasons is approved."

"This isn't the way I thought this was going to be at all," Roxy said. "I thought he was just getting a commission. I don't think I like this."

"How soon can I expect to get out?" Lowell asked.

"In six months, you'll be out. You can believe that. You got it from me."

"OK," Lowell said.

"You little shit," MacMillan said, angrily. "When I was your age, I would have given my left nut for a commission."

"May I be excused, Captain?" Lowell said, getting to his feet.

"Now wait just a minute!" Roxy said. "Mac, you stop this crap right now. This is *my* party. *I* asked Craig here for a party, and we're going to have a party. You guys just leave your differences at the goddamn door."

"No, you can't be excused," MacMillan said. "The general and Mrs. Waterford are due here in ten minutes. You will stay here, and you will act like you're having a good time. You understand me?"

"Now there's a direct order if I ever heard one," General Waterford said from the edge of the veranda. "But I don't see how you could possibly enforce it, Mac."

Lowell and MacMillan stood up.

"Good evening, Craig," Mrs. Waterford said. She walked up to him and gave him her hand. "How nice to see you."

"Good evening," Lowell said. He wondered how much of the exchange the Waterfords had heard. There were no signs that they had heard any of it except the last angry remark MacMillan had made.

"I understand that you're to be commissioned," Mrs. Waterford said. "Congratulations. I think you'll make a fine officer."

He looked at her, wondering if she was simply being gracious, or whether she actually meant what she was saying.

"Thank you," he said.

A cut-in-half, fifty-five-gallon barrel on legs was carried onto the veranda by two German maids. Major General Peterson K. Waterford removed his tunic, his necktie, and rolled up his sleeves. He put on a large white apron, on the front of which was stenciled the face of a jolly chef in a chef's hat and the legend, CHIEF COOK AND BOTTLEWASHER. Next he built a charcoal fire, and then personally broiled steaks. While he was cooking, he drank several bottles of beer, from the neck.

The steaks were excellent, thick, charred on the outside and pink in the middle. Roxy MacMillan provided baked potatoes, a huge salad, and garlic bread.

They talked polo. MacMillan, who knew nothing about polo, had nothing to say, and this pleased Lowell.

What the fuck, Lowell thought, sometime during the evening. I will play polo, and I will get out of the army six months early, and in the meantime I will be an officer. What have I got to complain about?

[ONE]
Bad Nauheim, Germany
24 May 1946

The Army of Occupation, recognizing the need for personal vehicles, and unwilling to pay what it would cost to ship tens of thousands of civilian automobiles from the States, had run excess-to-needs jeeps through the Griesheim ordnance depot. These were rebuilt to military specifications, except that the vehicles were painted black rather than olive-drab. They were sold to the post exchange for the cost of rebuilding $430, and resold to enlisted personnel who had expressed a desire to purchase such a vehicle for private transportation and who had been lucky enough to have their name drawn from a drum usually employed for bingo games at the service club. Private Craig Lowell's first (and as it turned out, his last) visit to the service club had been to witness the raffle. His had been one of ten names drawn.

Private Craig Lowell, in a Class "A" OD uniform, parked his black jeep behind division headquarters and met Captain Rudy MacMillan in the basement coffee shop. MacMillan told him to take off his Ike jacket. When Lowell had handed over his jacket, MacMillan laid it on the table, and unpinned the enlisted man's insignia (a U.S. and a representation of a World War I tank stamped on round brass discs) from the lapels. He reached out his hand and dropped them into Lowell's hand.

"Souvenir," he said. Then he ripped open small cardboard packages. He pinned small, unbacked, U.S. insignia to the upper lapels, a representation of a World War I tank to the lower lapels, and a single golden bar on the epaulets of the Ike jacket. He handed the jacket back to Lowell. By the time Lowell had shrugged into it, MacMillan had pinned a gold bar to the front of a gabardine overseas cap with officer's braid sewn along its seams.

He tossed Lowell's woolen enlisted man's overseas cap into the wastebasket.

"You won't need that anymore," he said. He handed Lowell the officer's cap. "You tuck that under your belt," he said. "You do not tuck it in your epaulet."

"Yes, sir."

He led Lowell back through the coffee shop, into a corridor, and to an elevator.

They rode up to the fourth floor, walked down a hotel corridor, and came to a corner suite, converted into offices.

"Good morning, Sergeant," MacMillan said to a master sergeant behind a desk. "I believe Colonel Webster expects us."

"Oh, he expects you all right," the master sergeant said. "You've really made his whole day with this, Captain."

"Yours not to reason why, Sergeant," MacMillan said. "Yours but to have everything all typed out."

"He called the general, you know," the sergeant said.

"I thought he might," MacMillan said. "I'm sure that the general reassured the colonel of Lowell's splendid, all-around qualifications to become an officer."

The sergeant looked at Lowell with amused contempt. He shook his head, then picked up the telephone.

Fuck you, Lowell thought. Fifteen minutes from now, you will have to call me "sir."

"Captain MacMillan is here, Colonel," he said. There was a reply. "Yes, sir."

He hung up the telephone.

"I gather the colonel is composing himself," he said, wryly. "He said to get everything signed."

MacMillan nodded. The sergeant got up. "You'd better sit down," he said to Lowell. "There's a lot of paperwork."

He handed Lowell a pen and handed him the first of an inch-thick stack of forms, each of which had to be signed. Lowell's fingers actually became cramped before he was finished, and by the time he was done, his signature, never very legible, had deteriorated into a scrawl.

There was a five-minute wait after all the papers had been signed. The sergeant major and MacMillan discussed someone Lowell had never heard of, an old friend from long ago. The telephone rang.

"Yes, sir," the sergeant said. He listened. "Yes, sir," he repeated, and hung up the telephone.

"Gentlemen," he said, "the colonel will see you now." He stood up and held open the door.

Lowell marched into the large room on MacMillan's heels. When MacMillan stopped, he stopped. When MacMillan saluted, he saluted.

"Good morning, Colonel," MacMillan said. The colonel ignored him.

"You are Craig W. Lowell?" the colonel said to Lowell.

"Yes, sir."

There was a look of utter loathing in the colonel's eyes. He hadn't liked it when the army had directly commissioned engineers, transportation experts, college professors, and other professionals in War II. He was furious with the idea of this young pup being made an officer simply because General Waterford wanted to play polo with him.

"I thank you for your opinion, Colonel," the general had said, when he telephoned him to protest. "But I want him commissioned."

Colonel Webster, a portly, dignified man, stood up.

"Come to attention," he said. "Raise your right hand and repeat after me: 'I, your name . . .' "

"I, Craig W. Lowell . . ."

"Do solemnly swear, or affirm . . ."

"Do solemnly swear, or affirm," Lowell parroted, "that I will defend and protect the Constitution of the United States against all enemies, foreign and domestic; that I will bear true faith and allegiance to them; that I will obey all orders of the President of the United States and the officers appointed over me, according to the regulations and the Uniform Code of Justice; and that I will faithfully discharge the duties of the office which I am about to assume. So help me, God."

The colonel lowered his hand. With infinite contempt, he said, "Congratulations, Lieutenant, you are now a member of the officer corps of the United States Army. You are dismissed."

MacMillan saluted, and Craig Lowell saluted. They performed an about-face. They started to march out of the office.

"I'm going to have your ass for this, MacMillan," the colonel said.

MacMillan did not respond. They marched out of the outer office and went back down the corridor to the elevator. MacMillan didn't say a word until they were back in the basement.

"The general," he said, "will be free about 1430. Adjust your schedule accordingly."

"Yes, sir," Lowell said.

"Until you get your feet on the ground, I suggest you keep your ass out of the line of fire," MacMillan said.

Lowell nodded his understanding.

"Don't look so goddamn scared," MacMillan said. "You're a survivor. You'll be able to handle this with no sweat."

Lowell nodded his head, because he knew MacMillan expected him to. In point of fact, however, he was not scared. Colonel Webster was obviously furious that he had been commissioned, and obviously held him in contempt; but Webster understood that Lowell hadn't had any more choice in the matter than he did. MacMillan's ass was in the line of fire, not his.

As he walked across the parking lot to his jeep, a technical sergeant threw him a crisp salute, and barked, "Good morning, sir."

Second Lieutenant Lowell returned the salute.

"How are you today, Sergeant?" he said.

I'll be a sonofabitch, he thought. I did that splendidly.

When Lowell drove back to the stable, climbed the stairs to his rooms, and pushed open the door, the bed had been stripped of sheets. When he opened his wall locker, it was empty. He turned around in confusion and found himself facing Ludwig, the groom, who was smiling broadly.

"I have taken the liberty of having the lieutenant's luggage packed and sent to the bachelor officer's hotel," Ludwig said to him. The lieutenant will find his boots and breeches in the officer's locker room."

"The word got around quickly, didn't it?" Lowell asked.

"Will the lieutenant accept the best wishes for a long and distinguished career from a former Rittmeister of the 17th Westphalian Cavalry?"

"Is that what you were, Ludwig?" Lowell asked.

Ludwig nodded.

"Well, thank you," Lowell said. "But I'm afraid my 'long and distinguished career' is liable to end as quickly as it began. When, for example, the French ride all over us."

"I think you're going to do very well," Ludwig said. "The ponies are coming along very well. And they're eighty percent of the game."

"You've played, haven't you?" Lowell asked, with sudden insight.

"Yes," Ludwig said. "And one day, perhaps, I will be able to play again." He was trying, Lowell realized, to sound more cheerful than he felt.

"For God's sake, don't let the general hear you say that," Lowell said, "or you'll wind up as a second lieutenant."

"I would be happy to be a second lieutenant," Ludwig said. "That sounds so much better than Unterwachtmeister."

"What the hell is that?"

"I have been accepted by the Grenzpolizei, the border police, as an Unterwachtmeister. The same thing as a PFC."

"I don't understand that," Lowell said. "What are you talking about?"

"I'm a soldier, as you are a soldier, Lieutenant," Ludwig said. "For me it was either the French Foreign Legion or the border police. The Legion is full of Nazis, so it's the border police."

"You're wrong about that, Ludwig. I'm no soldier."

Ludwig smiled at him, shook his head, then nodded. "Yes, you are," he said. "And I would suspect that in time you'll be a very good one."

Lowell changed the subject. Ludwig's compliment embarrassed him. Not for himself, because the notion that he would become a good officer was absurd, but for Ludwig, who had been a bona fide officer in a losing army, and was now reduced to a stable boy paying outrageous compliments to a nineteen-year-old.

"You're quitting? When?"

"I will stay until after you play the French," he said. "I would like very much to see my team beat the French." He held open the door, and bowed Lowell through it, half mockingly.

None of the other players said anything when Lowell walked into the locker room to change into riding clothes except to nod hello. If the Germans already knew of the change in his official status, Lowell thought, certainly the officers must know.

They don't want to burn their fingers, Lowell thought, by getting too close to the fire.

MacMillan is probably right, he thought, as he pulled on his boots. I am a survivor. He thought about what Ludwig had said about his being a soldier, and in time a very good soldier. It was a compliment, very flattering. And a blivet, which is defined as five pounds of horseshit in a one pound bag.

He walked out of the locker room and to his string.

"Guten Morgen, Herr Leutnant," the exercise boy said, smiling from ear to ear as he gave him a hand up on the chestnut mare.

[TWO]

It was a brilliant, splendid spring day, ideal for polo, and they played until eleven, saving the better ponies for the afternoon session when the general would play. There were three polo players, Lowell decided: the general, Fat Charley, and Private Lowell. The others played at polo, and there was a difference.

He smiled. He corrected himself. The three polo players were the general, Fat Charley, and *Lieutenant* Lowell. He wondered why he had not just been equipped with a gold bar when it was time to play the French, and told to behave like an officer. On the surface, that would seem to be a lot simpler solution to the problem. Probably, Lowell decided, it was another example of contorted military ethics. Falsely identifying him as a commissioned officer and gentleman would not be gentlemanly; hanging a commission on him when he was wholly unqualified to be an officer was something else. There was no question, now that he thought about it, that he was in fact an officer. All those papers he had signed, and Colonel Webster's unconcealed rage as he had administered that very impressive oath, left no doubt.

Fat Charley, sweat-soaked, red-faced, finally called the session off. Lowell had just scored a goal, and was at the opposite end of the field from the grooms and the three-quarter-ton truck on which the Veterinary Corps officer and his troops, and the troops with the towels and the ice water, waited and watched. Lowell rested his mallet over his shoulder and started down the field at a walk.

Fat Charley cantered up to him, turned, and rode beside him.

"Nice shot, Lowell," he said.

"Luck," Lowell said, modestly, although it had been, in fact, a damned good shot, a full stroke at the gallop that had connected squarely and sent the ball through the goalposts like a bullet.

"Could I catch a ride to lunch with you?" Fat Charley asked. "I've got to stop by my office a moment."

"Certainly, sir," Lowell said. Fat Charley, Lowell had learned by eavesdropping on his fellow polo players, had been with General Waterford in the war. He was an armor officer. But he had been detailed to the Corps of Military Police, and was the Constabulary's provost marshal. The idea was that he would become provost marshal general, which called for a major general. There was no way the establishment was going to let some asshole cop commissioned from civilian life be named a general officer.

There was an exception to that, Lowell had also learned. The European Command provost marshal was Brigadier General H. Norman Schwartzkopf, formerly Colonel Schwartzkopf of the New Jersey State Police. Schwartzkopf had been the man who had caught the kidnapper of Colonel Charles A. Lindbergh's baby, and was second in fame only to J. Edgar Hoover. The next provost marshal of the U.S. Army would be Schwartzkopf, and Fat Charley would be his replacement.

Only after Fat Charley had asked him for a ride to lunch did Lowell consider that as an officer he could no longer eat as a transient in the enlisted mess of the Signal Battalion, which was near the stables. And only a moment after that did he realize that Fat Charley had thought of that before he had and was helping him to ease the problem of transition.

Whether Fat Charley really had business at his office (a one-and-a-half-story brown stone building that reminded Lowell of a gas station) or whether that had simply been an excuse to have Lowell accompany him, he was in the building no more than three minutes.

He came out and heaved himself into the jeep beside Lowell, leaning back on the seat, his right booted leg outside of the jeep body and resting on the horizontal rear portion of the fender.

"The Bayrischen Hof," Fat Charley began without preliminaries, "is one of three hotels for bachelor officers, most of them company grade. Most senior officers are both married and have their dependents here. At lunch, the dining room feeds the married men who don't want to go home for lunch. Some of them stop in the bar for a drink or two on the way home. Dinner, and the bar afterward, is generally for the bachelors and transients. Now that the antifraternization ban has been lifted, you generally find frauleins, of all kinds, from the wholly respectable to the other end of the spectrum, in the dining room and bar."

Lowell nodded. He didn't say anything, because he didn't know what to say.

"It seems to have been decided," Fat Charley went on, "that if young officers are going to get falling down drunk and make asses of themselves over girls who are available for a pound of coffee or a couple pairs of stockings, it's better to have them do it where they're out of sight of the troops."

They were at the Bayrischen Hof by the time he'd made his little speech. Fat Charley pointed the way to the parking lot, and then led the way through the rear door of the four-story Victorian hotel to the dining room. He walked to a table occupied by a military police captain, who stood up at his approach.

"Have you room for a couple of old horse soldiers?" Fat Charley said, slipping into a chair. "Captain Winslow, Lieutenant Lowell."

They shook hands. A German waitress immediately served coffee, and laid a mimeographed menu before them. Lowell saw, a little disappointed, that the food was the same food served in the enlisted mess. When Fat Charley left beside his plate thirty-five cents in the paper script they used for money, Lowell did likewise.

"Lowell," Fat Charley said, when they had finished eating, "if you want to make sure you're properly checked in, I'll have another cup of coffee with Captain Winslow."

"Thank you, sir," Lowell said. "Nice to have met you, Captain."

"I'll see you tonight, probably," Captain Winslow said. "I live here, too."

As he walked across the dining room, he heard Fat Charley say to Winslow that he had "just arrived. Nice boy. Fine polo player."

The sergeant at the desk went with him to his room, a pleasant, airy double room on the top floor. He told him how the laundry was handled, and advised him to make sure he locked up his cigarettes and other goodies, because the krauts would sure as hell steal anything that wasn't nailed down.

Fat Charley was waiting in the lobby when he came down from his room.

[THREE]

The general showed up, with MacMillan, in a liaison aircraft precisely at 1430. His polo players were waiting for him, with the better ponies; and ten minutes after the general landed, the first chukker began.

At one point in the game, when the jeep horn sounded the end of the fourth chukker, Lowell found himself alone with General Waterford at the far end of the field. They walked their mounts back together.

"It's you, Fat Charley, and me," the general said. "Think it over, and then tell me who else we should play with."

By God, Lowell thought, here I am, on my first day as a second lieutenant, and the general is already asking my advice.

When the game was over, there were cocktails at the general's van, served by the general's orderlies and attended by such officer's ladies as happened to be in the area. He was introduced to Mrs. Fat Charley. She was very much like Mrs. Waterford, Lowell thought.

Afterward, Lowell drove to the Bayrischen Hof, and went to his room. He took a leisurely shower and then spent the hour and a half until the bar opened reading *Stars & Stripes* and listening to his radio.

The other polo players, when they came in, acknowledged his presence in the bar with a nod or a word, but none joined him where he sat at the end of the bar, and he was not invited to join any of the groups at their tables.

They're afraid of me, Lowell realized, or at least they don't know what to do with me. It is easier to stay away from me.

At six o'clock, after two beers, he went into the dining room and ate alone. Then he got in the jeep and drove across the park to the municipal auditorium, which like most of the useful buildings in Bad Nauheim, had been requisitioned by the army. He bought a ticket for twenty-five cents, and sat in the officer's loge, and watched a Humphrey Bogart movie.

After he'd returned to the Bayrischen Hof, he intended to go right to his room; but Captain Winslow, to whom he had been introduced at lunch, saw him passing through the lobby and called out to him. After Winslow had bought him a beer and he had bought Winslow a beer, Winslow offered the information that Fat Charley and the general and Winslow's father had been classmates at West Point.

Soon after that Lowell's eyes fell upon a tall, blond, dark-eyed fur-line at a table with another fur-line and two officers. The officer with her groped her, or tried to, under the table. His reaction was ambivalent. He thought that his new status would give him opportunity to rent a little pussy himself, something as good looking as that, something he had been reluctant to do so far because he had nearly been nauseated by the technicolor VD movie he'd been shown on arrival in Germany. Renting one of the fur-lines on the street for a box of Hershey chocolate bars or two boxes of Rinso was something a reasonable man just did not do. Renting one in an officer's hotel, however, might be something else again. Certainly, he reasoned, the army must take some measures to insure that the officer corps in an official officer's billet did not contact gonorrhea, syphilis, or even crabs.

He was also offended and angry that a nice-looking young girl like that should have to permit herself to be pawed by a drunken oaf like the captain at the table.

Then he told himself that it was none of his business, and said good night to Captain Winslow, who seemed to be a decent sort, and went to bed.

At midnight, there were sounds of crashing glass, and a feminine scream, and shouted male oaths, and of opening and slamming doors. He got out of bed and went to the door and stuck his head out.

The girl he had seen being groped in the bar was huddled against the wall at the end of the corridor, hurriedly fastening her clothes. Her blond hair, which she had worn in a bun at her neck, was now hanging loose and mussed. It made her look very young; and her wide blue eyes showed terror. The oaf Lowell had seen pawing her in the bar, dressed in only his skivvies, was being urged back into his room by two other officers and the sergeant from the desk downstairs.

As soon as they had the oaf inside his room, the room next to Lowell's, the sergeant turned to the girl and in broken German told her to get her hustling little ass out of the hotel, right goddamn now, and don't come back.

She scurried like a frightened animal down the corridor, past Lowell. There was shame and anger and terror and helplessness all at once in her eyes. She was entirely too good looking, Lowell thought, to be a whore. Whores are supposed to look lewd, lascivious, and tough. This one looked like somebody's kid sister. He thought about that. She looked like Cushman Cuming's little sister. What the hell was her name? The one he always mispronounced: Penelope. He had once seen Pen-ell-oh-pee Cumings in her nightgown with her boobs pushing out in front.

He watched as the whore fled down the stairs beside the elevator.

Lowell closed his door. He could hear, but not completely understand, the drunken outrage of the oaf next door. For some reason, he was as excited as he had been when he had seen Cush's kid sister in her nightgown in Spring Lake. He had been ashamed when that had given him a hard-on, and he was embarrassed now that what had just happened had also given him a hard-on.

He walked to the French windows and opened them, then looked out the window to the street below.

In a moment the fur-line came out of the hotel, walking quickly. She stopped on the sidewalk, looked both ways, and then hurried across the street into the municipal park. She disappeared into the shrubbery. She was probably taking a short cut through the park, Lowell thought. And then he saw that she had stopped twenty yards inside the park and was leaning on a tree.

What she is going to do, Lowell decided, is wait for a GI or an officer to come down the street, and offer herself. Strangely excited, he decided he would watch.

Two soldiers came down the sidewalk. The girl didn't move from her tree. Then an officer walking from another of the hotels to the Bayrischen Hof walked past her. She didn't approach him either.

There was a tightness in Lowell's chest, an excitement. He turned from the window, took his trousers from the chair where he'd laid them, and began to dress. He ran down the stairwell and walked past the knowing eyes of the sergeant on duty at the desk and into the street.

He entered the park. She wasn't leaning on the tree where he had last seen her, and for a moment he felt like a fool. Then he saw the edge of her dress behind the tree. She had seen him coming and was avoiding him.

"Guten Abend," Lowell said. She stepped from behind the tree, and stood clutching her purse against her chest. She smiled at him, a smile so forced it gave him a pain in the stomach. He saw that she had combed her hair. It was now hanging down past her shoulders. Damn it, she did look like Cush's sister.

"Guten Abend," she said, softly, barely audibly.

"He was drunk," Lowell said. She said nothing. "Are you all right?" She said nothing. "Can I take you home?" Lowell asked.

"I am very expensive," she said, after a moment's hesitation, in English, as if she was embarrassed.

Lowell was suddenly enraged. He had meant what he said; it was not a euphemistic phrase for "Wanna fuck? How much?" He had been offering to *take her home. Period.* He reached in his pocket, took what paper script his hand found, and thrust it at her.

She took it, counted it, nodded, her head bent, and jammed the money into her leather purse. He found himself looking at the purse. It was an alligator purse, a good one. But it was a woman's purse, not a girl's. It was obviously not hers. He counted the money as she counted it. He had given her fifty-five dollars, five or ten times the going rate.

She looked at him, met his eyes. There was defiance in them. Defiance and fear.

"Even for that much money," she said, in English, "I will not do anything with the mouth." She spoke decent rather than GI English, he realized. The partially understood complaints of the oaf suddenly came into focus. He had wanted her to blow him; she had refused. He turned around and started to walk out of the park.

"Where do you go?" she asked.

"To get my jeep," he said. "To take you home."

"It would be better that we go to your room," she said.

He had been torn between wanting to screw her, wanting to help a young woman in distress, and wanting to confirm his own wisdom and righteousness by telling himself he wouldn't touch a syphed-up kraut slut like that with a ten-foot pole.

Now he wanted to fuck her. He desperately wanted to fuck her. To impale her. To fuck the ass off her. Was it, he wondered, because she looked so much like Cush's practically certified virginal sister? That was a pretty disgusting thing to consider. Was he really, deep down, some sort of pervert, who wanted to mess around with little girls?

This was not a little girl, he reassured himself, no matter what she looked like. She might look about sixteen years old, with those blue eyes and that innocent little face, but she was as much a certified whore as Cush's sister Penelope was a certified virgin.

He waited until she caught up with him, then took her arm and hustled her across the street and into the hotel. The sergeant at the desk looked up, recognized the girl, and started to say something.

"Stay out of this, Sergeant," Lowell heard himself say, surprised at his boldness.

"I don't want any more trouble in here tonight, Lieutenant," the sergeant said, backing down.

"There will be no trouble," Lowell said. He got the girl in the elevator, down the corridor past the oaf's door, and into his room.

She looked around the room. She looked at him, very intently. She went into the bathroom, and he heard the water running and the toilet flushing, and when she came out, she was naked save for a pair of cheap cotton underpants. Her breasts weren't very large, he saw, and he could hardly make out the nipples, but they stood out erectly in front of her. She was pale, and thin, but she had very feminine hips.

She walked to the bed, flipped the covers down, and lay down on it. He looked at her. She reached down and hooked her hands in her pants and raised her hips and slipped them down. The tuft of hair at her groin was no wider than his thumb. She met his eyes, and then turned her head to the side.

She just remembered to act modest and shy, Lowell decided. He had no way of knowing, of course, that she had just told herself that she was glad, now she was about to do it, that the first time she did it would be with a young man, and a good-looking young man, too, and not the captain who had wanted to commit a perversion with her, and had beaten her when she refused.

Lowell stripped standing where he was, letting his clothes fall into a pile on the floor. When he was naked, he went to the bed and lay down beside her.

She would not look at him. He put his hand to her breast. It was as firm and warmed as it looked. By now, he thought, his hard-on should be tickling his chin. But it hadn't even started to thicken, much less stand up.

He slid his hand down her body to her crotch. There was no response in her, either. He might as well be patting a dog. He put his hand to her breast again. She rolled over on her back and spread her legs. He got between them. Nothing. He had a limp, useless dick.

He rolled off her, out of the bed, went to the bathroom and pumped himself furiously. Nothing. He stayed in the bathroom five minutes, thinking lewd thoughts, manipulating himself, all to no avail.

What it was, he thought, was shame for thinking that way about Cush's sister. Jesus Christ, for his first whore, why did he have to pick one who looked like a nice girl, and made him feel like a slobbering pervert?

He didn't know what to say to her when he came out. When he finally did open the bathroom door, she was gone.

Humiliated, furious, he tried to go to sleep. He tossed and turned for forty-five minutes, got out of bed, went to the bathroom, and began to masturbate. His penis thickened instantly, and immediately afterward, he felt the birth of his orgasm. He came all over the back of the toilet seat and the floor, and before he was able to go to bed, he had to get down on his hands and knees and wipe it all up with toilet paper.

[**FOUR**]

The girl came into the bar of the Bayrischen Hof the next night, ten minutes after Lieutenant Lowell had come in. He had spent the afternoon being measured for pink-and-green uniforms, which would be made to order. ODs from the quartermaster officer's store would be altered to fit him perfectly. He had bought additional items of uniform. A leather-brimmed, fur-felt officer's cap. A gabardine trench coat. Three pairs of pebble-grained chukka boots. Two pairs of tanker's boots. After he had bought the jeep, he had been out of money. He'd wired home, asking for a thousand dollars. The reply, a telegraphic authorization to draw a thousand dollars from the American Express office, had come within forty-eight hours. It had been in his pocket, uncashed, during the hectic form-a-polo team days. He had taken it to be cashed that afternoon.

When he presented it, at first he thought something was wrong. The clerk had taken the telegram and gone into a rear office. The manager had come out, smiling.

"Forgive me," he said. "But this cable draft is to *Private* Lowell."

"I've just been commissioned," Lowell said. "I've got an ID card . . ."

"That won't be necessary at all, Lieutenant Lowell," the manager said. "But there is something else."

He handed him another telegram.

J. FRANKLIN POTTS
GENERAL MANAGER
AMERICAN EXPRESS ACTIVITY GERMANY

INFO COPY
AMEXCO BAD NAUHEIM

IN RECEIPT GUARANTEE OF HONOR DRAFTS UP TO $1000.00 PER CALENDAR MONTH ISSUED BY PRIVATE CRAIG W. LOWELL HQ US CONSTABULARY BAD NAUHEIM AGAINST US, MORGAN GUARANTY NEWYORK OR CRAIG POWELL KENYON AND DAWES, NEWYORK. UNDERSTAND

LOWELL IS GRANDSON OF GEOFFREY CRAIG, CHAIRMAN OF BOARD, CRAIG POWELL KENYON AND DAWES. TELETYPE CONSTITUTES AUTHORITY TO DO SO.

ELLWORTH FELLOWS
GENERAL MANAGER, AMEXCO, EUROPE, PARIS

"If there is anything we can ever do for you, Lieutenant Lowell, please don't hesitate to ask."

"That's very kind of you," Lowell said.

"As I said, anything that we can do, anything at all."

Lieutenant Craig Lowell smiled smugly to himself as he walked out of the AMEXCO office toward the PX. Grandpa was passing out a thousand a month because he was under the impression Craig was being a well-behaved little private. Wait till the old man found out he was an officer.

That started him thinking of home. He thought there was six hours' difference between Bad Nauheim and Cambridge. That meant it was eight o'clock in the morning in Cambridge.

His peers, his chums from St. Mark's, his new friends from Harvard—those the provost had decided were Harvard material "worth salvaging," unlike those like himself who were not—were at that very moment lined up in their ROTC uniforms on the grass about to do a little close-order drill. If he should somehow manage to have himself miraculously transported to Cambridge, they would have to come to attention, salute, and call him "sir."

How amusing.

He decided he would have a photograph taken and send it to someone, Bunky Stevens, probably. "Having lovely time, wish you were here."

As he was fitted for his pinks and greens, and waited for change to be made after paying the bill, he daydreamed of home. He had not allowed himself to dwell on that subject very often. The cold truth of the matter was, he had been quite terrified of the army. The power of the corporals in basic training over him had been the most frightening thing to happen to him in his entire life, including the death of his father. From the moment he had raised his hand in the induction center, the previous February, five months ago, he had ceased being who he was, a Lowell, and had become, as indeed the corporal had lost no time at all in telling him, a miserable pissant. He had been advised to give his soul to Jesus, because his ass now belonged to the army.

He had been so terrified of basic training that for the first time in his life he had made a conscious, consistent effort to behave and to deliver what was expected of him. He had become, if not a model soldier, then the next best thing, a nearly invisible one. He had not called attention to himself. He had neither talked back nor whined. On the rifle range, at the last moment, he had remembered to miss. If he shot High

Expert, of which he was perfectly capable, he knew that he would have been taken out of the pipeline at the end of training and made into a marksmanship instructor.

Eight hours a day of Garand rifles going off in one's ear for the indeterminate future would be an awful way to pass one's penal servitude. He had been terrified on receipt of orders to proceed to Camp Kilmer for further shipment to Germany, and had spent his entire seven days' delay-en-route leave at Broadlawns on Long Island, half drunk, refusing to think about the future.

The troopship to Bremerhaven had been a floating Dante's inferno, a two-week horror. Only when he had arrived in Bad Nauheim and been assigned to the Constab as a clerk-typist had life begun to resemble at all the life he had known, and that similarity was limited to having sheets on the bunk, a place to take a bath, and food served on plates.

He had been in Germany only a week, and at the Constab only two days, when he came to understand that the venereal disease rate among the troops seemed to be the constant preoccupation of the Army of Occupation. Even the army radio station had commercials.

A GI solemnly pronounced: "Six fifteen hours, Central European Time. Remember, soldier! VD walks the streets tonight! And penicillin fails once in seven times!"

The army's solution to the problem was clean and wholesome sports, apparently in the theory that the troops would be exhausted to the point where they would not be interested in fornicating with frauleins. Every sport known to Western civilization was played, on command. Including, to his surprise, golf.

He had gone out for golf. At home, on the lawns of Broadlawns, which connected with the fairways of Turtle Creek Country Club, he had been whacking the ball around since he learned how to walk. The first time he played the Constab links, with some really awful clubs, he'd gone around the nine-hole course in 35, one under par. He had been posted to the golf team, and eventually named caddy master.

That was the turning point. He had moved out of the barracks into the golf course clubhouse. Slightly more civilized living. And then the polo came along. And now he was an officer and a gentleman.

He was a little annoyed with himself for his fear and concern. There was no reason why things should be different in the army—it was, after all, nothing more than a reflection of the society it served. He was what he was, a Lowell, and eventually he would come out on top.

Other people might have to spend their time washing tanks, or digging holes, or whatever; other people might have to wait, as the sign in the American Express office said in large letters, for a THREE WEEK OR MORE DELAY TO CASH PERSONAL CHECKS. He would spend his time playing golf and polo, as an officer, and would have his bank drafts honored at sight.

And soon it would be over, and he could go home. Certainly, as an officer, there would be a cabin on the returning troop ship, not a sheet of canvas between pipes in a hold thirty feet beneath the waterline.

He would, of course, wear his uniform when he got home. For a couple of days, until his civvies caught up with him. Pinks and greens, of course. Perhaps even the riding crop, or would that be a bit much? The pinks and greens, he decided. No riding crop. At Jack and Charley's 21 Club. Bunky Stevens would still be a college boy, down from Cambridge. He would be an officer, returned from overseas.

Second Lieutenant Craig W. Lowell moved his beer glass on the bar in the officer's mess of the Bayrischen Hotel, making little circles, dreaming of home.

"May I zit here?" the whore from the night before said timidly.

Goddamn, the last person in the entire fucking *world* I want to see right now!

He looked at her, met her eyes. Jesus Christ, how can she be a whore? She's even better looking than Cush's little sister. She's a goddamned certified beauty, that's all there is to it.

"Yes, of course, you may zit dere," Craig Lowell said, getting to his feet. He immediately regretted mocking her English and was relieved that she hadn't seemed to notice.

"Zank you," the whore said.

"Well," Craig Lowell said.

"I vaited in duh park undil I see you come in."

"Would you be more comfortable in German?" Craig Lowell said, in German.

"Oh, yes," she said, and she looked at him, and there was gratitude in her eyes. "I thought that you had spoken German last night, but I wasn't sure. I was so upset."

"May I offer you a drink?" he asked.

"A Goke-a-Gola, *bitte schön*," she said.

What do I say now? How did a nice girl like you wind up in a place like this?

He ordered the Coca-Cola from the bartender, in German.

"Jawohl, Herr Leutnant," the bartender said.

"Do you live here?" he asked. Do you like Radcliffe?

"I used to live not far," she said. "Marburg. A very lovely little university city. You must see it before you go home."

She sounds like the goddamned Chamber of Commerce.

He looked at her and saw her naked in his bed, with the thumb-sized tuft of pubic hair. He closed his eyes.

"I vill go," she said. "I am you making uncomfortable."

"No!" the refusal burst out of him. "You will stay. You will have dinner with me." That seemed to scare her. He smiled. "We agreed to speak German, don't you remember?"

"Yes," she said.

The oaf, the captain from the night before, sat across the dining room from them and sneered at Lowell's naiveté. What kind of a whore was it that wouldn't give you a blow job?

He asked her if she would like to go to the movies. She accepted. It was the same Humphrey Bogart movie. He sat beside her and once took her hand. It was limp and cold in his.

In the jeep, when he reached for the ignition switch, she stayed his hand.

"We must talk," she said.

"About what?"

"I will go with you," she said. "But not just for one night. You understand?"

"No."

"I must do what I must do," she said. "But not for one night."

"Why must you do it?"

"My father is missing," she said. "There is no work. The state has taken over my home."

"What about your home?"

"My home has been requisitioned," she said.

"Where's your mother?"

"My mother no longer lives," she said. "She did not want to live, the way things are now."

Lowell decided he didn't want to know what she meant by that.

"I must have money, and I cannot get a job," she went on. "I have nobody. So I will do what I must do. But not for one night." He didn't answer. "After a while, perhaps, I will do what you like with my mouth."

"Oh, for Christ's sake!" Craig Lowell said. She was offering to blow him.

"But we must have an arrangement," she said.

"What kind of an arrangement?"

"You will give me one hundred dollars a month, and you will buy me things in the PX that I can sell on the black market," she said. She looked at him. "I will be good to you," she said.

He didn't reply.

"You have already given me $55," she said. "For only $45 more, and the things from the PX, you can have me for a month."

"You can keep the money I gave you," Craig Lowell said. "And I'll take you home." This had gone far enough. He was getting in over his head in an impossible situation.

"I don't have anyplace to go," she said, and there was desperation, even something close to terror, in her voice.

"What do you mean, you have no place to go? Where did you go last night?" Christ, if she's playing on my sympathies, she's doing one hell of a good job of it. How can a gentleman, like myself, fail to respond to a homeless waif? And then he was ashamed of himself for mocking her.

"To the park," she said, matter-of-factly.

"You spent the night in the park?"

She nodded, lowered her head. "If you want, I will do it with the mouth." It was total resignation, utter submission. And he knew she was telling the truth about the park.

"Shut up, goddamnit!" he said. He started the jeep and turned it around furiously. "I'll tell you what I'm going to do. I'm going to let you spend the night with me. Nothing will happen between us. I'll give you some more money. Tomorrow, you find someplace to stay. And I will see what I can do about getting you a job."

She wept silently, wiping her eyes.

When they came close to the Bayrischen Hof, she told him to stop the jeep. She jumped out and ran into the park. He waited, sure somehow that she was coming, unable to do what his logic told him to do, unable to put the fucking jeep in gear and get out of here.

She came back with a suitcase. Like her purse, it was a quality piece of goods. It was old, but it was good leather, and there was even the vestiges of gold initials.

"I had it hung in a tree," she said.

Craig Lowell had never felt before the humiliation he felt marching through the lobby of the Bayrischen Hof with his fur-line and her worn-out pigskin suitcase, before the eyes of the officers, before the eyes of the desk clerk sergeant who had thrown her out the night before.

In the room, she asked if she might take a bath. He nodded.

The prick in him, as he thought of it, came out when he had a mental image of her naked in his bathtub. He was paying for it; goddamnit, he had the right to see her in her bathtub. He had the right to do anything he goddamned pleased with her. She had even *offered* to blow him!

He did not enter the bathroom.

He put on clean underwear (he usually slept naked) and a cotton bathrobe. He waited until she came out, in a nightgown that went down to her ankles.

He went to his trousers and gave her five twenty-dollar script certificates.

"Tomorrow, you will find someplace to live," he said. "And this will carry you through until you've straightened yourself out."

Tears ran down her cheeks. She took the money.

"Zank you very much," she said. "God bless you!"

Oh, shit! That's all I had to hear!

They got in bed. They both faced outward, their backs to each other. After a long time, he went to sleep. He was not going to screw her. For one thing, she probably had syphylis, gonorrhea, an army of crabs, and God alone knows what else. For another, he was a Lowell, and a gentleman, and gentlemen did not take advantage of women in distress.

He woke up slowly, halfway into a wet dream. He had been touching Marjorie Carter's magnificent breasts, and suddenly he was awake and in bed with a real woman.

Her. He was really awake now, and excited. Her nightgown had riden up over her hips. He had wrapped his arm around her in his sleep. His hand was resting against her stomach. He had the World's Prize-Winning Number One Hard-On.

He very carefully lifted his arm and withdrew it.

"I'm awake," she said, softly, in German.

"Huh?" Craig Lowell said.

She rolled onto her back.

"I said I'm awake," she said. She looked up at him, and spread her legs.

He crawled between her legs. This time it didn't go down. This time it was ready.

But it wouldn't go in. Where the hell was her hole? He spit on his fingers, rubbed it on the head, used it as a probe, felt it slip in.

He gave a massive thrust. It went all the way in. She yelped, softly, her hand in her mouth, biting her knuckle. It was easier now. It went in and out, in and out. She was making grunting sounds in her throat, half groans, half whimpers. Her midsection began to respond to him. She took her hand from her mouth and locked her arm around his neck, nearly choking him. She thrashed under him, calling upon Jesus, Mary, and Joseph.

He came.

He rolled off her and ran into the bathroom and washed himself, as he had been instructed to do in the technicolor VD movies. Now he was going to have clap and syphylis and crabs and Christ knows what else.

When he went back in the bedroom, she was curled up in a fetal position, not looking at him. When he got in bed, she got out, and he heard her doing whatever it is women do in the bathroom afterward. Then she came back and very quietly got into bed.

At first light, it happened again. Same goddamn thing. He woke up with his thing as rampant as it had ever been, pressed up against the crack of her ass.

The second time, he found the hole without much trouble, and she moved against him even more frenziedly, and she didn't make those yelping noises. And the second time, he told himself, what the fuck, I've already caught it. He didn't jump off her and go and wash his privates.

She said, when she had stopped breathing hard, "What is your name?"

"Craig," he said.

"I am Ilse," she said. "Ilse Berg."

When she had gone to the Civilian Personnel (Indigent Personnel) Office of the U.S. Constabulary to seek a job as a translator, the American had asked her her name, and she had told him Greiffenberg. He had asked her to spell it, and he couldn't understand her pronunciation, so finally he said, "Fuck it. From now on, fraulein, your name is Berg."

He wrote Berg down on her application, and she was afraid to correct him. Maybe he would, as he said, let her know in a month or two about a job. It didn't matter what her name was anymore.

She put out her hand to Craig, in the European manner, and shook his. She told herself that she had really been lucky. She had found an Ami who was kind and gentle. He was a nice person, she thought, and she thought that he acted a lot younger than he really was. He acted as if he was no more than eighteen or nineteen, and he must be older than that, for he was an officer. She promised herself that for as long as he kept her, she would do her best to live up to her end of the bargain.

It was preposterous, of course, to think that anything could come between them.

When he came back from the polo field that afternoon, she was waiting across the street from the Bayrischen Hof for him. When he stopped, she came gaily tripping across the street and got in the jeep and directed him three miles out of Bad Nauheim to a farm. She had rented a tiny two-room apartment. There was a tiny table. Somewhere she had found a rose, and put it in a small vase. There was a bed. She showed it to him proudly, and then turned. They looked at each other for a moment, and then, without a word, they started taking off their clothes.

[**FIVE**]
Baden-Baden, French-Occupied Zone, Germany
4 July 1946

The polo field was in sight of the Grand Hotel, and it was one of the oldest polo fields on the Continent, built to accommodate the English aristocracy whom had brought the game from India and then taken it with them to the Continent. It had been turned into a vegetable garden during the war, and the grass wasn't anything like either General Waterford or General Paul-Marie Antoine Quillier, his French counterpart, remembered from before the war, but it was, Waterford realized, a much better field than the field at Bad Nauheim.

The French, of course, had tried to get them drunk the night before at a dinner in the hotel, and afterward at a bar; but Waterford had seen that coming, and the only one who had defied his edict to stay sober was young Lowell.

He had decided to forgive Lowell. For one thing, Lowell was young; and there really wasn't much else for him to do with his elders around but drink. Primarily he was forgiving Lowell because the boy was playing better with what certainly must be a classic hangover than the others were playing in their physical prime.

They were five goals up on the French in the fourth chukker, when the French number three, with an offside neck shot, sent the ball toward the American goal. A good shot, twenty yards in the air, bouncing along the field for another ten yards and then picked up by the French number one, General Quillier, with an offside foreshot, which drove it another forty yards toward the American goal.

The players galloped past the spectators, past the band of the U.S. Constabulary in their chrome-plated helmets—its three trumpeters on their feet with instruments near their mouths—past the band of the Deuxième Division Mécanique of the French—with its bass drums draped in leopard skins, its Algerian mountain goats with gilded horns—past the tents set up to serve lunch and champagne, past the limousines of the generals, the staff cars, the personal automobiles, toward the American goal, behind which sat the L-5 Stinsons.

The American number four, Fat Charley, galloped up behind General Quillier. Leaning forward, standing in his stirrups, he passed him, raised his mallet over his head and swung it in a wide arc, a beautiful backhand that stopped the bouncing ball and sent it shooting in the other direction.

The American number three, Lieutenant Lowell, spun around in his headlong charge, changed direction, and galloped at the bouncing willow ball. He raised his mallet, then swept it down in a vicious arc so swift the whistling sound of the mallet was audible over the clatter of the pounding hooves. He drove the ball toward the French goal.

There was a muted round of applause from the ladies and gentlemen.

The three trumpeters of the U.S. Constabulary band, their eyes on their general, sounded the charge.

The American number one, Major General Peterson K. Waterford, coming from across the field at a gallop, misjudged the speed of the bouncing ball. He almost overrode it, but saved his shot by making an offside tail stroke, his mallet coming from the far side of his mount under the tail, as he galloped past it. The ball was twenty yards ahead of him almost immediately, just time for him to raise his mallet for an offside foreshot. It was a clean blow. The ball went ahead of him in a straight line, hit the grass, rolled, stopped.

He raised his mallet again, urged his mount to go even faster. The trumpeters sounded the charge again. His mallet came down again in a swift arc. The crack of the maple head of his mallet on the willow ball was clear and crisp.

He watched the trajectory of the ball, then looked over his shoulder. In perfect position to back him up, in case he missed, was his number three, at a gallop, his mallet resting casually over his shoulder. He wasn't going to miss the sonofabitch.

He raised his mallet, heard his trumpeters sound the charge again, then swung his mallet and connected. He looked up to see the ball heading straight for the unprotected goal. He spurred his pony into pursuit.

Major General Peterson K. Waterford appeared to have lost his stirrup. He fell forward against the neck of his mount, as if he had lost his balance. The pony, still at the gallop, went through the goalposts.

The bell rang. Good goal.

The general's pony, at the last moment before running into the nearest of the Stinsons, veered to the right. General Peterson K. Waterford was unhorsed. He fell heavily to the ground, landing on his shoulder, skidding on his face.

His number three, Lieutenant Lowell, made what appeared to be an impatient shake of his hand, twisting his wrist free of the mallet loop. He reined in his galloping mount and was off the animal before it recovered from its abrupt stop. He ran the ten feet to General Waterford, knelt beside him, and rolled him over on his back. He saw that although General Waterford's eyes were on him, they didn't see him.

General Quillier was next to arrive, dismounting as quickly as had Lowell. He took one look at General Waterford's eyes and crossed himself. Then some of the others came up, with Fat Charley nearly last. And finally, on foot, red-faced, puffing from the exertion, Captain Rudolph G. MacMillan.

QUARTIER GENERAL DE L'ARMEE D'OCCUPATION DE L'ALLEGMAGNE
4 JULY 1946

TO:HEADQUARTERS
UNITED STATES ARMY FORCES, EUROPE
FOLLOWING FROM BADEN-BADEN

MAJOR GENERAL PETERSON K. WATERFORD DIED SUDDENLY AT 1508 HOURS PRESUMABLY HEART ATTACK MORE FOLLOWS.

MACMILLAN, CAPT.

OPERATIONAL IMMEDIATE
HQ USFET
WAR DEPT WASH ATTN CHIEF OF STAFF
INFO HQ U.S. CONSTABULARY

IN RECEIPT UNCONFIRMED REPORT SIGNED MACMILLAN CAPT THAT MAJOR GENERAL PETERSON K. WATERFORD DECEASED 1508 HOURS THIS DATE AT BADEN-BADEN.

CLAY, GENERAL

OPERATIONAL IMMEDIATE
HQ USFET
WAR DEPT WASH ATTN CHIEF OF STAFF
INFO HQ U.S. CONSTABULARY

DEATH OF MAJOR GENERAL PETERSON K. WATERFORD CONFIRMED AS OF 1530 HOURS. GENERAL WATERFORD SUFFERED CORONARY FAILURE WHILE PLAYING POLO AT BADEN-BADEN. MRS. WATERFORD PRESENT. FURTHER DETAILS WILL BE FURNISHED AS AVAILABLE.

CLAY, GENERAL

[SIX]
Bad Nauheim, Germany
4 July 1946

HEADQUARTERS
UNITED STATES CONSTABULARY
APO 109 US FORCES

GENERAL ORDERS 4 July 1946
NUMBER 66

The undersigned herewith assumes command of the United States Constabulary as of 1615 hours this date.

Richard M. Walls
Brigadier General, USA

General Walls had been known as "the Wall" when he had played football for the Academy because there had been few people ever able to push past him on the football field. He had weighed 220 pounds then. He was, twenty-five years later, ten pounds heavier. He was the Constab's artillery commander, and upon official notification of the demise of the commanding general, he had acceded to temporary command by virtue of his date of rank.

He was at the headquarters airstrip when the first L-5 Stinson from Baden-Baden arrived. Captain MacMillan hauled himself out of the front seat of the little airplane, straightened his uniform, and marched over to the Chevrolet staff car. He saluted crisply.

General Walls did not smile when he returned MacMillan's salute.

"All right, MacMillan," he said. "Let's have it."

"The general seemed all right through the first three chukkers, sir," MacMillan said. "In the last few moments of the fourth chukker, he appeared to have lost his balance, and then he fell off the horse. When I reached him, sir, he was dead."

"Mrs. Waterford?"

"Mrs. Waterford was among the spectators, sir. As soon as possible, sir, I had the frogs TWX USFET."

"Subject to Mrs. Waterford's approval, of course, Captain, it is my intention to hold a memorial service for General Waterford at 1400 hours tomorrow."

"Yes, sir."

"How is Mrs. Waterford bearing up?"

"Very well, sir. Fat Charley . . . Colonel Lunsford is with her. They were classmates, sir, as I'm sure the general knows."

"I have spoken with General Clay," General Walls said. "The Air Corps has made available a C-54 to take Mrs. Waterford to the States. And the general's remains, if that is her wish."

"I believe Mrs. Waterford wishes the general to be buried at West Point, sir," MacMillan said.

"You've already asked, have you? You are an efficient sonofabitch, aren't you, MacMillan?" General Walls said. "All right, Captain, here it is. As a token of my respect for General Waterford, and my personal regard for Mrs. Waterford, you may consider yourself in charge of all arrangements until the general's remains leave the command."

"Thank you very much, sir."

"And then find yourself a new home, Captain," the general said.

"Sir?"

"You hear well, Captain," the general said. "General Waterford may have found you amusing, or useful, but I don't."

"Would the general care to be specific?" MacMillan, standing now at rigid attention, asked.

"The list of your outrages, MacMillan, is a long one. What comes to mind at the moment is that golf player you arranged to have commissioned. Shall I go on?"

"No, sir, that won't be necessary."

"I won't have someone like you in any outfit I command. In my judgment, medal or no goddamned medal, you are unfit to wear an officer's uniform. You are a scoundrel, MacMillan. A commissioned guardhouse lawyer. Is that clear enough for you?"

"Yes, sir, the general has made his point."

[ONE]
Drop Zone Carentan
Fort Bragg, North Carolina
5 July 1946

Major Robert F. Bellmon, Assistant Branch Chief, Heavy Drop Loads Division of the Airborne Board, Fort Bragg, North Carolina, was regarded by his peers, and by the four bird colonels and sixteen lieutenant colonels senior to him, with suspicion and even contempt. He had been reduced to major in one of the first personnel cutbacks—"without prejudice"—but everyone knew that not all officers promoted beyond their age and length of service had been reduced in grade.

But even if he had just been caught in a rollback and was a good armor officer, what was such a good armor officer doing volunteering for airborne? Why would armor permit a good armor officer to go to Parachute School and then on to Ranger School? The answer was clear, and the proof was his assignment to the Airborne Board as the armor specialist.

There was nothing that anyone could put a finger on to *prove* their suspicions of Bellmon—he certainly did his work well enough—but two things about him were perfectly clear. There was nothing that airborne was planning to do that wouldn't be known to Fort Knox immediately. He was armor's spy in the airborne camp. That was perfectly clear. Airborne had their spies at Knox, too. That was the way the game was played. The second thing that was clear was that Bellmon was not, and would never be, one of them.

He went through the things that were expected of him: membership in the Airborne Association, wearing his parachutist's wings when no other qualification badge adorned his uniform, and as sort of a symbolic gesture that he wasn't really armor, having himself detailed to the General Staff Corps for the duration of his assignment to the Board.

They suspected, however, and they were correct, that he was laughing at them.

Major Bellmon thought a lot of things in the army were laughable. He had once gotten himself in trouble as a young captain by laughing out loud at the uniform General George Patton had designed for armor troops. He had once enraged one of the members of Eisenhower's SHAEF staff by pronouncing *Shayfe* as *Sheef*, and then going onto explain that a sheef was something somebody who lisped put on when he wished to diddle somebody.

A photograph had been circulated among senior airborne officers. The commanding officer of the Parachute School at Fort Benning, as a courtesy to a field-grade officer, had sent a photographer aloft in the C-47 to chronicle Major Bellmon's fifth (qualifying) jump. Instead of grim determination and great seriousness, the photographer had returned with a print of Major Bellmon going out the door holding his nose, his eyes tightly shut, his right hand over his head . . . a small boy jumping into deep water.

And he was amused now, although he kept his thoughts to himself. He was sitting in a jeep (another of his idiosyncrasies was that he drove his own jeep; the assigned driver had to perch in the back seat) at Drop Zone Carentan. Other jeeps and trucks were gathered at the edge of the drop zone. There were a half dozen officers and twenty-five enlisted men. They all wore field jackets. The Airborne Board, like the Armor Board, the Artillery Board, and the Infantry Board, was a subordinate command of Army Ground Forces. The insignia of Army Ground Forces was a circle with three horizontal bands of color, blue for infantry, gold for armor, and red for artillery. But since all the personnel of the Airborne Board were airborne qualified, they sewed above this insignia a patch lettered *Airborne*. All this amused Major Bellmon.

A captain walked over to the jeep.

"The aircraft is airborne at Pope Field, Major," he said.

"Thank you," Bellmon said.

The test today was to drop, from a specially modified C-113 aircraft, an M24 light tank. The tank was firmly chained to a specially built platform, which in turn was chained to the floor of the C-113. When the aircraft appeared over the drop zone, the chains fastening the tank platform to the floor of the aircraft would be removed. A drogue parachute would be deployed from the rear of the airplane. When its canopy filled, it would pull the tank on its platform out of the rear of the aircraft. Then three enormous cargo parachutes would be deployed. They would, in theory, float the tank and its platform to the ground. On ground contact, the platform was designed to absorb shock by collapsing. The chains holding the tank to the platform would then be removed, and the tank driven off.

One of the weaknesses of a vertical envelopment was that you couldn't drop the necessary tanks, large-bore artillery, or engineer and other heavy equipment. This weakness was in the process of being rectified. Bellmon thought they had as much chance of solving the problem as they did of becoming ballet dancers.

Three minutes after the captain announced the aircraft was airborne, Bellmon got out of his jeep and walked to the drop zone. He saw that there were still and motion-picture cameras in place. And an ambulance. And even a three-man tank crew, to drive the tank away once it had landed.

He walked over to the tank crew. They came to attention.

"Stand at ease," he said. "How are you?"

"Good morning, Major," they chorused.

"What are you giving in the way of odds?" Bellmon asked.

"Not a fucking chance in hell, sir," the tank commander said.

"Oh, ye of little faith!" Bellmon said.

The airplane, a twin-boom, squatish aircraft whose boxlike fuselage had given it the name "Flying Boxcar," appeared in the distance. It approached and made a low-level pass. Someone set off a smoke grenade to indicate the direction and velocity of the wind. The aircraft made a low, slow turn and approached again, descending to a precise 2,000 feet altitude over the ground.

Bellmon raised his binoculars to his eyes and watched. The drogue chute came out the tail. Then the tank on its wooden platform. One by one, three huge cargo chutes filled with air and snapped open. The tank swung beneath them.

"Well, that much worked," Major Bellmon said.

One of the three parachutes began to flutter, and then lost its hemispherical shape.

"Sonofabitch ripped," one of the tank crewmen said. "I coulda told them that."

A second parachute ripped. The tank, which had been suspended horizontally, now hung from only one chute and was heading for the earth vertically. The third chute failed.

There was absolute silence as the tank plummeted toward the ground, trailing three shredded parachutes. It landed on its rear with one loud crash, and then fell over, right side up.

"I don't think you'll be needed today, fellas," Major Bellmon said. He walked quickly away. He sensed that the tankers were about to be hysterical, and he didn't want to be in the position of having to make them stop. He walked to his jeep, got behind the wheel, and drove out to where the tank had fallen.

The tank cannon had been in its travel position: turned to the rear and locked in place over the engine compartment. Some force, either of being jerked out of the airplane, or the opening shock of the cargo chutes, had torn it free from the mount. When the tank had hit, the high-tensile-strength steel in the gun barrel had been bent in a U.

It was too much for Major Bellmon. As he reached for the jeep's ignition switch, he started to snicker, then to giggle, and finally he laughed out loud. It took him a long time to get the jeep started and moving.

"Get on the horn, Tommy," he said to the driver, as the jeep turned onto the dirt road leading back to Fort Bragg. "And tell them we're on our way back in."

The driver turned to the radio, mounted above the right rear wheel well, and communicated with the Airborne Board.

"Major," he said, in a moment. "The post commander wants to see you as soon as possible."

"The *post* commander?"

"Yes, sir."

"Do you think somebody already told him that I was laughing?" Major Bellmon asked.

Post headquarters was in one of a line of three-story brick buildings that Bellmon remembered from before the war as enlisted men's barracks. He parked his jeep, told the driver to get himself a cup of coffee, and entered the building from the rear.

The commanding general's office overlooked the post theater and senior officer's brick quarters. Bellmon, after announcing himself to the general's secretary, peered out the window of the anteroom to see what was playing at the movies, convinced that it would be at least fifteen minutes before the general would see him.

"Come on in, Bob," the general said, behind him. That was unusual, too. Normally an aide would tell him that the general would see him. The general did not welcome visitors personally. "Where the hell have you been anyway?" the general asked, touching his arm as they entered the office.

Bellmon started to snicker.

"Something funny?"

"Forgive me, sir," Bellmon said. "They were dropping an M24. It landed right on the tube, and bent it into a U. I guess I have a perverse sense of humor."

The general didn't reply to that.

"The reason I asked, Bob, is that you had a call from the chief of staff, and nobody could find you."

"Sir," Bellmon said, "if I've caused you any inconvenience . . ."

"Not my chief of staff, Bob. *The* chief of staff."

"I don't understand, sir."

"When he couldn't get you, he got me. It is thus my sad duty, Bob, to inform you that Major General Peterson K. Waterford died suddenly at 1500 hours, German time, yesterday. We were old friends. I'm sorry."

"Do you know what happened, sir?"

"Heart attack," the general said. "Playing polo against the French. At his age."

"Jesus Christ!"

"I thought perhaps you would like to tell Barbara yourself. I'd be happy to . . ."

"I'll tell her, sir," Bellmon said. "Thank you."

"I've alerted Caroline. I thought I would give you a few minutes with Barbara and then send her in."

"Thank you very much, sir."

"Well, I guess he went the way he would have wanted to go. Playing polo."

"I was thinking just that, sir."

"My aide is laying on your plane reservations, and he'll be in touch. I'll come up for the funeral, of course."

"Thank you, again, General," Bellmon said.

"He was a little unusual, Porky Waterford," the general said, and his voice broke, and there were tears in his eyes, "But goddamn him, he was one *hell* of a soldier!"

[TWO]

The president of the Airborne Board walked into Major Bellmon's small office to find him standing with a coffee cup in his hand and looking out of the window.

"Bob, I called your quarters and they said you were here. First of all, I'm terribly sorry; and secondly, I certainly didn't expect to see you here."

"Thank you, sir," Bellmon said. "Caroline, the chief of staff's wife, is with her. She's something like an adopted aunt to her . . . wanted me out of the house. And then there was a call from the Air Corps, General Deese, who was a classmate of General Waterford. He's sending his plane. He insisted we take it. So I had time to kill, and this seemed to be a good way to kill it."

"Anything we can do, of course. I've sent Janice over to your place."

"A soldier's death, sort of," Bellmon said. "Playing polo. *Polo!*"

"A soldier should die with the last bullet fired in the last battle," the colonel said. "I guess this is close. Why don't we have a drink?"

"I've got the Ranger honor graduates coming in," Bellmon said. "I don't want to breathe booze all over them."

"I'll take them," the Airborne Board president volunteered.

"If you don't mind, sir, I'd rather handle it. It's either that, or look out the window."

"I understand," the president of the Board said. "However, if you change your mind, I'll be in the building most of the afternoon."

"Thank you, sir."

"I understand the M24 drop was a failure," the president said. "Any ideas?"

"I think we better find a better way of air-landing our tanks," Major Bellmon said.

"Let me have your thoughts in a memo, Bob," he said. "When all this is over, of course."

"Yes, sir."

Bellmon's secretary, a civilian woman whose services he shared with three other officers, put her head in his door and knocked on the door frame. Bellmon looked at her.

"You've got five lieutenants to see you, Major."

"I'll get out of your hair, Bob," the president said. "Again, I'm very sorry."

"Thank you, sir," Bellmon said. He nodded at his secretary. "Send the first one in, please."

First Lieutenant Sanford Felter, Infantry, United States Army, his cap tucked under his upper left arm, marched into Major Robert F. Bellmon's office, stopped three feet from his desk, saluted crisply, and announced: "Lieutenant Felter reporting to Major Bellmon as ordered, sir."

Bellmon smiled as he returned the salute, but there was no recognition on his face or in his eyes.

"Sit down, Felter," he said, indicating a straight-backed, upholstered chair. "How do you take your coffee?"

"Black, sir, please," Felter said.

Bellmon looked much better than the last time Felter had seen him. His face and his body had filled out, and the unhealthy brightness was gone from his eyes. Bellmon filled a china cup from a restaurant-style coffee pot and walked around his desk and handed it to Felter.

"Congratulations, obviously, are in order," Bellmon said. "I was nowhere near being the honor graduate when I went through the course. As a matter of fact, I was way down the numerical list."

"One of my classmates, sir," Felter said, "developed a theory that small people, having less weight to carry around, should be handicapped."

Bellmon laughed, and looked at Felter with new interest. That wasn't the sort of remark he expected from a young lieutenant. It wasn't flip, or arrogant, but self-confident.

"He has a point," Bellmon said, chuckling. "What I'm going to do, now, Felter, is take a quick look at your record. I'm telling you that, because I don't want you to think I'm waging psychological warfare by making you wait for me as I do it. I just didn't have a chance to do it before."

"Yes, sir," Felter said.

Bellmon found the service record interesting. Even fascinating. He would never have suspected that this little man, this little Jew, had ever marched in the Long Gray Line. But there it was, the first entry on his service record:

1Jan45 Hon Disch f/Corps of Cadets USMA (Class of 46) for purp of accept comm.

2Jan45 Comm 2ndLt Inf AUS Asgd Trans Off Det, USMA West Point NY

2Jan45-19Jan45 En Route 40 US Armd Div, APO 40, NYNY

19Jan 45 40MP Co, 40 US Arm Div (Dy as Asst O-in-C POW Interrogation Div)

23Apr45 Ofc of Mil Govt For Bavaria (Dy as Captured Documents Evaluation Off)

3Jul45 Prom 1st Lt, Inf AUS DOR 1Jul45 (Compl 6 mos satis comm svc)

17Aug45-4Oct45 En Route ZI (Incl 40 Dys Ret from OS lv)

5Oct45 Basic Inf Off Crs, USA Inf School, Ft Benning Ga

2Apr46 Dist Grad, Basic Off Crs USA Inf School Ft Benning Ga

21Apr46 Qual as Prchst, USA Inf School, Ft Benning Ga

23Apr46 USA Ranger School, Ft Bragg NC

2Jul46 Honor Grad USA Ranger School, Ft Bragg, NC

"I see you were with Hell's Circus," Bellmon said. Felter was not wearing the division patch on his right shoulder, as his wartime service entitled him to do.

"Yes, sir."

"Did you ever happen to meet General Waterford?" Bellmon asked.

"One time, sir, for about fifteen minutes."

"I'm sorry to tell you, Lieutenant," Bellmon said. "that General Waterford died yesterday. Playing polo, of all things."

"I'm sorry to hear that, sir," Felter said.

Bellmon had a sudden urge to challenge this self-confident little Jew.

"Why do you say that?" he demanded. "If you only saw him once for fifteen minutes, why would you have any feeling about his death, one way or the other?"

"I suppose I was considering what his loss means to the army, sir," Felter said. "General Waterford was recognized to be one of the better large armored force commanders."

Bellmon nodded, impressed that the reply had come without thinking, that Felter had not been offering condolences to curry favor.

"Yes, he was," he said. "I'm curious to hear your plans for your career, Felter. Do you plan to stay? Are you going to apply for regular army?"

"Yes, sir," Felter said.

"Since you left the Academy, you don't have a college degree. What do you plan to do about that?"

"I am enrolled in the Extension Department of the University of Chicago, sir. I hope to have my degree in a few months."

"You're talking about getting a degree by correspondence? Through the mail?"

"Yes, sir. I'm going for a degree in political science."

"Commendable," Bellmon said, dryly. The little bastard had an answer for everything. Then he suddenly realized that he was being hard on him for no good reason. Because he was a Jew? Or because his own father-in-law, who he really liked, maybe even loved, had just dropped dead, and he was upset by that?

"Felter, I apologize," Bellmon said. "I've been picking on you. For what it's worth, I have just had a death in the family. That's no excuse for picking on you, but that's what happened. I'm sorry."

Felter did not reply.

"Lieutenant," Bellmon said, smiling at him, "in token of the U.S. Army's profound appreciation of the splendid showing you have made at John Wayne High School, also known as the U.S. Army Ranger School, an effort, a real effort, will be made to give you your choice of assignment. There are about twenty-five different vacancies."

"Yes, sir," Felter said.

"You seem neither outraged nor amused at my somewhat irreverent reference to the Ranger School," Bellmon said.

"I've heard it called that before, sir," Felter said.

"And what was your reaction? Amusement, or outrage at the mocking of the sacred?"

"Amusement, sir," Felter said. He ran his hand over his closely cropped hair, which was already starting to thin. The movement served to shade his face. Bellmon looked at him very closely.

"And are you amused now, Felter?" Bellmon asked, and there was ice in his voice. He was furious with himself for not having recognized Felter immediately.

"Sir?"

"Do you find this situation amusing?"

"I don't quite know what you mean, sir," Felter said.

"You know precisely what I mean, Lieutenant. We have met before, haven't we?"

"Yes, sir."

"You did not elect to remind me," Bellmon said. "May I ask why?"

"I was offering the major the option of remembering me," Felter said. He paused, then added: "Or not."

"What happened to you when we got back?" Bellmon asked, after a moment. He ran his hand nervously over his head.

"I was ordered not to discuss Task Force Parker," Felter said. "And then I was sent to Munich."

"Did you hear what happened to me?"

"I heard the major was hospitalized," Felter said.

"In the nut ward," Bellmon said. "Did you hear that?"

Felter just perceptibly nodded his head.

"Did you elect not to remind me of our previous meeting because you believe I was temporarily bereft of my senses at the time?"

"I have examined the Katyn material," Felter said. "I believe the Russians executed the Polish prisoners."

"Where did you examine it?" Bellmon asked, surprised.

"The Polish government-in-exile, what used to be the Polish government-in-exile, presented it to Congress. The hearings are a matter of public record."

"But you took the trouble . . ." Bellmon said.

"I was interested," Felter said.

"And have you discussed either the Katyn business or Task Force Parker with anyone?"

"Not until today, sir."

"Not even with your wife?"

"No, sir. My wife is a sensitive woman."

"Similarly, Lieutenant Felter, I have not discussed what happened with anyone."

"Yes, sir."

"I was reduced in grade shortly after the war ended, Felter. That might have been because I was too young for the grade I held. I have been led to believe that my name is number fourteen on the next promotion list to lieutenant colonel. I will still be a rather young lieutenant colonel. Does that suggest anything to you?"

"It would suggest that there is no question concerning the major's stability," Felter said. "Or his discretion."

"There are some things, Felter, which should not be discussed unless one is absolutely sure of the audience."

"Yes, sir."

"You and I are not alone, Felter," Bellmon said.

"Yes, sir."

"You demonstrate a rather unusual understanding for someone of your rank and length of service," Bellmon said. He let that sink in. Then he smiled. "You may even be able to grasp what a crock of shit the ranger philosophy is."

Felter smiled.

"Well, I owe you one, anyway, for keeping me from getting blown away the day I was liberated. Tell me what you've been thinking about your career."

"I don't know quite what to say, sir," Felter said.

"Where do you what to be twenty years from now? In 1966? By then you should be a major, possibly even a lieutenant colonel. Battalion exec? What?"

"Sir," Felter said. "I think I would be suited to be an intelligence officer."

"Why?"

"I have a flair for languages. I speak German and Polish and Russian. And a little French."

"Russian?"

"My mother's family, sir."

"There is more to intelligence than linguistics," Bellmon said. He had just realized that while he had planned to kill some time by making the expected remarks to a bunch of dumb lieutenants, he was now faced with the opportunity to offer some genuine advice to a lieutenant who was obviously anything but dumb, and to whom, in fact, he owed his life.

"Yes, sir, I understand that," Felter said.

"The truth of the matter, Felter, is that most of the good intelligence officers in the last war—and I would suppose in all wars—were civilians in uniform. The mental training which makes for a good regular officer in peacetime is not often valuable in the intelligence business. What I'm saying, I suppose, is that we need very bright people to be intelligence officers, but that there is no place in the peacetime army for a bona fide intellectual."

"Sir, are we going to have a peacetime army?"

"Take that further, Felter," Bellmon said. "Explain yourself."

"I saw in the newspaper last week that we've taken over for the English in Greece, sir," Felter said. "That's hardly garrison duty."

There was a moment's silence as Bellmon sifted through a manila folder on the desk before him.

```
TELECON MEMO

Record of Telecon Between G-1 This Hq and Office of the Adjutant
General, War Dept (Col J C McKee & Lt Col Kenneth Oates)

Colonel Oates stated that the Chief of Staff had approved a re-
quest from the Commanding General, United States Army Mili-
tary Advisory Group, (USAMAG-G) for 86 company grade combat
arms officers to serve as advisors to the Royal Greek Army. If
possible, such officers should have a knowledge of the Greek
language, combat experience, and be willing to serve a minimum
tour of one year in hardship conditions. A levy of two officers
has been laid upon Fort Bragg (including all subordinate
units). Col. Oates further states that he must have the names
of selected officers within 24 hours. Volunteers will proceed
as soon as possible via mil air to Frankfurt, Germany, for
transshipment to Athens.
```

"Where else in the world do you see trouble spots, Felter?" Major Bellmon asked. "Just for conversation, of course."

"Sir, I think I'm talking too much," Felter said.

"Where else, Lieutenant?" Bellmon said. "If you haven't learned by now, it's high time you did, that when you open your mouth, you better be prepared to finish what you started to say."

"Yes, sir," Felter said. "India, sir. With their independence. Indochina, against French colonialism. China, where the communists are probably going to win. That may have implications for Indochina, too. Korea. The Philippines. Palestine, I don't want to forget that."

"Tell me about Palestine," Bellmon said.

"The Zionists are not going to give up. And neither are the Arabs. They will not tolerate a Jewish state."

"Whose side are you on?" Bellmon said.

Felter was sure now that his mouth had got him in trouble.

"I'm Jewish, as well as a Jew," he said. "My sympathies lie with the idea of a Jewish state."

"And if you were ordered to Palestine, on the side of the English, for example, against the Zionists?"

"I don't know, sir. I would probably resign."

"Don't say that to anyone else, Felter," Bellmon said. "Never let the enemy know of your options until you have to." He paused. "A classmate of mine is over there. Resigned his commission. Fighting for the Zionists."

"And you don't approve, sir?"

"No, Lieutenant, I don't," Bellmon said. "Does that make me in your eyes a bigot? An anti-Semite?"

"No, sir. But it illustrates my point about Palestine being a trouble spot. There's very little room for reason on either side. In a way like northern Ireland, which is another trouble spot."

"I hadn't even thought about Ireland," Bellmon confessed.

Having said that, he realized that Felter's assessment of the world was very much like his own. Charitably, it was realistic; or cynical. Like his own.

"Your next assignment will be with troops," Bellmon said, formally. "Junior officers need the responsibility of command. The following are vacancies available to you: 1st Cavalry Division, Dismounted, Kyushu, Japan; 187th Regimental Combat Team, Airborne Hokkaido, Japan; 24th Infantry Division, Hawaii; 5th Infantry Division, Fort Riley, Kansas; 82nd Airborne Division, here at Bragg; Any of the infantry basic training centers; 1st Infantry Division, Germany; Trieste United States Troops . . . that's the old 88th Mountain Division . . . in Trieste. They call it TRUST. Those are your options, Lieutenant."

"Sir, I heard that we're going to send company-grade officers to Greece. Would that be considered duty with troops?"

"Where did you hear that?"

"From some of the men in class, sir. A number of them have volunteered."

"Volunteers are apparently being solicited from officers with combat experience," Bellmon said. "You have none. At least officially."

"If I have to spend time with troops, sir," Felter said, "as part of my education, I would prefer to spend time with troops who are engaged."

"What are you after, Felter, a reputation as someone spoiling for a confrontation with the Godless Red Hordes?"

"I believe it is an officer's duty to learn as much as possible about potential enemies," Felter said.

"It is, of course," Bellmon said. "The trouble, historically, is that few people have been able to identify the next enemy in time to do anything about it. What if you're wrong?"

"You and I, Major," Felter said, "already know the Soviet Union is our enemy."

"Watch who you say things like that to, Felter," Bellmon said. "A lot of people think the Soviet Union is just a friendly bear."

Felter nodded.

"It's a hardship tour, Felter," Bellmon went on. "No dependents. Your wife will be denied the opportunity to live high on the hog in an Army of Occupation."

"I understand, sir," Felter said.

Bellmon picked up his telephone and told his secretary to get Colonel McKee on the line. When, a moment later, the telephone rang, Bellmon turned the receiver from his ear so that Felter could hear both sides of the conversation.

"Sir, this is Major Bellmon. I have one of your two company grades for Greece."

"Who's that?"

"A lieutenant named Felter. He was honor grad of the ranger school. He wants to go, and I think we should send him."

"I don't think so, Bob," Colonel McKee said. "For one thing, I've already got a couple of people who were 'encouraged' to volunteer. What did your guy do wrong?"

"Nothing, sir. As I said, he was honor grad of the ranger course. He wants to go."

"Bob, I'm not getting through to you. We're dumping people to Greece, not awarding it as a prize. It's a lousy assignment."

"Lieutenant Felter wants to go, Colonel. As honor grad, he is more or less entitled to pick his assignment."

"There's something you're not telling me, Bellmon. But I'm not going to ask. OK, you want this guy shanghaied to Greece, consider him shanghaied. Give me his full name, rank, and serial number."

[THREE]
West Point, New York
9 July 1946

Major General Peterson K. Waterford was laid to his final rest in the cemetery of the United States Military Academy at West Point. When the volleys had been fired, when the trumpeter had sounded the last taps, when the flag, folded into a triangle with no red showing, had been placed in Mrs. Waterford's hands by the Chief of Staff of the United States Army, the funeral party moved to the quarters of the Commandant for refreshments.

Major Robert F. Bellmon sought out Captain Rudolph G. MacMillan.

"I haven't had the chance before, Mac," he said, "to express my thanks. My mother-in-law's told me what a help you've been."

"What the hell, I was awful fond of the general," MacMillan said, embarrassed.

"And he of you," Bellmon said.

The Chief of Staff of the United States Army walked up and joined them.

"I've got to be getting back, Bob," he said. "But I didn't want to leave without saying good-bye and God bless, and without thanking you, Captain MacMillan, for all you've done for Mrs. Waterford."

"My privilege, sir," Mac said.

"You were with Porky a long time, weren't you?" the Chief of Staff said. He was a tall thin man, one of the few four-star generals then entitled to wear a Combat Infantry Badge, which General of the Army Omar Bradley insisted should go only to soldiers who had functioned well in ground combat. More than one general who'd been awarded one by orders he had signed himself had been told to take it off.

"No, sir," MacMillan said. "Not long at all. But Colonel . . . I'm sorry, *Major* Bellmon and I go back a long way."

"Mac and I were in the stalag, together, General," Bellmon said.

"Oh, of course. I knew there was something." His eyes dropped to the blue-starred ribbon topping MacMillan's display of fruit salad. "You are *the* MacMillan."

"The one and only," Bellmon laughed.

"And now what happens to you?" the Chief of Staff asked. "You're sort of left hanging, aren't you? Where would you like to go?"

"Anywhere they send me, sir, of course," MacMillan said.

"Oh, come on, MacMillan. The army owes you something," the Chief of Staff said.

"Sir, now that you bring it up," MacMillan said, "I was about to ask Major Bellmon if he could find a home for a battered old soldier."

"You got a spot for MacMillan, Bob? Where are you . . . oh, yeah. The Airborne Board. I *heard* about that."

"I think, sir," Major Bellmon said, "that we could find something to keep Mac occupied."

"I also heard—out of school, of course—that you're not going to be at Bragg much longer," the Chief of Staff said. "Among other things, I. D. White wants you at Knox. Why don't I just—?" He stopped in midsentence and made a barely perceptible movement of his head. A brigadier general walked over. He was a distinguished-looking officer with silver hair, and he wore the gold cord of an aide-de-camp.

"Tom, Major Bellmon will call you with the details," the Chief of Staff said. "The idea is to have Captain MacMillan assigned to Knox. Tell the G-1 to find something suitable for him to do there, will you?"

"Sir," MacMillan said, "the minute I get near personnel types, they want me to make speeches. Can it be arranged to sneak me into Knox?"

The Chief of Staff laughed.

"Sneak him into Knox yourself, Tom. I understand the captain's problem."

"Yes, sir," the aide-de-camp said. "Sir, we're going to have to be moving on."

"Let me say good-bye to Mrs. Waterford," the Chief of Staff said. "Get the car."

[FOUR]
McGuire Air Base
Wrightstown, New Jersey
10 July 1946

Sharon Lavinsky Felter was ashamed of herself because she hated her husband on the very day he was going away.

It wasn't that she didn't love him. She loved him as she had loved him for as long as she could remember. But it was possible, she had learned, to love and hate the same man at the same time.

She hated Sandy when he was being an officer, when he was giving orders she had to obey, and not listening to her, or even caring what she thought about anything.

They had ridden to McGuire, she and Sandy, and her mother and father, and Mama and Papa Felter, in a brand-new Buick Super two door. Now especially, with him going away, she needed a brand-new Buick Super two door like she needed a third leg. For one thing, she wasn't that good a driver, and for another, the Buick seemed to want to get away from her almost as if it had a mind of its own.

She had had no say about the Buick at all. He couldn't tell her father or his, or especially his mother what he'd told her ("The question is not open for discussion"), so he'd listened to their objections: All that money. Sharon didn't *need* a car. There was the Lavinsky's perfectly good 1938 Plymouth to carry her anywhere the Old Warsaw Baker's Dodge panel truck couldn't take her. If he had to have a rich man's car, he could buy one when he came to his senses and came home.

He heard the objections and ignored them.

"Try to understand this, Sharon," he said to her. "I'm getting a little tired of repeating it. I am a regular army officer."

He had told her that thirty-five times. She didn't really understand what that meant, but he had been very pleased with himself when the letter had come in the mail. They'd had to waste one whole day going down to Fort Dix, where he got another physical examination, and then was sworn in. But he was still a first lieutenant, and he wasn't going to get any more money, and the only difference she could see was that they gave him a new, shorter serial number.

Regular army officers, she tried to understand, had different obligations from reserve officers on extended active duty. And for reasons she could not understand, one of these was apparently that they had to have a rich man's car, a new one, just sitting around so that in case one was needed in a hurry, there it would be.

"We can afford it. For the couple of hundred extra dollars, I would rather have the reliability of a Buick. If I didn't think we needed it, or I didn't think we could afford it, we wouldn't buy it. Now let it be, Sharon."

He made her drive from Newark to McGuire Air Base, although that was the last thing she wanted to do. "Otherwise," he said. "You would never drive it. And I want you to know that you can."

It was crowded in the Buick, as big as it was, with Sharon and Sandy and Papa Felter in the front, and Sharon's mother and father and Mama Felter in the back. And with Sandy's luggage in the trunk, the front of the Buick was high up and Sharon had trouble seeing over the bull's-eye ornament on the hood.

And there was a lot of tension in the car, although everybody naturally tried to hide it. The Felters and the Lavinskys were really angry with Sandy, angry and hurt by his behavior and confused by it.

So far as they were concerned, he had done his part by going off to the war when he could have stayed safe and sound at West Point. Then when he had, thank God, come home in one piece, he had done more than his part by not taking the honorable discharge he had been offered.

Sharon had agreed with everything Mama Felter had said to Sandy, when she really laid it into him. Sandy could be anything he wanted to in life. God had given him the brains to be a doctor or a lawyer, or anything else he wanted to be. There was the GI Bill of Rights, which would pay for his education; and the bakery was coming along nicely, so there would be money for them to get a little apartment of their own and maybe even start a family while he was still in school, if that's what he and Sharon wanted to do. He had everything a reasonable man could ask for, and he was throwing it all away like a little boy running off to the circus. A soldier! Who did he think he was, Napoleon, because he was so short?

Papa Felter tried to shut Mama Felter up and calm things down. What Sandy was doing, he said, was proving himself, because he was small. After a while, he would come to his senses; he wasn't old yet. He said that Sandy had never had the time to sow any wild oats, the way he'd gone off to the war. Papa Felter said they should stop worrying, and be glad that he hadn't started drinking, or gambling, or chasing women, or whatever, the way most young men did.

After a while, Papa Felter said, Sandy would see things for what they were, and he would come to his senses. He had every confidence in that. For the time being, if it made Sandy happy to jump out of airplanes, and eat snakes in the jungle the way they made him do in ranger school, they would just have to go along with him.

That was all very nice, but it wasn't much help to Sharon. She wasn't asking much. She had been perfectly content in their room in Columbus, Georgia, outside Fort Benning, and in the little apartment in Fayetteville, North Carolina, outside Fort Bragg. As it said in the Bible, "Whither thou goest, I will go." If Sandy had wanted her to go with him to the North Pole, she would have gone and been happy, but that wasn't this. This was a whole year, maybe more, with her working in the bakery and Sandy doing God alone knows what in Greece. *Greece!*

Everybody in the car was torn between being mad at Sandy and feeling sorry for Sharon, and feeling sorry for the both of them.

When they got to McGuire Air Force Base, Sandy directed her to park the Buick Super in an area designated DEPARTING PERSONNEL PARKING.

He picked up his two heavy Valv-Paks and walked into the passenger terminal with his wife and his parents and his wife's parents trailing reluctantly behind him.

"Well, look who's here," he said, softly, as much to himself as to Sharon when he stepped inside the door.

"Who's here, Sandy?" Sharon asked.

"Some of my classmates," he said. "I heard about that. They report in early, and then take another two weeks in Germany when they get there."

She didn't know what he was talking about, but she could see who he was talking about. There were twenty second lieutenants in the waiting room wearing Class "A" tropical worsted summer uniforms—shirt, tunic, trousers, and brimmed cap—and twenty young women, all dressed up with flowers pinned to their dresses and suits, looking like brides.

Sharon deeply loved her husband, and wouldn't have swapped him for any man in the world, but being honest about it, when you looked at him in his khakis, Sandy looked like somebody delivering from the delicatessen.

"Honey, why didn't you wear your TWs?" Sharon asked.

"If you're going to have to spend eighteen hours in an airplane seat in a uniform," he said, just a trifle smugly, "you wear khakis."

He picked up the two Valv-Paks and walked across to the desk. Sharon trailed after him.

"Lieutenant," the sergeant said, scornfully, looking at the heavy Valv-Paks, "you're going to be way over weight."

"Take a look at my orders, Sergeant," Sandy said, unpleasantly.

The sergeant read the orders Sandy handed him.

"OK, Lieutenant," he said. "My mistake."

Sharon became aware that several of the second lieutenants were looking at them. She thought it was because Sandy was wearing khakis.

"It'll be just a couple of minutes, Lieutenant," the sergeant said. "Stick around the waiting room."

"Thank you," Sandy said. Then he took Sharon's arm and marched her over to the second lieutenants and their wives.

"Hello, Nesbit," Sandy said. "Pierce. O'Connor."

"I'll be damned, Felter," one of them said. "It is you."

"You'll be damned, *sir,"* one of the others said. "Note the silver bar." He put out his hand.

The third one smiled broadly, and said, "Sir Mouse, sir, may I present my wife?"

"How do you do?" Sandy said. "And may I present mine?"

One of them, as they were all shaking hands, told his wife that "Lieutenant Felter was with us at the Academy for a while." Sharon saw the explanation confused the wife. And she didn't like it when people called Sandy "Mouse," even though he told her he didn't mind.

"Deutschland bound, are you, Mouse?" one of them asked.

"Greece," Sandy said.

"Greece?" he responded, incredulously.

"There's a Military Advisory Group there," Sandy said.

"I didn't know that," he said.

Despite the fact that she knew Sandy was right that there was no sense in mussing a tropical worsted uniform on an airplane, Sharon wished that Sandy had worn his anyway. Or at least put on his other insignia. All he was wearing was his silver lieutenant's bar on one collar and the infantry rifles on the other. He was wearing regular shoes, even though he was entitled to wear paratrooper boots. He wasn't even wearing his parachutists' wings and boots or his Ranger patch.

Sharon could tell from the way the others talked to him, the way they looked at him, that they didn't think very much of him, either. Sad Sack Felter is what he looked like, two pastrami on rye and a side order of cucumber salad, double cream in the coffee. And meeting the young West Pointers and their wives confirmed what

Sharon had suspected. Sandy said going to Greece was a great opportunity for him. The others didn't think it was such a great opportunity; they didn't even know the United States had soldiers in Greece. They were going to the 1st Division and the Constabulary in Germany.

And they were taking their wives with them. Right on the same plane.

When she and Sandy walked over to their parents, Sharon sensed that the West Pointers were whispering about them.

Then the plane was announced.

Sharon's mother and Mama Felter started to cry out loud when Sandy kissed them. Sharon kept her tears back until Sandy climbed the stairs and disappeared inside the plane. Then she cried on her mother's bosom.

In the car on the way home, Papa said something terrible. He didn't know he said it. He was just thinking aloud. Papa said, "I suppose if you have to send somebody to get shot, it's better to send a Jew."

Sharon told herself that Sandy was the smartest boy she had ever met. If she believed that, she would have to believe that he would come to realize that what he was doing was the wrong thing for him, for them; and then he would come home and they could build a life together.

When he missed her, Sharon decided, that's when he would decide he was wrong.

[FIVE]
Bad Nauheim, Germany
11 July 1946

Colonel Charles A. Webster, the Constabulary's adjutant general, entered the office of the commanding general, Brigadier General Richard M. Walls, to bring certain personnel actions to the general's attention. General Walls had received no word regarding his future. He did not know if he would be given command of the Constab permanently or whether a major general would be sent in to take General Waterford's place. He had therefore been commanding the Constab from the same office from which he had commanded the Constab artillery, rather than moving into Waterford's office at Constabulary headquarters.

"I'm afraid I've let this slip, sir," Webster confessed, handing General Walls a teletype message. "I sort of hoped they would just forget us."

"What is it?"

"USFET laid a requirement on us for two combat-qualified officers to send to Greece. They also have to speak Greek."

"And?"

"I found people with those qualifications, but their commanders don't want to give them up."

"What the hell is going on in Greece?"

"I really don't know, sir. As I said, I thought if I just let it slip, they'd forget us."

"And what's the problem?" Walls asked. He read the TWX from USFET:

```
PRIORITY
FROM USFET 10 JULY 1946
COMMANDING GENERAL U.S. CONSTABULARY
ATTN: ADJUTANT GENERAL.

(1) REFERENCE TWX 55098. 27 MAY 1946.
(2) YOU WILL IMMEDIATELY FURNISH NAMES OF TWO OFFICERS
    SELECTED FOR TRANSFER TO US ARMY MILITARY ADVISORY GROUP,
    GREECE, REQUESTED IN REFERENCED TWX.
(3) YOUR ATTENTION IS INVITED TO REQUIREMENTS SPECIFIED IN
    REFERENCED TWX. SELECTED OFFICERS SHOULD BE OF COMBAT
    ARMS, GREEK SPEAKING, AND AVAILABLE FOR HARDSHIP TOUR OF
    NOT LESS THAN ONE YEAR. VOLUNTEERS ARE PREFERRED.

                              BY COMMAND OF GENERAL CLAY
```

After General Walls read the TWX, he pushed it back to Colonel Webster. "Let me think about it a minute, Charley," he said. "I really hate to give up officers with combat experience. If the balloon should go up with the goddamned Russians, how the hell am I expected to fight with an officer corps that never heard a shot fired in anger?"

"That brings us to Lieutenant Lowell, sir," Webster said. "Does the general intend to bring him before a board of officers for dismissal from the service?"

"That fancy-pantsed sonofabitch hasn't been an officer long enough for us to make that judgment," General Walls said. "Not to speak ill of the dead, that was really going too far, even for Waterford. Where's MacMillan? Did he find a new home?"

"Yes, sir. We got a TWX yesterday. He's assigned to Knox. He won't even be coming back."

"I would like to be able to send that sonofabitch to Greece," General Walls said. He looked up at Colonel Webster. An idea had been born. He reread the TWX.

"As I read this thing, Colonel," he said, "it says volunteers are preferred. 'Preferred' is not the same thing as 'required,' is it? And it also says that officers 'should be' of combat arms, Greek speaking, and available for a hardship tour. I would say that Lieutenant Lowell is available for a hardship tour, wouldn't you, Colonel?"

"Yes, sir, I would," Webster replied. "If the general decides not to board him out of the service."

"And he is presently detailed to a combat arm, isn't he?" General Walls asked. There was a pleased tone in his voice.

"Yes, sir, he is."

"Pity he doesn't speak Greek, but two out of three isn't bad, is it, Colonel?"

"Not bad at all, sir."

"Who else can you think of, offhand, Colonel, who also meets these requirements?"

"I heard from the CID, General, that there's a captain in the 19th they think isn't entirely all man, if you follow me."

"Anybody else?"

"There's a lieutenant in Combat Command A who's been writing some rubber checks."

"Send the fairy," the general said. "Anything else, Colonel Webster?"

"Not a thing, sir. That takes care of all the loose ends I can think of."

"Get both of them out of the Constabulary this afternoon, Colonel," General Walls said.

[SIX]

The military police duty officer came into Fat Charley's office in the provost marshal's building that Craig Lowell thought looked like a gas station.

"I thought I should bring this to the colonel's attention, sir," he said.

"What is it?"

"Colonel Webster just called, and said he was speaking for the general, and I was to send every available man to locate and arrest Lieutenant Lowell and bring him to his office."

Fat Charley thought a moment, and then he dialed Colonel Webster's number.

"Charley, what is this business about an arrest order on Lieutenant Lowell?"

"The general wants him out of the Constabulary this afternoon, Colonel."

"Where's he going?"

"He has been selected for assignment to Greece," Webster said, somewhat triumphantly.

"For Christ's sake, Charley, I saw that TWX. It says combat-experienced officers who speak Greek. It's not that boy's fault Waterford handed him a commission."

"Would you care to discuss it with the general, Colonel?"

"No," Fat Charley said. "I'll have him at your office in an hour, Colonel."

"Thank you for your cooperation, Colonel," Colonel Webster said.

Fat Charley hung up the telephone. He reached for his hat. "Is your driver outside?"

"Yes, sir. You know where to find Lowell?"

"I think so," Fat Charley said. "Have you issued an arrest order?"

"The duty sergeant put one out before I got this," he said. "Should I cancel it, sir?"

"No, you better let it stand," Fat Charley said. "I'm on Walls's shit list enough as it is without making things worse."

[SEVEN]

Forty-five minutes later Lieutenant Craig W. Lowell marched into Colonel Webster's office.

"Sir," he said, saluting. "Lieutenant Lowell reporting to Colonel Webster as ordered."

"You may stand at ease, Lieutenant," Colonel Webster said. "Lieutenant, this interview will constitute official notice to you of inter-theater movement orders. Regulations state that personnel notified of such orders be further informed that failure to comply with such orders constitutes desertion. Do you understand the implication of what I have just told you?"

"Yes, sir."

"By command of General Clay, Lieutenant, you are relieved of your assignment to the U.S. Constabulary, and are transferred to Headquarters, United States Army Military Advisory Group, Greece, effective this date. You will take with you such fatigue uniforms, field gear, and shade 33 uniforms as are necessary for an extended period of duty in the field. Shade 51 uniforms, and any household goods you may have, to include any personal vehicles, will be turned into the quartermaster. Such items will be stored for you at no expense to you at the U.S. Army Terminal, Brooklyn, New York, until such time as you complete your assignment, or request other disposition of them. You will procede from here to Rhine-Main Air Corps Base so as to arrive there for shipment by military air no later than 1800 hours this date."

"Yes, sir."

"Have you any questions?"

"Sir, I'm a little short of cash. May I have time to stop by American Express?"

"As part of your out-processing, Lieutenant, a partial payment of $100 will be made."

"Sir, I don't believe that will be enough money."

"You won't need money where you're going, Lieutenant," Colonel Webster said. "Any other questions?"

"No, sir."

"Captain Young, of my staff, will accompany you through your out-processing. If you have no further questions, that will be all, Lieutenant."

"Yes, sir."

Lowell saluted, did an about-face, and marched out of Colonel Webster's office.

Captain Roland Young, Adjutant General's Corps, who had rather relished the notion of personally running this disgrace to the uniform the hell out of the Constab, was annoyed and frustrated when he led Lowell into the corridor outside the adjutant general's office and found the provost marshal waiting for them. He could hardly tell the provost marshal to fuck off, even if the word was out that the provost marshal, like other members of Waterford's palace guard, was in hot water himself.

"I've sent a jeep for Ilse," the provost marshal said to Lowell. "They should have her here in a couple of minutes."

Captain Young thought that Colonel Webster would be very interested to hear that the provost marshal, in direct contravention of Constab (and for that matter, Theater) regulations, had ordered the transport of a German female in an official army vehicle.

"Thank you, sir," Lowell said. What the hell was he going to do about Ilse?

"What is the lieutenant's schedule, Captain?" Fat Charley asked.

"The lieutenant, sir, is to report to Rhine-Main no later than 1800 hours," Captain Young said.

"Amazing how efficient you paper-pushers can be when you want to," Fat Charley said.

Captain Young thought that Colonel Webster would be interested in that sarcastic remark, too.

"Is there anything I may do for the colonel, sir?" Captain Young asked. "There's not much time to go through the processing."

"I don't have anything else to do, Captain," Fat Charley said. "I think I'll just tag along with you."

The saddest part, Fat Charley thought later, was that in Lowell's room in the Bayrischen Hof, the two of them had looked like Romeo and Juliet. She cried and Lowell was teary-eyed, and they exchanged promises. They even dragged him into it. He offered to forward letters to Lowell, and to receive them for Ilse from Greece. And he assured Lowell, man to man, that he would keep an eye on her.

He would keep an eye on her, all right. He was convinced that what that eye would see—despite her tearful promises, despite the three hundred dollars Lowell had borrowed from him and handed over to her, despite what she probably believed herself at the moment—was that in two weeks she would be sharing some other junior officer's bed.

[EIGHT]
Rhine–Main Air Base
Frankfurt am Main, Germany
11 July 1946

Military Air Transport Flight 624, a passenger-configured C-54, landed at Rhine-Main twenty-two hours after takeoff from McGuire Air Base at Fort Dix, and after fuel stops at Gander, Newfoundland, and Prestwick, Scotland.

There was a welcoming delegation of officers and their ladies for the officers who were being assigned to Germany, and Transportation Corps people to handle those who were going beyond Frankfurt. Felter's khaki uniform was mussed, and he needed a shower, but clean uniforms and a bath were not among the facilities offered.

Felter was informed that the Athens plane was scheduled for departure at 1800 hours. It was 1500, three in the afternoon, German time. That meant he had at least three hours to kill. He could take the shuttle bus running from Rhine-Main to the

Hauptbahnhof in Frankfurt, have a couple of hours in Frankfurt, and return to Rhine-Main with plenty of time to make the flight.

The last time he had seen Frankfurt, he thought as the bus took him into town, it had still been smoldering, and he had been riding in the sidecar of a "liberated" Wehrmacht motorcycle.

When he got off the bus, he saw a white-and-black GI sign on a German hotel, the Am Bahnhof, identifying it as a bachelor officer's quarters. It followed that a BOQ in a hotel would have a mess. There had been an in-flight lunch between McGuire and Gander (a bologna sandwich, an apple, and a container of milk) and another (identical) between Gander and Prestwick. He had had nothing to eat since Prestwick.

He had just about reached the door of the Bahnhof when a nattily attired MP stepped in front of him and saluted.

"One moment, please, sir," he said. "May I see your identification, please?"

Felter handed it over.

"Would the lieutenant please come with me, please?" the MP said.

"What's this all about?"

"You are being detained, sir, for being in violation of USFET uniform regulations."

"I'm in transit," Felter said.

"Would the lieutenant please come with me, sir?" the MP said; and with movements as stiff as the Chocolate Soldier, he indicated the Bahnhof. Inside the Bahnhof was an MP station commanded by a first lieutenant.

The MP lieutenant wore parachutist's wings and the insignia of the 82nd Airborne Division. Felter remembered that the 82nd had left in Europe one regiment, the 508th, to guard the headquarters of the Army of Occupation, He now noticed that the lieutenant wore crossed rifles, not crossed pistols. He was an airborne infantry officer pressed into service as an MP.

"Lieutenant, you're a mess," the paratrooper said to him. "Have you got some sort of excuse?"

"I'm en route from Bragg to Greece," Felter said.

That caused some interest. For a moment, Felter thought he was going to be able to straighten this whole thing out.

"What were you doing at Bragg?"

"Ranger School," Felter said.

The lieutenant looked significantly at Felter's bare chest. Felter reached in his pocket and took his parachutist's wings from a collection of coins and held them up and smiled.

The lieutenant did not smile back.

Lieutenant Felter signed an acknowledgment that he was in receipt of a copy of a delinquency report, AG Form 102, the original of which would be sent through official channels to his commanding officer. He was delinquent in that he was in an unauthorized uniform, cotton khaki, where wool OD shade 33 or tropical worsted with blouse was specified. He was, moreover, without a necktie. He was not wearing qualification insignia (parachutist's) as required. In the Comments section, it was further pointed out that the uniform he was wearing was mussed and unmilitary, and that the subject officer was not freshly shaven.

A telephone call was made, and some senior military policeman decided that the thing to do with him, since he was in transit, was to transport him back to Rhine-Main, and turn him over to the air base duty officer, who could keep an eye on him until his plane left.

A Ford staff car was dispatched for that purpose.

It was, Felter thought, the first time that he'd been on report since he was a plebe.

The MP lieutenant marched him into the passenger terminal, where he telephoned for the duty officer, and then waited until he showed up and could sign for the "detainee," as if the detainee were a package. Then Felter was led to a small waiting room which held two other officers, a field artillery captain and an armored second lieutenant, tall, blond, muscular, in a superbly fitting uniform. He looked entirely too good to be true. He looked, Sanford Felter thought, like a model hired to pose for a recruiting poster.

"Keep your eye on this one, too, Captain," the duty officer said. "See that he gets on the Greasy Goddess." The captain nodded, but did not speak until the duty officer had left.

Then he said, "Sit down next to him, Lieutenant," and indicated the too handsome, too perfect lieutenant.

Felter did as he was told. The two lieutenants examined one another, and formed first impressions. While there were exceptions, of course, Felter had come to believe that officers who looked like movie stars seldom lived up to their appearance. Moreover, from the moment Major Bellmon had let him listen in to the telephone call at Bragg, when the officer Bellmon was speaking to thought that Bellmon wanted him shanghaied to Greece, Felter had come to understand that so far as most people in the army were concerned, an assignment to Greece was one step above being cashiered.

There was something in the field artillery captain's attitude that suggested that whatever had seen him assigned to the U.S. Army Military Advisory Group, Greece, it was not of his choosing, nor to his liking. He had, Felter was sure, been shanghaied. It was an easy step from there to conclude that the second lieutenant in the custom-tailored uniform and the hand-made jodhpurs was also being shanghaied. It was not at all unusual for second lieutenants, even West Pointers, to go wild when they first became officers. Drinking generally got them, but there were variants of this. Fast cars, women, gambling. Or a combination of all those things and more. Even before he learned his name, it was Sanford Felter's first judgment of Craig W. Lowell, that Lowell had done something to outrage the system, and had been banished.

Lowell's assessment of Felter was equally nonflattering. Felter was not physically impressive. His hair was already thinning. His khaki uniform was baggy on him. He was, Lowell concluded, one of those Jewboys, who had scored 110 on the Army General Classification Test and qualified for Officer Candidate School. He had somehow managed to get through OCS (when there was a shortage of second lieutenants, it was difficult to flunk out) and had been commissioned. Once assigned as an infantry officer, he had obviously been unable to cut the mustard, and they had gotten rid of him.

"Felter," Felter finally said, putting out his hand to Lowell.

"Lowell," Lowell replied, shaking his hand. Felter saw the field artillery captain get up and walk to the window, obviously to spare himself the business of introductions. He turned to look at Lowell again.

"I think you have just been snubbed," Lowell said.

Felter chuckled. "Where are you from?" he asked.

"New York," Lowell said.

"I'm from Newark," Felter volunteered.

"What did you do wrong?" Lowell asked.

"According to the DR," Felter said, "I have violated every known uniform regulation. And, in addition, went unshaved."

"I meant before," Lowell said. "Why are they sending you to Greece?"

"Actually, I volunteered for the assignment," Felter said.

Lowell didn't reply. Felter understood that Lowell didn't believe him.

"What about you?" he asked.

"Apparently things are terribly fucked up in Athens," Lowell said. "And General Clay decided I was the only man who could straighten things out."

Felter chuckled.

"What about you, Captain?" Lowell called across the room. "What shocking breach of military behavior did you commit?"

"When I have something to say to you, Lieutenant," the captain flared, "I'll let you know. Now you just sit there, and keep your goddamned mouth shut."

Lowell insolently clapped his hand over his mouth.

"Are you looking for trouble, Lieutenant?" the captain flared.

"What are you threatening, Captain?" Lowell said. "That you'll have me sent to Greece?"

The captain glared at him.

"Just shut the fuck up," he said, finally.

"Yes, sir," Lowell said, and started to say something else. Felter shook his head, "no." Lowell said nothing else.

A jeep came for them thirty minutes later, and carried them far down a taxiway to a Douglas C-47, which bore the insignia of the European Air Transport Command. Below the cockpit window was a well-executed painting of a nearly nude, large-breasted female and the words THE GREASY GODDESS II.

The aircraft had its nylon-and-pole seats folded against the walls of the fuselage to accommodate a half dozen large crates strapped to the floor. Forward, behind the door to the cockpit, was a pile of canvas mail bags. Running down the center of the fuselage ceiling was the cable to which static lines were hooked, and the red and green lights used to signal the jumpmaster were mounted by the door. The plane was equipped to drop parachutists. Felter wondered, idly, if it had been used for that purpose in the war.

The crew chief asked for their names, and wrote them on the manifest. He handed a copy of it to a ground crewman. He walked forward; and almost immediately, the plane shuddered as the engines were started. The crew chief came back, closed the door, and spoke to them briefly.

"When we get up, you can probably find a mail bag soft enough to sleep on," he said. He steadied himself by putting a hand, palm up, against the ceiling. The Gooney-Bird was already taxiing to the runway.

They refueled late at night in Naples, and then flew on through the blackness to Athens.

VII

[ONE]
Athens, Greece
12 July 1946

They landed at Elliniko Airfield as dawn broke. They were met at the airport by an American sergeant who wore British Army boots and who carried a Thompson submachine gun slung over his shoulder. He led them to the first British Army truck either of them had ever seen. The captain got in the front seat and they got in the back of the truck and were driven into Athens. Peering awkwardly out the back, Lowell saw a waterfront.

"We're on the coast," he announced. "What is that, the Mediterranean?"

Felter shook his head.

"That's the Saronikos Koplos," he said.

"The *what?*" Lowell asked, chuckling.

"Saronikos Kolpos," Pelter repeated. "Greece is sort of a peninsula here between the Ionian Sea and the Aegean. At the bottom is the Sea of Crete. What we're looking at is the Saronikos Kolpos."

"Lieutenant, sir," Lowell said, now actually laughing, "you are a fucking *fountain* of information."

Despite himself, Felter smiled at Lowell. Lowell was obviously a fuck-up, and Felter accepted as gospel that an officer was judged by his associates. He had intended to treat Lowell with correct remoteness—in other words ignore him, let him sense he didn't want to become a buddy. But he could not do that, and neither could he bring himself to pull rank on the handsome young second lieutenant.

"I know what that is," Lowell said a few minutes later, pointing out the rear of the truck at the Acropolis. "That's the Colosseum."

"Acropolis, stupid," Felter corrected him.

"Acropolis, Colosseum, what's the difference?"

"Culture as we know it comes from this one," Felter said, not really sure if he was having his leg pulled or not. "And they fed you Christians to the lions in the other one."

"I'll be *god*damned!" Lowell said, in mock awe.

They passed the Grande Bretagne Hotel, then drove to the rear of it and stopped. They entered the building through a rear door around which had been erected a sandbag barrier. A major was waiting for them. He showed them the dining room and told them where to find him after they had had breakfast.

Breakfast in the elegant but seedy dining room of the Grande Bretagne was coffee, bread, reconstituted dried scrambled eggs, and very salty bacon from 10-in-1 rations.

Afterward, they sought out the major, who turned them over to a florid-faced, middle-aged lieutenant colonel of artillery who didn't bother to disguise his disappointment in them. He told them they would receive their assignments later that day, after they had been "in-processed."

They were given some additional immunization injections and provided with a bottle of pills by an army doctor, a young captain, who warned them not to so much as brush their teeth in water that had not had a pill dissolved in it.

They were given a brief lecture by a major of the Signal Corps on the role of the United States Army Military Advisory Group, Greece. A captain of the Adjutant General's Corps, an old one, twice as old as the starchy little prick who had rushed Lowell out of the Constab with such relish, took from them their next of kin and home address, and provided them with a printed LAST WILL AND TESTAMENT.

The elderly AGC captain didn't say anything, just raised his eyebrows, when Craig Lowell elected to leave all his worldly goods to a fraulein named Ilse, in Germany. Fraulein Ilse, it was the captain's solemn judgment, would not be the only fur-line to be enriched by the death of some kid whose cherry she had copped. Fuck it, it was their life, and their money, and in the captain's judgment, there wasn't all that much difference between a kraut cunt and some greedy goddamned relative in the States.

However he had to tell Lowell there was no way the army would let him leave his GI insurance to a German lady; beneficiaries not next of kin had to be U.S. citizens.

They were then taken to the fourth floor of the Grande Bretagne, where a ballroom had been converted into a supply and arms room. They were issued British Army helmets, the notion being that the silhouette of standard U.S. Army helmets was too close to that of the Wehrmacht and Red Army helmets with which some of the communist guerrillas were equipped. There was no mistaking the silhouette of a British Army helmet. It resembled a flat-chested woman, the captain of ordnance in charge of the arms room told them.

They were given their choice of weapons.

There were M1 Garand .30–06 rifles and .303 British Lee-Enfields and 7.92 mm German Mausers, even a few 7.62 mm Russian Moissant Nagants.

There were U.S. .30 caliber carbines, M1 and M2.

There were .45 ACP Thompson submachine guns and 9 mm British Sten submachine guns.

There were standard issue .45 automatics, .455 Webley revolvers, .38 caliber Smith & Wesson revolvers, 9 mm Luger pistols, and even a half dozen .32 ACP Browning automatic pistols. These were made in Belgium but bore the Nazi swastika on their plastic grips right below the place where the words BROWNING BROS OGDEN UTAH USA had been stamped in the slide.

"Things are a little fucked up," the ordnance officer, an old leathery-faced chief warrant officer, told them. "Eventually, the Greeks will have all U.S. Army stuff, and there won't be any problem. But right now, what the troops have is English and captured kraut stuff. Lugers, Mauser rifles, Schmeisser machine pistols. Now that's the thing to get your hands on, if you can. Best goddamn machine pistol ever made. Naturally, none of them ever get back this far, and when they do, the brass grab them. The Sten gun isn't worth shit.

"The M1, the Garand, has it all over the Lee-Enfield .303, but there's goddamn little .30–06 ammo in clips up where you guys are going. Plenty of .30–06 for the machine guns, so if you want to try to reuse your clips, that's your option."

Lowell remembered trying without much success to reload the spring steel clips for the Garand on the rifle range at Fort Dix.

"I can give you all the clipped .30–06 you want here, but you're going to have to carry it with you," the old warrant officer went on. "Now the Webley .455 ain't worth a shit either, and that .38 S&W shoots a .38 S&W as opposed to a .38 *Special.* That's *really* not worth a shit. There's nothing beats an army .45 if you can shoot one, but there's Lugers if you want. Plenty of 9 mm all over."

"What do the regulations say we're supposed to draw?" Lieutenant Felter asked, politely.

"They haven't made up their mind yet, Lieutenant," the warrant officer said. "There's one school of thought that says you're a technical advisor and a noncombatant, and don't have to go armed at all. Nobody believes that shit. Now, if you should want to draw a U.S. Army weapon for protection against burglars, or whatever, you can have a .45 and either an M1 or a carbine or a Thompson. But you have to sign for them.

"You don't want to sign for a weapon, you can take your choice of anything else. One pistol and one rifle or a Sten. They're not on paper."

Lieutenant Felter took and signed for a Colt .45 and a Thompson submachine gun. The captain from the 19th Armored Field Artillery took and signed for a .45 and a carbine. Lowell had fired the Thompson "for familiarization" at Fort Dix and hadn't been able to keep it from climbing off the target. He was therefore afraid of it and signed for an M1 instead. Giving in to an impulse, he also took a 9 mm Luger. He had never held one in his hands before. For that matter, it was the second pistol he had ever held in his hands at all. He had also fired "for familiarization" the Colt .45 at Fort Dix and had been unable to hit a three-by-four target at twenty-five yards with it.

Had he wanted to, however, he could have fired High Expert with the Garand. He had been surprised at how he had taken to the Garand. The legendary recoil, which had frightened him and the other trainees, had turned out to be far less uncomfortable than that of the 12-bore Browning over-and-under his grandfather had given him for his twelvth birthday. He had spent long hours firing the Browning on the trap range his grandfather had built behind his house on the island. He had understood the Garand from about the fifth shot he had taken with it; and by the time their week on their range was over, he felt quite as comfortable with it as any gun he had ever fired. If he had to take a shot at somebody, which seemed beyond credibility, he would do it with a Garand. He took the Luger because he had always wanted one. It looked lethal. All self-respecting Nazi bad guys in the movies, and sometimes even Humphrey Bogart and Alan Ladd, used Lugers. But the idea that he would actually shoot it at somebody was as ludicrous as the grade B movies.

Lowell took a sealed oblong tin can marked "320 Rounds Caliber .30–06 Ball in Clips and Bandoliers" and two loose bandoliers of Garand ammunition. The ordnance warrant officer gave him two cardboard boxes of pistol ammunition. The printing on them was in German: *Für Pistolen -08 9 mm deutsche Waffen und Munitionsfabrik, Berlin. 50 Patronen.*

It wasn't quite credible, despite the evidence in his hands, that the pistol and the ammunition for it had been intended for use by the German Army.

They were fed lunch, 10-in-1 ration Beef Chunks w/Gravy, in the elegant dining room of the Grande Bretagne. Afterward, they found their names on a mimeographed Special Order of Headquarters, U.S. Military Advisory Group, Greece, which had been slid under their door. Felter and Lowell had been assigned to share a room. The field artillery captain's rank had entitled him to a private room, next door.

"Shit," Lowell said, when, sitting down on the bed, he read his orders. His name and the captain's were on the orders together. They were being assigned to the Advisory Detachment, 27th Royal Hellenic Mountain Division. Felter had been assigned to Headquarters, USAMAG(G), to something called DAB, Operations Division.

"What the hell is DAB?" Lowell asked.

"I think it means Document Analysis," Felter replied. "Probably Document Analysis Branch." He could tell from the confused look on Lowell's face that Lowell knew no more than he had before his reply. "I'm sort of a linguist," Felter said.

"No kidding?"

"My parents came from Europe," Felter said. "I picked up German, and Russian, and Polish."

"I had a German governess," Lowell said, in German.

"They need people who speak German," Felter replied in German. "They told me most of the maps are German and that what I'll be doing is adapting them for us. Didn't you tell that AG captain you spoke it?"

"I told him I didn't speak it," Lowell said, still in German.

"Well, go tell him you can. You can stay here," Felter said. "You're going to get yourself killed with one of the divisions."

"Why do you say that?" Lowell asked.

"You don't really think that ROTC and Basic Officer's Course qualified you for what you'll be doing, do you?"

"I was directly commissioned," Lowell said. "I don't know what they teach in ROTC or Basic Officer's Course."

"Directly commissioned as what?" Felter asked.

"Actually, so that I could play polo on a general's team," Lowell said.

"Am I supposed to believe that?"

"It happens to be the truth," Lowell said.

"You've had no duty with troops?" Felter asked.

"I was thrown out of college, so the draft board got me," Lowell said. "And then I had basic training, and then I was the official golf pro for the U.S. Constabulary golf club, and then I played polo," Lowell said.

"You're absolutely unqualified for duty as an advisor to troops on the line," Felter said.

"And you are?" Lowell asked. Felter let that pass.

"You're liable to get killed. Don't you understand that?" Felter asked.

"Ever since I put on this officer's uniform," Lowell said, "with a rare exception here and there, people have gone out of their way to let me know they think I'm something of a joke as a man. I'm rather tired of it. I intend to see if I am, or not."

"You don't know what the hell you're saying," Felter said.

"You too, you see? Even you."

"I'm a professional soldier," Felter said, somewhat solemnly.

"Sure you are," Lowell said, sarcastically.

"Listen to me, stupid," Felter said. "I was at West Point. I was in on the last days of the war. For what it's worth, I'm even a Ranger."

"No shit?" Lowell asked. He was dumbfounded. "Christ, you don't look like it."

"Thanks a lot," Felter said. They smiled at each other. Felter got up.

"Where are you going?"

"I'm going to tell the adjutant you speak German," Felter said.

"No, you're not," Lowell said. "Leave things alone. It's important to me."

Felter, standing by the door, looked at him.

"If you're a West Pointer, and whatever else you said, a Ranger, what are you doing here?" Lowell asked.

"I asked for this assignment," Felter said.

"Why?" Lowell asked.

"For the experience," Felter said.

"I want the experience, too," Lowell said. "Please mind your own business, Felter."

"Good God!" Felter said. "Have you got notions of glory, or what?"

"I just want to see what happens," Lowell said, simply. "And, figure it out. It would be your word against mine about whether or not I speak German."

Felter looked at him for a moment, and then walked to where Lowell had rested his M1 Garand against the wall beside the bed.

"Do you know how to use one of these?" he asked.

"Actually, I'm pretty good with one of them," Lowell said. "But I'd be grateful if you'd show me how that Luger works."

"Why did you take a Luger if you don't know how it works?" Felter asked, throwing up his hands.

"I already know I can't shoot a .45 worth a shit," Lowell said, simply. "And I thought the Luger was prettier."

"Jesus, you're insane!" Felter said. Then he picked up the Luger. "Come over here, Lieutenant. I will show you how this works."

"Thank you, sir. The lieutenant is very kind, sir." He smiled at Felter. "Are you really a Ranger, you little bastard?"

"Yes, I am, you dumb shit," Felter said.

[TWO]

At midnight, there was a boom. Lowell, who had been sleeping fitfully dreaming of Ilse, sat up in bed and turned the light on.

"Douse the light!" Felter ordered in a fierce whisper. Lowell saw him, .45 in hand, standing against the wall. He turned the light off and started to giggle before it sank in that the boom had been a shot and that they had been issued weapons and what the army called "live ammo" and that they were in Greece and there was a revolution going on.

He slid out of bed, and groped in the dark for the Garand. He found it in the corner of the room. He took an 8-round clip from the cloth bandolier and opened the action. It made an awful amount of noise. When he slipped the clip into the action, it sounded like a door slamming. His heard was pounding. He stood between the beds, the M1 at his shoulder, covering the door.

There was a rap on the door. Lowell's finger tightened on the trigger before he realized if somebody was going to burst in to murder them in their beds, it was unlikely he would knock first. He took his finger off the trigger, but kept it inside the stamped metal loop of the trigger guard, and kept the rifle at his shoulder.

"Duty officer!" a voice called.

Felter jerked the door open. Light from the corridor flooded the room.

The duty officer saw Lowell, and Felter, poised for action. He put his hands up, half mockingly, in surrender.

"I guess you heard it," he said. "Where did it come from?"

"Next door, I think," Felter said, lowering his pistol. Lowell had no idea where the sound had come from. The duty officer turned and walked further down the corridor. Felter went after him, and Lowell followed, feeling foolish, carrying the Garand at port arms.

There was no answer to the duty officer's knock at the field artillery captain's door. He pushed it open.

"Shit!" he said. He went into the room.

Lowell looked over Sanford Felter's head. The field artillery captain who had been kicked out of the Constab along with Lowell had lain down on his bed, put the muzzle of his .45 in his mouth, and blown the top of his head all over the brocade wallpaper of his room. His face bore a startled look. His eyes were wide open, as if he was looking at them.

Craig Lowell barely made it back to his room and the toilet bowl before throwing up.

He was still throwing up when the duty officer came into their room and picked up the telephone.

"Sorry to bother you at this hour, Colonel, but I think maybe you'd want to come up to 707. That new captain just blew his head off."

He looked in at Lowell, sprawled sick and scared on the floor.

"You all right?" he asked, and there was genuine concern in his voice.

Lowell nodded his head.

[**THREE**]

A sergeant came to their table in the dining room the next morning and told Felter that the adjutant wanted to see him.

Felter and Lowell said good-bye, shaking hands.

"Be careful," Felter said. "For God's sake, don't do anything foolish."

"Same to you," Lowell said.

They were both aware of and surprised by the emotion they felt at parting.

Felter started to ask Lowell one final time if he wanted him to tell the adjutant he spoke German, but he decided against it. He would make up his mind when he saw the adjutant.

Thirty minutes later, Felter walked into the room where Lowell lay on the bed, waiting for word that it was time to leave. Lowell said nothing as Felter walked into the room. Felter went to the closet and took out his Valv-Paks.

"The army, in its infinite wisdom, has decided to save your ass," Felter said.

"Goddamn you, I told you to keep your mouth shut," Lowell said, angrily, sitting up on the bed.

"I have just been appointed a replacement for the captain," Felter said. "We're both going to the 27th Royal Hellenic Mountain Division . . . whatever the hell that is."

[**FOUR**]

It was almost exactly two hundred air miles from Athens to Ioannina on the northern shore of Lake Ioanninon. There the headquarters of the 27th Royal Hellenic Mountain Division was located. It was just over twice that distance by road. They averaged twenty-five miles per hour over the road in a Dodge three-quarter-ton weapons carrier.

The road was mostly dirt, or more accurately, stones, and narrow; and it wound around one precipitous granite mountain after another. From time to time, they passed through small villages of whitewashed stone houses perched precariously to fit whatever flat space had been available when they had been built.

They were twenty-six hours on the road, stopping overnight at Preveza on the Ionian Sea, because, as the sergeant driving the truck told them, the commies held the roads at night.

Headquarters of the 27th Hellenic was in a two-story whitewashed stone building with walls eighteen inches thick. It was further reinforced to the level of the second floor by a mound of sandbags tapering toward the top. A pair of swarthy-skinned, unshaven Greeks wearing British Army uniforms were on guard outside. British .303 Lee-Enfield rifles were slung over the shoulders. They watched without expression as Felter and Lowell removed their bedrolls, their packs, their luggage, and the cases of ammunition from the back of the truck.

A competent-looking American master sergeant in British woolen battle trousers, a crumpled GI khaki shirt, and British hobnailed boots waved them inside the building. He did not salute.

"The colonel'll be back for supper," he said. "You want something to eat?"

When they nodded, he said, "We have Greek and GI rations. The Greek gives you the shits until you get used to it. The GI rations make you sick, period."

A Greek woman with a scarf around her head and in a voluminous black shirt served them lamb stew on tin plates, black coffee, and a large chunk of dark bread.

The colonel, when he showed up, turned out to be a wiry red-haired lieutenant colonel wearing the crossed flags of the Signal Corps.

"My name is Hanrahan," he said. "You'll be working for me." Then he switched to Greek, and, watching them carefully, talked for about thirty seconds. Then he shook his head in disgust when it was obvious that neither of them understood a word he was saying.

"That was too much to expect, I guess," he said, in English. "There's probably five thousand officers, Greek-Americans, who would give their left nut to come over here. And what do I get? No offense, gentlemen, but this is a fucked-up war."

He showed them a map. They were thirty miles from the Albanian border. Numbers on the map indicated the height of various mountain peaks from 5,938 feet to 8,192 feet. Lowell knew they were high, but he hadn't thought that high.

"Our mission," Colonel Hanrahan said, "is to keep the bastards from shipping supplies from Albania into Greece. There's no way in hell we can block every goat path, but we can block the roads. We do this from emplacements on hilltops, like something in the *Lives of the Bengal Lancer*. Little forts. They have machine guns for self-protection and mortars to cover the roads.

"The way it's set up is that I'm the advisor to the division. There are three regiments, each of them with three American officers—two majors and a captain. Each battalion has an advisor, supposed to be a lieutenant, but most of them are noncoms. And there are noncoms with some of the companies.

"There's nothing we can tell these people about fighting. They've really got a hard-on for the communists. Vice versa, of course. They learn quick, but most of them don't know diddly shit about vehicles, jeeps, trucks, and especially tracked vehicles. That's where you'll come in, Lieutenant."

"Sir, I don't know anything about tracked vehicles," Lowell confessed.

"That figures," the colonel said. "And what's your speciality, Lieutenant?"

"I just finished Ranger School," Felter said.

"Great. We need Rangers here about as much as we need armored officers who don't know anything about tracked vehicles."

"Sir, I can handle some tanks. Drive them, I mean," Felter said. "I've had familiarization training."

Hanrahan looked at Felter with renewed interest.

"Where did you get that?"

"At West Point, sir."

"You went to the Academy?" Hanrahan was now really interested.

"For two years, sir."

"Why did you march away from the Long Gray Line, Lieutenant?" Hanrahan asked, dryly.

"I was commissioned as a linguist, sir."

"What languages?"

"Slavic, mostly, Colonel. German. Some French."

"Greek?"

"No, sir. I hope to learn it here."

"You will," Hanrahan said. "I can use your Russian, Lieutenant."

Felter nodded, but said nothing.

"I have nothing against West Pointers, Lieutenant," Hanrahan said. "Despite the fact that I too am a product of Beast Barracks."

There was no reaction, though Hanrahan looked closely at Felter's face.

"We're getting a steady supply of ammunition for the 81 mm mortars, and for the 4.2 inchers," Colonel Hanrahan went on. "They fly it in by English seaplane, which can just about manage to land on the lake. We're building up supplies of American small arms ammunition. And we're starting to get some M1s. What I think I'm going to do with you guys is send you around to the companies, one at a time, with either a GI who speaks Greek, or a Greek who speaks English. You will instruct their officers and noncoms in the M1. They will instruct their men. When they know how to take it apart and put it together again, you bow out. They know all there is to know about shooting.

"We got a couple of armored sergeants here . . . all the noncoms are good men, by the way. You guys just leave them alone, understand? The sergeants will teach you what they can about the M8 armored car, Lieutenant. Keeping them running is your job from here in. Got it?"

"Yes, sir," Lowell said.

"Either of you have any questions?" the colonel asked.

Lowell said nothing. The colonel looked at Felter. "You look as if you have something on your mind, Felter. Let's have it."

"Sir," Felter said. "I just wondered about you being Signal Corps."

"I'm detailed infantry, Lieutenant, if that's what's bothering you. But I'm Signal Corps. I came to Greece in 1942 as a second john to operate a radio station for the OSS. And I stayed. And when the war was over I went home. And now they've sent me back, because I know these people, OK?"

"I didn't mean to sound out of line, sir," Felter said.

"Felter, when I think you're out of line, you'll know it," the colonel said. For the first time, he smiled at them. Lowell was warmed by it, and smiled back.

"If you knew what I was thinking, Lowell, I don't think you'd be smiling," the colonel said. "For what I was thinking was that instead of the trained, combat-experienced, Greek-speaking officers I was promised, I just inherited two lieutenants, one even dumber than the other."

"I would say, sir," Lowell said, "that that would be a reasonable statement of the situation."

"And I was smiling because it had just occurred to me that while Felter demonstrated his dumbness by asking what a flag waver is doing here, you were too dumb to notice anything was wrong."

But his smile was still warm.

"If you can remember that," he said, "that you *are* dumb, and keep your mouth shut and your eyes open until you see how things are, and if you can use that M1, you just might stay alive."

He reached into the drawer of his battered desk and came out with a strange-looking bottle and three small water glasses.

"The cocktail hour, gentlemen," he said. "The booze is known ouzo. It tastes like licorice. After a while you get used to it."

He poured the liquid in glasses and handed each of them one.

[FIVE]

No. 12 Company, 113th Regiment, 27th Royal Hellenic Mountain Division consisted of a Greek captain, a pair of lieutenants, three sergeants, a half dozen corporals, sixty-three other ranks, and an Alabama-reared Greek-American sergeant. The force was just about equally divided between two rock fortresses on either side of a narrow road winding down a valley.

The Greek-American sergeant, who gave his name as Nick, was a pudgy young man in his mid-twenties with curly blond hair. He wore no helmet or any other headgear. He wore GI OD trousers, a GI sweater, and over that a British battle jacket. Like everybody else, he wore hobnailed British boots. On the shoulder of the British battle jacket was the Greek cross, above which were superimposed, in Greek and English, the words *America.* He had a .45 automatic jammed into his waistband; and a Browning automatic rifle was slung over his shoulder.

As the American sergeant walked over to the half-track in which Lieutenant Craig Lowell had driven up the mountainside, Lieutenant Lowell was quite as impressed with him as he had been with the corporal who had called him a "miserable pissant" on his first day of basic training.

The difference, Lowell realized, was that *I* have been sent up here to command *him.* A chain of thought ran through his mind, triggered by the .30–06 caliber Browning automatic rifle the sergeant had slung over his shoulder.

The BAR was actually a light machine gun which could empty its 20-round magazine in the time it took to fart.

The weapon, in the hands of somebody who knew how to shoot it, was of the same quality as the Garand. In other words, one hell of a fine weapon. Private Lowell had taken a great deal of pleasure on the Fort Dix, New Jersey, rifle range in mastering the BAR; and his proficiency had both awed and annoyed the corporal who hated college boys generally and handsome college boys from Harvard in particular.

The BAR was a heavy sonofabitch, not the sort of thing one carried fifty feet further than one had to. Sergeant Nick Whatever he said was not carrying it around for the hell of it and certainly not to impress anybody. Furthermore, the sergeant had removed the bipod normally fitted to the barrel to steady the weapon when it was being fired. That suggested that he carried the BAR frequently and as a personal weapon. And *that* suggested two things: that the sergeant was really a soldier, and that there was something to shoot at.

For the first time, he realized the absurdity of his position. He had no business being here as a private soldier, and absolutely none as an officer. He wondered why he wasn't terrified. In fact, he was excited. They call that naiveté, he thought. Also known as stupidity.

The sergeant touched his hand to his eyebrow in sort of a salute, and Lowell returned it as casually. He had one further thought: that is the kind of salute an experienced sergeant throws a second lieutenant fresh from Officer Candidate School. If this sergeant had any idea that I know about ten percent of what the bottom man in any OCS class knows, he would be thumbing his nose at me.

The sergeant looked in the back of the half-track. There was a case of sixteen M1 rifles, plus cases of ammunition, cases of mortar shells, tin cans of .303 British ammunition, and cases of rations.

"Are those M1s for us?" the sergeant asked.

Lowell looked at the sergeant and wondered what would happen if he told him the truth: "See here, Sarge. Talk about fuck-ups. I don't know the first fucking thing about being an officer. What I would like to do is have you take over, tell me what to do, and see if you can keep me from getting hurt."

"Are those for us, Lieutenant?" the sergeant asked again.

"Right," Lieutenant Lowell said, getting out of the truck. "The idea is that I'm to give basic instruction to the officers." He didn't sound as unsure of himself as he thought he would.

"It's about time we gave these guys something to fight with," Nick said. "Come on in the CP; I'll introduce you to the officers." He took Lowell's arm and led him into a bunker built of sandbags laid around enormous granite boulders.

The commanding officer was an olive-skinned man with a flowing black mustache. There was a five-inch scar on his right cheek. He was the toughest-looking man Lowell had ever seen. This guy's going to see right through me, Lowell thought. When the captain offered his hand, his calloused grip was like steel. Incongruously, he smiled at Lowell as if he was really glad to see him.

The other officers were shy.

The captain with the black mustache put his hand on Lowell's shoulder and led him through the rear exit to the bunker. Outside was a mortar position, a 3.5 inch mortar with cases of ammo stacked for use. It was in a natural depression in the boulders, and like the bunker itself, reinforced with sandbags to fill in spaces between boulders. There were rifle-firing positions around its perimeter.

Still smiling broadly, the captain unslung his Lee-Enfield rifle.

"He says," Nick translated, "that this is what they have now, and would you care to try it?"

"Thank you," Lowell said, and took the Lee-Enfield and examined it. He had never seen one up close before he had seen them in the arms room in Athens.

The broadly smiling captain rattled off something else.

"He says he *wants* you to try it," Nick said.

"What am I supposed to shoot at?" Lowell asked.

The captain seemed to understand that. He took the Enfield back, dropped into an almost prone position in one of the firing positions and aimed down into the valley. There was a small concrete kilometer marker beside the road. Lowell thought it must be at least two hundred yards away.

With sign language, the captain indicated that that was what he meant. He lay down and very quickly pushed the safety off and fired. Lowell realized that around here people always carried a round in the chamber.

A chunk flew off the kilometer marker. The captain got to his feet, rapidly worked the action of the rifle, and handed it to Lowell with another of his broad smiles, which by now Lowell suspected were anything but sincere.

"I guess he wants to see if you know what the fuck you're talking about," Nick said.

Lowell lowered himself into the firing position.

I'm going to miss that goddamned thing, and then what the fuck am I going to do?

He fired. There was a puff of dust in the middle of the road. He had missed by six feet.

He furiously worked the action, chambering another round, and fired again. He missed again and was horribly humiliated. Both the American, Nick, and the Greek captain were smiling at him. He was supposed to be an expert, and he couldn't hit a foot square target at two hundred yards. He looked at the Enfield's sights, and realized he hadn't the faintest idea how to change them.

"Hand me my M1," he said. When he put the Garand to his shoulder and pushed the safety off, he thought for the first time that he had not fired it. It was not zeroed. It would have been better to have kept the Enfield and try to hit the goddamned kilometer marker with Kentucky windage.

It was too late for that now. He looked at the M1's receiver, twisting it slightly to examine the sight.

"I've never fired this sonofabitch before," he said, so that Nick could hear him.

Nick looked at him with contempt in his eyes. Lowell understood that he wasn't just humiliating himself but Nick, too, for he was an officer.

And then Lowell knew what to do. "Tell the captain," he said, handing the M1 to Nick, "that it would be too easy for me to use this weapon, because it is mine."

Nicks' eyebrows went up, and he said nothing.

"Tell him I am going to take an unfired M1 from the case," Lowell said, "and zero it with three shots, and then blow that goddamned marker away."

"I hope for both of us that you can produce," Nick said, and then he smiled confidently and spoke in Greek to the captain.

"Tell him to pick any of the rifles," Lowell said. Nick led the captain to the crate of M1s. The captain looked over the four Garands in the top rack and picked one out. Then he handed it to Lowell. Lowell opened the action and peered down the barrel. It was thick with preserving oil.

Lowell set the elevation at two hundred yards.

"Tell the captain the barrel is oily," he said. "And that I will clean it by firing twice."

Nick repeated the message in Greek. Lowell put a clip in the Garand, pushed the safety off, and shot twice in the air. Then he took up a sitting position.

"Tell the captain that for a short distance and a target that large, it is not normally necessary to use the prone position."

"Use the prone position, for Christ's sake. Hit that fucking road marker," Nick said, wearing a broad smile. "Once these guys figure you for a phony or a candy-ass, you're finished."

"Tell him what I said, Sergeant," Lowell said, smiling warmly at Nick, and then decided to go for broke. "And tell him that a good shot normally doesn't have to use a sling."

Nick spoke to the Greek captain.

"Tell him I will now fire three rounds for zero," Lowell said. He aimed very carefully, let out half his breath, held it, and squeezed the trigger. By pure coincidence, the sights were almost in zero. The bullet strike was vertically on the target, but two feet to the right.

He aimed and fired the rifle again. The second strike was within a couple inches of the first.

Lowell motioned the captain over, pointed to the sight.

"Tell him that sometimes only two shots are necessary for zero," he said. Nick repeated the message. "Tell him that I am moving the sight to the right twelve clicks, and that each click, at that distance, moves the impact two inches." He held up his fingers to illustrate. The captain, smiling with transparent insincerity, listened to the translation and nodded his head.

"And now tell him that I am going to demonstrate how to remove a partially emptied clip from the weapon," Lowell said. Nick made the translation. Lowell ejected the unfired six cartridges and their clip and put a full clip in the weapon.

"Shit, Lieutenant," Nick said. "I hope you can pull this off."

Lowell put the Garand to his shoulder, lined up the sights, held his breath, and squeezed off the first round. Dead on. A chunk of concrete flew into the air. He then emptied the rifle, firing as quickly as he could line the sights up on the shattered remnants of the concrete road marker. When he was finished, it was difficult to see the road marker; horizontally, about half of it was shot away, and four more inches or so off the left side.

With an entirely delightful feeling of triumph, Lowell gave Nick an idiot grin and then stood up. With a ceremonious bow, he handed the Garand to the captain and then motioned him to sit down in the firing position. He knelt over him, and fed a clip into the weapon.

The captain fired one shot, and then the rest of the clip, rapid fire. He flashed another magnificent smile, got to his feet, and handed Lowell the M1.

"Sonabitch!" he said. He reached over, patted Lowell's cheek, and then kissed it. Then he weighed the Garand appreciatively in his hands.

"That don't mean nothing, Lieutenant," Nick said. "Shit, they even hold hands! You just impressed the shit out of him, is all."

The Greek captain smiled at the American lieutenant. The American lieutenant smiled back. He smiled so broadly his cheek muscles began to ache. The captain, with an elaborate bow, waved him back to the bunker. He said something else.

"He says he would be deeply honored if you would show him how the magnificent rifle works, so that he and his men may kill many godless communists with it," Nick said. He watched Lowell's face for his reaction.

"They mean that, Lieutenant," Nick said. "I'm glad you didn't think it was funny."

Lowell felt a strange exhilaration.

"Please tell the captain that I would be honored to attempt to show a magnificent shot such as he is how the U.S. Army rifle functions," he said.

[SIX]
Coordinates C431/K003
Map, Greece, 1:250000
22 July 1946

To tell the truth, if it wasn't for Ilse he wouldn't mind this at all, Second Lieutenant Craig W. Lowell thought. It was like something out of the movies. The days were pleasantly warm, and the evenings were pleasantly cool, and there was nobody jumping on his ass at all.

The simple truth of the matter was that he liked being an officer. Not a polo-playing officer, but a real officer. He had been given a duty, a real military duty, and he took no small pleasure in being able to discharge it, in the realization that he was meeting his responsibility—and well.

It wasn't even as if he were a marksmanship instructor in basic training. He was teaching the teachers. Through him and him alone, first No. 12 Company, and ultimately the entire 113th Regiment, 27th Royal Hellenic Mountain Division, would be instructed in the proper use of the M1 Garand rifle.

Even Felter acknowledged that Lowell knew what he was doing, and Felter really was a West Pointer and a Ranger, even if he didn't look like it. Lowell was smugly proud that he had his company, No. 12 Company, completely qualified with the M1 when Felter was still taking his company's M1s out of their crates. Felter was a good man obviously (otherwise, how would he have gotten to be a Ranger?), but he wasn't a good teacher. Not a leader of men.

In all modesty, Craig Lowell believed that he had demonstrated his leadership ability by his courses of instruction in the M1. He had first demonstrated to each little group of trainees that with it he could blow the balls off a horsefly at two hundred yards. This established his personal credentials. Then he had blown away road markers firing the weapon as fast as it would fire, thus establishing the weapon's credibility. After that, with Nick standing beside him translating his short, simple sentences into Greek, it had been a snap. They wanted to learn, and they soaked up the information like a blotter. It was completely unlike basic training had been. Nobody in basic training had given a shit for the M1 rifle. That was, Craig Lowell decided, because it had not been presented to them properly. By the time they actually got to fire it, they were so sick of looking at it, cleaning it, and dry-firing it that they wouldn't have liked it if it had dispensed ice-cold beer.

Later Felter had needed Craig's help with his own company; and he'd been glad to give it. Then Felter had called Colonel Hanrahan and told him that he was having trouble but Lowell was doing splendidly, and that it would seem to make sense to have Lowell continue doing what he did so well so that he could return to see about the tracked vehicles.

Hanrahan had gone along with the suggestion. And now Felter was back at Ioannina, while Lowell had the Garand rifle training of the whole regiment to himself. It was rather strange, Lowell thought, about Hanrahan and Felter both having gone to West Point. He had always associated West Pointers with people like General Waterford and Fat Charley. His kind of people, so to speak. There was no question that Hanrahan was a good officer, but he behaved less like Fat Charley than like an Irish police sergeant.

But there was no question about it, as difficult as it was to believe, both Hanrahan and Felter had at one time marched up and down the drill field at West Point in those funny hats with what looked like a pussy willow bouncing around on top.

Lowell had become rather close to Nick. If Nick suspected that Lowell's knowledge of the military had come entirely from basic training, he hadn't made that plain. Aware that he had impressed Nick just about as much as he had impressed the Greek captain with that first day's marksmanship exhibition, Lowell had decided that what Nick didn't know wouldn't hurt him.

They shared a stone hut in the No. 12 Company area, taking turns boiling their eggs for breakfast, but eating the rest of their meals with the Greek officers. At night they read by the hissing light of a Coleman lantern. Nick could read Greek, so he got to share the Greek newspapers that came up and a few Greek magazines and what few books there were. The only thing in English to read was an occasional week-old *Stars & Stripes* from Germany and a shelf of field and technical manuals. For lack of something else to read, Lowell read the field and technical manuals. Some of them had as much application to what they were doing as the *Saturday Evening Post*, but some of them Lowell found fascinating.

The Infantry Company in the Defense, for example, spelled out in minute detail what 230 officers and men were supposed to do from the emplacement of the .30 and .50 caliber machine guns to the number and placement and depth of "field sanitation facilities, or latrines." Much of the information didn't precisely apply here, but a surprising percentage of it did. Lowell discreetly checked and learned that No. 12 Company's machine-gun emplacements more than met the criteria established "by the book."

Nick saw nothing unusual in Lowell's spending his evenings reading field manuals. Nick probably presumed that officers ordinarily passed their free time expanding their professional knowledge. He did not, in other words, give any sign that he suspected Lowell was discovering for the first time the meaning of such terms as "beaten zones" and "fields of fire" and "ammunition units," and what, precisely, a foxhole was beyond being a hole in the ground in which one took shelter.

Their routine was fairly constant. Every day, late enough in the morning to be warm enough to take the open-jeep trip in relative comfort, Lowell and Nick visited another company along the line. There they'd instruct the officers and senior noncoms in the M1 rifle. Afterward they would share a late lunch with the officers of the company they were visiting, before returning to No. 12 Company. There Lowell would fool around with the Zenith Transoceanic radio (thank God I bought that, Lowell thought; I would go insane without it) or play a little chess to pass the time with the Greek officers.

Sometimes, not always, he could pick up the American Forces Network on the short-wave band. That always triggered memories of Ilse, which sometimes depressed him and sometimes cheered him. He missed her terribly and worried about her; and he had to keep pushing back the fear that she would find somebody else. Other times, he was able to tell himself that he had found the woman who would share his life. When his year here was over, he would be reassigned to Germany, and they would be together again for good.

God, did he miss her! He had a mental image of Ilse on the banks of the Lahn River. That was only three weeks ago! And there hadn't been one letter in all that time.

What was she doing now?

Telling some new guy that she cost a hundred a month, plus rent on their apartment, plus the stuff he could get out of the PX?

Spreading her legs for somebody else? Oh, *shit!*

He forced that thought from his mind. He had read a line from a biography of General George S. Patton: "Never take counsel of your fears." There was obviously a good deal of sense in that, Lowell thought, and reminded himself again that if he had to be in the army, this was the place to be. Broadening. That's what it was. A splendid learning experience.

There came the peculiar burrup-burrup ringing sound of a U.S. Army EE-8 field telephone. A head appeared at the door to the bunker, said something in excitement, pointed to the right.

The Greek captain ran to a firing position, dropped onto his belly, and put field glasses to his eyes. He peered intently, and then suddenly turned and gave orders.

"What the hell is going on?"

"They got a report of bearers," Nick said.

The enemy! It's about time!

"Sometimes they make a mistake and get seen," Nick said, as he walked quickly to a firing position. He set the Browning automatic rifle in place in one of the rifle-firing points and peered off at what appeared to Lowell to be a bare expanse of rock.

Then Lowell saw something move. It was five hundred yards away if it was an inch.

The captain said something that Lowell somehow understood meant, "there." He gave more orders. Soldiers were working on the 3.5 inch mortar now, shifting the weapon, moving its baseplate.

The captain gave another of his insurance man smiles to Lowell and waved him to an empty firing position.

There was more movement in the valley below, things flitting between the huge boulders, casting shadows. You had to look carefully the first time, but almost immediately your eyes began to catch small movements, and you could see there were people out there, coming down the side of the mountain, moving slowly, but *there.*

The enemy!

There was the crack of the captain's M1, followed a moment later by a sharper sound, the burst from Nick's BAR. Lowell found himself peering through the sights of his rifle. Goddamned fool. Even if he saw anybody out there, he couldn't hit them. But he put his left hand on the sight of the M1 and cranked the knob, and the sight clicked as it rose up.

If one were to be completely honest, he was willing to admit there was something just a bit frightening about all this. Presumably, they, the enemy, will shoot back.

There came the roar of the 3.5 mortar going off behind him, and he felt the blast and his ears hurt. When he looked through the sights again, swinging the rifle from side to side, seeing nothing, he was trembling.

Nick's BAR went off and there was another shot from a rifle. And then there was an explosion out there, the dull crump of the mortar round landing. He saw by the smoke that it was far wide of the mark. The captain said something viciously sarcastic, then turned to his Garand again.

There was suddenly an awful pain in Lowell's bladder. I absolutely have to take a piss, he realized.

There came the sound of bullets passing overhead, remembered from the pits of the rifle range at Fort Dix. It was all rather amusing then, because the greatest care had been taken to insure that the bullets whistling overhead, however thrilling, would be harmless. There was no such intent here. There was also the sound of ricochets, not unlike the sound in the movies, but infinitely more threatening.

There came the noise that a kitchen knife makes when a large fat Negro, smiling broadly, swings it from behind his head and slices a red ripe watermelon in one fell swoop. On the porch of the mess hall at Camp Kemper. The Negro cook's name had been Ellwood. That is what came to Craig Lowell's mind when he heard the noise.

He turned and saw Nick sprawled on his back on the sunbaked pebbles. He had a shattered watermelon for his head. Second Lieutenant Craig W. Lowell threw up, and when he had finished heaving, became aware that he had shit in his pants. A moment later he had also voided his bladder.

He pulled his arms over his head. I am going to die here. I am going to have *my* head blown off. Oh, those dirty *bastards!*

He pushed himself a half inch closer to the top of the rocks protecting him, then an inch, then four inches, to get his head over the top, to *see* them, the dirty bastards. He saw a flicker of yellow flame out of the corner of his eye, and turned his head. There were two of them, lying prone, behind a light machine gun. The gun was on a bipod with a shoulder stock, rather than on a tripod. They were sweeping the position with short bursts of fire, so as not to over heat the barrel.

Where the fuck is my rifle?

He slid down and then crawled backward to where he had dropped the M1, grabbed the muzzle, and pulled it up to him.

Two bullets hit the rocks in front of him, high. They sent splinters into his face, stinging him, before ricocheting with a low whistle. He had a faint impression that he could see one at the top of its apogee.

He slid up on the rocks, laying his hand on a flat spot, laying the forearm in his hand. Fecal matter slid down his inner thigh. *Shit!*

He placed his cheek on the stock. He couldn't see the fucking sights! He was crying. He took his hand from the pistol grip and the trigger and wiped his eyes with his knuckles, then with his fingers, and blinked. The sights came into focus.

The machine gunner paused and then started swinging the muzzle back toward Lowell's position. The M1 jumped against Lowell's face. The loader let go of the belt of ammunition and collapsed. The machine gunner looked down at him, and then got to his knees and scooped up the machine gun in both arms. Craig shot him as he stood erect; again, as he wobbled; again, as he went back on his knees; and then, finally, very deliberately, in the head.

That'll teach you, you sonofabitch!

The M1's action was open, smoking slightly, giving off a faint bitter smell of gunpowder and burned oil. Following the example of the Greeks, Craig had wedged the leather rifle strap between the two rows of cartridges in two clips. He pulled one of them loose. The cartridges came out and spilled against the rocks, making a clinking noise. Trembling, he pulled the second clip loose. The cartridges didn't fall out, but they were out of their proper position.

Fuck it!

He laid the empty M1 down and ran over to Nick. Nick's eyes were wide open, very bloodshot, and blood ran out of his nose, ears, and mouth. The rear of his skull was shattered open. Lowell bent over him and felt the bile rise in his throat. He took BAR magazines from Nick's pouches and ran with them to the firing position. Then he went and got Nick's BAR and ran back, dragging it by the barrel, the stock banging on the rocks behind him. He dropped onto his belly, breathing heavily, eyes full of sweat again, and pulled the 20-round magazine from the BAR. Though there were cartridges in it, he threw it away anyway, and charged the BAR with a fresh magazine.

He rested the front end of the BAR where he had fired the M1. There were two more men at the machine gun now, one picking up the ammo cans, the other scooping up the machine gun itself.

The BAR jumped in his hands. Two short bursts. There were now four dead men at the machine gun. No. Three. One of the bastards was still alive! The BAR jumped again in his hands.

And then one more man came to the machine gun. Didn't you get the message, you sonofabitch? The BAR jumped again, and then stopped. Empty. Lowell ducked behind the rock, pulling the BAR down with him. He changed magazines, then got back in position.

Nothing moved. And there were no yellow flickering muzzle blasts. Just the bluish white clouds of smoke, followed a moment later by the *crump* as the sound of mortar shell's detonation reached them.

The shit was drying, caking, on his leg. He could smell it. He threw up again, dry. There was nothing left to come out of his stomach. He felt faint and rested his cheek on the rock, smelling the tung oil on the BAR stock as he stared at the empty .30–06 shell casings scattered around him.

When there was quiet, he carefully aligned eight cartridges in a clip and loaded the M1; and leaving the BAR where it was, he went back to Nick. He pulled off his Ike jacket and placed it over Nick's shattered head.

The Greek captain came over to him and made the sign of the cross over Nick, and then, with tears in his eyes, he held Craig Lowell's head against his chest, and very gently kissed the top of his head.

Lowell went to the stone hut he had shared with Nick, took out his bedroll, and took from it all his spare underwear. Then he went to the water barrel, and took off his boots and his pants and dipped a T-shirt in the water barrel and wiped the feces off his legs.

It took a long time. He thought that he was going to be sick again. Then one of the Greeks came up to him. He handed him a pair of Greek (actually English) woolen pants, well worn but clean. And then he handed him a British battle jacket. It had his second lieutenant's bar and his tank on the collar points.

"Thank you," he said. The Greek soldier nodded and pointed to the left epaulet.

There was a cheap, gray metal pin pinned to it. The insignia of the 113th Regiment, 27th Royal Hellenic Mountain Division. The Greek, who was a pockmarked old fart who needed a shave, reached out and tenderly ran his rough hand over Lowell's face and said something to him. Lowell had no idea what he said, but he smiled and nodded his head. The Greek bent over and picked up the shitty trousers and skivvy shorts and the T-shirt Lowell had used as a shit wiper and carried them off.

[SEVEN]

Second Lieutenant Craig W. Lowell, wearing mostly a Greek uniform, was leaning on the stone and sandbag walls of his hut, puffing on his next to last cigar when Lt. Colonel Paul T. Hanrahan and First Lieutenant Sanford T. Felter drove into No. 12 Company's area. Hanrahan was driving.

When the weapons carrier stopped, Hanrahan got from behind the wheel and looked at Lowell, who made no move to get off the wall. Hanrahan glanced at the body, which was under a sheet of canvas now. A crucifix rested on top of the canvas. Then he walked toward Lowell.

When he was ten feet away, Lowell pushed himself off the sandbags and saluted. Hanrahan returned the salute as casually.

"You all right, Lieutenant?" Hanrahan asked.

"I'm alive, Colonel."

"What happened to your face?" Hanrahan asked. Lowell unconsciously put his fingers to the already formed scabs on his face.

"Stone splinters, I think," Lowell said.

Colonel Hanrahan put his finger out and touched the regimental insignia on his epaulet.

"They *give* that to you?" he asked. The implication was clear, Lowell thought. I am wearing something I should not be wearing.

The Greek captain, seeing what Hanrahan had done, came up and, taking him by the arm, led him behind the bunker where the dead of the engagement were laid out in two rows. On one side were the Greeks, under cheap cotton flags. On the other the enemy were on their backs with nothing covering them. Captured weapons and supplies were piled between them. The Greek captain led Hanrahan to the end of the line where five bodies lay in a group. A machine gun and some small arms and some supplies were at their feet.

Lowell had seen the bodies before, but only then, when he saw the captain indicating him, did he understand why these bodies and the machine gun were in a special group. These were the men he had killed.

I don't feel a fucking thing, he realized. Not one fucking thing. If I'm supposed to be all upset because I have taken human life, I'm not.

"The captain seems to think you're pretty hot stuff, Lowell," Lt. Colonel Hanrahan said, coming back to him. "A regular Sergeant York."

"We're going to need another interpreter up here, Colonel," Lowell said.

"There's one coming with the trucks to get the other bodies and this stuff," Hanrahan said. "I wanted to come get Nick myself."

They had brought with them in the weapons carrier an American flag and a locally made cheap pine coffin, which was already splitting. Lt. Col. Hanrahan and Lieutenant Felter carried it to the tarpaulin-covered body. Hanrahan and Lowell picked Nick up and put him in the coffin, and then Hanrahan got on his knees and nailed the flag to it. Finally, Hanrahan and Lowell hoisted the coffin into the weapons carrier.

"I'll take care of writing the next of kin," Hanrahan said. It was the first Lowell had even thought about that.

"Thank you, sir," he said.

"And I'll send you some clothes with the other trucks."

"Is the mail coming up with the trucks?" Lowell asked.

Hanrahan pointed to Lt. Sanford T. Felter, who, looking ashamed, handed Lowell his only mail. It was from the Constabulary officer's club. He owed a twenty-five dollar initiation fee and three months dues of ten dollars per month. Unless the bill was paid within seventy-two hours, it said, his commanding officer would be notified.

"The mail is terribly fouled up," Felter said, lamely.

"Yeah, sure it is," Lowell said.

[**EIGHT**]

After his junior officer had passed satisfactorily, more than satisfactorily, through his first engagement, Paul Hanrahan was not surprised that he immediately started going Greek. Although Hanrahan would never have said it out loud, it was the Brotherhood of Arms. Probably without knowing it, and certainly without thinking about it, Lowell had joined the tribe. The tribe happened to be Greek. He wanted to be like the others, so he dressed like them, thought like them, acted like them.

Within a month, to the disgust of many of the American officers at Ioaninna, Lowell was far over the line. He had helped himself to a supply of British uniforms from a building full of British surplus at Ioannina. A Greek mama washed it for him to get rid of the awful smell of the British antimoth preservative. He wore a second lieutenant's bar pinned to one collar point, and a U.S. was on the other. These were the only things that distinguished him from a Greek officer.

Under the battle jacket, he wore an open khaki shirt, a GI sweater, and a silk scarf. In one of the Greek companies he instructed, he had acquired a black leather belt and Luger holster the Germans had left behind. The buckle was a solid brass affair, cast with the words GOTT MIT UNS in inch-high letters.

Probably to mock Felter's parachute wings, Hanrahan thought, he had moved the 113th Regimental pin above his breast pocket from his epaulet. Felter had gone Greek only in that he wore British boots and no necktie. Hanrahan sensed that the only reason Felter was wearing his parachutist's wings was that he had noticed Hanrahan wearing his own.

Felter was spending most of his time around the division and regimental headquarters. His fluency in Russian fitted in perfectly with Hanrahan's personal obsession. Lt. Col. Red Hanrahan took personal umbrage at the Russian insistence that the Greek revolution was nothing more than an internal affair and that they had nothing to do with it. He was determined to capture one of their Russian counterparts (they could hear them on the radio) and personally take the sonofabitch to Athens.

Lowell got back to Ioannina once or twice a week to sleep overnight, to run messages and errands from the regimental advisors, and to get an American ration meal. And, Paul Hanrahan knew, to wait for a letter that never came.

Paul Hanrahan often thought that if he could get his hands on the little German bitch who had dumped Lowell, he could have cheerfully choked her.

Lowell had received two letters from his mother, both of them still addressed to Private Lowell. She wrote that she remembered Athens from her honeymoon, and she gave him the addresses of restaurants he simply shouldn't miss. While he was there, she wrote, he should take advantage of the opportunity and take a week's cruise among the Greek islands.

Lowell never got around to answering his mother's letters.

The letter he was waiting for took seven weeks to come. The civilian mail service between Greece and Germany was practically nonexistent, and the APO service apparently wasn't much better.

Dear Craig,

After waiting for a month, I know why you haven't written to me. I understand completely. I want to thank you for being so kind to me, and I want you to know that I will ever remember you with most fond thoughts. Your little German friend,

Ilse

Craig Lowell had no way of knowing, of course, that two weeks after he had left Germany, General Walls had called Fat Charley into his office and with great delight told him he stood relieved. When Lowell's letters to Ilse arrived in Germany, care of Fat Charley, they were duly forwarded by the Army Postal Service, surface shipment, to Headquarters U.S. Army Recruiting District, Pittsburgh, Pennsylvania, to which Fat Charley would report for duty six weeks after landing in the States.

It was only the night that Craig finally got Ilse's letter that Sanford Felter heard the whole story about how Craig had met Ilse. He learned, too, that Lowell was only nineteen years old and had lasted at Harvard College only three months before being placed on indeterminate suspension.

Sanford Felter wrote Sharon about it the next day—after he'd sobered Lowell up and sent him out of Ioannina lying in the back of an ammo carrier.

He told her that he really felt sorry for Lowell because of the girl. The thing was, despite everything, despite his good looks and his wealthy background and all, and even the way he'd become almost famous for his icy courage under fire, Craig was really just a boy who had been taken in by a German girl. She obviously was interested in him only for what he could bring her from the PX.

He had offered a prayer for Lowell, Sanford wrote, because the kid was likely to do something very foolish in his mental condition. It made me realize, he added, how good God has been to me in giving me a fine woman.

He wrote, too, that he had come to really respect and admire Colonel Hanrahan; but, because he didn't think she would either understand or care, he hadn't gone into much detail.

Hanrahan had sought out Felter's company the night before. An ad hoc social night, Hanrahan thought privately, of the Ioannina Chapter, West Point Protective Association. He needed somebody to talk to; and he guessed correctly that he could talk to Felter in confidence.

In Felter's room, over a cup of tea, they talked of many things, what they were doing, their wives, the Greeks, and, of course, the Future of the Army.

He asked Felter, and Felter told him, why he had volunteered for Greece. And then Felter had put the question to him, and Hanrahan had enough ouzo aboard to answer him.

"What about you, Colonel?" Felter said. "Why are you here?"

"The function of an officer in peacetime," Hanrahan said, "is to prepare to fight the next war. That seems pretty goddamned simple to me, but most people I know don't understand it."

"You don't mean that we're going to fight here," Felter replied, "nor that our next war is going to be a guerrilla war, do you?"

"Award the short lieutenant the cement bicycle," Hanrahan said. "No, I don't. What I'm talking about is leading other people's troops."

"Mercenaries? That's the reason the Roman Empire fell."

"I don't mean mercenaries. I mean helping people fight their own wars. Phrased simply, Felter, whether we like it or not, we're going to have to keep the Russians from taking the world over. And since there's no way we can match them man for man, we have to use other people's troops. We're the most sophisticated society in the world, and we have enough people to train other people."

"That's not mercenaries?"

"Pay attention. I said 'to fight their own wars.' It is to the Greeks' advantage to keep the Russians out. And their own men are doing just as good a job, probably a better one, than the 82nd Airborne could do. We give them the equipment, and we train them to use it."

"You think this is the future, then?"

"I want to be a general just as much as anybody else who went to school on the Hudson, Felter. And I am not noble. If I thought the way to get to be a general was to be at Bragg playing paratrooper again, that's where I would be. I intend to be *the* fucking expert when it comes to fighting other people's wars with other people's soldiers."

Then he realized that he was talking too much, even to Felter, and went to bed.

Neither did Sandy Felter tell Sharon that he had written a staff study for Colonel Hanrahan, an intelligence estimate actually, concerning the situation. He wasn't sure if Colonel Hanrahan would have the time to read it, and if he did read it, what he would think of it. He might just laugh at him.

Sanford Felter had taken the facts as he saw them and come up with what he thought was a very likely course of enemy action.

The thin line that the 27th Royal Hellenic Mountain Division had stretched across its portion of the Albanian border was growing more and more effective as time passed. Many pathways across the border from Albania had been dynamited and rendered impassable. All roads wide enough for trucks were now covered by mortars, machine guns, and even by 37 mm mountain cannon in a few places. The enemy was no longer able to infiltrate supplies across the border with reasonable impunity, or with a rate of losses he could afford to pay.

Behind the thin line of the mountain division, however, the same paths were open as they had been for thousands of years. The same paths and a great many caves.

If he were the enemy, Sanford Felter reasoned, rather than send supplies piecemeal across the line, he would breach the line. In a sudden attack, he would take out a couple of the little fortresses guarding the roads. Once they were out of the way, he would send truckloads of supplies through. The trucks would be lost, but if they penetrated a couple of miles behind the mountain division's lines, and guerrillas were waiting to hide the supplies in the mountains, the trucks could be considered expendable.

And certainly the Russian-supported guerrillas and, more importantly, the Red Army advisors on the other side of the border would be influenced by the basic Red Army tactic, which was massive attack. In this case, probably with mortars.

A massive, hour-long attack by mortars against positions which heretofore had not been subject to more than an occasional round, would probably succeed, the valor of the Greeks not withstanding.

To Sandy's immense pleasure, Colonel Hanrahan sent the study to Athens with the comment that he found it very interesting and was taking appropriate measures, within the limits of his assets, to help the mountain divisions resist such an attack.

There weren't very many assets available to the senior U.S. Army advisor to the 27th Royal Hellenic Mountain Divison. But he organized what he had as best he could—three M8 armored cars, six half-trucks, two six-by-sixes, and five weapons carriers—into a mobile light armored column *cum* ammo train.

The vehicles and the men were now set aside and parked, awaiting the attack Felter prophesied. They were identified, and on receipt of a signal, their drivers would be given orders to report to a designated location. There a basic combat load of ammunition for the vehicles and troops and a load of mortar and small arms ammunition to resupply the fortresses under attack had been cached.

Lt. Col. Hanrahan didn't actually make these arrangements himself. He received and approved the arrangements made by Lieutenant Felter. He had come to admire Felter, a process which began with something close to paternal amusement. Felter was the archetypical West Point lieutenant, taking himself and his mission very seriously. But unlike most young lieutenants, Felter made very few mistakes. He neither left important things out, nor had to be cut down to reality. It occurred to Hanrahan one day that the only thing wrong with Felter was that he looked like a mouse. Hanrahan was regularly furious with himself for not being able to remember his first name; he kept calling him Sidney. He thought of him as the Mouse, and had not been surprised to learn from Felter that they had called him "the Mouse" at the Academy.

Once he had given Mouse Felter the go-ahead to set up his relief column, Felter had presumed that he would be in command should it be necessary to actually employ the column. At first, Hanrahan had thought the idea ludicrous, but had not hurt Felter's feelings by telling him so. But as Felter's analysis of the enemy's intention seemed more and more plausible, the idea of letting the Mouse have the command seemed more logical. Felter had run several dry runs: gathering the vehicles together, loading them up, forming the column. He worked the kinks out, made alternative arrangements and additions (the incorporation of three ambulances, for example) and so turned an idea into a working arrangement.

And then Hanrahan got the failed ring-knocker, and that blew the Mouse out of the saddle.

Once a week, or perhaps every ten days, a Stinson L-5 flew into Ioannina and picked up Hanrahan and flew him to Athens. Sometimes they wanted to see him in Athens; more often he went to Athens to plead for more supplies. And sometimes he went and flew back the same day because that way he could pick up the mail sacks and maybe a couple of bottles of whiskey.

The ring-knocker was a captain, a large man with a mustache. Hanrahan had noticed him before they were introduced. The captain was standing beside his luggage in the lobby of the Grande Bretagne. He was obviously new because he was wearing a complete OD uniform, his trousers tucked into new GI combat boots. He was also wearing his ribbons, including something Colonel Hanrahan had never seen before. It was an Expert Combat Infantry Badge without the silver wreath. All the captain was wearing was the blue part with the flintlock.

They looked at each other with frank curiosity. Hanrahan had gone Greek. His only item of U.S. issue uniform from his Limey helmet to his Limey hobnailed boots was a khaki shirt, to whose collar points were pinned the silver oak leaf of his rank and the gold letters, U.S. Everything else was British. He carried a Schmeisser submachine gun in his hands, not because he thought he would need it in Athens, but because there was a possibility the puddle jumper might have to land en route. And some of the areas between Ioannina and Athens were firmly in the hands of the bad guys. The captain was armed with a .45 in a regulation web belt, and a .30 carbine rested against his canvas Valv-Pak.

Lt. Col. Hanrahan had the distinct impression that the captain did not approve of him. He was, obviously, out of uniform. Hanrahan smiled at the mental image of what had happened back in Germany when they'd gotten Felter's delinquency report back. It had come down through channels. From Frankfurt Military Post to Headquarters, U.S. Forces, European Theater; and then because the U.S. Army Military Advisory Group, Greece, was under the Deputy Chief of Staff for Operations, U.S. Army, in the Pentagon, it had gone to Washington. And then been flown to Greece.

One lousy little lieutenant had been caught in an improper uniform because he was halfway through a forty-hour plane trip from the States. And some chickenshit, nattily uniformed MP officer, for the sake of all that was sacred to the chair-warmers, in the name of General Clay, had ordered that the "subject officer's commanding officer report by endorsement hereon the specific corrective disciplinary action taken."

Van Fleet had thought it was funny. There was a note in his handwriting paper-clipped to the official "Your Attention Is Invited to the Previous Indorsement"

"Red. If you have enough wood for a gallows, hang him. Failing that, I suppose shooting to death by musketry will have to do. Van Fleet, LT GEN."

Red Hanrahan had not chuckled at the whole thing and thrown it in the waste-basket, as General Van Fleet obviously expected him to do. For some reason, he kept it. And a day after it arrived, he put it into his typewriter.

```
                    8TH IND

HQ US ARMY MILITARY ADVISORY DETACHMENT
27TH ROYAL HELLENIC MOUNTAIN DIVISION IN THE FIELD

TO:HQ US ARMY MILITARY ADVISORY GROUP, GREECE
   c/o U.S. EMBASSY
   ATHENS, GREECE
   1. The serious transgressions by First Lieutenant Sanford
T. Felter against good order and discipline enumerated in the
basic communication have been considered at length by this
headquarters.
   2. After due and solemn consideration, and acting upon the
advice of my staff, I have decided to slap subject officer
lightly upon each wrist.
                                   Paul T. Hanrahan
                                   Lt. Colonel, Signal Corps
                                   Commanding
```

He sent it to Athens in the next mail bag, thinking it would give the general a chuckle, and that the general would then chuck the whole ludicrous thing away. But a week later, there came in the mail bag a carbon copy of the ninth indorsement:

9TH IND

HQ US ARMY MILITARY ADVISORY GROUP, GREECE
THE UNITED STATES EMBASSY
ATHENS, GREECE

TO:HEADQUARTERS, U.S. FORCES, EUROPEAN
THEATER

APO 757, US FORCES

PERSONAL ATTENTION GENERAL LUCIUS D. CLAY

The commanding general, US Army Military Advisory Group, Greece, heartily concurs in the corrective disciplinary action re: 1st Lt S.T. Felter detailed in the previous indorsement.

BY COMMAND OF LIEUTENANT GENERAL
JAMES VAN FLEET
Ward F. Doudt
Colonel, General Staff
Adjutant General

Clay was going to have to do something about that, when he got it. And it was unlikely that he would try to lecture Big Jim Van Fleet about the necessity of having officers properly uniformed and closely shaven. What would probably happen would be that Clay would simply pass the "Your Attention Is Invited to the Previous Indorsement" back down to the chickenshit MP, and that, it was to be hoped, would cause the bastard to lose some sleep.

Lt. Col. Red Hanrahan went into see the G-1, the personnel officer, first thing. He could see no reason why the entire goddamned United States Army could not arrange to make an infrequent shipment of PX items to the 27th Royal Hellenic Mountain Division's advisors. All he wanted was razor blades, shaving cream, and maybe a couple of lousy boxes of Hershey bars.

The G-1 expected this routine complaint. He listened to it patiently, waited for it to end, promised again to do what he could, and then said: "Say, Paul. I just thought of something. I've got a new officer for you. And I don't think he's left yet." A sergeant was dispatched to the lobby and returned with Captain Daniel C. Watson, the officer Hanrahan had noticed earlier.

Hanrahan took a certain perverse pleasure in being introduced as the man Captain Watson would be working for. It changed the captain's attitude about 180 degrees.

"What is that thing on your chest, Captain?" he asked, with a smile.

He was informed that it was the Expert Infantry Badge, as opposed to the Expert Combat Infantry Badge. So far as Colonel Hanrahan was concerned, the CIB was the only medal that meant a shit. What this ring-knocker was wearing was a qualification badge. He could shoot every weapon in the infantry arsenal, jump over barbed wire, throw hand grenades at a target, and probably make a fire by rubbing two sticks together.

After the captain had gone (to be carried to Ioannina in a supply convoy), Hanrahan asked to look at his service record. The G-1 was a little reluctant, but finally produced it.

Captain Watson had gone ashore in North Africa with the 1st Division as a platoon leader in the 18th Infantry. He had next gone to a hospital. There was no record of a Purple Heart, and there was no award of the Expert Combat Infantry Badge. You got the CIB for ninety days in combat, or unless you were taken out of combat sooner by getting shot, in which case the CIB and the Purple Heart came automatically and together.

Hanrahan looked up from Captain Watson's service record and met the eyes of the G-1.

"Battle fatigue," the G-1 said.

"I don't want him," Hanrahan said. "I'll send him back, and you can find a job for him here."

"For Christ's sake, Paul," the G-1 said. "You know how that happens."

The G-1 wore both the CIB and the ring. Hanrahan knew that another ad hoc meeting of the West Point Protective Association had just been called into session.

"He paid for it," the G-1 went on. "He spent the war running basic trainees. He's still a captain. His classmates are all majors, at least, for Christ's sake. He deserves another chance."

"Why?" Hanrahan asked, simply.

"I can show you his 201 file if you like," the G-1 said. "Once a month, from the time he went to the hospital, he requested combat duty. Every goddamned month, Paul. A career shouldn't be ruined by one incident."

Hanrahan suspected that that was a slip of the tongue. The G-1 hadn't used the word "incident" without some reason. The captain, Hanrahan decided, had either cowered in a hole, or run. The Association of Graduates of the United States Military Academy at West Point had taken care of one of their own. He had been adjudged to be suffering from battle fatigue. If you just lose it, they don't use the word incident. What the hell, he had been close to running himself a dozen times.

"OK," Hanrahan said. "We'll give him a second chance."

"Let's go get some lunch," the personnel officer said. "I understand for a change that we're having gravy with meat chunks."

When Captain Watson reported to Ioannina the next day, the Expert Infantry Badge was missing from his breast. Hanrahan assigned him as assistant G-3 (Plan and Training), sending the captain who held that post up to one of the regiments. Watson worked like hell; Hanrahan was willing to grant him that. He lorded it over Felter, but Hanrahan figured not only that the Mouse could take it, but that two enthusiastic ring-knockers deserved each other.

In the next two months, Second Lieutenant Lowell had only one run-in that required Colonel Hanrahan's personal attention. Righteously indignant, Captain Watson had reported to Colonel Hanrahan that Lieutenant Lowell "in his cups" had told him to go fuck himself when Captain Watson had suggested that not only was he making a spectacle of himself in the officer's mess, but that he had never seen a dirtier, more disreputable uniform.

Hanrahan had jumped all over two asses about that. He told the Duke, as he had come to think of his gone-Greek handsome young lieutenant, that the next time he talked disrespectfully to a senior officer he would personally kick his ass; and he had explained to Captain Watson, with exquisite sarcasm, that it was his position as commanding officer to exercise a modicum of tolerance vis-à-vis the behavior of a nineteen-year-old officer who was almost daily exposed to enemy fire, and who by his personal valor had earned the respect and admiration of the 27th Royal Hellenic Mountain Division.

"The officer of whom we are speaking, Captain, manages to get back here about once a week. While I deplore, of course, any action on the part of any officer which might tend to bring discredit upon the officer corps of the United States Army, I must confess that if I hadn't had a bath or a decent meal in a week, I myself, might be tempted to take a little drink when I came back here."

Watson took the rebuke as if he had had his face slapped. Hanrahan, after a day or two, came to the conclusion that perhaps it was getting through to Captain Watson what the fuck the army was all about. After eight years in uniform.

The next week, Watson had come to him with the request that he be given responsibility for the armored supply column. The request came as a surprise, but the captain's arguments were soundly based. And if the bad guys did try to bust through the lines, Hanrahan would prefer to have the Mouse here, to listen to the Russian frequencies and perhaps hear something of interest.

The Mouse took the news of relief without a word, but there was a deep disappointment in his eyes that shamed Hanrahan. The next time Hanrahan had a couple of drinks too many he told the Mouse about Watson being given a second chance. In the morning, when he remembered what he had done, he was furious with himself.

Although he looked for it, he could not detect any change in the Mouse's attitude toward Captain Watson. He was, in fact, so helpful to Watson that Watson came and asked if Lieutenant Felter might not be assigned as his deputy. "In case the balloon does go up, it would be better to have a backup American officer."

So ordered.

VIII

[ONE]
The Greek–Albanian Border
6 September 1946

The balloon went up three weeks later. Hanrahan had felt in his bones that it was about to happen.

There had been intelligence reports from Athens about movements from the interior of Greece toward the Albanian Yugoslavian borders—an unusual amount of donkey-wagon traffic. Line-crossers reported to Athens and Athens reported to Hanrahan that there was an unusual amount of truck traffic in Albania. The number of reported attempted (and successful) infiltrations declined.

The Mouse had hit it right on the head. Hanrahan wondered how much longer he himself would have taken to figure it out.

There were reports from all over the line, first of sniper fire, then of mortar fire. The same reports had come in for the past five days. Nothing had happened. The fire had simply died down. The Greeks felt that they were teaching the Reds a lesson with their counter-mortar fire. Granting the Greeks could drop a 76 mm mortar round in a latrine hole at 1,000 yards, Hanrahan didn't think this was the case.

And then Captain Watson had come into Colonel Hanrahan's room.

"Lieutenant Lowell is on the radio, sir," he said. "He wants to speak to you."

If Captain Watson was piqued that Lieutenant Lowell hadn't wanted to talk to him, he gave no sign.

What the hell was Lowell's radio code? Hanrahan couldn't remember.

"Duke, this is Pericles Six, go ahead."

"I'm with Pegasus Forward, Colonel. We're under heavy mortar attack."

Pegasus Forward was No. 12 Company, 113th Regiment. Ever since Nick had been killed, Lowell had sort of adopted No. 12 Company, and vice versa. He was technically assigned to the headquarters company of 113th Regiment, but he spent his nights at the front with No. 12 Company. Hanrahan had learned that through Lieutenant Lowell's dedicated efforts, No. 12 Company had more than its fair share of what creature comforts were available. These he'd mostly stolen from the American officers at division.

Hanrahan had not responded to the complaints. So far as he was concerned, the key to success in an operation like this was for distinctions between the Americans and the Greeks they were advising to disappear. This wasn't the British Indian Army; the Greeks were not second-class citizens. The Greeks had to believe that, within reason, their American advisors lived as they did. Lowell was doing that. It was possible that his behavior would shame some of the other American officers into copying him. Lowell was proof of the colonel's theory. He was the only junior officer in the division who matter-of-factly issued orders directly to Greek soldiers, and more important, had his orders obeyed. If Greek troops didn't like their American officer, they weren't insubordinate; they were simply unable to comprehend what the American wanted unless it was translated for them by one of their own officers. Yet they seemed to have no trouble whatever understanding what Lowell told them to do in his really awful, hundred-word Greek vocabulary.

Hanrahan stepped to the map, checking his memory that No. 12 Company's two rock fortresses were on either side of a truck-capable road.

"When did it begin?" Hanrahan asked.

"About twenty minutes ago," Lowell's voice crackled over the radio. "They took out our signal bunker."

"What are you using?" Hanrahan asked. Across the room, his eyes met those of Mouse Felter, who was standing, his arms folded on his chest, watching and listening.

"The M8 radio, Colonel," Lowell said. The Duke doesn't know diddly shit about proper radio security, Hanrahan thought. And then he thought that it didn't really matter. "Pericles Six" was obviously known to the Russians as the American advisor's radio code.

"What's your situation?"

"I'm holding," Lowell's voice replied. "But we're running through a lot of ammunition."

Goddamned Greeks, Hanrahan thought. They regarded an incoming mortar round as a slur on their masculine pride, that had to be answered with a barrage.

"I'm holding?" Hanrahan said, a little annoyed. Lowell was not the commanding officer. He was just the goddamned advisor.

"Captain Demosthatis bought it," Lowell said. "I assumed command."

"How many other casualties?"

"All the officers," Lowell said. "They've been hitting us pretty hard."

"Mount your operation, Captain Watson," Lt. Col. Hanrahan ordered. Then he pressed the microphone button: "Duke," he said, "give them tit for tat. I'll run some ammo up there to you." He spoke conversationally, calmly, although his stomach was in painful knots.

"We can't get out of here, Colonel," Lowell said, and even in the frequency-clipped voice that came over the radio, Hanrahan could hear fear, perhaps even terror in his voice. "They got the motor pool, and when I came out to use the radio in the M8, the tires were all blown."

"No sweat, Duke," Hanrahan replied. "They can't get through your mortars, and we'll get some ammo up to you right away. I've already given the order."

"You better send some officers, too," Lowell said. "I took a little shrapnel coming out to the M8."

Hanrahan's stomach twisted again.

"Well, boy, you just take it easy. We're on our way. What they're trying to do is get some trucks down your road. We know all about it, and we're ready for it."

"Annie Oakley clear with Pericles Six," Craig Lowell's voice, for the first time using the correct radio procedure, came over the radio.

"The cavalry's on the way, Duke," Hanrahan said. "I promise you. Pericles Six, out."

He wondered if the message had gotten through. He wondered why Lowell had suddenly broken off radio contact.

He looked around the room. Felter, having checked it, was loading a 30-round magazine into his Thompson submachine gun.

"Sidney," he said.

"Sir?"

"Nothing," Colonel Hanrahan said. "Get moving."

"Colonel, it's *Sanford,"* Felter said, gently, shaming Hanrahan again. Then he put his Limey helmet on his head and left the G-3 office.

Carrying the Thompson under his right arm like a bird hunter, Felter trotted across the parking lot toward the sandbagged ammo bunker, where several vehicles had already shown up. They were being hurriedly loaded by Greek soldiers. He heard the peculiar sound of a half-track behind him. When he turned to look, he saw the driver's face peering out the windshield. The armor plate which could be lowered to protect the driver was in the propped-open position. Felter waved the half-track into position in the column line.

Next he saw the command jeep, an innovation of Captain Watson's that Lieutenant Felter did not approve. The jeep held their communications radios and had a .50 caliber machine gun mounted on a pedestal. Captain Watson apparently thought of it as his horse. He was going to lead his troops like Light-Horse Harry Lee. Bugler, sound the charge!

When the column had been Felter's, he had the third half-track in line as the command vehicle. The radios would be protected, and so would the commander. If the column were ambushed, the first thing they would take out would be the lead vehicle. The way Watson had it set up, they would lose their communications and their commander to the first bad guy with a machine gun or a grenade.

Felter had tried to set up another group of radios in his half-track, but Watson had caught him at it and told him it wasn't necessary. He had also taken the opportunity to pointedly remind Felter that he was the column leader, and that simple courtesy, as well as regulations, dictated that Felter consult with the commander before taking any action on his own. A fellow West Pointer should know that.

A General Motors six-by-six, and then another, appeared, and troops poured out the backs. They joined the lines of men handing ammo cases hand-to-hand from the bunkers. The trucks, which carried a 2.5 ton load (and for that reason were also known as "deuce-and-a-halfs") were "new." They had seen World War II, and had been rebuilt in ordnance shops in Germany. The American supply line was beginning to operate.

Felter didn't like the way Watson was running around, excited, almost hysterical. He reminded himself that he knew something about Captain Watson that he shouldn't know. He wished Colonel Hanrahan hadn't told him about the captain's record.

In ten minutes, the column was loaded and ready. Watson stood up in the front seat of his jeep and gave the forward sign.

"Charge!" Felter thought, sarcastically. The drivers of the vehicles behind him had been racing their engines for two minutes, ready to go. They would have followed Watson's jeep the moment it moved. They didn't need a hand signal.

The half-track jerked into motion. He felt like a fool. He was almost knocked off his feet, because he had been standing up like Watson himself.

He could hear the sound of the mortar barrage, even over the roar of the engines, long before they reached the site of No. 12 Company. As they grew closer, however, the blurred sounds became more distinct, and there were separate noises now, cracks, and crumps, and *barooms*, and the rattle of small arms fire. Felter thought they were "marching to the sound of the musketry," but he couldn't remember which famous general had said that.

They were close enough now to make out the differing sounds of Enfields, Mausers, and Garands, of .30 and .50 caliber machine guns; and they were close enough to be able to detect glowing light as mortars were fired and as their shells landed. There was a low-hanging yellow cloud of dust around the next curve of the road.

Felter leaned over and lowered the armor plate over the driver's windshield. The driver would now have to steer by peering through a slit in the plate. He started to lower the armor plate on his side, and was suddenly thrown against the windshield. The half-track had lurched to a stop.

When he regained his balance, he stood up on the seat. There was a small cloud of yellow-and-black smoke on the road, fifty yards in front of Captain Watson's jeep. That had been a long round, Felter knew, a fluke. Watson's jeep should now move on.

Watson's jeep did not move on. Watson jumped out of his jeep and ran to the side of the road, the down side, and stood behind a boulder taller than he was. He looked around for Felter, and when he saw him, signaled him to join him.

Felter left the half-track by climbing over the windshield onto the hood, and then down over the bumper and the winch in front. He carried the Thompson in his right hand. As he ran toward Captain Watson, another mortar round landed, thirty yards further down the slope from where Captain Watson stood, a hundred yards toward the firefight. Another wild round, the Mouse thought, wondering if he was going to get wiped out by a mistake made by some worker in an ammunition factory.

"We can obviously go no farther in this fire," Watson said. "I intend to set up a defense line at the ridge of that hill." He pointed to the rear.

"They're waiting for this ammunition, Captain," Felter said.

"They've been overrun," Captain Watson said. "Isn't that obvious?"

"I don't think so, sir," Felter said, politely. "I can hear their mortars and automatic weapons."

"Well, then, Lieutenant," Captain Watson said, sarcastically, "if you're so sure, why don't you just reconnoiter on your own?"

"Yes, sir," Felter replied, accepting the sarcasm as an order. He ran back onto the road, and signaled the driver of Captain Watson's jeep to pick him up. The half-track behind the jeep moved as soon as the jeep did. Felter held out his hand, ordering it to stop.

He jumped into the jeep.

"Felter!" Captain Watson shouted at him. "Come back here!"

Lieutenant Felter pretended not to hear him.

The jeep carried him three hundred yards down the road. The positions of No. 12 Company were under heavy fire, wrapped in smoke and dust. But they weren't overrun. He could see muzzle flashes, and somehow his eye caught a mortar round at the apogee of its arc. No. 12 Company was returning fire, all right.

Felter studied the two little fortresses and the road leading to them through his binoculars. The road had been literally hacked out of the mountainside. It was one-way, just wide enough to take a half-track. But there was an advantage to that. If a mortar shell hit above the road, the shrapnel would be thrown sideward and upward. If one hit the slope of the mountain below the road, only a small amount of shrapnel would be thrown so as to strike anything on the road.

It would take a direct hit to knock out one of the column's vehicles. Even if that happened, they could simply push the disabled vehicle off the road and out of the way.

When he was sure of his position, he ran back to his jeep. The driver already had it turned around.

Captain Watson was where he had left him. For some reason, he had drawn his .45 and was holding it in his right hand, limp, at his side.

Felter got out of the jeep and ran over to him.

"They're under fire, sir," Felter reported. "But they have not been overrun. And the amount of enemy fire actually landing on the road up there is negligible."

"If they have not yet been overrun," Captain Watson said, in a strained voice, as if forcing himself to speak, "it is just a matter of minutes until they are. And this column cannot survive the fire being brought upon the road."

"Yes, it can, Captain," Felter said, very calmly. "Everything's going to be all right, Captain." Captain Watson looked at him as if he had never seen him before. "We're expected up there, Captain," Felter said, talking slowly and reasonably. "The colonel told them we would be there. They need our ammo. Sir."

"I'm not going to be responsible for this column being wiped out in any childish display of heroics," Captain Watson said, very clearly, as if he had rehearsed what he was going to say.

The Greek captain who served as interpreter, and who rode in the first half-track, came running over.

"Is there something you can tell me to tell the men?" he asked. "Is something wrong?"

"Nothing's wrong, Captain," Felter said. "We're moving out."

"We are *not moving out!*" Captain Watson said, firmly, loudly. "We are withdrawing." The Greek captain looked from one to the other American.

"Captain, among others, Lieutenant Lowell is on that hilltop," Felter said.

"I'm sick of you, and everybody else, telling me about Lieutenant Lowell," Captain Watson said, his voice very intense. "Lieutenant Lowell this, Duke Lowell that."

Felter felt himself, despite everything, smiling. Captain Watson sounded like Sharon when she was angry.

"Don't you smile at me, Jewboy," Captain Watson said. "Don't you ever smile at me!"

"Sir, I respectfully request permission to take two of the tracks to the hill while you form a fall-back line," the Mouse said.

"Denied!" Captain Watson sputtered. He was waving his .45 around. "You have your orders, and you will carry them out. Tell the drivers to turn around!" he said to the interpreter.

The interpreter looked at Felter. There was contempt for Watson in his eyes.

"I'll ride in the first track," Felter said to the interpreter. "We'll leave the wheeled vehicles here until we see what the situation is."

"Felter, I give the orders!" Captain Watson said, almost a shout.

"Sir," Felter said, "I have been ordered by Colonel Hanrahan to reinforce Number 12 Company. I intend to carry out that order."

"You'll obey *my* orders!" Captain Watson said, and now his voice was shrill.

"Everything's going to be all right, Captain," Felter said, calmly. He raised his hand over his head and made a "wind-up" gesture. Starters on the tracks ground.

"Goddamn you, this is mutiny!" Captain Watson said.

Felter ignored him. He started back to the road.

There was the booming crack of a .45 going off. Felter kept walking. There was another shot, and this time Felter heard the bullet whirring beside his head. He stopped, paused motionless a moment, and then turned around.

"One more step and you would have been a dead man," Captain Watson said. He was holding the pistol in both hands, pointing it at Felter.

They looked at each other for a long moment. Finally Captain Watson got control of himself. Trembling, he lowered the pistol, fumbled to get it back in its holster.

"Get these goddamned vehicles turned around!" he said to the interpreter.

Lieutenant Felter raised the muzzle of his Thompson submachine gun and pulled the trigger. Captain Watson fell over backward, struck by six .45 caliber bullets traveling at approximately 830 feet per second. And then his body started to slide down the mountainside.

The interpreter looked at Felter.

"Pass the word to the drivers that if a vehicle is disabled, they are to push it off the road," Felter said.

"Yes, sir," the interpreter captain said.

[TWO]

Lt. Colonel Paul T. Hanrahan leaned forward and held up the sheet of paper in his portable typewriter and read what he had written. He looked across his desk at Lieutenant Sanford T. Felter, who sat in a straight-backed chair, his fingers locked together in his lap, staring at nothing. Hanrahan felt very sorry for him, a pity mingled with a surprised admiration. It wasn't the sort of thing he would have expected from Felter. Then Hanrahan ripped the sheet of paper out of the typewriter, took a pen from a pocket sewn to the upper sleeve of his British battle jacket, and signed his name.

"Sidney," he said. "Excuse me, *Sanford.*"

Lieutenant Felter stood up.

"Yes, sir?"

"Read this, Sanford," Lt. Col. Hanrahan said. "Read it aloud."

Felter took the sheet of paper, and started to read it.

"Aloud, Felter," Hanrahan said. "I said, 'read it aloud.' "

"Dear Mrs. Watson," Felter read, in a strained voice. "By now you have heard from the War Department about the death of your husband. Please forgive the bad typing, but I wanted to get this letter out to you as soon as possible. It will be flown out of here with a young officer who was wounded in the same engagement in which Captain Watson gave his life.

"Captain Watson was commanding a relief column dispatched to relieve a Greek Army unit under heavy enemy attack. Heedless of the personal danger to himself, Captain Watson elected to lead the column in a jeep. En route to the scene of action, the convoy was ambushed by guerrillas. Captain Watson was struck by automatic weapons fire which killed him instantly, and I am sure, painlessly.

"I'm sure you will take some small comfort in knowing that, inspired by Captain Watson's personal example of courage, the junior officer under him rallied his troops and saw the mission brought to a successful conclusion.

"Captain Watson's courage and personal example were an inspiration to his men. I know of no finer epitaph for a soldier than to say that he died leading his men into battle.

"The officers and men of both the 27th Royal Hellenic Mountain Division and the U.S. Military Detachment join me in expressing their sorrow at the loss of your husband and their comrade-in-arms. I have been advised that Captain Watson has been recommended for a decoration by the commanding general of the 27th RHMD.

"Sincerely yours, Paul W. Hanrahan, Lieutenant Colonel, Signal Corps, Commanding."

Felter looked at Lt. Col. Hanrahan.

"I'm not sure I can live with this, sir," he said.

"You will live with it, Lieutenant. You will live with it the rest of your life. As I will live with the knowledge that if I had done what I knew should be done and had refused to accept him up here, he would still be alive. The subject is closed, Felter. I don't wish to discuss it further."

There came the sound of a multiengined airplane.

"That must be the Sutherland," Colonel Hanrahan said. "I guess we better go say good-bye to the Duke."

"People know, Colonel," the Mouse said. "Captain Chrismanos saw me. Lowell was there when we brought the body back. He asked me what had happened and I told him."

"The subject is closed, Mouse," Hanrahan repeated. "Closed. Finished."

He took Felter's arm and led him out of his office. They walked over to the infirmary, another of the stone buildings reinforced with sandbags. There was a sign over the door: "The Mayo Clinic G&O Ward."

"How is he?" Hanrahan asked the young American doctor, as if Lowell weren't lying on the stretcher, awake.

"I'd like to get a little more blood in him," the surgeon said. "He lost a hell of a lot. We need some type O-Positive. I was about to have a look . . ."

"I'm O-Positive," Felter said.

"You look pretty shaken, Mouse," the doctor said. "I think you're right on the edge of shock."

"I'll give him the blood," Felter said. "I'm all right."

"You sure you got enough to give away?" Lowell asked.

"Get on with it, doctor," Hanrahan ordered. "They don't like to leave that Sutherland sitting here any longer than they have to."

Felter rolled up his sleeve and lay down on the operating table.

When they were connected and left alone for a moment, he looked down at Lowell, below him on the stretcher on the floor.

"If they send you home, will you go see Sharon?" Felter asked.

"You gutsy little sonofabitch," Lowell said. "I've been thinking about you blowing that yellow bastard away. I would never have thought you would have had the balls."

"What I'm afraid of is that I really shot him because he called me Jewboy," the Mouse said. "I shouldn't have done it."

"Christ, *I'm* glad you did," Lowell said. "I was scared shitless up there. Better him than me. What the hell is the matter with you?"

"Will you go see Sharon?" Felter asked again, to change the subject.

"They're not going to send me home. They're sending me to Frankfurt, for Christ's sake. I'll be back here in a month."

"But if they do, will you?"

"Yeah, sure."

"You've got the address?"

"Burned in my memory," Lowell said. "The Old Budapest Restaurant. How could I forget that?"

"Warsaw Bakery," Felter corrected him, even though he knew Lowell was pulling his leg. "Are you in pain, Craig?"

"No, believe it or not. It feels like it's asleep. Doc says it will start to hurt after a while. He gave me some pills."

"You'll be all right," Felter said. "You were very lucky, Craig."

The doc and the colonel came in and watched as the blood flowed between them. Then they were disconnected, and a couple of Greek soldiers picked up Lowell's stretcher and carried it to the wharf and manhandled it into a rowboat. The doc rode out with him in the rowboat to the Sutherland seaplane and saw that the crew chief knew what to do with him. He wasn't really in any danger. His arm and shoulder had been sliced open with shrapnel, and he'd lost a lot of blood, but the doc doubted that there would be any trouble once they got him in a bed and started a penicillin regimen and got some decent food in him.

When the doc got back to shore, the Mouse had passed out and was on the stretcher.

[THREE]
New York City
8 September 1946

The very existence of the United States Army Advisory Group, Greece, posed certain delicate administrative problems for the United States Army, especially when one of its members got himself shot up.

There was no war, ergo, there could be no wounds, no Purple Hearts. Personnel of USAMAG(G) were "injured" not "wounded."

The entire Standing Operating Procedure-Notification of Next of Kin, U.S. Army Military Advisory Group, Greece, Personnel, was classified CONFIDENTIAL. The next of kin were to be advised by the most expeditious means, by a notification team consisting of a chaplain and another commissioned officer. In the case of company-grade officers, where possible, the notification officers would be a grade senior to the injured officer. They would exercise judgment in imparting specific information to the next of kin. The implication was that the next of kin be told as little as possible beyond the fact that their next of kin had been "injured"; his condition; the prognosis; and the medical facility (normally the 97th General Hospital in Frankfurt) to which he had been sent for treatment.

A brand-new olive-drab Plymouth four-door sedan, driven by a sergeant and carrying a major of the Adjutant General's Corps and a lieutenant colonel of the Army Chaplain's Corps bounced off the Governors Island ferry and headed up past the Battery to the West Side Highway. It crossed Manhattan on 57th Street, past Carnegie Hall, and then turned up Park Avenue. It turned left on 60th Street, and left again on Fifth Avenue, and finally stopped before a large apartment building overlooking Central Park. The doorman of the building, after a moment's indecision, walked across the sidewalk and opened the door of the staff car.

"On whom are you calling, gentlemen?" he asked.

"Mrs. Frederick C. Lowell," the major said.

"You mean Mrs. Pretier," the doorman corrected him.

"No, I mean Mrs. Frederick C. Lowell," the AGC major insisted.

"Mrs. Frederick Lowell is now Mrs. Andre Pretier," the doorman said. "Does Mrs. Pretier expect you, gentlemen?"

"No, she does not," the AGC major said. "This is official business."

Mrs. Pretier could not come to the telephone—she was dressing—but Mr. Pretier gave the doorman permission to pass the gentlemen through to the elevator.

Mr. Pretier, who despite his name was a sixth-generation American, came to the door on the heels of the maid.

"My name is Pretier, gentlemen," he said. "What is it you wished to speak to my wife about?"

"We would prefer, sir," the major said, "to speak to Mrs. Pretier personally."

"Well, if you insist, and it won't take long. We're on our way out, so to speak. Can I offer you something?" He raised his martini glass.

"No, thank you, sir," they said in unison, the chaplain a bit more sternly because he was a Southern Baptist and as such a total abstainer.

Mrs. Janice Craig Lowell Pretier entered the living room, which overlooked Central Park, a few moments later. She swirled through the door to show off her dress to her new husband, and stopped at the bar where she picked up a martini glass.

"Aren't you *darling*, darling," she said. "Just what I need before I face those awful people."

Her eyes fell upon the two officers standing at the entrance to the thirty-five by fifty foot room holding their uniform hats in their hands. Both were impressed by the room and its furnishings, and made just a little uneasy by the opulence and what it represented.

"What's this?" Janice Pretier asked with one of her winning little smiles. "Oh, it's about the *jeep,"* she added. "I thought someone would show up eventually about that."

"Ma'am?" the AGC major asked.

"Three weeks ago," Mrs. Pretier explained, "someone in the army in Brooklyn telephoned to say there was a jeep over there, and could I come for it. It must be my son's. He's a soldier, you know, but I haven't . . ."

"Ma'am," the AGC major said, "we're here about your son. Your son is Lieutenant Craig W. Lowell, is he not?"

"And that's something else strange I've wanted to ask somebody about. One day he's a private playing golf in Germany, and the next thing I hear is that he's a lieutenant in Greece. A lieutenant is an *officer*, isn't he?"

"Yes, ma'am," the AGC major said.

"Then what's this all about? My son is just a *boy*. You people really shouldn't have drafted him at all."

"Mrs. Pretier, your son has just been recommended for the award of the second highest medal the King of Greece can bestow."

"Craig? You must be mistaken. A medal? What for? You people must have your wires crossed or something."

"No, ma'am, if your son is Craig W. Lowell, there's no mistake," the major said. "And I'm afraid I have some disturbing news, as well," he added.

"Disturbing? What do you think this has been so far? What are you talking about?"

"I'm afraid, ma'am," the chaplain said, "that your boy has been injured. He's in no danger—"

"Injured? What do you *mean, injured?"*

"He's suffered some cuts on his shoulder and arm," the chaplain said. "He is in no danger."

"Surely, this must be some ghastly mistake," Mr. Pretier said.

"And how did that happen?" Mrs. Pretier asked, icily, no longer smiling, now holding the major and the chaplain personally responsible for damage to her baby.

"It seems that Craig," the chaplain said, "was wounded in action . . ."

"Wounded in *action?* What are you *talking* about? The war is *over.*"

"There is a revolution in Greece, ma'am," the major said.

"What's that got to do with my Craig?" she asked.

"Your son is assigned to the American Military Advisory Group in Greece," the major said.

"I don't understand any of this," Mrs. Pretier said. "Andre, darling, get Daddy on the phone, like a dear, will you?"

He went to the telephone and dialed a number.

"Lieutenant Lowell had been flown to the 97th General Hospital in Frankfurt, Germany, for treatment," the major said. "It is one of the finest hospitals in the world. The treatment is unsurpassed."

"I still think this is some horrible mistake, a nightmare. You are actually standing there and telling me my son has been *shot*, and is in a hospital?"

Andre Pretier carried the telephone to his wife. She snatched the handset, which had a silver sheath over it, from his hand.

"Daddy? Daddy, there are two soldiers here in the apartment, and they've got some crazy story about Craig being shot and being in a hospital in Greece or Germany or someplace; and Daddy, here, you talk to them."

The chaplain was closest to her. She thrust the phone at him.

"This is Chaplain Foley of First Army Headquarters, sir. I understand that you are Lieutenant Craig Lowell's grandfather. Is that the case, sir?"

"I was going to go in the service myself," Andre Pretier said to the major from the Adjutant General's Corps. "But they found a heart murmur."

[FOUR]
Frankfurt am Main, Germany
9 September 1946

The ambulance, a civilian-type Packard rather than a GI ambulance, rolled without stopping past the guard at the gate of the 97th General U.S. Army Hospital on the eastern outskirts of Frankfurt.

The huge, attractive hospital was a rambling, four-story structure, built just before World War II. The ambulance drove to the Emergency entrance, turned around carefully, and backed in.

A nurse and two medics who had gone to Rhine-Main Air Base to meet the plane got out; and four medics, in hospital whites, rolled a stainless steel body cart out to the ambulance. Between them, they got the patient out of the ambulance and onto the cart and rolled him quickly through automatically opening glass doors.

An officer of the Medical Service Corps met them right inside the door. His eyes rose when he saw the patient was holding a holstered German luger against his chest with his one good hand.

"Have you got a permit for that gun?" the Medical Service Corps captain demanded. "Is it registered?"

"Registered?" Second Lieutenant Craig W. Lowell said, incredulously. He started to laugh, but it hurt. "Oh, shit," Lowell said, shaking his head.

"I'll have to ask you to give me that pistol, Lieutenant," the captain said.

"Fuck you," Craig W. Lowell said.

"Watch your language, Sonny boy," a middle-aged nurse dressed in operating room greens said, walking up to the wheeled cart. A green mask hung around her neck, a green cap covered most of her gray hair, and her feet were in hospital slippers.

Lowell looked up at her.

"There's a lady present," she said.

"Sorry," he said.

She put her fingers on his wrist, and took his pulse. She snapped her fingers, and a younger nurse pushed a flask of fresh blood on a wheeled stand up to the body cart. The older nurse snapped her fingers again, and one of the medics handed her an alcohol wipe. Moving with speed born of skill and experience, she found his artery, slipped a needle into it, and watched until the blood began to flow into him. Then she signaled for the medics to start wheeling the body cart.

"What about that pistol?" the Medical Service Corps captain asked.

There was no reply.

The middle-aged nurse walked rapidly down the highly polished linoleum of the corridor, past the emergency examining rooms, directing the cart with one hand behind her. They came to a bank of elevators. After a moment a door whooshed open. There were three people on it, one in whites, two in uniform.

"Out," the middle-aged nurse said, gesturing with her hand.

The body cart, and the fresh blood stand, and the nurse and the two medics pushing the cart got on the elevator. There was no room for the captain. When the door started to close automatically, he put out his hand and held it open.

"He can't bring that pistol in the hospital," he said to the middle-aged nurse, who was a major in the Nurses Corps.

"Not now, goddamn it," she said. "Not in his shape. I'll take care of it later. Let go of the door."

The door closed, and the elevator started to rise.

She looked down at Lieutenant Lowell.

"Relax," she said. "I just did that to get him off your back about the gun. How do you feel?"

"Shitty," he said, "now that you've asked."

"I'm going to give you a bath anyhow," the nurse said. "Washing your mouth out won't be much extra work."

"Sorry," he said.

The elevator stopped and the door whooshed open.

"What happens now?" Lowell asked, as they rolled down another corridor.

"Well, the first thing we're going to do is get that cruddy uniform off you," she said. "And give you a bath. And pump some blood in you."

"I'm hungry," he said.

"And then we'll see what else you need," she said.

"You're not going to knock me out," he said.

"We won't? Get this straight, Sonny boy: I'll do whatever I damned well please to you."

"I'm not going to let you knock me out and grab the pistol," he said.

"What's with that pistol, anyway?" she asked.

"It saved my ass, and I intend to keep it," he said.

She looked down at him with surprise in her eyes, but said nothing. The cart was rolled into a private room. The orderlies moved him from the cart onto the bed. She saw his face go white from the pain.

"We'll just cut that jacket off," she said to him. "It won't hurt that way."

"I want the jacket, too," he said. "I want the jacket and the pistol. The rest of it you can have."

What she should do, she knew, was give him something to knock him out. And cut his clothes off, and give him a bath, and take the pistol. He was probably going right up to the OR anyway.

"You've got a hard head," she said, and bent over him and pulled the intravenous needle from the inside of his wrist. Then she reached for the holstered pistol he clutched to his breast.

"I'll put it under your mattress," she said. The young nurse with the whole blood looked at her in surprise when she did exactly that.

"Help me to get his jacket off him," the operating room nurse said. "And then send for one of the Schwestern to help me undress him and give him a bath. For reasons I can't imagine, it embarrasses healthy young men to be undressed by a healthy young woman."

She was pleased when the boy in the filthy, blood-soaked uniform chuckled. She wondered what had happened to him.

"Major, really," the nurse in the crisp whites and the starched cap and the lieutenant's bar said.

"Good God," the operating room nurse said. "You're lousy. Where the hell have you been, anyway?" She looked at the young nurse. "He's going to have to be deloused before we do anything else."

The young nurse left the room. Two middle-aged German nurses, called *Schwestern*, sisters, came in and matter-of-factly, impersonally, efficiently, stripped him, deloused him, and then bathed him in alcohol. The major pulled off his bandages, looked, and put them back. The blood transfusion apparatus was hooked up again.

"You need a haircut and a shave, too," the major said. "But that can wait."

"I'm hungry," he repeated.

"If we have to put you under," the major said, "you'll just throw up all over the recovery room."

"I was sewn up at Ioannina."

She picked up the telephone and gave a number. She asked for a colonel, and then said, "OK," and hung up. A few moments later, a doctor in surgical whites pushed open the door.

"I thought you were going to prep him and bring him right up."

"It looks to me like the guy in Greece knew what he was doing," the major said. "I just called up to ask you to look at him."

"How do you feel, Son?" the doctor asked, very tenderly raising the loosened bandages and examining the sutures.

"I'm hungry," Lowell said.

"Well, that's a good sign."

"He was lousy," the major said.

"I don't see any point in opening him up now," the doctor said. "Not until we get some X rays, anyhow. And let's get some more blood in him. Are you in pain?"

"I feel like I was run over by a locomotive," Lowell said.

"What happened?"

"I forgot to duck," Lowell said.

"Let's get some more blood in him," the surgeon said. "And get him something to eat. We'll have another look in the morning. I asked if you were in pain. You want something for it?"

"Hell, yes."

The surgeon scribbled an order. He smiled down at the bed. "You're going to be all right," he said. "Sore, but all right."

The ward nurse, a captain, had come into the room. The surgeon handed her the orders. The immediate care of the patient was no longer the responsibility of the operating room nurse. She left the room, and started toward the elevators. Then she changed her mind, and turned around, and walked to the kitchen.

"Hello, Florence," the dietician said. "What brings you here?"

"You got a steak in the cooler?" she asked. The dietician, a captain, raised her eyebrows. "You're about to get an order for a high-protein, low-bulk meal for 505," the operating room nurse said. "505 is about thirteen years old. He came in lousy, skinny as a rail, just about out of blood, and stitched up like a baseball. I figure we can do better for him than a couple of poached eggs on toast."

"All right, Florence," the dietician said. "I'll see to it."

"Thank you," the operating room nurse said. She picked up the telephone and gave a number, and when it answered, she said, "This is Major Horter. If anybody wants me, I'll be with the multiple shrapnel case in 505."

Major Horter walked back down the corridor to the PX refreshment stand. She reached into the flap of her operating room whites and took a dollar in script from her brassiere and bought two Cokes from the attendant. Then she went to 505.

"Chow's on the way," she said, handing him one of the Cokes.

"Thank you," he said.

"There's a phone line to the States," she said. "You got a number, I'll call your mother or somebody and tell them you're all right."

"No," he said, immediately, firmly. Then he smiled. "Thanks, anyway."

"By now, she's going to have a telegram, or they sent somebody to tell her," Major Horter said. "She's liable to be worried."

"When Mother heard I was in Greece," he said, "she sent me a list of restaurants I shouldn't miss. The less she knows about all this, the better off she'll be."

The ward nurse came in carrying a tiny paper cup on a tray.

"What's that?" Major Horter asked. The ward nurse told her.

"I'll give it to him, after he's eaten."

"He's supposed to have it now," the ward nurse said.

"He's an emergency surgical patient, and I'm the Chief Emergency Surgical nurse," Major Horter said, flatly. "OK?"

"Yes, ma'am," the ward nurse said, snippily. She set the tray and the pill on the bedside table and marched out of the room.

"You're a real hard-nose, aren't you?" Lowell said to her.

"Takes one to know one," she said. "You want a cigarette?"

"I don't use them, thank you," he said. "I smoke cigars."

"You're not old enough to smoke cigars," she said.

He shrugged.

When the WAC from the kitchen brought him his steak, Major Horter cut it up for him, and fed it to him, piece by piece. When she asked him if he wanted the bedpan, he said he could make it to the toilet, and she realized that unless they put somebody in the room to hold him in bed, he was going to try it the minute he was alone, so she helped him to the john, and smoked a cigarette until he was finished, and then she helped him back in bed.

"You want me to clean your Luger?" she asked. He was surprised at the offer.

"It's not the first one I've ever seen, Sonny boy," she said. "I got one in a leather case with a shoulder stock. Captain from the 2nd Armored gave it to me. I know how to clean a Luger."

"Please," he said.

"Who'd you shoot with it?" she asked, idly.

"He was supposed to be a Greek. But he was blond. He was probably a Russian," he said. "Sonofabitch sneaked up behind us and started throwing grenades."

"Is that what happened to you? A grenade?"

"No," he said. "I'd been hit two hours before that."

She gave him his medication. Then she took the Luger from under the mattress and wrapped it up in his bloody, dirty British battle jacket. She stood by the side of the bed and waited until the narcotic got to him and his pupils dilated and his eyelids fell. Then she lowered the top of the bed, and walked out of the room.

She went to the dressing rooms for Operating Ampitheaters Four and Five, and put the battle jacket in the linen sterilizer, giving it fifteen minutes at 500 degrees to kill the lice and whatever else it was infested with. Then she took it and the Luger, now wrapped in surgical towels, to her rooms. She filled the bathub, added Lux and got down on her hands and knees and scrubbed the battle jacket. The rinse water was still dirty, so she filled the tub again, and left the jacket to soak overnight. She took her baths in the OR dressing room anyway.

Then she took the Luger and removed the magazine. There was one round in the magazine, and when she worked the action, another 9 mm case came flying out. Then she took it apart, cleaned it and oiled it, wrapped it again in the surgical towel, and put it in the top drawer of her dresser under her khaki shirts.

On the way to see him in the morning, she stopped by the PX and got a really weird look from the clerk when she handed him her ration card, and said she wanted a box of the best kind of cigars.

[**FIVE**]

"Dearest Sharon," the Mouse wrote from Ioannina, "you remember what Scott Fitzgerald wrote about the rich being different from you and me. I want you to remember that if Craig Lowell comes to see you. I don't know why I said 'if.' He said he would come to see you, and I think he will. I will be surprised and I guess hurt if he doesn't, because I have come to think of him as a friend, probably the best friend I have ever had, and I don't think he would have promised to come see you unless he meant it.

"What happened to him sounds like a movie starring John Wayne.

"I already wrote about him sort of adopting one of the Greek companies up near the border. I don't know if Colonel Hanrahan knew what he was doing or not. If he did know, he looked the other way when Craig stole anything that wasn't nailed down, as they say in the army, and carried it to 'his' company. Food, liquor, clothing, fuel, and even an oil heater from the senior (U.S.) officer's quarters here.

"He was up with 'his' company when there was a large attack on it. The communists were trying to overrun the forts. They used a lot of mortars; and a large number of people, including all the Greek officers, were killed or wounded. Craig was badly wounded himself. But he took command (which is really unusual, since the Greeks normally won't take orders from anyone but another Greek) and held out until we were able to get a relief force up to help. When they got there, there were only twenty-eight men left alive (out of 206), and they were nearly out of ammunition.

"When they got Craig back here, the doctor had to give him five pints of blood. He'd lost that much. They flew him out of here on a Royal Air Force seaplane to an army hospital in Germany. The doctor said he will be all right, but when I first saw him, I was frightened for him. He was gray.

"He thinks he'll be coming back here, but Colonel Hanrahan doesn't think so. Colonel Hanrahan thinks they will probably, eventually, ship him to the United States. Colonel Hanrahan is usually right, which means that you will probably soon get to meet the fellow I've written so much about. I don't want you to judge him by first impression, and I want you to warn Mama and Papa beforehand that he will certainly say something that will either hurt them or make them mad, or both. The language Craig uses—and sometimes it's really *raw*, honey, if you know what I mean—I guess is some kind of a defense mechanism, to hide his feelings, but you had better be prepared to be shocked. You'll have to remember that he doesn't mean anything by it. Tell Mama and Papa that.

"I want you all to be very nice to him. I don't think he has many friends, and not much of a family either. I really don't understand his relationship with his mother. He just doesn't seem to care about her at all. And she feels the same, from what I've seen, about him.

"That's all I have time for now, except to tell you that Colonel Hanrahan liked an intelligence analysis I drew up for him, and is going to put something about it in my efficiency report. I told him that I wanted to be an intelligence officer, and this will probably help me.

"And tell Papa that Colonel Hanrahan said he would have me flown to Athens for the Holy Days. And never forget even for a second, that I am

"Your *faithful* and loving husband, Sandy also known as the Mouse I don't even mind anymore)."

[SIX]
Headquarters, War Department
Office of the Surgeon General
The Pentagon, Washington, D.C.
13 September 1946

"Within the hour," the surgeon general of the United States Army said, "I'm delighted to be of service, Senator." He broke the connection with his finger, and then tapped the phone to get his secretary on the line.

"Ask Colonel Furman to come in here right away, will you, please, Helen?"

Colonel William B. Furman, Medical Service Corps, Chief of Administrative Services, Office of the Surgeon General, appeared ninety seconds later.

"Get on the phone, Bill," the surgeon general said. "Call the 97th General Hospital in Frankfurt, and get me a complete rundown on the medical condition of a soldier named Craig W. Lowell."

"Do you have his rank and serial number, sir?"

"No serial number. But he's either a lieutenant or a private, if that's any help," the surgeon general said, smiling. And then he thought a moment. "And, Bill, when you get his rank and serial number, send a TWX. Medical condition permitting, space available, have him put on the next medical evacuation flight to Walter Reed."

"He's somebody important, I gather, sir?"

"I just had the senior senator from New York on the phone. He leads me to believe that Private Lowell, or Lieutenant Lowell, whatever he is, owns just about a square mile of downtown Manhattan Island," the surgeon general said.

"I'll get right on it, sir."

[SEVEN]

The commanding officer of the 97th General Hospital was an old friend of Major Florence Horter. They had served together three times before, and it was unofficial but rigid Standing Operating Procedure that when the hospital commander scheduled an operation, Major Florence Horter was scheduled as his gas-passer; and if the Medical Corps officers who were board-certified anesthesiologists felt slighted, tough teat.

Major Horter, in a green blouse and pink skirt, and wearing all of her ribbons, walked into his office.

"What the hell is going on, Flo?" the hospital commander asked.

"About what?"

"With you and this kid from Greece," he said. "Don't tell me May and December."

"Don't be a horse's ass," Major Horter exploded. "He's a nice kid, that's all."

"And that's why you're taking him off on a weekend pass? Two days after you tell me, and I TWX the surgeon general, that he shouldn't be airlifted for at least a week?"

"How'd you find out about that?" she asked, curiously.

"It doesn't matter," he said. "What the hell is going on?"

"OK. He's got a girlfriend. Or he had one. He can't find her, and we're going to look for her."

"A girlfriend, or a fraulein?"

"Both," she said.

"The policy of this command is to discourage emotional involvements between troops, especially officers, and frauleins."

"Tom," Major Horter said. "This boy is going to go look for that girl whether or not the army likes it. You want to get involved with an AWOL charge?"

"I can call him in here and scare him a little," the hospital commander said.

"He won't scare," Major Horter sad. "Not only is he a boy who thinks he's in love, but he's a real hard-nose."

"Where are you going to look for the fraulein?"

"Bad Nauheim," she said.

"OK, Flo," he said. "But for Christ's sake, remember he's got friends in high places."

"I don't think he's got a friend in the world, except maybe me and this fraulein," she said. "You're forgiven for that May and December crack, Tom."

"What the hell was I supposed to think? All of a sudden, you start acting like a . . ."

"Maybe a frustrated mother, Tom," she interrupted him. "Leave it at that."

Major Florence Horter had a brand-new 1946 Packard Clipper two-door sedan. When she drove it up the curved road to the main entrance of the 97th General

Hospital, Craig Lowell was standing there waiting for her, his arm in a sling, his Ike jacket worn over his shoulder. She thought again that he looked very, very young. Maybe not thirteen anymore. But his age. Nineteen was still a boy.

She dreaded what he was likely to find in Bad Nauheim. It wasn't that she blamed the German girls for jumping into bed with these kids. Under the circumstances, that was to be expected. Sex was all they had to get by. It wasn't the first time in history that had happened, nor would it be the last.

It was just that this damn fool of a young man really believed that he had found the exeception that proved the rule. That *his* fraulein had been a virgin—he'd even told her that, and he obviously believed it—and that she was different from all the others.

What he was liable to find, if he found her at all, was that she had simply substituted some other young jackass for him, and that if she was everything he said she was, she had the new jackass convinced that he had been the first and that she was in love with him. Again, she didn't blame the girl. If she was one of these German kids who had lost everything in the war, and couldn't find a job, a young American officer with a ticket in his pants to the land of the big PX would look pretty appealing to her, too.

She just didn't like to think what being forced to face facts would do to Craig Lowell. She didn't care if Lowell was a personal friend of Harry S Truman himself, the bottom line was that he was the loneliest kid she had ever met and that he was betting his entire emotional bank account on one hell of a long shot. An impossible long shot. This race had been fixed, and Lowell had a ticket on the wrong horse.

When they got to Bad Nauheim, he directed her to the outskirts of town and down a dirt road to a farmer's house. She went with him to the door. She didn't speak German, but she understood enough to understand what the farmer and his wife told him. The girl was gone, had been gone for a long time, right after he had left, and they didn't know where she had gone.

Then they went back into Bad Nauheim, to the provost marshal's office. The provost marshal Craig Lowell was looking for was long gone. No one he asked had ever heard of a fur-line called Ilse Berg. Then they drove across Bad Nauheim to one of the BOQs, and they sat in the lobby and waited until the bar opened so he could ask the bartender. The bartender was new, and he couldn't remember a fraulein with that name—hell, he never got their names—or meeting the description Lowell gave him.

"There's one more thing we can try," he said, when they were in the Packard again. "She was from Marburg. She was always trying to get me to go to Marburg, and see the house she lived in before the war. She said it was a castle."

"Haven't you had enough?" Florence Horter said. "You're kicking a dead horse."

"I want to try it," he said. "If you don't want to take me, why don't you just take me to the railroad station?"

They drove to Marburg, and put up in a transient officer's hotel right in the middle of the medieval city. A smart-ass sergeant asked them if they wanted adjoining rooms.

In the morning, a sympathetic sergeant at military government called the German police, who told him there was no Berg family with a daughter named Ilse in Stadt, Land, or Kreis Marburg. Then he went to the military government files and came up with a 1940 city register. There were seventeen Bergs, none of them with a female child named Ilse. And there was no castle named Berg. *All* castles, or most of them, anyway, were called "Berg Something."

"Like the Administration Building for the Kreis," the MG sergeant said. "That's Schloss Greiffen*berg.*"

"Thanks a lot," Lowell said. "I really appreciate your courtesy."

"How'd you hurt your shoulder, Lieutenant?" the sergeant asked.

"You know what they say, Sergeant," Lowell said, bitterly. "It's not sex that's bad for you. It's the running after it that kills you."

They started back to Frankfurt am Main. He didn't say anything at all until they were back on the autobahn; and when she stole looks at him, she saw that he was really thinking this whole mess through. The proof came when he told her about some little Jewish lieutenant in Greece, who had not only saved his ass on the hillside, but who had given him blood later.

"He was like you, Major," Lowell said. "He had my fraulein pegged and didn't know if he should tell me or not." He put a cigar in his mouth, and lit it with the cigarette lighter. He laid his head back against the seat and blew smoke rings. He looked, for a while, as if he might cry.

"She wasn't the first girl in your life," Florence Horter said. "She won't be the last."

"As a matter of fact," he said, "she was the first. But she won't be the last." He sat up, and jammed the cigar defiantly in the corner of his mouth.

"Now, don't go off half shot, chasing every skirt in sight just to prove you're a man," Florence Horter said.

He gave her a dirty look, and she thought she was about to be told off. He had to be mad at somebody, she decided, and it might as well be her.

But he surprised her. He chuckled.

"C. Lowell," he said, raising the arm in the sling. "One-armed broad chaser." Then he cursed. He had moved the arm too far.

"Watch the sutures, damn it," Major Horter said.

"Yes, ma'am," Lowell said. "Major, sir."

When they got to Frankfurt, a little after five thirty, and saw the curved white bulk of the I. G. Farben Building looming out of the rubble, Major Florence Horter took her hand from the wheel and pointed at the building which housed Headquarters, U.S. Forces, Europe Theater.

"How would you like to buy me a steak in the O Club?"

"I would be honored, ma'am," he said.

"If you stared soulfully into my eyes," she said, "and maybe held my hand a little, it'd give everybody something to talk about."

They attracted more than a little attention when they walked into the officer's club dining room, a large, glass-walled, high-ceilinged room. For one thing, she thought, Lowell was a rather spectacular sight with his arm in a sling and his Ike jacket worn over his shoulders like a Hungarian cavalryman. Even without that, he would have attracted attention simply for being a tall, handsome, muscular young man. And finally, here he was in the company of a frumpy field-grade nurse, nearly old enough to be his mother.

He was, she saw, totally oblivious to the looks they got.

She didn't like it when he gulped down the first scotch and water, and then had two more before he even opened the menu, but then she decided that maybe he was entitled to get a little drunk; and in his condition, she didn't think it would take much booze.

It took a lot more to get him high than she thought it would, and something else surprised her. He did not, as she expected, start either to feel sorry for himself about his fraulein or to get nasty about her. He ran off at the mouth a little, but there wasn't one self-pitying word about the fraulein.

They stayed in the officer's mess until it closed at midnight, and then drove back to the 97th General Hospital compound. It was only after she had dropped him in front of the main entrance that she remembered that his pass had expired at 2400. The door would be locked, and the OD would have to let him in and take his name. She figured she could talk the OD out of writing him up, but decided the hell with it. By the time it worked its way through channels, he would have been evacuated to the States. She parked her car and went to her room.

The duty officer had taken a chance and gone to bed right after midnight; and so he was annoyed to see the young second lieutenant standing outside the locked glass doors. He gave the kid verbal hell as well as writing him up for being AWOL.

When he handed Lowell his copy of the delinquency report, Lowell asked, very politely, whether he had been born chickenshit, or whether it was something he had learned in the army. The OD snatched the delinquency report from Lowell's hand.

"You will consider yourself under arrest, Lieutenant," he said.

"Fuck you," Lowell said, cheerfully.

The OD called the sergeant of the guard, a middle-aged sergeant-technician, and told him to "escort this officer to his ward and inform the nurse on duty that he is under arrest."

"Will you come with me, please, Lieutenant?" the sergeant asked, kindly.

"Certainly." Lowell said. "Anything to oblige."

When they were out of sight of the OD, the sergeant asked him what had happened.

"That wasn't too smart, Lieutenant," the sergeant said after Lowell had told him. "But I'm glad somebody finally told that sonofabitch off."

They walked up the wide, curving stairs to the mezzanine and the bank of elevators.

The German night maintenance force—the gnomes, as they were known—were scrubbing the marble floors on their hands and knees. They made Lowell uncomfortable. There was something degrading about it. He walked quickly to the elevators to avoid looking at them.

"Craig?" a soft voice asked hesitantly, disbelieving. He paused, but didn't completely stop walking.

"Craig," the voice said. "Oh, my God, you've been hurt!"

He stopped and turned.

"Yeah, I've been hurt," he said.

"Craig!" It was a wail now, of anguish.

Ilse was kneeling, erect, but kneeling, behind a bucket. She had a scrub brush in her hand. She was wearing a shapeless black smock of some kind, and there was a faded blue rag wrapped around her head.

"I'll be a sonofabitch," Craig Lowell said, unaware he had said it.

Ilse got awkwardly to her feet, putting the scrub brush in her bucket. She wiped her hands on her dress.

"I am happy to see you again," she said. "I didn't know that you were here, or perhaps I would have asked per . . ."

"Oh, Jesus Christ," he said, and it came from the depths of his soul. "What are you doing with that fucking bucket?"

He ran toward her, his eyes filled with tears, and he was drunk, and he slipped on the slippery wet marble and went crashing to the floor. He got the stitches in his chest and in his shoulder, and as he felt the blood warm his skin, he thought: They won't be able to put me on that fucking air evac plane now.

Ilse screamed and a nurse came running and took one look at him and said, "You opened your goddamned stitches."

Other people came running, a wardboy, and another nurse and a doctor.

When they got him onto a wheeled cart, he reached for Ilse's hand, and held it. She looked so terrified he was afraid she would faint.

The doctor said, "What's that all about?"

"This is my girl," Lowell said.

"She can't come with you now," the doctor said. "You're bleeding like a stuck pig."

"She either comes," Lowell said, "or I will wake up everyone in the fucking hospital."

"OK, Romeo," the doctor said. "If that's the way you want it." They were rolling him down the hospital corridor now, toward the elevator. "What were those stitches put in there for, anyway?" the doctor asked.

"I was hit in Greece," Lowell said.

"Oh, you're the multiple shrapnel case," the doctor said. "I've heard all about you."

They were in some kind of an emergency room now, and they stopped the cart and Lowell looked up at Ilse, who was crying and smiling at once, and he felt a pin prick and the next thing he knew he was in the hospital bed, with Major Florence Horter looking down at him. She was still in her Class "A" uniform skirt and khaki shirt.

"You're disaster prone, you know that?" she said. "A walking accident."

"I found my girl," he said. "She was here all the time, goddamnit. Scrubbing your goddamned floors."

Major Florence Horter just nodded. She didn't trust herself to speak.

[EIGHT]

HEADQUARTERS
WALTER REED US ARMY HOSPITAL
Washington, D.C.

SPECIAL ORDERS
NUMBER 265

27 Sept 1946

EXTRACT

****

41. 2ND LT LOWELL, Craig W FinC (Det Armor) 0-495302, Det of Patients, WRUSAH, is plcd on CONVALESCENT LEAVE (not chargeable as Ord Lv) for pd of thirty (30) days, and WP Home of Record, 939 Fifth Avenue, New York City NY. Off auth per diem. Off auth tvl by personal auto. TCS. TDN. Off will report as req to U.S. Army Hosp, Governors Island, New York, NY as nec for outpatient treatment. AUTH: VO, The Surgeon General.

****

FOR THE HOSPITAL COMMANDER
James C. Brailey
Colonel, Medical Service Corps
Adjutant

Lowell rode in a taxicab from Walter Reed to the station. His right arm was still in a sling, but he could bend it and get it into the sleeves of his shirt and Ike jacket. The wound on his chest had stopped suppurating, and while there was still some suppuration from the wound on his arm near the elbow—a slimy, bloody goo—all he had to do to it was to keep putting fresh bandages on it to keep it clean. He was to exercise it every day.

He had five twenty-dollar bills, crisp new ones, in the breast pocket of his jacket.

No one seemed to know where his records were, so they had given him a partial payment and told him that he could get another from the finance officer on Governors Island by showing his orders and his ID card.

He had a canvas bag from Frankfurt, bought with the partial pay Florence Horter had arranged for him at the 97th General. The bag held two changes of underwear, two khaki shirts, a razor, a tube of shaving cream, and a styptic pencil. Over the underwear and below the shirts was the Luger. The German belt and holster had simply rotted away, but he had kept the GOTT MIT UNS brass buckle. The battle jacket was in Germany. Florence Horter had said there was no point in his taking it with him, and he had agreed.

He bought his ticket, boarded the train, and went to the club car. He was disappointed that they refused to serve drinks until the train left the station. A salesman came and sat down in the opposing chair and took out his briefcase and started to use it as a desk. Lowell was relieved; he would not be expected to talk.

When the train started moving, he ordered a bottle of ale from the waiter and drank most of it down immediately. He was parched. Some soldiers got on the train in Baltimore, but none came into the club car. A great many soldiers got on the train in Trenton, and a dozen came into the club car.

Lowell thought that it was almost exactly a year before that he had gotten on the train at Trenton, Private Craig W. Lowell, ordered from the U.S. Army Replacement Training Center (Infantry), Fort Dix, N.J., to the U.S. Army Overseas Personnel Station, Camp Kilmer, with seven days' delay-en-route leave.

Like these guys, probably.

A group of four troopers obviously fresh from basic took over a four-man table and called for drinks. One of them pulled down his tie, unbuttoned his jacket, and slumped down in the chair.

It must be the ale, Lowell thought. That trooper's behavior annoys me more than I am willing to bear in silence.

He got up and walked to the table.

"Pull up your tie, button your jacket, and act like a soldier," he heard himself say.

He was met with eight hostile, scornful eyes. Nobody moved.

"I won't tell you again," Lowell said.

"Yes, *sir!*" the one with the loose tie and open jacket said. There was a snicker from one of the others. But the tie was pulled up, and the jacket buttoned.

"Thank you," Lowell said. He returned to his seat. For some reason, he was very pleased with himself, even though he couldn't imagine why he had done what he did.

The train backed into Pennsylvania Station, so that the parlor cars and the club car were close to the end of the platform. Long before he could get up and get off the train, he saw his grandfather, a tall, heavy, mustachioed man in a chesterfield and homburg, standing just outside the wrought-iron gate. A man in gray chauffeur's livery stood beside him.

When he finally managed to leave the train, and his grandfather saw him, there was a smile on his face. He took his homburg off and held it in his hand as Craig walked up.

"Well," the Old Man said, "home is the soldier, home from the wars." He put his hand out. Craig Lowell hugged him. His grandfather, he thought, was the only one in the family worth a shit.

"You don't have any luggage?" his grandfather asked, rather ceremoniously putting the homburg on his head.

"Let me have that, sir," the chauffeur said, reaching for the canvas bag from the Frankfurt PX.

"I'll carry it, thank you," Lowell said.

The car, a 1940 Packard with a body by Derham, the front seat exposed to the elements, was parked in the 33rd Street entrance to the station. A policeman, standing near it, touched his cap as they approached. Lowell's grandfather waved Craig into the car first. Inside, it smelled of leather and cigars. His grandfather leaned forward in the car and took a cigar from a box mounted beneath the glass divider.

"May I have one of those?" Craig asked.

"Yes, of course," his grandfather said. He looked indecisive for a moment, and then handed him the cigar he held. "I've already clipped it," he said. "Would you like me to light it for you?"

"Just hand me the lighted match, please," Craig said. His grandfather struck a regular kitchen match on the sole of his shoe and handed the flaming match to Craig.

"How long have you been smoking cigars?" he asked.

"Since I was ten," Craig said. "My father caught me smoking a cigarette and made me smoke a cigar, so I would get sick. But I didn't get sick; I liked it. What he did was teach me to smoke cigars, not give up smoking."

"I didn't know that," his grandfather said.

"Where are we going?" Craig asked.

"I thought we'd have some lunch," his grandfather said. "Porter wanted us to come downtown, but I thought you would be going out to Broadlawns . . ."

"Porter?"

"I thought it would be appropriate, under the circumstances, to have Porter welcome you home. It's such a trip in from the Island that I didn't think you'd want your mother to endure it."

Lowell wondered if that meant his mother was drunk again, or flying high on her pills.

"I had hoped to have a talk with you alone," Lowell said.

"I was under the impression you liked Porter."

"Porter is an asshole," Lowell said.

"You're not in the company of soldiers now," the Old Man corrected him. "Watch your language, Craig."

"You told him to come," Craig said, an accusation.

"I telephoned to tell him you had returned to this country, and he said that I should by all means bring you to lunch when you got to New York."

"What is he doing downtown?" Lowell asked.

"Working for Morgan and Company," his grandfather said. "I thought he could use the experience."

Geoffrey Craig had had two children, a son and a daughter. Porter Craig was the son of his son, now deceased, and Craig Lowell the son of his daughter. There were no other children or grandchildren.

The Packard limousine pulled to the curb before a building just off Fifth Avenue on 43rd Street. The chauffeur ran around the front and opened the passenger door. Geoffrey Craig got out, and then turned to help Craig. They walked up a shallow flight of stairs, and the older man held open a door for his grandson.

"Good afternoon, Mr. Craig," the porter said. He went to a large board which listed the names of every member of the club and had a little sliding tag device to indicate if they were in the building.

Lowell looked up at the board and saw *Craig, Porter* below *Craig, Geoffrey.*

"Porter belongs?" he asked. The Old Man nodded.

"I thought you had to be at least sixty," Craig said.

He got a withering look from his grandfather. Porter Craig at that moment walked into the foyer of the club. He was a slightly chubby man of indeterminate age. He was actually, Craig thought, twenty-nine or thirty. He could have passed for twenty-five or forty.

"Well, hello, Craig," he said, with forced joviality. "How the hell are you, boy?" He grabbed Lowell's shoulders.

"Watch the goddamn shoulder," Lowell said.

"Sorry," Porter Craig said, jerking his hands away.

The porter appeared with a claim check.

"I'll be happy to take that bag, sir," he said.

"I'll keep it, thank you," Lowell said.

"Does Craig have to sign the guest book?" Porter Craig asked.

"I believe he does," the older man said.

"Sign it for me, then, Porter," Lowell said.

"Yes, of course."

They walked up a wide flight of stairs and took chairs around a small table.

A waiter took their drink order.

"Ordinarily, I don't," Porter Craig said. "But this is rather a celebration, isn't it?"

When the drinks were served, a scotch sour for the Old Man, a scotch and soda for Porter, and a bottle of ale for Lowell, Porter Craig raised his glass and said, "Welcome home, Craig."

"Thank you," Lowell said. He wondered what Ilse was doing at precisely that moment. It was half past one here. It was half past six, already getting dark, in Germany.

"Granddad tells me you're going out to Broadlawns and get your strength back," Porter Craig said.

"I don't know if I am or not," Lowell said.

"Because of Pretier, you mean?" his grandfather asked. "Actually, he's rather a decent sort, Craig."

"If he can put up with Mother," Lowell said, "he's either a saint or a masochist."

"That's a remark in extraordinarily bad taste," his grandfather said.

Lowell shrugged, but made no apology.

"Your mother expects you," his grandfather said. "You're going to have to go out there."

Lowell shrugged again, this time in agreement.

"I'll go see her," he said.

Lowell finished his ale, and looked around for the waiter.

"Is that good for you?" his grandfather asked.

Lowell looked at him and raised his eyebrows.

"I'm a big boy, now," he said.

"With a chip on your shoulder," Porter Craig said.

"Porter, Craig has just gone through a terrible experience," their grandfather began, and was interrupted when another guest stumbled over the canvas bag from the PX in Frankfurt. He didn't fall down, just lurched, regained his balance, and gave the trio a dirty look.

"What in the world do you have in that bag," Porter Craig asked, "that you refuse to check it?"

"A change of underwear, a razor, and a pistol," Craig said.

"What are you doing with a pistol?" his grandfather asked.

"You'll go to jail," Porter Craig said. "Didn't you ever hear of the Sullivan Law? Pistols are illegal."

"Not for an officer, they're not," Lowell said.

"I've been curious about that," Porter Craig said. "Are you really an officer? How did you become an officer? You're only nineteen. And you didn't finish school. The last I heard, you were expelled and drafted, and the next thing, you show up in an officer's uniform . . ."

"Just who the hell do you think you are, Porter, the FBI?" Lowell asked.

"Porter's curiosity is natural," their grandfather said. "I'm more than a little curious myself."

"You have a right to be," Lowell said. "So far as I know, that temporary guardianship order is still in effect."

"And I don't?" Porter Craig asked.

"Fuck off, Porter," Craig Lowell said, conversationally. Heads turned.

"Lower your voice," the Old Man said. "Porter, under the circumstances, I think that it might best if Craig and I talked privately."

Porter Craig, red-faced, tight-lipped, got to his feet and fled from the room. He didn't even say good-bye. Grandfather and grandson locked eyes.

"I realize now that bringing him here was a mistake," the older man said.

"I've never liked that sonofabitch," Craig said. "And one of the things that came to mind when he gave me the phony dear-cousin welcome downstairs was that I no longer have to put up with his bullshit."

"You have proved that you are a man," his grandfather said. "That language is unnecessary. Please remember that you are a guest in my club. A club to which your father belonged."

"I'm sorry," Craig said, sounding genuinely contrite.

"We'll say no more about it," his grandfather said. He took a wooden match and struck it and handed it to Craig, whose cigar had gone out. "Do you like that?"

"Really good."

"I've had some put down at Dunhill's," his grandfather said. "They make them in Nicaragua, of all places. I'll have some sent out to Broadlawns, or, if you like, you can stop by on your way to the Island and pick up whatever you need. I'm taking a cab downtown, so that you can have the Packard."

"Thank you," Lowell said.

"And now, I hope, we can conduct our conversation in a civilized manner," his grandfather said. "Do you feel like telling me what has happened to you?"

"All right," Lowell said, and he told his grandfather the whole story, leaving out any reference to Ilse.

"If I didn't think it would set off a stream of obscenity," the Old Man said, when he had finished, "I would tell you that I am not only proud of you, Craig, but happy for you. You seem, finally, to have grown up."

Lowell smiled broadly.

"Is something funny?" his grandfather asked.

"Grandpa, you just fell into the spider's web," Lowell said.

"How do you mean?"

"I want my majority," Lowell said.

"I don't quite understand."

"I want to go back to court with you, and have that temporary guardianship order revoked, and then I want another order granting me my majority."

"Would you mind explaining why?"

"It's a little embarrassing for me, as an officer and a gentleman by act of Congress, to be legally a minor child."

"We can talk about this later," his grandfather said.

"No, we're going to talk about it now," Lowell said.

"Let's get something to eat first," his grandfather said.

"Fine. We can talk while we eat," Lowell said.

They walked out of the library into the dining room and ordered.

"Even if I were willing to go along with this majority business," his grandfather said, "what makes you think the court would?"

"For one thing," Lowell said, "you seem to generally get what you're after in court. And for another, according to the law of the State of New York, one of the times maturity can be granted is when the minor child is commissioned as an officer in the armed forces."

"You've consulted an attorney, I gather?" the Old Man said, dryly, looking at the plate of Dover sole the waiter had laid before him.

"I've asked one a couple of questions," Lowell said.

"The only possible motivation I can come up with is that you have the misguided notion you're qualified to manage your financial affairs, that you want your trust fund now."

"I didn't say that," Lowell said. "I don't know the first goddamned thing about money. I don't give a damn about managing the trust fund. I want some money from it, say another thousand a month, but that's all."

"They're making available a thousand a month now, aren't they?" Lowell nodded. "And that's not enough?"

"I told you, Grandpa, I'm a big boy now. I don't need you or anyone else telling me how much money I need."

"And," the Old Man said, sharply, "if I don't think it's wise to go along with this idea of yours?"

"Then I'll just have to find some hungry shyster lawyer," Lowell said.

They locked eyes again. Finally, his grandfather snorted.

"And I think you'd do that," he said. "Let me understand what you're asking. You want your majority. You want an income of two thousand a month from the fund. Actually, it's funds, plural. And you will permit me to retain the management of the funds?"

"I'd be grateful to you if you would," Lowell said.

"You'd put that in writing, of course?"

"I'm prepared to trust you, as one gentleman to another," Lowell said, smiling at his grandfather. "But if you insist on having it in writing . . ."

"By God, you have grown up," his grandfather said, smiling back at him. "I'll have it in writing, though, since you don't mind."

"If you can't trust your own grandfather, who can you trust?" Lowell asked, in mock innocence. The Old Man laughed.

"It's a pleasure doing business with you, sir," he said, and laughed. Then he said: "It will take a couple of weeks. I'll look into it."

"All it takes is for us to show up the judge's chambers. I want it done this week," Lowell said.

There was one more locking of eyes. Then his grandfather shrugged his shoulders.

"If it's that important to you," he said, "I'll start the wheels rolling as soon as I get to the office."

Lowell thought that this confrontation between them was very different from their last. At that time, when an appeal to emotion had failed to achieve the desired result, the Old Man had resorted to shouts, arm-waving, and a threat that Lowell had known was empty (he'd seen his father's will) to cut him off without a dime. He would not be the only young man who had ever thrown away the advantages to which he had been born to die in the gutter, his grandfather had shouted.

Obviously the Old Man wanted something this time. What it was came out over the Brie and crackers with which they ended their meal. His grandfather told him that Andre Pretier was good for Craig's mother. She was off the bottle, he reported with surprising candor. She wasn't on pills. There had been few "incidents," and he wanted it kept that way. The way the Old Man put it, Lowell thought, it had been rather ungentlemanly of him to have caused the notification team to go to the apartment on Fifth Avenue and upset his mother.

The limousine was waiting for them at the curb when they went back out onto 43rd Street. Lowell had always wondered how the chauffeurs managed it, considering the traffic and the other limousines that had passengers at the same place.

"I can get a cab out to the Island," Craig said.

"Nonsense," his grandfather said. "Besides, you're going to stop at Dunhill's and get cigars."

"I would hate to have anything get in the way of your little chat with your legal counsel, Grandfather."

The Old Man chuckled. Then, seeing a cab, he put his fingers in his mouth and gave out with a whistle that pierced the noise and bustle of midtown Manhattan. The cab pulled to the curb, and his grandfather got in.

Then Lowell got into the limousine.

"Dunhill's and then Broadlawns, is it, sir?" the chauffeur asked.

Three weeks ago today, Lowell thought, I was living in a sandbagged hut in the mountains of Greece.

And three weeks ago today, Little Craig nearly got his little ass blown away.

"Please," he said to the chauffeur, and then reached for another of his grandfather's cigars.

[NINE]

Gardeners were at work wrapping the shrubbery in anticipation of the first frost when the Packard rolled through the gates of Broadlawns. The house itself was not visible from the road. He didn't see anybody in the gate house, but there must have been someone there, for his mother was standing on the veranda in front of the long, rambling, two-story brick house when they got there. Obviously expecting him. With a tall, rather elegant man standing beside her.

Andre Pretier. His mother's husband. Well, if she had to buy a husband, she had bought a good-looking one, a gentlemanly type.

When the chauffeur had to help him out of the car, his mother put her hand to her mouth. Her hair was solid gray, worn short. She had a ragged cashmere sweater over her shoulders.

"Oh, darling!" she said, when he walked up to her. "Are you all right?" She gave him her cheek to kiss. He remembered the smell of her perfume.

"Is that the best you can do?" she asked.

He embraced his mother somewhat gingerly. She had been drinking—he could smell the gin—but she was not drunk, and that was an improvement. She looked healthier, too.

"And this is Andre," she said.

Pretier gave him his hand.

"Welcome home, Craig," he said. "I hope that we can be real friends. I'd really like that."

"Thank you," Craig said.

"Let's get inside before we catch a cold," Craig's mother said.

A tall, light brown butler stood inside the door.

"Welcome home, sir," he said. "May I take your bag?"

"Thank you," Lowell said.

"I expect Craig would like a drink," Pretier said. "Come on in here," he said, gesturing toward the sitting room. "We've had a fire laid. First of the year. I always like a fire, don't you?"

Very handy, Lowell thought, to warm your shaving water.

The butler wheeled up a cart.

"What will you have to drink?" Pretier asked him.

"Ale, please," Lowell said.

"I don't believe we have any ale, sir," the butler said.

"We'll have to have some in the future," Andre Pretier ordered.

"Scotch and soda, please," Craig said.

"We have your little jeep," his mother said. "Andre went to Brooklyn and picked it up for you himself. That and your trunks."

"That was very nice of you," Craig said to Andre Pretier. "Thank you very much."

"I was happy to do it," Andre Pretier said. "I want you to feel welcome here, Craig."

"Thank you," Lowell said again, taking the drink from the butler.

He didn't recognize any of the servants. When she had been at the sauce, or on the pills, or both, she had run off a lot of servants. These were West Indians, blacks who spoke a British accented English.

Lowell wondered if Andre Pretier knew that he wanted Craig to feel welcome in his own house. Lowell's father's will had given his mother use of the house for her lifetime, or until she remarried, whereupon it would pass to the Aforementioned Trust for the Benefit of Craig W. Lowell, together with all furnishings. She had married Pretier, and now all this was his.

"Well," Andre Pretier said. "As the Spanish say, my house is your house."

Craig looked at him, wondering if he meant what he was saying, and if so, why he had brought it up the moment he had walked in.

"You just let us know what you want, and we'll do our best to provide it," Pretier went on. "If you'd like to just lie about and do nothing, or if you'd rather get together with your friends, a party or a dinner or whatever, just speak up."

"We want you to be happy, dear," his mother said. "We're so glad to have you back after your accident." He was looking at Pretier when she said that, and Pretier winked at him. The message was clear. Let her think you had an accident.

"Thank you," Craig said.

"Did Grandpa give you lunch?" his mother asked.

"Yes," Craig said.

"Would you like something to eat now? A sandwich and a glass of milk?"

"No, thank you."

"Would you like a cigarette, Craig?"

"I'd like a cigar," he said. "Grandpa got some for me, from the humidor at Dunhill's."

"Oh, I'm afraid my baby is gone for all time," his mother said brightly. "Smoking cigars."

"We kept the boat, the power boat, in the water," Andre Pretier said. "I thought you might feel up to using it. Some of the days are really quite warm."

"What boat?"

"My boat," Andre Pretier said. "I had her brought down from Bar Harbor."

"That would be very nice," Craig said.

"I've become quite the sailor," his mother said. "Haven't I, darling?"

"Yes, my darling, you have," Andre Pretier said.

When the butler handed him his scotch and soda, Craig said, "There was a package of cigars from Dunhill's in the car. Would you get me a box, please?"

"I've sent someone for them, sir," the butler said.

"I hope you're not smoking too many of them," his mother said.

"I understand that they're supposed to be better for you than cigarettes," Andre Pretier said.

"Don't be silly, darling," his mother said. "How could they be?"

Andre Pretier did not press the point.

"I don't mean to cast a pall on your welcome, Craig," he said, "but what are the arrangements for medical treatment?"

"I'm going to go into New York," Craig said. "To Governors Island. Tomorrow."

"Do you have to?" his mother asked. "There are perfectly good doctors we can call here."

"Craig is a soldier, darling," Andre Pretier said. "Soldiers do what they're ordered to do." He smiled at Craig. "I'll tell the chauffeur," he said. "Have him stand by, so to speak."

"You know, even with him sitting there in his soldier suit," his mother said, "I really can't believe that he is a soldier." She smiled at her son. "Do you have to wear it all the time?"

"No," he said. "As a matter of fact, I'd like to change out of it right now."

"I'm sure you would," she said. "But finish your drink, first."

The butler held out an open box of cigars to Craig. After he had taken one, the box was placed on the coffee table. Andre Pretier bent over him and held out a match.

"That's vulgar, darling," his mother said, when he bit the end off and spat it out. "Grandpa has a little knife he uses. If you're going to smoke cigars, you really should get one of those little knives."

"They call them cutters, I think," Andre Pretier said.

"You should have gotten one when you were at Dunhill's," his mother said. "Why didn't you think of it?"

Craig drained his drink.

"I think I'll change clothing," he said. "Will you excuse me?"

"We've put your things in your old room, darling. Remember?" his mother said.

"Yes, of course," he said.

He walked up the thickly carpeted stairway to the second floor, and down a wide corridor toward his old room, actually two rooms, at the end of it. A maid was vacuuming the carpet. She shut the machine off and smiled at him shyly until he passed. He had a mental image of Ilse kneeling by her scrub bucket in the 97th General Hospital.

He went into the bedroom of the small suite and took the sling off very carefully. Then he took off his jacket and his necktie and his shirt and pulled off his T-shirt. The shirt stuck to dried whatever it was leaking from the bandage at his elbow.

He rang for a servant.

The butler came right away. Craig told him to bring bandages and gauze and Mercurochrome.

When the butler came back, Andre Pretier was with him.

"Your mother thought I might be able to help," he said. When he saw the bandages, he said, "I'd rather your mother didn't see that."

"Me, too," Lowell said. He pulled the adhesive tape loose and held his arm out for the butler to rebandage.

"They said that if there was suppuration, they would probably keep me in the hospital on Governors Island for a couple of days," Craig said. "How do you want to handle that?"

"Why don't you just say you're spending a couple of days with friends?" Andre Pretier said. "That way she won't worry."

"Why don't you tell her I called and said that?" Craig said.

"I think that would be best," Andre Pretier said. "And now I'll go down and tell her that Kenneth is perfectly capable of helping you."

When Pretier had gone, Craig asked Kenneth to pack a bag for him, enough clothing for a week or ten days, one uniform, the rest civilian clothing, and to put it into the car he would be using in the morning.

He had breakfast alone the next morning. The Master and Madame, Kenneth told him, seldom rose before ten; and then they had breakfast in their room. After he had breakfast, he walked out the front door where the chauffeur was waiting, holding open the rear door of an ornately sculptured automobile Craig didn't recognize.

"What is this thing, anyway?" Craig asked.

"It is a Delahaye with a body by Fortin," the chauffeur said. "It is Mr. Pretier's automobile."

"Very nice," Craig said. "Have you been with Mr. Pretier long?"

"Oh, yes, sir."

Well, that seemed to confirm it. Pretier had money of his own. He had not married Craig's mother for her money. He wondered why he had married her.

"I want to go to the Morgan Guaranty Trust on 53rd Street first," Craig said. "And then to the Federal Building."

"And then to Governors Island, sir?"

"No. After the Federal Building, we're going to Newark," Craig said.

[TEN]

In Newark, after they'd driven past the Old Warsaw Bakery on the corner of Chancellor Avenue and Aldine Street and he knew he'd found what he was looking for, he told the chauffeur to drop him at the corner and that he wouldn't need him anymore.

There was a line of people waiting to buy bread and rolls; and two pictures of the Mouse were over the cash register, one in his cadet uniform, one in pinks and greens. Two little American flags were crossed proudly above them.

He set his bag down on the tile floor and after a moment sat on it. He waited there for about five minutes until the line went down. Then the slight, pleasant-faced, shy-appearing woman with her black hair in a bun, dressed in a too-large white baker's smock saw him for the first time.

She looked at him very strangely, and then she came from behind the glass display cases and walked up to him. He stood up.

"Craig?" she asked.

"Sharon?"

Sharon Lavinsky Felter stood on her tiptoes and kissed Craig Lowell on the cheek.

"Sandy wrote you'd come," she said. "I'm so glad you did."

A couch in Felter's flat over the bakery opened up into a double bed, and he slept in that.

Three days later, he took a cab from the Felters' flat back into New York, although Mr. Felter had offered to drive him anywhere in the world he wanted to go.

He met his grandfather at the Borough of Manhattan Court House, where a judge took about five minutes to declare him an adult in the eyes of the law. Next he went to the Federal Building and picked up his passport, then to LaGuardia Airport where he caught Trans-World Airlines Flight 307, a Lockheed Constellation, New York—Paris, with a stopover at Gander Field, Newfoundland.

He told the captain in the embassy in Paris who handled entry permits for the American Zone of Occupied Germany that he was a student who wished to visit his aunt, Major Florence Horter, at the 97th General Hospital in Frankfurt. The captain telephoned Major Horter to verify his story. She met him at the Hauptbahnhof in Frankfurt. She was alone.

"I wasn't sure that you were going to get away with this," she said. "And I didn't want Ilse to get upset."

"I said I'd be back in about a month," he said. "It's twenty-six days. I'm back. And anyway, Ilse's pretty tough."

"Ilse's four months' pregnant," Major Horter said. "Chew on that for a while, Sonny boy."

[ELEVEN]

Craig W. Lowell and Ilse von Greiffenberg were married by the pastor of St. Luke's Protestant (Lutheran) Church in Frankfurt am Main, with Major Florence Horter as their only attendant.

The pastor had mixed feelings about the whole thing. For one thing, the groom's great good spirits were at least partially inspired by alcohol. The bride was obviously pregnant. He had serious doubts if they had considered all the ramifications of marriage, temporal and spiritual.

But they seemed to be in love; and at least the American was trying to do the right thing. There were literally thousands of girls bearing the children of American soldiers who would not marry them.

After the wedding, the newly married couple went to Oberursel. There after a long and frustrating search, Ilse and Major Horter had found a small, but clean, apartment where Ilse would wait until her immigration papers were processed. The groom undressed, and Major Horter changed his dressings while the bride looked on, making little noises of sympathy.

Then Major Horter left the couple with her wedding gift to them, three bottles of Moët champagne, and a book, *So You're Going to Have a Baby?*

Before she left, Major Horter and Lieutenant Lowell went shopping in the Frankfurt post exchange for all the things Ilse would need while she waited to go to America. Ilse was a German national, and German nationals were prohibited by regulation from entering post exchanges. She waited in the car, nervously twisting the four-carat diamond ring on her finger. She knew it couldn't be real—where would Craig get that kind of money?—but she thought that it was beautiful anyway.

[ONE]
Student Officer Company
The United States Armor School
Fort Knox, Kentucky
30 October 1946

Student Officer Company, The Armor School (SOC-TAS) was a collection of two-story wooden barracks painted yellowish white with green shingled roofs. They were spread out to conform to the contours of the low hill on which they had been built, and were generally centered around a two-story administrative building and a single-story orderly room. The latter was two standard orderly rooms built together. A standard mess hall capable of seating 750 troops had been converted to form slightly more luxurious dining facilities for officers (instead of twelve-man plank tables, there were four-man tables covered with oilcloth). It was placed on the edge of the cluster of buildings overlooking the classroom buildings built on the flat land below.

Each of the student BOQs was identical. They were slightly longer than standard enlisted barracks. There were six suites on each side of a corridor running down the center of the buildings. Each suite contained two bedrooms, each furnished with an iron bed, a chest of drawers, a desk, a straight-backed chair, and an armchair. A bath, consisting of a water closet, a double sink, and a tin-walled and concrete-floored shower, connected the two rooms of each suite. In each barrack, one of the two-room suites had been set aside for use as a "recreation room," which was a euphemism for bar.

Having been assigned to Room 16-A of Building T-455, Second Lieutenant Craig W. Lowell lifted his luggage—a canvas Valv-Pak and a nearly new leather suitcase, stamped with his father's initials—from the back seat of a Chevrolet sedan. He found Building T-455 and then, on the second floor, Room 16-A. He had some trouble making his key operate the lock on the door, but he finally managed to get it open. He walked into the room and looked around at the bed, the desk, and the armchair. He tossed the suitcases on the bed, and one by one unpacked them. He hung the uniform and the civilian clothing in the doorless closet, and then put his shirts and his linen in the chest of drawers. When the suitcases were empty, he put the suitcases in the closet.

He opened the door, found the bath, urinated, and then, after a moment's hesitation, knocked on the door opening to the other room.

"Come!" a deep voice called.

He stepped inside, smiling. He was surprised to see a very large, very black man lying on the iron bed, dressed only in a pair of white jockey shorts.

"Surprise, surprise!" the black man said to him. When Lowell didn't reply, he added, "You're not in the wrong place, white boy; but then, neither am I."

"My name is Craig Lowell," Lowell said.

"And I know what you're thinking, Craig Lowell," the black man said to him.

"Do you?"

"Hell, they put me in with a dinge!" the black man said.

"What I was actually thinking was that you're the biggest coon I've ever seen," Lowell said. "Excuse me, black boy." He pulled the door closed and went back through his room and outside. He got back in the Chevrolet and went to the PX and bought a Zenith Transoceanic portable radio to replace the one that had gotten blown away at No. 12 Company. That accomplished, he went through the PX scooping up things he thought he would need, from shaving cream to shoe polish to half a dozen paperbacks from the newsstand rack. He put everything in the car and then found the liquor store. He bought scotch and gin and vermouth and asked for ale, but there was none. Then he went back to the PX and bought a carton labeled, "A complete set of household glassware," and put it in the car. Finally, he drove back to Room 16-A of Building T-455.

He put away the things he had bought, unpacked his complete collection of glasses, rinsed out one, and poured scotch into it. There was probably ice around somewhere, he thought, but he decided against going to look for it. He had grown used to iceless whiskey in Greece. He diluted it with water from the bathroom and then unpacked the Zenith from its box. He put the empty glass carton and the empty radio carton in the hall and pulled the desk across the floor next to the bed, so he could put the radio on it. Then he plugged it in, went through the broadcast band, found nothing he liked, and finally got some classical music, fuzzy, with static, but listenable, on the 20-meter band. He lay down on the bed and picked up one of the paperbacks.

There was a knock at the bathroom door.

"Come," Lowell called.

The black man, still in his underwear, stepped inside the room.

"You aren't the biggest white boy I've ever seen," he said. "But you're not actually a midget, yourself." Lowell said nothing.

"Phil Parker," the black man said.

"Hello," Lowell said.

"I thought you went to ask for alternate accommodations," Parker said.

"I went to get booze," Lowell said. "You want scotch or gin, help yourself."

"Thank you," Parker said. He poured scotch in a glass. "You always drink it without ice?"

"I do when I don't have any ice," Lowell replied.

Parker picked up the pitcher which came with the complete set of household glassware and walked out of the room. When he returned the pitcher was full of ice.

"You are a man of many talents, Phil Parker," Lowell said, holding up his glass. "Where did you get the ice?"

"There's a rec room, read bar, down the hall," Parker said, dropping two cubes into Lowell's glass. He met Lowell's eyes. "I would have gone to the Class Six myself, except I thought common decency required that I stick around until someone moved in here. In case, for some reason, having seen me, he might want to move out."

"You want to go half on a refrigerator?" Lowell asked. "I don't want to keep running down the hall for ice like a bellboy, and I do like a cold beer sometimes."

Parker looked at Lowell for a moment before replying. The easiest thing to do was take him at face value as a man who wasn't a bigot. But he had been down that road before. A belief in racial equality sometimes was a fragile thing in the face of peer pressure.

He decided to take a chance. There was something special about this guy.

"There's something you should know about me," Parker said. "Before we become bosom buddies."

"What's that?"

"I'm going to be the honor graduate of this course," Parker said.

"Why in the world would you want to do something like that?" Lowell replied, astonished.

"I'm dead serious, Lowell," Parker said. "That's what you do, if you're colored, and a regular army officer," Parker said. "You do better than the white guys, just to stay even with them."

"Regular army? Funny, you don't look stupid."

"Actually, I'm a near genius," Parker said. "But it may be necessary for me to study at night once in a while. I become violent when someone disturbs me when I am studying. I thought you should be forewarned."

"Do you know where we could buy a refrigerator?" Lowell asked. "The PX?"

"That's not the way it's done," Parker said.

"It's not?"

"Give me a minute to clothe my magnificent ebony body," Parker said. "And I will show you how an old soldier does it."

When Parker returned, he was in fatigues. They had been tailored to fit his body and were stiffly starched. They were not anywhere near new. His boots were highly polished. His insignia and his brass buckle gleamed. He looked, Lowell thought, as if he were ready to stand inspection. Then he changed his mind. He looked as if he were accustomed to wearing a uniform. He thought it was likely that Parker (it was hard to tell how old he was) was a former enlisted man, a career sergeant who had gone to OCS. That would explain both the old soldier's appearance, and his announced intention to be the honor graduate. Lowell thought of Nick.

He was convinced of the accuracy of his assessment of Lieutenant Parker both by Parker's car, a gleaming 1941 Cadillac sedan with a Fort Riley auto safety inspection decal on the windshield, and by what happened next. Parker drove them to the Class Six, the liquor store, where he bought scotch and gin and vermouth, and two bottles of good bourbon. In the car, he made Lowell pay for one of the bottles of bourbon.

Then they drove to the Post Quartermaster Household Goods Warehouse. Parker found the small office used by the noncom in charge of the warehouse.

"Can I help you, Lieutenant?" the sergeant asked.

"I hope so, Sergeant," Parker said to him, closing the office door and setting the two bottles of bourbon in their brown paper bags on the sergeant's desk. "I have a small problem."

"What would that be, Lieutenant?" the sergeant asked, pulling the paper bags down to see what kind of liquor they contained.

"My roommate here has an unusual medical condition," Parker said. "Unless he has a cold beer when he wakes up in the morning, he suffers from melancholy all day."

"I've heard about that disease," the sergeant said.

"So I thought, in the interests of the health of the junior officers, you might be able to see your way clear to issue him a means to keep his beer cool."

"I think something might be worked out, Lieutenant," the sergeant said. He slid the bottles of bourbon off the desk top and into a drawer. "You got wheels?"

They drove back to the Student Officer Company with a refrigerator precariously balanced in the open trunk of the Cadillac. They carried it upstairs to Parker's room.

"I don't think I will be having many visitors," Parker said. "And that means no one will see this refrigerator. If no one sees it, no one will ask any questions, such as, 'How come that lieutenant has got a refrigerator, and I don't?' "

Lowell chuckled. "What were you, Parker, before you were commissioned?"

Parker looked at him, as if surprised by the question.

"If you must know, I was cadet major," he said.

"West Point?" Lowell asked, in surprise.

"Bite your tongue!" Parker said. "Norwich."

"Norwich?"

"You've never heard of it," Parker said flatly. "I'm not surprised. But to widen your education, Norwich for a hundred years has provided the army with the bulk of its brighter cavalry, and now armor, officers."

"I've never heard of it," Lowell repeated.

"It is not, Lowell, what you're thinking," Parker said.

"What am I thinking?"

"It is not a Mechanical and Agricultural College for Negroes with an ROTC program," Parker said. "I was the only colored guy in my graduating class."

"Where is it?"

"Vermont," Parker said. "And where did you go to school? Yale?"

"Harvard."

"How come you're not artillery? I thought Harvard had artillery ROTC."

"I'm not ROTC," Lowell said.

"There is no way a slob like you could have gotten through OCS," Parker said.

"I was directly commissioned," Lowell said.

"What kind of an expert are you?" Parker asked.

"I know how to play polo," Lowell said.

"So why aren't you playing polo?" Parker asked. He didn't seem at all surprised at Lowell's announcement.

"The general I was playing for dropped dead," Lowell said.

"Waterford?" Parker said. "I heard about that. My father and Waterford were pretty good friends."

"Your father was in the army?"

"Mah daddy, and mah gran'daddy, and mah gran'*daddy's* daddy," Parker said, in a mock Negro accent. "White boy, you now runnin' around with a bona fide member of the army establishment, Afro-American division."

"What the hell are you talking about?"

"If you don't know, then I can't explain it to you."

"Try."

"My antecedents have been slurping around in the army trough since, right after the Civil War, they chased the Indians around the plains. They used to call them the 'Buffalo Soldiers,' " Parker said. "My father and my grandfather retired as colonels. My great-grandfather was a master sergeant."

"I'm awed," Lowell said.

"So after fucking around with you for a while, wondering what to do with you, they decided to send you to Basic Officer's Course?"

"Yeah."

"Well, under my expert tutelage, Lieutenant," Parker said, "you may just be able to get through."

There was no overt act of racial discrimination from the first day. The 116 white second lieutenants in Basic Armor Officer's Course 46–3 simply ignored the five black, two Puerto Rican, six Filipino, and three Argentinian officers. And Lowell, the white one who lived with the big coon.

On his part, Parker ignored the four second lieutenants who were black, the Puerto Ricans, and three of the six Filipinos, the three who had gone to West Point. The other three he tolerated. The Argentinians stuck to themselves, eventually moving out of the BOQ entirely to rent an apartment in Elizabethtown, where many of the married second lieutenants also lived.

It was a week before Phil Parker saw Lowell without his T-shirt, and thus the scars, which resembled angry red zippers running up his chest and over his shoulder.

"What the hell happened to you?"

"I walked into a fan," Lowell replied.

"The hell you say," Parker replied.

[TWO]

The day after Parker saw Lowell's fascinating and unexplained scars, Parker learned that Lowell was married, and to a German girl, and shocking him far more, that Lowell's Chevrolet was the Hertz rent-a-car he had picked up at the airport on his way to Fort Knox and simply kept.

It was a Saturday morning, and when Parker went into Lowell's room to wake him for breakfast, Lowell wasn't there. On the way to the mess hall, Parker saw the Chevrolet parked outside a building housing a dozen pay booths for the use of enlisted men undergoing basic training.

When he looked in the car, to make sure it was Lowell's (there was no question about that; Lowell's helmet liner and several of his books were on the back seat), he came across the rental documents from Hertz.

He went in the telephone building and found Lowell sitting on a couch, waiting for something.

"I'm calling my wife," Lowell volunteered when Parker crashed into the seat beside him.

"Why don't you call her collect from the phone in the BOQ?"

"She's in Germany," Lowell said, and while they waited for the international call to be completed, Lowell told him about Ilse.

"Hey, if there's anything I can do," Parker said, "like a little money for a plane ticket, or something. Just speak up. Unscrew your left arm at the elbow and the Friendly Phil Parker Small Loan Company will leap to aid you."

"Money's not the problem," Lowell said. "It's the fucking Immigration Service. They're waiting for the CIC to clear her. They have to be sure she wasn't a Nazi. For Christ's sake, she was sixteen when the war was over." He looked up at Parker. "But thanks, Phil. I appreciate that." There was such gratitude in Lowell's voice, in the look in his eyes, that Parker was embarrassed. He changed the subject.

[**THREE**]

Craig Lowell was sitting on his bed dressed in his shorts with his back up against the headboard. He had a glass of scotch whiskey in his hand, a large black cigar in his mouth, and a copy of *The Infantry Company in the Defense* in his lap. He was no longer as awed by the manual as he had once been, and he had just concluded that if some unsuspecting neophyte placed his air-cooled .30s where the book said they should be placed "for optimum efficiency," he was going to get his ass rolled over the first time he faced an enemy equipped with grenade launchers. At that moment there was a knock at the door.

"Come!" he called.

"Are you decent?" a female voice called.

"I am neither decent nor clothed," he called back. "There is a difference. Wait a minute."

He got out of bed and went to the closet and wrapped himself in a silk dressing gown. Like the luggage, it had belonged to his father, and he had helped himself to it when he returned from Germany and spent his last two days of leave at Broadlawns. He had heard the female outside giggle at his remark, and that pleased him.

He had wondered what King Kong was doing about his sex life, and now he was about to find out.

When he pulled the door open, he was facing an attractive woman in her late twenties or early thirties. She was white, and that surprised him.

"Yes, ma'am?" he said.

"I'm Barbara Bellmon," she said. "I'm looking for Phil Parker."

She was wearing a wedding ring. What was a respectable-looking, even wholesome-looking, married white woman knocking on King Kong's door for? Whatever it was, it was none of his business.

"I'm sorry," he said. "Phil went over to the library. He should be back in an hour, or maybe longer."

"Oh, damn," she said. "Look, I'm an old friend of his. Could you give him a message for me?"

"Certainly."

"Message is simple and classified Top Secret," she said. "Message follows. Bob gets his silver leaf back effective Saturday. Party at the house at 1830. Appearance mandatory."

"Got it," Lowell said. "I'll tell him as soon as he gets back."

"Translated, that means my husband got promoted and I found out before he did," she said.

"How would one offer congratulations under those circumstances?"

"Very simply," she said. "Come to the party with Phil."

"You say you're an old friend of Phil's?"

"I used to baby-sit for him when he was in diapers," she said. "And his father and my husband are very close."

"That would be Colonel Parker," Lowell said, trying to put it all together.

"Colonel Parker and, as of Saturday, *Lt. Col.* Bellmon," she said. "We're all old friends."

"How nice for you," Lowell said.

"I didn't get your name," she said.

"Lowell," he said. "Craig Lowell."

"Well, Craig Lowell, you just tag along with Phil on Saturday night. All you can eat, and more important, all you can drink."

"That's very kind, but I'll be out of town," he said.

"Some other time, then," she said.

At the prescribed hour, Second Lieutenant Philip Sheridan Parker IV presented himself at the quarters of Bob and Barbara Bellmon, a small frame house near the main post, above which a large sign read: "Second-Chance Bellmon's Party."

Barbara Bellmon saw him first, and kissed him on the cheek.

"My, how you've grown, Little Philip," she said.

"And you're a colonel's lady now, again, and not supposed to go around kissing second johns before God and the world," he said.

"Where's John Barrymore?" she asked.

"Who?"

"Your roommate, the one with the silk dressing gown, Harvard accent, and stinking cigar."

"Lowell," Phil Parker said, grinning at the thought of an encounter between Barbara Bellmon and Lowell. "That's right, you met him, didn't you?"

"I invited him to the party."

"He didn't say anything to me," Parker replied.

"Strange man," she said. "Most second lieutenants jump at a chance of free booze."

"He's strange, but he's a good guy, Barbara," Parker said. "He's got money, I think."

"Doing his two years?"

"If he has to serve that long," Parker said.

Bob Bellmon saw him then.

"Jesus Christ, look at this! The last time I saw it, it wasn't an inch over six feet."

"Congratulations, Colonel," Parker said.

"I've been waiting for you," Bellmon said. "We're going to call your old man. If it wasn't for your old man, I wouldn't be here." He grabbed Phil's arm and led him into the crowded living room and to the telephone, and they placed a call to Colonel

Philip Sheridan Parker III, Retired, in Manhattan, Kansas, and the name of Craig Lowell didn't come up again.

[FOUR]

The next Saturday, very early in the morning, Lieutenant Phil Parker was introduced to Ilse Lowell on the telephone. Later, over breakfast in the main post cafeteria, Lowell asked Parker if he had any plans, or whether he would be free to go to Louisville with him.

"What's in Louisville?"

"I've been thinking over what you said about getting a car."

"Perhaps you are not then quite as dense as the evidence suggests," Parker said. "You want to go look at cars?"

"No, I want to buy one," Lowell replied, as if the question was a strange one.

"What kind of car?"

"A Packard."

"A Packard? Packards are driven by movie stars and uppity niggers," Parker said.

"Somebody in Bad Nauheim had a Packard," he said. "A convertible. Ilse said it was the most beautiful automobile she had ever seen."

"Obviously the lady has taste," Parker said. "But have you got the pocketbook to support it?"

"Yeah, Phil," Lowell said, "as a matter of fact, I do."

They went into Louisville in uniform, because Parker had been informed that the Brown Hotel would serve colored officers in uniform. They dropped off the rental car at the airport, had lunch with several drinks in the Brown Hotel, and then went to the Packard dealership on Fourth Street.

The salesman on duty, fully aware that the basic pay of second lieutenants was just over $310 a month, didn't even bother to pitch the two young officers. They had obviously come in solely to gape the Rollson-bodied 1941 convertible on the showroom floor. They certainly couldn't afford a car like that; but on the other hand, they were officers, even if one of them was a nigger, and were unlikely to get the seats dirty or do something else to harm the car.

The 180 convertible had been turned in three months before on a new Packard Clipper by the proverbial Little Old Lady. It had been up on blocks during all of World War II, and there was only a little over 9,000 miles on the clock.

The sales manager had decided to hang on to it to draw customers into the showroom. They weren't making cars like that anymore, and Packard wasn't even going to have a convertible in the line until next year's lineup. The sales manager hung a $6,500 price on it, which was about a thousand more than the car had cost when it was new. He would take a chance, he said, that someone would walk in with more money than brains and pay it. If no one bought it for, say, three or four months, then he would decide what to do with it. In the meantime, it would draw potential customers to the showroom floor.

It was an enormous automobile, built on a 138-inch wheelbase, and was bright yellow, with the Packard stylized swan in chrome sitting on top of a massive grill. The headlights were separate, and the front fenders held spare tires.

The two young soldiers examined the car from front to rear for about three minutes, and then the white one walked over to where the salesman sat in an armchair.

"Can I help you?"

"I just might be interested in that," the white kid said.

"That's $6,500," the salesman said.

"I'll give you six even," the kid said.

"Have you got any idea what the payments would be?" the salesman said. "We'd need a third down, that's more than two thousand, and . . ."

"I'll give you a check for six thousand," the young lieutenant said, interrupting him.

He seemed perfectly serious. Since the sales manager normally didn't come in on Saturdays, the salesman called him at the golf course and told him he had a soldier from Fort Knox who was prepared to write a check right then for six grand for the convertible.

The check he offered was on the Morgan Guaranty Trust of New York. The price was all right, but there was a large question about a second lieutenant having enough cash in his checking account to cover the check. It was finally decided to accept his offer, and to tell him that the car would have to be "gotten ready" and unfortunately there was no one around on Saturday to do that. They would be happy to deliver the car out to Fort Knox on Monday after it had been "gotten ready." That would also give them a chance to call the Morgan Guaranty Trust and see if the check was any good, or whether, as the sales manager half suspected, it was just one more crazy soldier boy from Fort Knox just fucking around with half a load on.

The car was delivered Monday afternoon. It was waiting for Parker and Lowell when they came back to the BOQ to find the academic standings for the first two weeks of the course posted on the BOQ bulletin board.

Parker, Philip S IV was first, with an average of 98.7.

Lowell, Craig W was third, with an average of 97.9.

Parker was delighted. Lowell was amused. He understood why he was getting such good grades. For one thing, the course material was rather simple. It was, in effect, a basic training course for officers upon first entering the army. Lowell had had enlisted basic training, and for all intents and purposes he had been running a company in Greece. Parker had gone to Norwich, a military college. And they had studied, not very hard, nor very long, but apparently long enough and hard enough to be able to beat the tests.

They had a couple of drinks to celebrate and then decided to get a steak at the main post officer's club to "test" the yellow Packard convertible. They put the roof down, and snapped the boot in place, and then, for a joke, Parker insisted on riding in the back seat.

They were both astonished at how often and how snappily they were saluted. Not only by enlisted men, the only people required by military custom to salute second lieutenants, but by officers as well, even one full bird colonel.

It was obviously the car, they decided over their drinks and steaks; and they were correct but not in the way they thought.

Two weeks after the convertible was delivered, Lowell ran into Captain Rudolph G. MacMillan at the Class Six store.

Lowell was coming out of the store with his arms full of booze and ale. There was no way he could salute.

"Hello, Captain MacMillan," he said.

"I'll be damned," MacMillan said. "What the hell are you doing here?" He turned and followed Lowell into the parking lot. The Packard was parked next to a Ford coupe. MacMillan opened the door of the coupe, so that Lowell could unload his whiskey and beer. Lowell put the whiskey and beer in the Packard. He didn't have to have the door opened, for the top and windows were down.

"I don't know why I'm surprised, but I am," MacMillan said, when he realized his error. "That's the sort of thing I should have expected from you, rich boy."

"It's nice to see you, too, Captain," Lowell said.

"Why aren't you in Greece?" MacMillan asked.

"The real question, Captain, sir, is why am I still in the army. Do you remember telling me, sir, that you'd get me out of the service?"

"You know what happened," MacMillan said. "I asked you how come you're not in Greece?"

"I didn't like it there," Lowell said. "People were shooting at me."

"And so you pulled some strings and got out?"

"That sums it up neatly, sir," Lowell said.

"You're in Basic Officer's Course?"

"That's right," Lowell said.

"Maybe you'll learn something," MacMillan said.

"As you told me, Captain, I don't know enough about the army to make a pimple on a good corporal's ass. That was just before you told me I would be able to get out of the army."

"I hope they run your ass off over there," MacMillan said.

"Actually, sir, I'm number three in my class."

MacMillan's face flushed. He looked as if he was going to say something, but he simply turned around and walked away.

"Captain MacMillan," Lowell called; and when MacMillan ignored him, he called his name again so loudly that MacMillan, aware others in the parking lot were looking, had no choice but to turn around.

Lowell saluted crisply. "It was very nice to see you again, Captain MacMillan," he said. "Please extend my best wishes to Mrs. MacMillan, sir."

MacMillan returned the salute and walked into the Class Six store.

It was a week after his meeting with MacMillan before Lowell understood why he and Phil Parker had been so enthusiastically saluted while riding around in the

Packard and why MacMillan had made the crack about the car. The major general commanding Fort Knox also drove a Packard convertible. It was also yellow, but it was a 120, and not nearly so ostentatious as Lowell's 180. They had been saluted in the belief that the car was the commanding general's personal vehicle. It was now believed that Lieutenant Lowell was not only guilty of a breech of etiquette which decreed that lieutenants do not drive automobiles as expensive as the commanding general, but that he (and Parker) were intentionally mocking him (because Parker rode in the back seat with the roof down in the winter, grandly returning the salutes).

They stopped putting the top down, and when they went to the main post, they now went in Phil's old Cadillac; but the damage was done. They had been identified as smart-asses, and there was nothing they could do to alter that perception.

Lt. Col. Bob Bellmon, when he heard about the two wise-ass lieutenants in SOC, one of whom was a nigger who had gone to Norwich, called Phil Parker on the telephone.

"Phil," he said. "A word to the wise should be sufficient. Get yourself a new roommate. I'll speak to the SOC commander, if you like."

"With all respect, sir, I wish you wouldn't do that."

"Goddamn it, Phil, I know that you weren't mocking the general. But the general doesn't know that."

"Sir, neither was Lowell."

"Bullshit."

"Sir, Lowell is my friend."

"Your friend is a wise-ass, and he's going to hurt your career."

"I'll have to take that risk, sir."

"Your loyalty, Phil, is commendable," Bellmon said, dryly. "Don't say you weren't warned."

[**FIVE**]

Even the continued ranking of Second Lieutenants Parker and Lowell at or very near the head of their class did nothing to reduce their ostracism. The word was out that they were a couple of smart-asses, and that was that. They even had a goddamn refrigerator in their room; they thought they were too good to drink with everybody else in the rec room.

But what really pissed their classmates and their instructors was what happened at the retreat parade. There was a regular once-a-month formal retreat parade, at which people got medals and citations, and heard their retirement orders read. Student Officer Company marched over to the main post in formation, a hell of a long walk, especially since nobody in SOC was going to get a medal or a citation, or be retired.

When they had roll call in the SOC area, Lieutenant Lowell did not answer when his name was called. The tactical officer even asked the nigger if he knew where he was, and the nigger said, "No, sir."

So they marched over to the main post without him. While they were walking at route march, before they got near the main post and the tac officer started calling cadence, it was whispered about that the smart-ass nigger lover had finally fucked up. He should have known there would be roll call and that he would get caught ducking the formation. He'd have a hard time explaining by indorsement hereon (which is probably the way they would handle it) why he had absented himself without authorization from a scheduled formation.

But when they were all lined up, and the school commandant stood up in front and bellowed, "Persons to be decorated, Front and center, March!" there was the nigger lover, right at the head of the line. And when the adjutant stepped to the microphone and called, "Attention to orders," it was something none of them had ever heard before.

"His Most Gracious Majesty, Philip, by the Grace of God, King of the Hellenes, is pleased to bestow upon Lieutenant Craig W. Lowell, United States Army, the Order of St. George and St. Andrew with all the rights and privileges thereunto pertaining, in token of His Most Gracious Majesty's appreciation of Lieutenant Lowell's outstanding valor and military prowess while attached to the 27th Royal Hellenic Mountain Division."

It wasn't even a regular-sized medal. It was about the size of a coffee cup saucer, and the VIP from Washington didn't pin it on him, he hung it over his shoulder on a purple ribbon six inches wide.

"Hey," one of his classmates asked *sotto voce*, "who the fuck are the Hellenes?"

"The Greeks, you clod-kicking hillbilly," Lieutenant Parker informed him.

Smart-ass nigger.

For a couple of days, the citations for his medals (they'd also hung a U.S. medal on him, an unimportant one, the Army Commendation Medal, called the Green Hornet) were on the SOC-TAS bulletin board, and then somebody tore them down.

[SIX]

When he finally got word that Ilse had her visa, Craig Lowell went to the orderly room and asked the Student Officer Company commander for a few days off. He wanted to look for an apartment for his wife, he said, and then he wanted to go to New York to meet her plane. He was sure, he said, that he could make up what academic work he would lose. His overall average so far was 98.4.

"You're in the army, Lowell," the major who was his company commander said. "Even if you don't seem to fully understand that. Don't let that goddamn medal go to your head. You can't just take off whenever you feel like it to handle your personal affairs. I can see no reason why an adult female can't get off one airplane and onto another by herself. And when she gets here, you'll be given two hours off, like everybody else, to go by post housing."

"Sir, I hadn't planned to live on the post," Lowell said.

"Quarters are available, Lieutenant. You will live on the post. Is there anything else?"

When he told Parker what that chickenshit sonofabitch had said, Parker said it was what he should have expected for being a nigger lover. And he fixed the business about quarters (probably with a couple of bottles of bourbon; Lowell never knew how for sure). The day before Ilse was scheduled to arrive, he took him to the company-grade family housing area, where barracks had been converted into apartments. A neat little painted sign LT LOWELL was on the door of one of them. When they went inside, it was full of brand-new furniture from the quartermaster warehouse. All they had to do was push it around where it looked best.

Parker didn't go with him to meet Ilse at the airport in Louisville, and he was sort of glad that he didn't. Because when he saw Ilse coming awkwardly down the steps from the plane, as big as a house, looking frightened and pale, and when he hugged her, both of them cried, and he wouldn't have wanted Phil to see that.

Ilse told him that Sharon Felter and the elder Felters had met her plane. Then they had driven her to someplace called Newark and put her on the plane to Louisville.

He was disappointed with Ilse's reaction to the Packard. She said it was beautiful all right, but with her pregnant and his mother sick, he must be really out of his mind to think they could afford something like that.

"Liebchen," Lowell said. "I've got a lot of money. *We've* got a lot of money. Much more than most people do."

"I know," she said, and he understood that she didn't have the first faint idea what he meant. It was not the time to get into it, not now.

Ilse was pathetically pleased with the apartment and the furnishings, and he wondered how she would have reacted if he had gone through with his original notion to call Andre Pretier and tell him he was married, and would Andre either meet his wife's plane or at least send a chauffeur and a car and see that she got on the Louisville plane.

If Sharon hadn't seemed so delighted that she could go and meet the plane, he'd have had to do something like that; and if learning that her baby was married unduly upset his mother, fuck it. She was going to have to find out sooner or later anyway. She was about to be a grandmother.

But Sharon had really wanted to go meet the plane, and the problem of how and when to tell his mother—and for that matter, his grandfather—about Ilse could be delayed for a while.

Ilse smiled, but she really didn't understand the flowers Parker had sent to the apartment—a huge horseshoe, with the words DEEPEST SYMPATHY in gold foil letters on a purple sash hung on it. Ilse didn't understand, if that was what Americans sent to a funeral, why Craig thought it was so funny.

Ilse's nearly joyous reaction to the crappy little apartment with its veneer furniture and thin rugs (Lowell thought the shag living room carpet looked like an enormous bath towel) made him face what he thought was an unpleasant truth about his wife. She wanted him to think she came from a good background—that *von* Greiffenberg bullshit—but when he pressed her for details, she didn't want to talk about her family. She'd tried once to tell him her father had been a count and a colonel, and that the castle in Marburg (it was more of a villa than a castle; didn't she know the difference?) was the house she had grown up in.

If that was so, why was she broke? Why was she in Bad Nauheim, doing what she was doing? The truth to be faced was that she was lying through her teeth about her father (or else he had been a Nazi, which was something else to consider). She was ashamed that she had been a whore (or at least that she had been willing to be a whore, and would have been one if he hadn't come along), and so she was making up stories. So what was wrong with that?

She probably thought, he decided, that he was telling her a lie, too, about having a lot of money.

The truth of the matter was that he didn't give a damn if she had been raised in a cave by pig farmers. And he hadn't exactly been honest with her, either, when he'd told her his mother was sick, and that that was the reason she couldn't meet the plane and her daughter-in-law. His mother didn't even know he was married. He had enough problems as it was, without having his mother flip her lid and causing trouble.

He had not completed an overseas tour, so he was eligible for one when he graduated from Basic Officer's Course. With a little bit of luck, he would be sent to Japan or Alaska, someplace where he could take her with him. But he could also be sent to Korea where you couldn't take dependents, or back to Germany, maybe even to the Constab. You couldn't have German nationals as dependents in Germany.

She might find herself as alone here as she had been in Germany.

The thing to do was say nothing that was liable to upset her. Especially now, just before the baby was to be born.

[SEVEN]

Mrs. Ilse von Greiffenberg Lowell was delivered of a seven-pound four-ounce son at the U.S. Army Hospital, Fort Knox, Kentucky, two days before her husband was graduated, third in his class, from Basic Officer's Course.

Ilse was so happy that she was afraid something would go wrong, she told her husband. She was so happy that she wept when a sterling silver teething cup was delivered to the hospital with a card reading, "Love, Mother Pretier." She didn't suspect at all that it had been sent by her husband.

All she cared was that the baby was healthy and that Craig wasn't going to be sent overseas, the way Phil Parker was. Craig had been assigned to the Armor School as an instructor in the Tank Gunnery Division. They were sending Phil all the way to Japan.

The child was christened at post chapel number three following the rite prescribed by the Episcopal Church. It was necessary to have two godfathers and one godmother. Because it was of obvious importance to Ilse, and because he didn't know anyone else he could ask, he called Roxy MacMillan and explained his problem. Roxy said that she would be delighted, and so would Mac, but when they got to the chapel, she said that Mac had been called away. So Peter-Paul Lowell's godfathers had the same name. His godfathers were Lt. Philip Sheridan Parker IV and Colonel (Retired) Philip Sheridan Parker III. Phil's father had come down to Knox from Kansas for the graduation parade. He remembered Knox, he said, when it had six buildings and four outhouses, and he wanted to see how it had changed.

Colonel Parker stayed with the Bellmons, and when Bob Bellmon told him of his concern about Phil's roommate, Parker said that he had actually rather liked Lowell, but in any event it was all over now.

[EIGHT]
Fort Knox, Kentucky
18 October 1947

First Lieutenant Sanford Felter returned from the U.S. Army Military Advisory Group, Greece, with two Green Hornets for his outstanding administrative skill (which was fairly routine for a first john who had spent his entire tour with one of the divisions,) and with the Legion of Merit, which was unusual. He was also decorated by the Greek government with the Order of Knight of St. Gregory, First Class.

In the Comments section of his last USAMAG-G efficiency report, he was described as "a small in stature, erect officer who has constantly demonstrated a grasp of military affairs beyond that expected of an officer of his grade and experience. He is unhesitatingly recommended for command in the grade of captain in combat. However, this officer has indicated a preference for a career in military intelligence and in the opinion of the rating officer would make an outstanding intelligence officer." The efficiency report was "enthusiastically endorsed" by Lt. Gen. James Van Fleet, USAMAG-G Commanding General.

On the morning of his fifth day in the apartment over the Old Warsaw Bakery on the corner of Aldine Street and Chancellor Avenue in Newark, N.J., the mailman delivered a thick manila envelope, registered, return receipt requested. It contained a hundred copies of Paragraph 33, Department of the Army General Order 101:

****

33. FIRST LIEUTENANT SANFORD T. FELTER, 0-357861, INFANTRY, Transient Officer Detachment, Camp Kilmer, N.J., is placed on temporary duty and Will Proceed to U.S. Army Language School, the Presidio, San Francisco, Calif, to undergo Course No. 49-002 (Greek Language). Off will report no later than 5 January 1948. Upon completion of course of

instruction, Off is further placed on TDY and WP to the Infantry School, Fort Benning, Ga., to undergo Course No. 49-444 (Advanced Inf Off Course). Upon Completion of course of instruction, Off is transferred in grade and WP to the U.S. Army Counterintelligence Center, Camp Holabird, 1019 Dundalk Avenue, Baltimore 19, Md. to undergo Course No. 49-101 (Classified). Upon reporting to Fort Holabird, Off will be detailed Military Intelligence and all further personnel actions will be under the Assistant Chief of Staff, G-2, Hq, Dept of the Army. Off will be in per diem status while attending the Army Language School. Off will be in Temporary Change of Station status while attending the Inf School. Assgmt to Fort Holabird is PCS. Off auth tvl by private auto. Off is auth to be accompanied by dependents at no expense to govt to the Presidio and the Infantry Center. Tvl of dependents and household goods to Ft Holabird is auth from Newark, N.J.

FOR THE CHIEF OF STAFF
Edward Witsell
Major General, The Adjutant General

When he knew what his orders were, and after he had been home two weeks, he and Sharon loaded all their clothes in the Buick Super and started out for the Presidio, via Fort Knox, where Craig Lowell was stationed.

Craig and Ilse and the baby (Peter-Paul, like the candy bar, and called P. P. for a couple of reasons) were living in a converted barracks near Godman Field and driving an enormous old yellow Packard convertible. Despite the car (which was, after all, nearly six years old), Sandy wondered if maybe Craig had just been telling stories about having a lot of money. Their quarters were furnished with strictly GI furniture, and Ilse didn't seem to be expensively dressed. But then the very first night when they were playing gin rummy and the pencil broke, Sandy went to the GI desk to get another. When he opened the drawer he found five uncashed paychecks and a statement from the Morgan Guaranty Trust in New York showing a checking balance of $11,502.85 and was a little ashamed of himself for doubting Craig.

He also saw a signature block on a training schedule for the Department of Tactics. Craig was a gunnery instructor in the Tank Gunnery Division of the Department of Tactics. The signature block was:

Robert F. Bellmon
LT. COLONEL, ARMOR
DEPUTY DEPARTMENT COMMANDER

He asked Craig what he looked like, and Craig described him.

"Why do you ask?" Craig then asked.

"I know him," Sandy said. "I was—" he stopped. "He's the officer I asked for the Greece assignment."

"That sounds like him, the chickenshit sonofabitch," Craig said, bitterly. "He's prick enough to let a dumb lieutenant volunteer to get his balls shot off."

Sharon and Ilse were embarrassed at the outburst, and especially at the language, and Sandy let it drop.

The next night, however, while Craig was off running a night-fire exercise (he would have liked to have seen that, but Craig told him that with Chickenshit Bob around, there was no chance), he took Sharon to the movies (Ilse didn't like to put P. P. in the officer's club nursery and begged off). When they came out, after he'd thought it over carefully, he decided it was the right and proper thing to do to pay a courtesy call on Colonel Bellmon.

Lt. Col. Bellmon had been assigned quarters near the parade ground on the main post, not far at all from the theater. They were two-story brick houses, looking like something from an Andy Hardy movie. Middletown, U.S.A.

Sharon was a little nervous. She really had no experience with the army at all, just the two dances she'd gone to at West Point. And the truth of the matter was that the only confidence that Sandy had was in the training he'd received at West Point in "Customs of the Service" as a yearling. Calls were required of junior officers upon their seniors when reporting for duty. Cards, one corner turned up, were deposited on a tray provided for that purpose in the foyer of quarters. Calls were encouraged, but not required, upon senior officers with whom one was acquainted, when visiting officially, or unofficially, other posts and stations.

As he walked up the concrete walk between the closely cropped sections of lawn, Sandy suddenly remembered the rest of it. Wives were expected to wear gloves and hats. Sharon had a hat on, but no gloves. Well, it was too late to do anything about that.

He stood under the porch light and took a card from his wallet. It was a little smeared. He'd bought a hundred of them, but the only time he had ever used one was to put it on the mailbox at the bakery so he would be sure to get his mail.

But there was nothing he could do about that, either. He turned up the corner of the card the way you were supposed to and rang the bell.

A tall, attractive woman wearing a turtleneck sweater and slacks answered the door.

"Hello," she said cheerfully.

"Good evening," Felter replied and thrust the card at her. She smiled, and he saw tolerance in the smile. He was being gently laughed at.

"You're reporting in, Lieutenant . . ." She read the name. "Felter?"

"No, ma'am. I'm passing through. I just wanted to pay my respects to Colonel Bellmon."

She turned. "Bob!" It was a shout. "Come in, please. I'm Mrs. Bellmon."

They stood awkwardly in the foyer. Colonel Bellmon, a plaid sweater over his khaki shirt, a glass in his hand, came into the foyer. For a moment, Sandy was afraid he wouldn't remember him. Or wouldn't want to.

"Felter," Colonel Bellmon finally said. "I'll be damned."

"Yes, sir."

"Well, come in," Bellmon said. "I'm glad to see you. You've been assigned to Knox?"

"No, sir," Sandy said. "Sir, may I present my wife?"

"It's a pleasure to meet you, Mrs. Felter," Bellmon said. "I gather you've introduced yourself to Barbara? Barbara, Lieutenant Felter was in on Task Force Parker."

The women shook hands. Barbara Bellmon looked at Felter with new interest.

"You say you've been assigned here?" Bellmon said, leading them into a well-furnished living room. There was a silver-framed photograph on the mantelpiece of Major General Peterson K. Waterford sitting erect on a horse.

"No, sir, I'm just passing through. I'm on my way to the Presidio to the Language School."

"Well, I'm glad you stopped in to see me," Bellmon said, and he sounded perfectly sincere. "I often wondered what happened to you in Greece."

"It was a very interesting assignment, sir," Felter said. "That's why I came. To thank you."

"I'm glad to hear that," Bellmon said. He looked thoughtful. "I'm really not just saying that, Felter. I've often wondered about it. The truth of the matter is, I had learned an hour or so before I talked to you that my father-in-law had just dropped dead." He gestured toward the framed photograph on the mantelpiece. "I wondered if I was in full possession of my faculties, is what I'm saying."

"I think it was a good assignment, sir," Felter said.

"And now you're going to the Presidio. And from there, no doubt, to Dundalk High?"

It took Felter a moment to catch up on that, to remember that the U.S. Army Counterintelligence School was located at 1019 *Dundalk* Avenue, Baltimore 19, Maryland.

"Yes, sir," Felter said. "Via the Infantry School. Advanced Officer's Course."

"Fine, fine," Colonel Bellmon said. Mrs. Bellmon arrived surprisingly quickly, Sandy thought, with a tea tray. That made him feel better. If her husband were really not glad to see him, there would be no tea tray.

"And what brings you to Knox? Certainly not just to see me."

"No, sir, I have a friend here," Felter said.

"Who's that?"

"Lieutenant Craig Lowell, sir," Felter said. "I believe he works for you."

"I'm disappointed in you, Felter," Bellmon said. "Until you said that, I had an image of you as one more responsible member of the Long Gray Line. You met him in Greece, I gather?"

"Yes, sir."

"The Duke is not one of Bob's favorite lieutenants, I'm afraid," Barbara Bellmon said, laughing.

"He has managed to antagonize just about everybody on the post," Bellmon said. "Me, most of all."

"I'm sorry to hear that," Felter said, realizing that it didn't surprise him. He regretted bringing up Lowell's name. "Can I ask what he's done?"

"What Bob cannot stand is being outwitted," Barbara Bellmon said, laughing. "It destroys his image of himself."

"I can't stand being mocked," Bellmon said. "I'm a soldier, and I don't like to see officers mock the army." Then he softened. "But you're right, honey, that bastard has outwitted me."

"Tell him what he did," Barbara Bellmon said. "You're making it sound as if he ran off with army funds."

"Do you know about the medal?" Bellmon asked. "The one he got the Greeks to give him?"

"Yes, sir," Felter said. "I was there when he earned it."

"You were? What's it for?"

"He assumed command of a Greek company after the Greek officers were killed," Sandy said. "And, although he was pretty badly wounded, he kept the communists from breaking through our lines."

"You know that for a fact?" Bellmon asked, sharply.

"Yes, sir. I was with the relief column."

"Goddamn it," Bellmon said. "He did it again. When I asked him where he got it, he said it was for his contribution to Greco-American relations."

Barbara Bellmon laughed heartily.

"Goddamnit, that's not funny," Bellmon said.

"I think it's hilarious," Barbara said.

"It is not funny to mock decorations for valor," Bellmon said. "That's not funny at all."

"You're being unfair, Bob," Barbara Bellmon said. "Tell them the whole story."

"OK," Bellmon said. "I'll tell you my assessment of your friend, Felter, and you correct me where I go wrong. Before he was assigned to me, he had already earned himself a reputation as a smart-ass while he was in Basic Officer's Course. The general is very proud of his Packard automobile. A yellow convertible. So your friend shows up in a bigger, fancier yellow Packard convertible. You can imagine how the general liked that."

"I thought it was funny," Barbara Bellmon said.

"The general didn't," Bellmon said. "And neither did I. If you think about it, that's a pretty expensive little mockery. I hate to think what his monthly payments were on that Packard."

"Sir?" Felter said, hesitantly, and Bellmon looked at him. "Sir, Lowell is well off. I mean, he's rich. He can afford a Packard or anything else he wants to drive."

"Oh," Bellmon said. "Well, that explains a lot, I suppose."

"Tell him about the medal," Barbara Bellmon said.

"Well, the general passed the word that he wanted your friend off the post ninety seconds after he finished Basic Officer's Course. He was going to send him to Korea. He was assigned to the Department of Tactics, and I put him to work as a gunnery instructor, having found out that he didn't know anything at all about tank gunnery. I figured that just might humble him."

"And it turns out, Lieutenant," Barbara Bellmon said, "that he seems to have some mysterious, otherworldy ability to control projectiles in flight. He *wills* a hit. He promptly became the darling of the enlisted men, those old sergeants who think second lieutenants are useless. His students have constantly done much better than any other lieutenant's students. But that's still not the story of the medal."

"But it is of the sergeants," Bellmon said. "Now, certainly, I don't hate all Germans. There are good Germans and I'm the first to admit it. But the facts are that the German girls who marry Americans are, by and large, looking for a meal ticket. So far as I know, Mrs. Lowell is a lady in every respect."

"I'm glad you said that," Barbara Bellmon said, icily.

"I like Ilse very much," Sharon said, suddenly. It was the first time she had opened her mouth. "I like her and I feel sorry for her. She lost her father in the war, and here she is all alone with a baby."

"I like her, too," Barbara Bellmon said. "What little I've seen of her. Sometimes, Bob, you make me sick."

Felter picked up on that. It meant acceptance of them by Mrs. Bellmon. Otherwise she would have kept her mouth shut and told her husband off when they were alone.

"Be that as it may," Bellmon went on, obviously uncomfortable, "she is an officer's lady, and she is not supposed to find her friends from among the enlisted wives. And second lieutenants are not supposed to run around with the sergeants, either."

"Put yourself in that girl's shoes, Bob," Barbara Bellmon said. "How would you like to go to a party and have all the women make it pretty clear to you that they think you're a prostitute who latched on to an American meal ticket?"

"How terrible for her!" Sharon said.

"It's your job, Barbara," Bellmon said, "to stop that sort of thing."

"When I had the chance, I did what I could," Barbara Bellmon replied.

"The point is, she didn't give you the chance, because she didn't go to officer's ladies meetings. And your friend, Felter, never went to the officer's club or to official parties."

"And socialized with the enlisted men," Felter said. He wasn't surprised to hear that. In Ioannina, he could get away with that because of the circumstances. He could not get away with it in a garrison situation, where the customs of the service, the rigid distinctions between officers and enlisted men, were rigidly observed.

"I called him in," Bellmon went on, "and had a little talk with him. I didn't like his attitude at all, but there was nothing I could put my finger on. My father told me that before the 1928 Manual for Court-Martial, there was an offense called 'silent insolence.' If that was still in effect, I could have had him tried. All I could do, however, under the circumstances, was let him go. But then I wrote him a DF . . ."

"Excuse me?" Sharon interrupted. "A what?"

"A DF," Bellmon explained. "It stands for distribution form. The next stop down from an official letter, and one step up from a note."

"I'm sorry, I must sound stupid," Sharon said.

"Don't be silly," Barbara Bellmon said.

"Anyway, I wrote him a DF telling him that it was considered important for officers to participate in the social activities of their organization, and that I expected him to appear, in the prescribed uniform, at all subsequent such events."

"And he didn't show up?" Felter asked.

"Oh, did he show up!" Barbara Bellmon said. "General Dowbell-Howe of the British Royal Tank Corps was given an official dinner. The invitations said dress uniform with medals. That meant the general and the chief of staff and a couple of the senior colonels came in dress blues. Bob doesn't even have any. Everybody else came in pinks and greens. Your friend, Lieutenant, shows up in mess dress. God only knows where he got it, but he showed up in it. Wearing his medals. The Army of Occupation Medal, the Army Commendation Medal, and this enormous thing pinned to the jacket and a purple sash. His Greek medal. He looked like something out of Sigmund Romberg operetta."

"I don't know what mess dress is," Sharon said.

"A little jacket like a bartender's," Barbara said. "With a vest. White tie and stand-up collar. The trousers have colored stripes, gold for armor in his case. And a cape. With a yellow lining. God, he was spectacular!"

"I sent him home the moment I saw him and told him that I expected to have on my desk, in writing, at 0700 the next morning, his explanation for his conduct," Bellmon said. There was a touch of a smile at his face. "Why he was out of uniform."

"And your friend sent him a copy of the regulation which encouraged the optional wearing of mess dress at all official functions at which dress uniform was required."

"Sir, is it possible that he was trying to comply with his orders to the best of his ability?" Felter said, loyally. "I mean, where I would have to think a long time about buying mess dress uniform, Craig wouldn't have to worry about it. He'd just order it."

"I don't think so, Felter," Bellmon said. "He was doing it on purpose. He's a real guardhouse lawyer when he wants to be."

"Tell him about the pistol range, Bob," Barbara said. "That really did it."

"ARs, as you know, call for the annual qualification by commissioned personnel with the .45," Bellmon said. "Lowell, as a token of the affection and respect in which he is held by his seniors, was named range officer for the Tactics Department."

"And he ran it exactly by the book," Barbara Bellmon said, chuckling.

"You really think he's funny, don't you?" Bellmon said.

"Honey, he reminds me of my father," Barbara said. "Think about it, you know he does. Fancy uniform. Always making waves."

"What your friend Lowell did, Felter, was certify that thirty-eight of the fifty-one officers of the Tactics Department had failed to qualify."

"Now, wait a minute," Barbara Bellmon said. "You stood up for him for that.

You said you would have done the same thing, if you had the courage, when you were a lieutenant."

"I never had the smart-ass reputation Lowell does," Bellmon said. "When the colonel heard about it, he was furious. He'd already lost one full day's duty from fifty-one officers, and now he was going to lose a full day's duty from the thirty-eight who had failed to qualify. He was convinced Lowell had failed them on purpose."

"So he sent them back out and thirty-one failed the second time around," Barbara said.

"Mrs. Bellmon," Felter asked, "your father was General Waterford, wasn't he?"

"Why, yes, he was."

"Unless I'm mistaken, Mrs. Bellmon," Felter said, "it was General Waterford who commissioned Lowell."

"What did you say?" Col. Bellmon said.

"I said, I think General Waterford is the one who commissioned Lowell from the ranks."

"Your friend pulled some smart-ass guardhouse lawyer trick and had himself commissioned as a finance officer," Bellmon said. "I checked. I wondered where he got a commission."

"Why would my father do that?" Barbara Bellmon asked, visibly interested.

"As I understand it, Mrs. Bellmon," Felter said, "General Waterford wanted Lowell to play on his polo team. And he couldn't, because he was a private."

"Oh, that sounds like Daddy!" Barbara Bellmon said, and really started to laugh. "Call me Barbara, Lieutenant, please."

Bellmon jumped to his feet and went to a telephone on a small table by the door. He dialed a number. "Roxy," he said. "This is Bob Bellmon. Is Mac there?" There was a pause. "Sorry to bother you at home, Mac. But I have just heard an incredible story that I want to check out. What do you know about General Waterford commissioning Lieutenant Lowell?" There was a much longer pause. "I wish I had known this earlier, MacMillan," Colonel Bellmon said, coldly. "I can't imagine why you didn't think I would be interested." Then he hung up.

He nodded at Barbara, who laughed out loud again, and then he said to Felter: "Score one for you, Super Sleuth. And that damned MacMillan knew it all the time and never said a word to me."

"MacMillan," Barbara said, chuckling again, "knew of the high esteem in which you held Lieutenant Lowell. He wanted to put as much distance between himself and Lowell as he could. I think that is known, darling, as covering one's ass. And we know how good Mac is at that, don't we?"

Bellmon gave his wife a dirty look.

"Well, now," Barbara Bellmon went on, brightly. "Now that we know that he and Daddy were friends, we'll have to have Lieutenant and Mrs. Lowell to dinner, won't we? I wonder how that's going to go over with the colonel?"

Bellmon frowned a moment, and then smiled. "Since the colonel thinks your father was at least as infallible as the Pope, it should be very interesting." He reached over and patted Felter's knee.

"Felter, you never cease to amaze me," he said. "You're a fountain of information nobody else has."

[NINE]

Barbara Bellmon, who was the daughter and granddaughter of a general officer, and who regarded her present role in life as simply marking time until Bob got his stars, made up with great care the guest list for the "little dinner" she arranged for the lieutenants and their wives.

First of all, she wanted to do something nice for the Lowells, especially for the wife, who had been treated shabbily. And she knew that Bob liked Felter and Felter's wife and that he wanted to introduce him to the establishment here. It would be obvious to everyone that since the Felters and the Lowells would be the only junior officers present that they were someone of whom the Bellmons thought a great deal.

Captain and Mrs. Rudolph G. MacMillan were not on Barbara Bellmon's guest list. Barbara felt sorry for Roxy, who would quickly get the point of not being invited. Roxy was incapable of cutting someone or hurting someone's feelings. MacMillan had simply, with his usual skill, protected his ass. Lowell was on some people's s-list, and MacMillan didn't want to get splattered. Sometimes, Barbara could not stand MacMillan. He was supposed to be an officer and a gentleman. But he was only an officer, as he had proved here.

MacMillan, she knew, would work his way back into Bob's good graces. For one thing, he had a skin like an alligator. More important, she knew she would never be able to completely break him off from Bob. They'd been in the damned POW camp together, and Bob had some absurd notion that he had failed Mac when they were there. He would carry Mac on his back, get him out of scrapes, as long as they were in the army.

There was going to be an element of humor, too. Barbara could hardly wait until the colonel, who referred to Lieutenant Lowell as that "blond-headed pissant," found out the pissant had been a lot closer to her father than the colonel had ever been.

There would be some dropped jaws from the other lieutenant colonels, too, when they saw Lowell and his German wife. And they would probably drop even further when they saw that the Bellmons were having as their guest of honor a slight, already balding little Jew, who would deliver a little talk after dinner on the functioning of the U.S. Army Military Advisory Group, Greece.

Barbara decided that she would call Lieutenant Lowell's quarters and ask his wife and Felter's to "help" her with the arrangements for the dinner. She didn't need any help, but if they came early, she could brief them on who was who at the party. Neither one of them, obviously, had had any experience at all in dealing with either the wives of senior officers or the senior officers themselves. And that was an important part of the army.

Barbara had no way of knowing that Craig Lowell's reaction to her request was that she had a lot of goddamned nerve asking her guests to help set up her stupid party. Fortunately, Sandy Felter correctly guessed Barbara Bellmon's motives, and he drove the women to the Bellmons' quarters at five in the afternoon and then spent from five fifteen to six forty-five, when it was time for them to go to the party, keeping Lowell from drinking.

After Barbara had finished her briefing, Bob Bellmon went out of his way to be charming to the young women. He complimented them on their looks and opened a bottle of Rhine wine for them, partly because Lowell's wife was German and partly out of concern that if he gave either of them anything stronger, they would get tight.

"What part of Germany are you from, Mrs. Lowell?" he asked, as he poured the Rhine wine.

"Hesse," Ilse said.

"Oh, I know Hesse," he said. "Where in Hesse?"

"A small city," Ilse replied. "Marburg an der Lahn."

Of course, he thought. Marburg was near Bad Nauheim, where she apparently had met Lowell. And then he thought of something else, and the thought pleased him.

"Oddly enough, Mrs. Lowell," he said, "both my wife's father, General Waterford, and myself, had a good friend from Marburg."

"Did you really?" Ilse asked.

"A German officer. He had gone to the French cavalry school at Samur with General Waterford; and when I was captured, he was the commandant of my prison camp. A really fine man. His name was von Greiffenberg."

"What did you say?" Ilse said, barely audibly.

"I said my friend's name was Peter-Paul von Greiffenberg," Bellmon repeated.

"Herr Oberst Bellmon," Ilse said, *"Oberst Graf Peter-Paul von Greiffenberg war mein Vater."*

"Oh, my God!" Bellmon said.

Sharon, thinking she had to translate, said, "She said the officer you said was your friend was her father, Colonel."

"I speak German," Bellmon said, more sharply than he intended. Then, much more loudly than he intended, he called his wife's name.

Barbara came quickly into the living room.

"What's the matter?" she asked. She saw the look on Ilse Lowell's face and on her husband's. Ilse was fighting back tears.

"Mrs. Lowell," Bellmon said, "would you please be good enough to tell my wife who your father was?"

"My father," Ilse said, speaking slowly and precisely in English, "was an officer the colonel tells me he knew and that your father knew."

Barbara looked at her husband.

"Von Greiffenberg," he said. He pointed his hand at Ilse. "That's Peter-Paul von Greiffenberg's daughter."

"My God!" Barbara said.

"Goddamnit, he did it to me again!" Bellmon said.

Barbara looked at him in confusion for a moment, until she took his meaning.

"Don't be an ass," she snapped. "How was he to know you knew him?" Then she saw the worried look on Ilse's face. "Ilse, honey," she said, "it's all right. It's just that Bob really admired your father, and he feels like a fool because you've been here so long, and so alone, and he didn't know who you were."

Lieutenants Lowell and Felter arrived at the Bellmon quarters at the same time as did the colonel and his lady. The colonel was surprised to see Lowell, but not nearly as surprised as he was by how Bellmon greeted them.

"My wife tells me, Lowell, that there was no reason for you to presume that I knew your father-in-law. Somewhat against my better judgment, I have decided to go along with her reasoning."

"I have no idea what you're talking about, Colonel," Lowell said.

"Colonel Graf Peter-Paul von Greiffenberg is who I'm talking about, Lieutenant," Bellmon said. "Your father-in-law. And one of the finest officers it has ever been my privilege to know."

Lowell looked at him and saw he was dead serious. So Ilse was telling the truth about her father being a colonel after all, he thought. I'll be goddamned!

Barbara heard his raised voice and came rushing up. She smiled broadly at the colonel and his lady.

"The most wonderful thing has just happened," she said. "We've just learned that Mrs. Lowell's father was an old and dear friend of my father's and of Bob's. He was the commandant of Bob's prison camp."

"Mrs. Lowell's father?"

"Was Colonel Count Peter-Paul von Greiffenberg!" Barbara said.

"Extraordinary," the colonel said. "Well, how about that!"

There were cocktails and then a sit-down dinner, after which Bob Bellmon, not feeling much pain, repeated the story of the extraordinary coincidence.

"As some of you know," he said, "I was liberated from Russian internment by Task Force Parker, Colonel Philip Sheridan Parker III. The man who located us, Lieutenant Sanford T. Felter, is the man we're honoring tonight. He's just returned from Greece, and I've asked him to tell us what's going on over there."

Lieutenant Felter, once he was called on, spoke with a surprising lucidity about the functioning of a military advisory group. With great skill he traced the Greek operation from the beginning until he had left it. Barbara decided that Bob was right. Felter was as smart as a whip, a far better officer than he looked capable of being.

She was worried about Lieutenant Lowell. He had had entirely too much to drink, from the predinner cocktails through the postdinner brandy, and was now sitting with the brandy bottle before him, leaning back on the legs of his chair, listening with what looked like interest to Felter's little speech.

And then Felter lit the fuse.

"My service in USAMAG-G was entirely on the staff," he said. "Lieutenant Lowell was on the line. I'm sure he could offer something of value to add to what I've said."

"You got it, Mouse," Lowell said, waving his hand drunkenly, deprecatingly. "I can't think of a thing to add. Thank you just the same."

One of the lieutenant colonels was drunk, too. Delighted with his own wit, he said, "Since you've found fault with everything in the Department of Tactics, Lowell, I'm surprised you didn't find a good deal wrong with the way General Van Fleet ran the Greek operation."

"Van Fleet did a superb job with the crap they sent him," Lowell replied, matter-of-factly.

"General Van Fleet, you mean, Lieutenant," the lieutenant colonel snapped, before he was shushed by his wife.

"Big Jim," Lowell said, agreeably, helping himself to more brandy. *"That* Van Fleet. Superb officer."

"I would be interested in your assessment of the line, Lieutenant," the Colonel, Bob's boss, said. If Lowell was good enough for Porky Waterford, perhaps he had made too hasty a judgment of him. After all, the boy did get that fancy medal and was married to the daughter of a German officer who was an old friend of Waterford's.

"I don't think so," Lowell said, pleasantly.

Lowell let the chair fall forward onto its four legs. He drained his brandy glass and stood up. Barbara exchanged glances with Bob. There was nothing that could be done now except pray.

"There were, as I see it, two major errors in the way we handled Greece," Lowell began, now dead serious. "The first was that we tried to superimpose our ideas and our organization on theirs. We simply presume that we know all there is to know about organization and that everybody else is doing it wrong. Bullshit.

"The second error, which compounded the first, was in the selection of officers. I was rather typical of the officers we sent over there. I was absolutely unqualified, and I wasn't alone. We had a motley collection of incompetents other people were happy to get rid of. We had the failures, the ignorant, and the cowardly."

"See here, Lowell!" one of the guests protested.

"By the time I left," Lowell went on, undaunted, "and I wasn't there long, we had gotten rid of most of the incompetents. They had been shipped home, sometimes in a box or put to work counting rations, or shot for cowardice. Or, as in my case, somehow learned their job by doing it."

"Wisdom from the mouth of a babe," one of the colonels snorted.

"What did he say about getting shot for cowardice?" a wife asked in a loud whisper.

"The next time you gentlemen mount an operation like that," Lowell went on, "I respectfully suggest that you send your best officers, not your worst, officers whose knowledge of warfare goes beyond the field manuals." They were glowering at him. It was not the position of a second lieutenant to publicly challenge the conduct of a military operation.

Mimicking a lecturer at the Armor School, Lowell said, "I will now entertain questions until the end of the class period."

There was absolute silence for thirty seconds. Then the colonel, ice in his voice, said: "I can't let that comment about cowardice go unchallenged. On what do you base that allegation? You're not speaking from personal knowledge?"

"Yes, sir, I am," Lowell said.

"You felt someone was a coward? Is that what you're saying?"

"I *suspected* someone was a coward," Lowell said. "Another officer was forced to make that judgment."

"In what way?"

"In order to complete his mission, the officer to whom I refer—a West Pointer, by the way—felt it necessary to remove his cowardly commanding officer. Who was also, come to think of it, a West Pointer."

"What do you mean, *remove?*"

"He cut him down with a Thompson is what I mean, Colonel," Lowell said, very simply.

"I think," Lt. Col. Bellmon said, after a long moment in which he decided that Lowell was telling the truth and that the situation was about to get out of control, "that we should have a nightcap on the porch, gentlemen."

Later that night, sleeping on the fold-down bed in the living room of Lowell's apartment, Sharon softly asked Sandy if what Lowell had said about one officer shooting, *murdering*, another officer in cold blood was true.

"Yes, it was," the Mouse said. "But I don't think Craig did himself any good by telling those officers that story. Those things happen, honey, but you just don't talk about them." He had a mental image of the Thompson bucking in his hands, of Captain Watson tumbling down the mountainside.

Sandy Felter suddenly rolled on his side and grabbed Sharon and pulled her to him, and despite her protests that they would wake the baby and Craig and Ilse and that she didn't *want* to, not *here*, he took her. He had never done anything like that before, and he was ashamed of himself, even if Sharon, afterward, thought it was kind of funny and teased him about not drinking any more brandy.

[TEN]

Shortly after the dinner at Lt. Col. Robert Bellmon's quarters, Second Lieutenant Craig W. Lowell was transferred from the Tank Gunnery Division of the Armor School to the U.S. Army Armor Board. The Board, which was on, but not subordinate to, Fort Knox, was the agency which tested new tanks and other armored force vehicles.

Lowell was now viewed by the establishment at Fort Knox in a different light. He was no longer a smart-ass guardhouse lawyer who'd managed to somehow wangle a commission and had thereafter thumbed his nose at the army. Despite his indiscreet remarks at the Bellmons' party, he was a young man from a very prominent family whose potential had been recognized by no one less than Porky Waterford himself. In addition, he was married to the daughter of a German aristocrat who had been a colonel and an old friend of Waterford.

And Porky's judgment about the boy's potential had certainly been vindicated. The medal the Greeks had given him was the second highest one they awarded. It was understandable that a young man who had commanded a company in combat would tend to be a little bored with Basic Officer's Course and would say things he really shouldn't have said. Under the circumstances, it certainly spoke well for him that he had done so well in Basic Officer's Course, graduating third, with a 98.4 grade average.

Bellmon had a little chat about Lowell with Colonel Kenneth J. McLean, president of the Armor Board. McLean had not been at the dinner at which Lowell had made the speech, but he had been in North Africa with General Waterford. Colonel McLean said he could always use a bright young buck like that. The commanding general approved the transfer.

Lowell was assigned as an assistant project officer on the 90 mm high-velocity tube project for the M26. The original M26, which was to eventually replace the M4A4 as the standard tank, had come with a 75 mm cannon. The army had learned a healthy respect for the German 88 mm cannon, and a U.S. 90 mm high-velocity tank tube was designed and manufactured and was now under test by the Armor Board. If successful, it would make the M26 the most powerfully armed tank in the world.

The testing was rather simple in nature. The tube was fired under all possible conditions to see what broke. At that point ordnance engineers, military and civilian, came up with a fix.

Three M26 tanks, each under a lieutenant and crewed by senior noncoms, were under the general supervision of a lieutenant colonel, who handled the engineering and the other paperwork. Lowell became one of the three lieutenants.

The other lieutenants had heard that the president of the Board had requested Lowell's transfer from the school. That spoke well of him. So far as the noncoms were concerned, a second john with a CIB who had been an enlisted man was hardly your standard candy-ass shavetail, and Lowell's subsequent behavior (no chickenshit) and performance (that sonofabitch really knows how to fire a tube) confirmed their judgment of him.

The officers' ladies of the Armor Board, having heard that Colonel McLean had requested Lowell's transfer from the school, and having seen Mrs. Lowell together with Mrs. Bellmon at the commissary and at lunch with her in the officer's club, concluded that Ilse Lowell was the exception that proved the rule about frauleins; and they went out of their way to welcome her to Board social activities.

Lowell himself was delighted with his new duties. The M26s he'd been firing at the school had had to be treated with the utmost care to prevent breakdowns. During their four-week course of instruction, each tank crew in training had fired precisely thirty-two rounds of 75 mm ammunition. It was incredibly expensive and tough on the tube itself, and every round had to count. The absolute reverse was true at the Board. He and his crew picked up a tank at the maintenance building in the morning, drove the sonofabitch as fast as it would go out to the firing ranges and the torture-rack testing area, and then fired as many (sometimes twice as many) rounds in a day as he had fired in the whole four-week course at the school.

One of their problems was the necessity to constantly replace the M4 tank hulks and the worn-out trucks used for targets. They literally blew them into little pieces.

For lunch, they would pile into jeeps and three-quarter-ton trucks and drive five miles through the woods to the Fort Knox Rod and Gun Club for hamburgers and beer. There they'd fill out the forms that Testing Evaluation Division gave them to gain data on the M26A2 (90 mm high-velocity tube).

They were generally finished for the day at half past two or a quarter to three; and by half past four, Lowell had returned to his apartment. He took a shower, played with P. P., maybe fooled around with Ilse a little, and then they went together to the commissary or the PX, and maybe took in a movie. P. P. was a good baby. You could take him to the movies, and you never heard a peep out of him.

Craig actually looked forward with regret to his coming release from active duty, at the completion of his two years of commissioned service. He had to get out, of course. For one thing, it made absolutely no sense to stay in. If he stayed, they wouldn't let him stay at the Board. They'd send his ass overseas and make him officer in charge of counting mess kits or something. He wasn't even sure he could have stayed if he wanted to. The army was cutting back on the number of reserve officers on active duty. The only way to stay was to go regular army; and to do that, you needed a college degree.

What he had, he realized, was a very pleasant way to spend the last six months of his service. He should be, and was, grateful for that.

On a Thursday afternoon, when he had about two months to go, Colonel McLean was waiting for him at the door of the cavernous maintenance building, when he came barrel-assing back to the barn from a day on the range.

He signaled the driver to stop when McLean put up his hand. He climbed down from the turret and signaled for the driver to go park the beast.

"Good afternoon, sir," he said to Colonel McLean. McLean put his hand on his arm.

"There's been some bad news for you, Craig," McLean said. "Your grandfather's passed on. Your cousin Porter Craig telephoned."

It wasn't like the school where those chickenshit bastards wouldn't even let him go to New York to meet Ilse. By the time he got back to the barn, the Board had really taken care of him. He had leave orders and reservations on the plane. Mrs. McLean was in the apartment, Ilse had their bags packed, and all he had to do was take a shower and get dressed and go down and get in the colonel's car. That way he wouldn't have to worry about his car while he was gone. "Let us know when you're coming back, and we'll have somebody to meet you."

Mrs. McLean insisted on going into the airport with them, carrying the plastic bag filled with diapers and stuff for P. P. that Ilse normally carried over her shoulder.

"I have reservations," he said. "Two, round trip to New York. The name is Lowell."

"Oh, Craig, I didn't think about money!" Ilse said. Mrs. McLean started to open her purse.

Lowell handed over his Air Travel card.

"First class," he said to the reservations clerk.

Ilse wanted to say something; but with Mrs. McLean there, she didn't.

"Do you have enough cash, Craig?" Mrs. McLean asked.

"I've got enough for a cab," he said. "That's all I'll need." Then he decided to hell with that, too. Truth time.

When he had the tickets, and knew when they would be in New York, he walked to a pay phone and called Broadlawns, collect.

Porter Craig finally came to the phone. He wondered what Porter was doing there. Was his mother on the sauce again with the Old Man dead?

"I'm leaving Louisville in about ten minutes, Porter," he said. "We get in at nine twenty. Will you have somebody meet me?"

"Why don't you just take a cab?" Porter said. "The house is full of people."

"Goddamnit, Porter, send a car and a chauffeur," he snapped. "Nine twenty. Eastern Airlines Flight 522." He hung up. He saw the look in Mrs. McLean's eyes and the bafflement in Ilse's.

P. P. acted up on the plane, probably sensing that something was wrong. All he wanted to do was be cradled in silence; everytime that Ilse started to talk, to ask questions, he started to fuss. Lowell was grateful. He didn't want to explain anything. He would explain afterward.

A chauffeur in gray livery was waiting at LaGuardia when the DC-6 landed.

"I've got to change him," Ilse said, as the chauffeur walked up to them.

"Lieutenant Lowell?" he asked, touching his cap.

"Is there somewhere Mrs. Lowell can change my son?" Lowell asked him.

Ilse looked at the chauffeur in confusion, in disbelief.

"Yes, sir," the chauffeur said. "If you'll follow me."

On the second floor of the terminal building, the chauffeur pushed open an unmarked door. Inside was a private lounge. There was a stewardess or somebody behind a desk. When she saw the young officer walk in, she stood up.

"May I help you, Lieutenant?" she asked, barring his way.

"This is Mr. Craig Lowell," the chauffeur said. The hostess looked at him. "Mr. Geoffrey Craig's grandson," the chauffeur said.

"Oh, please come in," the hostess said, "And this is Mrs. Lowell?"

"Mrs. Lowell has to change our son," Craig said.

"Right this way, Mrs. Lowell," the hostess said, and took Ilse's arm and led her away. Ilse looked actually frightened, Craig thought.

Lowell handed the chauffeur the baggage checks.

"The car is at entrance three, sir," the chauffeur said. "Would you like to meet me there? Or should I come back?"

"I'll meet you there." There was a bar in the VIP lounge. Craig ordered a double scotch and drank it neat.

The limousine was a Chrysler LeBaron with a stretched body. Craig wondered idly who it belonged to.

Ilse didn't ask questions on the way to Broadlawns. P. P. had upchucked, she said, and he had a fever. But when they passed inside the gate at Broadlawns, she asked where they were.

"They call this place 'Broadlawns,' " he said. "My mother lives here."

There were a half dozen cars on the circular drive before the house. Most of them were limousines, with their chauffeurs chatting in a group off to one side. When they walked up to the door, it was opened for them by the West Indian butler.

"Good evening, Mr. Lowell," he said. "Madam. The family is in the drawing room."

The family and some other vaguely remembered faces were scattered around the drawing room; but the center of attention was his mother, who was sitting on a couch facing the door to the foyer.

When she looked at him, he saw that she was drunk.

"Craig," she said, getting unsteadily to her feet, "Pop-Pop is gone."

The she saw Ilse standing behind him holding P. P. A look of confusion, of bafflement, clouded her face.

"I don't believe . . ." she began.

"Mother, this is Ilse," Craig said. "The baby is Peter-Paul. He's your grandson."

"I don't understand," his mother said, plaintively.

"My God!" Porter Craig said.

"This is my wife, Mother," Craig said. "And our son."

"But you never said anything," his mother said. She walked unsteadily over to Ilse and stared frankly at her.

"I'm sorry about your father, Mrs. . . . Mrs. . . ." Ilse could not remember the name of the man Craig had told her his mother had married.

"You're foreign," Mrs. Andre Pretier accused.

"Ilse is German, Mother," Craig said.

"Yes, I can see she is," his mother said. She turned to face him. "How dare you? How could you do this to me?"

"For Christ's sake!" Craig said.

P. P. struggled, turned, and threw up what looked like a solid stream of vomitus that splashed on the carpet.

"My God!" Porter Craig said.

"Andre!" his mother shrieked, turning around to look desperately for her husband. When she located him, she screamed, "Do something."

"What, darling, would you like to have me do?"

"Get that goddamned woman and her squalling brat out of my house!" she screamed, and then ran into the corridor and up the stairs.

"Craig," Porter Craig said, "you really could have handled this whole thing better."

"When I want your fucking advice, Porter," Craig exploded, "I'll ask for it."

"Craig!" Ilse said. "I want to go."

"I really think that would be best," Andre Pretier said. "Under the circumstances. Until your mother has had a chance to adjust to this."

"Craig," Ilse repeated, just over the edge of tears, "I want to go."

"Everyone seems to forget that this is my house," Craig said. "I'll go if and when I goddamn please."

"Craig, for God's sake!" Porter Craig said. "What did you expect, when you just walked in like this, with that woman?"

"That woman, you pasty-faced cocksucker, is my wife!"

"You can't talk to me that way!" Porter said.

"Oh, my God, Craig, please," Ilse said. "Take me out of here."

"Go to the apartment," Andre Pretier said. "I'll call and tell them you're coming." Lowell glared at him. "Craig, you know your mother. Staying here will just make things worse."

"Where are they going to bury him from?" Craig asked.

"Saint Bartholomew's, of course," Porter Craig said. "He was on the vestry."

His mother reappeared at the doorway, hysterical.

"Get out, get out, get out!" she screamed, tears running down her cheeks.

"You see what you've done," Porter Craig said.

The butler was standing by the door across from his mother. His face was expressionless.

"Have the chauffeur put my things back in the car," Craig Lowell ordered. "And then telephone the Waldorf and get me a suite. Have them get me a doctor."

[ELEVEN]

Ilse whimpered all the way into New York City, and she refused to go either to the funeral home to see the body or to Saint Bartholomew's for the funeral service. He tried to tell her that his mother had nothing against her and that it could just as easily have gone the other way, that she could have welcomed Ilse and P. P. into the family. He tried to tell her that he had had no way of knowing which way his mother would go; and for that reason, he had put off the meeting until it could no longer be put off.

Ilse didn't seem to have been hurt by him, by what he had and had not done; and she certainly wasn't angry with him. She just wanted to get out of New York and go home, and she didn't want to see any of his family. He didn't blame her.

He sat next to his mother during the funeral, and he rode with her to the cemetery; but she didn't speak to him. She was on Cloud Nine, he realized. Tranquilized like a zombie.

When Andre Pretier and Porter Craig came to the suite in the Waldorf after the interment, Ilse fled into the bedroom and wouldn't come out.

They asked about the baby, and Craig told them the doctor said there was nothing wrong with him. He was teething, and the plane ride had upset him.

Andre Pretier said that if he had known who actually owned Broadlawns, he would have been in touch before to see what could be worked out in the way of renting it or, if Craig wished, having it appraised so that he could buy it.

Craig believed him.

"We can let Broadlawns ride," he said. "I was angry, and I shouldn't have said what I said."

"I understand there have been certain bequests in grandfather's will," Porter said.

"I understand, unless he was lying to me, that we split everything right down the middle," Craig said.

"We'll have to get together and talk things over," Porter Craig said.

"Steal what you can while you can, Porter," Craig said. "You've got two years."

"What is that supposed to mean?"

"Grandpa wanted me to go to Wharton, Porter," Lowell said. "I think I will. It's a two-year course. And then I'll be back."

"You're going to Wharton," Porter Craig said, tolerantly, patiently. "Wharton is a graduate school, Craig. You'll have to take a degree, Craig."

"Two things I learned in the army, Porter," Lowell said, even more dryly sarcastic, "is that 'when there's a will, there's a way' and 'there's an exception to every rule.' You ever think about that? Who knows? I just might be the next chairman of the board and chief executive officer."

[ONE]
Headquarters, U.S. Army Counterintelligence Corps Center
Camp Holabird
1019 Dundalk Avenue
Baltimore 19, Maryland
15 August 1948

First Lieutenant Sanford T. Felter spent the eighteen months following his visit to Craig Lowell at Fort Knox in school. First there was six months at the U.S. Army Language School at the Presidio of San Francisco. Next came six months at the Advanced Infantry Officer's Course at Fort Benning, Georgia. And finally there was to be six months at the CIC Center, "Dundalk High," in Baltimore.

The Army Language School was, and is, the best language school in the world. The instructors are persons wholly fluent in the language to be taught; and for many of them, the language they teach is their mother tongue.

From the first day, all instruction is in the language to be learned.

"Good morning, Lieutenant," Felter's advisor said. "What I have just said was in Greek, in case you didn't know. Hence forth, all instruction will be in Greek. The Greek phrase for 'repeat after me' is—" and he gave the phrase. "Repeat after me: Good morning, Major."

"Good morning, Major," Felter said in Greek.

"Very good," the major said in Greek. "That means very good."

"Yes, sir," Felter said in Greek. "I know. I picked up a lot of it while I was in Greece."

"Can you read it as well?"

"Yes, sir. I read it a little better than I speak it. I'm told I have a terrible accent."

Following a written and oral examination, Felter's service record was amended to add "Greek language proficiency: Fluent, written and oral." Permission was received from the adjutant general, with the concurrence of the assistant chief of staff G-2, to submit Lt. Felter to instruction in the Korean language, in lieu of Greek.

The Felters shared a neat little brick duplex with a Chinese American lieutenant from Hawaii who was an instructor in Cantonese. Orally, there was a great difference between the two languages, but there was, Felter found, a strong similarity in their written forms.

Felter was graduated from the Korean language course "with distinction," and as a result of an examination, he was also determined to be "fluent" in written Cantonese and "semifluent" in spoken Cantonese.

They drove back across the country. Sharon was pregnant (it had probably happened *that* night at Fort Knox; the Mouse prayed that the alcohol in his blood would not affect the fetus), and the trip was punctuated by frequent stops for her to spend a day in a motel bed.

The quarters available to first lieutenants attending the Advanced Officer's Course at Fort Benning were nothing like the duplexes in the Presidio. And the philosophy of instruction seemed to be to physically exhaust the students in one overnight field training exercise after another. Finally, Sandy convinced Sharon that it would be better for the baby if he moved into the BOQ and she went home to Newark.

The only pleasant memory the Mouse had of Fort Benning was the day he was called into the Student Officer Company orderly room and told by a visibly surprised major (who knew he was en route from the Army Language School to the Counter-intelligence center and had logically concluded he was one more pencil-pushing Jew-boy) that a general order from the Department of the Army had been received awarding him the Expert Combat Infantry Badge and the Bronze Star with "V" (for Valor) device for his service in Greece.

Years later, Felter learned that Big Jim Van Fleet had gone from Greece to Washington and patiently demanded over a period of six months, day after day, that the army owed those who served with divisions and regiments in Greece more than the hypocrisy of an Army Commendation Medal. He finally wore the bureaucracy down.

Camp Holabird was much nicer than Fort Benning. There were no quarters on the post for junior lieutenants, but Holabird was right in Baltimore in the Dundalk section, and he and Sharon and Sanford Felter, Jr., spent the time in a nice little rented apartment.

It was like going to civilian work, and the duty hours were eight to five. Baltimore was close enough to Newark so that his father and mother could drive down and spend an occasional weekend with them, or sometimes his mother would come alone on the train. And it was just a couple of hours from Philadelphia where Craig was enrolled in the Wharton School of Business; and so they saw a lot of the Lowells. When, his curiosity aroused, he asked Craig how he'd gotten into Wharton, without having an undergraduate degree, Craig had said they made an exception for people who owned banks.

Some of the things Felter learned in the CIC Center were fascinating, and some of them were sort of funny. Privately, he thought of parts of it as the Official U.S. Army Burglar and Safecracker School.

But the life was good. For one thing, there were a lot of Jews there. During the war and immediately afterward, there had been a lot of Jewish refugees from Hitler in the CIC; and even now there were still enough Jewish refugees from Germany getting drafted who spoke German and were needed in the CIC.

There were enough practicing Jews for a Sabbath service under a rabbi-chaplain at the post chapel, and the Mouse and Sharon also participated in the congregational activities. There weren't that many Jewish officers, but because most of the CIC people worked in civilian clothes or with the blue-triangle U.S. Civilian insignia on their uniform, there were far less restrictions against being friendly with enlisted personnel than there were at other places in the army.

For a while Sandy was worried that he had been categorized as a Jew and would wind up in Germany chasing Nazis and doing security checks on German girls who wanted to marry Americans. But in his fourth week of training, while the others were being instructed in the filing system of the National Socialist Democratic Worker's Party, he and a major who had never before spoken to him were taken to a small office and began a course which explained the inner administrative procedures of the Russian State Security Service.

He learned that the Jewish personnel who were bound for Germany and the de-Nazification program were referred to as "the temporary help" and was a little worried that it was an anti-Semitic comment. But he thought it through. That's all they really were. They were not involved in the business he was being trained for. What the temporary help were involved in was the punishment of the Nazis. The Nazis no longer posed a threat to the security of the United States. The communists did.

When he was graduated, he was given a special $350 allowance to buy civilian clothing and a little leather folder with a badge and his photograph on a plastic identification card reading: "The bearer is a special agent of the United States Army Counterintelligence Corps." They also issued him a five-shot Smith & Wesson. 38 Special revolver with a two-inch barrel.

He was first assigned to the 119th CIC Detachment, First Army, which was in an office building on West 57th Street in New York City. He wanted to rent an apartment in New York, but Sharon said there was no sense throwing money away. They could live with his parents, and besides he would hurt his mother's feelings.

So every morning, early, he would ride the bus to Pennsylvania Station in Newark and take the commuter train to New York and the subway up to West 57th Street.

What the 119th CIC Detachment did mostly was run complete background investigations on people who wanted to get a Secret or a Top Secret security clearance. Special agents went around to where they lived and asked questions, and they went to their schools and talked to their teachers.

Felter did that for a couple of months, and then he was named deputy agent in charge of the detachment, which meant that he handled all the administration. There were thirty-six special agents, most of them sergeants, with a couple of warrant officers and one other officer. Everybody was in civilian clothes.

It wasn't what he had envisioned it would be like as an intelligence officer, and he began to wonder if he had been letting his imagination and his ego run away with him when he had thought he was going to do something important. Nevertheless, there didn't seem to be anything he could do about it.

And then, all of a sudden, he was called to a meeting at First Army Headquarters on Governors Island and introduced to a gray-haired man with an accent like Craig Lowell's. The man bought him lunch and talked German, Russian, and Polish to him. Felter knew he was being checked to see how well he spoke those languages, but he had no idea why.

And then the man said, "A friend of yours told me you can be a mean sonofabitch on occasion, Felter. Is that true?"

"I can't imagine who would say that about me," Felter said, truthfully.

"Paul Hanrahan," the man said, "is our mutual friend."

"Oh, Colonel Hanrahan. He said that about me?"

"He sends his best regards," the man said.

"Where is he now?" There was no reply to the question.

"Felter, how would you like to go to Berlin for a couple of years?" the man said.

"Oh, I'd like that," Felter said.

[TWO]

Mr. and Mrs. Sanford T. Felter and little Sandy flew to Germany on Pan American Airways. As a Department of the Army civilian employee, accountant, GS-9 (equivalent, if he had been an officer, to captain), employed by something called the office of Production Analysis, Mr. Felter was entitled to company-grade officer quarters, a PX card, and other privileges, including access to the U.S. Army Hospital for himself and his family.

For three months he debriefed line-crossers from East Germany, at first with regard to the placement of Russian military formations. Then, as he acquired knowledge of East Germany and Poland, he began to specialize in information regarding the Volkspolizei, the paramilitary East German police force.

From there he moved naturally to a position immediately under the station chief himself. This entailed the recruitment of Germans and others who—because they hated the Russians, or else for the money—were willing to cross the border the other way to provide specific answers to his (or Washington's) questions regarding various facets of East German military and economic activity.

Sharon liked Berlin. Zehlendorf, where they lived, hadn't suffered the destruction other parts of the city had; and their quarters were the nicest they had had so far, even nicer than the duplex at the Presidio.

But she really didn't understand when he told her that he was sorry, but he wanted her to discourage the overtures of friendship from the wives of officers he had known at West Point. They would obviously be curious to know what he was doing and that awkward question could not be answered. Neither did Sharon understand why she had to have a driver for the car and was forbidden to leave the little compound in which they lived on foot, unless Sandy or the "driver" she had been assigned were with her.

"Karl is a very nice man," she said. "And I know he wasn't a Nazi. But he scares me. Why does he have to carry a gun, Sandy? Why are you carrying a gun, Sandy?"

He could hardly tell her that the reason that she had been assigned a "driver" and that he was never without a gun was that the bastards on the other side often expressed their displeasure with their American counterparts by staging hit-and-run automobile accidents or by throwing acid in their children's faces.

Sharon spoke German, of course, and that made it easier for her to make friends with the German women who worked with Sandy, and even with women she met when she shopped. She adjusted.

When it became evident that the East Germans had every intention of transforming their border guard and the purely military elements of the Volkspolizei into an army (as, indeed, the West was transforming the Grenzpolizei, the customs/border guard, into a new Wehrmacht, ultimately to be called the Bundeswehr), Felter, on his own initiative, began compiling a dossier on its potential officers. The station would also get one from the Gehlen Organization, of course. Felter thought it would be good to be able to compare the two.

Many of the officers would obviously come from the present officers of the Volkspolizei, but there were not enough of those to lead an army. That left the Russians with two options: They could promote beyond their abilities officers and noncoms presently serving in the Volkspolizei whose loyalties to communism generally and the Kremlin specifically were beyond question; or they could draw upon the pool of captured officers they still (despite weak, pro forma, denials to the contrary), held scattered all over the Soviet Union.

Felter made regular inquiries concerning these officers, for it would not have surprised him if Katyn had been repeated many times in the blank expanses of northern Russia. Though he was never able to pin anything down, he heard rumors of large-scale massacres; and that buttressed his belief that the Soviets had decided upon another plan of action. If a man were confined to hard labor for many years and then offered the chance to put on again an officer's uniform—and particularly if he were not required to take an oath of allegiance to a communist state per se, but simply to a German government—he could be quite valuable to the Soviets.

Such men couldn't be trusted with command, of course. That would take someone of sound ideology. But there were any number of staff positions that needed filling, and filling them with qualified officers would free ideologically sound officers for command.

The Soviets ran the risk, of course, that among these "nonpolitical officers" would be some whose imprisonment had politicized them against the Soviet Union and their East German vassals. Such officers would be susceptible to approach from the West, either for purely ideological reasons or purely selfish ones. The Russians would watch for such men carefully, but two, or ten, or a hundred would slip through their net. Sandy Felter was determined to catch as many of them as he could.

This sort of thing was technically the responsibility of the Gehlen Organization, and any activities in this area by Sandy were supposed to be coordinated with the Gehlen Organization. The prescribed channel to effect liaison was through his station chief to the Gehlen man serving as liaison with him. Sandy Felter, with nothing to go on but a gut feeling, did not trust the Gehlen Organization liaison man, although the man enjoyed the full support of the station chief.

Fully aware that what he was doing was twice forbidden (going out of channels and establishing what were known as "private files"), he began to collect the names of prisoners known to be alive in the Soviet Union. When he had the names of fifty-three such officers in the grades of major through colonel, he carried them with him to the Gehlen Organization's compound in the American Zone outside Munich. And then he took a chance. He gave them to a fat analyst who looked for all the world like a jolly butcher. He told him the names were from a private file and that he hoped to expand the file. The fat jolly German told him that he could not, of course, accept material out of channels, but if Felter would come back in fifteen minutes, he would return his list to him.

When he picked up his list, there was stapled to the back of it three pages—photocopied—of a similar list. Where the names on the added list were duplicated on Felter's list, there was a brief biography of the individual name and a file number.

In the months that followed, he furnished the jolly butcher with two hundred more names, and he received in return more than one hundred other names he did not have. One of the names rang a very loud bell.

```
Greiffenberg, Paul.(?) Oberstleutnant(?) NKVD # 88-234-017.
   Sicherheitsdienst Folio Berlin 343-1903. Camp No. 263, Kyr-
   tymya(?) 18Mar46. (File 405-001-732).
```

He picked up the Berlin telephone book. There were twenty two people (including all spelling variations) named Greiffenberg. Paul was Ilse's father's middle name. P. P.'s name was Peter-Paul, with a hyphen. It had been Oberst, not Oberstleutnant. It had been *von* Greiffenberg, not plain Greiffenberg, and there were twenty-two plain Greiffenbergs in Berlin, so the name was not uncommon. Most importantly, Bellmon had told him that Oberst Graf Peter-Paul von Greiffenberg had been shot down by the Russians outside Zwenkau. It was highly unlikely that what he had was anything more than a coincidence.

But he asked for File 405-001-732, a routine request for information from the Gehlen Organization, sent through his station chief to the Gehlen man.

The station chief didn't pay attention when the request was sent in, but when the file in due time arrived, he blew his top and ate Sandy's ass out. He told him to stick to what he was supposed to do, keep up on the Volkspolizei, and forget about long-time prisoners.

"For Christ's sake, Felter," the station chief concluded, "The last note on this guy is March 1946. By now he's probably been shot. They do that, you know."

Felter never got a chance to look at File 405-001-732; and the next time he got to the Gehlen Organization, the jolly fat butcher was not there. You did not ask where people were.

He kept building up his list, however; and whenever he had a chance to debrief a returned long-time prisoner, he always brought up the name of Colonel Graf Peter-Paul von Greiffenberg. Nobody had ever heard of him.

[THREE]
Philadelphia
21 April 1949

Craig Lowell, in a tweed jacket, a tieless white button down-collar shirt, gray flannel slacks, and loafers, walked across the campus of the University of Pennsylvania to the MG, Ilse's car, in the parking lot. The enormous old Packard had gone shortly after they'd come to Philadelphia. Ilse didn't like to drive it, for one thing, and for another, he rather disliked having people stop and stare at it when he drove it around town.

He bought a Jaguar. He wanted the Jaguar, but he didn't like the trade-in offer the dealer made, so he did something impulsive with the huge yellow automobile. He had it delivered to Broadlawns with a red ribbon tied to the hood ornament, and a card taped—along with the bill of sale—to the wheel:

Dear Andre,

Thanks for everything. Try to stay on the black stuff between the trees.

Fondly,
Craig

Andre liked classic cars, and he had done well by his mother. Ilse thought that it was a very nice thing for him to do. Ilse was about as afraid of the Jaguar as she had been of the Packard. And one day, when he had the Jaguar in for service, Ilse had walked out of the showroom and stared into the adjacent showroom.

"That's sweet," she said. "Are they very expensive, Craig?" she said about the car on the showroom floor. So he'd bought her an MG-TC with wire wheels. It made you feel as if you were being dragged along the ground in a bucket.

Ilse was coming along well. He couldn't be happier. They took an apartment high up at 2601 Parkway, nothing fancy, just enough for them; and Ilse furnished it in something called Danish Modern. He didn't know or care about things like that, but if it made her happy, great.

The apartment had three bedrooms, a kitchen, and an enormous living room on two levels. He went to a used office furniture place and bought a huge desk, some bookcases, and a lamp that moved around on swivels. He also rented a typewriter from IBM. The bills for the apartment and the typewriter, and what the GI Bill didn't pay for at Wharton, went into his Trust. As a married veteran with two dependents the government sent him a check for $134.80 a month. He gave that to Ilse for pocket money. The estate of Geoffrey Craig sent him a check every month, and a much larger check every three months. He played around with the stock market with the larger check, what was left of it after it passed through the hands of the accountant; and he lived on the monthly checks. When the checking balance got out of hand, he put the excess in the market, too.

He turned down business propositions from Porter Craig. He told him he would wait to get into that until he was through Wharton and in New York when he could look at everything and see where things stood.

Porter had been obliging as hell from the time he'd seen him in the Waldorf right after the funeral. He was obviously kissing ass for his own reasons, but some of it was useful. For instance, Porter had put him up for the Rose Tree Hunt, on the Main Line. He didn't intend to hunt, but they played some half-assed polo, and there were bridle paths.

Ilse was riding. And she rode well. And she gradually started to tell stories about riding as a child in Germany with her father. Not all the women at Rose Tree were horse's asses. Some of them were actually rather nice, and Ilse had moved into those circles. Unhappily, his fellow students at Wharton were generally a pain in the ass, fiercely ambitious pencil-pushers. But he held his own against them academically, and he came to form the nasty arrogant opinion that if those morons were the competition he was going to have to face when he went to New York, then he was not going to have a hell of a lot of trouble.

Giving Andre the Packard had been rather like casting bread upon the waters. He was sure Andre was responsible for the armed truce that now existed between him and his mother. His mother and Andre had been to see them twice, once when they first moved into the apartment, and next a couple of months ago, when the Pretiers were on their way to the Palm Beach place.

Ilse, who was as hardheaded as a rock, was never going to completely forgive his mother for the scene at Broadlawns, but she had decided that a baby needed a grandmother and possibly vice versa, so she watched carefully as his mother would play—briefly—with P. P. It was hardly a scene, Grandma and Child, that would wind up on a cover of the *Saturday Evening Post*, but it was something.

In the campus parking lot Craig Lowell stepped around a panel truck and found himself six feet from the muzzle evacuator on a 90 mm tube on an M26. Somebody was moving the turret. It was the cleanest M26 he had ever seen. Behind the tank was the recovery vehicle that had obviously carried it onto the campus. And behind that was an M24 light tank, a couple of M8 armored cars, some trucks, and a couple of jeeps.

The Pennsylvania National Guard was recruiting on campus.

"You want to look inside?" a captain in ODs asked him.

Lowell smiled and shook his head, "no." But then, he decided, what the hell. He laid his briefcase on the fender and climbed up over the drive wheel. He waited until some potential recruit, smiling with delight, climbed out of the commander's turret, and then he swung his legs through the hatch and dropped inside.

They'd stationed a master sergeant inside. Christ, the inside was spotless. The paint wasn't even chipped. It must be brand new, or damned near brand new. The master sergeant showed him the breech of the tube, and the place where they stored the rounds and the driver's seat.

Craig sniffed and smelled the familiar smells, and then he smiled and hoisted himself out of the commander's hatch.

"Like to drive something like that?" the captain asked him, with a smile.

Craig smiled back and nodded, "yes."

"Give me two minutes of your time," the captain said, "and let me explain our program to you."

Somehow reluctant to get off the tank, Lowell nodded.

If he would enlist in the Guard—either in the Tank Company or the Reconnaissance Company, which also had vacancies—he would be trained to drive and operate a tank at the regular Tuesday evening meetings, half past seven to half past nine. Then in the summertime, there were two weeks active duty for training. During these two weeks he would receive the same pay and allowance the regular army got. After he had gone to enough Tuesday Evening meetings and had completed one summer camp, he would be eligible to enter Advanced ROTC; and on graduation he would be commissioned a second lieutenant in the army reserve.

"I've already got a reserve commission," Craig said.

"You do? As what?" the captain asked.

"First john," Craig replied. "Armor." He jerked his thumb at the M26. "M26 platoon commander." He had been promoted to first john the day before he had been released from active duty.

"School training? You been through Knox?"

"I taught M4A4 gunnery at Knox," Lowell said.

"No experience on these, then?"

"I was an assistant project officer at the Armor Board for that 90 mm high-velocity tube," Lowell said. "I know a lot more about that hot noisy sonofabitch than I really want to."

"We can use you," the captain said.

"No, thanks," Craig said.

"Get you a promotion to captain," the captain said. "What the hell, it's a day pay for two hours on Tuesday."

"No, thanks," Craig repeated. "But thank you just the same."

The captain gave him his card and said he should think it over. No obligation, he said, just come by the armory on Broad Street some Tuesday and see what it's like.

The first sergeant was a Fairmount Park cop. None of the platoon leaders had ever served a day on active duty. They were graduates of the One Night a Week for a

Year, Plus Two Weeks at Summer Camp PANG OCS. The supply sergeant was Colonel Gambino's brother. Colonel Gambino had served two years as a major and then light bird in War II. He had commanded a Transportation Corps truck battalion, after being directly commissioned because of his experience with heavy trucks. Gambino and Sons had for years had the garbage hauling contract for the north end of Philadelphia.

"I'll tell it to you straight," Colonel Gambino said. "I felt like a fucking fool at Indiantown Gap last summer. We had nine tanks, and we couldn't get one of the fuckers out to the firing range without the fucker breaking down."

"What about the one I saw out on the campus?"

"I borrowed it, and a guy to run it, from the 112th Infantry in Harrisburg."

"You got spare parts?"

"I got a fucking warehouse full of spare parts. What I don't have is anybody who ever saw a fucking M26 before. I did all right with the M4A4s we had."

"I think I can get the M26s running for you," Lowell said.

"You get them fuckers running, you're a captain."

"I'm a captain and Tank Company commander, and *then* I get them running," Lowell said.

"I already got a company commander. He's the S-4's brother-in-law. I can hardly fire him."

"If you want me to get your tanks running, Colonel," Craig Lowell had said, quite sure of himself, "you're going to have to."

HEADQUARTERS
111th INFANTRY REGIMENT
PENNSYLVANIA NATIONAL GUARD
305 North Broad Street
Philadelphia, Penna.

SPECIAL ORDERS 15 May 1949
Number 27

EXTRACT

****

3. 1st Lt Craig W. LOWELL, 0-495302, Armor, U.S. Army Reserve (Apt. 2301, 2601 Parkway, Phila Penna) having joined, assigned Tank Company, 111th Inf. 28th Inf Div, PANG for dy.

4. 1st Lt. Craig W LOWELL, 0-495302, Armor PANG, is Promoted CAPT PANG with DOR 15 May 1949. (Auth: Letter, Hq, The Adjutant

General PANG, Subj: One Grade Promotion of Officers to fill PANG vacancies, dtd 11 Feb 1949.)

****

BY ORDER OF COLONEL GAMBINO
Max T. Solomon
Major, Armor, PANG
Adjutant

HEADQUARTERS
111th INFANTRY REGIMENT
PENNSYLVANIA NATIONAL GUARD
305 North Broad Street
Philadelphia, Penna.

GENERAL ORDERS
Number 3

15 May 1949

The undersigned assumes command effective this date.

Craig W. Lowell
Captain, Armor, PANG

While it proved impossible to get all nine M26s ready for firing in time for summer camp, Captain Lowell got all of them running well enough to be driven from the armory to the railhead, and then from the railhead at Indiantown Gap to the training area.

He found one competent mechanic and two half-assed mechanics in the company; and the four of them—Lowell happily up to ears in grease—got the turrets and the traversing mechanisms and the range finders and the sights and the tubes themselves ready on three tanks. There was no way that all nine tanks could be gotten into shape with the time and the people he had.

There was a simple dishonest solution to that. He fired nine functioning tanks by firing the same three functioning tanks three times over. The regular army inspecting staff was so surprised that any of the 111th Infantry's M26s ran and fired at all that they didn't notice (or pretended not to) that the paint on the vehicle identification numbers was fresh and a little runny, as if the numbers underneath had been painted over.

Everybody was happy, from the division commander down to Captain Lowell. When he came back from summer camp, he loaded Ilse and P. P. in the car and they went down to Cape May, N.J., and rented a cottage on the beach for the rest of the summer until he went back to school. Every Tuesday night, he got in the Jaguar and drove back to Philly for drill at the armory.

What he was thinking of doing, when he finished school in January and they moved to New York, was join the New York National Guard. What the hell, some people played tennis for a hobby and some played golf. What he would do for a hobby is play soldier.

He'd straightened out the Fairmount Park cop who was his first sergeant, and the first sergeant straightened out the platoon sergeants while Captain Lowell straightened out the platoon commanders. Tank Company, 111th Infantry, PANG, was arguably the sharpest company in the regiment, possibly even in the division; and Lowell could not remember anything else that had given him so much pleasure since he had taught the Greeks of No. 12 Company how to fire the Garand.

It might be a little childish, but so what? If he was going to spend the rest of his life computing potential return on capital investment, getting out in the fresh air and getting his hands dirty would probably be very good for him.

[FOUR]
The American Sector
Berlin, Germany
21 May 1950

Lieutenant Colonel Bob Bellmon came through Berlin as part of some visiting general's entourage and looked up Sandy Felter. Bellmon was now in the Pentagon, assigned to the Office of the Deputy Chief of Staff for Operations.

He called Felter and offered to take Sharon and Sandy out for dinner, but they had him instead to their quarters. Sandy offered to send a car to pick him up, but Bellmon said he had a car and it wouldn't be necessary.

Felter was curious about two things: How did Bellmon come into possession of his quarters' telephone number, which wasn't listed in the Berlin Military Post telephone directory, and how did he know where he and Sharon lived? The compound was not listed either.

Sharon, sensing that Sandy liked Bellmon and that Bellmon was important to their future, made a special dinner, and even arranged for one of the maids to take care of Little Sandy after he'd been shown off, so that he wouldn't be a nuisance. After dinner she tried to leave them alone twice, in case "they wanted to talk," but each time Bellmon made her stay. The third time she asked, Bellmon said, "I really would like a couple of minutes alone with him, Sharon."

Sharon said she'd go see how Little Sandy was doing.

Felter offered Bellmon a brandy and set the bottle in front of him.

"How'd you get my quarters' number, Colonel?" Sandy asked, aware that he was putting Bellmon on the defensive. I am no longer an innocent young lieutenant, he thought.

The telephone number had come from Red Hanrahan, Bellmon told him, and that amounted to an announcement that Hanrahan was also in Washington. Hanrahan, Bellmon said, sent his best wishes and had asked about Duke Lowell.

"I haven't heard from him since he got out," Bellmon said. "Have you?"

"Sharon hears from Ilse all the time," Felter said. "He made captain in the Pennsylvania National Guard."

"Oh, Jesus Christ!" Bellmon said. "God help the National Guard."

In the mistaken impression that Felter knew MacMillan, Bellmon said that Mac had gone to helicopter school, and that he had been assigned to Tokyo. "MacArthur likes the notion of having another Medal of Honor around, I suppose. They can exchange war stories."

"Is he working for MacArthur?"

"He's assigned to Supreme Headquarters," Bellmon said. "I think he's too smart to get close to MacArthur. Good Soldier Mac avoids getting too close to the flames if at all possible."

Then he asked, surprisingly, "You like working in civilian clothing, Sandy?"

"It's all right." There was more to the question than idle curiosity. "Colonel Hanrahan ask you to ask me that?"

Colonel Bellmon ignored the question.

"How are you getting along with your station chief?" he asked, instead.

Felter didn't answer the question.

"He asked to have you replaced," Bellmon said. Felter wondered if the visit of Colonel Bellmon was social, if Hanrahan had known he was coming to Berlin and had asked him to have a word with him, or whether Bellmon's role with DCSOPS had an intelligence connection of its own, and he was here officially.

Whatever the case, Felter was sorry Bellmon had told him what he had. Not because the station chief had stuck a knife in him, but because it might tend to cloud his judgment about the station chief.

"If I were in a position to ask for his relief," Felter said, flatly, "I would. And I would be justified. He's not."

"The story is that you're putting your nose in the wrong places," Bellmon reported.

"An intelligence officer has to walk a narrow line between putting his nose every place he can and interfering with somebody else," Felter replied. It had just occurred to him (and he wondered why it hadn't occurred to him before) that the only two officers in the army to whom he could say exactly what was on his mind were Hanrahan and Bellmon. Hanrahan because of their Greek service, Bellmon because of Katyn and Task Force Parker.

"You don't think you've gone over the line?" Bellmon asked. Felter shook his head.

"The only time I came close to it was asking for a file on a Soviet prisoner, a man named Greiffenberg."

"Greiffenberg? Our Greiffenberg?"

"I don't know. The one I found is a lieutenant colonel," Felter said. "And plain, without the 'von.' "

"Do you think it's possible he's still alive?"

"About one chance in two hundred," Felter said. "I thought it was worth checking out. But I was very careful. The file I asked for was purely routine. I checked that out. It had been offered to everybody. CIC. DIA. Even the Office of Naval Intelligence."

"What was your information? Where is your Greiffenberg?"

"I had fairly reliable information that there was an Oberstleutnant Paul Greiffenberg at a labor camp in Siberia. There are twenty-two people with that name in the Berlin phone book."

"How did it come up?" Bellmon asked.

"I've been compiling a list, a private file, on potential East German Army staff officers. The reason I checked was obviously personal. Not really personal. A gut feeling. Sometimes I go on my gut feelings. Ilse Lowell's maiden name was Greiffenberg, and her father is missing."

"Ilse's father is dead," Bellmon said. "The Russians shot him the day before you and Phil Parker showed up at Zwenkau."

"You see the body?"

"They shot all the Germans," Bellmon said.

"The reason I asked is that I found out they usually didn't shoot Oberstleutnants and better. Not even the SS equivalent. Not right off, anyway, the way they blew your people away."

"I didn't see the body," Bellmon said. "I didn't want to see it. But I think other people did."

"The operative word is 'think,' " Felter said.

"You don't happen to have a photograph?"

"I never got to see the file," Felter said. "My station chief sent it back."

"Why did he do that?"

"I was being put in my place," Felter said.

"What would you do if you found out?" Bellmon asked.

"Tell Craig and let him decide," Felter said.

"If the Russians knew he knew about Katyn," Bellmon said, "he'd be dead."

"Yes, he would," Felter said.

"Does your station chief know you know about Katyn?"

"I've never discussed it with him."

"What's he got it in for you then for?"

"Maybe he doesn't like Jews," Felter said. "But it's probably because I make him nervous. He's not too bright. Just bright enough to know it. He relies pretty heavily on Gehlen's liaison man."

"And you don't?"

"No."

"You're not going to be replaced," Bellmon said. "Unless you want to be. You want to come work for me in the Pentagon?"

"Not right now, but thank you."

"Something you want to finish here?"

"Yes."

"I gather it's important?"

"I think so."

"Red thinks you're pretty levelheaded, Sandy," Bellmon said.

"I think I am, too."

"When you're ready to leave here, let me know. I can use you, and a Pentagon tour wouldn't hurt your career."

"I gather you're doing something interesting?"

"Something right down your line, as a matter of fact."

"Maybe a little later," Felter said.

"Doing something foolish now would be liable to ruin your career," Bellmon said.

"I could always go join the Pennsylvania National Guard," Felter said, and they laughed out loud; and that was the end of the conversation.

[FIVE]

Felter thought about it a good deal in the days that followed. The only way his station chief would have enough balls to actually ask that he be replaced would be if someone encouraged him to do so. And that meant the man from the Gehlen Organization. One more improbable, unreliable, gut feeling to add to the question. Reliability Factor: Zero.

He also had a gut feeling about his loss rate, but he really had nothing to go on there, either. So far as his loss rate went, he was losing fewer agents than was to be expected (he should have lost more), but he was suspicious about the *quality* of the people he did lose. He wasn't losing the quick-money people. He was losing the people who had too much experience to be casually rolled up the way it seemed to be happening.

In the most recent case, one of his German associates recruited a former Dresdener who had been a black marketer and who for a price was willing to go back to Dresden.

When Felter submitted the memorandum and request for funds to the station chief, he identified the Dresdener as a former captain of the Sicherheitsdienst who had been in Munich. The memorandum also gave the date when he would cross the line.

An agent-in-place reported to him three days later that the agent had been rolled up in East Berlin as he boarded the bus for Dresden. They hadn't even asked for his papers. They had been expecting him. They knew what he looked like, and they knew where to look for him.

The station chief listened carefully and thoughtfully to Felter's analysis of the probable explanation for that and then told Felter there was no way *his* German associate, who had been vouched for by General Gehlen *personally*, was a double agent.

What had happened to Felter's Dresdener was just one of those things. For all Felter knew, they had been looking for him. It was against the law to be a black marketer in East Germany, too. "And in the future, Felter, just put the facts in your memorandums. I've been charged with making analyses."

The facts were, as Felter saw them:

(a) He had arranged for *his* German associate to be out of Berlin, and he was sure that he had stayed out, from the time he had brought the agent's name up. His associate had not known whether Felter had put the Dresdener to work or not.

(b) He had typed up the memorandum and request for funds himself, rather than have his clerk do it, and he had omitted to make the usual copies for the file, and he had personally carried it to the station chief.

(c) It was unlikely that the station chief was a double agent.

(d) His agent had been rolled up; they had expected him.

A month from the day Lieutenant Felter entertained Lt. Col. Bellmon at dinner, Colonel Luther Hollwitz, who despite his Germanic roots, was a native-born Soviet citizen at that time serving as deputy chief of station for the NKVD in Berlin, crossed into the American Zone at Check Point Charley, at the wheel of a 1940 Opel Kapitan. He drove to the subway station at the intersection of Beerenstrasse and Onkel Tom Allee in the West Berlin suburb of Zehlendorf in the American sector. He walked a block to the Hotel zum Fister, drank a glass of Berliner Kindl Pilsener in the small dining room, and then walked up the stairs to Room 13. Two minutes after he entered the room, he was joined by the liaison officer assigned to the Office of Production Analysis by the Gehlen Organization. They shook hands perfunctorily, in the European manner, and then sat down in facing, identical rattan armchairs.

Something came crashing through the window, which opened onto a small fenced-in courtyard. Colonel Hollwitz and the liaison officer from the Gehlen Organization had just enough time to identify the object which had come flying through the windowpane. It was a World War II German Army field grenade, the kind the Americans called the "Potato Masher," because it looked like that kitchen utensil.

By the time he heard the dull explosion, Sandy Felter had already dropped from the fire escape to the ground, jumped onto his bicycle, and pedaled through the alley to the sidewalk in front of the Hotel zum Fister.

Like the other people on the sidewalk, he stopped when he heard the explosion. Like the other people on the sidewalk, he looked around, registered surprise and curiosity, and then, shrugging, went about his business. He eased his bicycle over the curb, and rode slowly away.

When the Kriminalpolizei investigated the incident, they located sixteen people who had been in the immediate vicinity of the Hotel zum Fister at the time of the explosion. Not one of them remembered the young man on the bicycle.

Within thirty-six hours, the bodies had been identified, and the decision made "at the highest levels" that the files of the Office of Production Analysis had been wholly compromised.

The station chief was immediately flown out of Berlin to the United States. The Office of Production Analysis was closed down. The entire contents of its office—personnel, files, desks, tables, even the telephones—were taken under Military Police escort to Templehof Field and loaded aboard three C-47 aircraft of the Military Airlift Command. They were flown to Munich and then trucked to Garmisch-Partenkirchen near the Austrian border. The U.S. Army maintained a recreational area there for its forces. Other agencies of the army and the United States government had taken over salt mines there—literally miles of labyrinthine passages—for other purposes.

The man who had bought Felter lunch at Governors Island was there also, ostensiby a Special Services Lt. Colonel in charge of the army's recreation area. And there too was Colonel Red Hanrahan.

"I'm a little disappointed in you, Felter," Hanrahan said. "Was that really necessary?"

"I thought so," Felter replied. "It was two lives versus thirteen. We would have had to give Hollwitz back. By the time I would have been able to make my case to my station chief, there is no telling what damage would have been done."

"Why a hand grenade?" the man who had bought him lunch inquired, with polite curiosity. "What if it had been a dud, as old as it was?"

"I rebuilt the detonator," Felter said. "And replaced the charge with C-4."

"How thoughtful of you," the man from Governors Island said dryly.

"What happens to me now?" Felter asked.

"You'd be surprised to know how far up this went," Hanrahan replied. "Before it was decided that you had done what had to be done, under the circumstances."

"That doesn't answer my question, sir, with all respect."

"Do you know how to ski, Felter?" the man from Governors Island asked.

"No, sir."

"You'll have plenty of opportunity to learn," the man from Governors Island said. "We're going to keep you here, on display, and wait and see if the NKVD has figured this out."

"What about my family?" Felter asked.

"I'm sure you considered that before you acted on your own," the man from Governors Island said. "To answer the specific question: If we shipped your family home, they would know for sure, wouldn't they?"

Hanrahan said: "That decision came from way up, too, Mouse."

"I think they're going to blame it on the Gehlen Organization," Felter said. "They know that we normally hire out this sort of thing. When they find out this wasn't done on a contract, they'll think Gehlen."

"Unless they've got somebody else inside Gehlen who knows different," the man from Governors Island said.

"The only man in Gehlen who knows they didn't do it is Gehlen himself," Hanrahan said. "He's very embarrassed by the whole affair."

"What am I going to be doing?" Felter asked.

"No matter what happens," Hanrahan said, "you can't work covert any more. So we're going to put the Sphinx on your lapels and put you to work overt in uniform. You'll get your promotion on time, next month I think. The standard procedure, what would normally happen to someone like you whose operation was blown.

"You could, of course, resign," the man from Governors Island said.

"Is that a suggestion, sir?" Felter asked.

"No, it's not," he said. "But it's an option you can consider. You mentioned your family."

"I believe," Felter repeated, "that they're going to blame it on Gehlen."

Lieutenant and Mrs. Felter were assigned quarters on the second floor of a two-family, steeply roofed villa in Garmisch-Partenkirchen. Lieutenant Felter was assigned duty as an instructor (Soviet Army Organization) at the European Command Intelligence School and Center.

The day after he received his promotion to captain (Sharon was very angry with him; she simply could not see why he had to pay for his own promotion party, which cost nearly three hundred dollars), he learned that the station chief had been struck and killed by a hit-and-run driver on Collins Avenue in Miami Beach, Florida.

[SIX]

Captain Craig W. Lowell, Commanding, Tank Company 111th Infantry, PANG, submitted his resignation on 14 December 1949, to take effect 16 January 1950, the day after he would graduate from Wharton and move to New York. Colonel Gambino was sorry to see him go, and said that he would be happy to ask around and see about getting Lowell a job in Philly if he really wasn't dead set on living in New York.

Lowell thanked him, but said he had to go to New York.

When he went home that night from the armory, he stopped in a bar on North Broad Street and had a couple of drinks with his first sergeant, enough drinks so that when he got home he had enough courage to tell Ilse what he was really thinking.

He didn't want to go to New York, he said. Spending the rest of his life making money he didn't need, becoming another Porter Craig, was a frightening prospect that became more frightening as the time to go to New York came closer. Ilse said she didn't really want to go to New York either.

He gathered his courage and told her what he really wanted to do was go back in the army. What did she think about that?

She said that she thought he should do what he really wanted to do. She would be happy no matter what he decided.

He spent three days writing and rewriting and polishing a letter to the adjutant general. Subject: Application for Recall to Active Duty.

He included with it, as attachment one, a letter from the dean of students at the Wharton School of Business, stating that although he had been admitted as a special student, he had undergone the curricula prescribed for candidates for the degree of Master of Science, Business Administration. Had he had the requisite baccalaureate degree, he would have been graduated as an MBA, summa cum laude; and if, at any time within the next five years he acquired such a baccalaureate degree, the Wharton School of Business of the University of Pennsylvania would, on application, award the MBA degree to him.

He included a letter from Colonel Gambino, who wrote that Captain Lowell was the finest company-grade officer he had ever known, and that he recommended him without qualification as a superb leader of men, as an outstanding administrator, and as a maintenance officer of proven ability. Gambino didn't believe all of this bullshit, of course, and he suspected correctly that Lowell thought of him as a dumb wop. But fair's fair: The snotty fucker had taken over the fucked-up tank company, straightened it out, got the fucking tanks running and the tubes shooting, and brought back a fucking SUPERIOR rating from summer camp.

After thinking it over carefully for a day and a half, Lowell's letter to the adjutant general included this sentence:

"4. The undersigned is aware that he is underage in grade and is willing to accept a reduction to first lieutenant in the event this application for call to extended active duty is favorably acted upon."

When there was no reply, he went through with the move to New York. Porter Craig was helpful. He personally took Craig and Ilse around and showed them half a dozen apartments in properties owned by the estate. Ilse wasn't enthusiastic about any of them.

"I know," Porter said. "The Mews."

"What the hell is a Mews?" Craig asked.

Porter showed them. Ilse was enthusiastic. The Mews, a block off Washington Square in the Village, was a row of town houses on a cobblestone alley. The whole block was owned by the estate, which meant the alley itself was a private street, like Shubert Alley. A private security guard kept the public out. You could park your car in front of the place when you didn't want to put it in a garage.

Ilse thought it was a good omen that the Mews weren't quite finished. She could pick the color of paint she wanted and decorate it herself. Until it was ready, they moved into a suite at the Fifth Avenue Hotel, a block away.

Lowell went to work downtown. Porter Craig very gently suggested that he spend some time looking around, to get a feel of the operation, and see if some facet of it didn't really interest him. Porter had taken over Geoffrey Craig's office, but their grandfather's name was still on the door. What he was doing, Craig realized, was waiting until it became evident to Craig himself that Porter should assume the chairmanship of the board. Geoffrey Craig had been chairman of the board and chief executive officer. Porter was functioning as "acting" chairman of the board. Logically, since Porter knew more about what was going on than Craig did, he should become chairman, and they could give Craig a title, maybe president, which would reflect his share of the holdings, but leave Porter in charge.

Porter had obviously decided, and Craig rather admired him for it, that he should lean over backward to avoid an awkward confrontation. Craig had already come to the same conclusion, that Porter was obviously better qualified to run things than he was, and that a confrontation would be likely to cost both of them money. The thing to do, he decided, was let Porter have his way, but not to hand it to him on a silver platter. Let him sweat a little, first.

Craig went to the 169th Infantry, NYNG, to see what he could do about joining the New York Guard. They had their full complement of officers, he was told, fully qualified. They would enter his name on a waiting list, but frankly, Mr. Lowell, we just don't believe that any vacancies are going to occur for which you would be qualified as a captain. Your chances would be much better if you were willing to apply for a second lieutenant's table of organization position. We really feel that first lieutenants should have between three and seven years of commissioned service, and our junior captain has eight years. You have two years of active service, and a year in the Guard. You see my point, I'm sure.

When he told Porter, over lunch, about this, Porter laughed gently at him.

"You really should have come to me," Porter said. "If you really want to be a weekend warrior, I'll have a word with the governor."

"I need a recommendation from you to the governor?"

"All I would do, Craig," Porter said, "is remind the governor who you are."

"You mean who I am in terms of how much Grandpa left me?"

"All right, if that's the way you wish to put it."

"I'm a qualified armor officer," Craig said.

"By your own account, your qualifications didn't seem to awe Colonel Whatsisname."

"Fuck it," Lowell said. "To hell with it."

"If you change your mind, let me know," Porter said. "Although, for the life of me, I can't imagine why you would want to waste your time doing that."

"I said, fuck it, let it go," Craig said.

"If you're not going to be a soldier, don't you think it's time you cleaned up your language?" Porter asked.

Lowell looked at him, half angry. He smiled. "Very well," he said. "Diddle you, Porter."

"That's an improvement," Porter said, and they laughed together.

The army finally got around to answering the letter Craig had sent to the adjutant general.

HEADQUARTERS
DEPARTMENT OF THE ARMY
OFFICE OF THE ASSISTANT CHIEF OF STAFF
FOR PERSONNEL
The Pentagon, Washington 25, D.C.

15 May 1950
201-LOWELL, Craig W Capt
0-495302

Mr. Craig W. Lowell
Apt 2301
2601 Parkway
Philadelphia, Penna.

Dear Mr. Lowell:

Thank you for your letter of 17 December 1949, volunteering for extended active duty.

A careful review of your records, and the personnel requirements of the Army for the foreseeable future has been conducted by this office.

Under present policy, no applications for extended active duty from commissioned officers who have not been awarded a bachelor's degree from a recognized college or university are being accepted.

Furthermore, your total commissioned service and time in grade as a first lieutenant does not meet the established criteria for your present grade of captain. Your records will be reviewed sometime during the next fiscal year by a panel of officers who will recommend to the Assistant Chief of Staff for Personnel whether or not you should be retained as captain, Army of the United States, in a reserve capacity, terminated, or offered a commission in a grade commensurate with your age, length of service, and other factors. You may expect to hear from them directly in approximately six (6) months.

Under these circumstances, obviously, your application for recall to extended active duty cannot be favorably considered.

Thank you for your interest in the United States Army.

Sincerely yours,

John D. Glover

Major, Adjutant General's Corps
Deputy Chief, Reserve Officer Branch
(Armor) ODCS-P

He was sorely tempted to write Major Glover and tell him to stick his commission up his anal orifice, but he decided, finally, fuck him. It wasn't worth the time or effort.

[SEVEN]
Garmisch-Partenkirchen, Germany
30 May 1950

Garmisch was nice, really beautiful, but there were some problems. There weren't very many permanent party personnel, and the commissary and PX were small. There was only a small medical detachment, known as the Broken Bones Squad, to handle skiing accidents; and there was not even a dentist.

What the permanent party did was drive into Munich, about one hundred kilometers (sixty miles) to the north. A U.S. Army General Hospital there provided pediatricians for Sanford, Jr., and obstetricians for Sharon now that she was that way again. There was also a huge commissary with a much wider selection than the one in Garmisch had; and, of course, the Munich Military Post PX was the largest in Germany.

Sandy arranged his classes so that he was free after 1100 on Fridays. That allowed him to get into Munich to the hospital by half past two. He had bought a 1950 Buick Roadmaster sedan, two months old, from a captain who had been a ski instructor. He'd broken his leg and been shipped home. Sandy got it at a good price, and he liked having a big car. The way some of the Germans drove, it was better to be in a big car in case of accident.

There was a standard routine when the Felters went to Munich. First, he dropped Sharon at the hospital and then he went to the commissary with the shopping list. Then he went back to the hospital and picked up Sharon and Little Sandy, and they went together to the PX. They spent the night in the Four Seasons Hotel, and then drove back to Garmisch late Saturday mornings. He didn't like to be on the roads at night if he could avoid it, and the Four Seasons was a good hotel—run by the army—where you could get a really fancy meal at a very reasonable price.

It was a Friday afternoon in early June, the first really nice spring day they'd had. Sandy dropped Sharon off at the hospital (Little Sandy didn't need to see the pediatrician, so he had him with him), and then he drove to the commissary.

He parked the Buick, then got out and somewhat awkwardly locked it, holding Little Sandy in his arms so he wouldn't run around the parking lot in front of a car.

And the fat jolly butcher from the Gehlen Organization appeared out of nowhere and said: "Oh, what a pretty little boy!"

"Why, thank you," Sandy said. "I think so."

"He looks just like my grandson," the jolly fat butcher said, and took out his wallet and held it open for Sandy to look.

It wasn't a picture of a little boy. It was a picture of a tall, skinny man in worn work clothing.

"That was taken ten days ago," the butcher said. "At Vyritsa, near Leningrad. If nothing goes wrong, processing takes about ten days. We'll keep you posted."

"You're sure this is the one?"

"My dear Felter," the man said, "please believe me. That is Colonel Count Peter-Paul von Greiffenberg."

"No offense," Felter said. "But this is a little personal, too."

"So I understand," the jolly butcher said, enjoying Felter's surprise. "Our mutual friend thought that Colonel Robert F. Bellmon would be interested in the gentleman's homecoming, and asked me to ask you if you would be good enough to give him the word."

The fat jolly butcher put his wallet away, and started making cootchy-cootchy-coo sounds to Little Sandy. Then he said, "Our mutual friend would like both of you to know that while we make a mistake once in a while, most of the time we're pretty efficient."

Then he tipped his hat and walked away.

[EIGHT]
Marburg an der Lahn, Germany
24 June 1950

He was tall and skeletal. His eyes were sunken and his skin was gray, and he had other classical signs of prolonged malnutrition. The suit that Generalmajor (Retired) Gunther von Hamm had insisted on giving him in Bad Hersfeld to replace the rags he had from the Russians hung loosely on his shoulders and bagged over his buttocks, which were nothing more than muscle and bone. The shoes hurt his feet, although he couldn't understand why that should be. They were quality leather, even lined with leather. Gunther had said that the government was paying pensions again and that he really could afford to give him clothing, money, and whatever else he needed until his own retirement and back pay came through.

He had been riding in the dining car since lunch. He had felt a little faint, and he hadn't wanted to walk back to his second-class compartment. He'd asked the waiter if he could stay, and the waiter had been more than obliging. The waiter had seen returnees like him before. They made him uncomfortable, and if one of them wanted to sit at a dining car table, that seemed little enough to ask.

He had broken the rules. He was supposed to go to a returnee center in Cologne, but when the train had stopped at Kassel, the first stop after crossing the border, he had just gotten off. He had had enough of centers and processing. He'd hitchhiked to Bad Hersfeld and found Gunther and Greta by the simple expedient of looking for their name in the phone book.

Gunther had picked him up in his Volkswagen, and he could tell from the look in Gunther's eyes how bad he looked—and something else: Gunther did not have good news for him.

He got it that night: His wife was dead, a suicide. His daughter was believed to have gone to relatives in East Germany. Gunther said the Red Cross was very helpful in circumstances like these, in establishing contact across the East/West German borders.

He knew that Gunther didn't believe a word he was saying.

So he had come home to nothing.

He had felt too weak to go on just then, and so he imposed on Gunther's hospitality for four days. They fed him, and they tried to talk of pleasant things. And then he had announced, and he would not be dissuaded, that he was feeling fine now and wanted to go to Marburg. He had no place else to go, and there was no sense putting it off.

Kassel appeared to have really taken a beating. He remembered the Americans had come up north to Kassel through Giessen. Out of the foggy recesses of memory, he recalled seeing a communiqué. American armored forces had taken Giessen and were proceeding in the direction of Kassel.

If they had done this to Kassel, what had they done to Marburg, which was on their only possible route north?

The train reached the Marburg railyards all of a sudden, surprising him. The area didn't seem to have suffered any damage at all.

He got up and picked up the cardboard suitcase, tied shut with strings. He remembered to leave a tip for the waiter. There was new money; deutsche marks had replaced reichsmarks. He really had no idea what they were worth. Gunther had given him five hundred deutsche marks, to be paid back when he got his affairs in order.

He looked at the money, and decided that five marks would be a suitable tip. There was a little strip of silver inlaid in the paper. He had noticed that with interest.

He laid the five marks on the table and got up and walked carefully out of the dining room and stood in the vestibule. The waiter came after him and gave him his five marks back.

"Welcome home, *mein Herr*," he said.

"Thank you very much," he said. That was very touching. Do I look that bad?

He could see out the open vestibule window now. There *wasn't* much damage. People were playing soccer on the old soccer field. Whatever else had happened, the twin spires of St. Elizabeth's Church were there, rising above the trees.

Next the old city came into view. There was no damage. How incredible. It looked exactly as it had looked the day he left! As he had so often thought of it in memory.

And then they were in the station, and the train was slowing. He waited until it had completely stopped. He stepped between the cars into the vestibule from which the steps had been lowered, then got carefully, awkwardly off.

He was still holding the five marks in his hand. He put it into his jacket pocket, or tried to. The pocket was still sewn shut. He put it in his trousers pocket. Just having money was a strange feeling.

The people made him feel strange. They were all so fat, they were all so *rosy*.

There were two men on the platform, watching the arriving passengers go down the stairway to the tunnel leading to the station. Policemen. He knew a policeman when he saw one. They were looking at something, probably a photograph, held in their hands.

They can't be expecting me, he thought. No one knows about me. No one knew about me coming until I arrived. My name wasn't even on the list of returned prisoners.

But the policemen, nevertheless, looked at him very intently when he walked past them and started down the stairs. Probably because I was so long a prisoner. Policemen don't like prisoners; whether they are criminals or prisoners of war, it makes no difference.

They know, he thought, with something close to terror. They know I didn't go to the center in Cologne, as I was ordered to do. They have come to arrest me.

He sensed, rather than saw, that the policemen were coming down the stairs behind him. There was a feeling of terror. So close, and am I to be arrested again? But why? There didn't have to be a reason. The state provided any reason it wanted. It was not necessary to satisfy a prisoner that he was being justly detained.

He went up the stairs into the station. The general outline of the station was familiar, but there was something new. He wondered about that. The glass, of course. The doors were now all glass. Before they had been wooden doors with glass panels. Now they were huge pieces of thick glass. Much nicer. The station had obviously been bombed; and when they'd rebuilt it, they had put in new doors, making them all glass.

He wondered why they didn't break, with all the use they obviously got.

He had probably been wrong about the policemen. They hadn't arrested him. Why should they? They had just happened to come down the stairs when he did.

He reached the glass doors. The door was automatic, and he watched it close. He put his hand out to push it open again. Before he touched it, the door opened away from him with a whoosh. How did they do that?

He stepped outside. Way down Bahnhofstrasse, he could see the Cafe Weitz. It was still in business. How interesting.

Somebody snapped their fingers behind him. He started, turned his head, and saw one of the policemen, with a subtle but unmistakable gesture, pointing him out to someone else, someone ahead of him.

What do they want to arrest me for?

How much can I be punished for not going to the center in Cologne?

Then he thought: It's probably nothing more than a debriefing. The military wants to debrief me on what I saw in Russia. I saw the inside of an office in a logging camp in a swamp and nothing more. I could tell them, "I saw nothing of military significance at all." But they wouldn't believe him. They would insist on a full interrogation, according to regulation.

He bristled then. They should have sent an officer to do this. I am entitled to that courtesy. They should have sent an officer in uniform, not policemen.

There was an enormous car at the curb. He read what was spelled out in chrome on the trunk lid. Ford Super Deluxe. It didn't look like the Ford automobiles he remembered.

A tall man who looked like a policeman was leaning on the car, and now he stood up straight and took off his hat and stepped in front of him.

"Herr Graf?" the man asked in a Berliner's accent. It had been a long time since he had been addressed as Herr Graf. He was afraid of the policeman.

"Herr Oberst Graf von Greiffenberg?" the policeman asked again.

"Yes," the Graf said. "I am the Graf, and formerly Oberst."

"Herr Oberst Graf, will you come with us, please?"

Resistance was obviously futile. There were three of them, and he was tired and weak. He got in the back of the Ford. One of the policeman got in beside him and the other one in the front.

With squeal of tires, the car made a U-turn and drove past the soccer field. Policemen always drove too fast, he thought.

"See if you can raise them from here, Ken," the driver of the car, the man in charge, said. He spoke in English. It had been a long time since he had heard English spoken.

The other man in the front seat picked up what looked like a telephone.

"Umpire, Umpire," he said. "This is Home Base. Do you read, over?"

"Home Base, this is Umpire. Read you five by five, go ahead."

"I'll be damned," the man driving said.

"Umpire, Home Base," the man with the telephone said. "We have the eagle in the bag. I say again, we have the eagle in the bag. Heading for the autobahn."

"You're Americans," he said.

"Yes, sir, Colonel," the man driving said. "We're American. We've been looking all over for you."

The radio went off again a few minutes later.

"Home Base, Umpire, do you read??"

"Go ahead, Umpire."

"You'll be met at the autobahn. Black Buick Roadmaster. Confirm."

"Understand black Buick at the autobahn."

"Roger, Roger. What's the eagle's condition?"

"Feathers are a little ruffled, that's about it."

"Umpire clear with Home Base."

There was an even more enormous automobile waiting for them at the autobahn. A little Jew got out of it and walked over to the Ford and opened the door. He put his hand out.

"My name is Felter, sir," the little Jew said. "I'm here to meet you at the request of an old comrade-in-arms. We've been looking all over for you, sir."

"Who would that be?" he said, stiffly. "What old comrade-in-arms?"

"Colonel Robert Bellmon, sir," the little man said.

The Graf straightened. So Bellmon had made it, had he?

"This is very kind of Colonel Bellmon," the Graf said. "But if it is permitted, I would prefer to be in Marburg."

"If you will, sir," the little Jew said, "please come with me. I have a car, here, sir," Captain Sanford T. Felter said.

The Graf was not used to arguing with authority.

"Very well," he said.

The Jew's Buick Roadmaster was the biggest automobile the Colonel Count von Greiffenberg had ever seen. The softness of the seats was incredible. They were like a very comfortable couch.

"May I be permitted to inquire where I am being taken?"

"Kronberg Castle, sir. Colonel Bellmon, and some others, are waiting for you there."

"Some others?"

The little Jew didn't answer that question.

"It'll take us just about an hour, sir," he said.

Colonel Graf Peter-Paul von Greiffenberg dozed off.

The last time Colonel Graf Peter-Paul von Greiffenberg had been to Kronberg Castle was at a reception given by Prince Philip of Hesse. Now, he was not very surprised to see, it had been taken over by the Americans. To judge by the officers he saw, they were using it as some sort of rest hotel for their senior officers.

The little Jew opened the door for him and led him into the hotel.

"If you'll come with me, please, sir," he said.

The inside of the castle was just as luxuriously furnished as it ever had been.

"Colonel, if you'll just sit here a moment, I'll go get Colonel Bellmon," the little Jew said, ushering him into an armchair.

"Get this gentleman whatever he wants," the little Jew said to a waiter.

"What can I get you, sir?" the waiter asked.

"Nothing, thank you," he said. "I think I'll walk around. If I may."

"Of course, sir."

He walked into what used to be the library. It was still the library, and through its French doors he could see the rolling lawn. He went to look out.

He saw Bellmon. Bellmon and a tall, good-looking young man were driving golf balls. The colonel was perversely pleased that the little Jew had not been able to find Bellmon. He considered walking through the French doors and just going up to him. And then he decided he had better wait. He was, in effect, Bellmon's guest.

There was a blond child, a boy, a beautiful little thing, being attended by a middle-aged woman in an army nurse's uniform, and a blond young woman, obviously the child's mother. The young woman looked too young to be a general's wife, but she had a coat, mink, he thought, and clothes and jewelry that made it plain she was not a junior officer's wife.

She belonged, the colonel decided, to the tall blond man driving golf balls with Colonel Bellmon. There was something about him that smelled of money and position.

Then the little Jew appeared and walked quickly over to Colonel Bellmon.

Bellmon dropped his golf club and started into the building. The young man went to the young woman. They started for the building. It must be Bellmon's son and daughter. That's who it had to be.

Colonel Count Peter-Paul von Greiffenberg turned and faced the door through which Bellmon would appear. He would, he told himself, not lose control of his emotions. He would be what he was, an officer and a gentleman.

Bellmon entered the room and saw him and, the colonel knew, recognized him. But he did not cross the room to him. Do I look that bad?

The young woman in the mink coat, clutching the child in her arms, came into the room. She gave the child to the handsome young man. And then she crossed the room, and looked into his eyes.

"Papa?" she asked.

The Captains

I

At approximately 0500 Sunday, 25 June 1950, Koreans awakened Major George D. Kessler, USA, Korean Military Advisory Group advisor to the 10th Regiment at Samch'ok and told him a heavy North Korean attack was in progress at the 38th parallel.

U.S. ARMY IN THE KOREAN WAR, VOL. 1, P. 27
OFFICE OF THE CHIEF OF MILITARY HISTORY, U.S. ARMY, WASHINGTON, D.C., 1961

[ONE]
Seoul, Korea
25 June 1950

The 38th parallel bisects the Korean peninsula. From a point near Ongjin, on the Yellow Sea, to another near Yangyang on the Sea of Japan, the parallel stretches just over 200 miles.

If the forces of the Immun Gun, the Army of the People's Democratic Republic of Korea, had been spread out equally across the 38th parallel, there would have been one Immun Gun soldier every twelve feet. There were 90,000 of them. And one in three of these was a veteran of the Chinese Communist Army, which had just sent Chiang Kai-shek fleeing to the island of Formosa.

They were not, of course, spread out across the line. They were formed in Russian-style military organizations. There were seven infantry divisions, one armored brigade, equipped with the Russian T34 tank which had stopped Germany's best, a separate infantry regiment, a motorcycle regiment, and a brigade of the Border Constabulary, the Bo An Dae, North Korea's version of the Waffen SS.

They had 150 tanks in all, and 200 airplanes, large quantities of 76 mm self-propelled howitzers, and even more 122 mm truck-drawn howitzers. They were "advised" by a large contingent of Russian officers and technicians, and they were equipped with Russian small arms.

They also had boats, and they made two amphibious landings behind the South Korean lines between Samch'ok and the 38th parallel on the Sea of Japan in coordination with an attack by the 5th Infantry Division on the 10th Regiment of the Republic of Korea's (ROK) 8th Infantry Division.

The 2nd and 7th North Korean Infantry Divisions attacked the understrength ROK 6th Division at Ch'unch'on. The 3rd and 4th North Korean Infantry Divisions, reinforced by the 14th Tank Regiment, attacked the ROK 7th Division at Uijongbu. The North Korean 1st and 6th Infantry Divisions, reinforced by the 203rd Tank

Regiment, attacked the ROK 1st "Capitol" Division (less the 17th Infantry Regiment) at Kaesong on the route to Seoul and Inchon. And on the extreme left of the front, that peaceful Sunday morning, the North Korean Border Constabulary Brigade and the 14th Infantry Regiment attacked the ROK 17th infantry Regiment, which held the Ongjin peninsula on the Yellow Sea.

[TWO]
Ongjin Peninsula, Korea
0400 Hours
25 June 1950

When, without warning, the positions and the headquarters of the 17th Infantry Regiment of the Capitol Division were brought under artillery, mortar, and heavy automatic weapons fire by the Border Constabulary of the People's Democratic Republic of Korea, the three American officers—a captain and two lieutenants—of the U.S. Army Korean Military Advisory Group were asleep in their quarters on a knoll overlooking the regimental headquarters, a sandbag bunker erected on the near side of one of the hills.

Their quarters, now fixed up to be as comfortable as possible, had once been a farmhouse. The floor was baked mud, through which vents carried heat in the winter, a device alleged to be the world's first central heating system. The walls were mortared stone, eighteen inches thick, and the roof was of foot-thick thatch.

Because they recognized the need to do so, the three made a valiant effort to live as much like their Korean counterparts as they could, yet there were things in the ex-farmhouse to be found nowhere else in the 17th Infantry. There was a General Electric refrigerator and a Zenith combination radio-phonograph and a Sears, Roebuck three-burner electric hotplate, all powered via a heavy rubber-covered cable by a skid-mounted GM diesel generator. And there was a Collins BC-610 radio transmitter and an RCA AR-88 communications receiver, used for communication with KMAG in Seoul, forty-five or fifty miles, as the crow flies, to the east.

For all practical purposes, the 17th Infantry (Colonel Paik In Yup commanding) was on an island, although the Ongjin peninsula was of course connected with the peninsula of Korea. When the Great Powers had partitioned Korea after War II, they had made the 38th parallel the dividing line. The Russian and Red Chinese-backed People's Democratic Republic lay north of it, while the American-backed Republic of Korea lay south.

The 38th parallel crossed the Ongjin peninsula very near the point where it joined the Korean peninsula; the line was fortified on both sides, and there was no land passage between the Ongjin peninsula and the rest of South Korea. All commerce (what there was of it) and all supply of the 17th Infantry had to be accomplished by sea.

It was generally agreed among the three American officers assigned to the 17th that if the gooks north of the parallel started something, they were really going to be up the creek without a paddle.

Seconds after the first artillery shell whistled in from North Korea, it was followed by another and another. Simultaneously, there came the different whistle of incoming heavy mortars, and off in the distance, the dull rumble of heavy machine guns. It was apparent that the shit had indeed hit the fan.

The three officers dressed hurriedly, in crisply starched fatigues and highly shined combat boots (laundry and boot polishing were available for three dollars per month, or the equivalent in PX merchandise) and picked up their personal weapons. Technically, as instructors of the 17th Infantry, they were supposed to be unarmed. But the North Koreans were capable of infiltration, and the South Koreans were capable of stealing anything not firmly embedded in concrete; personal weapons to defend themselves against either happenstance were as necessary to their survival as the water purification pills and toilet tissue (1,000 sheets per roll) that reached them at irregular intervals via the South Korean Navy's LSTs.

The senior instructor, clutching a U.S. .30 caliber carbine in his hand, announced that he was going over to the CP to see what the fuck was going on. His two subordinates, one armed with a carbine, the other with a privately owned Smith & Wesson .357 Magnum revolver, turned to firing up the diesel generator (shut down at bedtime because of the horrific roar it made) and to warming up the BC-610 and the AR-88 radios.

By the time the generator had been running long enough to warm up the radio tubes, the senior instructor was back from the 17th Infantry's command post.

"Any luck?" he asked the lieutenant at the microphone. The lieutenant shook his head, "no." The captain took the microphone from him.

"Victor, Victor, this is Tahiti, Tahiti," he said into the mike. And he said it again and again without response for fifteen minutes as artillery whistled in to explode deafeningly, sending white-hot fragments of steel ricocheting off the foot-thick stone walls of the hootch, until the voice radio operator on duty at KMAG returned from taking a leisurely crap secure in the knowledge that absolutely nothing was going to happen at 0400 on a Sunday morning in the Land of the Morning Calm.

"Tahiti," a bored voice finally came over the AR-88's speaker. "This is Victor. Read you five by five. Go ahead."

"Where the fuck have you been?" the captain demanded, furiously. And then without waiting for a reply, he went on. "Victor, stand by to copy Operational Immediate, I say again, Operational Immediate."

The radio op's voice was no longer bored: "Victor ready to copy Operational Immediate. Go ahead."

"From Tahiti Six to KMAG Six, 17th ROK under heavy artillery mortar and heavy automatic weapons fire since 0400. Believe ground assault will follow shortly. All KMAG personnel at CP. Advise. Signature is Delahanty, Captain. You got that?"

"I got it, Tahiti," Victor said. "Stand by."

[THREE]
Headquarters
Korean Military Advisory Group (KMAG)
Seoul, Korea
25 June 1950

The commanding general of KMAG had boarded a ship the day before in Pusan to go home; his replacement had not officially assumed command. The slot called for a brigadier general, and there had been no rush among the army's one-star generals to ask for the command. Korea, "Frozen Chosen," was generally recognized to be the asshole of the globe, and serving as senior advisor to its raggedy-assed army was not considered to be a desirable assignment.

Pending the assignment of a new general, command had been temporarily vested in the KMAG chief of staff, a colonel of artillery. When the word of the North Korean invasion reached him, when it became apparent that it was not an "incident" but a bona fide invasion of South Korea by a four-pronged land assault across the parallel and by two amphibious invasions on the east coast, the colonel had serious doubts that anything could be done to stop it. The only American troops in South Korea were his, and they were not organized in any kind of military formation that could be committed to combat. And while the colonel believed that the South Korean Army would fight, he knew better than just about anyone else that they didn't have much to fight with.

That made evacuation, or withdrawal, or whatever word one wanted to use for getting the hell out of Seoul, the only reasonable action to take. Doing that was not going to be easy. There were a thousand problems to be solved almost immediately, and among these was what to do about those three poor bastards stuck on the Ongjin peninsula with the ROK 17th Infantry.

The only sure way to get them out was by air, by Stinson L-5, a single-engine aircraft used by the army to direct artillery fire from the air, to supervise movement of armored or logistic columns, and as sort of an aerial jeep. But it would take either three L-5s, or three flights by one L-5, because the tiny aircraft were capable of carrying only one passenger at a time. Furthermore, the colonel realized that he had better things to do with his L-5s. They were not only the best eyes he had, but they were absolutely essential to carry messages. Communications, never very reliable, had already started to go out, probably because of sabotage. He was very much afraid that he was going to have to leave the three KMAG instructors to fend for themselves.

And then the colonel remembered that there was a Supreme Commander, Allied Powers (SCAP) L-17 Navion sitting at Kimpo Airfield. One of MacArthur's palace guard, a colonel in military government, was enamored of a State Department civilian lady at the Embassy, and had arranged to fly over from Tokyo to see her. It was a four-passenger airplane, big enough to pick up the three officers at the 17th ROK Infantry CP. The colonel considered begging the use of it from the SCAP colonel, but decided not to do that. The SCAP colonel, probably still asleep in the arms of love, might very well decide that the Big Picture required his immediate return to the Dai Ichi Building. There was time, the colonel decided, for the L-17 to rescue those poor bastards on Ongjin, and then fly the SCAP colonel out.

He motioned a master sergeant to him.

"Take a jeep and go out to Kimpo, and find the pilot of a SCAP L-17, and ask him to go get the officers with the 17th ROK," he said. "If he won't do it, you get him on the horn to me. At pistol point, if you have to."

[FOUR]
Kimpo Airfield
Seoul, Korea
25 September 1950

Captain Rudolph G. "Mac" MacMillan, Army Aviation Section, Headquarters, Supreme Commander, Allied Powers (SCAP), had flown one of SCAP's L-17 Navions to Seoul from Tokyo the day before, landing just before noon after a two-day, 1,000-mile flight.

MacMillan was Scotch-Irish, out of Mauch Chuck, Pennsylvania. He had enlisted in the army ten years before, at seventeen, after two years in the anthracite coal mines where everybody else he knew worked out their lives. He had no idea what the army was going to be like, but it couldn't be worse than the mines. The possibility of becoming a commissioned officer and a gentleman had never entered his mind. His vaguely formed dream then was to get up to corporal in four years, so he could marry his sweetheart, Roxy, and maybe up to staff sergeant before he had thirty years in. With a staff sergeant's pension, he had dreamed, he could save enough money to buy a saloon, and then he and Roxy would be on Easy Street.

World War II had changed all that.

There were three L-17s in the fleet of army aircraft assigned to the U.S. Army of Occupation in Japan. The Navions (from North American Aviation) had been bought "off-the-shelf" with funds reluctantly provided by Congress, less to provide the army with airplanes than to assist North American Aviation in making the transition from a manufacturer of warplanes (North American had built thousands of P-51s during World War II) to a manufacturer of light aircraft for the civilian market.

The L-17 Navion bore a faint resemblance to the P-51. There was a certain sleekness in the Navion that no other light aircraft, except perhaps Beech's "Bonanza," had; and the vertical stabilizer of the small aircraft looked very much like the vertical stabilizer of the P-51. But it was a civilian airplane, despite the star-and-bar identification painted on the fuselage and the legend US ARMY painted on the sides of the vertical stabilizer.

The seats were upholstered in leather, and the instrument panel, probably on purpose, looked like the dashboard of a car. There were four seats under a slide-back plexiglass canopy. There had been a notion among certain North American executives that all it was going to take to fill America's postwar skies with Navions flown by business executives and salesmen, and even by Daddies taking the family out for a Sunday afternoon drive through the skies, would be to convince the public that the Navion was nothing more than a Buick or a Chrysler with wings. They had designed the Navion to fit that image.

An airplane, of course, is not a car, and the idea never caught on as people hoped it would, but a number of Navions were built, and about forty of them were sold to the U.S. Army. They were used as transport aircraft for senior officers who wanted to fly, for example, from Third Army Headquarters in Atlanta to Fort Benning when there was no convenient (or available) means to do so by commercial airlines.

Some of the Navions were sent to the army overseas, to Germany and the Panama Canal Zone, to Alaska and Japan. Unofficially, they were assigned on the basis of one per lieutenant general and higher. By that criterion—which worked in the States and in Europe—Supreme Headquarters, Far East Command, U.S. Army, Japan, should have received but two L-17 Navions, for there were only two officers in the Far East in the grade of lieutenant general or above.

Lieutenant General Walton H. Walker commanded the Eighth United States Army, the Army of Occupation of Japan. Above him was General of the Army Douglas MacArthur. Custom, not regulation, dictates the rank of senior officers immediately subordinate to a five-star general. When General of the Army Dwight D. Eisenhower commanded the Army of Occupation of Germany from the Farben Building in Frankfurt, his chief of staff had been a full, four-star general, who himself had a three-star lieutenant general for a deputy. Five other lieutenant generals were scattered through the command structure.

When five-star General of the Army Douglas MacArthur had requested a suitable officer to serve him as chief of staff in the Dai Ichi Building in Tokyo, the Pentagon could find no officer suitable to serve the Supreme Commander except a lowly major general, Edward M. Almond, whose most distinguished previous service had been as the commanding general of a division in the Italian campaign whose troops were almost entirely black.

MacArthur rose above that studied insult, as he rose above others, including the somewhat unequal distribution of L-17 Navion aircraft. Headquarters, European Theater got thirteen of the winged Buicks, and Headquarters, Far East Theater got three. MacArthur simply made the L-17s availble to whoever needed aerial transportation around Japan and to Korea.

At the lower echelons, however, among the brigadier generals and the colonels in the Dai Ichi Building, and especially among the small corps of army aviators, use of the L-17 became a matter of prestige, of privilege, of honor.

The SAC (for Supreme Allied Commander) army aviation officer, a full colonel, and his deputy, a lieutenant colonel, flew most of the missions in the L-17s. With the exception of Captain Rudolph G. "Mac" MacMillan, the other pilots permitted to fly the tiny fleet of L-17s were the other lieutenant colonel aviators, and a few, especially well-regarded majors.

MacMillan, who frequently got to fly one of the L-17s, was a special case. He had several things going for him, even though, having learned to fly only four years before, he was a newcomer to army aviation. For one thing, in 1940, Rudy MacMillan had brought prestige to the Department of the Philippines by winning the All-Army Light-Heavyweight Boxing Crown. The contests had been held that year at Fort McKinley, near Manila; and MacArthur, then Marshal of the Philippine Army, and a boxing fan, had watched MacMillan train, and had personally awarded him the golden belt.

MacMillan had not been with MacArthur in the Philippines during the war—which always granted a special cachet—but he had done the next best thing. He'd won the Medal of Honor. If there was one little clique around General MacArthur for whom he did not try to conceal his affection, it was those few men entitled to wear, as Douglas MacArthur himself wore, the inch-long, quarter-inch-wide piece of blue silk, dotted with white stars.

MacMillan's award had been for his "intrepid gallantry and valor in the face of overwhelming enemy forces." MacMillan had been trapped on the wrong side of the river during Operation Market-Garden, his fifth jump into combat with the 82nd Airborne Division. He didn't learn that he had been awarded the Medal, or the battlefield promotion to second lieutenant and officer and gentleman, until some months after the action. He spent some of that time in a German POW camp in Poland, and some of it escaping from the camp and leading twenty-two others on an odyssey to freedom that earned him the Distinguished Service Cross to go with his new gold bars and the Medal.

So no one had really been surprised, when the orders were cut for Colonel Jasper B. Downs, General Staff Corps, Hq, SCAP, to proceed by army aircraft to Seoul to confer with KMAG, that Captain MacMillan had been assigned as his pilot. A flight to Seoul was a good deal.

Mac MacMillan had come to Seoul with instructions from Mrs. Roxanne "Roxy" MacMillan, the twenty-eight-year-old redheaded woman to whom he had been married for a decade, to get her eight yards of a really nice green silk brocade. Roxy wanted some to make herself a dress, and some to send home to her sister in Mauch Chuck, Pennsylvania.

There were a number of things available in the enormous Tokyo PX that were unavailable in Korea. If you knew what you were doing, you could make the Seoul trip with one extra, nonsuspicious Valv-Pak full of the right things, and come home with an empty Valv-Pak and a nice stack of either Army of Occupation script or real green dollars; or if you liked that kind of stuff, with the Valv-Pak full of silk brocade, maybe wrapped around some three-hundred-year-old vase.

When the master sergeant from Headquarters, Korean Military Advisory Group (KMAG), burst into MacMillan's room at the bachelor officer's hotel at Kimpo Airfield, the silk brocade was in his Valv-Pak, wrapped around a nearly transparent china tea set MacMillan had been solemnly informed was at least three hundred years old.

In his bed was a large-breasted blond he had not planned on, but who had been at the Naija Hotel roof garden when he'd gone there for a drink, and who had soon made her desires known. Mac MacMillan's philosophy was that while he didn't go running after it, he didn't kick it out of bed either. He always wore his wedding ring.

If he was going to get a little on the side, it was better to screw a commercial attaché, or something like that, an American broad from the Embassy who had as much to lose as he did, than fuck around with either the nips in Tokyo, or the slopes here.

But he was embarrassed when the master sergeant came barging into his room at the BOQ and caught him in bed with her like that.

"What the hell?" he said, sitting up in bed. "Goddamnit, Sergeant, didn't anybody ever teach you to knock?"

"Captain, the North Koreans are attacking all over the goddamned parallel."

The blond looked at him in disbelief for just a minute, saw that he was serious, and covered her mouth with her hand.

"Oh, my God!" she said.

"Jesus Christ!" MacMillan said, and got out of bed and picked up his shorts where he'd dropped them on the floor.

"Are they coming here?" the blond asked, holding the sheet in front of her, more frightened now than embarrassed or outraged.

"It's no raid," the sergeant said. "It's a war, that's what it is."

"Jesus Christ," MacMillan said again. He pulled his tropical worsted Class "A" trousers on, and then dipped into the nearest of his two Valv-Paks and came up with a small Colt .32 caliber automatic pistol. He ejected the clip, confirmed that it contained cartridges, replaced it, and put the pistol in his hip pocket.

"The colonel sent me to ask you to pick up three officers on the Ongjin peninsula," the master sergeant said.

"Why?" MacMillan asked, as he put on his shirt.

"Because they're cut off, is why," the sergeant said.

"I got my own colonel to worry about," MacMillan replied.

"Unless you go get them," the sergeant said, "they're gonna get run over."

"I didn't say I wouldn't go get them," MacMillan replied. "What I said was that I got my own colonel to worry about."

"What happens to me, Mac?" the blond asked. She was now out of bed, her back to the men, picking up her underpants from where she had dropped them the night before.

"The sergeant will take you into Seoul to the Embassy, or wherever you want to go," Mac said. "If I were you, I'd go to the Embassy first."

"All right," she said, as if making a decision.

"The guys at Ongjin know I'm coming after them?" MacMillan asked.

"We told them we'd try to get somebody up there," the sergeant said.

"That's not what I asked," MacMillan said angrily.

"Their radio's out," the sergeant said.

"Which means they could already be rolled over, doesn't it?" MacMillan said.

"We have to try," the sergeant said.

"*We* have to try?" MacMillan said. "Shit!"

There was a peculiar whistling sound outside. MacMillan's face screwed up as he tried to identify it. Then there came the scream of propellers on aircraft flying low.

"Goddamnit, they're strafing the airfield," MacMillan said and went to the window, pushing the curtain aside. He saw a Russian-built YAK fighter pulling up after a run on the terminal building across the field. "Shit, if they get the Navion, we'll all be walking," he said.

The blond, oblivious to the amount of thigh she was displaying, hooked her stockings to her garters, pulled her dress down, and slipped into her shoes. MacMillan sat down and put on his shoes and socks.

"Let's go see if I still have an airplane," he said. He put his leather-billed cap on, picked up his two Valv-Paks, and walked out of the BOQ.

The Navion, parked across the field from the air force and civilian terminals of the airfield, was intact. MacMillan put his Valv-Paks in the plane, one in the luggage compartment, one in the back seat, and then turned to face the blond and the sergeant.

"I want you to find my colonel," he said. "Colonel Downs, he's in the Naija Hotel. Tell him what I've done and that I should be back here, if I can still get in here, in an hour. If I can't get in here, I'll go down to Suwon."

"Yes, sir," the master sergeant said. He had just noticed the fruit salad on MacMillan's tunic. He didn't think much of army aviators, and wondered if this one was really entitled to wear the blue ribbon with the white stars on it.

"You'll be all right," MacMillan said to the blond. "They've got an evacuation plan, in case something like this happens."

She raised her face to be kissed. It turned into a passionate embrace. MacMillan was grossly embarrassed. She was hanging on to him like that not because she was horny, but because she was scared.

He freed himself, stepped up on the wing, and crawled into the cabin. He busied himself with the preflight checklist, not looking up until he heard the sounds of the jeep starting up and driving away.

Then he got out of the cabin again and walked around the plane, making the preflight. After that, he got in again and cranked it up. When the propeller was turning and the engine smoothing out, he closed the canopy, released the brakes, and moved onto the taxiway.

There was no response when he tried to call the tower, so he simply turned onto the active and pushed the throttle to the firewall. Even if he was taking off downwind, he had enough runway to get it into the air.

He took off toward the city, made a steep, climbing turn to the right, passing over the KMAG Skeet and Trap Club on the banks of the Han River, and then changed his mind about the altitude. The YAK fighters might come back. He lowered the nose and flew at treetop level through the low mountains until he reached Inchon and the sea. Then he pointed the Navion's nose toward the Ongjin peninsula.

[FIVE]

MacMillan made a power-on approach to the command post of the 17th ROK Infantry Regiment. With his flaps down and the engine of the Navion running at cruise power, he had two options. If he saw the Americans he had come to fetch, he could chop the throttle and put the Navion on the ground. If he didn't see the Americans, or, as he thought was entirely likely, he saw North Koreans, he could dump the flaps and get his ass the hell out of there.

There was nobody in sight as he flew over the command post, and he had just about decided the unit had been rolled over when he spotted three people furiously waving their arms and what looked like field jackets at the far end of the short, dirt runway. He was too far down the runway by then to get the Navion on the ground, so he went around again, came in even lower, dropped his landing gear, and when he was halfway down the dirt strip, touched down. He hit the brakes as soon as he dared.

Now that he was on the ground, rolling toward the three men, he could see they were Americans. As he taxied toward them, he wondered where the hell everybody else was. And then there was an explosion which both shook the Navion and sprayed it with dirt and rocks. He had landed at the 17th ROK Regiment thirty seconds before they blew up the CP.

The first of the three Americans scrambled onto the Navion's wing before MacMillan had finished turning around and before he had the canopy open. He lurched to a stop, unlatched the canopy, and slid it back on its tracks. One by one, almost frenziedly, the three American officers climbed into the cockpit.

MacMillan was pleased to see that the last man to climb in was the senior of the three officers. The senior officer would most likely be the last. But it wouldn't hurt to ask.

"Is that all?" MacMillan shouted, over the roar of the engine.

The officer beside him vigorously shook his head, "yes."

MacMillan turned to slide the canopy closed. There was a pinging noise on the side of the fuselage. He turned around and rammed the throttle to the firewall. The Navion began to move. The officer beside him slid the canopy home and latched it in place. The Navion lifted off the ground. MacMillan pulled the wheels up and then immediately pushed the nose down to put a rise off the end of the dirt strip between him and the machine gun.

Sixty seconds later he was over the water and safe.

He thought that if Roxy's silk brocade and the nearly transparent, 300-year-old tea set got shot up, she'd really be pissed.

With the canopy closed and the engine throttled back to cruise, conversation was possible.

"Captain," the major said, "thank you very much."

"My pleasure," MacMillan said.

MacMillan realized there was going to be a confrontation between him and Colonel Jasper B. Downs, Deputy Chief, Office of Military Government, Headquarters, Supreme Commander, Allied Powers, the minute he touched down at Kimpo Airfield in Seoul.

Colonel Downs was sure to be waiting for "his" L-17 to land, more than a little pissed that "his pilot" had taken the aircraft assigned for his use on a flight without his permission. Colonel Downs was very much aware of his status as a senior member of the SCAP staff. In the present emergency, the chair-warming sonofabitch would see his duty clearly: He would be obliged to return to his headquarters immediately.

Fuck him.

It was not that Captain MacMillan was in the habit of frustrating the desires of his seniors, or for that matter, even privately questioning any orders he received. It was simply that he thought of himself as a warrior, and of Colonel Downs as a rear-echelon desk trooper. For the first time since he had arrived in the Far East—for that matter, for the first time since he had been in a drainage ditch in Belgium in the closing days of War II—MacMillan was sure of what he was doing.

As far as he was concerned, there were only two kinds of soldiers. There were those who lost their heads at the sound of hostile fire, and those who didn't. The warriors and the chair-borne. MacMillan believed himself to be a warrior, despite his present status as an army aviator. He had won the Medal as a paratrooper. And perhaps more important, General of the Army Douglas MacArthur, SCAP himself, was a warrior. He'd gotten the Medal in War I, and he liked to have people with the Medal around him.

All of these things combined to convince Captain Mac MacMillan that there was nothing really to worry about with Colonel Jasper B. Downs, even if the chair-warming sonofabitch would be waiting at Kimpo with his balls in an uproar.

MacMillan's prediction that Colonel Downs would be impatiently, even furiously, waiting for the Navion to return was quite accurate. Moreover, Colonel Downs was accompanied by Miss Genevieve Horne, a Foreign Service officer attached to the U.S. Embassy, Seoul, to whom (with, of course, the permission of the ambassador) he had offered transportation out of Korea. Obviously, there were going to be few cultural exchanges in the near future (Miss Horne was deputy cultural attaché), so her presence was not only not essential to the conduct of the Embassy's affairs, but actually an impediment to it. Flying her to Tokyo in the L-17 would not only insure her safety, and take advantage of passenger space that otherwise would be wasted, but would also give the colonel and Miss Horne the opportunity to spend some time together in Tokyo before she had to go back to Seoul after this incident with the North Koreans blew over.

Colonal Downs was therefore more than a little annoyed when he and Miss Horne and her luggage arrived at Kimpo Airfield and found his L-17 was gone. While it would be an exaggeration to say that Colonel Downs panicked when he couldn't find either the L-17 or anyone who knew what had happened to it, it would not be an exaggeration to say that he was enraged when he finally learned where the L-17 was. And when the plane touched down, he was quite prepared to give Captain MacMillan the benefit of his thinking.

Also waiting at Kimpo Field were two officers from KMAG, bearing with them a note scrawled on a message form by the acting commander, KMAG, authorizing them to commandeer any KMAG aircraft for the purpose of conducting an aerial reconnaissance of the land approaches to Seoul. While they knew full well that the L-17 was not assigned to KMAG, they approached it nevertheless the moment it taxied up before the army hangar. If the pilot was not impressed with their authority to commandeer, perhaps he would listen to reason.

MacMillan did just that, over the violent protests of Colonel Downs, which included both a recitation of the urgent need of his services at the earliest possible moment in Tokyo and a direct order to Captain MacMillan that he make immediate preparations to board himself and Miss Horne and fly them there.

"I'll split it down the middle," MacMillan said to the KMAG captain. "I'll take one of you guys with me for a recon. One hour. No more. The other one stays here and sits on that fuel truck. I don't want anybody blowing it up while I'm gone."

"Goddamnit, MacMillan," Colonel Downs said, with mingled disbelief and rage, "I've given you a direct order, and I expect to be obeyed."

"While I'm gone, Colonel," MacMillan replied, "you ask the lady to get what she really has to have into one of those suitcases. We can't take all of them."

Colonel Downs resisted the temptation to tell MacMillan what he intended to do with him when they got back to Tokyo. If he went too far, MacMillan conceivably would not return to pick him up at all. He could settle his hash in Tokyo. Congressional Medal or not, captains do not go around refusing to obey direct orders from colonels.

MacMillan actually gave the KMAG officer a two-hour recon flight. It took that long, and that's all there was to it. He landed at Kimpo again at a quarter past one, and it was another forty-five minutes before he could refuel the Navion and take off for Pusan.

MacMillan took on thirty gallons of gasoline in Pusan, more than enough for the Pusan-Kokura leg of the flight over the Straits of Korea, but not enough to fill the tanks. He was over Maximum Gross Weight as it was. If he had topped off the tanks, he'd never have gotten the Navion into the air.

When he landed at Itazuke Air Force Base near Kokura, he noticed unusual activity and had some trouble getting somebody to fuel the Navion. The ground personnel were too busy with fighter aircraft to bother with a little army liaison airplane.

It was nearly 0300 hours when MacMillan landed the Navion at Tachikawa Airfield at Tokyo. The long ride had done nothing to calm Colonel Downs's rage, and possibly it had been fueled by the last, long, Itazuke-Tachikawa leg, during which he had ridden in the somewhat cramped back seat. Miss Horne had requested that she be allowed to ride up front, and of course there was no way he could refuse her. Neither had he been able to participate in the long conversations she had had with MacMillan, because they were conducted via earphones and microphones, and the back seat was not equipped with them.

He would have been even more disturbed had he been able to eavesdrop on the conversation.

"Can I ask a personal question?" Miss Horne had asked MacMillan, over the intercom.

"Sure."

"Isn't that the Congressional Medal of Honor?"

"Yeah," MacMillan replied and actually flushed.

"I really don't know what to say," she said. "I've never met anybody before who had the Congressional Medal."

"There's a bunch of them around," MacMillan said.

"Oh, no, there's not!" Miss Horne insisted, touching Captain MacMillan's arm for emphasis.

"Yeah, there is," MacMillan insisted.

"I feel a whole lot better, I don't mind telling you," she said, "with someone like you around. I was really getting worried back there at Kimpo."

"There was no reason to be worried," MacMillan said. "I wouldn't have taken those KMAG guys on that recon flight if I didn't think there was time to do that and pick you up, too."

"Jasper, I mean, Colonel Downs was very worried." MacMillan said nothing.

"I suppose," Genevieve Horne said, "that someone like yourself thinks clearly under stress. I mean, I wish I had known who you were before you left us standing on the field."

"I have this rule," MacMillan said. "I never leave pretty women stranded."

She chuckled with pleasure.

"I'll bet your wife has to watch you closely around women," Genevieve Horne said.

"She tries hard," MacMillan said.

"And does she always succeed?"

"Not always," MacMillan said. "I took a course in evasive action one time."

"If it wasn't for the circumstances, I'd say that meeting you has been quite an experience, Captain MacMillan."

"Does the colonel watch you pretty closely?" MacMillan asked.

"I don't think he's going to have much time to do that," she said.

"You'll be staying at the State Department's transient hotel?"

"And probably bored out of my mind," she said.

"Maybe I could do something about that."

"I'm pretty good at evasive action myself," Genevieve Horne said.

Colonel Downs knew only that a conversation was taking place. He had no idea what was being said. He passed the time composing and relishing the words he would say to MacMillan as soon as they were on the ground at Tachikawa and out of the airplane:

"Captain MacMillan, you will consider yourself under arrest to quarters. You will go directly to your quarters and remain there until you receive further orders."

He would later explain to Genevieve Horne the gravity of Captain MacMillan's offense against good order and discipline; he simply could not ignore it.

Colonel Downs was not given the opportunity to discipline Captain MacMillan for disobedience of a direct order, however. The L-17 was met by a half dozen officers, the senior of them the special assistant to the SCAP chief of staff, a full colonel senior to Colonel Downs and with whom Colonel Downs had previously had personality clashes.

The special assistant to the SCAP chief of staff informed them they were wanted immediately in the G-3 Conference Room at the Dai Ichi Building to render a firsthand report of what they had seen in Korea; they were the first eyewitnesses to be available. The airplane itself would immediately return to Kokura, carrying three SCAP staff officers. The 24th Infantry Division at Kokura had already received an Alert for Movement order, just in case it would be necessary to intervene in Korea.

At the Dai Ichi Building, to Colonel Downs,'s enormous surprise, considering the hour (it was 0415 when they got there), the Supreme Commander, Allied Powers was in the G-3 Map Room, studying a map. He was dressed in a zippered leather jacket and an ancient, washed-smooth khaki shirt and trousers.

"What say you, Mac?" the SCAP said to MacMillan. "Is that the faint rattle of musketry I hear over the far hill?"

"I think we got us a war, General," MacMillan said to MacArthur. "You don't send tanks on a border incident."

"But do we *know* there *are* tanks? Or is this something somebody has heard, and repeated with dramatic amplification?"

"I counted 112 myself, General," MacMillan said. "In just two places."

"Be good enough, MacMillan," the Supreme Commander said, placing a hand on MacMillan's elbow and leading him to an enormous map of Korea, "to show me precisely where they were." And then he remembered Colonel Downs, or very nearly: "Howard, isn't it?"

"Downs, sir," Colonel Downs replied.

"I presume you were with Mac, Colonel Downs?"

"No, sir," MacMillan said. "I asked the colonel to stay behind at Kimpo to make sure we would have fuel to get back here."

"Did you confer with the KMAG staff, Colonel?" MacArthur asked.

"No, sir," Colonel Downs replied. "There wasn't time, sir."

"You have nothing, then, to contribute?" MacArthur replied. He did not wait for an answer. He simply turned his back to Colonel Downs and examined the map while MacMillan showed him where he had seen the Russian-built T34 tanks heading toward Kaesong, Uijongbu, and Ch'unch'on.

II

[ONE]
Hotel Continental
Paris
28 June 1950

Mr. and Mrs. Craig W. Lowell, their three-year-old son, Peter-Paul, and Mrs. Lowell's father, Count Peter-Paul von Greiffenberg (who had, only a few days earlier, been released from a Siberian concentration camp) had been placed in a four-room suite on the fourth floor of the hotel. The master bedroom's windows opened on both the Rue de Castiglione and the Rue de Rivoli. The other rooms, a sitting room and two bedrooms, opened on the Rue de Rivoli and the Tuileries beyond.

When the telephone rang, Mr. and Mrs. Lowell were asleep in their bed. Mrs. Lowell, a blond, pert-breasted woman of twenty-one, was naked save for a pair of flimsy pale blue underpants. Mr. Lowell, a large, smoothly muscled, mustachioed man of twenty-three, was completely naked. During the night, the sheet that had covered them had been kicked to the bottom of the bed, and in her sleep, Mrs. Lowell had turned on her side and curled up for warmth. Her husband lay sprawled on his stomach, one hand resting possessively on his wife's leg.

He was instantly awake when the telephone rang, rolling over on his back and reaching out for the old-fashioned telephone on the table beside the canopied bed. As he brought the instrument to his ear, he sat up and swung his legs out of bed.

"Yes?" he said, and then remembering where he was, added, *"Oui?"*

"Did I wake you up?" his caller asked, concern in his voice.

"Hold on, Sandy," Lowell said. "I want to change phones. Ilse's asleep."

He placed the ornate handset gently on the bedside table and stood up, crossing the room to a chaise longue, where the maid had laid out his dressing gown. The dressing gown was silk, and there was a large monogram embroidered over the breast. It had come from Sulka's, across the Rue de Castiglione from the Hotel Continental. But the monogram was not Craig Lowell's, and the first time that he had ever been in Sulka's was late the previous afternoon, when they had arrived in Paris, and had gone there—mainly because it was the closest store—to get his father-in-law some underwear and some off-the-shelf shirts.

The dressing gown had belonged to Lowell's father. Like the five-piece matched set of leather luggage stacked by the door awaiting a porter to carry it off for storage, it had just been too good to give to the Salvation Army, although the Salvation Army had been given his father's shirts and shoes and underwear.

At home he never wore a dressing gown, or even a bathrobe. So far as he was concerned, a man was either dressed or he wasn't, and there was no reason for an intermediate step. Ilse had packed the dressing gown for him, so that his barbarian beliefs would not be evident to the people who worked in hotels. Ilse was concerned about things like that, he had come to decide, not because she was concerned what anyone would think about her, but about him.

As he jammed his arms into the sleeves of his father's dressing gown, he was glad that she had packed the damned thing. Otherwise, he would have had to get dressed before going to the phone in the other room. Either get dressed, or run the risk of giving the shock of her young life to Mademoiselle Whatsername, the nurse the bank had arranged to meet them in the hotel.

It was not that he believed that Mademoiselle had never seen the undressed male form. It was the zippers and extra assholes that upset people the first time they saw him.

The zippers and the extra assholes, so called because that was what they resembled, were the result of what the official medical records had termed "moderate to severe lacerations of the torso and upper arm, caused by shrapnel from artillery and/or mortar projectiles" and "two (2) penetrating entrance and exit wounds, in the upper left arm and extreme upper left torso, at the arm juncture, caused by small arms fire, either rifle or light machine gun."

The wounds had long since healed, but his body would be marked forever.

He started for the door, but then stopped. He went back to the bed and very tenderly pulled the sheet on the bed over his wife. He thought again, as he had the very first time he had ever looked at her asleep in his bed, that she looked like a child, much too young, too innocent, to be in bed with a man.

He walked into the sitting room, and was surprised, almost startled, to see his father-in-law sitting on the floor with his son. The older man was wearing one of the shirts they'd bought at Sulka's the day before. Its collar was opened and the sleeves rolled up.

Christ, Lowell thought, he looks like a fucking cadaver.

"Good morning," he said.

"I hope we didn't wake you up," his father-in-law replied.

P. P. smiled at his father.

You don't have to talk, Squirt, his father thought. That smile of yours would charm the balls off a brass monkey.

"No, I have a call," Lowell said. "I'm going to take it out here."

He sat down on one of two opposing couches and picked up the telephone on the coffee table between them and told the operator to put through the call on the bedroom phone.

"Where are you?" he asked.

His caller told him.

"OK," he said. "You're nearly here. Look out the window, and you can see the Opera. It's a straight shot from the Opera here. You'll see a big thing in the middle of the street about two blocks away. That's right in front of the Ritz. Go around it.

The street dead-ends on the Rue de Rivoli two blocks beyond. And that's it. We're on the right side, on the corner. I'll order up some breakfast."

He hung up the telephone.

"Captain Felter," he explained to his father-in-law. "He's at American Express."

His father-in-law nodded. Lowell went into the bedroom, hung that phone up, and then returned and picked up the extension and asked for the desk.

"This is Mr. Lowell," he said. "Captain Felter and his family are about to arrive. They're my guests. I don't want them given a bill for anything, including gratuities. You understand?"

When he hung up the phone again, his father-in-law said, "You are very gracious. Perhaps even generous to a fault."

"I'm rich," Lowell said. "It's easy to be gracious and generous if you're rich."

They smiled at each other.

"Besides, I owe Sandy a lot, and he's a hard guy to pay back."

"I owe him a great deal, too," his father-in-law said.

Lowell walked to the door and examined a box with five porcelain buttons, and selected one and pushed it, to summon the floor waiter.

He turned and looked at his son and his father-in-law. P. P. had gotten off the floor and was standing behind his grandfather, with his arms locked around his neck.

"Found yourself a new pal, have you, Squirt?"

"Grosspapa," the child said.

The old count smiled.

"Yeah," Lowell said. "Grosspapa." He looked at his father-in-law. "What am I going to call you?" he asked.

"Whatever you like," the count replied.

"To Ilse," Lowell said, "you're 'Papa.' To the squirt, you're 'Grosspapa.' But how about us? I'd feel a little uncomfortable with 'Dad,' and I don't think you'd like calling me 'Son.' "

"You say what you think, don't you?" his father-in-law replied.

"How about 'Colonel'?" Lowell asked.

" 'Colonel' would be fine. And you?"

"How about calling me 'Craig'?"

"Whatever you like," the older man said, adding, "Craig."

"Grosspapa," P. P. said.

"He's your mama's papa," Lowell said. "And your Grosspapa. And to me, he's the Colonel. How's that grab you?"

"He's Mama's papa?" the boy said, as if surprised.

"Right," Lowell said.

"And *my* Grosspapa," the boy said, possessively.

The Colonel looked on the edge of tears.

The floor waiter knocked discreetly at the door, and was told to enter.

"Good morning, gentlemen," he said.

"What we're going to have to have," Lowell said, "in about fifteen minutes, is breakfast for, let me see," he counted on his fingers, "six. Plus two children. An American breakfast. The Felters are Jews, so we'll skip bacon and ham. How about rump steaks? Fried eggs, pommes frites, steaks. Orange juice. Milk for the kids. Bread, as well as croissants. And coffee. Bring some coffee and croissants right now, would you please?"

"Thank you very much," the floor waiter said, bowed, and left.

Lowell glanced at his father-in-law. There were tears in his eyes, and a tear ran down one cheek.

"Take it easy, Colonel," Lowell said, gently.

"Everything has happened too quickly," he said.

"Yeah," Lowell said, uncomfortably.

"I keep wondering if I have gone mad," the colonel said. "Or if I will wake up."

"There's a corny American expression, Colonel," Lowell said. " 'All's well that ends well.' "

" 'Corny'?" the colonel asked.

"Trite," Lowell said.

"You learn to lower your expectations," the colonel said. "Until you are pleased that your dream of being warm, or not hungry, has come true."

"I expect," Lowell said, uncomfortably.

"I don't mean to make you uncomfortable, Craig," the colonel said.

"Don't be silly," Lowell said.

"I used to dream of food," the colonel said. "Of beef and butter. Of real coffee."

Lowell said nothing.

"I'm hungry!" P. P. announced. "When do we eat?"

"Are you really hungry?" Lowell said.

"I'm really hungry."

"We'll have some nice liver in just a few minutes," Lowell said.

"You will not! I heard you! You said steak!"

"Do you like steak for breakfast, P. P?" the older man asked.

"It's all right," the child replied, having considered it.

"Steak for breakfast," the colonel said. "My God!"

Lowell said nothing.

"When I came back," the colonel said to Lowell, "I got off the train in Bad Hersfeld, and saw an old comrade of mine. He told me that my wife had taken her life and that he believed my daughter had gone to East Germany to look for relatives. He tried to encourage me by saying the Red Cross was very good about finding people in such circumstances."

"Well, that's all behind you, Colonel," Lowell said.

"I told myself that I would do what I could to find her, to do what I could for her," the colonel went on. "And then, this . . ."

"Yeah, well, what the hell," Lowell said.

He was relieved when the floor waiter rolled in a tray with a coffee service and a plate of croissants on it.

"You get one croissant, P. P.," Lowell said to his son. "To hold you until breakfast comes."

"Why can't I eat now?"

"Because Uncle Sandy and Aunt Sharon are coming, and we're going to wait for them."

He watched as his father-in-law very carefully buttered a croissant and ate it with tiny bites, savoring each morsel.

There came another knock at the door.

"Entrez!" Lowell called.

The door opened.

A slight, balding man pushed the door open and peered cautiously in.

"Come on in, Sandy," Lowell said, walking up to him, and putting his arm around his shoulder.

"Guten Morgen, Herr Oberst Graf," the little man said, in fluent, vaguely Berliner-accented German.

When Peter-Paul von Greiffenberg had returned to Marburg an der Lahn after five years of Soviet captivity, Sanford Felter had been waiting for him at the railroad station. Not, as the count had first believed, as one more policeman to take away his freedom again, but to take him to a reunion with his daughter, and a son-in-law and grandchild he knew nothing about.

Lowell stepped behind Sandy Felter, kissed his wife, and snatched Sanford T. Felter, Jr., aged two, from his mother's arms.

"Thank God, he looks like you, sweetheart," he said.

"Craig!" Sharon Felter said. She was a dark-haired, light-skinned, slightly built woman with large dark eyes.

"One ugly bald man in a family is enough," Lowell said.

"Herr Oberst Graf," Felter said. "May I present my wife?"

"You must forgive my appearance, Mrs. Felter," the older man said, bowing over her hand. "I am honored."

"Oh, we've heard so much about you," Sharon said. "Oh, forgive me. I didn't say it. Welcome home!"

"Thank you," he said.

"Ilse's asleep," Lowell said. "Go throw her ass out of bed, Sharon."

"I will not!" Sharon said. "Craig, really, sometimes . . ."

He walked to the bedroom door.

"Hey, Ilse! Up and at 'em! Sandy and Sharon are here."

"You didn't have to do that," Sharon said, walking to the bedroom door. "Ilse, I told him not to."

And then she went into the bedroom and closed the door after her.

"Breakfast is on the way," Lowell said. "Or it's supposed to be. Help yourself to some coffee."

"We ate before I called," Felter said.

"Well, you're just going to have to eat again. I know your idea of breakfast. A hard-boiled egg and a stale roll."

Felter shook his head, and then opened a briefcase. He took out a manila folder and handed it to Lowell.

"What's this?"

"The colonel's service record," Felter said. "A certified copy, anyway, and the findings of the Denazification Court."

"I don't understand," the colonel said.

"American law forbids the immigration of Nazis, Colonel," Felter explained. "You have to be cleared. This will clear you."

"How the hell did you get that overnight?" Lowell asked.

"I didn't get it overnight," Felter said. "I worked on that damned thing for years."

"Hey, buddy," Lowell said. "Thanks."

"You're welcome," Felter said.

"Captain Felter suspected for some time that you were alive, Colonel," Lowell said to his father-in-law. "He's really the one who got you out."

"How does one express his gratitude for something like that?" the colonel asked.

"As briefly as possible, please," Felter said, with a smile.

"Take off your coat and stay a while," Lowell said.

"Your thugs grabbed our luggage the minute we pulled up outside," Felter said. "At least I hope they were your thugs."

"Meaning what?"

"Meaning I hope you know where to find our luggage, what room we're in, that sort of thing."

"I think you're down the hall. Get on the phone and ask."

"What do I say? 'This is Mr. Felter, where am I?' " Felter asked, and chuckled.

Lowell laughed. Felter took off his coat and hung it on the back of a chair. Then, as discreetly as he could, he reached in the small of his back, withdrew a Colt .45 pistol, which he slipped into the briefcase, and then set the briefcase on the floor beside the couch.

"You've heard of the Mafia, Colonel?" Lowell asked.

"The Mafia?"

"The fraternal order of Sicilian gangsters? They always go around carrying guns."

"I don't believe Captain Felter is a gangster," the colonel said.

"Captain Felter is a spook," Lowell said.

"I don't know what a spook is," the colonel said.

"He's an *intelligence* officer," Lowell said, with mock awe. "Which is not quite the same thing as an intelli*gent* officer."

"Oh, Christ, Craig!" Felter said, exasperated.

"I think you're embarrassing the Captain, Craig," the colonel said.

"I'm used to it, Colonel," Felter said. "He has been embarrassing me from literally the first day I met him."

"You'll have to pardon my near total ignorance of my son-in-law," the colonel said. "When was that?"

"We were on our way to Greece," Lowell said. "In 1946. I was being sent there in disgrace, and Felter, demonstrating that he is indeed fit to march in the Long Gray Line, had volunteered for the assignment."

"The Long Gray Line?" the colonel asked, and then remembered. "Oh, yes, of course. West Point. You're a West Pointer, Captain?"

"I went there for a while," Felter said.

"And you, too, Craig?"

Lowell laughed. "Good God, no. I was a reserve officer, just long enough to do my time and get out. Sandy's the one who has the Pavlovian response to the sound of a trumpet. As anyone who knows will tell you, Colonel, I was a lousy soldier."

"Well, some men take to it, and some don't," the colonel said, graciously.

"The military establishment heaved an enormous sigh of relief when they were finally able to kick me out the gate," Lowell said.

Felter looked between the two of them, and saw that Colonel Count Peter-Paul von Greiffenberg, three wound stripes, recipient of the Iron Cross with Swords and Diamonds, the eleventh of his line to go to war for his country, accepted what Craig Lowell had said about his military service at face value.

"I'm sorry, Craig," Felter said. "I can't let that stand."

"What?" Lowell said.

"Colonel, when your son-in-law was nineteen years old, attached to the Greek Army as an advisor, the unit with which he was serving . . ."

"Knock it off, Sandy!" Lowell interrupted him.

"The unit with which he was serving," Felter went on, relentlessly, "Number 12 Company of the 27th Royal Greek Mountain Division, was attacked by a reinforced regiment of Russian-trained Albanian and Greek troops. All the Greek officers were killed. This 'lousy soldier' your daughter married assumed command, although he was at the time shot full of holes. When the relief column reached his position, there were only twelve men left alive. But they held their position, inspired by this 'lousy soldier.' He's such a 'lousy soldier' that they gave him the Order of St. George and St. Andrew."

"You've always had a fat mouth, you little shit," Lowell said.

"Craig!" Ilse von Greiffenberg Lowell said, shocked as she came in the room. "What's the matter with you? After what Sandy's done for us, how dare you talk to him that way?"

"It's all right, Ilse," Sandy Felter said. "It sounded worse than it really was."

"They're always saying cruel things to each other," Sharon Felter said. "They sometimes make me sick to my stomach. You'd never know how much they love each other, the way they talk to each other."

"Oh, shit," Lowell said. He walked quickly to Felter, wrapped his arms around the smaller man, hoisted him off the ground, and planted a wet and noisy kiss in the middle of his forehead.

"Put me down, you overgrown adolescent!" Felter demanded.

"Say 'pretty please,' you little prick," Lowell said. He squeezed Felter in his arms until Felter gave in.

"Pretty please, you big bastard!" he said. Lowell, laughing, set him down.

"Now, if that doesn't prove I love him, what does?" Lowell asked.

"I'm ashamed of you, Craig," Ilse said, but she was smiling.

The floor waiter, trailed by three busboys, arrived with the breakfast, and started to set up the breakfast table.

Felter watched them, and then, out of the blue, said: "Speaking of war, I just heard on AFN that that's not a border incident in Korea, but a real invasion."

"What's not a border incident?" Lowell asked.

"According to AFN—" Felter said, and then digressed to explain. "AFN is the U.S. radio station in Germany, Colonel, and according to the news broadcast I heard just now, what they first said was a border incident is now a real invasion. Seoul is about to fall."

"Have a nice war, Sandy," Lowell said.

"What a terrible thing to say!" Ilse snapped.

"He doesn't mean half the things he says," Felter said. "If you understand that, you can learn to put up with him."

"Can we eat now?" P. P. asked.

[TWO]
Washington, D.C.
5 July 1950

By direction of the President, the Secretary of the Army was authorized and directed to call to active duty for the duration of the Korean police action 2,500 company-grade officers of the various arms and services then carried on the rolls of the inactive reserve.

The officer corps of the United States Army is composed of four components. There is the regular army, those officers whose profession is arms, who meet the criteria established by the Congress for the regular army, and who plan to serve until retired. The number of regular army officers is provided by law. Before World War II, the number of officers on active duty who were not regular army was minuscule. During World War II, the percentages were reversed, and only a few officers could be recognized—by their shorter serial numbers—as regular army.

The bulk of regular army officers come from the United States Military Academy at West Point, and from the other service academies: Virginia Military Institute, Norwich, the Citadel, Texas A&M, and a very few others. But it is possible for individuals, normally reserve officers on active duty, to apply for integration into the regular army, and some are accepted.

The second component of the officer corps of the United States Army is the corps of officers assigned to the National Guard. Technically, these officers hold commissions granted by the governors of the various states, since in peacetime the National Guard is under the control of the various governors. These officers simultaneously hold reserve commissions in the United States Army.

The third component is the reserve officer corps, which is in turn composed of four components:

(1) Reserve officers on extended active duty: those who plan to remain in uniform until retired. These officers serve at the pleasure of the Congress, and they enjoy no guarantee of service until retirement (as do officers holding a regular army commission).

(2) Reserve officers on active duty: generally involuntary, such as those officers called to active duty after graduation from a Reserve Officer Training Corps program at a college or university. They serve on active duty for a specified period of time.

(3) Reserve officers of the organized reserve: those officers assigned to a reserve unit, which meets one evening a week or one weekend a month. They also serve two weeks of active duty for training in the summertime. These officers receive a day's pay and allowances for each training session and earn retirement credit for such service.

(4) Inactive reserve officers: those reserve officers who hold commissions, but are not members of the active army, the National Guard, or the organized reserve. They undergo no training and receive no pay.

The officers the army wished to call to duty for the Korean peace action were officers in the last category, the inactive reserve.

Whenever possible, such involuntarily recalled officers were to be given a thirty-day notice so that they could wind up their personal affairs. It was recognized, however, that due to the critical situation in the Far East, this would not always be possible.

A critical shortage of company-grade officers existed in the combat arms. In the absence of a pool of officers recently graduated from the various service schools, who could be assigned to troop units, it was decided that a pool should be formed from the ranks of the inactive reserve of officers meeting the following criteria:

(a) Of appropriate grade and age. (You need young men in the line units.)

(b) Combat experience. (When you get right down to it, somebody who has heard a gun go off in his ear is really the best guy to lead troops in combat; there's no substitute for combat experience.)

It was argued that calling such officers to active duty, particularly when it was not going to be possible to give them even thirty days to wind up their personal affairs, was not really fair to the officers in question. For one thing, they had already been shot at. For another, not only had they not been getting paid the way other reserve and National Guard officers had been paid (a day's pay for two hours' "training" once a week), but they had been specifically assured that if they kept their commissions in the inactive reserve, they would be called to duty only in the event of an all-out war, and only after the National Guard and active reserve had been called to duty.

It was one of the tougher decisions the Commander in Chief was forced to make. He made it based on his own experience as a captain of artillery. It was a goddamned dirty trick on the officers involved, and he knew it. But there was another side to the coin. Sending troops into battle under inexperienced officers when experienced officers were available was inexcusable. The first duty of an officer—whether a lieutenant or a captain or the Commander in Chief—is to the enlisted men. That was a basic principle of command. He could not justify not calling up the best qualified officers simply because they had already done their duty. They were needed again. They could save some lives. It was a dirty goddamned trick on them, but that's the way it was going to have to be.

[THREE]
Kokura, Japan
7 July 1950

The well worn but immaculate jeep of First Lieutenant Philip Sheridan Parker IV, the commander of the third platoon of Tank Company, 24th Infantry Regiment, 24th Infantry Division, rolled up before the barracks housing his platoon. Parker slid gracefully out of the vehicle.

The lieutenant, whose skin was flat black and whose features brought to mind an Arab in a flowing robe, was six feet, three inches tall and carried 225 pounds without fat. He walked quickly up the walkway to the barracks. He was dressed in stiffly starched fatigues and wore a very small fatigue cap squarely on the top of his head. Around his waist was a World War I pistol belt, from which dangled a swiveled holster holding a Model 1917 Colt .45 ACP revolver.

He had just learned that his platoon would not deploy to Korea with the rest of the company, but would take possession of some new tanks first. The division ordnance officer had learned of the presence of eight M4A3 medium tanks in the Osaka ordnance depot, where they had undergone conversion of their main armament from a 75 mm cannon to the new, high-velocity 76 mm cannon. In addition, the tanks had undergone Depot Level IRAN, or Inspect and Repair As Necessary. This had meant an almost complete rebuild. Thus, in their moving parts, they were new tanks.

The ordnance officer, after first receiving assurance that he was welcome to the M4A3 tanks, had made his discovery known to the division commander. The division commander had first told the ordnance officer to send someone to Osaka to take physical possession of the tanks. He then decided to assign them to the tank company of the 24th Infantry Regiment, the other two regiments of the division already being in the process of deployment to Korea. The regimental commander of the 24th Regiment had told the tank company commander of the availability of the tanks.

The tank company commander had decided to give the medium tanks to the third platoon. For one thing, Lieutenant Parker had recently come onto the promotion list for first lieutenant, having completed the requisite time in grade. For another, the company commander was of the opinion that Lieutenant Parker was the best of his three platoon leaders. And finally, Parker had had experience with the high-velocity 76 mm tube at Fort Knox. Having made his decision, he called Parker in and told him.

Parker pushed open the left of the double wooden doors of the barracks and started up the stairway, taking them two at a time. His platoon was housed in two twenty-five-bed squad bays on the third floor of the tank company barracks. He knocked on the door of the private room of the platoon sergeant, Sergeant First Class Amos Woodrow, and when Woodrow came out, followed him into the nearest of the squad bays.

"Atten-hut!" Sergeant Woodrow called, and the troops, who had been reluctantly packing their personal equipment in footlockers (which would be stored by the quartermaster during their Korean deployment), came to attention.

"Go next door and get the other guys," Woodrow ordered, pointing his finger at the trooper nearest him. The trooper, a slight little man who lived in mingled fear and awe of both his platoon sergeant and his platoon commander, scurried out of the room.

Parker thought that Sergeant Woodrow would be a good man to have along with him. He wasn't overly impressed with many of his troops, and some really worried him, but Woodrow was obviously a first-class noncom.

Sergeant First Class Amos Woodrow also approved of Lieutenant Parker. Sergeant Woodrow was thirty-eight years old, and had been a soldier since 1942. He had served with the 393rd Tank Destroyer Battalion in the Normandy campaign, had been wounded and hospitalized, and then had served a tour with the only Negro unit in the Constabulary in the Army of Occupation of Germany, the 175th Armored Field Artillery Battalion, where he had been crew chief and section leader of a self-propelled 105 mm howitzer.

Sergeant Woodrow liked Lieutenant Parker's style.

On Parker's fifth day with the platoon, Corporal Ezikiah Lavalier had called Corporal Franklin Roosevelt Taylor a motherfucker when Corporal Taylor had accidentally sprayed him with a water hose while washing an M24.

"Well, Taylor," Lieutenant Parker had said, "I must confess that I am both surprised and very disappointed to hear that."

"Suh?" Corporal Taylor had said, popping to rigid attention.

"I would never have thought that of you, Taylor," Lieutenant Parker had gone on smoothly.

"I don't know what the lieutenant's talking about, sir," Taylor had said, uneasily.

"Didn't you hear what Corporal Lavalier called you?" Parker had inquired innocently.

"Oh, that," Taylor, visibly relieved, had replied. "That don't *mean* nothing, Lieutenant, sir. We just talks like that."

"Oh, then, it doesn't *bother* you? You don't mind someone saying that about you?"

"It don't bother me none, Lieutenant," Taylor had reassured him.

"Well, I guess that just goes to show how different people are, doesn't it?" Parker had said, and walked away.

That night, in the regimental NCO club, Sergeant Thaddeus J. Quail, the two-hundred-pound assistant mess sergeant, had conversationally requested of Corporal Taylor: "Motherfucker, hand me them peanuts."

"Watch your mouth, nigger," Taylor replied sharply. "Don't you be calling me no motherfucker."

"Who you calling nigger, nigger?"

"Let me spell it out for you, nigger. You're a nigger, but I ain't no motherfucker. You got that straight?"

Whereupon Sergeant Quail punched Corporal Taylor in the mouth. When the participants in the brawl had been separated and returned to their orderly room by the division military police, Lieutenant Parker had been the officer of the day. The charge of quarters had summoned Sergeant First Class Woodrow from his room.

When he got to the orderly, both Sergeant Quail and Corporal Taylor were standing to attention before Lieutenant Parker's desk. Corporal Taylor had lost a tooth, and there was half-dried blood on his lip.

"Rank has its privileges, Sergeant. You may give me your version of what happened first," Lieutenant Parker had told him, in his dry manner.

"Sir," Sergeant Quail said, uneasily, "me and Taylor had a little argument."

"I see. What about?"

"He called me a nigger, that's what he done, and I ain't taking that from nobody," Quail said righteously, and then remembered to add, "sir."

"What he done," Taylor said, equally righteously, "was to call me a motherfucker. That's what he done, Lieutenant, that's what started the whole thing."

"Is that true, Sergeant? Did you accuse Corporal Taylor of having sexual relations with his mother?" Lieutenant Parker asked.

"I didn't say *that*," Sergeant Quail said. "I just called him, friendly-like, that."

"What's 'that'?"

"You called me motherfucker, and you know you did, and other people heard you, nigger!" Corporal Taylor said.

"See, there he goes again!" Sergeant Quail said, righteously.

"The term 'nigger,' " Lieutenant Parker said, reasonably, "comes from the African country of Nigeria. The way it began was the same way people started calling people from Poland 'Polacks' and people from Hungary 'Hunkys.' It is not very nice, and I don't like it myself. In fact, I become very angry when someone calls me a 'nigger,' and I sympathize with you, Sergeant Quail. Under the circumstances, I have been known to lose my temper myself."

"But he called *me a motherfucker*, Lieutenant," Corporal Taylor said, in equally righteous indignation. "A motherfucker is a *lot* worse than a nigger."

"Yes, it is," Lieutenant Parker agreed.

There was a long, long pause, during which Lieutenant Parker appeared to be seriously considering the problem. Then he took the 1928 *Manual for Courts-Martial* from the desk drawer.

He consulted the index until he was quite sure that both sinners knew what the volume he held in his hand was, and then found the applicable Article of War.

"Whosoever shall use provoking language to another in the military service shall be guilty of conduct prejudicial to good order and discipline," he read slowly and solemnly, "and shall be punished as a court-martial shall direct." He looked up at Sergeant Woodrow.

"Sergeant Woodrow," he said, "you're an old soldier. Would you say that calling someone a name that suggests he's having sexual relations with his mother is provoking language?"

"Unless it were true, sir," Woodrow said, "it would be."

"Goddamn, you know that's not true," Taylor said, shocked.

"I didn't *mean* it that way, Lieutenant," Sergeant Quail said. "And Taylor knows I didn't. And anyway, he called me a nigger."

"I'll have to give this matter some thought," Lieutenant Parker said. "I want to talk it over with Sergeant Woodrow, to decide whether a court-martial would be in the best interests of the service. Until we reach a decision, you two stay away from each other, and away from the club."

Thereafter the incidence of one soldier of the third platoon of the 24th Infantry Regimental Tank Company suggesting incestuous activity on the part of another soldier dropped dramatically, although there were several fistfights unreported to official authority.

Sergeant Woodrow thought Lieutenant Parker had class. He had not been surprised to learn subsequently that Parker was one of the old breed, that Parkers in the service went back to the Buffalo Soldiers of the Indian wars.

Other soldiers, all Negro, of shades ranging from Parker's flat black to light pink, came into the squad bay and lined up in a half-circle around Lieutenant Parker.

"Atten-hut!" Woodrow called again. As soon as they were still and quiet, Parker gave them at ease.

"Everybody try to pay attention. I've got some news," he said.

The troops didn't seem to care. Parker saw that at least four of them were quite drunk.

"Hey, Lieutenant," one of the tank commanders called, "Where did you get the go-to-hell six-shooter?"

"My grandfather carried it in France," Parker said. "In World War I."

"While he unloaded ships?" a voice from the rear of the group said. Parker recognized him. Staff Sergeant Sidney, a light-skinned troublemaker.

"Stand to attention," Parker said softly. Slowly, almost defiantly, the soldier, a staff sergeant, stood to attention.

"Your ignorance shows, Sergeant Sidney," Parker said, softly. "So I will take time we should be spending doing more important things to tell you things you should know. My grandfather served as a captain with the 369th Infantry Regiment. They fought at Château-Thierry. My grandfather was awarded the Croix de guerre by the French government. The regiment, whose troops were all Negro, received the Distinguished Unit Citation. The regiment were soldiers, not stevedores. I will not have them slandered by anyone, especially by anyone with your attitude. Do I make myself clear?"

Sergeant Sidney didn't reply.

"Do I make myself clear, Sidney?" Parker said. There was now menace in his voice, although he didn't raise it.

"Yes, sir," Staff Sergeant Sidney said, after a moment.

"Don't open your mouth again until I give you permission," Parker said, and waited a long moment. Then he said, "You may stand at ease."

The room was now absolutely silent.

"There are eight M4A3 tanks, with the high-velocity 76 mm tube at Osaka," Parker said. "I have been told that if I can guarantee we can use them, the third platoon can have them. Who here besides Sergeant Woodrow has had any M4 experience?"

A dozen hands went up, including Sergeant Sidney's.

"How well do you know the M4A3, Sergeant Sidney?"

"I was school-trained at Knox," Sidney said.

"OK. There will be a bus out in front of the barracks in an hour. Make up a list of the others with M4 experience. And have them ready to go when the bus shows up."

"Sir," Sergeant Sidney protested, "we were told we could have the night off, before going on the ship tomorrow."

"You'll be in Osaka tomorrow," Parker said. "We're going there tonight."

"I've got to say good-bye to my girl, Lieutenant," Sergeant Sidney said.

"I'm sorry," Parker said. "There won't be time for that. We have to go to Osaka, take delivery of the A3s, get them on ship board, and rejoin the rest of the regiment in Korea."

Sergeant Sidney said nothing. But there was a look on his face that annoyed, even angered Parker. But there was nothing he could do about it now.

"We're going to turn our M24s over to the other two platoons," Parker went on. "They'll serve as spares. I'll answer questions, but you're warned that I don't know much more than what I've told you."

Sergeant Sidney was not outside the barracks when the bus came, nor was he anywhere to be found.

"Turn the sonofabitch in as AWOL to miss a movement, Lieutenant," Sergeant Woodrow said. "Let him do six months in the stockade."

"I think Sergeant Sidney would much rather be doing push-ups in the stockade than getting shot at in Korea," Parker said. He was embarrassed that he hadn't thought ahead and had Woodrow keep an eye on him.

"What good would he do us in Korea?"

"He's school-trained on the A3," Parker said. "Can you find him, do you think, Sergeant Woodrow?"

"Yes, sir, I know just where to look."

"I would hate to see the career of a good soldier like Sergeant Sidney ruined by his having missed a shipment, Sergeant," Parker said. "Do you think you could reason with him?"

"Has the platoon sergeant the platoon commander's permission to speak informally, sir?" Sergeant Woodrow asked.

"Yes," Lieutenant Parker said.

"I'll have that nigger motherfucker on the boat if I have to break both his legs," Sergeant Woodrow said.

"Carry on, Sergeant," Parker said.

[ONE]
New York City
10 July 1950

Craig W. Lowell was not surprised to find Andre Pretier's chauffeur waiting for him beyond the glass wall of customs at LaGuardia, but he was surprised when the chauffeur told him that Pretier was in the car.

Andre Pretier was Lowell's mother's husband. Not his stepfather. They had been married after Craig had been drafted into the army in early 1946, following his expulsion for academic unsuitability from Harvard. While the chauffeur collected his luggage, Lowell looked for and found the car.

It was a Chrysler Imperial, with a limousine body by LeBaron, a long, glossy vehicle parked in a tow-away zone. There was an official-looking placard resting against the windshield, bearing the seal of the State of New York and the word "Official." Craig had often wondered if Pretier had been provided with some sort of honorary official position by some obliging politician, or whether he or his chauffeur (who had been with him for twenty-five years) had just picked it up somewhere and used it without any authority, secure in the knowledge that airport and other police asked fewer questions of people in custom-bodied limousines than they did of other people.

The first Pretier in America had come as a member of the staff of the Marquis de Lafayette during the American Revolution. He had stayed after the war and founded the shipping (and later import-export) company which was the foundation of the Pretier fortune. He had been at Harvard with Lowell's father, and there, incredibly, become enamored of the woman who was to become Craig Lowell's mother, an infatuation that was to last his lifetime. He had proposed marriage precisely one year and one day after Lowell's father had been buried.

Andre Pretier leaned across the velour seat of the Chrysler and offered his hand to Lowell as he bent to enter the car.

"I didn't expect this," Lowell said. "Thank you, Andre."

"We had to take your mother to Hartford," Pretier said.

Oh, shit, that's all I need, Lowell thought.

Hartford was the euphemism for the Institute of Living, a private psychiatric hospital in Hartford, Connecticut.

Pretier handed Lowell a small crystal bowl, a brandy snifter without a stem.

"Bad?" Lowell asked.

Pretier threw up his hands in resignation.

"She simply can't take strain, or excitement," Pretier said.

"What was I supposed to do, Andre?" Lowell asked, sharply. "Tell my father-in-law to stay in Siberia?"

"I don't think that had anything to do with it," Pretier replied, not taking offense at Lowell's outburst. Lowell had often thought that the real reason he disliked his mother's husband was that Andre Pretier rarely, almost never, took offense at anything, no matter what the provocation.

"What set her off, then?"

Pretier threw his hands up in frustration again.

"I don't really know. She . . . uh . . . had a relapse in the city."

"A spectacular relapse?"

"I'm afraid so," Pretier said. "They had her at Bellevue."

"She's all right, now?" Lowell asked.

Pretier nodded. "I thought you had enough on your hands," he said. "Otherwise I would have called."

"She didn't start asking for me?" Lowell asked.

"She was sedated rather heavily until today," Pretier said.

"Medically, or because I was due in?"

"Both."

"And you think I should go to Hartford?"

"I would be very grateful if you would," Pretier said. "The doctors think it would be beneficial, if you could find the time."

How the fuck can I refuse, when you put it that way? Lowell thought. What decent, true-blue American boy could refuse to go see his loony mother in the funny farm when that would both be beneficial, according to the doctors, and make her long-suffering husband very grateful?

"Of course," Lowell said. "When?"

"I didn't think you would want to take the train," Pretier said. "I've arranged for a plane."

"That's very kind of you, Andre," Lowell said. He reached up and helped himself to more cognac.

His mother, a tall, rather thin, silver-haired woman, didn't seem especially pleased that he had flown to Hartford to visit her, and she didn't ask more than perfunctory questions about what had taken place in Germany and France.

"You said he was a count, didn't you?" she asked. "Didn't I hear that someplace?"

"Yes, he is."

"And lost everything in the war, doubtless, so that we'll have to support him?"

"Actually no, Mother," he said. "The von Greiffenbergs are from Hesse, which is in the American Zone. He didn't have his property confiscated."

"We'll see," she said, closing the subject. She didn't like being told that the father of the foreign doxy her son had dragged home from Europe wasn't after her money as well as his.

A little ashamed of himself (she was, after all, a sick woman in a hospital), he refused to drop the subject.

"Actually, Mother, the reason I'm here is that he gave me a power of attorney to claim his property here."

"What property here?"

"The government has it, under the Enemy Alien Property Act. Some money, some securities, even some art."

"And you really think the government will give it up?"

"So the lawyers tell me."

"We'll see," she said.

It was after ten when he finally got to his house on Washington Mews, a private alley near Washington Square in Greenwich Village. Andre had suggested that he spend the night at Broadlawns on Long Island, the rambling estate that Craig had inherited from his father, and that he now rented to the Pretiers, because Andre refused to live there without paying. But Lowell wanted to go home to the town house that Ilse had decorated, to sleep in their bed, to be at least that close to her.

There was no one home at 11 Washington Mews. Their servants had been given the time off while he and P. P and Ilse were in Europe, and he had to go through the complex procedure of first unlocking the door and then racing up the stairs and down the corridor to his bedroom to put another key into the burglar alarm, to deactivate it before it rang both Pinkerton's and the police precinct. Otherwise a platoon of police cars with howling sirens would descend on Washington Mews.

He turned off the burglar alarm and then went back downstairs to get the one suitcase he had with him and which he had dropped at the door. He remembered seeing some mail on the floor, too.

There were five or six letters, which he tossed unread onto the hall table, and the yellow envelope of a telegram. He almost tossed that with the unopened letters, but then decided it might be a cablegram, rather than a telegram, some just remembered bit of information his father-in-law thought he should have in order to better handle his affairs in New York.

He opened it. It wasn't a cablegram. It was a telegram.

WASH DC (GOVT RATE) JUL 7 1950
CAPTAIN CRAIG W. LOWELL 0-495302
11 WASHINGTON MEWS
NEW YORK CITY
FONE & DELIVER

BY DIRECTION OF THE PRESIDENT, YOU ARE ORDERED TO REPORT TO FORT GEORGE G. MEADE, MARYLAND, NOT LATER THAN 2400 HOURS 12 JULY 1950 TO ENTER UPON AN INDEFINITE PERIOD OF ACTIVE DUTY IN CONNECTION WITH THE KOREAN PEACE ACTION.

EDWARD F. WITSELL
MAJOR GENERAL, US ARMY
THE ADJUTANT GENERAL

[TWO]
Pusan, Korea
12 July 1950

The third platoon of Tank Company, 24th Infantry Regiment, debarked from the USNS *Private Albert Ford* at Pusan four days after the rest of the company had arrived.

Lieutenant Parker had a premonition that he was going to be very much alone in this police action, this show of force, or whatever it was. He was worried, even frightened by the prospect. He had never heard a shot fired in anger, had never issued an order involving life and death. Parker was quite as innocent—as virginal—at war as most of the troops in his platoon.

On the other hand, he had heard a good deal about war, about the unpredictability of human reaction to it. He had often heard that sometimes it was the apparently strong who turned out to be unable to handle their fear; who, if they didn't actually collapse under fire, were unable to think clearly, who couldn't make rational decisions. He wondered if that would happen to him.

There was no question in his mind that so far as junior armor officers were concerned, he was as well trained as any. He was, like his father before him, a graduate of Norwich University, a small institution little known outside Vermont and the army. Norwich had been providing the army with regular cavalry officers for more than a century. Norwich second lieutenants "coincidentally" were given regular army commissions on the same day West Point graduates got theirs; "coincidentally" it had as its president a retired West Pointer general officer of cavalry; and "coincidentally" it had a faculty for the military arts and sciences provided by the army to the same criteria as the faculty to West Point.

There was a gentleman's agreement going back to the time that Sylvanus Thayer had become Commandant of West Point. The cavalry establishment, in and out of uniform (and in and out of uniform, cavalry has been, since the first warrior mounted a horse, the service of the wealthy and powerful), would not fight the Corps of Engineers and the infantry and Sylvanus Thayer and West Point; and the West Point establishment, in and out of uniform, would not only see that Norwich graduates were given regular cavalry commissions but would regard them as professional and social peers.

Similar gentleman's agreements existed between the West Point establishment and the Citadel (assuring that the regular officer's corps of all the arms and services had a fair leavening of well-bred Southerners) and the Texas Agricultural and Mechanical College (assuring that both the regular artillery and the reserve officer's corps were liberally laced with Aggies). The relationship between the West Point establishment and the Citadel and Texas A&M was much better known, because the relationship between Norwich and the West Point establishment was seldom discussed.

After graduating from Norwich and entering upon active duty, Lieutenant Parker had attended the Basic Armor Officer's Course at Fort Knox, Kentucky. He had graduated "with Great Distinction"—that is to say, as the honor graduate of his class—but Fort Knox had not been entirely the beginning he had hoped to make on his career. Socially, it had been a disaster.

He had shared a BOQ suite (two two-room "apartments" sharing a shower and toilet) with a second lieutenant who had attracted the wrath of the military social establishment like a magnet draws iron filings. He was not a West Pointer, nor even someone commissioned from the Reserve Officer's Training Corps or Officer Candidate School. The man was Second Lieutenant Craig W. Lowell.

Parker had thought of Lowell a good deal since this Korean business had started. Lowell was in New York, a civilian, and working in the family business, which was modestly described as an investment banking firm. Parker had wondered if Lowell would be recalled and decided that he probably wouldn't be. And he'd really wondered, now that he was actually going to war, if he would be able to function as well as Lowell had functioned in Greece.

No one would have thought that Lowell would be a good soldier, a good officer, but he had wound up with the second highest decoration for valor the Greek government gave. On the other hand, everyone would expect a Norwich graduate to at least "do his duty," and possibly serve with distinction—especially the son of a Norwich graduate who had commanded a tank destroyer battalion across North Africa and Europe, the grandson of a colonel who as a captain had commanded a company of the 369th Infantry in War I, and the great-grandson of a master sergeant who had fought Indians with the 9th Cavalry and gone up Kettle Hill in Cuba with Teddy Roosevelt. Philip Sheridan Parker IV told himself he would be satisfied if he didn't shit his pants and run when he first round came his way.

[THREE]

When the platoon assembled on Pier One in Pusan, Staff Sergeant Sidney was present and accounted for, although complaining of pain from injuries suffered in a fall in the shower. Perhaps because of the "fall in the shower," he seemed ready to do what was expected of him, and Parker put him to work—still another time—checking the machine guns on the M4A3s and the personal weapons.

It took about two hours to unload the M4A3s from the hold of the *Albert Ford* and another hour to fuel and arm them. Parker found a supply of 76 mm high-velocity rounds in a warehouse directly across from where the *Albert Ford* was tied up; and in the belief that ammunition supply would be a problem (so far as he knew, he had the only medium tanks in Korea), he ordered that as many cases of the ammunition as possible be tied to the outside of the tanks.

Sergeant Woodrow disappeared for thirty minutes during the off-loading procedure and returned with a General Motors six-by-six truck and a Dodge three-quarter-ton ambulance without the Red Cross insignia painted on its sides. The trucks bore bumper markings identifying them as belonged to the 25th Infantry's Headquarters and Service Company. The bumpers were spread with track grease and then covered with dirt from the pier so the markings could not be read. When the platoon moved out, both trucks, loaded as heavily as possible with 76 mm ammunition, were placed in the column after the first two tanks.

Five hours later, coming around a bend in a narrow, tar-covered road, Lieutenant Parker came on the regimental headquarters. It consisted of a tent fly erected by the side of the road to shade the headquarters staff from the hot sun, and the regimental headquarters' vehicles, halfheartedly camouflaged across the road.

There was also one M24 tank. When Parker saw it, he thought he might be in luck; it was possible the company commander was at the command post.

He was not. And the M24 was all that was left of the first and second platoons of the tank company.

"My report to division said that Captain Meadows and the others are missing and presumed dead or captured," the regimental commander said bitterly. "I have, however, been reliably informed that the captain, was seen together with several of his officers and approximately seventy men, on foot headed in the general direction of Pusan."

"I don't quite follow you, sir."

"I mean they bugged out, Lieutenant. They turned tail and ran. Is that clear enough for you?"

"What are my orders, sir?"

"Render what assistance you can to the 3rd Battalion," the colonel said, pointing out their location on a map laid on the hood of a jeep. "The last time I heard, they were in this general area."

The colonel was obviously distraught. And it was equally obvious that the colonel, if he did not expect Parker and his men to run like the others, at least would not be shocked or surprised if they did.

"I presume, sir, the orders are to hold that line?"

"Those are my orders, Lieutenant," the colonel said.

Parker went back to the road and climbed in the turret of his M4A3. He put on his helmet and adjusted the radio microphone in front of his lips.

He looked around at his force: a few tanks, manned by frightened, inexperienced, inadequately trained black men. And they were supposed to take on the whole North Korean Army? It was absurd on its face. What was going to happen was that they were all going to get killed. Unless they ran.

But then he had another thought. This was not the first time a few black men had faced an enemy superior in numbers—and probably in skill. Master Sergeant Parker of the 9th Cavalry had fought and beaten Chiricahua Apache, and had lived to run up Kettle and San Juan hills with the Rough Riders.

The cold fact was that if he didn't do this right, if he didn't come through now as his heritage and his training required, the men with him would die.

It was clearly better to die fighting than die running.

He pressed the mike button.

"Wind 'em up," he heard himself say. "Charge the machine guns. Load the tubes with a HEAT round. The bad guys are about a mile from here."

He was frightened. He laid his hand on the wooden grips of the 1917 Colt revolver. So this was what it was all about. Not knowing what the fuck you were supposed to do, or how the fuck to do it.

Had his father and his grandfather gone through something like this?

"Move out," he said to the microphone. The M4A3 jerked under him.

Around the next bend, he could see men on foot coming down both sides of the road. When he got close to them, he told the driver to slow. He put binoculars to his eyes. He could see nothing, except a haze that might be smoke residue from incoming rounds—or which might be haze, period.

A lieutenant flagged him down. Parker ordered the tank driver to stop. The lieutenant climbed with difficulty over the tied-on cases of 76 mm ammo.

"Turn around," he said. "They're right behind me." There was terror in the lieutenant's eyes.

"I don't see anybody back there," Parker said.

The lieutenant looked over his shoulder.

"The colonel told me to tell you to secure your positions," Parker said. "Reinforcements are on the way. We're the first of them."

"I'm not going back up there."

"Tell your men to climb on my tanks," Parker said. "You'll have to show me where to go."

The lieutenant looked at him out of wide eyes.

"Tell them," Parker said, again, softly. "Everything's going to be all right."

For a moment, he thought that he had won.

"Fuck you," the lieutenant said, not angrily. A man who had made his decision. He jumped off the tank.

His men had gathered in a clump around Parker's tank, watching. Paying no attention to them at all, the lieutenant resumed walking toward the rear. Parker pulled the Colt from its holster, pointed it at the sky, and pulled the trigger.

The noise was shocking, hurting his ears.

The lieutenant turned and looked at him.

"Get your men on the tanks," Parker ordered.

The lieutenant looked at him for a long moment, and then deliberately turned his back and started walking.

I'll fire a shot into the ground beside him, Parker thought; but even as he raised the pistol, he knew that wouldn't work. The sights lined up on the lieutenant's back. He pulled the trigger. The old pistol leapt in recoil. The lieutenant fell spread-eagled on the ground, tried to rise, then fell again and didn't move.

Parker looked at the men gathered around his tank. His eyes fell on a sergeant.

"Have your men climb on the tanks, Sergeant," Parker shouted. "You are now under my command."

The sergeant didn't move. Parker tried to put the Colt back in its holster. He missed. He could hear the pistol clattering around in the hull. He hoped it wouldn't land on its hammer and fire. He put his trembling hands on the handles of the .50 caliber machine gun, and—awkwardly—trained it on the infantrymen on the ground.

"Mount your men, Sergeant," Parker ordered.

"OK," the sergeant said, softly, and then raised his voice. "On the tanks," he shouted. "Everybody on the tanks."

Parker touched his throat microphone.

"If anyone jumps off, shoot him," he ordered. "Move out!"

A half mile further down the road, he came on the defense positions. There were twenty men manning them. Another sergeant ran out when the tanks approached.

"Is there an officer here?" Parker asked.

"No, sir, he bugged out," the sergeant said.

"You're in command?"

"I guess so, Lieutenant."

"Put these men to work," Parker ordered. "If any of them try to leave without my specific order to move, shoot them."

The sergeant, a wiry little black with an acne-scarred face, came to attention and saluted.

"Yes, sir," he said.

"I'll see you're decorated for this, Sergeant," Parker said. Then he touched the throat microphone. "Woodrow, put the tanks in a defensive position."

"Yes, sir," Sergeant Woodrow's voice came back.

"Let's take a run up the road a little and see what we can see," Parker said to his driver.

There was no response. Parker looked into the tank interior. The driver was handing the old Colt up to him.

"You really shoot that bastard, Lieutenant?" the driver asked.

Parker looked at him a moment before he nodded his head.

"Get back in the saddle," he ordered. "I want to see what's up ahead."

"Yes, sir!" the driver said. He dropped back into the hull. In a moment his voice came over the intercom. "OK, Lieutenant."

"Scouts forward," Parker said, almost to himself.

"Right up the fucking road, Lieutenant?" the driver asked, as the tank began to move.

"Right up the fucking road," Parker replied.

Another half a mile further forward, they came across six M24 light tanks. Five were facing forward, one toward the rear. They formed a half-circle.

"Maybe they're booby-trapped," the driver said, putting Parker's thoughts into words.

"Yeah, and maybe they're not," Parker replied. "Maybe they were just left here." He thought for a moment. He touched his throat microphone again. "If anybody shoots at me, return the fire," he said. "I'm going to go see."

He hoisted himself out of the turret, climbed down the tracks, and ran to the nearest M24, the one facing to the rear. The hatches were open, but there was no sign of damage at all. He climbed onto the hull, looked down into the driver's seat, and then stood on the hull and looked into the turret. Finally, he climbed into the turret. There was ammunition for the tube, and the machine guns were cocked and ready to fire. Just to be sure, he dropped into the driver's seat and tried to start the engine. It cranked but wouldn't start, and for a moment, Parker thought it was out of fuel. But the gauge showed half full. Perhaps a fuel line stoppage. He wondered if he remembered enough from watching mechanics to clear a fuel line stoppage.

And then the engine caught. It ran roughly for a moment or two and then smoothed out. He put it in gear and drove it to where his M4A3 sat and climbed out.

He ordered the gunner and the loader from his tank. He installed the gunner in the M24 and told him to go back to where the rest of the platoon was in place and to tell Sergeant Woodrow to send four crewmen back, anyone who thinks he can drive an M24.

"You always wanted to be a tank commander," he said to the loader, the junior man in a tank crew's hierarchy. "You go get one of those M24s, and its yours . . . as commander."

"Jesus Christ, Lieutenant!" the loader said, unnerved.

"Go on," Parker said. "I don't see why we should give our tanks to the enemy, do you?"

"No, sir," the loader said, and he ran toward the parked tanks.

Parker climbed into the M4A3 and took the gunner's position. He strapped on the throat microphone.

"You're the commander," he said to the driver. "Until we get some people back up here, I'll have to fire the tube."

He put his eyes to the rubber eyepieces of the gunsight. He moved the turret from side to side. There was nothing out there but a bright summer Korean day.

In fifteen minutes, crewmen from his M4A3 showed up, clinging to the hull of the M24 he had taken over. Five minutes after that, the last of the M24s had driven past him on the way to the defensive positions. He watched the last one depart, and then took a final look through the sight.

He saw movement, and then quite clearly saw crouching figures coming onto the road at a right angle from the left, and then following the road in his direction, in the ditches on either side.

He touched the throat microphone.

"I'm going to fire one round in this thing," he said. "The minute I do, turn it around and shag ass."

"Gotcha, Lieutenant," the driver said. Parker aimed the cannon. HEAT rounds were High Explosive, Anti-Tank, not very effective against personnel. What he needed was a cannister round. But he didn't have a cannister round.

He took aim at a concrete drain abutment and pressed the trigger. The round went whistling over it, to explode harmlessly five hundred yards away. Immediately, the driver spun the tank around on one track and hightailed it for the rear.

Furious, Parker climbed awkwardly into the turret of the lurching tank, skinning his hands and knees. He stood on the seat, grabbed the handles of the .50 caliber machine gun, and spun the turret around to face the rear. By the time the turret swung, they were around a corner in the road; and there was nothing for him to fire at.

When he got back to where he had left Woodrow and the platoon, he didn't know what to do with the M24s. He was unable to raise the regimental CP on any of the tank radio frequencies.

He walked over to Sergeant Sidney's M4A3. Sidney was sitting with his legs straddling the tube.

"Sidney," Parker said, "take one of those M24s and go back to regiment. Tell the colonel we have six of them and ask him what to do with them. And get us a radio frequency."

Sidney looked at him as if he were very sleepy. He nodded without saying a word and climbed off the cannon barrel. It was not, Parker decided, the time to remind Sidney that when sergeants were given an order by an officer, they were supposed to say, "Yes, sir."

Twenty minutes later, the regimental commander showed up, driving a jeep himself.

Parker climbed off his tank, walked to the jeep, and saluted.

"Where did you get the tanks, Lieutenant?" the colonel asked.

"I found them on the road, sir," Parker said. "They had apparently been abandoned. I'm going to need crews for them."

"Who are these other men?" the Colonel replied, not responding to the request.

"I think they're from Item Company, sir," Parker replied.

"That figures," the colonel said. "I recognized the body of Item Company's commander on the road on the way up here."

It took a moment before Parker realized the colonel was talking about the lieutenant he had shot.

"There's no other officer up here?" the colonel went on.

"No, sir."

"OK," the colonel said. "I don't have any communications to give you, but I'll try to get word to you if there's a further withdrawal." He corrected himself: "*When* there is a further withdrawal."

"Yes, sir."

"In the meantime, do the best you can," the colonel said. "You've got the ball."

"Sir, what about crews for the M24s?"

"That's your problem, Lieutenant. You're the company commander."

"Sir?"

"You heard me. You're Tank Company commander, and if that's what's left of Item Company, you're also Item Company commander. Your orders are the same as mine. Do what you can with what you've got."

"Yes, sir."

"I wouldn't spend a lot of time digging in," the colonel said, as he cranked the jeep engine. "Apparently, we're not the only ones suffering from bug-out fever."

Parker saluted, a reflex action, as the jeep pulled away. The colonel was too preoccupied with other matters to remember to return it.

"Sergeant Woodrow!" Parker called. Woodrow came running up.

"What's the word, Lieutenant?"

"I've just been named company commander. This is apparently the company."

"Yes, sir."

"That makes you first sergeant," Parker said. "Of our people and these infantry types. The tanks are ours, but we're going to have to find crews for them."

"I'll get right on it, Lieutenant," Woodrow said. He touched his right hand to his forehead, a sloppy movement of his arm and wrist until the fingers touched the eyebrow, then a crisp movement, almost a jerk of the hand two inches away from the forehead. It wasn't a parade ground salute, but it was a salute rendered with respect, from a first sergeant to his company commander on the battlefield. Their eyes met for a moment.

"Thank you, First Sergeant," Lieutenant Parker said, the faintest suggestion of emotion in his voice. "Carry on."

[FOUR]
Tokyo, Japan
18 July 1950

The assignment of officers in the grade of captain rarely comes to the attention of very senior officers. But there are exceptions.

"Is there something else, VanAntwerp?" the Supreme Commander, Allied Powers asked of one of his colonels, who lingered momentarily after the other officers had left the SCAP conference room after the reading of the daily communiqué.

"Sir," the colonel said, "I'm concerned about MacMillan."

"Oh? Where is he? I haven't seen him about lately."

"In Korea, sir, flying an L-5."

" 'General,' " the SCAP quoted Captain MacMillan on his return from Korea immediately after hostilities began, " 'I think we got us a war.' " The SCAP smiled. "MacMillan is a warrior, Colonel. He lies dormant, like a hibernating grizzly, until he hears the blare of the trumpet and the roll of the drum, and then he comes alive again."

"General, MacMillan has the Medal," the colonel said.

"You are implying?" SCAP asked.

"That there would be a good deal in the press in the event Captain MacMillan should be killed, or turn up missing, or fall into the hands of the enemy."

SCAP thought that over for a moment.

"Yes," he agreed, nodding his head. "Recommendation?"

"That Captain MacMillan's contribution to the tactical situation as an L-5 pilot is no greater than any other pilot's. His loss at this time would have unfortunate public relations aspects."

"Recommendation?" SCAP asked again.

"That he be assigned other duties."

"Recommendation?"

"That he be returned to the Zone of the Interior for training as a helicopter pilot. Initially, particularly if the general saw fit to decorate him for his services, specifically his rescue under fire of the three KMAG officers from the Ongjin peninsula, he would have a definite public relations value."

"Order him home, Colonel," SCAP said. "Silver Star, you think?"

" 'General of the Army Douglas MacArthur,' " the colonel quoted from the photo caption he would release, " 'himself holder of the Medal of Honor, is shown awarding the Silver Star to Captain Rudolph G. MacMillan. It was the third award of the Silver Star to MacMillan, who won the Medal of Honor in World War II. MacMillan was decorated for his heroic service as an army aviator in the opening days of the Korean conflict . . .' "

"Yes," the SCAP said. "Arrange it, Colonel."

"Yes, sir."

IV

[ONE]

Captain Craig W. Lowell, Armor, U.S. Army Reserve, 11 Washington Mews, New York City, having been ordered—by telegram, by direction of the President of the United States—to report to the United States Army Reception Center, Fort George G. Meade, Maryland, not later than 2400 hours on 12 July 1950 for an indefinite period of active duty in connection with the Korean conflict, rolled up to the MP shack at the gate at 2330 hours.

He had checked into the Lord Baltimore Hotel in Baltimore shortly after two that afternoon, after driving down from New York City in his Jaguar XK120 convertible coupe. Someone from the office had called, and when he walked up to the desk and gave his name, an assistant manager appeared almost instantly, introduced himself, said how pleased they were to have him in the house, that they had a nice, quiet little suite for him, and if there was anything, anything at all he could do to make Mr. Lowell's stay more pleasant . . .

"Thank you," Lowell had said. "There is."

"How may we be of service?"

"That's full of uniforms," Lowell said, pointing to the canvas Valv-Pak at the feet of the hovering bellman. "I'm going to need everything washable in it washed and everything else pressed, practically immediately."

"It will all be ready for you in the morning," the assistant manager said.

"I need it by eight o'clock tonight," Lowell said.

"That may be a little difficult," the assistant manager said.

"I'm sure you'll be able to manage," Lowell said. "I'll keep the suite, even if I don't get to stay in it, until I tell you otherwise. Bill it to the firm, marked for my personal account."

"Certainly, Mr. Lowell," the assistant manager said.

Lowell motioned the bellman over, gave him ten dollars, and told him to take care of the uniforms that needed washing and pressing. And then he went in the bar and had a couple of drinks and tried to work up enough courage to call the Hotel D'Anglais in Monte Carlo, where Ilse, P. P., and the colonel were waiting for him, and to tell Ilse what had happened.

He had talked to her three times since he'd been in the United States and hadn't been able to tell her. He knew that not having told her posed another problem. She would be hurt.

He decided, again, that he would wait until he knew something. When he realized he was getting as tight as a tick tossing down the scotches, he left the bar and went down Baltimore Street and went in the first movie theater he came to.

He fell asleep and woke up with a stiff neck and his right leg painfully asleep.

He went back to the hotel, went into the hotel dining room, and had a split of California burgundy with a large slice of rare roast beef and then went to the desk and got the key to the suite.

There were two message slips under the door. Both said the same thing. He was to call Porter Craig in New York City. Porter Craig was his cousin and chairman of the board of Craig, Powell, Kenyon and Dawes, Investment Bankers. Porter Craig was ten years older than Craig Lowell. He was Groton and Harvard and the Harvard School of Law. He did not get as much exercise as he would have liked, and was getting a little thick at the middle. He was also getting a little thin on top, and there was the suggestion of the jowls he would have in later life. If it were not for the coldness in his eyes, Porter Craig might have looked kindly.

Porter Craig's reaction to Lowell's telegram from the adjutant general of the United States Army was contemptuous anger. He would have a word with the senator, and that would be the end of it. It was absolutely outrageous that they should ask him to serve again. He had done his share.

The truth of the matter, Lowell knew, was that Porter was overreacting. In his heart of hearts, he would much prefer that Craig Lowell be gone from Craig, Powell, Kenyon and Dawes. Knowing that had shamed Porter, and his reaction had been to demand that Lowell accept the influence he could bring to bear against the army.

"You're going to have to let me do this, Craig, before you report. Once you report, getting you out will be infinitely more difficult than keeping you out. You understand that?"

"I'll let you know when I need you, Porter," he had told him.

He did not return Porter's calls now.

He undressed, showered, and shaved, aware that it was something of a symbolic ritual, and then he dressed in his uniform, except for the green tunic. He laid this on the bed and pinned the twin silver bars of a captain on the epaulets, the U.S. and armor insignia on the lapels. He looked at his ribbons, and replaced them in the leather insignia box. And then he took from the insignia box a miniature, unauthorized, and thus very popular version of the Expert Combat Infantry Badge and pinned that over the breast pocket.

He put the tunic on, buttoned it, and closed the belt, then took an overseas cap and put that on. He examined himself in the mirror. He saluted his image.

"Captain Lowell," he said. "Reporting for duty, sir." And then he said, "Shit!"

Then he called the desk and told them to have the car brought around and to send a bellman to his room. A moment after he hung up, he called back and told them to send up a bottle of Haig and Haig Pinch with the bellman.

When the bellman showed up, Lowell told him to take the uniforms on their hangers and to lay them out either in the trunk of the Jaguar or behind the seat, so they wouldn't get mussed, and to put the Valv-Pak and the briefcase on the passenger side seat.

"I'll be in the bar," Lowell said. "Acquiring some liquid courage."

"My brother-in-law got called up, too," the bellman said. "Poor bastard."

"Your brother or me?" Lowell asked.

"Both of you," the bellman said.

Lowell thought again of calling Ilse and decided against it, then had two drinks in the bar before walking out of the hotel lobby and getting directions to Fort George G. Meade from the bellman. After that he got in the car and drove off.

The MP at the gate came to the car, saluted, and bent over.

"Reception center," Lowell said.

"Stay on this road, sir," the MP said. "One point three miles. You'll see a sign."

"Thank you."

"That's a real fine set of wheels, Captain," the MP said, and saluted again.

It was, Lowell thought, his second visit to Fort George G. Meade, Maryland. He had previously reported here after a postcard had informed him that his friends and neighbors had selected him for induction into the armed forces of the United States.

That was so much bullshit. He had been drafted because he'd been given the heave-ho from Harvard, cancelling his academic exemption.

He had arrived the first time by chartered bus, after a train ride from New York. He remembered the sergeant who had been waiting for them at the reception center, who had been displeased with the speed with which Private Lowell had gotten off the bus and into ranks, whose spittle had had sprayed Private Lowell's face as he screamed in his ear that he personally doubted that such a pile of shit could ever be turned into a soldier.

This time, when he reported to the reception center, a sergeant got to his feet when he walked in the building and actually smiled at him. He then assigned a corporal to take him to the BOQ. The corporal collected five dollars for BOQ fees, to pay for the orderly who had made up the bunk and who would sweep the floor and clean the latrine he was to share with the three other officers in the two bedroom, one latrine suite.

No bugles were blown the next morning, and neither did some bull-chested cretin amuse himself by lifting the end of his bunk and letting it slam back to the floor. No one screamed, "Drop your cocks and pick up your socks, it's reveille!" at the top of his lungs.

A sergeant came in and turned on the lights.

"There will be an orientation formation at 0800, gentlemen," he said. "If you want breakfast, the officer's open mess feeds from now on. The big white building the other side of the parade ground."

But there were other painful similarities. The impersonal physical examination, so much meat on the hoof being examined by bored doctors. The arm stiff from the tetanus shot, like seven others administered whether or not it was needed, because that speeded up the processing.

The forms to be filled out.

The false hopes: "They can't send all of us to Korea. When this bullshit is over, we'll be assigned somewhere counting mess kits."

"Shit, I haven't been near the army for five years. I'm not qualified to command a squad, much less a company."

"I've been working for the Chase Manhattan bank. I'd be of much greater use as a finance officer than in a line company. I don't know anything anymore about a line company."

"That fucking war is going to be over in six months. Just as soon as Truman gets the balls to drop the A-bomb on them."

The first thing that the Adjutant General's Corps captain (who would interview Captain Lowell and determine his assignment) thought when he saw him was that, if he were not wearing the "Bloody Bucket" shoulder patch from the 28th Infantry Division, Pennsylvania National Guard, Lowell could have easily been mistaken for a regular, or what was known as a "career reserve" officer. He *looked* like a soldier, not like most of the other recalls, who generally showed up in a uniform that looked as if it had been stuck in an attic trunk for a half decade—if, indeed, they showed up in uniform at all.

Captain Lowell's Class "A" green tunic and pink trousers were immaculate and perfectly tailored. His feet were shod in the highly polished, pebble-grained jodhpurs normally worn only by regular armor—or armored cavalry—officers who felt their appearance justified the extraordinary cost. He wore no ribbons on his breast; it was bare save for the miniature, unauthorized version of the wretched silver flintlock on a blue background, the Expert Combat Infantry Badge.

"You're one of the unfortunates, Captain Lowell," the AGC captain said to him with somewhat forced joviality. "Your service record seems to have been mislaid between here and Fort Benjamin Harrison."

At Fort Benjamin Harrison, in Indiana, in enormous, file-filled warehouses, the army maintains the records of officers and enlisted men not on active duty.

"Where does that leave me?" Captain Lowell asked.

"Well, what we're going to do for you fellows is make up a temporary service record, and 201 file, and then correct it when the real thing catches up with you. I don't suppose you've kept your own 201 file?"

"As a matter of fact, I have," Lowell said. He reached onto the floor beside him, picked up a softly gleaming, saddle-leather attaché case bearing his initials in gold. "May I?" he asked, placing it on the captain's desk and opening it. He took out two inch-thick folders, their contents held in place by metal clips. "Everything's in there," he said.

The AGC captain flipped quickly through them.

"May I have these? They'd certainly be a help."

"You may make certified true copies of anything you want," Captain Lowell said, "but you can't have them."

The AGC captain didn't like that at all. He spent the next fifteen minutes reading through the files.

"You've had a very *interesting* career, haven't you?" he said, finally.

Lowell didn't reply.

"Captain, how would you feel about a detail to infantry?" the AGC officer asked.

"I wouldn't like that at all, Captain," Captain Lowell said, flatly.

"You've got to look at the big picture," he said. "There aren't that many vacancies for armor officers of your grade."

"Great, send me home."

"You've had service—according to your record, distinguished service—as an advisor to an infantry unit. And we need infantry company commanders. You have the Expert Combat Infantry Badge."

"Cut the bullshit," Captain Lowell said, unpleasantly.

"Now wait a minute!"

"I'm not going to take a voluntary detail to infantry. If I'm detailed to infantry, I will make a stink you wouldn't believe. I'm a qualified armor officer."

"Not as a captain, you're not. You're not a graduate of the Advanced Armor Officer's Course."

"Neither am I of the Advanced Infantry Officer's Course," Lowell said.

"I don't really need your permission, you know."

"Yes, you do, you chair-warming sonofabitch, or else you wouldn't have called me in here to feed me your line of bullshit."

"Have a seat, Captain Lowell," the lieutenant colonel in charge of Recalled Officer's Classification and Assignment said, and then he said to the AGC captain, "I'll handle this, Tom."

He spent fifteen minutes going over Captain Lowell's personal 201 file.

"You're very young to be a captain, you know," he said, finally.

"Yes, sir, I suppose I am," Lowell said.

"We need infantry company commanders," the lieutenant colonel said.

"I hope you find them, sir," Lowell said.

"What have you been doing as a civilian, Captain?" the colonel asked.

Lowell took a moment to reply. The colonel looked up at him.

"I'm an investment banker," Lowell said.

"I'm not entirely sure what that means," the colonel said.

"Did you have a title of some sort?"

"Vice-chairman of the board," Lowell said, distinctly.

"The name of the firm?"

"Craig, Powell, Kenyon and Dawes," Lowell said.

"I don't know the name," the colonel said. Lowell didn't reply.

"In New York City?"

"Twenty-three Wall Street," Lowell said.

"Paid pretty well, I suppose," the colonel asked, idly.

"Is that an official request for information, Colonel?" Lowell asked.

"Yes," the colonel said. "I guess it is."

"I drew a hundred thousand," Lowell said.

"Captain," the colonel said, more in resignation than anger, "if I have to tell you this, I will. It's a court-martial offense, the uttering of statements known to be false in response to an official inquiry. According to your own 201 file, you were graduated from the Wharton School of Business just about a year ago. And now you're telling me . . ."

Lowell reached forward slightly and nudged the telephone toward the colonel. "Use my name and call collect, Colonel," he said. "You asked for the information and I gave it to you. I inherited half the firm from my grandfather."

The colonel looked at Lowell for a long moment.

"You were originally commissioned in the Finance Corps," he said. "Is that what this is all about? You want to go back to the Finance Corps?"

Lowell chuckled.

"Colonel," he said, "I would be outright disaster in the Finance Corps."

"But you were originally commissioned in the Finance Corps?"

"That was simply an expedient means of getting me into an officer's uniform," Lowell said. "I never stepped behind the counter of a finance office."

"You won a battlefield commission?" the AGC lieutenant colonel asked.

"First they handed me a commission," Lowell said. "The battlefield came later."

"I think that needs an explanation," the lieutenant colonel said.

Lowell hesitated a moment before replying.

"You know who General Porky Waterford was, I presume, Colonel?"

"Yes, of course. He had the 40th Armored Divison, 'Hell's Circus,' during War II. You were with 'Hell's Circus'?"

"I wasn't in the Second World War," Lowell said. "I was drafted after the war and sent to the Army of Occupation in Germany. To the Constabulary, which Porky Waterford commanded."

"And?"

"It was important to the general that his polo team play the polo team of the French Army of Occupation, and win."

"I don't quite follow you," the lieutenant colonel said.

"I play polo, Colonel," Lowell said. "In those days I had a three-goal handicap. The general wanted me to play on his team against the French. I could not play because French officers will not play with enlisted men. I was a PFC."

"And you're telling me you were commissioned just so you could play polo?"

"I made a deal with Waterford's aide, a captain named MacMillan. I would take the commission, as a Finance Corps second john, and play polo, and within six months I would be out of the army."

"There was an officer named MacMillan who won the Medal," the lieutenant colonel said.

"That's Mac," Lowell said. "But that well-laid plan didn't quite work out the way it was supposed to."

"What plan?"

"To get me out of the army," Lowell said. "While we were playing the French at Baden-Baden, General Waterford dropped dead. He had a heart attack in the saddle, going for a goal. So that ended the polo, and that ended my chances to get out of the army the same way I got my commission, in other words, somewhat irregularly."

"Frankly, Captain, if this incredible yarn of yours is true, I don't understand why they wouldn't have been happy to separate you. As quickly as possible."

"I hadn't been an officer long enough to be given an efficiency report," Lowell went on. "So they got rid of me. They sent me to the Military Advisory Group in Greece, apparently in the belief that if luck failed them, and I didn't get killed, the Advisory Group would get stuck with throwing me out of the army."

"What did they do with you in Greece?"

"I wound up as advisor to Greek mountain infantry company. For all practical purposes, I commanded it."

The lieutenant colonel looked closely at him. Lowell met his eyes.

"Then I got hit," Lowell said. "And they sent me home. To the Basic Armor Officer's Course, where officers who had never heard a shot fired in anger told me all about what I could expect if I should ever get in combat. But I came out of Knox, out of the army, trained as tank officer."

"What do you want, Captain?" The AGC lieutenant colonel asked.

"If I have to go to war again, I want to go as an armor officer."

"You have been around the army long enough to know that what counts is what the army needs, not what the individual would like."

"I have no intention, sir, of taking a detail to infantry," Lowell said.

"What's wrong with the infantry?" the colonel asked.

"Right now, the infantry in Korea is being sacrificed for time. I don't intend to be part of that sacrifice."

"That could be interpreted as an admission of cowardice," the colonel said.

"I readily admit to being a coward," Lowell said. "But I'm not a fool."

"Captain Lowell," the colonel said, "the personnel requirements of the army are such at the moment, due to the situation in Korea, that there is a surplus of armor officers, and a shortage of infantry officers. To meet the requirement for infantry officers in Korea, the army is detailing a number of armor officers to infantry, selecting those who have infantry experience, and for whose service as armor officers there is no projected need. You have been selected as one of those officers, Captain Lowell. That is all, you are dismissed."

HEADQUARTERS
U.S. ARMY RECEPTION CENTER
FORT GEORGE G. MEADE, MARYLAND

SPECIAL ORDERS
NUMBER 187 — 14 July 1950

EXTRACT

****

18. CAPT Craig W. LOWELL, ARMOR, 0-495302, Co "B" USARC, Ft Geo G Meade, Md, is detailed INFANTRY trfd and will proceed USA Inf Sch Ft Benning, Ga, for purp of attending Spec Inf Co Grade Off Crse # 50-5. On completion trng off will report to CG Ft Lawton, Wash, for air shpmt to Hq Eight US Army, APO 909 San Fran Calif for asgmt within Eight US Army. Five (5) Days delay-en-route leave authorized between Ft Benning and Ft Lawton at Home of Record, 11 Washington Mews, New York City NY. Off is *not* entitled to be accompanied by dependents. Off auth storage of personal and household goods at Govt Expense. S-99-999-999. Auth Ltr, The Adj Gen dtd 1 Jul 50, Subj: Detail of

Surplus to Needs Armor, Artillery and Signal Corps Officers to Infantry.

****

BY COMMAND OF
MAJOR GENERAL HARBES
Morton C. Cooper
Lt. Col, AGC
Acting Adjutant General

[TWO]
Fairfax, Virginia
15 July 1950

Lt. Colonel Robert F. Bellmon, Armor (Detail, General Staff Corps), Chief of the Tank and Armored Personnel Carrier Section of the Tracked Vehicle Division of the Office of the Assistant Chief of Staff for Operations, had caught himself making six stupid mistakes in a two-hour period in his office in the Pentagon, and had decided to call it quits.

He knocked at the office door of his boss, a brigadier general, who looked up and smiled, but did not speak.

"With your permission, sir," Bellmon said, "I'm going to hang it up. I'm spending more time correcting the stupid mistakes I'm making than I am doing anything worthwhile."

"You've been reading my mind, again, Bob," the general said. "Honest to God, I was just about to get up and run your ass out of there. You've been putting in too much time."

"Thank you, sir," Bellmon said. "I'll see you in the morning, General."

"No, Colonel. You will see me Friday morning. You will take tomorrow and the day after tomorrow off."

"I'll be all right in the morning, General," Bellmon protested.

"Indulge me, Bob," the general said. "Take a couple of days off. Get drunk. Charge your batteries."

"I'll really be all right in the morning, General."

"Splendid," the general said. "Then you will be able to enjoy your morning ride through the Virginia hills, or your golf game, or for that matter, whatever indoor sport strikes your fancy. Goddamn it, I told you Friday."

"Yes, sir," Bellmon said. "Good afternoon, General."

"You tell Barbara what I said," the general said.

"About indoor sports, General?" Bellmon asked, with a smile.

"Leave, Colonel!" the general said, and pointed his finger out the door.

Bellmon went to Pentagon Parking Lot A64-B and found his 1948 Buick convertible (as far as he was concerned, the last of the good ones) and started home.

He started to plan, for he was by nature a planner. The statement of the problem was that he was exhausted, physically and, more important, mentally. Since he had returned from Europe, summoned off leave when the Korean balloon went up, he had been putting in eighteen-hour days of logistic chess. He had been trying to find and move and arrange for the inspection and repairs of sufficient tanks to equip the forces presently in Korea, those in Japan about to go to Korea, those in Hawaii about to go to Japan and/or Korea, those in the United States about to go to Hawaii, Japan, and/or Korea, and those about to be formed.

He loved the challenge. Not as much as he would have loved to command one of the tank battalions, of course, but as the next best thing. It was a bona fide intellectual challenge, even more fascinating than chess, because the available supplies and the requirements for them changed literally hourly.

He had done a good job, shuffling around literally billions of dollars' worth not only of tanks and personnel carriers, but the support for them, human and material. This had exhausted him. He'd reached his limits.

He would be all right in the morning, but the general had been dead serious. He was not to report back to work before Friday.

With a little bit of luck, he could get the kids to go to bed early, and then he'd feed Barbara a couple of martinis, and they could make whoopee tonight. That's what he needed. Dr. Bellmon's prescription for Colonel Bellmon's exhausted condition: three martinis and a piece of tail.

Twenty minutes after he left the Pentagon, he reached the split rail and fieldstone fence of "the Farm." There was no name on the mailbox by the drive and no sign. There was only an old mule-drawn plow, painted black, sitting on the fieldstone fence, clearly visible.

It was a question of being discreet. The Farm was far too luxurious a place for a lowly lieutenant colonel to live in without comment. Unless, of course, one knew the circumstances. The truth was that it was indeed a farm. It had been a farm in great financial distress when Bellmon's grandfather had bought it, when he was a major assigned to the War Department in 1909. Major (later, Lieutenant General) Thomas Wood Bellmon had seen the place as a good investment. Its lands could be farmed on shares, or rented out, and the income would pay the mortgage. In effect, it gave him a rent-free place to live while stationed in Washington, at the expense of having to drive an hour each way to the State, War and Navy Building on Pennsylvania Avenue next to the White House.

The Farm had long since been paid off (it had twice changed hands by inheritance) and it now contained 480 acres more than it did when Major Bellmon had bought it. It was more than self-supporting. All but the seven acres around the house itself, these in woods, were rented out.

When a Bellmon (Bellmon's two older brothers were general officers) or a Waterford (Bellmon's wife was the daughter of the late Major General Peterson K. Waterford and she had two brothers who were officers, one army, and one, God forgive him, a flyboy) was stationed in the Washington area, he occupied the house. When none was in the area, it was rented out to old friends. The rent charged was the housing allowance, which wouldn't come close to paying what the Farm was worth, but did pay for repairs, taxes, and upkeep, more important, it kept somebody in the house to see that the pipes didn't burst or that someone didn't steal all the furniture.

The house itself was three or four times as large as the original Virginia farmhouse Major Bellmon had bought forty-one years before. Additions had been made. The original house, now the left wing, was converted into a study. The house now had nine rooms, four baths, a swimming pool, a garage, an outbuilding where the kids played, and even a trap range overlooking a valley.

There was a similar establishment, Casa Mañana, owned by the family in Carmel, California. There was no rule that said that simply because you were an officer you had to raise your family in the really dreadful family housing found on most camps, posts, and stations. There was an unwritten law that you could live comfortably—in keeping with your means—and discreetly. Hence, no sign at the gate to the estate. Just the old plow, painted black.

"Turn in, General at the old plow on the fence. The house is a quarter mile down the dirt road. We generally have a nip about seven, and eat around 2000."

Bob Bellmon blew the horn as he approached the house. This annoyed Barbara greatly, but the kids liked it. He parked the Buick convertible beside Barbara's Ford station wagon and the jeep, and got out. He was surprised and pleased to see her, and the kids, a boy and a girl, waiting for him at the door.

Just like a Norman Rockwell cover on the *Saturday Evening Post*, he thought, and then was annoyed with himself for being a cynic.

"You and that damned horn," Barbara said, as she gave him her cheek to kiss. He quickly squeezed her buttocks.

"I am ordered to take two days off," he said.

"It's about time he saw how exhausted you were," Barbara said, in reference to the general.

"I don't know if he did or not," Bellmon said. "I asked for the time."

"Well, either way," she said.

They went into the house. He hung the tunic carefully on a hanger in the hall closet, and put the brimmed cap on the shelf above.

"Make me a very cold, very large martini," he said. "While I change."

"Drink now, change later?" she asked.

"No, change now, drink lots later," he said.

"Is it going to be one of those days off?"

"And aren't you glad?" he said.

"Uh huh," she said. "And guess who's going to choir practice?"

"God loves me," Bellmon said, and went upstairs to change. What more could a man ask, he asked himself rhetorically, than for two days off, a cold martini, a wife who likes to fool around, and a priest of the Episcopal Church who schedules children's choir practice at precisely the right time.

When he came down, the kids and Barbara were gone. She had taken them early to choir practice, he realized, or had in some other manner gotten rid of them. He would have to make his own martini. That seemed a small enough price to pay.

Ten minutes later, he heard the crunch of automobile tires on the road and decided it was Barbara coming home. If he had planned ahead, he thought, he could have greeted her at the door starkers and played "Me Tarzan, You Jane" with her on the living room floor.

It was probably better this way, he thought. Drag it out a little.

The bell—a real, old-fashioned, hand-twisted door bell—rang.

"Christ!" he said. "Who the hell?"

He opened the door.

Craig W. Lowell stood outside his door. He wore gray flannel slacks, a white shirt, and a cravat, like an English duke in the country.

This was bound to happen, Bellmon thought. Something—something like Craig W. Lowell showing up out of nowhere—was bound to fuck up his fun.

"Hello, Craig," he said, forcing himself to smile. "What brings you traipsing down my country lane?"

"I heard that beggars are offered booze," he said.

"Come on in," Bellmon said, putting his hand on his arm. He didn't like Craig W. Lowell. Barbara did. For reasons he couldn't begin to understand, Barbara automatically forgave Lowell for things that would have seen her terminate a lifelong friendship with somebody else. Barbara's father, General Waterford, and Lowell's father-in-law, just returned from Russian imprisonment in Siberia, had gone to Samur, the French cavalry school, together before War II.

Lowell's father-in-law, Colonel Count Peter-Paul von Greiffenberg, had also been the commandant of the POW camp where Bellmon had been confined. Von Greiffenberg and Bellmon had become friends, separately from the colonel's relationship with General Waterford.

Until von Greiffenberg had shown up alive in Marburg a month before, Bellmon had believed that he was dead. Bellmon was delighted that von Greiffenberg had survived, not only for himself, but for the colonel's daughter. Bellmon liked Ilse von Greiffenberg Lowell very much.

It was Craig W. Lowell that he disliked.

"What can I make you?" Bellmon asked.

"Scotch," Lowell said. "Please. Barbara home?"

"Not at the moment," Bellmon said, going behind the bar in the living room to make Lowell a drink. "How's the colonel making out?" he asked.

"He's taking the waters in Monte Carlo," Lowell said, dryly, "while I work on his financial affairs."

"When did you come back?"

"On the seventh," Lowell said.

"And when are you going back to Europe?"

"I wish to hell I knew," Lowell said. He took the scotch from Bellmon and raised the glass to him. "Mud in your eye, Herr Oberstleutnant," he said.

"Who's here?" Barbara called from the front door.

"Come and see," Bellmon called back.

Barbara took one look at Craig W. Lowell and squealed with pleasure. "You look like an advertisement for fairy cigarettes in *Town and Country*," she said. She went to him and kissed him on the cheek. "I thought you'd be in the south of France."

"Obviously, no," Lowell said. "I have the strangest feeling that I walked in here in the middle of Bob's Day."

You sonofabitch, Bellmon thought, furiously. How dare you say something like that to me in the middle of my living room?

Barbara collapsed in laughter, infuriating her husband even more.

"How could you tell?"

"He was pawing at the ground when he opened the door," Lowell said. "And then he seemed even less joyous to see me than he usually does."

Barbara laughed.

"What brings you way the hell out here?" she asked. "I'm delighted to see you, of course, and we insist you stay for dinner and the night . . . (Goddamnit, I knew she'd do that, her husband thought) . . . but I'm surprised."

"I couldn't stay the night," Lowell said. "Thank you just the same."

"You tell me why not," Barbara insisted, taking her husband's martini glass and sipping from it.

"That would put Bob in the awkward position of harboring a deserter," Lowell said. They looked at him in confusion.

"If that's supposed to be funny, I missed the punch line," Barbara said.

"It's not funny. I've deserted."

"Deserted what?" Bellmon asked.

"I've been ordered to Benning," Lowell said. "To go through some quickie course for reserve officers they're going to send to Korea to get slaughtered, and I've decided I'm not going."

"You're serious, aren't you?" Barbara asked.

"You were recalled?" Bellmon asked.

"There was a telegram waiting for me at the house," Lowell said.

"Ordering you to Benning?"

"Ordering me to Meade, where some pencil-pusher told me that I was now in the infantry."

"There's a shortage of infantry officers," Bellmon said. "So I'm told."

"You're not serious about not reporting, are you?" Bellmon asked.

Lowell took an airlines ticket folder from his pocket.

"Ten forty-five to London, with connections to Monte Carlo," he said.

"They'll court-martial you, you realize?"

"Possibly."

"What do you mean, 'possibly'?" Bellmon snapped. "That's absence to avoid hazardous service. They can shoot you for that."

"Come on, Bob," Lowell said. "I'm not much of a soldier, I admit, but I know better than that. They haven't, at least officially, shot anybody since they blew away that Polack, Slovik."

Lowell looked at Barbara, and handed her his glass.

"I could use another one of these," he said.

"Sure," she said. "I'm sorry you had to ask."

"Why are you telling me all this, Craig?" Bellmon asked. "You don't think there's anything I can do to help you, do you?"

"Yeah, as a matter of fact, since you ask, Colonel, I do," Lowell said.

"And what would that be?"

"You could get on the telephone, and convene an ad hoc meeting of the West Point Protective Association, and find somebody to cancel that detail to infantry."

"What makes you think I could do something like that, even if I wanted to?" Bellmon demanded angrily.

"Because otherwise, I'm gong to make a big stink."

"That sounds like a threat," Bellmon said.

"No threat. Statement of intentions."

"I'm trying to control my temper," Bellmon said. "I think you had better leave before I no longer am able to."

"Hear him out," Barbara said, her voice flat. She handed Lowell the drink he had asked for, and when her husband said nothing else, she went on: "What do you want from Bob, Craig?"

"I don't want to be sent to Korea as an infantry officer, and get myself killed."

"The killing of officers comes with war, Lowell," Bellmon said, icily.

"Killing and slaughter are two different things," Lowell said.

"What kind of a stink are you going to cause?" Barbara asked, sounding as if she were idly curious.

" 'Craig W. Lowell, New York banker, charged with desertion,' " he said. " 'Decorated hero says he is will not go to Korea as untrained cannon fodder.' "

"You'd do that, too, wouldn't you, Lowell?" Bellmon asked, the contempt in his voice shocking even his wife.

"You bet your sweet ass I will," Lowell said.

"I can't pretend to understand what you're thinking," Bellmon said. "What made you think you should bring me into this."

"It's not that hard to figure out," Lowell said. "I figured it out between Fort Meade and Washington. I fucking near . . . sorry, Barbara, that just slipped out . . ."

"I've heard the word before," Barbara Bellmon said.

"I was nearly killed in Greece, you will recall."

"And returned a decorated hero," Bellmon said.

"I shouldn't have been on the goddamned mountaintop, Robert," Lowell said. "One of you professionals should have been there."

"I grant the point, but so what?"

"So once is enough," Lowell said. "I came through that. But I am not going to put myself in a position again where I am unqualified to lead untrained troops. And get my ass blown away at the same time."

"I'm beginning to understand your warped thinking," Bellmon said. "But you had better understand, Lowell, that the army is bigger than you, or me, and that individual desires have nothing to do with anything. You better get back in your car and proceed as ordered, to Benning."

"You're not refusing to go to Korea, are you, Craig?"

"As an infantry officer, I am."

"He's bluffing," Bellmon decided, and announced, "He's desperate and bluffing. You're really despicable, Lowell."

"Certainly desperate and probably despicable, but not bluffing," Lowell said. He drained his glass and laid it on the bar. "Sorry you had to get involved in this, Barbara," he said.

"Where are you going?" Barbara asked.

"I'll send you a postcard from the Riviera," Lowell said.

Barbara pushed the lever on a flop-open telephone directory.

"What are you doing?" Bob Bellmon asked.

She dialed a number.

"Colonel Bellmon calling for General Davidson," she said. She handed the telephone to her husband. "You can either tell him to send the MPs to Washington National," Barbara said, "to stop a deserting captain. Or that you found out that the system grabbed an armor officer who's badly needed in Korea and threw him into the infantry."

He took the phone from her without thinking.

"I'll do nothing of the kind," he said.

"Who's Davidson?" Lowell asked.

"Deputy Chief of Staff, Personnel. He was my brother's roommate at the Academy," Barbara Bellmon said.

"General," Lt. Col. Bellmon said to the telephone, "I really hate to bother you personally with this, but I don't know how else to handle it. And it's further made delicate because the officer involved is a close friend of my wife's. The point, sir, is that the net you threw out to snag infantry officers snagged an armor officer we really need."

Barbara Bellmon and Lowell watched Bob Bellmon as he spoke. Then he said, "One moment, please, sir," and turned to Lowell. "Let me have your orders, Lowell."

Lowell handed him his orders. Bellmon read them over the telephone.

"Thank you very much, sir," Bellmon said, finally. He handed Lowell his orders back. "I'll have Captain Lowell remain at Fort Meade until the paperwork comes through."

"Now," Barbara Bellmon said, "let's have a friendly drink."

HEADQUARTERS
U.S. ARMY RECEPTION CENTER
FORT GEORGE G. MEADE, MARYLAND

SPECIAL ORDERS
NUMBER 191 18 July 1950

EXTRACT

****

1. So much of Para 18, Spec Orders 187 this Hq dtd 14 July 1950, pertaining to the detail of CAPT Craig W. LOWELL, ARMOR, 0-495302 to INFANTRY is rescinded. AUTH: Telecon, Deputy, the Asst Chief of Staff, Personnel, Hq Dept of the Army & Acting Adjutant Gen, this Hq, 17 July 1950.

2. So much of Para 18, Spec Orders 187 this Hq dtd 14 July 1950, pertaining to the trans of CAPT Craig W. LOWELL, Armor 0-495302 to the USA Inf Sch, Ft Benning Ga for tng, and for trans to Hq US Army Eight is rescinded. AUTH: Telecon Asst Chief of Staff, Personnel, Hq Dept of the Army & CG, US Army Reception Center & Ft Geo G Meade, Md. 16 July 1950.

3. CAPT Craig W. LOWELL, ARMOR, 0-495302 Co "B" USARC, Ft Geo G Meade, Md., is trfd and will proceed US Army Outport, San Francisco Calif International Airport, San Francisco Calif by the most expeditious military or civilian air transport for further mil or civ air shipment (Priority AAAA-1) to Hq 73rd Med Tank Bn, 8th US ARMY in the field (Korea). This asgmt is in response to TWX Hq SCAP re critical shortage Co Grade Armor Officers dtd 3 July 1950. The exigencies of the service making this necessary, off is *not*, repeat *not*, auth delay en route leave. Off is *not* entitled to be accompanied by dependents. Off auth storage of personal and household goods at Govt Expense. S-99-999-999. AUTH: Telecon Asst Chief of Staff, Pors, Hq Dept of the Army Wash DC & Acting Adj Gen this Hq 17 July 1950.

****

BY COMMAND OF
MAJOR GENERAL HARBES
Morton C. Cooper
Lt Col., AGC
Acting Adjutant General

[THREE]
The Naktong River
South Korea
24 July 1950

Lowell took the Pennsylvania Railroad to New York, a TWA triple-tailed Lockheed Constellation to San Francisco, a United DC-6 to Honolulu, and another DC-6—this one Pan American—to Tokyo via Wake Island.

He called Ilse from New York and told her what had happened; and when he hung up, he went to the VIP lounge and got wordlessly as stiff as a board before boarding the plane. When he called her again from San Francisco, it was ten hours later, and her father had apparently talked to her, because she was not hysterical, only weeping and trying to be brave. He got the colonel on the line, and the colonel said that whatever he did, he was not to worry about Ilse and Peter-Paul. He would take care of them. The colonel wished him God speed.

He called Porter Craig from San Francisco and told him what was happening, and asked him to personally make sure (which meant getting on a plane and going to Europe) that Craig, Powell, Kenyon and Dawes was doing everything possible to get the colonel's affairs straightened out as quickly as possible. He told Porter to personally make sure that Ilse understood that his army pay would be more than adequate for his needs, and that his salary from the firm would continue.

"I don't want her skimping and scraping, Porter, you understand?"

"Good God, Craig, don't worry about her. She's family, for God's sake!"

For some reason, that short sentence from Porter Craig, whom he generally thought of as a three-star horse's ass, reassured him.

"Yeah, Porter, she is," he said, his voice tight.

"You take care of yourself, old boy," Porter said. "Since you insist on going through with this, the least I can do is put your mind at rest about your wife and child. Andre does very well with your mother. You're the one we're all concerned about."

"Yeah, well, you keep your sticky fingers out of the till, Chubby," Lowell said and hung up because he was afraid he was going to start crying.

An army bus met them at Tachikawa Airport outside Tokyo and drove them through really stinking rice paddies and sooty industrial areas to a military base, Camp Drake. He was assigned a BOQ, issued a footlocker for his Class "A" pink and green and tropical worsted and khaki uniforms (which would be stored at Drake while he was in Korea), then issued a steel helmet, a .45 Colt pistol with a web belt, a holster, three magazines, a magazine holder, a first aid pouch, and, for reasons he didn't understand, a compass. He was told that in the morning he would be issued new fatigues and combat boots and taken to the range to fire the .45. In the meantime, he was restricted to the BOQ and the officer's open mess.

There was a telephone center in the mess, and he put in another call to Ilse.

While he was waiting for it to go through, at 0310 Tokyo time, a sergeant came and found him.

"I thought you'd gone over the fence to Tokyo for the night, Captain, when I couldn't find you in your BOQ."

"I'm trying to call my wife," Lowell said.

"I got a car outside, Captain," the sergeant said, uncomfortably. "There's a C-54 going to K1—that's Pusan—at 0400. With that priority of yours, you've got to be on it."

The C-54 was an old and battered cargo plane. He rode to K1 airfield, on the southern tip of the Korean peninsula, stretched out on the pierced aluminum floor.

There was no one to meet him, and the air force types in the crowded terminal had only a vague idea where he might find the 73rd Medium Tank Battalion.

"If you can't get them on the phone, Captain, there's no fucking telling where the fuck they are."

Lowell picked up his now nearly empty Valv-Pak (it held only four sets of fatigues, underwear, a second pair of tanker's boots, his toilet kit, and the 9 mm Pistole-08, the German Luger he'd carried in Greece) and walked out of the terminal.

His first impression of Korea was that it stank. Later that day he was to learn it stank because the Koreans fertilized their rice paddies with human waste. His second impression was that the U.S. Army in Korea was in shitty shape. There was an aura of desperation, of frenzy, even of fear. They were getting the shit kicked out of them, and it showed.

He hitchhiked a ride in a three-quarter-ton ammo carrier into Pusan itself, and asked directions of an MP.

"They're somewhere up near the Naktong, I think," the MP told him. "Everything's all fucked up."

The MP flagged down an MP jeep for him, and they carried him to the outskirts of town to the main supply route, a two-lane, once-macadamized road now reduced to little more than a rough dirt trail by the crush of tanks and trucks and artillery passing over it.

Lowell tried vainly to catch a ride with his extended thumb and finally stopped another three-quarter-ton ammo carrier by stepping into the middle of the road and holding up his hand like a traffic cop.

Two hours later, he was at the command post of the 73rd Medium Tank Battalion (Separate), on the south bank of the Naktong River.

The command post was new; it wasn't even completed. Soldiers, naked to the waist, sweat-soaked, were filling sandbags with the sandy clay soil and stacking them against a timber-framed structure built into the side of a low hill.

The unfinished structure, however, was already in use. When Lowell walked inside, a very large sergeant was marking on a celluloid-covered situation map with a grease pencil; a GI manned a field switchboard; and, most importantly, a wiry lieutenant colonel and a plump major were crowded together at a tiny, folding GI field desk, examining what Lowell thought was probably an inventory of some kind.

He walked up to the desk and waited until they became aware of his presence. The major spoke first.

"Something for you, Captain?"

Lowell came to attention, saluted, and said: "Captain C. W. Lowell reporting for duty, sir."

The wiry little lieutenant colonel returned the salute. "Got your orders, Captain?" he asked, and Lowell handed them over. The lieutenant colonel read them carefully, and then passed them to the major.

"You have a personal copy, Captain?"

"Yes, sir."

"Let's take a little walk," the lieutenant colonel said. He stood up and put his hand out. "I'm Paul Jiggs," he said, dryly. "Commander of this miraculous fighting force."

Lowell shook his hand.

"Major Charley Ellis," Jiggs continued. "S-3. We don't have an exec at the moment. He got blown away before he got here." Lowell was aware that Colonel Jiggs was watching his face for his reaction to that somewhat cold-blooded announcement. He tried to keep his face expressionless. Major Ellis offered his hand and gave Lowell a smile.

"We won't be long, Charley," Colonel Jiggs said. "Do what you think has to be done."

"Yes, sir," Major Ellis said. Colonel Jiggs put his hand on Lowell's arm and led him out of the half-finished bunker, around it, and to the crest of the hill against which it was built.

"That's the Naktong," he said, indicating the river. "If they get across that, it'll be Dunkirk all over again, except that we're not twenty miles from the White Cliffs of Dover. It will be a somewhat longer swim across the Sea of Japan."

"And are they going to get across?" Lowell asked.

"Of course not," Jiggs said, sarcastically. "If for no other reason than my magnificent fighting force is digging in to repel them. I say magnificent, Captain, because the 73rd Medium Tank Battalion, Separate, didn't even exist a month ago. It sprang miraculously from the ground to do battle for God and country, manned with rejects, clerks, gentlemen from various Army of Occupation stockades, and equipped with junk from various abandoned ordnance depots. Do you get the picture?"

"Yes, sir, I think so," Lowell said.

"You will forgive me, Captain," Colonel Jiggs said. "There is nothing personal in this. But I confess a certain disappointment in what I got in response to a desperate request for experienced company commanders. In my innocence I was hoping to get a battle-experienced company commander. And what I get is a National Guardsman, to judge by that Bloody Bucket patch on your sleeve. And—forgive me, Captain—a captain who doesn't look either old enough to be a captain, or to have earned that CIB he's wearing."

Lowell flushed but said nothing.

"And who is, moreover, to judge by his orders, either someone with friends in high places, or a fuck-up, and most probably both." When Lowell didn't reply, Colonel Jiggs went on. "I solicit your comments, Captain. And please don't waste my time."

"What would you like me to say, Colonel?" Lowell asked.

"For example, tell me how old you are?"

"Twenty-three, sir."

"How the fuck did you get to be a captain at twenty-three?"

"The truth of the matter, Colonel, is that I made a deal with a regimental commander in the Pennsylvania National Guard. If he would make me a captain, I would get his M46s running. He did, Colonel, and I did."

"That figures," Colonel Jiggs said. "The goddamned National Guard has M46s, and here I sit with a motley collection of M4s!" Then he looked at Lowell. "How did you get to be an expert with the M46s?"

"I was assigned to the Armor Board. I was project officer on the 90 mm tube project."

"How the hell did you get an assignment like that?"

Lowell didn't reply.

"Not important. I'll take your word about that. I have been promised, in the oh, so indefinite future, that we'll be given M46s. If we're both alive when that happens, we'll be able to see if you're an expert or not. Tell me about that CIB you're wearing. Did you get it in War II? That would mean, if you're twenty-three, that you are a very young veteran indeed of War II."

"I came in the army in 1946," Lowell said. "I got the CIB in Greece."

"Doing what?"

"I was an advisor to the 27th Mountain Division."

"They didn't have tanks in Greece," Jiggs said.

"I didn't say they did, Colonel," Lowell said.

"You want to explain those fascinating orders of yours? How come the Assistant Chief of Staff, Personnel, took a personal interest in your assignment?"

"No, sir, I do not," Lowell said.

"Are you influential, Lowell, or a fuck-up?"

"Both, sir," Lowell said.

For the first time, Colonel Jiggs smiled at him.

"Do you think you're qualified to command a tank company, Lowell?"

"No, sir," Lowell said. "I can probably command a platoon all right, but a company would be more than I can handle."

"Is that so? Are you modest, Captain Lowell?"

"A realist, sir."

"You're a captain. Platoon leaders are lieutenants."

"You can have the railroad tracks," Lowell said. "I think I can hold my own with a platoon, if you'll give me one."

"It doesn't work that way at all. Captain, you now command Baker Company. Get your ass up there, look around, get settled, and I'll be up either later today, or in the morning, and we'll have another little chat."

"Yes, sir."

"That's all, 'Yes, sir'?" Jiggs asked.

"Yes, sir," Lowell said.

[FOUR]
Company "B" 73rd Medium Tank Battalion (Separate)
Naktong River, South Korea
24 July 1950

The jeep driver who came from Baker Company to pick him up was a staff sergeant who needed a shave and whose fatigues were streaked under the arms, between the legs, and down the back with grayish-white. At least they were taking salt tablets, Craig Lowell thought; at least they *had* salt tablets to take.

He was aware that the staff sergeant was examining him with contempt and resignation. The staff sergeant had seen the Bloody Bucket patch of the 28th Infantry Division, Pennsylvania National Guard, sewn to Lowell's now sweat-soaked fatigue shirt.

"You taking over, Captain?" the staff sergeant asked. When enlisted men dislike officers, they address them by their rank and avoid the use of the term "sir."

"Yes, I am," Lowell said.

"Just get in from the States?"

" 'Just get in from the States, *sir?* " Lowell corrected him. "Yes, Sergeant, I just got in from the States, and I'm a chickenshit candy-assed National Guardsman who will bust your ass down to private the next time you fail to call me 'sir.' 'Captain' will not do."

"Shit," the sergeant said, and Lowell turned, surprised, to glower furiously at him. The sergeant was smiling at him. "You a mind reader, Captain? *Sir.*"

"You can bet your regular army ass I am," Lowell said.

"Most of the replacement officers show up in brand-new fatigues," the sergeant asked. "Did they run out of them over there, too?"

"I don't know. They didn't issue me any."

The sergeant nodded his understanding. He had not called Lowell "sir," but there was no longer surly disrespect in his tone of voice. Lowell let the failure to call him "sir" pass.

"The company's short of clothing?" Lowell asked, as the jeep bounced up a narrow, rocky road.

"We're short of everything," the sergeant said, and this time he remembered and added, "sir."

"What do you do?" Lowell asked.

"I lost my tank," the sergeant said. "Sir."

"What happened?"

"Sonofabitch collapsed of old age," the sergeant said, "Engines won't take this fucking heat. Nothing takes this fucking heat long."

"What's the company doing?" Lowell asked.

"Sitting on this side of the Naktong, waiting for the gooks to cross it."

"Using the tanks as pillboxes?" Lowell asked.

"That's about it, sir," the sergeant said, seemingly surprised that a replacement officer would know enough to ask that kind of a question.

"Have the tracks been exercised? Will they run if they have to?" Lowell asked.

"Some of them," the sergeant replied. "And some of them won't."

"Maintenance?"

"Shit!" The disgust and resignation was infinite in the single word.

They came to the command post. As at the battalion CP, a sandbag bunker was being built against the side of a hill. There was a field kitchen set up under a canvas awning, called a "fly," and behind it was a grove of tall, thin poplars. There was an enormous mound of fired 75 mm shell casings and beside it an equally large mound of the cardboard tubes and wooden cases in which the shells had been shipped from the ammo dumps. There were three eight-man squad tents set up on the bare, baked ground; and sandbag-augmented foxholes—one-man, three-man, and one large enough for eight people—had been dug around them. They were intended to provide protection during mortar and artillery barrages, Lowell realized; but they were dug in the wrong places.

The realization that he had spotted something wrong pleased him. It was a suggestion, however faint, that he knew more than whoever was presently in charge here.

"The lieutenant's in there, probably, Captain," the staff sergeant said. Lowell looked at him. When Lowell's eyebrows raised in question, the staff sergeant added the required "sir."

"You're learning," Lowell said, smiling at him. "You're learning."

The staff sergeant had indicated the sandbag bunker, but Lowell didn't go there when he got out of the jeep. He walked first to the eight-man tents and stuck his head inside them, one at a time. In each were sleeping men, stretched out on folding canvas cots. There was a strong smell of sweat in each tent.

Lowell then walked up the gentle slope of the hill against which the CP bunker was being built.

At the military crest (just below the actual crest) of the hill, eight M4A3 Sherman tanks had been emplaced so that in their present position, or by moving them no more than ten feet, their tubes could be brought to bear down the far side of the hill, which sloped gently down to the banks of the Naktong River. Four hundred yards to his left, Lowell saw a bridge, both rail and road, that had been dropped into the river.

He walked to the nearest M4A3. Its crew members, sweat-soaked, were either sitting or lying on the ground in its shade. Two of them were shirtless, and all of them were dirty, tired, and unshaved. None of them moved when he walked up. He looked down at one crewman until he reluctantly got to his feet.

"What shape is this thing in?" Lowell asked.

"It overheats," the crewman said. Lowell looked at him curiously as if he didn't understand.

"It overheats," the crewman repeated. "Gets hot. Fucking filters are all fucked up, and so's the radiator."

"From now on, you say 'sir' to me, soldier," Lowell said.

"It overheats, *sir*," the soldier said. "You some kind of inspector or something? *Sir?*"

"I'm your commanding officer," Lowell said. "What do you plan to do about cleaning the filters? About flushing the radiator?" Lowell went to the tank and stood on the bogies and ran his hand into the slots in the armor over the engine. "And about getting the mud and crud out of there?"

"You work on it in this heat, *sir*," the crewman said, impatiently explaining something quite obvious to a moron, "you either burn your hand, or you get heat stroke."

"Have you checked the water in the batteries today?" Lowell asked.

"Yes, sir," the crewman said.

"Then it could be reasonably expected to start?" Lowell asked.

"It would probably start, yes, sir."

Lowell quickly climbed onto the side of the tank and then dropped into the hatch over the driver's seat. The temperature inside the tank, which had been exposed to the sun all day, was probably 120 degrees, possibly even higher. His body was instantly soaked in sweat. The batteries sounded weak when he started the engine. By the time he had it running and the engine smoothed down enough to move it, the lever—exposed through the open hatch to the direct rays of the sun—was too hot to hold. He squirmed around and got a handkerchief from his pocket and used it to keep his hand from being burned.

Then he raced the engine to signal he was going to move, locked the left track, and threw the right into reverse. The M4A3 backed out of its position. When he had it pointing in the right direction, he drove it quickly down the hill, past the field kitchen, and ten yards into the grove of poplars, crushing them under the tank. Then he got out of the tank.

By the time he walked back to the field kitchen, his presence had been made known to the acting company commander, who was waiting for him. The acting company commander was a thin first lieutenant in salt-streaked fatigues. He needed a shave.

"Are you Captain Lowell, sir?" he asked.

"Get yourself a shave and a clean uniform, Lieutenant," Lowell said, cutting him off in midsentence. "And then report to me properly."

He turned his back on him and looked up the hill to the revetment from which he had driven the M4A3. The crew was standing up now, looking down to see what the hell was going on. Lowell pointed at them, finger and arm extended, and then made a fist with his hand and pumped it up and down over his head, the signal to "form on me." Hesitantly at first, the crew of the M4A3 started down the hill, eventually breaking into a little trot.

"Yes, sir?" the man he had spoken to on the hill said.

"You're the tank commander?"

"Yes, sir."

"Do you know in which of those squad tents the mess sergeant is asleep?"

"Yes, sir," the tank commander said, baffled by the question.

"Ask the mess sergeant to report to me, please, Sergeant," Lowell said. "And then take those tents down, slit the seams, and rig a sunshade where I parked your tank. Then flush the radiator and the filters. When you've done that, you and your crew can get some sleep."

"Rip the tent up?" the tank commander asked, incredulously.

"A fightable tank is liable to keep us all alive, Sergeant," Lowell said. "That makes more sense to me than providing a place for the mess sergeant to sleep."

"Yes, sir," the tank commander said, more than a little pleased that this new company commander was going to throw the mess sergeant's ass out of bed.

The mess sergeant, a fat, heavily sweating, nearly bald man in his middle thirties, his fatigue shirt unbuttoned, his feet jammed into laceless combat boots, approached Lowell a few minutes later, his bluster fading as Lowell met his eyes.

"The captain's got to understand that other people, I mean not just the cooks and KPs, use them tents."

"Not anymore they don't," Lowell said. "What have you got cool to drink, Sergeant?"

"We ain't got any ice or anything like that, Captain," the mess sergeant said, "if that's what you're asking."

"Get me what you have, please," Lowell said, coldly.

The mess sergeant waddled to a Lister bag and returned in a moment with a canteen-cup full of water. Lowell took it, tasted the water, and spit it out.

"That's the purifier, Captain," the mess sergeant said. "Can't do nothing about that."

"You can purify drinking water by boiling it," Lowell said. "Water purification pills are intended for use only when there's no other means available. Why is it that I don't see water boiling?"

There was no reply that could be made to that. The mess sergeant flashed Lowell a wounded look.

"You do know how to make GI strawberry soda, don't you?" Lowell asked.

"Sir?" the mess sergeant replied, baffled by the question.

"You heat cans of strawberry preserves and gradually add water which has been boiled," Lowell said. "It's not much, but it's a hell of a lot better than that chemically flavored horse piss you're handing out. Put someone to work on that right away."

"Sir, I don't know if we got any strawberry preserves," the mess sergeant said.

"Then make it out of what preserves you do have," Lowell said, icily. "And if you don't have any preserves, Sergeant, then go steal some."

The acting company commander returned, in a clean, unpressed fatigue uniform. His face was bleeding from his shave. He walked up to Lowell and saluted, holding the salute as he recited, "Sir, Lieutenant Sully, Thomas J. I've been acting company commander."

Lowell returned the salute, very casually.

"My name is Lowell, Lieutenant," he said. "I herewith assume command. Please see that a general order so stating is prepared for my signature."

"Captain, we was never even issued a typewriter," Lieutenant Sully said.

"In that case, Lieutenant," Lowell said, "find someone who prints very neatly. Where is the first sergeant?"

"Captain, we've been taking turns, twelve hours on and twelve off. He's sleeping."

"Where?"

"In the bunker, sir."

"Have we got a field first?"

"Staff Sergeant Williams, sir. The man who picked you up at battalion."

"Oh, yes," Lowell said. He looked around and located Staff Sergeant Williams, and made the "form on me" signal to him by pumping his fist over his head.

"Yes, sir?" Sergeant Williams said.

"You've heard what I want done with the squad tents?"

"Yes, sir. Ripped up into sunshades."

"Colonel Jiggs will be here either later today or in the morning," Lowell said. "By the time he gets here, I want the tents gone, and I want those latrine holes somebody dug where the tents are, filled up. You got that?"

"Yes, sir."

"I'm now going to see the first sergeant," Lowell said. "I want to see him privately. I'm curious to see if he's as fucked up as everybody else I've seen around here."

He walked to the sandbag bunker and disappeared inside.

"Jesus Christ!" Lieutenant Sully said. "Who the fuck does he think he is? Patton?"

"I don't know, Lieutenant," Staff Sergeant Williams replied thoughtfully. "I got the feeling he knows what he's doing. Maybe a little inspired chickenshit is just what this outfit needs." Then he realized what he had said. "No offense, Lieutenant."

The mess sergeant reappeared.

"Lieutenant," he said. "The only preserves we got is little bitty cans, one to each case of 10-in-1's. You really want me to open all them cases like he said?"

"What I want, Sergeant Feeny," Lieutenant Sully said, "is beside the point. What's important is that the company commander told you to boil water and make drinks out of preserves. If I were you, from what I've seen of our new company commander, I'd get the lead out of my ass and do what he told you to do."

At first light the next morning, Lt. Col. Paul T. Jiggs got in a jeep and drove to Baker Company.

Baker Company's troops were shaving, using their helmets as wash basins. They were all wearing their fatigue jackets, and they were all wearing their .45 pistols in their shoulder holsters. Canvas flys protected all the tanks on the line from the sun.

When he saw Captain Lowell, the Bloody Bucket of the Pennsylvania National Guard was gone from his fatigues. Captain Lowell was standing in the mess fly, watching the mess sergeant (significantly, the mess sergeant himself, not one of the cooks or one of the troopers in KP) scramble powdered eggs. Lowell was bareheaded.

He had a German Luger stuck in the waistband of his trousers. He was puffing on a large, black cigar.

When he saw Colonel Jiggs, Lowell took the cigar from his mouth and, smiling broadly, threw him a salute that was cocky to the point of insolence.

"Good morning, sir," he said. "Would the colonel care for some breakfast?"

"I've eaten, thank you," Jiggs said.

"Then how about a cool glass of GI strawberry soda? I regret we have no orange juice, but the sergeant's working on that."

"I think that would be very nice," Colonel Jiggs said.

I'll be damned, he thought, if this kid doesn't seem to know exactly what he's doing.

[ONE]
Frankfurt am Main, Germany
30 August 1950

The black Buick Roadmaster (carefully waxed and polished from the day, six months before, it had been delivered at the European Exchange Service Automobile Center) signaled for a right turn, slowed, and turned off the northbound lane of the autobahn and into the EES service station at the Frankfurt am Main turnoff.

It rolled slowly up to the pumps. The driver, already balding though still a young man, operated the electrically powered windows and told the attendant to fill it up with high test and to please check under the hood. He operated the hood release latch, and then put his uniform cap on, opened his door, and got out. There were captain's bars on the epaulets of his green tunic and the crossed rifles of infantry on the lapels. There was the flaming sword on a blue background shoulder patch, the insignia of the European Command. But there was no fruit salad on his breast, nor parachutist's wings, nor other qualification badges. He was a small man, short and small-boned, obviously Jewish.

There was fruit salad in a drawer in his dresser in his quarters. There was a Bronze Star for his performance as a POW interrogation officer, and a second Bronze Star for his participation in Task Force Parker, which had liberated several hundred officer prisoners in the closing days of World War II. There was a set of silver parachutist's wings, and a small strip of cloth with the word "Ranger" embroidered on it. There was even a ring, a ring-knocker's ring, with USMA 1946 cast in gold around an amethyst.

But the captain was in the intelligence business, and a balding little Jew wearing a Ranger patch and jump wings and a West Point ring and a couple of Bronze Stars would stand out in a crowd. Intelligence officers try very hard not to stand out in a crowd.

A woman, smaller even than the captain, opened the right rear door of the Roadmaster and emerged with an infant in her arms. She wore black pumps, a small black hat, and a simple black dress. There was a brooch on her breast, and a gold Star of David hung from a thin gold chain around her neck.

The captain opened the right front door of the Roadmaster and plucked a male child from a steel-and-plastic seat hooked over the automobile seat. He sniffed.

"He didn't wait," he said.

"He's still a baby, Sandy," the woman said. "And it was a long ride."

She took the boy from him and with a child in each arm walked to the ladies' rest room. The captain went around to the trunk and took out a rubber and canvas bag used to store soiled diapers. Sharon did not believe in the new disposable diapers. Not only were they criminally expensive, she believed they irritated the baby's skin. She would flush the diapers in the toilet, then put them in the rubber bag to take home. After the bag had been removed from the trunk, the captain would leave the trunk open for at least an hour, and then spray the interior with an odor killer.

The captain carried the diaper bag to the door of the ladies' rest room. He set it outside the door, knocked at the door to let Sharon know he'd brought her the bag, and then went into the men's rest room. When he came out, he went out to the service island, watched the attendant check the oil, the water in the window washer reservoir and the radiator, and the hydraulic fluid in the transmission, power brakes, and power steering. He took a notebook with an attached pencil from the glove compartment and made precise entries regarding the servicing of the Buick, including a computation (to two decimal places) of miles per gallon.

Except for his uniform and the fact that they were on the autobahn outside Frankfurt, Germany, they could have been a typical American couple out with the children for a ride, and stopping for gasoline on the highway.

Sharon finished the necessary business with the children in the rest room. As she put the older child in the front seat, and then got in the back seat with the baby, the captain paid for the gasoline with both U.S. Forces of Occupation scrip (used in lieu of "green dollars") and gasoline ration coupons. Then he got behind the wheel, and they drove into Frankfurt am Main.

The parking lot behind the Frankfurt Military Post chapel was half full of cars, many of them (like the Buick Roadmaster, which carried a MUNICH MILITARY POST tag) with tags from outside Frankfurt: Nuremberg, Heidelberg, Bad Tolz, Berlin, Stuttgart, even Salzburg and Vienna.

It was a gathering of American Army Jews, a regular, every other month affair, held in rotation by every group of Jews large enough to be entitled to the services of their own rabbi, and functioning as a sort of unofficial congregation.

There were services, of course, and tours of the areas where they met, but the real purpose was fellowship, to be with their own kind. The captain had told his wife that actually the real purpose was gluttony. She had pretended shock, but giggled, for the captain was close to the truth. Each "congregation" tried valiantly to outdo the other in the kind and variety and, of course, quality of the food served during the two-and-a-half-day "get-togethers." Stuttgart, at the moment, was the undisputed victor. At the Stuttgart get-together, in addition to the roast chicken and the chopped liver and the gefilte fish and all the rest, there had been fresh orange juice and a fruit salad and two kinds of wine . . . all imported, who knew how, from Israel.

As the captain parked the Buick, three GI buses, former six-by-six trucks with bus-like bodies fixed on them, pulled into the parking lot. That was for the cultural tour of Frankfurt, scheduled for this afternoon. After sundown the services would begin.

As soon as they were out of the car, women from the Frankfurt congregation converged on them to take the children and turn them over to the care of the *goyim*, more formally known as the Frankfurt Military Post Protestant Women's Fellowship, who ran an around-the-clock nursery for the Jews when they got together, in exchange for similar services from the Jewish women.

Sharon went off with the women and the suitcases full of clothes and diapers. The captain stood by the Buick, not quite knowing what to do. The Chaplain (Major) Rabbi of Frankfurt Military Post, a large and jovial redheaded man, went to rescue him.

"Welcome, welcome," he said. "I'm Rabbi Felter."

The captain looked at him and laughed.

"I'm Captain Felter," the captain said. "How have you been, cousin?"

The rabbi laughed. "I wondered what you would look like," he said. "I saw your name on the roster. Munich, right?"

"Right," Felter said.

"Mrs. Felter get taken care of all right?" the rabbi asked. Captain Felter nodded. "Well, come on, we'll get you your name tag, and then I'll get you, kinsman, a special treat. Some bona fide Hungo-Israeli slibovitz. One up on Stuttgart."

The rabbi, a demonstrative man, put his hand on the small of Captain Felter's back. And then he withdrew it as if he had been burned. The smile on his face changed from happy to strained. He looked down at Captain Felter.

"You really think you need that here, today?" he asked. Felter met his eyes.

"You said something about slibovitz, Rabbi?" he replied.

"Right, just as soon as we get you your name tag."

A large-breasted woman sat behind a folding table.

"Who do we have here, Rabbi?" she asked.

"This is Captain Felter," the rabbi said. The woman flipped through a box and came up with two neatly lettered name cards, with safety pins on their backs.

"Captain Sanford?" she said. "And Mrs. Sharon?"

"Right," Captain Felter said. "Thank you."

Rabbi Felter took the captain's name plate and pinned it on the flap of his breast pocket. He examined it to see it was straight, and he read it:

```
CAPT Stanford T. 'Sandy' Felter
(Sharon)
Office of Agricultural Evaluation (Bavaria)
Hq, EUCOM
```

Bullshit, the rabbi thought. Office of Agricultural Evaluation, my ass. Not with a .45 automatic under his tunic; not with that icy look he gave me when he knew I had felt it. The rabbi smiled.

"On to the first authentic bona fide Hungo-Israeli slibovitz ever exported from Israel. Stuttgart, eat your heart out!"

[TWO]

Two hours later, after an enormous lunch that he knew would give him indigestion for the rest of the week, Captain Felter detached himself from the group being given a tour of the just reconstructed Temple Beth-Sholem. Before Hitler (and now, again) it was the most beautiful synagogue in Frankfurt.

He walked down the wide steps and started toward the corner. And then a taxi appeared, a Mercedes sedan with a checkered border running around its middle. He flagged it, and it pulled to the curb. The driver rolled down the window.

"Will you take me to the Farben Building?" Felter asked, in English.

"Get in," the driver said, and reached over the seat back and opened the door. The cab headed for the I. G. Farben Building, but when it reached Erschenheimerlandstrasse, it turned left rather than right.

"How have you been, my friend?" the driver asked, in German.

"Until I had lunch, I was doing fine," Felter replied, in accentless German. "And you, Helmut?"

"We just came back from holiday," the driver said. "Went to a little country hotel outside Salzburg. Got some clean air."

The taxi drove to a recently refurbished office building overlooking the Main River. There was an underground garage. The taxi drove to the door of an elevator and stopped, and Felter quickly got out and entered the elevator. He pushed the 8th floor button, and when the elevator began to rise, said, rather loudly: "The Baker's Boy just got on."

A female voice came over a hidden speaker: "Good afternoon. Isn't it lovely out?"

The elevator stopped, and the door opened. Felter saw a pleasant-faced, gray-haired woman sitting behind a receptionist's desk. A sign hung on the wall behind her, the legend engraved in either glass or lucite: "The West German Association for Agronomy".

"Go right in," the woman said. "He's been waiting for you."

She pushed a button beneath her desk, and there was the sound of a solenoid receiving an electrical impulse. When Felter pushed on a steel door covered with a wooden veneer, it moved effortlessly inward, permitting him to pass, and then closed with a clunk like a bank vault after him. Inside were two other doors, again sheathed in wood veneer. As he approached one, there came again the sound of a solenoid being activated. Beyond the second door was a large, sunlit room furnished in light oak.

A bald, stout, benign-looking man in his shirt-sleeves crossed the room to shake Felter's hand, and to offer him a drink or coffee.

"I've just had some of the first Hungo-Israeli slibovitz ever exported," Felter said. "What I need is an Alka-Seltzer."

"How about some peppermint schnapps?"

"God, no. That would make it worse."

"Try the schnapps, Sandy," the bald man said. "The peppermint is good for you."

He went to a bar, concealed in a cabinet, and poured a long-stemmed glass three-quarters full of peppermint schnapps and handed it to Felter.

"This is going to take some time," the bald man said. "You want to take off your coat?"

Felter unbuckled his tunic belt, and then unbuttoned the tunic and took it off and hung it up. The bald man waved him into a chair, and handed him a two-button switch.

"Left stops the projector," the bald man said. "Right operates the dictating machine."

"I remember," Felter said. He sat down in the chair and then sat up and reached behind him and laid the .45 automatic on the table beside the dictating machine.

"Der kleine Kapiton und die grosse Kanone." The bald man chuckled. "Do you really need something that large, Sandy?"

"I can't hit the broadside of a barn with a snub-nose," Felter replied, "and if you hit something with a .45, that's it."

The bald man went to his desk and pushed several buttons. Heavy curtains closed over the windows, and a beam of light from a motion picture projector flashed on the wall. The frozen image of a railroad station appeared on the wall.

"It's all yours, Sandy," the bald man said. Felter pushed one of the buttons on his control. The frozen images began to move. The camera focused on a man coming out of the station. Felter froze the image, stared at it for a moment.

"That's him," he said. "No question about it." He said the man's name and then pushed the button which sent the images into motion again. It took half an hour for all the film, generally in segments no longer than sixty or ninety seconds, to be shown.

"Very interesting," he said, when the projector died, and the curtains whooshed open again. "What the hell do you think it is?"

"Obviously," the bald man said, "I was hoping you could tell me."

"Off the top of my head," Felter said, "what it looks like to me is that somebody needs to be convinced he's playing with the big boys. Step Two is that if they are willing to send him in to convince that somebody, then that somebody is somebody worth convincing. I don't like that."

"What do you think of Karl Neimayer?" the bald man asked.

"I was afraid to bring his name up to you," Felter said.

"Have you got somebody on him?"

"That would violate the solemn agreement between the United States and the Federal Republic of Germany," Felter said.

"Have you got somebody on him, Sandy?"

"Next question, Gunther?"

"I have been reluctant to really watch him, Sandy," the bald man said. "Especially since I know other people are watching him, too. I can't afford to have a parade following him around. And, I submit, neither can you. We have a certain commonality of interest here, Sandy."

"Not admitting, of course, that I have anybody on Neimayer, what do you propose?"

"Simply that it would make a lot more sense to have one of yours on Neimayer alternating with one of mine, than to have both of ours on him at the same time."

"It would be our ass if we were caught," Felter said. "You know that."

"I can really trust my man," the bald man said. "Can you really trust yours?"

Felter thought that over a moment.

"Yes," he said. "He reports that he's had to break it off several times, for fear Neimayer would be too suspicious. I could put it to him that this would be a solution. They'd have to know each other."

"Deal?" the bald man asked. "They can take turns watching him?"

"Deal," Felter said.

He wrote a name and a telephone number on a scrap of paper and handed it to the fat man. "He knows my handwriting. Have your man give him this."

"Dieter Stohl," the bald man said, "is my man."

"Jesus," Felter said. "I never would have guessed."

"Thank you," the bald man said. "I thought you would have. Or are you attempting, again, to convince me how inept you are?"

"Gunther . . ." Felter said, mockingly, holding his hands out before him in a gesture of helplessness.

"You almost got away with it," the bald man said. "As long as I have been in this business—and theoretically should know better—I constantly have to remind myself that you generally know three times as much as you want me to think you know."

"You overestimate me," Felter said. "All I am, Gunther, is an American *schlemiel* playing spy."

"Sure, you are," Gunther said and smiled. "And I am the Virgin Mary."

"If there's nothing else, I have to get back," Felter said. "Do I get a cab ride?"

"There's one other thing," the bald man said. He laid a pinkish manila folder in Felter's lap. Felter read it.

"Oh, shit!" he said.

It was an extract of criminal police records, from Kreis Marburg and Kreis Bad Nauheim, of Land Hesse. It detailed the arrest for soliciting for the purposes of prostitution, and for frequenting premises known to be used for prostitution, of Ilse von Greiffenberg, also known as Ilse Berg.

"There's no record of conviction for prostitution," Felter said. "All this means is—"

The bald man interrupted him: "That she was picked up for hanging around the Tannenburg Kaserne in Marburg and the officer's hotel in Bad Nauheim, where she was trying to keep from starving. The countess had just killed herself. She was sixteen. I'm not condemning her, Sandy."

"Yes," Felter said, "that's all it means." Then he looked at the stout German and met his eyes. "You owe me, Gunther," he said. "I want this, every last goddamned copy of it, jerked from the files and burned."

"This is the next to the last copy of it," Gunther said. He took it from Felter, walked to one of the cabinets along the wall, slid it open, and dropped it into the open mouth of the small gray machine. There was a whirring noise, and from the bottom of the machine, tiny chips of paper, no larger than a character on a typewriter, poured out in a stream into a paper bag with BURN printed in two-inch-high red letters on it.

" 'The next to the last copy,' is what you said," Felter said.

"You have it," the bald man said.

"*I* have it?"

"The Americans. An application on behalf of the lady in question for accreditation as an authorized dependent was made."

"I made it," Felter said. "Or I had it made. Her husband, who incidentally is my best friend—"

"Then a very fortunate man," Gunther interrupted him.

"—is a reserve officer," Felter went on, "who was recalled and shipped almost immediately to Korea."

"So I understand," Gunther said. Felter looked at him in surprise.

"How did you get involved?" he asked.

"I must confess—and don't be angry, Sandy—that I decided, from the way you got the count out of Germany, the rapidity with which he was given an entry visa to France, that you knew something about him that we didn't."

"I explained that to you, Gunther," Felter said. "He has high-placed friends. My involvement was personal, not in the line of business."

"So you told me. But you must admit that it is rather unusual for someone released from a Russian POW camp who crosses the East German border at four one afternoon, to be in a suite in the Hotel Continental in Paris at five thirty the next day."

"Do you also know what time I arrived?" Felter asked, dryly.

"At eight twenty-five in the morning, the next day," Gunther said.

"I'm impressed," Felter said. And then went on: "Ilse's husband is a very wealthy, very powerful man, who generally gets what he wants, when he wants it. He wanted his wife reunited with her father in relaxing circumstances, and he was able to arrange that. That's all there is to it. We're not interested in the colonel, Gunther, really, we're not."

"We are," Gunther said.

"Why? Will you tell me?"

"He was about the only active participant in the von Klaussenberg bomb plot who wasn't even suspected. A very clever man, Oberst Graf von Greiffenberg."

"Why are you interested?" Felter asked. He was surprised. He hadn't known that von Greiffenberg had been in on the plot to blow up Hitler. Now that he heard he was and thought about it, he wasn't surprised. But he was surprised that he didn't know about it.

"People like you and me and the count, my friend, are always in demand," Gunther said.

"I don't think he'd be interested," Felter said.

"You can never tell, though, can you, until you ask? I don't think he came home from five years in Siberia with a profound admiration for Marx, Lenin, or Peace Through Socialism."

"As you say," Felter said, "you never can tell."

"Just as a precautionary measure, we flagged the count's file," the bald man said, "asking that we be notified of any activity. We have a reliable man in the Kreis office in Marburg an der Lahn. A devoted pensioner."

"And he's the sonofabitch who dragged this out of the sewer?"

"Your army, my friend," the bald man said. "Your CID, Criminal Investigation Division, seems fascinated with prostitution and vice. They're the ones who requested a records check on Frau von Greiffenberg-Lowell."

"And your sonofabitch self-righteously gave it to them."

"No, my sonofabitch found out about it, and sent me the copy we just shredded, and checked carefully to see that was all of it."

"Sorry," Felter said. "I just . . ."

"I think when the Graf gets his affairs in order, he'll find that the man who has been so obliging to your CID has been helping himself to the Graf's assets while the Graf was in Siberia. His motivation, apparently, was to keep the Graf from prosecuting and making public his daughter's shameful past."

"Are we sure there's only one copy left?"

"There are no copies anywhere in German files," the bald man said, flatly, so there could be no chance of misunderstanding him.

"Now, I owe you one, Gunther," Felter said. He reached over and picked up the .45 automatic and slipped it into the skeleton holster in the small of his back. He put his tunic on, and then his hat, and shook the bald man's hand. "Thanks again, Gunther."

In English, the bald man said, "It's always a pleasure doing business with you." He wrapped an affectionate arm around Captain Felter's shoulders, and walked with him through the two steel doors to the elevator.

[**THREE**]

The Mercedes taxicab took Captain Felter to the former headquarters of the I. G. Farben chemical cartel, carefully spared from wartime bombing in order that it might serve as an American headquarters. A WAC sergeant at the visitor's desk directed him to the Office of the European Command Provost Marshal General.

From the relaxed attitude of the personnel in the provost marshal general's outer office, he sensed the PMG was not in his office.

"I'd like to see the provost marshal general, please," Felter said to the Military Police Corps lieutenant colonel.

"I don't think you have an appointment, Captain," the lieutenant colonel replied, almost gaily. "The PMG only makes appointments when he plans to be here."

Felter took a leather folder from his breast pocket and held it before the lieutenant colonel's face.

"Who is the most senior officer I can see?" he asked.

"We don't see very many of those around here," said the lieutenant colonel. Unconscious that he was doing so, he stood up and nearly came to attention. "If you can tell me what you're after, perhaps I could help you," he said.

Ten minutes later, a florid-faced man in uniform, but wearing the insignia of a Department of the Army civilian employee, carried a thick manila folder into the outer office of the provost marshal general.

"Is this the entire file?" Felter asked. The florid-faced man looked to the lieutenant colonel for guidance. "I mean, is this all the notes, the drafts, leads, whatever?"

"Answer the man," the lieutenant colonel said. "He has reasons for asking."

"No, sir," the florid-faced man said. "That's not all. That's as far as we got. I mean, we're not finished."

"Get me the rest," Felter said. "Everything. And if you prepare a receipt, Colonel, I'll sign it."

"You're taking the file with you?" the florid-faced man asked, surprised.

"Yes, I am," Felter said.

"Colonel," the florid-faced man said, "that's a working file." He looked at Felter. "You know what's in it?"

"Yes, I know what's in it," Felter said. "That's why I came for it."

"Well, then, look. It's not just one of those routine things where we don't give this dame a clean bill and a PX card. The guy that married her's an officer. We have to bring the CIC in on this. They're going to want to see that file, too. To make their determination. In case he goes for a Top Secret clearance."

"And the CIC would bring it to our attention in good time," Felter said. "The problem being that their good time would be far too late to do us any good."

"I see what you mean," the lieutenant colonel said, solemnly.

"Well, what do we do about not giving her a PX card?" the florid-faced man said.

"If it would make things any easier for you, I'll give you a memorandum—presuming you can have someone here type it up for me—"

"Of course," the lieutenant colonel said.

"Stating that I have the file, and that there is nothing in it of a detrimental nature which would preclude the issuance of dependent credentials," Felter went on.

"And you'll deal with the CIC?" the lieutenant colonel asked.

"Yes, of course."

"But there *is* detrimental material," the florid-faced man insisted.

"No," Felter said, slowly, carefully. "There is not."

"For Christ's sake, Dannelly," the lieutenant colonel said, "can't you see there is more to this case than some fraulein peddling her ass before she got some stupid jackass to marry her?"

Felter looked at Dannelly's florid face and solemnly nodded his head.

"I'll go get the notes and stuff," Dannelly said.

Felter went directly from the Office of the Provost Marshal General to the basement of the Farben Building, to the Classified Documents Vault. They knew him there, but even though he was not seeking access to the vault itself, just to the general area, they first compared his signature and thumb print with the signature and thumb print on file.

"We don't see much of you guys," the lieutenant colonel on duty said. "What can we do for you, Felter?"

"I want to use your shredder," Felter said, "and get rid of some stuff that's over-classified."

"You need a witness to the destruction?"

"No," Felter said. "But I would like to witness the burning."

He walked to the shredder, a larger, noisier one than the shredder in the bald man's office. He put a fresh burn bag under it, and fed the CID's report on Lowell, Ilse Elizabeth (B. von Greiffenberg), German National (Dependent Wife of Captain LOWELL, Craig W. 0-495302 Armor, USAR) into the shredder. When it was shredded, he took the burn bag out behind the Farben Building and handed it to a burly uniformed MP who threw it into a raging fuel-oil incinerator.

Then he walked over to the Frankfurt Military Post chapel and sat in the Buick and waited for Sharon and the others to come back from their tour of the rebuilt synagogue and the other cultural attractions of Frankfurt am Main.

[FOUR]
Sangju, South Korea
11 September 1950

The company clerk of Tank Company, 24th Infantry Regiment, 24th Infantry Division, walked into the Old Man's office and laid two thin stacks of paper in front of him, the white original and the yellow carbon.

"Here the sonofabitch is, sir," he said.

"Sit," the company commander ordered. "I will read it. If there are no mistakes, strike-overs, or other manifestations of your gross incompetence as a company clerk, you may then have a beer, like the rest of those who are righteous and efficient in our assigned tasks."

The young, light-tan sergeant smiled at his huge company commander. The Old Man knew how much he hated being drafted to be company clerk.

"You understand, of course," the Old Man went on, "why you have to wait for your beer? If you can't do it sober, what would it look like . . ."

"That sonofabitch is perfect, sir," the young tan sergeant said.

The Old Man read it very carefully.

MORNING REPORT TANK COMPANY 24TH INFANTRY REGIMENT
11 SEPT 1950

PRESENT FOR DUTY: OFFICERS	WARRANT OFFICERS	NONCOM OFFICERS	ENLISTED
1	0	16	102

ABSENT IN HOSPITAL	2 OFF 0 WO	54 EM
ABSENT WITHOUT LEAVE	0 OFF 0 WO	36 EM
ABSENT AND PRESUMED KILLED IN ACTION OR MISSING	4 OFF 1 WO	104 EM
CONFINED PENDING COURT-MARTIAL	1 OFF 0 WO	3 EM

ORGANIZATION RELIEVED VICINITY SANGJU KOREA AND PLACED IN EIGHTH ARMY RESERVE EFFECTIVE 0001 HOURS 11 SEPT 1950

ABRAHAM, CHARLES W SGT RA 12379757 PREV REPORTED MIA CONFIRMED KIA 30AUG50

FOLLOWING BREVET PROMOTION VERBAL ORDER COMMANDING GENERAL 24TH INFANTRY DIVISION CONFIRMED AND MADE MATTER OF RECORD:
1ST LT PARKER, PHILIP S IV 0-230471 TO BE CAPT EFFECTIVE 10SEP50 THE EXIGENCIES OF THE SERVICE MAKING IT NECESSARY AND THERE BEING NO OTHER QUALIFIED OFFICER AVAILABLE, UNDER THE PROVISIONS OF AR 615-356

FOLLOWING TWO BREVET PROMOTIONS VERBAL ORDER COMMANDING OFFICER 24TH INFANTRY REGIMENT CONFIRMED AND MADE MATTER OF RECORD:
SFC WOODROW, AMOS J RA 36901989 TO BE 1ST SGT EFFECTIVE 29JUL50
S/SGT SIDNEY, EDWARD B RA 16440102 TO BE M/SGT EFFECTIVE 29JUL50.

FOLLOWING FIFTY-THREE BREVET PROMOTIONS VERBAL ORDER COMMANDING OFFICER TANK COMPANY 24TH INFANTRY REGIMENT CONFIRMED AND MADE A MATTER OF RECORD SEE ATTACHMENT ONE HERETO

FOLLOWING OFF ATTACHED AND JOINED FROM 8TH US ARMY REPLACEMENT COMPANY 11SEPT50
1ST LT STEVENS, CHARLES D 0-498566
1ST LT DURBROC, CASPAR J 0-3490878
1ST LT PORTERMAN, JAMES J 0-4017882

```
2ND LT WITHERS, ALLAN F 0-4119782
WOJG KENYON, ALGERNON D RW-39276

FOLLOWING 102 EM ATTACHED AND JOINED FROM EIGHTH ARMY REPLACE-
MENT COMPANY 11SEPT50 SEE ATTACHMENT TWO HERETO
                                        PHILIP SHERIDAN PARKER IV
                                        CAPTAIN, ARMOR
                                        COMMANDING
```

The large black man looked at the small tan man.

"I'm awed," he said. "I am awed."

"Thank you, sir."

"But no beer," Captain Parker said.

"No beer?"

Captain Parker reached into a duffle bag.

"A literary type such as yourself deserves more than common beer," he said. He handed him a bottle of scotch.

"Ah, hell, I couldn't take that, Captain. I know they only gave you three bottles."

"Don't argue with me, Sergeant," he replied. "I'm a captain now, you know."

As this exchange was taking place, the officers listed in the morning report were gathered in the Operations Room of the S-3 section of the 24th Infantry Regiment.

"I wanted to have a word with you gentlemen before your transport arrives," the regimental commander said to Lieutenant Stevens, DuBroc, Porterman, and Withers.

They were dressed identically in brand-new fatigue uniforms, still showing the creases from packaging. They also wore brand-new combat boots, and each carried a .45 Colt Model 1911A1 automatic pistol in a shoulder holster.

"I'll begin by saying that what I have to say to you is not to go any further than these walls." The walls to which he referred were those of a stuccoed frame building, three stories high, which four months before had been the Pusan Normal School.

"An officer, during his career, serves in many challenging assignments. There is no assignment more challenging, however, than service with colored troops. I can think of no test better designed to test the leadership qualifications of an officer. You may consider yourselves fortunate to have been given such an assignment, no matter what you may be thinking at the moment.

"You may have heard certain rumors about the combat effectiveness of this regiment. Unfortunately, most of what you have heard, discounting the inevitable exaggeration as a story makes its way around, are true.

"Some of our troops have run in the face of the enemy. Some of our troops have abandoned their positions and their equipment and given in to panic. There have been instances of outright cowardice. I will not deny there is a good deal of mud on the regiment's colors.

"Which brings us to the basic question, why? And the answer to that, gentlemen, not to mince words, is leadership. This regiment has been poorly led, from the platoon level to the command level. I am the fourth commander of this regiment since it was committed to this conflict, so the failures of leadership fall as heavily on senior officers as junior.

"It is my intention, gentlemen, to restore the good name of this regiment. I regard my assignment here as a challenge, almost as a compliment to me. My superiors apparently feel that I am capable of leading this regiment in such a manner that what has happened so far will be ascribed by the historians to the confusion that is an inevitable by-product of turning a garrison duty unit into a combat unit.

"The regiment has been badly mauled in the opening days of this conflict. Average unit strength is approximately sixty percent of the authorized table of organization and equipment. Until the last couple of days, requirements elsewhere have denied us replacement personnel.

"You gentlemen are the vanguard of the new and revitalized 24th Infantry. In one way, the fact that the unit to which you will be assigned will have an entirely new complement of officers and have as replacements more than fifty percent of its strength, may be viewed as an advantage. You will have the opportunity to mold it in your image, gentlemen. I am sure you will rise to the challenge. Are there any questions?"

"Sir, you said, 'an entirely new complement of officers'?" Lieutenant Stevens asked. He had already determined that he was the senior officer. He had interpreted that to mean he would be the company executive officer, but with "an entirely new complement" he might be company commander. If you served in combat with a company for thirty days in a position senior to your rank, you could be promoted to that rank.

"A slip of the tongue. There is one officer presently assigned to Tank Company," the colonel said. "I'm sure that at least one of you will outrank him. He made first lieutenant in May."

Lieutenant Stevens found this very fascinating information indeed.

It had been the division commander's intention to call the regimental commander to inform him of his decision to make Parker a captain, which would permit him to remain in command. From everything he'd heard about Parker, he was a first-class officer and not only deserved the promotion but was obviously qualified to command (he had lived through the last two months). But something had come up every time he was about to reach for the telephone and tell him of his decision.

Lieutenant Stevens rode in the front seat of the ambulance without Red Cross markings, wondering if that wasn't somehow illegal. An ambulance was an ambulance. Taking one . . . it was probably stolen . . . and painting the red cross over and using it like a truck was something you could expect from a bunch of niggers.

One of the first things he would do in command would be to get rid of it. If they wanted to be treated like white men, it was time they understood they would be expected to behave like white men.

Tank Company was located six miles from the regimental command post, in a village called Chinhae. Lieutenant Stevens was momentarily pleased when he saw the first sergeant, a tall erect colored man in a crisply starched uniform, who approached the ambulance, came to attention, and saluted.

"Sir, may I welcome you to Tank Company?" the first sergeant said. "We've been waiting for you gentlemen for a long time."

"Thank you, Sergeant," Lieutenant Stevens said. "Will you have someone take care of our personal gear? Is that the way to the orderly room?"

"Yes, sir," the first sergeant said. Stevens knew that he had zinged him. Good. The important thing to do was establish your control. Then you could be a nice guy. Within reason, of course. Give a nigger an inch and he'd take a mile.

Tank Company had apparently taken over some sort of Korean country inn, something like a hotel. The floor was of woven straw. There was a sign lettered with a wax crayon, tacked to the wall. SHOE LINE. BARE FEET BEYOND THIS POINT.

Some nigger's sense of humor, obviously mocking the sign erected at regimental boundaries: HELMET LINE. HELMETS WILL BE WORN BEYOND THIS POINT.

Well, he had no intention of paying a bit of attention to that. He marched down the tatami-covered corridor until he came to another sign. CP.

He slid a sliding door open. There was a nigger buck sergeant sitting in front of a typewriter, his face making it perfectly obvious that the device was entirely too complicated for him to grasp. He looked up at Lieutenant Stevens and the other officers and his eyes widened.

"Don't you come to your feet, Sergeant, when you see an officer in here?" Lieutenant Stevens demanded. He was rather pleased with himself. He was establishing his position on military courtesy much sooner than he thought he would have an opportunity to do so.

The sergeant jumped to his feet. "Sorry, sir," he said. "The Old Man says not to, and we haven't had many officers around here." He paused, smiled, and added, "We ain't been inside all that much, either."

"Watch it in the future, Sergeant," Lieutenant Stevens said, with what he thought was just the proper mixture of sternness and paternalism. "Where is your officer?"

"In his office, sir," the sergeant said, nodding to another sliding door.

Lieutenant Stevens slid the door open. He saw a very large, very black man, naked to the waist, sweating, standing looking out the window. He held a can of beer in his hand.

"Ah, you must be the replacement officers," he said. "Come on in and have a beer." He waved at a metal container on the floor. It bore a red cross on all of its visible sides, and the words HUMAN BLOOD—RUSH.

"Just what the hell is going on around here?" Lieutenant Stevens asked.

"I beg your pardon?" the half-naked nigger asked in that phony Harvard a lot of them, in Lieutenant Stevens's experience, affected.

"Are you by any chance an officer?" Lieutenant Stevens demanded.

"Yes, I am," the nigger replied, amused. "Who are you?"

"I'm Lieutenant Stevens," Stevens said.

The half-naked black man with the can of beer stopped smiling. He looked Stevens up and down, and then looked beyond him at the other officers.

"Is that a West Point ring I see on your hand, Lieutenant Stevens?"

"As a matter of fact, it is," Stevens said. "But I asked who the hell you are."

"I find it difficult to believe," the half-naked nigger said, in his Harvard accent, every syllable precisely pronounced, "that an officer exposed to all the opportunities afforded by the United States Military Academy at West Point is unaware of the protocol involved in reporting to a new command. I presume, therefore, there is some excuse for your lack of military courtesy."

"I believe I'm in command here, Lieutenant Parker," Lieutenant Stevens said.

"Oh?" Parker said, his tone of voice suggesting idle interest. "I haven't been informed of my relief."

"I'm informing you now," Stevens said.

"I see," Parker said. "And where am I supposed to go? Regiment? Did you happen to bring me a copy of my orders?"

"You'll stay here, so far as I know," Stevens said. "What I'm saying, Lieutenant, is that I'm senior to you."

"I was promoted captain today," Parker said. "Were you promoted captain before that?"

Stevens felt his stomach contract into a knot.

"There's apparently been some sort of mix-up," he said.

"Sir," Parker said.

"Sir," Stevens said.

"Well, now that the air is cleared," Parker said, "have these officers sit down, lieutenant, and remove their foot gear. There's a sign outside that you should have read."

Stevens and the others just looked at him.

The sergeant who had been behind the typewriter came into the room without knocking.

"Here's your shirt, Captain," he said.

"One of the beer cans was frozen," Parker said, conversationally. "It exploded." He turned his back on the others and tucked his shirt in his trousers. "And when you have removed your shoes, gentlemen," he went on, "you can go back out and try reporting to your new commanding officer as the customs of the service dictate."

Stevens heard the nigger warrant officer chuckle. His face flushed, he sat down on the woven straw tatami and took off his boots. Deeply humiliated, carrying his boots in his hands, he went back down the corridor past the SHOE LINE sign, dropped off his boots, and then made his way back to Parker's office.

When the four officers and the warrant officer were shoeless, Stevens marched them into Parker's office.

"Sir," he said, saluting. "Lieutenant Stevens and other replacement officers reporting for duty."

Parker casually returned the salute.

"Stand at ease, gentlemen," he said. "Welcome to Tank Company, 24th Infantry." He met the eyes of each man. "As we have just established, I am Captain Philip Sheridan Parker IV, the commanding officer. There are some things I think you should know. First of all, about me. I am not only regular army, but I am a fourth generation army brat. For the past two months, I have been the only officer physically present for duty. I am still alive, and in command, and that should impress you as de facto proof that I am qualified to command this unit.

"Secondly, Tank Company has the distinction of being the only unit in the regiment which has not, at least since I've been in command, run in the face of the enemy. Through a process of attrition, our strength, until Eighth Army saw fit to send us replacements today, was down to one officer, sixteen noncoms and 102 enlisted men. Each of these men, and especially the noncoms, has been tried in battle and found worthy. The first sergeant pointed out to me this morning that none of our platoon sergeants or tank commanders held a rank higher than corporal when we entered combat. The majority, in fact, were privates first class.

"I have no way to judge the quality of the replacements, officer or enlisted. I have full confidence in the men I had before you and the enlisted replacements arrived. Having seen here what the effects of poor leadership are, I have no intention of seeing either the combat effectiveness of this unit destroyed, or equally important, losing the lives of any of my men by placing in a position of command any officer until I am satisfied that he is, indeed, qualified to take command.

"I am, therefore, going to turn each of you over to a platoon sergeant. You, Lieutenant Stevens, will be turned over to First Sergeant Woodrow. Until such time as they, in their exclusive judgment, decide that you are qualified, you will, with the insignia of rank removed, function as a tank crewman, and perform such other duties as you may be assigned."

"You can't do that!" Stevens protested.

"Any officer who fails to measure up will be relieved. There is a pool of officers who have been relieved in Pusan. I understand they are engaged in unloading ships, as stevedores," Parker went on.

"What about me, Captain?" the warrant officer asked.

"Were you a company clerk before you got your warrant?"

"I was a battalion personnel sergeant," he said.

"OK. You can relieve Sergeant Foster," Parker said. "If you can find a typist in the replacements, you can have him. All of our morning reports for the past two months have to be redone. Foster can help you do that. When he's finished, I promised him a tank."

He looked at each of them again, one at a time, slowly.

"With the exception of Lieutenant Stevens, you are dismissed," he said. "Tell Sergeant Foster I said to turn you over to Sergeant Woodrow."

Confused, shaken, angry, they saluted awkwardly in sort of a contagious reaction, and filed out of the office. Stevens remained.

"I presume, Lieutenant," Parker said, "that in addition to being regular army, you are a career soldier?"

"Yes, sir," Stevens said.

"You won't have much of a career if I relieve you, Lieutenant," Parker said. "Oh, eventually, I'm sure the West Point Protective Association would take care of you.

They would have the records changed. But you and I know, Lieutenant, don't we, that you would forever be identified as the guy who was relieved in the nigger tank company? Officers who are relieved while serving with a nigger tank company very seldom make general, Lieutenant." Parker let that sink in a moment, and then he went on.

"If you cross me, you'll be lucky to make light bird in twenty years. I know the rules of this game, and I know them better than you do." Parker paused. "I don't expect a reply, Lieutenant, and you are dismissed."

VI

[ONE]
Company "B" 73rd Medium Tank Battalion (Separate)
Pusan, South Korea
2 September 1950

The Old Man, also known as "the Duke," and sometimes as "Deadeye"—none of these appellations ever to his face although he was fully aware of and rather pleased by what the troops called him—walked down the trench to the command post. He had a cigar jammed into the corner of his mouth, and he carried an M1 Garand rifle in the crook of his arm, for all the world like a hunter out for an afternoon's sport.

Forty-five minutes before, a six-by-six had deposited replacements—one lieutenant and four troops, two sergeants and two privates first class—at the CP, and they were nervously waiting to meet their new commanding officer.

Baker Company was in the hills, north and west of Pusan, its M4A3s dug into the shale of the mountains, surrounded by sandbag revetments. Where possible, a roof of logs and sandbags was built over them. They were, for all practical purposes, pillboxes. Their function was to protect the line with direct fire from their 75 mm cannons and their machine guns.

The M4A3s seldom moved from their positions. The engines were regularly run, and they received regular maintenance, and the tanks were moved a few feet once or twice a day to keep the tracks lubed; but the troops had been fighting more as infantrymen than as tankers, the distinction between them being primarily that the infantrymen were periodically relieved, if only for a brief period, while the tankers had yet to leave the lines. The heat was brutal, and there was little ice.

S/Sgt William H. Emmons, Jr.:

We had ice. God knows where the Duke got it, but he got it; and we had enough to cool, if not chill, our drinking water, and the strawberry preserve soda, and the daily booze ration. It was so fucking hot that sometimes the beer cans exploded before we could get them cooled. The food was C and 10-in-1 rations, high protein, left over from World War

II and generally inedible. When the Duke took over, the company was suffering from dysentery, heat rash, heat exhaustion, and low morale, primarily because we were under intermittent fire twenty-four hours a day (not continually, just enough to keep our nerves taut, or to drive us over the edge) and the only thing we had to look forward to was more of the same.

When the Duke walked in the CP bunker, the first sergeant called "Atten-hut!" and the replacements stood straight and tall.

"Rest," the Duke said, and then: "What have we here? Visitors?"

"Sir," the lieutenant said, saluting, "Lieutenant Monahan reporting for duty with a detail of four."

The Duke returned the salute.

"What about that, First Sergeant?" the Duke said. "The lieutenant has manners."

"Yes, sir," the first sergeant said. "I noticed that."

"But you don't," the Duke said. "You haven't offered these gentlemen a libation, have you? Shame on you, First Sergeant."

"I beg the captain's pardon, sir," the first sergeant said, as if he was all shook up by the criticism. Then he turns to the replacements: "May I offer you gentlemen a small libation?"

I admit, I didn't know what a fucking libation was until I met the Duke, but the buggy look they gave the soldier was because you don't expect first sergeants to pass out booze anywhere, much less in a bunker about fifty yards from the fucking front line.

"Sir?" the replacement lieutenant asked, baffled.

"We have martinis, scotch, bourbon, and some really dreadful rum," the Duke said.

"Not for me, thank you, sir," the replacement lieutenant said. He was not about to make a fool of himself. The troops shook their heads and mumbled, "No, thank you, sir."

"I think I'll have a martini, First Sergeant, if you please," the Duke said.

"I just happen to have some made, sir," the first sergeant said. "And with the captain's permission, I will have one myself."

"Of course," the Duke said.

Then he asked the replacements for their orders, and by that time the first sergeant had taken a blood flask from a Medical Corps insulated cooler. He also took two martini glasses from the cooler. The blood flask, which had a rubber gasket sealer, was filled with a transparent fluid, which the first sergeant carefully poured into the martini glasses.

The replacements watched this wide-eyed.

"I regret, sir," the first sergeant said, like an English butler, "that we seem to be out of both olives and onions."

"The exigencies of the service, First Sergeant," the Duke said.

They raised their glasses to each other.

"To Baker Company, 73rd Medium Tank," the Duke said.

"You play ball with Baker Company," the first sergeant replied.

"Or you get the bat stuck up your ass," the Duke finished. They sipped their martinis.

The Duke turned to the replacements.

"We give you an option around here, gentlemen," he said. "You get two drinks, or two beers, a day. You may take less, but no more. Would you like to know what happens

to anyone, but especially noncoms and officers, who take more than their daily sauce ration?"

"Yes, sir," the replacement lieutenant said, after he realized he was expected to reply.

"Pray tell the lieutenant, First Sergeant," the Duke said.

"You get the bat stuck up your ass," the first sergeant said. And then it was too much, and the Duke broke up and laughed, and the first sergeant laughed, and that made it all right for the rest of us to laugh.

"Welcome to Baker Company," the Duke said. "I'm the Generalissimo of this ragtag rolling circus. My name is Lowell. You may call me 'sir.' "

The goddamned Duke had class, there was no question about that. That regular business of giving the replacements a drink (some took it and some didn't know what the fuck was going on and didn't) did a couple of things. It made them feel at home; it made them feel they were in sort of a special outfit; and it got the Duke's point across, that nobody could afford to get sauced.

That fucking M1 he carried was one more proof. The .30 caliber M1 Garand was the standard weapon of the infantry soldier. It was looked down upon by tankers, both as a tool of the infantry dogfaces and as a heavy unwieldy weapon which kicked like a fucking mule. Very few noncoms, and even fewer officers, even in the infantry, carried one.

They were practically fucking unknown in a tank company, for Christ's sake, except for such shits and feather merchants as the cooks and the truck drivers. The basic weapon for tank crews was the .45 caliber M3 submachine gun, called the grease gun because that's what it looked like. Tank crewmen were also armed with the Colt Model 1911A1 automatic pistol. If they could get one, the tankers, officers, noncoms, and troopers armed themselves with the Thompson .45 caliber ACP submachine gun, "the Thompson" or "tommy gun," which was sometimes available for purchase at a going rate of $100; or with a carbine, either the M1, which was a semiautomatic shoulder weapon firing what was really a pretty hot pistol cartridge, or the M2 carbine, which had a lever permitting full automatic fire. Both versions were generally equipped with two curved, 30-round "Banana" clips, taped together upside down, so that as soon as you blew away thirty rounds, all you had to do was pull the empty magazine out, turn it over, and slam the other, loaded magazine back in.

Comes the Duke, comes Deadeye, right out of the National Fucking Guard, and just about as soon as he had the mess sergeant's fucking tent torn down to make sunshades for the tanks, he takes a Garand away from one of the assholes in the kitchen, and gives him his Grease Gun for it.

And then he zeroes the sonafabitch, just like he was on some fucking basic training rifle range back in the land of the big PX, getting down on his goddamned belly, doing everything but wrapping the strap around his arm, and zeroes the sonofabitch, shooting holes in a fired 75 mm casing he set up by pacing off two hundred yards right behind the line.

There's the company, tearing down tents, and ripping them up, and filling in latrines and foxholes that had been dug someplace he don't like, and here's the mess sergeant boiling a thirty-gallon pot of water and stirring strawberry preserves around in it, and here's practically everybody else working on the tanks (and the fucking gooks are going to hit us for sure, just as soon as it gets dark) and here's the Duke on his belly like some basic trainee, going through that up-two-clicks, right-three-clicks, zero bullshit with a fucking Garand.

For reasons of their own, the gooks didn't hit us that first night the Duke took over. They hit us the next night.

The way it worked, back then, was that they would wait until it got dark, or as dark as it was going to get, and then they'd throw mortars at us, and some artillery—not much, they weren't in much better shape, supply-wise, than we were, and I guess maybe they knew they were pissing in the wind, since we had the bunkers and the tanks.

So they'd lay in a barrage, and then they'd lift it, and then they'd start down to the edge of the river from their positions on the other side. Some of them had boats and floats, but you could practically walk across the Naktong River where we were.

Once they lifted the mortars, they wouldn't shoot their small arms until they were across the river. I guess they knew it wouldn't do them any good. And we didn't shoot back, either, until they were across the river and actually starting to come up the slope to our positions.

We were in pretty shitty shape as far as ammo went. We needed what they called "canister," which is sort of a super shotgun shell. Sonofabitch is filled with ball bearings; and when it goes off, it really blows troops away. Naturally, since we needed canister, what the bastards sent us was HEAT, which means High Explosive, Anti-Tank, and which is great if you're shooting at tanks but is next to fucking worthless if you're shooting at people. I mean, using HEAT against troops is like shooting fucking flies with a .45, you get my meaning?

So what we did was call in artillery, and sometimes we got it and sometimes we didn't, so what we usually wound up doing was firing the light weapons on the tanks. Thirty and fifty caliber machine guns. Now, the machine guns on a tank are air-cooled, which means that when you start firing one of them steady, the barrel heats up—I've seen them glow like coals—and pretty soon you have to change the sonofabitch, which is a pain in the ass when it's cold, not to mention glowing red goddamned hot, and when people are coming up the hill shooting at you.

So the way it worked was we waited until they were across the river and then opened fire. If we got artillery, fine. And if we didn't, we did pretty well just with the machine guns and with what canister rounds we did have.

Like I said, the first night that the Old Man had the company, the gooks didn't hit us. So we knew they would the second night.

So right after dark, the Old Man shows up in the positions. He's puffing on this big black cigar, he's got this fucking Garand in his arms, with a couple of extra clips to the strap, and, so help me, Christ, he's got a hand grenade in each pocket of his fatigue jacket. And he's dragging Lieutenant Whatsisname? The little fucker who got blown away two, three days later. The one who had been acting CO, after Captain Dale got it, until the Duke showed up. Sully was his name. Thomas J. Sully.

Anyway, the Duke's got Sully with him, and Sully explains what usually happens, and the Duke listens, and asks a couple of questions, and then Sully says that maybe it would be a good idea if they went back to the company CP, so they could be there when the gooks start coming.

The Duke looks at me—we were standing by my tank, you see—and he says, "The radios in that rusty tub work, Sergeant?" and I tell him. "Yes, sir, most of the time," and he asks me can I come up with enough wire to run an extension between the commander's cupola comma panel and the platoon bunker, and I tell him sure.

"Do it," he says, and then he tells Sully he thinks he'll stick around up here, and if Sully wants to go back to the CP, he can. Sully thinks it over, decides the Duke is out of his fucking mind, and shags his ass off the hill.

So then we sat and waited for the gooks. The Duke asks us about where we come from, and whether we're married or not, the usual officer bullshit, and sure enough, thirty, forty minutes later, the gooks start throwing mortars at us, the way we knew they would.

It lasted maybe five, ten minutes, and then it lifted. And when it lifted, no Duke. I figured he got smart and went down the hill. I had a BC scope, you know what I mean? They're like binoculars and a periscope put together? You can see over the edge of someplace without exposing your head. It stands for Battery Commander's scope, I think. Anyway, I had a BC scope set up in the bunker, and I was looking through it. It was full moon, or nearly, and I could see pretty good.

Sure enough, down their hill they came, first their point men, and then two guys maybe ten feet behind him, and then four, five guys behind them. Making sort of a triangle, and heading toward us.

The gook point man was a good three hundred, maybe three hundred fifty yards from us.

And then I hear, right over my head, three shots. Bang Bang Bang. Thirty caliber, but too far apart to be a machine gun. I am just wondering what the fuck our new National Guard commander is up to when I notice that the gook point man and one of the two guys behind him is down.

That sort of upsets the gooks, and they all fell down, and started shooting up the other side of the river, the bank, I mean, right across from them, where they figure we stuck an outpost. They blow the shit out of it with their small arms, and even call mortars in on it. Now I know we don't have anybody down there, so it has to be the Duke. So I go outside, and there he is, sitting on top of the bunker, this time with the strap of the M1 around his arm, and wearing a shit-eating grin.

"I think they see ghosts, Sergeant," he said. "Better they battle ghosts than us, wouldn't you say?"

So I told him he was pretty good with the Garand, and he said, " 'Pretty good'? Sergeant, I'm magnificent!" You see what I mean, class?

So what happened after that was that we picked one guy, the best shot, from each platoon, and made him a sniper, and the Duke actually came up later with real sniper's rifles, '03A4 Springfields, and M1Cs, which is an M1 with a cheek piece on the stock and a four power scope. And after that, let me tell you, the gooks didn't walk across the Naktong like it was a fucking street. They still came, but by Christ, they came careful!

Sgt. Jared Mansfield:

The Old Man had been called to battalion, and they talked about what was going on, even though he was called to battalion at least once a day. The Old Man, for all practical purposes, was the battalion S-3 (Plans and Training Officer). The S-3 was an ineffective old fart who couldn't find his ass with both hands. If he didn't have the Old Man showing him how to pour piss out of a boot, the outfit would be as fucked up as that nigger division had been. But they talked about the Old Man being at battalion again because there was nothing else to talk about. They wondered if he would be able to steal some more beer, or if there would be mail.

The Old Man returned from battalion at 1530. In his jeep were three bags of mail, six cases of beer, and one case of Coca-Cola. He carried one of the cases of beer into the CP himself, and the first sergeant and the clerk and the radio operator went out to collect the rest.

The Old Man walked to where the executive officer was sleeping. It was a bed made from an air mattress suspended on communications wire woven between the tree trunks that also served as pillars to hold up the plank-and-sandbag roof of the bunker. He gently touched his arm.

"The mail is here," he said. The XO swung his feet off the bed, and got to his feet.

"Send for runners for the mail," the Old Man said. "And then we'll have an officer's call. Noncoms are invited, but I want at least a sergeant left in each platoon."

"Yes, sir."

"There's a little beer, and one lousy case of Coke," the Old Man said.

Runners from the platoons came quickly and stood impatiently as the company clerk went through the first-class mail pouch, breaking the mail down into platoons.

The three platoon leaders and the chief warrant (who was supposed to be the administrative officer, but who had been a motor sergeant before taking the warrant exam and was now happily functioning as the motor officer) drifted into the command post as soon as they had determined if they had, or didn't have, mail in the bag.

"You, Tommy," the Old Man said to the second platoon leader, "are a fucking disgrace to the officer corps."

"Yes, sir," the second platoon leader replied, "I am. Does that mean, I hope, that the captain is thinking of sending me home in disgrace?"

"Where the hell have you been, anyway? What have you been rolling in?"

"We pulled the power package on Twenty-Two, sir. The transmission was losing fluid. When we pulled it, we found out why. The housing was cracked."

"All over you?"

"Yes, sir."

"Have you got it running?"

"Yes, sir."

"Is everything else running?" the Old Man asked and looked at each officer in turn and finally at the chief warrant. The chief warrant reported that everything was running, and that he had managed to get three complete, in-the-crate, power packages and three complete, in-the-crate, sets of tracks.

"Not individual tracks, Captain. Complete sets. Two complete tracks in a box. Christ only knows where they found them."

"I don't suppose," the Old Man said, innocently, "that they'd fit an M46?"

"No, sir," the warrant officer replied, and looked curious.

"OK, then," the Old Man said, "sometime in the next four days, put them on the tanks that need them most."

"I thought about that, sir," the warrant officer said. "I thought I'd wait until we lose one. What the hell, there's no sense in replacing a track until it goes."

"Make up your mind where you want to put them, but I want them put on the tanks that need them most, and as soon as you can get to it. What about the wheels?"

"The jeeps are all running, sir, and in good shape. The both of them," the warrant officer said. There were four jeeps in Company "B." Two were authorized. Two had been "borrowed" when their drivers had left them momentarily unattended. The Old Man obviously knew about the two stolen jeeps, but said nothing about it.

"We're being relieved," the Old Man announced.

"Jesus, it's about time," one of the platoon leaders said.

"As soon as it gets dark," the Old Man went on, "a Korean captain and a platoon leader, and one platoon, will come up. They'll be sneaked up. The idea is not to let the bad guys know we've been relieved by Koreans. They will be followed by another platoon tomorrow, and the third platoon the day after tomorrow. As soon as they have been checked out to my satisfaction, our platoons, one at a time, can come off the hill."

"What about the equipment, Captain?" the chief warrant officer asked.

"We'll turn our tanks over to them," the Old Man said.

"And go through the whole business of getting everything in fairly decent shape again? Why the hell can't the slopes bring their own tanks, and let us keep ours?"

"I made the same passionate speech to Colonel Jiggs," the Old Man said. "He heard me out, and then he said, 'OK, if you feel that strongly, you can keep your tanks, and I'll give the M46s to the Koreans.' "

"M46s? No shit!"

"So I said, 'Yes, sir, I know the stalwart men of Baker Company would much prefer their spotless and shining M4A3s to dirty new M46s.' "

There was laughter, and then the lieutenant that the Old Man had jumped on spoke up.

"What's the catch, Captain?"

"My orders are to insure that everybody is checked out in the M46, and to prepare for an attack," the Old Man said.

"Attack? Whose stupid idea is that? Walker's?"

The reference was to Lt. Gen. Walton "Bulldog" Walker, the Eighth Army commander, who shared a surname with a Company "B" cook.

"It came to him when he was slicing Four Ways," the Old Man said, referring to the field ration meat, which could be used in four ways.

There was more easy laughter.

"Goddamn, Captain, every other slant-eye in the world is out there. And what are we supposed to do for support? They even pulled the Third Marines out of here."

"I will bring your solemn assessment of the situation to the colonel's attention," the Old Man said. "But in the meantime, at least until he sees the error of his ways, I'm afraid we're just going to have to go along with him."

There was laughter.

"Tell the troops," the Old Man said, "but make sure you also tell them I'm going to be the judge of whether or not the Koreans are capable of relieving us. That's all."

[TWO]

They left the bunker. The Old Man made a levitating signal with his hand to the company clerk, who had sat down again behind the typewriter.

"Yes, sir," he said.

"I would be profoundly grateful for a sheet of paper and an envelope," the Old Man said.

The executive officer gave him some with *Officer's Open Mess, Fort Shafter, Hawaii* printed on it in golden ink. The Old Man rolled the paper into the typewriter, carefully X-ed out Fort Shafter, Hawaii, and typed in "Fortress Lowell, South Korea.

Then he typed, very rapidly, as if he had been thinking for some time about what he was going to say.

My Darling Ilse,

I have a few moments between golf and the cocktail hour, and I thought I would pass it dropping you a note instead of dancing with the ladies, although I know my actions will break their hearts.

There was no mail from you today, and I could cheerfully boil in oil the bureaucrat who decided that since we can mail letters post-free from here to America, there was no point in sending any stamps here. My letters, as you've noticed, have to make a stop at the firm, so that they can be remailed to you. God only knows what has happened to your letters to me. I have had only one, the one you sent to Fort Lawton, since I got here. The others are probably en route by sea, via the Suez Canal and mysterious India.

Despite that, my morale is reasonably high. as high as any man denied the pleasure of the company of his wife and son can be. I have a fine company, as I've written before, good officers, good noncoms, and a few unmitigated sonsofbitches.

They've apparently finally gotten the supply system into gear, for today I was informed that we will be reequipped with M46 tanks starting tomorrow. Your father will be able to explain that they have a 90 mm tube, as opposed to the 75 mm on the M4A3s, a lower profile, and are generally a far better tank all around.

What I suppose I'm leading up to saying, *Liebchen*, and please don't misunderstand me, is that although I bleed at being separated from you and P. P., I really would much rather be here, doing what I'm doing, than I would be at the firm. In some strange, perverse way (and I wouldn't tell anyone else this), I feel as if I belong here, in the sandbags, surrounded by weapons, and the sometimes really ghastly smell of the army.

I'm a good officer. I say that with all modesty. I don't think it's anything that I do. I just seem to be able to understand the system, and the people that make it up, and to make the whole thing fit together like a jigsaw puzzle or a well-oiled clock. There is no question in my mind (or in the colonel's either; he as much as told me) that Baker Company is the most efficient in the battalion. We seem to work together. The company is alive. I'm proud of it and of being part of it, and most of all for knowing that I'm responsible for it.

So, *Liebchen*, I'm going to take up the offer you made me in Philadelphia, when you said I could go back in the army. We'll be here about a year, I would judge, and then I'll be coming home to you. I'll take a month's leave in Germany.

I won't write how much I miss you and P. P., because I'm a big boy now and big boys aren't supposed to cry. You won't mind me saying that I adore you, though, will you?

All my love

He signed his name with a grease pencil, licked the envelope, and only then remembered he hadn't addressed it. The address still tore him up.

Mrs. Craig W. Lowell
Schloss Greiffenberg
Marburg an der Lahn, Germany

Schloss meant "castle" in German; it sounded as if the mailman rode a horse and wore a suit of shining armor.

He folded that envelope smaller, so that it would fit inside the envelope which would take it to the firm, for remailing to Germany.

"I have to beg one more envelope," he said. He looked at the company clerk. "You got one I can have, Stu?"

"What's the postage to Germany, Captain?" the company clerk replied.

"I have no idea."

"I wrote my mother, Captain, about the trouble you were having writing to Mrs.

Lowell, and she sent me a bunch of stamps for you. They're fifteen-cent ones. I'll put two of them on, to make sure." He reached out his hand for Lowell's envelope.

"Why, thank you very much," the Old Man said. "And thank your mother for me, too, please, Stu." The Old Man turned, so that neither the exec nor the company clerk would see that his eyes, for some reason, had suddenly started to water.

[THREE]
Washington, D.C.
6 September 1950

Rotary Wing Course 50–4 (Special) had been established at Fort Sam Houston, Texas, by verbal order of the Secretary of the Army in order to meet a requirement of the highest priority from Eighth United States Army, Korea (EUSAK). From the very first days of the Korean conflict, it had been quite clear that rotary-wing aircraft, specifically the Bell H13 and the Hiller H23, were ideally suited for use as battlefield ambulances. They saved lives.

Within two weeks of the commencement of hostilities, enterprising army aviators had fitted locally fabricated litter racks to the skids of the few helicopters available, turning them into aerial ambulances.

Technically, such modifications were aerodynamically unsound, for with a pilot, and two wounded men in the litter racks, both aircraft were over maximum gross permitted weight. They were also illegal, because they had not been approved by the air force, which had, under the Key West Agreement of 1948, sole engineering responsibility for army aircraft.

The aerial ambulances worked. To hell with the engineers, and screw the air force.

Both the H13 and the H23 helicopters were designed to carry a pilot and a passenger, each with an estimated weight of 180 pounds. It was believed, furthermore, that carrying an approximately 180-pound weight in the only position the litter racks could be fitted would severely affect the weight and balance characteristics of the aircraft. Carrying two such weights would not only further increase the imbalance, but would raise the aircraft's gross weight beyond the point where it could fly safely, if indeed at all.

On the other hand, loading a critically wounded soldier onto a helicopter litter rack meant that he could be flown quickly, and in relative comfort, to a Mobile Army Surgical Hospital (MASH) where his life, 95 times out of 100, could be saved. That statistic stood out: If a wounded soldier arrived alive at a MASH, the odds were 95–5 that he would live.

Too many wounded men had arrived dead at the mobile hospitals after a two-hour-long ride over battered and potholed roads in the standard army ambulances—Dodge three-quarter-ton truck frames with square bodies capable of carrying five litters.

Notwithstanding the established principles of aerodynamics and the Key West Agreement of 1948, which forbade the army to do much more with airplanes than use them as aerial jeeps, the H13s and the H23s shuttled back and forth between the battlefield (known now as the main line of resistance, or MLR) and the mobile hospitals and saved lives. The call went out for many more helicopters, and the pilots to fly them, as quickly as possible.

The aircraft themselves were easier to come by than the pilots to fly them. Bell and Hiller went on a three-shift, twenty-four-hour-a-day production schedule. It was decided that for convenience in maintenance and parts supply, Hiller H23s should be used exclusively in Korea, at least until things straightened out. As a result, H23s from the army worldwide were hastily shipped to the Far East. They would be replaced, according to plan, by Bell H13s as they came off the production line.

Pilots posed a greater problem. There were few helicopter pilots in the army when the war broke out, and the pool of chopper pilots available in the reserve was negligible or non-existent. An unusually well-qualified pilot is required to teach someone else how to fly, and the few highly qualified pilots around had quickly been ordered to Korea.

Contracts were let to engage the relatively small number of civilian helicopter pilots as instructors, and applications for helicopter pilot training, from commissioned and warrant officers, were quickly processed and approved, the criteria being essentially that the applicant could pass the rigid standards of a flight physical.

The Medical Corps, to spare its physicians from administrative matters, had established a corps of administrators, called it the Medical Service Corps, and issued them caducei with the letters MSC superimposed on them as lapel insignia. When the first medical evacuation helicopters were assigned to the Medical Service Corps, so were the pilots that came with them.

Then the Medical Corps, which had always been admired, but had never had much of a dashing military reputation, entered the political arena. The surgeon general received permission to gather together at the Army Medical Center, at Fort Sam Houston, in San Antonio, Texas, sufficient numbers of its helicopter pilots to train *other* Medical Service Corps officers to be helicopter pilots. It also received authority to increase the number of Medical Service Corps officers it was permitted to have. Care of the wounded has always been given the highest priority within the army, and it was given here.

Almost immediately, however, it became apparent that if the Medical Corps got all it asked for in the way of instructor pilots and training helicopters, there would be an insufficient number of either available elsewhere in the army to train the helicopter pilots required for other missions. It was decided to return helicopter training to the artillery, where it had been before Korea, and to make available to the Medical Corps as many spaces as possible in the classes.

It was also decided that the training underway at San Antonio would be permitted to continue until such time as the Artillery School at Fort Sill was prepared for the massive influx of student pilots. In the meantime, a certain small number of officers of other arms and services would be sent to Fort Sam to undergo flight training with the medics.

Despite what he had been told in the Far East (that he was being sent home in order to go to chopper school), Captain Rudolph G. MacMillan quickly learned by phone what the candy-asses in the Pentagon really wanted to do with him. First, they wanted to put him on display for a couple of months as a hero. Then, maybe, they could talk seriously about "finding him a space" in a rotary-wing transition course.

Well, screw that! He wanted to get back in the goddamned war before it was over.

He hung up the telephone, went upstairs in Roxy's mother's row house on Railroad Street in Mauch Chuck, Pennsylvania, and took a green tunic from the closet. He laid it on the bed, pinned his ribbons on it—all of his ribbons, including the one which sat alone and on top of all the others, the blue-silk, star-spotted ribbon of the Medal—and then hung the tunic on the hook in the back seat of his brand-new 98 Olds "Rocket" and started out for Washington.

Lt. Colonel Robert F. Bellmon, who had been in the Polish stalag with him, was assigned to the Office of the Assistant Chief of Staff for Operations. If Bellmon couldn't do him any good, there were other people. Before he became a talking dummy for the assholes in PIO, he would complain right up to the top, as far as the Chief of Staff, if that was necessary.

Bellmon laid it on the line, and told MacMillan what he suspected. They wanted him out of the Far East because of the Medal. They didn't want anybody with the goddamned Medal to get blown away. A dead hero is worse, public relations-wise, than an ordinary dead soldier. He had been sent home to get his ass out of the line of fire, not to become a chopper jockey.

"I can probably get you out of the hands of public relations, Mac," Bellmon told him. "But you better get used to the idea that you're going to sit out the rest of this war. They're not going to send you back to the Far East, period."

Colonel Bellmon walked MacMillan down the labyrinthine corridors of the Pentagon to the office of a classmate assigned to the Office of the Assistant Chief of Staff, Personnel. He introduced Mac to him as an old and dear friend, who had been in the stalag with him, who had been in the Far East, and who was now in the clutches of the people in public relations.

Bellmon seldom asked for favors. Colonel Bellmon's classmate was prepared to do anything within reason for an old and dear friend of Bellmon's, particularly one with the Medal, short, of course, of sending him back to the Far East.

It posed no problem at all. An infantry captain at Benning, an assistant instructor in the Department of Tactics, would receive notification that because of space limitations, his orders to attend helicopter flight training at Fort Sam Houston had been cancelled, and that he was being rescheduled for a subsequent class, details to follow.

Captain Rudolph G. MacMillan would receive orders directing him to report for helicopter pilot training at the U.S. Army Medical Center, Fort Sam Houston, San Antonio, Texas.

Afterward, Bob Bellmon insisted that Mac spend the night at the Farm. Barbara, Bellmon said, would not forgive Mac for not bringing Roxy with him to Washington, but he would just have to face up to that.

They stopped and bought steaks on the way to the Farm, and grilled them, and talked about how General Waterford, despite the long hours he had spent concealed by charcoal smoke, was probably the world's worst steak broiler, personally responsible for the destruction of more good meat than any other human being.

"Good God, Mac!" Bellmon said, suddenly. "You don't know about Colonel von Greiffenberg, do you?"

"What about him?"

"He's back," Bellmon said.

"I thought he was dead," MacMillan said. "I heard—*you* told me—that the Russians blew him away just before you got liberated."

"That's what I thought. So did everybody else. But he showed up alive. The Russians had him in Siberia."

"Well, I'll be goddamned," MacMillan said, pleased. "That's damned good news." And then his face clouded. "And what about Lowell?"

Craig W. Lowell was not one of Captain Rudolph G. MacMillan's favorite people. Despite what Lowell had done in Greece, in MacMillan's judgment Lowell was a candy-ass who should never have been commissioned.

"I've seen him twice lately," Bellmon said, looking at his wife to signal her to keep her mouth shut.

"And?" MacMillan asked.

"Once, in Germany. He was there, of course, to meet the colonel when he came across the border," Bellmon said.

"I'm glad for Ilse," Mac said. "Roxy and I always liked her. I never could figure what she saw in Lowell, but she was all right."

"And then we saw Captain Lowell," Barbara said. "When he stopped by on his way to the Far East."

"Captain Lowell?" Mac asked, disbelieving.

"What do you think about that?" Bellmon asked.

"How the hell did he arrange that? He can't be more than twenty-four or twenty-five years old?"

"Twenty-three, actually," Bellmon said. "He went in the National Guard, and arranged to get himself promoted. He's good at that sort of thing, you may have noticed."

"Ah, that makes me sick. He's got no more right to be a captain than Roxy does. What's he doing? Playing golf at Camp Drake?"

"There is a pool of misfit officers, relieved officers, incompetent officers, in Pusan," Lieutenant Colonel Bellmon said. "They are engaged as stevedores, I understand. I devoutly hope that Lowell is among them."

"That's a filthy, rotten thing to say!" Barbara said, furiously.

"Your friend Lowell is a thoroughly rotten man," Bellmon said.

"You've got no right to say anything like that," she said.

"After his coming here the way he did," Bellmon said, as angrily, "I have the perfect right."

"The reason you don't like Craig, darling," Barbara Bellmon said, icily, "is because he has the balls to do things you don't. He won't let the system crap on him, and call it 'cheerful willing obedience to orders.' You don't like Craig, darling, because he makes you realize that you're more of a clerk than you like to admit."

She jumped to her feet, spilling her drink in the process, and stormed inside the house.

"Jesus, what was that all about?" Mac asked.

"I was just thinking," Bellmon said, "that my wife, when she is angry, is really her father's daughter."

"Jesus, yeah," MacMillan said. "That sounded just like one of the general's tantrums, didn't it?"

"I'll give her a couple of minutes to cool down," Bellmon said. "And then I'll go get her."

Goddamn that bastard Lowell, he thought. He can cause trouble when he's ten thousand miles away.

[FOUR]
Brooke U.S. Army Medical Center
Fort Sam Houston, Texas
10 September 1950

When he reported for duty at Fort Sam, MacMillan's breast pocket was bare of all ribbons and qualification badges except his aviator's wings. He did not want to call attention to himself at all, just get through this bullshit as quickly and as smoothly as possible. If his orders had not identified him as a fixed-wing, instrument qualified aviator, he would not have worn his wings either.

Fixed-wing aviators, he learned on arrival, had no set program. They would be rotary-wing students until such time as they had been adjudged competent, entry-level helicopter pilots, or until it became clear that they were never going to master safe flight in rotary-wing aircraft.

Fixed-wing qualification is no indicator at all of an individual's potential as a chopper jockey. Helicopter piloting is the most difficult of all flying in terms of coordination; and numbers of splendid fixed-wing pilots have never been able to make the transition.

MacMillan's instructor had long before learned that it was quite necessary to destroy the ego and self-confidence of a fixed-wing pilot about to undergo rotary-wing training in order to make him pay attention. The quickest and surest way to do that was to take him for an orientation ride and let him see for himself how difficult it was and how embarrassingly inept he was at it.

A fixed-wing aircraft is controlled, simplistically, by the stick and the rudder pedals. Climbing is accomplished by pulling back on the stick, descending by pushing forward on it. Turns are accomplished by moving the stick from side to side and by depressing one of the rudder pedals. Straight and level flight can often be accomplished simply by removing one's hands and feet entirely from the stick and rudder pedals, and letting the plane fly itself.

Helicopter flight is somewhat more complicated. There are pedals which function essentially like rudder pedals, but they are *not* rudder pedals, and taking one's feet off them entirely will immediately start the helicopter's fuselage spinning. It is necessary, using the "rudder pedals" (which actually control the small, counter-torque rotor mounted vertically in the tail), to maintain an equilibrium between opposing forces.

There is a "stick" between the legs, and it too has major differences from the stick on a fixed-wing aircraft. What it actually does is tilt the "rotor cone" in the direction it is moved. The rotor cone is the arc described by the rotor blades as they revolve. Imagine an empty, very wide-mouthed, very shallow ice cream cone. If the cone is tilted forward, it tends to move the helicopter forward; tilted to the rear, it tends to move the aircraft to the rear. It can be tilted in any direction.

The helicopter pilot's left hand is simultaneously occupied by a third control. A motorcycle-like rotary throttle is held in the curled fist. The straight piece of aluminum tubing on which it is mounted also controls the angle of the blade. In other words, it adjusts the "bite" the rotor blades take of the air as they spin around the rotor head. The steeper the bite (angle of attack), the more lift is provided. And the steeper the angle of attack, the more power is required. Constant throttle adjustment is required. An instrument in front of the pilot has two separate needles, one indicating rotor speed, and the other engine rpm. The needles are supposed to be superimposed, within a small range indicated by a green strip on the dial.

For purposes of comparisons, when the pilot of a fixed-wing aircraft is poised for takeoff, he simply pushes the throttle forward to "take off power." Then he steers the airplane, as it gathers speed down the runway, by use of the rudder pedals and stick. At a certain point, the speed of the air passing over his wings generates sufficient lift to literally lift the airplane off the runway.

A helicopter pilot, on the other hand, must first acquire lift by judicious application of engine power and simultaneous raising of the cyclic control. The instant the helicopter leaves the ground, he must establish and maintain equilibrium between opposing forces by use of the "rudder pedals" to keep the machine from starting to spin, and then adjust the position of the rotor cone to control the direction of flight—even if that direction is not to move at all: the most difficult of all flight manuevers, the "hover."

Having accomplished all this, the helicopter is still not in a flight condition, but in an intermediate step called "transitional lift." What this means is that the helicopter is sort of floating on a cushion of air compressed between the rotor blades and the ground. When he climbs higher, or when he moves off in any direction, he "loses the cushion" and instantaneous compensatory movements of all the controls are necessary.

The easiest way to convince anyone of what a hairy bitch chopper driving is—but especially a well-qualified fixed-wing pilot—is by demonstration rather than explanation. And once the student pilot is convinced that he has a hell of a lot to learn, as he inevitably is when the chopper instantly gets away from him, he then becomes a docile and dedicated student.

Captain MacMillan's instructor pilot spent thirty minutes showing him the mechanical construction of the Bell H13. Then they climbed inside the plexiglass bubble, where he spent another fifteen minutes explaining the controls and the layout of the instrumentation. He figured he would give this guy, who seemed pretty cocky, a thirty-minute demonstration to convince him beyond any doubt, reasonable or otherwise, that he was really going to have to bust his ass before he could fly a chopper.

Following the instructor's step-by-step instructions over the intercom, MacMillan fired up the engine, and checked the instruments one by one to make sure the indicators were all within the safe operating range ("in the green") indicated by stripes of green tape on the instruments.

"Now," the IP said, "it's going to get away from you. Expect it to. Just don't overreact. Try to figure out how you're under-or over-controlling." MacMillan nodded. "Ease up, very gently, on the cyclic; and remember, you're controlling the throttle."

MacMillan nodded again and did as he was told. He picked the bird straight up. He didn't like the feeling, so he picked it up another couple of feet. He tried out the rudder pedals, to see how sensitive they were. Then he looked over, unaware that he was in a near perfect hover, just out of ground-effect.

"Now what?" he asked his instructor pilot.

"How much bootleg chopper time do you have, MacMillan?" the IP demanded. He did not like being made a fool of.

"None," MacMillan replied. "I've always been afraid of the goddamned things. Can I try to fly it?"

"Be my goddamned guest," the IP said. He had never until this moment believed there was such a thing as a natural helicopter pilot. MacMillan dropped the nose, moved across the field ten feet above it, and then, increasing the pitch, soared into the air, a disgusting look of pure pleasure on his face.

[**FIVE**]

This time, Bellmon's classmate in the Office of the Assistant Chief of Staff, Personnel, was not so obliging. There was absolutely no chance of MacMillan being returned to the Far East, much less to Korea, as a chopper pilot.

"For one thing, you're a returnee. You have to spend a year in the States," the lieutenant colonel told him.

"I'll waive that," MacMillan said. "Jesus Christ, Colonel. They want to make me an IP. I couldn't take that."

The lieutenant colonel showed him the letter from SCAP in the Dai Ichi Building, addressed somewhat baroquely to "My Dear Comrade Ellsworth" (the Assistant Chief of Staff, Personnel, who was not fond of his first name and signed himself "E. James Brockman") and containing the SCAP's reluctant conclusion that Captain MacMillan's assignment to duties "which would place him in the jeopardy of the instant situation in Korea" would not be in the overall best interests of the army.

"As painful as it will surely be for a warrior of MacMillan's caliber to turn a deaf ear to the sound of the battle trumpet," SCAP wrote, "I'm sure that, once the situation is explained to him, he will discharge his training or administrative duties with the same dedication he has so often demonstrated under fire."

"Bullshit," MacMillan said. "I'll quit flying before I let them make me an IP."

"General Brockman said to give you a choice between here and Fort Polk," and lieutenant colonel said.

"Polk? In Louisiana? What the hell's going on there?"

"It was just reactivated as a basic training center."

"Oh, Jesus Christ, Colonel!"

"Where you would be aide-de-camp to General Black."

"Black's a pretty good general," MacMillan said. "What the hell did he do wrong to get sent to Fort *Polk?*"

"Korea's an infantry war," the lieutenant colonel explained. "They're not going to send any armored divisions over there. I suppose the thinking is that if the balloon goes up . . . in Europe, I mean . . . he could activate an armored division at Polk."

"What would I be doing here?" MacMillan said. "I'm almost afraid to ask."

"Presidential Flight Detachment," the lieutenant colonel said. "Flying choppers."

"I heard about that," MacMillan said. "And I heard you needed a thousand hours, minimum, no-accident chopper time."

"To fly the President or the VIPs you do," the lieutenant colonel agreed.

"So what would I be doing?"

"You would be very decorative around the White House," the lieutenant colonel said. "Especially in a dress blue uniform or mess kit. Wearing your medals, not your ribbons." He paused, and then said, wryly: "You'd really be something in a mess kit, MacMillan."

The mess kit was an ornate, formal dress uniform for evening wear. Most officers hated it.

"Did anybody bring my name up to General Black?" MacMillan asked.

"You're OK with him, if that's what you're asking. He said that after you get a little more experience, he'll even let you fly him around in your whirlybird."

VII

[ONE]

Schloss Greiffenberg
Marburg an der Lahn, Germany
12 September 1950

Peter-Paul Lowell, half shy and half glowering, his bunched fists pulling his mother's skirt off her hips so that it was evident she was wearing only a half slip, looked at the woman his mother was affectionately embracing.

"Got a kiss for me?" Sharon Felter asked, squatting down to his level. He buried his face in the familiar warmth of his mother's tweed skirt.

"Aunt Sharon's known you since you were a tiny baby," Ilse von Greiffenberg Lowell said. "Give her a kiss."

Peter-Paul von Greiffenberg Lowell, known as P. P., stuck his tongue out at Sharon Felter and then let go of his mother's skirt, turned and ran up the shallow stairs and into the open door of the large villa.

"A chip off the old blockhead, I see," Sandy Felter said to Ilse, and kissed her on the cheek. Felter was in civilian clothing. In civilian clothing few people suspected he was a soldier. He looked more like a lawyer, a CPA, a member of any number of sedentary professions.

Felter raised his head toward the Schloss, which was enormous, although not quite the sort of building that comes to mind with the word "castle."

"What time is the changing of the guard?" he asked.

"It's even larger than I remembered," Ilse said. "And it's even worse because most of the furniture is gone."

"What happened to it?" Sharon asked, innocently. Ilse was embarrassed. "Did I ask the wrong question?"

"I think Ilse found out that the furniture was 'liberated' by the Americans," Sandy said.

"It's not important," Ilse said. "What are we standing here for? Come on in, I'll get you something to eat and drink."

"I need the you-know-what," Sharon said. "My kidneys can't take thirty miles of cobblestone roads."

Ilse took her and the Felter kids off to the toilet. Sandy Felter was left alone in what obviously had been the library. The walls were lined with empty shelves, and in a corner, obviously awaiting a rail to roll along, a library ladder rested against the wall.

"My dear Captain Felter," a male voice cried in English, "you must forgive my manners. Have you been left all alone?"

"It's very nice to see you again, Graf von Greiffenberg," Felter said, in German.

"You are our first guests," the Graf said. "Which seems, under the circumstances, and despite the condition of the house, very appropriate."

"You're very kind to have us," Felter said.

The change in the Graf von Greiffenberg since Felter had seen him last was remarkable. On June 26—he remembered the date because it was the day the North Koreans had come across the 38th parallel—he had met the Graf at the Marburg exit of the autobahn. Less than thirty-six hours before that, the Graf had come across the East-West German border, finally released from Russian imprisonment. The Gehlen Organization kept people at the border points, and an hour after he had crossed, while he was still en route to the returned prisoner camp, Felter had been informed by telephone of his release.

The colonel had taken it upon himself to get off the train at Bad Hersfeld to see an old friend, and they'd had a hell of a time finding him, even with agents of the U.S. Army Counterintelligence Corps enlisted to locate him. The CIC had found him. They had agents waiting for him when he walked out of the bahnhof in Marburg. Felter had been notified, at Kronberg Castle, the U.S. Army VIP guest house outside Frankfurt am Main, where he had been waiting with Lt. Colonel Bob Bellmon and Craig and Ilse Lowell, and he'd gone and picked him up.

The cadaverous, musty smelling survivor of five years in Siberia—five years under an "official" death sentence, five years of not knowing if today they would take him out and garrote him, or shoot him, or run over him with a truck, or otherwise take his life in an "accident" or "while trying to escape," five years of not knowing what had happened to his family, or if he still had a family—had been reunited with his daughter at Kronberg Castle. He learned not only that she had survived the war, but that she had married and borne a son. And that his daughter's husband was a wealthy investment banker with sufficient political influence to have a French entry visa waiting, so that the colonel could be flown by chartered aircraft to Paris, where he would "be more comfortable."

The Graf von Greiffenberg was still thin, three months later, but no longer cadaverous. His eyes were no longer either sunken or bloodshot, and he smelled, Sandy thought, of expensive soap and aftershave. He was dressed in a blue, open-collared shirt, gray flannel slacks, and American loafers. But he was, Sandy thought with one corner of his mind, obviously both German and an aristocrat. Somewhat nastily, Felter thought that money could indeed work miracles—and was ashamed of himself as quickly as the thought popped into his mind.

The Graf looked around the room, and gestured at the empty shelves.

"I missed my books, most of all," he said. "In the East. And I miss them now. Furniture can be replaced. Walls can be repainted, floors refinished. But there were books in this room that simply . . ." He cut himself off, and went to a cabinet beneath the empty shelves, opened it, and came out with a large, leather-bound book and put it in Felter's hands. "The Nazis, and then Americans, and finally the democratically elected government of Land and Kreis Marburg left me this," he said. "Ironic, isn't it?"

Felter took the book and opened it to the title page.

"Russian," the Graf said. "They didn't take the Russian books."

"Reminiscences of the Crimean Campaign," Felter read. "By Major General the Grand Duke Alexander Alexandrovich, Commander of His Imperial Majesty's Kiev Guard."

"My late wife's kinsman," the Graf said. "Great, great uncle, I think." He spoke in Russian, then said what he was thinking. "Your Russian, my dear Felter, is better than mine."

"My great, great, great uncle," Felter said with a smile, "was probably a conscript in the Grand Duke's infantry."

"And do you find your command of Russian valuable in your military career, my dear Felter?"

Felter met his eyes, and paused a moment before replying. "Often of great value," he said.

"I no longer know anyone whom I might contact," the Graf said. "But I have thought, over the years, that my knowledge and experience might be of some use."

"I'm sure it would be," Felter said. "Perhaps after you get your feet on the ground, and the word gets around that you're home, something will turn up."

"Perhaps," the Graf said. "Forgive the imposition, after everything you've done for me, Felter, but I was hoping that you . . ."

"I have reason to believe that you won't have to ask for work, Colonel," Felter said.

The Graf was pleased. He nodded, and changed the subject. He had been determined to bring the subject up with Felter, who was an intelligence officer, but he was afraid that he would appear too eager, and be thought an anticommunist zealot. At the upper echelons of what he wanted to do, there was no room for zealots. He wondered what Felter knew, but he knew he should not, could not ask. He would have to let them come to him.

"Ilse heard from Craig today," the Graf said. "A letter mailed five days ago in Korea, delivered here today. The world is shrinking."

"What did he have to say?" Felter asked.

"His unit is about to be reequipped with M46 tanks," the Graf said. "The . . . what is that marvelous word you Americans use? The *pipeline*. Craig wrote that 'the *pipeline* was apparently finally in place and beginning to spew forth a cornucopia of materiel.' "

"Craig should have been born a hundred years ago," Felter said.

"Why do you say that?"

"In the days when noblemen raised their own regiments," Felter said.

"Yes," the Graf said and smiled.

"Colonel the Duke of Lowell's Squadron of Dragoons," Felter said. He chuckled. *"They* would have ridden unscathed through the Valley of Death at Balaclava."

The Graf chuckled with him.

"They call him that, you know," Felter said. "They call him 'the Duke' and he loves it."

The Graf laughed out loud. "I didn't know that, but it doesn't surprise me at all."

Sharon Felter and Ilse Lowell appeared at the door to the library, and saw the two men laughing. They looked at one another, and wordlessly agreed not to disturb them. They turned and walked back down the wide corridor. Ilse Lowell put her head into the kitchen (like the rest of the house, it showed the signs of rehabilitation: mason's and painter's and carpenter's tools and equipment put away over the weekend) and asked a plump, gray-haired woman if she would make tea, "and ask Rosa to serve it in the garden."

Then the two women went into the garden and sat down at an obviously new wrought-iron table under a striped umbrella. Ilse took a cigarette from her purse, held it up in offer to Sharon, and when Sharon shook her head, "no," put the pack back in her purse.

"Go ahead," Sharon said, "if it makes you feel good."

Ilse lit the cigarette. She told Sharon of the letter she'd had that morning from Craig. A maid, Rosa, delivered tea, which was actually a selection of cold cuts (all beef and veal, in deference to the Felters) and cheese and breads, in addition to the tea.

Sharon surreptitiously examined the bread, and found it without fault. It occurred to her that she was a long way here from the bakery on the corner of Chancellor Avenue and Aldine Street in Newark, New Jersey, where she had grown up two doors down the street from Sandy.

Sharon Lavinsky had been a year behind Sandy Felter all the way through school; she literally could not remember a time when she did not sense they belonged together. And she had known that Sandy was someone really special, smarter and stronger than anybody she had ever known.

His brains had gotten him into West Point. The congressman had gotten in trouble about passing out appointments to the service academies, and had announced that from now on he would make all appointments on the basis of competitive examinations. Sandy walked away with the exam, getting fifteen more points than the man in the second place.

Sandy's parents and Sharon's parents were of a mixed mind about Sandy taking the appointment when it was offered to him. With a brain and an academic record like his, he could really make something of himself: a doctor, a lawyer, even a judge. Even a dentist or a CPA was better than being a soldier. On the other hand, the war was on, and as long as he was at West Point, he would be safe. Sandy was the Class of 1946, and by then the war would be over and he wouldn't have to go.

What the Felters didn't know, nor the Lavinskys, nor even Sharon herself, was that Sandy wanted to go to West Point because he wanted to be a soldier. He was going there to go to war, not to get out of it. His parents and hers, and Sharon herself, began to suspect this after a while, but they told each other that he would grow out of it, that he would come to his senses.

Sharon believed this. When they went up the Hudson to see him in his plebe year, he looked like a dwarf around the others, most of whom looked like football players. He didn't look as if he belonged.

And then he did something that made everybody, Sharon included, think he had lost his mind. When he came home on his Christmas leave in 1944, he told her that if she loved him, she was going to have to trust him to do what he thought was right. At first, Sharon thought he wanted them to do something together they shouldn't. She thought about it a moment, and decided that if that's what Sandy really wanted to do, all right.

But it wasn't that (Sharon and, she was sure, Sandy, too, went virginal to their wedding bed). It was a lot worse than that. Sandy, who was always reading anything he could get his hands on, had come across an army regulation which authorized the direct commissioning of linguists. He spoke Russian and German and Polish and had studied French for four years in high school, so he spoke that, too, although not as well.

They tried to talk him out of it at West Point, and actually got pretty nasty about it, he told her, before they finally gave in. But they gave in.

On 1 January 1945, while the Battle of the Bulge was still raging in Europe, Cadet Corporal Felter was discharged from the Corps of Cadets of the United States Military Academy at West Point, and immediately commissioned into the Army of the United States as Second Lieutenant, Infantry (Detail: Military Intelligence as Linguist). They swore him in at the breakfast formation, and the band played "Army Blue" ("We Say Farewell to Kay-Det Gray and Don the Army Blue") and "Dixie." Then, as the Corps of Cadets marched off to breakfast, Second Lieutenant Felter was driven to the railroad station. At four that afternoon he was over the Atlantic, en route to the 40th Armored Division, "Hell's Circus."

When Sandy came home, he insisted they get married in the chapel at West Point. If their rabbi wanted to marry them, fine; otherwise, they would be married by an army chaplain. They would have the reception in the Hotel Thayer, which was a hotel owned by the army. He told her that it would be important to her later, to be able to say that she had been married at West Point.

So they had been married at West Point, in a very nice ceremony. A few of the members of Sandy's old class, '46, showed up. They said that as far as they were concerned, Sandy was still one of them, and they gave him a '46 class ring, and they gave Sharon a miniature of it. That made it better.

Sandy hadn't gone back to West Point, although he could have, because he had found out he could get a college degree by correspondence from the University of Chicago. Sharon went with Sandy to Fort Benning, where he went through the Parachute School, and then to Fort Bragg, where he went through the Ranger School.

"I'll probably never jump out of another airplane," Sandy told her. "And they don't want me in the Rangers. But that's part of the game, and I have to play it."

"What game?" she'd asked him.

"The army is like the boy scouts," he said. "They have a system of merit badges. The more merit badges you have, the better. I'll get jump wings from Benning, and a little strip with 'Ranger' on it at Bragg, and then I'll have as many merit badges as someone of my age and rank is supposed to have. That's the way the game is played."

So he became a paratrooper and a Ranger, and Sharon thought they would probably spend two or three years at Fort Bragg, while Sandy did what young officers were supposed to do—two years, preferably three, duty with troops.

But as the honor graduate of the Ranger School, he was given his choice of assignments, and he chose what Sharon thought was the worst one. He volunteered for duty with something called the U.S. Army Military Advisory Group, Greece (USAMAG-G). Dependents were not authorized in Greece. She would be left behind again, for a year, maybe more.

Sharon's mother cried, and said Sandy had a devil in him, and Sandy's mother was ashamed of what her son had done to Sharon. But he went. Greece was where he met Craig Lowell. Sandy wrote (often every day) and he told her about Craig. At first, to tell the truth, he hadn't liked Craig Lowell. Lowell had been sent to Greece as some kind of punishment, and Lowell didn't like the army. But as the letters kept coming, Sharon detected that Sandy was changing his mind about Lowell, and that they were becoming friends. Sharon was pleased that Sandy had found a friend. All of his life, he had really been friendless.

Sandy also wrote that he was an administrative officer, in charge of supplies. He painted a picture of himself safe behind a desk, but when he sent a roll of film home, and she got it back from the drugstore, she knew he was lying to her. Four of the pictures on the roll were of dead people. One of them showed a large, blond, good-looking young man who looked American. He was holding a Garand rifle in his hand, smiling proudly like a hunter in Africa, with his foot on the chest of a dead man with a long mustache and a bullet hole in the middle of his forehead.

The same young man was in other pictures on the roll; in one of them he was sitting with Sandy at a table, holding his fingers up in a V behind Sandy's head in a picture of six people. Sandy was carrying a gangsters' tommy gun and the young man was carrying a rifle, and Sharon knew two things: The good looking young man was Sandy's friend Craig Lowell, and what Craig Lowell and Sandy were doing was fighting a war, no matter what Sandy wrote he was doing.

Sandy wrote her that he felt sorry for Craig, that as smart and as tough as he was, he had been taken in by a girl in Germany, a girl of low morals who was making a fool of him. She hadn't written him once since he'd come to Greece, and Lowell was nearly crazy over it.

And then there had been a letter from Sandy saying that Craig had been "injured" and that he would probably be sent home, and would come to see her. He warned her not to bring up the fraulein he'd gotten into the mess with.

Three weeks later, in the Old Warsaw Bakery, glancing out the plate-glass window while she waited on customers, Sharon saw a limousine, even fancier than the Cadillac limousines the funeral homes used, turn off Chancellor Avenue. Sharon went over to the window to see if it was going to stop.

It pulled to the curb halfway down the block, and a chauffeur in a gray uniform ran around and opened the door and a young man got out. Limping a little, the young man started to walk toward the bakery, carrying the suitcase, and Sharon Lavinsky Felter went back behind the counter, so that Sandy's friend Craig Lowell wouldn't know that she had seen him get out of a fancy limousine.

The next week was tough on Sharon. Craig, who slept on the couch in the Felters' apartment, talked about nothing but Ilse. He said he was waiting for his passport, so he could fly to Germany and marry her. Sharon was very tempted to tell Craig that Sandy—who was generally right about things like that—felt he was being made a fool of, but she couldn't bring herself to do it.

Craig flew to Germany, and came back married, and told Sharon his Ilse was pregnant. He said he didn't give a shit what anybody else thought, including Sandy. He knew Sandy thought Ilse was a kraut whore, but it was important to him that Sharon know that Ilse was a good woman.

Craig asked Sharon if she would meet Ilse when she came to New York from Germany, and see that she got on a plane to Louisville. Craig was in the Basic Armor Officer's Course at Fort Knox, near Louisville, and he didn't think the bastards would give him time off to come to New York to meet Ilse himself.

The first thing Sharon thought when she looked into Ilse Lowell's tear-filled eyes was that when Sandy was wrong, he was really wrong. This was no whore. This was an seventeen-year-old girl who was six months' pregnant and thoroughly terrified.

"Could I kiss you?" was the first thing Sharon Felter had ever said to Ilse Lowell.

In the Lavinsky Chevrolet on the way to New Jersey, Ilse said there had been "a terrible mix-up about the ticket." When she got to Rhine-Main, they had a First Class Royal Ambassador Drawing Room in the Skies ticket waiting for her.

"I asked what the difference in price was," Ilse said. "And would you believe it was two and a half times the price of a regular seat? I made them give me the difference back. We're going to need all our money for the baby." She opened her purse and displayed the money.

Sharon had decided that if Ilse didn't know Craig was rich, it was not her business to tell her. And she was pleased, too, to have the proof that Ilse hadn't gone after Craig because he was rich.

Peter-Paul Lowell was born in the U.S. Hospital at Fort Knox, Kentucky, shortly before his father graduated from the Basic Officer's Course. Sandy and Sharon saw him for the first time there, when Sandy came home from Greece and they were on their way to the Army Language School at the Presidio in San Francisco.

They later figured out that it was in the guest bedroom of Lieutenant Lowell's quarters (a converted barracks) that she and Sandy had started Little Sandy.

After the Language School, Sandy had gone to the Counterintelligence Corps (CIC) Center at Fort Holabird in Baltimore. The general's wife there had all the ladies in for a tea, and then given them a little speech saying the best way they could help their husbands' careers from now on was not to try to share it; not to ask questions; not even to think about it, just to provide a warm nest.

At first she'd liked the CIC. Sandy was assigned to the detachment in New York

City. He wore civilian clothes, and they lived with his parents on Aldine Street. He went to work every morning just as if he was a businessman, even carrying a briefcase. That had lasted about five months.

Just after Craig had gotten out of the army, and he and Ilse were in Philadelphia where Craig was enrolled in the Wharton School of Business, Sandy and Sharon and Little Sandy went to Berlin.

The only question she'd asked Sandy was if he was still in the CIC and he told her no, he wasn't. She didn't like Berlin. Physically, it was all right. They had a very nice house in Zehlendorf. There was even a yard man and a driver. The yard man was never very far from his wheelbarrow, and in the wheelbarrow were a two-way radio and a submachine gun. The driver carried a gun, and Sandy carried a gun.

And then, all of a sudden, they left Berlin and went to Garmisch-Partenkirchen, in Bavaria. Sandy put his uniform back on, but he still carried a pistol all the time, under his uniform, and they lived in a compound surrounded by barbed wire. They had tried to hide the barbed wire, but it was there, and Sharon had never grown used to it.

She did not ask, or allow herself to think much, about what Sandy was doing. They were together, and he was happy, and she was happy, too.

For a while, it had looked like everything was perfect. Sandy had found out that Ilse's father wasn't dead after all, and then he had found out that he was going to be released by the Russians. He'd talked to her about that, asked her advice.

"What do I do, Sharon? Do I tell her? So that she can be here when her father comes across the border? Or do I wait until he does? In case something goes wrong?"

"Are you sure of your information?"

He thought about it a minute. "My sources are reliable."

"Then you'd better tell her," Sharon told him, and he did. And Craig and Ilse and P. P. had flown over, and were waiting for her father when he came home, after all that time in a Soviet prison camp in Siberia.

Everything was just perfect for them, and then the army had called Craig back in, and just about the next day sent him to Korea.

"At least," she had told Sandy, "if something happens to Craig, Ilse has her father."

Sandy said something funny: "Craig is not the kind that gets killed in a war, Sharon. He's the kind that thrives on it."

Sharon didn't believe that. She was nearly as worried about Craig as Ilse was, and she wondered why, whether it was for him or for Ilse. She concluded that it was because of Ilse, and when she asked herself why that was, she realized that Ilse was the first real friend she had ever had, too, the first friend she had loved, rather than just gotten along with.

"Why don't you and P. P. come and see us for a couple of weeks," Sharon asked. "Bavaria, the mountains, are just beautiful this time of the year."

"Do you have room?" Ilse asked.

"All the room we'll need."

"I'd like that," Ilse said, and Sharon was pleased for the both of them.

And she was pleased for everybody when she saw Sandy and the colonel having such a good time together. It was a crying shame that Craig had to be so far away, in Korea.

[TWO]
Pusan, Korea
12 September 1950

The harbor of Pusan was crowded with ships. There were gray warships and troop ships and supply ships of the U.S. Navy, and a motley assortment of civilian ships—cargo ships, tankers, even two passenger ships. And the white-painted hospital ship, the USS *Consolation.*

A steady stream of lighters moved between the inadequate piers and the ships, off-loading all sorts of supplies. Only when there was something aboard that could not be off-loaded into a lighter or a barge was a ship given pier space. Even the troops disembarked by climbing down rope cargo nets into small boats and Coast Guard landing barges.

Lt. Colonel Paul T. Jiggs, commanding officer of the 73rd Medium Tank Battalion (Separate), stood on the wharf of Pier One and watched as M46 medium tanks were off-loaded.

Teams of Ordnance Corps technicians, who themselves had often been in Korea only a day or two, had gone out to the transport when she was still waiting her turn to come to a pier, and had readied the tanks for instant movement. They ripped the protective coverings from the engines, charged the batteries, and fueled the tanks, then started the engines and ran them long enough to make sure they would run.

An M46 weighs forty-four tons. The ship that had carried them from San Francisco, as huge as it was, leaned toward the pier as each tank was hoisted from her holds and swung over the side. It straightened again when the tank's weight was on the pier.

Ordnance noncoms got in the tanks before the cables were taken off, and started the engines. Then, when the cables were free, being hauled up and back over the holds, they drove the M46s off the pier.

The tanks were freshly painted. They looked new. They *smelled* new, as the paint burned off their exhaust manifolds. They were fresh from ordnance depots across the United States. But they weren't truly new tanks. They were M26s which had been rebuilt, incorporating a new turret cannon, a high-velocity 90 mm tube with a muzzle brake and a powder fume extractor; a new power train, a brand-new GM Allison combined cross drive and steering unit that made the M46 considerably easier to drive (all the driver had to do was push a "joy stick" in the direction he wanted to go, and that was it—wrestling the double levers of an M4A3 would soon be an thing of the past); and a new, more powerful Continental 12-cylinder engine.

The M26 with the new cannon and new engine and new power train were reborn as the M46, the Patton, named after the general.

Colonel Jiggs had come to Pier One to see for himself that the M46s were indeed on hand, and not the wishful figment of some G-3 planner's imagination. The reason was that the M46s being taken off the ship, and driven off the pier, were Colonel Jiggs's M46s.

He had come to Pier One from a meeting with the deputy chief of staff and the assistant chiefs of staff, G-1, G-3, and G-4 (Personnel, Plans and Training, and Supply) at the forward headquarters of the Eighth United States Army. He had learned that, as of 0001 hours that morning, the 73rd Medium Tank Battalion, (Separate) had become the 73rd Heavy Tank Battalion (Reinforced).

Instead of three line companies and a headquarters and service company, he would now command five tank companies, all M46s with that beautiful 90 mm high-velocity cannon; one cavalry troop, equipped with M24 light tanks, for reconnaissance purposes; two batteries of 105 mm howitzers, self-propelled (howitzers mounted on an M4 chassis); an ordnance ammo platoon; an ordnance maintenance platoon; a Transportation Corps truck company; a Signal Corps communications platoon; a medical team detached from the 8005th MASH; and two companies of mechanized infantry.

The ordnance types unloading the tanks before his eyes belonged to him, although they didn't know it yet.

73rd Medium Tank had become a combat command in everything but name. Its size made it a command calling for a full colonel, possibly even a brigadier general. But they were giving it to him.

"I'm not going to sit here with my thumb up my ass wondering," he had told them. "Do I get to keep this beautiful pocket division you're giving me, or am I going to be relieved as soon as I get it organized?"

"If you can get it together and keep it together for the next month, Paul," the assistant chief of staff had told him, "it's yours."

Jiggs had nodded, deciding the assistant chief of staff would not have said that if it weren't true. He had done a damned good job with the 73rd, and they knew it. He was entitled to a chance with this pocket armored division they were setting up.

"You want to borrow some staff officers?" the assistant chief of staff said. "That's a lot of spaghetti to hold on one fork."

"No, sir," Jiggs said. "My staff is fine the way it stands."

"Anything you need, Paul," the G3 said. "Speak up. Quickly."

"Thank you, sir."

[THREE]

When the last of the forty-two M46s had been off-loaded onto Pier One, Lieutenant Colonel Paul T. Jiggs drove back to the command post, slowly, knowing what he had to do, wondering if it was the right thing, wondering if he could carry it off.

When he was almost at the command post, he made a U-turn on the main supply route and drove a mile back to the MASH. He found the commanding officer, an old acquaintance, but not an old friend, in one of the wards and asked him for a few minutes of his time.

There was no problem. The MASH commander was as much an old soldier as he was a surgeon. He didn't even ask any questions. He simply nodded his head and agreed to do what Jiggs asked. It was the kindest way to do an unkind thing that had to be done for the overall good of the army.

Jiggs then drove back to his CP and went to the S-3 (Plans and Training) section. The S-3, looking somewhat haggard, was bent over thick mounds of paper on his desk, a sheet of three-quarter-inch plywood set on two-by-four sawhorses. It was a moment before the S-3 was aware that Jiggs was standing by the desk.

"Yes, sir?" he said. "Sorry, Colonel, I was pretty deep in that."

"Get your pot, Charley," Colonel Jiggs said. "I want you to take a ride with me."

Jiggs drove them out of the battalion area, down the main supply route (MSR) back toward Pusan, and then turned off onto a finger of land looking down on the ships crowding Pusan Harbor. It was a wet and miserable day, raining, and yet warm enough for the putrid stink from the rice paddies to be heavy in the air. A shitty smell, Colonel Jiggs thought, to go with a shitty job to do on a shitty day.

"Charley," he said, when he had stopped the jeep and turned sideward on the seat to face him, "how much service do you have?"

"Sixteen years, Colonel."

"I want to talk to you about you," Jiggs said.

"Yes, sir?" There was the faintest suggestion of concern, even alarm, in Major Ellis's voice.

"As of 0001 this morning," Jiggs said, "we are, in everything but name, a combat command. Our morning report strength tomorrow will be two and a half times what it was today."

"That sounds like good news, sir."

"Not for you, it isn't," Jiggs said, finally biting the bullet. Shit, get it over with. "You can't handle it."

"I'm sorry you feel that way, Colonel," Ellis said. "I've tried to do my best."

"That hasn't been good enough," Jiggs said. "We both know that Lowell's been carrying you."

"I'm afraid I can't accept that, sir," Ellis said. "Certainly, Captain Lowell has been a great help to me, but—"

"Let me make my position clear," Jiggs interrupted him. "You are going to be relieved. That's been settled. The only question is how."

"Sir," Ellis said, "I will protest my relief."

"Are you that stupid?" Jiggs said, trying to sound more angry than he really felt. He really felt lousy, not angry.

"I resent that, sir," Ellis said.

"Resent it all you want," Jiggs said, "but get it through your head that I've got you by the balls. Don't you threaten me with an official complaint."

Ellis seemed to be forming several replies, but in the end he said nothing.

"What I really have in mind, Major, is the good of the unit. Above all else. And I know you're the same kind of a soldier—the outfit comes first."

"I like to think of myself that way, Colonel."

"Now, I can relieve you as of this moment, Ellis, and you can complain to Walton Walker himself, and you'll stay relieved. If you think that through, you'll know I'm right."

"You have that prerogative, sir."

"To do that, it would be necessary for me to write an efficiency report on you that would keep you from getting any other responsible assignment, and more than likely, would see you finishing out your twenty years with stripes on your sleeve."

Ellis looked at him, met his eyes, but said nothing for a moment. Finally, he said: "I've tried to give you my best, Colonel."

"I know you gave me your best, and I'm grateful to you for doing it; but your best simply has not been good enough."

"You're talking about Lowell, of course," Ellis said. "Colonel, he's a graduate of the Wharton School of Business. He's got a mind like a goddamned adding machine. I have to work at it, look things up. He remembers them."

"I have never for a moment believed you weren't giving me the best you had to give, Charley," Jiggs said. "But it's not good enough."

"I appreciate your breaking this to me as gently as you could, Colonel," Major Ellis said after a moment. "I won't bitch. You knew I wouldn't."

"I'm not through, Charley," Jiggs said. "I want more from you. And I'll tell you what I'll do for you in return."

"What else can you want? I've already agreed to cut my own throat."

"I want Lowell as my S-3," Jiggs said.

"The minute you relieve me, G-1 will send you a replacement. And if they've doubled the size, more than doubled the size, of the outift, they're liable to send you a light bird. Two light birds, one to be your exec. Or, shit, you're liable to get ranked out of your job."

"I've been promised the job for thirty days. They didn't say it, but if I get through the next thirty days, I'll get an eagle. If I don't . . . up the creek."

"In any event, there's no way you can make Lowell your S-3," Ellis said.

"If my S-3 is Absent in Hospital," Jiggs said, "I can give him the job temporarily. And after thirty days, I can promote him."

"Is that what all this is about? Getting a promotion for Lowell? Christ, he's not old enough to be a captain."

"What this is all about is providing the outfit with the best S-3 I can," Jiggs said, rather coldly.

"I'm sorry," Ellis said. "I'm a little shaken. I hadn't expected any of this. Shit, what am I going to tell my wife?"

"If you want to, you can tell her you're having a little trouble with your back, which is why you're in the hospital. Give me a month in the hospital, Charley, and I'll give you a good efficiency report and have you sent home."

"That won't work," Ellis said. "They won't keep me at the MASH. They'll either send me back here, or to Japan."

"I've got that fixed," Jiggs said. "I know the MASH commander."

"You know what's funny, Colonel?" Ellis said. He didn't wait for Jiggs to reply. "Now that it's out in the open, I'm not ashamed. Goddamnit, I did my best."

"Yes, you did," Jiggs said. "This would have been a lot easier for me, Charley, if you hadn't."

[**FOUR**]

Back at the MASH, Colonel Jiggs found a sergeant and sent him to fetch the MASH commander.

"This is Major Charley Ellis, Howard," Jiggs said. "Treat him right."

"We'll start him off with a shot of medicinal bourbon," the MASH commander said. "And then a hot bath, and then we'll see what's wrong with his lower back."

Ellis reached over and shook Jiggs's hand before he got out of the jeep. Jiggs watched him walk toward the Admitting Tent. Ellis turned and looked at him. Jiggs raised his hand in a crisp salute. Ellis returned it just as crisply, and then went inside.

Jiggs turned his jeep around and drove to the CP.

He saw the sergeant major.

"Put Major Ellis's shaving gear, other personal stuff, in a bag and have someone—you, if you have the time—carry it to him at the MASH. Then ask Captain Lowell to come here."

"He's in S-3, Colonel," the sergeant major said.

"Well, then," Colonel Jiggs said, "we won't have to send for him, will we?" Then he went into S-3 and informed Captain Lowell that he was now acting S-3 of the 73rd Heavy Tank Battalion (Reinforced).

VIII

[**ONE**]
Pusan, South Korea
12 September 1950

The S-3 sergeant of the 73rd Medium Tank Battalion (Separate) was Technical Sergeant Prince T. Wallace, RA 33 107 806, of Athens, Georgia. Prince Wallace was a tall, heavy, barrel-chested man of thirty-one. He had been drafted during World War II, served in the North Africa, Normandy, and French campaigns, and had commanded the third tank in the task force under Colonel Creighton W. Abrams in the relief of Bastogne. As a master sergeant, loaded with points for long overseas service, and with decorations for valor and for having been three times wounded, he had been among the first of the troops repatriated and discharged after the war.

He enrolled under the GI Bill of Rights at the Valdosta State Teacher's College in his native Georgia, and completed a year of college training. By then he had come to the conclusion that he really didn't want to be a schoolteacher, and that the prospect of three more years in college was something he didn't want to face. He also decided that he really missed the army, so he went to Fort MacPherson, in Atlanta, and reenlisted.

Since he had been out of the army more than ninety days, he had lost the right to reenlist as a master sergeant. He reentered the army as a private first class and underwent an abbreviated basic training course at Fort Bragg. He was then assigned to the G-3 section, Headquarters V Corps at Bragg, as a clerk-draftsman. He applied for Officer Candidate School, was accepted, and was promoted to corporal before his orders to the OCS at the Ground General School at Fort Riley, Kansas, came through.

In his fourth month at OCS, it seemed quite clear to him that in the shrinking army there was going to be less and less room for officers who did not have a college degree. Looking into the future, he saw himself as a first lieutenant, possibly even a captain, who would be "nonselected" for retention on extended active duty as a reserve officer. There was no way he could qualify for a regular army commission because he did not have a college degree, and no way that he could see to get a college degree. Five or ten years down the road, he would be starting out as an enlisted man again, for the third time.

There was a third possibility for an army career, one which posed few risks. That was appointment as a warrant officer. An "officer" is correctly a "commissioned officer." That is to say, he has a commission, signed by the President of the United States, naming him an officer. Corporals and sergeants are called "noncoms," from noncommissioned. They have no commission. They issue orders under the authority of a commissioned officer. Warrant officers have warrants. They too are not officers (they cannot command), although they are entitled to a salute from enlisted men and their own juniors; and the pay of the four warrant officer grades (Warrant Officer Junior Grade, and Chief Warrant Officer Grades Two through Four) is identical to that of second lieutenant through major. Warrant Officers live in BOQs, eat at officer's messes, and are addressed as "sir" by enlisted men.

Warrant officers were traditionally expert in some military skill, from Explosive Ordnance Disposal to Enlisted Pay. Traditionally, noncommissioned officers in the top two enlisted grades were offered appointment as warrant officers, either directly, because of some skill they had, or as the result of competitive examination. Being made a warrant, and thus accorded the respect paid to an officer, was sort of the unofficial bonus paid to noncoms of long and faithful service. They spent their last few years in an officer's uniform, and were retired with the pay of a captain or a major.

Prince Wallace thought that was the way he would like to go. He would become an expert S-3 sergeant, highly skilled in the planning of military operations and the training required to carry them out, and he would, sooner or later, get his warrant. He would thus have the good life of the officer without the responsibility, and without running the risk of being busted back to the ranks.

Corporal Prince T. Wallace, having voluntarily resigned from Officer Candidate Status, was ordered to the Far East Command (FECOM) and ultimately assigned to the S-3 section of the 7th Cavalry Regiment, First Cavalry Division (Dismounted) on the island of Hokkaido, again as a clerk-draftsman. He was ordered to the First Cavalry Division's NCO Academy, and as a reward for having graduated at the top of his class, promoted sergeant. He was reassigned to First Cavalry Division (Dismounted) Headquarters, as Noncommissioned Officer in Charge (NCOIC) of the Logistics Section, Office of the Assistant Chief of Staff, Plans and Training, G-3. In the vernacular, he was now the First Cav's G-3 logistics sergeant.

A year later, he was promoted staff sergeant, and it was as a staff sergeant that he prepared to deploy to Korea when the gooks came across the border in June 1950. He made it as far as the dock, where his visibly and unashamedly furious G-3 informed him that those miserable sonsofbitches at Eighth Army (Rear) had grabbed him as cadre for some about-to-be-formed tank battalion, and how the fuck they expected the First Cav's G-3 section to function without trained people was something he didn't understand.

Staff Sergeant Prince T. Wallace made a good first impression on Lt. Colonel Paul T. Jiggs, newly appointed commander of the 73rd Medium Tank Battalion. Sergeant Wallace looked like a soldier. His hair was cropped closely to his skull, and his face was cleanly shaven. His fatigue uniform was starched and tailored to fit him like a second skin. His boots glistened.

For a couple of days, Lt. Colonel Jiggs toyed with the notion of making Wallace either the first sergeant of Headquarters and Service Company, or the sergeant major of the battalion itself. He had met both those senior noncommissioned officers and found them wanting.

But he had also met his S-3, Major Ellis, and formed the instant opinion that the man was going to need all the help he could get. Staff Sergeant Prince T. Wallace, who had been logistics sergeant for the First Cavalry Division G-3 section, was obviously the man to give him that help.

Colonel Jiggs took Staff Sergeant Wallace for a ride in his jeep and explained the situation to him. What the battalion needed was a good S-3 sergeant, even more than a sergeant major or a Headquarters and Service Company first sergeant. You could pick up sergeant majors and first sergeants anyplace; S-3 sergeants, *good* S-3 sergeants, were goddamned hard to find. Jiggs told Wallace that he recognized it was costing Wallace a couple of stripes, for the TO&E slot for an S-3 sergeant was only a technical sergeant, paygrade E6, as opposed to the paygrade E7 authorized for first sergeants and sergeants major. Staff Sergeant Wallace told Lt. Col. Jiggs that he understood the situation, and would do his best as the S-3 sergeant. Lt. Colonel Jiggs that same afternoon went to G-1 at Eighth Army and made an obnoxious prick of himself until the G-1, just to get rid of him, came through with authority to promote Staff Sergeant Wallace to technical sergeant, paygrade E6, immediately.

Jiggs's snap judgments of both Major Ellis and Sergeant Wallace were quickly vindicated. Without Wallace, Ellis would have fallen flat on his face. Ellis tried hard, but he just couldn't hack it. Jiggs tried very hard to have him replaced before the 73rd went to Korea, but there was simply nobody else around.

The first time Captain Craig W. Lowell met Technical Sergeant Wallace, he too formed a snap judgment, but not quite the "now *there's* a *noncom*" judgment of Lt. Colonel Jiggs. What Captain Lowell decided, when he became aware of Technical Sergeant Wallace's eyes surreptitiously on him, was, "Why, that big sonofabitch is as queer as a three-dollar bill."

Captain Lowell's snap judgment, like that of Lt. Colonel Jiggs, was one hundred percent on the money.

Captain Lowell had also decided that it was none of his business, that Wallace was Ellis's problem, and that unless he found out (and he would certainly make no special effort to find out) that Tech Sergeant Wallace was taking teenaged PFCs and corporals into the bunkers, he would not only say nothing but go out of his way to keep from even raising his eyebrows.

At first, Wallace was not very impressed with Captain Craig W. Lowell (except, of course, physically: Wallace thought Lowell was handsome to the point of beauty—like a fucking statue). He did not think it set a good example for an officer, particularly a company commander, to go around without his helmet, and with a Garand slung from his shoulder (two clips of ammo clipped to the strap, like a common rifleman) and a German Luger stuck in the waistband of his trousers instead of the .45 in a shoulder holster considered de rigeur for line-company tank officers. Captain Lowell, moreover, was doing a number of things either without permission or in direct contravention of regulations and the standing operating procedure (SOP).

Sergeant Wallace knew for a fact that Baker Company was drawing comfort rations (cigarettes, toilet paper, writing paper, beer, Coca-Cola, razor blades, and shaving cream) from both Eighth Army (where they were supposed to get them) and from the Korean Communications Zone depot (which supported the rear echelon troops not assigned to Eighth Army), where Captain Lowell had convinced the supply officer that his company wasn't getting anything from Eighth Army.

Wallace subsequently learned that the noncoms of Baker Company were actively engaged in the black market, almost certainly with Captain Lowell's tacit (and probably active) permission. The company's supply sergeant regularly took loads of fired brass 75 mm shell casings into Pusan, where instead of turning them in to the ordnance salvage dump, he bartered them with a Korean black marketeer. In return he would get Korean handicrafts of one form or another (most often things like cheap OD-colored cotton jackets with "I know I'm going to heaven, because I've served my time in hell—Korea 1950" embroidered on them, or pictures of women with grotesquely outsized bosoms, painted on black velvet; but also some really rather beautifully engraved brass dishes, bowls, and ashtrays, made of course from the fired shell casings). The handicrafts themselves were then bartered. As a result, Baker Company always had ice from the Quartermaster Ice Point; it had its own movie projector and a steady supply of 16 mm films from Eighth Army Special Services; and most outrageous of all, Sergeant Wallace knew for a fact, it had its own rolling brothel, operating out of the back of an ambulance. The girls were actually delivered to the troops manning the tanks on the line, and plied their profession in the rear of the ambulance, which was equipped with a mattress, sheets, water for washing, and illuminated by a red night-light from a tank.

On the other hand, as Sergeant Wallace had to admit, Baker Company had the highest percentage of tracked vehicle availability in the battalion; the lowest incidence of heat exhaustion; an almost negligible VD rate; and most important, the highest combat efficiency. Captain Lowell lost fewer men, wounded or KIA, than any other company commander in the battalion; and Baker Company regularly killed more of the enemy than anybody else, because somehow Baker Company's tanks started when they were supposed to start, ran when everybody else's had succumbed to either overheating or old age, and fired whatever had to be fired.

However, it wasn't until Captain Lowell had started "helping out" in S-3 (when Major Ellis had been "snowed under"), that Sergeant Wallace really changed his mind about Captain Lowell. He came to respect Lowell, not only for his professional competence, but for his extraordinary tact and compassion in dealing with Major Ellis. Only he and the colonel, Sergeant Wallace was sure, were aware of what a square object in a round hole Major Ellis was. When he looked at Major Ellis, Sergeant Wallace saw himself (if he had gone through OCS and taken a commission) assigned duties he was simply not equipped to handle, which would have doubtless put him in grave risk of being knocked back to the ranks, if not thrown out of the army entirely.

Technical Sergeant Wallace had been in ths S-3 bunker when the colonel came in and told Major Ellis to get his pot and go for a ride with him. He sensed that something unpleasant was happening, but he wasn't sure what. After Captain "Deadeye" Lowell came in (with his M1 cradled in his arms like a hunting rifle and that German Luger stuck in his belt) and asked, "Where's the Boss?" he realized Captain Lowell didn't know either.

If anything was going to happen to Major Ellis, Sergeant Wallace knew that Captain Lowell would be among the first to know. When he told Captain Lowell the colonel had taken Major Ellis away, Captain Lowell seemed genuinely surprised. He went to one of the folding tables and asked Sergeant Wallace to get him the Wheeled Vehicle Status Report from the safe. Captain Lowell had been very careful about not asking for the combination to the safe; access to the material inside was limited to the commanding officer and the S-3 and, if the S-3 chose, to the S-3 sergeant. Company commanders, even one "helping out" as much as Captain Lowell did, were not supposed to have the combination.

Captain Lowell spent an hour with the Wheeled Vehicle Status Report, and finally came up with a list of vehicles, by serial number and date, to be turned in to the newly established Ordnance Wheeled Vehicle repair facility. The list was neatly typed; Captain Lowell typed nearly as neatly, as fast, and as accurately as Sergeant Wallace himself did.

"When the major returns, Sergeant Wallace, would you tell him those are my recommendations for the overhaul cycle?"

They both knew that Lowell's recommendations would be accepted entirely and without question. But they were playing the game. Wallace was delighted that Lowell had done the overhaul list; if Major Ellis had started on it, it would have been an all-day decision-making process. Major Ellis worried so much about making the wrong decisions and looking like a fool that he took forever to make any decision.

"Sir," Sergeant Wallace said, "may I ask the captain a somewhat personal question?"

"Shoot," Captain Lowell said.

"I've been wondering why the captain doesn't use a holster for the Luger, sir."

"Very good reason," Lowell said, with a smile. "Because it won't fit in a .45 holster. I'm aware that it offends your sense of propriety, Sergeant Wallace, but I don't know what to do about it."

"I have the most remarkable houseboy, sir, Kim Lee Song," Sergeant Wallace said. He saw Lowell's eyes tighten, and he thought: *He suspects.* But he went on. "He has connections to get things made of leather, sir. I don't mean the garbage you can buy along the side of the road. I mean quality goods."

"You think he can have a holster made for this?" Lowell said.

"I'm sure he could, sir," Wallace said.

Lowell pulled the Luger from his waist and handed it butt first to Wallace.

"There's a round in the chamber," he said. "Be careful with it." Then he reached in his pocket and passed over an oblong piece of brass. "I want that mounted on the holster somewhere," he said. Wallace looked at it, and after a moment recognized it as a German Army belt buckle. The words GOTT MIT UNS were cast into it.

"It came with the pistol," Lowell said, "and I want it on the holster."

It was, Sergeant Wallace recognized, something Lowell was not prepared to discuss.

"Yes, sir," Wallace said. "I understand."

"If Major Ellis wants me," Lowell said, "I'll be at the company."

"Yes, sir," Sergeant Wallace said.

A few moments later Colonel Jiggs entered the bunker. Sergeant Wallace called "attention," and the enlisted men jumped to their feet. Lowell continued what he was doing; his back turned to Wallace, he was tucking his shirt in his trousers.

"Rest," Jiggs said. "I was about to send for you, Lowell," he added.

"Yes, sir," Lowell said. "You caught me on my way out."

Jiggs took Lowell's arm and led him deeper into the bunker to Major Ellis's desk, and then handed him a piece of paper. Lowell's eyebrows went up as he read it. The colonel said something to him that Wallace couldn't hear, then patted Lowell on the arm, and walked out of the bunker. Lowell looked over at Wallace, and then sat down at Major Ellis's desk. He had never done that before, and Sergeant Wallace again sensed that something was up. Lowell motioned with his finger for Wallace to come over.

"Yes, sir?" Tech Sergeant Wallace asked.

"Major Ellis has been hospitalized with a lower back condition," Lowell said, his voice devoid of intonation. "I have just been named acting S-3."

"May I ask the captain how long the major will be gone?"

"At least thirty days," Lowell said.

"But it is not anticipated that a replacement for the major will be assigned?" Wallace asked.

"If anyone asks, Sergeant, we expect that the major will return tomorrow. Between you, me, and the colonel, however, the major will be gone at least thirty days."

"I'm sure the captain will be able to hold things down."

"You really think so, Wallace?" Lowell said. "Here's something else between you, me, and the colonel." He handed Wallace the small piece of paper Colonel Jiggs had handed him. It was a message form, and it had been filled out in pencil:

FROM: CG, ARMY EIGHT

TO: CO, 73RD HV TNK BN

MESSAGE: PREPARE TO MOVE REINFORCED COMPANY STRENGTH FORCE 75 MILES DIRECTION SUWON ON LINE PUSAN KOCHANG SUWON ON TWO HOURS NOTICE. EXPECT MOVEMENT ORDER WITHIN SEVEN DAYS.

WALKER
LT GEN

"We have been augmented by a bunch of troops," Lowell said. "The colonel is going to send a list over as soon as he has it copied. As soon as we have it, I want you to take a three-quarter-ton truck and go collect their company clerks."

"Sir?"

"Who knows more about a company than the company clerk?" Lowell asked. "And besides, most of them can type, and we're going to have a lot of typing to do around here in the next couple of days."

"Yes, sir," Wallace said.

"Wait a minute, Wallace," Lowell said.

"Sir?"

"I don't want anybody to know about this, or anything I do, or anything I tell you to do, but you, me, and the colonel."

"Of course, sir."

"From what I've seen of you, you're one hell of an S-3 sergeant, and I would miss you. But the minute you open your mouth, you're going to be back inside a tank. You understand me?"

"Yes, sir," Tech Sergeant Wallace said.

"I have enough trouble with the colonel as it is," Lowell said with a smile, "without having other people feed him arguments."

"I understand, sir."

"I'm glad you do, Sergeant Wallace," Lowell said. "You're a big sonofabitch, and if I can't get you to play ball with me, I'd frankly hate to have to stick the bat up your ass." He paused. "I would, of course. It would be difficult, but I would."

"I believe the captain and I understand each other, sir," Wallace said.

[TWO]
Near Chinhae, South Korea
13 September 1950

Captain Philip S. Parker IV, commanding Tank Company, 24th Infantry, turned his jeep into a bowl in the terrain formed by a nearly complete circle of low hills, and stopped.

He looked up the rim of the bowl, examining the positions of his tanks. They were placed at more or less regular distances along the rim, right in with the infantry. Here and there were multiple .50 caliber machine guns, mounted on half-tracks, manned by artillerymen who had arrived in Korea expecting to sit on a hilltop someplace waiting for enemy airplanes and instead found themselves sitting between tankers and infantry-men on the front line.

Parker also looked at the dirt roads leading to his tanks and the half-tracks, as he did almost every day. He was looking for deterioration in the roads. He wanted to be sure that if they had to move the vehicles (if they had to bug out, in other words), they could.

He was an unimportant company commander, who had no idea of the big picture, but he had a gut feeling that things could not continue as they were. Either the North Koreans would get off their ass, and mount an offensive which would succeed in breaking through the Pusan perimeter, or the Americans would get off theirs and really counterattack.

There was some reason to believe the latter would be the case. There had been some replacements and some resupply. He had been astonished and pleased to see a column of brand-new M46 tanks rolling through Pusan one day. If there were M46 tanks, they could counterattack. He had experienced a moment's wild hope that he would be reequipped with M46s, but then had faced reality. The 24th Division—and his regiment—were on the Eighth Army shitlist. They were unreliable.

Eighth Army was not about to turn over new M46 tanks to the niggers. The niggers would more than likely promptly turn them over to the gooks, the way they had when they first came.

Even Tank Company of the 24th Infantry had given most of its tanks away before Parker had assumed command. That's what they would remember, not that after Parker had assumed command, Tank Company of the 24th hadn't lost one tank, or bugged out an inch without being ordered to do so.

It was known, Parker thought bitterly, as guilt by association, and there wasn't one fucking thing he could do about it.

He was a fourth-generation cavalry soldier, and he was convinced that he had fought as well, and been as good an officer, as his ancestors. But so far as Eighth Army was concerned, he was just one more nigger.

His father had warned him to expect this sort of thing. He had pointed out that the appellation "Buffalo Soldiers," applied to the 9th and 10th (Colored) Cavalry in the Plains and Indians war, had had nothing to do with the bison that roamed the plains, but had been a derogatory reference to the short, bristly, buffalo-like hair on the heads of the Negro troops.

He was surprised when an incoming artillery round detonated about seventy-five yards from where he sat in his jeep. You could usually hear them coming in. He hadn't heard this one until it went off. It was probably a single harrassing round, designed more to keep everybody nervous than for any other purpose. But you never could tell, and it never hurt to be careful. So far he had gone without so much as a scratch, even when things had been really hairy for a while. He had lost half the people he'd come to Korea with.

He reached down and flipped on the jeep's ignition switch, moving his right leg up so that he could tromp on the gas pedal at the same time. He felt something slippery.

What the fuck am I sitting in?

He looked down and saw that the seat was covered with something red, and that it was all over his pants. It was a moment before he realized what it was. He'd been hit; that red stuff was his blood.

He argued with himself: I didn't feel a thing. How can I be hit, if I didn't feel a thing? How can I be hit if I don't feel a thing *now*? But there was no goddamned question about it: that was blood.

He continued to start the engine. It didn't hurt him to move his leg. He put the jeep in gear, and drove to a battalion aid station, built against the slope of the hills, a sandbag-covered shack with a Red Cross sign leaning against it.

He blew the horn and a medic came out, and he waved him over to the jeep.

"Yes, sir?"

Parker pointed to the seat, and to his blood-covered rear end.

"What the hell happened?" the medic asked.

"I'll be goddamned if I know," Parker said.

"You got hit, Captain," the medic pronounced professionally.

"No shit," Parker said, sarcastically.

"Looks like a piece of shrapnel," the medic said. "Hurt much?"

"No," Parker said.

"It will," the medic said, matter-of-factly. "I think we better get you onto a stretcher, so's we can get you over to the MASH. Way you're bleeding, you're going to have to go to the MASH."

It didn't hurt even to get out of the jeep, and to walk into the aid station. But almost as soon as he was face-down on a stretcher, and the medic had cut his fatigue pants away from his buttocks, it began to hurt. It began to hurt like hell.

The battalion surgeon, who had been asleep, was summoned, and he took one look at Parker's rear end and said that he wasn't in any danger. He would probably be back on duty in a month or six weeks, maybe sooner; but in the meantime, he could expect that it was going to hurt like hell.

"You better get some blood in him," the surgeon said to the medic. "And slap a compress on his ass. They can do the rest at the MASH."

Parker could cheerfully have kicked the surgeon in the balls.

Where were you wounded in the war, Daddy?

Why, Son, your heroic daddy caught one in the ass.

Shit!

[THREE]
Headquarters, 73rd Heavy Tank Battalion (Reinforced)
Pusan, South Korea
14 September 1950

Surprising neither Lt. Colonel Paul T. Jiggs nor Technical Sergeant Prince C. Wallace, Captain Craig W. Lowell built Task Force Bengal, as the "reinforced company" was now known, around Company "B." Lowell was still officially the Baker Company commander, despite his "temporary" assignment as battalion S-3 ("pending the return of Major Ellis from the hospital"); and he transparently hoped to be given command of Task Force Bengal. If it was built around his company, his chances of that happening were obviously enhanced.

"You will notice, Sergeant Wallace," Lowell said, "that the word 'reinforced' in reference to the company to be reinforced has not been defined. The amount of reinforcement is being left to our judgment, that is to say, my judgment. I intend to err on the side of generosity."

Orders were drawn augmenting Company "B" by one platoon of M46s from Able Company and another from Charley Company; and by a platoon of light M24s for "reconnaissance."

" 'Reconnaissance' my ass; we'll use them to guard the fuel and ammo trucks," Lowell said. "We're going to reconnoiter by fire, with Wasps."

" 'Wasps'?" Sergeant Wallace asked. He had never heard the term before.

"What you do is mount another .50 in the back of a weapons carrier," Lowell said. "And you make sort of a turret for the one in the back, and the one in the front, out of sandbags and old fuel drums. Then you barrel-ass down the road, shooting at anything that moves or that looks like it could be a machine gun or artillery emplacement. The natural tendency of people being shot at, Wallace, is to shoot back. And while they're shooting back at the Wasps, we blow them away with the M46s."

"But what about the people in the Wasps?"

"They run like hell at the first shot," Lowell said. "That makes them a lousy target, and at the same time their evasive action keeps the bad guys from thinking about the tanks, which can then, almost at their leisure, blow them away."

"Does the colonel know about the Wasps?" Wallace asked.

"Not yet," Lowell said.

"What do you think he will say when you tell him?"

"He will probably be just as enthusiastic about the Wasps as I am about the overly melodramatic name he's chosen for this little excursion of ours."

"I don't know, Captain," Wallace said, doubtfully.

"Do you understand what's really going on here?" Lowell asked.

"Maybe it would be better if you told me," Wallace replied.

"Well, take a look at the map. There is no railhead at Koch'ang. It is not a major road hub. The river is fordable at this time of year, so there's no bona fide necessity to grab the bridge. Which poses the question, why the fuck are we going to Koch'ang in the first place?"

"Forgive me, Captain. Because we're ordered to?"

"That, too, of course. But why the order?"

Wallace shrugged his admission of ignorance.

"To see what Eighth Army is facing behind the lines," Lowell said. "We're being sent out to see how far we can get before we get blown away."

"You're not suggesting that they're sacrificing us, are you?"

"They don't use that word, but don't you believe they give a shit what happens to us, just so they get the information they think they need."

"That's a brutal assessment."

"They call this war, you know," Lowell said dryly. "It's a perfectly reasonable thing for them to do. The question then becomes what do we do after we do what we are ordered to do."

"You've lost me," Wallace admitted.

"OK. We're ordered to Koch'ang. So we get to Koch'ang. Then what?" Wallace looked at him in confusion. "Look at it this way," Lowell went on. "Eighth Army is willing to spend us to find out how strong the North Koreans are between here and Koch'ang. OK, so we do that. Quicker than they think. So that leaves us in Koch'ang. So then we come back? That doesn't make any sense. To come back directly, I mean. Let's stay behind the lines and raise hell until we have to come back."

"We'd have to be supplied by air."

"Only with ammo. We can take enough fuel and rations with us. Make up a two-day ammo requirement. Triple ration for all the guns. Regular ration for small arms, except for .50 caliber. I want a lot of that."

"Yes, sir," Sergeant Wallace said. "But the colonel's not going to like this."

"Let's present him with a fait accompli and let him shoot that down."

"Yes, sir," Sergeant Wallace said. He was glad again that he hadn't taken a commission. Coming up with something like Captain Lowell had would have been impossible for him. He would never have dared to suggest, much less try to accomplish, something like Captain Lowell was doing. He wondered why he wasn't sure that Colonel Jiggs would shoot Captain Lowell down.

While Wallace prepared the lists of ammo requirements, Lowell studied the maps. He triumphantly laid a proposed route before Wallace.

"This is what we'll do," he said. "It'll take us only the twenty-four hours, maybe less, that backtracking down our original line of advance would. We can take the airdrop either at Koch'ang, or better yet, here in this area."

"Yes, sir," Sergeant Wallace said, not wanting to argue with him, and not wanting to agree either.

"This'll turn Task Force Bengal—Jesus, what a lousy name—into a real tiger," Lowell said.

He laughed hard at his own pun, and it was contagious. Wallace joined in.

"I thought," Colonel Jiggs said, "that Task Force Bengal had a certain flair to it." They had not seen him come in.

Captain Lowell was embarrassed, Wallace saw, but he was not silenced.

"I've just been having a fascinating chat with Sergeant Wallace, sir," Lowell said. "He has come up with some very interesting ideas."

"Is that so?" the colonel asked. Wallace had no idea what Captain Lowell was talking about.

"The sergeant," Lowell said, "was pointing out on the map to me how we could turn this probing mission into a real, oldtime, behind the lines cavalry raid." At that point, Colonel Jiggs realized whose ideas Lowell was advancing, but he winked at Wallace and didn't interupt Lowell.

"I've underestimated you, Sergeant Wallace," Lt. Colonel Jiggs said. "If I didn't know better, I would think that these ideas came from the fevered brain of someone who had gone to the Wharton School of Business."

"I have an idea or two of my own, Colonel," Lowell said.

"I'm sure you do," Lt. Colonel Jiggs said. "Just so that Wallace doesn't get all the glory."

"Wasps," Lowell said.

"I beg your pardon?"

"What you do is mount .50s in three-quarter-ton trucks," Lowell began.

"And you have a vision, do you, of riding in the lead, what did you say, 'Wasp'? Leading, so to speak, this grand and glorious cavalry sweep?" Colonel Jiggs's remarks got to Lowell. He realized the colonel was mocking him, and he shut up.

Then the colonel said, "It might work. But have you got time to set something like that up?"

"Baker Company's got five ready to go, Colonel."

"You will ride in a tank," Colonel Jiggs said. "In an M46, not an M24, and you will be no closer to the point of the column than the fourth vehicle."

"May I infer from that that the colonel has decided I am to be allowed to command the column?" Lowell asked.

"Captain Lowell, where else am I to find someone who devoutly believes he is the combined reincarnation of George Armstrong Custer and George Smith Patton? Or dumb enough to try what you obviously intend to try?"

"Thank you, Colonel," Lowell said, and Sergeant Wallace saw that he said it humbly.

"Why 'Wasps'?" Colonel Jiggs asked.

"They sting," Lowell said. "You know, like a wasp."

"What an overly melodramatic nomenclature," Lt. Colonel Jiggs said dryly. "Why, that's nearly as bad as Task Force Bengal."

"My head, sir," Lowell said, "is both bloody and bowed."

"I came in here with one thing on my mind," Lt. Colonel Jiggs said. "Now I have three things. First, if you really think that you can go further and faster than anyone else does, you'd better think about what kind of supplies you'll need to have air-dropped."

"Sergeant Wallace has just about finished drawing up our requirements, sir," Lowell said.

"I can have them for you in an hour, sir," Wallace said.

"OK. That brings us to Item Two. Don't you plan on going along to the Little Big Horn, Wallace. After the Indians do in Custer here, I'm going to need you."

"I'd really prefer to go along, sir. I'm a tank comm—"

"Goddamnit, *I'd* really prefer to go along, too," Colonel Jiggs snapped. "You stay, Wallace, and that's it."

"Yes, sir," Wallace said.

"Item Three," Colonel Jiggs said, and took a message form from his pocket and handed it to Lowell. Lowell read it, and handed it to Wallace.

```
FROM: CG, ARMY EIGHT
TO: CO, 73RD HV TNK BN

AT 0425 HOURS 15SEP50 FOLLOWING LIFTING OF A THIRTY MINUTE
ARTILLERY BARRAGE TASK FORCE BENGAL, AUGMENTED AS YOU SEE FIT
FROM FORCES AVAILABLE TO YOU, WILL PASS THROUGH THE LINES AND
ATTACK ON THE LINE PUSAN KOCHANG SUWON ENGAGING TARGETS OF
OPPORTUNITY BUT WITH PRIMARY MISSION OF REACHING KOCHANG AS
SOON AS POSSIBLE.
                                                      WALKER
                                                      LT GEN
```

[FOUR]
Pusan, South Korea
0415 Hours
15 September 1950

Task Force Bengal began to actually form only when the artillery barrage began at 0355 hours. The various components of it—a dozen tanks here; the self-propelled howitzers there; the dogfaces on their six-by-sixes; the Signal Corps radio trucks; the ammo trucks; the fuel trucks—had formed separately; and when the barrage began, they started to converge on the departure point.

Captain Lowell was already there, of course, and the first sergeant of Baker Company (who was going) and Technical Sergeant Wallace (who wasn't) stood on the road like traffic cops, making sure the vehicles were in line where they were supposed to be.

When the barrage started, the sky had been dark, and the flare of the cannon muzzles had been almost exactly like a lightning storm. But as the barrage continued, the sky grew lighter; and the artillery was less visible. It was still audible, however, a ceaseless roaring as the shells passed overhead.

Colonel Paul T. Jiggs, to his fury, had been summoned by a messenger from Eighth Army Forward. He had been afraid that Task Force Bengal was about to be scratched. But that wasn't what Victor Forward wanted him for.

He raced up to the head of column, where he found Captain Craig W. Lowell leaning on an M46. There had been changes to the M46 since Lt. Colonel Jiggs had last seen it the previous afternoon.

It was now named. ILSE had been painted on the turret. What the hell, that was his wife; he was entitled. But what pissed the colonel was the guidon flying from one of the antennae. It was the guidon of Baker Company, a small yellow flag with a V-shaped indentation on the flying end. As originally issued, it had read "B" and below that "73." Baker Company of the 73. The yellow identified it as cavalry, or armor.

Someone had carefully lettered "Task Force Lowell" on the guidon.

Jiggs controlled his temper after a moment. He knew where the change had come from. Lowell hadn't done it. His troopers had done it. They had been shoving everyone's nose in the dog shit ever since they had been picked as the nucleus of Task Force Bengal, and especially since the word had gotten out that their CO, the Duke, was to command.

Lowell stood erect and saluted as Colonel Jiggs walked up. He was as worried as Jiggs that the last-minute call had meant the operation had been either delayed or scratched.

"I like your guidon, Lowell," Colonel Jiggs said.

"That wasn't my idea, Colonel," Lowell said, embarrassed.

"Of course not," Jiggs said, sweetly, letting him sweat. He handed him a sealed manila envelope. "Signal Operating Instructions," he said.

"It goes?"

"It goes."

"Thank God! I was scared shitless when they called you to Victor Forward."

"And something else, Lowell, which explains a whole hell of a lot."

He handed him a message form.

FROM: SUPREME COMMANDER
TO: ALL US FORCES IN KOREA

AT 0200 HOURS 15SEP50 ELEMENTS OF THE FIRST U.S. MARINE DIVISION, AS PART OF THE X UNITED STATES CORPS, LT GEN EDWARD M ALMOND, USA, COMMENCED AN AMPHIBIOUS INVASION OF THE KOREA PENINSULA AT INCHON NEAR SEOUL.

MACARTHUR
GENERAL OF THE ARMY

"It's about time we got off our ass," Lowell said.

"So what you are is a diversion," Jiggs said. "The more hell you can raise, the better."

"Diversion, hell. I'll head for Seoul!"

"First try to get to Koch'ang, Captain Lowell," Colonel Jiggs said.

Lowell looked at his watch.

"I better get cranked up, Colonel," he said.

"First get to Koch'ang, Captain," Jiggs said.

"Yes, sir."

Colonel Jiggs put out his hand.

"Try to stay alive," he said. "And remember, you are not George Patton."

Lowell looked at him for a moment, and then he smiled. He put his fingers in his mouth, whistled shrilly, and caught the attention of the driver of the M46 behind his. Then he extended his index finger, held it over his head, and made a "wind it up" signal. A starter ground, and an 810 horsepower engine burst into life.

"Watch it, Craig," Colonel Jiggs said, laying a hand on his shoulder. "I want you and everybody else back alive."

Lowell was embarrassed by the emotion. He nodded his head, and then started to climb up the bogies and onto the M46 he had just named ILSE.

The barrage stopped precisely on schedule. And precisely on schedule, Task Force Bengal began to roll across the line of departure.

Lowell went first. He would put his Wasps out front only after he had gotten behind the enemy lines.

Lt. Colonel Jiggs stood where Lowell's tank had been parked, waving his hand and even sometimes returning salutes, as the task force rolled past him, vehicle after vehicle, seemingly forever.

At that moment, he hated Captain Lowell, who was taking his troops into battle, while he had to stay behind to wage war with the chair-warmers at Eighth Army.

[FIVE]
57th U.S. Army Field Hospital
Giessen, Germany
23 September 1950

Major T. Jennings Wilson, QMC, Chief, Winter Field Equipment, U.S. Army General Depot, Giessen, had been awake in his private room on the top floor of the hospital since daybreak, even before they brought him his breakfast.

He was horribly hung over, and it hurt him to breathe. He'd either broken some ribs when he slammed into the steering wheel, or at the very least, given himself one hell of a bruise. His knees were sore, too. They had probably slammed against the dashboard. Goddamned kraut!

Major Wilson had searched his memory. He was a little confused. Christ, anybody would be confused, but he didn't think they'd taken a blood sample, so he was probably safe from a charge that he was drunk. He didn't remember things clearly from the moment of the crash until he sort of came to in the X-ray room.

He did remember some things. He remembered getting out of the Oldsmobile, after the crash and looking at the Jaguar long enough to see that the woman driving it was dead, and that the car had kraut license plates. That was going to cause him trouble. There weren't that many krauts with enough money to drive Jaguars, and that meant it was the kind of kraut who would probably sue the shit out of him in a German court, before German judges. Did the German courts have juries? If they did, obviously there would be German jurors, who would not only find him guilty, but sock him with a million dollars' worth of damages.

Fuck it, that's what you bought insurance for. That was the insurance company's problem, not his. His problem was getting through this without seeing his career go down the toilet. The army got hysterical when you got in a wreck involving a German national. It was bad for German-American relations, and the army was going ape-shit lately about German-American relations. The bullshit they were passing out was that the U.S. Army was a "guest" of the German people.

Bullshit. The U.S. Army was here because they'd beat the Germans in War II.

He went over and over in his mind what had happened, and by the time the MPs showed up, he was reasonably sure that he was home free. Oh, there were going to be problems, of course. He was going to need a new car. The Olds was demolished; the whole fucking front end was gone. And he knew he could count on trouble with the insurance company. They were going to have to pay for this, of course, but then, sure as Christ made little apples, they were going to cancel his insurance. Or jump his premiums.

And he'd probably given Dolores fits. He remembered that the doctor who had examined him had said that his wife had been notified and told that she should wait until today to see him, that they wanted to keep him under observation for twenty-four hours. Dolores sometimes went off the deep end when something like this happened. She wouldn't understand that it was just one of those things that happens sometimes. He was sorry about the kraut woman, naturally. Nobody likes to be involved in a fatal accident. It was a goddamned shame, and he was sorry about it, but things like this happened, and it seemed to be his turn to have it happen to him.

He knew the MPs would get involved. They investigated every accident. And when it was a bad one, like this one, they sent Criminal Investigation Division, CID, agents to do the investigating. CID agents were MP sergeants who wore civilian clothes, the army equivalent of police detectives.

Major Wilson was not surprised, either, that the CID agents who came into his room were wearing officer's pinks and greens. All they wore was officer's U.S. insignia on the lapels. No insignia or rank or branch of service. Just the officer's uniform permitted to civilian employees in Civil Service Grade GS-7 or better. What the hell, pinks and greens looked good, and if he had been an MP sergeant, he'd probably have done the same thing.

"Major Wilson?" the older of the two CID agents asked.

"That's right," Major Wilson replied.

The credentials of a CID agent, a leather folder carrying a badge and a plastic-covered ID card, were flashed in his face.

"I'm Lieutenant Colonel Preston, Major Wilson," the older of the two CID agents said. "And this is Agent MacInerney."

Major Wilson wondered, fleetingly, if he really was a light colonel, or whether that was some sort of technique they used, making believe they ranked you to get you off balance. He decided it didn't matter. What was important for him was to handle these two very carefully.

"How do you do, sir?" Major T. Jennings Wilson said, politely.

"I guess you know why we're here, Major," Preston said. "To talk to you about the collision yesterday afternoon."

"I understand," Major Wilson said.

"And I'm sure you're aware of your rights under the 31st Article of War? I mean, I'm sure you know that you don't have to say anything to us that would tend to incriminate you? Or, for that matter, that you don't have to talk to us at all?"

"Yes, of course," Major Wilson said. "I'll answer any questions you have, Colonel. Any that I can."

"Thank you for your cooperation," Preston said. "I guess the best way to go about this, if you don't mind doing it this way, would be for you to just tell us what happened, in your own words. Would that be all right with you?"

"I'll do my best, sir," Major Wilson said.

"And the best place to start, of course," Preston said, "is at the beginning. I understand you were in Bad Hersfeld. Is that so?"

"Yes, sir," Major Wilson said. "I was in Hersfeld for the past two days. I was with the G-4 of the 14th Constabulary. I'm chief of the Winter Equipment Division of the Depot, and I was up there trying to get a line on the requirements of the 14th for the upcoming year."

"I see," Preston said. "And you were coming back here when this happened?"

"I almost made it," Wilson said, wryly. "Yes, sir, that's right."

"When did you leave Hersfeld?"

"After lunch," Major Wilson said.

"Have you got an approximate time?"

"Oh, say, and I really don't remember, precisely, 1400, something like that. It was really a working lunch."

"And you drove straight through? You didn't stop anyplace?"

"I drove straight through."

"Then you made pretty good time, didn't you? The collision took place at 1630, according to the German police."

That idle question worried Major Wilson. Of course he had made good time. And the only way to make good time was to speed. What were these bastards up to? Were they going to divide the miles traveled by the time it took, and then charge him with speeding? He had heard they were capable of chickenshit like that. But then he thought that through. To do that, they would need witnesses to swear that he had left at a precise time, and he didn't think anybody could truthfully swear to the time he'd left the club in Hersfeld.

"Yes, sir," he said. "I guess I did. There was hardly any traffic on the roads."

"Tell me what you remember about the accident," Preston suggested.

"Well, truthfully," Major Wilson said, "not much. It all happened so quickly."

"You remember where it happened?" Preston asked.

"Yes, of course. About four, five miles out of Giessen. There's a series of curves in the road there, S's, I guess you'd call them. You really have to take them slowly. Well, as best as I recollect, Colonel, I was in the second or third curve, when all of a sudden this kraut comes around the curve in the other direction, coming out of Giessen, I mean to say, going like the hammers of hell. A Jaguar. You know how those krauts, the ones with enough money to drive a car like a Jaguar, drive."

"Go on."

"Well, that's all there is to tell. I tried to get out of her way, but she was on my side of the road, and there was nothing I could do."

"You say the Jaguar was speeding?"

"Going like hell," Major Wilson said.

"What about you?"

"Hell, I know that road, sir. I wasn't going more than thirty-five or forty."

"Had you been drinking, Major?"

"To tell you the truth, I had a couple of drinks over lunch at the club in Hersfeld. I know, duty hours and all that, but I'd put in a tough day and a half."

"A 'couple' is two," Preston said.

"I think two is all I had, sir," Major Wilson said.

"The collision, Major Wilson, is under investigation by both the army and the German police."

"Well, I'm not surprised," Major Wilson replied.

"Why do you say that?"

"Well, the obvious reason. They get an American officer in front of a German court, an American carrying all the insurance they make us carry, and they can walk away with a bundle. You could hardly call it a trial by my peers."

"You'll be tried by your peers, Major. I think you can count on that."

"Well, that's good news," Major Wilson said. "I'll take my chances before an American court-martial any time. We know how crazy these krauts drive."

"I don't think I'm making myself clear," Preston said. "You're going to face a civil suit in the German courts. And criminal prosecution by a court-martial."

"I don't understand, sir."

"Your story doesn't wash, Major," Preston said. "For openers, we already have statements from the waiter of the officer's club in Hersfeld. You had five drinks, not two, at lunch. And then at a quarter to four, you stopped at the Gasthaus zum Golden Hirsch in Kolbe and drank two bottles of beer, to wash down two drinks of Steinhager. They remember you clearly because you were offensive when they had no American whiskey to offer."

"I deny that, of course," Major Wilson said.

"Let me go on," Preston said, icily. "The Jaguar wasn't speeding. We know that for two reasons. One, we know that the Jaguar entered the highway approximately one hundred yards from the point of impact. There is an intersection there with a back road, which leads, as you probably know, to the commissary and PX at the QM Depot. The Jag had taken that road. We have witnesses. Two, the gear shift lever of the Jag was locked into second gear by the impact. A Jag won't do more than thirty-five or forty, wide open, in second gear. And we can't prove it, of course, but we consider it unlikely that a woman with a child beside her is going to run her car flat out."

Without really thinking what he was saying, Major Wilson said: "Those krauts drive crazy, and everybody knows it."

"You're wrong about that, too, Major," Preston said. "The woman you killed when you came around that turn at between sixty-five and seventy miles per hour, on the wrong side of the road, isn't what you can really call a 'kraut.' She was a naturalized American citizen. And she was the wife of an American officer named Lowell, who's in Korea."

Major Wilson looked at Preston with horror in his eyes.

"I hope they hang your ass, Wilson," Preston said.

"Colonel . . ." the other CID agent said, trying to shut him up.

"I'd like to prosecute you myself, you shitheel," Preston said, having lost his temper beyond redemption. "They won't let me. But you better get yourself a good defense counsel, because I'm going to do whatever I can to send you to Leavenworth."

The other CID agent took Preston's arm and pushed him out of the room. Major T. Jennings Wilson looked at the closed door for a moment, and then he leaned over the side of the bed and threw up.

[SIX]
Near Osan, South Korea
25 September 1950

The L-5 came out of the mountains just behind Ch'ongju, and flew over the main supply route running through the valley, now jammed with lines of trucks and artillery. It flew around the mountains to Ch'onan. By then the build-up, as the supply line stretched, was less visible. Instead of backed-up traffic, there were small convoys of trucks, some accompanied by tanks, some quite alone. Here and there fires burned. There had been some resistance. The colonel wasn't sure how much of the smoke was from battle, or from what the North Koreans had set afire as they retreated.

Less frequently, in the crisp early morning skies, he could make out the sites of obvious battles. There were smoldering Russian T-34 tanks down there. Once they had learned how to handle them, the T-34s had stopped being invincible. After Ch'onan, the main supply route ran through the coastal valley which went all the way up to North Korea, past Inchon, where on September 15, nine days before General Ned Almond had led the X Corps ashore.

The colonel looked at his map. Twenty kilometers, about fourteen miles, to P'yongt'aek, and again that far from P'yongt'aek to Habung-ni. When he looked out the window, he saw a burning M46, but a hundred yards beyond it, not only the smoldering hulks of four T34s but the bodies of their crews. There had been a fight there, one that would never be recorded in the history books, because the war had passed it.

He had, Colonel Paul Jiggs thought, a bird's-eye view of the battlefield. He corrected himself: a Godlike view. Not here, because what had happened here was finished and done; but on other battlefields he would use an aircraft to see what was going on, while it was going on. To command troops he could see, not troops he had to pray would be where he thought they were. To literally look over that next hill and see what the enemy was up to.

He had the airplane because of Lowell, and he had frankly thought when Lowell requisitioned it that Eighth Army would tell him to piss up a rope. Tank battalions were not authorized aircraft, either for artillery spotting (tank cannon are normally used to engage targets that can be seen by the tank crew and therefore aerial fire direction is not considered necessary) or for purposes of liaison or personnel transport. More than likely he could have written a staff study, justifying the assignment of a light aircraft to the 73rd Heavy Tank (Reinforced) on the basis of its size and intended mission. But that would have taken two weeks to write and six months to be reviewed and acted upon.

Lowell had found a better way. He had found that observation aircraft were authorized to the artillery on the basis of one-half aircraft and one pilot per firing battery. He had presented a requisition on that basis to Eighth Army, and they had approved it, as they would have approved a requisition for two tons of chocolate ice cream: If you can find it, then you're welcome to it. And then Lowell had found it.

The 119th Artillery (Self-Propelled) had lost two of its batteries to the 73rd Heavy Tank (Reinforced). They were in support of IX Corps, and their airplanes had gone into the IX Corps aircraft pool. An official request to IX Corps to relinquish one L-5 and two pilots for it would have been honored, of course. Say, in six months.

Lowell had driven a jeep to the IX Corps airstrip and commandeered an L-5 and two pilots on the spot. Lieutenant Taddeus Osadachy, a 235-pound Polish-American from Hazelton, Pennsylvania, known as "the Gorilla" because of certain facial features some found unattractive, was dispatched in the L-5 with one of the pilots, and Lowell brought the other one back in the jeep. The pilots didn't mind at all, but the IX Corps aviation officer and the IX Corps chief of staff were apoplectic, and had submitted an official complaint through channels.

In the meantime, 73rd Heavy Tank had the L-5, and had used it from the moment Task Force Bengal had crossed the line in order to maintain contact and to fly out the wounded. Lowell had been rampaging through the enemy rear for nine days. He was now nearly halfway up the peninsula. The radio truck had long since been blown away, and about the only reliable communication they had was with the L-5.

Colonel Jiggs picked the microphone from the side of the window, checked to see that the radio was tuned to armor frequency, and then squeezed the mike button.

"Bengal Forward, this is Bengal Six."

To his surprise, there was an almost immediate response. He hadn't expected contact on the first try.

"This is Bengal Forward. Go ahead."

"What are your coordinates, Bengal Forward?" the colonel asked.

"I don't think I'm supposed to say over the radio," the voice replied, "but the Duke said when we stopped that we were about three miles from Habung-ni."

"Let me speak to Bengal Forward Six," the Colonel said. Goddamned kids got half the message. This kid had the message that you weren't supposed to give your coordinates over the radio in case the enemy had captured a map and would be able to locate you with it. So what he did was announce their location in the clear.

"The Duke's helping them refuel," the radio operator said.

"Can you get a message to him?"

"Roger."

"Tell him to hold where he is. This is Bengal Six. You got that?"

"Yes, sir, Colonel, I got it," the radio operator said.

"Is there someplace up there we can land?" Colonel Jiggs asked.

"You could land on the road, I suppose, if the tanks weren't all over it," the radio operator said.

"Then get the tanks off the road," Colonel Jiggs replied, patiently.

"You mean right now?"

"I mean right goddamned now. We'll be there in about five minutes."

"I'll tell the Duke, Colonel," the radio operator said.

"You do that, Son," the colonel said. He hung the microphone back in its hook and bent his head to the side, leaning it against the plexiglass, so he could see further forward that way. It didn't help. The road was empty and still.

And then, a moment later, there they were.

Twenty-five, thirty (he'd started out with thirty-eight M46 tanks were pulled off on both sides of the narrow dirt road. In between the tanks were self-propelled howitzers. The tracked vehicles, tanks, and howitzers had left just enough room on the road for the ammunition and fuel trucks to pass. At the tail end of the column were the M24s, which had been put into use as guards for the fuel and ammo convoys.

Standard tactics prescribed the use of light tanks to reconnoiter ahead of the main force. Lowell was using them in exactly the opposite way, having them bring up the rear. It was a good thing Eighth Army hadn't had time to look closely at Task Force Bengal before it set out. Eighth Army would have shit a brick if they had seen Lowell's Wasps, all their gunners volunteers, the three-quarters loaded at least a half-ton over the truck's rated weight capacity with .50 caliber ammo.

Now Lowell was kind of a hero with Eighth Army. He was really fucking up the enemy's rear. They didn't know which way to run, for at any time they could encounter Lowell's tank column. Even Eighth Army had started calling it Task Force Lowell, first as a joke, and now routinely.

From the air, Jiggs thought, Task Force Lowell—he corrected himself, Task Force *Bengal*—while impressive, was not nearly as impressive as it had been when it had passed through the lines of the 24th Division. That had really been something to witness. They had come down the MSR at full bore, buttoned up, engines roaring, tracks chewing up the road, antennae whipping in the air.

Colonel Jiggs, watching it from the air now, indulged in a little self-pity, thinking that's where he should be, in the first M46, leading his troops. The temptation to assume command himself had been very strong, especially when Eighth Army had changed its mind again and again, each time adding to the Task Force's mission. They were his troops, and it was only fair that he should command them, not some kid who thought he was Patton.

But there were two inarguable facts. Lowell was a splendid commander who could think on his feet, and he continued to prove it. Besides, what was left of Task Force Bengal wasn't really much more than a company. It was amazing he had that much left, but the point was that what was left wasn't much.

And somebody, somebody with rank, had to stay behind and run the store. Somebody with a little rank had to be there to demand trucks and fuel and, as it turned out, four additional airdrops of fuel and ammo when Lowell had run faster and farther than even he thought he could. Jiggs's job was in the rear on the radio and the telephone, shaking his brand-new silver chicken in people's faces.

The colonel thought that nobody—except the troops themselves—had ever thought they'd get this far forward, this fast. Where the lead tank was stopped was the point of the advance of the Eighth Army in its breakout from the Pusan perimeter.

There was activity now on the ground. Trucks began to pull out from where they had been parked, and to head back to the M24s which would guard them on the road back to P'yongt'aek. The tanks started their engines, generating clouds of blue smoke, and pulled up close to the three-quarter-ton Wasps and the lead tank, leaving room on the road for the L-5 to land.

"Can you get in there?" Colonel Jiggs asked the L-5 pilot, the man Lowell had kidnapped, a young lieutenant fresh from civilian life in the States, a man he hardly knew.

"Yeah," he said, thoughtfully. It wasn't disrespectful. At the moment he was just making a professional pilot's judgment, unaware that he was back in the army. "I'll come in from the north. I hope to Christ the bad guys aren't dug in up there. With machine guns, I mean."

He dropped the little plane to no more than a few feet off the ground. They flashed by the trucks, the empty stretch of road, and then the tanks. Then the pilot stood the L-5 on its wing and made a 180 degree turn. They passed over the tanks so low that Colonel Jiggs was genuinely concerned that they would hit the radio antennae. Then they touched down on the dirt road and bounced for perhaps two hundred yards. The pilot stopped the plane and then raced the engine, turning the aircraft around at the same time. Then he taxied back up the road to the rear of the tank column.

The commanding officer of Task Force Bengal, of the 73rd Heavy Tank Battalion, walked, not ran, to where the L-5 had stopped and Colonel Jiggs was climbing out.

Without disturbing the M1 on his shoulder, Captain Lowell saluted. The salute was one half of one degree short of insubordination.

I know what you're thinking, you poor bastard, Jiggs thought. You think I'm here to grab your glory, to lead the column myself.

"How goes it, Lowell?" the colonel said.

"We're ready to roll again, Colonel," Lowell said. "Has something come up?"

"You've really done a bang-up job, Lowell," Colonel Jiggs said. "I know that. More important, Eighth Army knows it."

Lowell didn't even reply.

"I've got a couple of things for you, Lowell," Colonel Jiggs said.

Lowell's eyebrows rose in curiosity, but he didn't say anything. Colonel Jiggs reached in his pocket and came out with a major's gold oak leaf.

"This belongs to Charley Ellis," the colonel said. "He said to tell you you owe him a drink."

"That's nice of him," Lowell said. "I think I would have stayed pissed at me, under the circumstances."

"He's grateful to you," Jiggs said wryly. "Having him named battalion inspector general was a stroke of guardhouse lawyer genius, Lowell."

Lowell smiled, but said nothing.

"You've earned that leaf, Lowell," Colonel Jiggs said, but he did not shake hands or make a formal speech of congratulations.

"Is that all, sir?" Major Lowell said.

"I'm afraid not, Major Lowell," Colonel Jiggs said. The suspicion was instantly back in Lowell's eyes. "I had to make a decision whether to give you this before you made the join-up, or after. I decided that you should have it as soon as I could get it to you." He handed Lowell a folded sheet of teletype paper.

PRIORITY
HQ EUROPEAN COMMAND
FOLLOWING PERSONAL FROM GENERAL CLAY FOR GENERAL WALKER
EIGHTH UNITED STATES ARMY KOREA.

BULLDOG, DEEPLY APPRECIATE YOUR RELAYING FOLLOWING SOONEST TO CAPTAIN CRAIG W. LOWELL, 73RD HEAVY TANK YOUR COMMAND. QUOTE I DEEPLY REGRET TO INFORM YOU THAT ILSE WAS KILLED INSTANTLY IN AUTOMOBILE CRASH NEAR GIESSEN SIXTEEN THIRTY EUROPEAN TIME 22 SEPTEMBER. PETER-PAUL UNHARMED AND WITH HIS GRANDFATHER. LETTER WITH DETAILS EN ROUTE AIRMAIL. SHARON AND I SHARE YOUR GRIEF. SANFORD T. FELTER CAPT UNQUOTE. BULLDOG, FURTHER PLEASE ADVISE THIS OFFICER THAT ALL FACILITIES OF EUROPEAN COMMAND ARE AT HIS DISPOSAL IN THIS PERSONAL TRAGEDY. FINALLY, BULLDOG, ALL OFFICERS AND MEN EUROPEAN COMMAND THRILLED AT YOUR BREAKOUT. BEST PERSONAL REGARDS SIGNED LUCIUS END PERSONAL MESSAGE FROM GENERAL CLAY TO GENERAL WALKER.

SUPPLEMENTAL
FROM SUPREME COMMANDER UNITED NATIONS COMMAND TO GENERAL WALKER EIGHTH ARMY PERSONAL PLEASE CONVEY TO CAPTAIN LOWELL THE PERSONAL CONDOLENCES OF MYSELF AND MRS. MACARTHUR.

MACARTHUR
GENERAL OF THE ARMY

"Oh, *shit!"* Major Lowell said.

The colonel handed him the cap of his flask. It held an ounce and a half of scotch.

"I'm sorry, Lowell," Colonel Jiggs said.

"Shit, even General MacArthur's sorry," Lowell said. Tears were streaming down his cheeks. He drank down the scotch, gasped, coughed. The colonel filled the flask top again, and offered it to Lowell, who shook his head in refusal. The colonel drank it himself.

"Are you all right, Major?" the colonel asked.

"Yes, sir," Lowell said. "Everything's just fucking hunkydory."

"You want to take a few minutes?" the colonel said. "The war will wait."

Lowell didn't even reply. He saluted and started walking up the line of tanks. He had his head bent, and the colonel presumed he was crying. But as he passed each tank, he raised his hand, finger extended, over his head and moved it in a circle. One by one, the tank engines burst into life.

The colonel got back in the L-5, put the earphones on.

"All right," Lowell's voice, tear-choked, came over the radio. "Let's get this fucking show on the road."

"Say again that last transmission," someone replied.

"What I said, Sergeant Donahue," Lowell's voice came back, nearly under control, "was to have the bugler sound the fucking charge!"

The three-quarter-ton Wasps, their gunners in their homemade turrets immediately test-firing the .50s, jerked into motion. The lead tank, Lowell's, the M46 named ILSE, moved out after them. When it had gone fifty yards down the road, the second tank began to roll. Colonel Jiggs waited until they had all gone, and until the dust on the road had settled enough for the L-5 pilot to take off. Then he leaned forward and asked how much fuel there was.

"About an hour, Colonel."

"We'll wait ten minutes, and then take off. That should give us enough time to see what happens."

Thirty minutes later, in the air, when he was sure, Colonel Jiggs tuned the radio to the command frequency and picked up the microphone.

"Victor, Victor, this is Bengal Six."

"Go ahead, Bengal Six."

"Stand by to copy Operational Immediate," Colonel Jiggs ordered.

"Victor ready to copy Operational Immediate."

"To Commanding General, Army Eight," Jiggs dictated. "Operational Immediate. Personal for General Walker. Task Force Lowell, I say again, Task Force Lowell, I spell, Love Oboe Whiskey Easy Love Love, 73rd Heavy Tank, Major Craig Lowell, effected join-up with elements of X United States Corps at 0832 Hours near Osan. Recommend immediate award of Distinguished Service Cross to Major Lowell. Signature is Jiggs, Colonel, commanding 73rd Heavy Tank. You got that?"

"We got it, Colonel."

"OK," Colonel Jiggs said. Then he said to the pilot, "Now we can go home."

[ONE]
The Farm
Fairfax County, Virginia
28 September 1950

Barbara Waterford Bellmon thought of it privately as "Belt Time." It was the time of day, between four thirty and five, when she had a little belt. The kids' problems were taken care of for the day, dinner was well underway, all her parental and wifely obligations for the day satisfied. She took a shower and did her face and her hair, and had nothing more to do but wait for her husband to come home from the Pentagon.

She then made herself a drink, generally a stiff scotch with just a little ice, so that she could taste the whiskey; and she settled herself on the couch before the fireplace, spread the newspaper out beside her, curled her feet under her, and read the newspaper at her leisure.

There was a fire in the fireplace today; it was getting chilly enough for a fire in the fireplace, and she liked that. Her man would come to the cave from a day battling dragons and dinosaurs and find his mate waiting with a fire.

Bob Bellmon came home to a drink and a meal and a smile, rather than to a recitation of what had gone wrong in the Bellmon household. Barbara was proud that she was able to do that much for him. He was still working sixty or more hours a week riding a desk, and she felt sorry for him.

She had a thought that somewhat shamed her. It looked as if the Korean War was about over. That meant Bob wouldn't have a chance to go there to take command of a battalion, that he would have sat out this war at a desk in the Pentagon. Was it wrong to feel sorry for him? Was it wrong to think it a shame that the war was going to be over so soon (MacArthur had been quoted as saying the "enemy was near defeat; the troops should be home by Christmas")? Was there something wrong with her, that she wanted her man to have his chance to go to war?

She flipped the pages of the *Washington Post*, scanning them quickly, reading what looked interesting. A story on the editorial page caught her eye, and she read it.

"My God!" she said, and read it again. And then she shook her head, and smiled, and looked up at the ceiling. And then she jumped off the couch and slipped her feet into loafers, and ran to the front door.

"Bobby!" she shouted. "I have to go to the store for a minute, I'll be right back!"

There was no response.

"Bobby!" she screamed.

Robert F. Bellmon III replied: "I heard you."

"When I talk to you, you answer me!"

"Yes, Mother," Bobby replied, resignedly.

God, she thought, he really is his father's son!

She went out of the house, pulling a sweater over her shoulders against the chill, and got in the Ford station wagon and drove three miles to the crossroads store. There was a stack of seven newspapers on a battered wooden table outside. She picked them all up, laid a dollar bill under the rock that had held them in place, got back in the car, and drove back to the Farm. She entered the house by the kitchen door, laid the newspapers on the kitchen table, and took a pair of scissors from a cabinet drawer.

One by one, she opened each newspaper to the editorial page, cut out the story that had caught her eye, and then neatly stacked the papers on the table, so that Bobby could bundle them up for the boy scout newspaper collection.

Then she took the seven copies of the story and carried them into the library. She took a roll of Scotch tape from the desk drawer, and began to stick the stories up all over the house. She put one on the glass in the front door and one on the glass of the kitchen door, just in case Bob came in the house that way. She stuck one to the mirror in the hall, where Bob would take off his tunic and hat. She stuck one to the mirror over the bar, one to the mirror in the downstairs bathroom, in case he would take a leak on his arrival home, another in their bathroom, and the last one to the mirror over her chest of drawers in their bedroom.

Then she went back and made herself another stiff scotch, sat down on the couch, and waited for Bob to come in.

KOREAN REPORT: The Soldiers

by John E. Moran
United Press War Correspondent

SEOUL, SOUTH KOREA September 26 (Delayed) (UP)—The world has already learned that Lt. General Walton Walker's Eighth Army, so long confined to the Pusan perimeter, has linked up with Lt. General Ned Almond's X United States Corps, following the brilliant amphibious invasion at Inchon.

But it wasn't an army that made the link-up, just south of a Korean town called Osan fifty-odd miles south of Seoul; it was soldiers, and this correspondent was there when it happened.

I was with the 31st Infantry Regiment, moving south from Seoul down a two-lane macadam road, when we first heard the peculiar, familiar sound of American 90 mm tank cannon. We were surprised. There were supposed to be no Americans closer than fifty miles south of our position.

It was possible, our regimental commander believed, that what we were hearing was the firing of captured American anti-aircraft cannon. In the early days of this war we lost a lot of equipment. It was prudent to assume what the army calls a defensive posture, and we did.

And then some strange-looking vehicles appeared a thousand yards down the road. They were trucks, nearly covered with sandbags. Our men had orders not to fire without orders. They were good soldiers, and they held their fire.

The strange-looking trucks came up the road at a goodly clip, and we realized with horror that they were firing. They were firing at practically anything and everything.

"They're Americans," our colonel said, and ordered that an American flag be taken to our front lines and waved.

Now there were tanks visible behind the trucks—M46 "Patton" tanks. That should have put everyone's mind at rest, but on our right flank, one excited soldier let fly at the trucks and tanks coming up the road with a rocket launcher. He missed. Moments later, there came the crack of a high-velocity 90 mm tank cannon. He was a better shot

than the man who had fired the rocket launcher.

There was a soldier in front of our lines now, holding the American flag high above his head, waving it frantically back and forth. Our colonel's radio operator was frantically repeating the "Hold Fire! Hold Fire!" order into his microphone.

His message got through, for there was no more fire from our lines and no more from the column approaching us.

The first vehicles to pass through our lines were Dodge three-quarter-ton trucks. These mounted two .50 caliber machine guns, one where it's supposed to be, on a pedestal between the seats, and a second on an improvised mount in the truck bed. They were, for all practical purposes, rolling machine-gun nests.

Next came three M46 tanks, the lead tank flying a pennant on which was lettered Task Force Lowell. The name "Ilse" had been painted on the side of its turret. There was a dirty young man in "Ilse" 's turret. He skidded his tank into a right turn and stopped. He stayed in the turret until the rest of his column had passed through the lines.

It was quite a column. There were more M46s, some M24 light tanks, fuel trucks, self-propelled 105 mm howitzers, and regular army trucks. We could tell that the dirty young man in the turret was an officer because some of the tank commanders and some of the truck drivers saluted him as they rolled past. Most of them didn't salute, however. Most of them gave the dirty young man a thumbs-up gesture, and many of them smiled, and called out, "Atta Boy, Duke!"

When the trucks passed us, we could see that "the Duke" had brought his wounded, and yes, his dead, with him. When those trucks passed, "the Duke" saluted.

When the last vehicle had passed, the dirty young man hoisted himself out of his turret, reached down and pulled a Garand from somewhere inside, and climbed down off the tank named "Ilse."

He had two days' growth of beard and nine days' road filth on him. He searched out our colonel and walked to him. When he got close, we could see a major's gold leaf on his fatigue jacket collar.

He saluted, a casual, almost insolent wave of his right hand in the vicinity of his eyes, not the snappy parade ground salute he'd given as the trucks with the wounded and dead had rolled past him.

"Major Lowell, sir," he said to our colonel. "With elements of the 73rd Heavy Tank."

We'd all heard about Lowell and his task force, how they had been ranging between the lines, raising havoc with the retreating North Korean Army for nine days. I think we all expected someone older, someone more grizzled and battered than the dirty young man who stood before us.

At that moment our colonel got the word that the young soldier who had ignored his orders to hold fire and two others near him had been

killed when one of Lowell's tanks had returned his fire. The death of any soldier upsets an officer, and it upset our colonel.

"If you had been where you were supposed to be, Major," our colonel said, "that wouldn't have happened!"

Young Major "Duke" Lowell looked at the colonel for a moment, and then he said, "What would you have us do, Colonel, go back?"

There shortly came a radio message for Major Duke Lowell, and he left his task force in Osan. He had been ordered to Tokyo, where General of the Army Douglas MacArthur was to personally pin the Distinguished Service Cross to his breast.

Barbara Bellmon heard Bob's Buick on the stones of the driveway. She pretended to be fascinated with the newspaper spread out on the couch beside her. She heard his footsteps before the front door, and knew that he was reading the newspaper story.

She heard him come in the house. He said nothing to her, and she wouldn't have looked at him if her life depended on it. She heard him go to the bar, where another newspaper clipping hung where he couldn't miss it. She heard him pour himself a drink. He said nothing.

"Oh, for God's sake, Bob," she said, finally. "Don't be such a lousy sport. You were wrong about Craig. Admit it!"

"Lowell didn't go to Japan to get the DSC," Bob Bellmon said. "He went there to go on compassionate leave."

"He doesn't get the medal? What do you mean, compassionate leave?"

"He got the DSC," Bellmon said. "But I don't think he cares one way or the other."

"What are you talking about? What's this about compassionate leave?"

"On September 22," Bob Bellmon said to his wife, "while Ilse was driving home from the commissary at the Giessen Quartermaster Depot, a major, who was drunk, ran head on into her."

"Oh, my God!" Barbara said, faintly, almost a wail.

"Killing her instantly," Bellmon went on.

"P. P.?" Barbara asked, in a hushed voice, her hands in front of her mouth.

"He was thrown clear, and bruised somewhat, but he's alive."

"Oh, my good God!" Barbara repeated. "What can we do?"

"Not a hell of a lot," Bellmon said. "I spoke with the count on the telephone, and Felter sent flowers to the funeral in our name."

"What can we do for Craig?"

"Craig is probably already in Germany," Bellmon said.

[TWO]
Fort Polk, Louisiana
18 April 1951

Major General Ezakiah Black was a good soldier. When he was given an order, he said, "Yes, sir," and without bitching performed that duty to the best of his ability. He had been ordered to assume command of the U.S. Army Replacement Training Center, at Fort Polk, and immediately devoted his best effort and most of his thought to taking a steady stream of enlistees and draftees and recalled reservists and turning them into soldiers.

Fort Polk, a hastily built World War II training camp, had been on "standby" status (for all practical purposes, closed) since the end of War II, when it had been last used as a separation center. The Louisiana National Guard had used a small portion of Polk for summer camp, and there was a small caretaker detachment stationed there. But the post looked like a ghost town when General Black arrived. The parade ground was grown up in weeds, the wooden buildings all needed paint, and the macadam roads had simply deteriorated.

There were problems with sewerage, with electricity, with the telephones, with dry rot in barracks and office buildings, with fuel storage tanks. Anything subject to deterioration from disuse or the elements had deteriorated. The Corps of Engineers let millions of dollars' worth of contracts to bring things up to at least minimal standards, but the post was really not ready when the first trainload of draftees arrived.

Getting it ready, getting the operation running smoothly, was for a month a bona fide challenge to General Black's managerial skills. But after that, the job was a great goddamned bore.

There was a basic nine-week cycle. Recruits arrived, spent a week getting their shots and their uniforms, getting tested, given orientation lectures. Then they started on the eight week, Phase I, of their basic training.

There were six hundred men in each cycle. When the pipeline was full, that meant 4,800 men in one week or another of Phase I. About half of each graduating class remained at Polk for Phase II training as infantrymen. The others were sent to Phase II training in other branches, artillerymen to Sill, tankers to Knox, Signal Corps to Monmouth, and so on. When the first group was in the third week of training, Black was informed his weekly input would be doubled, and that was followed by another burst of frenzied activity to double the number of barracks, and to have their stopped-up toilets fixed, their leaking roofs repaired, and their smashed windows replaced.

But that was it. Things calmed down, and there really wasn't a hell of a lot for a major general to do except follow the course of the war in Korea and keep an eye on Germany, which was where the Russians would strike if they came in.

General Black began to divide his day in two. In the morning he dealt with what he thought of as the current situation. In the afternoons he planned for the future. If the Russians came in, he would be expected to form and train an armored division. He planned, quite unofficially, to do just that. He went over the assets of the post and determined where he would house an armored division, where he would have firing ranges, fuel dumps, beer halls, and garbage dumps.

He went further than that. He started looking around for the equipment an armored division would need. He visited, officially and unofficially, the quartermaster depots and the ordnance depots and the general depots. He looked around the onpost warehouses at Knox and Sill and Benning, to see what they had stored away.

One of the things he had inherited when he got the basic training camp was an army aviator. All he knew about Captain Rudolph G. MacMillan, when MacMillan was proposed to him as an aide-de-camp, was that he had the Medal, that he'd picked up a Silver Star Medal (his third) in the opening days of the Korean War, and that Jesus H. Christ MacArthur himself had written the Deputy Chief of Staff, Personnel (DCS-P) to keep him out of the war. That was enough for Black. Another soldier they didn't want for this war needed a home, and he had a home to give him.

They sent him an airplane pilot, but didn't give him an airplane to go with him. No aircraft, his G-4 had been informed, were available at the moment. They would be sent to Fort Polk when they were available. He didn't think MacMillan stood a chance in hell of getting airplanes or helicopters, but he gave him permission to scrounge for one.

MacMillan disappeared. When General Black asked the G-4 if he had sent him someplace, the G-4's reaction had been one of righteous outrage.

"The general is not aware that Captain MacMillan is in the Panama Canal Zone?"

"No, I'm not," Black said, and stopped himself just in time before he finished aloud the question in his mind: "The Panama Canal? What the *hell* is he doing in Panama?"

"Captain MacMillan informed me, General," the G-4 said, "that he was traveling to Panama VOCG." (Verbal Order, Commanding General.)

"I wasn't aware that he had left," General Black replied, wondering why he had impulsively covered for MacMillan. Because he was entitled to special consideration because of the Medal? Or because the S-1 was such a fucking sissy?

MacMillan returned from Panama with three Hiller H23/CE helicopters. General Black knew so little about helicopters that it wasn't until later that he learned they were not supposed to be flown over such great distances. They were supposed to be disassembled and shipped. MacMillan, with two borrowed Panama Canal Zone aviators, had flown them up, in 150 and 200 mile jumps, via Nicaragua, Costa Rica, Honduras, and Mexico.

It was the first excitement General Black had had recently, and it amused him. MacMillan had learned that the H23/CEs, specially modified versions of the H23 for use in mapping operations by the Corps of Engineers (hence, the CE designation), were in Panama, and not being used, because their pilots and the mapping crews had been sent to Korea.

He had gone down there and talked Panama into turning the machines over to him on the basis that while they were doing Panama no good at all, they could be put to "temporary" use as aerial ambulances at Fort Polk. MacMillan then found two helicopter mechanics who could be transferred and arranged for the medical evacuation helicopters and the mechanics to be assigned to the post hospital, where they would be unlikely to be discovered and even less likely to be taken away if they were.

Next, he arranged for the Medical Corps to assign two helicopter pilots to fly the "med-evacs" and turned one of the H23/CEs—now properly adorned with Red Crosses—over to them. The other two machines he kept, hinting that since there was a parts supply problem, he was going to use one of them for cannibalization. That is, it would furnish parts to the other helicopters, the one at the post hospital and the one which now permitted General Black to travel anywhere on the enormous Polk reservation in comfort and in a matter of minutes, rather than after an hour-long ride down bumpy roads that wouldn't take a staff car.

MacMillan next turned up (in Alaska) a five-passenger Cessna LC-126, an airplane designed for operation in the "bush" of Alaska and Canada. With the first money to fight the Korean War, the army had come up with a new airplane it thought it wanted, another "bush" airplane, a DeHavilland of Canada "Beaver." It was being "user tested" in Alaska, and doing splendidly; and Alaska hoped that by giving one of their old LC-126s to Fort Polk, they would thus be able to plead that they should be allowed to keep a "Beaver" after the user test.

While nothing had been said to General Black about his frequent trips to other posts and the supply depots, he had been a little uneasy. While he had the authority to order himself anywhere he wanted to, it being presumed that he knew what was official business and what was not, copies of the orders he issued to himself for travel to Forts Knox and Benning and the supply depots at Atlanta and Anniston and Lexington were routinely sent to Fourth Army Headquarters at Fort Sam Houston. Eventually, somebody was going to ask him about it, and tell him, either officially or unofficially, that when it was time for him to start gathering the logistics for an armored division, he would be told; and until then, he should not be making a nuisance of himself.

The LC-126 MacMillan had brought back from Alaska and which no one seemed to know about (officially or unofficially) was an ideal means to make his "visits," and traveling in it could be performed without putting himself on orders.

So General Black came to spend a good deal of time in MacMillan's company, visiting the widespread activities of the basic training operation in the H23/CE and traveling to other posts and the supply depots in the LC-126. He learned a good deal about MacMillan that he hadn't known before. General Black, as a colonel and then as a brigadier general, had commanded Combat Command B of the late Major General Peterson K. Waterford's "Hell's Circus" in Europe. He knew about Waterford's son-in-law, Bob Bellmon, being a prisoner. MacMillan had been in the stalag with Bellmon; and at the time Porky Waterford had bought the farm (he had dropped dead playing polo, which everybody who knew him thought was the way Porky would have wanted to go out), MacMillan had been his aide-de-camp.

In General Black's opinion, MacMillan was not overendowed with brains, but he knew how to keep his mouth shut, and there was no question about his scrounging ability. They became, if not quite friends, then a good deal more like pals than a general and his dog robber normally are.

MacArthur sent Ned Almond in with X Corps at Inchon, as brilliant a maneuver as General Black had ever seen. Walker had finally broken out from the Pusan perimeter, and in the first maneuver of General Walker's that met General Black's approval, had sent a flying column, a battalion-sized M46 force, racing around behind the enemy lines. It was a classic cavalry sweep, destroying the enemy's lines of communication, keeping him off balance, and then finally linking up with X Corps.

Almond and X Corps had been on the Yalu when the chinks came in. Black and MacMillan had been at the Lexington Signal Depot.

Almond had pulled X Corps, with all its equipment, all of its wounded, and even its dead, off the beach at Hamhung on Christmas Eve, 1950, after the chinks had chewed up Eighth Army again. Black and MacMillan had spent Christmas Eve in the Prattville, Alabama, Holiday Inn, forced to land there by weather on the way home from a "visit" to the Anniston Ordnance Depot.

Truman relieved MacArthur. General Black was really of two minds about that. MacArthur was right, of course. There is no substitute for victory. But Truman was right, too. Soldiers take orders, and they stay out of politics.

In March 1951, General Black learned that MacMillan had not been using the third H23/CE as a source of "unobtainable" parts to keep the other two flying. When he thought about it, he realized that he should have known that if MacMillan could scrounge entire helicopters, he would have no trouble scrounging parts to keep them flying.

On a Saturday afternoon, drinking a beer on the back porch of the general's quarters after a basic training graduation parade (the general always felt bad watching the trainees march proudly past; in a month, a lot of those handsome, tanned, toughened young men would be dead), MacMillan said if the general didn't have anything important to do on Sunday morning, say about 0900, he had something he wanted to show him.

The general had absolutely nothing to do on Sunday morning.

At exactly 0900, MacMillan fluttered down in the third H23/CE into the general's backyard. There was something hooked up to the skids, and when the chopper was on the ground, the general saw that there was an air-cooled .30 caliber machine gun on the right skid, and four tied-together 3.5 inch rocket launchers on the left.

"What the hell is all this, Mac?" General Black asked, but he got in the helicopter.

"The cavalry rides again, General," MacMillan said. "C Troop of the 7th Cavalry, Second Lieutenant George Armstrong Custer—that's you—has just been ordered to check out a story that Sitting Bull is moving an armored column around the Little Big Horn River. You and your first sergeant, that's me, 1st Sgt. John Wayne, ride out together."

"You're starkers, MacMillan," General Black said, but he was smiling.

MacMillan picked up the H23/CE, not far, not more than fifty feet off the ground, and flying no more than ten feet over the top of the pine trees that covered the Polk reservation, flew out to the Distance Estimation Course.

While located in the range area, the DEC was not a firing range. What it was was a field 1,000 yards long and 400 yards wide on which worn-out trucks and jeeps and even two ancient M3 tanks from War II had been scattered among pill boxes, foxholes, and trenches. Basic trainees were required to estimate how far away the various battlefield targets were from their positions.

"Geronimo, Geronimo," MacMillan's voice came over the intercom. "This is Geronimo Forward. Enemy force consisting of three jeeps, three trucks, and two M3 tanks spotted 1,000 yards from Little Big Horn. Engaging."

"You're in your second childhood, MacMillan. You know that?" General Black said.

"Watch this," MacMillan said. He zoomed low over the DEC, and came to a hover 200 yards from the M3 tank hulks. There was a sudden, frightening whoosh two feet below General Black's feet, followed by an orange flash. A 3.5 inch rocket flashed away, and passed fifty feet over the M3.

"Maggie's Drawers, MacMillan," the general said, making reference to the red flag waved on firing ranges to indicate a complete miss.

"I haven't had very much practice," MacMillan said. "I had one hell of a time stealing these rockets from ordnance."

There was a second roar and a second burst of smoke.

The 3.5 inch rocket hit the M3 hulk's chassis. The hulk seemed to lift, just barely, off the ground, and then settle again. In the split second he had to look before MacMillan moved the helicopter, almost violently, to engage the second M3, General Black saw a cratered hole in the M3, right in front of the driver's hatch. MacMillan hit the second M3 with both of his two remaining 3.5 inch rockets. Then he moved the helicopter 150 yards from the remains of an ancient GMC six-by-six truck.

The .30 caliber machine gun on the other skid began to chatter. There was surprisingly little noise, but General Black felt the entire helicopter vibrate, alarmingly, from the recoil. He was frightened for a moment, but then fascinated as he watched MacMillan move the tracer; stream (every fifth round in a normal belt of machine gun ammo was a tracer; from the steady stream of tracers here, Black realized that MacMillan was firing all tracers) across the ground and into the old truck.

Finally, the ammunition all gone, MacMillan zoomed off from the truck, and flew back to the nearest M3 hulk, where he put the H23/CE gently on the ground, and turned to look at General Black.

"I'm not the brightest guy in the world, General," MacMillan said. "How come I had to figure this out?"

General Black didn't reply. He got out of the H23/CE and examined the crater hole in the M3's hull. And then, impulsively, he hoisted himself onto the tank, and then onto the turret, and lowered himself inside. He'd fought, briefly, in M3s in North Africa as a technical liaison officer with the British, teaching them the M3. The older models, this one, had had riveted hulls. When they were hit, the hulls came apart, and the rivets rattled around the interior of the hull, killing the crews. Later models were welded. The British had called it the "Priest," because the side-mounted cannon made it look something like a pulpit in a church.

The M3s had been replaced by the M4s, and that's what he'd commanded in Europe. And now they were gone. The task force that Walker had sent north from Pusan had had M46s. And now Bulldog Walker was gone. Bulldog bought the farm, in a jeep accident, on Christmas Eve in Korea. And here he sat at Fort Goddamned Polk, Louisiana, giving basic training and dreaming of an armored division he knew goddamned well wasn't coming.

The interior of the M3 didn't stink as bad as he thought it would. There was evidence of animal life, squirrels probably; he didn't think there would be rats.

He squeezed himself into where the driver's seat had been. That 3.5 rocket had blown a neat hole right through the hull. If this had been an operational tank, it would be a dead tank now.

He heaved upward, and with effort got the driver's hatch to open on its rusty hinges. He saw a jeep coming hell bent for election across the field. He ducked back into the hull. Let them think it was MacMillan, alone. Let Mac get rid of them, and they could fly home, and he could consider the ramifications of rocket-armed choppers.

MacMillan certainly was not the first one to think of arming choppers, he thought. But, under that goddamned Key West Agreement of 1948, the army was forbidden armed aircraft. In 1948, when the Defense Department had been formed, and the Air Corps, previously a part of the army, had become a separate service, they'd held a meeting at Key West and defined the roles of the army, the navy (which included the Marine Corps), and the new air force. The air force, logically enough, had been given responsibility for things that flew. They had promised to support the army with air power as needed. It was, on the surface, a logical arrangement, except that it was the air force that decided what the army needed in aerial support, not the army. And the air force was far more interested in spending its budget on intercontinental bombers and rockets than on supporting the dogfaced soldier. Arming aircraft was the air force's—and only the air force's—privilege. The air force was not about to waste money developing armed helicopters when they had the capability of atomizing the enemy. It was General Black's solemn opinion that the Key West Agreement was goddamned stupid.

He thought that it was likely that MacMillan was the first one to actually try rockets and machine guns on choppers. The other people who had thought about it were also smart enough to know about the Key West Agreement and afraid to violate it.

There was the sound of angry voices outside. What the hell was that all about?

General Black stuck his head out of the commander's hatch. A tall, thin light bird, whose name he could not recall, but whom he remembered was the range officer, was giving MacMillan hell. Unauthorized use of the ranges, firing on a range that wasn't supposed to be fired on at all, was absolutely, unquestionably, against regulations.

"Colonel," General Black called out. The skinny light bird, his face still contorted with rage, snapped his head in the direction of the general's voice. For a moment, until he recognized the general (who had left his fatigue cap in the H23/CE), he glowered at the partner in crime of the idiot who had befouled his range.

Then he saluted, literally struck dumb. The last person in the world he expected to see crawling out of a derelict M3 was the post commander.

"I thought you might be interested to see what Captain MacMillan's rocket did to the interior of this," General Black said, conversationally. He hoisted himself out of the hatch, and made room for the skinny light bird to climb in. Then he jumped to the ground.

"I've seen enough, Mac," he said. "Let's go home."

[THREE]
Fort Polk, Louisiana
1 May 1951

HQ DEPT OF THE ARMY WASH DC
CG FT POLK LA (ATTN: MAJ GEN E. Z. BLACK)

INFO:CG USARMYFOUR FT SAM HOUSTON TEX
CCG USARMYEIGHT KOREA

1. TELECON BETWEEN VICE CHIEF OF STAFF, USA: DC/S-PERSONNEL HQ DEPT OF THE ARMY AND MAJ GEN E. Z. BLACK, CG US ARMY REPLACEMENT TRAINING CENTER AND FORT POLK LA 2030 HOURS WASH TIME 30 APR 1951 CONFIRMED AND MADE A MATTER OF RECORD.

2. MAJ GEN E. Z. BLACK (LT GEN DESIGNATE) IS RELIEVED OF COMMAND US ARMY REPLACEMENT TRAINING CENTER AND FT POLK LA EFFECTIVE 0001 HOURS 2 MAY 1951, AND WILL PROCEED BY FIRST AVAILABLE AIR TRANSPORTATION TO HQ FAR EAST COMMAND TOKYO JAPAN FOR FURTHER ASSIGNMENT WITH USARMY-EIGHT AS COMMANDING GENERAL XIX US CORPS (GROUP). GEN BLACK IS AUTH A PERSONAL STAFF OF FOUR.

FOR THE CHIEF OF STAFF
RALPH G. LEMES
BRIG GEN, USA
DEPUTY THE ADJ GEN

[FOUR]
Kwandae-Ri, North Korea
8 May 1951

Master Sergeant Tourtillott, a heavyset man in his forties, with a full head of curly silver hair, a Thompson submachine gun resting against his hip, and presenting a picture of a doglike devotion to General Black's protection that he didn't intend (although his devotion to General Black was in fact, doglike; he had been with him since Africa), stood by the rear door of the XIX Corps Conference Room and waited for the general to appear.

He did. He wore fatigues, tanker's boots, and a .45 automatic in a shoulder holster.

"Gentlemen," Master Sergeant Tourtillott called out, "the Commanding General. Atten-hut!"

Fifty officers rose to their feet.

General Black, wearing three stars on each of his collar points, walked into the room, trailed by Technical Sergeant Carmine Scott, his clerk.

"Be at ease, gentlemen," he said.

There were three armchairs in the center of the front row of chairs. One was occupied by the deputy corps commander, a major general, and the other by the corps artillery officer, a brigadier general. The center chair was obviously intended for General Black. Black walked to the chair, and smiled at Sergeant Scott.

"General," he said to the brigadier general, "would you mind giving Scotty your chair? He takes notes for me, and he has to be next to me."

"Somebody get the sergeant a chair," the corps artillery officer called out, moving his own chair to make room.

"General, you're going to have to listen carefully to what I say," General Black said. "I didn't say, 'Get Sergeant Scott a chair.' I asked you to give him yours."

Flushing with mingled anger and humiliation, the corps artillery officer signaled for a colonel to give up his chair. Sergeant Scott sat down next to the general and took out a stenographer's notebook and three pencils. He held the two spares in the same hand as the notebook, and poised the third over a blank page.

"Get on with it," General Black said.

The deputy corps commander went to the stage-like platform.

"On behalf of the officers and men of XIX Corps, General, welcome."

"Thank you," Black said.

The briefing, designed to inform the new corps commander of every possible fact concerning his new command, went on for an hour and a half.

General Black leaned his head toward Sergeant Scott every few moments and spoke softly to him. Sergeant Scott, his head moving almost constantly to signal his understanding of what was being said, scribbled steadily in his stenographer's notebook.

Presentations were made by the General Staff, G-1 (Personnel), G-2 (Intelligence), G-3 (Operations), and G-4 (Supply). They were followed by the Special Staff (the medical officer; the provost marshal; the ordnance officer; the signal officer; the transportation officer; the aviation officer; the civil affairs and military government officer; the finance officer; the chemical officer; and the special services officer).

When it was all over, General Black got to his feet and turned and faced the roomful of officers.

"Gentlemen," he said, "I am a simple soldier. When I was a cadet at Norwich, I was told, and I believed, and my subsequent career has proven true, that the essence of command is to make sure the troops have confidence in what they are doing. Troops must have faith in their officers. Officers build and maintain that faith in a very simple manner: They never lie to their troops; they never ask them to do something they cannot do themselves, or are unwilling to do themselves; and they never partake of creature comforts until the last private in the rear rank has that creature comfort. If you'll keep that in mind, I'm sure that we'll get along."

And then he walked out of the room, with Master Sergeant Tourtillott and Technical Sergeant Scott trailing along after him.

One by one, the General Staff officers presented themselves in his office. Prompted by Technical Sergeant Scott, working from his notes, General Black asked each of them specific questions and issued specific orders. He asked each of them if they had questions. None of them did, until he got to the adjutant general.

"We seem to have a problem, sir, with Captain MacMillan," the adjutant general said.

"Already? For Christ's sake, he hasn't been here seventy-two hours."

The adjutant general handed General Black a TWX.

HQ DEPT OF THE ARMY
CG XIX US CORPS KOREA

REF: PARAGRAPH 6, SPECIAL ORDER 87, HQ USA REPL TNG CNTR & FT POLK LA DTD 1 MAY 51.

(1) CAPT RUDOLPH G. MACMILLAN, 0-367734, INF, HAVING BEEN RETURNED TO THE ZI AFTER COMBAT SERVICE IN THE KOREAN CONFLICT, IS NOT ELIGIBLE FOR FURTHER SERVICE WITHIN EUSAK UP OF POLICY LETTER 285-50, OFFICE OF THE ASSISTANT CHIEF OF STAFF, PERSONNEL.

(2) IN VIEW OF CAPT MACMILLAN'S PREVIOUS DISTINGUISHED RECORD, AND THE UNDESIRABILITY TO EXPOSE HIM TO THE HAZARDS OF COMBAT AGAIN, NO REQUEST FOR WAIVER IS DESIRED.

(3) THIS MSG WILL SERVE AS AUTHORITY TO ISSUE ORDERS

REASSIGNING CAPT MACMILLAN TO HQ MIL DISTRICT OF WASHINGTON FOR DY WITH PRESIDENTIAL FLIGHT DETACHMENT.

FOR THE ASSISTANT CHIEF OF STAFF, PERSONNEL
RICHMOND HULL
LIEUT COL AGC
ASSISTANT ADJUTANT GENERAL

"Tourtillott," General Black called out, "get MacMillan in here."

"He's down at the airstrip, General," M/Sgt. Tourtillott replied.

"Get in a jeep and go get him," Black ordered.

When he handed MacMillan the TWX, and took a look at his face, General Black's carefully rehearsed speech vanished from his mind.

"Tourtillott, get back in your jeep and go get the aviation officer," General Black said.

"You're not going to pay any attention to this thing, are you, General?" MacMillan asked.

"Just keep your mouth shut, Mac, for once," General Black said.

The aviation officer, a full colonel, appeared ten minutes later in a crisp fatigue uniform.

"What took you so long, Colonel?" Black asked.

"Sir, I was in a really rotten flight suit," the aviation officer said.

"Try to remember for the future, Colonel," Black said, "that when I send for you, it's very likely that I have something on my mind more important than the cleanliness of your uniform."

"Yes, sir."

"Do you know Captain MacMillan?" Black asked.

"Yes, sir. I just met him. He was explaining the general's rotary-wing requirements, sir."

"Colonel, have you got any flying missions that don't get any closer than, say, five miles to the MLR?" General Black asked.

"I don't think I quite understand the question, sir."

"Think about it," General Black said, nastily.

"Yes, sir," the aviation officer said; and then, having thought about it, said, "Yes, sir," again. "We operate TWA, sir. Teeny-Weenie Airlines. We supply radio relay stations, and weather stations, and an outfit on the East Coast at Socho-Ri that supports a South Korean intelligence outfit."

"The aircraft involved do not get closer to the line than five miles. Is that a correct statement?"

"Yes, sir."

"Tell me about the outfit supporting the South Korean intelligence outfit," General Black said. "How far are they from the line?"

"About ten miles south of it, sir."

"And is there any reason MacMillan couldn't stay with them?"

"No, sir. They're right in with a radio relay station. One of ours, I mean."

"OK, Mac," General Black said. "Here it is. You quarter yourself with the Americans over on the coast. You occupy your time flying back and forth between here and there, never getting any closer to the line than five miles, thereby freeing one of the colonel's pilots and permitting me to assure those who are worried about your health that you are in no danger whatever."

"General, what about my aerial cavalry?" MacMillan protested.

"Take it or leave it, Mac," General Black said. "You either fly these supply missions for the colonel here, or you pass out hors d'oeuvres in the White House."

"I'll stay here, sir," MacMillan said.

"I'll have your ass if I find you've flown anything, anywhere, that the colonel hasn't told you to fly, and I'll have the colonel's ass if you do and he doesn't tell me. Have I made myself quite clear, gentlemen?"

"Yes, sir," MacMillan and the aviation officer said in unison.

"Colonel," Black said to the adjutant general, "send the following TWX to the Deputy Chief of Staff for Personnel, Headquarters, Department of the Army: 'Captain Rudolph G. MacMillan has been assigned essential noncombatant duties.' "

"Sir, you can't do that," the adjutant general said.

"I beg your pardon?" General Black said, as if he didn't believe that he had heard correctly.

"The regulation . . . I read it before I brought this to your attention, General . . . is quite clear. MacMillan's remaining here would be in clear violation of the regulation."

"Let me tell you something, Colonel," Black said. His normally ruddy face had turned white with anger, but he had control of his voice. "I don't know how you got to be a colonel without learning this, but since you apparently have, I'll try to embed it in your memory: Regulations and policy are for the *guidance* of a commander. Nothing more. Don't you *ever* tell me again that I can't do something because it's against regulations. I *command* this Corps, which is a horse of an entirely different hue than *administering* it to the satisfaction of some pencil-pusher in the Pentagon. Now, is that clear enough for you, or will it be necessary for me to have to make you write it a hundred times on that goddamned blackboard of yours?"

"It's perfectly clear, sir," the adjutant general said, faintly.

"You are dismissed, gentlemen," the XIX U.S. Corps commander said.

[ONE]
Socho-Ri, South Korea
22 May 1951

It took Mac MacMillan about three days to figure out what was going on at Socho-Ri. It was a low-level intelligence outfit. It was attached for rations and quarters to XIX Corps (Group), but it wasn't assigned to Eighth Army, or to the nearly autonomous X Corps. It was assigned to Supreme Headquarters, United Nations Command.

That explained the willingness of the XIX Corps (Group) aviation officer to assign a Beaver solely to supply the needs of the 8045th Signal Detachment. It was easier to simply turn a Beaver over, and thus insure their satisfaction with the quality of the support they were receiving from XIX Corps (Group), than to have Supreme Headquarters, United Nations Command breathing over their shoulders.

The XIX Corps (Group) aviation officer must be similarly pleased with the assignment, MacMillan realized. That freed one of his pilots for other duties.

MacMillan would have preferred to have been given command of a company of parachute infantry (the 187th Regimental Combat Team was in Korea). Failing that, any infantry company. Failing that, he would liked to have flown artillery spotting missions in an L-5 or the new L-19 Cessna they were supposed to be getting. And failing that, he would have preferred to be General Black's personal chopper jockey.

All of those things were obviously out of the question, which caused him to examine the 8045th Signal Detachment with great care. The commanding officer was a captain of the Signal Corps, but Mac outranked him, if it got down to that. There were three other officers, and a flock of sergeants, but only a very few lower-ranking enlisted men.

What they were doing was maintaining communications with intelligence agents—mostly Korean, though with a rare American involved—in North Korea. Most of the communications were by radio. But there were some messages that had to be carried by hand. And sometimes there was film that also had to be hand-carried out. In addition, the agents themselves had to be taken in—in other words, landed secretly on the beaches of North Korea—and when the time came, picked up from the beaches and taken home.

In that process, MacMillan saw his opportunity to make a greater contribution to the war effort than flying a Beaver back and forth between Socho-Ri and the XIX Corps (Group) airstrip.

There was an exhilaration he had almost forgotten when he thought about being behind enemy lines. He'd done that six times, five jumps into enemy-held terrain, and one odyssey across Poland when he'd left the POW camp. He was just about as good at that as he was at anything else.

There was no reason he could see why he couldn't go with the people planting and extracting agents, and while they were doing what they did, he would blow up railroad bridges, tunnels, and generally make a nuisance of himself.

But there were going to be some problems.

If General Black heard about it, he would find himself on the next plane to the White House Army Aviation Detachment. And he had given Black his word as an officer and a gentleman that he wouldn't fly within five miles of the front, so he couldn't use an airplane. But the important word there was "fly." He hadn't given his word about walking or riding or going on a boat.

The second problem was the detachment commander. He was under the impression that Mac had been assigned to him as an airplane driver, period. He judged army aviators the way most people in the army did, including MacMillan; he thought of them as commissioned aerial jeep drivers. So Mac began to cultivate the Signal Corps captain, to let him know that he was not your run-of-the-mill asshole aviator.

And then, an omen literally out of the fucking blue, that problem solved itself. A Navion landed unannounced on the dirt strip running parallel to the beach at Socho-Ri. The strip wasn't on charts, and it wasn't supposed to be used, but a Navion made one pass over the village and then touched down.

MacMillan and the Signal Corps captain went down to run whoever it was the hell off. And then the canopy opened.

"Well, look what the fucking cat drug in!" MacMillan called.

"Jesus Christ, the world's ugliest Scotchman," Lt. Colonel Red Hanrahan, the Navion's sole passenger, said. He jumped off the wing root and embraced MacMillan.

Lt. Colonel Hanrahan was the officer in charge of the operation, back in Tokyo. Mac had known him for years. As a second lieutenant, when MacMillan had been a corporal, Hanrahan had been MacMillan's platoon leader when what was later to become the 82nd Airborne Division was two provisional companies of volunteers jumping out of small airplanes with civilian parachutes.

Hanrahan had left the 82nd Airborne under mysterious circumstances. MacMillan had learned he'd been in the OSS, in Greece during the German occupation, and that he'd later been in Greece after the war when Lowell had been there.

"What the hell are you doing here?"

"General Black sent me over to make sure your people got treated right, Red," MacMillan lied, and purposefully used Hanrahan's nickname, rather than his rank, in the correct belief that Hanrahan would not correct him, and that this would awe the shit out of the Signal Corps captain.

Right on both counts.

The next time the Signal Corps captain planted an agent, MacMillan went along for the ride. The captain was not about to tell the colonel's asshole buddy he couldn't.

What this outfit needed, MacMillan decided, was some better equipment than the Korean junks they were using. What they needed was something fast, maybe a junk powered by a diesel. Maybe double diesels. Maybe even a PT boat. He had heard there were some PT boats at the U.S. Navy Yard in Yokohama. He'd have to come up with some excuse to get to Japan, and look into that. He knew where there were a couple of Marine diesels. Just to try his feathers, he flew to XIX Corps, and submitted a requisition through the XIX Corps G-2, saying it was from the outfit—the Supreme Headquarters, United Nations Command's outfit—in Socho-Ri.

Eleven days later, a GI tractor trailer delivered two marine diesels to Socho-Ri. There was a Korean shipyard further down the coast. MacMillan acquired a junk they didn't have much use for, for a truckload of gasoline in five-gallon jerry cans. XIX Corps (Group) gave him whatever fuel he asked for and asked no questions. For an additional 1,000 gallons of gas, the Koreans installed the diesel engines and reinforced the junk in several places, so that MacMillan could mount .50 caliber machine guns.

He ran into General Black one time at the XIX Corps (Group) airstrip.

"You staying out of trouble, Mac?"

"Yes, sir."

"You been flying any closer to the front than you should be, to get to specifics?"

"To be specific, sir, I never fly closer than ten miles to the front."

That same night, he blew up the first of what was to be more than seventy North Korean railroad bridges.

[TWO]
Ch'orwon, North Korea
20 May 1951

Headquarters, IX U.S. Army Corps, Eighth U.S. Army, had established itself in a ravine off the main supply route about six air miles (fourteen by road) from the main line of resistance. The commanding general and his staff had been put up in quonset huts, and the General Staff and the Technical Services (including the four messes, field-grade officers, company-grade officers, first three graders, and enlisted men) in tropical buildings, that is to say, sheet steel buildings on poured concrete slabs.

Four huge diesel generators provided electricity. There was a water purification plant, a laundry, and two shower points, one for enlisted men and company-grade officers, and a second for field-grade and senior officers. The general officers (three of them, the commanding general, the chief of staff, and the artillery commander) had their own mess and shower.

There was an airstrip, serving both C-47 aircraft and the light aircraft: Stinson L-5s, Cessna L-19s, Navion L-17s, DeHavilland L-20 Beavers, and Hiller H23 helicopters organic to IX Corps and its subordinate commands. There was the 8404th Military Police Company to provide security and the 8319th Transportation Car Company to provide jeeps and light truck transportation. The 8003rd Army Band played twice a day, at the reveille formation and at retreat, and also provided popular music at the IX Corps recreation center to which troops on a roster basis were brought from the front lines for a day's recreation, including hamburgers and ice cream sodas.

It was, in other words, what Colonel Thomas C. Minor felt was a *proper* headquarters, one in keeping with the requirements of a senior command, one from which he, as assistant chief of staff, G-1 (Personnel), could bring order from administrative chaos. The smooth functioning of the army (not only here, in the field but the army worldwide) depended on adherence to regulations.

Personnel-wise, the major problem was twofold. In the confusion which had been rampant since the police action started, commanders had seen fit to ignore army regulations under the authority granted them (an error, in Colonel Minor's judgment) to do whatever they considered necessary for the discharge of their mission in combat. They had been particularly blind to regulations regarding both enlisted and officer promotions, and in the assignment of officers without regard to suitability and qualification and even date of rank.

Enlisted men had gotten off the ships as privates and privates first class and five *months* later, as the result of a *series* of highly irregular and often blatantly illegal promotion policies, had become master sergeants and first sergeants. One of the first things Colonel Minor had done upon taking over as assistant chief of staff, G-1, three weeks before was to stop that. There would be no promotions above staff sergeant below division level and no promotions to the first two enlisted grades without Corps, that is, *his* permission. God alone knew what havoc had already been wrought on the Enlisted Personnel Picture worldwide by promoting draftees to master sergeant. The Enlisted Personnel Picture was sort of the colonel's own ball of wax. Before coming to Korea, he had been Deputy to the Chief, Enlisted Personnel Division, Manpower Section, Office of the Assistant Chief of Staff for Personnel, Headquarters, Department of the Army in the Pentagon. He knew, probably better than anyone else in the army, what was going to happen to carefully thought-out Enlisted Promotion Programs (promotion from private to master sergeant should, it had been decided, take a minimum of twelve years active service) if every other soldier who went to Korea as a PFC came home as a technical sergeant or higher. That had had to be stopped, and Colonel Minor had stopped it.

The officer personnel situation was even worse. The subordinate commands of IX Corps were riddled with officers who held down table of organization and equipment positions for which they were totally unqualified, or who had been promoted with little or no consideration being given to qualification or time in grade, or both.

On the other hand, the careers of many officers who had previously been quite good, and even outstanding, to judge by their service records, had been ruined by the whim of combat commanders, who had relieved them on the spot without so much as a moment's warning and sent them packing. Officers were entitled by regulation to counseling before any action—much less relief—which might be considered detrimental to their careers could be taken.

Colonel Minor, during a visit to the 73rd Heavy Tank Battalion (Reinforced), had seen something even worse, insofar as good order and discipline were concerned: Apparently with the approval and certainly with the knowledge of the battalion commander, there was an obscenity painted on the turrets of the tanks. It was even worse than obscenity, even though it was certainly that. It was clearly prejudicial to good conduct and order. The army functioned on cooperation between separate commands. There was simply no justification for the philosophy of the 73rd Heavy Tank Battalion (Reinforced) which was painted on the turrets: YOU PLAY BALL WITH THE 73RD, OR WE'LL STICK THE BAT UP YOUR ASS.

The general had agreed with him about *that.* Just as soon as he had returned to the IX Corps CP and briefed the general on what he'd seen, the general had authorized him to send a TWX absolutely forbidding the painting of any obscene or vulgar word or term or drawing on army property.

Colonel Jiggs's response to that order had been right on the edge of insubordination. Colonel Minor had decided he wouldn't carry *that* tale to the general. He would wait until the general visited the 73rd Heavy Tank Battalion (Reinforced), and saw for himself that the only thing Colonel Jiggs had done was paint over one word.

There was still outrageously emblazoned over the turrets of the 73rd's M46 tanks the legend, "You play ball with the 73rd or we'll stick the bat up your XXX." There was no mistaking what the painted-over word was.

The second thing Colonel Minor had seen at the 73rd Heavy Tank Battalion that he never thought he would see in this man's army was the S-3. For one thing, he was barely old enough to vote. For another, he was a National Guardsman. For another, not only had he not attended the Command and General Staff College, a normal prerequisite for staff duty, he hadn't even attended the Advanced Armor Officer's Course. When Colonel Minor was as old as Major Craig Lowell, he had been looking forward to his promotion to *first* lieutenant.

Another proof that Colonel Jiggs was a fool was his blunt statement that his Boy Wonder was the best S-3 he had ever known as well as a superb combat commander. It was the sort of thing one could expect from an officer who had relieved fifteen officers without so much as counseling any *one* of them, just *ruined* their careers. He had actually led the breakout from the Pusan perimeter with lieutenants commanding companies and sergeants commanding platoons, and the whole task force under the actual command of his Boy Major.

The Boy Major had been awarded the Distinguished Service Cross for his part in the breakout. Immediately, in the emotion of the moment—rather than after calm, deliberate collection and evaluation of the facts, the way it was supposed to be done.

So far as Colonel Minor was concerned, that was ample reason to relieve Colonel Jiggs as summarily as he had relieved the others "for lack of judgment in a combat situation."

But Jiggs had been lucky. His breakout, thanks to the cooperation of the enemy, had been successful. And so had his withdrawal from the Yalu when the Chinese came in. The 73rd Tank had come out of *that* smelling like a rose. Just luck. If General Almond had been as impressed with the 73rd Heavy Tank Battalion as they would have you believe, he would never have given it up to IX Corps. He had been very glad to get rid of it probably, if the truth were known. Let somebody else clean up the mess they had made for themselves.

Jiggs was a sonofabitch; there was no mistake about that. When Colonel Minor had sent a fully qualified major to be the 73rd Heavy Tank's S-3, instead of being grateful to Minor, he had called Minor to protest; and when Minor had told him that he was simply complying with regulations and policy, as well as the general's personal directive to him to make sure that the IX Corps officer corps was brought up to snuff, Colonel Jiggs had announced that he was going to personally protest to the commanding general.

At first Minor had thought that was just an idle threat, but his friend, the assistant to the Secretary of the General Staff, a fine young lieutenant, had telephoned him the night before to say that Colonel Jiggs had requested and been granted a personal interview with the general.

Colonel Jiggs was up there in the White House now with the general, and God only knows what allegations and outright untruths he was making.

One could not permit oneself to dwell on things like that. One was far better off simply putting them out of one's mind and going on with one's duty.

He was still thinking about how the administration of the army could really be fouled up unless there was someone in charge who knew precisely what he was doing, when his General Staff telephone buzzed. The general had a special telephone circuit, giving him instant communication with his General Staff. When he dialed 1, the G-1's (Colonel Minor's) telephone rang.

"Minor, sir," Colonel Minor said, catching it before it had a chance to ring again.

"Come up, will you?" the general said, and hung up.

Colonel Minor strapped on his web belt and .45 and then stepped in front of the mirror to make sure that his face was clean, that his camouflage parachute scarf was properly folded around his neck, and that the sandbag cover on his helmet was still drawn tautly. And then he walked quickly up the hill to the White House.

[THREE]

Colonel Jiggs was with the general when Colonel Minor reported, saluting crisply and remaining at attention until told to stand at ease. He was pleased to see that Jiggs was wearing his pearl-handled, gussied-up, chrome-plated .45 in a civilian shoulder holster. The general wasn't going to like that. He would have thought that Jiggs would have had more sense than to wear it.

"You know Colonel Jiggs, of course, Colonel," the general said.

Jiggs, who was sprawled in a most unmilitary fashion in one of the general's folding canvas chairs, made no move to get up or shake Minor's hand, and when Minor started toward him, he *waved* at him.

"I've had the pleasure," he said, sarcastically.

"Colonel Jiggs is a bit upset about his S-3," the general said. "Let's hear your side of it."

A *bit upset*, Colonel Jiggs thought, was the fucking understatement of the year. What he would like to do is ram a shovel up the ass of this paper-pushing sonofabitch, and then spin it around and jerk his chickenshit guts out with it.

"I can't imagine why there is any cause for concern, sir. I've managed to acquire for Colonel Jiggs a fully qualified major, who was second in his class at Leavenworth. He has four years in grade as a major, and this assignment is right for him at this point in his career and right for the 73rd Tank, who obviously needs a fully qualified officer."

"And did Colonel Jiggs tell you that he was perfectly satisfied with his present S-3?" the general asked.

"I believe the colonel mentioned something along those lines."

"I told you, Colonel," Jiggs said, "that Lowell is the best S-3 I've ever known, that I couldn't do without him, and that if you persisted in this business, I would take it up with the general," Jiggs said. "Don't tell me you've forgotten our little discussion so soon, Colonel."

Jiggs got a dirty look from the general, and reminded himself again that he would gain nothing by losing his temper.

"He is not really qualified, Colonel, no matter how well he's been able to fill in the breach," Colonel Minor said, reasonably.

"Sir," Jiggs interrupted, "Major Lowell did so well that we gave him the DSC."

"I consider that award, given under those circumstances, somewhat questionable," Colonel Minor said.

"Fortunately for the major, then," Jiggs said icily, "we'll just have to go with the decision of General Walker. General Walker gave Major Lowell his DSC."

"Be that as it may—" Minor began.

"I have just told the general," Jiggs interrupted him again, "that in addition to the DSC, I got him the DSM for the way he pulled us out of North Korea when the chinks came in."

He had not told the general that the last man in the world he expected to see on the Yalu was Major Craig W. Lowell. He would have bet his last dime, right after the link-up, that he, as well as the U.S. Army, had seen the last of Major Craig W. Lowell.

He had started getting what the army called "senatorial inquiries" about Lowell right after Lowell had been flown out of Seoul and put on compassionate leave. He'd gotten four or five of them a day. Lowell had a lot of friends in very high places, and those friends were not at all concerned that the army was in a war. They wanted Lowell instantly returned to the United States on the first available air transport, and they wanted his application for release from active duty, on compassionate grounds, approved yesterday.

At first Jiggs had been a little pissed. The army took care of its own. The wheels to get an officer whose wife had been killed home to his child had already been in high gear when Lowell arrived in Osan. He had been in Germany five days later.

But then he realized that under the same circumstances, if he had the clout, he would have done exactly the same thing.

And then, not quite a month later, Major Lowell had walked into his tent in North Korea.

"You should let a fellow know where you've moved," he said.

"What the fuck are you doing back here?"

"I'm here for duty, Colonel, if you'll have me," Lowell said, and there had been something in his eyes that had kept Jiggs from asking any further questions.

It wasn't until later, until just before the chinks came in, that he got an answer. They had an hour or so alone and a bottle of scotch, and Jiggs had asked him if he was hearing from Germany.

"I get a letter a week," Lowell said. "Teutonic efficiency."

"Is your boy getting adequate care?" Jiggs asked.

"He's surrounded by relatives," Lowell said. "He lives in a castle. In the castle in which his mother is buried. And her mother. And his side of the family going back five hundred years."

It had poured out of him then, and Jiggs had sat and listened.

His mother was in and out of mental hospitals. His father was dead. His only blood relative was a banker he couldn't stand. The only home life, as Colonel Paul T. Jiggs understood the term, had been with the German girl he had married.

"So there I sat, Colonel," Lowell had told him, "in a crypt. Like a goddamned Boris Karloff movie. With a bottle of scotch. Looking at a piece of marble on which somebody had chiseled Ilse Elizabeth Lowell, Gräfin von Greiffenberg, 1929–1950, Requiescat in Pace. My wife was behind that fucking piece of marble, and I was thinking that I was never, really never, going to see her again. And then, as drunk as I was, I had a clear thought: I didn't belong in that goddamned crypt. And neither did I belong in the States, which everyone from my fucking cousin to my father-in-law was telling me was best thing for me, under the circumstances. I suddenly realized where I belonged."

"You don't mean here?" Jiggs asked.

"Yeah, ain't that a bitch? That's just what I thought."

"You're going to stay in the army?"

"Don't laugh. It's the only home I've ever really had. The only friends I have are soldiers."

"There are worse ways to spend your life," Jiggs said.

"Investment banking being high on that list. What do you think my chances are for a regular commission.?"

"You should be a shoo-in," Jiggs had told him. "They don't pass out that many DSCs. And not many people get to be majors at twenty-four."

"You think I can keep the majority?"

"I think so," Jiggs had said. He had vowed then to do what he could, and he had, and now this paper-shuffling asshole was trying to shove another asshole into Lowell's job.

"As far as I'm concerned, Colonel," Colonel Jiggs said, relatively calmly, "an officer who had demonstrated his skills in a mess like the bug-out from the Yalu is a hell of a lot more qualified than the number-two man at C&GS."

Colonel Minor's silence, as he well knew, eloquently said, "So what?"

"And where is it your intention to assign this outstanding young major?" the general said.

"That did pose a problem, sir," Colonel Minor said. "As you point out, Major

Lowell is very young. As a general personnel policy, it is ill-advised to put an officer in a position where he is younger than his subordinates."

"What do you plan to do with him, Minor?" Jiggs said.

"I thought I would bring him here, sir," Colonel Minor said. "And give him some staff experience at this level of command."

"Where?" Jiggs pursued. The general gave him a pained look.

"In civil affairs and military government, actually," Colonel Minor said.

"That's going to look great on his service record," Jiggs said, sarcastically. "From S-3 of a combat command to civil affairs."

You're a fine one to talk about careers, Colonel Minor thought. The way you *ruined* careers of regular officers by summary relief. He said: "He's a National Guardsman, he really doesn't have a career."

"He's applied for the regular army, and I have heartily endorsed his application," Jiggs said.

"If he is accepted into the regular army, it will be as a first lieutenant, possibly even a second lieutenant, considering his age . . ." Minor said.

"In which case, I have recommended that he be retained on active duty in his reserve grade," Jiggs said. "I don't want that boy's career ruined by a tour as a civil affairs officer."

"I would hardly say ruined," Minor said.

"I don't really much care what you would hardly say, Colonel," Jiggs snapped.

"Take it easy, Jiggs," the general said.

"I beg your pardon, sir," Jiggs said.

"How much time has he got to do in Korea?" the general asked.

"About four months, sir," Jiggs said. "He's been here ten months, maybe eleven."

The general suddenly stood up and walked to a connecting door.

"John, can you come in here a minute?" he said. A very small major general in a starch-stiff set of fatigues walked into the room. Jiggs jumped to attention.

"John, we have a problem officer," the general said. "According to Colonel Minor, he's wholly unqualified to be what Colonel Jiggs says he is, the best S-3 he's ever known."

The little general looked amused.

"Do I have to take sides, sir?" he asked.

"He's also the young buck who ran that cavalry sweep through South Korea during the breakout. So he's only got about four months to go in Korea," the general said. "Jiggs is afraid that a tour in civil affairs, which is what Minor recommends, would look lousy on his service record."

"Jiggs is right," the little general said.

"You need an aide," the corps commander went on. "Presuming the chemistry is all right, would you be interested in him?"

"What do you think, Jiggs?" the little major general asked.

"I think Major Lowell would make the general a very fine aide-de-camp, sir."

"OK," the corps commander said. "I've just done my Solomon act for today. You two may go."

"How soon do I get him?" the small major general asked.

"Today, sir, if you like," Jiggs said. "Colonel Minor has been very efficient in sending me his replacement."

"One more thing," the small major general said. "Knowing you, Jiggs, I just have to ask. Is he housebroken?"

"Not only that, sir, but he can read and write. He wrote, for example, our battalion motto."

The little general laughed. "If that's going to go in the history books, you're going to have to have it translated into Latin. The general and I were talking about that last night. It belongs at C&GS, of course, as a morale booster. But how are you going to put it in the manual?"

"Cooperation with the 73rd Tank Battalion is expected and anticipated," Colonel Jiggs said. "Our disappointment will be manifested by the violent insertion of a sports implement into the anal orifice."

"Good to see you, Jiggs," the little general said, chuckling. "Come on up and have dinner sometime." He looked at the corps commander and got silent approval to leave.

Jiggs came to attention.

"Thank you, general," he said.

"OK, Jiggs," the corps commander said, "I hope you're satisfied."

"Yes, sir. Thank you very much," Jiggs said, and saluted and walked out of the general's office.

Well, you win some and you lose some. That was about a tie, Colonel Minor thought.

XI

[ONE]
Kwandae-Ri, North Korea
18 August 1951

"E. Z., I hate to speak to you like a battalion commander to an overzealous shavetail," the Supreme Commander, United Nations Command said to the commanding general of the United States XIX Corps (Group). "But you are obviously in need of guidance."

"With all due respect, sir, has the Supreme Commander ever heard of the phrase 'the blind guiding the blind'?" Lieutenant General. E. Z. Black replied.

"When the last Supreme Commander gave the faintest hint that something would please him. . . ."

"With all due and profound respect, sir, you ain't the last Supreme Commander."

"*His* subordinate commanders fell all over themselves," the Supreme Commander went on, "in the eagerness to make him happy. This is known in some circles as 'cheerful and willing obedience to the lawful orders of a superior officer.' "

"Will you settle for 'senior' officer?" the XIX Corps (Group) commander asked, innocently.

"If you understand that that's an order, I will," the Supreme Commander said.

They were sitting alone at the fieldstone bar of the general officer's mess of XIX Corps (Group), a room known as the Jade Room after the XIX Corps' radio code name, Jade. They were drinking, neat, twenty-four-year-old Ambassador scotch, brought to Korea by the Supreme Commander, United Nations Command.

"I've only been here a couple of months, Matt," Lieutenant General E. Z. Black said. "It's not time for me to take an R&R."

"A couple is two," the UN Commander said. "You've been here four. During which time you have put in eighteen-hour days, seven days a week. And you're not, although you sometimes act like one, a twenty-three-year-old cavalry lieutenant any more."

"Woman works from sun to sun, but a gen'rul's work is never done," General Black said.

"I don't know why the hell I'm arguing with you," the Supreme Commander said. "Now, whether you want to accept it as your due for breaking your ass straightening out XIX Corps in half the time I thought it would take you—and I mean that, E.Z., you've done a hell of a job—or the concern of an old friend who doesn't want you dropping dead of a heart attack brought on by overwork, you will take seven days rest and recuperation leave in connection with TDY to Tokyo. This is an order."

General Black sipped at his scotch, then raised his glass to the Supreme Commander, giving in.

"The troops call it 'I and I,' " he said. "For 'Intercourse and Intoxication.' I'm a little old for that."

"As Georgie Patton once said, 'A soldier who won't fuck, won't fight,' " the Supreme Commander said.

"That wasn't Georgie, that was Phil Sheridan," the XIX Corps commander said.

"You have reservations at the Imperial Hotel for seven days, starting next Friday."

"Why then?"

"Because that's the soonest Marilyn could get over here," the UN Commander said.

"Marilyn's coming over?" General Black asked. Marilyn was Mrs. Black.

"I called her up. And told her I felt duty bound to report that word had reached me you were carousing with Oriental ladies."

"You're capable of that, you bastard," the XIX Corps commander said.

"And since Marilyn is flying halfway around the world to save her marriage, the least you can do is show up at the Imperial, sober, shaven, and wearing a smile."

"It'll cost a fortune to fly her way out here," E. Z. Black said.

"You cheap sonofabitch," the Supreme Commander said. "You've got more money than Carter has liver pills."

"I don't know how well this is going to sit with the troops," E. Z. Black said. "They don't get their wives to come out here."

"They're not lieutenant generals, either. For Christ's sake, E. Z., they like that sort of thing. *Their* general is supposed to be somebody special, to do special things. About the only way you can tell a general officer from a PFC these days is because the general is usually older and fatter."

"It smacks of special privilege," E. Z. Black insisted. "It is special privilege."

"Let me worry about that," the UN Commander said, and his voice showed impatience. "If you weren't rich, E. Z., you wouldn't think twice about it. You lean so far over backward, you're always falling on your ass."

"OK, OK," General Black said. "You win."

"Your Supreme Commander may not always be right, but he's always your Supreme Commander," the UN Commander said. He looked at his watch. "Time, isn't it?"

"Yes, sir," Lieutenant General E. Z. Black said. The intimate conversation between friends was over. It was the responsibility of the XIX Corps (Group) commander to insure that the schedule of the visiting United Nations Commander was followed. He didn't even finish the inch of 24-year-old scotch in his glass.

"Finley!" he called, and in a moment a full bird colonel wearing the insignia of an aide-de-camp to a three-star general stuck his head into the Jade Room.

"Anytime, General," Colonel Finley said.

The two general officers put on their headgear—a helmet with a taut sandbag cover in the case of the XIX Corps commander, a stiffly starched fatigue cap for the UN Commander—checked to see that their buttons were buttoned and that the gold buckles of their special general officer's leather pistol belts were properly centered on the bellies, then walked out of the Jade Room.

A platoon from each battalion of the units assigned to XIX Corps (Group) were lined up on one side of the small parade ground between the rows of prefabricated tropical buildings. Each platoon had the national colors, and there was a sea of divisional and regimental flags and company guidons. Before the assembled troops was a three-cannon battery of 105 mm howitzers.

The moment the two general officers appeared before the headquarters's Quonset huts, the band began to play. First "Ruffles and Flourishes" and then "The Star-Spangled Banner." When that was over, the cannons fired, fifteen rounds, the prescribed tribute to a four-star general officer.

Then both general officers climbed into a glistening jeep, which bore a four-star plate on both bumpers. Steel railings permitted both of them to stand up. The jeep started off, followed by a half dozen other jeeps containing lesser officers. As they reached the assembled troops, an order was shouted, and all the flags except for the national emblem dipped in respect. Both general officers saluted, holding the salute as the jeeps slowly passed before the troops and dipped colors.

At the end of the line, they completed their salute, and then sat down and drove across the oiled dirt road to the XIX Corps (Group) airstrip where an Air Force C-47 sat waiting.

The aircraft had already been loaded with the baggage of the visiting party. All that remained now was for them to board the plane. The last to board was the UN Commander. He returned the salute of the XIX Corps commander, made a final personal remark ("Marge'll want to have you and Marilyn to dinner, of course"), and then got on the airplane. The door closed, and the engine starters began to whine.

The XIX Corps commander's jeep driver looked at General Black for instructions.

"We'll wait until they get off the ground," the XIX Corps commander said, as he lowered himself into the front seat.

The C-47 got its engines going and taxied down to the far end of the runway.

The XIX Corps commander suddenly had a crisp and clear image of his wife. He could almost smell her, could almost feel the softness of her breasts against him, see her still shapely legs flashing under her skirt, see her (it still excited him, after all these years) rubbing her breasts when she took off her brassiere.

The C-47's engines roared, and it came racing down the runway toward them.

It had been General E. Z. Black's intention to stand in the jeep and render a final hand salute as the C-47 passed over them. That was now quite impossible. If the XIX Corps commander stood up, it would be immedately obvious to the two dozen or more senior officers and enlisted men standing near him that their commander had a hard-on.

Sitting down, the XIX Corps commander waved an informal farewell to the United Nations Commander.

[TWO]
Tokyo
24 August 1951

The 1941 Cadillac limousine (which had been MacArthur's) picked up Lieutenant General E. Z. Black at the Imperial Hotel a few minutes after the UN Commander's personal car, a Buick, had picked up Mrs. Black to deliver her to the UN Commander's quarters for cocktails with the headquarters ladies.

It drove him to the Dai Ichi Building, where an MP who must have been six-feet-six opened the door for him. A bird colonel, one of the UNC's aides, saluted and smiled and escorted him into the building, through the lobby, and into an elevator.

They rode to the third floor, and then walked down a corridor to a conference room. There were chairs at the enormous table for thirty people, but there were only a handful in the room. Someone called "attention" when E. Z. Black walked in the room, which told him that the UNC wasn't here yet.

"Rest," E. Z. Black said. He identified, as well as he could, the people in the room. The only two he recognized were the UNC's G-2 and a colonel, whose name for the life of him he could not recall, but whom he recognized as a spook, an army officer on sort of permanent TDY to the CIA.

Then he remembered the name: Hanrahan. He had met Hanrahan at a party at

Jim Van Fleet's quarters in Washington. He had been introduced as a civilian, but Van Fleet had quietly informed Black that Hanrahan had been one of his people in Greece and was one of the officers the army had sent over to the CIA. A good man, Van Fleet had told him. For Jim Van Fleet, that was a compliment of the highest order.

Black walked over to him.

"Hello, Red," he said. "Nice to see you again."

"I'm flattered the general remembers me," Hanrahan said.

"I see you've reenlisted," Black said. He wanted Hanrahan to know that he knew.

There was also a captain, a little Jew, who wore a CIB and parachutist's wings and the crossed rifles of infantry.

"Why don't you sit down, General?" the aide-de-camp said. "I'm sure the general will be along in a moment."

An interior door opened, and the UN Commander walked in. Everyone came to attention without formal order.

"Sit down, gentlemen," the UNC said, and took a seat at the head of the table. "Howard, get us some coffee, and then secure the place," he ordered.

A master sergeant, who had apparently been waiting outside, rolled in a tray with a silver coffee service, and then left the room, closing the door behind him.

"Do we all know each other? Hanrahan, have you met General Black?"

"I know Colonel Hanrahan, General," Black said.

"And do you know Captain Feldman?" the UN Commander asked.

"It's Felter, sir," the captain said. "How do you do, General?"

Captain Felter was wearing a ring. General Black took a good look at it when Felter crossed the room to shake his hand. I'll be goddamned, he's a ring-knocker, E. Z. Black thought. Will wonders never cease?

"Before I turn this over to Colonel Hanrahan," the UN Commander said, "I want to officially announce this meeting is classified Top Secret/Mulberry. Everyone present is so cleared."

What the hell is "Mulberry"? General Black wondered.

Hanrahan got to his feet. "To get right to the heart of the matter, General Black, I'm afraid we're going to take one of your assets away from you."

"What asset is that?"

"The 8045th Signal Detachment," Hanrahan said.

General Black had to think a moment before he could identify the 8045th Signal Detachment. His troop list, the list of units assigned to XIX Corps (group), filled three single-spaced typewritten pages, everything from the "40 US Inf Division" through the "8807th Ordnance Ammo Bn" to the "8656th Signal Pigeon Platoon." He was finally able to sort out the 8045th Signal Detachment as the outfit where he had cached Mac MacMillan. They were the people over on the East Coast at Socho-Ri, the radio relay outfit also charged with supporting a South Korean intelligence operation of some sort.

After he had been over there about a month, flying an L-20 "Beaver" back and forth between the Jade CP and the East Coast, MacMillan had asked that he be assigned to them rather than to headquarters. They needed an old soldier assigned to them, Mac had said, one who knew how to deal (the General had read "scrounge") with Eighth Army and Korean Communications Zone (KCZ) supply depots on their behalf. They were doing a hell of a lot, MacMillan had said, with very little; and with adequate supplies, they could really earn their pay.

He had given in. There had been repercussions to his "Captain MacMillan has been assigned essential noncombatant duties" TWX, and it would be better if he were able to honestly say that MacMillan was assigned to some unimportant rear area Signal Corps unit, rather than to XIX Corps (Group) Headquarters.

He had smiled on learning from the XIX Corps (Group) aviation officer that the first thing MacMillan had scrounged on behalf of the 8045th Signal Detachment was an H23 helicopter to go with the Beaver.

"Otherwise known as 'MacMillan's Floating Circus,' " Colonel Hanrahan said.

"You know Mac, don't you, Colonel?" General Black said, smiling. "I didn't have the heart to send him home. So I sent him over there."

"I found it very interesting, General Black," the UNC said, dryly, "that I knew virtually nothing about the little operation of yours until Colonel Hanrahan brought it to my attention."

"It was hardly worth bringing to the general's attention," General Black said. "A couple of officers, a handful of men, who when they were not otherwise occupied with a radio relay mission, were helping, I guess, now that I see him here, Colonel Hanrahan."

" 'Helping Hanrahan,' as you put it, E.Z.," the UNC said, "is not all they've been up to."

"I'm afraid you've lost me, sir," Black confessed.

"You mean you don't know about the blowing up of railroad tunnels, the knocking down of bridges?"

"No, sir," Black said. Goddamn that MacMillan! He should have known that MacMillan's silence was proof that he had not quietly accepted an assignment that put him on ice.

"What about the PT boat, E.Z.?" the UNC asked, obviously enjoying his discomfiture. "Did you know about that?"

"I knew he got a boat from the navy," Black said, somewhat lamely. Before he had asked for a transfer, MacMillan had asked for permission to scrounge a boat from the navy, to "make it easier to get around."

Hanrahan was smiling broadly.

"I didn't know it was a PT boat," General Black went on. "I thought maybe an LCI, or an admiral's barge, or something."

"But you did know about Task Force Able, didn't you, E.Z.?" the UNC asked.

"Yes, sir. That was explained to me as a logistic convenience. If the Signal Detachment and the Koreans were under a joint command, they'd have an easier time getting logistic support."

"Persuasive chap, this Major MacMillan, isn't he?" the UNC said, dryly.

"I didn't hear about that, either," General Black confessed. "The last I heard he was Captain MacMillan."

"That just came through, General," Hanrahan said. "Mac doesn't know about that yet, either."

"I plead guilty and throw myself on the mercy of the court," General Black said. He sensed that he was in over his head here, and wondered what the hell it was all about; what MacMillan had done to get all this attention.

"General," Black said, deciding to get it all out in the open, "I have probably indulged MacMillan more than I should have."

"Indeed?" the UNC said, with a strange smile.

"Yes, sir. Hell, what he is is an old-time regular army sergeant. He's a good officer, but I suspect that he would really be happier to be first sergeant at Scofield Barracks. Sending him home to be a hero on display at the White House would kill him. What the hell, he was in a kraut prisoner cage with Porky Waterford's son-in-law. He won the Medal going in, that and a commission, and he won the DSC breaking out. He got another Silver Star, his third, the day this war started. If I've given him special consideration, I plead guilty. But I'd probably do it again for him tomorrow. What I don't understand is how this got all the way back to you."

"What about the Chinese junks, E.Z.?" the UNC asked. "Do you know about those, too?"

"I know about one of them," Black said. "Until just now, I thought it was a supply vessel for the Koreans."

"He has two, Colonel Hanrahan informs me," the UN Commander said. "And has a third under construction. He has paid for them with gasoline. Do you have any idea where MacMillan could lay his hands on enough gasoline to buy three ocean-going, very fast, multiple-engined, diesel-powered junks?"

"No, sir, I don't."

"I am really impressed, General," the UNC said, "with this demonstration of your firm hand on the logistics pipeline."

"As General Black is aware," Colonel Hanrahan said, "the Koreans are running an intelligence operation out of Socho-Ri. The point is, that the intelligence operation is really a diversion for another intelligence operation."

"I don't understand that at all," General Black said.

"Under cover of infiltrating low-level operatives, General, we have been inserting, and withdrawing, more important people."

"I still don't understand," Black admitted.

Hanrahan thought it over before replying.

"I don't think there is any harm in telling you that we're dealing with the Chinese, via their forces in North Korea," Hanrahan said. "I really can't go any further than that, General."

"OK," Black said. "I get the picture."

"So MacMillan was one of those things that sometimes happens," Hanrahan said. "When I found him over there, the first thing I thought was to get him out of there as quick as I could. I've known Mac a long time, General. I knew there was no way he was going to sit there and fly rations back and forth for long."

"No, that's not exactly his style, is it?" General Black said.

"And then it occurred to me to let him run a little wild," Hanrahan said. "The more trouble he caused, the more activity there was, the greater chance that our people could be concealed in the general confusion. You follow me, sir?"

"Yes," General Black and the UNC said together. Black was not sure to whom Hanrahan had addressed his remark.

"So I'm responsible for a good deal of MacMillan's success," Hanrahan said. "I got him the PT boat, for example."

"I see," the UNC said.

"What has happened now," Hanrahan said, "is that things are getting a little out of hand." He was obviously choosing each word with care. "At a time when our operation is in a critical place." He paused, and then went on: "We sent a submarine offshore to pick up one of our agents. They sent a team in rubber boats. They had just about reached shore when MacMillan blew up a railroad tunnel about a hundred yards away."

"And your people got hurt?" General Black asked.

"No, they weren't hurt," Colonel Hanrahan said. "The agent we were picking up had enough sense to go back in the bushes when the tunnel went up. And there was, of course, an alternative pickup plan. But when the sub went back, they weren't sure if they were going to have to fight off the North Koreans or what the sub commander referred to as 'pirates.' "

"OK," General Black said, "I get the picture. Colonel, you can take my word for it that as soon as I can get to a radio, MacMillan's private army will be disbanded, and Captain . . . *Major* . . . MacMillan will be on the next plane to the States."

"That isn't what we have in mind, General," Colonel Hanrahan said.

"Oh?"

"There has been a good deal of resistance from State, the State Department, about our using submarines. World opinion is apparently against submarines. They seem to be afraid that the other side can stage a sinking which would make us look bad."

"Go on," General Black said.

"After the incident where the submarine extraction party arrived precisely at the moment MacMillan was blowing up a tunnel, State managed to convince the . . . State has been successful in having us forbidden the use of submarines in any further operations of this nature."

"I see," General Black said.

"Which leaves us with MacMillan, and his junks, as our only asset," Colonel Hanrahan said.

"So you're going to take over MacMillan, and his junks, and presumably whatever else you need?" the UNC asked.

"We're going to take over direction of the MacMillan operation, General," Colonel Hanrahan said. "The operation will continue, much as it has, but under our supervision. He will go on doing very much what he has been doing, with this major change in priority. Inserting and withdrawing our people takes priority. It's as simple as that."

"I understand," General Black said.

"Now that I've been faced with the fact that submarines are no longer available to us," Hanrahan said, "I think maybe State is right. MacMillan can, for example, go in with twenty people, and come out with nineteen, leaving an agent on the shore—or pick one man up at the same time he's blowing a bridge—with a much lesser risk of being discovered, or even suspected, than if we use a sub. The Chinese are clever. They know you don't use subs unless what you're doing is very, very important."

"You think MacMillan is capable of handling this for you?" General Black asked.

"That's where Captain Felter comes in," Hanrahan said.

General Black had been wondering about the role of the little Jew with the West Point ring.

"We've got a radio crew coming in from the States with some really fancy radio-teletype cryptographic equipment," Hanrahan went on. "We'll have a direct link between Washington and Captain Felter, and Felter can give the word to MacMillan."

"I have a rude question to ask," General Black said. "And there's nothing personal in this, Captain, believe me. But if this operation is as important as you tell me it is, isn't Captain Felter a little junior for all that responsibility?"

"Washington wants one of their own men on the scene, General," Colonel Hanrahan said.

"What's he doing in an army uniform if he's one of yours?" General Black said.

"Captain Felter thinks of himself as a soldier, General," Colonel Hanrahan said, somewhat tartly. "Like myself, he has declined an offer of civilian employment with the agency to which we are attached. I had Captain Felter sent from Germany. I can think of no other officer as well qualified to handle this operation. Captain Felter was with me in Greece."

"E.Z.," the UNC said, cutting off the exchange, "the real purpose of this meeting, my presence here, is to impress on you the importance of Hanrahan's mission. And to tell you that the word I got, when Colonel Hanrahan was 'attached' here, was that what Hanrahan wants, Hanrahan gets."

"Yes, sir," General Black said. "I understand, sir." He turned to Felter. "Anything we've got you can have, Captain," he said. "And if you run into any trouble with MacMillan, as you're liable to, you come to see me."

"I can handle Major MacMillan, sir," Captain Felter said, matter-of-factly.

[THREE]
Kwandae-Ri, North Korea
30 August 1951

Captain Sanford T. Felter, wearing the crossed flags of the Signal Corps (and without his Combat Infantry Badge, his parachute wings, and his West Point Class of 1946 ring) went to Korea with Lt. General E. Z. Black at the conclusion of the general's

R&R leave. General Black's L-17 Navion met them at K16 in Seoul and flew them to the XIX Corps (Group) airstrip.

General Black's aides-de-camp met the Navion. General Black's junior aide was instructed to have Captain Felter equipped with field uniforms and to have him standing by the General's office no later than 1600. General Black's senior aide was told to contact Major MacMillan at the 8045th Signal Detachment and have him at the general's office no later than 1530.

Then General Black went to his quarters and changed into his fatigue uniform. He had—wondering if it made him some sort of a pervert—stolen a handkerchief from his wife. He sniffed its perfume and then carefully wrapped it in plastic and slipped it into his breast pocket. He wondered how long the perfume would last.

He then underwent a two-hour briefing by his G-3 on what had happened in his absence. When it was finished, MacMillan was waiting for him. When they walked through the outer office of General Black's personal office, Captain Felter was already there, dressed in mussed fatigues, brand-new combat boots, and looking, General Black thought, like the Israeli version of Sad Sack.

"You miserable sonofabitch," General Black said to MacMillan, "not only did you make a three-star horse's ass out of me in front of the Supreme Commander, and in front of a professional spook named Hanrahan, but you broke your word to me. You gave me your word you wouldn't go within five miles of the MLR."

Very lamely, MacMillan explained: "I said I wouldn't *fly* within five miles of the line."

"You're a goddamned guardhouse lawyer, that's what you are. That's a bullshit excuse and you know it is. I meant, and you know I meant, that you were not to stick your ass in the line of fire."

"Goddamnit, General," MacMillan said, now shamed that he had been caught, "I'm paid to be a soldier. Take the fucking Medal back and let me go to a line outfit."

General Black was wholly unaccustomed to having that sort of language directed to him by a very junior major, who didn't even know he was a major. His face whitened, but in the end he concluded that not only was there something wrong with a personnel system that ordered an officer out of combat solely because he had performed superbly in combat previously, but that, under identical circumstances, he would have done exactly what MacMillan had done. Probably not as well, General Black decided. But he would have tried.

"At least you could have told me about the goddamned submarine, Mac," General Black said, taking a bottle of the 24-year-old Ambassador scotch from his desk drawer and pouring two drinks. He looked up at MacMillan. "Why didn't you?"

"Well, I figured the general had enough on his mind," MacMillan said.

"Your escapades have come to the attention of the highest authorities," General Black said. He and MacMillan upended the shot glasses, swirling the scotch around in their mouths, then swallowing it, together, as if it had been rehearsed. "God, that's good whiskey."

"I'm really sorry if I got you in trouble, General," MacMillan said. "I really am. I never thought anybody would find out."

"Congratulations," General Black said, pouring more 24-year-old scotch into their glasses.

MacMillan looked at him in confusion.

"You are now a field-grade officer, Mac," Black said.

"No shit?" MacMillan asked, pleased and surprised.

"The UNC is going to give us a parade," Black said. "You get the gold leaf pinned on your shirt, and I will be awarded the Horse's Ass Medal with crossed swords and diamonds for letting a dumb shit pull what you pulled on me."

"We're not in trouble," MacMillan said, relaxed and smiling.

"You know Colonel Red Hanrahan?" the General asked.

"Yes, sir."

"Hanrahan is so impressed with your little operation that he's taking it over."

"Where does that leave me?"

"Did you happen to notice that captain sitting outside? The one who looks like Sad Sack?"

"His name is Felter," MacMillan said. "I've never met him, but I know who he is. He's in thick with Red Hanrahan. And Bob Bellmon, too. What's he got to do with this?"

"You're now working for him, effective immediately," General Black said.

"He's CIA? Since when is the CIA getting involved in blowing up bridges?" MacMillan asked.

"Who said CIA? I didn't use that word."

MacMillan shrugged. "Hanrahan's CIA."

"They're going to use your operation as a cover for them," General Black said. "Putting their people in and getting them out."

"That's all?"

"They have priority of mission," General Black said. "You take your orders from Captain Felter."

"I can handle that. I was afraid you were going to put me behind a desk."

"I should," General Black said. "If you get yourself knocked off running around like John Wayne, Mac, my ass will be in a crack."

"I have no intention of getting myself killed," MacMillan said.

"Watch yourself, is all I'm saying. I mean it, Mac. I don't want to find myself in a position explaining why I allowed a Medal of Honor winner to get himself shot."

"Yes, sir. Is that all you've got for me?"

"Not quite," the General said. He gave MacMillan the rest of the bottle of the 24-year-old Ambassador scotch.

MacMillan put the whiskey in a musette bag and walked out to pick up Captain Felter.

"I thought I knew who you were," he said, putting out his hand. "But I wasn't sure if I should admit it."

"It's nice to meet you, Major," Felter said, shaking his hand.

"You heard about that, too, huh?"

"I heard. Congratulations."

"Yeah, well. You keep your mouth shut, and your nose clean, and you can't help but get promoted," MacMillan said.

"I saw Colonel Bellmon, Colonel and Mrs. Bellmon, in Washington. They asked to be remembered to you, if I saw you. I said I didn't think I would see you."

"Yeah, I'll bet she sent her best regards," MacMillan said. "And speaking of asshole buddies, I saw an old friend of yours the other day. Lowell. Would you believe that pissant is a major?"

"I heard he was."

"He just got himself named aide-de-camp to the chief of staff at IX Corps."

"You heard what happened to Ilse?" Felter asked.

"Who? Oh, you mean that kraut he married. I never could remember her name. Yeah, I heard. Tough."

"Yeah," Felter said. "Tough."

"I've got a Beaver at the airstrip," MacMillan said. "Whenever you want to go."

"I'm ready anytime you are," Sandy Felter said.

"I want to stop by the PX and buy some major's leaves," MacMillan said. "But that's all I have to do. You got the time, we could run over to IX Corps and see Lowell. Take us about an hour."

"I'd like to see him, of course," Felter said, "but I don't think we're going to be able to find time for that. Or that it would be a good idea, even if we could find the time."

Macmillan recognized the rebuke.

"Hey," he said, "I got the word. I mean *I got the word.* But put your mind to rest. There aren't half a dozen people aside from my people who know what we're doing. The word is that we're a radio relay outfit. My guys tell that story when they get to the IX Corps for the PX and a steak and whatever. What I'm saying is that I don't let anything get in the way of my mission, either."

"Sorry," Felter said, after a moment. "You tend to get paranoid in my line of work."

[FOUR]
Socho-Ri, South Korea
30 August 1951

An hour later, as darkness fell, MacMillan dropped Task Force Able's L-20 De-Havilland Beaver out of overcast skies and landed on a dirt road fifty yards from the Sea of Japan, near the village of Socho-Ri.

The inhabitants of the village had been evacuated. The thatch-roofed, stone-walled houses had been fumigated and taken over as living quarters. The three American officers, twenty-seven American enlisted men, and seven Korean officers occupied the seven best houses, one of which served as a mess hall, bar, and transient quarters. These houses were surrounded with concertina barbed wire and were known as the compound.

The senior Korean officer, Major Kim Lee Dong, had been a lieutenant in the Imperial Japanese Army, with long service in China. Among other duties, he had been charged with housekeeping. He had levied upon the women's section of the Republic of Korea for mess personnel, selecting from the more than two hundred eager volunteers for special duty forty women who understood that members of an elite unit expected more of their mess support personnel than cooking, washing, and tending the furnaces of the hootches. Presuming the performance of their duty was satisfactory, they could expect not only a triple ration to do with what they wanted, but supplemental pay as well.

MacMillan, once he had assumed command of Task Force Able, had arranged for the Korean military personnel, officer and enlisted, to be placed on the American ration return. Inasmuch as Task Force Able was considered to be combat unit on the line (MacMillan had arranged for that determination, too), each individual on the ration list was authorized a ration and a half, plus a comfort ration of cigarettes, toilet paper, candy bars, and even writing paper and envelopes. There was a special ration of two cans of beer per day.

While the appetites of the Americans were phenomenal by Korean standards (the breakfast menu of Task Force Able, for example, was fruit juice, coffee, reconstituted milk, cereal, eggs to order, bacon, ham, biscuits, toast, butter, jam and marmalade, and fresh fruit), there was invariably enough food left over (indeed, uncooked) to provide mess personnel with an additional source of income via the black market, even after augmenting the Korean ration.

A jeep and a three-quarter-ton truck met the DeHavilland L-20. The American driver of the truck, the mess sergeant, supervised the off-loading of that day's ration of fresh fruit and fresh meat (picked up while MacMillan was at XIX Corps) so that the fucking slopes wouldn't make half of it disappear before it got to the fucking kitchen, while the Korean driver of the jeep drove MacMillan and Felter to the club in the compound.

The club was crowded with American enlisted men, most of them sergeants, and all of them somewhat older than the teenagers who constituted the bulk of enlisted men in Korea. They were at the bar. A captain and a warrant officer were sitting before a table reserved for officers, drinking beer and bourbon.

"Gentlemen," MacMillan said, "this is Captain Felter, who has been attached to us as an advisor. And I am, in case you are all blind, Major MacMillan, your new field-grade commanding officer."

He said it loud enough for everybody in the building to hear, and they all came over to congratulate him.

"I suppose I'm stuck to buy all you thirsty bastards a drink," MacMillan said. "Just make sure you beer drinkers don't get a sudden scotch urge."

"Welcome, Captain," the captain who had been sitting at the table said, once the commotion died down a little. "Welcome to MacMillan's Floating Circus."

Felter was experiencing a strange emotional experience. He took a moment to analyze it, to try to explain it, as he shook the captain's and the warrant officer's hands. Then he knew what it was. He didn't feel at all like a stranger here. It was

Ioannina, the 24th Royal Hellenic Mountain Division, the U.S. Military Advisory Group, Greece, all over again. It was as if, instead of having come to an obscure village in the middle of nowhere, he had come home.

"I'm going to move Felter in with me," MacMillan said. "Which means you'll have to move out, Paul." The captain's face registered surprise. "The 'advice' Felter is going to give us is advice we're going to follow," MacMillan added. "Get the message?"

"I don't want to move the captain out of his quarters," Felter said.

"My pleasure, Captain," the captain said. "Besides, MacMillan snores."

Without asking, a Korean girl in army fatigues delivered a liter bottle of Asahi beer and a glass and set it before MacMillan.

Felter spoke to the girl in Korean. She was visibly surprised, and giggled, and covered her mouth with her fingers. Then she scurried away and returned in a moment with a bottle of white wine. Felter thanked her in Korean.

"I'm impressed, Felter," MacMillan said. "There aren't many people who speak Korean."

"I get by," Felter said, shyly.

The sliding door opened and a heavyset Signal Corps captain, followed by a slight warrant officer stepped inside the room.

"Who the hell are they?" the captain who had lost his room to Felter asked. There were few visitors to Socho-Ri, and no welcome ones.

The newcomers looked around the room, saw the officers at their table, and walked over to them.

"What can I do for you, Captain?" MacMillan asked, not very friendly.

"Hello, Captain," the newcomer warrant officer said, putting out his hand to Felter. "Nice to see you again."

Felter got to his feet and shook the warrant officer's hand and said it was nice to see him, too. It was evident to MacMillan that Felter hadn't the foggiest idea who the warrant was.

"We're looking for Captain Felter," the captain said. "I see we found him."

"Can I help you?" Felter asked.

"I got two commo vans for you," the captain said.

"Oh, yes," Felter said. "I didn't expect you so quickly."

"I've got orders to get the net in by 2000," the captain said. "You want to tell me where to put it?"

"I really don't know," Felter said, looking at MacMillan.

"Mr. Davies is my commo officer," MacMillan said. "Maybe he can help."

"I need a place to rig some ninety-foot antennae," the captain said.

"Go show him where, Davies," MacMillan said. Davies got to his feet and so did Felter. They left the room. The newly arrived warrant officer sat down in Davies's chair.

"I'm crypto," he said. "I don't know diddly shit about antennae, fortunately. Hey, honey, get me a beer, will you?"

"I gather you're going to be with us?" MacMillan asked, almost sarcastically.

"It looks that way, Major," the cryptographic warrant officer said.

"Mac," the captain said, "just who the fuck *is* that little Jew?"

"I told you," MacMillan said, "he's here as an advisor. From above."

"But who the fuck is he?"

"I'll tell you who he is, Captain," the cryptographic warrant officer said. "That's Mouse Felter."

"Is that supposed to mean something?" MacMillan asked.

"He's one mean little son of a bitch, for one thing. I wouldn't recommend letting him hear you call him a little Jew, Captain."

"Why do you say he's mean?"

"I was with him in Greece. I don't think he remembers me. I was an EM then. But I remember him."

"What did he do mean in Greece that so impressed you?" MacMillan asked.

"I'm not sure I should talk about it," the warrant officer said.

"Goddamnit, you started it, now finish it," MacMillan said sharply. He was more than a little curious to know what the warrant knew about Felter.

"Well, we had a captain who didn't want to relieve some Greeks stuck on a hill," the warrant officer said. "They was dropping mortars on the road. And the Mouse figured he should at least try. There was some kid American lieutenant on the hill with the Greeks."

"The kid's name was Lowell, right?" MacMillan said.

"Yeah, you know about it, huh?"

"Doesn't everybody who's been in the army more than two weeks?" Mac replied. Guessing it was Lowell was a wild shot. It had hit the fucking bull's-eye.

"I have nine years, six months, and four days, Major, sir," the captain said. "And I don't know about it."

"Tell him," MacMillan said, grateful that he would now hear the rest of the story himself.

"When this captain lost his nerve, and not only wouldn't go up the hill, but told the Mouse he couldn't go either, the Mouse blew him away with a Thompson," the warrant officer said. "Just like that." He made the stuttering sound of a Thompson.

"No shit?" the captain said.

"No shit," the warrant officer said. "Don't fuck around with him, he's meaner than shit."

Unknowingly, Captain Sanford T. Felter had jut been raised 95 Brownie points in the opinion of Major Mac MacMillan.

[FIVE]

It took just over three hours to erect the antennae required. Felter stayed on the site until the network was in, and then saw to it that the enlisted men were fed and given places to sleep. Then he went to the club and asked if he could have an egg sandwich or something. When he'd eaten that, and drunk a Coke, he said that he was going to turn in, that it had been a long day, and would someone please show him where to go.

MacMillan summoned the waitress who had served them before, with whom Felter had spoken in Korean. He signaled for her to go with Felter.

Felter followed the girl to the thatch-roofed house. She showed him where the latrine was and the heated shower. He thanked her and went to the latrine, and then took a shower. Then he sat down at the folding wooden desk and took out his pen to write Sharon a letter.

There was movement behind him. For some reason, he was startled. He pushed himself sideward off the chair, rolled on the floor, and when he came up, he had his Colt .45 automatic, cocked, in his hand.

It was the Korean girl. She was no longer wearing the army fatigues. She was dressed in a flimsy nylon robe, so short that he could see her nylon panties and the tuft of black hair beneath.

He had frightened her; she yelped, almost screamed.

"You frightened me," he said, laying the pistol on the desk. "I'm sorry."

"I'm sorry," the Korean girl said. "I did not mean to displease you."

"You didn't displease me," he said. "Is there something I can do for you?"

"You don't like me?"

"Oh," Felter said, finally understanding. "I have a wife."

"Here?"

"No, in America."

"But here you need a woman."

"I don't need a woman," he said.

"You want, maybe, a boy?" she asked. "I go ask . . ." She had switched to English.

"You can speak Korean with me," Felter said.

"If you don't want me, the major will send me away," the girl said.

"Well, you go tell Major MacMillan that I said I want you to take care of me," Felter said. "You tell him I said that."

"You are a great gentleman," she said. "I will take very good care of you." She made a deep curtsy, and then backed out of the room.

Felter sat back down at the table, and began to write.

Dearest Sharon,

Well, here I am in Korea. I have been put in charge of a small radio station on the Sea of Japan. It's far from the front lines, so I am in no danger at all. As a matter of fact, the only bad thing about this place is that there's no indoor plumbing. There's a shower, but when you have to go, you have to use a place in the backyard.

It is a small detachment of men, to operate the radio station, and to provide transportation of people and supplies along the coast. They have two Chinese junks, just like the ones you see on postcards, and I hope to get a ride in one tomorrow or the day after.

I will write more tomorrow, when I've had a chance to look around. I'll close now, because it's been a long day, and I'm very tired.

I love and miss you and our children very much. Many kisses and hugs to you all.

Your adoring,

Sandy

P.S.: There is a major here named MacMillan, who knows Craig. He told me that Craig is now an aide-de-camp to the chief of staff of IX Corps. I'd like to see Craig, but it's a long way from here, and I don't see how I'll be able to make the trip anytime soon. I was glad to hear that he won't be in combat anymore.

XII

[ONE]
Ch'orwon, North Korea
23 August 1951

Major General John J. Harrier, Chief of Staff, IX Corps, pulled the sheet of paper from his sergeant major's typewriter, gave what he had written a quick glance, took a pen from a pocket sewn to the sleeve of his stiffly starched fatigue jacket, and wrote, "I Love You, Johnny," on the bottom of the page. He put an envelope into the typewriter and addressed it to his wife, then folded the letter in thirds and put it in the envelope. He tossed the letter in the mail drawer, the upper of four stacked open boxes on the sergeant major's desk, and stood up.

He picked up a can of Schlitz beer, drained it, and then put the empty can in the sergeant major's wastebasket. He looked at his watch. It was nearly eleven. He had hoped that the beer would make him sleepy. It had not.

Maybe, he told himself, if he took a little walk it might help him sleep. The corps commander and the chief of staff took turns making middle-of-the-night visits to the IX Corps Operations Room. Tonight was Harrier's turn to sleep through. It made no sense to be off-duty, so to speak, and wake up two or three times in the middle of the night.

General Harrier picked up his soft leather pistol belt and Colt .32 ACP automatic pistol and strapped it around his middle. He went into the outer office. The duty officer stood up.

"Sit," General Harrier said. "I'm going to take a little walk before turning in. I should be in my quarters by midnight."

"Yes, sir," the duty officer said. "Good night, General."

General Harrier walked down the hill from the White House on the path that led past Colonel's Row. Colonel's Row was actually two rows of one-man tents, twenty in all, in which the fourteen full colonels of Headquarters IX Corps and the six aides-de-camp for the Corps' three general officers were housed, the latter for the convenience of the generals, not as a special privilege for the aides-de-camp.

As General Harrier walked past Colonel's Row, he was surprised to hear the staccato sound of a typewriter. He located the tent from which the sound came from faint cracks of light around the door of one of them; the others were dark, their occupants either on duty or off in one of the messes. It was coming from the tent of his junior aide, Major Craig W. Lowell.

So far as aides-de-camp went, Major Lowell was a mixed blessing. Harrier had suspected that would be the case from the moment he had first laid eyes on him. First of all, he had not reported for duty immediately, as Colonel Paul Jiggs had implied he would. It had been six days after the session in the corps commander's office, between Jiggs (a fine officer, in Harrier's opinion) and Minor (a fine paper-pusher; necessary, of course, but not really what General Harrier thought of as a fellow soldier), over Minor's purely chickenshit intention to assign Lowell to civil affairs.

"I expected you some days ago, Major," Harrier had said to Lowell when he finally showed up.

"Sir, it took me some time to brief my replacement."

The implication was that training an S-3 of a tank battalion on the line was more important than being a dog robber. That was true, but most officers would have rushed to duty with a general.

Lowell, moreover, had arrived somewhat out of uniform. Because of the heat around tanks, made nearly unbearable in the heat of the Korean summer, Jiggs's battalion (it was more like a combat command) had special, unofficial permission to wear their fatigue jackets outside of the trousers and to roll up the sleeves. Not only had Lowell reported for duty so dressed (unofficial protocol in the army would have seen him showing up in the uniform prescribed for his new organization), but wearing, instead of either a web pistol belt and a .45 or an issue shoulder holster (prescribed only for tank crews, but worn by most tank officers), a German Luger in a nonissue shoulder holster. On the holster was a shiny brass medallion reading GOTT MIT UNS.

Before he had suggested that Lowell take the rest of the day off to get himself settled and into uniform, Harrier had given him Speech Three, in which he traced the role of aides-de-camp in the military from the days when they were general officer's messengers on horseback to the present, when the assignment of aides to general officers had a dual purpose: to relieve the general officers of bothersome details, and to give the aides an intimate glimpse of the duties and responsibilities of general officers.

The next day, Lowell, in proper uniform, had served briefly as Harrier's senior aide. That same day, Lieutenant Colonel Edmund Peebles had arrived from duties as executive officer of the 35th Infantry Regiment to become General Harrier's senior aide-de-camp. As General Harrier in his bones knew there would be, there was an instant personality clash between the two men.

Colonel Peebles was infantry, West Point, and thirty-eight years old. He had not been given command of an infantry battalion, and he suspected, correctly, that service as a regimental exec was not going to be worth as many Brownie points at promotion time as command of a battalion would have been. His performance as senior aide to General Harrier was about his last chance to make bird colonel. Peebles knew he was never going to command a regiment, but he was perfectly willing to settle for a silver eagle as a staff officer.

He knew the way to convince the general of his talents in a staff position was to function in a staff position, and the obvious way to do that was to make sure the junior aide was fully occupied with household chores, so that he wouldn't have the chance to function as a staff officer.

Unfortunately, but unavoidably, Major Lowell looked at Lieutenant Colonel Edmund Peebles, his immediate superior, through the eyes of a commander and saw in him the same things Peebles's other commanders had seen, the things that had kept him from command. Peebles was a good officer, providing someone told him what to do. He was incapable of making important decisions quickly, and often not at all.

Moreover, Lowell was generously endowed with self-confidence. He was, after all, a twenty-four-year-old major. He saw his role as aide-de-camp to General Harrier as Part Two of the functions of an aide: to see how upper echelon command worked, as training for the day when he would wear stars. Arranging the general's itinerary or composing rosters of people who would be invited to dinner in the IX Corps general officer's mess or seeing that the general's jeep was polished were not what he was there to do. Whenever Peebles assigned him such duties, Lowell delegated them to lieutenants and sergeants.

Major Craig W. Lowell was, in his own mind, a commander en route from a junior command (and Task Force Lowell, which had earned him the nation's second highest award for gallantry, the Distinguished Service Cross, was by any standard a more important command than an infantry battalion) to a larger one. Lowell had quickly seen that Colonel Peebles was en route from one desk to another.

Paul Jiggs had accepted General Harrier's vague invitation to "come to dinner" by showing up the day after the session in the corps commander's office and had used the opportunity to tell Harrier what a splendid young officer he was getting for his aide: that rare combination of logistician and combat commander. Jiggs was not given to undeserved praise, and there had been other evidence of Lowell's popularity as a commander. There had been a steady stream of officers and noncoms who, having completed their tours, had scrounged a jeep and driven to IX Corps to say so long to Lowell, their former commander, before going home.

They had come singly and in twos and threes as they'd gotten their orders, and it had been impossible not to hear their often drunken and sometimes quite emotional reminiscences.

"I'll never forget the day this chickenshit baby face took over the company. Goddamn, did he shake us up!"

"So, finally, after running all up and down the goddamned peninsula for nine days, we finally make it to Osan, and we're almost there, and some dumb fucking infantryman can't tell the difference between an M46 and a T34, and lets fly with a bazooka at us. Well, shit, one of the tanks blows him away, and we finally make the link-up. So there's this full bull infantry colonel, and *he's* pissed, believe it not, because this dumb fucker of his has taken a shot at us and gotten himself blown away, and he jumps on the Duke's ass, and he says, 'Major, if you had been where you were supposed to be, this wouldn't have happened.' So the Duke looks him right in the eye, and says, 'Colonel, what would you have us do, go back?' "

"So we're making the bug-out from the Yalu, and we just barely get our ass off the beach at Hamhung, and there we are on this goddamned troop ship, assault ship, whatever the fuck they called it. It was Christmas Eve, and for the first time in a month, six weeks, we're warm and we get a bath and something besides fucking 10-in-1 rations, and the Duke comes down in the hold with a couple of the officers carrying a couple of cases of 90 mm HEAT, and this Swabbie officer flips his lid, and says, 'The Major should know that he can't bring live ammo into a personnel compartment.' The Duke tells him not to worry, it ain't ammo, it's booze. Goddamn, that made him even madder. I don't know how the Duke handled it, but the 73rd Heavy Tank had a drink on Christmas Eve, the night we come off the beach with all our equipment and our wounded and even our KIAs, and fuck the navy and its regulations."

Harrier especially remembered the warrant officer, a great big bull of a man. Lowell had told him later he'd been his S-3 sergeant, and he'd gotten him the warrant. Mean-looking son of bitch, looked like he could chew spikes and spit out tacks. He stood there with the tears running down his cheeks as he said good-bye, and finally ended up hugging Lowell. For a moment, it had looked to General Harrier like he was going to kiss Lowell.

General Harrier suspected that Lt. Colonel Peebles was one of those officers who based their philosophy of command on the belief that all an officer can expect from his subordinates is obedience and that most good commanders are hated and feared by their troops (a commonly held belief, inspired by George Patton, and one with which Harrier disagreed). Harrier was also aware that Peebles deeply resented Lowell's troops, especially the officers, taking the trouble to come by and say "so long."

It had been necessary to get Major Lowell out from under Colonel Peebles before there could be trouble. Harrier had arranged for Lowell to work with the Secretary of the General Staff and for his sergeant major to handle the dog-robbing tasks for him. Lowell was shortly to go home, anyway, and Harrier decided he was entitled to go home without having an official run-in with Peebles.

Idly curious to see what Lowell was up to, pushing a typewriter at midnight in his tent, General Harrier turned off the pebble path, walked to Lowell's tent, and pushed open the door.

Wearing nothing but his drawers, Lowell was sitting before a typewriter, his fingers flying over the keys, and for a moment General Harrier thought he was writing a letter. Then he realized that was wrong. Lowell was retyping something. There were sheets of carbon in the typewriter, and all sorts of official-looking documents strewn on the folding table and on Lowell's cot, which he had dragged beside the typewriter.

General Harrier watched him for a moment, and then he said, softly: "We have typists, you know, to do that sort of thing."

Lowell instantly stood up.

"Sorry, sir, I didn't know it was you. I thought it was Colonel Peebles."

"What the hell are you doing, anyway?" Harrier asked, and walked to look at what was in the typewriter.

"This is the staff study for the organic air section, sir," Lowell said.

"I'm touched at your dedication," the general said, dryly.

"You said as soon as possible, sir," Lowell said.

"What I meant to suggest was that you apply the whip to the typing pool," the general said, "not do it yourself."

"Well, sir," Lowell said, "the truth of the matter is, I've made several changes in your study. While the typists are typing yours, I'm typing mine. It was my intention to present both of them to the general for his consideration, sir."

"You have *improved* what I gave you, Lowell?" the general asked. "Is that what I hear you suggesting?"

"There were several areas I thought perhaps the general had overlooked," Lowell said.

"Why don't you tell me about them now?" the general said, dryly sarcastic. "You might save yourself a lot of typing."

The air section had simply evolved. According to the tables of organization and equipment, aircraft—either airplanes or helicopters—were provided only to tactical organizations. L-5s and L-19s were assigned to the Corps for messenger service as aerial jeeps; to the Corps of Engineers for aerial survey; and to the Medical Corps for use as ambulances.

As far back as World War II, it had been obvious to some officers that there were other uses for light aircraft. Patton had ferried an entire infantry battalion across the Rhine River, one man at a time, in the back seat of two-man L-5s taken from tactical units and pooled for that specific purpose.

Once the Korean War had started, the need for more and more aircraft within the army had become immediately evident. The commander of the X Corps at Inchon, General Ned Almond, had had to borrow a helicopter from the Marines to make his way around Korea.

So far the solution to the problem had been unofficial. There were far more aircraft and pilots than the tables of organization and equipment (TO&E) provided. They were just carried as "excess."

The "excess" aircraft and pilots had been pooled at division and corps to provide aerial support to the headquarters and to units which were not provided with aircraft. The aircraft and their pilots, however, remained assigned to the units which were authorized on the TO&E. When a division was shifted from one corps to another, or relieved, their aircraft and pilots left with them.

For some time General Harrier had wanted to make the assignment, the authorization, official, but had put off doing anything about it until he had Lowell dumped in his lap. The boy came with a reputation as an S-3. OK. Let him do it. He told the Secretary of the General Staff to get it done and had not been at all surprised when the SGS had given it to Lowell to do. Working from General Harrier's detailed draft, Lowell was supposed to prepare the final version of the staff study, the basic army document for a change in policy, which Harrier would sign and send off on its lengthy bureaucratic journey to the Pentagon.

Given Major Lowell's seldom hidden belief that the army (with a few exceptions such as himself) was equipped with staff officers who were less than fully competent, General Harrier was not surprised that Lowell had made changes in his arguments and his proposals. Harrier was also aware that there were few majors who didn't believe they had better solutions to a given problem than the one proposed by a general. So it came as no surprise to General Harrier that Lowell would try to "improve" on the work of a man literally old enough to be his father and who had been an officer when he was born.

What surprised General Harrier was that when he read Lowell's version of the staff study he had to admit there *had* been improvements to his original proposals and the arguments in favor of them. There was no mistaking it; it was excellent staff work, and Harrier recognized it as such.

There were some places where Lowell was dead wrong, too, and Harrier pointed them out to him.

"We'll go with your version," Harrier finally said. "As changed. Have it typed up."

"Yes, sir."

"To tell you the truth, Lowell—and I'm aware I'm running the risk that your head will swell even larger—that was pretty clear thinking. Perhaps you're not quite as incompetent as Colonel Minor suggests."

"Thank you, sir."

"I meant that, Lowell, just the way I said it. *Have* it typed up. All work and no play makes Lowell a dull boy. Go down to the club and get yourself a drink."

"One of the reasons I did this, General," Lowell said, simply, "was to keep myself out of the club."

"Oh?"

"It's a good thing I'm not rich," Lowell quipped. "I could very easily become a drunk."

Harrier was concerned. Jiggs had told him about Lowell's wife. The day he'd earned himself a footnote in the history books with Task Force Lowell, the day he had become a twenty-four-year-old major, there had been a TWX telling him he was a widower. Maybe he was into the sauce and worrying about it.

"But you *are* rich," General Harrier said. "I just got the report of your Top Secret background invesigation. Fascinating reading."

Lowell didn't reply.

"Getting yourself a reputation as a teetotal, a drudge," General Harrier said, "could do your career as much harm as being rich. A lot of business is transacted at an officer's club bar. You can tell a man, at the bar, that he's as full of shit as a Christmas turkey, and get away with it. You can't do that in an office."

"Yes, sir," Lowell said.

"Your trouble, Lowell, if you do stay in the army, is not going to be doing your duty," Harrier said. "It's going to be concealing your opinion that most people are horse's asses."

Lowell didn't reply.

"Most of them are, Lowell," General Harrier said. "But you can't let them know." He smiled at the young officr. "Good night, Lowell."

"Good night, General."

[TWO]

When General Harrier left Lowell's tent he started to walk back up the hill toward the White House and the general officer's quarters. Then he changed his mind about going to bed. He wasn't sleepy. He walked to the sandbagged G-3 operations bunker. The MP guard on duty outside was standing more or less erect with his Thompson submachine gun in the proper sling-arm position rather than sitting down on the sandbags with the Thompson on his lap, so Harrier knew that someone senior was inside.

"Good evening, sir," the MP said, giving him a crisp hand salute.

"Good evening, Sergeant," Harrier said, and walked inside. Inside, there was the sound of the smaller, separate diesel generator that provided power for the Ops Center, and the clatter of a teletype machine. The G-2 and G-3 were in the Ops Center, and so was the general.

"Insomnia," Harrier explained his presence. "Tomorrow night, I won't be able to keep my eyes open."

He walked to the enormous situation map, and one of the G-2 sergeants told him what was going on. Not much. With the exception of some harassing and intermittent artillery fire on the positions of the 45th Division, and a couple of platoon-sized probing patrols against the 187th Regimental Combat Team, the front was quiet.

The bureaucrats were at work, however, General Harrier thought. The teletype machine was still clattering. He turned to look at it. The general was watching it, and possibly something was up, for the general waited until the lengthy message had been completely transmitted and then tore it from the machine himself. He carried it to one of the two upholstered chairs facing the situation map, sat down, and started reading the three-and-a-half-foot length of yellow teleprinter paper.

General Harrier went and sat in the other upholstered chair and waited patiently for the general to finish reading the TWX. The general snorted, swore, and made unbelieving faces as he read the document, and Harrier knew that whatever it was, the general didn't like it. Finally, he handed the yellow sheet of paper across the small table between the chairs to Harrier.

"When I was a G-3," the general said, "I moved an entire infantry division from North Africa to Sicily with a shorter Ops Order."

Harrier glanced at the heading of the TWX in his hands.

FINAL ITINERARY: THE WAYNE BAXLEY AND HIS ORCHESTRA USO TROUPE.

Harrier began to skim over the TWX. In infinite detail, it listed the members of the USO troupe, by age, sex, and assimilated rank, ranging from the lowest stagehand, who would be accorded the privileges of a lieutenant while in Korea, to Mr. Wayne Baxley and Miss Georgia Paige, the movie star, who would be treated as VIPs, that is, provided with quarters and transportation normally reserved for major generals. Then, in fifteen-minute segments, it traced where the troupe would be from the moment it landed at K1 Airfield outside Pusan until it boarded the transport planes which would fly it back to Tokyo from K16 (Kimpo) outside Seoul thirteen days later.

But the general was not finished: "Furthermore," he said, "I entertain very serious doubts that these troupes really do anyone any good."

"Sir?" General Harrier asked, to be polite. The general wanted an audience.

"The alleged purpose of these USO things is to raise troop morale," the general said.

"I thought it was to remind the troops of the girls they left behind," General Harrier replied. "For whom, along with Mom's apple pie, they are allegedly fighting."

"It reminds them of girls, all right," the general said. "And, if you get right down to it, that's pretty damned cruel, maybe even perverse."

Harrier was surprised to realize that the general was quite serious.

"They bring these girls over here, and get them to prance around the stage wearing just enough clothes to keep them from getting arrested, and that reminds these healthy, horny young troopers of girls all right. And then we tell them they can look, but they can't touch. Now, that's cruel *and* perverse."

"I really hadn't thought of it that way," Harrier said.

"In terms of efficiency," the general said, "it would be cheaper to do what the French do."

"From what I've heard," General Harrier said, chuckling, "that solution occurred to Paul Jiggs, too."

The reference was to the French custom of providing brothels to troops on the line, and to the rumor that the ambulances of the 8222nd Ambulance Platoon attached to the 73rd Heavy Tank Battalion (Reinforced) had carried warm female bodies to the MLR as often as they had carried wounded bodies away from it.

"Shame on you, General," the general said. "Those were volunteer native nurses, bringing what comfort they could to the troops."

There was general chuckling, involving the sergeants as well as the colonels and the generals. The general took notice of it.

"It's a good thing I know you guys don't talk about what you hear in here at the NCO mess," he said. "It always breaks my heart to send a good G-2 or G-3 sergeant down to walk around a QM dump with an M1 on his shoulder."

The sergeants laughed.

"Well, what about it?" the general asked one of the G-3 sergeants. "Do the troops get any good out of these USO shows?"

"Even if all I can do is look, General," the sergeant replied, "that's better than nothing."

"OK, so I'm wrong," the general said.

"General," the G-2 sergeant said. He was a thin man in his early thirties. "You know what pisses the troops off? The way the women wind up with the officers. I mean, in the messes."

"Well, damn it, that's not my fault. They tell us where to feed them," the general said. He pointed to the TWX. "Hell, they even tell us who we have to assign as escort officers. Did you see that, Harrier? Paragraph 23. Or somewhere along in there."

General Harrier found Paragraph 23 on the long sheet of teleprinter paper.

```
23. In order to facilitate the movement of the Troupe through
its itinerary,each Corps (and the XIX Corps, Group) will
assign one officer, preferably an aide-de-camp, in the grade of
major or above as escort officer for the Troupe while it is
within the respective Corps area. (Or the area of the XIX
Corps, Group). Such officer will report to the Wayne Baxley
Troupe Escort Officer (Col. Thomas B. Dannelly, or his
designate) two (2) days before the Troupe is scheduled to
arrive at the respective Corps (or at the XIX Corps, Group) and
will remain attached to the troupe until it departs the
respective Corps (or the XIX Corps, Group).
```

"What do you think about that?" the general asked. Harrier handed the TWX to the G-3, who, it occurred to him, had been too polite either to ask for it, or to read it over Harrier's shoulder.

"Sorry, Charley," General Harrier said, and then responded to the general's question. "I presume, General," he said, "that the press of urgent military duties has, regrettably, made our aides unavailable for anything else, no matter how worthy an enterprise."

"What do you propose?" the general asked.

"Let the special service officer handle it," Harrier said. "Let him go himself, if it comes to that."

"No," the general said. "Do you know that they actually run an after-operations critique on these things? And if we didn't give up one of the aides, there would be a paragraph in there saying we had failed to comply with paragraph such and such, and some chair-warming sonofabitch with nothing better to do would have us replying by indorsement stating our reasons. It will be less trouble to send them an aide."

"Yes, sir," Harrier said.

"Just keep those people away from me, Harrier, while they're here," the general said.

"Away from you, sir?"

"Another paragraph in there 'strongly recommends' that the commanding generals entertain them at dinner. As of right now, General, entertaining visiting movie stars and band leaders is the responsibility of the chief of staff."

"Yes, sir," Harrier said.

"Just get them in here, and out of here, with no waves," the general said.

"Yes, sir," Harrier said. "Sir, the chief of staff has always believed it is his duty to bring to the corps commander's attention facts of which the corps commander may not be aware."

"Such as?"

"Does the name Georgia Paige register with the general, sir?"

"That the one who goes around without a brassiere?" the general asked.

"Yes, sir."

"What about her?"

"Does the corps commander really wish to forego the opportunity to reconnoiter that anatomical terrain personally?"

The general laughed.

"The chief of staff is herewith advised," he said, "that in his heart of hearts, the corps commander is like any nineteen-year-old trooper in the Corps. If he can't have it, he doesn't want to have it waved in his face."

"Does the chief of staff have the corps commander's permission to look, sir?"

"You ought to be ashamed of yourself, Harrier," the general said, and laughed again. "Just keep those boobs away from me."

"Yes, sir," Harrier said.

General Harrier took a pencil from his pocket and bent over the sheet of teletype paper.

"Action: SGS," he wrote. "Maj Lowell. Harrier." He held the teletype in the air, and the commo sergeant came and took it from his hands. Major Lowell was the junior field-grade officer among the six aides-de-camp. Junior officers get the dirty jobs.

Christ, knowing Lowell, General Harrier thought, he was liable to wind up getting his hands on the magnificent boobs of Miss Georgia Paige. She really had a gorgeous set. General Harrier had seen her picture on the posters announcing the coming of Wayne Baxley and His Orchestra. He wasn't that old.

It had been a flip, irreverent thought. And then he had a somewhat sobering thought: Maybe a woman was what Lowell needed. Lowell had never taken an R&R. He'd been in Korea since he'd returned from the compassionate leave he'd taken right after his wife had been killed. Was it "devotion to duty," an unwillingness to leave his duties? Harrier didn't think so. It was probably that he was afraid he was going to lose control. He was holding it all in. He couldn't do that forever. Maybe he could get himself laid.

Bullshit. These people didn't come over here to fuck the troops. They come to entertain them, and to get their names in the papers.

The odds against Major Craig Lowell, or any soldier, getting into the pants of Georgia Paige, or any of the other women in the Wayne Baxley Troupe, were probably precisely the same as they would be if they paid a ticket to see them in the Paramount Theater in New York. On the order of two million-to-one.

[THREE]
Kwandae-Ri, North Korea
30 August 1951

When Lieutenant General E. Z. Black walked out of his office into the office of the Secretary of the General Staff of the United States XIX Corps (Group), he found that officer, a thirty-five-year-old major, having words with another officer who looked just about old enough to be a lieutenant, despite the gold major's leaf on his fatigue jacket collar.

That aroused General Black's curiosity, as did the fact that the young major wore a nonstandard holster with a German Luger in it. And then, when the SGS saw General Black and shut off the conversation and got to his feet, and the young major came to attention, he saw that he was wearing some very interesting insignia, the two-starred aide-de-camp's insignia on the other collar point, and the triangular armored force insignia with the numerals 73 where the armored division number was supposed to go.

"Go on," General Black said, "I can wait. Take care of the major."

"Sir," the SGS said, "I just informed the major that we have no Major MacMillan here."

"And?" General Black said.

"And I asked the major if he was inquiring on behalf of General Harrier, and he tells me he's inquiring personally."

"What do you want with MacMillan, Major?" General Black asked.

"He's an old friend, sir," Lowell said. "I was under the impression he was your aide, sir."

"He was," General Black said. "But I'm afraid he's not available. I can get word to him, if you'd like, that you were here to see him."

"Thank you, sir," Lowell said. "It's not important. I just happened to be here and thought I'd take a chance and try to look him up."

"Is General Harrier coming here?" General Black said.

"No, sir. Not that I know."

"You just came to see Mac, is that it?"

"No, sir. I'm here about the USO troupe."

The young major was obviously less than thrilled about being baby-sitter to the movie stars. Understandable. He was a tank officer.

"How long were you with the 73rd Heavy Tank?" General Black said.

"About eleven months," the young major said.

"Then you were in on Task Force Lowell?"

"Yes, sir," the young major said, with a funny kind of a smile.

"Well, when you go home," General Black said, "you can remember that, and forget the USO baby-sitting."

"Yes, sir."

"You have the advantage of me," General Black said. "You know my name, but I don't know yours." He put out his hand.

"Lowell, sir," he said.

"You're Lowell?" General Black said. "That Lowell?"

"Yes, sir. I had the task force, if that's what you mean."

"What are you doing as a dog robber?" General Black asked.

"I've got a couple of months to go before I rotate, sir. And when they sent in a qualified S-3, Colonel Jiggs found a home for me."

"And now you're baby-sitting the USO? Jesus Christ!"

Lowell didn't say anything.

"I gather you're not tied up with them now?" General Black asked.

"No, sir. I've got a transportation truck company due here by 1800, to move the troupe baggage. The air force is going to pick up the movie stars at 0745 tomorrow."

"In that case, you've got time for a cup of coffee?" General Black said. "I read that after-action report. You gave a lot of people fits using M24s as supply guards, and armored trucks to take the point."

"I hope I didn't give you a fit, sir."

"Hell, no," Black said. "The way to use armor is to hit as hard as you can with the most you've got, not telegraph your punches."

He threw a stack of papers to the SGS.

"See if you can keep people from bothering me for the next forty-five minutes or so," he said to the SGS, and then he motioned Major Lowell into his office ahead of him.

General Black was bored. If they wouldn't give him an armored force to command, and since he was too old, anyhow, to command a tank force in a classic cavalry maneuver, the next best thing was to do it vicariously. He wanted to talk to this young officer, full of piss and vinegar, who had proved pretty goddamned clearly that there was still a place for cavalry and a balls-to-the-leather attitude in the age of nuclear warfare.

"You can either have coffee, Major," Lt. General Black said, "or a belt of this." He held up his last bottle of 24-year-old Ambassador scotch.

"I think the booze, sir," Major Lowell said.

"I was afraid you'd say that," General Black said. "The most dangerous place in the world to be is between a bottle of booze and a thirsty cavalryman."

He poured Lowell three inches in a glass.

"Christ," he said, "from what I read in the after-action report, I'd have really liked to have been along on that operation. Tell me, Major, where did those armored trucks—what did you call them, 'Wasps'?—come from?"

Lowell sat down without being asked to, sipped on the general's splendid scotch, and told him about the Wasps and Task Force Lowell.

[FOUR]

When Miss Georgia Paige saw the blond young major enter the XIX Corps (Group) general officer's mess with the corps commander himself, it confirmed the feeling she had had in their first, ninety-second encounter: This was somebody special.

He had reported to Colonel Dannelly, the troupe escort officer, during lunch. He had looked at her long enough, Georgia thought, to be disappointed to see that she wasn't brassiereless under her khaki shirt. That was the first thing they all checked to see. That no-bra business had been a stroke of pure genius on the part of Tony Ricco, her press agent. It had even gotten her on the cover of *Life* long before her career had reached the point where *Life* would have paid any attention to her at all, much less put her on the cover.

It had been a little embarrassing when Tony had called to her in front of all those people in the studio to blow on the nipples so they'd stand up, but that had been what really made that photograph take off when they handed it out to the press, and then used it in the advertising. *The New York Times* and the *Chicago Tribune* wouldn't use the picture without airbrushing the nipples sticking up under the shirt, but Tony had gotten press mileage out of that, too.

Georgia was aware that her nipples were the first thing men thought of when they saw her. The good-looking young major had been no different from the others about that, but there was something different about him. Maybe because after he'd looked and saw that she was wearing a bra, he had just stopped paying attention to her.

He even refused Colonel Dannelly's invitation to sit down and have some lunch. He said that he had a friend he wanted to look up, if he could. She had been disappointed, and that had surprised her. What the hell difference did it make? Christ, there were enough good-looking young men in her life, some of whom actually liked women. What was one soldier, more or less?

She had been curious to meet this general. Her father had told her that he was one of the legendary generals from World War II, one of the tank generals under somebody named Waterford (whom she had never heard of) and Patton, whom everybody had heard of. And this general, unlike the other ones, seemed to have gone out of his way to avoid meeting with the troupe. That had made Wayne mad. Wayne Baxley was very conscious of being a star, leader of what he really believed was "America's Favorite Orchestra," and he considered it his right and due to be fawned over by the brass. She wondered if this general had really been as busy as his flunkies said, or if he just didn't want to be around Wayne Baxley and the other "stars." There had even been some question as to whether he was going to show up on this last night.

But here he was, and the young major was with him, and it was obvious to Georgia that Colonel Dannelly couldn't figure that out.

"It's a pleasure to meet you, Mr. Baxley," the general said. "We're happy to have you with us."

Wayne Baxley, oozing charm, replied that he always tried to do whatever he could for the boys in uniform. He told the general that Bob Hope had told him he was Number Two in terms of miles traveled to entertain the boys in uniform. Georgia thought that was so much crap, and wondered if the general believed him. For one thing, she didn't think that Bob Hope would be seen in public with Wayne Baxley, and if they had actually met, she was sure Baxley had called him "Mr. Hope" and hovered around him the way the brass here was hovering around this general. Finally, Wayne got around to introducing her.

"And every GI's dream girl, General, Georgia Paige," Wayne said. Georgia was surprised he hadn't called for a round of applause.

"How do you do, Miss Paige?" the general said. He had not looked to see if she was wearing a brassiere.

Then the general said: "I suppose, Lowell, you've met our guests?"

"Yes, sir," the good-looking young major said.

He looked at her, and then away, as if embarrassed to be caught looking. Georgia flashed him one of her warmest smiles, but it was too late. He was examining the stones in the fireplace of the general's mess.

A sergeant walked up to them with a tray full of drinks.

The general took a drink, and then he leaned over and spoke softly into the sergeant's ear. Georgia shamelessly eavesdropped: "Put Major Lowell beside me," he said. The sergeant nodded.

For a moment, Georgia wondered if the general had something going with the young major. He was pretty enough. And then she discarded that notion, reminding herself this was the army, not show business, and the army was funny about faggots. Wayne had given a speech to the fairies, telling them that if anyone started fooling around with the soldiers, he would have to answer to him.

The way they were seated at dinner was with Georgia between two generals, the one, Black, her father had told her about, and the other a major general (two stars), one rank lower than Black. The young major was on the other side of General Black, and Wayne Baxley on the side of the other general. Where he was just about completely ignored by both generals, even when he went into his drunken Italian harmonica player routine.

The general spent dinner talking about tanks, and some task force, and the other general listened in to that conversation. And the young major had trouble keeping his eyes on the general, and off of her, which made her both feel better and worry a little. Could he tell she was interested, or was he finally aware that she was a movie star?

After dinner, of course, Dannelly moved in as quickly as he could when they were standing around the bar with brandy and coffee. She stayed with the general, because it was obvious that Major Lowell was wanted there. She was surprised how much: When Colonel Dannelly "suggested" that Lowell might like to watch them take the stage down after the last show, so that he could see what was involved, the general had shot that idea down.

"I'm sure he didn't get to be a major at his age without knowing how to load a trailer truck," General Black said. "And if you can spare him, we haven't finished our conversation."

"Certainly, sir," Dannelly said. "I'm sorry, sir."

"How old are you, Major?" Georgia heard herself asking. "You look a little young to be a major."

"Twenty-four," he said.

"Christ," General Black said, "I knew you were young, but not that young." Then he looked at Georgia. "George Armstrong Custer was a brigadier general when he was twenty-one, Miss Paige," he said. "But that was during the Civil War. You see very few twenty-four-year-old majors these days. As a matter of face, you see practically *no* twenty-four-year-old majors." The subject seemed to fascinate him. He turned back to Lowell. "Jiggs get you the leaf after Task Force Lowell?" he said.

"Actually about two hours before we linked up," Lowell said.

"Oh, you were with Task Force Lowell, were you, Major?" Colonel Dannelly asked.

"That's why they called it Task Force Lowell, Colonel," General Black said, sarcastically.

"What's a Task Force Lowell?" Georgia asked.

"This young man took thirty-eight M46 tanks, Miss Paige," General Black said, "and some self-propelled artillery, and using them as an armored force is supposed to be used—which hasn't often happened in this war, unfortunately—ran them around the enemy's rear, disrupting his lines of communication, blowing up his dumps and his bridges, for nine days. Phil Sheridan couldn't have done any better."

Georgia had no idea who Phil Sheridan was. But it was obvious that the general, for different reasons, was as favorably impressed with this blond young man as she was.

The young major sensed Georgia's eyes on him, looked at her, and blushed.

All of a sudden, it occurred to Georgia Paige that when these people talked about George Armstrong Custer, they weren't thinking of Errol Flynn playing a role, but a real person. General Black, who was obviously impressed with the young major, had *really* known and fought with General Patton. The young man who blushed when he looked at her, had actually done whatever the general had said he had done, "disrupting lines of communication, blowing up dumps and bridges."

Confirmation came when they were walking from the general's mess to the outdoor theater where they would give the final performance in the XIX Corps (Group) area.

"Well, that explains what he's doing as an aide," Colonel Dannelly said.

"The blond kid, you mean?" Wayne Baxley asked. "I didn't get to hear much of that conversation."

"What were you saying, Colonel?" Georgia asked.

"Every once in a while, a really outstanding young officer turns up," Dannelly said. "One that they know is going to be a general. So they give him assignments to train him. Working as a general's aide is one of them."

"You mean, they could look at that kid and tell he's going to be a general?" Wayne asked, disbelievingly.

"He's halfway there already," Colonel Dannelly said. "I feel a little foolish. I should have known who he was. He's wearing the 73rd Tank patch."

Midway through her act (which consisted of a couple of minutes of repartee with Wayne Baxley, most of his "humor" a mixture of innuendo and wide-eyed staring at her boobs, followed by three vocals, during which she had the chance to slink around the stage in a dress cut incredibly low in the back to remind everybody that she was the one who went braless), she looked into the wings and saw Lowell standing there in a shadow.

She sang the rest of the song to him, looking over the microphone right at him, wondering (the thought somewhat shocking her) if he screwed as well as he fought. She normally didn't have thoughts like that, and even if she was attracted physically to some man, she didn't think words like "screwing." She was a little bit afraid of him, she realized. Now that she thought of it, she didn't believe he was twenty-four. They had been pulling Dannelly's leg. She was twenty-three. He had to be older; otherwise, how could he make her feel like a foolish girl?

He was gone from backstage when she finished her act, and she didn't see him again that night, although she hung around the general's mess until it was late, hoping he would show up.

He wasn't at breakfast either, and when she asked Dannelly where he was, Dannelly said he'd flown ahead to IX Corps to make sure the trucks with the troupe's portable stage and all the props had arrived safely.

When the C-47 landed at the IX Corps airstrip, she looked out the window for him. He was sitting on the hood of a jeep. When the door of the airplane opened, and the photographer's flashbulbs started going off, he was standing to one side. Their eyes met. Georgia smiled. She had a funny feeling in the pit of her stomach. Down there.

He knows, she thought. And I should be embarrassed, but I'm not.

At lunch, when they had a rare moment alone, Georgia realized she had to get him away from the others. She had an idea.

"I've never been close to a tank," Georgia said, winsomely.

"They're all on the line," he said. "You're not permitted up there."

"Please," she said. For some damned reason it was important.

"I'll see if I can get one down here for you to see," he said.

"Thank you," Georgia said.

She touched him then for the first time, letting her hand rest for a moment on his lower arm. He was warm and muscular.

He was also (although perhaps with the exception of Captain Sanford T. Felter, who was his best friend, no one would believe it) very inexperienced with women. Certainly none of the men in the 73rd Heavy Tank would believe that the Duke had known only two women sexually in his life. There had been an afternoon session in a sailboat just before he had been expelled from Harvard College. He got so excited finally getting her white shorts off, finally seeing what one really looked like, that his loss of virginity occurred on the second stroke.

When he had been sent to Germany, where women were quite literally available for a half-box of Hershey bars, or a box of Lux form the PX, he had remained chaste, less from a sense of morality than a sense of horror of what would happen to him, down there, if he caught something. The army had prepared a technicolor training film with a lot of footage taken in Walter Reed Army Medical Center, in the ward where patients suffering from the third stage of syphilis were treated. There was a lot of footage of suppurating open ulcers on the genital organs. Eighteen-year-old Private Craig W. Lowell had been convinced. He took his sexual gratification through masturbation, thinking of the girl at college, and what it had looked like, felt like, in the thirty seconds it had been all his.

And then there had been Ilse. He hadn't been able to get it up with her the first time he tried it with her. But it had finally worked, and he had fallen in love, and if you are nineteen and in love, you don't cheat on your beloved. Not even if you are an officer serving with the 24th Royal Hellenic Mountain Division, and women are provided to take care of the officers.

And certainly not if you are an officer and a gentleman and an Episcopalian off in a war. As a happily married husband and father, you are aware of sexual drives, certainly, and what a strain abstinence is. You might possibly arrange for a group of Korean women to be examined by the battalion physician, but you don't have anything to do with them. What you do, if you're an officer and a gentleman and a faithful husband and father, is jerk off in a Kleenex feeling just a little ashamed that the imagery is that of your wife.

And when some drunken fucking quartermaster major in an Oldsmobile comes racing down a cobblestone road on a rainy afternoon, and wipes out your wife, then you just don't have any urges. The only thing it's now good for is to piss. It will probably never work again. It's better that way. What the hell, they had better than three years together. He had known it was too good to last. But he had thought that he would be the one to get blown away over here, not that some fucking QM asshole would wipe her out.

He didn't even think of women. He thought he would never think of women again.

And then, when Georgia Paige had leaned over to pick up something from a table, thirty seconds after he met her, and he saw the white of her brassiere down her open collar, it all came back. The photographs of her with her nipples standing up against the material of her shirt. Knowing that they were there, six feet away, right under that white brassiere.

And what was under her underpants, the outline of which he could see through her tight khaki pants.

And part of his brain telling himself he was a fucking fool. For one thing, she was a famous movie star, and what the hell would she want with him, especially after she found out how old he was. Maybe, if she'd thought he was thirty, he could have succeeded in making a pass at her. But if she did fuck him, then that meant she would fuck anybody, that the only difference between her and the Koreans in the ambulance was that she was white and didn't smell of kimchee.

"I tried to find a tank," he told her. "There aren't any in reserve that I could get."

"You mean there's no extras at all?"

"I mean there's only so many hours on their clocks, and I wasn't going to order one down here that they may need tonight."

That just slipped out. For Christ's sake, what was the matter with him? She wasn't some goddamned sergeant he could tell off like that.

"I'm sorry," he said.

"I shouldn't have asked," she said. "I'm sorry."

"All it is is a big tractor with sides," he said. "Nothing but a big steel casting one tracks. You're not missing anything."

"I want to see what you do," she said. His heart beat very heavily, once, twice, three times.

"I'm sorry," he said.

"Take me up there," she said.

"Out of the goddamned question," he said.

She braided her hair and pinned it on top of her head. In the jeep, there were two steel helmets and two ponchos. She drove. The MPs didn't look at jeep drivers, he said.

They got to the helmet line, and he folded the top of the jeep down and laid the windshield flat on the hood, and showed her how to drape the poncho over the steering wheel. The rain on the helmet sounded like rain on a tin roof.

They went up the side of a mountain at four miles an hour, the transmission in low-low. There were fireworks overhead, beautiful orange streaks that seemed to float through the sky. He told her they were harassing and intermittent .50s, and that for every orange tracer she saw, there were four bullets she couldn't see.

A soldier with a submachine gun pointing out at them from under a poncho stepped in front of them.

"Who the fuck are you?" he asked, and then he saluted. "Jesus Christ, Major, we didn't expect to see you back up here."

"You didn't," he said. "OK?"

"You got it," the soldier said.

"Where's Baker Company?"

"Right here," the soldier said. "You're right in the middle of it."

There was a sound like a freight train right over their heads.

"That's that motherfucking 8 incher," the soldier said. "Cocksuckers try to see how close they can come."

The soldier looked at her, idly curious, in the dim red glow of a shielded flashlight.

"Jesus Christ, I don't believe it," he said.

"That's why you didn't see me, OK?"

"Hey, Miss Paige," the soldier said, "I'm sorry about the language, but this is the last fucking place . . . Sorry."

"It's all right," she said.

"She wants to see a tank," Lowell said. "Where's Blueballs?"

"Second down the line," the soldier said. "You going to take her in the CP?"

"If you guys can keep your mouth shut," Lowell said.

"Hell, Major, you know we can."

"Don't leave your post," Lowell said. "I'll have somebody relieve you."

They gave her coffee and doughnuts in the CP, and apologized for not having any milk. Somebody had a box of flashbulbs, so they crowded everybody they could together in the pictures, until the bulbs were used up.

And when everybody in Baker Company, 73rd Heavy Tank, had either shaken the hand of, or gotten the autograph of, or been kissed by Miss Georgia Paige, Lowell took her back out in the rain and showed her Blueballs. That's what she thought he had said, and there it was, painted on the turret in yellow: BLUEBALLS.

"That's quite a name," she said.

"It used to be called something else," he said. "But then the colonel said we had to use names with a B."

"What was it called before?"

"I forget," he said. And then he said, "Ilse."

"Who's Ilse?" Georgia asked, jumping on that. "Your girl?"

"I used to be married to a girl named Ilse," he said.

"I'm sorry," she said.

"She's dead," he said. "She was killed in a car crash."

"While you were here?" She knew that, somehow.

"Yes," he said.

"Oh, honey," she said, "I'm so sorry." She put her hand on his arm.

The crew climbed out of Blueballs, and then helped her climb up on it.

Lowell went in first, then put his hands on her hips and lowered her inside. It was white inside, dirty, and smelled of burned powder and burned electrical wiring and oil. There were 90 mm cannon shells in racks, and boxes of machine-gun ammunition, and leather helmets.

"This was yours?" she asked.

"Yes. From Pusan to the Yalu," he said. There was deep pride in his voice.

"Blueballs?" she asked.

He blushed again.

"For the reason I think?" she asked.

He didn't reply. She put her hand out and touched his cheek.

"We better get out of here," he said. "They'll be looking for us."

He put his hands on her hips again and hoisted her half out of the turret. She could feel his hands trembling.

"Wait a minute," she said, and found a footing on something, then pulled furiously at her khaki shirt and jerked the brassiere out of the way. Then she lowered herself back down inside the tank, until her breasts were at the level of his face, and he could suckle at her famous nipples.

XIII

[ONE]
Ch'orwon, North Korea
5 September 1951

Miss Georgia Paige's good intentions to keep her personal life and her professional life separate vanished as she stood in the door of the C-47 which would take her, and the other members of the Wayne Baxley troupe, from the IX U.S. Corps airstrip to K16 at Seoul and eventually, via Tokyo, home.

Dressed in a khaki shirt (fetchingly unbuttoned almost to her navel) and khaki trousers, with a fatigue cap perched on top of her head, she smiled and waved for the photographers, and actually turned to duck her head and enter the aircraft. But then she jumped off the airplane and ran weeping into the arms of an impeccably dressed young major, clinging tightly to him, her face first buried against his chest, and then raised to kiss him.

The hundred or more troops gathered to watch the troupe make its departure applauded, whistled, and cheered. Wayne Baxley finally had to get off the C-47 to get her, wearing a broad "Ain't that touching" smile on his face for the benefit of the photographers, but actually furious in the knowledge that photographs of her smooching that goddamned Lowell kid were the ones that would make the papers, not those taken of himself.

In the door, finally, tears streaming down her face, Georgia Paige threw Major Lowell a kiss and mouthed the words, "I love you."

And then Wayne Baxley pulled her inside, and the door was closed. The C-47's left engine kicked into life with a cloud of blue smoke and the plane taxied to the end of the pierced-steel planking landing strip and took off.

It was the first time an oral expression of love had passed between the young officer and the young actress. They had, however, frequently expressed their affection physically following Georgia's uncontrollable urge to offer Lowell her breasts in the turret of Blueballs. They had spent that night making love on Lowell's narrow cot in his tent on Colonel's Row, getting no more than an hour's sleep at a time, one or the other of them waking to lightly stroke and awaken the other, and then to join their bodies and fall asleep entwined together.

At 0400 Georgia had "sneaked" back into the VIP Quonset hut on the hill, past one of the guards who had an enormous knowing grin on his face. If she was going to fuck some officer, the enlisted men were generally agreed, Major Lowell was the deserving one. The Duke had class.

At 0530, Major Lowell had carried a tray with toast and coffee and jelly from the general's mess to the VIP Quonset in case one of the VIPs had wakened early and wanted toast and coffee. Only one of the VIPs was awake, and she was not interested in toast and coffee. She was fresh from her shower, and at 0535 she and Major Lowell were making the beast with two backs in the somewhat wider and more comfortable bed with which the VIP quarters were equipped.

At 0615, when the corps commander entered his mess after his ritual first-thing-in-the-morning check of the situation map, he found Major Lowell and Miss Paige, heads close together, having breakfast, and saw what looked very much like the imprint of human teeth marks on Major Lowell's lower neck.

The Wayne Baxley troupe gave a 1030 performance near the 8077th MASH for MASH, ordnance, engineer and chemical units in the immediate area. A second performance on the same stage was given at 1430 for personnel of the 223rd and 224th Infantry Regiments of the 40th U.S. Infantry Division, and their immediate supporting units, the 555th Artillery Group and the 73rd Heavy Tank Battalion (Reinforced). The 73rd lived up to their reputation, as reported to Colonel Minor by the captain he had dispatched to "keep an eye on things."

Many of them were drinking, the captain reported, and long after the performance was over, four military policemen were found tied up and less their trousers. They had made the mistake of remonstrating with the tankers over the beer and whiskey.

The 73rd had sent a tank to the performance, God only knows why, and the obscenity painted on the turret ("Blueballs") was certainly going to appear in press photographs, for Miss Paige had obligingly agreed to pose for photographs with the men of the 73rd and their tank. What was worse, they had appeared with a hand-lettered sign three feet tall and twenty feet long, with the legend "Georgia Paige Can Play with Our Bats Anytime."

Colonel Minor realistically concluded it could have been worse. With Colonel Jiggs having gone home, and Major Lowell now at Corps Headquarters—the two of them replaced by a colonel and an S-3 who understood the necessity of strict discipline—things were a lot better than they had been, even considering the beer and whiskey drinking and the vulgar sign. While there was obviously a good deal yet to be done, the 73rd Tank Battalion was considerably less a uniformed group of thugs and madmen than it had been.

Neither Miss Paige nor Major Lowell appeared for dinner that night in the general's mess, but they turned up in the general's six-by-six van, loaded for use as the star's dressing room, when the troupe showed up at the new location for the performance for troops of the 24th Infantry Division that night.

On the final day in the IX Corps area, after the daytime performances intended to entertain troops who for one reason or another could not attend the earlier ones, there was no evening performance. It was believed that now that the troops had received their creature comforts, it was all right for the brass to be entertained. The troupe entertained in the field-grade officer's mess. Those who had hoped to meet Miss Paige personally were to be disappointed, however. She disappeared immediately after performing, claiming to have a headache.

A rumor circulated that the chief of staff's aide, that boy-faced major, was fucking the ass off her, but this was generally discounted. General Harrier, not to mention the general, wouldn't stand for something like that, and anyway, why would someone like Georgia Paige want to fuck a lowly major?

The general, entering the chief of staff's office three hours after the C-47 had carried the Wayne Baxley troupe away, smiled warmly at the chief of staff's junior aide-de-camp, and politely observed that he looked a little peaked. "You getting enough sleep, Lowell?"

Twenty-two times. Twenty-two times for sure. Maybe twenty-three or twenty-four. Sometimes, it was twice in a row. He had lost count, although he tried very hard to remember each time. Jesus, he had never believed you could really fuck that often. But all she had to do was touch it, and it popped up like a spring, ready to go.

At 1500 on the day the troupe departed, General Harrier told Major Lowell that he had obviously been working around the clock, and why didn't he just knock off for the rest of the day and come in in the morning with his eyes open.

Lowell lay on his cot, half dozing, half dreaming of Georgia, but he didn't sleep. And by 2000, he came back to earth. He got dressed and went up to the White House and went to work. It was amazing how goddamned much paper could accumulate in five days.

By midnight Lowell had cleaned up the work that had accumulated while he had been off baby-sitting the USO troupe and falling in love. He went to his tent and got undressed. He realized he wasn't sleepy, and that if he didn't want to toss and turn for an hour, if he wanted to get some sleep, he would need a drink. Booze always made him sleepy. But there was no booze in the tent. He would have to go get a drink. He put on a fresh, stiffly starched fatigue uniform and started for the general's mess.

He realized he didn't want to go there. For one thing, General Harrier was liable to be there, and Harrier had told him to get some sleep. Or the general would be there, and the general's innocent crack about whether he had been getting enough sleep hadn't been innocent at all. He didn't want to see the general, or any of the other aides, especially Peebles. That left the field-grade mess.

But he didn't want to go there, either. At this hour of the night, the only people in the field-grade mess were going to be field-grade drunks, the majors and lieutenant colonels who really had nothing to do the next day they couldn't do hung over. And they could be counted on to make a pitch to the chief of staff's aide-de-camp, either for some specific, invariably idiotic personal project, or just on general principles, so they would have a friend in high places.

To hell with that, too. He kept walking, and headed for the company-grade mess, where his drinking companions would be lieutenants and captains and a few majors who preferred that company to the more prestigious company they could find in the field-grade mess.

There was an enormous black man sitting alone at the bar, hunched over a drink.

Lowell walked up behind him, deepened his voice, and said: "I really hate to drink with ugly niggers."

Captain Philip Sheridan Parker IV, after a moment's absolutely rigid hesitation, turned slowly on his stool to the right, cold fury on his face. As he turned to the right, Lowell moved out of his line of sight. Parker suddenly swung around the other way.

"Jesus Christ, look at you!" Phil Parker cried out. He grabbed Lowell by the ears and kissed him wetly in the middle of the forehead. "Oh, my God, a major! How the hell did you do that?"

"I cheated," Lowell said.

"What the hell are you doing here?" Parker asked, as Lowell slid onto the stool beside him.

"Slumming, actually," Lowell said. "How the hell goes it, King Kong?"

"How's Ilse? And P. P.?"

"Ilse's dead, Phil," Lowell said.

He was shamed to realize that he hadn't thought of Ilse, or P. P., at all in the last ninety-six hours.

"Oh, my God!" Parker said, in anguish. "How the hell did that happen?"

"Automobile accident, in Germany," Lowell said. "In September. Just about a year ago."

"For Christ's sake, you should have written," Parker said, angrily. "Goddamn, that's awful."

"That's the way things go," Lowell said.

"So you came back in the army?"

"I was here when it happened," Lowell said. "Some quartermaster asshole in Germany got drunk and ran head on into her."

"My God, Craig, you know how sorry I am!"

"Yeah, thanks," Lowell said.

"A year ago?" Parker asked. "You were here a year ago?"

"Yeah. I'm about ready to rotate." He thought: And now I have a reason to go home. I have someone to go home to.

"Seventy-third Heavy Tank?" Parker asked softly.

"Yeah."

"I should have known that was you," Parker said. "But I asked around and they said the task force commander had been a major, and in my innocence, I decided there was no way you could have been a major."

Lowell didn't want to talk about that, and he didn't want any more of Parker's sympathy about Ilse. It made him very uncomfortable.

"How long have you been here?" he asked.

"From the beginning," Parker said. "I had the first M4A3s in Korea."

"Company commander?"

"Tank Company, 24th Infantry," Parker said. "And I was so proud of myself for making captain. I should have known you'd one-up me."

"Just a natural recognition of my genius."

"But you went home, when . . . it happened, I mean?"

"I went to Germany," Lowell said. "It turned out that Ilse's father really is a colonel and a count. P. P. is with him."

Phil Parker was naturally curious about that. It was a long time before Lowell could change the subject again.

"You haven't told me what you're doing here. If my tour is just about over, you should have been sent home a long time ago."

"They're having a general court-martial," Parker said.

"And you're on it?" Lowell said. "Great, it will give us some time together. I'm dog robber for the chief of staff."

"I'm not on it," Parker said. "I'm the accused."

"What the hell did you do?"

"I am charged with violation of the 92nd Article of War," Parker said.

Lowell searched his memory for what that meant.

"Article 92 is murder-rape," he said, after a moment. "What happened, Phil? Some nurse change her mind?"

"I'm charged with murder," Parker said.

"If this is some kind of joke, Phil, I miss the point."

"No joke, Craig."

"You want to tell me about it?"

"Not particularly."

Lowell grabbed the bottle from the bar.

"I'm taking this with me, Sergeant," he said to the bartender. "Put it on my bill."

"Major, you can't do that," the bartender said.

"Sergeant, I'm not supposed to do it. There's a difference between 'not supposed to' and 'can't.' " He took Phil Parker's arm. "Let's go, King Kong," he said.

"Where are we going?"

"Colonel's Row," Lowell said. "Try to behave."

They didn't go directly to Colonel's Row. They stopped by the company-grade officer's tents, where Parker shared a squad tent with three other officers. Parker took a large manila envelope from beneath his air mattress, and when they were in Lowell's tent handed him a thick report, bound together with a metal fastener.

"Once they have decided to go through with the court-martial," he said, "they have to let you know what they have against you."

He gave the document to Lowell.

SECRET

HEADQUARTERS
EIGHTH UNITED STATES ARMY
OFFICE OF THE PROVOST MARSHAL

17 August 1951

SUBJECT: Report of Investigation into Allegations Concerning Captain Philip S. Parker IV, 0-230471

TO: Judge Advocate General
Eighth United States Army

1. Attached hereto are interviews conducted with various personnel by agents of the Criminal Investigation Division, OPM, Eighth Army, in connection with certain allegations concerning the conduct of subject officer.

2. These interviews are summarized as follows:

a. CPL Francis F. YOUNG, RA 32777002, formerly assigned to Company "I," 24th Infantry Regiment, 24th Division, was interviewed at the Tokyo Army Hospital where he is undergoing treatment for wounds. YOUNG stated that on or about 14 July 1950 near Sangju, Republic of Korea, during retrograde movement, he saw a "tank officer" shoot to death with a "six-shooter" LT Ralph J. ROPER, Commanding Officer of "I" Company. ROPER was then making his way to the rear. Troops then accompanying ROPER were returned to the line. It has been established that CAPTAIN PARKER (then 1LT) was in the vicinity at the time, and that he carries, as a personal weapon, a revolver believed to be a 1917 Model Colt .45 ACP. YOUNG, however, on being shown a photograph of PARKER, was not able, or was unwilling, to positively identify PARKER as the officer who shot ROPER to death.

b. LT ROPER was initially carried on the rolls as Missing in Action and Presumed Dead. Attempts to locate his remains by Quartermaster Graves Registration Service following the breakout were only recently successful.

c. 1LT Charles D. STEVENS, 0498666, Tank Company, 24th Infantry Regiment, was interviewed at Tokyo General Hospital, where he is undergoing treatment both for burn injuries received in combat and neuropsychiatric division, related the following: On 16 September 1950, shortly after he joined Tank Company, 24th Infantry Regiment, in the vicinity of Tonghae, Republic of Korea, he was serving as a crew member of an M4A3 tank. This was apparently part of an on-the-job training program instituted by PARKER in contravention of regulations. STEVENS was serving as a loader on a tank commanded by 1SGT Amos T. WOODROW, RA 36901989.

Tank Company, 24th Infantry, PARKER commanding, had participated in an unsuccessful attack by the 24th Infantry against the enemy near Tonghae. After an initial penetration of enemy lines, heavy enemy mortar and artillery fire made it impossible for 2nd Battalion, 24th Infantry, to cross a rice paddy and take up positions in support of Tank Company, then commanded by PARKER.

PARKER was in radio communication with 2nd Battalion, and the interchange between them was audible to STEVENS over the tank intercom system. PARKER informed 2nd Battalion that he was in control of former enemy positions and would hold until such time as 2nd Battalion could make their way to him. STEVENS described PARKER'S judgment of the security of his position as unsound, stating that they were under severe artillery and mortar fire, and that it would be only a matter of time until all the tanks involved were destroyed. 2nd Battalion advised PARKER by radio to withdraw, stating that another attempt would be made following an artillery barrage.

At this point, a tank commanded by SFC Richard M. OGLEBY (ASN unknown) was struck by enemy artillery fire which destroyed its right track and severed its radio antennae. The tank, however, remained operable, if immobile, and continued to engage the enemy. The damage to SFC OGLEBY'S tank was reported by WOODROW to PARKER by radio. PARKER then ordered WOODROW to leave his tank, make his way to the disabled tank, and order its crew to abandon the damaged vehicle. WOODROW complied with this order and STEVENS assumed command of that tank. In making his way to the damaged tank, WOODROW was struck and killed by mortar fire.

STEVENS reported that WOODROW had been killed by radio to PARKER. PARKER then ordered STEVENS to move his tank, and to recover WOODROW'S body, and then to proceed to the damaged tank to evacuate its crew.

STEVENS reported that, in his judgment, PARKER'S order was sucicidal, and he requested reconsideration. PARKER repeated the order. At this time STEVENS overheard a radio message to PARKER ordering him to withdraw to the departure line. Presuming this order superseded PARKER'S order, STEVENS ordered the driver to back out of the position, and to withdraw as ordered. (The driver was SGT Quincy T. ARRANS, JR., RA 14375502, a newly assigned replacement.)

STEVENS states that PARKER, observing this movement, went on the radio and said, "Hold in place, you yellow sonofabitch, or I'll blow you away," or words to that effect. STEVENS attempted to relay this order to ARRANS, but, probably because of a defective intercom, ARRANS did not hear the order, and continued to move the tank.

At this point, STEVENS'S tank was struck by what he believes to be a HEAT round fired by PARKER. It struck the right rear track, and fragments penetrated the engine compartment, severing fuel lines and setting the tank on fire. ARRANS successfully exited the burning tank, but was killed a few minutes later by mortar fire. STEVENS, in exiting the tank, suffered second and third degree burns over 25 percent of his body. He extinguished the flames on his clothing, and sought shelter in a ditch.

At approximately this point, enemy artillery and mortar fire decreased to such a level that the Commanding Officer of 2nd Battalion chose to mount a second assault, which was successful. STEVENS was located by medics of the 2nd BATTALION and evacuated, in a semiconscious condition, to the 8048th MASH.

d. SGT Lowell G. DABNEY, RA 35189632, Tank Company, 24th Infantry Regiment, was interviewed at Tokyo General Hospital where he is undergoing treatment for wounds suffered in the same engagement. DABNEY was the gunner of the WOODROW-STEVENS tank. He had joined Tank Company as a Private after his unit, "I" Company, 224th, had been involved in the incident described in the YOUNG interview.

(1) He stated that he heard PARKER order WOODROW to send STEVENS from the tank over to the disabled tank, and that STEVENS refused to comply with WOODROW'S order, whereupon WOODROW left the tank, leaving DABNEY in charge.

(2) When WOODROW was hit, DABNEY stated he left the tank to offer what aid he could.

(3) That the moment he left the tank, it began to withdraw, and was a moment later struck by an enemy mortar in the engine compartment, which set it ablaze.

e. Records of the 8112th Ordnance Company indicate the tank, which was recovered after this action, was struck with a HEAT round, probably of American manufacture.

f. Attempt to garner further information from other personnel of the Tank Company, 24th Infantry Regiment, by agents of the CID have been generally unsuccessful. Apparently no other personnel heard the radio traffic referred to, or if they have knowledge of such traffic are unwilling to relate it. CAPTAIN PARKER has declined to answer questions of any sort, claiming the protection of the 31st Article of War.

LaRoyce J. Wilson
Colonel, Corps of Military Police
Provost Marshal

1st Ind

HQ EIGHT US ARMY 23 Aug 51
201-PARKER, Philip S (Capt) 0-230471
TO: Commanding General, IX US Corps

For appropriate action and reply by endorsement hereto

FOR THE COMMANDING GENERAL
Steven G. Galloway
Colonel, Judge Advocate General's Corps
The Judge Advocate General

2nd Ind

HQ IX US CORPS 1 Sep 51
201-PARKER, Philip S (Capt) 0-230471
TO: Commanding General, Eight US Army

1. In consideration of subject officer's performance in Korea, which included a battlefield promotion to the grade of Captain, and the award of the Silver Star and Purple Heart Medals, he was offered the opportunity to resign from the service for the good of the service under the provisions of AR 615-365.

2. Subject officer has declined to submit his resignation.

3. A board of officers convened under the provisions of the 31st Article of War has considered the allegations made against subject officer, and has recommended that he be tried by General Court-Martial for murder and attempted murder.

4. This headquarters will try subject officer before a General Court-Martial and your headquarters will be advised of their decision.

FOR THE COMMANDING GENERAL
Thomas C. Minor
Colonel, Adjutant General's Corps
G-1

"Pure chickenshit," Lowell said. "Why the hell didn't you resign?"

"I'm a soldier, Craig," Philip Sheridan Parker IV said.

"And you're innocent, right?"

"They have their facts straight," Parker said. "Or almost."

"And you're going to just walk in there and lay down, right?"

"I'm going to do whatever happens."

"Why don't you resign, if you're not going to fight it?"

"Because I would rather be cashiered for doing what I did, than have people think I resigned because they found out I was a thief, or queer . . . or any of the other reasons they let people resign for the good of the service."

"You're liable to wind up in Leavenworth, you realize that?"

"I've considered that."

"Well, we can't have that," Lowell. "We'll just have to beat this court-martial."

" '*We'll*' have to beat it?" Parker asked, chuckling.

"Shit, if they throw you in Leavenworth, then it would be just me against the system," Lowell said. "I don't want to be all alone."

"And you've already figured out a way to beat the court-martial, right?"

"No," Lowell said, "but I just figured out who to ask." He looked at Parker, and their eyes met, and they both were embarrassed by the emotion.

"Christ," Lowell said, after a moment, "that's the trouble with you junior officers. Take our eyes off you for thirty seconds, and you've stuck your dick in the fan."

[TWO]
Beverly Hills, California
9 September 1951

The moment the Pan American DC-6 rolled up before the terminal building at Los Angeles International, and Wayne Baxley looked out the window and saw the reporters, print and television, rushing out to the plane, he realized bitterly that the scene the big-teated cunt had staged at the IX Corps airstrip just before they left would grab her all the press.

There was no chance the press was there to meet him. Standing in the middle of the assembled press corps was the cunt's wop press agent, holding a copy of the *Los Angeles Times* over his head in both hands. The *Times* was carrying the same photo he had seen in the *Honolulu Reporter-Gazette* when they had refueled there, a three-column photograph of Miss Georgia Paige, tears running down her cheeks, in the embrace of a soldier.

Wayne Baxley had no trouble reading the headline: GEORGIA SAYS GOOD-BYE TO HER GI. *"Georgia,"* for Christ's sake, as if everybody knew her by her first name. He wasn't a GI, either, goddamn it, he was a goddamned officer. The story in the Honolulu paper had made it even worse:

SOMEWHERE IN NORTH KOREA September 7 (AP)—He was just one of the more than a hundred combat-weary GIs who slipped out of the trenches and sandbag bunkers of this battle-torn land to say good-bye to Georgia Paige as she left for home after entertaining the troops. Then the actress whose pictures adorn every fox-hole here became just another American girl as she ran weeping into the arms of her GI, who was going to have to stay here and fight while she went off to what the GI's call the "land of the big PX."

There were cheers and applause and more than a few teary eyes in battle-weary faces as the girl all the GIs dream of clung desperately to one of their own. Wayne Baxley, whose band was part of the Paige USO Troupe, finally had to separate the young lovers and put her on the plane. Georgia turned in the door of the Air Force transport for a final look at her GI, and then the door closed, and the GI vanished in the crowd before anyone could learn his name.

It wasn't a goddamned band, for God's sake. It was the Wayne Baxley Orchestra. And it wasn't the cunt's USO troupe, it was the Wayne Baxley Orchestra Troupe. She was just fucking excess baggage.

Wayne Baxley had a hard time smiling as he made his way through the reporters and photographers. He declined to be interviewed, asking the boys for their understanding. It was a long way home from Korea, and he and the orchestra were tired.

He knew himself well enough to know that if he said anything to the press, he was liable to tell them just what he thought of that big-boobed publicity stealing cunt.

In the studio-sent limousine on the way to Beverly Hills, Mr. Tony Ricco, Miss Georgia Paige's press representative, leaned over and kissed Miss Paige on the cheek.

"I'm proud of you, baby," he said. "How the hell did you manage the tears."

"Fuck you, Tony," Miss Paige said, angrily,

"What the hell's the matter with you?" Mr. Ricco inquired. "Don't tell me you've got the hots for this guy?"

"I've got the hots for him," she said. "OK?"

Mr. Ricco put his hands up in front of himself, as if to ward off an attack.

"How long does it take to get a roll of film developed?" Miss Paige inquired.

"Couple of days," he said. "What kind of film?"

"You can do better than a couple of days," Georgia Paige said. "Like today, Tony." She handed him a roll of 35 mm film.

"What the hell is this anyway?" Tony asked. "A picture of Mr. Lucky?"

"Yeah, and they're personal, Tony. Just get them souped and printed and give them to me. Craig's going to be mad enough about that story in the papers."

"Why should he be mad?" Tony asked, in honest bewilderment.

"You wouldn't understand," she said.

"Try me," he replied.

"He's not just a GI," Georgia said. "He's an officer."

"I'm glad that wasn't in the papers," Tony said. "It's better that Mr. Lucky's an enlisted man."

"What I want you to do," Georgia said, "is count the people in the pictures, and get them to make me up two eight-by-tens for each one. I promised the kid who took them I'd do that."

"Whatever you say, baby," Tony said.

"And get it done today," Georgia said. "With what I spend on publicity photos, they can do that for me right away."

"I'll take care of it," Tony said.

When the first print came off the drum dryer, Tony saw that he had something special. For one thing, dumb luck probably, the pictures were perfectly exposed and focused. For another thing, they were taken right up on the line. There was a sign: YOU ARE UNDER ENEMY OBSERVATION FROM THIS POINT FORWARD. And the GIs looked like combat soldiers. They looked like combat soldiers who couldn't quite believe that Georgia Paige was right there with them.

"Marty," Tony called out, "make me another set. One of each, eleven-by-fourteens."

Then he picked up the telephone and called the Time-Life LA Bureau.

"Bob," he said, "how would you like, exclusively, some first-class color shots of Georgia actually on the front line?"

[THREE]
Socho-Ri, North Korea
10 September 1951

It wasn't that Major Craig Lowell said that he was on the official business of Major General Harrier. It was simply that it was presumed that he was, when he showed up at the airstrip and announced he had to go find a major over in the XIX Corps area, and that he'd better go in a chopper, in case there would be no landing strip for an L-19.

Half a dozen aviation section pilots were sitting around operations on homemade couches. The only difference between them, Lowell thought (as he often did), and the half dozen GIs who sat around the office in the motor pool was that the clowns who flew the puddle jumpers and whirlybirds had benefitted from an aberration in the system which decreed that people who flew little two-seater $15,000 airplanes and $75,000 choppers had to be officers. M46 tanks, which cost $138,000 and had a crew of four, were commanded by staff sergeants.

Major Lowell had once been heard to say that army aviators had to back up to the pay table. It had not endeared him to the army aviators, but there wasn't much they could do about it. He was both a major and the aide-de-camp to General Harrier.

"Fortin," the operations officer called to one of the pilots, "take Major Lowell where he wants to go."

Finding MacMillan wasn't all that difficult. He was an aviator, and they all knew each other. When they touched down at the XIX Corps airstrip, Lowell sent the chopper jockey inside to ask where MacMillan was. He was back out in two minutes.

"He's at a strip on the East Coast, Major," he said. "But you're supposed to have special permission to land there."

"You got it," Lowell said. "Let's go."

Thirty minutes later, the H23 fluttered down at Socho-Ri. A competent-looking technical sergeant carrying a 12-gauge trench shotgun drove up to the chopper in a jeep and politely informed them that this was a restricted area. If they were broken down, he added, he would relay any messages they had, but they couldn't leave the airstrip.

"I'm here to see Major MacMillan," Lowell said.

The sergeant, with a perfectly straight face, said that there was nobody named MacMillan around Socho-Ri.

"I don't have time for any of your cloak-and-dagger bullshit, Sergeant," Lowell said. "I know MacMillan is here. And what happens now is that we're going to get in that jeep and you're going to take me to see him."

The sergeant examined Lowell closely and thoughtfully for a long moment before he made up his mind, and gestured with the shotgun toward the jeep.

The sergeant drove them to a small village, now surrounded by a double row of concertina barbed wire. There were guards, armed with Thompson submachine guns and the trench shotguns, but they didn't stop the jeep when it passed through the gate in the barbed wire.

They stopped before the largest of the thatched-roofed, stone-walled houses.

"This is where you want to go, Major," the sergeant said.

Lowell entered the building. There were several enlisted men and a warrant officer inside, and a table with nonstandard communications radios.

"Major," the warrant officer said, "I don't think you're supposed to be in here."

"Where's the commanding officer?" Lowell demanded. The warrant officer indicated a closed door. Lowell walked to the door, knocked on it, and then pushed it open without waiting for an invitation.

"I'll be damned," he said.

"Well, hello, Craig," Captain Sanford T. Felter said, moving his hand away from the .45 Colt automatic that lay on the desk beside a manila folder imprinted with the words TOP SECRET in three-inch-high red letters.

The two men looked at each other without saying anything else for a moment.

"You're not supposed to be here," Felter said. "But I guess you know that."

"If I had known you were here, I would have been here sooner," Lowell said.

"Yes," Felter chuckled, "I know you would have. That's why I didn't let you know that I was."

"I never got a chance to really thank you," Lowell said, "for what you did when Ilse. . . ."

"No thanks are necessary, Craig," Felter said. "You know that."

"I owe you," Lowell said. "Don't forget that."

"How are you doing, Craig?"

"All right," Lowell said. "Actually, how I'm doing is that I'm in love with a movie star named Georgia Paige. But I don't think now is the time to tell you about that."

"Craig," Felter said, "you really shouldn't be here. You shouldn't even know about this place."

"Funny," Lowell said, "I thought we were on the same side of this war."

"You don't understand," Felter said.

"I understand you're a spy," Lowell said. "But don't worry. I have a Top Secret clearance myself."

"It would be better if I came to see you," Felter said.

"I'm here to see MacMillan," Lowell said. "You're an unexpected bonus."

"What do you want with him?" Felter asked, rather coldly.

"A friend of mine is up before a general court-martial," Lowell said.

"And you think that MacMillan will be able to come up with some clever little trick to get him off?" Felter asked, sarcastically, almost angrily.

"Yeah. That's what I hope," Lowell said. "MacMillan is the best guardhouse lawyer in the army." He was growing annoyed with Felter.

"I know what you're going to think, and say, before I say this, Craig," Felter said, "but you're going to have to do without MacMillan."

"You want to tell me why?"

"Because what we're doing here is more important than your friend in trouble," Felter said. "And you know me well enough to know I wouldn't say that unless I had to."

"If I wasn't desperate, I wouldn't be here."

"I'm sorry, Craig," Felter said. "It's a matter of priority."

"What my friend is accused of is shooting an officer who refused to fight. You know how that happens sometimes." The look in Felter's eyes was frightening. They locked eyes for a long time.

"You can talk to MacMillan," Felter said, finally; and it was, Lowell realized, the voice of command, a decision beyond argument. "But you are not to involve him. I don't want any attention directed to us through him. You understand that?"

Felter called in one of the sergeants and told him to take Lowell to MacMillan. MacMillan was aboard one of the junks Lowell had seen as the H23 prepared to land. From the air, it looked like any other junk. Up close, he saw what it really was. There were mounts for .50 caliber machine guns bolted to the deck, foreward and aft. There were radio antennae mounted to the masts, and through an open hatch, Lowell saw large diesel engines.

MacMillan himself was sitting on the deck of the aft cabin with three Koreans, all of them carefully inspecting belts for .50 caliber machine guns. MacMillan seemed neither pleased nor surprised to see Lowell, although he got to his feet when he saw Lowell and broke out a bottle of 12-year-old scotch. And he said, after a moment, what he was thinking: "Jesus Christ, what are you, twenty-three?"

"Twenty-four," Lowell said. "Me being a major bothers the shit out of you, doesn't it, Mac?"

"Yeah, I guess it does," MacMillan said. "You're a long way from the golf course at Bad Nauheim, aren't you, PFC Lowell?"

"I would never have guessed that you, Captain MacMillan, sir," Lowell said, a little annoyed, "would end up as a pirate."

"I don't think this is really auld lang syne time," MacMillan said. "What do you want, Lowell?" But before Lowell could start to reply, MacMillan said something else. "Felter told me what happened to your wife. Sorry about that, Lowell. What did you do with the kid?"

"He's in Germany. His grandfather came home from Russia."

"I wrote Roxy and told her, and she wrote back and said I should send her your address. I never got around to it, but what Roxy wants to do is offer to help. You need anything?"

"Not for the boy," Lowell said. "But a friend of mine is in trouble. You remember the big guy I ran around with at Knox?"

"Man Mountain Coon, you mean?"

"They're going to put him before a general court-martial," Lowell said.

"Charged with what?"

"In the early days over here, he blew away an infantry officer when he wouldn't fight."

MacMillan sipped deeply at his drink before replying. "I heard of that happening," he said, "to people you wouldn't believe."

"I need some help," Lowell said.

"For openers," MacMillan said, "You start by saying, he *is accused* of blowing this guy away. You don't admit it if he did it on the White House lawn with the President watching."

"The first thing I thought about," Lowell said, "was getting on the telephone and having a criminal lawyer sent over from the States. But then I thought that might make him look guilty. And then I thought of you."

"You don't need a high-priced lawyer for the trial," MacMillan said. "That pisses the court off. Later, on appeal, is when you need the real shysters."

"You sound pretty sure they'll find him guilty."

"Is he?"

"He did what they say he did."

"That doesn't necessarily mean he'll get convicted of it," MacMillan said. "But the thing you have to keep in mind is that general courts generally know what the convening authority wants done. If the general who convened the court wants your friend hung, he'll probably be found guilty."

"Shit!" Lowell said.

"Well, it's no big deal," MacMillan said. "Even if they sock him with a death sentence, it won't be carried out; aside from rapists and criminal types, the army has executed only one man since the Civil War. What will probably happen, the worst that will happen, is that the court-martial will find him guilty, sentence him to death, or life, to make the point that you aren't supposed to go around shooting people, and the general, on review, will commute death to life, or life to twenty years, and he would be out, with good behavior, in maybe five, six years."

"How do we keep him out of jail at all?" Lowell asked. "I don't care what it costs, Mac."

"Money won't do you any good here," MacMillan said. "Maybe later. The best thing you can do is check around and find some reserve judge advocate officer, who's really pissed about being called back in the service and doesn't give a shit for his army career or efficiency report. Get him to defend your friend. He may be lucky. But even if he's not, a good civilian lawyer can generally get anybody off on appeal. Somebody is bound to fuck up something in the paperwork."

Sandy Felter showed up on the junk as they were killing the last of the twelve-year-old scotch. Lowell wondered if he had really come to drive him back to the airstrip, now that he was finished, or if he had come to let him know his time was up. But on the way to the airstrip, Felter said, obviously sincere: "Hey, I'm sorry about the reception."

"Forget it."

"What we're doing here is important," Felter said. "It comes first."

"In other words, nice to see you, but don't come back?"

"Yeah."

"I won't."

"I hope your friend comes out all right," Felter said.

"But you really don't give a damn one way or the other, do you?" Lowell asked.

"No, I guess I don't, when you get right down to it."

"What if it were me?" Lowell asked.

"I don't know," Felter said, honestly.

"If you had to do it again, Sandy, would you blow away Captain Whatsisname?"

Felter gave him another incredibly cold look, one almost of hate, and certainly of contempt.

"You don't understand, do you?" he said. "I didn't do what I did to save your neck. I did it because that officer was interfering with the mission."

"No, Sandy, I guess I don't," Lowell said. He put out his hand, and they shook hands, and they smiled at each other, but it was as if it was between strangers.

XIV

[ONE]
Ch'orwon, North Korea
15 September 1951

Major Craig W. Lowell was aware that he was not only on the shit list of Major General John J. Harrier, but that he was about to become the ne plus ultra persona non grata of the IX Corps chief of staff.

The trouble he was in, in other words, was not one half the trouble he was going to be in.

He wasn't sure if he had gone slightly crazy, or if the reverse was true, that he had finally come to his senses, but the bottom line, in that quaint vernacular of Wall Street, was that he really didn't give a damn.

At the moment, it seemed to him that the army, which was having a shit fit about what had happened when Georgia had been in the Corps, was acting quite childishly. Morality and propriety had been offended, and he was the guilty party. It reminded him somewhat of the time his school had been in New Jersey playing tennis against Peddie and had been entertained by the students and faculty of Miss Beard's School in Orange, where he had put Ex-Lax on the candy plates. It had given seven or eight fifteen-year-old girls diarrhea, and sent the head into a frenzy.

The only difference seemed to be that the head at St. Mark's hadn't known who had put the Ex-Lax on the candy plates, and the head here knew who the sinner was.

There had been a lightning bolt from the Pentagon. A heavy manila envelope, sealed and stamped BY OFFICER COURIER, had been sent from the Pentagon in the hands of a replacement lieutenant colonel, brought from the Dai Ichi Building in Tokyo to Eighth Army Headquarters by the warrant officer courier carrying the week's cryptographic codes, and from Eighth Army to IX Corps by the Eighth Army commander's junior aide-de-camp, who personally put it in the hands of the corps commander.

The corps commander had then opened it and summoned the chief of staff, and both of them had then solemnly contemplated a short, square piece of notepaper, the letterhead of which was a representation of a full general's four-star flag, flying in the breeze.

The message was brief: "The Chief of Staff desires your comments on the article on pages 73–78 of *Life* magazine, enclosed."

Life had somehow come into possession of the roll of film Georgia had taken at the 73rd Heavy Tank Battalion and then carried with her back to the States. *Life* had run a full-page photo showing Georgia, wearing body armor, standing with a group of tankers. There were eight tankers, six enlisted men and two officers, including Major Craig W. Lowell. Behind them was Blueballs.

They were good photographs, and the name "Blueballs" was clearly legible. So was what the troops of Baker Company—in mockery of the air force practice of painting kills on the side of the aircraft fuselages—had painted on the turret: eight silhouettes of Russian-built T34 tanks, with an X drawn through them, signifying the eight confirmed kills made by Blueballs (five of them when it had been "Ilse" on the way up the peninsula, and three by later commanders). There were also, for a laugh, silhouettes of ox carts, Korean papa-sans, and people in wheelchairs, with X's indicating they had been wiped out, too.

There was a large line of type superimposed on the picture:

GEORGIA PAIGE VISITS THE FRONT LINES.

The caption beneath the picture read: "Her world-famous bosom hidden beneath a bulletproof vest, her long locks in braids, Hollywood's hottest new star slipped away from the USO troupe entertaining troops in the rear areas to visit this tank battalion on the front line 'somewhere in North Korea.' "

The other five pages showed Miss Paige while an unshaved GI poured bourbon in her canteen cup; autographing a copy of the famous erect-nipples photograph stapled to a company situation map; kissing one soldier while a line formed behind him; and being helped down from Blueballs by two eager soldiers. Her shirt was improperly buttoned, as if she had had it off. Lowell was in most of the pictures, sometimes looking at Miss Paige as if she gave milk, and wearing his German Luger in the shoulder holster with the GOTT MIT UNS belt buckle gleaming.

Lowell had been called in by General Harrier to answer for his sins. There had been a recitation of them.

"There seems to be absolutely no question, Major Lowell, that, in direct violation of regulations, and showing less common sense than that expected of a corporal, you actually took that woman up to the front."

"No, sir," he said. "I mean, yes, sir. I took her up there."

"What were you thinking?"

He could hardly have told the general what he was really thinking.

"I regret any embarrassment I have caused, sir."

"That's not good enough, Lowell. I can't remember ever having been so humiliated by the actions of one of my officers."

"With all respect, sir, I fail to see how my actions could humiliate you."

I am, after all, a fucking major, and I don't think they expect major generals to go around holding majors by the hand.

"There you are, for all the world to see, wearing an unauthorized weapon, in an unauthorized shoulder holster, with a Nazi motto on it."

"God is with us" is a Nazi *motto? Does he really believe that?*

"And standing in front of a tank with an obscenity painted on it."

"I repeat, sir, my regret for any embarrassment I may have caused you."

"And I repeat, Major, that's not good enough!"

"Yes, sir. What would the general have me do, sir, to make amends?"

"Just close your damned mouth," General Harrier had said. "When I want a reply, I will ask for one."

There followed a long pause.

"What I really would like to do to you, Lowell," General Harrier finally said, "is stand you before a court-martial for conduct unbecoming an officer and a gentleman!"

I wonder where it says in Amy Vanderbilt that what I've done is ungentlemanly.

"With the press around here, however, that would only result in even greater embarrassment to the army."

You're goddamned right it would. The army would really look silly if you tried to throw a court-martial at me.

"You stand relieved as my aide," General Harrier said. "Your behavior will be reflected in your efficiency report. Until your orders are issued, you will remain in your tent except for meals. You will come here to empty your desk between the hours of 2000 and 2030 tonight. Aside from that, I don't want to see you around this headquarters again. You are dismissed."

"Yes, sir," Lowell said. He saluted and about-faced, then walked down to Colonel's Row.

When he went back that night to clean out his desk, he saw how the general had replied to the Chief of Staff. The letter had been typed and then placed on the aide's desk, so that he could give it to the general for his signature first thing in the morning.

Hq IX Corps
APO 708
San Francisco, Cal.
16 Sept 51

Dear General Malloy:

The Corps Commander has asked me to reply to your note regarding the article in *Life* magazine. My junior aide-de-camp, Major Craig W. Lowell, was the IX Corps Escort Officer for the Baxley USO Troupe while they were in the IX Corps area.

Major Lowell, who, you may recall, commanded Task Force Lowell during the breakout from the Pusan perimeter and the link-up with X U.S. Corps, is a responsible combat commander who would not, obviously, endanger the life of Miss Paige by taking her (or any other civilian) into a position where there would be any danger of enemy action.

When the Baxley Troupe performed for troops including the 73rd Heavy Tank Battalion (Reinforced) near the 8077th MASH, some troops of "B" Company, 73rd Heavy Tank, Major Lowell's former command, and without specific permission to do so, brought one of the "B" Company tanks from the line to the 8077th MASH area. I can only presume that they hoped their former company commander would be able to get them special consideration to pose with Miss Paige in photographs; in any event, this obviously transpired. Enclosed are photographs of Miss Paige, the tank Bluebell, and troops of Baker Company taken at the time, and which were not published in *Life*.

Both this unauthorized movement, and the very questionable "humor" of the lettering and symbols on the tank in question were brought to my attention by the IX Corps G-1, Colonel Thomas C. Minor. I am attaching a copy of his report, including photographs of the tank in question, together with the copy of my letter to the CO, 73rd Heavy Tank Battalion, directing him to immediately correct the spelling of the name of Bluebell, and to obliterate all symbols except those of the eight T34s Bluebell has been officially credited with killing.

We have, obviously, as you are well aware, no control over what *Life* magazine, or any other publication, chooses to say. However, what responsibility there is for this unfortunate incident is clearly mine. I have counseled Major Lowell, informing him that his special consideration for troops of his former command was ill-advised and unseeming.

I stand ready, of course, to answer any other questions you might have.

Sincerely,
John J. Harrier
Major General

Lowell checked his uniform. His aide-de-camp's insignia were gone, and the crossed sabers of cavalry superimposed on an M46 tank were back. The Luger and the shoulder holster were locked in his footlocker, as were his tanker's boots and his tanker's shoulder holster. He had gone to supply and drawn a standard web belt and holster. He was, he decided, in the perfect uniform prescribed for a field-grade officer "awaiting assignment" at IX U.S. Corps.

Then he walked up the hill to the White House, and entered the office of the Secretary of the General Staff.

"I thought that you were told to stay in your quarters until you got your orders," the SGS, a normally pleasant, just promoted to full bull colonel, said.

"Yes, sir."

"I sent you orders sending you home an hour ago," the colonel said.

"Sir, I am in doubt as to which orders I should obey," Lowell said. "And am coming to you for clarification." Then he laid a letter on the Secretary of the General Staff's desk. It was signed by First Lieutenant Bennington T. Morefield, Judge Advocate General's Corps, and informed him that he was to hold himself available to appear as a witness for the defense in the case of *The United States of America v. Captain Philip S. Parker IV*.

[TWO]
Ch'orwon, North Korea
16 September 1951

Major General John T. Harrier went into the office of the corps commander, and closed the door.

"Major Lowell has not left the Corps, sir," he said. "He has been summoned as a witness in Captain Parker's court-martial."

The general thought that over a moment, and then he asked: "As a witness for the defense?"

"Yes, sir."

The general thought that over a moment, too; then he said: "I think that it would be a very good idea, John, if you attended the trial. I want to avoid, of course, any suggestion of command influence on the outcome. But I think it's entirely appropriate that everyone concerned be aware that this case is of special interest. I would hate to have the trial disrupted by the irrational behavior of anyone."

"Yes, sir."

"What the hell has Lowell got to do with that trial, anyway? I wasn't even aware they were acquainted."

"I don't know, sir."

"Keep me advised," the general said.

Despite what he had said about wanting to avoid "any suggestion of command influence," there was no doubt in Harrier's mind that the General wanted Parker hung. He wondered why. Some personal feeling that Parker deserved punishment?

Racial prejudice? There was *something*, otherwise they could have sent any other officer in the headquarters to "keep him advised."

When the general's chief of staff walked into the courtroom, the court would draw the obvious conclusion, that having decided to court-martial Parker, the general wanted a report on anyone who appeared to be trying to frustrate that desire.

Harrier walked down the hill from the White House and entered the tropical building with the sign SILENCE: COURT IN SESSION outside. There were two MPs outside the building, who saluted him, and two more inside the building, who pulled the door to the courtroom open for him.

He walked in and tried to make himself as inconspicuous as possible in the rear of the small room. It was like trying to hide an elephant, he thought, under a tulip.

He was surprised at the initial steps of the trial. He had been a defense counsel in his younger days, and he would not have stricken from the court, on preemptory challenge, the two officers Lieutenant Bennington T. Morefield struck from it. They were a bird colonel and a lieutenant colonel, both wearing the Combat Infantry Badge. He would have kept them, as probably being sympathetic to another combat officer.

And he was surprised at Lieutenant Bennington T. Morefield's behavior during the prosecution testimony. He had expected objection to practically everything the CID agents said, as well as the quoting of arcane legal principles which would be beyond the understanding of the court-martial officers.

He did nothing of the kind. He didn't challenge the facts at all. The court could have no question in their minds that Captain Parker did in fact shoot the officer of the 24th Infantry who couldn't find it in himself to stand and fight. The facts concerning who shot up the tank, the second charge, were even more clear, and General Harrier was surprised that Morefield didn't even try to muddy those waters, to try to form a reasonable doubt, as much as he could, as Harrier would have done had he been in his place.

But this JAG lieutenant didn't. He as much as admitted that Parker had indeed blown the other tank away.

The only thing he did, Harrier realized, was impress upon the court that the enlisted witnesses against Captain Parker testified against him with great reluctance and thought rather highly of him.

He asked each of them the same question: "Now, I realize that no one wants to go into combat, but if circumstances made it necessary for you to go back into combat, under the circumstances in which these events allegedly occurred, would you be in any way reluctant to serve under Captain Parker?"

And the answer was always the same: "No, sir."

"Even if the allegations against Captain Parker are true?"

"No, sir. Or yes, sir. I mean, Captain Parker is a good officer."

"You would have no fear that Captain Parker would go berserk and turn any weapons under his control on you, instead of the enemy?"

"No, sir."

When the defense's turn came, Morefield introduced classified after-action reports, which painted a clear picture of confusion, chaos, and cowardice on the battlefield, and which in three instances mentioned that Tank Company, 24th Infantry, had held its positions when the rest of the regiment had "withdrawn without orders."

Score one for the defense, Harrier thought.

The next round, Harrier concluded, was lost. Colonel Howley, the regimental commander, who should have gone to bat for Parker, didn't. Howley hadn't brought the charges against him. The goddamn provost marshal had. Either Howley hadn't known, at the time, what Parker had done—which was damned unlikely—or he had known and lent his tacit approval as something made necessary by the situation. If that was the case, he had a moral obligation to help Parker now. But Colonel Howley apparently lost his nerve once he got on the witness stand. If it had been his intention to do Parker any good, he failed. All he testified was that Parker was a good tank company commander.

On cross-examination, he discounted the chaos, confusion, and cowardice. He probably thinks it was a reflection on him, Harrier decided. Colonel Howley stated that he could conceive of no situation in which he, or any other combat commander, would have to resort to shooting an officer on the field of battle.

(Three years later, sitting on a secret Selection Board for Brigadier Generals, General Harrier would cast a nay vote regarding Colonel Howley. A single "nay" vote is sufficient to deny an officer the star of a general officer.)

"The defense calls Major Craig Lowell," Lieutenant Bennington T. Morefield said, softly.

It occurred to Harrier for the first time that the officers on the court just might interpret Lowell's appearance the wrong way; they might decide he was appearing with the blessing of himself and the command structure. Harrier felt the eyes of the members of the court flicker over to him, wondering if this was indeed a message from on high.

Lowell's salute to the court-martial would have done credit to a cadet at West Point. His uniform was crisply starched and his boots glistened. The Combat Infantry Badge with Star (Second Award) glistened on his chest.

"Major Lowell," Lieutenant Morefield said, "you have been called as a character witness in this case. You know the accused? And if so, will you point him out?"

Lowell pointed to Parker.

"Let the record show that Major Lowell pointed out the accused Captain Parker," Morefield said. Then he turned to Lowell. "Major, you don't know what happened on the dates in question, do you?"

"No, sir."

"You don't know any more about what really happened than I do, than the officers of the court know, than my learned opponent, the prosecutor, excuse me, the trial judge advocate, knows, do you?"

"No, sir."

"What we're all trying to do here today, Major, is to reach the facts in this case. And once we have the facts, to weigh them, to decide whether or not Captain Parker's actions were detrimental to good military order and discipline."

"Objection!" the trial judge advocate said, jumping to his feet. "What we are trying to determine here is whether or not the accused is guilty of violation of the 92nd Article of War, murder."

The president of the court looked thoughtful.

"I'll sustain that objection," he said. "The court will ignore in its deliberations Lieutenant Morefield's last comment."

"With all respect, sir, I invite the court's attention to the 92nd Article of War, which states that murder, and also rape, are offenses in that they are detrimental to good military order and discipline. Shall I read the Article, sir?"

"We can read it ourselves, thank you," the president said, icily, and when he read it, said: "I don't quite understand your point, Lieutenant."

"Sir," Morefield said, slowly, carefully, "the Congress in its wisdom has decided that the federal statutes which govern behavior of the civilian populace are not applicable to the military. Hence, the 1928 *Manual for Courts-Martial* and its precedent Articles of War. The difference, sir, is that under federal law, and the laws of the several states, murder, to use that as an example, is considered to be an offense against—a commonly used phrase—'the peace and tranquility' of the community. Military offenses, on the other hand, as the Congress has carefully spelled out, are those actions which are 'detrimental to good military order and discipline.' "

"I think that's nonsense," the trial judge advocate said. "Murder is murder."

"Are you trying to tell me, Lieutenant," the president of the court asked, "that murder is sometimes justified in order to preserve good military order and discipline?"

"What I am saying, sir, is that an action necessary to preserve good military order and discipline cannot be an offense."

"That's absolute nonsense, and you know it!" the trial judge advocate said furiously. "I've never heard such absurd reasoning!"

"The objection has been sustained," the president said.

"Sir, with all respect, the defense enters an objection for the record, and in order that the appellate authorities might have all the facts clearly before them, should there be a conviction at this level, the defense respectfully requests that the court reporter read back from his notes what my statement was, the objection to it, my counterargument, and the court's final decision."

The court reporter read the whole thing back.

Clever as hell, Harrier thought. Morefield is giving them another chance to think over what he said. And there's that threat of review.

General Harrier had been curious when Captain Philip S. Parker IV, on being advised that a Board of Inquiry had recommended his trial before a general court-martial and that the general had approved the recommendation, had requested that Lieutenant Bennington T. Morefield, Judge Advocate General's Corps, 45th Division, be assigned as his defense counsel.

Whatever he was, Parker wasn't stupid, and there had to be some reason he had asked for the services of a specific lieutenant, when he would have been able to pick any of the majors and lieutenant colonels of the IX Corps JAG office to defend him.

General Harrier had made discreet inquiries about Lieutenant Morefield, and learned that he was regarded as a smart-ass Harvard Law School type. He had been a deputy U.S. attorney in New York before being called into the service, where he had promptly earned a reputation at Fort Polk, Louisiana, for getting his accused off. Lieutenant Morefield had been sent to Korea with a subtle recommendation that his background and experience suited him for duty as a prosecutor.

Harrier said nothing to anyone about what he had learned about Parker's defense counsel. For one thing, if the IX Corps JAG had been doing his job, Morefield would be assigned here as a prosecutor, where he could have been sent down to the divisions as necessary to prosecute the serious cases. That the JAG would be facing a smart-ass Harvard lawyer was the JAG's own fault.

Furthermore, General Harrier believed that the accused was indeed entitled to the best possible defense. He privately hoped that Parker would beat the charge, although he realized that his chances were slim to do so. For one thing, he was obviously guilty as charged, and for another, the officers picked for the court were well aware the general believed he should be found guilty, *pour encourager les autres.*

"I thank you for your indulgence, sir," Morefield said.

"Get on with it, Lieutenant," the president said impatiently.

"Major Lowell," Morefield said, "I notice that you are wearing the Expert Combat Infantry Badge with a star, signifying that it has been awarded to you twice."

"Yes, sir."

"You earned both awards as an officer?"

"Yes, sir."

"Which means, then, that on two different occasions, you have commanded troops in combat?"

"Yes, sir."

"Where?"

"Here and in Greece," Lowell said.

"Have you ever been a tank company commander?"

"Yes, sir."

"You were in fact, the commanding officer of Task Force Lowell, which effected link-up with the X Corps when Eighth Army broke out of the Pusan perimeter?"

"Yes, sir."

"For which, I understand, you were given the Distinguished Service Cross?"

"Yes, sir."

"I also understand that you have been decorated with the Distinguished Service Medal for your performance of duty as S-3 of the 73rd Heavy Tank Battalion during retrograde movement from the Yalu River in December 1950?"

"Yes, sir."

"You have, then, experience in combat in the attack *and* the retreat?"

"Yes, sir."

"I also understand that you were awarded the second highest medal for valor bestowed by the Greek government, the Order of St. George and St. Andrew, for your behavior above and beyond the call of duty in Greece. Is that, also, true?"

"Yes, sir."

"Were you a tank commander, a commander of armored forces, in Greece?"

"No, sir."

"What did you command in Greece?"

"I was an advisor to a Greek regiment."

"But you were decorated for your performance as an infantry company commander, were you not?"

"Yes, sir."

"How did that come to be, Major?"

"I assumed command when the Greek officer was killed, sir."

"And you led troops who were not even legally subject to your orders? So well that their King decorated you?"

"They gave me a medal," Lowell said, obviously embarrassed.

"You could fairly be described, then, as a young officer whose experience of command in combat, as well as whose personal valor, has seen him promoted to a rank unusually high for someone of his age. Would that be a fair statement?"

"Objection!" the trial judge advocate said. "For what it's worth, the prosecution will stipulate that Major Lowell is an outstanding, valorous young officer. But I don't see what that has to do with this case."

"Thank you," Morefield said smoothly. "Major, I want to ask you a hypothetical question. On the field of battle, in the midst of 'chaos, confusion, and cowardice,' to use the phrase from the after-action reports, can you imagine a situation where the maintenance of good military order and discipline would require a summary execution?"

"Objection!" the trial judge advocate said.

"Yes, sir, I can," Lowell replied.

"Objection sustained," the president of the court said. "The court will not consider defense counsel's last question, or the response to it, in its deliberations."

"I have no further questions," Morefield said softly. "Your witness."

The trial judge advocate was surprised at having the witness turned over to him. He had expected Morefield to keep pursuing the notion that combat demanded extraordinary measures. But he stood up and walked over to Lowell.

"We know each other, Major, don't we?" he asked.

"Yes, sir."

"I'm a little confused, Major," the trial judge advocate said. "I was under the impression you were aide-de-camp to General Harrier."

"Not any longer, sir."

"Oh?"

Lowell said nothing.

"Why aren't you aide-de-camp to General Harrier any longer, Major?"

"I believe that I was found wanting," Lowell said.

Harrier decided that line of questioning had backfired on the trial judge advocate. He saw quickly stifled smiles on the faces of several members of the court. The word was out: Lowell was in trouble for fucking the movie star. That was a sin, of course, but it was the sort of sin that paled in comparison with the recitation of Lowell's military virtues that Morefield had brought to the court's attention.

" 'A soldier that won't fuck won't fight!': General Philip Sheridan," thought Major General John Harrier.

"In other words, despite the picture Lieutenant Morefield has painted of you as a truly extraordinary officer, Major, you were relieved of your duties as aide-de-camp to the general because you were unable to perform them satisfactorily?"

"I don't believe the general was concerned with the performance of my duties, sir," Lowell said, dryly.

One of the officers on the court guffawed. There were chuckles. The trial judge advocate finally realized he was marching in the wrong direction, and changed the subject.

"I would like to ask you this, Major," he said. "Would you have this court believe that you, personally, would summarily execute an officer, or a soldier, simply because you felt he had not measured up to your standards on the battlefield?"

"That's not what I said, Captain," Lowell said. "We weren't talking about my standards."

"What exactly, then, did you say?"

"Please have the reporter read back my question, and Major Lowell's response, from the record," Morefield said, getting to his feet.

That was done.

"Now, to get back to my question, Major," the trial judge advocate said. "Would you, or would you not, personally shoot someone, officer or enlisted man, out of hand?"

"I would do so reluctantly, sir," Lowell said. "But to answer your question: If someone's cowardice threatened my mission, or was threatening the lives of my men, yes, I would."

"I put it to you, Major, that anyone who feels he may take the law into his own hands is unfit to wear the uniform of an officer of the United States Army."

"Objection!" Morefield said.

"Sustained," the president said. "That wasn't a question, Colonel, that was a statement."

"I have no further questions for this . . . *officer,"* the trial judge advocate said. He made *officer* sound like an obscenity.

"A couple of question on redirect," Morefield said. "Major Lowell, you seem to have no question in your mind that you would, as the prosecution puts it, summarily execute someone under the circumstances described. Is this a philosophical position you have taken, or is it based on experience?"

"It's based on experience, sir," Lowell said.

"Go on."

"I was once in a situation where I was the beneficiary of such a decision," Lowell said. "An officer had been ordered to relieve my unit. He elected not to. His second in command was forced to shoot him and assume command."

"*Forced* to shoot him?"

"Yes, sir. If he hadn't, we would have been overrun and wiped out. More important, two missions would have failed. Ours on the hill, his to support us. He had to do it."

"And what happened to the officer who was forced to take this action?"

"Nothing," Lowell said. "He is presently serving."

"Mr. President," the trial judge advocate said.

"Just a minute," the president of the court said. "I can't permit you to make an unsupported statement like that, of that magnitude . . ."

"Mr. President, Major Lowell is under oath," Morefield said.

"Major Lowell, you have made a charge against the entire disciplinary structure of the army," the president said. "I am now going to ask you for the name of the officer who has taken the law into his own hands and ask you if he is available to this court. Is he in Korea?"

"Sir," Lowell said, "he's in Korea. But I won't give you his name."

"What did you say?"

"I am unable to give you his name," Lowell said.

"Unable or unwilling?"

"I respectfully decline to do so, sir," Lowell said. "His action saved my life. I can hardly repay that by subjecting him to the same sort of difficulty Captain Parker is in."

"Sir," the trial judge advocate said angrily, "I respectfully request that the witness be ordered and directed to reply to the question."

The president of the court looked at Lowell for a long time, and then up and down the table at the faces of the court.

"The court," he said finally, and with finality, "will not consider in its deliberations anything Major Lowell has said regarding his personal experience with a combat situation in which an officer allegedly shot another officer."

That did it, General Harrier decided. Parker will beat it. Parker and Lowell have come across as good commanders who had the balls to do something unpleasant that had to be done. The trial judge advocate looks to them like some noncombatant who is digging up something that should have been left buried.

The general, he thought, is really going to be pissed.

Screw him. Of all the officers under whom John Harrier had served in his military career, the general was the one who had given him the most difficulty in being a loyal subordinate. He was one of those who had managed to rise to high rank by delegating embarrassment and failure, and assuming responsibilities for other men's successes.

Once that thought had come forward in his mind, General Harrier grew really angry. Chickenshit sonofabitch hadn't even had the balls to call Lowell in and eat his ass out. "Get him out of the Corps, John," he said. "Quietly. And since he's yours, you reply to the Chief of Staff."

He was going to sacrifice that kid's career over a couple of photographs in a goddamned magazine.

[THREE]

A victory party was held in Major Lowell's tent on Colonel's Row. Lieutenant Bennington T. Morefield finally took enough of the Haig and Haig Pinch to say what was on his mind.

"I hope that the two of you realize you're both through in the army," he said. "Unless you want to pass the time until you're retired in one idiot job after another."

"You think it's that bad?" Parker asked, surprised.

"May I speak freely?" Morefield said, with infinite sarcasm, and then went on immediately. "So far as you're concerned, Captain, you have ceased being a safe and responsible token nigger. From this day forward, you're going to be the nigger captain who beat a general court for murder with a smart-ass civilian lawyer."

"I've never thought I was anything *but* a nigger captain," Parker said. "I can live with that. My father spent thirty years as a nigger officer. I have no illusions."

"Oh yes you do, you dumb shit," Morefield said. "You think that by trying just a little harder than anybody else, you can make it. You think that since your father did that and got to be a colonel, you can do it, and because 'times have changed' you can probably even make general."

"I was found innocent, wasn't I?"

"You were acquitted. There's a difference. Lowell and I got you off. That's not being found innocent. No one thinks you didn't blow those people away. You won't ever be given another command, and neither will Lowell."

"You don't seem to understand," Parker said. "We have both proved ourselves as company commanders."

"You proved nothing," Morefield said. "Can't you *see* that? The fact that I managed to convince those guys that you should not be locked up for doing something they could see themselves doing, doesn't mean that they're patting you on the back. They felt sorry for you, that's all. And when the time comes to pick somebody to command a battalion, they're going to pick anybody but the nigger who blew the people away when he had a company, and almost got locked up for it. Can't you see that?"

Neither Phil Parker nor Craig Lowell replied. Morefield went on.

"And you, *Major*, do you *really* think the army is going to give a command to an officer who stood up in a general court-martial and announced that he can find nothing wrong with shooting people who get in his way?"

And still there was no reply.

"I'm not getting through to either one of you, am I?" Lieutenant Bennington T. Morefield said. "OK, fuck it. Forget I said anything."

"I don't think we got through to you, Morefield," Parker said.

"Try again," Morefield said, sarcastically.

"I'm not sure if I can," Parker said. "It sounds so simple that it's hard to comprehend. We're soldiers, the Duke and I. *Soldiers*. What do we do for a living is lead people in combat. We do it well. And leading people in combat is what the army is all about."

"Get it through your head that what you might be able to do isn't going to count," Morefield said. "They're not going to give you the chance."

"I happen to have a little more faith in the army than that," Parker said.

Morefield didn't reply. He just swung his head back and forth. There was nothing more he could say. And then he thought of something to say.

"Look at it this way," he said. "You're a danger to the army, the both of you, exactly as the guys who got in your way were a danger to the army. The difference is that they're not going to have to shoot you to get rid of you. They're going to stick you away in some bullshit job, and do it with pleasure. But they're going to keep you from posing any further danger to the army. You better believe that."

Goddamn him, Craig Lowell thought. He's right. He sees the army much clearer than Phil does. The sad thing is that I see it, now, like he does. It's time for me to go home and grow up.

He realized sadly that that was really the last thing in the world he wanted to do, even if Georgia Paige was waiting for him in Los Angeles.

[ONE]
The People's Democratic Republic of Korea
0205 Hours
16 November 1951

The junk lay dead in the water, a mile offshore a deserted stretch of the North Korean coast. Despite a weather report to the contrary, the night was cloudless, and the light from a half-moon was far brighter than expected.

Captain S. T. Felter, dressed in a black rubber wet suit, watched silently as two eight-man aviation life rafts were inflated. Their yellow color had been designed to provide the greatest visibility under all conditions of light, and their designers and manufacturers had done their job well. All attempts to paint over the yellow had failed; the paint either immediately flaked off, or, in the case of one initially promising experiment, promptly ate through the rubberized fabric.

Shrouds had been sewn by female members of the Korean Army, sort of slipcovers made of black cotton. They were draped over the curved sides of the rafts and laced in place with the grommets and rope designed to permit downed aviators to climb aboard.

Once the rafts had been inflated, and the shrouds laced in place, the rafts were carefully lowered over the side of the junk. Two Korean Marines slid down ropes and climbed into the rafts. Next, strapped to a four-foot square of plywood to provide stability, two three-quarter-ton-truck batteries were lowered by rope, and the plywood carefully put in position so that the flexing of the inflated boat would not chafe through the rubberized canvas.

Finally, the electric motors, which operated almost silently, were lowered from the junk and fixed in place on the bouncing rafts. A third Korean Marine in a wet suit, his face blackened with what was actually lipstick, manufactured with a black rather than red pigment, slid down the rope into one of the converted life rafts.

"You better put some more of that crap around your mouth," Rudolph G. MacMillan said to Captain Sanford T. Felter, who was known as "the Mouse," though only behind his back. "You look like Al Jolson."

The Mouse vigorously spread the black lipstick around his mouth with his fingers. "Better?"

"Yeah," Macmillan said.

The Mouse stepped to the rail of the boat and carefully lowered two walkie-talkies into the rafts, and then the weapons—two fully automatic carbines, their stocks cut off at the pistol grip, a Thompson .45 caliber submachine gun, without the butt stock, and a Winchester Model 1897 trench gun. Each item was wrapped in heavy plastic.

Felter turned and looked at MacMillan. Then he shrugged. There really wasn't anything to say. He grabbed the rope and slid down it into one of the rafts. Over the sound of the water lapping at the junk's hull came the sound of a click; then, faintly, the hum of an electric motor. Water churned under the end of the rafts.

By the time they passed around the bow of the junk, the four men in them were lying flat on their stomachs, so that nothing above the sides of the rafts could be seen.

MacMillan walked to the high stern of the junk and followed the boats as long as he could through night glasses. He could see them far longer than he wanted to. He was half sure he could see the phosphorescence of the waves breaking on shore. He had a gut feeling that something was going to go wrong.

He stepped into the cabin, closed the door, and lit a cigarette. He took two puffs, nervously, and then crushed it out and went back outside. He looked through the night glasses again, and wondered if he could really still make out the two rafts, or whether it was simply his imagination.

Fifty yards offshore, just as they could detect the action of the breaking waves, there was another click, and the hum of the electric motors stopped. Two of the Korean Marines, chosen for their height, quietly slipped into the water, trying to find the bottom with their feet. One of them raised his arm straight above his head and pushed himself to the bottom. Only his hand remained above the water.

Felter slipped into the water and whispered in Korean, "A little further in should do it."

They pushed the rubber rafts another ten yards toward shore. The Korean Marine could now stand on the bottom, his head out of the water. Felter was still in over his head. He swam a few strokes, tried it again, and then swam another few strokes. He could now make his way to the beach, walking in the trough of the waves, letting the crests lift him off his feet. He looked over his shoulder. The Korean Marine who was to accompany him was to his left, a few feet behind him.

As they came closer to the beach, he bent his legs further and further, so that only his head was out of the water. Toward the end, he was nearly in a squatting position.

He took a look up the beach, and down it, and then signaled to the Korean Marine. He came smoothly, but not quickly, out of the water, and then, without taking his foot completely out of the water, so there would be no splashing sound to be heard above the crash of the waves, walked out of the water and onto the beach. He ran across the sand into a small valley between dunes. There was only about fifteen feet of hard-packed sand, and then the dunes. The dunes were more rock than sand, the granite mountains of Korea meeting the Sea of Japan.

He took up a position behind a rock and unwrapped the Winchester trench gun. He pulled the exposed hammer back with his thumb. There was already a round in the chamber, and silence was important. He heard the click-clack as the Korean Marine opened the action of the carbine, just far enough to check to make sure there was a round in his chamber.

He pulled up the elastic cuff of his wet suit sleeve and stole a quick look at the luminous face of his watch. They were fifteen minutes early. As much as it terrified him to spend so much time ashore early, he had learned that unless he was at the rendezvous point when the agent to be picked up arrived, the pickups had a habit of taking off to try again another day.

It was better to be early. The risk to the whole operation was less that way. This operation was important. They were bringing out a Red Chinese colonel who was chief of staff to a Red Chinese lieutenant general. The Red Chinese lieutenant general, who had been educated at Southern Methodist, had come to the painful decision that Mao Tse-tung was not China's savior, and that his Stalinist policy of exterminating the middle class was as wrong, as sinful, as impractical, as Stalin's had been.

It was believed the lieutenant general would be useful.

He heard the sound of a jeep engine.

A *jeep?*

He crawled around the rock, far enough out onto the narrow strip of sand to look both ways.

A jeep's blackout lights were coming down the beach.

The Mouse crawled backward behind the rock.

With the light from that damned moon, he realized, they had decided they could patrol the beach by vehicle using blackout lights only, without running the risk of being seen from offshore and fired upon.

And, Felter realized, there was enough light for them to see that the smooth sands had been disturbed, if not the actual footprints.

The jeep was close enough now so that he was aware of the peculiar whining noise of the transmission in four-wheel drive.

Then they saw where the sand had been disturbed. The jeep stopped. The brakes squealed; the jeep needed a brake job.

"In there," a Korean voice said.

"I will call the lieutenant," another voice said.

Shit, a radio.

"Now!" Felter said, in a whisper.

He and the Korean Marine fired almost at once. The blast from the muzzle of the short-barreled riot gun was painfully yellow. Felter fired twice, to make sure. One of the Koreans screamed, a painful wail. Felter fired a third time, and the scream stopped abruptly.

The Mouse stepped toward the jeep, to make sure everyone was dead. He was falling. He had no control over his left leg. He fell against the rear of the jeep, then fell to the ground. His shotgun fell onto the sand, and he thought, now I'll be up all night cleaning the damn thing.

All of a sudden, he was aware that his leg was asleep. He put his hand down the leg. His fingers felt something wet and warm. He put his fingers in front of his face. It was blood.

The Korean Marine bent over him.

"What's the matter with you?" he asked.

"I've been shot," Felter said.

If he had been shot, then he had been shot by the Korean Marine. A stockless carbine, fired full automatic, had a life of its own.

"Are we going to go?" the Korean Marine asked. It was really a question. It was not a request.

"If the pickup was anywhere around here," Felter said, "he heard that shooting. He won't be coming."

The Korean Marine nodded.

Felter pulled himself to his feet by clinging to the jeep. His face passed the left rear bumper. 1CAV. Half the vehicles in the North Korean Army had been captured from the 1st Cavalry. They called them the "Chinese Quartermaster." God*damn* the 1st Cavalry, Felter swore mentally. Erect now, he took a step toward the water. And then another, and then he crashed heavily onto the sand.

There was a shocking pain in his knee now, and he screamed in pain. The Korean Marine came back to him. There was a question on his face. The orders were clear. The wounded were to be shot, rather than have them fall into North Korean hands. Torture cannot force answers from dead men.

"Help me into the water," Felter said. "Maybe I can swim."

He was a little ashamed of himself. He had issued the eliminate-the-wounded order. Now that it applied to him, he was unwilling to live up to it.

The Korean Marine straddled him, grabbed him under the armpits, and ran awkwardly with him to the water's edge. Felter scurried into the shallow water like a crab, until he was deep enough to feel the water start to buoy him up.

He remembered he had left MacMillan's shotgun on the beach.

Without thinking, he kicked both his legs. He screamed and got a mouthful of water and choked. He got into a somewhat erect position, his head out of the water, and threw up. And then he pushed himself back into the water, out toward the rafts. He bit his lip to keep from screaming again. The undulation of the water moved his knee—he knew now that he had taken a carbine bullet in the knee—so that the broken bones grated against one another.

He saw, momentarily, the Korean Marine swimming strongly away from him. He isn't supposed to do that, Felter thought, angrily. He is supposed to kill me before he leaves me.

He felt nauseous, and wanted desperately to throw up, but forced the urge down by sheer power of will. He swam using his arms only, trying at the same time to press his legs together in the hope that that would keep the wounded knee from flexing.

At least he could get into deep water, so that when he passed out, he would drown.

The damned trouble was that when he was reported missing, Sharon would keep hoping. If that damned Korean Marine had done what he was supposed to have done, then she would know.

The pain, as incredible as it was, was getting worse. He screamed and water filled his mouth, and he felt himself losing consciousness. And then something jerked his head, grabbed him by the hair. He wondered if it was a shark. There were sharks in these waters, and sharks were attracted by blood, and when you were bitten by a shark, you weren't supposed to feel it.

Something pulled at his knee. It *must* be a shark, he thought. They take successive bites at people. He wondered how long it would take him to die.

He felt himself slowly, but inexorably, losing consciousness.

He was throwing up. He was throwing up everything he had ever eaten. That meant he wasn't dead. He smelled the peculiar smell of the rubber of a raft. He was in a raft, his face pressed against the curved sides, his face smeared with his vomitus.

He rolled over on his back. He screamed again when the knee twisted.

And then there were fireworks in the sky, a brilliant white light.

Oh, shit. Illuminating rounds. Now they'll get the junk, too.

There was the crump of mortars now, the whistles of the descending rounds, a flash of light and a somewhat muffled roar as they exploded.

Oh, Jesus, I hope the junk is getting out of range.

He could hear its diesels, roaring, the mufflers cut out. There was no sense in running quietly now. The thing to do was get away.

The sound grew louder and louder. He turned again, in the direction of the sound, and he screamed again when the knee was twisted, and this time he didn't swim up from the blackness. He settled into it, felt its comforting blackness close in over him.

[TWO]

The first thing MacMillan thought when he saw the illuminating flare was that it was American. He'd seen enough of the sonsofbitches to recognize an American flare when he saw one. Then he realized that while they might have been manufactured in the United States for the United States Army, they had not been fired by United States troops.

"Sonofabitch," he said. He put his binoculars to his eyes and searched the shoreline. Just as the first mortar round whistled out of the sky and landed, exploding on the surface of the water seventy-five yards away, he picked out the little rubber raft.

He stepped to the controls, jerked the lever which cut out the mufflers, and with the other hand shoved the throttles forward. The diesels roared.

"Get those fucking sails down!" MacMillan shouted.

The sails would slow the junk down, acting as air brakes, rather than the opposite, when he got the junk up to speed.

If he ran into a sandbank, he thought, that would be all that anybody would write. But it never entered his mind not to try to get Felter and the Korean Marine off the beach.

A second and third mortar round landed. The first landed in the spot where the junk had been thirty seconds before. The second landed in his wake, now a double cocks's tail of water churned up by the powerful diesels.

He spun the wheel to the left, and then to the right, and then straightened the junk up.

The Koreans were having trouble with the rigging.

"Cut the goddamned ropes!" MacMillan shouted, at the moment the forward sail fluttered down the mast. The second followed a moment later.

Now, he thought, he could get some goddamned speed.

"I take? I take?" the Korean Marine who was nominally the junk's skipper asked.

"Yeah," MacMillan said. "We pick up. You understand?"

The Korean looked at him out of his dark, expressionless eyes. He nodded his head.

MacMillan stepped away from the wheel and the throttles. He went to a .50 caliber machine-gun ammo box, to which a hasp for a padlock had been welded. He unlocked the padlock with a key hanging from his dog chain, opened the ammo box, and took from it a manila envelope. He tore it open. Inside was a cover sheet stamped TOP SECRET. Below that, the Signal Operating Instructions in case of emergency. This was clearly an emergency.

He found what he was looking for. He went to the radio, switched in the channel assigned, and picked up the microphone.

"Mulberry, Mulberry," he called. "This is Balaclava, Balaclava."

He was surprised when Mulberry came right back.

"This is Mulberry, go ahead."

"Condition Yellow," MacMillan said. "Condition Yellow."

The pitch of the diesels stopped. They slowed to idle. What the fuck was going on?

And then their pitch increased again, and he felt the junk slow. The Korean Marine had slowed the engine to shift into reverse, and was now racing them to stop the junk in the water. They were obviously about to try to pull Felter and the Korean Marine out of the water.

But even over the roar of the diesels, he could hear the incoming mortars. He ducked involuntarily as he heard the whistle of one that he knew was going to be close.

It landed on the port side. If that's where the rubber boat was, that was the end of them.

Two other mortar rounds landed in the water. MacMillan heard the whistle of their shrapnel overhead.

What the fuck was taking them so long to get Felter and the Marine back aboard?

He saw the body basket he had scrounged from the navy being lowered over the side. One of them, *at least* one of them, had been hit.

There came the whistle of mortars again.

The first two missed. The third landed on the high forward deck and blew away the .50 caliber mount and the Korean Marines who had been manning it.

"Balaclava, Mulberry," the radio said. They had apparently gotten the message, "Condition Yellow," which meant the mission had been detected. "Do you require assistance, over?"

Shit, what a dumb fucking question.

"Mulberry, Mulberry. This is Balaclava," MacMillan said to the radio. "Condition Orange. I say again, Condition Orange." "Condition Orange" meant "Under attack, require assistance."

The navy body basket came over the side. MacMillan ran to see who it was. Three more mortar rounds came in, landing where they had been. The North Korean on the mortars simply had never seen a junk that could move like this one. Otherwise they would have been blown out of the water long before this.

The body basket held Felter, who was unconscious and bleeding badly from a wound in his knee. He'd thrown up and pissed and shit his pants, and he stank; and he almost made MacMillan sick to his stomach.

They were headed out to sea now, the diesels roaring, the junk crashing into the waves. In a little while, they would be safe from the mortars. But that didn't mean safe. The North Koreans would probably come after them with patrol boats, or planes, and they would shell them when they were within range of shore batteries.

MacMillan put a tourniquet on Felter's leg, put a Korean Marine beside him to hold it, and ran back to the controls.

"Right out to goddamned sea!" he ordered, gesturing toward the open sea.

The Korean skipper didn't like that. He would have preferred to run along the coast, away from the North Korean patrol boats. But he did as he was told, and he didn't have much time to consider whether Major MacMillan was wrong.

Another three mortar rounds bracketed the fleeing junk. One of them landed amidships, and a piece of shrapnel struck the skipper in the stomach and passed out his back, severing his spinal column. He flopped around on the deck for fifteen seconds before he lay still.

MacMillan caught pieces of the same round. One sliced a chunk out of his left thigh, and the other opened a neat gash in his forehead. He had to wipe the blood out of his eyes to find the microphone.

"Mulberry, Mulberry," he said to the microphone. "This is Balaclava, Balaclava. Condition Red. I say again, Condition Red."

Condition Red was the code phrase for "Vessel damaged, in immediate danger of sinking."

Then MacMillan hobbled over to the controls. Slapping a compress on the hole in his thigh, he steered the junk straight out into the Sea of Japan.

[THREE]
USS Charles Dewey, DD404
Latitude 41 Degrees 17 Minutes
Longitude 129 Degrees 21 Minutes
0235 Hours
16 November 1951

"Ambrose," the radio said. "This is Hammerhead."

Ambrose was today's radio call sign for the USS *Charles Dewey*, DD404, a destroyer attached to Destroyer Squadron K-06, radio code Hammerhead.

"Go ahead, Hammerhead," the radio operator reported.

"Ambrose, stand by to copy Operational Immediate."

"Hammerhead, Ambrose ready to copy Operational Immediate." The radio operator got half out of his swivel chair and pushed a switch. "Skipper . . ." he began, and then the radio spoke again. The operator put his fingers on the typewriter keys.

"Ambrose, Operational Immediate follows: Execute Balaclava. End message. Acknowledge."

"Ambrose copies Operational Immediate, Execute Balaclava."

"Roger, Ambrose. Hammerhead, clear."

"Ambrose, clear."

"You get that, Skipper?" the radio operator asked.

"I got it," the skipper's voice came over the intercom. "Stand by."

It was half past two in the morning. The skipper was dressed in his skivvies, and had been asleep. He went to his bulkhead safe, and worked the combination. It took him three tries. He took out a vinyl zippered pouch, not unlike a bank deposit pouch. There were a half dozen sealed envelopes in it. He went through them until he came on one marked BALACLAVA. He tore it open. There was a cover sheet, a dashed red line surrounding the edge of the sheet reading TOP SECRET. He lifted the cover sheet. He stepped to the intercom.

"Sparks?"

"Yes, sir."

"Get on 225.35 megacycles. Identify yourself as Florence Nightingale. Establish contact with United Parcel. Get their position."

"Two twenty-five, thirty-five, got it, Skipper," the radio operator said. He spoke to the microphone: "United Parcel, United Parcel, this is Florence Nightingale."

There was no response, so he made the call again. This time there was a reply.

"Florence Nightingale, this is United Parcel. Go ahead," MacMillan said.

"United Parcel, Florence Nightingale," the radio operator said. "What is your position? I say again, what is your position?"

"Florence Nightingale, Fox Item Item George Fox Able. I say again, Fox Item Item George Fox Able."

"Understand Fox Item Item George Fox Able," the radio operator said. "Stand by."

The skipper, still in his skivvies, rushed from his cabin to the bridge. He jammed the heel of his hand against a palm-sized brass knob by the passageway door. A bell immediately began to clang.

The speaker, who had been leaning against the starboard compass, stood erect and pressed his microphone switch.

"General Quarters, General Quarters," he said. "This is no drill. This is no drill."

The skipper looked at his chart table. The officer of the watch indicated their position with the points of his dividers.

"Steer one three zero," the skipper ordered.

"One three zero it is, sir," the helmsman replied, spinning the wheel to port.

"Have the engineer give us emergency military power," the skipper said. The engine room telegraph clanged, and the officer of the deck picked up the telephone to the engine room. "Emergency military power," he said.

The destroyer heeled sharply. The skipper almost lost his balance. He regained it and went to the intercom.

"Sparks, advise United Parcel Florence Nightingale is en route at flank speed. Estimate one hour and five minutes."

"Aye, aye, sir. Skipper, they advise they are on fire and about to lose power."

"OK, Sparks, thank you," the skipper said.

"Somebody in trouble, Skipper?" the officer on the deck asked.

"You heard it," the skipper said. "I'm going to get my pants on."

"Seas are smooth, Skipper," the officer of the deck said. "They can take to the boats."

"I don't think 'a wooden sailing vessel bearing the appearance of a junk' is able to have any small boats," the skipper said. "I hope they can all swim."

[FOUR]
Kwandae-Ri, North Korea
0240 Hours
16 November 1951

One of the sixteen radio teletype machines in the XIX Corps (Group) Communications Center rang a bell and immediately began to type out a gibberish series of five character words both on the roll of yellow teletype machine paper and on a strip of perforated tape which spilled out the side of the machine. One of the operators on duty waited until there was about two feet of perforated tape dangling from the machine.

Then he carefully ripped it off and walked across the room to another machine. He inserted the tape in a hole, pushed a switch, and watched as the machine began to swallow the tape. A moment later, the keys of the machine clattered into life.

```
OPERATIONAL IMMEDIATE
TOP SECRET MULBERRY
FOR JADE SIX PERSONAL
BALACLAVA REPORTS CONDITION ORANGE. PREPARE TO RENDER
ASSISTANCE WHEN REQUESTED.
```

"Captain," the operator said. The communication officer on duty, who had been reading the *Stars and Stripes* at his desk, laid it down and walked to the cryptographic machine. The operator went to the clattering radio teletype machine and ripped off another length of perforated tape and inserted it in the cryptographic machine. It began to clatter again.

```
OPERATIONAL IMMEDIATE
MULBERRY BUSH NUMBER 2
BALACLAVA REPORTS CONDITION ORANGE.
```

The communications officer picked up a telephone and dialed a number.

"Black," a voice answered on the second ring. Jesus, the Old Man himself. The communications officer wondered if he had dialed the wrong number.

"General, I was trying to get Colonel Newburgh," he said. "This is the comm center, Captain Tailler."

"What is it, Captain?"

"I've got a Mulberry Operational Immediate coming in, sir. Colonel Newburgh requested that he be informed whenever that happens."

"OK, Captain," Lt. General E. Z. Black said. "Thank you very much. I'll be right down. Try the G-3 Operations Room for Colonel Newburgh."

General Black entered the comm center. A moment later, Colonel Newburgh—who, the troops said, because of his silver brush mustache and curly hair, looked like a model in a booze ad in *Esquire*—walked in. The commo officer handed the two Operational Immediates to General Black, who read them and handed them to Colonel Newburgh.

The machine began to clatter again. In foot-long lengths, the operator tore the perforated tape from the teletype machine and fed it to the crypotgraphic machine.

OPERATIONAL IMMEDIATE
MULBERRY BUSH NUMBER 3
BALACLAVA SIX WOUNDED LEG AND HEAD BALACLAVA FIVE WOUNDED LEG AND FACE.

"Six is Felter, right?" General Black said.

"Yes, sir," Colonel Newburgh said. "MacMillan is five."

"Goddamn him!" General Black said.

OPERATIONAL IMMEDIATE
MULBERRY BUSH NUMBER 4
EXECUTING OPERATION BALACLAVA. USS DEWEY DD404 EN ROUTE POINT CHARLES. ETA ONE HOUR FIVE MINS

"Get in touch with that destroyer," General Black said softly. "See if they have a medic aboard. Send it in the clear. Encrypting takes too long."

One of the commo sergeants sat down at a radioteletype keyboard and rapidly typed out:

FROM JADE
TO HAMMERHEAD
QUERY: DOES BALACLAVA HAVE MEDIC ABOARD? SIGNED BLACK LT GEN.

"If they have a doctor aboard," General Black said, "what about other facilities? Get the aviation officer up here, Carson."

Colonel Newburgh picked up the telephone and dialed a number from memory. There was no answer. He broke the connection and dialed another number.

"This is Colonel Newburgh," he said. "Where is Colonel Young?" There was a reply, and then Newburgh said, "Please wake him up and ask him to join me in the comm center immediately." He hung up the telephone.

OPERATIONAL IMMEDIATE
MULBERRY BUSH NUMBER 5
BALACLAVA SIX SUFFERED SEVERE LOSS OF BLOOD TYPE AO.

"Carson, take care of that," General Black said.

Colonel Newburgh picked up a telephone and dialed 1. An operator came on the line.

"Get me Massachusetts Six," he said.

```
HAMMERHEAD TO JADE SIX
USS DEWEY CARRIES MEDICAL OFFICER ABOARD. NO INFORMATION
AVAILABLE RE STOCKS OF BLOOD. SUGGEST TRANSFUSION POSSIBLE.
```

"This is Carson Newburgh, Doctor. I want you to put enough Type A and AO blood to treat two seriously wounded men in a jeep and get it to the Jade airstrip right now. You had better send a surgeon, too, if you have one available," Colonel Newburgh said to the commanding officer of the MASH serving the nearest division to XIX Corps (Group). Colonel Daniel Young, the XIX Corps (Group) aviation officer, out of breath, ran into the comm center. He walked up to Colonel Newburgh.

"Yes, sir."

"Young," General Black called from across the room, "what time is daybreak?"

"It's 0442, sir," Young said. General Black looked at his watch.

"Sir," Colonel Young said, "I only need daylight to land. I can take off anytime."

"Carson, show Young where he will have to go," General Black said.

"Yes, sir."

[FIVE]
Point Charles
0405 Hours
16 November 1951

"Skipper," the officer of the deck said, and the skipper went and lowered his head into the black eyepiece of the radar.

"Bring us around to one twenty-five," the skipper ordered.

"One twenty-five it is, sir."

"I see a hell of a lot of smoke, Skipper," the officer of the deck said.

"And we're five miles away," the skipper said.

"Captain?" the loudspeaker said.

"Go ahead."

"Operational Immediate from Jade, sir. Helicopter en route with blood and surgeon aboard. Estimated time of arrival thirty minutes."

"Acknowledge the message, Sparks, and tell the doctor."

"Aye, aye, sir."

[SIX]

The destroyer seemed to settle on her stern as her engines went to full reverse.

"I'll be a sonofabitch," MacMillan said. "Here comes the goddamned cavalry."

He was sitting on the deck, beside Felter. The stern of the junk was on fire. There weren't many visible flames, just a hell of a lot of dense greasy smoke from the burning diesel fuel. For some reason it just sat there and burned rather than exploding or even spreading, and MacMillan idly wondered why.

There were only six people left alive. He and Felter had been wounded, Felter pretty badly, himself lightly, and the others were unhurt, unless you counted a burned hand as a wound.

The junk was dead in the water, and seemed to be slowly sinking, although it was hard to tell.

MacMillan gently shoved Felter's shoulder. He wanted to tell him that a destroyer was now inching its way through the ocean toward them. Felter woke up, as if he had been asleep, and moved, and then screamed.

MacMillan, who had the hypo ready, jabbed it into his arm. It worked quickly. He threw the empty syringe over the side, and then, after a moment, the three full ones he had in his hand. It had been his intention, if the fire reached them, to give Felter several of the hypos. Enough so that he wouldn't feel the flames.

The destroyer loomed over them, so close that MacMillan was genuinely concerned they would be overturned, and drowned at the last goddamned moment.

And then people were coming down knotted ropes. They wore those silly-looking navy steel pots and life preservers. One of them was an officer, getting tar or whatever it was on the ropes all over his clean, starched khakis.

"Over here," MacMillan said.

"I'm from the *Dewey,*" the navy officer said.

"You got a doctor aboard?"

"Yes, we do."

"You better take care of him," MacMillan said, indicating Felter in the body basket. "He's in pretty bad shape."

"You don't look so hot yourself, sir," the navy officer said.

"I'm all right," MacMillan said and got to his feet and passed out.

He woke up in a bed. From the way the destroyer was rolling, he knew they weren't moving. His trousers had been cut off him, and there was a bandage on his leg, although he was still dirty.

Temporary dressing, he decided, while they work on Felter. He felt his forehead, and found another bandage.

He sat up in the bed, and saw that he could see out an open door. The junk, still burning, was three hundred yards away. He swung his feet out of the bed, and made it to the door just in time to meet a doctor, an army doctor, coming in.

"What the hell's the matter with you?" the doctor said. "Get your ass back in bed."

"Why aren't we moving?"

"They just got orders to destroy the junk," the doctor said.

MacMillan was pleased that it took five rounds from the destroyer's 5-inch cannon before the junk finally rolled over and sank beneath the surface of the Sea of Japan.

Only then did he permit the surgeon to have a look at his leg and face.

"You haven't mentioned Felter," he said, as the surgeon cleaned the wound in his leg. "Does that mean he didn't make it?"

"He's got a pretty badly torn-up leg," the doctor said. "But he'll make it."

"Where are we going now?"

"Pusan," the doctor said. "To the hospital ship *Consolation.*"

"Am I that bad hurt?"

"No. Not at all. You'll be sore. You lost a chunk of meat, but it was mostly fat. No muscles, I mean. You were lucky."

"Then why do I have to go to a hospital ship?"

"Because General Black said that I was to permit nothing whatever to interfere in any way with your recovery to the point where he can put you on a plane to the United States at the earliest possible moment," the doctor said.

MacMillan laughed, deep in his belly, loudly.

[SEVEN]
Pusan, South Korea
0900 Hours
17 November 1951

The U.S. Navy hospital ship *Consolation*, her sides and superstructure a brilliant white, a Red Cross thirty feet square painted on each of her sides, floated sedately in Pusan Harbor.

Captain Rudolph G. MacMillan, dressed in hospital pajamas and a bathrobe, watched as a powerboat, known as the Captain's Barge, glistening brass and spotless white paint and polished mahogany, put out from Pier One in Pusan and made its way to the *Consolation*'s landing ladder. Two sailors in spotless white uniforms and a lieutenant junior grade stood on the landing platform. The sailors secured the boat to the landing platform, and the lieutenant held out his hand for the passenger of the barge. The passenger jumped onto the platform at the bottom of the landing stair without help. The lieutenant saluted.

"Welcome to the *Consolation*, General," he said. "The captain's waiting for you." He gestured up the stairs.

Lt. General E. Z. Black walked briskly up the stairs, trailed by an aide-de-camp.

When he reached the top of the stairs, six sailors blew on long, narrow brass whistles.

Lieutenant General E. Z. Black smiled and saluted.

A navy captain in a white dress uniform, complete with sword, and a navy captain in dress whites without a sword took two steps forward and saluted.

"Permission to come aboard, sir?" General Black asked.

"Permission granted," the captain with the sword said. General Black threw a crisp salute to the national colors flying on the flagstaff aft. Then he saluted the two captains again. He spotted MacMillan, and smiled, which relieved MacMillan.

"Don't think I came to see you, you disobedient sonofabitch," General Black said. All was right with MacMillan's world. If the general were really mad, he would have been icily formal.

"Welcome aboard, General," the captain with the sword said, a little confused by the interchange between the general and the major. "It isn't often we're honored by the presence aboard of a senior army officer."

"Thank you very much," General Black said. "You know why I'm here?" he asked but didn't wait for a reply before going on. "I want to make sure that nothing gets in the way of Major MacMillan's prompt return to the ZI. And I want to check on Captain Felter."

"Felter's got problems, General," MacMillan said solemnly.

"What kind of problems?" General Black asked. He directed the question to the captain without a sword.

"There's not much left of his knee, sir. After consultation, we have concluded that amputation of the leg is indicated."

"I'm sorry to hear that," General Black said.

"Felter doesn't want it cut off, General," Mac said.

"What do you mean, he doesn't want it cut off?" Black asked sharply.

"He says he'll take his chances, and he won't let them cut it off," MacMillan explained. "He made me promise I'd tell you."

"What the hell does he expect me to do about it?" Black asked, very uncomfortably.

"There's a psychiatric problem involved with the loss of a limb, sir," the hospital ship commander said.

"I suppose there would be a problem," General Black said. "But is 'psychiatric' the right word?"

"I don't know what other word to use," the navy physician said. "By definition, Captain Felter is, at the moment, deranged."

"Because he doesn't want his leg cut off, he's crazy? Is that what you're saying?"

"Not that we believe him, of course, General," the hospital ship commander replied. "Or that it would affect our decision if we did, but he has threatened me personally, and any other medical officer involved, with physical violence if we proceed with the procedure."

"If Captain Felter threatened your life, Doctor," General Black said, "I would take it very seriously."

"I had hoped, sir, that you might have a word with him."

"Is their no way his leg could be saved?"

"Not here, sir. Possibly at San Diego Naval Hospital. Just possibly. The damage is severe."

"But there's a chance it could be saved at San Diego?"

"I don't think anyone could restore that knee, General. At best, his leg would be stiff for the rest of his life."

"I think I would rather have a stiff leg than no leg at all," Black said. "Why don't we send him to San Diego?"

"It's against policy, sir."

"What do you mean, against policy?"

"We are fully equipped here to render general hospital treatment. We provide such treatment."

"But you just told me they could save his leg at San Diego," General Black said.

"I said they might be able to, sir," the captain said. "If he were there. But he's not there. He's here and it's against policy to transfer patients between facilities of equal capability."

"I have never, in twenty-nine years of military service," General Black said, "heard such unmitigated bullshit." His aide winced. MacMillan smiled. Both had been treated before to an E. Z. Black rage.

"General, there is no cause for . . ."

"Shut your mouth, Captain," E. Z. Black said. "If I want any more bullshit out of you, I'll squeeze your head like a pimple." He turned to the aide-de-camp.

"Give your pistol to MacMillan," he said. The aide did as he was ordered.

"If any of these butchers get within fifteen feet of Felter, Mac, shoot them," Black ordered. He turned to the aide. "You get back in this jackass's Pirates of Penzance rowboat," he said, "and go ashore, and get on the telephone to United Nations Command, and you tell them I have two officers aboard this floating abattoir that I want transferred immediately by air to the U.S. Army General Hospital in Hawaii. You got that?"

"Yes, sir."

"And then you come back out here, and you make personally sure, at pistol point if necessary, that they put Felter and MacMillan on the plane."

"Yes, sir."

"I intend to make a formal report of this encounter, General Black," the captain without a sword said.

"So do I," Black said. "And when I'm through with you, you pasty-faced sonofabitch, you won't be allowed to put a Band-Aid on a soldier's pimple. You'll be back in the VD ward of Charity Hospital in Havana, treating syphilitic whores. Where, goddamnit, you obviously belong."

He turned to MacMillan.

"I presume you know where I can find Felter, Mac?"

"Yes, sir."

"Take me there."

"I'll be happy to escort the general," the hospital ship commander said. He had regained control of his temper after remembering that that morning's *Stars & Stripes* had reported that the President had recommended Black for his fourth star.

"You keep out of my sight!" General Black snarled. "Lead the way, Mac."

"Right this way, General," Major MacMillan said.

XVI

[ONE]
Los Angeles, California
2 January 1952

The bellman at the Beverly Wilshire Hotel set the two Valv-Paks immediately inside the revolving door, where they would be out of the way and convenient to carry back outside. It was the bellman's professional judgment that the man in the somewhat rumpled clothing would not be staying. He admitted to not having a reservation.

On the other hand, the desk would try to fit him in. Whenever possible, the hotel tried to do what it could for servicemen. The bellman knew the tall, rather good-looking man was a serviceman, because the Valv-Paks were stenciled in black with his name and rank.

He could see where "CAPT" had been obliterated with black paint, and "MAJ" added. MAJ XXXX C W Lowell 0-495302.

"May I have the pleasure of serving you, sir?" the desk clerk asked. He thought that the young man before him was rather interesting. His clothing, a tweed jacket and gray flannel trousers, was mussed, as if he had slept in it, or it had been stored or something, but it wasn't cheap clothing. And the man himself looked a bit *worn*, as if he had been drinking, or gone without sleep. But he was beautiful.

"Can you put me up?"

"You don't have a reservation?" It was more a statement of fact than a question.

"No," he said. "I'd like a suite. For a day at least. Possibly longer."

"I'm afraid there's very little available, without a reservation, Mr. . . ."

"Lowell," he said. "C. W. Lowell. Major C. W. Lowell."

"Yes, of course. *Major*. Forgive me." He didn't look old enough to be a major. But he probably looked marvelous in a uniform. "Let me see what I can do for you," the desk clerk said, with a warm smile. He checked his file. "I do have a cancellation. A nice room on the fourth floor, front."

"If that's the best you can do," Lowell said. Good God, did they have a union rule? That you had to be a faggot, have a phony English accent, and smell like a flower shop to get a job as a desk clerk?

"Front!" the desk clerk called, and told the bellman to take Major Lowell to 407. Then he checked the registration card to see where Major Lowell was from. It told him hardly anything at all.

"C. W. Lowell, Maj USAR, c/o The Adj Gen, The Pentagon, Wash DC," it said, and his purpose for being in Los Angeles was "personal."

The bellman was pleasantly surprised with the newest guest of the Beverly Wilshire Hotel. He had expected two dollars, a dollar a bag. He got instead, a twenty dollar bill, from a thick wad of twenties (the bellman had been in the service and guessed, correctly, that Major Lowell had just been paid; the army paid in twenty dollar bills).

"I've got a lot to do," Major Lowell said to him. "And not much time to do it in. First order of business is to get me a bottle of scotch, either Johnny Walker Black, or Ambassador, something like that, and some soda. Will twenty take care of you and that?"

"That'll take care of it fine, sir," the bellman said, snatching the twenty.

"I've got to commune with nature," Lowell said, pointing to the bathroom. "If I'm still in there when you bring the scotch, stick around. I've got more for you to do."

When he came out of the bathroom, the bellman had not yet returned. He emptied his trouser and jacket pockets, and then took off his clothing, down to his underwear, sat on the bed, and reached for the telephone. The bellman came in.

"Open that up and make me a light one," Lowell said. To the telephone he said, "Please get me Mr. Porter Craig at Craig, Powell, Kenyon and Dawes at 22 Wall Street in New York City. I'll hold."

The bellman opened the bottle of Ambassador 12-Year-Old and made the maior a drink and handed it to him. The major reached for the stack of twenty dollar bills tossed casually on the bed and came up with two more.

"Take that jacket and pants and have them pressed," he ordered. "It's worth ten bucks to me to have that done immediately. How you split that with the valet is up to you. The rest of it is to get me a box of good cigars, Upmann Amatistas, if the tobacconist has them. If not, any good, large Cuban cigar. If they have them, get Ring Size 47. If not, the larger the better."

"Upmann Amatistas," the bellman said. "The larger the better. Yes, sir."

Lowell turned his attention to the telephone. The number was ringing.

"Craig, Powell, Kenyon and Dawes, good afternoon."

"Long distance is calling Mr. Porter Craig."

"I'll connect you with his office."

"Mr. Craig's office, good afternoon."

"Long distance is calling Mr. Porter Craig."

"I'm sorry, Mr. Craig isn't in at the moment."

"Find out where he is," Craig Lowell said.

"May I ask who is calling?"

"Craig Lowell."

"Sir, if you wish to speak to the party on the line, I'm required to charge you for the call."

"OK. OK. Where is Mr. Craig?"

"I'm sorry, sir. Mr. Craig is in conference and cannot be disturbed."

"Tell him I'm on the phone," Craig Lowell said.

"I'm sorry, I can't disturb him, sir. He left specific word."

"Goddamn it, woman, you tell him I'm on the line!"

"One moment, sir."

"This is Mr. Lucas. I'm Mr. Porter Craig's administrative assistant. With whom am I speaking?"

"Craig Lowell. Get him on the line."

"One moment, please, Mr. Lowell."

There was a pause, and then a voice with the somewhat nasal, somewhat clipped intonations of a Wall Street investment banker out of St. Mark's School, Harvard College, and the Harvard School of Business Administration.

"Craig! How are you, boy?"

"Christ, you're harder to get on the phone than God."

"The girl in the office is new, Craig. She didn't know who you were. You really didn't have to swear at her."

"Porter, I've had enough bullshit in the last twelve hours to last me a lifetime. I don't need any more from you."

"Where are you, Craig?"

"Los Angeles. In a six-by-six-foot cubicle in the Beverly Wilshire."

"You're home then. Welcome home, boy!"

"I need some influence out here, Porter. Who do we have out here?"

"What kind of influence?"

"I need a movie star's unlisted telephone number for one thing," Craig said.

"That can be arranged, I'm sure. Any movie star in particular? Have you been partaking of the cheering cup, Cousin?"

"Not yet. I asked you who we have out here."

"I never know with you. Are you serious about the movie star's telephone number?"

"Dead serious."

"Then Ted Osgood is your man. He's keeping an eye on our participation in *The Fall of Carthage* at Magnum."

"How large is our participation?"

"If you had been reading the tons of paper I've been sending to you, you would know."

"I've had other things to do."

"Two point five million; thirty-seven point five percent."

"That's the guy I want."

"Well, he's right there in the Beverly Wilshire with you. Call him and tell him who you are, and I'm sure he'll get any telephone number for you that you might want."

"He probably wouldn't answer his phone, either," Lowell said. "You call him, and you tell him who I am. Tell him to speak to the management and get me out of this closet, and then tell him to arrange a car for me, and then to meet me. I'll either be in my room, the bar, or the barbershop."

"I'll call him as soon as you get off the line. Anything else? When are you coming East?"

"When you opened our safety deposit box, did you find my passport?"

"Yes. I remember seeing it."

"Well, get it out, and check it to see if it's still valid. If it's not, get it brought up to date."

"Craig, I think you have to do that yourself."

"Porter, arrange it. Call that goddamned senator of yours."

"It'll take a couple of days, I'm sure," Porter Craig said. "I gather you're going to Germany?"

"Of course, I am."

"Then what, may I ask, are you doing in Los Angeles?"

"You may not ask," Lowell said. "Porter, I really would like to see this Mr. Osgood within the hour."

"I'll do my best," Porter Craig said. "You'll stay with us, of course, when you're in New York."

"I'll let you know when I get my feet on the ground."

"Do you need any money?" Porter Craig asked.

"I probably will," Lowell said. "I'm presuming your man Osgood can get a check cashed for me."

"Of course."

"So long, Porter."

[TWO]

Mr. J. Theodore Osgood, Senior Vice President, Entertainment & Recreation Division, Craig, Powell, Kenyon and Dawes, Inc., drove up to the Bevery Wilshire Hotel in a limousine arranged for him by his financial counterpart at Magnum Studios immediately after Mr. Porter Craig's telephone call. Mr. Osgood was not anxious that it get back to Mr. Craig that the car he had rented for his business use while in California was a red Chrysler LeBaron convertible.

He spoke first with Mr. Hernando Courtwright, the hotelier, and told him that it was very important that one of his guests, a Major Craig Lowell, be immediately provided with at least a suite, and preferably one of the better ones. He confided to Mr. Courtwright that Major Lowell, like Porter Craig, was a grandson of the founder of Craig, Powell, Kenyon and Dawes, whose estate had been equally divided between them.

Mr. Courtwright went with Mr. Osgood to the barber shop, where they waited patiently for Major Lowell to emerge from under a hot towel, and then introduced themselves. Mr. Courtwright apologized for the mix-up at the desk—they sometimes made monumental errors of judgment—and informed Major Lowell that his luggage had already been transferred to Penthouse Three.

Mr. Osgood said that an automobile was on its way to the Beverly Wilshire Hotel, and that since Mr. Craig had relayed no preference, he had taken the liberty of ordering a Jaguar coupe.

That earned Mr. Osgood a very pained look, confirming Mr. Craig's announcement that, frankly, Craig Lowell was sometimes a very difficult sonofabitch, and had to be handled with the finest of kid gloves. He was sure for a moment that the Jaguar was going to be unsatisfactory. But, finally, Lowell had nodded his head and said, "Thank you."

"I understand you may be running a little short of cash," Osgood said next. "Now, while I'm sure the hotel will take your check . . ."

"Our privilege," Mr. Courtwright said.

"No numbers were mentioned, so if you like," Mr. Osgood went on, "I'll call our correspondent bank . . . actually, as you know, it's more of a subsidiary . . . and tell them you may be stopping by."

"I'll just need some walking around money, thank you."

"And then, I understand, there was the matter of an unlisted telephone number."

"Georgia Paige," Lowell said. He felt like a goddamned fool about that. He'd simply presumed her number would be in the book, and when he'd gotten off the airplane from Tokyo, he'd tried to call her, to tell her he was home. There was a number, but it was unlisted, and the operator would not give it. So he'd sent a telegram to the house in Beverly Hills, telling her he was home, and asking her to telephone him, any hour of the day or night, at the transient field-grade officer's BOQ at Fort Lewis. He included the number. There had been no call.

So he decided the next thing he would do would be to arrive in LA unannounced and simply take a cab to her house. She had already written, in some detail, what kind of a welcome home present he could expect when they were together again. He flew from Seattle to LA wallowing in that scenario. What she would we wearing. How quickly he would take it off of her, and where. And what they would do when he had her clothes off.

When he got to the house in Beverly Hills, there was no one there but a Mexican couple, about equal in size at 300 pounds, neither of whom spoke English. They were absolutely unable to comprehend his gestures that Georgia was his beloved and he wanted to speak to her on the telephone. He had already paid the cab off, so he had to walk away, carrying both goddamned bags. After about a mile, some cops came along, and after more or less politely insisting that he prove he was indeed a field-grade officer of the U.S. Army and not a burglar with two Valv-Paks full of somebody else's silver and jewelry, they found a cab for him.

"All you would have had to do is ask," Mr. Courtwright said, picking up the telephone and asking to be connected with his secretary.

"And, if Osgood here hadn't shown up," Major Lowell said, "you would have politely told me to go piss up a rope."

"Major Lowell is just home from Korea," Mr. J. Theodore Osgood offered in extenuation.

Courtwright smiled and wrote Georgia Paige's unlisted number on his business card.

"She's not home, Major Lowell," J. Theodore Osgood said. "They're shooting *Unanswered Prayer*. I passed the sound stage on my way off the lot."

"Can you get me into wherever she is?" Lowell asked, as the barber finished his shave and began to rub something oily onto his face.

"Yes, of course," Osgood said. "I'll call ahead if you like and have a pass ready for you at the gate."

Osgood didn't use the telephone in the barbershop. He used a house phone in the lobby and he telephoned his counterpart at Magnum Studios and told him that Craig Lowell, who was likely to be hard to handle, was coming to the studio to see Miss Georgia Paige. He had no idea why.

When Lowell saw the car provided for him, he wasn't surprised. The goddamn Jaguar was identical to Ilse's. He had impulsively shipped it to Marburg an der Lahn because she so loved that car. She had been driving it when the drunken quartermaster asshole had slammed into her.

As he drove to Magnum Studios, he had a clear mental image of Ilse sitting on the passenger seat with P. P. in her arms, and with her legs innocently arranged so that he could see her pants. Sex and motherhood.

"Major Lowell," the man waiting for him at the gate said, "I haven't had the opportunity to meet you before, and I'm happy to now. I'm John Sanderland, and I'm Magnum's Vice President, Finance."

"I see you spent some time in Philly, Mr. Sanderland," Lowell said. Sanderland was wearing the insignia of alumni of the Wharton School of Business at the University of Pennsylvania.

"Doesn't everybody?" Sanderland said.

" '49," Lowell said.

"Hail fellow, well met," Sanderland said delightedly. " '40." Perhaps, he thought, Major Craig W. Lowell wouldn't be as difficult as Osgood suggested.

They drove onto the lot. It was Lowell's first visit to a motion picture studio. He was somewhat disappointed to see that it looked more like a factory than anything else. Then he realized that it was a factory, the word actually being a shorter form of "manufactory," a place where things are made by hand.

There was a red light flashing over the door of one of the warehouse-like buildings, and what looked like a retired cop, in a private policeman's uniform, standing in front of it with his arms folded. Lowell had seen enough movies about Hollywood to know the flashing red light meant that they were "shooting" inside.

The private cop did not step out of the way, however, as Lowell expected him to, when the red light went off.

"Closed set," he announced. "You got to have a pass."

"I'm a vice president of this corporation," Sanderland said.

"I don't doubt that for a minute, Mister," the guard said. "But you still got to have a pass. The set is closed."

"Oh, for Christ's sake!" Sanderland said, but they had to get back in Lowell's car and go to the Administration Building for passes. When they returned to the sound stage, the red light was flashing again, and they had to wait ten minutes in the hot sunshine for it to go off again.

"They weren't shooting that long," Sanderland said, angrily, as he hauled back on the heavy, soundproof door. "They just didn't want to be interrupted."

"What the *fuck* is this?" a man screamed in a high-pitched voice, as they entered the sound stage.

Lowell, who had been looking for Georgia and had just seen her across the wide, cluttered room, was startled. Then he became aware that the screaming man was pointing at him.

The excited pansy recognized Sanderland. "What the *fuck* do *you* want?" he demanded of him. "And *who* the *fuck* is *he?"*

Lowell looked across at Georgia. She seemed to be running away. No wonder, with this sewer-mouthed pansy screaming his head off.

"You say 'fuck' one more time, Slats," Lowell said, "and I'll wash your filthy fucking mouth out with fucking soap."

"*Who*ever this cocksucker *is*, Sanderland," the skinny man said, "get him off *my* fucking set!"

Without much apparent effort, Lowell spun the skinny man around, marched him to a red fire bucket mounted on the wall, and dunked his head in it.

A man in a business suit who had been rushing toward the door when the incident started, now gestured to two burly laborers. They restrained the skinny man when Lowell turned him loose.

"What the hell is going on around here?" he demanded of Sanderland.

"Major Lowell," Sanderland said, "this is Mr. Berman, the producer of this film. Mr. Berman, Major Lowell is from Craig, Powell, Kenyon and Dawes, and he seems to object to your director's characterization of him as a cocksucker."

"I'm walking, Sanderland," the skinny pansy screamed. "I'm walking. That's it. I'm finished." The laborers let him go, and he stormed, dripping, across the set.

"I'm not saying that wasn't a good idea, Major," Mr. Berman said. "I just hope you realize what that gesture cost us."

"I have no idea," Lowell said. "But whatever it was, I'll be happy to pay it."

"I don't think so," Mr. Berman said. "It will be two days before our director will feel the muse has returned sufficiently for him to resume the practice of his art. We're budgeted at thirty-nine five a day. Are you really willing to pay nearly eighty thousand dollars for the privilege of washing out that mouth, even considering how foul it is?"

"Hell, I'm sorry," Lowell said, feeling like a fool.

"May I ever so politely inquire what we can do for you on this closed set?" Berman asked, sarcastically.

"I came to see Georgia Paige," Lowell said.

"Indeed? Might I inquire why?"

"We're friends," Lowell said.

"Well, in *that* case," Berman said, sarcastically, "why don't you go over to her dressing room? She has nothing else to do at the moment but entertain friends. Not now. And probably not tomorrow. And probably not on the day after tomorrow, either. That should give you plenty of time for a friendly visit." Berman gestured to a small house trailer on the far side of the building.

Aware that eyes were on him, Lowell started to walk toward it. He heard Berman ask Sanderland who he really was, and part of Sanderland's reply. Then there was an explosion immediately behind him, and by reflex action, he threw himself on the floor. He couldn't control it. He hit the dirt even as one part of his mind told him that the explosion was a bursting light bulb, maybe a big one, but a light bulb only, dropped from somewhere up above.

Shamed and furious, he got to his knees and looked upward. A burly man was sliding down a ladder, a look of concern on his face. He reached Lowell just as Lowell stood up.

"Hey, I'm sorry," he said.

"About as sorry as I am for dunking the other wise-ass in the fire bucket," Lowell said.

"No," the man said. "Hey, I mean it. I dropped the bulb to say 'hurray for you.' I didn't know you jump the way people like you and me jump when you think a sudden noise is incoming."

"You got me, you bastard," Lowell said, smiling. "You really got me."

"You looked as shocked as our director," the man said, "when you ducked his head in the fire bucket."

He looked over the man's shoulder. Georgia was standing there, looking at him unbelievingly.

"My God," she said, "Is that *you?*"

She came and he hugged her. She raised her face to his and he kissed her. Her lips were warm, but not as hungry as they had been on the IX Corps airstrip. He remembered that he had felt her heart beating then. She hadn't pressed herself close enough against him now for him to feel her heart beating, and neither were her arms holding him the way they had on the airstrip.

It wasn't the homecoming embrace he had held in his mind.

Sanderland came up to them.

"You should have told me you knew Major Lowell, Georgia," he said. "I would have treated you differently."

"How so?" she asked, somewhat confused that Lowell knew Sanderland.

"I would have treated you with greater respect and offered you less money."

"What the hell are you talking about?"

"You've often told me you'd like to meet one of the money men from New York," Sanderland said. "To tell him off. So here's your chance."

"Is he putting me on?" Georgia asked, looking at Lowell. Then she thought it over. "I get the feeling he's telling me the truth."

"Does it matter?" Lowell asked.

"He must be telling the truth," she said. "Otherwise you couldn't have gotten on the set. Why didn't you tell me you were coming?"

"I tried. I got out two days before I was supposed to."

She dismissed him for something more important.

"Where's Derek?" she asked.

"He went home," Sanderland said.

"What do you mean, 'he went home'?" she snapped. "We're not finished."

"Your friend gave him a shampoo," Sanderland said. "In a fire bucket."

"I don't believe any of this conversation," Georgia said, smiling, showing her red gums and perfect teeth. "What the *hell* are you talking about?"

"Derek talked dirty in front of your friend, and your friend washed his mouth out by dunking his head in a fire bucket," Sanderland said.

Georgia Paige immediately decided this was the truth.

"Great!" she exploded. "Great! Thanks a lot!"

She glowered at Lowell for a moment, and then walked quickly across the building toward the trailer Berman had pointed out to him.

"Now we're even," Sanderland said. "*That* cost you."

"Go fuck yourself," Lowell said to him, and walked across the floor to the trailer. He knocked, but there was no reply. He pushed open the door and went inside. Georgia was lying on a chaise longue, legs spread, her head resting on her hands. Lowell walked up to her and looked down.

"I'm sorry," he said.

"You don't understand," she said. "I have been working myself up all day for this shot. And then I don't get to make it."

"I'm really very sorry," Lowell said.

She looked up at him and smiled and held her arms out to him. She held him against her, but when he tried to touch her breast, she pushed him gently but firmly away.

"Not here," she said. "Let's get the hell out of here."

He didn't even get a chance to watch her change clothes. A gray-haired woman came into the trailer without knocking, gave Lowell a dirty look, and jerked her thumb toward the door. It took her fifteen minutes to change clothes, during which a steady stream of people entered and left the trailer, while he stood around outside.

He had to follow her to the house in Beverly Hills, trailing a studio Cadillac limousine in the Jaguar. Her house, he decided, was probably entitled to the term mansion. The banker in the recesses of his brain suddenly came to life. She hadn't been successful that long. He had read in a fan magazine that her father was in the insurance business in Ohio, and that she'd gotten her start in the movie business while acting in plays at the University of Ohio. Her rise, the fan magazine had said, had been "meteoric." That meant that it was only recently that she had been making a lot of money, and that meant the house was hers only technically. The money for the house had probably come from the First Federal Savings and Loan of Beverly Hills.

They'd driven past that. The houses in Beverly Hills, Lowell thought, deserved much larger lots than they had been given. He had a quick mental image of the gate at Broadlawns, and the drive inside the gate. He came to the conclusion (which he shamefully acknowledged to be snobbish) that Beverly Hills, generally speaking, was a high-priced housing development, Levittown for the affluent.

When they finally got inside her house, there were half a dozen people there, including a man she introduced as her press agent, and whom Lowell disliked on sight. It was a very long time before they were rid of them, and the press agent lingered longest.

And then Georgia said she was hungry, and that Consuela, presumably the 300-pound Mexican, wasn't there. So they went to the Villa Friscati on Sunset Boulevard. A steady stream of people stopped at their table, all of them ignoring him after finding out that he was a soldier.

They finally made love about nine thirty, but it wasn't what it had been in Korea, and she threw him out, saying that despite what he'd done, Derek might want to shoot the next day. That meant she would have to get up at half past four and needed her sleep.

"When are you going to be finished with this movie?"

She told him. Six weeks, maybe seven. When she saw the look on his face, she asked if something was wrong.

"I was hoping you would go to Germany with me in a couple of days."

"Germany? Why do you want to go to Germany?" And then she remembered. "Oh, yeah. Your little boy is there. I forgot about him."

They put a good face on it. They discussed it calmly and logically. He would go to Germany and do what he had to do about the little boy. And by that time, the picture would be nearly done, or maybe, if nobody else ducked Derek's head in a fire bucket, finished. And then they would have some time to be together and really talk things over.

But they both knew when he walked out of her door at a quarter past ten on his first night home that they had both been kidding themselves.

[THREE]
Walter Reed U.S. Army General Hospital
Washington, D.C.
16 February 1952

Sharon and Sandy had been expecting Craig ever since the flowers had arrived. The flowers were fifty dollars' worth of carnations, stuck into a five-foot chicken-wire horseshoe, and with the gilt letters spelling out GRAND OPENING glued to a purple six-inch-wide sash. It took up a whole corner of Sandy's private room.

He arrived the following Saturday, about four o'clock in the afternoon, in a pink-and-green uniform, complete with all his decorations. Sandy was surprised to see that. Lowell normally wore only his Expert Combat Infantry Badge. He was struck again with the realization that Lowell looked the way an officer was supposed to look.

"You little bastard," Lowell greeted him, "I thought I had taught you how to duck. What happened to you, anyway?"

"I thought the man said 'stand up,' " Felter said. "So I stood up. And here I am."

The men shook hands. Sharon stood beside Lowell, and very naturally, Lowell put his arm around her shoulders. Sharon leaned against him.

"I didn't know," Lowell said. "I ran into MacMillan at Knox. He told me."

Felter nodded.

"So how are you doing?" Lowell asked, awkwardly.

"I'm in what they call physical therapy," Felter said. "Once in the morning, and once in the afternoon, they give me a bath, and then they torture me."

Sharon suddenly shook loose from Lowell and went to the bedside table. Sandy was embarrassed.

"Look," she said. She handed him a lidded leather box six inches by three. Lowell opened it, looked down at the Distinguished Service Cross, and then unfolded the copy of the citation.

HEADQUARTERS
DEPARTMENT OF THE ARMY
WASHINGTON, D.C.
AWARD OF THE
DISTINGUISHED SERVICE CROSS

4 January 1952

By Direction of the President of the United States, the Distinguished Service Cross is awarded to MAJOR SANFORD THADDEUS FELTER, 0-357861, Infantry, U.S. Army.

CITATION: During the period 30 August-16 November 1951, MAJOR FELTER (then Captain), while engaged in military operations of the highest importance, repeatedly, without regard to his own possible loss of life, demonstrated valor above and beyond the call of duty. His actions reflect great credit upon himself and the United States Army. Entered the Military Service from New Jersey.

Lowell folded the citation and put it back in the case, and then snapped the case shut.

"Well," Lowell said, "at least they gave you the leaf. You can spend that."

"That's a terrible thing to say," Sharon flared. "That makes you sound as if you're jealous, Craig!"

"Why should he be jealous?" Felter said. "Look close, honey. He's got one of his own."

"I don't care if he does or not," Sharon said. "You shouldn't make fun of a decoration."

"Oh, I'm proud of him," Lowell said. "MacMillan told me all about it."

"You're kidding," Felter said.

Lowell, beaming at him, shook his head, "No."

"Damn him!" Felter said. "He knows better than that."

"He has this odd notion, Sandy, that we're on the same side."

"That has nothing to do with it," Felter said, and threw both hands in the air.

"Well, I guess you could write him a letter of reprimand," Lowell said.

"You know what he did, Craig?" Sharon asked.

"Certainly, I do," he said. "I'm a major in the U.S. Army. They tell me everything."

"Then you tell me," she said. "Sandy won't. All I know is that he wrote and told me he was running a radio station, and the next thing I know, Colonel Hanrahan came to the house and told me he was here."

"Well, Sharon—" Lowell said.

"Goddamn it, Craig!" Felter interrupted.

"First of all, Sharon," Lowell said, "he did a fine job of cutting the VD rate among the troops."

Sharon blushed. "Oh, Craig!" she said.

"And then he got everyone in the unit to make a contribution to the Red Cross. The army is really interested in a hundred percent contribution rate to the Red Cross."

"So tell me about you," Sandy said.

"How's P. P?" Sharon asked.

"With his grandfather," Lowell said. "I spent thirty days in Marburg."

"How is he?"

"Surrounded by kraut aristocrats," Lowell said, "who will probably, in time, be able to forgive him for being half-American."

Sharon looked disturbed, and Lowell saw it.

"There's a whole family there, aunts and uncles, cousins, second cousins twice removed. Most important, women. How the hell could I care for him?"

"Sandy and I talked about that," Sharon said. "If you could see your way clear to letting us have him. You know we love him, Craig."

"Jesus, you know what that means to me," Lowell said, emotionally. "But I think the thing to do with him is what's being done. You've got your own kids, and I don't know what the hell I'm going to be doing. And they are his family. They're making sure that he doesn't forget how to speak English. I guess what I'm saying is that they're taking good care of him."

"I understand," Sharon said. "Maybe, when you get remarried . . ."

"You seem pretty sure about that," Lowell said, making a joke of it.

"You're even younger than Sandy," Sharon said. "You'll get married again."

"I put you on warning, lady, that if you start matchmaking . . ."

"I'm not impressed," Sharon said. "You should get married again."

"I don't think so," Lowell said, surprisingly firmly. Sharon let it drop after saying, "I'd love to see him again. Have you got a new picture?"

While she was looking at P. P. in the arms of his father, Sandy said: "I asked before, what are you doing?"

"You will be delighted to hear, Major, that I am on my very good behavior—

you will note the medals—and trying very hard to make the right impression on my peers and superiors."

"What are you doing?"

"Killing time until I get out," Lowell said, "at the Advanced Officer's Course."

"I thought you put in for regular army?" Sandy asked. "What did you do, change your mind?"

"It was changed for me," Lowell said. "The application hasn't come back yet. They are probably trying to find the right words to reject it."

"Why would they reject it?"

Lowell said, obviously quoting verbatim, " 'While this officer has demonstrated outstanding ability at command at the company level, it is obvious that he sometimes acts impulsively and without adequate consideration of all factors concerned. It is to be hoped that as he matures, he will acquire the stability of personality necessary for command at the battalion level. In the meantime, however, the undersigned cannot in good conscience unreservedly recommend him for such command.' "

"Who did that to you?" Felter asked, disturbed.

"That's the efficiency report I got from His Excellency, the IX Corps commander."

"What did you do? Did it have something to do with your friend's court-martial?"

"You don't want to talk about this," Lowell said.

"What did you do?" Felter pursued.

"I got up in a general court-martial and testified that I could indeed see circumstances in which an officer is justified taking another officer out of a situation," Lowell said. "The corps commander had decided that he wanted to put my friend in jail. He was piqued when the court let him go, and blamed it on me."

"I heard he was acquitted," Felter said. "But no details. What happened to him?"

"He's at Knox with me," Lowell said. "Captains and lieutenants who have heard very few guns go bang in anger are teaching us how to command tank companies by the book."

"That's obviously a waste of your time," Felter said. "But I don't suppose there's anything you can do about it."

"Not that I can think of," Lowell said dryly.

"So you withdrew your application for the RA? Is that what you meant when you said you were killing time until you can get out?"

"No. I figured I'd let them squirm trying to turn me down. I meet every single criterion, and then some. I'm not even giving them a chance to say that I've been a wise-ass in class. I'm getting 4.0's, which is more difficult than I would have believed."

"You never had any trouble with school," Felter said.

"We had an interesting class problem last week," Lowell said. "A brand-new one. It seems that when the Eighth Army in Korea broke out of the perimeter, a reinforced tank company was sent as a task force to disrupt the enemy's lines of communication and eventually to effect link-up with X Corps. It was rather a challenge to offer constructive criticism, to improve the operation. I thought it was done right the first time."

"You're kidding," Sharon said.

"Oh, no," Lowell said. "But, just to prove how cooperative I am, I came up with a long list of improvements to the way it was done. If I had done any of them, I would still be tied-down fifty miles from Pusan, attempting to coordinate liaison with supporting arms and services." He paused, and chuckled, adding, "Especially if I had waited for confirmed intelligence to give me the strength of assaulted units."

"It's something out of Franz Kafka," Sandy said sympathetically. "Well, what *are* you going to do?"

"I can only answer that negatively," Lowell said. "I'm not going to go back to the bank. Aside from that, I really don't have plan one."

"When do you get out?"

"In five months," Lowell said. "Now, what happens to you?"

"I've been selected for the War College," Sandy said.

"I thought you had to go to Command and General Staff first," Lowell said.

"Sandy made that on the five percent list, too," Sharon said, proudly. "Major and the War College on the five percent list."

"I took C&GS by correspondence," Sandy said. "In Korea. It was either C&GS or a course in how to upholster your own furniture."

"And then what?"

"Here," Sandy said. "We bought a house in Alexandria. A hundred dollars down and a hundred dollars a month for the rest of our natural lives."

"What are you going to be doing here?"

"The same sort of thing I've been doing," Sandy said, uncomfortably.

There came a light in Lowell's eyes, and Sandy Felter was sure he knew what it was. Lowell was going to apply for Intelligence.

They let the subject drop, talked of other things.

Two months later, shortly before he was to be released from the hospital on limited duty, an agent of the Counterintelligence Corps showed up at Walter Reed, flashed a badge, and said he was conducting an investigation into the character of one Major Craig Lowell, who had given Major Felter as a reference.

"Could you, without reservation, recommend him for a position of great trust and authority?"

"I could, and do," Felter said. "But I think I know what this investigation is really all about, and the answer to the real question, 'Would Craig Lowell be any good as an intelligence officer?' is 'No, he would not.' "

"That's pretty strong, Major," the CIC agent said. "What do you base that on?"

"The one thing an intelligence officer cannot be is impulsive," Felter said. As the words came out of his mouth, he felt like a hypocrite. He had several times acted impulsively. Who was he to criticize Lowell?

"Rephrase," he said. "An intelligence officer must know how to restrain his impulsive urges. Major Lowell does not have that characteristic."

"That sort of thing would be decided by the people who evaluate his application,

Major," the CIC agent said. "They'll want to know what you think of him as an officer. They'll determine if he's liable to make a good intelligence officer."

"I'm one of the guys who sits on those boards," Felter said. He rolled over on his hospital bed, and opened his shaving kit, and took out a well-worn leather folder. He opened it and showed it to the CIC agent.

"I didn't know that about you, Major," the CIC agent said.

"There's no reason you should," Felter said. "When you make up your Report of Interview, make sure it includes the information that I revealed my duty assignment to you, and my statement that recommending that Major Lowell not be considered for an intelligence assignment was personally difficult for me. He's my best friend."

The CIC agent nodded his head.

"And the next time you find yourself wishing that you were through with backgrounds, and 'really doing something in intelligence,' " Felter said, "remember this interview. That isn't the only decision I've had to make that makes me a little ashamed of myself."

[FOUR]
Fort Knox, Kentucky
17 May 1952

When Major Craig Lowell was informed by the adjutant of Student Officer Company, the Armor School (SOC-TAS), that his application for integration into the regular army had been approved, and that, presuming he could pass a precommissioning physical examination, he would be integrated into the regular army as a first lieutenant, with adjusted date of rank 24 July 1950, and that he would be permitted to continue on active duty as a reserve officer in the grade of major, he simply nodded his head.

He had toyed with the notion of endorsing the correspondence "insert your RA commission violently upward into your anal orifice."

But when the commission was actually tendered, even though he told himself that he knew better, he thought perhaps he was at least partially vindicated, that if they were really out to hang his ass, they would have thought of some excuse not to offer the RA commission.

His application for intelligence was still in. Certainly Sandy would have said a number of good words about him, and he had the Greece experience, and that would certainly be a hell of a lot better than going back to the bank.

His application for assignment to intelligence duties came back with an endorsement saying that "no vacancies exist at the present time for an officer with your qualifications nor are any anticipated in the foreseeable future, and therefore reapplication is not encouraged."

He swallowed that.

Captain Philip Sheridan Parker IV was honor graduate of Advanced Officer's Course 52-16. He was given a replica of a Civil War cavalry saber and a one year's free membership in the Armor Association. He was assigned to Fort Devens, Massachusetts, as assistant dependent housing officer.

Major Craig Lowell, who was .05 grade points behind Captain Parker (3.93 and 3.88, respectively, out of a possible 4.0), received permanent change of station orders to proceed to the Bordentown Military Academy, Bordentown, New Jersey, as deputy to the army advisor to the Junior ROTC Detachment at the private military high school for boys.

XVII

[ONE]
New York City
16 October 1952

When Porter Craig, president and acting chairmen of the board of Craig, Powell, Kenyon and Dawes, returned to his office from the Luncheon Club on the 38th floor of the Morgan Guaranty Trust Building, where he had lunched with his cousin, Major Craig W. Lowell, he sat down at his desk and swiveled the high-backed leather chair so that he could look out the huge plate-glass window at lower Manhattan Island and the Hudson River. He put his feet up on the marble window sill, and sat with the balls of his fingers touching, as if praying.

Then he suddenly spun the chair around, pushed the concealed button on his desk which activated a microphone concealed in the cigar humidor, and told his secretary to get the senator on the telephone just as quickly as she could.

"Porter Craig, Senator. Thank you for taking my call. I know what a busy man you are."

The senator replied that it was always a pleasure to speak with his good friend, and asked how he might be of service to his favorite man on Wall Street.

"I've just had lunch with my cousin, Craig Lowell," Porter Craig said. "And let me make clear to you this telephone call is my idea, not his. I'm quite sure that he would be furious if he even suspected I would pass what he told me any further. Or in any way interfere in his affairs."

"I remember the name," the senator said. "He was in the army in Greece, as I recall, five or six years ago? Was wounded, and something of a hero, wasn't he?"

"That's the man."

"Your grandfather asked me to find out what I could about his condition. I was, of course, happy to be of assistance. Now, what about him?"

"He's about to resign from the army," Porter Craig said. "And while I would, of course, be delighted to have him here with me in the firm . . . he's a Wharton graduate, and smart as a whip, and I can't really see why he stayed in the army at all, frankly."

"But apparently, he did," the senator said. He was beginning to sense the reason behind the call.

"And did rather well, I must say. He's a major, which I understand is truly extraordinary for someone his age."

"He was just a boy, I recall, when he was in Greece."

"He's hardly more than a boy now," Porter Craig said. "Twenty-five."

"Extraordinary," the senator said.

"He's just back from Korea," Porter Craig went on. "Looking like a young Patton. He has the Distinguished Service Medal and the Silver Star, and God knows what else. There's barely room for his ribbons on his uniform."

"Indeed," the senator said. He wished Porter Craig would make his point.

"I suppose that's what makes me angry enough to bring this to your attention," Porter Craig said. "It seems to me that he's entitled to more from the army, because of what he's done for the army, than is apparently the case."

"Go on," the senator said.

"He told me that he's about to resign."

"Did he say why? It would appear to me that with a record like that, he should have a brillant career ahead of him."

"I suspect that he may have risen a bit too fast," Porter Craig said. "I suspect there may be some jealousy involved."

"I'd be surprised if there were not," the senator said. "But surely, he can rise above that?"

"The reason he gives for resigning from the army is that he thinks he has been removed from consideration for meaningful advancement."

"Why does he think that?"

"Because of the assignment they've given him."

"Which is?"

Porter Craig was not about to be brought to the point until he was ready to make it.

"And it's not only Craig who has been, in my judgment, rather shoddily treated. He just graduated, with honors, from the Army School at Fort Knox, second in his class. The honor graduate, Senator, if you can believe this, has been assigned as a dependent housing officer in Massachusetts. Craig, who was second in his class, has been assigned to Bordentown Military Academy, where he says he is in the charge of the sergeant who is teaching the little boys how to march."

"That doesn't seem to be a very satisfactory assignment for a bright young major, does it?" the senator asked. "Nor a very wise expenditure of the taxpayer's dollar?"

"I didn't think so," Porter Craig said. "That's why I called you. I would not ask for special treatment, and he certainly wouldn't ask for it himself. But I don't think I am asking for special treatment when I bring what I consider an outrageous waste of the taxpayer's dollar to your attention."

And just incidentally, the senator thought, keep Cousin Craig from coming home again and claiming his half of Craig, Powell, Kenyon and Dawes, Inc.

"You don't happen to know the number of the course he attended at Fort Knox, do you?" the Senator asked.

"No, I'm afraid I don't."

"Well, I can find out," the senator said. "I'll get back to you, Porter. I understand the situation. Sometimes, you have to call the military to attention."

"As I say, I'm not seeking any special treatment for my cousin," Porter Craig said. The senator was annoyed.

"But if it could be arranged to keep him in the army, fine, is that it?"

There was a long pause.

"That would seem to sum it up rather aptly, Senator," Porter Craig said finally.

"I'll see what small influence I have on the Pentagon can do for you, Porter," the senator said. "In the meantime, try to talk him out of submitting his resignation."

[TWO]
Washington, D.C.
19 October 1952

The senator met the Vice Chief of Staff of the United States Army at a cocktail party and dinner given in honor of the junior senator from Iowa at the Occidental Restaurant by the American Farm Machinery Foundation.

"Tell me, General," the senator said, laying a fraternal arm around the Vice Chief of Staff's shoulders, "how is your new personnel system working out? Is it getting round pegs in round holes, or are you still trying to make bakers out of candlestick makers and vice versa?"

The Vice Chief of Staff of the U.S. Army knew the question was not idle.

"So far as I know, Senator," he said, "it's working out very well."

"The right officer in the right assignment, right?"

"We try to do our best, Senator," the Vice Chief of Staff said.

"And how often does that work?"

"How about ninety-nine times out of a hundred?"

"You don't mean to say?"

"Have you something specific in mind, Senator?" the Vice Chief of Staff asked.

"I was wondering about the school system, as a matter of fact," the senator said.

"What, sir, were you wondering?"

"Whether it's really worth all the money it costs the poor taxpayer."

"Well, if a man can't drive a truck when we get him, and we need truck drivers, we have to teach him how to drive one. It's as simple as that."

"I was thinking more of the officer-level schools."

"What level?"

"The Advanced Officers' Courses. Are they really necessary?"

"Absolutely."

"And you can put their graduates to work, doing what they're trained to do?"

"We can, and we do."

"You don't mean to say!"

"Yes, sir."

"And after they're trained, right into that little round hole, right? Presuming it's a little round officer?"

"To the best of my knowledge, Senator," the Vice Chief of Staff said. He wondered what the hell the senator was leading up to.

"If we were playing poker, General," the senator said, "would you bet on that hand? Or would you want to see if you could draw some better cards?"

"I've got all the cards I need, thank you, Senator," the Vice Chief of Staff said.

"I'll call," the senator said. "Get out your little notebook, Son," he said to the silver-haired, full bird colonel aide-de-camp of the Vice Chief of Staff.

"I didn't hear the bet," the Vice Chief of Staff said with a broad smile that showed just faint signs of strain.

"You're telling me you're assigning officers so that their service, in terms of their records and the expensive education the taxpayer has bought for them, will give the taxpayer the best possible return on his investment," the senator said. "I'm betting you're not."

"But what's the bet?"

"Just a fun game, between friends," the senator said. "Now, just for the hell of it, let's find out—picking something out of the air, you understand—how you assigned the two officers at the top of their class at the last Advanced Officers' Class at Fort Knox. The last class, I believe, was Number 52-16. You write that down, Son, so we all remember. I would be very interested to know who they are, what kind of records they have, what their assignments are, and why they were made."

"You get that, Dick?" the Vice Chief of Staff said to his aide.

"Yes, sir."

"Put it in writing, General," the senator said. "You're a silver-tongued devil, you are, always making me think you said something you didn't say."

[THREE]
Fort Devens, Massachusetts
25 October 1952

In addition to his other duties, the assistant dependent housing officer at Fort Devens, Massachusetts, had been assigned as assistant club officer. The club officer himself, a major of the Transportation Corps, set a fine table, as they say, but he wasn't much with the books. Taking care of the books was just the job for a jigaboo captain who had been the honor graduate of the Advanced Course at Knox.

When four telephoned calls, spaced at precise forty-five-minute intervals, failed to raise Captain Philip Sheridan Parker IV at his bachelor officer's quarters number, his caller, somewhat embarrassed that he hadn't thought of this before, told the long distance operator to try to locate Captain Parker at the officer's club.

There was the sound of a barroom.

"Officer's open mess, main bar room, Sergeant Feeney, sir."

"Long distance is calling Captain P. S. Parker," the operator intoned.

"I'm not sure if he's here," the sergeant said.

"Look for him," the caller said, flatly.

"I beg your pardon?" the sergeant-bartender said.

"I said, look for him," the caller repeated.

"May I ask who's calling, please, sir?"

"This is Colonel Philip Sheridan Parker," the caller said.

There was a long wait, and then the click of an extension telephone being lifted.

"Captain Parker, sir."

"You may get off the line, Sergeant," Colonel Parker said.

The background sound of the barroom vanished.

"Hey, Dad, how are you? Is anything wrong?" Phil Parker asked, concern in his voice.

"Nothing is wrong. Is this telephone relatively secure?"

"Nobody else is on it, if that's what you mean. You sound upset, Dad. Is something wrong?"

"Have you been considering resignation?"

Phil Parker hesitated a moment before replying. "The thought has run through my mind," he said. "I haven't done anything about it."

"I'm glad to hear that," Colonel Parker said.

Phil didn't reply.

"Have you been drinking?" Colonel Parker asked.

"No, but that's one thought that really has been going through my mind." And then he understood the reason for the question. "Oh," he said. "In addition to my other duties, I am assistant club officer. I've been going over the books. That's why I'm here."

"I would like to suggest that you put off any action with regard to resignation for a while," Colonel Parker said.

"Dad, I have no intention of spending my life fighting with dependent wives about grease spots on kitchen walls, or counting bottles of whiskey and A-1 sauce in officer's clubs. A classmate of mine is in the shipping business in Boston. He's offering me a hell of a lot of money, and the chance to live for a couple of years in Africa."

"You're a soldier," his father said.

"I'm beginning to have serious doubts about that," Phil Parker replied.

"I had a telephone call late this afternoon from an officer with whom I served in Europe. I am not at liberty to provide his name."

"And?"

"This officer is also a soldier," Colonel Parker said. "He leads me to believe that your situation is not quite as hopeless as you might think."

"Club officers are in short supply," Parker said.

"Two things are about to happen," Colonel Parker said. "You are about to be transferred, within the next couple of weeks, from Fort Devens."

"No kidding? Where am I going?"

"He didn't say," Colonel Parker said. "But he said that you are also going to be offered an opportunity which will provide a chance for you to get your career back on the tracks."

Phil Parker didn't reply.

"I will not bore you with maudlin tales of unpleasant assignments I had," Colonel Parker said. "You're a man. You'll have to make your own decisions. I would suggest, however, that whatever you're thinking of doing can wait for three months."

"You're not going to tell me who called?"

"Nothing more than to tell you he is a general officer for whom I have a good deal of respect. And affection, too, if that seems germane to you."

"I don't understand how he knew I was thinking of resigning," Phil Parker said. "I haven't mentioned that to anybody."

"We go back a long time together, Phil," Colonel Parker said. "He once dissuaded me from resigning."

"OK, Dad. I'll wait a while."

"Your mother said to tell you the young lady in the photograph is quite handsome."

"And what do you think?"

"I have been wondering if there is something significant in your having sent her photograph at all."

"She's really something special," Phil Parker said. "I met her at the Pops."

"The orchestra? Is that what you mean?"

"Yes," Phil said.

"Who introduced you?" his father asked.

"You really want to know?" Phil said, and chuckled. "Well, what I did, Dad, was walk up and hand her my card. I said I'd call her. Her date didn't like that at all. But he wasn't large enough to react violently."

"L'audace, l'audace, toujours l'audace," Colonel Parker said, a faint chuckle in his voice.

"She's a pathologist," Phil said. "What do you think about that?"

"A medical doctor?"

"At Harvard Medical School," Phil said. His father heard a touch of pride in his son's voice.

"I'm impressed," Colonel Parker said. Then, bluntly, "What kind of an officer's wife do you think she'd make?"

"Because she's a doctor, you mean?"

"Because she's a Negro," his father replied.

"They say 'black' now, Dad."

"You've thought about that, however?"

"Oh, yeah," Phil Parker said. "Her parents don't think much of soldiers."

"Few people do," Colonel Parker said.

"I've got to throw that into the equation, too, Dad."

"Contemplation of marriage is the one exception to the rule that any action is better than none," Colonel Parker said.

"I'll let you know what happens," Phil Parker said.

"Don't act hastily, Philip," his father said. "Whatever you do."

[FOUR]
Bordentown, New Jersey
23 October 1952

The Bordentown Military Academy took pride in the medical care, routine and emergency, it provided for the Corps of Cadets. The medical staff included a full-time physician, given the brevet rank of major, and four registered nurses, one brevet captain and three brevet first lieutenants.

Since no member of the Corps of Cadets happened to be confined in dispensary with any of the illnesses which strike boys in either their immediate postpuberty or teenage years, Evelyn Wood, R. N., was not required to remain in the eight-bed dispensary, but was instead required only to be in white uniform, to remain on the campus, and to keep the school switchboard operators and the duty officer aware of her location.

Her crisp white uniform was carefully laid on top of her red-lined nurse's cape, and her underthings were laid on top of the uniform, all of it on one of the two small upholstered chairs provided for each of the bedrooms in staff quarters number two.

Evelyn Wood herself, when the telephone rang, was lying naked on her stomach between the legs of Major Craig W. Lowell, who was the duty officer and similarly obliged to remain on campus in a location where the telephone operator could immediately locate him.

At the first ring, he reached down and gently but firmly disengaged Nurse Wood's mouth, and then turned on his side and reached for the telephone.

"Duty officer," he said. "Major Lowell."

She understood his concern, but she really would have taken great pains not to bite it off. Slightly piqued, she thought that at least he could have said, "Excuse me."

Evelyn Wood had seen Major Craig Lowell the day he reported for duty, a week late, for the fall semester. She wasn't exactly proud of how far she'd had to go to get them where they were, but on the other hand, there weren't that many good-looking single men who drove red Lincoln Continental convertibles around Bordentown, and desperate measures had been necessary.

He simply hadn't been interested in her at first. She had hoped that she would have a chance to meet him, more or less alone, somewhere on the campus, at the movies, someplace like that, but the only times she saw him were in staff quarters, and then he had looked right through her.

He spent his weekends off campus, leaving just as soon as he could on Friday afternoons and returning very late on Sunday.

What she'd had to do was lie in wait for him in the dispensary, when he was the duty officer and required to check on the dispensary twice during his tour of duty. She'd told him that since he had to be up anyway, he should come by her quarters after she finished her tour at midnight, and she would give him a cup of coffee.

He hadn't come. Instead, he had telephoned her quarters and told her to come to his, unless what she really had in mind was coffee.

That had been really humiliating, going down the corridor in her dressing gown, a shameless admission that what they both had in mind was s-x, instead of making a friendship that might result in courtship, and only then, possibly, s-x. She had really been tempted to turn around and tell him to go to hell.

But she had gone to his quarters and ten minutes after she walked in the door, she had been in his bed, and God, he was good there. Once they'd started, it was really actually better than it would have been the other way. There was something very exciting about not putting up any phony modesty and pretense. When she got turned on, *anything* went, and anything she wanted to do was fine with him.

She found out that he was a widower with a little boy, and the idea of an instant family finally had given her cause for concern, until she realized, feeling something like a fool, that he hadn't come within a hundred miles of suggesting anything like making anything of their relationship.

He took her out sometimes during the week, on her two nights off, to Trenton, and once to Philadelphia. He took her to really nice places, as if money didn't mean a thing to him. It would have been nicer if she had more seniority and got weekends off, but she didn't, and she hadn't really expected him to hang around the campus. He still went to New York or someplace every weekend.

All she could hope for, Evelyn Wood told herself, was that their relationship would gradually ripen. She knew he liked her.

"Is that you, Craig?" a woman's voice asked. It was familiar, but he couldn't place it.

"Who's this?"

"I'm crushed that you don't remember," she said. "This is Barbara Bellmon."

"Well, I'll be goddamned," he said.

"Probably," she said. "What are you doing? Can you talk?"

"Sure. What's on your mind?"

"Actually," she said, "Bob wants to talk to you." He heard her say, "Craig is on the line, honey."

"How are you, Lowell?" Bob Bellmon said a moment later. It wasn't at all hard to detect that he wasn't thrilled with the prospect of talking to him.

"Why I'm fine, Colonel," Lowell said. "May I offer my congratulations? I saw in the *Army-Navy Journal* that they've finally given you your silver chicken."

"Thank you," Bellmon said, stiffly. "Very kind of you."

"How may I be of service, Colonel?" Lowell asked lightly, enjoying Bellmon's discomfiture.

"In point of fact," Bellmon said. "Your name came up at lunch today."

"My ears haven't been burning," Lowell said. "What was said about me?"

"In the opinion of the officer with whom I had lunch . . ."

"Who was that, Colonel?"

"I'm not at liberty to say," Bellmon said. "A senior officer, who somehow knew that I know you."

"And what did this anonymous senior officer have to say about me?"

"He holds the opinion that there was something of an overreaction to that business with you and the movie star."

"You're talking about my efficiency report?"

"Yes, of course I am."

"That efficiency report was a result of my testifying for Phil Parker in his court-martial."

"That's not the story I get."

"Well, Bob, that's the story."

"Your case, as you are probably well aware, has been brought to the attention of a very senior officer by one of your politician friends."

"Now, I really don't know what you're talking about."

"You're denying it?"

"Yes, I'm denying it. I've been thinking about having a word with my senator—my cousin's got one in his vest pocket—about getting me permission to resign, but so far I haven't talked to him."

At that point, he thought of Porter Craig.

"My cousin may have done something like that," he said. "But, believe me, Bob, I didn't."

There was a pause before Bellmon went on.

"In any event, your case was brought before a senior officer by a senator."

"The one you had lunch with, no doubt?"

"I had lunch with his aide-de-camp," Bellmon said.

"And?"

"As I said, he feels there has been an overreaction to what happened to you in Korea."

"I wish you would get to the point," Lowell said.

"You'll shortly receive orders to Sill," Bellmon said. "To an assignment more in keeping with your experience and abilities."

Now Lowell paused before replying.

"What about Phil Parker?" he asked.

"Phil's going to Sill, too."

"Virtue, I gather," Lowell said, "is its own reward. Thanks for calling me. I appreciate it."

"I can't accept credit for something like that," Bellmon said. "It was pointedly suggested to me that since we were such old friends, that I make the call."

"What do I have to do, Bob," Lowell flared, "to get in your good graces? Win the goddamned Medal? There's two sides to the Korean story, believe it or not!"

"Both of you stop it," Barbara Bellmon said angrily, apparently on an extension. "Craig, he told me again and again he thought you got a raw deal in Korea."

"I apologize, Lowell," Bellmon said.

"You apologize, '*Craig*,' " Barbara Bellmon said firmly to her husband.

"I apologize, Craig," Bellmon said dutifully.

"Now I'm embarrassed," Lowell said. "You don't owe me an apology, Bob. I know I grate on your nerves. I can't help it."

"Daddy grated on his nerves, too, Craig," Barbara said. "You're in good company."

"That's right, that's right," Bob Bellmon said righteously. "You and Porky Waterford are two of a kind, Lowell."

" *'Craig,'* " Barbara corrected him again.

"I'm a full colonel," Bellmon said. "He's a lousy major. I can call him anything I want to call him."

It was a joke, and they all laughed. And they talked of P.P., and Lowell promised to come by the Farm on his way to Sill, when he got his orders. Finally, he hung up.

He rolled over onto his back.

"What was that all about?" Evelyn Wood asked, smiling at him, stroking him.

"I'm about to be sprung from durance vile," Lowell reported.

"I don't know what that means," Evelyn said. "You're going somewhere?"

"Right."

"Where?"

"Fort Sill, Oklahoma," he said. He smiled happily. "Now where were we?"

Damn, she thought, as she took him in her mouth again. She should have known it would turn out like this.

XVIII

[ONE]
The Artillery School
Fort Sill, Oklahoma
New Year's Day, 1953

The United States Air Force traces its heritage to the aviation section of the Signal Corps in the days before World War II. Army aviation traces its heritage back to the Civil War, when Thaddeus Lowe provided the army with balloons, from which Union Army artillery fire was directed against the Confederate Army of Northern Virginia attacking Washington.

The vast bulk of army aircraft (as opposed to *Army Air Corps* aircraft) in World War II, almost all of them Piper Cub L-2s or Stinson L-5s, were assigned to the artillery for the same purpose, aerial direction of artillery fire.

It was natural, therefore, that artillery took over the role of pilot training. Artillery observers were trained at the same time as the gunners were trained, on the huge Fort Sill reservation.

In both separate batteries, and as part of armored formations, a large portion of U.S. Army artillery is self-propelled; that is, the cannon are mounted on tracked tank chassis.

Major Craig Lowell thought there was nothing really unusual about his assignment to the Office of the G-3 (Plans and Training) of the Army Artillery Center, Fort Sill. It was the sort of assignment to which he was entitled. He was an armor officer with S-3 experience. He knew tracks, and how to teach people to operate and maintain them.

Neither was it surprising, only a pleasant coincidence, that Phil Parker should have been called from passing out dependent housing at Fort Devens for assignment to Sill, following what Lowell thought of as "the conditional pardon." It was a logical place for him to be assigned, too. Parker was made motor officer, tracked vehicles, in the Self-propelled Artillery Department of the Artillery School. His job was to make sure that sufficient self-propelled tracks were available to carry out the training missions prescribed by the G-3.

They weren't in armor, but it was the next best thing. The BOQs were ghastly, perched so that the sand of Sill was blown into everything by the never-ending wind. Regulations did not permit bachelor officers to live off post, that privilege being reserved for officers with dependents, for whom no housing was available on the post.

It was a question of semantics. They were not confined to the post, but they would not be paid a housing allowance since BOQs were available to them.

Lowell, on his third day at Fort Sill, after investigating the available hotel accommodations and rental housing nearby, and finding them just about as bad as the BOQs, had thrilled a salesman at Lawton Realty by making a five-thousand-dollar down payment on the demonstration model of the Holly Crest Split-Level ($26,500) in the Lawton Heights subdivision, sufficient to get quick approval of the mortage at the First National Bank of Lawton. He then gave him another check for the furnishings, which were on sort-of-a-loan from Oklahoma Home Furnishings.

All that was required to move in was a visit to the department store for sheets, towels, and that sort of thing, and to the grocery store.

It did cause some raised eyebrows from the neighbors, first when the wives came bearing gifts for the wife, and learned there was no wife, and next when an enormous black captain also moved in.

They didn't look like fairies, but you couldn't tell anymore, these days.

There was some talk like that until the next Friday, when a tall and elegantly dressed black woman got out of a taxi and smiled at the horseshoe of flowers propped against the door with a ribbon reading, "WELCOME TO THE WILD WEST, ANTOINETTE." She had been mailed a key, since Phil couldn't get off during the day to meet her at the plane.

Antoinette, despite her parents' protests that doctors of medicine or not, nice girls don't fly thousands of miles to spend weekends with a soldier, was a frequent guest at 2340 Bubbling Creek Lane, and she was there when the telephone call came on New Year's afternoon. So was Harriet Albright, the assistant vice president at the First National Bank of Lawton. Harriet, a redheaded divorcée, had been thrilled at the prospect of "burning some steaks" at Major Lowell's house, after having been informed by the Morgan Guaranty Trust—of whom she had made the necessary inquiries relative to granting a mortage—that there was no question whatever regarding his credit rating, and even after he had carefully pointed out to her that his roommate was colored, and that they had as their house guest, his roommate's fiancée, who was also colored.

Harriet had never been personally prejudiced herself, and there weren't that many bachelors around whom a vice president of the Morgan Guaranty Trust would describe as "very rich."

Craig was in the kitchen with Antoinette, having just tasted Antoinette's Pommes Frites d'Alsace, when the pale yellow telephone matching the wallpaper went off in his ear.

He was on his fourth martini, and feeling better than he had felt in a long time.

"Hello," he said to the telephone.

"Major Lowell, please," an obviously military voice said.

"What number are you calling, please?" Lowell said. He had no intention of running out to the post to do something that damned well could wait until Monday morning.

"The number I got from information," the caller said. "Is that you, Lowell?"

"Yes, sir."

"My name is Roberts. We have a mutual acquaintance, Bob Bellmon."

"Oh, yes, sir."

"I've been looking for you, and for Captain Parker, since Thursday," Roberts said. "I presume he's there with you?"

"Yes, sir."

"My wife and I would like to call on you, Major," Roberts said, and it was clear from the tone of his voice that whatever this was about, it was not social. "Would in an hour be convenient?"

"Could you give me some idea what this is all about . . . is it Colonel?"

"Lieutenant Colonel," Roberts said. "I'm the deputy post aviation officer."

"Colonel, we're in the middle . . . we're about to have dinner."

"I'll give you an hour and a half then," Colonel Roberts said. "2340 Bubbling Creek Lane, isn't it?"

"It's the house with the 'Sold' sign nailed to the 'Furnished Model' sign on the lawn," Lowell said.

Antoinette laughed at him.

"Why don't you take that down?" she asked.

"It beats a street number all to death, doesn't it?"

Antoinette laughed, and then she said: "Every time I have my girlish dreams of getting you two out of the army, and into respectability, I have this nightmare: I see that 'For Sale/Sold' sign, and I remember you're not really housebroken, socially speaking. It's probably better my parents haven't met either one of you."

"I'll have you know," Lowell replied, "you beskirted chancre mechanic, that Congress has decreed that Phil and I are gentlemen."

He patted her on the bottom, and then he went in to where Phil was mixing another pitcher of martinis and told him what was about to happen.

An hour and fifteen minutes after his telephone call, Lt. Colonel and Mrs. William Roberts got out of their Mercury coupe and walked up to the door of 2340 Bubbling Creek Lane. Colonel Roberts pushed the doorbell, and he and his wife could hear the first eight notes of "Be It Ever So Humble." Mrs. Roberts giggled.

Lowell opened the door. He was dressed in a polo shirt and slacks.

"Colonel Roberts, I presume," he said.

"I *love* your doorbell," Mrs. Roberts said, with a wide smile.

"Wait till you see the wallpaper in the downstairs lavatory," Lowell said. "It's an artistic rendition of that famous statue in Belgium of the little boy doing you know what."

"Fantastic!" she said, and she and Craig Lowell smiled at each other.

"Please come in," Lowell said. Roberts shook his hand, but didn't say a word.

Captain Philip Sheridan Parker IV, who had been on the couch with Dr. Antoinette Ferguson, got up.

" 'I just can't get over,' as they say," Mrs. Roberts said, " 'how big Sweet Little Philip has grown!' "

"I beg your pardon?" Parker said.

"I have been brought along on Bill's recruiting expedition as proof that at least he's married to someone friendly," she said. "I knew you at Riley before the war. My folks and yours still exchange Christmas cards. I'm . . . I was . . . Jeanne Whitman."

"Oh, sure!" Parker said, his face widening with a smile. "How's your father?"

"Fine. And yours? My parents are out in Carmel."

"Mine are still outside the gate at Riley," Phil said. He turned to Antoinette. "Mrs. Roberts, may I present Dr. Antoinette Ferguson? And this is Mrs. Albright."

"Doctor of medicine?" Colonel Roberts asked. "Or of philosophy?"

"I'm a pathologist," Antoinette said.

"And Harriet is a banker," Lowell said. "Make sure you mention that when you write his mother."

"Our neighbors refer to this place as Respectability Hall," Parker offered.

"I'll bet they do," Colonel Roberts said. "Well, now the small talk is out of the way, why don't you regale the ladies, Jeanne, with stories of the Old Army while I talk to these two?"

"I'm really sorry to break into your party this way," Jeanne Whitman Roberts said, "but there's no stopping Bill when he gets this way."

"Is there somewhere we can go?" Roberts asked.

"Can I fix you a drink?" Lowell asked.

"I'm a little afraid you've had too many already," Roberts said bluntly.

"And I intend to have at least one more, Colonel," Lowell said coldly. "Phil and I have fixed up the third bedroom as sort of an office. We can go up there." He picked up the martini pitcher, poured a drink and held it out to Roberts. Roberts paused, and finally gave in and took it. Lowell offered another martini to Phil Parker, who shook his head, "no." Then Lowell poured one for himself and waved Roberts up the stairs.

"OK, Colonel," he said, when Roberts had helped himself to the only upholstered chair in the room, "what's this all about?"

"I've got a couple of questions to ask you," Roberts said. "And do me the courtesy of giving me straight answers." Both Phil and Craig nodded.

"What do you think, by and large, of army aviators?" Colonel Roberts asked.

Phil Parker shrugged his massive shoulders. "Not much," he said. "I mean, I never thought of them much, period. But now that I am thinking of them, per se, I don't think much of them, either. Is that straight enough for you, Colonel?"

"Lowell?" Roberts asked, without replying.

"I have always wondered why the army feels it can turn a half-million-dollar tank and command of a four- or five-man crew over to a sergeant, and on the other hand has to have a lieutenant or a captain—or even a major—flying a two-seater, fifteen-thousand-dollar airplane."

"In other words, you don't think much of army aviators, or, for that matter of army aviation?"

"You want it straight?" Lowell asked. "OK. There's obviously a place for airplanes in the army. God knows, there's nothing better for column control. I've used them myself. I've even wondered why the hell we can't put rockets on some of those little planes. Maybe even on choppers. They'd be good tank killers. But that's not what's happening. Army aviators are a collection of commissioned aerial jeep drivers playing air force."

"You don't think much of the typical army aviator, is that what you're saying?"

"No offense intended, Colonel. But you asked for it. And there it is. I'm like Phil. I don't think much of them, period, except to wonder why the hell they should be officers."

"A good many aviators leave a good deal to be desired," Roberts said. "A number of them, in fact, are officers who got into some scrape in their basic army, saw the handwriting on the wall, and came to aviation because it was either into army aviation or out of the army."

"Tell me, Colonel, have our reputations preceded us?" Lowell asked.

"I know a good deal about the both of you," Roberts said. "Including the bad."

"And since we are such certified fuck-ups, you're here to recruit us for army aviation?" Lowell challenged. "I don't think I'm quite that fucked up, Colonel, thank you just the same."

"Shut up, Craig," Phil Parker said, sharply. "The colonel is a guest in our quarters. We didn't expect visitors, Colonel. We've been drinking."

"It doesn't seem to make you forget that you're supposed to be an officer and a gentleman," Roberts said. He glowered at Lowell as if waiting for an apology. He didn't get one.

"Flight classes at the aviation section of the Artillery School consist of thirty-two officers," Roberts said, after a long, tense pause. "In the event that, during the first two weeks of flight training, something causes an officer to drop out of flight school, Fort Sill is authorized to replace those officers from qualified officers already present at Fort Sill. The training schedule, as you can understand, Major Lowell, will have to go on regardless of the number of officers present to take the training."

"And you just happen to have lost two of your students, is that it?" Phil Parker asked.

"Well, I'm sorry this has been a wild-goose chase for you, Colonel," Lowell said. "But before I would become an aerial taxi driver, I would resign."

"There are nineteen officers at Fort Sill at the moment on the waiting list," Roberts said, undaunted. "Ready and willing to take flight training."

"Then why do you want us?" Phil Parker asked.

"Because, in your case, Captain Parker, you have been identified to me as a solid and stable officer, from a long line of soldiers, who was given a raw deal in Korea."

Parker didn't reply. Roberts looked at Lowell.

"And you, Lowell, I want you because of what's written in your Counterintelligence Corps dossier."

"I don't understand," Lowell replied.

"You have political influence at the highest levels," Colonel Roberts said, "and you will continue to have it, no matter which party holds temporary power, because you are, through inheritance, not because you did anything at all to earn it, obscenely rich."

"I have never attempted to use my financial position," Lowell said, slowly and distinctly, so that Parker, recognizing this as a sign of fury, looked at him with concern, "in any way whatsoever to seek special privilege in the army."

"You were relieved of your duties at the Bordentown Military Academy, Major, by the Vice Chief of Staff, at the request of the senior senator from New York."

"I was presented that as a *fait accompli,"* Lowell said. "My cousin arranged that. He doesn't want me in New York."

"I believe that," Roberts said. "But nobody else will. And I notice you didn't complain that you were receiving special treatment."

"Oh, *shit!"* Lowell said. "I should have known something like this would pop up."

"It's not the end of the world," Roberts said.

"If you know about it, Colonel," Lowell said, "it will be all over the fucking army."

"Your political influence is one thing that makes you attractive to me," Roberts said. "I was not overly impressed with that grandstanding ride you took out of Pusan. You're lucky you didn't get the whole task force wiped out."

"Colonel," Lowell said, "don't talk to me about Task Force Lowell. I was there, and you weren't, and that was the proper use of tanks in that situation."

"You enjoy command, don't you?" Roberts asked. "Pity you'll never get another one in armor."

"You seem a good deal more sure of that that I am, Colonel," Lowell said."

"Don't take my word," Roberts said. "But what about Paul Jiggs? Would you take his? Or Bob Bellmon's?"

"You've been talking to them?"

"They've been trying to sell you to me, Major. And you're doing a very good job of unselling yourself, political influence or no political influence."

Lowell just looked at him. Their eyes locked. Finally, Roberts picked up the telephone. "Operator, get me Colonel Paul Jiggs, at the National War College, in Washington, D.C."

Lowell reached over and broke the connection.

"I'm a little surprised that Colonel Jiggs would bring up the political business," he said.

"I shouldn't tell you this, because you're arrogant enough," Roberts said. "But I finally seem to be getting through the layer of smart-ass, and I'll take a chance. Jiggs said that you're a splendid combat commander, a splendid S-3, and a three-star wise-ass. He said that with luck, you may grow out of being a smart-ass, and that I'm going to need both commanders and planners, and that I'm not going to get many to volunteer."

"What you're suggesting is that I could get a command in army aviation," Lowell said. "Of what? A reinforced platoon of Piper Cubs?"

"How about a company of rocket-armed helicopters?"

"You're a dreamer, Colonel," Lowell said. "The air force won't stand still for that."

"I see entire divisions, entirely transported and supported by army aircraft," Roberts said. "That's what I dream."

"A vast armada of L-19s, Beavers, and H13s filling the sky," Lowell said, sarcastically.

"I told you to watch your lip," Phil Parker said.

"That's my brain talking, not the booze," Lowell said.

"OK," Roberts said. "Paragraph Four. Conclusions. Where you stand now, Major Lowell, is as an officer far too young for the grade you hold, with an efficiency report that will hang around your neck the rest of your career. There is no way, *no way*, that you will *ever* command a tank battalion, and you're smart enough when you're sober to know that. And when your time comes to be considered for lieutenant colonel, if you last that long, and the choice is between you and some officer whose efficiency report does not state he acts impulsively and cannot be recommended for command, you know who will be promoted."

"You've been reading my efficiency reports, too, huh? You get around, don't you, Colonel?"

"Yeah, I do," Roberts said. "I'm generally as unpopular with my peers as you are with yours."

"Who's going to promote an officer who spent ten years flying a Piper Cub?" Lowell asked.

"In ten years, I don't intend that the army will be flying Piper Cubs," Roberts said. "And when they start picking *aviation* battalion commanders, they'll have to pick them from aviators. By your own statements, you consider most army aviators mediocrities and misfits. Against that kind of competition, you just might not have to go from being the youngest major in the army to the oldest, Lowell."

"What's in it for you, Colonel?" Lowell replied.

"I told you. Both Bob Bellmon and Paul Jiggs have been touting you as the best G-3 type I can get. That and the political influence."

"You keep saying 'I,' " Philip Sheridan Parker said. "You sound like you own army aviation."

Roberts gave him a cold look.

"Right now, I'm one of the three officers on active duty who were in the first class, the 'Class Before One,' before they numbered the classes for liaison pilots. The other two are about to retire. To the considerable surprise of my classmates, who to a man felt that I had thrown away my career, I have been promoted with them. Right now, I'm one of the very few people with the vision to see an air-mobile army. Yeah, Captain, I guess you could say I have a certain possessive feeling toward army aviation."

"You really think you can get away with it?" Lowell asked.

"I hope I can," Roberts said. "I work pretty hard at it."

"What do you think, Phil?" Lowell asked.

"He sure do talk it up, don't he?" Captain Philip Sheridan Parker IV said, in a thick Negro accent. "He make a *fine* casket salesman. He make it sound like you *need* the solid bronze."

"I've got to do a lot of things I don't like to do," Roberts burst out, furiously. "But I don't have to take being mocked by assholes like you two."

"Colonel, you have really sprung something on me I didn't expect," Lowell said. "I'd like to think it over. When do you have to know?"

"Right goddamned now," Roberts said, still red in the face and furious.

"I saw my father on the way out here," Phil Sheridan said. "He said that I was making the same mistake a lot of people were making." Confused, both Lowell and Roberts looked at him. "He said that armor wasn't cavalry, and he said that there will always be a place on the battlefield for cavalry."

"What the hell is that supposed to mean?" Roberts asked.

"He said it didn't come down from Mount Sinai engraved on stone that cavalry has to be mounted on a horse," Parker said. "What you said before, Craig. About arming helicopters? What the hell is that, a fast-moving lightly armed force, unrestricted by roads, but cavalry?"

"You think the man has a point?" Lowell asked.

"What happens to me next?" Parker asked. "There aren't many field-grade motor officers around. Count me in, Colonel."

"Don't be impetuous," Lowell said. "This needs some thought. If we fuck this up, Philip my lad, we would really be finished. How soon do you need an answer, Colonel?"

"Right goddamned now," Roberts said. "I need two bodies at the airfield at 0800 tomorrow. Yours or somebody else's."

"Well, in that case," Lowell said. "I think I'd better have another martini."

"What the hell kind of an answer is that?" Colonel Roberts demanded.

"It mean," Captain Philip Sheridan Parker said, again in his thick Negro accent, "look out aviation! Here come duh Duke and King Kong!"

Roberts was still mad. "I hope you two bastards don't think you're doing me a favor," he said. But he got up and put out his hand to both of them.

[TWO]

Antoinette didn't seem impressed one way or the other when they came down from their meeting with Colonel Roberts and told her that they were about to soar off into the wild blue yonder, starting at 0800 the next morning. But when they tapered off from the martinis into wine spritzers, she became what Lowell thought of as a royal pain in the ass.

When Harriet finally went home, she got even worse. And then, surprising the both of them, she made a pitcher of martinis, and when asked about the pitcher, said she was in a good mood to drink at least one pitcherful, and possibly two.

"Would you tell me why you're being such a bitch?" Phil Parker asked.

She finished the martini she was drinking before she replied.

"Why am I being such a bitch?" she said. "Right. Good question."

"You're drunk, for Christ's sake!" Phil said to her.

"In vino veritas," Antoinette said.

"Ergo sum," Lowell said.

"E pluribus unum," Parker said. He and Lowell laughed.

"Screw you, Phil!" Antoinette snapped, furiously. And then she started to cry.

"What the hell is the matter?" Phil asked, half angry, half concerned.

"Well, excuse me, kiddies," Lowell said. "Little Craig is going to go tuck it in."

"You stay!" Antoinette ordered.

"What the hell have I done?" he asked, but he sat back down.

"I've had enough of this," she said.

"Of what, honey?"

"Of being a damned camp follower."

"I'm sorry you feel that way," Phil said.

"I'm not like that redheaded tramp of yours, Craig."

"Harriet? Hey, Slim, if Harriet is the problem, it's solved. I've had about all of her I can stand myself," Lowell said. "And now may I go to bed?"

"No," she said. "That's not what I mean. What I mean to say is that I can't go on like I am. I have to make up my mind."

"About what?" Phil asked.

"Every time I come out here, I convince myself that I'll be able to talk you out of the army, and get you home to Boston. And every time, nothing happens."

"Nothing will, Toni," Parker said softly. "I'm a soldier. That's what I do."

"And I'm a doctor," she said. "That's what I do."

"And ne'er the twain shall meet?" Phil said.

She looked at him, and with tears streaming down her cheeks, nodded her head.

"I've had enough of this maudlin bullshit," Lowell said, and got up.

"Watch it, Craig!" Parker said, angrily.

"Either she loves you and wants to marry you and bear your children, or she doesn't. It's as simple as that. You two can fight about it all night for all I care, but for Christ's sake, if she gets hysterical, throw some water on her. I need my sleep."

He stormed out of the room and went upstairs.

Five minutes later there was a knock at his door. Captain Philip S. Parker IV and Miss Antoinette Elaine Ferguson, M.D., wished him to be the first to know that they were to be joined in holy matrimony.

"In a couple of weeks, Craig. Just a little ceremony. My folks and Toni's, and that's about all. You, too, of course."

"But not Harriet?"

"No," Toni said, and leaned over and kissed him. "Not Harriet."

"I suppose this means I'll have to find someplace else to live, doesn't it?" Lowell said.

"This is your home, dummy," Parker said.

"I'll make you a good deal on it," Lowell said, "if you agree to rent me a room. This one."

[THREE]
Fort Sill, Oklahoma
14 January 1953

Chaplain (Lt. Col.) James Jackson "Brother Jack" Glover, Fort Sill's senior chaplain, was a Southern Baptist from Daphne, Alabama. He naturally reflected the "mores of his background," as he thought of it, but he prided himself on keeping his feelings about colored people to himself. They were all God's children, after all, and this wasn't Daphne, Alabama, but the U.S. Army. There was no room for prejudice in the armed forces of the United States, and he did whatever he could, whenever he could, to condemn bigotry.

Having said that, there was really no phrase Brother Jack could think of to better describe the colored officer who had come to his office five days before than "an uppity nigger."

His door had been open to him, and his heart, and he had been willing to render unto him precisely the same services that he would render to any of his Protestant military flock, regardless of color.

He had tried to explain to him that marriage was a sacrament and that it should not be entered into lightly and not without a lot of prayer. He had told him that he had regularly scheduled marriage counseling sessions and that he would be happy to schedule the captain and his young lady for the next one.

"Chaplain, all I want from you is to tell me when I can have the chapel in the next five days. I intend to provide my own clergyman, and I'm really not interested in counseling. I've given this marriage a good deal of thought for a long time."

"But has your young woman?"

"My 'young woman,' Chaplain, is a doctor of medicine, and she's given the matter even more thought than I have."

"Captain," Brother Jack had told him, "my marriage counseling sessions have the enthusiastic support of the general. It is official command policy that officers and enlisted men be encouraged to participate before assuming the responsibilities of marriage."

"With all respect, Chaplain, when can I have the chapel?" he asked, not even bothering to conceal his impatience.

Brother Jack would not have been surprised if the colored captain's intended had turned out to be a white woman. There was a certain class of white women, mostly Yankee intellectual types, who really chased after big black bucks like this one. But she was a coon, too. She had brought their wedding license to the chaplain's office two days later, after he'd told the colored captain that he would have to see the marriage license before he could turn the chapel over to a civilian clergyman. Good-looking woman, Brother Jack thought. Obviously had a lot of Arab—or white—blood in her. Not one of your flat-faced jungle bunnies. Maybe she really was a doctor. That's the way she signed the marriage license, anyway.

Then things started happening that really began to bother Brother Jack, though the way the liberals were running things and ruining the army, the last thing he wanted was a run-in with the NAACP about picking on the colored.

The first thing that happened was that he walked into the chapel and found the general's aide snooping around. When he asked him what he could do for him, the general's aide said all he knew was that the general had told him to come to the chapel and make sure things were up to snuff.

Brother Jack could hardly call the general and ask him what he was worried about, but just to be sure, he called in all the chaplain's assistants and had them give the chapel a good GI party, top to bottom. It didn't need it, of course, but a chapel could never be too clean.

The next thing that happened was that Mrs. Roberts, the wife of the head aviator, came to the chapel and started nosing around herself. She told him that an old friend of hers was being married there, and she wanted things to be first rate.

He wasn't really surprised when the friend turned out to be the colored captain.

He expected that the civilian minister who was going to perform the ceremony would be in touch with him, but that didn't happen; so Brother Jack called the president of the Lawton Ministerial Association, of which he was a member, and asked him who would be a likely candidate among the colored clergy to marry a colored officer and his fiancée. He got three names, and called all three of them, but they had never heard of a Captain Parker.

On the morning of the wedding, Brother Jack went by the chapel just to make sure things were all right. There was a self propelled 155 mm cannon, a Long Tom on a tank chassis, parked in front of the chapel. He didn't know what was going on, and he went to the driver and asked him what he was doing, and the driver told him all he knew was that he had been told to bring the vehicle to the chapel, and that the general's aide would meet him there.

And then things really started to happen. Two panel trucks showed up from Lawton loaded with flowers; and then Mrs. Roberts started to arrange them all over the chapel. The obvious thing to do, to show her he had no prejudice, was to help her with that, and that's what he was doing when he saw the front door of the chapel open, and a major wearing a sword came in.

"I got the sabers, Chaplain," the major said. "Where's the condemned man?"

The major's name was Green, and he said that he was president of the local chapter of Norwich graduates, and he just wished to hell they'd given him a little more time; all he could come up with on such short notice was twelve officers, including himself. Brother Jack had never heard of Norwich, and didn't know what he was talking about, and moreover, Major Green had obviously been at the bottle. You could smell it four feet away.

And then what really put the cork in the bottle, the chapel door opened again and a major general came in. Brother Jack saw the stars first, and only afterward the silver crosses on his lapels. There is only one man in the U.S. Army who wears the two stars of a major general and the crosses of Christ: the Chief of Chaplains.

Mrs. Roberts ran and kissed him on the cheek.

"Father Dan," she called him, even though Brother Jack knew for a fact that he was Episcopalian, not Roman Catholic. "I'm glad you could make it."

"Not only that, I came in style," he said. "E. Z.'s here, too."

"Where?"

"The bar at the club is open," he said. "Where else?" Then he saw Brother Jack. "I really hate to just jump in on you like this, Chaplain," he said, "but I went through War II with the colonel, Colonel Parker, that is, and I christened the groom, so I figured that it was my duty to marry him."

"We're honored to have you here, sir," Brother Jack said. "Is there anything I can do?"

"Nothing but clean up the mess afterward," the Chief of Chaplains said, cheerfully. "I know this chapel. I was stationed here. The reason the organ is new is because the old one, when I was here, used to collapse once a month."

Then the guests started to arrive. Including the officer the Chief of Chaplains had identified as "E. Z." E. Z. turned out to be the newly appointed Vice Chief of Staff of the United States Army, General E. Z. Black.

The Vice Chief of Staff of the U.S. Army smelled as heavily of booze as did Major Green.

Fair's fair, Brother Jack decided, admitting that the very brief Episcopalian wedding ceremony had a lot of class, even if it meant the minister didn't have much of an opportunity to exhort the bride and groom on their responsibilities to God and the community as man and wife.

And he really liked the officers lined up outside the chapel afterward, with their sabers forming an arch over the newlyweds. He hadn't been able to find out what this Norwich Association was, but he made a note to look into it. Maybe he could get them to do the saber thing regularly. It added a nice military touch.

The self-propelled 155 mm cannon was a disaster, as Brother Jack knew it would be. First, when they started it up, it made so much noise you couldn't hear the organ music during the recessional. Next, it frightened the bride, when the groom and she got into it. And when she rode it to the officer's club, she got grease all over her white dress.

And, as Brother Jack knew very well it would, it just tore up the macadam road in front of the chapel and all the way to the officer's club, where there was a party that could only be described as drunken.

But he couldn't say anything to anyone about that. For what happened was that the Vice Chief of Staff of the U.S. Army, a four-star general, obviously in his cups, had called out to the groom's father (whom Brother Jack had learned was a retired colonel). "Come on, Phil," the Vice Chief had said, "it's our last chance, probably," and then ordered the driver and the commander of the self-propelled 155 mm off the vehicle and had driven Captain and Mrs. Philip Sheridan Parker IV to their reception at the officer's open mess.

The Majors

I

[ONE]
Washington, D.C.
10 March 1954

The black four-door Buick Roadmaster carried Virginia license plates. Attached to the plates was a strip of metal on which was stamped "Alexandria 1954," as proof the owner had paid his 1954 Alexandria city automobile tax. The car showed none of the other decalomania, however, that many of the cars in the Washington, D.C., area showed, thus identifying them as military personnel attached to the Military District of Washington, or as employees of the federal government authorized to park in Section B, Parking Lot III, of the Department of Labor, or so on.

There was nothing about the car, in other words, that made it appear to be anything but the car of someone who lived in Alexandria, Virginia. But when it turned off Pennsylvania Avenue, the normally closed gates of 1600 Pennsylvania Avenue were open, and the two guards on duty touched their caps in salute and waved it through without stopping it either to examine the driver's identification or to telephone to see if he was expected, though it was late at night.

The driver proceeded to the entrance nearest the Executive Office Building, the ornate old Army-Navy-State Department Building. Two marines, in dress blues, came out to the car before it had stopped.

"I'll park it for you, sir," one of them said to the driver.

"If you'll come with me, sir," the other one said.

The man who emerged from the car was a small, prematurely bald, rather skinny man wearing a baggy suit, white shirt, nondescript necktie, and black shoes. He was the antithesis of memorable.

When the marine headed away from the elevator that went to the Command Operations Room, the small man asked him where they were going.

"To the quarters, sir."

The small man did not reply.

When he got off the elevator which opened on the wide entrance corridor of the living quarters, the Secret Service agent on duty nodded to him.

"You're to go right in," he said.

"Thank you," the small man said politely, as he passed through the double door the agent held open for him.

There were two men in the room. One of them, a brigadier general whose tunic was adorned with the heavy golden cord, the *fourragère*, identifying the military aide-de-camp to the President of the United States, was bending over the back of a fragile, gilt chair. In the chair sat a balding, bespectacled man wearing a tattered sweater. On the sweater was sewn a large "A."

"That was quick," the President of the United States said.

"There's not much traffic this time of night, sir."

"We're drinking," the President said, indicating a silver tray on which whiskey bottles sat. "Will you have something? Or coffee?"

"Coffee, please, sir, black," the small man said.

The military aide walked out of the room.

"I spoke with John an hour or so ago," the President said. "He sends his regards."

"Thank you, sir."

"I only recently learned that you were classmates and friends," the President said.

"Acquaintances, sir," the small man said. "And he is '44. I would have been '46."

The President nodded, and then smiled. "He leads me to believe it can get a little chilly in Korea."

"The troops call it 'Frozen Chosen,' sir," the small man said.

A black man, a U.S. Navy chief steward, wearing a starched white jacket, came into the room with a silver pot of coffee and two cups and saucers. He left, closing the door behind him. The aide did not return.

The President poured coffee into one of the two white china cups, and then said, "I think I'll have a little of that myself," and poured the second cup full. "Reinforced, of course," he said, splashing bourbon into the cup. He held the bottle over the second cup and looked at the small man.

"Please," the small man said.

"Help yourself, Major," the President said, and went to a table and opened a folder. He took from it a stapled document, the cover sheet of which was stamped, top and bottom, with TOP SECRET in inch-high red letters. Red stripes ran diagonally across the cover sheet.

He waited until the small man had seated himself, rather awkwardly, on a low, red leather couch and then he handed it to him. The small man put his cup and saucer down, held the cover sheet out of the way, and carefully read what the President had given him.

COPY *1* of *3*
DUPLICATION
FORBIDDEN

TOP SECRET
(QUINCY),
THE JOINT CHIEFS OF STAFF
THE PENTAGON
WASHINGTON 25, D.C.

8 March 1954

EYES ONLY
VIA FIELD-GRADE OFFICER COURIER
TO: Commander in Chief
U.S. Forces, Far East
The Dai Ichi Building, Tokyo, Japan
INFO: The President
The White House
Washington, D.C.

By direction of the Chairman of the Joint Chiefs of Staff, the President concurring, you are authorized and directed to appoint Lieutenant General E. Z. Black, USA, as your representative to meet with the Commander in Chief, French forces in French Indo-China at Hanoi, as soon as possible. The purpose of the meeting is to determine if augmentation of French forces by American forces no longer required for operations in Korea would permit the French, in the immediate future, to sustain their operations at Dien Bien Phu, and ultimately to suppress Viet Minh/Communist insurgent forces currently threatening French control of Indo-China.

It is emphasized that General Black's mission is solely to evaluate the present military situation. He is *NOT* authorized to commit U.S. forces, of any type, for any purpose.

For planning purposes only, it is contemplated that the following U.S. forces might be made available for service in French Indo-China, should United States intervention be determined to be feasible and desirable:

Elements, Eighth U.S. Army, as follows:

1st U.S. Cavalry Division (Dismounted)
40th U.S. Infantry Division
187th Infantry Regimental Combat Team (Air-borne)
8058th Mobile Army Surgical Hospital
555th Artillery Group
Command and Support units to be determined

Elements, 20th U.S. Air Force, as follows:

433rd Air Transport Group
2055th Air Control Squadron
2057th Meteorological Squadron
271st Fighter Wing
107th Fighter Bomber Squadron
707th Bomber Squadron (Augmented)
Command and Support units to be determined

Elements, Pacific Fleet, as follows:

Four attack transports
Fleet oiler
Task force, elements to be determined, but including:
Aircraft carrier with three fighter squadrons and one fighter-bomber squadron aboard
Escort vessels
Ships of the line to be determined

Inasmuch as it is anticipated that should American augmentation of French forces occur, General Black would be placed in command, you are authorized and directed to designate such general or flag officers as General Black may desire, representing the forces named above, to accompany him to Hanoi, or such other place as he may deem necessary.

In view of the politically sensitive nature of General Black's mission, it is directed that his party travel in civilian clothing by chartered civilian aircraft. This letter constitutes authority for the expenditure of whatever discretionary funds are necessary. Waiver of normal passport and visa requirements has been received from the French Colonial Administration.

General Black will make a daily report, to be encrypted in French Indo-China, and transmitted via officer courier to Tokyo for radio teletype transmittal to the Chairman of the Joint Chiefs of Staff. 20th Air Force has been directed to make courier aircraft available.

On completion of his discussions with the French authorities, General Black will prepare a report, to be encrypted in French Indo-China, and transmitted in like manner. *NO*, repeat *NO*, copies of this report are to be retained in the Far East, and all notes and other material used in its preparation are to be destroyed.

General Black may select whatever staff he desires to accompany him.

FOR THE CHAIRMAN, THE JOINT CHIEFS
Edmund C. Williams
Major General, USMC
Secretary of The Joint Chiefs of Staff

"Yes, sir?" the small man asked, when he had finished reading.

"You read that pretty carefully," the President said.

"Yes, sir."

"I was led to believe you wrote it."

"I drafted it, sir, for the Joint Chiefs. They might have changed it."

"Did they?"

"Not significantly, sir."

"How's your health, Felter?" the President asked.

"Fine, sir."

"I mean, really. Not officially. Are you fully recovered?"

"Yes, sir."

"I understand the only way you can get into Dien Bien Phu is by parachute. You feel up to that?"

"Yes, sir,"

"I want you to go to Indo-China with General Black," the President said, "and then detach yourself, quietly, from the official party, go to Dien Bien Phu, see what shape they're in, positions, supplies, morale, the whole business, and then come back here and tell me what you find."

"Yes, sir."

"I want you to take someone with you, sort of a backup. A soldier, preferably. Do you know someone like that?"

Major Felter thought a moment.

"Yes, sir, I know just the man. He's at Fort Knox."

"Tell me about him."

"Major, Armor," Felter said. "He had five combat jumps in World War II as a pathfinder. And was given the Medal. He wasn't wounded in World War II."

"MacMillan?" the President asked. "He was with you when you had your misfortune in Korea, wasn't he?"

"Yes, sir."

The military aide to the President of the United States returned to the room. Major Felter realized that there must be a hidden button somewhere that the President had pressed to summon him.

"Major Felter's volunteered to go, Charley," the President said. "Get the show on the road."

"Yes, Mr. President."

The President sat down at a table and took a sheet of notepaper and quickly scrawled something on it.

"This may come in handy, Major," he said, handing it to him. Major Felter read it.

"Yes, sir, I'm sure it will."

"Every soldier's ultimate ambition, Felter," the President chuckled. "Commander in Chief." He put out his hand. "Go with God, Major," he said.

[TWO]
Hq XIX U.S. Corps (Group)
Kwandae-Ri, North Korea
12 March 1954

The air force C-47 gooney bird which touched down daily at the XIX Corps (Group) airstrip had six passenger seats. They were up front in the cabin just behind the bulkhead separating the cabin from the cockpit. The rest of the cabin was given to cargo transportation, and sometimes the sick, on litters. Not the wounded; they passed their way through a Mobile Army Surgical Hospital (MASH) on their way to more complete medical facilities via a separate aerial evacuation system.

The gooney bird carried mail bags, and priority air freight, and milk. Fresh milk, from a herd of dairy cattle in Japan whose output had been contracted for by the U.S. Army Veterinary Corps, and was dispensed by the U.S. Army Quartermaster Corps at the direction of the U.S. Army Medical Corps to pregnant dependent women, dependent children under the age of five, and those soldiers whose gastrointestinal difficulties indicated a daily ingestion of fresh milk.

There were two means of aerial travel from XIX Corps (Group) in North Korea to Eighth U.S. Army Headquarters in Seoul, South Korea. One was by light army aircraft; Cessna L-19s, observation and liaison aircraft which would carry one passenger; and DeHavilland L-20s, "Beavers," of Teeny-Weeny Airlines, which carried six passengers. In addition, there were two North American "Navions" at XIX Corps (Group), but these were generally reserved for the corps commander, Lieutenant General E. Z. Black, or one of the other five general officers assigned to the corps.

The second means of aerial transportation was the milk-run gooney bird, which stopped at XIX Corps (Group) as its last stop on a round-robin flight from K16 (Kimpo) in Seoul to the three corps (I, IX, and X) and one corps (group) (XIX) on the front lines.

The C-47 gooney bird was faster and more comfortable than the light army aircraft and thus popular with senior officers. Officers at I, IX, and X Corps, however, which were closer to Seoul, sometimes found that if they tried to get to Seoul on the milk-run gooney bird, they got no further than XIX Corps (Group) where they were bumped (Rank Hath Its Priviliges) by senior XIX Corps (Group) officers and left to get to Seoul the best way they could. This was because XIX Corps (Group) was, in everything but name, an army, with an army-sized complement of senior officers. Consequently, the low man in a milk-run passenger seat was seldom any more junior than a lieutenant colonel.

There were three full bull colonels and three light birds in the seats of the milk-run gooney bird when it touched down at the XIX Corps (Group) airstrip. A young lieutenant, who looked as if he was torn between pleasure and worry about brass-hat wrath, climbed up the folding step to make his announcement.

"Gentlemen," he said. "I'm sorry. You've been bumped."

There was some grumbling, and after a moment, a full bull colonel in his late fifties asked incredulously, "Certainly, Lieutenant, not all of us?"

"Yes, sir," the lieutenant said. "All of you."

When they had collected their gear and climbed back out of the gooney bird, the three full colonels stood by the wing. They had each separately concluded that it was highly unlikely that there were six full colonels, each of them senior in grade to themselves.

A jeep, top down, drove up to where the gooney bird sat at the extreme end of the narrow dirt runway. The jeep held four passengers, all enlisted men, one more passenger than regulations prescribed. In addition, there was a motley collection of luggage, some GI barracks bags, some canvas Valv-Paks, and three civilian suitcases. While authorities generally looked the other way at Valv-Paks, regulations proscribed civilian suitcases in Korea. They were supposed to be entrusted to the Quartermaster Corps in Japan for safekeeping.

The enlisted men—a middle-aged master sergeant, a sorrowful-faced technical sergeant, a baby-faced staff sergeant, and a buck sergeant—got out of the jeep, and with the driver, formed a human chain to load the luggage onto the aircraft. Buried under the personal luggage were several GI equipment cases. When all the luggage was on board, the enlisted men climbed onto the airplane.

When they did not emerge after sufficient time for them to have stowed and tied down the luggage and equipment cases, one of the colonels, curiosity aroused, went to the aircraft door and looked inside. The enlisted men were seated in the seats the brass had just been ordered to vacate.

The colonel climbed aboard the C-47 and went to the middle-aged master sergeant.

"What the hell is going on here, Sergeant?" he demanded.

"Sergeant Greer is in charge, sir," the middle-aged master sergeant said, nodding his head at the baby-faced staff sergeant, who, having taken off his stiff-crowned "Ridgeway hat" (after Gen. Matthew Ridgeway, who had found the issue fatigue cap unmilitary and stiffened his with cardboard), looked even younger.

The colonel went to Staff Sergeant Greer, whom he now remembered having seen around the general's office.

"You're in charge, Sergeant?" the colonel demanded. "Is that correct?"

"For the moment, sir, yes, sir," Staff Sergeant Greer replied.

"Presumably you're on orders?"

"Yes, sir."

"May I see them, please?"

"No, sir."

"What do you mean, 'No, sir'?" the colonel demanded, furiously.

"We ready to go, Greer?" a voice called out. The colonel saw a full colonel, one he recognized, Colonel Carson Newburgh, officially the XIX Corps (Group) headquarters commandant, the man in charge of housekeeping. The colonel was also aware that Carson Newburgh was a good deal more influential than military housekeepers usually are. He was a reserve officer, a Texan, an Aggie, an oil millionaire. He had gone across Africa and Europe with E. Z. Black. E. Z. Black had gone into combat in North Africa with the "Hell's Circus" Armored Division as a major. When Eisenhower had stopped Hell's Circus on the banks of the Elbe, twenty-four hours—no more—from Berlin, E. Z. Black had been a major general, commanding. Carson Newburgh had been with him there, too, as a light bird. And he'd come back on active duty when Black had been given XIX Corps (Group) in Korea.

He was the only man in Korea who dared to call Ezakiah Zachariah Black "E. Z." to his face.

"You got the boss's bags," baby-faced Staff Sergeant Greer called back, "then we're ready."

The colonel made his way back down the cabin of the gooney bird. Colonel Carson Newburgh gave him a faint smile and a curious look. The colonel had hoped to avoid meeting General Black. He did not.

General Black got on the airplane, and then turned around. Leaning out the door, he pointed a finger at another master sergeant, this one enormous, black, and sad-faced. "Goddamnit," Lieutenant General E. Z. Black said, "I told you why you can't go."

"Yes, sir," the master sergeant said.

"Take a goddamned R&R," General Black said. "That's an order, Wesley, goddamnit, not a suggestion."

"Yes, sir," the master sergeant said.

"Greer, goddamnit, speaks French, and you don't," General Black concluded. "You'd be excess baggage."

"Yes, sir," the master sergeant said. "I understand I'd be excess baggage, sir."

"Oh, shit," General Black said. "Get on the goddamned airplane."

"Yes, sir," the master sergeant said, and with surprising grace for his bulk, climbed aboard.

General Black's eyes fell on the colonel. They were icy cold.

"Just debarking, sir," the colonel said.

General Black met the eyes of Colonel Newburgh.

"Wesley's been with me longer than you have," General Black said, defensively.

"Yes, sir," Colonel Newburgh said, smiling broadly.

"That will be twenty dollars, thank you kindly, Colonel Newburgh, sir," baby-faced Staff Sergeant Greer said.

"Goddamnit, Greer, did you actually bet I'd bring him along?" General Black asked. "Am I that goddamned predictable?"

"To those of us who know and love you so well, sir," Staff Sergeant Greer said, unctuously.

"Go to hell, Greer," General Black said. "Well, what are we waiting for? Let's get the show on the road."

The enormous black master sergeant was waiting impatiently at the door for the colonel to get off the aircraft. When he did, he effortlessly pulled the heavy door closed and then settled himself on the floor for the takeoff.

[THREE]
K16 Air Base
Seoul, South Korea
12 March 1954

The milk-run gooney bird from XIX Corps (Group) came in low over the Han River bridge, which had been dropped into the river in the early days of the police action and which the engineers had subsequently repaired so that it was partially usable, and touched down at K16. The pilot contacted ground control. Instead of being ordered to proceed down the taxiway to the terminal, he was ordered on a roundabout trip around the airfield, up and down taxiways and across runways, and finally ordered to stop before an unmarked hangar on the civilian side of the field.

"What the fuck are they doing?" he asked of his copilot. The copilot didn't reply. Instead, he pointed out the windshield to a man in a light gray flight suit who was making the standard arm signals (a finger pointing, and a hand making a cutting motion across his throat) ordering him to shut down the port (passenger door side) engine.

Unless the pilot's eyes were failing him, the man performing this buck-sergeant, ground-handler operation wore the star of a brigadier general and the wings of a master aviator.

The pilot cut the port engine.

Lt. General E. Z. Black and his party debarked the aircraft and disappeared through a small door in the huge hangar door. The buck general ground handler made a get-it-out-of-here signal with his hand.

"Air Force 879," ground control said in the pilot's earphones. "Take taxiway eleven to base operations."

Inside the hangar was a China Air Transport (CAT) DC-4. The pilots, standing by the wheels, were American. General Black was not surprised. CAT was an offspring of American involvement with Chiang Kai-shek's China, starting with the American Volunteer Group (the Flying Tigers) before the United States was officially involved in World War II.

The air force brigadier general came in from outside and walked to General Black and saluted. Black shook his hand.

"We about ready to get this show on the road?" General Black asked.

"No, sir," the air force brigadier said. He handed General Black a sheet of yellow teletype paper.

URGENT
HQ USAF WASH DC
TO: CG K16 AFB

DELAY DEPARTURE CAT SEOUL-HANOI CHARTER FOR TWO ADDITIONAL PASSENGERS ENROUTE VIA MIL AIR. AUTH: WILLIAMS, MAJ GEN USMC JCS.

"Jesus H. Christ!" General Black exploded. "I should have known goddamned well those bastards would send somebody from the Pentagon, or the goddamned State Department, to snoop."

"I don't have anything else, General," the air force brigadier said. "No names. Not even an ETA." (Estimated Time of Arrival.)

"What the hell," Black said. "I don't have anything better to do anyway than sit around a goddamned hangar with my finger up my ass."

"Would the general like a little belt?" the brigadier asked.

"The general would dearly love a little belt," Black replied. "But I don't think this is the time or place."

The enormous black master sergeant whom Black had taken along at the last minute came up.

"General," he reported, "I've got your civvies unpacked. They're kind of messed up."

"Isn't everything?" General Black replied. "Where are they, Wes?"

"On the airplane," the sergeant replied.

"Everybody else is here?" Black asked the air force brigadier.

"Yes, sir," he replied. "Here and in civvies." He pulled the full-length zipper of his flight suit down, revealing a shirt and tie and brown tweed sports coat.

"I will change clothes," General Black announced. "And if the goddamned snoops haven't shown up by the time I'm finished, then I *will* have a little belt."

General Black boarded the DC-4 and walked up the aisle to the front, where his orderly had unpacked a footlocker rushed priority air freight from the United States. Two suits, both of them mussed and creased from long storage, and an equally mussed trio of shirts had been laid across one of the seats.

He picked the least mussed of the suits, and changed out of his uniform. He understood the necessity of wearing civilian clothing—the shit would really hit the fan if the press found out the Americans were thinking of saving the French's ass in Indo-China—but he didn't like it. Particularly since his civvies were mussed up.

When he was finished, he stepped into the aisle.

"Gentlemen," he said, "may I have your attention, please?"

There were five army officers, four generals and the colonel commanding the 187th Regimental Combat Team; four air force generals, two admirals, and a dozen others, officers or enlisted technicians.

The middle-aged master sergeant in General Black's party was a cryptographer; the technical sergeant was a cartographer familiar with French military maps; the buck sergeant was a court stenographer Black had brought along to take precise notes; the baby-faced staff sergeant fit no precise military description. Black had often told Colonel Carson Newburgh that S/Sgt Greer was the official court jester. But he was more than that. He had been a buck sergeant with the 223rd Infantry Regiment when he had been sent to XIX Corps to function as a court reporter in a personnel hassle. Carson Newburgh had kept him on for his clerical skills, and somehow he had become part of the inner circle, gradually assuming greater and greater responsibilities and discharging them without fault. He had earned the jealous ire of his enlisted seniors. There had been a choice of getting rid of him, or keeping him and giving him the stripes commensurate with his responsibility, and despite his youth and length of service. They had kept him, and made him a staff sergeant, and Black had never regretted the decision.

A wall of faces filled the aisle. General Black's eye fell on S/Sgt Greer.

"Sergeant Greer," he said, "is there any reason why you're still wearing your uniform?"

"Sir," Greer replied immediately, "I thought that I would wait until we got where we're going, and *then* I'd muss my civvies up."

General Black was not the only senior officer in a storage-mussed uniform, and the remark was met first with a muted chuckle, and then a couple of snorts, and finally outright laughter.

"Gentlemen," General Black said. "You have just met Sergeant Greer. Unless there are objections, he'll handle all enlisted arrangements and problems. As you may have sensed, Greer is a past master at taking care of Number One. Colonel Newburgh will handle the officers. I don't think we'll have any problems. The French can be quite charming when they want something. I really hate to bring this up, but the situation is delicate, and I think I have to. This whole affair is very secret for what should be obvious reasons. I have to tell you, and this is an order, that you are not to tell anyone, wives, superiors, anyone, where we are, have been, or what we did while we were there. This is just as important as a situation where an air force major general, in London, found himself a lieutenant colonel the next morning after he talked too much.

"Item Two: No one, myself included, is authorized to promise, or even suggest, anything to the French. We're there to assess the situation and that's all.

"Item Three: We are about to be joined by two VIPs. That's why we're sitting here. I don't know who they are, or what they want. When I find out, I'll tell you."

"General?" the air force brigadier who had met the gooney bird interrupted.

"Go," General Black said.

"A jet bomber that nobody expected is about to land from Honolulu. They asked that I be informed. It's probably our VIPs."

"Thank you."

Ten minutes later, the hangar doors began to creak open. A tug hitched itself to the nosewheel of the DC-4 and it was pulled outside. A jeep, painted in a black-and-white checker-board pattern and with a huge checkerboard flag flying from its rear came across the field. Two men in flight suits got out of it, each carrying a canvas Valv-Pak. General Black saw them out the window.

"I'll be goddamned!" he said.

The two newcomers got aboard. The pilot of the DC-4 immediately started his engines, and the transport lumbered down the taxiway. Then, after a brief pause to test the engines, the plane turned onto the runway, gathered speed, and took off.

When they had reached altitude, the newcomers made their way forward, to where General Black was seated alone. Colonel Newburgh and the air force brigadier came with them.

Both men were army officers, both majors, one a muscular, ruggedly handsome Scot, the second a slight, bespectacled Jew.

"Well, Felter," General Black said, "I see they put you back together again."

"Yes, sir," the little Jew said. "Nearly as good as new. You know how grateful I am."

"And where the hell did you find that?" General Black said, pointing to the Scot. "I thought I was rid of him, once and for all."

"Colonel Bellmon said he didn't care what I did, or where I went, General," the Scot said, "just so long as I stayed out of trouble. So here I am."

"And what are you going to do here?" General Black asked, innocently.

"We're going to very quietly go have a look at Dien Bien Phu," Major Felter said.

"That's not on the program," the air force brigadier said flatly, confirming what Black had suspected, that the brigadier was his counterpart even though he was outranked by the air force major general aboard.

"Yes, sir," Major Felter said. "I know."

"You can't visit Dien Bien Phu without General Black's permission," the air force brigadier said. "And I would strongly suggest he not give it."

Felter looked at Black and the air force brigadier. Then he reached into his pocket and handed Black a squarish white envelope. Black read it, and nodded, and then handed it to the air force brigadier general. It was a handwritten note on engraved stationery.

THE WHITE HOUSE
WASHINGTON

10 March 54

Major Felter is traveling at my request. He is to be given whatever assistance he requires.

DDE

"And does Mac have friends in very high places, too, Felter?" General Black inquired.

"Well, sir," Major Felter said, "he knows you and me."

"Goddamnit, Mac," General Black said. "I know I shouldn't be, but I'm glad to see you." He grabbed MacMillan's hand in both of his own.

[ONE]
Dien Bien Phu, French Indo-China
17 March 1954

Including the smell, which was so foul he was really afraid that he might throw up, there was a hell of a lot about this escapade that was very familiar to Major Rudolph G. "Mac" MacMillan.

The airplane was American, a good old faithful Douglas C-47 gooney bird. The frogs had been using it to evacuate their wounded. That's where the stink came from, from blood and piss and rotting flesh and shit. The first thing a body did when it was dead was crap its pants, when the sphincter muscles relaxed. The frogs were evacuating only their badly wounded.

The chutes, main and reserve, were American, but Mac MacMillan wasn't at all sure they could be trusted. He suspected that the frogs who had packed them had not paid as much attention to the fine points of packing or to the condition of the chutes themselves as the riggers in an American airborne outfit would have. The uniforms the frogs were wearing were American, too: GI fatigues and web equipment, weapons, everything but the boots. The boots were native frog boots.

The kid didn't even have boots. He wasn't even a parachutist, so obviously he didn't have jump boots. He was going to jump in regular Class "A" uniform oxfords, the kind the army called "low quarters." The kid was apparently a gutsy little bastard, but he was scared, and Mac knew it. Mac had had a lot of experience over the years with scared people.

The kid was some kind of superclerk for General Black, and when Black had learned that they were going to Dien Bien Phu, he had sent the kid along.

"If you think you could learn something, Greer," was the way Black had put it. "For all I care, you can go along."

For a young sergeant working for Lieutenant General E. Z. Black, that was the same thing as a direct order. So the kid had come along on this little excursion thinking that he was going to be flown in and out. When the frogs said they would have to jump in, he'd said OK, he'd jump. He said he'd always wanted to try it anyhow. That was so much bullshit. The kid was scared shitless. But there was nothing anybody could do about that. Anything that anybody said to him would only make it worse. What was going to happen would happen, and he couldn't do a damn thing for him.

Mac MacMillan's boots were standard American jump boots, not GI but Corcoran's. It was accepted as an article of faith among parachutists that Corcoran jump boots not only took a higher polish than GI jump boots, but that you stood much less chance of breaking your ankles when you landed. MacMillan had started wearing Corcoran's when there had been no GI jump boots, when somebody in the Quartermaster Corps had done something right for once and had asked the Massachusetts shoe manufacturer to come up with a pair of boots that would be suitable for crazy people who were planning to jump out of airplanes.

The first order had been issued to the members of the battalion of the 82nd Infantry Division that had been designated as a Test Battalion (Parachute). Mac MacMillan, recent All-Philippines boxing champion, had joined up because they were going to pay him another fifty bucks a month to jump out of airplanes. He had just gotten married and needed the money.

He hadn't had those boots a month when some thieving sonofabitch slit his duffel bag at Benning and stole them. When he went to the supply room and looked at the non-Corcoran jump boots they wanted to issue him, he remembered hearing that the "good" boots were being sold in the PX. Every pair of jump boots he had ever owned since then he had bought either at the PX or direct from Corcoran in Massachusetts.

He thought that if anybody had told him a month ago when he bought the pair he was wearing now that he would be jumping in them into some frog outpost in some asshole corner of nowhere, with Sandy Felter, some kid sergeant making his first jump, and a dozen frogs, he would have told him he was out of his fucking gourd.

"Something on your mind, Mac?" Felter asked him, sticking his head so close because of the noise that MacMillan could smell his toothpaste.

"Geronimo! You little bastard," MacMillan said.

"Geronimo!" was what John Wayne had shouted as he went out the door in a war movie about paratroops. Everybody knew about that. MacMillan, who had been a parachutist since 1940, and on whose wings there was barely room for the five stars he had earned, one a time, on five jumps into combat, had never heard anybody else yell "Geronimo!"

Felter smiled.

"You didn't tell me this is what you had in mind," MacMillan said, gesturing around the airplane. "You said 'inspection trip,' shitface."

"You love it," Felter said.

"You may love it, you little prick," MacMillan said. "I've been here before."

"That's why I brought you along," Felter said.

"I'm going to get you for this, Sandy," MacMillan said.

Major Sandy Felter was one of the few people for whom Major MacMillan felt both affection and admiration. Felter had been responsible for one of MacMillan's very few philosophical observations: *You can't tell what a warrior looks like.*

Felter was even a West Pointer, though he rarely wore his ring. He was Class of '46, but he hadn't been there when the rest of the Class of '46 had thrown their hats into the air on graduation day. He'd resigned from the Corps of Cadets to take a direct commission as a linguist. As a POW interrogation officer with Major General "Porky" Waterford's "Hell's Circus" Armored Division, he had learned the location of a group of American officer prisoners-of-war being moved on foot away from the advancing Russians.

Task Force Parker (Colonel Philip Sheridan Parker III) had been formed to go get them, and Felter had gone with them. By the time his classmates were admiring themselves in their brand-new second lieutenant suits, Felter had been a first lieutenant with a Bronze Star for the Task Force Parker operation, and the admiration of Porky Waterford, whose son-in-law, Lt. Col. Bob Bellmon, had been one of the rescued American officers.

MacMillan had been in the stalag with Bellmon, as a technical sergeant, the senior NCO of the American enlisted men imprisoned with the officers. That had been before he had learned that his behavior in Operation Market-Basket, where he had been captured, had earned him both a battlefield promotion to second lieutenant and the Medal.

Just after the Germans marched the officers off to the west, leaving the enlisted men to fend as well as they could, MacMillan had led an escape in an odyssey across Poland that had earned him the Distinguished Service Cross to go with the Medal. He'd heard about Felter when he and Bellmon had got together in the States.

And he'd heard about Felter's activities with the U.S. Army Advisory Group to Greece from another old buddy, Lt. Col. Red Hanrahan, who had been with Mac at Benning, jumping out of airplanes before there had been an 82nd Airborne Division. Felter had been sent to Greece as a Russian language linguist, and had wound up commanding a relief column that had stopped a major Albanian border-crossing operation. Hanrahan had refused to confirm the rumor that it had been necessary for Felter to blow away the American officer in charge, who'd turned yellow and wanted to run. So far as MacMillan was concerned, if the story wasn't true, Hanrahan would have said so.

And MacMillan had personal experience with the little Jew. In Korea, MacMillan had run an irregular outfit, Task Force Able, and Felter had dropped in one day with orders from above that Task Force Able was now in the spy business, and would take its orders from Felter. Felter wasn't expected to do anything more than sit behind a desk and run the show. But he was a warrior, and he'd spent as much time behind North Korean lines as any of the agents, and he'd damned near got himself blown away when one operation went sour.

He'd taken a nasty wound in the knee, that damned near cost him his leg, and had shown a lot of guts in dragging himself off the beach and back into the water, willing to drown rather than be captured; he knew too much to be captured.

Sandy Felter was MacMillan's kind of man. He was a warrior.

The jumpmaster came down the aisle and hesitantly gestured to MacMillan.

"Talk to him, prick," MacMillan said. "You speak frog."

Felter spoke to the jumpmaster in French, then switched to German. The eyes of the jumpmaster half smiled.

"He wants to know if you have jumped before," Felter said, smiling.

"Oh, Jesus, that's all I need, a kraut jumpmaster in the frog airborne!"

"Somebody's going to understand English, Mac, for God's sake!" Felter said, torn between amusement and genuine concern.

"Find somebody who does, and tell him I want to go home," MacMillan said. Then he looked up and met the jumpmaster's eyes and said, in not bad German: *"Ja, ich war ein Fallschirmjäger im zweiten Weltkrieg."*

The jumpmaster didn't seem surprised that MacMillan had been a paratrooper in War II. *"Und der Bub?"* he asked.

MacMillan replied that *"der Bub,"* the boy, was a virgin, but that he would take care of him.

The jumpmaster nodded.

"Ungefähr fünf Minuten," he announced. He wore the stripes of a company sergeant major and the unit insignia of the Third Parachute Regiment of the French Foreign Legion.

The jumpmaster gave the commands in French, but they were still all very familiar to MacMillan.

"Stand up," the jumpmaster said. And the parachutists—the legionnaires and Felter, MacMillan, and Greer—got up out of their aluminum and nylon sheeting benches and stood up, fastening the chin harnesses of their helmets, checking the position of their scrotums relative to the straps that ran between their legs, and making whatever adjustments were necessary.

"Check your equipment," the jumpmaster ordered. The buddy system. Major Rudolph G. MacMillan, Armor, USA, checked the harness and other equipment of Staff Sergeant Greer, trying not to make a big deal of it, and then checked Felter. Finally, Felter checked MacMillan.

"Hook up!" They snapped the hooks of their static lines around the stainless steel cable running along the roof of the cabin, and tugged on it to make sure it was secure and that the spring-lock opening had closed as it was supposed to.

"Stand in the door!"

The jumpmaster put Felter and MacMillan second and third on line, and Greer after them. MacMillan changed that. He unhooked his static line and put it behind the kid's, and then got in the line behind Felter and Greer. It would be better to have the kid in the middle.

First man in the stick was a Foreign Legion corporal. He was a Frenchman, a foreigner in his own army (no Frenchman can serve in the Foreign Legion) because he had believed that National Socialism was the wave of the future and had gone off with ten thousand other Frenchmen into the Charlemagne Legion of the Waffen SS. The Charlemagne Legion fought with distinction in Russia, and died in the battle of Berlin, but Unterfeldwebel François Ferrer had been one of the lucky ones. He hadn't died, and he had made his way west and gone into French captivity, but as a German with a Waffen SS paybook. Being in the SS was bad, but not as bad as being a member of the Charlemagne Legion. Once the war was over, there was a rebirth of fervent patriotism in France.

One day they had taken him from the POW enclosure and carried him to Marseilles, and he had thought he had been found out and would be tried as a traitor. He had been found out, but what they did was drop him off without a word before the recruiting office of the Foreign Legion.

He was a corporal again. The Legion carried him on their rolls as Franz Ferrer, and in 1957, when he'd done his twelve year hitch, he would be eligible for French citizenship. The Legion didn't care where you came from. If you gave the Legion twelve years, and lived through it, and wanted to try Civvie Street, they would see to it that you got the proper papers.

The legionnaire did not feel sorry for himself. He had enlisted in the Charlemagne Legion of the Waffen SS to fight communists, and that's what he was doing now.

The gooney bird's pilot throttled the engines back and lowered the flaps. They were six or seven hundred feet over thickly forested mountains, approaching a valley.

There came a sound, a dull, metallic pinging, like a full garbage can being kicked. The gooney bird lifted its left wing and started to bank to the right. A faint trail of smoke began to flow off the left wing. It grew larger, darker.

"Oh, *shit!*" Major Mac MacMillan said.

The dense cloud of dark smoke began to glow, then burst into orange. There were flames now, furious flames.

MacMillan let go of the stainless steel static line cable and with both hands pushed Corporal Franz Ferrer out of the door. He didn't have to push Felter. Felter had figured out what was happening. He went out the door a split second after the legionnaire.

MacMillan grabbed Staff Sergeant Greer's shoulders and shoved him, with a mighty heave, through the door.

MacMillan felt himself falling backward into the gooney bird as the door side of the airplane went high. He managed to get one hand on the leading edge of the door; otherwise he would have fallen across the cabin. The C-47 was in a steep diving bank to the right. MacMillan pulled himself closer to the door; got both hands on it; and finally, using all his strength, pulled himself through it.

His static line caught momentarily on the doorsill, then slid to the rear. MacMillan thought he would slam into the tail assembly. But it passed a foot from his face. A moment later, he felt the barely perceptible tug as the static line pulled first the cover off and then the pilot chute from his main chute. Soon he felt the chute deploying, sensed that it was out of the bag, that it was opening. At the moment when his experience taught him to expect the opening shock, he felt it.

He had spun around and around, and when the canopy filled and the risers grew taut, he was facing in the direction where he could see the C-47. In a gentle, graceful curve, the left engine nacelle an orange ball of fire, it flew into the forest canopy, disappeared for a moment, and then exploded. No one else got out.

MacMillan twisted his head to see what had happened to Felter and the kid and the frog corporal. There was only one parachute canopy still in the air. That was Felter. He had gone out before the kid, but soaking wet the little bastard didn't weigh 130 pounds. He would take a little longer getting down.

MacMillan saw the frog corporal's canopy and the kid's hanging from treetops. Then he saw Felter's canopy lose its fullness. Felter was down in the trees, too.

MacMillan looked between his feet, put them together, and bent his knees to protect his balls. In that instant he hit the first upper branches. He closed his eyes and put his arm over them as protection against a branch getting him in the eyes.

And then, amid the sounds of breaking branches, recoiling from painful slaps and punches at his head and legs and body, he was down. He opened his eyes. He was thirty feet up in a tree, maybe forty.

It was very, very quiet.

He got himself swinging, hoping the chute wouldn't rip free and he wouldn't suddenly find himself dropping to the ground, and in time was able to grab a branch he thought would hold his weight. He climbed on it, hit the quick release on his harness, and stood there for a moment, hanging on to the tree trunk with both arms.

He heard movement, fifty yards away, a hundred, who knows. The thing to do was get out of the goddamned tree.

He climbed to within twenty feet of the ground, beneath which there were no branches. He hung from the lowest branch and dropped. The landing was surprisingly soft; the ground was covered with rotting vegetation. It smelled like a septic tank.

He sat a moment and considered his position. This wasn't his goddamned war. Personally, he wasn't all that fond of the French, and he didn't give a shit if they owned Indo-China or not. He was a neutral. The Viet Minh, Sandy had told him, were run by a guy named Ho Chi Minh. All during War II, the United States had had an OSS detachment with Ho Chi Minh. Ho Chi Minh might hate the frogs, but he might like Americans.

If Ho Chi Minh's people saw him in this frog jump suit, they would naturally decide that he was a frog. MacMillan unzippered the jump suit and climbed out of it. Beneath it, he wore a Class "A" (less tunic) summer uniform. Including decorations. Sandy Felter had told him to wear his decorations. Frogs were big on medals, and Mac had the big medal, the Medal of Honor. The reason they were all in goddamned Class "A" tropicals was that they were sort of sneaking into Dien Bien Phu.

If it had come to the attention of some of the big frog brass that they were going to take a look at Dien Bien Phu for themselves, instead of relying on the word of *le Général* that everything was peachy keen, he more than likely would have tried to stop them. So they had had breakfast in the Cercle Sportif in their Class "A" tropical worsteds, so the frogs could count noses, and then they had sneaked off to the airport, where Felter, somehow, had it fixed for them to get on the gooney bird bound for Dien Bien Phu.

He started walking in the direction of the noise he thought he had heard. He kept sinking into the rotting vegetation and cursed, thinking he had ruined what were damned near new jump boots.

He heard voices after a while, and they damned sure weren't American or French. Sort of sing-songy. He moved quietly, with a skill learned stalking deer and an occasional bear in the woods around Mauch Chuck, Pennsylvania, and honed as a pathfinder in North Africa and Sicily and France and Germany. Then he dropped to his hands and knees and scurried across the ground like an insect. Finally, he dropped flat on his belly and crawled. He thought he was fucking up a nearly new set of TWs, too.

There were three Chinks, or whatever they were, dressed in black pajamas, and they had the frog, the one he'd pushed out the door. The gooks were armed with Chink submachine guns and one GI carbine, and knives. They had the frog tied to a tree, spread-eagled, and what they were doing was working on him with the knives.

They had slit his cheeks and his chest, and he was covered with blood. The reason he wasn't screaming was because they had his mouth stuffed full of the rotting shit from the jungle floor.

Then they pulled his pants off. He tried to scream, and almost made it, when he realized what the gooks were going to do now.

MacMillan had thought the stories they had been told in Hanoi about the Viet Minh cutting people's cocks off and stuffing them in their mouths was so much bullshit.

MacMillan reached in the back pocket of his trousers and took out a Colt .32 ACP pistol. Very carefully, he took the clip out and checked it, and then he silently replaced it and very carefully worked the action, chambering a cartridge.

Shit, a lousy .32 automatic against three guys with submachine guns and a carbine!

He inched himself around the trunk of a large tree. Two of the Viet Minh guys were working on the frog, the dirty bastards really enjoying themselves, and the third was looking vaguely in MacMillan's direction. Fifteen yards away. Maybe even less. But the vegetation was so thick!

MacMillan rested his left arm against the tree trunk, held the pistol in both hands, and aimed right at the gook's nose. It hardly made any noise going off, the sound swallowed by the dense, moist vegetation. The gook, for a moment, seemed surprised. Then blood gushed out of his right eye, and he sank to the ground. MacMillan turned the pistol on the other two, got off a hasty shot, and then another, and then he rolled back, so the tree trunk would give him protection.

There came expected bursts of fire from the Chink submachine gun. Two bursts. Two guns? Or one burst from two guns?

Then something else. Two shots, evenly spaced. *Boom! Boom!*

Loud shots. Certainly not a pistol. Nor a rifle. It sounded more like a shotgun. What the hell were the Chinks, or whatever they were, armed with? All he'd seen were the Chink submachine guns. Were there more gooks than he'd seen? A couple of perimeter guards, maybe?

"It's OK, Major," the kid called out. "They're all down."

MacMillan very cautiously edged around the tree. The kid was untying the frog.

MacMillan stood up, and walked over and looked at the dead, holding the little .32 automatic out in front of him. He felt a little foolish when he got close enough for a good look. One of the Chinks had half of his head blown off, and the other one's entire midsection was a mass of bloody pulp.

It was a shotgun; no other weapon would have made a wound like that. He looked at the kid. He had the frog loose now, and was picking something up from the ground. A sawed-off shotgun.

The frog, blood streaming all over him, bent over and picked up one of the submachine guns. He walked to the body of one of the Viet Minh and emptied the magazine into his crotch.

MacMillan walked over to the kid and took the sawed-off shotgun from him. It was really a sawed-off people killer, not just what was left after somebody took a hacksaw to a 12-gauge Winchester Model 12. Even the magazine tube and the mechanism to work the action had been cut down. Instead of five in the magazine and one in the chamber, this wouldn't hold more than two shells in the magazine. The stock behind the pistol grip had been cut off. What was left wasn't a hell of a lot bigger than a .45.

"Very nice," MacMillan said.

"I was an infantryman before I was a dog robber," the kid said.

"What the hell did you shoot the first one with?" the kid asked. MacMillan held out the little .32 Colt.

"Don't knock it, it worked," he said. And then he thought of something else and grew angry. "Especially when you're supposed to be unarmed."

"Yeah," the kid said.

"Where did you have that?" MacMillan asked. "I didn't see it."

The kid didn't answer. There was a sound in the forest. The kid dropped to his knees, holding the sawed-off people killer in front of him. MacMillan, holding the .32 out, realized that the kid had only one shell left.

"Hold your fire," Felter called out, from somewhere in the thick vegetation. "It's me."

He came into sight a moment later, tucking a .45 automatic into his belt at the small of his back under his tropical worsted tunic.

"You miserable little prick!" MacMillan said, as Felter walked into the small natural clearing. "God*damn* you!"

Felter ignored him and knelt before the Frenchman, who was now sitting down, resting his back against a tree.

"He's going to bleed some more," he said. "What happened to him?"

"The Chinks were about to feed him his own cock," MacMillan said.

"Viet Minh, Mac," Felter corrected him. "Are you all right, Sergeant?"

"Yes, sir," Staff Sergeant Greer said.

"He saved our ass with his shotgun," MacMillan said. "You owe us one big fucking apology, Felter."

"Because of the gun, you mean?" Felter asked, smiling.

"You're goddamned right," MacMillan said. " 'No guns, Mac. Not even that little Colt of yours. We're neutral observers.' "

"I didn't think for a minute that you'd pay a bit of attention to me," Felter said. "That was for the record."

"Bullshit!" MacMillan said.

"Off the record, Sergeant," Felter said, "I'm glad you misunderstood my instructions."

"He must have had that thing stuck inside his pants," MacMillan said. "Take a look at it."

Staff Sergeant Greer handed over the sawed-off shotgun.

"That's very nice," Felter said. *"Very* nice. Where'd you get it?"

"I made it," Greer said.

"When we get out of this," Felter said, "I'd like you to make one for me."

"Are we going to get out of this?" Sergeant Greer asked.

"At this point, Sergeant," Felter said, "we place ourselves in the capable hands of Major MacMillan. He's actually quite good at dealing with situations like ours."

"Fuck you, Sandy," MacMillan said. He walked over and had a look at the frog, to see if he was up to doing what they would have to do to keep alive.

[TWO]
Hanoi, French Indo-China
17 March 1954

Les cocktails were served by *le Général Commandant des Forces Françaises en Indochine* and his staff, to Lieutenant General E. Z. Black, USA, and his staff in the Cercle Sportif's upstairs lounge. The cocktails were served by soldiers, enormous, jet-black Senegalese in French service, who wore white jackets, billowing trousers, and red hats, soft, but something on the order of a fez. Following cocktails, *le dîner* would be served in the main dining room.

The French officers were in full uniform, despite the civilian clothing the Americans wore in the now obviously absurd notion that by so doing they might conceal their presence in Hanoi.

General Black was not in a good mood. What the goddamned French actually were having the gall to ask for was troops, and airplanes, and ships, but mostly troops, infantry troops, to fight their goddamned colonial war under French officers. They had the experience in dealing with communist insurgents, they said, and the Americans didn't, and Indo-China *was* part of France.

Black had slipped a note to Newburgh at the conference table:

"Take a list of names, so we'll know where we can find experienced officers the next time we need to lose a war."

He had, of course, behaved himself during the conference. He had been the soul of military charm and tact, and tried to explain the difficulty that General Eisenhower, *President* Eisenhower, would have in getting Congress to agree to send American troops to Indo-China at all, much less to serve under French officers.

He had made it through lunch without incident, and through the afternoon session, but here, with a couple of drinks in him, Colonel Newburgh was just a little worried about Black. He had encountered him at the urinals.

"I have just figured out what all those medals the frogs are wearing are," Black had said to him. "The brass one with the naked lady on the horse is for the Phony War. The one with the massed flags is for losing the battle of the Maginot Line, and the one with the triple-barred cross is for shelling the Americans when we came ashore at Casablanca . . ."

"Take it easy, E. Z.," Newburgh said, sternly. "It'll be over soon."

"You know when I was happiest, Carson?" Black said, zipping his fly. "When I was a full bull colonel, hoping for a buck general's star to retire on in the by and by, and had nothing to worry about but commanding Combat Command A. Just a soldier, none of this smiling bullshit."

"I suppose George Washington felt the same way about the French and Indian Wars when he was asking Congress for money and troops."

"French and Indian Wars? Goddamn right. *He* knew who the enemy was."

"Prepare to smile," Newburgh said, chuckling. "Smile!"

"I'll go charm the sonsofbitches, Colonel," Black said. "A good soldier goes where he is told to go, and does what he is told to do, and he smiles." He leered insanely at Colonel Newburgh. "Smile satisfactory, Colonel?"

"Try to hide the fangs a little more," Newburgh said.

It was very difficult.

A major general waited outside in the lounge to tell General Black that while he was sure *le Général* didn't remember him, he remembered *le Général* from the glorious days when *le Général* had Combat Command A of Hell's Circus, and had "assisted" *le Général* LeClerc's 2nd (French) Armored Division in their preparations to liberate Paris.

It was Lieutenant General E. Z. Black's professional opinion that (a) there had been no military requirement whatever to take Paris in the first place; it could have been easily bypassed, and Von Choltitz, the German commandant, had been perfectly willing to declare it an open city if they had bypassed it; and (b) that if it was in the best interests of the United States to take the goddamned place, they should have permitted Hell's Circus to take it. Combat Command "A" of Hell's Circus (which he just coincidentally happened to command) had been poised on the outskirts of Paris, ready to roll around or through (whichever was ordered) when the radio had come from SHAEF ordering him to stand in place and let LeClerc pass through him.

General E. Z. Black's smile was rather strained when a French colonel came to the French major general and spoke into his ear in what he thought was a whisper.

The C-47 on which the two American officers and the American sergeant had been trying to get into Dien Bien Phu had been shot down. There were no survivors.

The French major general was obviously torn between telling General Black what he had just heard, or passing this sad responsibility to *le Général Commandant.*

"General," General Black said, in his fluent French, "please be so good as to offer my apologies to *le Général Commandant.* The men lost to your enemy were all personal friends of mine, and I must see about informing their families of this tragedy."

Lieutenant General E. Z. Black and Colonel Carson Newburgh left the Cercle Sportif in the Rolls-Royce the French had assigned for his use. They went to the American Consulate on the Rue General Marneaux, got the cryptographer, and sent the URGENT radio to the Joint Chiefs of Staff reporting that Majors Sanford T. Felter and Rudolph G. MacMillan and S/ Sgt Edward C. Greer had been aboard a French C-47, trying to get to Dien Bien Phu, had been shot down, and were presumed dead.

Then General Black and Colonel Newburgh went to the villa they had been assigned by *le Général Commandant*, and they drank all of one, and part of a second, quart bottle of Haig & Haig scotch whiskey.

[THREE]
Dien Bien Phu
French Indo-China
21 March 1954

"What we're betting on," MacMillan said, "is that they're soldiers."

"Blooded troops, is what you mean," Felter said.

It was six in the morning and they were in the jungle, overlooking one of the outposts of the French garrison at Dien Bien Phu. They were in what in World War I would have been called "no-man's-land." The French emplacements were two hundred yards ahead of them, across a relatively open area strung with barbed wire, and probably mined, and torn up by literally a hundred thousand artillery and mortar shells. The Viet Minh emplacements were behind them, over the crest of a line of hills, out of sight and safe from direct, line-of-sight rifle and machine-gun fire from the French.

They had spent the last four nights crawling through the Viet Minh lines on their bellies, literally inches at a time. They had made it—although privately none of them thought they would—but it hadn't solved their problem. They were within two hundred yards of French protection, but it might as well have been two hundred miles.

So far as the French were concerned, anybody out there in the jungle was Viet Minh. The moment the French saw movement out there, they would bring the area under fire. From the shot-down trees, and the countless craters in the ground, a generous expenditure of ammunition to repel a ground attack was the standard French tactic.

The problem, then, was to let the French know that they were out there, and friendly, without having the French blow them away.

MacMillan's solution to the problem was unusual, but neither Felter nor Greer could think of a better idea.

They would start a fire, using dried leaves, twigs, and limbs from the shot-down trees. The French would naturally bring this under fire. So the fire would have to be started slowly, in order for them to get away before the firing started. The fire would be large. It would continue to attract French attention. After they had brought the fire site under enough small arms and mortar fire to have blown away anybody close to it, they would crawl back to it, stand up, put their hands over their heads, wave their arms, and walk slowly toward the French lines.

They would either be permitted to enter the French lines, or they would be blown away.

If they stayed where they were, they would be blown away by the Viet Minh, probably after the Viet Minh had cut their cheeks open and fed them their cocks.

"Fuck, it," S/Sgt Greer said, "let's do it. Light the sonofabitch."

" 'Light the sonofabitch, please, sir,' Sergeant," Major MacMillan said.

"With all respect," Greer replied, as he started to crawl away, "fuck you, Major."

It went almost exactly as planned. The fire was lit; the fire site was brought under fire by the French; the mortar fire was lifted; they crawled back to the fire site; then gathered their courage and stood up.

They held their arms over their heads and walked, waving their arms toward the French positions. The French did not open fire on them. They had walked perhaps fifty yards when the French opened up.

They dove to the ground, and spent ninety seconds, which under some circumstances can be a very long time, trying to make themselves as thin and flat as possible. And then they realized that the machine-gun and rifle fire was ten feet in the air, and that the mortars were arcing down to the ground and exploding between them and the Viet Minh positions. The frogs' fire was covering them!

They got up and ran toward the French emplacements, and made it unhurt, except for Greer, who caught a piece of mortar shrapnel on his right leg, outside, about ten inches from his crotch.

[FOUR]

The Dien Bien Phu hospital was, of course, underground. Despite the fact that everybody knew it was impossible, the Viet Minh had manhandled American 105 mm howitzers, captured in the early days of the Korean War, up into positions overlooking the French positions, and kept them under a steady barrage of fire. Sometimes one shell every ten minutes, sometimes fifty shells in one minute.

The French were living underground, and their hospital was underground.

The piece of shrapnel which had caught Ed Greer had sliced his skin open like a jagged knife, but had not stayed in his body. The wound had been sutured shut, and he had been given, by injection and orally, medicine to resist infection and pain. The doctor who had treated him, after professing astonishment and joy that the American spoke French, told him that the greatest risk of infection was not from the shrapnel wound, but from the leech and other insect bites, and that "after you're out of here, take a lot of baths with antibacteriological soap."

He was put to bed for the night in a private room, a small cubicle equipped with a U.S. Army hospital bed, an American Coleman gasoline lantern, two canteens of water and a glass, and copies of months-old French and Indo-Chinese newspapers.

Felter and MacMillan came to see him. MacMillan explained the situation precisely, if not with overwhelming tact.

"We're going to party with the officers," he said. "That leaves you out. You can party with the troops, if you like, but if you're smart, you'll stay where you are in the clean bed. The troops here sleep on the ground. They're going to try to get us out of here in the morning, or the next day."

"I'll stay here," Greer said.

"Got you some clothes," Felter said. He hung a set of Foreign Legion jungle pattern camouflage fatigues on a nail driven into one of the white-painted tree trunks which supported the hospital bunker roof.

"You want something to drink?" MacMillan asked.

"Please," Greer said.

"I'll see what I can do."

Ten minutes later, the legionnaire the Viet Minh had tied to the tree came into his room accompanied by two other very drunk legionnaires. Greer was sure that one of them was an American, although he denied it and said he was a Belgian. He was either American, or he'd lived in the States long enough to acquire a perfect command of Chicago English. He was a sergeant, and he had been brought along to translate by the company sergeant major, who didn't know that Greer spoke French.

"Franz told us what you did for him," the "Belgian" legionnaire said. "And the sergeant major says that now that you nearly got yourself killed in this sewer, and jumped into here, you are now one of us."

They sat him up in bed, put the camouflage fatigue jacket on him, pinned parachutist's wings on it, the company sergeant major kissed him on both cheeks, they both saluted him, helped him out of the jacket, handed him two unlabeled bottles of red wine, and left, staggering.

Greer drank about half a bottle of wine, from the neck, while reading *Paris Match* and *Le Figaro* by the hissing light of the Coleman lantern. Then he turned it off and went to sleep, naked under the damp sheet.

He woke up when he sensed the nurse's flashlight probing the room, but didn't move until he heard the hiss of the Coleman as she lit it. Then he turned his head and looked up at her.

A blond, her hair was parted in the middle and drawn tight against her skull. She wore the legionnaire's jungle fatigues. Thirty, Greer judged. Maybe not that old. A woman would turn old quick here.

"I will bathe your leech bites," she said, in English.

"Je parle français, Mademoiselle," Greer said.

She asked him how he came to speak French, and he told her that he had been with a carnival, and there had been some French acrobats. She asked him what he had done with the carnival, and he lied and told her his father had owned it.

And all the time, she dabbed at the leech bites and the insect bites on his backside with cotton-soaked alcohol, pulling the sheet off him when it was necessary to work below his waist. He smelled the alcohol, of course, but it was overwhelmed by the smell of her perfume.

By the time she had worked her way down to his calves and ankles, he had a prize-winning erection.

"Roll over," she said.

"That would be very embarrassing for both of us, just now," Greer said.

She laughed, and handed him a towel.

He told himself that he was embarrassed, and that it would go down naturally under the circumstances, which were, after all, nurse-patient, rather than romantic.

She found a bite they hadn't noticed before under his armpit, and worked on that, and then she worked her way down his body. The hard-on did not go down. She worked around it, down his legs. She rebandaged the sutured shrapnel wound.

"You still have it hard," she said, level voiced.

He blushed. She chuckled, deep in her throat.

"It is nothing to embarrass," she said.

Her hand was on his stomach, an inch or so above the tent his erection was making of the towel.

"There are thirty-nine women here," she said. *"French* women. Five of them are married, three to officers and two to sergeants. That means thirty-four women for several thousand of mens."

"Those are pretty good odds," he said.

"We have enough with the Viet Minh without fighting among ourselves over men," she said. "And we are not whores."

He had no idea what she was leading up to.

"I only once in a while wish a man," she said. "But if I were to have to do with a man here, it would cause difficulty."

He nodded.

"You understand?" she asked.

He met her eyes.

She slid her hand under the towel, held him, chuckled appreciatively. She picked the towel off him with the other hand, and hung it over the rail at the foot of the bed.

"No move," she said, and let go of him, and got out of her Foreign Legion fatigue pants, and climbed onto the bed and straddled him and guided him into her.

He had never had anybody do that to him before, and he never forgot it.

The plane that came to get them out the next day crashed on landing, and then there was fog the day after that, and no plane; so it was the third day before they ran out to a gooney bird in the midst of an artillery barrage, got in it, and were soaked with the clammy sweat of fear until it got down the runway and into the air out of range of the Viet Minh's heavy .50s.

[FIVE]
The Embassy of the United States of America
Taipei, Formosa
25 March 1954

Lt. General E. Z. Black returned from dinner with the ambassador as soon as he could without giving offense. He had declined the offer of the VIP guest house and had been assigned quarters in the main Embassy building instead.

When the marine guard saluted him, even though he was in civilian clothing, Black asked him if he had happened to see Sergeant Greer.

"Yes, sir," the guard said. "He's in the attaché's office, sir."

"What's he doing there?" Black wondered out loud.

"Sir," the guard said, "he told the officer of the day that he was acting under your orders."

"Yes, of course," General Black said. "That's on the third floor, right?"

"Yes, sir," the marine said.

He had inquired of Greer's whereabouts out of some vestigial (perhaps parental?) concern that Greer would celebrate his safe return with whiskey and wild, wild women. What he had hoped to learn was that Greer hadn't left the Embassy, not that he had invoked his name and was up to God alone knows what in the attaché's office.

It wasn't hard to find the attaché's office. Its door was the only one in the long corridor from which light spilled into the corridor.

There was a soldier from the Embassy, a technical sergeant in his late thirties, perhaps even his early forties, in the outer office. Greer had installed himself at the secretary's desk, and was furiously pounding her IBM electric typewriter.

The Embassy sergeant came to attention the instant he saw General Black. Sergeant Greer glanced up at him, and then resumed his typing, finishing the line or the paragraph or whatever, before finally standing up.

Greer was in a new khaki uniform. When they thought he was dead, they had packed up his personal gear and his uniforms and sent them home. When MacMillan, Felter, and Greer finally returned from Dien Bien Phu, the three had been wearing French Foreign Legion jungle fatigues. The khakis had probably come from the military attaché's supply room here.

Greer's sleeves now held chevrons with one more stripe. He has just as many stripes, General Black thought, as the sergeant who has been sent to keep an eye on him, a man twice his age. Greer was also wearing a set of French parachutist's wings, and pinned to the epaulets of his khaki shirt was the regimental badge of the *3ième Régiment Parachutiste de la Légion Étranger*. He could probably get away with wearing the jump wings, General Black thought, but the Foreign Legion regimental crest had to go. But now, he decided, was not the time to tell him so.

"You about finished, Greer?" General Black asked, when Greer had finally found time to come to attention.

"Another half a page, General," Greer said. He picked up a stack of paper from the secretary's IN basket and handed them to General Black. Then he sat down, put a sheet of paper in the typewriter, and resumed his furious typing. He was finished, tearing the page from the typewriter with a reckless flourish, before General Black had read what Greer had given him.

"This would have waited until morning," General Black said, as he read. It was his final report on the Hanoi Conference. He corrected himself. Not exactly. His nineteen-year-old technical sergeant, fresh from vanquishing the enemy on the field of battle, had taken it upon himself to "improve" the draft Col. Carson Newburgh had written, and which he had just about decided to transmit.

I should jump all over his ass, Black thought, but the truth was that the boy had cleaned it up, removed what could have been ambiguities.

"I had planned to be hung over in the morning, General," Greer said. He had had his tie pulled down. He was now standing in front of a mirror, adjusting it in place.

Devotion to duty, General Black thought, wryly, may be defined as correcting your general's sloppy English before you go out and get drunk.

"Do you know what 'hoist on your own petard' means, Greer?"

"I'm afraid to ask."

General Black turned to the Embassy sergeant. "Can you get Colonel Newburgh on the horn for me?" he asked.

"Carson," he said when Newburgh came on the line, "Greer has made certain improvements to our document. Do you feel up to having a look at them now?"

Sergeant Wallace, the court reporter, was summoned, and the sergeant from the Embassy dismissed. It took more than an hour to make still further changes, until Colonel Carson W. Newburgh announced: "That ought to do it. We can sit around here from now on, just moving commas around. It looks good to me, E.Z."

"All right, Sergeant," General Black said. "Please retype it and have it encrypted and sent off. URGENT, I think. I don't think PRIORITY will hack it."

"It doesn't have to be retyped," Sergeant Greer said. Black glowered at him. "We're going to burn the goddamned original anyway," Greer said.

"Encrypt it the way it is, Sergeant Wallace," General Black said.

"We don't have a title for it, sir," Sergeant Wallace Black said.

" 'Report of Lieutenant General E. Z. Black to the Joint Chiefs of Staff,' " Sergeant Greer answered for him. " 'Subject: An Evaluation of the French Military Position in Indo-China, with Emphasis on the French Garrison at Dien Bien Phu.' "

Black thought a minute, and then nodded his head.

Sergeant Wallace took the report and went in search of the cryptographer.

"Your head is so large now, Greer, that I say this reluctantly," General Black said. "But you did a good job, and I appreciate it."

"And may the sergeant say, general, that the sergeant is delighted with the manner the general has chosen to show his appreciation?" He fondly patted his new chevrons.

"That's in lieu of a medal," Black said. "You deserve them."

"When I get the medal, do I have to give it back?"

"What medal?"

"Croix de Guerre," Greer said. "For preserving that Frenchman's most important possession. It'll probably say for valor, or some such bullshit, but that's what it'll be for. I thought you knew about it."

"The Pentagon won't let you accept it, Greer," Carson Newburgh said. "It would be embarrassing politically."

"Christ, and I always wanted to be a certified hero," Greer said.

"And those Foreign Legion regimental crests have to go, too," General Black said. "Have them put on a cigarette lighter, or something, but get them off your uniform."

Greer started to take them off.

"What about the wings?" he asked.

"I think he can keep those, can't he, Carson? As a qualification badge?" Newburgh nodded. "If anybody asks, say you took the French parachute course."

"I did, I did," Greer laughed. "The *quick* course."

"You know what we mean, Greer," Colonel Newburgh said.

"I'm sorry about the Croix de Guerre, Greer," General Black said. "The French pass out medals like samples, but they're generally pretty choosy about the Croix de Guerre."

"They also parade magnificently," Newburgh said, sarcastically.

"I thought about that," Greer said. "Maybe we're too quick to make fun of them. They need that bullshit. We don't."

"I don't follow you, Greer," Colonel Newburgh said.

"We haven't lost a war, yet," Greer replied. "They have."

Black looked at him intently. The same thought had occurred to him during the four days of the conference. It was not the sort of observation you expected from a sergeant. A nineteen-year-old sergeant.

"Now what, Greer?" Black said.

"Sir?"

"What are you going to do now?"

"Well, sir, the sergeant hoped that the general could see his way clear to placing the sergeant on, say five days' TDY right here in Taipei. To tidy up loose ends, so to speak."

"That would obviously explain those gorgeous wings you're wearing," Colonel Newburgh said.

"I am solemnly informed they work wonders with the ladies."

"You can have the TDY," General Black said. "But that's not what I was asking."

"I wanted to talk about that, too," Greer said. "But I didn't think this was the time or place."

"You want to stay in? You want to go to West Point?"

"Yes, sir, I want to stay in," Sergeant Greer said. "No, sir, I don't want to go to West Point."

"Why not?" General Black asked, somewhat sharply.

"Being a plebe would be a hell of a comedown after I've been a hero of the French Foreign Legion," Greer said, laughing.

Col. Carson Newburgh laughed. "Is that it? You think you're too good to be a plebe?"

"I don't think I'd last very long, Colonel," Greer said.

"How about Norwich?" Black asked. "I think I can get you a scholarship."

"Or A&M," Newburgh said. "I have some influence there." He was, in fact, a trustee and former president of the Alumni Association.

"How about a direct commission?" Greer asked. "As a first john?"

Newburgh looked at Black, who took a long moment to collect his thoughts before replying.

"If you had come to work for me as a lieutenant, Greer, I would write an efficiency report on you that would, unless you really fucked up, get your career on the right tracks."

"But?" Greer replied.

"You didn't. You're an enlisted man."

"I get your point," Colonel Newburgh said.

"Forgive me, sir," Greer said, disappointment evident in his voice. "I don't."

"You haven't had your card punched, Son," Newburgh said. "You've got to play the game by the rules. You shouldn't even be a tech sergeant."

"Sir, I was under the impression I was earning my keep."

"Technical sergeants are supposed to be thirty years old," General Black said. "Lieutenants, at least those who will have responsible careers, are supposed to come out of the Point, or A&M, or Norwich, or the Citadel. I can get you a commission, Greer, and you'd probably get to be a captain before somebody stuck a knife in your back. What we're talking about here is making you into a responsible senior officer, not somebody who puts in twenty years and retires."

"I couldn't put up with that West Point bullshit," Greer said.

"No," Black said, "I don't think you could, either. But you're going to have to get a college degree somehow, Greer. Or you might as well get out."

"Which brings us back to A&M," Colonel Newburgh said. "I can arrange a full scholarship, Greer, if it's a question of money."

"Thank you," Greer said, but from the tone of his voice, both Newburgh and Black knew that it was thanks for the offer, but not an acceptance of it.

"You tell me what you want," General Black said. "And you can have it. The commission, too, against my better judgment."

"I wipe out correspondence courses," Greer said. "Getting a degree isn't going to be a problem."

"There's a hurry-up program at A&M," Newburgh said. "Get your degree in three years. And a regular commission."

"Or, I can go to helicopter school," Greer said.

"Helicopter school?" Black asked, surprised. That was the first time that had been mentioned.

"Which means I get a warrant in six months. Then I go to the University of Chicago, which gives college credit for military experience, including flight school, and take some correspondence courses. Then I apply for a reserve commission, and a competitive tour for a regular commission."

"You'd have to take the Series 10 courses," Newburgh replied. Series 10 courses were correspondence courses offered to enlisted men. If successfully completed, the noncommissioned officer was then eligible to apply for a reserve commission.

"I already have," Greer said.

"How'd you do?"

"Three decimal nine," Greer said. Four decimal zero was perfect.

"Then what's this warrant officer helicopter pilot business?" Black asked.

"That's where the action's going to be," Greer said. "And the establishment is going to keep it for themselves. If I was a pilot before I took a commission, I'd be in already. Otherwise, I'm not sure I could get in."

"Then what's this bullshit about wanting me to commission you?"

"I was hoping I could get both out of you," Greer admitted. "A commission and flight school."

Carson Newburgh laughed.

"L'audace, l'audace, toujours l'audace," he said.

"Mais certainement, mon Colonel," Sergeant Greer said.

"I think you ought to shrink that oversized head of yours, Greer, and I think you're making a serious, perhaps fatal mistake in not going to either the Point, or A&M, or Norwich. But if the helicopter school is what you want, I'll see that you get it."

The middle-aged general and the teen-aged sergeant looked at each other.

"Thanks," Sergeant Greer said. There was more respect, and affection, in the one word than either General Black or Colonel Newburgh had ever before heard from Sergeant Greer.

"Take off, Greer," General Black said. "And five days is spelled Eff Eye Vee Eee. Not six, not seven, not even five and a half."

"The sergeant assures the general he will report as required, where required, and when required," Greer said. He saluted crisply, and then he left the room.

"If that little sonofabitch doesn't wind up either in the stockade or in the hospital with a terminal case of social disease," General Black said, "I think he'll do very well."

III

[ONE]
Ozark, Alabama
26 March 1954

Thirty minutes out of Atlanta, Southern Airways Flight 117, a Super DC-3, landed at Columbus, Georgia. Six of the twenty-one passengers who had filled the seats got off, and no one got on. Howard Dutton took advantage of the opportunity to take both of his heavy, bulging, worn briefcases from beneath the seats and put them on the empty seat beside him.

He was a stocky, square-faced man wearing rimless spectacles, a starched white shirt already well wilted, and a suit that seemed a half size too small for his body. He was always uncomfortable when his briefcases were out of his sight, for they, rather than the turn-of-the-century safe in his office, were really his private and confidential files. His wife, who was his secretary, had the combination to the safe in the office. She had orders, which he believed she followed faithfully, never to mess around in his briefcases.

His briefcases were rarely out of his sight, even at night, when he kept them at the side of his bed in his frame house on Broad Street. They contained his secrets. He now had the biggest, most important secret of his life in the double-strap briefcase.

There were two briefcases. The first he had had since he graduated from the University of Alabama. It closed with one strap. He had carried his books in the single-strapper through the University of Alabama Law School. He had bought the double-strapper after the war, when he had been in Washington as administrative assistant to the Hon. Bascomb J. Henry (D—Fifth District, Ala.), and the single-strapper just hadn't been big enough to hold all that he had to carry around.

He resisted the temptation to open the double-strapper and take out the papers which made the secret official. But he rested his hand, casually, on the double-strapper, while he smiled a no-thanks to the stewardess's offer of a Coke-or-coffee and a bag of peanuts.

Thirty minutes out of Columbus, the Super DC-3 landed again, at Dothan, Alabama, and taxied to the one-floor frame terminal building. From Dothan it would go to Panama City, Florida, and from Panama City to Fort Walton Beach, eighty miles down the coast, where the flight would terminate.

Three people got off at Dothan, two of them standing by the Super DC-3 while a ground crewman opened the door in the fuselage and removed their luggage. Howard Dutton had no luggage besides the briefcases. The single-strapper held two soiled white shirts, identical to the one he was wearing, a soiled sleeveless undershirt, soiled boxer shorts, and a soiled pair of black nylon socks.

Howard Dutton had gone from Ozark, Alabama, to the nation's capital, to the halls of Congress, to the seat of power, to deal with some of the most powerful men in the nation, with a change of underwear and two extra shirts, and he had returned victorious.

A warm feeling swept through him, instantly replaced by one of annoyance, concern, and a little anger. He had seen his daughter, Melody, standing inside the plate glass doors of the terminal. Howard Dutton dearly loved his daughter Melody, who was seventeen, and a senior at Ozark High School, and had been touched that she had driven all the way here from Ozark to meet her daddy.

But then he had noticed how Melody was dressed. Melody was wearing a white T-shirt, through which the brassiere restraining her pert young breasts was clearly visible, and a pair of blue shorts that were so short they reminded Howard, to his immediate shame, of the shorts worn by a whore in a Birmingham brothel he had gone to one drunken weekend when he was at the university.

That was a hell of a thing for a father to think about his own seventeen-year-old daughter, he thought, but the cold facts were that that's how the whore had been dressed. Melody, of course, was simply blind to what she looked like. She had never seen a whore, as far as he knew, and probably wasn't sure what one did. It was hot, and, still a child, she did what she had done when she had been a child. She took off as many clothes as she could.

Howard mentally cursed his wife. Wives were supposed to see about that sort of thing, make sure their daughters looked respectable when they went in public.

Melody ran out of the building and gave him a hug and a wet kiss.

"How's my favorite daddy?" she asked.

If it was anyone's fault that she was running around in public looking like a fancy lady in a Birmingham whorehouse, Howard Dutton decided, it damned sure wasn't this innocent child's.

"You shouldn't have come all the way here in this heat," he said. "You should have sent Clem." Clem was the janitor at the bank, an amiable elderly black man who sometimes drove the car.

"I was *bored* out of my *gourd*, Daddy," Melody said.

"That's the only reason, you were bored?"

"And I missed my favorite daddy," she said. She hugged him again. One of the other debarking passengers happened to be male, happened to see Melody hugging her daddy, and happened to appreciatively notice Melody's pink buttocks, about half of which were visible below the blue shorts.

Goddamned pervert! Howard Dutton thought. *Looking at an innocent young girl like that!*

He walked Melody around, rather than through, the Dothan Municipal Airport Terminal Building, to where she had parked the car, its nose against a cable strung between creosoted six-by-sixes stuck in the reddish clay. He set the double-strapper on the ground and opened the door of the 1951 Ford Super Deluxe. He tossed the single-strapper onto the back seat, and then picked up the double-strapper and tossed that onto the floor in the back.

"You want me to drive, Melody, honey?" he asked.

"No, I don't," she said. "You are one of the world's worst drivers."

He had been afraid of that, and would really have preferred to drive, but he knew that you had to force yourself to let them grow up, and driving cars was part of growing up.

He took off his suit jacket, its inner pockets sagging with the weight of still more paper, and carefully laid it on the seat back so that it wouldn't slide off the slippery plastic upholstery.

The senator had sent one of his assistants to take him to Washington National from the Capitol. In a 1953 Mercury four door. With an air conditioner. That air conditioner had really been nice in the muggy heat of Washington, and the muggy heat of Washington wasn't anything like the muggy heat here. He really wished he could have an air conditioner.

The 1951 Ford Super Deluxe belonged to the Farmers and Planters Bank of Ozark, of which Howard Dutton was president and chairman of the board. While the bank could well afford, financially, an air-conditioned Mercury for its president and chairman of the board, Howard Dutton could not afford, socially, to drive anything that suggested the bank was getting rich on the sweat of its depositors. Howard's father had taught him that. Depositors were just looking for some excuse to bad-mouth their bankers.

Maybe soon. Not right away, but soon, when everybody had a little more money, because of what he was doing for them, he could at least get a car with a goddamned air conditioner.

He decided that they would go home the long way. Indulge himself. For one thing, Prissy (for Priscilla, Mrs. Howard Dutton) had told him on the phone that Tom Zoghby had dropped dead. One moment, Tom had been talking with somebody (Dudley Claxton, he thought Prissy said) and the next moment he was dead on the floor. Right on the sidewalk in front of Zoghby's Emporium.

The minute he got home, of course, he would be expected to go see the widow and young Tom and the girls. There was no getting away from that, even if he had wanted to, but at the same time it wasn't the sort of thing you liked to do. That he liked to do. There were a lot of people who really got their pleasure rushing to console a widow and a bereaved family.

Tom had probably left his family well fixed, which was something. But still, there might be a need for some cash money, and he would have to have a word with young Tom (he wouldn't want to bother the widow) about maybe selling some of that land along County Highway 53.

He was suddenly shamed with the thought. That would be dishonest and unethical, now that he had the secret. He was surprised with himself; he wasn't, no matter what people thought, the kind of banker that went around taking advantage of widows and heirs. After a moment, he was able to convince himself that he had thought about buying the Zoghby land along Highway 53 without thinking about the secret. The secret was so new, that he just hadn't thought about it. He really hadn't been trying to take advantage of Tom's boy.

"Go up 84 toward Enterprise," he told Melody.

There were two ways to get from Dothan to Ozark. The short way was to turn left when leaving the airport, and then left again, and up US 231. The long way was to turn right when leaving the airport, and then right again, on US 84, toward Enterprise, and then, fifteen miles along, turn right again and cut through the Camp Rucker Reservation.

He was entitled, as a reward, both not to rush home to see the Widow Zoghby and to take a look at Camp Rucker. He was a banker and a lawyer, and he knew he didn't own Camp Rucker. But at the same time, he had a special relationship with it that nobody else could claim, not even Congressman Henry (May He Rest in Peace).

In 1934, under Roosevelt's Rural Reclamation Administration, the government had bought from Congressman Henry (and other people) 125,000 acres of worked-out cotton land, after they'd sent experts in who had decided the soil was so poor that nothing man could do was going to make it productive again for at least a generation.

Goddamned fools had cottoned the land, and just worked it to death, destroying the topsoil, so it blew away, and then, when the rains came, gullied it, so that it wasn't worth a damn for anything. Congressman Henry was as guilty as any of them, so you couldn't just say the dumb rednecks were getting what they deserved, reaping what they had sowed.

So the government had come in and bought it up, paying ten dollars an acre for land that was worth maybe a dollar, a dollar and a half, and they'd sent in the CCC, and stopped what they could of the worst gullying and planted it in loblolly pine, and said that in maybe fifty years they would think of clearing it again for planting. Maybe by that time they would have come up with some way to make topsoil or do something to clay that would make it grow things; and in the meantime they could timber it, twice, and get something out of it.

And then, six years after that, when the pines were head-high, World War II had come along (or was coming along, and everybody could see it coming) and the military was looking for places to build training bases.

The land was transferred to the War Department in late 1939, but it wasn't until late 1941, right before the Japs bombed Pearl Harbor, when Howard Dutton had been in his last year in the law school at Alabama, that they announced plans to make it a base. And it was nearly a year after that, November 1942, before they did anything.

Once they started, of course, they really got in high gear. When Howard Dutton left the Basic Officer's Course in Miami, in the Air Corps, all there was on what was still called "the Reclamation Land" was some surveyors' tapes and markers, but when he came back on leave three months later, there was Camp Rucker, named for General Rucker, who'd been a Confederate general.

In ninety days they'd built a military post, everything from barracks to a laundry to rifle ranges. All Howard Dutton had seen around Courthouse Square on his leave, before going over to the China-Burma-India theater as an Air Corps lawyer, was khaki uniforms. And, oh, how the money had rolled in!

Two divisions, eleven, twelve thousand men each, plus the support troops, had trained at Camp Rucker, and after they had gone off to war, they had changed it into a POW camp, and the place had held more than twenty thousand Italian prisoners from North Africa. They'd been lucky there, the Eyeties were glad to be out of the war, and they'd caused no trouble at all. They'd worked the farms. Hell, they'd even made out with the women, but nobody talked about that. There was something unpatriotic about the women doing that, with their own men off to war on the other side. But it happened, even if no one talked about it.

Right after the war, the place had closed down again, and where there had been twenty thousand soldiers, there was maybe a dozen enlisted men and a couple of officers, just watching the place, to make sure people didn't steal the place blind.

It had opened again for the Korean War, not the way it had been (they had trained a National Guard regiment from Wisconsin, not a division) and not for as long. It had closed down again in 1953, last year, with the Korean War still going.

And when the soldiers went, so had all that government money. When the camp was open, even with the Eyetie prisoners, they'd had to buy all sorts of things, mostly services, from Ozark and Enterprise and even Dothan. There were jobs, that was the thing, jobs ranging from fireman to barber, all kinds of clerks, people to work in the post exchange, fix the telephones, all the things the army needs and can't do for itself. The best kind of jobs, to a banker's way of thinking, ones that brought money into a community and took nothing out. If a factory opens, that means jobs, sure, but it also means you (the city) have to pay for firemen, and policemen, and sewers, and everything else people expect. But a military post either doesn't need that sort of thing or pays for it itself.

There was all kinds of idiotic talk going around about what to do with the post, when it closed down. Turn it into a university. Get industry to relocate on it. Even, when things got desperate, turn it into a prison. After all, they'd had all those Eyeties out there, so you knew that worked.

But those weren't answers and Howard Dutton knew they weren't. He had seen it from the beginning, from the day he'd come home from the war. War or not, the thing to do with Camp Rucker was keep it Camp Rucker, keep it filled with soldiers.

That was the reason Howard had gone to work on the congressman, gone off to Washington, instead of taking over from his father at the bank or opening a law practice. He had learned in the Air Corps that if there is a system, you can figure out how the system works, and then make it work for you.

That was his secret. He had made the system work the day he wanted it to work.

He didn't think of himself as a hypocrite. What he had done was going to make a lot of people rich around town, be good for the whole county. But it was also, and he knew this, and was not embarrassed by it, going to make him a rich man, too. Richer than he ever would have gotten at the bank. Much richer.

God helps those who help themselves. Say what you like. It was true.

US Highway 84 was a two-lane macadam road, nearly straight, running through gently rolling land between farms and untended land. Fifteen miles from Dothan, Howard Dutton told Melody to take the right turn at a fork. This was the "new road," built when they built Camp Rucker in ninety days from the time the first nail was driven. It cut across large patches of what the Rural Reclamation Administration had called "submarginal farm land" to Daleville, one of the oldest communities in the county.

Daleville was a ghost town when Melody drove her Daddy through it, in the Ford Super Deluxe. When the camp was open, Daleville was just outside the gate, and the single street was lined with cheap frame buildings that used to house laundries and dry cleaners and Army-Navy stores and hamburger stands and used car lots.

No bars or saloons. Dale County (named after the same Dale who had set up a store at the crossroads and named it Daleville) was Baptist dry. That's not dry, that means that there are no bars, and you can't get a drink in a restaurant or beer at the grocery store. You generally get your own beer when you're out of town in a wet county, and you get your whiskey in pint bottles from a bootlegger. But there are no public places to drink, where people can go and ruin their lives with the Devil's Brew.

A small general store was still open, and the one-room post office next door, and there were half a dozen worn-out pickups and as many battered old Fords and Chevvies on the weed-grown lot of one of the used car places, but everything else was closed down and boarded up and falling down. There were no soldiers and there was no business.

There was a sign at the deserted gate, where once MPs in white leggings and pistol belts had stood waving people through and saluting officers in their cars. The sign said: "Military Reservation—Do not leave marked route."

What that meant was that you were supposed to follow the one road, which ran on the fringes of the built-up area, and which led to the other side, to the road to Ozark. They didn't want people running around loose in the built-up area, where they could help themselves to toilets and wire and pipe and even the barracks themselves because they were just sitting there asking to be stolen.

Howard Dutton gestured with his arm.

"Drive around the sawhorses, Melody," he said. "I want to have a look around."

"Are we looking for anything in particular?" she asked.

"Just drive around the area behind post headquarters," he said.

To their left were enormous wooden garages, where once the rolling stock of infantry divisions, trucks and tanks and cannon, had been repaired. He knew, although he couldn't see it, that beyond the garages was a 2,000 bed hospital. A hundred or more single-story frame buildings connected with walkways to keep the patients out of the sun and rain as they were wheeled between the buildings.

A flag still fluttered from the flagpole in front of post headquarters, for the caretakers had taken over that one building for their headquarters and living quarters. The last contract issued for more than a thousand dollars by the purchasing office before it had closed was to bring electricity from Dale County Rural Electrification Agency lines to the post headquarters. The coal-fired generators which had provided electricity to the post when it was open were still there, and ready to run, but it was cheaper with just a dozen men on the post to string a line and buy electricity from REA.

The grass was cut right in front of post headquarters, but the parade ground in front was grown waist high with grass, and there was grass that high between the endless rows of barracks.

Melody drove past post headquarters to the field house, and around it, and down crumbling macadam streets through regimental areas. The barracks looked in good shape, except for flaking paint and broken windows here and there. Beside each of the two-story wooden buildings, there was even a supply of coal for their furnaces in small concrete-block caches. There were even lights in the fixtures over the doors, and hanging from lamppoles every block.

And then up ahead he saw an Army pickup truck blocking the road.

Melody stopped the Ford with its nose a foot from the pickup's fender and Howard Dutton got out of the car, a smile on his face.

"Oh, it's you, Mayor," the major driving the pickup truck said. He waved his hand. "Hi, Melody!"

Melody got out of the car and walked over to them. Howard Dutton wished she hadn't done that, with half of her bottom hanging out that way.

Howard Dutton was on his second term as mayor of Ozark. He had decided it was really easier to be mayor himself than to pick somebody for the job, and then have to watch every move he made.

"Hot enough for you, Major?" Howard Dutton said, extending his hand. He was always very charming to Major Feeler, the post commander, even though he thought Feeler was a fool, and sometimes wondered what Feeler had done to find himself with an idiot job like this.

"I was so hot," Major Feeler said, "that I went down to the pool at the officer's club. Dirty or not, I was going to have a swim."

"And you did?" Melody asked.

"Would you believe there was three snakes in that pool?" the major said, and they laughed together.

Melody said "Oook" and made a face.

"Anytime you want a swim, you should come to Ozark," Howard Dutton said.

There was a community swimming pool at the community house.

"I just may do that," the major said. "I saw the car driving past headquarters. If I'd known it was you, I wouldn't have chased you."

"I guess I'm violating the law," Howard Dutton said. "But I had a few minutes, and I wanted to get a last look at the place before they start tearing it down."

Major Feeler, very obviously, made up his mind before speaking.

"Maybe I shouldn't be talking out of school, Mayor Dutton," he said. "And I wouldn't want you to quote me."

"I appreciate your confidence, Major," Dutton said.

"I just heard from Third Army in Atlanta that there's a hold on the awarding of the demolition contract."

"Cancelled, you mean?" Dutton asked.

"No, sir. Just a hold."

"Isn't that interesting?" Dutton replied. "What do you suppose that means?"

"I don't know," the major said. "Maybe they figured it would just be cheaper to let it all fall down than to pay to have it torn down."

"You may well be right," Dutton said, seriously. "If you hear anything, I'd appreciate learning about it."

"I'll tell you anything I can, Mayor," the major said. "You know that."

The Farmers and Planters Bank of Ozark, at Dutton's direction, never pressed Major Feeler hard when he was late with his car payment.

"I appreciate that," Dutton said, and shook Major Feeler's hand. "I truly do. And now, I think, we've seen enough. Next time you get to town, you come and have a cup of coffee with me, you hear?"

"I'll do that," Major Feeler said. He got back in his GI pickup truck and drove off, waving as he did.

Dumb ass, Howard Dutton thought.

But he was smiling. Even that had gone well. The demolition contract was on "hold." That happened all the time, for any number of reasons.

The secret, the secret that Camp Rucker was not going to be torn down at all, but reactivated, was still a secret. There were still several days, maybe as much as a week, to do things before the word got out.

"Let's go home, honey," he said to Melody.

He was going to make enough money so that when Melody went off to college, she would really have a good time, without having to worry about what things cost, the way he had had to, when he was at the university. Maybe he'd get her a car, a convertible. Pretty girls like Melody deserved to ride around in convertibles.

[TWO]
Fort Knox, Kentucky
26 March 1954

"So there I was," Major Rudolph G. MacMillan said to Colonel Robert F. Bellmon, Assistant G-3 (Plans and Training), Headquarters, the United States Army Armor School and Fort Knox, Kentucky, "surrounded by howling savages, low on water, about out of ammunition, when, far away, I heard the faint sound of a trumpet sounding 'Charge.' "

Then he lowered his head, addressed the ball, and sank a thirty-two-foot putt on the eleventh hole of the Fort Knox officer's open mess golf course. He then raised his head and smiled warmly at Colonel Bellmon.

"So there I was," Colonel Bellmon said, "standing before the general, who had just handed me an URGENT radio, saying you were down and presumed dead, and the general said, 'You better tell Roxie.' "

Their eyes met.

"So I figured I'd wait until morning," Bellmon went on. "That wasn't the first time the Pride of Mauch Chuck had been reported presumed dead."

"I owe you," MacMillan said. "Some dumb sonofabitch from the CIA went and got Sharon Felter out of bed at three o'clock in the morning and told her. Complete routine, even a goddamned rabbi and a doctor."

"I know," Bellmon said. "I've talked to Felter."

"And what did Felter have to say?"

"He said he knew how close you and I are," Bellmon said.

Their eyes met for a long moment. Then Bellmon walked to his ball, wiggled into putting position, and stroked it. It hit the lip of the hole, half circled it, and then rolled two feet back toward Bellmon.

"You going to give me that?" Bellmon asked. MacMillan shook his head. "No." Bellmon shrugged, and then sank his putt. They walked to their clubs, mounted in two-wheel carts, and dragged them to the 12th tee.

There was a Coke machine there, inside a small gazebo. MacMillan fed it dimes, handed a Coke to Bellmon, and leaned on one of the pillars supporting the roof.

"We went over there nonstop in a bomber," MacMillan said. "From Andrews Air Force Base in Washington."

"Nonstop?" Bellmon asked.

"They refueled us in the air twice," MacMillan said. "Once over the West Coast, and again over Hawaii, or near Hawaii. Scared the shit out of me. What they do is fly up under the tanker, and then the tanker extends a probe, got little wings on the end of it to guide it. And then it meshes with a thing on the front of the bomber. We're going six hundred miles an hour, you understand. Very hairy."

"So you went where?" Bellmon asked.

"Seoul. K16. They were holding a civilian transport for us. CAT. You know, from Formosa. A DC-4. Everybody's there, in civilian clothing. E. Z. Black's in charge. Had an air force brigadier who was very unhappy when Felter told him we were going into Dien Bien Phu. Felter had a note from Eisenhower. That shut up the air force."

"I thought you said General Black was in charge."

"Black's people were told to stay away from Dien Bien Phu, and to wear civilian clothes," MacMillan said. "Jesus, that was funny."

"Funny?" Colonel Bellmon asked. "How funny?"

"Well, the whole operation is a big damned secret, see, very hush-hush. They even hid the CAT DC-4 in a hangar in Seoul, for Christ's sake, so nobody would see it. So we arrive in Hanoi. Only Felter and me are in uniform. Everybody else is in civvies. And there's half of the French Army out there, honest to God, Bob, a battalion of troops and a brass band. Cymbals, trumpets with flags hanging down from them, bass drums. Even a couple of goats with gold-painted horns. Full dress reception. Frog brass in dress uniforms. Our brass in mussed civvies, looking like they've been sleeping in their clothes. Except for a couple of the enlisted men. You know that big black orderly of Black's?"

"Sergeant Wesley," Bellmon said.

"Yeah. He must weigh three hundred pounds. Well, Black brought him along. And he's got this kid who works for him, a guy named Greer. He reminds me of Craig Lowell in the old days, except this kid knows what he's doing. Black sends him along to keep an eye on us. About as subtle as a Honolulu whorehouse madam. Well, the first thing the frogs tell us is that we can't land, we have to jump. And the kid is no jumper. But he says he's going even if he has to jump. And he does."

"Lowell, by the way," Bellmon said in a level tone, "just graduated from flight school. He and Parker."

Major Craig W. Lowell and Captain Philip Sheridan Parker IV bothered Lieutenant Colonel Robert F. Bellmon. But he was honest enough to admit to himself that it was probably because he couldn't simply dismiss them as a pair of wise-asses.

Parker was establishment, the fourth soldier to bear the name. The first Philip Sheridan Parker had been the son of a master sergeant who rode in the Indian Wars with General Philip Sheridan. His son, Colonel Philip Sheridan Parker, Jr., had been the senior "colored" tank officer in World War I. Colonel Philip Sheridan Parker III, of General Porky Waterford's "Hell's Circus" Armored Division, had commanded Task Force Parker that had saved Bellmon from whatever plans besides instant repatriation the Russians had for two hundred "liberated" American prisoners.

Lowell, if not antiestablishment, was certainly not *of* it. He came from a wealthy family, but had entered the army as a draftee after having been kicked out of Harvard. He had turned up in Bellmon's life, when MacMillan, serving at Bellmon's recommendation as aide-de-camp to General Waterford, had been ordered to produce a polo team from personnel assigned to the Constabulary in occupied Germany. And Craig W. Lowell was a three-goal polo player. There are not many three-goal polo players anywhere, and there had been none in the Constabulary except Lowell.

The idea of having the best polo team possible was General Waterford's obsession. General Waterford had graduated, in 1937, from the French cavalry school at Samur. Now he wished to play the French, both for personal reasons, and, Bellmon was sure, for reasons involving the prestige of the U.S. Army. If he was going to win playing the French, he was going to have to have PFC Craig Lowell playing as his number two.

French officers, however, do not play with enlisted men.

So General Waterford delegated the problem to Captain MacMillan. MacMillan arranged for Lowell to be temporarily commissioned as a second lieutenant in the Finance Corps. He would play polo, and then be released from active duty for the convenience of all concerned.

But on the day of the polo game against the French, Porky Waterford suffered a heart attack, dying in a way which would have met his approval: in the saddle, at the gallop, almost at the opposition's goal and about to score.

That left the problem of what to do with 2nd Lt Craig W. Lowell. He was not discharged, but instead swept under the rug. He was sent to Greece, where, it was believed, if he wasn't killed, at least he would be out of sight.

Forced into it, Craig W. Lowell took to soldiering as if he had been born to be a warrior. He came home from Greece with the second highest decoration for valor the Greek throne bestowed, the highest being reserved for Greek nationals. As Bellmon had heard from Red Hanrahan, Lowell had assumed command of a Greek Mountain Division company after the officers had been killed, and despite several serious wounds, repulsed a communist attack, personally killing more than a dozen of the enemy himself.

After that, Lowell got out of the army, and settled into his new home in Washington Mews with his wife Ilse, a girl he had met in Germany. But then was recalled for Korea. In Korea, he had commanded Task Force Lowell, which spearheaded the breakout from Pusan, earning himself a Distinguished Service Cross and a major's golden leaf. But at the moment of his greatest glory, he learned of the death of his wife in Germany.

Choosing to stay in the army, Lowell had a distinguished military career ahead of him. But the following year, he threw it away, first by cavorting with a visiting movie star in a way unbefitting an officer and a gentleman, and then by defending Philip Sheridan Parker IV, who was court-martialed for having found it necessary to shoot an officer who had lost control on the battlefield.

Bellmon genuinely believed that both Phil Parker and Craig Lowell should have resigned from the service. They had not. They had volunteered for army aviation, which Bellmon (and most other members of the establishment) regarded as a dumping ground for misfits and ne'er-do-wells.

"I heard about that," MacMillan said. "Where'd they send them?"

"Lowell went to Germany, Parker to Alaska. We seem to have gotten away from Hanoi."

"Yeah. OK. Well, this kid sergeant is a real sharp operator. He had just come back from leave in Hong Kong. Where he's bought civilian clothes. He's wearing a plaid suit with a suede vest, and he's bought clothes for Wesley too. Pin-striped, double-breasted suit. Looks like a nigger undertaker. So what we have here is Black's colored orderly and this kid who works for him looking like an advertisement in *Esquire*, and here's all the brass looking like a bunch of bums. So they play the Marseillaise and the Star Spangled Banner, and Black, in a tweed suit, troops the colors. And then they load everybody into limousines—a Rolls-Royce for Black, and old Packards and old Cadillacs from before War II for everybody else—and sirens screaming, they take us into town in a convoy.

"If Ho Chi Minh didn't know the Americans were coming, the frogs sure arranged for him to find out. Black gets taken to a frog VIP villa, him and Carson Newburgh, and the other generals are spread around among the other frog generals. The rest of us are taken to the Cercle Sportif, which is sort of a golf club, with a place where the frogs jump horses over fences. What do you call it?"

"Steeplechase?"

"I don't think so. But something like that. Anyway, it's pretty first class. So there's going to be cocktails at five o'clock and then dinner. And then the frogs find out that Wesley and the kid who works for Black, and the other technicians, the cryptographer, the map guys, are enlisted men. And the shit hits the fan. Christ, there are fifteen frogs running around flapping their arms and chattering like whores in a cathouse raid. *Enlisted men* in the Cercle Sportif! Napoleon will spin in his grave!"

"I thought you said they were in civvies?" Bellmon asked.

"They were. And they were all high-class troops, too. They weren't about to piss in the potted palms. But anyway, even Black gets involved in this. And he was pissed, too, let me tell you. They finally move them into a hotel in town, which means that they have to lay on transportation for them, to get everybody back and forth . . ."

"Tell me about the meeting," Bellmon said.

"I didn't get to go to the meeting," MacMillan said. "First thing in the morning, Felter takes my ass out to the airport. We're going to fly to Dien Bien Phu. We did. We just didn't land."

"No landing strip?"

"Oh, yeah. Under 105 and mortar fire. The only time they land is to evacuate people. The rest of the supplies go in by being kicked out the door. They don't even put the landing gear down. You know about Air America?"

"Something."

"They've got a bunch of ex-air force guys, and some Flying Boxcars, and they supply the place. Parachutist replacements jump in. It's safer."

"You got hit," Bellmon said.

"They got .50s on the hilltops. And some 20 mm stuff, too. I think they got us with .50s. It didn't blow up when it hit us, just set the goddamned engine on fire."

"So you went out the door?"

"There was a French Foreign Legion guy, a frog, which is unusual, in the door. I pushed him out, and then this Greer kid, and then I went out."

"Where was Felter?"

"You know Felter," MacMillan said. "He knows how to take care of Number One. He was out the door like a shot."

"But nobody else got out?"

"If we hadn't been standing in the door, we wouldn't have gotten out," MacMillan said. "It was hairy."

"Then what?"

"So we land in the trees. Smashed my goddamned watch. So I started sneaking around in the bushes, and I see that the Viet Minh, the communists, have caught the frog, and, honest to God, Bob, they're about to cut off his dick and feed it to him. So I shot one of them . . ."

"With what? You were specifically ordered to go unarmed."

"I shot them with that .32 Colt you gave me in the stalag," MacMillan said. "A goddamned good thing I had it, too. And then I ducked behind a tree, to kiss my ass good-bye, because the slopes I didn't blow away had Chink submachine guns. And then, all of a sudden, *Boom! Boom!*"

"What was that?"

"That's this Greer kid. He's got a sawed-off Winchester Model 12, loaded with single ought buckshot. He blew one slope's head half off, and a hole right through the other one. No shit, right *through* him. You could put your fist in the hole."

"Where was Felter?"

"After it's all over, the little bastard walks up, calm as shit, out of the jungle. He told me not to take a gun, but *he* had that goddamned .45 he always carries."

"And then you walked into Dien Bien Phu?"

"Walked is not the word. It took us four days. We crawled. We ran. We climbed trees. But we did very little walking. The legionnaire, who had been there before, made us hide all day, and move at night. Very hairy. The woods were full of gooks looking for us. We hid in trees. Got eaten alive by bugs. And then, and this was the hairy part, we had to get into Dien Bien Phu. They got a major base and a couple of outposts, separated, and as far as they're concerned, anybody out there in the woods is a bad guy. If it moves, shoot it."

"But you made it."

"Yeah."

"The French didn't see anybody get out of the C-47," Bellmon said. "That's when they sent the casualty cables."

"Anyway, we got there. You wouldn't believe that place, Bob. It's like what France in War I must have been. Everything underground. The gooks lay in harassing and intermittent all the time, and then, every once in a while, they shoot boom boom boom, twenty-four hours a day. So the officers stay half drunk, and the troops stay mostly drunk."

"Can they hold it?"

"No way," MacMillan said. "After we kept the gooks from cutting off his dick, the legionnaire told us whatever we wanted to know. I don't know how the hell they're doing it, but the communists are moving 105 howitzers . . . ours, incidentally, ones the First Cav lost in Korea . . . over those goddamned mountains by hand. And ammunition for them. More and more all the time. There's no way the frogs can hold Dien Bien Phu. The legionnaire told me that there's a couple of more cannon every day. Sooner or later, that's it."

"You didn't go to the meetings in Hanoi at all?"

"No, but Sandy got a report from Black, and I was there when he told him."

"Well?"

"The frogs are crazy. They want the First Cav, all right, and they want the 187th RCT, right now, but they want it under French command. They want to run the show."

"How did you get out of Dien Bien Phu?" Colonel Bellmon asked, half idle curiosity, half because he wanted to consider the ramifications of MacMillan's last remark.

"On an ambulance plane," MacMillan said. "Once you go into Dien Bien Phu, you stay there. Which is why they're not putting any more women in there. The only way to get out is on an ambulance plane. The gooks use the Red Crosses as aiming points."

"You say Colonel Black told Felter the French wanted command of American troops?"

"That's what he said," MacMillan replied. "That's when he started talking French.

He told them that there was absolutely no way the American people would stand still for putting American troops under French command, even if, which he doubted they would, they would stand still for Americans being sent there at all."

"And their response?"

"They would rather have their dicks cut off with dignity than admit that they had to have the Americans bail their ass out again."

"So what's going to happen, Mac?" Bellmon asked.

"Dien Bien Phu is going to fall," MacMillan said. "If we sent in a couple of divisions, maybe, just maybe, we could have it. Otherwise, it goes."

"What do you mean, 'it'?"

"All of it, the whole goddamned colony."

Bellmon didn't say anything for a long time.

"You want to play golf, Mac?" he said, finally.

"One more thing," MacMillan said.

"What?"

"Thanks for not running right over to Roxie when the cable came," MacMillan said.

"I figured you'd turn up," Bellmon said. "God takes care of fools and drunks and you qualify on both counts."

They locked eyes for a moment.

"So Lowell got through flight school?" MacMillan said, closing the subject.

"Not without difficulty, I understand, between us," Bellmon said. "He is not a natural-born aviator."

"The Duke generally hires people to do dirty jobs like that," MacMillan said. "They sent him to Seventh Army, huh?"

"Yeah, for a year. Basic utilization tour. Major Lowell will spend the next year being told what to do by lieutenants and captains."

"At least they'll be older than he is," MacMillan said, and then he walked out of the gazebo and thumbed a tee into the ground.

IV

[ONE]
Broadlawns
Glen Cove, Long Island, New York
12 April 1954

Only a few of the house's chimneys, and only if you knew where to look for them, could be seen from any point along the fence which enclosed Broadlawns. The fence, which enclosed 640 acres, more or less (a square mile, as nearly as they bothered to survey in 1768), marched around the property from the low waterline of Long Island Sound, up and down the rocks and boulders and the flat places and the hollows, and was broken only once, at the gate.

The fence was made of brick pillars, eight feet tall, between which were suspended two iron strips. Every eight inches along the iron strips was a steel pole, pointed at the upper end. The fence and the gate and the gatehouse had been erected as hastily as possible in the early days of the Civil War when one of Broadlawns's mistresses had been concerned that the draft riots in New York City, fifteen miles away, might spread to the country. She was in the family way at the time and had to be indulged.

There was one gatepost, to which a bronze sign reading BROADLAWNS was affixed. The other side of the gate was tied to the gatehouse, which was built of granite blocks, and made large enough to house ten or a dozen men and feed them, in case the draft riots did get out of hand, and it was necessary to protect the place in the country, as the family thought of it, with private policemen.

A policeman lived in the gatehouse now. He had been brought to the gatehouse as a baby, when his father had been in charge of the gate. He had grown up and gone to high school, and to Fordham University for two years; and then he had become a New York state trooper, and had risen to sergeant in twenty-eight years of service. He had retired to the gatehouse, and now his son was a state trooper lieutenant.

The retired state trooper sergeant had taken over the responsibilities of groundskeeper when the groundskeeper had died. He supervised the men who tended the grounds and the mechanic who kept the lawn mowers and other equipment running, and was responsible for just about everything on the place outside the house. Inside the house was the responsibility of the butler.

The retired state trooper and his son had been very helpful to the present owner of the house when he had been a young man with access to automobiles easily capable of exceeding the speed limits of the state of New York. There was only one arrest on the records, that for a 105-mile-per-hour chase by seven police cars, the arrest coming only when the car had blown a tire and rolled over. There was a limit to the sergeant's influence with his peers.

The house was visible from Long Island Sound, but it was so far back from the water, across broad lawns, that it appeared from the water to be smaller than it was. Even up close, standing in the drive, it wasn't very imposing. It was only when one was inside that the size and complexity of the house became apparent. It had begun as a farmhouse; and additions had been made to it, the most recent in 1919. There were now seven bedrooms, a library, a morning room, a drawing room, a living room, a bar, a small dining room, a large dining room, and a breakfast room.

Many people believed that Broadlawns was a private mental hospital, and others thought it belonged to the Roman Catholic Archdiocese of New York and was used as a retreat for clergy who had problems with alcohol or were otherwise mentally disturbed.

Developers, over the years, studying plats of the land, had often thought it would be a very desirable piece of property to turn into really classy, half-acre, maybe even three-quarters of an acre, plots. They had been informed the property was not for sale. The persistent ones, who believed that everything had its price, were advised by their bankers not to make nuisances of themselves. The people who had owned Broadlawns since 1768 did not wish to be disturbed, and since they were deeply involved in the real estate business around New York, they were not the sort of people small-potatoes developers could afford to antagonize.

Most of the property around Wall Street which was not owned by Trinity Episcopal Church was owned by the people who owned Broadlawns. And they had other property as well.

Broadlawns's butler was a West Indian, a tall, light-brown man with sharp facial features and graying hair. He wore a gray cotton jacket over gray striped trousers. When he walked into the bar to announce a call for Major Craig W. Lowell, his pronunciation was Oxford perfect, and somehow a bit funny.

"I beg your pardon, Major. The firm is on the line. They wish to transfer a call. Is the major at home?"

Major Craig W. Lowell, who was a little drunk, looked at him in annoyance.

"Did they say who?" he asked.

"No, sir," the butler said.

"Shit," Major Lowell said. He was a very large man, who wore his blond hair in a short, barely partable crew cut. He was blue-eyed, although his eyes turned icy sometimes when he was annoyed, as they did now and made him look older than his twenty-six years.

He unfolded himself from the leather armchair in which he had been slumped, his feet on a matching footstool, a cognac snifter cradled in his hands, and walked to the telephone on the bar. The butler beat him to it, pushed a button on the base of the telephone, and then picked up the handset and held it out to him.

"Thank you," Lowell said, and then to the telphone: "This is Major Lowell."

"I have a Major Felter on the line, Major," a voice Lowell recognized to be that of his cousin's, Porter Craig's, secretary said. "May I transfer it?"

"By all means," Lowell said.

He heard her say, "One moment, Major Felter, I have Major Lowell for you."

"Mouse, you little bastard!" Major Lowell said.

"I'm at LaGuardia," Major Felter said. "Where are you?"

"What the hell are you doing at LaGuardia?"

"I came to see you off," Major Felter said.

"Hold on, Mouse," Major Lowell said. He covered the mouthpiece with his hand and turned to face the other man in the room, his "stepfather," Andre Pretier. "Can I use your car?"

"Yes, of course."

"Mouse, go to the Pan American counter and give them my name," Lowell said. "Tell them I'm going to meet you."

"They have taxicabs," Major Felter said.

"Go to the goddamned lounge," Lowell said. "I'll be there in twenty minutes." He hung up before Felter could protest further.

"The chap they thought had been killed?" Andre Pretier asked.

"Uh huh," Lowell said. "He came to see me off."

"Will you see that we can take care of the major's guest?" Andre Pretier said to the butler.

The butler dipped his head, and walked silently out of the room.

"You want some more of this, Andre?" Lowell asked, holding up the bottle of cognac. Andre Pretier shook his head, "no."

"But help yourself," he said, and then he said: "Sorry, Craig. I seem to be unable to remember this is your house."

"Shit," Lowell said, and then he chuckled. "Sorry, Andre, I seem to be unable to remember one doesn't say 'shit' in polite company."

Andre Pretier smiled and raised his snifter in salute.

"May I make a suggestion?" Pretier asked.

"Yes, of course."

"You've had a bit of that," he said. "Are you all right to drive?"

The eyes turned icy again. But then Major Lowell said, "No, of course I'm not." He pushed a button, and in a moment, the butler reappeared.

"Would you ask Thomas to go to the Pan American VIP lounge at LaGuardia," Andre Pretier ordered, "and pick up a . . ."

"Major Sanford T. Felter," Lowell supplied.

"Yes, sir," the butler said.

The butler returned to the bar forty minutes later.

"Major Felter, Major Lowell," he announced.

Felter, wearing a baggy, ill-fitting suit, walked into the room. Lowell jumped out of his chair, hesitated awkwardly, then gave in to the emotion. He went quickly to the slight man, wrapped his arms around him, and lifted him off the ground.

"For God's sake, Craig!" Felter protested. Lowell set him down.

"I'm glad to see you, you little shit," Lowell said. "I thought you were pushing up daisies."

Andre Pretier got to his feet.

"Mouse, this is my stepfather," Lowell said. "Andre Pretier. Andre, Sandy Felter."

"A genuine pleasure, Major Felter," Pretier said.

"How do you do, sir?" Felter said, shaking his hand.

"What do you want to drink, Mouse?" Lowell asked.

"Have you got a Coke? Or ginger ale?"

"Can you imagine this teetotaling little bastard jumping into Dien Bien Phu, Andre?"

"For God's sake, Craig!" Felter protested again.

"The Mouse is a spook, Andre," Lowell said. "He sees Russian spies hiding behind every set of drapes."

"What are you celebrating?" Felter asked, coldly. He had seen that Lowell was drunk.

"Craig was in Hartford," Andre Pretier said. "Visiting his mother."

"How is she?" Felter asked.

" 'Progressing nicely' is the phrase they used," Lowell said.

"I'm glad to hear that," Felter said, politely.

"What that means is that she hasn't gone any further over the edge," Lowell said. He looked at Andre Pretier. "I have no secrets from the Mouse, Andre," he said. "But if that was out of line, I'm sorry."

"Not at all," Pretier said. "What we're doing for my wife, and Craig's mother, Major, is trying to get her the best help we can. It doesn't seem to be working as well as we had hoped."

"I'm sorry," Felter said.

"To get off that unpleasant subject, Mouse," Lowell said, "what brings you to Sodom on Hudson?"

"I wanted to see you off," Felter said. "I wanted to thank you for going to see Sharon."

"Shit," Lowell said. He smiled a little drunkenly at Andre Pretier. "There I go again, Ol' Sewer Mouth."

"Sharon told me what you did, Craig," Felter said.

"Christ, I hope not. You mean she told you I proposed?"

Felter shook his head resignedly.

"When are you going?" he asked.

"Half past ten," Lowell said. "Pan American has a sleeper flight to Paris. And then I'll catch the Main-Seiner to Frankfurt."

"Then I'm glad I decided to come today," Felter said. "If I had waited until tomorrow, you would have gone without calling. Exactly as you left the house an hour before I got there."

"Well, since you were still alive, I realized that Sharon wasn't going to marry me," Lowell said. "So there was no point in my staying for your great 'here I am home, straight from the mouth of death' scene."

"How did you find out, Craig?" Felter asked. "Sharon said you got there an hour after the notification team."

"Actually, it was closer to two hours," Lowell said. "I had a little trouble finding an air-taxi."

"And you're not going to tell me who told you?"

"So you can turn him in for breaking security?" Lowell asked. "No way, Mouse."

"OK, let it go," Felter said. "Tell me about flight school."

"There I was, ten thousand feet up, with nothing between me and the earth but a thin blond . . ."

"How much have you had to drink?" Felter asked.

"A bunch," Lowell said. "I wasn't prepared for Hartford."

"I tried to tell him, Major, that she probably wouldn't recognize him," Andre Pretier said. "But he insisted on going."

"Tell me about Dien Bien Phu," Lowell said. "What the hell were you and Mac doing there in the first place?"

"You know more than you should already, Craig," Felter said.

"I want to hear about you and MacMillan running around in the jungle," Lowell insisted. "After bailing out of a gloriously aflame airplane."

"I'm beginning to suspect who you talked to," Felter said.

"What happened, for Christ's sake?"

"Perhaps," Andre Pretier said, "it would be better if I excused myself."

Felter looked at him a moment.

"There's no need . . ."

"Excuse me," Andre Pretier said, and got up and walked out of the room.

"I'm not supposed to talk about this," Felter said. "And you know it. And I feel badly about asking him to leave his own living room."

"This is the bar," Lowell said, "not the living room. And it's mine, not his."

"God, you're impossible. You know what I mean."

"That's so much bullshit," Lowell said. "If you can't tell me, Mouse, who can you tell?"

"Maybe I will have a drink," Felter said. "Can I trust you to keep your mouth shut?" He answered his own question. "No, of course, I can't," he said. "But every spook has to have one weakness. You're mine."

He related what had happened at Dien Bien Phu, painting a picture of himself as a rear echelon chair-warmer being led to safety through the Indo-China forest by a French Foreign Legion corporal, one of the Army's most decorated parachutists, and a nineteen-year-old sergeant with a sawed-off shotgun.

Lowell automatically added Felter's role to their exploits. In his judgment, Major Sanford Felter was quite as accomplished a close combat warrior as MacMillan or anyone else Lowell had ever met in the service. He had seen Felter in action; in fact, he owed his life to Felter, who had blown away an officer who had stood in the way of a reinforcement column coming to Lowell's rescue during counterinsurgency operations in Greece.

A mental picture came into Lowell's mind of Felter in Indo-China in his tropical worsted uniform, the large .45 automatic he was never without held in front of him with both hands. He literally wasn't large enough, or his thin wrists strong enough, to fire the .45 with one hand. With two hands, firing slowly and deliberately, he seldom missed. He was literally a dead shot.

"So, with appropriate pomp and ceremony," Felter concluded, "during a barrage of 105 mm fire, cannon and ammo courtesy of the First Cavalry, we were formally inducted as honorary members of the *3ième Régiment Parachutiste* of the French Foreign Legion."

"Christ," Lowell said, "I wish I had been there." He wondered if he really meant that. He knew that his saying so had pleased Felter, for Felter had long had the notion (Lowell considered it unfounded) that Lowell was a natural-born combat soldier.

"They tried to give us the Croix de Guerre," Felter said. "Naturally, since we weren't supposed to be there in the first place, there's no way we'll be allowed to accept it."

"Christ, and what I've been doing, at enormous expense, is learning how to fly a whirlybird," Lowell said.

"Tell me about it," Felter said.

"Nothing to tell," Lowell said. "It's just as idiotic, having a major fly a helicopter, as I thought it would be. Like assigning a major as a jeep driver. I felt like a goddamned fool, when, with the band playing and flags flying, they pinned our wings on us."

"You don't believe that," Felter said, firmly.

"I don't know if I do or not, Mouse," Lowell said, drunk-serious. "I have to be periodically rebrainwashed; my faith wavers."

Felter glanced out the window and saw Andre Pretier walking on the wide lawn which stretched from the house down to the water's edge. He opened the French doors and walked out to him.

"I seem to have run you out of your own house," he said. "But I'm through talking about what I shouldn't have talked about, if you'd like to come back in."

"I understand," Pretier said. Felter led him back into the house.

"What we're talking about now is the importance of aviation to the army," Felter said. "I'm afraid it's not all that interesting."

"I don't even know what you're talking about," Andre Pretier said. "Craig, frankly, hasn't talked much about what he's been doing."

"He's been becoming an army aviator," Felter said.

"My ignorance is total," Pretier said. "I didn't know the army even had aviators."

"When the air force became autonomous, Andre," Felter began, and Andre Pretier sensed that Felter was relieved to have found a safe subject for conversation, "they began to devote most of their effort toward bombers and high-speed fighters, and to rockets. The army needs light aircraft, right on the battlefield. Since the air force was unable to provide them, the army was given authority to develop its own air service—army aviation. Craig is in on the ground floor."

"There are a few wild-eyed madmen around, Andre," Lowell said, wryly, "who envision entire divisions being airlifted by helicopters."

"I see," Pretier said. "And you saw, or see, enough merit in this theory to leave tanks? As Guderian saw enough merit in the blitzkrieg to change over to the German tank corps from signals as a colonel?"

"Would that it were so," Lowell said. "The cold truth, Andre, is that my last efficiency report in Korea was so bad that I had the choice between going to army aviation or turning in my soldier suit."

Pretier looked in surprise at Felter, saw the pained look on his face, and knew that Lowell was telling the truth.

"It wasn't quite that bad, Craig," Felter said.

"You know better than that, Mouse," Lowell said. "Cut the bullshit."

"But you were decorated in Korea," Pretier said, genuinely surprised. "Several times decorated. And promoted."

"That was before I fucked up," Lowell said, helping himself to more cognac.

"What did you do?"

"You are looking, Andre," Lowell said, making a mock bow, "at one of the few, perhaps the only, soldier in Korea who got into a sexual scandal with a white woman."

"I am *not* surprised," Pretier said, trying to make a joke of it.

"The establishment was almost as pissed about that as they were when I stood up in a court-martial and announced, under oath, that I could see a situation in combat where an officer has the duty to blow away another officer who is not doing his duty."

Andre Pretier looked at Sanford Felter again, and again got confirmation from the pained look on his face that Lowell was telling the truth.

"Who was the woman?" Pretier asked, choosing, he hoped, the least delicate of the two subjects.

"Georgia Paige," Lowell said.

"The actress?" Pretier asked. "The one who . . ."

"Goes without a bra?" Lowell filled in for him. "Yes, indeed, *that* Georgia Paige."

"And that is what you were doing in Los Angeles when you first came back?" Pretier asked.

"It didn't take long," Lowell said, bitterly, "for it to become painfully apparent that Georgia and I, to coin a phrase, were simply ships that had passed in the night."

"What happened, Craig?" Felter asked, and it was a demand for information from a friend that could not be denied.

Lowell didn't reply immediately. Felter wondered if he was thinking over his reply, or deciding whether or not to reply at all.

"We hit it off pretty good in Korea," Lowell said.

"How did you arrange that? In Korea, I mean?" Felter asked.

"I think she was carried away with the warrior image," Lowell said. "I showed her my tank, and that seemed to excite her."

"Come on!"

"Scout's honor, Mouse. That's where it happened. Some of the 'immature judgment' my efficiency report talks about was taking her up to the line, to my old outfit."

"That *was* immature," Felter said. "Also stupid."

"Be that as it may, it excited the lady," Lowell said. "And true and undying passion burst into flower. And I returned to the ZI full of youthful dreams. I would pick her up in L.A., and I would fly off to romantic Germany with her, where she would instantly form a fond attachment to my son. We would thereupon start looking for a small house by the side of the road, where we could be friends to man and start making babies."

"What happened?"

"For one thing, she was making a movie and couldn't get away for six weeks, and then when the subject of Peter-Paul came up, she said, 'Oh, yeah. Your kid. I forgot about that.' "

"Oh," Sandy Felter said, sympathetically.

"I began to wonder if she would really make the loving stepmother I believed she would," Lowell said. "Ah, shit, what's the difference?"

"Did she know you're rich?" Felter asked.

"We rich say 'well off,' Mouse," Lowell said.

Felter decided he was onto something.

"She wanted you to get out of the army, and you wouldn't do it?" he asked.

"We didn't get that far," Lowell said.

"But she knew you were 'well-off'?"

"I don't really know. She knew, of course, that I had some clout out there in movieland. The firm, by an interesting coincidence, was financing her movie. If we hadn't been, I don't think I would have been allowed near her. Christ, I had to pull in all the clout I had to get in touch with her. But that wasn't it, one way or the other. What it was was that I was such a goddamned fool that I mistook a marvelous piece of tail for love."

"I'm sorry, Craig," Felter said.

"I thought all my problems were over when Bellmon called me . . . oops, that slipped out, didn't it? . . . and told me you had gone to a hero's grave in far-off Indo-China. After a suitable period, as short as possible, I would marry Sharon, and all of my problems would be solved."

"I'm sorry to disappoint you," Felter said.

"Next time, don't get my hopes up," Lowell said. "Next time, stay dead."

"Somebody will come along, Craig," Felter said. "Aside from your morals, you're every maiden's dream."

"I know, I know," Lowell said. "But it embarrasses me so when they get on their knees and start kissing my hand."

"He's right, Craig," Andre Pretier said. "You'll find someone."

"I don't really think I want to," Lowell said. And then, quickly: "For Christ's sake. Let's start telling dirty jokes or something."

[TWO]
Aviation Detachment
Headquarters, Seventh United States Army
Augsburg, Germany
15 April 1954

Lieutenant Colonel Ford W. Davis, Commanding, Aviation Detachment, Headquarters, Seventh Army, happened to be in the outer office of the detachment when the civilian walked in. He was curious to the point of being annoyed. He didn't like what he saw.

The civilian was dressed in a mussed sports coat, and gray flannel slacks, a civilian-model trench coat hung over his shoulders. There was a silk foulard in the open collar of his white button-down-collar shirt.

A reporter, Colonel Davis decided. Probably an American, probably from the *Munich American*, a tabloid published by a bunch of wise-ass ex-GIs, catering to the enlisted men, a bunch of goddamned troublemakers always looking for a story that made the army generally, and the officer corps specifically, look bad.

Colonel Davis laid the file he had been reading on top of the file cabinet and walked over to where the civilian was talking to the sergeant major.

"What's going on?" Colonel Davis asked.

"This officer is reporting in early from delay-en-route leave, Colonel."

Davis looked at him. Colonel Davis was suspicious of tall, handsome men, particularly the kind that wore scarves around their necks and trench coats over their shoulders. The officer came to something like attention.

"Actually, sir," the handsome young man in the movie actor costume said, "I'm not coming off leave. I'd hoped to be able to get a PX card."

"When are you due off leave?"

"My orders call for me to report to Camp Kilmer 20 April, sir," he said.

"Then what are you doing here now?"

"I was married to a German, sir," the officer said. "I have a son here."

"How'd you get here?"

"I came commercial, sir."

Davis put everything together. As a general rule of thumb, only German whores married Americans. Officers did not marry whores. Not officers with any smarts. So what this young buck had done was marry a kraut whore, and he was smart enough to realize that meant he had ruined his career. What officers who fucked up their careers in their branch of service did was apply for flight school.

Colonel Davis was a career soldier, out of Texas A&M into the artillery. He had gone to flight school as an artilleryman in War II, when the primary function of army aviation was artillery fire direction, using Piper Cubs as airborne forward observation posts. In those days, there had been an "L" superimposed on pilot's wings, to differentiate between "liaison" pilots flying Cubs and "real pilots." Colonel Davis had been a liaison pilot in those days.

He'd stayed an army aviator, not because he was a fuckup, but because he and a tiny clique of others saw the future role of light aircraft in the army. The air force, when it had become a separate branch of the armed services, had made it clear they weren't going to bother giving the army what aerial services it would need. They were going to fight the next war with nuclear weapons dropped from 40,000 feet; with fighter planes flying at twice the speed of sound; with rockets, for Christ's sake, from space. They were not going to waste their time fucking around with the guys in the mud on the ground.

The army was going to have to have its own aerial capability, not only artillery direction and liaison—messenger—flights, but medical evacuation, probably by helicopter (Korea had proved that theory) and, eventually, an aerial transport capability in the fifty miles behind the front lines. What the army really needed was its own close support aircraft, low and slow and near the ground. They were a long way from that, but Colonel Davis believed that, too, would come in time.

He had stayed in army aviation because he believed in it.

And because he was a professional soldier, he had looked for and found the weaknesses in army aviation. If you don't know what's wrong, you can't fix it. He was sure he had found the greatest weakness in army aviation, but he had no idea how to fix it.

The weakness could be described simply: the officer corps of army aviation, like Ivory soap, was 99 44/100 percent pure incompetents, malcontents, ne'er-do-wells, and fuck-ups. Instead of throwing the incompetents out of the army, they were allowed to go to flight school. There was no question, looking at Handsome Harry standing here before him with a goddamned silk scarf wrapped around his throat, trying to look like Errol Flynn, that he was about to get one more fuck-up that nobody else in the army wanted, an officer so goddamned dumb that he had married a kraut whore.

"I don't know what you expected to find here," Colonel Davis said, icily. "But this is a military organization, and we expect that when newly assigned officers report for duty, they do so in keeping with the customs of the service. That is to say, in uniform."

"Yes, sir," Handsome Harry said.

"The sergeant here will sign you in," Colonel Davis said. "And see that you're installed in the bachelor officer's quarters. I did hear you use the past tense in reference to your marriage, didn't I?"

"Yes, sir."

"And then you will present yourself here in uniform and report for duty. Clear?"

"Yes, sir."

"You've given the sergeant major a copy of your orders?"

"Yes, sir."

"When you're through with them, Morgan, bring them in to me," Colonel Davis said, and then he turned away and walked into his office.

As he closed the door, he heard Handsome Harry say, his voice amused, "That, Sergeant, is what is known as starting off on the wrong foot."

Wise-ass prick thought it was funny, did he? He'd straighten his ass out in a hurry.

The first occasion Colonel Davis had to consider that perhaps he had made an error in his snap judgment of Handsome Harry was when the sergeant major came into his office a few minutes later and laid a battered, creased copy of Handsome Harry's orders on his desk. Colonel Davis glanced at them quickly, and then looked more closely.

"A *major?"* he said. "A *regular army* major? He doesn't look old enough to be a captain. And regular army?"

"No, sir," the sergeant major agreed. "He doesn't."

"Do we have his service record?"

"No, sir. It must be on the way. He wasn't due to report to Camp Kilmer until 20 April."

Colonel Davis looked at Handsome Harry's orders again, reading them carefully this time, to see what they could tell him.

HEADQUARTERS
THE U.S. ARMY ARTILLERY SCHOOL
FORT SILL, OKLAHOMA

SPECIAL ORDERS
NUMBER 87 20 March 1954

EXTRACT

****

31. MAJ Craig W. LOWELL, 0439067, ARMOR Student Off Det, Avn Sec, The Arty Sch, having successfully completed the prescribed course of instruction, and having graduated from Rotary Wing Aviator's Course 54-6, The Arty Sch, is designated an army aviator, effective 20 Mar 54. (H-13 and H-23 aircraft only).

32. MAJ Craig W. LOWELL, 0439067, ARMOR, is awarded Primary MOS 1707 (Army Aviator, Rotary Wing only) eff 20 Mar 54.

33. MAJ Craig W. LOWELL, 0439067, ARMOR MOS 1707 Stu Off Det, Avn Sec, The Arty Sch, is relvd prsnt asgmt, trfd and WP Hq US 7th Army APO 709 c/o Postmaster, NY, NY, for further asgmt with Avn Sec ARMY SEVEN as RW Aviator. Auth: TWX Hq DA Subj: Initial utilization assgmt newly designated RW Aviators dtd 3 Jan 54. Off will report in uniform NLT 2330 hrs 20 Apr 54 to USA Personnel Cntr, Cp Kilmer, NJ, for further shpmnt to US Army Europe via mil sea transport. Off auth thirty (30) Days Delay En Route Lv. Home of Record: Broadlawns, Glen Cove, Long Island, NY. Off auth trans of household goods and personal auto at Govt expense. Permanent Change of Station. Effective date change Morning Report 20 Apr 54. Tvl & mvmnt household goods and personal auto deemed nec in govt interest. Approp: S-99-999-9999.

****

EXTRACT

BY COMMAND OF
MAJ GEN YEAGER

OFFICIAL
Peter O. Romano
Captain, AGC
Asst Adjutant

Jerome T. Waller
Colonel, AGC
Adjutant General

All that Major Lowell's orders told Lieutenant Colonel Davis was that Lowell was a just-graduated chopper pilot. But between the lines, Davis could read that he was a fuck-up. Majors didn't go to army aviation unless they had fucked up by the numbers. What piqued Davis's curiosity was Lowell's rank, and his regular army status. He didn't seem old enough to be a major, and Davis would have given odds that he wasn't West Point, or one of the other trade schools, A&M, the Citadel, VMI. Maybe Norwich. Probably Norwich. He was Armor, and Norwich turned out large numbers of RA tankers.

Two hours later, the sergeant major announced Major Lowell.

"Send him in," Davis said.

Major Lowell marched into Lieutenant Colonel Davis's office. He stopped three feet from Davis's desk, raised his hand in a crisp salute, and announced:

"Major C. W. Lowell reporting for duty, sir."

Lieutenant Colonel Davis returned the salute.

"Stand at ease, Major," he said. Lowell assumed a position closer to "parade rest" than "at ease." He met Davis's eyes. At "parade rest" he would have looked six inches over Davis's head.

He was in a Class "A" uniform, "pinks and greens," a green tunic and pink trousers. The uniform, Davis saw, had not come off a rack in an officer's sales store. The fit was impeccable. Obviously tailor-made. Obviously expensive. But what impressed Lt. Col. Davis was the fruit salad.

Above Major Lowell's breast pocket was an Expert Combat Infantry Badge, a silver flintlock on a blue background, with wreath. A star between the open ends of the wreath indicated the second award of the CIB. Major Lowell had been to war, twice. Davis decided that he was obviously a good deal older than he looked, some freak skin and muscle condition that made him look twenty-four, twenty-five years old. Sewn to one shoulder of his tunic was the insignia of the Artillery School. Sewn to the other was a triangular Armored Force patch with the numerals 73. There was no armored division numbered as high as 73, so it must be one of the separate battalions. Davis recalled that a separate armored battalion had made the breakout from Pusan in the opening months of the Korean War.

That tied in with some of the fruit salad: UN Service Medal; Korean Service Medal, with three campaign stars; and the Korean (as well as American) Presidential Unit Citations worn over the other tunic pocket.

Immediately below the CIB were aviator's wings, obviously brand new. Below the wings were his medals. Distinguished Service Cross. That was the nation's second highest award for gallantry in action. He also had the Distinguished Service Medal. And the Silver Star with an oak leaf cluster signifying a second award. And a Bronze Star with "V" device, signifying that it had been awarded for valor. Two oak leaves on that. Did that mean he had four Bronze Stars or just three? Davis wasn't sure if they gave second "V" devices for second valorous awards. Purple Heart with three clusters. Wounded four times. Then there were ribbons signifying foreign decorations, four of those, and then the World War II Victory Medal (which didn't mean he had actually been in World War II; that hadn't been declared over until late in 1946, and if you were in the service then, you got the medal) and the Army of Occupation Medal (Germany).

They were very careful about how they passed out the DSC.

"I don't recognize some of those, Major," Lt. Col. Davis said.

Major Lowell said nothing.

"What are the foreign decorations, Major?" Davis asked, a somewhat menacing tone in his voice. "Korean?"

"Three of them are, sir."

"Tell me about them," Davis said.

Lowell bent his head and pointed to the medals. "This is the Order of St. George and St. Andrew," he said.

"Korean?" Lt. Col. Davis asked, a challenge.

"Greek, sir," Lowell said. "And this is the Korean Distinguished Service Cross, the Korean Military Medal, and the Tae Guk, which is the same as our DSM."

"If it was your intention, Major," Lt. Col. Davis said, "to dazzle me with your fruit salad, you have succeeded."

"Sir, regulations stipulate that decorations will be worn when reporting for duty in garrison."

"I didn't know that," Davis said, coldly. Lowell did not reply.

"How do you plan to handle it, Major," Davis asked, "when Camp Kilmer reports you AWOL as of 20 April?"

"Sir, I spoke with the AC of S, Personnel, a Colonel Gray, who informed me that a TWX from my receiving organization would clear that up."

"And you expect to be reimbursed for your commercial travel here?"

"No, sir."

"And you hoped to be continued on leave here in Germany, is that it?"

"Yes, sir."

"You made a mistake reporting in, Major," Lt. Colonel Davis said. "I'm very short of chopper pilots, even ones fresh from flight school. I am going to have to put you right to work."

"Yes, sir," Major Lowell said, immediately. That was the first thing Major Lowell had done of which Lt. Col. Davis approved. He had expected at the very least a delay while Lowell thought that over, and at worst a recitation of tragic facts that made his being on leave a humanitarian necessity. Lowell hadn't blinked an eye.

"You were with the 73rd Armor in Korea?"

"73rd Heavy Tank," Lowell said, making the correction. "Yes, sir."

"They were involved in the breakout from the Pusan perimeter?"

"Yes, sir."

"Were you with them, then?"

"Yes, sir."

"Tell me something, Major," Lt. Col. Davis asked, with deceptive innocence, "what is a regular army Major with nearly as much fruit salad as George Patton doing flying a chopper?"

Lowell met his eyes, and there was a pause before he replied.

"I came to the conclusion, sir, that my future as an armor officer was going to be less than I hoped."

"Fucked up, did you?"

"Yes, sir."

"And it was reflected on your efficiency report?"

"Yes, sir."

"And it was either into army aviation or out of the army?"

"Very nearly, sir."

"How much service do you have? Until you have your twenty years, I mean?"

"I've got five years and some months of active duty service, sir."

"You made major in five years?" Davis asked, disbelievingly.

"I was out for two years, sir. From 1948 until 1950. I was recalled for the Korean War."

"How old are you, Lowell?" Davis asked.

"Twenty-six, sir."

"And at twenty-six, you have had time to make major and then fuck up by the numbers?"

"That would seem to sum it up nicely, yes, sir."

"You say you have a son?"

"Yes, sir."

"Living with his mother here in Germany?"

"His mother is dead, sir. He lives with his mother's family."

"Do you think your responsibility toward your son is going to interfere with the performance of your duties here?"

"No, sir."

"See that it doesn't," Davis said. "I am one of those old-fashioned soldiers who believes that an officer's primary responsibility is to his duty. Those with personal problems which interfere with their duties should get out of the army."

"Yes, sir."

"You understand your position here, Major?" Davis asked, and went on without waiting for a reply. "You're on an initial utilization tour. The primary purpose of such a tour is to build up your flying time. By and large, you will be treated exactly as if you were a warrant officer or a second lieutenant. Your rank, during your initial utilization tour, is not going to buy you any privileges. You understand that?"

"Yes, sir."

"I'm going to send you down to Lieutenant Colonel Withers, who has the Rotary Wing Special Missions Branch," Colonel Davis said. "Read VIP."

"Yes, sir."

"Colonel Withers will teach you how to fly our way," Davis went on. "And after a long while, he might even let you fly passengers. Unimportant ones. Not the brass. The aides."

Lowell smiled and said, "Yes, sir."

"There is one thing you fuck-ups get when you come to army aviation," Colonel Davis said. "A clean slate. So far as I'm concerned, Major Lowell, your slate is clean. But the other side of that coin is that I dislike people who come to aviation because it's their last chance."

"Yes, sir," Lowell said.

"I'll certainly see you around, Lowell," Davis said. He got up and put out his hand. "You may consider yourself officially welcomed to the Seventh Army Flight Detachment."

"Yes, sir. Thank you, sir."

"You're dismissed, Major."

Lowell looked askance at him.

"Something?"

"It would help, sir, if I knew where to report to Colonel Withers."

Davis had forgotten the little ploy he'd made about needing chopper pilots so badly that Lowell would not get the rest of his leave.

"How much time, minimum, would you require to get your personal affairs straightened out?" he asked.

"My son is in Marburg, sir," Lowell said. "A day up there, a day there, and a day back. Three days."

"Take it as VOCO," Davis said. "Then it won't be charged as leave. And while you're gone, I'll speak to Colonel Withers. Maybe after we get you checked out in the local area, we can work a week or ten days' leave in."

"Thank you, sir," Lowell said. He saluted, did an about-face, and walked out of the office.

Davis wondered for a moment what Lowell had done to fuck up, and then put him out of his mind. He would make up his mind whether he was a Class "A" fuck-up (unsalvageable), or a Class "B" (just another mediocrity who had a bad efficiency report), or a Class "C" (salvageable and of potential use to army aviation in the future), after he'd read his service record and made some inquiries on his own.

It was not necessary for Colonel Davis to do the latter. The day after Major Lowell had reported for duty, Colonel Davis got a letter from the man recognized by the small group of professional soldiers in army aviation as the President.

The tiny nucleus of army aviators who were interested in more than getting their twenty years in for retirement were generally regarded with disdain by the others. They called them the Cincinnati Flying Club, a derogatory reference to the Society of the Cincinnati, membership in which was limited to descendants of officers who had served under George Washington in the Revolution. Lt. Colonel William R. Roberts, USMA '40, a graduate of the first class of liaison pilots ever trained. ("The Class Before One") was known, affectionately or disparagingly, depending on who was talking, as "the President of the Cincinnati Flying Club."

PO Box 334
Fort Sill, Okla.
20 March 1954

Dear Ford:

I have arranged to have sent to you one Major Craig W. Lowell, who graduated, barely (he is not a natural pilot) from RW 54-6 today. I personally don't like him, but in our present personnel situation, and because of considerable pressure applied to me by, among others, Bob Bellmon, I decided he's worth the risk.

In the opening days of the Korean War, Lowell, then a recalled National Guard captain, led the breakout from Pusan after the Inchon invasion. He's the Lowell of Task Force Lowell. It got him a major's leaf at twenty-two, and he subsequently covered himself with glory and medals in the dash to the Yalu and the withdrawal from Hamhung. Paul Jiggs, who commanded the 73rd, and who was last week given his first star, swears he is a splendid combat commander, and the best plans and training man—and oh, God, how we need them—he has ever known.

The bad news is that he has, Bellmon informs me, an efficiency report as bad as he's ever seen. He is on the s—tlist for two things: not recommended for combat command and lack of judgment.

The first thing that has him in trouble was standing up in a court-martial and announcing that he could see nothing wrong with an officer executing on the spot another officer who didn't measure up in combat. The accused in the trial was a young, Negro, Norwich-type captain who was accused of murdering an allegedly cowardly-in-the-face-of-the-enemy officer in the Pusan perimeter, and then turning his own tank cannon on another yellow one during the move up the peninsula. The connection becomes involved because he's Norwich, and because his father, Colonel Philip Sheridan Parker III, retired, commanded the task force from Porky Waterford's Hell's Circus which snatched Bellmon back from the Russians in the closing days of World War II.

Young Parker, incidentally, "volunteered" for aviation the same day Lowell did, and graduated with him. He has been assigned to Alaska, which is as far apart as I could arrange to have them separated.

The second thing that has Lowell on the spot is the scandal

he caused by taking Georgia Paige (the actress who doesn't wear a brassiere) up to the front when she was here with a USO troupe. Photos got out. The story is that Lowell was carrying on with her whenever they could find a horizontal place.

In any event, Lowell was assigned as an assistant professor of military science at Bordentown Military School, and Parker was assistant housing officer at Fort Devens. These are the sort of people from whom we must recruit.

One more thing about Lowell: he is obscenely rich, by inheritance, and has considerable influence in the Congress.

Further interconnection: Bellmon believes that the reason he is not at this moment among the missing in Siberia is because of the decent behavior, at considerable risk to himself, of the officer commanding the stalag. Our man Lowell, when he was in Germany early-on, married a German lady who turned out to be the daughter of Colonel Count Peter-Paul von Greiffenberg, who was at the time cutting down trees for the Russians in Siberia.

The count was released by the Russians in 1950, just in time to meet Lowell before he was sent to Korea. Lowell was in Korea about four months when a drunken quartermaster major (U.S.) ran into her car near Giessen and killed her. The boy is being raised by his grandfather. Grandfather is now Generalmajor von Greiffenberg of the Bundeswehr. Deputy Chief of Intelligence.

All of these details, Ford, so that you'll be aware of what we have in Lowell (and to a lesser degree in Parker). The potential to do us enormous good is there, but so is the potential for damage. My gut feeling is that if the trouble he's just been through hasn't taught him his lesson, we should get rid of him quickly and permanently, even if this enrages the armor establishment. It puts a heavy burden on you, and I'm sorry, but that's the way it is.

It will be announced in the next week or so that Camp Rucker, in Alabama, will be reactivated and designated the Army Aviation School. I have been there. There is one dirt strip, last used during War II as an auxiliary field by the air force. Whatever we need we'll have to build ourselves, which means begging for money. *But at least we have our own base!*

What we need are some senior people, for the next couple of years. I try hard, but evangelism doesn't seem down my alley.

Helen sends love to you and Betty.

Always, Old Buddy,

Bill

P.S.: In case you didn't notice, I was #34 (of 36) on the last colonel's list. I think that it should come through (in eight or nine months) in time so that the eagle will qualify me to take over the Aviation Board, which will be among the first activities opened at Camp Rucker.

Lieutenant Colonel Davis had indeed noticed the name of Lt. Col. William Roberts on the colonel's promotion list. His own name had been conspicuously absent. The fact that Bill Roberts was on it might be significant. And it might not. Roberts was West Point. His promotion might be because of the West Point Protective Association, which took care of its own, even the mad-eyed radicals of army aviation. But it *might* be because somebody in the Pentagon appreciated what he had done in the past, and what he might do in the future.

Davis wished that he had known about Lowell before he had assigned him to Withers. Withers had been a horse's ass even before he had discovered Jesus Christ as his personal savior at age forty-four, and what he was now was a religious fanatic. It would have been better to have kept Lowell closer to home, where he could be watched, and perhaps, if he turned out, taught something, perhaps even converted to the One True Faith. But it was too late now. And maybe what Lowell needed was a CO washed in the blood of the lamb.

[THREE]
Marburg an der Lahn, West Germany
15 April 1954

The major domo at Schloss Greiffenberg (it was more of a villa than a castle, having been built in 1818, after improvements in the tools of warfare had rendered battlements and moats obsolete; but a Graf doesn't live in a villa, he lives in a Schloss) was new and didn't know Lowell, and was unimpressed when Lowell told him who he was. He left him outside, with the door closed in his face, with the announcement he would "make inquiries."

A woman opened the door. An attractive, prematurely grayhaired woman who smiled and put out her hand, and spoke to him in English.

"My dear Major Lowell, you will have to forgive us. All Peter-Paul's man said was that 'there was an American at the door.' Please come in."

"Thank you," he said.

"Peter-Paul didn't expect you until next month," she said, and then she raised her voice, and called in German, "Liebchen, your Papa is here!"

Her voice was considerably less pleasant when she spoke to the major domo.

"Put Major Lowell's things in the room next to the child's, and the next time, don't be such a stupid ass. This American is the child's father."

She doesn't, Lowell realized, understand that I speak German. That could be interesting, or amusing.

The child didn't come. They had to go find him. Then he hid behind the woman's skirts.

"He's not used to you," she said.

Peter-Paul Lowell had been born in 1947. That made him seven, his father decided, a little old to be hiding behind a woman's skirts. Or is it that I am so formidable a figure?

"What do you say, Squirt?" he said.

The child didn't reply.

"I think, if I may say so," the woman said, "that it would be best to leave him alone. He has the von Greiffenberg hard-head."

"There's some Lowell in him, too," Lowell said. "Well, to hell with him. If he doesn't want the guns, I'll just give them to somebody else."

"What guns?" the boy said.

"It can talk, you see?" Lowell said. "The guns in the brown bag. The man took it upstairs to my room."

The boy fled the room.

"Major," the woman said. "Forgive me. What can I offer you to drink?"

"Scotch, please," he said.

"I think there's a little left," she said. "Peter-Paul has been waiting for you to come so that he can get you to buy liquor from the army."

"I didn't think to bring any," Lowell said. "And you forgot to tell me who you are?"

"Oh, just another of the displaced relatives Peter-Paul has taken in," she said. "This one from Pomerania. I'm Elizabeth von Heuffinger-Lodz. The countess and my mother were sisters."

I'll bet, Lowell thought, that there's a title that goes with that.

"As you gather, I'm the child's father," he said. "My name is Craig."

She shook his hand again.

I'd like to screw her, he thought, and then he wondered why that thought had suddenly popped into his mind. That would really be a goddamned dumb thing to do, even if she was interested, and there was no reason to suspect she would be.

Peter-Paul Lowell, P. P., came into the room as she handed Craig Lowell a drink. He had on a cowboy hat, a vest, a pair of chaps, on backward, a gun belt, and two enormous sixshooter cap pistols.

"You have your chaps on backward," Craig said.

"Excuse me?"

The European accent and the European manners of the boy made the father sad. He took a large swallow of the weak drink, and then dropped to his knees to show his son how a cowboy wore his chaps.

When he looked up at the woman, he saw her eyes on him. He had the feeling that she was surprised about him, for some reason. She probably expected me to come in here wearing Bermuda shorts, knee socks, and chewing gum, he thought.

[ONE]
The Pentagon
Washington, D.C.
15 May 1954

Major Rudolph G. MacMillan, wearing his pinks and greens with all his ribbons and overseas bars and the unit shoulder insignia of both the Armored Center (where he was presently assigned) and the 82nd Airborne Division (his most significant World War II assignment), very carefully opened the door of the men's room cubicle a crack and peered out. Then he closed the door carefully and slid the lock in place. A colonel had come in, one he didn't know, and he wasn't waiting for him.

Major MacMillan was off limits. The men's room in which he sat, trousers up, was a senior officer's latrine, reserved for colonels and better. Lieutenant colonels down to second lieutenants had their own latrines and the enlisted men had theirs.

MacMillan hated the Pentagon, and Pentagon types hated MacMillan types, as company clerks hated squad corporals. But squad corporals could take company clerks out behind the PX beer hall, or waylay them on their way home from the service club and kick the shit out of them when they misused their typewriters.

Corporal Rudolph G. MacMillan had kicked the shit out of a company clerk at Fort Benning in '41 for making a "clerical error" on his service record that kept him from getting the three stripes of a buck sergeant. And the company clerk had told the first sergeant, and the first sergeant had hauled him before the company commander, and both the company clerk and the first sergeant had been sure that he was going to come out of the company commander's office with bare sleeves, and with a little bit of luck, under arrest pending court-martial. But he had had his facts straight then, and he'd come out of the company commander's office as Sergeant MacMillan.

The company commander had made his decision, as Corporal MacMillan had bet his life he would, not so much on fairness, but on what was best for the company. What was right counted, but what *really* counted was what was best for the company.

What Major MacMillan was betting his life on now was the accuracy of his perception that the Pentagon was nothing more than an oversized orderly room. The majors and lieutenant colonels were company clerks who used their typewriters with far greater subtlety when they wanted to screw one of the field troops, and you couldn't grab one of the bastards by his shirt collar and bloody his nose. But a good soldier could still lay the facts out before the company commander, and if he had his facts straight, and what he proposed was good for the army, the Old Man, even if he wore the stars of a general officer instead of a captain's railroad tracks, would do what was best for the outfit.

The hydraulic door-closer whooshed again, and MacMillan cracked open the door of his cubicle again. A lieutenant general walked into the latrine and headed for the urinals, his hand dropping to part his tunic, to get at his zipper.

Major MacMillan pushed open the door of his cubicle and walked to the adjacent urinal. The general glanced at him casually, looked away, and then looked back.

"I'll be damned," the Deputy Chief of Staff for Operations of the United States Army said, shaking himself, tucking himself in, zipping himself up. "Mac MacMillan. How the hell are you, Mac?"

"A little nervous, General," MacMillan said.

"How so?"

They were shaking hands.

"I just punched a company clerk in the mouth, General," MacMillan said.

The general laughed.

"That was a long time ago, Mac. God, that was a long time ago."

"This was another company clerk, General," MacMillan said. "This one is a colonel."

"You're in trouble, Mac?" the general asked, seriously now.

"That'll be up to you, General."

"You didn't really punch . . . ?" the general asked. With MacMillan, the question had to be asked, and not only because when the general had first met Corporal MacMillan, Mac had been about to try out for the post boxing team.

"Figuratively speaking, of course, General," MacMillan said. "The way a major punches a colonel is to wait in a latrine for the general after the colonel has made it quite plain that the colonel has made up his mind and doesn't want to hear any more discussion of an issue. After the colonel has made it an order that I am not to bother the general."

"All you have to do, Mac, to talk to me, anytime, is to call me at the house."

"I'm not here as your friend, sir. I'm here as an officer."

The general's face suddenly turned stern. "If we weren't friends, Mac, I would ask you what the hell you're doing in the senior officer's crapper."

"General, the major requests fifteen minutes of the general's time."

"I heard you were being assigned," the general said. "Hell, I arranged it, Mac. You don't like your assignment, is that it? You don't want . . ."

"I'm a soldier, General. I go where I'm sent and do the best I can when I get there."

"Then what is it? I thought you'd be glad not to have to work here."

"Sir, the general, in my opinion, has made a mistake in setting that whole aviation development operation up the way he has," Major MacMillan said.

"Major," the general said, "I am now going back to my office. I will inform my secretary that I have given you an appointment—" he stopped and looked at his watch—"for fifteen minutes at 11:30. I will hear your arguments. Inasmuch as I made the decisions I have made on the advice of Colonel Gregory, I will ask Colonel Gregory to join us."

"Yes, sir. Thank you, sir."

"Or, after pointing out to you that Colonel Gregory will be your efficiency report rating officer, I will completely forget we ever had this little chat."

"Sir, I will be there at half past eleven."

At 11:28, Major MacMillan walked into the outer office of the Office of the Deputy Chief of Staff for Operations and told the receptionist that he had an appointment with the DCSOPS at 11:30.

It is said that the DCSOPS is the man who actually runs the army. Legally, he is coequal with the other deputies to the Army Chief of Staff—DCSPERS (Personnel), DCSLOG (Logistics), and DCSINT (Intelligence)—but as a practical matter, he is the one who makes the recommendations to the Chief of Staff (rarely overturned) about where and when and how the army will fight. Intelligence will tell him about the enemy; personnel will tell him how many troops he can have, and logistics will tell him about supplies. He adds these things up, and decides, taking into consideration the probable intentions and capabilities of the enemy, where to send the troops and their logistical support.

In peacetime, he decides whether the army needs tanks more than artillery, communications more than tanks, or, recently, whether the army needed an air mobility capability more than the tanks and cannon and rifles that armor, artillery, and infantry were screaming for.

When Major Mac MacMillan was shown into the inner office, both Colonel Arthur Gregory, Chief, Aviation Branch, DCSOPS, and Brigadier General Howard Kellogg, Assistant DCSOPS, were already there, sitting, the width of a cushion between them, on a red leather couch against the wall.

"Sir," Major Mac MacMillan snapped, bringing his stocky, barrel-chested body to rigid attention, "Major R. G. MacMillan reporting as ordered, sir."

The DCSOPS returned the salute with a casual wave of the hand.

"Stand at ease, Major," he said. "You know these gentlemen, I believe. You have fifteen minutes."

"With your permission, General," MacMillan said, and walked to the coffee table before the couch. He had a briefcase in his hand. Such had been his parade ground behavior and posture that none of the three officers noticed it until he set it on the floor and began to neatly lay papers from it in stacks on the table.

"Sir," he said, and both the Assistant DCSOPS and the Chief, Aviation Branch,

DCSOPS, noticed his use of the singular "Sir" instead of "Gentlemen." MacMillan was making his pitch to the DCSOPS, not to them. That violated the rules. But the DCSOPS was going along with him. It was going to be the Assistant DCSOPS and the Chief, Aviation Branch, DCSOPS, *vs.* Major MacMillan, with the DCSOPS himself hearing the case without a jury. God *damn* MacMillan! Medal or no goddamned medal, that was going too far.

"Sir," MacMillan said, "I am under orders to report to the president of the Airborne Board, Fort Benning, Georgia, for duty as liaison between the Aviation Section of the Airborne Board and DCSOPS."

"We know that, MacMillan," the Assistant DCSOPS said. MacMillan acted as if he hadn't heard him.

"In a very short time," he went on, "the Aviation Section of the Airborne Board will become the Aviation Board, shortly after the reactivation of Fort Rucker, Alabama. Aviation testing and development will then report directly to you, sir, rather than through the Airborne and Artillery Boards."

"We know all that," the Assistant DCSOPS said. "What I don't understand is why we're discussing this with you."

"And that's *Camp* Rucker, MacMillan," the Chief, Aviation Branch, said. "And I was under the impression that whole business was classified. What was your right to know?"

"Let him talk," the DCSOPS said.

"I will then become the liaison officer between the Army Aviation Board and the DCSOPS," MacMillan said. "In other words between army aviation and the army."

"Army aviation is a concept, not a branch of service, Major," the Assistant DCSOPS said.

"Yes, sir," MacMillan said. "That's my point."

"Your point then," the aviation officer said, sarcastically, "is lost on me."

"Let's hear him out," the DCSOPS said, somewhat icily.

"My efficiency report will be written by the president of the Aviation Board, and endorsed by Colonel Gregory," MacMillan said. "Whatever information you get up here will come from the president of the Aviation Board via Colonel Gregory."

"Have you a better suggestion?" Gregory asked, sarcastically.

"What's wrong with that, Mac?" the DCSOPS asked. He wasn't overly impressed with MacMillan's intellectual ability, but he knew that MacMillan knew what he was risking by coming here the way he had. MacMillan had paid his dues, the Medal aside, and he was entitled to a full, fair hearing before he paid the price. It had already become apparent to the DCSOPS that he could no longer be assigned to the Aviation Board; MacMillan had already burned that bridge.

"Both Bill Roberts and Colonel Gregory are members of the Cincinnati Flying Club," MacMillan said.

"You refer, I'm sure, to *Colonel* William Roberts," Colonel Gregory said, fury in his voice.

"The Cincinnati Flying Club?" the DCSOPS asked. "What the hell is that?"

"The old-timers, the *establishment* old-timers. They think army aviation belongs to them."

"Define establishment," the DCSOPS said.

"Regulars who stand a chance to make general," MacMillan said. "The WPPA. People like that."

The Association of Graduates and Former Cadets of the United States Military Academy at West Point was widely referred to throughout the army, by officers who had not been privileged to attend that school, as the West Point Protective Association, or WPPA. This appellation was disliked by members of the WPPA.

"I resent that, Major," Colonel Gregory said. "I deeply resent that."

"Make your point, Mac," the DCSOPS said. He now deeply regretted stopping in for a quick leak in the colonel's can. He had a private pisser in his office and he should have used it. He wondered for the first time how long MacMillan had stalked him in there. All morning, certainly. Maybe all week.

"The only information you're going to get, General," MacMillan said, "will be what the Cincinnati Flying Club wants you to hear."

"That's slanderous and insulting!" Colonel Gregory flared.

"Shall I stop, sir?" MacMillan asked.

"No, go on, Mac," the DCSOPS said. "You've already dug your grave. You might as well jump right in."

"Sir, you would be making a mistake to turn army aviation over to the Cincinnati Flying Club."

"MacMillan, I've heard about all I intend to take about the so-called Cincinnati Flying Club," Colonel Gregory said. MacMillan ignored him again.

"You need a separate outfit down there, General," MacMillan said. "Separate from the Aviation Board, separate from the Flying Club. Otherwise, the Flying Club will see that their guys get the command assignments, their projects get the money, and their ideas about how to use aircraft to support the ground troops get to be doctrine and get printed as field manuals."

There was silence for a long moment in the room. The DCSOPS knew that neither Gregory or his own Assistant DCSOPS would be able to let that accusation pass without rebuttal. He wondered what form it would take.

"A special unit, commanded, no doubt, by you?" the Assistant DCSOPS asked, sarcastically.

Ignore it, it'll go away. Ridicule it, it'll be ignored. Not bad, the DCSOPS thought, but it won't wash.

"By Bob Bellmon," MacMillan responded. "Or somebody like him. Somebody who's not artillery. Who's not in the Flying Club. But somebody who's also in the WPPA."

"Bob Bellmon's not even an aviator," the Assistant DCSOPS said, disgust in his voice. "And I resent, Major, your constant and insulting references to a West Point Protective Association."

"I could teach him, or anyone else, how to fly in a month," MacMillan said. "Flying's not as mysterious as some people would have you believe."

"Mac," the DCSOPS said, "you're going off half cocked. "You haven't thought this through."

"Yes, sir, I have," MacMillan said. "What we need down there is a Class II Activity of DCSOPS, maybe called 'Combat Developments.' Here it is."

A Class II Activity is an army unit stationed on a military post, which is not subordinate to the post commander, but instead to another—usually higher—headquarters. Hospitals, for example, "belong" to the Surgeon General, not to the commanding general of the post where they are located.

MacMillan handed the DCSOPS a thick sheaf of papers held together with a metal fastener. "Here's my proposed table of organization and equipment. Briefly, it consists of a commanding officer, an executive officer, some logistic and engineering officers, *and* a liaison officer. Plus the necessary enlisted technicians."

The DCSOPS took the material from MacMillan and started to read it. It was immediately apparent to him that somebody besides MacMillan had had a hand in it. It was a finished piece of staff work, and while MacMillan might be the warrior's warrior, he was anything but a staff officer. Whoever had done this for him knew what he was doing.

The DCSOPS thought it over for a moment, then grew angry.

"Mac, who put you up to this?"

"Sir?"

"Goddamnit, somebody did. You didn't write this." The DCSOPS had already made up his mind to hang the sonofabitch who, afraid to state his position publicly, had connived to get poor simple Mac to stand up for him.

"Those are my ideas, sir," MacMillan said. "I had a friend of mine help me put them down on paper."

"Who's your friend?" the DCSOPS asked.

"I can't tell you, General," MacMillan said.

"Why not?"

"Because he said I was committing suicide coming in here with this, and he wouldn't help me do that."

"What's his name, Mac?" the DCSOPS asked, weighing MacMillan's apparently honest reply in his mind.

"I gave him my word as an officer and a gentleman that I wouldn't say who he was, sir," MacMillan said.

MacMillan was incapable of making that up, the DCSOPS decided. He was so simple, such a virgin in this whorehouse of the Pentagon, that he actually believed in such Guidebook for Officers platitudes as the word of honor of an officer and a gentleman.

"I'm not asking you, Mac," the DCSOPS said. "I'm telling you."

"I'm sorry, sir, I can't do that," MacMillan said. He came to attention.

The DCSOPS looked at him a moment. Then he stood up and tossed the staff study in the lap of the Assistant Deputy Chief of Staff for Operations.

"You take a quick read of that," he said, and then pointed at MacMillan. "And you come with me."

He led MacMillan into his small conference room.

"Mac, I have to know who put you up to this," he said.

"Nobody put me up to it, General," MacMillan said.

"All right, then, who 'helped you with it.' I give you my word as an officer and a gentleman that I won't do anything to him, now or later. But I have to know."

"Why do you have to know?"

"Because what you've done is suggest that there is someone in the service, someone besides yourself—someone rather senior, I would judge, from that staff study—who feels that Colonel Gregory and the Assistant DCSOPS have made a serious error in judgment. Or less kindly, are trying to put something over on me."

"Hell, he's not senior," MacMillan said, chuckling.

"Who is he, Mac?" DCSOPS said. When there was no reply, feeling foolish, he repeated: "I give you my word, Mac, as an officer and a gentleman, that I won't do anything to him."

"His name is Lowell," MacMillan said.

"Rank? First name?"

"He's a major. Craig W. He just finished flight school."

"Lowell? That's the young buck who was screwing the movie star in Korea?"

"Yes, sir."

"And then got involved in Phil Sheridan Parker's boy's court-martial?"

"Yes, sir."

"No wonder he didn't want his name involved. He's got his ass in a deep enough crack the way it is."

The DCSOPS was relieved to find out what he had. And rather surprised that the Lowell kid—he recalled that he was only twenty-six or so—was capable of such good staff work. Pity he'd fucked up his career the way he had. The army had good staff officers and they had good combat commanders, but there had been a severe shortage of men who were both since Valley Forge. The Lowell kid had already made his mark as a combat commander. If he was also capable of staff work like this, he could have gone far and fast.

"It won't go any further, Mac," the DCSOPS said. "You have my word."

"Yes, sir," MacMillan said. "Thank you, General."

They went back into the large office. The DCSOPS looked at his assistant and raised his eyebrows in question. He was not surprised that the two of them were ready with a reply to shoot down MacMillan.

"Sir, we don't need an empire down there," the Assistant DCSOPS said. "Gregory's shop can handle anything that comes out of Rucker. The whole idea in sending Major MacMillan down there is to smooth things out, not make waves. A lot of people would be furious if we tried to shove something like this down their throats. *Armor* doesn't have a special operation for combat developments. *Infantry* doesn't have one. Why should aviation?"

"How do you respond to that, Major?" DCSOPS asked.

"The colonels and the majors at Knox and Benning who are planning for the next war commanded companies and battalions and regiments in the last one," MacMillan said. "There's nobody, *nobody*, in aviation with combat command experience."

Christ, the DCSOPS thought, he's right about that.

"It would be a slap in the face to those officers, myself included," Colonel Gregory said, "who have worked so long and so hard to get army aviation this far. The suggestion, frankly, infuriates me."

"I respectfully suggest that Colonel Gregory has made my point," MacMillan said. "The Flying Club will be furious if they don't get to spend all the money the army is about to pour into army aviation any way they want to. They mean well, General. But they just don't know about ground combat."

"Is that all you have, Major?" the DCSOPS asked. He saw that Colonel Gregory's face was livid with scarcely concealed fury.

"Yes, sir," MacMillan said, and came to attention.

"I'll look this over, Major," the DCSOPS said. "And have these gentlemen look it over and offer their comments."

"Thank you very much, sir," MacMillan said. "May the major consider himself dismissed, General?"

"You can go, Mac," the general said. MacMillan saluted, did a crisp about-face, and marched out of the office, dipping his knees just low enough to pick up his briefcase as he walked past the coffee table.

There was silence in the room for a moment. Then the Assistant DCSOPS chuckled as he leafed through the proposed table of organization and equipment.

"Well, he's got brass, I'll say that for him," he said. "This thing calls for a colonel, a light colonel, two majors, four captains, and a dozen lieutenants. *And* eleven aircraft."

"Eleven aircraft?" the aviation officer asked, a bitter tone in his laugh. "Only eleven?"

"A twin-engine Beech, two Beavers, three Cessna L-19s, two H-19s, an H-34, and two H-13s," the assistant DCSOPS said, reading from the proposed table of organization and equipment. "That's eleven."

"Mac's a nice fellow," Colonel Gregory said (*reverting*, the DCSOPS thought, *to the ridicule it and it'll go away tactic*). "Not too smart, but nice. Let's also give him a B-29, a squadron of P-51s, and maybe a C-54." He and the Assistant DCSOPS enjoyed their laugh.

"I was about to say have a couple of photocopies of that staff study made," the DCSOPS said. "But if there is only one copy, if it leaks, we'll know where it leaked. You take it first, Colonel Gregory, and list your objections to it, and then send it to me through General Kellogg."

"Does the general really intend to put this through the review procedure?" Colonel Gregory asked, in disbelief.

"The general does," the general said. "You and General Kellogg are it, Greg. Review it and get it back to me in a week, will you, please?"

"Yes, sir," the aviation officer said. "Will there be anything else, sir?"

"Yeah. No matter what I decide, MacMillan was right about the efficiency report. Fix it so you rate him, Greg, and I'll endorse it. I may not give him his empire, but I'm sending him down there to work for me, not the Aviation Board. Or what was it he said, 'the Cincinnati Flying Club'?"

[TWO]
Marburg an der Lahn
West Germany
23 December 1954

There was a side to Lt. Col. Edgar R. Withers's late-blooming rebirth in the Lord Jesus Christ which worked to Major Craig W. Lowell's advantage. Colonel Withers called Lowell into his office for a little private chat and told him, man to man, that he believed that Ilse's tragic death was the means the Lord had taken to test Lowell, to see if Lowell could measure up to his dual responsibility as a Christian to be both father and mother to the "poor lad."

Withers said he was going to arrange Lowell's duty schedule so that Lowell could make frequent trips to Marburg. He did that, and he even "understood" when Lowell got the spectacular speeding ticket.

Lowell had arranged through Craig, Powell, Kenyon and Dawes's London office to buy a Jaguar convertible "out of routine merchanting," in other words, without having to wait his turn on the waiting list. The Jaguar arrived in Germany two weeks after he ordered it, by coastal ship to Bremen, and he rode up to Bremen to pick it up on a troop train carrying military personnel to the army's maritime facility in Bremerhaven.

He had no sooner got on the Frankfurt-Munich autobahn when a Mercedes whipped past him doing at least ninety. He remembered having heard that there was no speed limit on the autobahn and shoved his foot to the floor.

He was arrested by military police near Hersfeld. The no speed limit did not apply to American officers. It applied only to the Germans. He shortly found himself replying by indorsement to the commanding general of Seventh Army, explaining why he had violated the command's 60-mile-per-hour speed limit by driving his personal vehicle in excess of 110 miles per hour on the autobahn near Hersfeld.

Withers was required to punish him. He could have fined him a third of a month's pay, and written a really nasty letter for his personnel file. He chose instead to "orally reprimand" him, the least of the punishments prescribed, and the oral reprimand consisted in bringing Lowell's attention to the fact that if he should kill himself on the highways, "the lad" would be an orphan.

While technically that was true, Peter-Paul Lowell would not have been left all alone in the world should his father wipe himself out on the autobahn.

Schloss Greiffenberg, now that the Graf von Greiffenberg had returned "from the

East"—the innocuous euphemism for Siberian imprisonment—was crowded with displaced Prussian and Thuringian and Pomeranian and Mecklenburgian kinfolk. All of them seemed to have had the foresight to either ship the family treasure out of East Germany before the Russians came, or even sooner to have opened numbered bank accounts in Zurich.

While they bemoaned the loss of their estates to the Bolsheviks, they were living as they had lived for centuries, in castles, tended to by servants, and with little to occupy their time but the investment of their capital—and the care of a little boy.

Elizabeth, the Pomeranian Baroness von Heuffinger-Lodz, Lowell soon learned, was the first among equals of his German in-laws. Shortly after he returned "from the East," not long after Ilse had been killed, Lowell's father-in-law was offered a commission in the Bundeswehr, Germany's new army. There were not all that many ex-colonels around whose opposition to Hitler was certifiable and thus were safe to lead a new German army.

There was no question about accepting the commission. It was his duty to *das Vaterland* to accept an officer's commission, as his ancestors had for seven hundred years. Lowell's father-in-law was now Generalmajor Graf von Greiffenberg, Deputy Chief of Intelligence.

It had seemed entirely logical to the Graf, with his daughter dead, and his American son-in-law at war in Korea, to turn the rearing of his grandson over to a widowed relative. That, too, had been going on in the family for hundreds of years. And when Craig Lowell thought it through, it seemed logical to him, too. The boy was obviously better off here than he would be "at home" in the United States, with a grandmother in a funny farm and the only other "logical" choice for his rearing Craig's cousin Porter Dawes and his wife. There would be time, Lowell had decided, to make the boy aware of his American heritage later. At the moment, his father was busy, trying as best he could to save his military career.

Herr Generalmajor (he was so addressed, or as "Herr Graf"; it was as if he had no Christian name) seemed confused about Craig's status as an army aviator. There had been two-seater Feisler Storche airplanes in the Wehrmacht, too, flown by people one didn't pay much attention to. It was hardly the sort of thing an officer and a gentleman did.

Lowell did not tell his father-in-law of his difficulty with the army. It wasn't that he was ashamed of what he had *done*—he had had a moral obligation to stand up and be counted when the army had tried to screw Phil Parker, and Ilse had been long dead before he had become involved with Georgia Paige—but rather that his father-in-law, for whom he had a great deal of respect, had simply presumed that Lowell, like himself, was an officer and an aristocrat, and Lowell really liked that.

It would have been awkward to acknowledge that he was on the shit list, or even that he was in trouble at all. As a result, Lowell found himself arguing the case for army aviation with a good deal more conviction than he really felt.

Herr Generalmajor didn't seem to be overly impressed with Craig's arguments, and often made references to Craig's "next command." There would be no "next command" in tanks, Lowell knew; and he doubted, in his dark moments, if there would ever be an aviation command more important than an aerial motorpool. Even if the dreamers had their way and eventually got their aviation battalions, he doubted that he would be given such a command.

Craig was determined, however, to be close to his son, which meant seeing him often, even if Ilse's relatives seemed to treat him sometimes as the vestige of an unfortunate alliance that would best be forgotten. Only his father-in-law and Elizabeth von Heuffinger-Lodz seemed to really accept him as a member of the family.

To solve Craig's time-in-transit problem, the Graf turned over to his son-in-law an enormous Mercedes sedan, equipped with the special license plates issued to general officers of the Bundeswehr. That kept the German police at a respectful distance, and the U.S. Army Military Police no longer had authority to control speeding German vehicles on the autobahn. Lowell rented a garage in Augsburg, leaving the Mercedes in it when he was on duty and the Jaguar there when he drove to Marburg.

His personal life in the military society at Augsburg was unsatisfactory, but he had expected that, and it didn't particularly bother him. He had decided against taking an apartment "on the economy," although the Generalmajor offered to help him find one. He didn't intend to stay in Augsburg when he had time off anyway, and he didn't want to call attention to himself.

He lived in the BOQ. Despite the notion that "initial utilization tour" aviators were assigned without regard to rank and branch of service, and that he was nothing more than a commissioned jeep driver, he was, de facto and de jure, a major, a field-grade officer.

Nonaviators disliked aviators, as a general rule. Not only were they regarded, once again, as nothing more than jeep drivers with commissions, but salt was rubbed into that wound by flight pay. Aviator lieutenants made as much money as nonflying captains.

The old-time aviators, the ones who ran the Seventh Army Flight Detachment and told Major Lowell when and where he was to fly, were required to pay to him the military courtesy captains and lieutenants are obliged to show to majors. They lived in company-grade, single-room BOQs, while "young Major Lowell" (how the *hell* did he get to be a *major?*) was assigned a field-grade officer's two-room suite. They might be flight examiners and his instructors in the finer points of helicopter flight, but they were the ones who pulled officer of the day and conducted inventories of the unit supply room. Majors are not expected to do that sort of thing.

Lowell made some friends among them, of course. They weren't all either commissioned cretins or fools. He understood a good deal of the resentment the old-timers felt toward the newcomers. As it became increasingly evident that army aviation was going to grow, it had become just as evident to the old-timers that after having taken all the crap they had all those years, the newcomers were about to take all the gravy.

A letter from MacMillan, eight lines long, and with six misspelled words, reported that a Combat Developments Office had been set up under the DCSOPS at Camp Rucker. Lowell felt more than a little uneasy about that, for Bill Roberts had written shortly afterward, bitterly reporting the same thing and saying it was the first step in the establishment's attempt to take over army aviation. It would be very embarrassing if Bill Roberts found out that Lowell had put MacMillan's thoughts into a presentable form. He had done it for MacMillan primarily because Mac was just back from the escapade in Indo-China, and somehow felt he was paying him back for taking care of Sandy.

Mac would have really looked like the dumb ass he was if he had submitted his proposals to the brass in the form they had been in when he had showed them to Lowell. But Mac had been right: the Army simply couldn't afford to turn a vastly expanded army aviation program over to the Cincinnati Flying Club. Not because the members of the Club weren't competent, for they were about the only people around aviation who were, but because there was not enough of them to go around. When they ran out of Cincinnati Flying Club members for responsible jobs, they would have to get people outside of aviation altogether, for the vast bulk of the other army aviators simply were unqualified.

The subject of the low quality of aviation officers as a personnel problem for the future had been the subject of several of Lowell's long letters to Bill Roberts. Roberts was now a full colonel at Camp Rucker and president of the Army Aviation Board. Lowell had suggested solutions, including the periodic reassignment of officers to their basic branch, so officers would know something besides flying. Roberts argued that what the army needed was a separate branch for aviation, Army Air Corps II. Lowell had concluded that Roberts was wrong and MacMillan right.

Lowell—after some time—finally acquired adequate skill as a pilot by the simple expedient of flying whenever he had the chance, and, where necessary, by using his rank to get the more interesting flights (ferrying brass around during maneuvers, for example). There was no longer any question in his mind that he was a competent pilot, but that was not the same thing as saying that he was a good one. He had to work at it. He could not swoop and soar like real aviators, who flew as if they had been born to fly.

It was during a brass-ferrying flight near Bad Tolz that he had his own rebirth of faith, not in Lt. Col. Edgar R. Withers's Lord and Savior, but in army aviation.

The brass hat he was chauffeuring was a brigadier general, the European Command's deputy quartermaster general. Like most technical service soldiers, the general took his role in the scheme of things very seriously. He was up at the crack of dawn, loaded down with steel helmet and field equipment, and had kept Lowell busy flying between one supply point and another.

Many of the supply points where the general stopped to jack up the troops were Class IV, POL, Petrol, Oil and Lubricants. One of them, inevitably, was engaged in refueling a tank battalion.

As Lowell made the approach to a field beside the road, he was at first—and automatically—critical. The M48s were too close to one another. If they were attacked by enemy tanks or aircraft, or if there was a fueling fire, one exploding tank would blow up others. The company commanders didn't know what they were doing, and neither did the battalion commander, or he would have straightened things out.

But the battalion commander *had* a battalion, Lowell reminded himself. Although

Major Craig W. Lowell had commanded a battalion-sized task force and he had fought so well with it that it was now in the textbooks, he would never be given command of one again.

He had another thought, as he prepared to land the H-13:

Christ! he thought. *If I had a couple of 3.5 rocket launchers mounted on the skids of this thing, I could take out two of those tanks and be gone before they knew what hit them!*

As quickly as the thought came to him, he shot it down. There was no way to mount rocket launchers on a helicopter's landing skids, and even if there was, there would be no way to aim them.

And just as quickly came the solutions. Rocket launchers had *no recoil.* They kicked up a lot of dust on the ground, but that wasn't recoil. A rocket's propelling charge recoiled against the atmosphere. They *could* be fired from choppers. And they could be aimed by aiming the whole airframe. A helicopter is capable of movement through all axes.

While the assistant quartermaster general was off shaking up his troops, Lowell made a sight for rocket fire. He took off his aviator's metal-framed sunglasses and snapped their lenses out. Then he bent them into a U at the nosepiece. Then he found his personal roll of toilet paper, invariably carried when playing soldier on maneuvers where one crapped where one found the opportunity. He unrolled it all, and took the paper tube on which it had been wrapped and shoved it through the bent frame. Finally, he taped it to the top of the control panel, and tried to line it up parallel to the center line of the H-13.

When the assistant quartermaster general got back into the H-13 and ordered himself transported to the next outpost of his logistic empire, Lowell made a mock rocket firing run over the parked tanks.

Sighting through the toilet paper tube would work!

"Major," the assistant quartermaster general asked, "what the hell was that strange maneuver you just made? You some sort of a hot-rodder?"

Lowell could think of nothing to reply that wouldn't make him look even more foolish in the general's eyes. He said nothing.

"Don't do anything like that again," the general said.

"Yes, sir," Lowell said.

"And take whatever that is you've got taped to the dashboard off," the general ordered. "It's unmilitary."

Unmilitary or not, Lowell thought, as he pulled off his ruined sunglasses and the toilet paper tube and threw them out the door, that's going to affect tank warfare even more than the 3.5 rocket itself did. It gets the rocket to the tank. And the army could swap one $75,000 helicopter for one enemy $500,000 tank. That would be a real bargain, even *if* the enemy got the chopper. By the time the tankers could get the turret-mounted .50 caliber machine gun in action, they wouldn't have time to engage it. Not until the chopper had fired its rockets. He said it in his mind again: the army could afford to trade choppers for tanks all day long.

That night he began to put it all down on paper. A thousand questions arose that would have to be answered. He started looking for the answers. He decided that before he even told Bill Roberts about it, he would have answers for those thousand questions, and maybe, if he could arrange it, he would be able to actually try firing rockets from a helicopter's skids.

Lowell wrote about it right away to Captain Phil Parker, telling Parker to keep his mouth shut. Lowell began to see rocket-firing helicopters as his way out of purgatory. He didn't want some sonofabitch from the Cincinnati Flying Club latching on to his idea and claiming it as his own.

When Phil replied, he said nothing whatever about Lowell's idea. He wrote that he had been granted a Special instrument Ticket, which meant that he was his own clearance authority. If he figured it was safe to fly, he could take off. Lowell had grown used to being replaced by an old-timer the moment the clouds looked threatening.

Lowell told himself that Phil was flying fixed wing. There was no such thing as instrument flight in helicopters, so it meant nothing. But then he realized that it did mean something: if they were given an instrument flight capability, rotary wing aircraft would be even better rocket launching platforms. He would have to check that out, too.

While Major Craig W. Lowell spent as much time at the controls as he could, as well as long hours working on his rocket-armed helicopter idea, and as much time as possible with his son, he did not enter into a life of dedicated monasticism. He was twenty-six, in perfect physical condition. The juices of life flowed.

There were a number of single American women around Augsburg, service club hostesses, civilian secretaries, and specialists of one kind or another at Seventh Army Headquarters, and he worked his way through them, bedding some of them, being refused by others, never letting it get serious.

He had no desire to remarry. He really hadn't met another woman with whom the idea of sharing his life had any appeal. But it was not true, as the O Club gossip had it, that he worked his way through *each* and *every* female at Seventh Army. There wasn't time for that many women in his life, even if being in his life meant squiring them to the Seventh Army officer's club and little more. After a while, too, the word got around among the women that all the aviator major wanted was somebody in his sack, and that marriage was the last thing on his mind. Dating Major Lowell painted them before other eligibles (even if the other eligibles weren't generally field grade and possessors of a red Jaguar automobile) as girls who had been tried and found either willing or undesirable.

His fluent, unaccented German, acquired from one of a long line of governesses who had acted *in loco parentis* for his "ill" mother, and perfected when Ilse had been alive, came back quickly, and that opened two other sources of females: the girls who hung around the military (these were not, despite their reputation, all semipro hookers looking for a meal ticket, but in many cases young women who simply found Americans more attractive than their German contemporaries) and the Germans in the Augsburg and Munich upper crust, to whom he was known as the widowered son-in-law of Generalmajor Graf von Greiffenberg.

While he didn't score nearly as frequently as the stories went, he scored enough so that his reputation preceded him. If he appeared with a redhead on his arm for the Tuesday Standing Rib Special at the officer's mess, you could bet that there would be a blond or a brunette the following week.

God only knows where he goes every weekend he can get off, went the talk. It was the general consensus that he used his weekends to diddle the married women whom discretion demanded he diddle at least one hundred miles from the flagpole. It became known that the sonofabitch had a Mercedes 280, with kraut plates, stashed in town.

This suspicious behavior came to the attention of the Counterintelligence Corps. A somewhat disappointed CIC agent, who had really felt that he was onto some sonofabitch on Moscow's, or at least Karlshorst's, payroll, reported that the automobile in question was the property of Generalmajor Graf von Greiffenberg of the Bundeswehr, and that a check of the subject's records indicated that Generalmajor Graf von Greiffenberg was the subject's father-in-law, and had been named guardian of the subject's minor child in the event of his death.

Only the CIC knew that Lowell was spending his weekends and his three-day VOCOs with his son and the Baroness Elizabeth von Heuffinger-Lodz, who was P.P.'s adoptive mother in everything but law. Otherwise, everyone but Lt. Col. Edgar R. Withers preferred to think his weekends were spent in carnal abandon with one straying wife, or oversexed secretary, or another. And the CIC is in the business of investigating people, not issuing character references. Lowell quickly earned a reputation as a swordsman, first class.

The thought of something happening between Lowell and Elizabeth had occurred to both of them and had been weighed and found, in the balance, absurd. They became friends instead.

Although he had passed the Bad Nauheim arrows on the autobahn every time he drove to and from Marburg, Lowell had never turned off for a look at the town where he had met Ilse, where he'd lived with her, where he had made her pregnant. He didn't, he admitted to himself, have the balls.

Elizabeth von Heuffinger-Lodz was responsible for him finally going back. When he arrived at Schloss Greiffenberg to spend Christmas, Elizabeth said she had heard that the army theater in Bad Nauheim was going to have a special Christmas program of cartoons and Walt Disney's *Fantasia* for dependent children, and could he arrange to take them? They could also visit the PX and get Peter-Paul things unavailable at any price on the German economy.

There was no way to refuse. He told himself that he was being foolish, anyway. That was all a long time ago. Sometimes, especially around Elizabeth, whose soft white skin and long, slim legs had their effect on him, he had difficulty even remembering what Ilse looked like.

When Elizabeth asked for the car, the chauffeur misunderstood, and was waiting in the courtyard, all dressed up in his livery, holding open the back door of the 280 for *Frau Baroness, Herr Major, and den süssen kleinen Peter-Paul.* It was easier to let him drive than to make a scene.

The chauffeur elected to take them into Bad Nauheim past the Bayrischen Hof.

It was a bright, crisp winter day, and as the Mercedes drove past the park where

Ilse had spent that first night, a jeep came the other way, and a young girl jumped out, legs flashing under her skirt, and ran into the hotel.

Lowell's heart leapt, and he just had time to be amused at that, when a mental image of Ilse lying naked under him, when he took her virginity, filled his mind. She had trusted him, given him her body, given him P.P., when she didn't have a pot to piss in. And here he was, with P.P., in a goddamned chauffeur-driven Mercedes, and she was rotting in her grave. It was so goddamned unfair!

Tears came without warning, his heart went leaden, and it was all he could do to keep from sobbing out loud. He looked away. His eyes fell on P.P., standing up on the back floor, looking out the window. He got control of himself, and let his breath out very slowly.

"She was here with you, wasn't she?" Elizabeth asked.

"Right in there," he said, and met her eyes, not caring that she could see his tears.

"And you loved her very much, didn't you?" Elizabeth asked.

"Yes," Lowell said, surprised at the depth of his emotion. "Very much."

"And you loved who, Papa?" P.P. asked.

"Your mother, P.P.," Lowell said.

P.P. was not interested in his mother, whom he only very faintly remembered.

"And now you love Tante Elizabeth?" P.P. asked.

"Right on the button, Squirt," Lowell said.

"Right on the button?" P.P. asked, confused.

Elizabeth took Lowell's hand in her gloved one, and held it tightly.

After they had taken P.P. to see the Christmas program, and then through the PX to buy him what Lowell later thought of as one each of everything in the toy department, they had dinner in the officer's open mess. Elizabeth was willing to acknowledge that only the Americans really knew how to make a steak, even if there were few other American accomplishments worth mentioning.

On the way home to Marburg, Lowell, convinced that he was now in charge of his emotions, directed the chauffeur to the farmer's house where he had lived with Ilse.

"What are we doing *here?*" P.P. demanded to know, looking at the small farmhouse.

"This is where you come from, Squirt," Lowell said.

"Oh, no, I don't either!"

"This is where your mother and I decided to have you," Lowell said.

"That must have been a *long* time ago," P.P. said. "Can we go in?"

"I don't think so," Lowell said. "Somebody else lives there now." He gestured for the chauffeur to start up.

P.P. fell asleep on the secondary highway to Marburg, lulled to sleep by the swaying of the softly suspended large car. Elizabeth pulled him over her and propped him up in the corner, and then slid over beside Lowell. She took his hand.

"I used to feel sorry for Ilse," she said. "Now I'm a little jealous."

"How do you figure that?"

"You loved her," she said. "That's more than Kurt and I had."

Without really knowing that he was doing it, Lowell put his arm around her shoulder and pulled her closely, affectionately, to him. And then, without thinking about that, either, he kissed her. First a gentle kiss, between friends. Then it became less than innocent, gentle. It was, for some reason, highly exciting.

"This is dangerous," he said.

"What harm can one night do?" she whispered.

He kissed her again, and was not at all surprised when her tongue darted at first teasingly, and then hungrily, into his mouth, or when she violently twisted her body around so that she could press her breasts against him, or when her hand dropped to his crotch.

But that night was the only time it happened. She didn't come to his room again over the holidays, and the next time he got to Marburg, three weeks later, she made it plain within the first couple of minutes that what had happened between them was a freak happenstance, and that it would never happen again.

But they remained friends. The other relatives said they were like brother and sister and privately talked among themselves how fortunate it was that Ilse's American seemed to understand how far better it was for Peter-Paul to remain with Elizabeth, and wasn't it a shame that they hadn't, you know, felt *that* way about each other?

Lowell was personally disappointed when his initial utilization tour was over and he remained assigned to the Seventh Army Aviation Detachment. He had hoped for assignment to one of the divisions, where his rank would demand he be given a staff position. That was obviously the reason he remained assigned to the detachment as an aviator; they didn't want to give him a responsible assignment.

He used his rank to insist that he be checked out in the new, fourteen-passenger Sikorsky H-34 helicopter, and he was the first of the new breed in Seventh Army to be allowed to fly it as pilot in command. That special privilege was generally recognized to be because the Seventh Army aviation officer had heard good things about Major Lowell from Colonel Bill Roberts, while he was in TDY in the States.

He also used his rank to have himself sent to Sonthofen for a ten-week cross-training course in fixed wing flight. He was now what they called dual rated, and sent a copy of his orders to Phil Parker in Alaska. Being dual rated made things more even between them, catching up with Phil now that Phil had the coveted Special Instrument Ticket. Parker responded with a Xerox of his flight log. He had gotten himself checked out, incredibly, by the air force in C-119 Flying Boxcars and C-47s on skis. Parker sent him a photograph in which he was kissing a stuffed polar bear. Lowell sent him a photograph, his head on Rommel's body, of himself as a field marshal, and then had Elizabeth pick out something really nice to send Captain and Mrs. Parker for their first baby, a girl.

[ONE]
Clayhatchee Springs, Alabama
17 January 1955

Darlene Heatter cleaned up the kitchen as soon as John went to work, washing the dishes, wiping the table clean, even mopping the floor. Then she made the bed and dusted the living room, and then she dressed the kids. Finally, she got dressed, a nice dress, not a Sunday dress, but nice all the same. She didn't like to go to the church, even when there weren't any services, unless she looked nice.

Darlene was an attractive woman, a few pounds shy of being plump. She had brown hair and brown eyes, and every once in a while she fantasized about having her hair bleached. She had been blond as a child, but then, when she was just starting high school, it had started to turn dark.

She'd put peroxide on her hair to keep it blond, but her mother caught her doing it and told her that only tramps and women who hung around beer joints bleached their hair. "If you want to look loose," she'd said, "you'll have to wait until you get married and leave home. As long as you live under my roof, you won't bleach your hair, or do anything else to make yourself cheap."

She'd thought about that encounter years later, when she actually did get married, and thought about being free to bleach her hair, but she hadn't done it. She told herself that she was now a young Christian married woman and no more free to look like a tramp than she had been in her freshman year of high school.

Darlene collected the kids and put them in the old pickup. The old pickup was a '47 Ford, red, with the back window gone and a crack in the front one, and pretty well rusted out in the bed from the fertilizer, which just about ate metal. The new pickup was a Ford. It wasn't really new, but it had belonged to the Hessia Peanut Mill supervisor, who hadn't really used it as a farm pickup, so it was the next best thing to a new one. Not worn out or eaten up by rust or anything.

She'd talked John into buying it, without turning the old pickup in as a down payment. They weren't going to give him anything for it, she told him (and that was true, they wouldn't have given him what it was worth, considering all the time he'd put in on it fixing it up and rebuilding it) and he really should have something to use as a spare. You never could tell what would happen, she said.

John was back out at Camp Rucker, thank sweet Jesus for that, and not only as a fireman, GS-2, but as a fire equipment vehicle operator, GS-3. It wasn't really a promotion, just that he was qualified for the higher job because of his experience and seniority. What it was, officially, was that he had applied for a new job instead of just getting his old one back.

It was sort of funny, he told her, because now that he was a fire equipment vehicle operator, GS-3, there weren't any fire equipment vehicles. Not real ones. They'd auctioned off the old fire engines (some man from Chicago had made the high bid and come all the way down to take them away) when the post was supposed to be closing down for good. The new equipment hadn't come yet, although the army had issued the purchase order for them, and they were supposedly being built. All the fire department at the post had to fight fires with until the new equipment was delivered were some regular trucks with water pumps on the back, and some regular water trucks, regular army trucks. John and some of the others had gone to Georgia, to Fort Benning, to get them. It was the first time John had ever ridden in an airplane.

When she arrived at the Clayhatchee Springs Church of God, a white frame building set on brick piers, nobody was there. She hadn't expected anybody to be there, and would have been disappointed and maybe even a little embarrassed if there had been. She got the door unlocked and turned her kids loose in the nursery and asked them *please* not to tear anything up. Then she went into the church office.

When she got to the door, it occurred to her for the first time that maybe they locked the office. She had keys to the church and even the food cupboards in the kitchen (because she was on the Hospitality Committee and the Ladies Altar Guild), but if they locked the office door, she would have been out of luck. She had no reason to have keys to the office.

The office door was open. And there was the typewriter, right on top of the pastor's desk, with an oilcloth cover over it.

A month before, right after John had gone back to work, Darlene had been in the post office to send some wrong-sized corduroy overalls for Johnnie back to Sears and Roebuck, and she saw the civil service announcements on the bulletin board next to the FBI's Ten Most Wanted Criminals posters.

Fort Rucker was hiring typists, clerk-typists, and typist-stenographers on a competitive examination, and you could write for application blanks or call a number somebody had written in the notice with a Magic Marker. There were vacancies from GS-1 through GS-5 for something they called secretary (stenotyping).

So she called, and the lady in the personnel office said that all you had to do to get taken on as a typist, GS-1 or GS-2, was be able to type. If you typed twenty-five words a minute, you could get hired as a GS-1. If you typed thirty-five words a minute, you could get yourself hired as a GS-2. They would teach you whatever else you had to know once you were on the payroll.

Darlene had given it a lot of thought. John had been a GS-2 before they closed the post, and they'd had all the money they needed. If she could get a job as a GS-1, now that he was a GS-3, that was probably the same thing as two GS-2 paychecks. That was all the money in the world.

The only trouble was that John probably wouldn't want her to work. He would tell her that she should be home with the kids. And she couldn't type; there was that little problem, too.

Darlene Heatter sat down at the pastor's desk and pulled the oilcloth cover off his typewriter. Then, from her purse she took a package of typing paper, wrapped in cellophane, for which she had paid twenty-nine cents in the Piggly Wiggly Superette, and a battered book, bound at the top, which she had borrowed from the Choctawhatchee regional library book-mobile: *Typing the E-Z Way.*

She put a piece of paper in the typewriter and lined it up. She'd already read the first part of the book, and understood what she was to do.

Darlene Heatter put her fingers on the keyboard, and very slowly but with firm strokes, she began to type: aaa lll aaa lll aaa lll alal alal alal lala lala la.

[TWO]
The U.S. Army Ground General School
Fort Riley, Kansas
23 February 1955

ROUTINE
HQ DEPT OF THE ARMY WASH DC
0905 21 FEB 55

TO: CG USA GGS AND FT RILEY KANS

1. THE DEPUTY CHIEF OF STAFF, USA, WILL PAY AN INFORMAL VISIT TO THE USA GROUND GEN SCH & FT RILEY KANS 24-25 FEB 1955.

2. GENERAL E. Z. BLACK, USA, AND HIS PARTY, CONSISTING OF ONE VIP CIV, TWO OFF, AND TWO EM, WILL ARRIVE VIA PRIVATE CIV AIRCRAFT AT APPROX 1100 HOURS FT RILEY TIME 24 FEB 55 AND WILL DEPART FT RILEY BY PRIVATE CIV AIRCRAFT AT APPROX 0900 HOURS FT RILEY TIME 25 FEB 55.

3. GENERAL BLACK DESIRES TO EMPHASIZE THAT HIS VISIT IS INFORMAL. THE V/CS USA DOES NOT, REPEAT NOT, DESIRE HONORS. HE DESIRES THAT ALL ACTIVITIES AT FT RILEY CONTINUE WITHOUT INTERRUPTION. HOWEVER, THE V/CS USA WILL, SHOULD THIS BE THE DESIRE OF THE CG USA GCS & FT RILEY, AND PROVIDING IT DOES NOT INTERFERE WITH PRESENT PLANS, PARTICIPATE IN GRADUATION CEREMONIES FOR WOCRW FLT TNG CLASS 54-4 ON 24 FEB 55.

4. THE V/CS USA DESIRES THAT HE AND HIS PARTY BE PROVIDED TRANSIENT QUARTERS OVERNIGHT. FIELD GRADE TRANSIENT QUARTERS

AND GROUND TRANSPORTATION ARE DESIRED FOR THE THREE (3) MAN CIV AIRCREW OF THE CIV ACFT.

5. PROVISIONS OF PARA 3.(B)1 THROUGH PARA 3.(b)16 STANDING OPERATING PROCEDURE NO. 1.3 WILL BE COMPLIED WITH.

BY COMMAND OF THE CHIEF OF STAFF:
EDWIN W. BITTER, MAJOR GENERAL, USA
SECRETARY, GEN STAFF, USA

The TWX posed several questions to Major General Evan D. Virgil, USA, Commanding General of the U.S. Army Ground General School and Fort Riley, Kansas, first and foremost of which was, "Why the fuck is Black coming out here?"

The Chief of Staff, U.S. Army, devotes most of his time to the Joint Chiefs of Staff, of which he is a member, and to the President of the United States, the President's cabinet, and to the Congress. The Vice Chief of Staff, who is also a four-star general, devotes his time to the U.S. Army.

And he has a role in the scheme of things should the balloon go up. If the balloon went up, it was entirely likely that there would be casualties not only in the executive branch of government, but in the Congress and in the Department of Defense as well. The line of succession to the man who has the authority to push the button descends through the Vice President to the Speaker of the House of Representatives, various other high elected officials, and only far down the line comes to the military.

As a practical matter, it was tacitly recognized that if the seat of government should go up in a nuclear mushroom, the order to push the button, when received from a four-star general or admiral, would be enough to convince the bright young men in the classified ordnance dumps that they could forego Standing Operating Procedure for Issue of Classified Weaponry and pass out the Nuclears and the Chemical, Biological, and Radiologicals.

It was agreed that the orders would come from the senior surviving four-star general or admiral. It was recognized that the order would be given by the first surviving four-star to be able to get through to the red phones connecting the brass to the men in the classified ordnance dumps.

The first thing the commanding general did on receipt of the TWX was call in his signal officer and instruct him to have radio telephone links with scrambling devices instantly installed in two separate locations, the VIP guest house and a secret concrete bunker, and to insure that each separate link was capable of communication with each of the seven places on the list he was provided.

Then he called in his aides and his sergeant major and put them to work. The junior aide was to see to transportation and quarters for the crew of a civilian airplane. The sergeant major was to make sure that the VIP guest house was made ready for the Vice Chief of Staff of the United States Army. The senior aide was placed in charge of having new programs printed for the graduation exercises of Warrant Officer Candidate Rotary Wing Flight Training Class 54–6, listing General E. Z. Black, Vice Chief of Staff of the United States Army as guest speaker. The Commanding General, USA Ground General School and Fort Riley, Kansas, would introduce the Vice Chief of Staff.

"And I want the band there, all of them, not the ragged collection of clowns I saw the last time," the post commander ordered. "And make sure we have a four-star flag for the platform. I don't care where you get one, get one. Uniform for all hands will be Class "A" with medals. No ribbons. Medals. The general staff will attend, and tell them I expect to see their wives. I don't know what flight training has laid on, but there will be a reception afterward. A cake. I want it done *right,* Scott."

"Yes, sir. I take the general's meaning."

"And get with Whatsername, the officer's wives' club advisor . . ."

"Mrs. Talley, sir."

"Tell Mrs. Talley what's going on and get her to make sure the WOC wives look like officers' ladies. No slacks. Hats and gloves, if that's possible."

"Yes, sir."

"Get your show on the road, we don't have much time."

At 1030 hours, the commanding general, the deputy commanding general, and their wives arrived at the Fort Riley airfield, driving past long lines of Cessna L-19s—used for training of fixed wing aviators—and long lines of Bell H-13 helicopters—used for training of rotary wing aviators. The commanding general's junior aide-de-camp and the sergeant major were already on hand, shepherding a line of olive-drab Chevrolet staff cars. The junior aide-de-camp had also arranged for a jeep with a radio tuned to the tower frequency to be on hand.

At 1050 hours, the radio in the jeep came to life.

"Ah, Fort Riley, this is Martin Three Zero Seven. I am five minutes out. I have General Black and party aboard. Request approach and landing."

"What the hell is a Martin?" the commanding general asked his deputy. The deputy shrugged his shoulders.

"Martin Three Zero Seven, Fort Riley," the tower replied. "You are cleared as Number One to land on Runway Four Five. The winds are negligible. The altimeter is two niner niner. Report on final."

"Understand Number One on Four Five," the aircraft replied.

A glistening black Cadillac came up beside the line of staff cars. A tall, erect black man in a gray suit got out of the car.

"See who the hell that is," General Virgil ordered.

"Sir, I believe that's Colonel Parker, retired," his aide told him.

"Oh, yeah. I wonder what the hell he wants?"

The tall, erect black man leaned on the fender of the gleaming black Cadillac and, shading his eyes, looked up into the sky.

An airplane appeared, far off, fairly low, and approached the field at a surprisingly high speed. It passed a mile to the left, banked steeply, and started its descent.

"Riley, Zero Seven on final," the radio said.

"Jesus, that's a B-26," the deputy commanding general said.

The airplane, a Martin B-26, a two-engine World War II bomber, was now making its approach. The flaps and landing gear were down. There was a screech as the tires touched, and almost immediately a deafening roar as the props were reversed and the throttles opened. The B-26 slowed very abruptly and started to turn around.

"Riley, Zero Seven on the ground at one minute to the hour. Taxi instructions, please."

"Zero Seven, a FOLLOW ME is en route to meet you."

A jeep with a huge FOLLOW ME sign mounted on its back seat raced out to the B-26, turned around in front of it, and then led the glistening ex-bomber to the line of staff cars. They could see what was painted on the vertical stabilizer now. There was a representation of an oil rig and the words: THE NEWBURGH CORPORATION.

The pilot taxied the airplane nose in to them and shut down the engines. General Virgil led the small procession over to the door, which unfolded from the side of the fuselage. He had a moment's glance at the paneled interior before the door was filled with the body of a huge black master sergeant. He came down the stairs with surprising grace for his bulk, casually saluted the two general officers, said, "Good morning, gentlemen," and then opened a cargo door to the rear of the passenger door and started to take out luggage. His tunic was pulled up as he stretched, and General Virgil saw that he had a .45 automatic in the small of his back.

And then General E. Z. Black got off the plane. He wore an overseas cap, rather than the leather-brimmed headgear normally worn by senior officers, and he wore it cocked to the left, in the armor tradition.

General Virgil saluted crisply. Black returned it idly.

"Good to see you, Virgil," he said. "But you didn't have to come out to meet me." He smiled and nodded at the wives. "Ladies," he said.

A full colonel and lieutenant colonel followed him off the airplane, then a tall, gray-mustached civilian, and finally a younger master sergeant, carrying a briefcase. The unmistakable bulk of a .45 in a shoulder holster was visible under his tunic.

"General, do you know General Young?" General Virgil asked.

"Yes, of course," Black said. "How are you, Young?" Then something caught his eye, and he walked quickly toward the tall, erect, black man.

"Look at this, Carson," he called over his shoulder. "We've been met by the local undertaker."

Colonel Philip Sheridan Parker III, retired, offered his hand to the Vice Chief of Staff of the U.S. Army. He got, instead, a bear hug.

"Slats, God, it's good to see you!" General Black said. The mustached civilian walked up and shook hands with Parker.

"I'm awed by your airplane, Carson," Colonel Parker said. "The last time I saw one of those, it dropped bombs on me. They said it was a mistake."

"I was right there with you, Phil," Carson Newburgh said. "Outside Bizerte. Don't be impressed with the plane. It belongs to the company."

General Virgil filed away for future reference the fact that the retired, outside-the-gate black colonel had friends in very high places.

The colonel, who wore the insignia (lapel pins with four stars and a golden rope through his epaulets) of an aide-de-camp to a full general, walked up to General Virgil.

"The general desires to attend the graduation ceremonies for WOCRW Class 54–6," he said. "But he desires to arrive just as they begin."

"I've, uh, taken the liberty, Colonel, of arranging for the general to address the graduating class," General Virgil said.

"I don't believe the general had that in mind," the aide-de-camp said. He walked over to General Black.

"You're scheduled, sir, to address the graduating class."

Black frowned, and then shrugged.

"Oh, what the hell," he said. "You want to hear me give a speech, Slats?"

"The general's speeches are usually something to hear."

"Virgil, I don't want to arrive until just before the graduation starts," General Black said. "We have—" he looked at his watch—"fifty-odd minutes. Where can I hide? Better than that, where can we all get a quick drink?"

"My quarters, sir. I'd be honored," the post commander offered.

"Let's open the club," General Black said. "I'll ride with Colonel Parker in his limousine, and the rest of you can meet me there."

They were distracted by the sight of the enormous master sergeant heading their way, more precisely, marching their way. He marched up to Colonel Parker, raised his hand in a salute far more rigid than the one he rendered to the post commander, and barked: "Colonel Parker, sir! Does the colonel remember the sergeant, sir?"

The tall, erect black man saluted, as if he knew he should not salute in civilian clothing, and then put out his hand.

"Of course, I do, Tiny," he said. "I'm just surprised they haven't put you out to pasture."

"Oh, they're trying to, Colonel," he said. "But I got the Vice Chief of Staff on my side, and I'll stay in for a little while longer."

"Come along with us, Wes," General Black said. "You can have a little eye-opener with us."

"No, sir," Master Sergeant Wesley said. "I'll have one with you and the colonel later. I'm going to go see Greer."

"He's not supposed to know we're here," General Black said.

"Hell, General, you know better than that. If it's going on here, Greer knows about it, and has already figured out how to make money on it."

"Indulge me, Sergeant," General Black said. "Do what I tell you."

Master Sergeant Wesley got behind the wheel of the Cadillac.

"You get in the back," he said to Colonel Parker. "It'll be like old times, me driving you someplace."

The master sergeant with the briefcase and the .45 in the shoulder holster got in beside Master Sergeant Wesley. General Black, Colonel Parker, and the mustached civilian, Carson Newburgh, got in the back. The Cadillac drove off.

"Call the club," General Virgil said. "Make damned sure it's open when he gets there."

"I already have, sir," his aide-de-camp replied.

General Virgil impatiently waited for his wife to get in the staff car, and then he took off in pursuit of the Vice Chief of Staff of the United States Army.

At ten minutes after nine the next morning, five minutes after he had watched the B-26 race down the runway, he put in a telephone call to a classmate at the United States Military Academy, presently assigned as Deputy to the Assistant Chief of Staff for Personnel.

"Howard, I just had the most interesting visitor out here."

"I heard he was going out there. What the hell was it all about?"

"Well, you ever hear of a Colonel Philip Sheridan Parker III, retired?"

"Sure. You mean you don't know him?"

"I know he's retired out here."

"His great-great-grandfather retired out there, when Riley was an Indian-fighting cavalry post. There have been Parkers around the army for a long, long time."

"He certainly seems pretty close to General Black."

"They go back a long way together. Parker had a tank destroyer battalion with Porky Waterford's Hell's Circus in Europe. Black had one of the combat commands. That's all it was, war stories week?"

"No. Black hinted strongly that he wanted to address WOCRW 56–4."

"What the hell is that?"

"The sergeants we taught how to fly and made warrant officers out of."

"Is that so? Any particular reason?"

"He showed a particular interest in one of them, a kid named Greer. Had him to dinner at the club, and then they partied all night in the VIP guest house with Black's enlisted men, that great big orderly and the guy with the gun and the briefcase. Very intimate affair."

"Very interesting," the Assistant DCSPERS said. "I'll find out who he is."

"I thought you might be interested."

"Yeah, thanks, Evan."

"Scratch my back sometime."

The Assistant DCSPERS called for the service record of Warrant Officer Junior Grade Edward C. Greer. He found it interesting. He was only twenty years old. They had to waive the age requirement for him to go to flight school. He had been a technical sergeant when he applied for the Warrant Officer Candidate Program. There were not very many nineteen-year-old technical sergeants, either, which was also interesting. Nor were there very many technical sergeants of any age to whom the French government wished to award the Croix de Guerre. The State Department had declined to give permission for him to accept it, but the request was in his record jacket.

The Assistant DCSPERS saw that WOJG Greer had been assigned to a Transportation Corps helicopter company for an initial utilization tour.

He called Colonel William Roberts at Camp Rucker, Alabama, and asked him if he could use a rather unusual warrant officer right from helicopter school. Roberts said that he could not. But he suggested that the Aviation Combat Developments Agency might be able to use him.

That name struck a familiar chord in the mind of the Assistant DCSPERS. He had that file pulled. He saw why it had stuck in his memory. They had sent Lieutenant Colonel (Colonel-designate) Robert F. Bellmon down there, with a delay-en-route assignment to the Bell helicopter plant, for a special senior officer's course in helicopter flight.

That was very unusual. But so was Bob Bellmon. He was Porky Waterford's son-in-law. He'd been a POW in Germany. The connection was complete. The Assistant DCSPERS told his secretary to cancel WOJG Greer's orders, and to have new orders cut assigning him to the Aviation Combat Developments Office, a Class II activity of DCSOPS, at Camp Rucker, Alabama.

He was pleased; he was able to send General Black, the Vice Chief of Staff, a personal note saying that he thought General Black would be pleased to learn of WOJG Greer's new assignment.

General Black was pleased; one of those chair-warming assholes in personnel had finally done something right, had recognized the boy's potential, probably because of the denied Croix de Guerre, and had gotten him a decent assignment as a consolation prize.

WOJG Greer was pleased; anything was better than an assignment to a Transportation Corps helicopter company.

And Colonel William Roberts was pleased; if there was one thing Colonel (designate) Bob Bellmon, two weeks out of helicopter school himself, didn't need, it was a chopper pilot not old enough to vote who had gone to flight school even more recently.

There were, Colonel Roberts thought, a number of interesting things he could do for Bob Bellmon in the future. Sending an incompetent newcomer to work for an incompetent newcomer was only scratching the surface of possibilities.

[THREE]

The first thing Barbara Bellmon said, in the lounge of the Hotel Dothan, when her husband met her there after she had surveyed the post and the available housing was, "I now know how Grandmother Sage must have felt when she arrived at Fort Dodge."

"Was it that bad?" Bellmon asked.

"Everything but hostile Indians," Barbara told her husband. Grandmother Sage had been her great-grandmother, a tall, wiry, leathery lady who had lived to ninety-seven. She had regaled her grandchildren with tales of what it had been like as a young officer's wife living on cavalry posts during the Indian Wars. Some of what she had told them had been true.

"Well, what are we going to do?" he asked. He meant, *What have you decided that we're going to do?* for the division of responsibilities between them gave her housing. She would arrange for it, and he would not complain.

"I thought about trailers," she said.

"Oh, Christ!" he said, earning the disapproving glare of the waitress who had approached the table for his order. "Is it that bad?" Then he turned to the waitress. "You ready for another?" he asked his wife, and when she shook her head, "no," he told the waitress, "Bring me a gin and tonic with a double shot of bitters, please."

"With what?" she asked.

"A double squirt of bitters," he explained. "I like them bitter."

"I'll ask," the waitress said. "But I don't think we have anything like that."

"Ask," he said. "And if you don't, it's OK."

"Welcome to the Wiregrass, you-all," Barbara said, softly, when the waitress was out of earshot.

"You aren't really serious about a trailer, are you?" he asked.

"I don't know what I'm serious about," she said. "I'm really discouraged. There's just no housing, period."

"But a *trailer?*"

"Trailers," she corrected him. "Plural. We'd need two."

"You're serious, aren't you?" he asked. "You're suggesting we rent two trailers."

"We'd do better buying," she said. "They cost about $10,000, for a nice one, and we'd need two, so that would be $20,000."

"Why do we need two?"

"We have children," she said. "Or have you forgotten? And unless you would like one or more of them sharing our bed, we'll need two trailers."

"I thought they made big ones."

"I'm talking about big ones. The little ones are for newlyweds."

"No houses?"

"The name of the game is screw the soldiers," she said. "The houses that are available are either tiny, or outrageously priced, or both."

"We need what?"

"Four bedrooms," she said.

"Dick and Billy could double up."

"Three bedrooms, if you are willing to have your children hate you."

"I'm willing," he said. "Can you find a place?"

"How about six bedrooms?" she asked. "I found an antebellum mansion we can have for $650 a month. Six bedrooms. No air conditioning. I guess in the olden days they had colored people waving fans at Massa and Mistress."

"Six hundred fifty bucks a month?" he asked. "That's a hell of a lot of money."

"That's what I thought," she said, sarcastically, "but I thought I'd better check with you."

"Where is it?"

"On Broad Street," she said, "in Ozark."

"Let me finish my bitterless gin and bitters, and we'll go look at it."

"It will be very conspicuous, Bob," Barbara said. "It looks like Tara in *Gone With the Wind*. And it's sort of a stock joke among the officers' ladies."

"How do you mean?"

" 'If I thought I could get somebody to buy the children, I'm desperate enough to rent the $650 mansion,' " she quoted.

"Oh," he said, and thought that over for a minute. "Oh, what the hell, honey, I'm a colonel, or will be next week, and there'd probably be as much talk if we rented, or bought, two trailers."

"God, I'm glad to hear you say that," she said.

"Why?"

"Because now I can tell you I gave the man . . . and the man is the mayor of Ozark, *and* a lawyer, *and* a real estate guy . . . a deposit for it."

The reluctance of the Bellmons, separately, to take the antebellum mansion at $650 per month was not because of the rent, although $650 was nearly three times Colonel Bellmon's housing allowance. The Bellmons thought of themselves as "comfortable." Most of their peers, if they had known the extent of their holdings in real estate and investments, would have considered them wealthy. This could be an awkward situation in the army, where most officers lived from payday to payday, and they took great pains not to rub their affluence in anyone's sensitive nostrils.

On the way to Ozark in Barbara's Buick (Lt. Col. Bellmon' drove a Volkswagen to work), he told her about WOJG Greer.

"I was assigned a new rotary wing pilot today," he said.

"Oh?"

"By an interesting coincidence, he's the sergeant, the ex-sergeant, who went into Dien Bien Phu with Mac and Sandy Felter."

"How did you arrange that?" she said.

"I didn't arrange it. Bill Roberts arranged it."

"That was nice of him," Barbara said.

"This is no favor," Bellmon said. "He stuck it in me."

"Explain," she said.

"I asked for an experienced warrant helicopter pilot, somebody who had experience in Korea, at the very least. I need experts, honey, not kids who just graduated from flight school."

"Oh," she said, understanding.

"This is the first shot at Fort Sumter," he said. "Open warfare will shortly follow."

"Why?"

"Because Roberts knows what a threat I pose to the aviation establishment," Bellmon said. "And he's a good enough soldier to know that the best defense is a good offense."

"I thought you were sort of friends," she said.

"We were, when I was a tanker, and he was trying to sell aviation to armor as a tool armor needed. But the minute I put on wings, I became a threat, a contender for control of aviation, and that he can't tolerate."

"I don't understand the rivalry."

"He's been studying revolutions," Bellmon said. "He understands that the first thing that usually happens after a successful revolution is that the leaders of the revolutionaries are stood against a wall and shot."

"That's a little strong, isn't it?" she asked.

"What any officer wants is command," he said. "What Roberts fears is that after all the work he's done to convince the brass that aviation is necessary, the commands are going to go to newcomers. Like me."

"Is he right?"

"Right now, the Aviation Board is hot stuff. They've got a bunch of money, and a bunch of people, and they're about to get a bunch of new aircraft, and everything that goes with them. They're going to get their pictures in the paper. But, and Bill Roberts is smart enough to know it, I have the clout. I'm going to be deciding what aviation is going to do with the equipment, and the capability. He knows, in other words, that he's already been shunted over to a support role."

"How come you're so important?" she asked, gently sarcastic.

"I've had a battalion," he said. "The brass trust people who have had commands. And they don't trust aviators. They don't take them seriously."

"Is that fair?"

"What's fair? It's the way things are. The only chance the Cincinnati Flying Club has to keep control of aviation, to keep as much as they can, is to discredit me, people like me. They'll try to make the brass believe that you can't turn over the decision-making to brand-new aviators, because we don't know what we're doing."

"Who's right?"

"That's the bitch, Barbara," he said. "We both are. I don't think the birdmen know, because they haven't been there, what the combat arms need, and what it takes to make a battalion work. And the birdmen don't think that we know, because we haven't been here, what aircraft are, and what they can do."

"So what happens?"

"Darwin. Survival of the fittest. After a good deal of internecine warfare."

"Then you'll win," she said, confidently.

"I'm not entirely sure about that," he said. "And I'm not entirely sure I should."

"Look at Mac," she said. "Trust Mac's instincts."

"What do you mean by that?"

"Mac is the legionnaire in the phalanx," she said. "Nature's natural warrior. No philosophical questions in his mind. He just wants to follow an officer who'll keep him alive and win the battles he's sent to fight. And he enlisted in your army."

"Maybe," he said.

"I remember, I was old enough, when Daddy and I. D. White and Creighton Abrams went to armor from cavalry," she said. "Everybody said they were throwing their careers away. That's what you're doing. They couldn't fight the last war on horses, and they probably won't be able to fight the next one with tanks, or with troops jumping in with parachutes. Army aviation is the answer, and you know it, and you know you're the guy best qualified to figure out how it should be done. Otherwise, you wouldn't have been given the job."

"Have you ever considered a career in the WACs?" he asked.

"I prefer to stand on the sidelines, wearing a big floppy hat, and with a rose in my teeth," she said.

She showed him where to park, before Howard Dutton's office on Courthouse Square in Ozark, directly across the street from the Confederate monument. And they went into Dutton's office, where they met his daughter Melody, and had a cup of coffee. Then they walked down Broad Street where Howard Dutton showed Colonel Bellmon the old Fordham place, which had sat empty for five years, and which he was now going to rent to Bellmon for $650 a month.

VII

[ONE]

Frankfurt am Main, Germany
17 April 1955

As regulations prescribed, Major Craig W. Lowell was given an efficiency report at the conclusion of his year-long initial ultilization tour as an aviator. It wasn't much of an efficiency report; it wouldn't do him much good.

It said that he had performed the duties required of him in an exemplary manner and had materially increased his skills and knowledge as an aviator. Aviators on initial utilization tours were expected to materially increase their skills and knowledge as aviators. Most of them worked hard at it.

The efficiency report also said: "Inasmuch as subject officer has been on an initial utilization tour during the reporting period, he has not been required to perform any functions of command. Consequently, the rating officer has been unable to evaluate his performance as a commander, or to form any opinion concerning subject officer's potential performance as a combat commander in his present or in a higher rank."

In effect, what the efficiency report said was that he managed to put in another year's service without either killing himself in a helicopter or getting into trouble.

What he had become, Major Craig Lowell thought, was a taxi driver to the brass. He was nowhere nearer to doing anything important than he ever had been. There was no reason that a second lieutenant, six months out of flight school, couldn't do what he was doing.

The brass preferred not be flown by second lieutenants. The more senior the brass, the more they could make this known. They felt more comfortable being flown by senior captains and majors and even lieutenant colonels than they did by second lieutenants.

It was Lowell's belief that the younger the pilot, the better. He had prepared a staff study (for Bill Robert's signature; his own signature would make the document meaningless) proposing that fifty enlisted men no older than eighteen years of age, who met the basic requirements for OCS in terms of physical and mental ability, be sent to flight school for training as warrant officer rotary wing aviators. Current practice was to send to flight school deserving noncoms of long and faithful service, technical and master sergeants only, which generally made them twenty-eight or thirty. The performance of the fifty boy pilots over a couple of years would either confirm Lowell's theory, or disprove it.

Roberts had reported that the staff study had caused fits all up and down the Pentagon, particularly with the Transportation Corps, whose senior officer, the Chief of Transportation, had only recently won a major skirmish to have L-20 Beaver and H-34 Choctaw companies designated Transportation Airplane and Helicopter Companies, on the lines of Transportation Truck Companies, and bluntly announced he didn't want a flock of teen-aged warrant officers running loose with his aircraft. The staff study had not been rejected, however. It was "being studied." Rumor had it being studied by the Secretary of Defense himself.

"When you inevitably get us shot down in flames, Lowell," Bill Roberts had written, "we will make a spectacular crash."

Today, leading a flight of eight Bell H-13s, Lowell had flown up the autobahn from Heidelberg to Rhine-Main Airfield outside Frankfurt, where they had topped off the fuel tanks. After they'd taken off, they'd cut directly across Frankfurt over the Bahnhof and then up Erschenheimer-Landstrasse to the grassy expanse in front of the enormous curved facade of the former I. G. Farben Building, now Headquarters, U.S. Forces, European Theater (USFET).

The seven other Bell H-13s flew in trail behind him in a V, each chopper flying two hundred feet behind and one hundred feet above the bird in front of him. They would make an intentional display of themselves when they all suddenly, and virtually simultaneously, swooped out of the sky to pick up a visiting one-star and his collection of colonels and lower hangers-on and ferry them to Heidelberg, to Headquarters, U.S. Army, Europe.

"All right," Major Lowell said to his microphone, "now let's do it right."

He put the H-13 into a steep turn to the left, his eyes on the white painted *H* of the helipad. He straightened the bird out, dropped like a stone, flared, and touched down. He looked out the plexiglass bubble. Six of the seven choppers were on the ground. The seventh was coming in very slowly, like a bather about to test the temperature in a swimming pool. There's always one sonofabitch who's a minute late and a dollar short, Lowell thought, and then started to shut the helicopter down.

A tall, quite handsome officer, with a glistening star pinned to his overseas hat (you didn't see many of them anymore; the generals had taken to wearing the new olive-green uniform, whose hat was generously provided with scrambled eggs on the brim—far more general-like than an overseas cap) came rapidly striding toward Lowell's H-13.

Lowell hadn't expected them for a good five minutes. But he unsnapped his harness, jumped out of the helicopter, ran under the still rotating blades, and held open the passenger door for the buck general with one hand while he saluted with the other.

The general looked him up and down and got into the helicopter. By the time Lowell got back in, the general had already found the headset and put it on.

"I'm Major Lowell, sir," he said. "Were we by any chance late?"

"No, you were thirty seconds early," the buck general said. "That was pretty spectacular, that swooping pigeons bit. Do you do that all the time, or just to impress visitors?"

"We practice all the time, sir," Lowell said. "So that we can impress visitors."

"One of your pigeons was late," the general said. "Did you notice?"

The other pilots reported in, one at a time, giving just their number, to signify their readiness to take off: Five. Two. Seven. Four. Three. Six.

The needles were in the green. Lowell picked up on the cyclic, swooping back in the air. He saw in the mirror that the rest of the flight had taken off when he did. Perfect. The general hadn't seen that, of course. Just the bastard who was late.

"You're smiling," the general said. "I suppose the rest of your flock got off the ground by the numbers."

"Yes, sir."

"Including Tailgate Charley?"

"Yes, sir."

"Now that we're in the air, don't you think it would be a good idea to ask me where we're going?" the general asked.

"I was informed the general's destination was Heidelberg, sir."

"There has been a change in plans. I want to go to Bad Godesberg. Can you do that, or are you going to have to fuel up someplace?"

"We have enough fuel for Bad Godesberg and a thirty-minute reserve, sir," Lowell replied. He pressed his microphone button and called Rhine-Main area control and told him of the change in flight plans.

"That swooping pigeon bit was very impressive," the general said, when he had finished. "Does it have some sort of bona fide military application, or is it like chrome-plating mess kits?"

"If the general can imagine each of these machines as capable of carrying eight fully armed infantrymen, the general can probably imagine that we can discharge a platoon and its basic load of ammunition in just about the time it took us to pick up the general's party, sir."

"And each of those machines could be flown by a teen-aged boy, right?"

That surprised Lowell to the point where he looked at the general.

"Yes, sir, I think they could."

"You *are* one of Bill Robert's acolytes, then?" the general said.

"I don't think of myself so much as an acolyte, General, as a monsignor to his bishop."

The general laughed. "You've heard about the teen-age pilots, then?"

"I was able to help the bishop draft the appeal to the heavens, sir."

"That suggests you wrote it," the general snapped. Lowell didn't reply. "Either you did, or you didn't," the general snapped. "Which is it?"

"I wrote it, General."

"Then you must be another of the recent recruits to peace on earth through air mobility," the general said. "Another bright young officer throwing his career away in a quest for the Holy Grail."

Lowell didn't trust himself to reply.

"Had second thoughts already, have you?" the general asked.

"No, sir," Lowell said, and then he thought, fuck it, this guy hates army aviation anyway. "I'm in army aviation because I don't have a career to throw away. And, with all respect, sir, I think a lot of people are going to eat their words about Colonel Roberts. He's right, and most of his critics are wrong."

The general said, dryly: "Your loyalty is commendable."

Lowell now knew that whatever he said would be wrong. He said nothing.

The general said, "That was a colorful phrase, didn't you think? 'Another bright young officer throwing his career away in a quest for the Holy Grail.' "

The reply came before Lowell could stop it.

"I don't frankly think much of it, General."

"But you will admit it's colorful? I mean, it has a good deal more class than, for example, 'you dumb fuck, you!' Wouldn't you say?"

Lowell had to chuckle. "Yes, sir, it does."

"General Simmons has always had a flair for the spoken word," the general said. "He just used that Holy Grail line on me, when I told him that I had turned down chief of staff of the 2nd Armored Division to assume command of the Army Aviation Center."

The general was smiling when Lowell looked at him in surprise.

"If you're a monsignor, Major, and Bill Roberts is a bishop, I guess that makes me the Pope." The general made the sign of the cross. "Bless you, my Son," he said. "Go and sin no more." He seemed highly pleased with himself.

After a moment, he asked: "I have two more questions, Major."

"Yes, sir."

"There was a Task Force Lowell in the breakout from the Pusan perimeter. That was you, correct?"

"Yes, sir."

"OK, those blanks are filled in. I've heard about you. Next question. As one old tank commander to another, are these things hard to drive?"

"General, they're a bitch," Lowell said.

"I was afraid you were going to say that," the general said. "Then your thesis is the younger the man, the easier he will be to train?"

"Easier to train, in better physical condition with quicker reflexes, and he can be retained on flying duty for a longer period of time, with consequent reduction of training costs."

"Final question," the general said. "When you can find time, I want you to write down this instantaneous discharge of ground troops from helicopters for me. Send it to me at Rucker, it's in Alabama someplace, I never heard of it. Mark the envelope 'personal.' "

"Yes, sir," Lowell said.

"My name is Laird," the buck general said. "My friends call me 'Scotty.' " He paused. "You can call me 'General.' "

Lowell smiled dutifully at General Laird, who was obviously delighted with his wit. Lowell had heard that 'you can call me General' line before. And then he remembered where. The first time he had ever seen a general up close, on the polo field at Bad Nauheim. That long ago. Before he had been an officer; before, even, he had met Ilse.

The general had been Major General Peterson K. "Porky" Waterford, then commanding the U.S. Costabulary, the Army of Occupation police force. He had used the same line on his newly formed polo team, which had consisted of the general, two full bull colonels, and PFC Craig W. Lowell, soon to elevate from draftee to second lieutenant, because "Call Me General" Waterford wanted to beat the French. The French played only fellow officers and gentlemen, and PFC Lowell happened to be a three-goal polo player.

Lowell spent long hours in the three weeks after he dropped Brigadier General Laird and his staff off at Bad Godesberg, writing and rewriting a draft field manual, *Helicopter Placement of the Infantry Platoon*.

It wasn't something he had just thought up; the idea had occurred to him a long time ago (and not, he readily admitted, to him alone). The difference was that he had done more than think about it. Encouraged by Bill Roberts's responses to other ideas of his, he had considered the problem as something real and immediate, as if it were going to happen tomorrow. The only imaginary thing in his proposal was the helicopter itself. The army had already begun to take delivery of Sikorsky H-34 helicopters which could, under ideal conditions, indeed lift eight fully armed troops and their combat load.

The yet-to-be-designed, much less built, helicopter described in *Helicopter Placement of the Infantry Platoon* was capable of carrying twelve fully armed troops under all reasonable conditions, plus five hundred pounds of supplies, and the machine was designed so that troops would be off-loaded through doors on both sides.

Lowell played the devil's advocate, trying as hard as he could to find fault with his own idea and its execution. But finally it was done, and he typed it up himself, with five carbon copies, as neatly, he thought, as any clerk-typist of questionable sexual persuasion could type it, each copy having a cardboard cover and bound together with a paper clip.

Typing the address gave him the biggest thrill.

```
Brig. Gen. Angus C. Laird
Commanding General
The U.S. Army Aviation Center
Camp Rucker, Alabama 36362
                         personal
```

Brigadier General "Scotty" Laird had *asked* for it.

Lowell sent a copy to Phil Parker in Alaska. A Xerox copy; he had forgotten about Phil until he was halfway through typing it up. Six weeks later, he got a Xerox of *Emplacement of the Infantry (Ski) Platoon in Arctic Conditions by Ski-Equipped UIA "Otter" Aircraft.*

Phil had adopted his idea to arctic conditions and had used as his imaginary aircraft a sort of super Beaver, a fourteen passenger DeHavilland single-engine Bush aircraft not yet in the army inventory.

It was the only response Lowell ever got to his proposal. Colonel Bill Roberts acknowledged receiving it, but made no comment. General Laird never even acknowledged receiving it. After several months, Lowell concluded that Laird had just been playing with him, laying some charm on a young officer, getting him to write up an idea that he never intended to seriously consider. He was bitterly disappointed.

And he wasn't doing a goddamned thing of importance now. He was still with the Seventh Army Flight Detachment. He had picked up a bullshit title, "Deputy to the Chief, Special Rotary Wing Missions Branch," but he was painfully aware that he was still playing commissioned jeep driver, ferrying people from one place to another in a flying jeep.

[TWO]
Dothan, Alabama
10 July 1955

Rhonda Wilson Hyde examined herself with pleasure in the mirror of the dressing cubicle in Martinette's Finer Ladies Wear in Dothan. She was wearing a matching set, bra, panties, and half-slip, all black. The half-slip was lace from the hem nearly halfway to the waist. The panties were nearly all lace, except where a strip of solid material was necessary here and there to hold them together, absolutely as fragile and delicate and transparent as it was possible to make them. The bra, while it looked as fragile as the panties, was really quite strong. It had to be to hold her breasts up the way it was, and yet it was surprisingly comfortable. It was also surprisingly expensive, even for Martinette's Finer Ladies Wear.

When she had taken the undies out of the sealed cellophane package—which meant that she would have to buy them—she would have bet the thin straps would cut painfully into her shoulders. And she thought the plastic, or whatever it was, that pushed up the half-cups (the tops were open; anyone looking down her dress could see her nipples) was going to dig into the bottom of her breasts and probably jab painfully into the flesh below. But that didn't happen. The bra was as comfortable as any she had ever worn. And sexy!

But God, if Tommy didn't show up, how was she going to pay for it? Doc would blow his cork if he got a bill from Martinette's for $79.95 plus tax. Dentistry wasn't a printing press for money, he would say. Again.

She turned around, looking over her shoulder into the mirror. There was something sexy about the black strap against her white back.

There was a knock at the cubicle door, and someone pushed on it. But it was latched.

"Telephone, Mrs. Hyde," the saleswoman said. "Your husband, I think."

Good God, it better *not* be Doc. She was supposed to be with her mother, and her mother was supposed to be having trouble with her back. She unhooked the latch and an arm holding a telephone appeared in the crack of the door.

"Hello?" Rhonda Wilson Hyde said, when she had the phone to her ear, her free hand pushing the door closed.

"Can you talk?" Tommy Z. Waters asked.

"Hello, darling," she said. "I'm nearly through. I should be home in about an hour."

"I'm up the street," Tommy Z. Waters said.

"How interesting!" Rhonda said. "I'll hurry."

Tommy Z. Waters hung up without saying anything else.

"Good-bye, darling," Rhonda Wilson Hyde said to the dead telephone. Then she opened the door wide enough to put her hand, and the telephone, through.

When the saleswoman took it from her hand, Rhonda latched the door so she couldn't "accidentally" come in. Rhonda wanted to wear the black underwear, and she didn't want the saleswoman to know. She put her own bra and panties in her purse, and paid for her purchase in cash.

The Downtowner Motel up the street was owned by the Downtowner Corporation, whose stock was split among three doctors, a lawyer (Howard Dutton), and a businessman, Tommy Z. Waters.

Five minutes from the moment he had hung up on Rhonda Wilson Hyde, she came through the door of the motel room and pushed it quickly closed behind her.

"I'm always afraid that someone will see me come in here," she said, leaning against the door.

He didn't reply. Cutting through the Downtowner Motel parking lot was a shortcut to the municipal parking lot on the street behind it. If someone you didn't want to see happened to be in the motel parking lot, or walking through it, you just kept walking to the municipal parking lot (where you had parked your car) or onto South Main Street, where the shops were.

Rhonda pushed herself away from the door and went to the refrigerator, where she opened the freezer compartment and took out a small, ice-crusted glass. She put two ice cubes in it, and then walked to where five bottles of liquor stood on a chest of drawers. She filled the glass with gin, added an olive from a jar, and stirred it with her finger.

"Oh, I need this," she said. "You don't want one?"

He shook his head, "No."

"Oh, Tommy, darling, do you have any money with you? I went out without bringing any."

That hadn't stopped her from shopping, he thought. She had three bags.

He took a folded wad of bills from his pocket, spread them out, and extended them to her. There was three, maybe four hundred dollars in the fan he extended to her. Fifties and twenties and tens. Resisting the temptation to take it all, Rhonda pulled two fifties from the fan.

The bra and the panties and the half-slip had cost *almost* that much. It was only fair that Tommy pay for them. She was wearing them for him. Doc would never see her in them. Well, maybe the half-slip, but never the bra and the panties. They would give Doc a fit. She was a respectable married woman, and respectable married women didn't wear open-cupped brassieres and transparent panties with everything showing.

She said thank you, and then tucked the two fifties in her purse, and then she said, "I've got to tinkle."

When she came out of the toilet, she was wearing just the brassiere and the panties. Tommy was already in the bed, naked, with his hands laced behind his head.

"Like it?" she said. "I just bought it."

"Jesus!" he said. "Jesus Christ!"

She was pleased at what he said, and what happened. His cock got stiff. God, he had a marvelous cock! She went and sat on the bed and lowered herself over him, so that he could get his tongue on her nipple.

Afterward, as always, she went to the john first, but this time when she came out, she was dressed.

"What's the hurry?" Tommy asked. That's what he was asking out loud, Rhonda thought. What he was really asking was, "Only once?"

Until recently, Rhonda was in no greater hurry to leave than Tommy was, unless she was late or something. Tommy, in fact, often disappointed her when he just jumped out of bed, Wham, Bam, Thank you, Ma'am. Just like Doc.

"I'm going out to the post," Rhonda said, examining her lipstick one last time in the mirror. "To see about a job."

"What kind of job?"

"I took nutrition at the university," she said. "There's an opening."

"What's Doc think about that?" Tommy Z. Waters asked.

"I haven't told him yet," she said.

She sat on the bed and kissed Tommy, just her tongue, so she wouldn't muss her lipstick, and she gave his thing a little pump, just for the fun of it, and then she walked out of the motel room, looking around to see if anybody had seen her, and then got in her car.

If she got a job at the post, she decided, that would be the end of the motel room. She was tired of it anyway. Doing it with Tommy was getting to be just about as boring as doing it with Doc.

When Rhonda got the telephone call from the civilian personnel office out at the post, asking if she could come out there for an interview that afternoon, she thought that she was actually going to get the job.

She'd heard about the job at the New Year's Eve party at the officer's club. The military medical and dental people had gone out of their way to be nice to their civilian counterparts. Inviting people who lived in a dry county to a New Year's Eve where Kentucky sour mash bourbon sold for forty-five cents a drink was about as nice as they could be. One of the officers at their table had been a Medical Service Corps officer who had had a hard time keeping his eyes off her boobies. She'd taken a couple of drinks in the afternoon, and that had given her the courage to wear her other open-cupped bra.

Either Doc was so dumb he didn't notice, or he just didn't care, because, despite the way she'd worried about it, he hadn't said a word about it to her. Anyway, the major from the Medical Service Corps had told her, sometime during the evening, that the hospital was looking for dieticians, Grade GS-5. Rhonda had picked right up on that. She had her degree in home economics from the University of Alabama, and she'd had a lot of courses in diet and nutrition, and things like that.

The major said it wasn't up to him to decide—if it was, the job was hers—but that the civilian personnel office made the decision. They went over applications from people and saw whether or not they met the requirements. So Rhonda had filled out the application (my God, the thing was six pages long, and even wanted to know if you had ever been arrested, or been a member of any political organization advocating the violent, or revolutionary, overthrow of the United States government) and mailed it off. And five weeks later, she got the call.

The civilian personnel officer turned out to be a woman, a skinny woman, a 30-AAA cup, training-bra type woman, not an officer, which had sort of disappointed Rhonda. Women aren't interested in well-dressed women; they just get jealous. What the civilian personnel officer, Mrs. Cawthorn, told her was that the dietician, GS-5, job was already filled and that she wasn't qualified anyway. Rhonda was just about to tell her she could have told her that on the telephone and saved her a trip all the way out here, when Mrs. Cawthorn said there was something else.

Something called the Aviation Combat Development Agency had an opening for an administrative officer, Grade GS-7. Rhonda wasn't qualified for that, either, but since she had a college degree, *that* made her eligible for what they called the intern program, which was how the government trained people straight from college with no experience. She could start as a GS-5, and if after a year's probation she learned to do the job, they would make her a GS-7. Mrs. Cawthorn said she wasn't offering her the job. All she could do was set up an interview for her with the executive officer, a Major MacMillan, and see if he was willing to take a chance on her.

Mrs. Cawthorn got on the telephone right then and called Major MacMillan. The major said he could see her if she would get to his office within fifteen minutes.

She had a little trouble finding the place, a converted barracks, and when she went inside, there was a secretary, a Mrs. Heatter, who treated her as if she was collecting money for Russian Relief or something.

"Do you have an appointment?" Mrs. Heatter asked.

"He expects me," Rhonda said. "Civilian personnel sent me over about the administrative officer's job."

Rhonda would have had to be blind not to see that Mrs. Heatter was something less than thrilled to hear that.

"Why don't you tell him I'm here?" Rhonda said, flashing a big smile at her.

Mrs. Heatter picked up her telephone (a funny looking telephone; Rhonda had never seen one like that before) and dialed just one number.

"Major, there is a Mrs. Hyde here, who says you expect her." Mrs. Heatter then rose and showed Rhonda into another office. "Mrs. Hyde, Major MacMillan."

After all that formal business, Rhonda expected an officer in full dress uniform, at least. The man who said, "Come in, please, Mrs. Hyde," was wearing what looked like a junior league baseball jacket. It was a violent shade of orange and had a snake embroidered on the front with the word MOCCASIN sewn above it.

He shook Rhonda's hand, took her application from her, and offered her a seat. Rhonda regretted all the emphasis she'd given on the application to her nutritional and food preparation experience. It made her sound like a short order cook.

"What the application doesn't show, Major," Rhonda said, flashing him a big smile, and leaning over so that if he wanted to, he could look down her dress, "is that I've been running my husband's office since we were married. All the administration, so to speak."

"Do you type, by the way?"

"No," she said, "not very well." She figured she could get away with that; he had looked down her dress. He was all man, she could tell that.

"That must make things tough in your husband's office," he said, and there was a sarcastic tone in his voice, but he left it there and went on: "Here's a copy of the job description. Why don't you take a look at it and see if you think you'd be able to do it?"

Rhonda sat back and read the job description with what she hoped looked like intelligent interest. When she felt Major MacMillan's eyes on her boobies again, she sat up and leaned over, her eyes still on the job description, to give him a better look. It was either the boobies or nothing; she didn't understand a word of the job description. She told herself that an office was an office, and once she got the job she could figure out what she was supposed to do. She really wanted the job. Major MacMillan was very interesting, indeed, and there would probably be other interesting men, as well.

"I'm sure that once I got my feet on the ground, I could handle this," she said, and flashed him a dazzling smile. "But I have to tell you that I've never had the chance to be around senior army officers before."

"Do you know what a Multilith is?" Major MacMillan asked.

"Yes, sir," she said. "We have one at the church."

All she knew about a Multilith machine was that it was a dirty machine that sat in the preacher's office.

"And you can run it?" he asked. "Or supervise the people that do?"

"Oh, yes, sir."

"I have to tell you, Mrs. Hyde, that this isn't an eight-to-five job," Major MacMillan said. "We would expect you to be available to come into work sometimes very early in the morning, and to work at night, and over weekends. If you're looking for an eight-to-five job, this isn't it."

"My time is my own," Rhonda said.

"What about your husband? And your children?"

"My mother takes care of the children when the housekeeper isn't there," Rhonda said.

"Now, don't tell me that now, and then come in two months and tell me you can't handle the hours."

"I wouldn't do that, Major MacMillan."

"Can you come to work tomorrow morning?"

"Yes, sir."

"About seven o'clock," he said. "We start early sometimes." He wasn't that hard to figure out. He just wanted to see if she meant what she said about being willing to come in early.

"Yes, sir," Rhonda said. That was going to cause trouble. Doc would be furious if she wasn't there to make his breakfast. Too bad. She had a job, and the prospects looked simply fascinating. Doc would just have to get used to making his own breakfast. Hell, they could hire a cook at what she was going to make out here.

[THREE]
Camp Rucker, Alabama
16 August 1955

Warrant Officer Junior Grade Edward C. Greer's gray U.S. Air Force issue flight suit was sweat-soaked and showed white lines where the salt tablets, ingested as protection against the heat, had passed out of his body. He carried a white plastic crash helmet loosely under his left arm as he knocked at the sill of the open door of the director, Aviation Combat Developments Agency.

"Come on in, Greer," Colonel Robert F. Bellmon said. The kid looked exhausted. Bellmon really hated to do what he had to do, eat the kid's ass out.

Greer saluted, not especially crisply, but, Bellmon thought, with a flair that represented what a salute was really supposed to be all about, a greeting between practitioners of the profession of arms, not, as most people believed, a symbolic gesture of servitude by the junior to the senior.

"You wanted to see me, Colonel?" Greer asked, but it was more of a statement than a question.

"Little warm outside, is it?" Colonel Bellmon asked.

"I mounted a thermometer on the instrument panel," Greer said. "It went to 125 degrees." Bellmon noticed that that, too, was a statement of fact and not a complaint.

Good lad, he thought. Then, fuck it. I'll eat his ass out later.

"I thought you would be interested in this," Colonel Bellmon said, and handed him the stapled together stack of correspondence:

HEADQUARTERS

U.S. ARMY AVIATION COMBAT DEVELOPMENTS AGENCY

CAMP RUCKER, ALABAMA

20 July 1955

SUBJECT: Request for Flight Training in, and 250 hours of, YH-40 aircraft flight.

TO: President
U.S. Army Aviation Board
Camp Rucker, Alabama

1. Inasmuch as the USAACDA is charged with determining the future role, if any, of YH-40 aircraft presently undergoing flight testing by the USAAB in the field forces, it is considered absolutely essential that the USAACDA have access to YH-40 aircraft at the earliest possible time.

2. Request is made herewith that the following personnel of the USAACDA be given, as soon as possible, flight training in YH-40 aircraft assigned to the USAAB. While training by USAAB personnel of all USAACDA personnel listed would be most desirable, should this pose an unusual burden upon the mission of the USAAB, the USAACDA requests the training of Major R.G. MacMillan to a level qualifying him as an instructor pilot, in order that he might accomplish training of the other USAACDA personnel who will be involved with the YH-40, WOJG Edward C. Greer and the undersigned.

3. The USAACDA will arrange to schedule training to meet any USAAB requirements.

Robert F. Bellmon
Colonel, Armor
Director, USAACDA

1st Ind

HQ USAAB, CP RUCKER ALA 23 JULY 1955
TO: DIRECTOR, USAACDA CP RUCKER, ALA

1. The USAAB board has been assigned three (3) YH-40 helicopter aircraft. No additional YH-40 aircraft will be made available in the forseeable future.

2. In order to insure that available aircraft will meet the testing requirements placed upon the USAAB by DCSOPS, it is the policy of the USAAB that only helicopter pilots of great experience will be assigned to fly YH-40 aircraft. Criteria established include seven (7) years experience as a rated aviator; 2,500 hours total flight time; 1,000 hours rotary wing flight time.

3. Further, the flight testing mission placed upon the USAAB by the DCSOPS is such that available flight time for the available aircraft is fully scheduled through 31 Dec 1955.

4. Consequently, the request of the basic communication must be denied.

5. Should the USAACDA wish to furnish the USAAB with any specific flight tests it wishes to have accomplished, the USAAB will make every reasonable effort to have such tests conducted by USAAB personnel already qualified in YH-40 aircraft. The USAAB feels this would be the most economical use of available assets in any case.

William R. Roberts
Colonel, Artillery
President

2nd Ind

HQ USAACDA CP RUCKER ALA 24 JULY 1955

TO: DEPUTY CHIEF OF STAFF FOR OPERATIONS, HQ DEPT OF THE ARMY WASH 25 DC

VIA: Chief Avn Br DCSOPS Hq DA Wash 25 DC

1. Attention is invited to basic communication and 1st indorsement thereto.

2. Unless USAACDA personnel are trained in YH-40 aircraft and YH-40 aircraft are made available for a minimum of 250 flight hours, the USAACDA will not be able to generate performance and other data on which to base its recommendations for the utilization of the YH-40 in the field force.

3. Request guidance.

Robert F. Bellmon
Colonel, Armor
Director

3rd Ind

AVN BRANCH DCSOPS HQ DA WASH DC 5 AUG 1955

TO: DCSOPS HQ DA WASH 25 DC

1. The situation described in 1st and 2nd Ind hereto has been investigated by the undersigned, and the following determined:

a. The three YH-40 aircraft assigned to USAAB for USAAB testing are barely adequate for that purpose, and production of additional aircraft in the foreseeable future will be assigned to the USAF for airframe stress and other testing, and to the Transportation Corps for the determination of maintenance and spare parts requirements.

b. The USAAB testing program would be severely hampered by the loss of any YH-40 flight hours, either by the loss of YH-40 aircraft to another agency, or in the event of an aircraft accident.

c. Prudence requires that the available YH-40 aircraft, which, because of their size and power, and because their flight characteristics are not now known, should be flown only by experienced aviators in order to reduce the possibility of their loss due to pilot error or inexperience to an absolute minimum.

d. With the exception of Major MacMillan, the USAACDA aviators for whom flight instruction in the YH-40 has been requested are recent graduates of flight school. Specifically, the provisions of AR 1-670 requiring a one (1) year initialization tour had to be waived in the case of both Col. Bellmon and WOJG Greer in order to permit their present assignment.

e. A review of USAACDA test programs (proposed) by the undersigned indicates that the great majority of such testing could be integrated into present USAAB test programs.

2. It is therefore recommended that the USAACDA be directed to effect such liaison with the USAAB as necessary in order to incorporate those test programs they feel are necessary into present USAAB test programs. This would insure a more efficient use of available assets, and simultaneously reduce, through the use of aviators of long experience, the risk permitting USAACDA aviators to pilot the experimental aircraft would entail.

Arthur D. Gregory
Colonel, Artillery
Chief, Aviation Branch

4th Ind

Office of the Deputy Chief of Staff for Operations, Headquarters, Department of the Army, Washington 25, DC, 11 August 1955

To: Commanding General, USA Aviation School & Camp Rucker, Ala.
Chief, Aviation Branch, DCSOPS, Hq DA Wash 25 DC
President, US Army Aviation Board, Camp Rucker, Ala.
Director, US Army Aviation Combat Developments Agency, Camp Rucker, Ala.

1. The Deputy Chief of Staff for Operations wishes to remind all concerned that the USAACDA was established at Camp Rucker for several reasons:

a. In order to provide the DCSOPS with an independent agency capable of basing its recommendations concerning the future of army aviation in the field forces on its own independent judgment.

b. In order that it would be in a physical position to receive what logistic and training support it required from both the US Army Aviation Board and the US Army Aviation School and Center.

2. The Deputy Chief of Staff for Operations believes that very little meaningful data concerning operation of YH-40 aircraft by personnel with little flight experience, as would be encountered in a mobilization situation, can be obtained

from test programs in which all of the aviators have seven (7) years flight experience, including 2,500 hours total flight time, and 1,000 hours helicopter experience.

3. The Deputy Chief of Staff for Operations has received permission from the Vice Chief of Staff to have twenty (20) graduates from the next two (2) Warrant Officer Candidate Rotary Wing Flight Classes assigned for a period of six months to the USAAB for utilization as pilots of YH-40 aircraft undergoing test. Aviators of great experience presently assigned to the USAAB will be assigned to monitor such flight testing, but will *not* participate in flight testing under normal circumstances. It is believed that the pool of aviators possessing seven (7) years and many thousands of hours of flight experience will not be large enough to man the field force envisioned for the future, and that therefore large numbers of inexperienced aviators must be trained.

4. The President of the USAAB is directed to train the officers listed in the basic communication as YH-40 pilots as soon as possible, and to make available to the USAACDA YH-40 aircraft for a minimum flight test program of 250 hours.

5. The Deputy Chief of Staff wishes to state that while he has found this correspondence interesting, he is sure that he will not again be required to devote his time to solving problems that should not have arisen.

BY ORDER OF THE DCSOPS:

Howard G. Kellogg
Brigadier General, USA
Asst DCSOPS

"Jesus H. Christ!" WOJG Greer said. "You sure as hell won that one, Colonel."

"Colonel Roberts went a little too far," Bellmon said. "It was both too obviously chickenshit, and too obviously a grab for power. He lost that fight, but he's smart and he won't make the same mistakes the next time we get into it. Even this, if you think it through, Greer, is not all peaches and cream. I'm really on the Flying Club's—" he caught himself just in time, deleted "shit," and concluded—"list, now."

"Fuck 'em," WOJG Greer said, cheerfully.

"Close your sewer of a mouth, Mr. Greer," Colonel Bellmon said, very sharply, and when Greer looked at him in surprise, added: "And stand at attention, too, please."

Greer came to attention, a look of bafflement vanishing as he froze his facial features.

Colonel Bellmon pushed a lever on his intercom. "Major MacMillan!"

"Yes, sir."

"Please report to me immediately," Colonel Bellmon said.

"On my way," MacMillan replied cheerfully.

MacMillan came into the office a moment later, walking like Groucho Marx, grinning broadly, and tipping off his fiber tropical helmet.

"Look what I found in the clothing store," he cried, happily.

It was too much for Colonel Bellmon. In the Frank Buck hat, and khaki short pants, MacMillan looked like a burlesque comedian.

"I asked you to report to me, Major," Bellmon said, icily.

MacMillan looked at him in surprise, and then saw he was serious. He sailed the Frank Buck tropical helmet out the door, came to attention, and saluted.

"Major MacMillan reporting as ordered, sir," he said.

MacMillan, Bellmon thought, didn't look much older than he had ten years before, when, as Technical Sergeant MacMillan, he had been with Bellmon in the stalag.

"The reason I have asked you gentlemen in to see me," Bellmon said, "is that it has come to my attention that you are guilty of conduct unbecoming to officers and gentlemen."

MacMillan and Greer stole quick, confused looks at one another.

"And the reason I have you standing here at attention is to convince you that I consider this whole matter quite serious."

"May I inquire what the colonel makes reference to, sir?" MacMillan asked, still at rigid attention.

"Your filthy mouth, Mac," Bellmon said. "And yours, Mr. Greer."

They both looked confused. Bellmon let them sweat a minute, and then went on.

"Mrs. Heatter was in here," Bellmon said. "In tears. Crying. She said she had to have a transfer."

"I'm not sure I follow you, sir," MacMillan said. "What was she crying about?"

"She said she liked her job, but that she was a Christian woman, and she could not continue to work under such conditions."

"What conditions, Colonel?" Greer asked. Bellmon thought he looked about sixteen years old.

"Your filthy goddamned mouth is what I'm talking about, Mr. Greer," Colonel Bellmon said. "Your constant blasphemy and obscenity."

"Yes, sir," Greer said.

"Just Greer's filthy goddamned mouth, Colonel?" MacMillan asked, too innocently. "Or my goddamned filthy mouth, too?"

Bellmon stared at MacMillan in disbelief. Was MacMillan actually daring to mock him?

And then he recalled his own words.

"Shit!" he said. They all laughed.

He got control of himself in a moment.

"Oh, stand at ease," he said. "But listen to me, you two. I'm serious about this. Mrs. Heatter was really in here. She was really crying, and she was really upset. I've got enough trouble without her filing a complaint with civilian personnel about you two."

"I don't know what the hell she's talking about," Greer said, seriously. "I know what she's like. She carries Bible study lessons in her purse and reads them when she eats lunch. You don't think I was making a pass at her, or anything like that, do you?"

That thought hadn't even occurred to Bellmon.

"She's the kind who thinks that 'hell' is a dirty word, Greer," Bellmon said. "So don't use it."

"I thought I was watching it," Greer said. "But yes, sir, I'll watch it even more closely."

"We're all guilty, I'm sure," Bellmon said. "But she especially complained about you, Greer."

"Not about me?" MacMillan said.

"She said you don't seem to care what kind of filthy language he uses," Bellmon said. "So you watch Greer, and I'll be watching you. Understood?"

"Yes, sir."

"Take a look at this, Mac," Bellmon said, and handed him the YH-40 correspondence.

"Jesus Christ," MacMillan said. "When Gregory and Roberts saw this, the shit must have really hit the fan."

Colonel Bellmon did not correct him, Greer noticed. Because it would have been necessary to eat his ass out if he had? Or because he had agreed with MacMillan's assessment and really didn't notice the language?

"So we're going to get a YH-40 to play with, are we?" MacMillan said.

It was another of MacMillan's classic examples of saying the right thing the wrong way. They weren't going to "play" with the YH-40. MacMillan knew as well as he did what they were going to do with it.

The YH-40 was a nine-passenger helicopter, powered by an 1,100 horsepower turbine engine. It was intended to replace the Sikorsky H-19 and H-34, which had a reciprocating gasoline engine—neither efficient nor entirely safe in helicopter operations. It was faster, smaller, and carried as many passengers (nine, without equipment) as the H-34. It was obviously going to be the helicopter with which the army would be equipped in the 1960s.

The "Y" in the designation stood for prototype, an acknowledgement that the production helicopters (the H-40s) would be different from the prototype YH-40s in detail. They would be changed to reflect what would be learned about them when they were tested.

It was Bellmon's job as director of the Aviation Combat Developments Agency to test the machine to see what it was capable of and to adapt this capability to what had become known as the "Flying Army." He would then request that changes be made to the machine so that it could better accomplish its duty.

Both looking after the changes and testing to see if the modified aircraft did what it was supposed to do was the function of the Aviation Board. They had tried and failed—by painting themselves as the only experts—to usurp Bellmon's responsibility and authority. The fight had gone as high as DCSOPS, and DCSOPS had cut the Cincinnati Flying Club off at the knees.

But getting a YH-40 for 250 hours was only the beginning of the fight. Bellmon could count on the Cincinnati Flying Club finding fault with any conclusion he reached which did not entirely agree with one of their own. He would have to be able to prove every point he made about the YH-40.

That was not, as MacMillan put it, getting a "YH-40 to play around with."

But Bellmon didn't correct him. He knew he hadn't heard the end of the battle with Colonel Bill Roberts. He felt very much alone, alone in a way neither MacMillan or Greer could understand. Right now, they were the only two people he could really count on. It would have made no sense to hurt Mac's feelings by correcting him.

VIII

[ONE]
The Officer's Open Mess
Camp Rucker, Alabama
22 August 1955

"Mrs. Hyde? I'm Barbara Bellmon," the woman said, walking briskly over to Rhonda with a smile on her face, and her hand extended. "I'm so glad you could come."

"It was very nice of you to ask me," Rhonda Wilson Hyde, Administrative Officer (Probationary) of the USA Aviation Combat Developments Agency said to the wife of the Director of the USAACDA.

"I thought we should get to know one another," Barbara Bellmon said. She led Rhonda into the barroom of the officer's open mess and waved her into a chair at a table. A GI waiter was immediately at their side.

"What can I get you, Miz Bellmon?" he asked.

"Oh, I think I'll have one of your wave-the-vermouth-cork-over-the-neck-of-the-gin-bottle martinis," Mrs. Bellmon said.

"Yes, Ma'am," the waiter said. He looked at Rhonda.

"The same for me, please," Rhonda said.

She liked this. Respectable married women in Dale and Houston counties did not go by themselves to a bar and order martini cocktails at lunchtime.

"I always like a martini before lunch," Barbara Bellmon said. "But I feel wicked if I do it at home."

"I know what you mean, Mrs. Bellmon," Rhonda said.

"Oh, call me 'Barbara,' please," Mrs. Bellmon said.

"And you call me 'Rhonda,' " Rhonda said, pleased with that too.

"We should have had lunch sooner," Barbara Bellmon said. "But I was out of town."

"Oh?"

"A wedding," Barbara Bellmon said. "Scotty Laird's sister's boy married my cousin Ted's daughter. That's pretty involved, I guess, isn't it? If you're an army brat, as I am, you simply presume that everybody knows who you mean."

" 'Scotty' Laird? Is that the general who's coming here?"

"Yes," Barbara Bellmon said. "We grew up together, as the kids did. Army brats seem to wind up married to each other."

"That sounds very nice," Rhonda said. She found it interesting that Mrs. Bellmon was a friend of the incoming post commander. She had certainly started off in the right circles.

The waiter delivered the martinis.

"Here's to you and your new job," Barbara Bellmon said, raising her glass.

"Why, thank you," Rhonda said, and took a sip of the really icy, *really* dry martini.

"Do you like your job?" Barbara Bellmon asked.

"I'm just learning it," Rhonda confessed. "But I'm fascinated. I've been on the long distance telephone more in the last two weeks than I've ever been in my life."

"I'm sure it's quite a change from what you're used to," Barbara Bellmon said. There was something in her tone that Rhonda didn't like, but she couldn't put her finger on it.

"Yes, it is," she said smiling.

"You'll quickly learn that the army is a small world of its own," Barbara Bellmon said. "Everybody knows everybody else."

"Your husband," Rhonda said, and then corrected herself, "Colonel Bellmon and Major MacMillan are old friends, I know that."

"They met in a POW camp," Barbara Bellmon said. "During World War II."

"That must have been tough on you," Rhonda said, sympathetically.

"We have a friend," Barbara Bellmon said, "Major Craig Lowell. I think you'd like him. Well, as proof of my small army world theory: the commandant of the stalag, which is what they call a POW camp, was a Colonel von Greiffenberg. He and my father had been classmates at the French cavalry school at Samur together."

"Was your father a soldier?" Rhonda asked.

"My maiden name was Waterford," Barbara Bellmon said.

It took Rhonda a second or two to pick up on that.

"General Waterford? The one with the tanks?"

"That's right," Mrs. Bellmon said.

"Well, my God, I'm impressed," Rhonda said.

"You shouldn't be," Barbara Bellmon said. "His friends called him 'Porky.' "

"You know, you just can't imagine anybody calling a *general* 'Porky.' "

"Only other generals called him that," Barbara Bellmon said. Rhonda wondered why she was getting this whole business, why Barbara Bellmon was trying to impress her with her army connections. Then she realized that if she had been the daughter of a famous tank general, a friend of Eisenhower and Patton and people like that, she'd want people to know, too.

"I'm really impressed," Rhonda said, truthfully.

"Well, I'm telling you what a small world it is," Barbara Bellmon went on. "After the war, my father met a young soldier who really impressed him, and he arranged for him to be commissioned."

That was the truth, Barbara Bellmon realized as she spoke, but it was not the whole truth and nothing but the truth. What had impressed her father about Private Craig W. Lowell was that he was a three-goal polo player.

"Can generals do that? I mean, make officers out of soldiers?"

Barbara Bellmon signaled the waiter for a second martini.

"Generals can do practically anything they want to do," Barbara Bellmon said. "That's why everybody wants to be a general." They laughed together.

"I was telling you about Craig Lowell," Barbara said. "Well, he married a German girl—" now that I admit I am stretching the truth, she thought, the distortions come so easily!—"and that's something that young officers just don't do. Like making a pass at their commanding officer's daughter. Or wife."

"I understand," Rhonda said.

"And who do you think the girl turned out to be?"

"I really can't guess," Rhonda replied.

"The daughter of Colonel, now Generalmajor, von Greiffenberg," Barbara Bellmon said. "They named their son after the general, who was then in a Russian POW camp. He wasn't released until 1950."

"But then everybody lived happily ever after? What a charming story!"

"Not really," Barbara Bellmon said. "When Craig was in Korea, the girl was killed in an automobile accident."

"Oh, how terrible!"

"Yes, it was. And what made it worse was that the man who killed her was also an army officer. A quartermaster major. He was cashiered, of course, but that didn't bring Craig's wife back."

"What happened to the baby?"

"He's being raised by his mother's family," Barbara Bellmon said.

"You really are just one big family then, aren't you?"

"Yes," Barbara Bellmon said, and then to the waiter: "Oh, that was quick!" The waiter set fresh martinis before them.

"I'm go glad you told me all of this," Rhonda said. "It helps me to understand so much!"

"There's one other thing you should understand," Barbara Bellmon said.

"What's that?"

"Army wives don't like to share their husbands," Barbara Bellmon said.

For a moment, Rhonda wasn't sure that she had heard right.

"I'm sure," she said, "that I don't know what you mean." She tried to sound as indignant as she could. While it was true that she thought that Colonel Bellmon was quite a man, and to be absolutely truthful about it, she had wondered what it would be like with him, that had been fantasy. She was not about to get involved with her boss. Especially since he had shown absolutely no interest in her.

"You know exactly what I mean," Barbara Bellmon said.

"I don't know . . ."

"You're not Bob's type," Barbara Bellmon said. "But on the other hand, if any man has it waved in his face often enough, he's going to take a sniff."

"I just don't know . . ." Rhonda protested.

"Mac MacMillan," Barbara Bellmon said, "is something else. He's not quite as bad as Craig Lowell, but he has been known to stray. When that happens, Roxy MacMillan is very unhappy. And when Roxy MacMillan, who is one of my very best friends, is unhappy, I'm unhappy. And if I'm unhappy, I can make things very unpleasant for you, Rhonda."

"You have no right to say these things to me!" Rhonda said.

"I have the right," Barbara Bellmon said. "I'm what they call the colonel's lady. And it's not all pouring tea, Rhonda. You'd better understand that, too."

Rhonda was now speechless.

"All I'm saying to you is stay away from the married men, officer and enlisted," Barbara Bellmon said. "If you're not getting what you need at home, and you can't find it off the post, stay away from our married men."

"I don't have to sit here and be insulted this way!" Rhonda said.

"If you want to satisfactorily complete your probationary period, you do," Barbara Bellmon said. "I'm holding all the aces. When my father taught me to play poker, he told me to go for the jugular."

She met Rhonda's eyes and held them for a moment.

"Have a go at young Mr. Greer," she said. "I'd rather have him involved with someone like you than have him get caught by one of the local belles."

Without thinking what she was saying, Rhonda said: "Greer is just a kid!"

"He's big enough," Barbara Bellmon said. "And they're supposed to be better when they're young. Just keep in mind, though, that Greer's part of the family. Sort of a little brother."

"I don't quite understand you."

"Get Mac to tell you about him sometime. They had quite an escapade in Indo-China together."

The waiter appeared.

"Your table is ready, Miz Bellmon," he said, handing her the check. Barbara Bellmon signed it.

"You know, of course, Rhonda," she said, "that when you complete your probationary period, you'll be eligible to join the officer's club." She met her eyes again. "Shall we have our lunch?" she asked.

"I'm famished," Rhonda said.

"Probably the martinis," Barbara Bellmon said and led Rhonda into the dining room.

[TWO]
Augsburg, West Germany
26 September 1955

Major Craig W. Lowell spent most of the morning (from 0950 until 1215 hours) of 26 September 1955 in the PX cafeteria at the Hersfeld Kaserne of the 24th Armored Cavalry Regiment, drinking nickle coffee from a china mug and reading the *Stars and Stripes* and *Cavalier* and *True* magazines.

Major Lowell had flown to Hersfeld a full colonel of the Ordnance Section of Headquarters, Seventh Army, who was uneasy being flown about by junior officers and who had requested Major Lowell as pilot. Once in Hersfeld, however, reasoning that since Lowell was not an ordnance officer and therefore had nothing to contribute to his business with the 24th's commanding and ordnance officers and was in fact nothing more than a pilot, the ordnance colonel had told Major Lowell to "go catch a cup of coffee somewhere, and I'll get word to you when I need you."

At 1215 hours, Major Lowell was summoned from the PX cafeteria to the officer's open mess by the ordnance colonel, who at that time had reasoned he had an obligation to see that his pilot was fed. Even if he was an airplane driver, he was a major, a field-grade officer; common military courtesy required that he be invited to eat with them.

Luncheon at the 24th Armored Cavalry officer's open mess was a little awkward for Major Lowell. The colonel commanding the 24th Armored Cavalry was there, as was his executive officer, his S-3 plans and training officer, his S-4 supply officer, and the commanding officers of Troops "A," "C," and "D." All of these officers were naturally armor officers, and most of them looked curiously at Major Lowell when the ordnance colonel introduced him as "my pilot."

Major Lowell was wearing the cavalry sabers superimposed upon a tank insignia of armor, an Expert Combat Infantry Badge (second award), and his aviator's wings. In contravention of regulations, he was not wearing any of the ribbons representing any of his many medals.

Lowell typically ran into two classes of armor officers, those who knew about Task Force Lowell and those who didn't. Of those who did know about it and knew that he had been its commander, eighty to ninety percent felt that both its reputation and the promotion and decoration of its commander were so much bullshit. These rather rejoiced to see that the army had finally caught up with him and thrown him out of armor on his ass. Those other armored officers (including a rare one here and there who had been in Task Force Lowell), who felt that it was one of the better operations in that fucked-up war in Frozen Chosen and that its commander fully deserved his Distinguished Service Cross and the gold leaf, were even more awkward when encountered. They were embarrassed to see the man who had led forty-four M46 tanks faster and further than anyone else reduced to flying a whirlybird.

Those two groups together consisted of perhaps ten percent of all armor officers. The other ninety percent had never heard of Task Force Lowell or of Major Craig

Lowell. They were cavalrymen, stationed in a fort on the enemy's border, ready at a moment's notice to heed the sound of the trumpet and charge off to do battle, and they thought as much of an armor major who arrived driving a helicopter as they would have thought, a hundred years before, of a cavalry major who arrived at Fort Riley driving a mess wagon. Any cavalryman who would do something so degrading wasn't very much of a cavalryman.

There were no officers present at luncheon who had served under Major Lowell at the time he led Task Force Lowell, but there were, he was sure, at least two officers who connected him with Task Force Lowell and would thus have something to talk about when he was gone. The commanding officer of the 24th Armored Cavalry was one of them.

"Didn't you at one time work for General Paul Jiggs, Major?"

Brigadier General, then Lieutenant Colonel, Paul Jiggs had been the commanding officer of the 73rd Heavy Tank Battalion, from which Task Force Lowell had been formed.

"Yes, sir."

"I thought so," the colonel said. He did not pursue the subject. He had pegged Lowell for who he was, and whether he had pegged him as a brilliant armor commander or a spectacular fuck-up didn't matter; Lowell either deserved better than being a fucking chopper jockey or he was a real fuck-up. In either case, his presence was an embarrassment.

After luncheon, Major Lowell returned to the PX cafeteria and sat there among the off-duty enlisted men and the dependent wives until 1515 hours, when a sergeant came and fetched him. The ordnance colonel now desired to be flown back to Augsburg.

Lowell told himself that this was just not his lucky day. It would not have been pleasant if the ordnance bird had wanted to RON (Remain Over Night), for that would have meant spending the night in the O Club of the 24th Armored Cavalry. On the other hand, since the ordnance colonel had decided that he did not wish to spend the night on the East German border, this meant Lowell would be back in Augsburg in time for the monthly formal dinner dance, which he would be expected to attend.

Lowell dreaded unit parties. Because they bored him out of his mind, he generally managed to have himself sent away on a RON flight when they were scheduled. This time, he thought as he parked the Bell H-13 and supervised its refueling, he would not be successful in ducking the formal dinner dance.

Dress, mess, or Class "A" uniform with black tie was the required uniform for formal dinner-dance affairs. Dress or mess uniform were recommended but not prescribed. Dress and mess uniforms cost a small fortune, and commanders were reluctant to make the junior officers spend the money.

It had occurred to someone at Seventh Army, however, that aviators were paid more money every month than their non-flying peers, and what better way for them to spend that money than on mess and/or dress uniforms? Once they got the flyboys into mess and dress, maybe the others would be shamed into buying the uniforms.

Major Lowell knew that he was expected to show up in at least a dress uniform.

He was a bachelor. Bachelor majors could afford uniforms. He elected to go in mess dress, which was the most elegant and most expensive of the options. He wasn't sure if he was trying to be a conscientious member of the staff, or whether he was doing it for himself. Perhaps it was just to remind himself—after the scornful looks of the armor officers at Hersfeld—that he had once been a pretty good tank commander himself, despite what he was now doing.

There are cavalry yellow stripes down the seams of armor officer's mess dress trousers, and the lapels are cavalry yellow. Each sleeve has golden cord, sewn in an elaborately curved pattern. Second lieutenants get one cord, colonels six. As a major, Lowell got to wear four golden cords. And a golden cummerbund.

He pinned his three rows of minature medals to the right lapel. Around his neck, on a three-inch-wide purple ribbon, he hung the saucer-sized medal which signified that he had been named to the Order of St. George and St. Andrew by the King of Greece.

He looked, he thought, like something from a Sigmund Romberg operetta.

He dined with the chaplains; a Baptist who was visibly uncomfortable in a place where the booze flowed like rivers, and the Roman Catholic, whom Lowell suspected of being a pansy. As soon as he decently could, he left them and went to the bar.

Though Lt. Colonel Withers had become a teetotal when he had been born again, he still believed in unit parties because they were family affairs. Withers came to him at the bar and, in the belief that he was skillfully killing two birds with one stone, suggested to Major Lowell that he dance with the officers' ladies.

The first three dances were uneventful. The fourth lady, the wife of a newly assigned captain, pressed her breasts and ungirdled belly against him. When this produced an involuntary reaction in his external reproductive anatomy, he made a valiant effort to withdraw from further close physical contact. This proved impossible to accomplish. The lady's midsection stayed riveted to his, and her fingers played with his ear. When the dance was over, she led him back to her table, hand in hand, her breast pressed against his arm. And then as he thanked her for the dance and politely nodded to her husband and the other captains and their wives, she loosened her hand from his and groped him.

He was profoundly grateful to Lt. Col. Withers for catching him at the bar after the dance. He was still in possession of ninety-eight percent of his common sense and recognized a dangerous situation when he saw one. He spent the rest of the party drinking plain soda water and listening to Lt. Col. Withers extoll the merits of membership in the Augsburg Military Post Christian Men's Club.

For the next week, he took his meals either in the unit messes, where dependents were not authorized, or on the economy, thus avoiding the club and the chance of seeing the captain's wife.

He learned that her husband, Captain Suites, was assigned to Special Rotary Wing Missions Branch. Captain Suites was an archtypical army aviator, who saw as his sole *raison d'être* the piloting of aircraft. He was personally an amiable moron, with a high-pitched giggle. Lowell dismissed him from thought after he'd given him a check ride and reported to the senior flight instructor (another amiable moron, a lieutenant colonel who affected highly polished half-Wellington boots and was seldom seen without his aviator sunglasses) that Captain Suites (pronounced "Soots") was safe to fly people from hither to yon in his H-13.

Lowell flew Monday, Tuesday, and Wednesday of that week: two missions, and four three-hour check rides. The next day, Thursday, he would have to spend at his desk. Lt. Col. Withers had learned of his paper-pushing skill and turned over to Lowell as much of it as he could. Since he would not be flying the next day, he could have a couple of drinks.

(Aviators were officially forbidden to drink more than one beer the night before flying. Lowell never even took the permitted one. The army's official opinion of his flying ability was a good deal higher than his own. He had no intention of taking off with alcohol dulling his senses or impairing his coordination, and drank only when he was not scheduled to fly.)

But he resisted the temptation to take a drink at the club. The lady who had groped him might be there. He went instead to the movies, and the movie turned out to be incredibly bad. He tried but failed to suffer through it and got up after an hour and walked out. Fate, he decided, had pointed him toward the booze. To avoid going to the club, he went downtown in the Jaguar and went to the Cafe Klug, an establishment catering to the wealthier Germans, where the patronage of Americans was discouraged both by the prices and a thoroughly nasty maitre d'hôtel who took great pleasure in making it clear that they would be far more welcome elsewhere.

He made an exception for Major Lowell, however. The unusual *Amerikaner* not only never showed up in uniform, but was reliably reported to be closely connected with some very important people indeed, a rumor supported by the fact that the major spoke impeccable high-class German.

Lowell was given an on-the-spot, maître d'hôtel's promotion to *Herr Oberst* and bowed into the premises. He went to the bar and ordered a triple Johnnie Walker Black. (A triple in the Cafe Klug, costing the equivalent in deutsche marks of $4.50, contained roughly as much whiskey as a thirty-five-cent single did in the officer's club.)

He sat there, half listening to the orchestra, dimly aware of inviting smiles from several women alone at the bar and thinking what he thought of as quasiphilosophical profundities:

There was a military version of *The War Is Over; Soldiers and Dogs Keep Off the Grass!* He stated it in his mind, and restated it, until he was satisfied; *When the War Is Over, Warriors Interfere with the Smooth Running of the Peacetime Army.*

He thought of others:

An Ambitious Officer Is Like a Brazen Prostitute; He Makes Ordinary People Uncomfortable.

If Men Ride Motorcycles Because It Is Symbolic Power Between the Legs, Then the Helicopter Is the Ultimate Motorcycle: Any Moron Can Get It Up.

Simple Problems May Be Corrected in the Army Provided the Solution Is Complex; Simple Solutions to Complex Problems Are Not Tolerated.

He had just ordered his fifth drink and told himself that it was the last when the maitre d'hôtel coughed behind him, and, his tone making it clear he hoped it wasn't really true, announced that the "lady" at the door said that she was joining the *Herr Oberst.*

"I thought," Mrs. Suites said in a somewhat hurt tone of voice, "that you would call."

He didn't reply, just put a question on his face.

"You did send Ken on that Remain Over Night, didn't you?" she asked.

She swiveled on her barstool, gave him a conspiratorial laugh over her shoulder, and swiveled back again. This time her knee pressed his groin.

"Aren't you going to buy me a drink?" she asked.

Without really thinking what he was doing, he signaled the barman to give her a drink.

[**THREE**]

"I have looked the other way, Lowell," Lt. Col. Edgar R. Withers said, "when your other escapades have been brought to my attention, but this time you've gone too far."

There is no way I can explain to this man—because he is incapable of understanding—that Phyllis Suites pursued me like a shark, Lowell thought. But it wouldn't matter if Lt. Col. Withers did understand what really had happened. If he saw Phyllis for what she was, a horny slut, I have still broken Army Commandments XI and XII; THOU SHALT NEVER DIDDLE A BROTHER OFFICER'S WIFE AND THOU SHALT NEVER, NEVER, NEVER STICK YOUR DICK TO THE WIFE OF A SUBORDINATE.

Phyllis was both: the wife of a brother officer and the wife of a subordinate. He said what he was feeling.

"I am deeply ashamed of myself, Colonel," he said.

"And well you should be, Lowell. What in God's name were you thinking about?"

There was no response to that. He couldn't think of a thing to say. He certainly couldn't tell the colonel, who was president of the Augsburg Military Post Christian Men's Club, that Phyllis Suites had overcome his nearly valiant efforts to avoid her and had run him to ground in the Cafe Klug. Or that he was half in the bag when she found him, and consequently paying less than usual attention to his ethical obligations as an officer and a gentleman. Or that he was suffering from the symptoms of close to six weeks' self-imposed celibacy and thus easy prey to the sinful lusts of the flesh. He had not thought of Phyllis Suites as a wife and mother when she grabbed his wang; he had thought that if she was so interested in the object, then it could be reasonably presumed that she would make a marvelous cocksucker. And so she had turned out to be.

"I was deeply ashamed of myself," the Colonel said, "when Captain Suites came in here and asked for my help."

Oh, Jesus Christ!

"I'm sorry, very sorry, that you have become involved, Colonel," Lowell said.

"I will interpret that to mean that you are sorry I am involved, and not that you're sorry only because you've been caught."

"Yes, sir."

"I'll tell you frankly, Lowell, that my first reaction was to bring you up on charges. If I have ever seen a case of conduct unbecoming an officer and a gentleman, this is it. You have betrayed your oath of office, and the entire officer corps."

Rather than being offended by having my ass chewed by this self-righteous, self-important little bastard, Lowell thought, I seem to be reveling in it. I deserve it. I really *am* a shit. I knew what an amiable jackass Suites is, the archtypical husband of the woman who plays around. For that reason I should have stayed completely away from his wife, even if that meant jumping out the goddamned window of the Cafe Klug when she came in there.

"Out of consideration for Captain and Mrs. Suites and their children, however—and it is their interests with which I am concerned, not yours—I have decided to keep the resolution of the mess you have generated unofficial."

"Yes, sir," Lowell said.

"I know that you don't think much of us who believe in the Lord Jesus Christ as our Savior, Lowell," the colonel went on. "But it's come to your defense. 'Judge not,' it says in the Bible, 'lest ye be judged.' I am aware that you have lost your wife and that your loss probably has made you bitter. What I have tried to do, therefore, is find a Christian solution to this problem."

There followed a sixty-second silence during which the colonel looked at Lowell with mixed loathing and compassion.

"A requirement has been laid upon us to provide a rotary wing aviator to the military attaché at the United States Consulate General in Algiers. The requirement is for company grade, but I have obtained permission to send you. You will be gone six months. You will leave in two days. That doesn't give you much time, I realize, but you'll have to make do with what you have. You will not, repeat *not*, make any attempt to communicate with Mrs. Suites in any way before you leave, and I think it would be a good idea if you took your meals in one of the unit messes."

"Yes, sir," Lowell said. "I'd like to thank you, Colonel."

"After you read your efficiency report, Major, you won't want to thank me for anything. Just be grateful that you weren't court-martialed. There is simply no excuse for your conduct."

[FOUR]
Ozark, Alabama
22 December 1955

Melody Dutton came by her father's office during her lunch period to pick up the 1953 Ford so that she could run up the highway to Brundidge to get something for her mother's birthday. "Daddy, if I had my own car," she said, "I wouldn't have to take yours and leave you walking."

"Honey," Howard Dutton replied, "you're still a little girl, and still in school."

"Oh, Daddy!" she said, in exasperation, but she smiled at him.

She was not a little girl. She was a freshman at the university. She was eighteen, soon to be nineteen. She was wearing a tight skirt and a loose sweater, the current fashion, and you could see, *anybody* could see, that she had a young woman's body. The young men were already sniffing around her.

He didn't know how he was going to handle that, when she got a young man, when she fell in love with a young man, when she left him for a young man. Howard Dutton had loved his Melody from the time she was in her crib, all pink and smelling good. Not that he didn't love Howard, Jr. (who was sixteen) or Marcia (who was fourteen). They were wonderful children, too, but not like Melody. He had to try very hard to be fair and decent and not to let it show how much more he loved her than the other two.

Melody was tall, lithe, blond-haired and blue-eyed, and gentle, shy, and loving. There was nothing that made him happier than to sit in the living room and hear her play something good, like Chopin, on the piano. Prissy had told him he was out of his mind when he bought her the Steinway. Melody wasn't a musical genius or a prodigy, or whatever, she was just a thirteen-year-old girl who'd had three years of piano lessons, and she didn't need a piano like that.

About the only thing he could do for Melody now, aside from what he was going to do today, was see her through college and set her up for marriage. The trouble with that was every time he really started to think about that, he was reminded that he was going to lose her.

It was God's way, Howard reasoned. God made teen-aged girls beautiful so they would attract the men and have babies and start the whole cycle all over again. Howard had once thought he would give away half of everything he owned, or would ever own, if he could have just one more year of things the way they were, without them changing. That was when Melody was thirteen, and they'd gotten the braces off her teeth, and she was just turning into a young woman, though young enough still to sit on his lap and snuggle up and let him kiss her on the top of her head.

That was five years ago. Five years from now, Melody would possibly be holding her own baby on her lap. He would be a grandfather and she would be a mother, and it made a nice picture, but he didn't like to think about it.

"I don't think he's busy, Tommy," he heard Prissy say. "Why don't you stick your head in and see?"

The way she should have done that was to push the button on the intercom and *ask him* if he was free. And she should have said, "Mr. Waters is here," and not called Tommy "Tommy." But she wasn't really his secretary, she was his wife, and she did things the way she wanted to do them, and not the way a secretary was supposed to.

"Come on in, Tom," Howard Dutton called. Tom Z. Waters was wearing an open-collared plaid sport shirt, a zipper windbreaker, white Levis, and oil-tanned, brass-eyeleted boots, not hunting boots, but the kind engineers and surveyors wear. He looked like an apprentice surveyor, Howard thought. The only way you stopped thinking about Tom Z. Waters as a nice young man—the kind you want to give a boost up the ladder—was after you had a look at his balance sheet, his 1040, and the contents of the safe in the office upstairs over Zoghby's Emporium.

"You about ready, Howard?" Tommy asked.

Howard nodded, and walked around his desk to the door.

"Tommy and I are going out to Woody Dells," Howard said to his wife.

"You're going to be out there all the rest of the afternoon?" Prissy asked.

"We've got a lot to look at," Howard replied. Goddamn, when he got his own private secretary, after they moved into the new bank, *she* damned well had better not ask him questions like that. All his private, personal secretary had better say was, "Yes, sir, Mr. Dutton," not ask him if he was going to be out all afternoon.

Parked at right angles to the curb was Tommy's GM carryall. They weren't going to be at Woody Dells all that long, and they wouldn't be going off the pavement, so they didn't really need the carryall. Another man would have come and picked him up in a car. But if he had come in a car, Prissy might have asked questions.

They drove out North Broad Street, out of town, crossed the highway, and drove two miles farther. They turned left and started down a steep hill. There was a sign, a regular-sized billboard. "WOODY DELLS," it said. "A Fine Place to Live. Homes from $19,550. FHA, VA, and Conventional Mortgages. Miller County Construction Company, Inc."

It had been a tree farm, loblolly pine planted in what the Rural Reclamation Administration had determined to be submarginal farmland—worked-out cotton fields.

There were two finished sample houses near the entrance (brick pillars, with split pine fencing running fifty yards the other side of the entrance). Each had a sign on the lawn saying, "FURNISHED SAMPLE. Sales Representatives on Duty." Another nearby had just the framing up. That would be another sample when it was finished.

Beyond the sample houses was a three-lane macadam road with concrete curbs and street signs reading Broad Vista Avenue. Two-lane macadam streets branched off it. There were signs of construction, bulldozers pulling out pine stumps and leveling lots, more bulldozers cutting more streets, pulpwood trucks hauling the pine off for the paper mills in Mobile, teams of men pouring concrete slabs, teams of rough carpenters putting up the frames.

"Is there anything out here you want to show me?" Tommy asked.

"No," Howard said, "I just needed a place I could say I was going."

"Thought so," Tommy said. He came to the end of the pavement, slowed almost to a stop, then drove over the edge. Engine groaning in low gear, he continued over a graded dirt road, ready for macadam, and then off that onto raw land, following the guttered tracks of pulpwood trucks.

"Where the hell are you taking me?" Howard asked.

"I used to shoot quail out here," Tommy said. "You'd be surprised how close we are to the highway."

He had no sooner said it that Howard saw the highway. He would have sworn it was at least a mile further on, and he'd walked these hills all his life. Tommy drove roughly parallel to the highway for a quarter mile, until he found a place where he could ease the carryall up the steep shoulder and onto the pavement.

Thirty minutes later, Tommy drove the carryall right into the garage of Dothan Ford and Mercury, and parked it in a service stall. Then they walked into the showroom.

There it was, right in front, where people driving by could see it. Flaming fire-engine red with highly polished chrome. The roof was down, and that canvas thing—whatever they called it—was snapped in place over the folded-down top. White sidewall tires and white vinyl seats. The entire works.

"Well, Mayor Dutton, what do you think of it?" the owner of Dothan Ford and Mercury said, shaking his hand. "You need a car like this, Tommy," he added to Tommy Z. Waters.

"Wish I could afford a car like that," Tommy Z. Waters said.

"If you'll give me the papers," Howard Dutton said, "I'll give you the check. Tommy's going to drive it home for me."

Potted plants and chrome-and-plastic couches were moved out of the way, and the double glass doors in the front opened. Tommy very carefully maneuvered the convertible out of the showroom. The tires squealed on the polished linoleum whenever he turned the wheel, and the exhaust sounded like a motorboat.

"Mayor," Tommy said. Tommy always called him "Mayor" when they were in situations like this, sort of a token of respect. "If it's all right with you, I'll just go along now."

"Be careful with it," Howard Dutton said.

"I'll be there with it at seven thirty sharp," Tommy said.

"You better be," Howard said.

He didn't give a damn, he *really* didn't give a damn what Prissy was going to say, and when Tommy showed up at seven thirty sharp, she was going to have plenty to say. What really mattered was that so long as she lived, Melody would remember that when she was eighteen, her daddy had given her a flaming red Ford convertible with white seats and every option that Ford made, including air conditioning and power seats. That's what she would remember, being daddy's girl, getting a fantastic Christmas present from her daddy.

To hell with Prissy.

IX

[ONE]
Camp Rucker, Alabama
22 December 1955

Major General Angus Laird walked out of his office and through the front door of post headquarters where a Bell H-13D two-passenger helicopter sat parked. It was a special H-13D. Although it was mechanically identical to every other H-13D in the Aviation Center fleet, it was painted white. The others were painted olive-drab. The seats were upholstered in white leather, and there was an eight-by-ten-inch red plaque mounted on either side of the cockpit with the two silver stars of a major general (Scotty Laird's second star had come in the month before).

The helicopter was the aviation evolution of Patton's jeep, General Laird had often thought. There was no mistaking whose H-13 it was. It was as flashy as they could make it. General Laird believed along with General Patton that generals should stand out visually from the troops in the ranks.

General Laird walked around the H-13 and made the preflight visual inspection. Then he got in the pilot's seat and fastened his lap and shoulder harness and put the earphones on over his cap with the two silver stars pinned to it. He threw the master switch and heard the gyros for the artificial horizon start to whirl. He adjusted the mixture and tuned in Ozark Army Airfield local control on the radio. He reached down and pulled up on the Engine Start switch. The starter whirred, and the engine coughed blue smoke and then started.

It was a lot more complicated to start than a jeep, he thought, but once you were in the air, it more than made up for it. It would have taken him thirty minutes to drive a jeep to Hanchey Field, where they were just starting to turn 3,500 acres of pine-covered clay and sand into the world's largest airport designed solely for rotary wing aircraft. He would be there in no more than ten minutes in the chopper.

The engine and transmission oil temperature gauges moved their needles to points on the circular dial where a strip of green tape indicated the proper operating temperatures.

The rotor was making its fluckata-fluckata-fluckata noise over his head. He pulled on the mike switch.

"Ozark local, this is Center Six."

"Go ahead, Center Six."

"Center Six on the ground at post headquarters. Request clearance for a low level flight to Hanchey Field," General Laird said.

"Ozark Army local control clears Center Six for a low level flight to Hanchey Field. Be aware of traffic in the area. Have a nice flight, General."

"Thank you," General Laird said. "Center Six light on the skids."

He picked it up, moved into transitional lift, and then out of ground effect. He lowered the nose and began to accelerate quickly across the parade ground. It was a wonderful feeling. God*damn*, it was like being a bird! He picked it up and flashed a hundred feet over a line of barracks in a climbing turn to the left.

The soaring was the best part. It was almost dreamlike. You just pulled up on the cyclic, and you had your own personal elevator.

He liked the feeling. He held the cyclic where it was and kept his eyes on the rotor rpm and the engine rmp needle indicators, which were both on the same gauge. The needles had to be superimposed. If you pulled too much cyclic, tried to take more power from the engine than it had to offer, you were in trouble. He wasn't running the risk of doing that. He wasn't a fool. He was well within what they called "the safe flight envelope."

He was over the pine forest now. He would be over the pine forest until he reached Hanchey Field.

His eyes flicked to the altimeter. The altitude it indicated was a couple of seconds behind where he really was. It worked on a diaphragm, and the dampening necessary made the indicator a couple of seconds slow. It was 1,000 feet, so he figured he was probably at 1,200 feet, maybe 1,300. High enough.

He just started to ease off on the cyclic when the engine above and behind him coughed. Coughed again. And died. The rotor and engine rpm needles split. The engine rpm needle swooped counterclockwise to zero. The rotor rpm indicator slowed less rapidly, but frighteningly.

What the hell?

He clamped the stick between his knees and pulled on the Engine Start switch. He heard it whine, thought he heard the engine cough.

In the last few seconds before the white H-13D struck the pine trees, Major General Laird knew what happened: *Carburetor ice! Carburetor ice! If you want to climb that fast, you are supposed to turn on the carburetor heat! Otherwise the carburetor intake, which is a venturi tube, loses temperature so rapidly that it freezes the moisture in the air passing through it and stops the fuel flow.*

He was going in. He reached forward and killed the Master switch.

Major General Laird and the white-painted H-13D hit the ground at a thirty-three degree angle at ninety knots. The helicopter sheared off the first two trees it hit and then struck a larger tree squarely in the middle. The trunk came through the plexiglass bubble and the instrument panel and crushed him against the seat. A fraction of a second later, the engine, torn loose from its mounts, smashed into the rear of the seat. He was probably dead before the gasoline rushed from the ruptured tanks through the remains of the bubble and soaked his flight suit.

WOJG Edward C. Greer was two miles away at the controls of an H-19. He had been in Montgomery, Alabama, at the Air War College, simultaneously running an errand for Colonel Bellmon and practicing low level flying. According to the standing operating procedure of the U.S. Army Aviation Center, aircraft commanders who wish to leave the area, or practice low level flight, were required to seek permission of the Ozark Army Airfield operations officer.

In the case of aircraft leaving the area, there was generally some officer trying to catch a ride, either to Montgomery or Atlanta, because of the lousy commercial service available from Dothan. In the case of aircraft wishing to practice low level flight, the operations officer generally directed the aircraft to areas on the post which were virtually flat.

Warrant officers junior grade were in no position to deny rides to senior officers or to protest that the whole purpose of practicing low level flight was to learn how to go between hills and mountains and over electric power lines.

The USAACDA policy, unofficial of course, was simply to ignore the U.S. Army Aviation Center standing operating procedure and to use one of their own. Greer had radioed the USAACDA operator when he was taking off from Ozark Army Airfield, and he telephoned him immediately upon landing at Maxwell Air Force to let him know he had safely arrived.

He had telephoned Mrs. Heatter just before he took off from Maxwell, and had been just about to reach for the FM radio to call in and say he was back on the Rucker Reservation when he saw the H-13D drop out of the sky.

He tuned the radio instead to 121.5 megacycles and called "MAYDAY! MAYDAY!" even as he put the Sikorksy into a steep, diving turn toward the crash site.

"Aircraft calling MAYDAY, go ahead."

"H-13 down halfway between Hanchey and the post," Greer reported. "No sign of fire. I'm landing."

"Down or crashed?"

"He went in from six, seven hundred feet, anyway," Greer said. "Crashed."

Greer raised the nose of the H-19, to lose speed, and then put it quickly on the ground, as close as he could to the wrecked H-13. He unfastened his harness and climbed out of the cockpit window. His foot missed the spring-loaded cover of the step in the fuselage wall. He pushed himself away from the helicopter and fell to the ground. He fell on his back, hard, and it knocked the wind out of him. It took him a moment to get it back.

Then he ran through the pines to the wrecked helicopter. Only when he was close enough to smell the avgas did he recognize the H-13D as the white-painted bird of the post commander. He saw the twisted frame, and the twisted body inside.

And he smelled the gas again.

Sonofabitch was very likely to blow.

If it blew, there wouldn't be enough left of the body to fill a fire bucket.

He ran to the machine, shuddered, and then threw up when he saw what the crash had done to the body. In moments, though, he steeled himself, reached in, and tried to tug the body loose. The release for the seat and shoulder harnesses was jammed. He reached into the ankle pocket of his flight suit and took out his knife.

The knife had begun life as a bayonet for a .30 caliber U.S. carbine. Sergeant Ed Greer had ground it down to half the original length even before he'd left the 223rd Infantry to go to XIX Corps (Group). It was as sharp as he could make it, and the only time he had ever had a chance to use it (running around in the goddamned Indo-Chinese jungle with MacMillan and Felter), it had proved to be as good a people killer as he hoped it would be. A lot better than that thin English Fairbairn commando knife a lot of people had thought was hot enough shit to pay forty-five bucks for.

He sliced through the shoulder and lap belts and pulled the body from the wreck. He grabbed it as well as he could under the armpits, and he was twenty yards from the wreck when it exploded.

And then the body burst into flame. Greer looked down in horror and saw that the front of his flight suit was on fire. So were his sleeves and his legs and even his leather flying gloves.

He pulled the gloves off frantically and started to work the long zipper that ran down the front of the USAF flight suit. His fingers fumbled, and terror swept through him. He calmed himself, put both hands to the opening of the flight suit, and ripped it open with brute force.

When he had it off, he started throwing sand on the flaming body.

When the ambulance helicopter arrived a couple of minutes later, they found him wearing nothing but jump boots, and charred skivvies. He was sitting on the ground near the body retching from an empty stomach.

[TWO]
Camp Rucker, Alabama
23 December 1955

HEADQUARTERS
CAMP RUCKER & THE ARMY AVIATION CENTER
CAMP RUCKER, ALABAMA

23 December 1955

SUBJECT: Christmas activities
TO: All subordinate units of USAAC
INFO: US Army Aviation Board
US Army Aviation Combat Developments Agency
US Army Signal Aviation Test & Support Activity

1. Mrs. Angus Laird has informed the undersigned that she and the other members of the family of the late Major General Angus Laird, while they appreciate the expression of sympathy implied, desire that General Laird's death in no way interfere with Christmas and New Year's activities previously scheduled at Camp Rucker.

2. No cancellation of activities scheduled to mark the Christmas and New Year's holidays is encouraged or desired.

3. A memorial ceremony honoring Major General Angus Laird will be conducted at Parade Field #2 at 0815 hours 26 December 1955. Participation of all USAAC subordinate units is expected. Participation by USAAB, USAACDA, and USASATSA is invited.

4. Major General Angus Laird will be interred at the cemetery of the United States Military Academy at West Point at 1600 hours 26 December 1955.

William F. Adair
Colonel, Corps of Engineers
(Acting) Commanding Officer

The army does not know how to cope with civilian dignitaries in matters of protocol. The tendency is to attempt to equate civilians of surrounding communities with their military counterparts.

Prissy (Mrs. Howard) Dutton barely knew Jeannie (Mrs. Angus) Laird, but when she and her daughter Melody showed up at Quarters #1 to pay their respects to the widow, they were immediately ushered into the room (which had been Scotty Laird's study) where the widow was surrounded by the senior ladies of the post. Prissy Dutton was the mayor's wife and thus Jeannie Laird's peer.

Jeannie Laird was glad to see her, not for the ritual expression of sympathy, but for the ritual offer to help in any way she could, which she was sure would follow.

"There is something," she said, "now that you mention it."

"Anything," Prissy said. "Anything at all."

"Do you have your car with you?" Jeannie Laird asked.

"We came in my daughter's car," Prissy said.

"I want to go over to the hospital," Jeannie Laird said. "And I want to do so as quietly as possible. Could I borrow your car? And perhaps Melody to drive me?"

"Certainly," Prissy said. "Would you like me to go with you?"

"No, what I want Melody to do, if you would, dear, is bring your car up to the kitchen door. And then I'll just run out and jump in, and no one will see me. We won't be gone long. But there is something I have to do."

In the Ford convertible on the way to the hospital, Jeannie Laird told Melody that the pilot of another helicopter had seen her husband crash, had immediately landed to see if he could help somehow, and in pulling General Laird's body from the wreckage, had been badly burned.

"I think they're going to decorate him," Jeannie Laird said. "But I wanted to thank him myself."

When they got to the hospital, Jeannie Laird sent Melody inside alone to ask what room WOJG Edward C. Greer had been assigned. When Melody found out, Jeannie Laird told her where to drive in the maze of hospital buildings.

"You sure know your way around here," Melody said.

"I've worked here three afternoons a week," Jeannie Laird said. "Two afternoons pushing the library cart around and one afternoon in the maternity ward teaching young mothers how to wash their babies." She paused. "I'm going to miss it," she said.

She showed Melody where to park the car, next to one of the interconnected single-story frame buildings, and then she led her inside through a door above which was written, "FIRE EXIT ONLY—NO ADMITTANCE."

Melody followed her down a polished linoleum corridor to a ward marked BURNS.

Melody didn't know what to do. She didn't want to see somebody all burned up, but she couldn't back out.

Jeannie Laird knocked at a wooden door, and without waiting she walked in.

There was a young man in the bed, both hands wrapped in white gauze. There was more gauze wrapped around his otherwise bare chest, and still more around his right leg.

The only clothing he was wearing was a pair of pajamas. The right leg of those was cut off above the knee. Melody could see the hair around his thing peeking out of the fly. She flushed and looked away. He didn't have any eyebrows. Where they were supposed to be, he was coated with a pink grease. She realized his eyebrows had been burned off. He didn't look old enough to have done what Mrs. Laird said he had done.

"Ladies, I am sorry to say I think you're in the wrong place," Greer said.

"I don't think so. I'm Jean Laird."

"Jesus!" Greer said, then: "Sorry."

"And this is Melody Dutton," Jeannie Greer said. "She was kind enough to drive me over here."

"Hi!" Melody said. Greer looked at Melody and nodded his head, just once.

"I wanted to thank you, Mr. Greer," Jeannie Laird said, "for what you tried to do for Scotty."

"Nothing to thank me for," Greer said.

"Everyone has been telling me he went quickly, without pain," Jeannie Laird said. Greer nodded. "If that happens to be true, I'd like to hear that from you. You saw it. No one else did."

"He went quick," Greer said.

"He was dead when you got there?" Jeannie Laird asked.

"Oh, yeah," Greer said. "He died when it hit."

"Then why did you . . . risk what you did, to do what you did?"

Greer looked at her a moment. Then he shrugged.

"Then you did what you did more for me, than for my husband?" Jeannie Laird asked. After a moment, Melody realized that what Mrs. Laird was asking was why Greer had risked his life to pull a corpse from a wreck. And then she understood why: because otherwise the body would have burned.

"I did it because I would want somebody to do the same thing for me," Greer said.

"If it makes you feel any better, Mr. Greer, Scotty would have done the same thing for you had the circumstances been reversed," Jeannie Laird said, and then, for just a moment, her voice broke and there was the suggestion of a sob. Then she got control of herself.

"I've brought you something, Mr. Greer," she said. She reached in her purse and came out with a battered silver flask. She handed it to him.

"I don't want that," Greer said, uncomfortably.

"If it wasn't for you, Mr. Greer," Jeannie Laird said, "it would have melted."

"Jesus Christ!" Greer said.

"I'm sure giving it to you would be what Scotty would want me to do with it," she said. She laid it on the bed. He picked it up awkwardly in his bandaged hands. Melody saw there were tears in his eyes.

"There's something in it," Greer said.

"Then I think we should drink it," Jeannie Laird said. "Don't you?"

"Why not?" Greer said. His voice broke.

Jeannie picked the flask up, opened it, and tilted it up.

"Good brandy," she said. "That was his medicine for everything."

She started to hand him the flask, and then saw how encumbered he was with the bandages. She held it to his mouth. He took a healthy swallow. Then Jeannie handed the flask to Melody. Melody didn't want to drink straight liquor, and she especially didn't want to do it from a dead man's flask. But she realized there was nothing she could do. She took a swallow. It burned her throat. It made her cough.

"I don't think your friend is used to booze," Greer said.

The door opened. Bob and Barbara Bellmon started to come into the room, but stopped when they saw Greer had visitors. They continued when they saw who it was.

"You all right, Jeannie?" Colonel Bellmon asked.

"We've just been having a little drink," Jeannie said. "Recognize this, Bob?"

"How well," he said.

"Scotty carried that for twenty years," she said. "Longer."

"I think you'd better hang on to it, Mrs. Laird," Greer said. "Thank you just the same."

"I've told Mr. Greer that Scotty would want him to have it. Do you think he would?"

"Absolutely," Barbara Bellmon said. "Absolutely."

Colonel Bellmon took the flask, shook it, and opened it.

"Here's to you, Scotty," he said, and took a large swallow, and then handed it to his wife. Barbara Bellmon took a large swallow, but said nothing.

They passed the flask between them, Melody included, until it was empty. Jeannie Laird and Barbara Bellmon took turns holding it to Greer's mouth.

"Now that it's all gone," Jeannie Laird said, "that probably wasn't the best thing we could do for Mr. Greer."

"I just checked with the flight surgeon," Colonel Bellmon said. "He'll be out of those bandages tomorrow except for his hands. He looks worse than he is."

"Hell, I was hoping for a thirty-day convalescent leave," Greer said.

"You've got it," Colonel Bellmon said.

"I was only kidding, Colonel," Greer said.

"I'm not," Colonel Bellmon said. "By the power vested in me by God and other senior headquarters, the hospital commander and the flight surgeon concurring, you are, as of midnight, on thirty-days' convalescent leave."

"Thank you," Greer said.

"Can I help you get home?" Jeannie Laird asked. She turned to Bellmon. "We can have him flown home, can't we, Bob?"

"He can be flown anyplace he wants to go," Bellmon said.

There was something about the reply that wasn't right, and Melody Dutton picked up on it.

"I'm going to have to get back to my quarters," Jeannie Laird said. She walked to the bed and shook Greer's wrist above the bandages. "Thank you again, Mr. Greer."

"I'm really sorry, Mrs. Laird," Greer said.

"If there's room for me," Barbara Bellmon said, "I'll catch a ride with you. Bob can pick me up over there."

In Melody's Ford, Mrs. Laird said, "A fine young man. He's just a kid. You expect warrant officers to be bald-headed and middle-aged."

"He's not old enough to vote," Barbara Bellmon said. "Or drink. You heard about him and MacMillan in Indo-China, didn't you?"

Jeannie Laird had not heard. Barbara Bellmon told her. And Melody Dutton was fascinated, awed. And then, because it gave them something else to talk about, besides Scotty Laird, Barbara Bellmon told Jeannie what else she knew about Warrant Officer Junior Grade Edward C. Greer.

"Bob got the CIC/FBI Complete Background Investigation report on him when he had to have a Top Secret security clearance," she said. "It reads like a cheap novel. He was raised in a carnival. His father ran a freak show. His mother, who never bothered to marry his father, ran off when he was four months old. He was raised by whatever women his father happened to be playing house with at the moment."

"That's terrible," Jeannie Laird said.

"And then by a court reporter in Indiana," Barbara Bellmon said. "The court reporter felt sorry for him and took him in when his father went to jail. She taught him to use one of those little machines . . ."

"Stenotype?"

"Right. And then he ran off and joined the army. He wound up working for E. Z. Black, and Black sent him to flight school."

"Then he doesn't have a family?" Jeannie Laird asked.

"Just his father, and he's still in prison," Barbara Bellmon said.

"Then where's he going on his leave?" Jeannie Laird asked.

"The BOQ, probably. Oh, we asked him for Christmas. And so did Roxy MacMillan. Mac is alive because of Greer, and Roxy can be very determined when she wants to be. I guess he feels uncomfortable with families."

Melody Dutton repeated the story that night at supper, leaving out the details she knew would drive her father and mother up the wall. In her version of the story, WOJG Greer was an orphan who had no place to go for Christmas.

As Melody thought she would be, her mother was touched by the story of an orphan with no place to go for Christmas dinner. She telephoned WOJG Greer at his BOQ the next day. WOJG Greer politely thanked her but told her that he had a previous engagement.

Melody next saw him at the memorial services for General Laird on Parade Ground No. 2. Mrs. Laird had seen to it that a seat had been reserved for him on the VIP stand, in the section reserved for "friends of the family."

Melody saw that someone must have dressed him in his dress-uniform, for his hands were still swathed in bandages. She saw that the Vice Chief of Staff of the U.S. Army, General E. Z. Black, who had been visibly bored when he was introduced to her father, wrapped his arms around Greer's shoulders when he saw him.

And she heard what he said, not able to entirely hide his emotions:

"Goddamnit, Greer, I'm glad to see you."

"Aw, shit, boss," Greer said, and then Greer and the Vice Chief of Staff of the U.S. Army laughed together.

And her mother went up to him, and said: "Mr. Greer, we're having a few people in for a buffet afterward. We'd like you to come. We'll take you back and forth, of course."

While her mother was talking to him, Greer was looking at Melody. That gave her a very strange feeling in the pit of her stomach, and when she saw him nodding his head, she felt her heart beat a little faster.

When the memorial ceremony was over, they transferred General Laird's flag-covered casket from the M48 tank on which it had come to the parade ground to the H-34 which would fly it to Ozark Army Airfield. There an air force transport waited to fly it to West Point along with all the generals who had come here for the ceremony. Afterward, Melody's mother went and led Greer by the arm to their Mercury.

He rode up in front with her father and didn't say a word all the way into Ozark. Melody saw that he had a scar on his neck. She wondered if he had gotten the scar as a boy, jumping over a fence or something, or whether he had gotten it as a soldier.

In the Dutton house, he made himself as inconspicuous as possible. Melody found him in her father's office, trying without much success to turn the pages of a magazine with his bandaged hands.

She got him a plate from the buffet and fed him. When their eyes met, she had a weak feeling in the pit of her stomach again.

"You're uncomfortable here, aren't you?" she asked.

He just looked at her and said nothing.

"Come on," Melody said. "I'll take you out to the post."

"Thank you," he said.

On the way to the post, she asked: "Where are you going to spend New Year's Eve?"

"At the club, probably. Not the main club. The annex."

"Who's going to hold your drink for you?" she asked.

"What do you want from me?" he asked.

"I was hoping for an invitation," she said.

"Why would you want to do that? Don't tell me you don't already have a date."

"You want to take me or not?"

"You're not my kind of people," he said.

"We won't know that until we know each other better, will we?" Melody replied.

"You wouldn't want to go to the annex," he said.

"I want to go to the main club with you," Melody said. "I'll pick you up and take you home. You can't drive, anyway."

"I drove to the parade ground," he said. "I can drive."

She interpreted that as an acceptance. After she dropped him by his car at the parade ground, she went home and called the boy she had had a date with at the Ozark Country Club. She told him she was sorry, but she wouldn't be in town.

She tried to call Greer three times between then and New Year's Eve, but he never answered the telephone. On New Year's Eve, she got dressed about half past six in an off-the-shoulder evening dress. She tried to call him again. This time his phone gave her a busy signal. When she kept trying, and still got the busy signal, she decided the phone was off the hook, whether by accident or intentionally.

When he didn't show up by seven thirty, she wondered if she had the courage to go out there. She worried that she was frightening him off. When it was time for her parents to go out to the post, and he still hadn't showed up, she lied to them. She told them he had called and was delayed, and that they should go out. She would be along later.

When he didn't come by half past eight, she went out and got in the Ford convertible, and crying, told herself that she was going to go out to his BOQ and really tell him off. If he didn't want to take her out, he should have been enough of a gentleman to tell her so, not let her get all dressed up and then not show up.

When she got to the post, she realized she didn't know where he lived. She turned around and went back to the MP house at the gate, where an obliging MP, who made it plain he thought she was something special as a woman, looked up *GREER, Edw C WOJG (USAACDA)* in the post telephone book. He lived in BOQ T-108, he told her, which was down behind the field house.

Melody found T-108, one of three identical two-story buildings in a row, without any trouble. And Greer's car was in the parking lot, the only one there.

His name was on a small cardboard sign stapled to a door on the second floor.

She knocked on the door.

"Go the fuck away!" he called out.

Melody flushed and started to turn to leave. But then she realized that he didn't know, couldn't know, that it was her.

She went to the door, and raised her hand to knock again. Then she changed her mind and pushed it open.

He was sitting in an upholstered chair, a magazine in his lap, a bottle of whiskey and a glass on a table beside him. A television set was playing.

When he saw her, he looked away. Then he got up and looked out the window. She saw that he was wearing a purple bathrobe and white pajama bottoms. A pair of white hospital slippers was in front of the chair. He had stolen them, she realized. Then she thought, if I knew he didn't have a bathrobe or pajamas, I would have bought them for him for Christmas.

"What the hell's the matter with you?" he asked, his back to her. "Coming to a BOQ?"

"I thought we had a date," she said.

"You thought that," he accused. "I didn't say anything."

"I broke my date to go with you," she said.

"Jesus H. Christ!" he said.

She started to cry.

"Oh, for Christ's sake!" Greer said. "What the hell is the matter with you anyway?"

"Why didn't you call me?" she asked. "You could have at least called me."

"I thought you'd get the message," he said. "Jesus, what do you want from me, anyway?"

"This is how you're going to spend New Year's Eve? All alone? Getting drunk by yourself? What's wrong with you, anyhow?"

"Look, Melody, or whatever your name is . . ."

"You know damned well what my name is!"

"Look, honey," he said, "you don't want to get involved with somebody like me."

"Why not?"

"Because I'm a fucking soldier, that's why," he said. "There's more," he added darkly.

"Your father's in jail, is that what you mean?"

"Who the hell told you that?" he asked, genuinely surprised that she knew. "Yeah, that's what I mean. Among other things."

"I'm not afraid of you," Melody said. "And I don't care about your father."

"Yeah, but just wait until His Honor the Mayor hears about it."

"Is that all that's bothering you?" Melody asked.

"That's just for openers," Greer said.

"Where's your uniform?" Melody asked. "I told my father and mother we'd meet them at the club, and we're going to meet them."

"What happens to me when he finds out?" Greer said. "About my father, I mean? And you can't tell me he's pleased with the notion of you going out with a soldier in the first place."

"Where's your uniform?" Melody asked, and when he didn't answer her (at least he hadn't told her to get out), she went looking for it. She found the BOQ consisted of two rooms, the room she was in, sort of a living room, and a bedroom. In the bedroom there was a doorless closet, which was covered with a cotton curtain. She pushed the curtain aside and saw that it was jammed full of uniforms.

"Which one of these?" she asked. She looked over her shoulder. He was standing in the doorway.

"What do you plan to do, dress me?" he asked.

She met his eyes. "Yes," she said. "You can't dress yourself."

"The blue one," he said. She turned and took a blue tunic and trousers from the closet.

"Jesus!" he said. "Just put it on the bed."

She laid the tunic on the bed.

"And get me a white shirt from the dresser drawers," he said. When she was sliding drawers open, he said: "Christ, you're even going to have to put my socks on."

"Sit down and I'll put them on," Melody said.

He sat down on the bed. She found socks in the chest of drawers and then remembered underwear. She found jockey shorts and a T-shirt in another drawer, and then thought about a necktie. She didn't know how to tie a man's necktie. What was she going to do about that?

She went to where he was sitting on the bed. He avoided looking at her. She squatted and forced a laugh, and said, "I don't have much experience doing this."

She tugged his sock on. She looked up at him, pleasure in her eyes.

"There!" she said. "One down and one to go!"

"Shit!" he said, and it was a cry of anguish. He twisted on the bed to get around her, to get up. When he did, she saw his thing, hard, erect, poking out of the fly of his pajamas.

He got that because he was looking down my dress at my breasts, she thought.

"Goddamnit, why don't you just get out of here?" he said, when he gained his feet.

"Obviously," Melody heard herself say, "because I don't want to."

"Don't tease me," he said. "Goddamnit, don't you tease me."

"I'm not going to tease you," she said.

"You know what's going to happen to your little schoolgirl's ass if you don't get it out that door, don't you?" he said.

Melody Dutton, as if she was in a dream, stood up, contorted her body, and reached behind for the zipper on her evening gown. The gown had a built-in bra, and when she stepped out of the gown, she was naked except for a brief pair of panties. Meeting his eyes, she slid them down off her hips. She went to him and untied the cord of his pajama pants. Then she lay on the bed.

"You dumb little shit," Ed Greer said to her no more than two minutes later. "What did you do that for?"

"I wanted to," she said.

"I never copped a cherry before," Greer said.

"How did it feel?" she asked, nastily, aware that she was close to tears.

"Oh, Jesus Christ!" he said, and hugged her to him, and it was all right.

"Did you hurt your hands?" Melody asked and sat up and held them gently in her own.

"Who cares?" he asked. She smiled down at him.

"It didn't hurt as much as I thought it would," she said. "In case you're wondering."

"But it did hurt?" he said.

"Not after a while," she said.

"You're sure?" he asked. "I mean, I didn't break anything, did I?"

Melody leaned over and kissed him.

"Happy New Year," she said.

"Jesus, your parents," he said. "They're at the club."

Howard Dutton *knew* the moment he saw Melody and the soldier with the burned hands walking across the floor to their table. There was a look in Melody's eyes (not guilt) that had never been there before. And there was proof later, the way they looked at each other, the way that Melody blushed a little.

Prissy didn't suspect a thing. That was to be expected. Prissy didn't have the brains she was born with. All Prissy saw in this boy was the orphan needing a family.

But Howard Dutton knew. While the boy went to the men's room, he'd told Melody he thought Greer was an unusual young man, and when Melody had said, "I'm going to marry him, Daddy," he wasn't all surprised.

Howard Dutton said—calmly—because he knew there was nothing else he could say, "We'll talk about it, honey."

And he decided that first off, they would have to get the boy out of the army. He didn't want Melody running off to the four corners of the world like a camp follower. He wanted her right here in Ozark. There was plenty of room for the boy. If not in the bank, then in one of the companies.

[ONE]
The Consulate General of the United States
Alger, Département d'Algérie, République Française
22 June 1956

Major Craig W. Lowell, with Sergeant William H. Franklin beside him, flew the Hiller H-23 over the desert due north from the foothills of the Atlas Mountains until he reached the Mediterannean. Then he turned right, several hundred yards out to sea, and flew along the beach and the coastal highway very low until he reached Algiers. He picked it up to a thousand feet then and flew directly across the city itself to the airport.

The crew chief came out while they were still shutting the bird down to deliver the message that the military attaché, a starchy infantry full bull colonel wanted to see Major Lowell right away. Then he said, in awe: "Holy Christ! Did you see that?" He pointed to the tail structure of the Hiller, where half a dozen bullet holes stitched the covering.

"Yeah," Sergeant Franklin said, dryly sarcastic. He was a tall, pleasant-faced, twenty-one-year-old black man. "I happened to be there when it happened."

"You better get a picture of that, too, Bill," Major Lowell said. "First a shot of the holes, and then rip the covering away and see what damage it did inside."

"Jesus Christ, Major," Sergeant Franklin said, examining the damage closely. In his dusty khaki shirt and shorts, he looked very much like the Norman Rockwell painting of an Eagle scout. "They came a hell of a lot closer than I thought they did."

"These things are a lot tougher than anybody believes," Lowell said. "And can take much more of a beating. As your properly focused, perfectly exposed movies are going to prove."

"Can I wait till I stop shitting my pants?" Sergeant Franklin said. He opened the side of a Paillard Bolex 16 mm motion picture camera, removed the exposed film it contained and reloaded it. Lowell had bought the expensive Swiss-made camera when the issue Eyemo camera had given Sergeant Franklin trouble. "Otherwise, the flick will shake a lot."

Lowell patted him on the shoulder.

"I am sure that you will do your usual splendid work," he said.

Franklin responded to the sarcasm in kind. "Yah, suh, boss. I does mah best foah you, boss."

Lowell affectionately punched his arm and got out of the helicopter and walked to his Jaguar. He started for the consulate, debating en route whether to report as he was—that is, in a short-sleeved, somewhat sweaty, open-necked tropical shirt and trousers—or to stop by his suite in the Hotel d'Angleterre on the Avenue Foch and change into something more in keeping with the formal atmosphere of the Consulate General. He elected to change uniforms. The military attaché was a starchy old bastard, and all he needed from him was a lousy efficiency report to go with the lousy efficiency report he'd received from Lt. Col. Withers.

He parked the Jag behind the elegant baroque villa that served as the Consulate building and had himself let in the back door by one of the Marine guards. When he saw that the military attaché had chosen that day to wear a white uniform, he was happy that he had changed into fresh tropical worsted tunic and trousers. He went through the prescribed ritual, "Sir, Major Lowell reporting to the military attaché as ordered," and standing at attention until given at ease. It seemed a little absurd in the baroque splendor of the villa, but he sensed the colonel expected it.

"Rest, Lowell," the colonel said. "Would you like a little something to cut the dust?"

"I would be profoundly grateful for a vodka tonic, sir."

"But you'll take a little neat scotch, right?"

"Yes, sir, with equal gratitude."

"How did it go?" the attaché asked, taking a bottle of scotch and what looked like Kraft cheese glasses from a drawer of the enormous mahogany desk.

"They put in a company and a half—a company, plus half the heavy weapons platoon and a signal section—in about five minutes. Against automatic weapons fire I would rate at medium to heavy," Lowell said.

"What kind?"

"German and U.S. light .30s, I think. A couple of Browning .50s."

"And they didn't get their whirlybirds shot down?"

"They all got in all right," Lowell said. "Several of them are going to have to be either repaired on site or destroyed. They won't fly."

"And you have all this in your movies, right?"

"Yes, sir."

"That really surprises me," the colonel admitted. "I would have given good odds that a good PFC with a BAR could knock those things out of the sky like a skeet shooter."

"I'm really impressed with how tough the H-21s are. For that matter, all of them: I took half a dozen hits in the H-23 and didn't know it until we landed."

"Sergeant Franklin all right?"

"Yes, sir. Have we got anything on hazardous duty pay for him?"

"Yeah, they turned it down. And they turned down flight pay, too. It's not authorized. What I'm going to do is up his housing allowance. The State Department pays for that, and they're willing to go along. In money terms, he'll do better than he would with flight and hazardous duty pay. It's not right; he should get credit for sticking his ass in the line of fire, but it's the best I can do."

"Thank you, sir," Lowell said. "I appreciate your efforts."

"You're not leaning on him, are you, Lowell? I mean, he really is a volunteer?"

"Yes, sir."

"I don't like to lean on troops," the colonel said, and then in the next breath: "What do you intend to do about your efficiency report?"

"Sir?"

"I've been waiting for your 'Exception to Rating and Indorsement,' " the colonel said.

"Colonel," Lowell said, "I'm guilty as charged."

"Bullshit," the colonel said. "You're guilty of getting your wick dipped, not of 'conduct suggesting a lack of the high moral standards required of an officer.' You'll never get rid of the gold oak leaf if you let that stay in your record."

"Sir, I don't know what I can do," Lowell said.

The colonel took a sheaf of paper and carbons from his desk drawer and threw it on the table.

OFFICE OF THE MILITARY ATTACHE
THE CONSULATE GENERAL OF THE UNITED STATES
ALGIERS, ALGERIA
APO 303, C/O POSTMASTER, NEW YORK, N.Y.

201-LOWELL, Craig W. Maj 0439067
21 June 1956

SUBJECT: Exception to the Efficiency Report of 30 November 1955 and the Indorsement Thereto

TO: Secretary of the Army
Department of the Army
Washington 25, D.C.

In the absence of any specific allegations concerning the moral conduct of the undersigned, the undersigned protests the entire tone of subject efficiency report and the indorsement thereto and requests that it be expunged from his record.

Craig W. Lowell
Major, Armor
Assistant Military Attache

1st Ind

Office of the Military Attache
United States Consulate General 23 June 1956

Algiers, Algeria, France
TO: The Chief of Staff
United States Army
Washington, D.C.

1. Recommend approval.

2. In the period subject officer has been assigned to the Office of the Military Attache, U.S. Consulate General, Algiers, Algeria, he has been under the close and personal supervision and observation of the undersigned. Not only has he demonstrated the highest personal standards to be expected of an officer, but has virtually daily risked his life in observing the operations of the French Army against the Algerian insurgents.

3. That his conduct has reflected credit upon the United States, as well as the United States Army, is made evident by the letter of commendation from the Consulate General (attached as Enclosure I) and by the citation accompanying the award to subject officer of the Legion of Honor, Class of Chevalier, by the Governor General of Algeria in the name of the French Republic. (Translation of citation attached as Enclosure II. The medal and the citation is currently being forwarded, through State Department channels, to the Office of Congressional Liaison, U.S. Department of State, requesting Congressional approval of the Award of a Foreign Decoration to a Serving Officer in Peacetime.)

4. It is clear to the undersigned, based on his twenty-nine (29) years of commissioned service that this officer has been grievously wronged in a personal vendetta, in all probability based on personal jealousy. Not only has this officer been promoted to his present grade long before his contemporaries, but is obviously destined, in the absence of petty chicanery against him, for much higher grade and responsibility.

5. The undersigned has been authorized to state that the Consul General concurs in this indorsement.

Ralph G. Lemes
Colonel, Infantry
Military Attache

The indorsement was already signed.

"I don't know what to say," Lowell said.

"Just don't believe any of that heroic diplomat bullshit," the colonel said. "And for Christ's sake, keep your pecker in your pocket from now on."

"You didn't have to do this," Lowell pursued.

"No," the colonel said. "I didn't."

It took four months to come back.

HEADQUARTERS
DEPARTMENT OF THE ARMY
WASHINGTON, D.C.

26 October 1956

Major Craig W. Lowell
Office of the Military Attache
The United States Consulate General
Algiers, Algeria, France
(Via Diplomatic Pouch)

Dear Major Lowell:

Reference is made to your letter of 21 June 1956, in reference to your efficiency report and the Indorsement thereof, covering your service while assigned to the Flight Detachment, Headquarters, Seventh United States Army.

The efficiency report and the Indorsement thereto has been expunged from your service record and the following substituted:

"While assigned to the Flight Detachment, Headquarters, Seventh United States Army, Major Lowell performed in a wholly satisfactory manner all the duties to which he was assigned.

"The exigencies of the service having made the rendering of an efficiency report covering this service impossible, it is directed that any personnel actions being based on Major Lowell's record consider his service while assigned to the Office of the Military Attache, U.S. Consulate General, Algiers, Algeria, as also applying to his service in Seventh Army."

The Secretary of the Army believes this to be an equitable resolution of the problem and has asked me to tell you that he extends every good wish for a successful career in the future.

Sincerely,
Ellwood P. Doudt
Major General
Special Assistant to the Secretary of the Army

Of the two acts, betraying a subordinate officer by screwing his wife, or making the chief of Rotary Wing Special Missions back down from the lethal efficiency report rather than make it public knowledge that Phyllis had dallied in his bed, the latter made Lowell feel more ashamed of himself. That was really conduct unbecoming an officer and a gentleman.

It made him more than a little ashamed of himself, for he was guilty as charged, and he was afraid that he hadn't seen the last of the chief of Rotary Wing Special Missions. If he was ever assigned under him (or even near him), he would get an efficiency report he couldn't protest.

His orders came a month after the letter from the Special Assistant to the Secretary of the Army.

HQ DEPT OF THE ARMY 16 DEC 1956
MILITARY ATTACHE
US CONSULATE GENERAL
ALGIERS, ALGERIA

MAJOR CRAIG W. LOWELL 0439067 ARMOR RELVD OFC MIL ATTACHE US CONSULATE GEN ALGIERS ALGERIA TRF AND WP VIA, MIL OR COMMERCIAL AIR TRAN FT LEAVENWORTH KANS RUAT CG US ARMY COMMAND AND GENERAL STAFF COLLEGE NOT LATER THAN 2400 HRS 6 JAN 1957 PURP ATTENDING USACGSC COURSE NO. 57-1. OFF WILL REPT OFC OF MIL LIAISON, THE PENT WASH DC EN ROUTE NLT 1200 HRS 29 DEC 1956. PCS. OFFICER AUTH TRANS PERSONAL AUTO AND HOUSEHOLD GOODS. NO REPEAT NO DELAY EN ROUTE LEAVE AUTHORIZED BECAUSE OF TIME LIMITATIONS.

FOR THE ADJUTANT GENERAL:
STANLEY G. MILLER
COLONEL, AGC

It was more than he had dared hope for. The year-long "Long" Course at the Command and General Staff College. If he ever was to get promoted before being "passed over" twice by a promotion board and thrown out of the army, or if he was ever to be given any kind of command or even a responsible job on a staff, he had to have C&GSC. Now that he had been given C&GSC, he realized that he had refused to think about his chances of a meaningful career. He had been living day to day.

He wondered why C&GSC had come through now. He suspected that it had something to do with his protesting the efficiency report. Maybe they had asked questions about him, unofficially, a telephone call here and there. He decided that that was probably it, and that he had been lucky, that the telephone calls had been directed to people, Paul Jiggs, for example, who would go to bat for him.

He had no idea what the OFC OF MIL LIAISON he was supposed to report to was. He had never heard of it.

Colonel Lemes asked what he intended to do with the Jaguar. Impulsively, Lowell offered to sell it to him and quoted a price he later found out was far below the market value. Colonel Lemes snapped it up. Lowell later wondered whether the colonel was just taking advantage of a bargain or whether he considered it a favor, tit for tat, a Jaguar at a bargain basement price in return for a salvaged career.

[TWO]
Washington, D.C.
29 December 1956

Lowell flew home via Paris on his first transcontinental jet. He spent the night at Broadlawns in Glen Cove and took the first flight he could catch to Washington the next morning. Just to stick the needle in, he telephoned his cousin Porter Craig and told him that he was going to decide, after discussing his future assignment in Washington, whether or not to stay in the army. Then he thought about that, and afraid that Porter would make another telephone call to the senator, called him back and took him off the hook.

The OFC OF MIL LIAISON turned out to be a small, three-room suite in the next-to-the-inner of the five rings of Pentagon offices. They were waiting for him and had a shiny staff car ready to take him back across the Potomac into Washington. The car went into the basement garage of a huge, monolithic building, where a squeaky clean young man in civilian clothes ritually offered his hand, identified himself as Captain Somebody, and took him in an elevator into a conference room on the fifth floor for what he said would be a "routine debriefing."

The squeaky clean young captain had a looseleaf notebook stuffed with paper. When they were joined by a secretary using a court reporter's stenotype machine, he opened the notebook and began to ask questions. Lowell was astonished at the amount of information the questions represented. They knew not only the names of most of the French officers with whom he had had contact, but a good deal about them as well.

Once the questions had been asked and answered, the lights were dimmed and a slide projector introduced. The slides had been made from the miles of film Sergeant Bill Franklin had made of French Army (in particular, the Foreign Legion's and the parachutists') actions against the Algerian insurgents. Each slide represented a question the film had left unanswered.

During the slide show, someone else came into the room, sat against the door, and watched without speaking. When the lights were finally turned back on, Lowell turned and saw the newcomer was Sandy Felter. He was in civilian clothing.

"Are you through with him, Captain?" Felter asked.

"Yes, sir," the captain said. There was something in the captain's demeanor, something in his tone of voice, that told Lowell he was paying Sandy Felter far more than the ritual courtesy paid by a captain to a major.

"Then I guess I'll take him home with me and feed him," Sandy said, walking over and putting out his hand.

"I didn't know you knew the major, sir," the captain said.

"Oh, yes," Felter said. "Major Lowell and I are old friends."

In Sandy's Volkswagen, on the way to the far reaches of Alexandria, Sandy said: "My neighbors don't know I'm in the army. In case it comes up."

"Super Spook, huh?"

"Nothing like that," Sandy said. And then changed the subject to ask about P.P.

Sharon laid out a full dinner; that meant she had known he was coming. *That* meant that Sandy had known he was coming. What the hell was he doing?

"Where did you get my film?" he asked. "I sent it to Bill Roberts."

"We asked Roberts for it and copied it," Sandy replied. That asked more questions than it answered.

There were two kids now, and Sharon was as big as a house with her third. She told him, after hearing about Elizabeth, that he had done the right thing to leave P.P. in Germany with her.

He spent the night on the Felter's couch, which unfolded into a bed. In the morning, Sandy drove him by his hotel where he changed into a fresh uniform and then over to the huge building again. Sandy parked the Volkswagen in a reserved spot near the elevator.

That meant he was important around here, Lowell realized, and then laughed at himself. He was becoming a spook himself, noticing details and reaching conclusions.

He wasn't in the building long. Overnight, what the stenotypist had taken down had been transcribed. He was asked to go over it, and make sure that the transcription and his answers were correct. Afterward, Felter appeared again and apologized for not being able to take him to the airport. He told him that when he got his feet on the ground at Leavenworth, he should plan to come to Washington and spend some time with them.

And then, almost idly, Felter asked if Lowell had had any thoughts about his replacement in Algiers.

Lowell was surprised at the question. What was Felter doing involved in officer assignments?

"I thought they had a school for attaché types," Lowell said.

"I don't want an attaché type," Felter said. "I want someone like you over there, who won't regard the assignment as a two-year cocktail party tour. I want somebody who'll really report on how the French are fighting that war. I suspect we're going to have one of our own to worry about pretty soon."

"You've answered your own question, Mouse," Lowell said. "You need a chopper jockey who's not afraid to get shot at. One who speaks French. Most important, one that nobody else wants."

Felter smiled at him.

"What business is that of yours, anyway?" Lowell asked.

"What business do you have, asking me what business I have?" Felter responded with a smile.

"Screw you, Mouse," Lowell said, affectionately. Then he hugged Felter and got into a plain (but obviously government owned) Chevrolet and was driven to Washington National Airport.

Sandy Felter returned to his office.

The reason Lowell had done so well with the French was that he was a gutsy combat type who spoke French fluently. Felter knew another gutsy combat type who also flew choppers and spoke French. Who was an honorary member of the *3ième Régiment Parachutiste de la Légion Étranger.*

He didn't know if the soldier could get a Top Secret clearance, and he was only a warrant officer, which wouldn't do. But a commission would be easy enough to arrange.

He called the office of Military Liaison in the Pentagon and told them he wanted the service record of WOJG Edward C. Greer on his desk within the hour.

[THREE]
Kansas City, Missouri
15 January 1957

The sales manager of Twin-City Aviation, serving Kansas City, Missouri, and its twin across the river, Kansas City, Kansas, was three-quarters convinced that he was wasting his time with his present "up," a walk-in customer who was making inquiries about either renting or buying an airplane.

He had walked in the door at half past eight in the morning, half an hour before Twin-City Aviation officially opened. He was, well, a little flashily dressed (there were not many people who had the balls to wear a silk foulard in an open-collared dress shirt around KC) and had announced that since he would be in the area for the next ten months or so, he had been thinking about either renting or buying an airplane to "get around."

The sales manager told him that he had certainly come to the right place, and just what sort of airplane did he have in mind?

The guy with the foulard and the tweed jacket with leather patches on the sleeves said he wasn't sure, that the whole idea had just occurred to him.

"You are a pilot, of course?"

"Yes," he said.

The sales manager looked out the window to see what kind of a car he was driving. A four-door Chevy. A new one. Did that mean anything?

It meant that he was a possible customer for a Cessna 172, a very nice little single-engine four-seater, with a complete set of Narco navigation equipment. Cruised out at 120 knots, burned about six gallons an hour.

"Be happy to take you up for a little spin," the sales manager said. "Now, I'm not trying to talk you into anything you don't want to do, but if you're going to be flying regular, renting is going to eat you up. We have to charge, you understand, for time you'd be sitting on the ground somewhere, in addition to the flight hours, which on a long term, regular basis, would run you $17.50 an hour.

"I've never flown a 172," the man said.

"Easiest airplane in the world to fly," the sales manager said. "You make a mistake, it gives you ten minutes to think it over."

"All right, let's try it," the man said.

They flew for fifteen minutes up the river to Leavenworth, and that was when the sales manager learned that the guy was in the army, at the school the army ran at Leavenworth for people they thought might be full colonels and generals.

"There's a fleet of H-13s and L-19s there," the guy said, "for proficiency flying. But I'm the junior aviator, which means I would have to get my proficiency time in from three to six on Sunday mornings."

"Oh, you're in the army, are you?"

"I'm a major. One of two in my class. Everybody else is a light bird."

Well, there goes the sale of this sonofabitch, the sales manager decided. There was no way a soldier could come up with the down payment on a 172, much less the payments, and *no way* he could afford the insurance and the maintenance. Not on army pay.

Well, what the hell, he'd probably spring for maybe ten hours of rental before he decided he'd better do his flying free, even if that meant—what was it he had said—"from three to six on Sunday mornings."

"Had about enough?" the sales manager asked, already making a 180 degree turn back toward KC.

"Yeah, this isn't going to do it."

"Look," the sales manager said. "There's a couple of Pipers around I could let you have, if you agreed to take, say, fifty hours over six months, for about $12.50 an hour. Nice little airplanes."

"That wouldn't do it either, I'm afraid," the major said.

They got back on the ground and parked the Cessna 172. The started walking back to the office.

"What's that?" the man said, turning to peer in the plexiglass window of an aircraft.

"That's an Aero Commander," the sales manager said. "Just got it in."

"Beautiful," Major Craig W. Lowell said. He had never seen one before. It was a sleek-looking, high-winged, twin-engined aircraft that looked, and probably was, fast. The one he was looking at was painted a high gloss white, with red trim.

"Gorgeous," the sales manager said. "That's a classy airplane."

"You say it's yours?"

"Until I can sell it, it belongs to me and the First National Bank of KC," the sales manager said.

"How about taking me up in this?" Lowell asked.

Jesus, the nerve of some people!

"If I had it as a rental ship, out for rent, which I don't, I'd have to charge a hundred an hour. You're looking at a hundred and twenty-five thousand dollars' worth of airplane, Major."

The major reached into his pocket, pulled out a folded wad of bills, and peeled off a hundred dollar bill.

"If you don't have anything else to do," he said. "I'd really like to take a ride in that."

What the hell, the sales manager thought. Why not? That way the morning won't be a complete loss.

"I'll get the key," he said, and pocketed the hundred dollar bill.

"It feels as if you're dragging your ass on the ground, doesn't it?" the major said, when they were taking off.

He didn't ask to fly the airplane, and the sales manager didn't offer to let him fly until the hour (well, forty-five minutes, who was looking at a clock?) was just about over.

He let the major land the airplane. He had a little trouble getting it on the ground. The Aero Commander's fuselage was eighteen inches off the ground, and that took some getting used to. For the first couple of landings, it was like you were going to fly right through the runway.

When they had it back in line and the engines were shut down, the sales manager could see the major was really reluctant to get out. He turned around in the copilot's seat and looked at the passenger compartment, with its elegant paneling, and ran his hand almost lovingly over the closest of the four glove-leather upholstered seats.

"This is a very fine airplane," he said.

"It sure is," the sales manager said.

"And frankly, I like the panel," the major said, turning to point at the instrument panel, which had a full array of the latest Aircraft Radio Corporation communication and navigation equipment.

That's very gracious of you, Mac, the sales manager thought, as he heaved himself out of the pilot's seat and then walked down the aisle to the door.

The major stayed another two minutes, which seemed a lot longer, before he got out of the copilot's seat and reluctantly got out of the airplane.

"What did you say it's worth?"

"It lists out, with all the equipment, at $129,480," the sales manager said.

"But you would take $125,000 cash, right?" the major asked, jokingly.

"Right," the sales manager replied, with a smile.

"How about $120,000, even?" the major said.

"As a special favor to you, I'd take $120,000 cash," the sales manager said. He was feeling pretty good. The bottom line was that he'd gotten nearly an hour in the Commander, which was a jewel to fly, and this guy had paid for it.

When they got back in the office, and the sales manager was getting paper and pencil out to rough out some figures for a fifty-hour use of a Piper, the major asked if he could use his telephone for a collect call.

"Sure," the sales manager said.

The major called a New York City number, collect to Porter Craig from Major Craig W. Lowell.

"Porter," he said, when his party came on the line, "I'm in Kansas City. Who do we do business with out here?"

Then he covered the mouthpiece with his hand and spoke to the sales manager: "You did say the First National Bank of Kansas City was your bank, didn't you?"

"Yeah," the sales manager said. "That's what I said."

"I'm about to write a rather substantial check, Porter," the major said. "Specifically, one for $120,000. And I don't want to wait until it clears. Would you call the First National Bank here and do whatever has to be done?"

The sales manager looked at him in confusion and disbelief. "I'm buying an airplane, Porter, is what I'm doing," the major said. "Have the bank call a Mr. Sewell at Twin City Aviation and tell him my check is good, will you?"

Then he asked the sales manager for a blank check and filled it out. It was for $120,000. Where the name of the bank was supposed to be, he had written Craig, Powell, Kenyon and Dawes, N.Y.C.

"What's this here, instead of the bank's name?" the sales manager asked.

"That's a bank. Or rather a firm of investment bankers," Major Lowell explained.

"Never heard of it," the sales manager said.

"Few people have," Major Lowell said. "Listen, I think it will take maybe thirty minutes to arrange for that check. I'm on my way to New Orleans. I'll need charts, and I'd like to read the Dash-One on that for a few minutes. Would it be all right if I took the keys and went out to it?"

The major was wrong about it taking thirty minutes to arrange for his check to be cleared. Five minutes later, the executive vice president of the First National Bank of Kansas City telephoned the sales manager of Twin City Aviation and told him the bank had received a telephone call from the chairman of the board of Craig, Powell, Kenyon and Dawes, the New York investment bankers, and that he could accept any check drawn against them by Major Craig W. Lowell, up to a quarter of a million dollars.

[FOUR]
Fort Benning, Georgia
15 January 1957

Lieutenant Colonel J. Peter Hawkins, Deputy Chief of the Platoon Tactics Branch, Tactics Division, of the U.S. Army Infantry School, had six months previously submitted (under the provisions of AR 615–301, and Department of Army Personnel Pamphlet 615–15) an application for consideration for assignment as a military attaché.

Shortly afterward, he became aware that he was the subject of a new complete background investigation, conducted among the military by personnel of the U.S. Army Counterintelligence Corps and in civilian areas by agents of the Federal Bureau of Investigation. Lt. Colonel Hawkins already had undergone a complete background investigation and held a Top Secret security clearance. That wasn't enough, apparently.

Two months before, he had been placed on orders to the 2nd Infantry Division in Korea. Although he presumed that to mean he had not been selected for duty as a military attaché, he had not been so officially notified. He had prepared to move to Korea, which meant that he had had to find off-post housing for his wife and children. Dependents were not authorized in Korea, and government quarters were authorized only for personnel assigned to a post.

He had purchased a four-bedroom, two-bath ranch house in the Riverview subdivision of Columbus, Georgia, taking over the mortgage from an ordnance major who had been reassigned to the Redstone, Alabama, Ordnance Depot.

And then his orders to the 2nd Infantry Division were cancelled. He received a telephone call from the Office of the Assistant Chief of Staff, Personnel, in the Pentagon, saying that he might expect other orders in the near future. The caller could give Lt. Colonel Hawkins no indication of what those orders might be.

Four days previously, there had been a TWX:

```
HQ DEPT OF THE ARMY
CG FT BENNING & THE INF CENTER, GA

IT IS ANTICIPATED THAT LT COL J. PETER HAWKINS 0386567 INF THE
INF SCHOOL WILL BE ORDERED TO AN OVERSEAS POST WITH FOURTEEN
(14) DAYS. DEPENDENTS WILL REPEAT WILL BE AUTH TO ACCOMP OFF.
TVL BY MIL AND/OR CIV AIR IS ANTICIPATED. OFF WILL INSURE
DEPENDENTS POSSESS PROPER PASSPORTS AND HAVE COMPLETED
IMMUNIZATION SERIES. THIS IS ALL THE INFORMATION PRESENTLY
```

AVAILABLE AND INQUIRIES ARE NOT DESIRED AND WILL NOT BE ENTERTAINED.

FOR THE ASST C/S PERSONNEL:
STEPHEN MASON
LT COL, AGC

And last night there had been a telephone call from the aide-de-camp to the post commander. He was to be at the army airfield at Fort Benning at 1000 hours. He was to be in a Class "A" uniform. He was to take with him enough linen and extra uniforms to spend three days away from Fort Benning. Transportation from Benning to where he was going would be by military air. The aide-de-camp had no further information.

When Lt. Colonel Hawkins went to Base Operations at 0915 the next morning and identified himself, they had no information to give him. They knew nothing.

At 0955 hours, Lt. Colonel Hawkins watched as a very unusual airplane taxied up to Base Operations. It was an Aero Commander. Colonel Hawkins had not known that the army had acquired any Aero Commanders, which were high-priced civilian business aircraft, the kind used by corporate big shots too impatient to take airliners. From the markings there was no question, however, that this was an army aircraft, for it was painted in army colors. But Colonel Hawkins had never seen any other army aircraft painted like this one. The paint was glossy, not flat, and most of it was gleaming white, not olive-drab. While it had the standard star-and-bars identification on the fuselage, the insignia looked much smaller than normal. The only place it said US ARMY was on the vertical stabilizer, high up, in letters no more than four inches tall.

A VIP aircraft, obviously. But there was no general officer's starred plaque mounted anywhere on the fuselage.

The door in the fuselage behind the high wing opened and an officer got out. He was wearing a Class "A" uniform, not a flight suit. There were wings on the tunic, so it was logical to presume he was the pilot, or copilot. In an airplane like that, obviously, flight suits were not necessary.

The pilot, a young captain, wearing the Military District of Washington shoulder insignia and a West Point ring came into Base Operations. He took one look at Lt. Colonel Hawkins and walked right to him. He saluted.

"Colonel Hawkins?"

Ask not, Lt. Col. Hawkins thought, *for whom the bell tolls. It tolls for thee.*

"Yes, I am," he said.

"Good morning, sir. Are you ready to go? Can I help you with your luggage?"

"Where are we going?" Lt. Colonel Hawkins asked.

"Let me have that bag, Colonel," the captain said, and then held the door out to the flight line open for him.

The captain stowed Colonel Hawkins's bag in the rear of the cabin and then walked forward.

"Good morning, Colonel," a little Jew in civilian clothing said. "I'm Sanford Felter."

"How do you do?" Lt. Colonel Hawkins asked, wondering just who the hell he was. There were two other passengers on the airplane.

"May I present General de Brigade des Fernauds?" the little Jew said, and then switched to French. *"Mon Général, je présente le Colonel Hawkins."*

Hawkins had kept up his French. Four years of it at the Point, further practiced when he'd been in Germany.

"I am honored, my General," Hawkins said in French.

"I am very happy to meet you, Colonel," the French brigadier said, in English.

"General des Fernauds is the military attaché," the little Jew said.

The Aero Commander was already moving.

"Everybody ready back there?" the pilot called. Lt. Colonel Hawkins slipped into a seat. He just had time to fasten the belt when the plane turned, the engines roared, and it began to race down the runway.

Lt. Colonel Hawkins realized he still had no idea where they were going.

Thirty minutes later, they landed at Camp Rucker, Alabama.

Out the window, Lt. Colonel Hawkins saw workmen erecting a sign on the Base Operations building: LAIRD ARMY AIRFIELD. He remembered hearing somewhere that the field had been renamed in honor of Scotty Laird.

The captain who had fetched him at Benning came down the aisle again, but before he reached the door it was opened from the outside and a warrant officer stuck his head in.

"I didn't know they let lousy civilians on military airplanes," he said.

"Bonjour, mon petit," the Jew said, smiling broadly, looking almost playful.

The warrant officer climbed inside and was followed by a major. Hawkins saw, with the surprise that comes even to old soldiers when they actually see one, the blue-starred ribbon of the Medal of Honor among the major's many other decorations.

"I swore I'd never get on another plane with you," the major said to the little Jew. "The last time, you nearly got my balls blown off."

"It's nice to see you, too, Major MacMillan," the little Jew said, with a wide smile.

"What the hell is all this, anyway? Bellmon's going to blow his cork when he comes back and finds both of us run off with you."

"Get on, sit down, and shut up," the Jew said to him. "Try to remember that you're supposed to be an officer and a gentleman."

When the warrant officer came into the cabin, he saw the French general.

"Pardonez-moi, mon Général," he said.

"Hello, Greer," the French general said. "It's good to see you again, my friend."

The warrant officer slipped into a seat across from Lt. Colonel Hawkins.

"Good morning, sir," he said, formally.

"Good morning," Lt. Colonel Hawkins said. The Aero Commander was already turning away from the Base Operations building.

Not two hours later, the Aero Commander turned off a taxiway at New Orleans

Lake Front Airport and parked beside a civilian Aero Commander. A tall man, blond and mustached, was leaning against its nose.

Felter was the first one out of the airplane. Lt. Colonel Hawkins followed him out the door.

Felter walked up to the civilian and they shook hands.

"I thought you were coming in commercial," Felter said to him. "What brings you here?"

"I just landed," the man said. "I heard your pilot give his ten-minutes-out report, and I had a hunch it was you."

"What did you do, rent a plane?" Felter asked, a hint of tolerant disgust in his voice.

"Actually, I just bought it," the man said. "Just this morning. What do you think?"

"I think that's more ostentatious than Patton's polo ponies," Felter said.

The tall man shook hands with the man with the Medal.

"What do you say, Mac?" he said.

"Did I hear you say you bought that?" MacMillan asked.

"Yeah, you like it?"

"Who are you going to get to fly it for you?" MacMillan asked, innocently.

"You must be Greer," Lowell said, putting out his hand. "Bob Bellmon tells me you're the final solution for MacMillan."

"And what's that supposed to mean?" MacMillan asked.

"A twenty-four-hour-a-day keeper to read road signs and menus for you, that sort of thing," Lowell said.

They were smiling, but Hawkins sensed that there was a degree of genuine hostility between them. Or maybe contempt.

"What's this all about, Mouse?" Lowell asked. "I appreciate getting an excuse for teacher to get out of school and an excuse to fly my new little bird down here, but I *am* a little curious."

"This is Lieutenant Colonel Hawkins," Felter said. "He's going to take your place in Algiers."

"Oh," he said. He put out his hand to Hawkins. "I'm Major Lowell, sir."

"How do you do?" Hawkins asked. He decided that he had not heard correctly or else that Major Lowell was joking about just having bought the civilian Aero Commander. Majors simply do not have that kind of money.

"Mon Général," Felter said, "may I present Major Lowell?"

"Mon Général," Lowell said, almost coming to attention before the general put out his hand to him.

"I'm happy to finally meet you, Major," the general said. "Especially under such circumstances."

"May the major inquire into the nature of those circumstances, *mon Général?"* Lowell asked.

"You have been a hero, again, Craig," Felter said. "And they are going to give you a medal, again."

Hawkins wondered just who the hell the little Jew could be. Probably someone from the State Department. He realized that he had just heard that not only had his application for attaché duty come through, but that he had been told where he was going. To Algiers.

They rode into downtown New Orleans in a Cadillac limousine with a Corps Diplomatique tag mounted above the license plate. They were taken to a turn-of-the-century mansion on Saint Charles Avenue. A brass plate mounted to the brick fence pillar identified it as *Le Consulat Générale de la République Française.*

They were ushered into the office of the consul general. Hawkins saw through French doors leading to another room that there was a buffet laid out, with half a dozen bottles of champagne in coolers.

"May I suggest, *Monsieur le Consul,"* the French general said, "that we have our little ceremony? And then we can have, perhaps, something to drink."

"Until just now," Lowell said to Felter, "I thought you were kidding."

The consul took a blue-bound folder from his desk.

Felter pushed the warrant officer and Major Lowell into line before the consul.

"Dans le nom de la République française!" the consul announced, dramatically. The French general came to attention.

He read a citation. For valor in action in leading survivors of a shot-down aircraft through enemy lines in the vicinity of Dien Bien Phu, French Indo-China, Major Rudolph G. MacMillan, U.S. Army, was invested with the Legion of Honor, in the grade of Chevalier. General des Fernauds pinned the medal of the Legion of Honor on MacMillan's tunic and then kissed his cheeks.

"Dans le nom de la République française!" the consul announced dramatically again. For his gallantry in action in flying a helicopter through intense enemy small arms fire to bring succor to French soldiers wounded in counterinsurgency operations in Algiers on at least twenty occasions, Major Craig W. Lowell was invested with the Legion of Honor in the grade of Chevalier.

"Dans le nom de la République Française!" the consul general announced, a third and final time. Majors MacMillan and Felter and Warrant Officer Greer were invested with the Croix de Guerre for their heroic rescue of a French Foreign legionnaire from the Viet Minh.

The champagne was served, and General des Fernauds raised his glass.

"To those we left behind," he said. Everyone raised his glass, and drank. Then the general dropped his glass to the carpet and ground it with his heel. Lowell and MacMillan, Felter and Greer, one a time, did the same thing. Lt. Colonel Hawkins was about to drop his glass—when in Rome, do as the Romans—when the consul stayed his hand.

"Only those who were there," he said, softly.

Hawkins was touched by the ceremony but wondered again why he had been brought all the way down here to witness it. And then he had the insight: somebody wanted him to know what was expected of him when he got to Algiers, and what was expected of him in Algiers was not taught at the Infantry School or at the Command and General Staff College. And then he had a second insight: the one who wanted him to know, the one who had arranged for him to come down here, was the little Jew.

[ONE]
Fort Rucker, Alabama
25 January 1957

Rhonda Wilson Hyde had "requested" Darlene Heatter to come in on Saturday to answer the telephones until noon, and there wasn't anything that Darlene could do about it.

It wasn't that she minded working; she got paid time and a half for overtime. It was just that she didn't like the way Rhonda Wilson Hyde was always ordering her around. But there wasn't anything she could do about it except act as if she didn't mind. Rhonda was the administrative officer and her immediate boss. The only person she could complain to was Colonel Bellmon. Though Darlene knew that she generally could get what she wanted from Colonel Bellmon, there was such a thing as wearing out your welcome.

Darlene was sure that things were going to catch up with Rhonda, anyway. It said in the Bible, "Judge not, lest ye be judged," and Darlene tried not to judge anyone, but there was no getting away from the fact that Rhonda Wilson Hyde was carrying on like a you-know-what.

About the only good thing you could say about her was that she wasn't fooling around with the married officers, just the bachelors, or else the married officers who were visiting USAACDA for a week or ten days without, of course, their wives.

At first, Darlene had thought that Rhonda was nothing more than a flirt, but she couldn't keep thinking that in the face of all the evidence. Rhonda *was* going to bed with them, and there was no denying a fact when it stared you in the face.

Darlene couldn't understand how a married woman could do that, go to bed with a man who wasn't her husband. Just going to bed for lust. The sinful lusts of the flesh. She had come across that phrase in a book of prayer from the Episcopal Church in the pastor's office when she had been learning how to type.

It was the work of the Devil, too. Sort of contagious, like a disease. Darlene had caught herself wondering what it would be like to do it with somebody other than John. Before she realized what she was doing, caught herself, and stopped, she had wondered what it would be like with Mac MacMillan, of all people.

She knew what had set that off: MacMillan and one of the other officers had been going into and out of the men's room at the same time. One going in while the other was coming out. MacMillan had put his hand right through one of the panels on the door, and they'd had to cut him out of it, to keep him from cutting his wrist any more than he had already cut it.

And Mr. Greer had laughed when he heard about it, and said, "What do you expect? Mac's built like a fucking tank."

The way they swore so much, the words were even usually used incorrectly. He didn't mean that a tank actually you know what. But that had started her thinking. Mac MacMillan *was* built like a tank. Large and powerful. Not that John wasn't all man or anything like that. But one of MacMillan's arms was about as big as one of John's legs, and his neck was about twice the size of John's and it was a perfectly natural thing for her to wonder if he was twice as big as John, all over. And what it would be like.

She was ashamed of herself when she realized what she was thinking, and she stopped herself right then. And every other time she had thoughts like that. She was a Christian wife and mother, and what she was thinking was sinful and indecent.

The temptation of Satan was awful. She had even thought of that when she was doing it with John. When she thought about it, sort of pretended that it was Mac on top of her, it made doing it with John better. It made her, you know, *convulse.* Or whatever it was called.

Maybe, she thought, it was the uniform. Uniforms were supposed to be appealing to women, and maybe that was it. They really had looked nice, the whole unit, when they'd been at USAACDA this morning.

They were giving Mr. Greer a commission as an officer, a promotion from the lowest grade of warrant officer to first lieutenant. Darlene thought it had something to do with the medals he and Mac had won in Indo-China.

When Colonel Bellmon had been up at Fort Benning, and Major MacMillan was acting as commanding officer, there had been a telephone call from the DCSOPS in the Pentagon in Washington, D.C., which was the boss of USAACDA, telling Major MacMillan that a plane would land at Laird Field, and take them someplace for a day or two.

When Colonel Bellmon came back from Fort Benning and found the both of them gone, he got sore and called the DCSOPS to find out what was going on. Because she just happened not to hang up after she'd placed the call for him, she heard a general tell him that it was combined politics and intelligence. The French were going to give them medals and a certain "unnamed Jewish major friend of yours" was involved. They would be gone no more than forty-eight hours.

Whatever it was, there had been a big party at the Pontchartrain Hotel that night, and they hadn't come back until late the next afternoon. And then in a private airplane. She'd overheard that conversation, too, when the control tower called and asked Colonel Bellmon if he expected a civilian Aero Commander to land. He'd said, no, he didn't, and then a couple of minutes later, the tower had called back and said that the pilot of the airplane was a Major Lowell and that he had Major MacMillan and Warrant Officer Greer aboard, so Colonel Bellmon had said it was all right for them to land and told the tower to pass the word to Major MacMillan that he wanted him to come directly from the field to his office.

Both Major MacMillan and Mr. Greer were a little drunk, or at least a little sick from being drunk. They said that Lowell had dropped them off at Rucker on his way back to Leavenworth and that Felter had taken some colonel she had never heard of back to Washington with him after the party in the hotel.

"Where did Lowell get the Aero Commander?" Bellmon asked.

"He bought it," MacMillan replied, laughing. "Where else?"

"And he's flying it, as drunk as you two are?"

"No, he stopped at midnight," MacMillan said. "He's not that kind of a fool."

The TWX about Mr. Greer getting promoted came in that night.

HQ DEPT OF THE ARMY WASH DC 0950 22 JAN 56
DIRECTOR, USAACDA CP RUCKER ALA

THIS TWX CONSTITUTES AUTH TO HON DISCH FR THE MIL SERVICE WOJG GREER, EDWARD C W727110 FOR THE PURP OF ACCEPTING A DIRECT COMMISSION AS 1ST LIEUTENANT ARMOR AUS AND CONCURRENT CALL TO ACTIVE DUTY. OFF WILL REMAIN ASGD USAACDA. OFF IS ALERTED FOR OVERSEAS SHIPMENT 26 JAN 1957. DA GENERAL ORDER 20 1956 IN PREPARATION WILL BE FURNISHED WHEN AVAILABLE.

BY ORDER OF THE DCS PERSONNEL:
EDMUND T. DALEBY
COLONEL, AGC

Normally, USAACDA didn't march in the regular Saturday morning parade on Parade Ground No. 2, but Colonel Bellmon had made them march this time. They would swear in Mr. Greer as an officer during the parade, and the colonel thought the unit should participate. Afterward, there was going to be a company party at Lake Tholocco, to say good-bye to *Lieutenant* Greer.

Everybody in the unit, civilians included, was invited, but Darlene didn't think that she would go, even when duty hours were over at noon, and she would be free too. There would be a lot of drinking, she knew. There was a whole jeep trailer filled to the top with iced beer, and that meant that there would be a lot of drunken people. Since she believed that the body was the temple of the Holy Spirit and that drinking was soiling that temple, Darlene didn't think she ought to go.

But Colonel Bellmon and Major MacMillan and a couple of the other officers came in after the parade. Colonel Bellmon seemed surprised that Rhonda Wilson Hyde had made Darlene come to work.

"We should have just had the switchboard refer calls to the staff duty officer," he said, and Darlene was glad that Rhonda Wilson had been caught doing what she had done.

"If you want to leave your car here, Darlene," Colonel Bellmon said, "you can ride out to the lake with us."

Since he expected her to go, there was nothing she could do about it, Darlene decided, and she sort of liked the idea of Rhonda Wilson Hyde seeing her show up out there with the colonel. She didn't have to drink any alcohol, she decided. There would surely be Coke and things like that out there. Maybe even some punch.

When she got there, she saw that it wasn't (except for the jeep trailer full of beer) very much different from a church picnic. A little more elaborate, maybe. Church picnics were generally covered dish. USAACDA was serving individual steaks cooked on charcoal with baked potatoes and baked beans. Mrs. Bellmon and the other officers' ladies had "arranged for" the food and drinks (in other words, paid for it), and the enlisted wives would help prepare and serve it.

Darlene helped the enlisted wives serve the food on the serving line, and then, because it was like a church picnic, she walked over to where the enlisted men, the privates and the technicians, had gone off by themselves, feeling a little out of place with the wives and children.

She knew how to make people feel comfortable, how to join in the fellowship with the others.

They had one of those enormous stainless steel kitchen pots, and it was full of fruit punch. She was glad to see that not everybody was drinking. The enlisted men smiled at her when she asked if she could have some of the fruit punch. When she sipped at it, she realized for the first time how thirsty she was and how good the punch was. She drank everything in the paper cup and held it out to be refilled.

"I'm absolutely dry!" she said.

[TWO]

Melody Dutton was absolutely furious with Ed Greer. She and her mother were trying to involve him as much as they could in the preparations for the wedding, and he just didn't seem to give a damn.

She had told him that the caterer from Dothan would be at the house from nine thirty Saturday morning and that she wanted him to help with the selection of the menu.

She knew that the whole idea of a big wedding made him uncomfortable, but they had talked that through. It was going to be more than just her reception, it was going to be a chance for people from all over the state to meet him, and that was going to be very important to him when he got out of the army and went to work as vice president of Dale County Builders, Inc.

He didn't know half the people he would have to know once he started to work, and the reception was as important to his future as anything Melody could think of.

Not only didn't he show up after that stupid parade as he had promised, but he didn't even call up and say he was tied up or something. There was no question in Melody's mind where he was. He was sitting drinking beer, in that stupid little bar, Annex 1 next to the BOQ, that's where he was.

When he finally showed up, she was really going to give him a piece of her mind.

The caterer waited as long as she could, and then she left. By then it was half past two in the afternoon. Just wait till he showed up!

Melody went to her room, took off her dress, and put on shorts and a T-shirt. Her mother had made her change into the dress before Mrs. Angie Gell, the caterer, had come. Mrs. Gell, who was from a fine old family, had her standards, and Melody should, in deference to them, put on a dress and look like a young woman about to be married, not like a tomboy.

Melody called the post number. When the operator came on the line, she asked for Annex 1.

"May I speak with Mr. Greer, please?" she asked, when one of his drunken cronies answered the phone.

"Not here, honey," the drunk said. "Would you settle for a lonely first lieutenant?"

Melody slammed the phone down in its cradle.

She wasn't going to have this out with him when he finally, in his own sweet damned time, elected to show up; she was going to have it out with him now.

She made the tires squeal as she backed the convertible out of the driveway (one of their wedding presents was going to be a new car; she had heard her father talking about that on the telephone). They were getting a house in Sunny Dale Acres and all the furniture, as well. She reminded herself angrily that Ed hadn't been very enthusiastic about that, either. She had had to pick out all the furniture herself. Ed said that he didn't know or care much about furniture. As long as it had four legs and a soft cushion, that was all he cared about.

She drove well above the speed limit (no Dale County deputy sheriff in his right mind would ticket Howard Dutton's daughter for speeding) until she reached the post. There she had to slow to thirty-five, because the MPs would give out speeding tickets, and they were a lot of trouble when you got one; you had to go to the federal courthouse in Dothan and pay it to a U.S. magistrate.

She jumped out of the car when she got to Annex 1 and went inside. The place was jammed with young officers and a bunch of girls she would just as soon not have had to say "hello" to, but Ed Greer wasn't there.

"Hey, Schatzie," one of them called to her as she was leaving. She hated to be called "Schatzie." Ed had told her that was what the soldiers called their German girl friends. Their frauleins. Ed had also told her that they called the frauleins "fur-lines," which Melody thought was really gross.

She turned to glower at whoever had called her name.

"I just remembered," a young warrant officer said, "that USAACDA is having a beer bust out at the lake. That's probably where he is."

"Thank you," Melody said.

That was just like him. He had told her about the beer busts. Once a month, the officers chipped in most of the money and provided the enlisted men with steaks and all the beer they could drink. That's where he was, out with the enlisted men swilling beer when he should have been arranging for the reception, which was just as important to him as it was to her. He preferred drinking himself silly on beer with the enlisted men to meeting his obligations and responsibilities to her.

Sometimes she just hated him!

It took her twenty-five minutes to find the USAACDA beer bust. There were three other beer busts, and she had to stop at each one long enough to find out it was the wrong one.

By the time she finally found the USAACDA beer bust, Ed was drunk. She could tell that from the bemused look on his face when he saw her. He was sitting on the hood of a jeep. The jeep was towing a trailer, and the trailer was full of huge chunks of ice and beer. The pine straw on the ground was just about covered with empty beer cans.

One of the enlisted men, a young sergeant, walked up to him just before Melody got to him and pointed to a group of GIs around a woman. Ed Greer laughed, and then grew serious.

"If the colonel finds out, he'll have your balls for breakfast," Melody heard him say.

"Hi," Melody said. Now that she was actually facing him, she really couldn't be angry.

"Hi," he said.

"If the colonel finds out what?" Melody asked.

"The troops have been feeding punch to our born-again Christian wife, mother, and Get-Thee-Behind-Me-Demon-Rum secretary," he said, and laughed.

"What's funny about that?"

"There's three half-gallons of vodka in that pot," he said. "Darlene is bombed out of her mind."

Melody looked over and saw Darlene Heatter, her face flushed, her hair mussed, with the group of GIs. Two of them had their arms around her shoulders. They were singing and laughing idiotically.

"And you think that's funny?" Melody snapped.

"It will do until something funnier comes along," Greer said.

"Why didn't you come and meet with the caterer?" Melody asked.

"A very good question," he said. He was really drunk, she saw. She had never seen him this drunk before.

"Or at least call and say you weren't coming?"

"You are looking at Old Mr. Ball-less himself," Ed said.

"What's that supposed to mean?"

"I didn't have the balls to call," he said. "As a matter of fact, before you showed up here—uninvited, I must point out—I was just about to decide that I would write you a letter."

"A *letter?* What kind of a letter?"

"A Dear John letter," Greer said, looking at her through somewhat fuzzy eyes. "In your case, a 'Dear Melody' letter."

"Saying what?" Melody asked. She had a sick feeling in the pit of her stomach.

"Saying, 'Dear Melody, dear sweet Melody, we have made one hell of a mistake.' "

"You're drunk," she said.

"Getting there," he agreed. "Getting there."

"If you have a point, I don't know what it is," she said.

"The army's sending me to Algeria," he said.

"The army's doing *what?"*

"Algeria," he said. "They're sending me to Algeria. Tomorrow."

"They can't do that!" Melody protested. "Your resignation was approved."

"I have withdrawn my resignation," he said.

"I don't believe any of this. Is this some kind of sick joke?"

"Believe it," he said. She knew then he wasn't lying.

"But why?" she asked.

"Because when I thought about it," he said, "I realized that I would much rather be a first lieutenant in the army than a vice president of Dale County Builders, Inc., despite the very nice fringe benefits."

"They offered to make you a lieutenant, if you'd stay?" she asked.

He put his hand to his collar point and exhibited it to her. There was the silver bar of a first lieutenant.

"Why didn't you talk this over with me?" Melody asked.

"Because you probably could have talked me out of it," he said. "And this opportunity wasn't going to knock again."

"What opportunity?"

"Algeria," he said. "Doing something important."

"I'm not important? Is that what you're saying?"

He didn't reply.

"We're supposed to be in love," Melody said.

"I thought about that, too," Greer said. "What we are is in lust. We've been fooling each other."

"How do you mean that?"

"You know what I mean," he said, mysteriously.

"We're supposed to be married on the tenth of February," she said. "What about that?"

He just looked at her and shrugged his shoulders.

"I'll be a laughing stock," she said.

"Sorry about that," he said.

"You never intended to marry me!" she accused, and now she was shrieking hysterically. "You bastard, you never intended to marry me! All you wanted was a piece of ass!"

"No. That's not true," Greer said. "I just finally stopped thinking about fucking and started thinking about the way things really are. We couldn't hack it, Melody. You're daddy's girl, and I'm a soldier."

"I hate you!" Melody shrieked. She didn't care that people were watching her. "You *bastard!"* she screamed.

She slapped his face and stormed toward her car. Halfway there, she turned around. Tears streaming down her face, she shook her fist at him. Then the fist turned into the finger. Then she screamed, "Fuck you!"

Then she got in the car and somehow got it started and put it in gear. With the wheels spinning on the pine straw, she started off.

Greer sat on the hood a moment longer and then tossed his beer can away. He walked over to the officer's table where there was whiskey. He made himself a scotch and soda in a paper cup.

MacMillan walked over to him, stood silently for a moment, then said:

"Does that mean the engagement is off?" he asked, innocently.

"Yeah, I suppose it does," Greer said, chuckling.

"You're not going to do anything foolish like get yourself shit-faced, are you?" Mac asked. "Sandy Felter frowns on drunks. What time are you due in Washington?"

"I'm on the 8:20 flight out of Dothan in the morning. I'll be in Washington National about 1500."

"You want me to get a plane and take you up there?"

"No, thanks anyway, Mac."

"Why don't you come over to the house tonight?" MacMillan asked.

"I've got to finish packing," Greer said. "Thanks anyway."

"Well," MacMillan said, "say hello to Felter. And don't do nothing heroic over there."

They shook hands. Greer walked to where he had parked his car. He was going to leave the car parked behind his BOQ. MacMillan would advertise it in the *Daily Bulletin* and sell it for him. Major Lowell (now *there* was a character—his own personal Aero Commander!) had talked to him at some length about what to expect in Algeria and had told him the smart thing to do for wheels in Algiers was buy a new Renault 4CV. With a diplomatic passport, he could get one tax free.

He was almost to the car when he saw Darlene Heatter. She was walking unsteadily toward the rest rooms. She would pass by the officers and their wives. He didn't give a damn about Darlene; so far as he was concerned, she could fall flat on her ass in front of Bellmon. But Bellmon would find out that the troops had been feeding her vodka-spiked punch. Bellmon would not think that was funny.

He caught up with her.

"Mrs. Heatter," he said. "I'm going back to the post. Can I offer you a ride?"

She looked at him uncomprehendingly for a moment, then smiled broadly.

"Why not?" she said, and took his arm.

He had a little trouble getting her into the car, she was that bombed.

"I feel so silly!" she announced, when they were on their way from the lake to the post.

"There was a lot of vodka in that punch you were drinking," he said. "In case you didn't know."

"I know," she said. "I figured that out myself."

"You did?"

"Yeah," she said. "When I started feeling so good, I figured that out myself."

"I see."

"I figured, since everybody else was doing it, why not?"

"And you like it?"

"It's different," she said. "But how am I going to go home?" She giggled.

Christ, now he was stuck with her. If she went home that way, her husband, another tee totaler, would cause all kinds of trouble. He decided he would take her to the snack bar and get her a cup of coffee and then dismissed that idea. She would be obviously drunk in the snack bar.

"If you'd like," Greer said, "I could make you a cup of coffee. In my BOQ."

She thought that over a moment.

"That's all you have in mind?" she asked.

He laughed.

"Word of honor. A couple of cups of coffee and you'll feel a lot better."

"Thank you," she said. "Thank you very much. If my husband ever found out about this, he'd kill me."

"Well, we'll just make sure he never finds out," Greer said.

She was unsteady on her feet going up the stairs to his room, and he was grateful that there was nobody in the BOQ corridors.

He installed her in one of the armchairs and got the electric coffeepot going. There were still two bottles of beer in the refrigerator, and he took one.

"I never tasted alcohol until today," Darlene said, when she saw him.

"Is that so?"

"And I've never tasted beer," she said.

"Don't you think you've had enough?"

"I want a taste of the beer," she said. He handed her the bottle. She took several swallows, licked her lips, and said it was good.

"If you drink the rest of that, the coffee won't do you any good," Greer said.

"So what?"

"What about your husband?"

"I was lying about him," she said. "He won't be home. He'll be at the fire station. Did you know that my husband is a fireman?"

"Yes, I did," Greer said.

"Well, he won't be home until nine tomorrow morning," Darlene said. "And the kids are at my mother's, so if I want to drink a beer, nobody has to know a thing about it."

"Help yourself," Greer said.

"Thank you, I will," she said, archly.

He took the last bottle of beer from the refrigerator and opened it. When he turned around again, Darlene was reading *Playboy.*

"I can't understand why girls pose for pictures like that," she said. "I mean, people they know would know."

"I guess they pay them," he said.

"I'm not a prude," Darlene said. "I know men like to look at naked women." She laughed. "And I guess women like to look at naked men, too. Somebody should start a magazine for women with naked men inside. I'd buy it."

Greer was suddenly alarmed. *Fuck the coffee*, he thought. *Just get her out of here!*

"You about ready to go, Darlene?" he asked.

"You trying to get rid of me, or what?"

"Don't you think you'd better start thinking about getting home?"

"I bet if I took my clothes off, you'd want me to stay," Darlene said. "I'll bet you would."

Greer didn't say anything.

Darlene stood up, and started to unfasten her blouse.

"What do you think you're doing?" Greer asked.

She had been looking down at her buttons. Now she looked, up at him.

"I just thought," she said. "You're going away tomorrow. For good."

"Yeah," he said. "I am."

"So nobody would ever know," she said. She lowered her head and looked at her fingers on the buttons, but she stopped moving the fingers. "You want to, or not?" she asked.

Fuck it, Greer thought. *It's probably just what I need.*

"Yes," he said.

[THREE]
The Pentagon
Washington, D.C.
1 June 1957

The Vice Chief of Staff of the U.S. Army caught the Chief of Staff of the U.S. Army as he was preparing to enter his black Cadillac limousine.

"I'm on my way to see the President, E. Z.," the Chief of Staff said.

"Fuck him, let him wait," E. Z. Black said. "This is important."

Shaking his head, smiling, the Chief of Staff took the sheet of paper extended to him. It contained just three names. There was a neat check mark by one of them.

"You think that's it, huh?" the Chief of Staff said.

"Yes, sir. That is my recommendation."

"There's going to be howls of rage," the Chief of Staff said. "Cries of favoritism, cronyism. They're going to read into this more than I think you intend."

"With a little bit of luck," General E. Z. Black said, "I'll be able to blame it on the outrageous interference of the Deputy Secretary of Defense on Internal Army Affairs."

The Vice Chief of Staff leaned over the roof of his limousine and scribbled his initials on the sheet of typewriter paper.

"Thank you, sir," General Black said.

"I'll be burned in effigy," the Chief of Staff said.

"They'll probably take your bust out of the Airborne Hall of Fame," General Black said. "Or use it for a dart board."

"Tell me. Because he's the best man? Or because you think aviation is the flying cavalry?"

"A little of both," Black said. "I've always been a little afraid of the airborne's idea of 'acceptable losses in the assault.' A tanker has been trained since he's a second lieutenant to conserve his assets."

"Yeah," the Chief of Staff said. "That's just what I decided. Right now, I mean. Trying to read your mind."

The Chief of Staff started to get into the limousine.

"Give my most respectful regards to our Commander in Chief," E. Z. Black said.

"I just might do that, E. Z.," the Chief of Staff said.

Because it had been far more political, the selection of a general officer to replace the late Major General Angus Laird as commanding general of the U.S. Army Aviation Center had been somewhat more difficult than the selection of a replacement commander for another of the combat arms or technical services schools would have been.

For one thing, there was no legally established aviation branch, and thus the slot was not reserved for an infantry general, as would have been the case had the commanding general of Fort Benning, the Infantry Center, suddenly died. Or for an artillery general, if the commander of the Artillery Center at Fort Sill had died. Or an armor general, had the commanding general's slot at Fort Knox suddenly come open.

As a matter of fact, it had been originally and rather universally believed that the new Rucker commander would not be an armor General. Scotty Laird had been armor, and logically—fairly—the new commander should not be. Now that armor had had its turn, it was now infantry's, or airborne's, or maybe even artillery's or, remotely, transportation's.

There are normally seven four-star generals on active duty. The Chief of Staff; the Vice Chief of Staff; the Commanders in Chief Europe and Asia; the Commanding General of Continental Army Command; and the Commanding Generals, U.S. Army Forces, Europe, and U.S. Army Forces, Far East.

Next down the line come the twenty-five to thirty lieutenant (three-star) generals, who command the eight armies, the larger corps, and serve as deputies to the four-stars. The Assistant Chiefs of Staff for Operations, Personnel, Logistics, and other general and special staff functions are normally lieutenant generals.

There are nearly two hundred major (two-star) generals and over three hundred brigadier (one-star) generals. It was from this latter group of more than five hundred one- and two-star generals, almost all by definition thoroughly qualified officers, that the selection would have to be made.

But numbers were deceiving. Not all of the five hundred brigadier and major generals were available for consideration. The technical service general officers were immediately eliminated from consideration. The Surgeon General and his subordinates were obviously out of the running, and so were the general officers who had spent their careers in the Finance Corps, the Signal Corps, the Ordnance Corps and the Quartermaster Corps. The Corps of Engineers made a halfhearted attempt to let it be known that it would not stagger the imagination to have an engineer general command Rucker, especially in view of the massive construction projects underway in Alabama.

The Transportation Corps made a serious attempt to gain the slot, coming up with a skillfully written staff study attempting to prove that aviation was really nothing more than an assemblage of flying trucks and jeeps. If the army of the 1960s, it argued, was indeed to be air mobile, then the bulk of the "aerial vehicles" would be flying trucks, as the vehicles of the present army were predominantly wheeled ones.

As vehicles of transportation, the Transportation Corps argued, it was simply logical to place the training of their crews and maintenance personnel under the Transportation Corps, which already had responsibility for wheeled vehicles and their serving personnel. They had an in-place, tested system, the Transportation Corps argued, that with obviously simple modifications could and should be adapted for army aviation. Finally, they argued, there was no place in the army better able to accept the thousands of warrant officer pilots than TC. When, for one reason or another, the warrant officer pilots could no longer fly, work would have to be found for them. Those who could not be absorbed in aviation-type functions could be employed in other TC rail, road and water operations.

The arguments advanced were logical, but the proposed TC equation lacked one essential ingredient. The Transportation Corps was a technical service, not a combat arm. While the odd TC officer, here and there, might have had to send out a truck convoy somewhere or other where it might come under fire, no TC officer had ever had to look his lieutenants in the eye and announce to them they were expected to lead their men over the next hill; or set the fuses to zero and fire point-blank; or push disabled tracks to the side of the road and keep moving.

There are three official combat arms—infantry, artillery, and armor—and a fourth, unofficial, but equally powerful politically, made up of officers of the three combat arms trained in the technique and philosophy of vertical envelopment, the airborne.

Airborne had always wanted aviation, and felt that it was logical for it to absorb it. Aviation was really nothing more than the evolutionary development of vertical envelopment. The helicopter, so to speak, was nothing more than an improved and vastly more efficient means for delivering the guy with the rifle safely behind enemy lines.

Infantry, although there were very few infantry generals who had not gone through the three-week jump school at Benning and who in consequence did not wear parachutist's wings, had by and large reached the consensus that airborne was so much elitist bullshit.

Their argument ran that it made very little sense to spend a great deal of time and money training people as parachutists only to lose somewhere in the neighborhood of twenty-five percent of them in parachute accidents before they fired a shot in combat. These accidents ranged from broken ankles, legs, and backs to electrocution and incineration on high tension power lines. This sin was multiplied when airborne tried to insist that airborne privates have Army General Classification Test scores of 100, only ten points below the AGCT required to send a man to OCS.

The function of an army, those disenchanted with airborne said, was not to die yourself but to kill the enemy.

Artillery's claim on the empty commanding general's office at Camp Rucker was by right of lineage. Army aviation had entered the army as Piper Clubs flying during War II as artillery spotters. It was theirs, they argued, and there was a corps of company and field-grade officers coming up who had spent their careers in aviation.

It was pointed out by the Signal Corps, however, that aviation, period, had entered the army, period, via the Signal Corps. The first aviator's "wings" had been a representation of the Bald Eagle clutching signal flags in his claws. There was no reason the Signal Corps should not send one of its generals to command Rucker. No one really took their bid seriously.

Armor maintained that aviation should be an armor function. For those who *really* understood military history and the lessons it taught, it was clear that the three combat arms were infantry (the man with the pike, or the bow and arrow, or the rifle, whatever the individual hand-held weapon); artillery, (the people who fired the catapults, the cannons, and the rockets); and cavalry (those who moved rapidly around the infantry and the artillery in battle, once on horses, presently in tanks, and quite obviously in the future on mechanical horses called helicopters). They were willing to grant that George S. Patton had made one mistake. He had gone along with the misguided when they wanted to change cavalry's name to armor. They pointed out that General I. D. White, who had gotten the 2nd Armored Division to the Elbe when General Porky Waterford was still hung up around Kassel, had thrown a famous I. D. White fit in the office of the Chief of the Staff after the war, the result of which was that cavalry sabers were superimposed on the tank in armor's insignia.

The arguments reduced the number of candidates to fill Scotty Laird's vacancy from nearly five hundred to about fifty. The selection process moved into the inner offices of the Pentagon. Further recommendations were not desired, nor would they be entertained.

The list was distilled down to three general officers, a straight-leg infantry major general, presently commanding the 1st Infantry—"the Big Red One"—Division in Germany; a jumping general, presently deputy commander, XVIII Airborne Corps, at Bragg; and a brigadier general, whom both the Chief of Staff and the Vice Chief of Staff (but few others) knew had just been selected for promotion to major general. The brigadier general was presently serving as Special Assistant to the Deputy Secretary of Defense for Research and Development.

At eight o'clock that same night, General E. Z. Black, Vice Chief of Staff of the U.S. Army, walked up to the charcoal grill erected in the garden behind Quarters No. 3 at Fort Meyer, Virginia.

A white-jacketed orderly was broiling steaks. A slight, erect man in civilian clothing watched him.

"Staying close to the fire, Paul?" E. Z. Black said.

"A cavalryman always knows enough to stay close to the food, General," Brigadier General Paul Jiggs said.

"And how are things in Research and Development?"

"I'm thinking about resigning and running for public office," General Jiggs said. "Obviously, politicians live much better than we do. They eat inside with linen on the table and everything."

Black laughed.

"I've got something for you, Paul," E. Z. Black said. He put something in Jiggs's hand. "Keep it under your hat until it's official."

Jiggs looked at the small silver pin in his hand. It was rank insignia: two stars joined together.

"Thank you, sir," he said.

"There's a catch, Paul. There's no free lunch."

Jiggs looked at him.

"Rucker and the Army Aviation Center," General Black said.

"I didn't think I was even being considered," Jiggs said. Black sensed that Jiggs's surprise was genuine.

[ONE]
Camp Rucker, Alabama
12 June 1956

HEADQUARTERS
THE U.S. ARMY AVIATION CENTER
CAMP RUCKER, ALABAMA

12 June 1956

The undersigned herewith assumes command of the United States Army Aviation Center and Camp Rucker, Alabama.

Paul T. Jiggs
Major General, USA
Commanding

[TWO]

On his third day as commanding general of the Aviation Center and Camp Rucker, Major General Paul T. Jiggs walked out the back door of the headquarters building and across the street and into the officer's open mess. He was trailed by his two aides-de-camp (one of whom he had brought from Washington, the other appointed that day; the latter had been functioning as unofficial aide to the colonel who had been in temporary command since General Laird's death) and a lieutenant colonel from the Department of Flight Training who had been named as the general's instructor pilot.

General Jiggs got in the cafeteria line, going to the end of it like everybody else instead of going into the dining room, where there was waiter service and a table reserved for the commanding general.

He put a bowl of gelatin with pineapple chunks embedded in it on his tray, then pork chops, no gravy, and held his hand up to refuse mashed potatoes. He took a roll, no butter, and a glass of water and a mug of coffee. He initialed the bill he was given by the cashier and found a table in the crowded cafeteria, uncomfortably aware that people were staring at him. They tried not to, but they did.

Apparently, Scotty Laird had not carried his own tray to eat with the peasants and had otherwise accepted the benefits of the myth that rank hath its privileges. Jiggs had already seen that the colonel who had been holding the fort had wallowed in the prerogatives of the base commander.

"Good afternoon," General Jiggs said to the adjacent table of second and first lieutenants, who responded—until he stopped them with a wave of his hand—by jumping to their feet.

The general's party joined him. They unloaded their trays and the junior aide collected all of them and put them on a tray table before sitting down himself.

The general's party became aware that something in the cafeteria dining room had caught the general's attention. He kept looking at something. They narrowed it down. The general's attention was drawn to two officers sitting at a table. One was a very large, very black captain, wearing stiffly starched fatigues and the Aviation Center insignia. The other was a young-looking major in a Class "A" tropical worsted uniform. One of General Jiggs's first official acts as commanding general was a change in the center uniform regulations. Wearing of tropical worsted uniforms during normal duty hours was discouraged. It was a good change, doing away with both chickenshit and high dry-cleaning bills. It was a lot cheaper to have khakis or fatigues washed and starched than it was to have TWs dry-cleaned. It was difficult in the Alabama heat to make a uniform last a full day before it became sweat-soaked.

The general spoke: "Across the room," he said, "are two officers. A major in TWs and a captain in fatigues. Do you see them?"

"Yes, sir," the general's party replied, almost in unison.

"I want you to carry a message to the major," the general said to the aide he had acquired since coming to Rucker.

"Yes, sir."

"You will tell the major that if he cannot afford to offer to buy the commanding general a cup of coffee, the general is willing to loan him the money to do so."

"Yes, sir," the aide said, confused, uneasy, getting to his feet.

"Wait a minute, I'm not through," General Jiggs said. "You will say to the captain that if he is indeed sweet little Phil Parker, the general will buy him a cup of coffee, too."

"Yes, sir," the aide said, and walked across the room. He returned almost immediately, with the major and the captain trailing him.

"Good afternoon, sir," they said.

"Long time, no see, Lowell," General Jiggs said.

"Yes, sir, it has been some time, hasn't it?"

"And you, Captain, were once known as sweet little Philip S. Parker, IV, am I correct?" he asked the six-foot-four-inch, 235-pound officer.

"Yes, sir."

"I'm an old friend of your father's," General Jiggs said.

"Yes, sir, I know."

"I was under the impression you were at C&GSC, Lowell."

"Yes, sir, I am."

"You're a long way from Leavenworth."

"I came to see Captain Parker, sir."

"Birds of a feather?"

"Yes, sir."

"What do I have you doing here, Parker?" General Jiggs asked.

"I'm an IP in Rotary Wing Advanced, sir," Captain Parker said.

"That's fascinating," General Jiggs said. "Are you any good at it?"

"I believe I'm competent, sir."

"As I was walking over here, it occurred to me that having a lieutenant colonel—no offense, colonel—detailed full time to teach me how to fly when I am not otherwise occupied was not a very efficient utilization of resources. Is there any reason, Colonel, why Captain Parker could not be detailed to teach me how to fly, permitting you to return to duties more appropriate to a senior officer?"

"Sir, I'd have to review Captain Parker's records," the lieutenant colonel said.

"He's either a competent instructor pilot or he isn't," General Jiggs said, his voice suddenly very cold. "Which?"

"I'm sure that Captain Parker is competent, sir," the lieutenant colonel said, uncomfortably. "But we like to take a little extra care with general officers, sir."

"Bullshit," General Jiggs said. "Captain Parker's father was my instructor in equestrianism at Riley when I was second john. I always told myself I'd get back at him someday. You arrange for it, Colonel."

"Yes, sir."

"How long do you plan to be AWOL from Leavenworth, Lowell?"

"I'd planned to turn myself in in the morning, sir."

"In that case, you'll be free to come to supper," General Jiggs said. "We eat at seven. At half past six, we serve drinks."

"Yes, sir."

"Are you married, Parker?"

"Yes, sir."

"Would it be convenient for Mrs. Parker?"

"I'll have to check, sir," Captain Parker said, a little uncomfortably.

"It's Dr. Parker, sir," Lowell said. "She's a contract surgeon at the hospital."

"If it would be convenient for *Dr.* Parker, I would be honored to make her acquaintance," General Jiggs said. "Now go finish your lunch."

General Jiggs ate two mouthfuls of pork chop.

"That was Captain Philip Sheridan Parker IV," he said. "A direct descendant of some of the first Negro soldiers in the army. His great, great, whatever it is, grandfather rode with Sheridan, and named his first-born after him. In the last great war to end all wars, that boy's father, Colonel Parker III, led an armored column into East Germany and snatched Bob Bellmon and two hundred other American officer prisoners from the Russians."

There was no reply.

"The other one is Lowell," General Jiggs said. "Anybody ever heard of Task Force Lowell?"

The aide he had inherited, who wished to remain assigned as an aide, had done his homework. In Korea, as a lieutenant colonel and later as a colonel, General Jiggs had commanded the 73rd Heavy Tank Battalion (Reinforced). A task force, Task Force Lowell, from the 73rd had made the breakout from the Pusan perimeter and linked up with General Ned Almond's X Corps after the landing at Inchon. It was described in the book the lieutenant had read as "a near classic utilization of an armored column in both the breakthrough, and in disrupting the enemy's rear." After he had read it, the lieutenant remembered reconstructing the operations of Task Force Lowell at the Point. They'd done it twice, once on the maps and the sand tables and again as an exercise in logistics: how to supply a fast-moving armored column with the almost incredible amount of fuel, ammunition, and other supplies it consumes, by whatever means are available.

"Yes, sir," he said.

"Tell them," General Jiggs said.

The word spread, beginning that afternoon, that all the rumors were true. Armor was taking over. The first party the general had thrown was pure armor. Some jigaboo captain, whose father had taught the general how to ride, no shit, a horse, back when there still was cavalry; Colonel Bellmon, armor, director of the Aviation Combat Developments Agency; Major MacMillan, the guy with the Medal; his exec, also armor. And some hotshot major from C&GSC who's the guy who flew into Laird Field in that red-and-white civilian Aero Commander. Also armor. Shit. The Armor Association would probably turn out to be worse for army aviation than the Cincinnati Flying Club and the West Point Protective Association.

[THREE]
19 June 1957
Oran, Algeria

The tourists, mostly members of Local 133, International Brotherhood of Master Machinists, Tool Makers and Die Cutters, United Automobile Workers of America, but including (to fill up the forty-four passenger buses used by African Tours, Ltd.) a trio of middle-aged schoolteachers; two rather willowy gentlemen from New Hope, Pennsylvania, who thought that Native Art was going to be important in their interior decorating business; and three others arranged for by the Oran office of American Express, gathered at 7:15 in the morning in the lobby of the Hotel de Normandie in Oran.

There was some confusion, of course, and someone, naturally, had overslept, and it was a few minutes after eight (not 7:30 *sharp*!) before the bus pulled away from the hotel. In thirty minutes the bus was out of Oran, which looked to most of the Americans not too different from European cities, except for the Ay-rabs in their dirty robes.

The bus—Dutch, diesel, enormous, with lots of glass and surprisingly comfortable and roomy seats—swayed not unpleasantly down the highway as the green of Oran and its environs turned into the brown of the desert.

Sidi-bel-Abbès, legendary home of the French Foreign Legion, was their first stop. It was something of a disappointment. The museum was interesting, but you can only take so many museums, and Local 133 had been on tour for sixteen days so far, and they had enough museums to last them awhile.

The legionnaires, except for their funny hats, looked disappointingly like Americans. Their uniforms were American khaki and U.S. Army work clothes, and they drove jeeps and Dodge three-quarter-ton trucks and GMC six-by-sixes, some of which, the machinists and tool and die makers agreed among themselves, *they* had made back in Detroit. The legionnaires were armed with good old U.S. M1 Garand rifles and Thompson .45 submachine guns and Colt .45 automatics.

And then something happened that made everybody really hate the goddamned French Foreign Legion. No sooner did they get out of Sidi-bel-Abbés, then they got stuck behind a French Foreign Legion convoy that moved down the road like a goddamned snail.

"Pass the sonsofbitches!" the machinists yelled at the bus driver, but the bus driver simply shrugged his shoulders.

It was not that there was any good reason to go faster, and they really couldn't have gone a hell of a lot faster on the narrow, winding roads. It was simply that they were part of their culture, and a vehicle in front of them going five miles an hour less than they were capable of going was almost insulting.

Not that it was uncomfortable in the air-conditioned bus. There was a refrigerator with soft drinks (Coke and some local orange soda that the Americans didn't like and some Algerian beer, which was nearly as bad). And the scenery was spectacular, if you liked rocks. Everybody oohed and aahed at first, and then they got bored with the mountains.

They went through Tiemcen to Geryville. They stopped in Geryville for lunch, and everybody was pleased with that. It gave them a chance to stretch their legs, take pictures of camels and great big Arabs on little tiny donkeys, and have a little lunch. And the French Foreign Legion convoy had disappeared. They wouldn't have to swallow their dust from here on in to wherever the hell they were going next. But when they left Geryville, the Legion convoy was on the road ahead of them again. Bastards!

They were going next to Colomb Béchar, via Ain Sefra. Fourteen miles out of Ain Sefra as the crow flies, and thirty-six miles out as the road wound its way up and around the mountains, four 105 mm artillery shells furnished by the United States of America as military aid to the Republic of France and captured by the *Armée Nationale pour la Libération d'Algérie* were detonated under the road.

The plan was to blow the shells when the bus was directly over them. The ANLA *sous-chef* who pressed the plunger had been well trained when he had been in the French Army, but he was a little nervous, and he pressed the plunger a half-second early.

The charge exploded under the bus's engine. The force was sufficient to send what was left of the engine sailing fifty feet into the air, and to neatly sever the bus's frame immediately behind the engine compartment. The driver and Mr. and Mrs. Rudolf Czernik, of Hamtramck, Michigan, who were riding in the forwardmost passenger seats, died instantly.

The back of the bus pushed what was left of the severed front of the bus approximately ten meters farther down the road before it dug into the macadam surface and stopped.

Six more tourists, including one of the interior decorators from New Hope, Pennsylvania, died in the initial explosion. Four others, riding near the front of the bus, suffered injuries that were to be fatal. Many others were injured, some seriously, some slightly.

But the ANLA plan to kill all on board was a failure: those to the rear of the bus were either unharmed, slightly injured, or simply badly shaken up.

Within moments of the explosion, legionnaires from a jeep which had been following the bus managed to get the rear door of the bus open. They began to unload first the unharmed passengers and then the injured passengers. The dead were left where they were.

The surviving passengers were herded into a ditch by the side of the road and told by a legionnaire with a heavy German accent to stay down and not move.

There was weapons fire now, the sharp crack of .30 caliber rifles and light machine guns, the heavier, booming crack of .50 caliber machine guns, the crumping boom of mortars. The noise was deafening. One of the members of Local 133, ignoring his screaming wife, crawled out of the ditch and reclaimed an M1 Garand and two bandoliers of ammunition from a legionnaire who lay in the road with half of his head blown off. He crawled back into the ditch, opened the action halfway to see if the rifle was loaded, and then crawled to the lip of the ditch.

He couldn't see anything, but he emptied the clip into the granite mountain above them, and then he loaded a fresh clip into the Garand. He turned to his wife: "Francine, for the love of God, shut the fuck up!"

The firing lasted about five minutes. The smell of gunpowder was in the air.

Then there was silence.

There came the sound of helicopters. The lithe, blond woman recognized that sound. Help was on the way. Help had come. She put her hand on her ankle. The pain made her want to scream. She had thought she had sprained it. She now realized, dully, that it was broken. It was already swelling and turning blue.

The sound of the helicopters came closer and closer, and then two flashed overhead. Over the sound of their engines and the fluckata-fluckata-fluckata of their rotors she could hear the sharp cracking roar of machine guns. She waited for the sound of helicopters landing. She had seen helicopters ambulances on television. If they had helicopters with machine guns, they were certain to have helicopter ambulances.

But there were no helicopter ambulances, and in about ten minutes the sound of the helicopters with the machine guns died out. The helicopters were now flying high, back and forth along the road.

Legionnaires had now formed a defensive line around the surviving tourists in the ditch. A legionnaire with a medical kit came over to her and looked a moment at the ankle and took a hypodermic needle from his bag. He smiled at her.

"I don't want that," she said. She hurt, she hurt as badly as she had ever hurt in her life, but she wanted to be conscious. She didn't want to be unconscious, not knowing what was going on, here in the middle of nowhere, where she didn't really know what had happened, only that she had almost been killed.

"No, *non,*" she said, then, "*nein,*" remembering that some of the legionnaires seemed to be German.

He pinned her hand painfully to the ground with his knee, grabbed her arm roughly with one hand, and injected her through her blouse sleeve with the other.

"Damn," she said, and then it was as if the lights and the sounds and everything else went off.

She became aware, first, of an old-fashioned ceiling fan turning and creaking above her. She focused her eyes on it. Then she smelled the smell of a hospital. It was disinfectant, what she thought of as chloroform, even though she knew that wasn't what it was.

Her mouth was absolutely dry. When she tried to lick her lips, her tongue was dry. She pushed herself up on her elbows. She had the worst headache she had ever had. Even her eyeballs hurt, as if something was pushing them from inside her skull.

There was a pitcher of something, probably water, and a plastic glass on a small table beside her. She rolled on her side to reach for it. Then she became aware of her leg. There was no pain, but it felt very heavy. She threw the sheet off her and looked.

She was in a rough white hospital gown. No buttons. It tied in half a dozen places. Whoever had tied her into it hadn't done a very good job. Her body was exposed from the waist down. She pulled the gown closed over her midsection and upper legs.

She wondered where her clothing was; there was no closet in the room. Her foot and ankle were in a dirty white plaster of Paris cast. She moved it from side to side. There was a dull pain, nothing that really bothered her.

She wondered where she was, and looked around for a button to call for a nurse, or a doctor, or somebody. She found it, but someone had tied it in a loop, for some reason just out of her reach.

She pushed herself upward on the bed and decided that she would sort of crawl up the headboard and reach the damned cord.

Then there was a knock at the door.

She slid quickly back into the bed, pulling the sheet over her, and tried to pull the hospital gown, which had ridden up, back down again. The sheets were thin, translucent, and she didn't want whoever it was at the door to see her hair down there.

There was a second knock.

"Come in," she called, and then she remembered something from her high school French. *"Entrez,"* she added.

He was an officer in a French Foreign Legion uniform, a parachutist's camouflage uniform. He was as deeply tanned as she had ever seen a man tanned. His muscular arms, exposed to the biceps by the neatly rolled up sleeves, were almost chocolate brown. His hair was bleached nearly white. His eyes were hidden behind gold-framed aviator's glasses. He was, she realized, the most handsome, sexiest, most masculine man she had ever seen.

He sort of backed into the room, as if finishing a conversation with someone in the corridor.

"Good afternoon," he began, artificially cordial, reassuring. "I'm Lieutenant Edward C. Greer, of the United . . ." He stopped in midsentence. "Holy shit!" he said.

She didn't say anything. Just waited for him to go on.

"United States Army," he picked up. "I'm temporarily stationed with the French Foreign Legion in Colomb Béchar. You're in a French Foreign Legion hospital. The doctors assure me that you are in no danger. Arrangements are being made to fly all the Americans from the tour out of here. It will take a few more hours to make the arrangements. In the meantime, if you will give me a name and address of someone you would like notified, the American consul general in Algiers will telephone them and assure them that you're all right."

She nodded.

"Except, of course," Lieutenant Greer said, "I don't need your address."

"I thought maybe you'd lost it," Melody said.

"If we can get you into a wheelchair," he said, "I can get you through on the radio. That would be better for your parents, if they heard from you, yourself, rather than one of those State Department assholes."

"I'm fine, Ed," Melody said. "How are you?"

"What the fuck are you doing here, anyway? Are you out of your mind?"

"I'm not here," Melody said. "Today I'm in either Strasbourg or Cologne, I forget which, looking at a cathedral."

"You almost got your ass blown off, you know that?" he said, angrily.

"You look pretty good yourself," Melody said. "That's a really nice tan."

"You're not telling me you came here just to see me?" he challenged.

"I'm queer for desert and rocks," Melody said.

"Hey, that was a long time ago," he said.

"Six months. I thought maybe six months would change things."

"There have been bandits in this area since before the time of Christ," he said. "While the French make every effort they can to police the area, obviously they aren't always successful."

"Those weren't bandits," Melody said. "Whoever it was, was trying to kill us."

"And the French Foreign Legion isn't exactly a police force, either."

"What was that, a speech someone told you to give?"

"His Esteemed Excellency, the Deputy Consul for Public Affairs himself," Greer said. "I told him he'd better come give it himself, but he said he was going to be needed in Algiers to handle the public relations end of this 'incident.' "

"What are you doing here?"

"Learning," he said.

"Learning what?"

"That escorting a civilian bus with a platoon of troops doesn't always guarantee the safety of the bus, for one thing," he said.

"Don't you care that I love you?" Melody asked.

"If that fucking charge had gone off a second later," Greer said, "we'd be sending what was left of you home in a rubber bag."

"Were you out there?" Melody asked.

"I was in one of the gunships," he said.

"Why didn't you land and help us?" Melody demanded.

"That was their game plan," he said. "They set that charge conveniently close to an area big enough to take a couple of H-21s."

"That's the one with a rotor at each end?" she asked.

"Yeah, the Piasecki. Flying Banana. We gave the French fifty, sixty of them. What we were supposed to do was lose our cool when we heard about the bus, and then rush in with H-21s and medical people. When we did that, they would knock out the H-21s."

"But we were civilians," Melody said.

"You were either French or American, which is nearly as good. You blow away one Frog *or* two Americans and you get a guaranteed ticket to heaven."

"Would that have bothered you?" she asked.

"Would what have bothered me?"

"If the bomb had blown me up?"

"What they're doing now," he said, "is sending patrols through the mountains over the airfield. As soon as they've been cleared, the air force is sending in a couple of transports from Morocco. They'll fly you to Algiers."

Melody started pulling open the bows fastening her gown.

"What the hell are you doing?" Greer asked.

"Looking," she said.

"You're all right. You must have slammed your ankle into a seat or something. You weren't hit."

"I may not have been hit," Melody said. "But I'm not all right."

"What's the matter with you?" he asked, and she heard the concern in his voice. Her nipples were standing up. She was glad for that. She knew he liked it when her nipples were erect.

"You tell me," she said. "You're the one who runs away from me."

"Hey, I thought that was all settled. Different folks. You're your kind of people, and I'm my kind of people. You want to close your goddamned robe? Before somebody comes in here, for Christ's sake!"

"Have you had a lot of girls since you came here?" Melody asked.

"What do you think?"

"Tell me."

"Lots of girls."

"You used to tell me I had the prettiest teats in the world," she said. "You find anybody with prettier teats, Ed?"

"Jesus Christ! You're really a fruitcake, you know that?"

"I went to bed with six different guys," she said.

"Shut up!"

"I fucked six different guys, some of them two and three times, and it was never like it was with you," she said.

"Goddamn you, will you shut up!"

"So I figured it was worth the trip over here," she said. "It took a little doing to get the money from my father. After what I got into with you, he decided I needed a keeper. I had a hard time ditching her. The cops in Coblenz are probably dragging the river for my body."

She looked up at him and forced a smile on her face, and then she saw his cold eyes and rigid jawline and that was too much. The whole trip, even nearly blown up, had been for nothing.

She let out a little howl, and threw herself on her side. "Get the hell out of here!" she said. "Leave me alone!"

She heard footsteps and figured that it was him, leaving the room. But then the bed sagged, and she knew he was sitting on it. She held her breath for a moment, and then rolled over to him, her arms out, reaching for him.

"Oh, baby," he said. "Jesus Christ, I've missed you."

"That's why you sent me all the letters, right? Not even a lousy postcard!"

"I just didn't want you to get into something you shouldn't," he said.

She moved her face to his, found his mouth. She put her tongue in his mouth, felt him shiver, as he always did. Then she thrashed around in his arms.

"Let go of me!" she said. He let go of her, surprised.

"What are you doing?" he asked.

"What does it look like I'm doing?" she asked, as she shrugged out of the hospital gown.

"Jesus, Melody, what about your ankle?"

"Fuck my ankle," she said. "Take your damned clothes off!"

[FOUR]
Extract from the Southern Star
Volume 87, No. 42
Ozark, Alabama
30 September 1957

OZARK, September 30—Mayor and Mrs. Howard Percy Dutton announce the wedding of their daughter Melody Louise, to First Lieutenant Edward C. Greer, United States Army, in Algiers, Algeria, September 28.

The previously scheduled nuptials, delayed because of Lieutenant Greer's reassignment from Camp Rucker, were conducted in the English Church in Algiers (Episcopal) by the Rev. Ronald I. Spiers, chaplain to the British Consulate General in Algiers.

Lieutenant Greer is an assistant military attaché at the United States Consulate General, Algiers, where the couple will reside.

XIII

[ONE]
Washington, D.C.
1 September 1957

At the conclusion of his first day on the job as Deputy Chief, Plans and Requirements Section (Fiscal), Aviation Maintenance Section, Office of the Deputy Chief of Staff for Logistics (DCSLOG), Major Craig W. Lowell caught a cab at the Pentagon and had himself driven to the Park-Sheraton Hotel.

He had arrived the night before from Frankfurt, and there were a number of things he had to do, starting with unpacking, thinking about getting a place to live, and getting an automobile.

But the first thing he did when he got to the Park-Sheraton was walk in the bar and order a very dry martini. He had reached the conclusion within an hour of reporting for duty that he was not going to like his new assignment at all. He was going to be a glorified clerk, despite his awesome title, and he was surrounded with horse's asses from his immediate superior, a Lieutenant Colonel Dillard, upward.

He quickly downed the first martini and was halfway through the second when the inevitable thought occurred to him: if he was going to have to spend his time moving paper around on a desk, he had might as well do that at Craig, Powell, Kenyon and Dawes, where he at least owned half the store.

He realized then that both the thought—and martinis—were dangerous at the moment. He set the martini down, scribbled his name on the bar check, and walked out of the bar and to the desk, where he asked for his key.

The desk clerk handed him a telephone message along with the key: "Please call Col. Newburgh." There was a number.

He didn't know a Colonel Newburgh, and he wondered how Colonel Newburgh, whoever the hell he was, had found him at the Park-Sheraton. The temptation was to crumple the message up and forget about it, but he knew he could not afford to offend any of his new superiors. He went to his room (there had been no suites available, something else that annoyed him) and took off his tunic, pulled down his tie, and dialed the number.

"Burning Tree," an operator announced, and for a moment, Lowell thought that he had dialed the wrong number. Burning Tree liked to refer to itself as the President's golf course. There were few colonels among its members.

"Colonel Newburgh, please," he said, however, just to make sure.

"May I ask who's calling?" the operator said.

"Major Lowell," he said.

"Colonel Newburgh is expecting your call, sir," the operator said. "He's in the steam room. Will you hold, please?"

In a moment, a deep, somewhat raspy voice said, "Newburgh, here."

"Major Lowell, sir," Lowell said. "Returning your call."

"Glad I caught you, Lowell," Newburgh said. "What I had in mind was a couple of drinks and dinner. I hope you haven't made other plans."

"Sir, do I know you?"

"We've met," Newburgh said. "And we have a number of mutual friends."

"May I ask who, sir?"

"Bob Bellmon, for one," Newburgh said. "Paul Jiggs for another. He is, that is, *Bob* is going to eat with us."

"That's very kind of you, Colonel," Lowell said. "What time?"

"I don't suppose you've had time to get a car. So if I sent mine for you, that'd give you half an hour to get ready . . ."

"I'll just jump in a cab," Lowell said.

"You know where it is?"

"I'm sure the cabbie will be able to find it," Lowell said.

"I'll leave your name at the door," Newburgh said. "Give them mine, and they'll pass you right in."

"Thank you," Lowell said, and hung up.

He took a shower and changed into civilian clothing, a tweed jacket, gray flannel slacks, a dress white shirt with a foulard in the open collar, and loafers. Then he took a taxi to Burning Tree Country Club.

"Major Lowell, as the guest of Colonel Newburgh," he said to the porter at the door.

The porter looked confused, checked his file, and announced: "I don't seem to have any record of that, sir. But I believe the colonel may be here, and if you'll be good enough to have a seat, I'll see about straightening this out."

"How about this?" Lowell said, handing the porter a card. It was the personal calling card of the executive vice president of the Riggs National Bank, who was also chairman of the Burning Tree House Committee. On it was written "Mr. C. W. Lowell. All privileges, pending action of membership committee."

"Oh, yes, sir," the porter said. "We've been told to expect you, sir. Go right in. I'm sure our manager would like to explain our facilities."

"Just point out the bar, please," Lowell said, with a smile.

"Yes, sir. Up the stairs, through the double glass door."

"Thank you," Lowell said, and found the bar.

There was a stand-up bar and a number of leather upholstered chairs before small tables. Lowell sat down at one of the tables. A waiter in a white jacket appeared immediately.

"Scotch, not much ice, and water," Lowell said.

"You're Mr. Lowell, sir?" the waiter asked.

"That's right."

"Your first night with us, sir, you're a guest of the club. And our manager just called to say he's tied up at the moment, but he looks forward to meeting you personally in just a few minutes."

"That's very nice," Lowell said. "Thank you very much."

When the waiter delivered his drink, a good stiff shot in one glass, a glass with ice, a bowl of ice, a small pitcher of water, and a plate of salted almonds, Lowell asked the waiter if he knew Colonel Newburgh.

"Yes, sir," the waiter said. "That's the colonel at the end of the bar, sir."

"Would you give the colonel another of what he's drinking, with my compliments?" Lowell asked.

"Yes, sir, Mr. Lowell, be happy to."

A minute later, Colonel Carson Newburgh, a tall, ruddy-faced man in his late fifties, in a splendidly tailored glen plaid suit, walked to Lowell's table. Lowell stood up.

"You one-upped me, Lowell," he said, offering his hand. "I guess I asked for it."

"What was the little game at the door?" Lowell asked. Newburgh sat down, and motioned for Lowell to sit.

"My intention was to teach by example," he said. "The point I was trying to make was that it is very hard for most people to gain access to these exalted premises. How'd you get in?"

"I had lunch with the chairman of the house committee in New York a month ago, and when he heard I was coming to Washington . . ."

"You're up for membership?"

"Yeah. He said the committee meets only once every three months."

"And decides which of the applicants, who applied two, three years ago, is the most worthy," Newburgh said.

"Some pigs," Lowell said, "as Mr. Orwell pointed out, are more equal than other pigs."

"It's nice to be rich, isn't it, Lowell?"

"It's way ahead of whatever is in second place," Lowell said. "I gather you are 'comfortable' too, Colonel?"

"I think you could say that," Newburgh said, and smiled at him.

"I'm really curious to know what this is all about," Lowell said. "Until you played games with me at the door, I thought my cousin was somehow involved, that he wanted me to meet the respectable people."

"No, the only contact I've had with Porter was to find out where you were staying," Newburgh said. "I don't really know him. But we have some mutual friends."

"So do we, you said," Lowell said.

"Bob Bellmon's coming over," Newburgh said. "He should be here right about now. I think the plane gets in at 5:55."

"Don't forget to leave your name at the desk," Lowell said.

"I won't have to," Newburgh said. "Bellmon's a member. His grandfather was a member."

"I shall have to remember to be nice to him," Lowell said. "Until after his chance to drop a blackball has passed."

"Barbara wouldn't let him do that," Newburgh said. "Barbara likes you."

"Just who the hell are you, Colonel?" Lowell asked. "And what the hell is going on?"

"My name is Carson Newburgh," he said. "As in the Newburgh Corporation."

"Then you *are* 'comfortable,' " Lowell chuckled.

"It's also been Lieutenant Newburgh," he said. "And since I did such a superb job as E. Z. Black's housekeeper in Korea, Colonel Newburgh."

"Now I know who you are," Lowell said. "Sure."

"And I know who you are, of course," Newburgh said, and chuckled. "You have been described to me as the consummate fuck-up."

"I've heard that," Lowell said.

"And also as a brilliant combat commander with a real genius for logistic planning."

"That would have to be Barbara Bellmon."

"Actually, it was Paul Jiggs."

"I'd love to be able to quote that to him, and use it as a lever to get me the hell out of the Pentagon."

"We now get to the point," Newburgh said. "You can, if you're willing to, make a greater contribution to the army sitting on your ass in the Pentagon than you made leading Task Force Lowell," Newburgh said.

Lowell's eyebrows raised in mocking disbelief.

"In case you're wondering," Newburgh said, smiling broadly, "why I called this little meeting."

Lowell chuckled, and held up his empty drink for a refill.

"What do I have to do?"

"One thing that will probably amuse you, and give you some satisfaction, and a number of other things that you will probably dislike intensely. Both are equally important."

"Tell me what will amuse me," Lowell said.

"There is an H-19 at Fort Lewis, Washington," Newburgh said, "that has been wrecked. Nearly totaled. You're going to have to find enough money in your appropriated-for-other-purposes funds to have it rebuilt, and do so without anyone knowing about it."

"And what happens to the H-19 when I do this? Some general has a flying command post?"

"Mac MacMillan gets a test bed for rocket-armed helicopters," Newburgh said. When he saw the look on Lowell's face, he added: "I told you that it would give you some pleasure."

"Is that why I got that paper shuffler's job?"

"That's part of the reason."

"Drop the other shoe, Colonel," Lowell said.

"From what I've heard about you from the Bellmons," Newburgh said, "and from my personal observations, you'd make a lousy politician. That's a shame."

"Why do you say that?"

"Because what the army needs from you is political influence."

"Porter refers to our distinguished solon as *our* distinguished solon," Lowell said.

"And I have one, actually three, too," Newburgh said. "But we need more than that."

"For what purpose?"

"To keep army aviation alive," Newburgh said. "The air force is going for the jugular."

"I'm not good at that sort of thing," Lowell said.

"No. But you're going to have to try. We'll help."

"I don't really know what the hell you're talking about," Lowell said.

"This town functions over Swedish meatballs and scotch on the rocks," Newburgh said. "More power is wielded at parties than in the Capitol buildings. It's pretty revolting, but that's the way it is."

"And where do I fit in?"

"The way you walked in here," Newburgh said. "I made my point with a demonstration, it seems, even if it wasn't the point I had in mind."

"I don't think I follow you."

"You plan to play some golf while you're in Washington, do you, Major Lowell?"

"Probably."

"Here?"

"Unless I can find someplace more convenient."

"Out there, Major, in Chevy Chase and Silver Spring, in the District itself, are several hundred congressmen, and God only knows how many thousand members of their staffs—and understand, Lowell, right away, that staffers are often more powerful than the men they work for—who can't get past the porter at the door to this place. And places like it. They would be deeply grateful to be asked to play golf with you, Lowell, and they would not risk losing your friendship by voting with the air force. Get the picture?"

"I get it, and I don't like it. I don't think it will work."

"It'll work."

"I wouldn't know our senator if he walked in the door."

"But he knows you, and you're going to be invited out by him. And you will go, and you will have a good time, and you will entertain him in return. And he will find himself sitting next to a very charming colonel, who will make our pitch in his ear."

"Jesus!"

"I don't want to wag the flag in your face," Newburgh said. "But this sort of thing is important, Lowell. And because you are—what did you say?—'comfortable'? Because you are comfortable, you can afford to do it."

Lowell looked at him for a long moment and then shrugged his shoulders.

"How do I start?"

"Call your friend at the Riggs Bank and tell him you want a nice little town house in Georgetown. Get one with a big kitchen and a big dining room. Nothing ostentatious, but efficient. Two or three in staff. Getting the picture?"

"A well-outfitted brothel," Lowell said. "I have the picture."

"And knock out the flip remarks. Act as if you like it."

Lowell put up his hands in surrender.

"That probably means drinking soda water with a squirt of bitters to give it a little color. Your guests can, and it is to be hoped, will, get drunk. You will not."

"Will I get an R&R?"

"Sure. Just take somebody valuable with you. Congressmen from Mobile, Alabama, love to go riding in Aero Commanders."

Newburgh raised his own glass over his head for a refill, and then he glanced at the door, and said, "Oh, there they are."

Lowell looked over his shoulder and saw Bob Bellmon, in uniform, walking into the bar beside a tall, muscular man in civilian clothing. He had never seen the muscular gray-haired man out of uniform before, and it was a moment before he recognized him to be General E. Z. Black, Vice Chief of Staff of the U.S. Army.

Lowell first thought that it was really very clever. Black's very presence lent credibility and authority to his new role as a lobbyist. (He had almost immediately had the irreverent thought that he was about to become the male Perle Mesta.) And Black's hands would be clean. The discussion was over. *Black* hadn't told him to wine and dine the provincial congressmen, or to take funds appropriated for one purpose and use them for another, probably illegal purpose. And rebuilding a wrecked H-19 with funds intended for something else, and then arming it, in violation of the Key West Agreement of 1948, which forbade the army to arm its aircraft, was certainly illegal.

But that wasn't why General Black had come to have a little chat with an obscure major.

An hour later, General Black lifted his eyes from the cracker on which he was spreading Camembert.

"I want you to stay away from Sanford Felter, Lowell," he said.

"Sir?"

"You heard what I said."

"May I ask why, sir?"

"Felter is our man in the White House," Black said.

"I don't know what that means, sir," Lowell said.

"I was about to say that it doesn't matter if you know or not—I gave you an order, and I expect it to be executed—but I suppose you are entitled to an explanation. Felter is the President's liaison man with the intelligence community. It's supposed to be a big secret, but he carries the rank of Counselor to the President. I don't want that role of his compromised in any way. Not by somebody making the connection between this lobbying activity of yours, or this armed chopper business. Clear?"

"Yes, sir," Lowell said. "But how do I explain this to Felter?"

"You're a bright fellow, Lowell," E. Z. Black said. "You'll think of something."

[TWO]
Georgetown, District of Columbia
4 July 1958

It was nearly midnight when Lowell's Eldorado turned onto his street, and he pushed the switch on the dash that triggered the automatic door-opening device on his town house garage. He'd had a little party for a small (30) group of people aboard a rented 55-foot Hatteras. They'd cruised the Potomac starting at half past five. Cocktails, a seafood buffet, and then champagne as they watched the fireworks.

He'd worked in the Pentagon most of the day, and the party had been a real pain in the ass. What he wanted now, desperately, was a drink. He got out of the Eldorado, pushed the button that closed the garage door, and entered the town house through the kitchen. The servants were gone, but there was a stack of bills awaiting his attention on the kitchen table.

He went out of the kitchen through the dining room, and then through the living room to the bar, where he found a bottle of scotch. He carried it back into the kitchen, mixed a strong drink with very little ice, and sat down at the table and wrote checks. While he wrote the checks, he had two more stiff drinks.

It was hot and muggy, and when he checked the thermostat, he saw that one of the servants, who didn't like air conditioning, had the temperature set at eighty. It came on with a thud, but when he climbed the stairs to his bedroom, it seemed as if every stair he took raised the temperature another two degrees.

It was too goddamned hot to even try to sleep. On an impulse, he took a pair of swim trunks from his dresser and carried them back downstairs with him. He undressed in the living room, throwing his clothes on a couch, went into the kitchen, and looked out the breakfast nook windows at the pool.

"What the hell," he said. "Why not?"

He turned on the floodlights and the underwater lights in the pool and walked into the backyard. The backyard was walled with a ten-foot brick fence. He walked down the terrazzo to the deep end of the pool, set his drink down on one of the umbrella-topped tables, and took a running dive into the pool.

Goddamned water must be ninety degrees, he thought. It was like jumping into a hot bath.

He climbed out of the pool halfway down and walked back to pick up his drink.

"Howdy, neighbor!" she called.

Shit, that's all I need. Constance.

Constance was his neighbor. Constance was the wife of a very important senator. The senator was sixty-eight, and said he was fifty-eight. Constance was thirty-odd and pretended she was twenty-two. Constance had short black hair which she wore pressed close to her skull.

He picked up his drink, put a smile on his face, and turned around.

"Howdy, neighbor!" he parroted. "I hope the lights didn't wake you up."

"Couldn't sleep," she said. Then she said, "Don't go away!"

What the fuck is *that* supposed to mean? he wondered.

He walked back to the house, stopping to look for a towel in the pool house. There was none. He went into the kitchen and toweled himself with dish towels. He hoped that Constance was not going to come over. He waited for the sound of the chimes, and when they didn't come in a reasonable time for her to have come over, he went and looked out the window. The street was deserted.

He could go to bed. The temperature would be lower, if not cool. He had to go to work in the morning and he needed his sleep.

"Hi!"

Constance, wearing a two-piece bathing suit that would have been appropriate for a late-blooming thirteen year old, came in from the kitchen.

"How did you get over the wall?" he asked, in surprise.

"Love always finds a way," she said.

He smiled at her and went to look. He was mystified.

"At the end by the house," she explained, coming to stand close to him. "They made sort of steps in the wall."

"I never noticed," he said.

"There's a lot you never notice," she said.

He smiled.

"Do you want to be wet outside or inside?" he asked, thinking he was being clever, offering her a choice between a dip in the pool or a drink. Constance chose to misunderstand.

"That's getting right down to the nitty-gritty right away, isn't it?" she asked. "Can I have a drink first, or should I just jump in bed?"

"Certainly, you jest!" he said, making that as much a joke as he could.

"I didn't mind you ignoring me when I thought you were queer," she said.

"You thought I was queer?"

"You're so beautiful, I thought you had to be," she said.

"I'm crushed," he said.

"And then I saw you paddling around with that newspaper reporter," she said. "And I just happened to notice that she left her car on the street all night."

"Engine trouble," he said.

"Certainly," she said.

"Would you like a drink?"

"I don't need one," she said. "But if it makes you feel any better."

He went to the kitchen to make her a drink. She followed him, and ran her fingers over a faint, fifteen-inch-long scar on his back.

"Where'd you get that?" she asked.

"A long time ago in Greece," he said.

"It's just enough to accent the rest of the perfection," she said. Her hand ran down his back and rested on his buttock. Either her fingers or her breasts coming out of the negligible top of her suit or the damp suit itself was enough to give him an erection. He was now afraid to turn around.

"Your britches are wet," she said. "If you don't get out of them, you'll catch your death."

"This conversation is getting dangerous," he said.

"Isn't it interesting?" she said.

"Neither one of us could afford anything like that," he said.

"What you couldn't afford, darling, is me going to my aging, impotent, but nevertheless insanely jealous husband and telling him you made improper and unwanted advances."

She moved her hand around to the front of his trunks, grabbed him, and chuckled deep in her throat.

"Take off your britches, darling," she said. "Like a nice boy."

[THREE]
Alexandria, Virginia
7 November 1958

The Cadillac Eldorado, which bore a District of Columbia license plate, a bumper-mounted decal authorizing the vehicle to be parked in Lot C-5-11 of the Pentagon parking area, drove slowly down Kildar Street while the driver swore aloud.

"These fucking rabbit hutches look all alike," he said.

And then he spotted a battered Volkswagen parked beside a Buick estate wagon. He turned off Kildar Street and pulled into the driveway and stopped behind the huge Buick and had a nasty thought: *Little Men Like Big Cars.* He had no idea why that thought had popped into his mind, and was immediately ashamed of himself.

The Deputy Chief, Plans and Requirements Section (Fiscal), Aviation Maintenance Sections, Office of the Deputy Chief of Staff for Logistics, was in uniform, the new olive-green shade 51 uniform. On his shoulder was the insignia of the Military District of Washington. There was a major's gold oak leaf on each epaulet. He wore the lapel insignia, a silver star on which was superimposed the national eagle, of the General Staff Corps, and on his tunic pocket was the insignia awarded to officers who have served a year on the Army General Staff. He wore no ribbons or qualification badges. Pinned to his tunic, above the left pocket was a name tag with white letters on a black background. It read LOWELL.

He got out of the Eldorado, let the heavy door swing closed of its own weight, and walked up to the door of 2301 Kildar Street.

The chimes played "Be it ever so humble" when he pushed the door bell, and as always, he winced.

Sharon Felter, a slight, feminine, black-haired woman wearing a full apron, opened the inner door. She squealed with pleasure when she saw him, and pushed open the screen door. She pulled him to her and kissed him, not quite on the mouth.

"Things never change," he said.

"What things?"

"The first time you ever kissed me, you smelled of freshly baked bread," Lowell said.

"Don't knock it, I could open a business."

"I would speak at that man you're married to," he said.

"He's not home yet, Craig," Sharon Felter said.

"I saw the pile of rust," Lowell said. "I thought he was here."

"Somebody from the office picked him up," Sharon said. "I think he had to go into Washington."

"But he is coming home?"

"He should be here any minute," she said. "Can I get you a drink?"

"Will you have one with me?"

She thought that over a moment, and then nodded her head. "To celebrate," she said.

"I suppose I'm expected to ask what you're celebrating."

"The visit of an old and dear friend, who, although he lives in Washington, might as well live in Anchorage, Alaska, or someplace, how often he comes to see us."

"I stand before you suitably shamed," he said. "But you know what would happen, if I did this very often? I would ply you with booze and carry you off into a life of sin."

"Would there be room for me?" Sharon replied. "You're not as young as you used to be, you know."

"Touché, Madame," Lowell said.

"What will you have to drink?" Sharon asked.

"Scotch, straight up," Lowell said. He was surprised when Sharon made herself a scotch on the rocks, a stiff one, not measuring the liquor.

"Has that man you live with been teaching you evil ways?" he asked, nodding at her drink.

"Doctor's orders," Sharon said. When she saw his eyebrows raise, she added: "Cross my heart."

"Is there something wrong with you?" Major Lowell asked, and the concern in his voice was intense and evident.

"Nothing, according to the doctor, that a little scotch and water won't cure."

"I'm not very good at games," he said. "And neither are you. What's wrong?"

"Tension. High blood pressure. Nerves. Lady's complaints," Sharon said.

"Because of what he's doing?" Lowell asked, almost angrily.

"All he does is work very hard," she said.

"Has he been up to his disappearing-act spy games again? Is that it? And don't tell Uncle Craig you're not supposed to talk about it."

"Just hard work," she said.

"Why he doesn't get the hell out of that business, I'll never know," Lowell said.

There was the sound of a car door slamming, and then of the front door opening.

"Hello, Craig," Sandy Felter said, coming into the kitchen. He was in a baggy, gray business suit. He did not seem either surprised or especially pleased to see Lowell.

"Let me guess," Lowell said. "This week, you're disguised as a bureaucrat."

"What brings you over here?"

"I heard you were out of town and thought it would be a splendid time to seduce your wife."

"Well, this was your chance," Felter said. "The kids are in Newark. You could have had her all to yourself if you'd come over earlier."

"I don't think either of you are funny!" Sharon said.

"From what I hear," Lowell said, "wife swapping is all the rage among up and coming D.C. bureaucrats."

"If anybody could check that out, you're the man," Felter said. "From what I hear, there have been so many women going into and out of a certain Georgetown town house the cops thought somebody had opened a store."

"Sandy!" Sharon said.

"He's just jealous, Sharon, that's all," Lowell said. "Some of us have animal magnetism, and some of us don't."

"And some of us are too smart to get involved with senator's wives," Felter said. He took off his jacket and opened the hall closet. The butt of a Colt .45 pistol was visible in the small of his back.

"That cannon makes your wife nervous, you know," Lowell said, as Felter took the pistol from its skeleton holster and laid it on the closet shelf. "From the time you leave until the time you walk back in, she has visions of you being ambushed by the NKVD in front of the Falls Church A&P. It's driving her to drink."

"I don't think that's particularly funny," Sanford Felter said.

"I wasn't trying to be funny. Before you sneaked through the door just now, in your inimitable imitation of Humphrey Bogart, I was saying to your wife that it was high time you stopped playing spy and went back to being a soldier."

"Just for the record, Craig," Felter said, coldly, "I am a soldier."

"In that bureacrat suit, you sure could fool me," Lowell said.

"To what do we owe the honor of your visit?" Felter asked, coldly.

"Enough!" Sharon said. "I don't know what it is with you two. You're closer than brothers, and you act like . . . I don't know what."

"How about brothers?" Lowell asked, innocently. There was a moment's pause and then Felter laughed.

"How about giving my little brother a belt?" Lowell asked. "He looks as if he can use one."

"Sandy?" Sharon asked.

"Why not?" he said. Sharon jumped up and walked quickly, into the kitchen to make her husband a drink.

"Mud in your eye," Felter said, taking a sip of his drink.

"Mazeltov!" Lowell replied. Felter looked at him and shook his head.

"You're amazing," he said. "Amazing. That came out anti-Semitic."

"Well, screw you," Lowell said. "I was simply trying to be charming."

"If you're trying to be charming, you want something," Felter said.

"Right," Lowell said.

"That figures, that figures," Felter said. "What?"

"I was dealing with one of your pals today," Lowell said.

"Oh?"

"Yeah. He came into my office, looked under the desk and in the wastebaskets to see if any Russians were lurking about, and flashed his badge on me."

"What kind of a badge?" Felter asked.

"CIC."

"Craig, I have nothing to do with the CIC. You know that."

"Creepy little bastard, drunk with authority," Lowell said. "He was asking questions about a friend of mine."

"What friend?" Felter asked.

"I want to know why he was asking the questions," Lowell said. He reached in his pocket and handed over a slip of memo paper. "That's the name."

"And what am I supposed to do with this?"

"Find out what kind of trouble my friend is in, and what I can do to help," Lowell said.

"You know I can't do anything like that!"

"Yes, you can. You may not want to, but you know you can."

"You can't believe I would even think about doing something like that," Felter said.

"Get on the goddamned phone and call somebody up," Lowell said.

"I'll tell you what I'm going to do," Felter said. "I'm going to go upstairs and take a shower. And I'm going to even forget that you asked me what you did."

"Kiss my ass, Sandy," Craig Lowell said. He stood up, and put his drink down.

"You're not leaving!" Sharon Felter said. There was an awkward silence. Sandy saw that Sharon was close to tears.

"No, of course not," Lowell said, after a moment.

"I'll make us another drink," Sharon said. Lowell saw that Sharon's glass was empty.

Sanford Felter walked up the stairs to his bedroom. The sonofabitch had no right to ask him things like that; he had no right to upset Sharon. God only knows what the human stud had been saying to her before he got home. Felter had noticed how quickly his wife had drained her glass.

God*damn* him!

Felter walked to the chest of drawers and unloaded his pockets. There were a couple of bills crumpled into a ball; a dollar or so in coins; a sweat-stained wallet; a leather folder containing a badge and a plastic identification card identifying him as a Deputy United States Marshal (which served, in case some zealous cop got curious, to justify the .45) and a plastic card, riveted to an alligator clip, containing his photograph, his name, and three diagonal red stripes. This granted him access at any time to any area of the Pentagon, the Defense Intelligence Agency, the State Department, and the CIA, as well as access to any information he might ask for.

In the classified files of DCSINTEL, where his service records were kept, was a copy of the Department of Army general order which had placed Major Sanford T. Felter, Infantry (Detail: Military Intelligence) of the Defense Intelligence Agency, on temporary duty with the White House. In the Eyes Only safes of the Secretary of Defense, the Secretary of State, the Director of the FBI, and the Director of the CIA, was a short note on White House notepaper:

THE WHITE HOUSE
WASHINGTON

Effective immediately, and until further notice, Major Sanford T. Felter, USA, is relieved of all other duties, and will serve as my personal liaison officer with the intelligence

```
community with the rank of Counselor to the President. This
appointment will not be made known publicly. Major Felter will
be presumed to have the Need To Know when this question arises.

                                                            DDE
```

There was a photograph on the dresser. It had been taken in Greece, near the Albanian border. It showed two very young officers. They were wearing American khaki shirts. The rest of their uniforms were British. The smaller of them, First Lieutenant Sanford T. Felter, twenty-two years old, cradled a Thompson .45 caliber submachine gun in his arms, like some bootleg era gangster. The taller of them, Second Lieutenant Craig W. Lowell, aged nineteen, had an M1 Garand slung over his shoulder like a hunter. There were two 8-round cartridge clips pinned to the Garand's leather strap.

Felter remembered, very clearly, other photographs that had been on that roll of 35 mm film. In an act of incredible stupidity, he had sent it home to Sharon to have it developed and printed. And when it came back from the Rexall drugstore on the corner of Aldine Street and Lyons Avenue, one block down from the Felters' bakery, Sharon, his wife of eight months, had seen what his room in Greece looked like and what the dog they had acquired somewhere looked like, and what his new friend Craig Lowell looked like. Two of the photographs had told Sharon much more about what he was doing in Greece than he wanted her to know. The two photographs showed Craig Lowell in the traditional pose of the successful big game hunter, smiling broadly, cradling his rifle proudly in his arms, kneeling on the fruits of the hunt. What he was kneeling on was a pile of three bodies. One of the bodies was looking at the camera with a look of surprise on his mustached face. There was a neat little .30 caliber hole in the middle of his forehead. The back of his head had been blown away.

Sharon had kept the print and the negatives until he came home, and then wordlessly given them to him. He had wordlessly burned them. Felter looked at the photograph of them together, way back then, and then he forced his eyes away and went into the bathroom and took a shower.

There was such a thing as pushing a friendship too far, he told himself. Craig expected too much.

As he soaped his balding head with Sharon's woman's shampoo (if he used soap, or regular shampoo, his skin flaked), he remembered how Craig W. Lowell had solved the problem of what he was going to tell Sharon and his mother and father and her mother and father about what he was doing in the hospital in Hawaii. While they were airlifting him from the hospital ship in Pusan Harbor to Hawaii, Craig, Porter, Kenyon and Dawes, investment bankers, had sent a nice young man around to Felter's Warsaw Bakery. The nice young man had a limousine, and the nice young man had traveled with them to Hawaii, just in case someone in the airlines hadn't gotten the word that the Felters and the Lavinskys were personal friends of the man who owned half of the firm that had just loaned the airline however many millions of dollars it took to make a down payment on a fleet of intercontinental transport aircraft.

And when they carried him into his room on the stretcher, they had all been there, and Sharon was hugging him and crying, and nobody could talk, except his mother.

"So, Sanford," his mother said, "you wouldn't believe our hotel. Would you believe we got two whole apartments? On the beach. You can look out from the porch and see these Hawaiian *schwartzes* riding on those boards. The Royal Hawaiian, yet."

And he remembered what Sharon had told him, after he'd come back from Dien Bien Phu. That Craig W. Lowell had sat in the chair where he was now sitting, swilling down booze and crying like a baby.

"In a way, Sandy, it was funny," Sharon said later. "Here we were, the widow and the orphans, and what we were doing was trying to make Uncle Craig stop crying."

"Shit!" Sanford Felter said. He stepped out of the shower, wrapped a towel around his waist, and went to his bed and sat on it. He opened the door of the bedside table and took out a black telephone with several buttons on it.

He dialed a number.

"Liberty 7-1936," a male voice said.

"Scramble Four Victor Twenty-Three," Felter said.

"Confirm Four Victor Two Three," the voice said, after a moment. "Go ahead."

Felter pushed the appropriate buttons on the special telephone.

"This is Felter," he said. "Get onto somebody in G-2 or the Defense Intelligence Agency and find out (a) why the CIC is investigating a man named Franklin, William B., and (b) what the investigation has come up with so far."

"Yes, sir," the male voice said. "Will you spell, sir?"

"Franklin, as in Poor Richard's Almanac," Felter said. The name rang a bell, but he couldn't put his finger on it. There were so many names.

"Yes, sir."

"I'm at my home," Felter said. "Get back to me here."

"Yes, sir."

Felter replaced the handset in the receiver without saying anything else. He put the phone back in the space under the bedside table. Then he stood up and walked back into the bathroom and put the towel in the hamper.

What he had done was absolutely a breach of the authority with which he had been entrusted. There was no other way to look at it. On the other hand, it was equally clear that he would get away with it. He reported to the President—and nobody else. Even if the directors of the FBI or CIA somehow heard about this, there would be no questions asked. For a long time now, he had been one of the very few who were given the benefit of any doubt.

He put on a sports shirt and a pair of slacks and went downstairs.

Craig was in the kitchen with Sharon. Sharon was making a salad. Craig was pressing roughly ground peppercorns into a steak with his thumb.

"So how were things in Germany?" Felter asked. "Is there any more whiskey, or did you two drink it all up?"

"How'd you know I was in Germany?" Lowell asked.

"I spoke to your father-in-law yesterday," Felter said. He found the bottle of scotch and made himself a drink. That killed the bottle. He was sure there had been four inches of whiskey in it when he'd gone upstairs. He saw that both his wife and Lowell had full, dark glasses.

"We took Peter hunting for his first time," Lowell said.

"Craig, you didn't!" Sharon said. "My God, he's only nine years old."

"He's a real kraut," Lowell said. "He loved it."

"He's a half-American, Craig," Sharon said.

"He finds that somewhat embarrassing," Lowell said.

"Oh, Craig!" Sharon said.

Felter pushed the curtain on the kitchen door aside to see how the charcoal was coming.

"You haven't started the fire," he accused.

Lowell snapped his fingers. "I knew there was something I had to do besides stick peppercorns in this."

It wasn't that funny, but Sharon and Craig thought it was.

It took forty minutes for the charcoal to achieve what Major Craig W. Lowell thought was the proper grayish hue. Time, Felter saw, for two more drinks. Sharon, he thought, is going to get sick to her stomach. Then, aware that he was being petulant, he enjoyed the notion that it would serve her right.

Lowell insisted on red wine to go with the meal. That was really going to make Sharon sick.

They had just about finished eating when the door chimes played "Be it ever so humble."

Felter drained his wine glass and went to answer it. A stocky, gray-haired man in a business suit, carrying a briefcase, stood before the door. Felter saw a black Chevrolet four-door sedan in the driveway behind Lowell's Eldorado. There was someone behind the wheel. He opened the door.

"Good evening, sir," the gray-haired man said.

"Come in, please, Colonel," Felter said, opening the door.

Felter led him into the dining room.

"You know Mrs. Felter, of course," Felter said.

"Ma'am," the colonel said.

"Colonel," Sharon said.

"This is Major Lowell," Felter said.

"How do you do, sir?" Lowell said. They shook hands, but the colonel did not offer his name, and Felter didn't use it.

"Can I offer you a glass of wine, Colonel? Or a drink?" Felter asked.

"Thank you, sir, no. I have the duty."

"You apparently have some answers for me," Felter said. The colonel looked uncomfortable.

"I rather doubt that either my wife or Major Lowell will rush to the nearest telephone to inform the Russian Embassy of this conversation," Felter said.

"Yes, sir," the colonel said. "Sir, I wasn't given much to go on, so I decided it would be best to bring you what I have myself."

"I'm sorry you had to drive all the way out here," Felter said.

"Sir, there are three Franklins, William, under investigation," the colonel said. He sat down at the table and opened his briefcase. "Two are routine background investigations. I have their summaries with me. The third, Lieutenant Colonel Franklin, who I would guess is the subject of your interest, has been, we believe, sexually compromised—we're not quite sure by whom—in Yokohama."

He laid three folders on the dining room table.

"Colonel Franklin's file, sir, is the thick one," the colonel said.

Felter nodded. He looked through the two thinner files, then pushed them toward Lowell. Their eyes met. Lowell selected one of the two thinner files and flipped through it quickly. Felter read the file concerning Lieutenant Colonel Franklin, who had apparently discovered at age thirty-six an interest in young, relatively hair-free male youths.

"Colonel," Felter said, "when you have finished this, would you be sure that I get a copy and otherwise be kept up to date?"

"Yes, sir," the colonel said. "Of course, sir. Sir, if there are any areas of particular interest to you?"

"Nothing your people are not presently covering very well, Colonel," Felter said. "I'm afraid that my concerns here amount to much ado about nothing."

"It never hurts to make sure, does it, sir?" the colonel said.

"It sometimes inconveniences people," Felter said. "Lowell, have you any questions for the colonel?"

"No, sir," Lowell said, straight-faced. "The colonel's people are obviously on top of the situation."

The colonel's pleasure was evident on his face.

"I feel rather bad about getting you all the way out here, when it turns out that there is no problem," Felter said. "Are you sure you won't have a drink? Or perhaps something to eat?"

"Thank you just the same, sir," the colonel said. "I have the duty."

The colonel stuffed the files back into his briefcase and Felter walked him to the door.

"Thank you again, Colonel," Felter said. "I'm very impressed with your response time."

"Thank *you*, sir," the colonel said.

Felter closed the door, walked into the kitchen, and made two drinks. He walked into the dining room and set one before Lowell. Then he sat down and stared at him. They stared at each other for a long time, and then they began to chuckle, and then to laugh.

There was a touch of hysteria in the laughter.

"Is that a private joke?" Sharon asked, pleased that they were laughing together.

"The things you get me to do, you bastard," Felter said.

"From now on, that poor fruitcake in Yokohama won't be able to take a leak without three creeps from CIC timing him with stopwatches," Lowell said.

"Are you going to tell me or not?" Sharon demanded.

"I don't know why the hell I'm laughing," Felter said. "It really isn't funny."

"There is an element of overkill, isn't there?" Lowell asked, chuckling.

"I'm getting mad, Sandy, I mean it," Sharon said.

"When Don Juan here was in Algiers," Felter explained, "he had a Signal Corps photographer sergeant named Franklin, William. The kid did his time, and got out of the army, and went back to Canton, Ohio, where, after a couple of months, he decided that he really didn't want to spend the rest of his life taking photographs of weddings. So he re-upped and put in for the warrant officer candidate helicopter pilot program. Before they give them their warrants, they give them a complete background investigation. The kid naturally listed Craig here as a reference. The kid figured that a field-grade officer of such an impeccable reputation was a good reference to have."

"So?" Sharon said.

"So MDW sent some sergeant in civilian clothes around to ask Major Lowell if he had, in fact, known Franklin, William B., and to inquire if he would recommend Franklin, William B., for a position of great trust and responsibility."

"Well, he could have been in trouble," Lowell said. "How was I supposed to know?"

"If he was a friend of yours, you could almost count on his being in trouble," Felter said.

"I still don't understand," Sharon said.

"What happened, honey," Felter said, "was that Don Juan did it to me again. I just put what is laughingly known as the intelligence community in high gear. The deputy chief of Army Counterintelligence rushed out here devoutly believing he was involved in a security matter of the highest priority. If he really knew what it was all about . . ."

"Hell, Sandy, you made his whole week. He'll be waiting for his boss at 0700 to tell him Super Spook himself told him personally he was impressed with his reaction time."

"I don't know why I'm laughing," Felter said. "Goddamn you, Craig, you're dangerous."

"Hand me the phone, Sharon, honey, will you?" Lowell asked.

"Don't you dare!" Felter said. "God knows who he wants to call."

"I'm going to call Franklin, that's who I'm going to call."

"No, you're not," Felter said.

"Why not?"

"For one thing, you're drunk," Felter said. "The last thing that kid needs now, two months before he graduates, is a telephone call from a drunken officer."

"*I'm* drunk? You're the one who could barely pronounce 'reaction time,' " Lowell said.

"Don't call him, Craig," Felter said. "You'd just make trouble for him."

"What Craig wants to do is see if he needs anything," Sharon said, somewhat thickly, defending him.

"Right. What's wrong with that?" Lowell demanded of Felter.

"You're just going to call attention to him," Felter said. "That's the last thing he needs right now."

"I'll call Phil Parker," Lowell said. "He's down there."

"Don't call anybody," Felter said. "Quit while you're ahead."

Lowell thumbed his nose at Felter and picked up the telephone.

Felter was pleased when Lowell could not complete his call to Captain Philip Sheridan Parker IV, and was limited to a brief, maudlin conversation with Dr. Antoinette Parker.

Antoinette assured him that she would have Phil check to see what, if anything, Warrant Officer Candidate Franklin needed, and then asked to speak to Sharon.

Lowell moved to an armchair in the living room while the women talked, and fell asleep. That solved another problem, Felter decided. Lowell was obviously too drunk to drive back into Washington. Virginia police were death on drunken driving. The chair was reclining. Felter got Lowell into a nearly horizontal position, loosened his necktie and belt, removed his shoes, and draped a blanket over him.

Sharon was still talking to Antoinette when he finished.

He waved at her, and went upstairs and got in bed.

He heard her come into the room ten minutes later, listened to the sound of her undressing, felt the bed sag as she got in beside him.

"You awake?" Sharon asked.

"I am now," Sandy replied.

"Antoinette wants us to come down there for New Year's Eve," Sharon said.

Felter didn't reply.

"I want to go, Sandy," Sharon said.

"It's a thousand miles down there," Sandy said. "You really want to go a thousand miles to sit around an officer's club full of drunks in dress uniforms?"

"Yes," she said.

"What did you say?"

"I want to go," Sharon repeated. "I want to walk into an officer's club with you, in uniform. I want to wear my West Point ring, and I want you to wear your West Point ring, and I want you to wear your uniform with all your ribbons and all your medals. I'm just a little sick of pretending the man I'm married to is an economic analyst for the goddamned CIA."

She's really drunk, Sanford Felter realized. Sharon rarely swore.

The confirmation of that analysis came when he rolled over and put his arms around her and found that she was naked.

"Surprise, surprise," she said.

"Not that I mind, of course, but what brought this on?" Felter asked.

"I got very horny, Sandy," Sharon said, solemnly, "when Colonel Whatsisname was here."

"Let me have that again?" he asked, amused. Her hand moved to his groin. "Women are turned on by strong and powerful men," Sharon said. She giggled as he started to grow erect. "Wheee!" she said.

He put his hand to her breast. It was firm and the nipple erect.

"You were the strongest man in the room," she said. "Stronger, Sandy, than that colonel. Stronger than Craig."

He was, he realized, deeply flattered. Even if she was drunk.

In vino veritas, he thought.

"But I never get a chance to show you off," she said. "I want to show you off, Sandy. I never get a chance to be an officer's lady. That's important to a woman. You're a man and you don't understand that."

"If you really want to go to Rucker, we'll go to Rucker," he said. He was a little ashamed of himself. Going to Rucker was a preposterous idea. What he wanted to do was screw. A stiff prick, he told himself, has no conscience.

Sharon was a good solid woman. This was the third time since they had been married that he knew for sure she was drunk. She had gotten drunk after they buried Craig's wife, and she had gotten drunk when her father died. When he thought about that, there was something unnerving about her being drunk now. Was 'her nerves' that serious a problem?

He put that thought from his mind. There was something wicked about her being drunk now and wanting him to screw her. He liked it. In the morning, she would be a little embarrassed about taking too much to drink, about what she was doing now. She would realize then that going to Rucker was really absurd.

She twisted away from him.

"What are you doing?" Sandy asked.

The bedside lamp came on.

"I want to see," Sharon said. "I want to watch!"

"You little vixen, you!" he said, and knelt between her legs. He could feel his excitement in his chest. He thought that it would be four days before the kids came back from Newark. He thought he would bring a bottle home some afternoon.

"Fuck me, Sandy!" Sharon hissed in his ear. "Fuck me good!"

He did.

When Sanford Felter went downstairs in the morning, Sharon was making Craig eat scrambled eggs, despite his protests that all he wanted was a cup of coffee.

She avoided her husband's eyes when he sat down at the table. She scrambled some more eggs and put them before him, with toast and grape jelly and grapefruit juice. Then she sat down at the table, and stirred her coffee.

"Craig," she said, "if Sandy can get off, will you take us to Fort Rucker for New Year's Eve? Antoinette asked us."

Lowell, surprised, hesitated before replying. Sandy knew that Craig didn't want to spend New Year's Eve at the Rucker officer's open mess any more than he did.

"Madame," Lowell said, "Lowell Airlines is at your beck and call."

Sharon looked at Sandy, met his eyes.

"The kids can stay with Mama Felter," Sharon said.

XIV

[ONE]
Fort Rucker, Alabama
11 November 1958

QUESTION: *What is a WOC?*
ANSWER: *Sir, a WOC is something one fwows at a wabbit.*

It had been rumored among both the staff of Warrant Officer Candidate Battalion, the U.S. Army Aviation School, and among the WOCs themselves that an amnesty would be granted by the commanding general to mark the Thanksgiving holiday. Major General Paul T. Jiggs, the post commander, who had otherwise earned a reputation as a starchy bastard, seemed to take some kind of a perverse pleasure in freeing WOCs from restrictions imposed by the WOC staff on whatever slim excuse he could find. Thanksgiving, to both the restricted and the restrictors, seemed to be just the sort of excuse the general would be pleased to have available.

Of the 254 WOCs in Companies A through D, thirty-two WOCs were under restriction of varying degree. Those WOCs whose academic grades were below acceptable standards, and who were guilty of no other offense against the rules and regulations, were restricted to the WOC area, but permitted to sign themselves out at the orderly room and visit the post exchange and the post theater. This authority specifically excluded visiting the post exchange cafeteria.

WOCs guilty of other violations were under progressively more restrictive restraints, in proportion to their offenses against the regulations. The most severe restriction imposed (beyond which punishment was expulsion from the WOC program) required that the WOCs, between the 0600 and 2200 hours, confine themselves to their rooms. During this period, dressed in a Class "A" uniform, they had the option of standing or sitting at their study desk. They were not permitted to smoke. Aside from a thirty-minute period during which they were permitted to read the daily newspaper, their reading material was limited to official textbooks and army manuals. The operation of radios, televisions, or other electronic amusement devices was proscribed.

The most common violation with which the WOCs on restriction were charged was "conduct unbecoming a warrant officer candidate and a gentleman." The specific charge was most often "use of vulgar and /or obscene and/or blasphemous language."

Ninety percent of the WOC class of which WOC William B. Franklin was a member consisted of regular army noncommissioned officers between the ages of twenty years and six months and twenty-six years and six months, and in the grades of E-5 through E-7, that is to say staff sergeants, sergeants first class, and master sergeants, or their technical counterparts, specialists five, six, and seven. There were tank commanders and cartographers, first sergeants and budget analysts, infantry platoon sergeants and medical corps x-ray technicians. There were aircraft mechanics and avionic technicians, photographers, small arms artificers, and even one farrier, who had come to flight school from Fort Meyers, Virginia, where he had been in charge of the horses used in the military funerals held half a dozen times a day at Arlington National Cemetery.

What they had in common, in addition to generally splendid physical condition, an average of 6.7 years of enlisted service, and Army General Classification Test (AGCT) scores averaging 123.6 (an AGCT score of 110 is required of officer candidates), was the desire to become both helicopter pilots and warrant officers.

They were old soldiers; they had been around. They knew that the pay scale for warrant officers was precisely that of officers in the ranks of second lieutenant through major. They would put up with whatever bullshit the army threw at them for six months, or however long it took, and they'd come out of it with a warrant, and it would be *sayonara* and *auf Wiedersehen* to the bullshit that went with being a goddamned EM. If they liked the life of an officer, they could wangle a commission and go for thirty, and if it turned out to be a pain in the ass, they'd just put in their twenty (drawing flight pay meanwhile) and retire at fifty percent of their base pay.

Getting through the bullshit was going to pose no problem at all. They weren't a bunch of fucking recruits, for Christ's sake. They knew the army game, and they knew how to play it. Cover your ass, keep your shoes shined, your pants pressed, your hair cut, and your mouth shut.

The army, for Christ's sake, was not going to fuck around with a bunch of old soldiers.

The orders which assigned them to the U.S. Army Aviation Center, Fort Rucker, Alabama, specifically forbade travel by private automobile and clearly stated that since the warrant officer candidates would be restricted to the barracks for the first six weeks of their training, "dependents are discouraged from accompanying sponsors."

Well, bullshit! Let the Old Lady drive the car, get a motel or a room someplace, and then it would simply be a matter of going over the fence at night to share the nuptial couch.

The orders which had sent them to Fort Rucker four months before further stated, specifically, that incoming students would report not earlier than 2000 hours and not later than 2200 hours, in Class "A" uniform, and that civilian clothing and other personal equipment would be turned in for storage to the quartermaster before they left their camp, post, or station to report to the Fort.

Sergeant Franklin had found a garage in Daleville, outside the gate, where he could leave his car and his civvies. He had taken a cab to the post, and had more or less expected to see what happened: starting at 2005 hours, a line of civilian automobiles owned by married noncoms appeared at the WOC area. Senior enlisted men, carrying for the first time in a long time a standard GI duffel bag, got out of the cars, perfunctorily kissed their wives, and marched up the sidewalk to the orderly room.

There they were greeted by cadre, corporals, and buck sergeants. They knew the routine. There was a roster. Their names were checked off. They signed in. They were given room assignments and informed that they were restricted to the company area.

They, like Franklin, were pleased with what they initially found. For one thing, they had BOQs. Regular goddamned officer's BOQs, a sitting room study with a desk and even a desk lamp. A bedroom with a real bed, not even a GI bed, a real bed, with a real mattress. There was a shower and a crapper, shared with the guy next door. It wasn't quite the accommodations Sergeant Franklin had had in the Hotel d'Angleterre in Algiers, but it was far more spacious and comfortable than he expected.

The guys next door were a surprise. Goddamned buck ass private recruits, fresh from Dix or Bragg or another basic training post, still showing the signs of the thirty-second haircut they'd got on their first day in the army. Bright kids, starry-eyed and bushy-tailed, but goddamned *rookies*. What the fuck they were doing here was something that would have to be figured out.

At 0600 the next morning, a somewhat scratchy phonograph recording of reveille was played over the public address system. This was almost immediately followed by the announcement, repeated twice, that the uniform of the day was Class "A" with ribbons and qualification badges. Breakfast would be served at the WOC mess. WOCs would form at 0625 hours in front of the barracks. They were told to determine among themselves who was the senior noncommissioned officer, and he would form the company. A member of the cadre would serve as guide for the march to the WOC mess.

Five master sergeants ambled outside at 0620. They were wearing immaculate uniforms and all their ribbons. They crisply saluted a five-foot-three-inch second lieutenant who was standing outside, and cheerfully barked, "Good morning, sir!" to him.

He returned their salute, gave them a half-smile, and stood watching with his arms folded.

They compared dates of rank, and it was determined that First Sergeant Kenneth G. Spencer, until three days before top kick of Dog Company, 508th Parachute Infantry, 82nd Airborne Division, was the ranking noncommissioned officer.

"What we'll do is have each of you take a platoon," First Sergeant Spencer said. "And you," he added to the fourth master sergeant, "will be the guide."

While it had been some time since some of the master sergeants had marched anywhere, they knew what the hell they were doing. When the rest of the incoming class came out before the barracks, they quickly formed them into three platoons, each headed by a master sergeant. The second john (who looked as if he had gotten out of the Point last week) gestured to the cadre corporal to present the roster to First Sergeant Spencer.

Roll was called.

First Sergeant Spencer performed an impeccable about-face, snapped his right hand to his right eyebrow in an impeccable demonstration of the hand salute, and barked: "Sir, all present and accounted for."

The shavetail returned the salute.

"Very good. March the men to the mess, Sergeant."

"Yes, sir!" First Sergeant Spencer said. He did another impeccable about-face.

The mess was a pleasant surprise too. Most school mess halls were pretty goddamned bad. This wasn't. There were four-man tables, each with pitchers of milk, condiments, table clothes, even napkins and flowers. More like an officer's mess than an EM mess hall. And the chow wasn't at all bad. Eggs any way you liked them, biscuits. First class.

Nobody had said anything about marching back to the company area, but First Sergeant Spencer had apparently decided it wouldn't hurt to play it safe and do things by the book, for when Franklin came out of the mess hall, Spencer was already there to form the troops again. When they were all assembled, he marched them back to the company area. Shiny Balls the Second John was waiting there for them. First Sergeant Spencer had guessed right. He had been expected to march the men back from the mess.

He formed the company into platoons, did an about-face, and saluted.

"Sir, the company is formed," he barked.

"Prepare the company for inspection in ranks, Sergeant," Shiny Balls the Second John said.

First Sergeant Spencer saluted, about-faced, stood at rigid attention and barked: "Open ranks, MARCH!"

The first rank took two large steps forward; the second rank took one large step forward. The third rank did not move.

"Dress right, *dress*. Ready. FRONT!"

First Sergeant Spencer followed Shiny Balls the Second John up and down the ranks. Shiny Balls stopped in front of each man, examined him from tip of cap to tip of shoes. Shiny Balls, thought Staff Sergeant William B. Franklin, really ate that inspecting-officer shit up.

Finally, it was over.

Shiny Balls stood in front of the company.

He reached inside his tunic and took from it something that First Sergeant Spencer had never seen before. It was Shiny Balls's collection of ribbons and qualification badges. Shiny Balls, Sergeant Franklin saw, wasn't quite the fresh-from-the-Point shitass he had appeared to be. Shiny Balls had his own collection of qualification badges. There was a CIB, and below the CIB a set of aviator's wings, and then, below a double line of four-abreast ribbons, a set of jump wings. There was a Silver Star and Purple Heart with a cluster among the ribbons. Franklin was surprised to see the patch of ribbons and insignia on Shiny Balls. The only other officer he'd ever seen with a set like that, which could be put on or taken off with such ease, was Major Craig W. Lowell; and Lowell had class.

"Gentlemen," Shiny Balls said, "my name is Oppenheimer, and I am your tactical officer. Now, ten percent of you, those who have joined us directly from basic training, will probably accept this without question. The other ninety percent of you, the noncommissioned officers, the backbone of the army, are doubtless at this moment entertaining certain questions.

"It is practically an item of faith within the noncommissioned officer corps that second lieutenants have a value on a par with a rubber crutch for a cripple, or lactation glands on a male camel.

"I believed this myself, gentlemen, when, before I was afforded the opportunity of an education at the United States Military Academy at West Point, I served as a platoon sergeant with the 140th Tank Battalion.

"Ninety percent of the commissioned officers with whom you will be associated during your stay with us, as well, of course, as one hundred percent of the warrant officers, have had service as noncommissioned officers.

"I would therefore like to make the friendly suggestion that any thoughts that any of you have regarding beating the system because of your vast and varied experience as soldiers in sundry assignments around the planet Earth should be dismissed as wishful thinking.

"We are going to teach you two things while you are here. We are going to teach you how to fly rotary wing aircraft. Since you are all in excellent physical condition and possess a degree of intelligence at least as high as that of officer candidates, and since flying, frankly, is not all that difficult, that phase of your training should pose no problem.

"We are also going to make a valiant effort to turn you into officers and gentlemen. An officer is someone charged with the responsibility for other men's lives; there is no greater responsibility placed on any human being. A gentleman is someone who has earned the respect of his peers and subordinates by his personal character. His word is his bond. He accepts and executes orders without any mental reservations whatever.

"There is no bed check here, gentlemen. There will be no guards posted to keep you from walking out the gate and spending the night with your wives in the Daleville Motel—or wherever else you have stashed them. When you are ordered to be in your quarters, you are expected to be in your quarters. Your very presence here means that you have given your word to faithfully execute all orders.

"You will not be punished, in other words, for going AWOL. You will be dismissed from the program as being unfit to be an officer and a gentleman because your word cannot be trusted.

"Neither do we function here on the buddy system. You will cover for your friends at your own risk. A gentleman is not a snitch who will run to his superiors to report the misbehavior of his peers. On the other hand, to give you a specific example, should it come to our attention that someone missed a formation, that someone failed to appear at the appointed time, at the appointed place, in the proper uniform, and that whoever was in charge of the formation covered for him, the result would be immediate dismissal for both individuals.

"That's all the explanation of how things operate that you're going to get, with this final exception. You will be marched from here to the quartermaster warehouse, where you will receive a complete issue of uniforms, from T-shirts and shorts to flight suits. Those uniforms will be adorned with the insignia prescribed for the various grades of warrant officer candidates, and with no, repeat no, other insignia of any kind. It will be impossible to tell, for example, a former first sergeant of a parachute infantry company from a former recruit E-1. And that, gentlemen, is the point.

"From the moment you put on those new uniforms until you graduate, or are dismissed, you can forget that you are a noncommissioned officer whom a grateful government has seen fit to equip with authority, and the symbols of that authority, as well as the symbols for whatever unusual contribution you may have made to the profession of arms in the past.

"You are all equal. What you are now, gentlemen, is WOCs. And what a WOC is, is something one fwows at a wabbit."

It was not, Staff Sergeant Franklin had decided, your typical bullshit welcoming speech.

[TWO]

By 21 November 1958, when Captain Philip Sheridan Parker IV marched into Dog Company WOC Battalion, Shiny Balls Oppenheimer, having completed eighteen months of satisfactory service, had received an automatic promotion to first lieutenant. His charges had gone through various stages of ground school, and phases I through IV of flight instruction. They would graduate just before Christmas, on completion of phase V (Light and Medium Transport Helicopter Operation Under Field Conditions).

Shiny Balls saw the Chevrolet staff car with the Collins VHF antenna mounted incongruously on its roof pull up before the company and correctly concluded that it was a messenger from On High; specifically, since only the post commander's staff car was equipped with the Collins antenna and the radios to go with it, an officer from the post commander's staff bearing amnesty for the WOC sinners.

He waited in his office for the little ballet to be carried out.

The WOC charge of quarters, at a little desk by the door, bellowed "Atten-hut" when the general's messenger entered the building. A moment or two later, the command was repeated as the general's messenger entered the orderly room.

"Sir," the WOC officer of the day barked crisply, "WOC Stewart, J. B., officer of the day, sir."

"Stand at ease," the general's messenger said. "Would you please offer my compliments to the tactical officer and inform him that I would have a word with him. My name is Parker."

The WOC officer of the day (the position was rotated daily among the WOCs) knocked at Shiny Balls's open door, was told to enter, entered, saluted, and said, "Sir, Captain Parker offers his compliments and requests to speak to the lieutenant, sir."

"Ask the captain to come in," Shiny Balls said, and prepared to stand up behind his desk.

"Sir," the WOC officer of the day said, at rigid attention, "Captain Parker, sir."

"Lieutenant Oppenheimer, K. B., sir," Shiny Balls said, saluting.

"Good afternoon, Lieutenant," Captain Parker said, returning the salute. He looked at the WOC officer of the day. "Be good enough to close the door when you leave," he said. The door was closed.

"It is the general's desire," Captain Parker said, "that your sinners be pardoned for all sins."

"Yes, sir," Oppenheimer said. "I suspected that might be the purpose of the captain's visit."

"I wish the announcement of the general's gracious gesture to be withheld from the troops until I have a word with one of them," Parker said. "One who is, I understand, a genuine, no question whatever about it, wise-ass."

"Who would that be, Captain?"

"Warrant Officer Candidate Franklin, William B.," Parker said.

Shiny Balls looked uncomfortable.

"May I say something, Captain?"

"Certainly."

"Now, I'm not trying to excuse what he did. It was wrong. I know it was wrong, and he knows it was wrong. But . . ."

"But?"

"He's a good man, Captain. Solid. And it isn't as if he had only 135 hours of flight instruction, if the captain gets my meaning."

"Your loyalty is commendable, Lieutenant," Captain Parker said, dryly. "And duly noted."

"Yes, sir. Shall I send for him, sir?"

"Just tell me where I can find him," Parker said. "I am going to have a word with him here, and then I am going to take him away from the company area for further counseling. You may make announcement of the general amnesty after we leave."

"Yes, sir," Shiny Balls Oppenheimer said. He turned to a chart on the wall and pointed out to Captain Parker the location of WOC Franklin's WOCQ. (WOCQ stood for warrant officer candidate's quarters. It was pronounced Wock You. It was far more often mispronounced.)

Captain Philip Sheridan Parker IV rapped once with his knuckle on the doorframe of WOC Franklin's WOCQ.

WOC Franklin, who had been sitting at his study desk, jumped to his feet.

"Sir, WOC Franklin, W.B., sir!" he barked.

"Stand at ease, Mr. Franklin," Captain Parker said. Franklin assumed the position of "parade rest" rather than the somewhat less rigid "at ease."

"My name is Parker," Captain Parker said. "In addition to my other duties, I am the post equal opportunity and antidiscrimination officer."

"Yes, sir," Warrant Officer Franklin said.

"It has come to my attention that you have been charged with, and are being punished for, a rather serious violation of flight safety rules."

"Yes, sir."

"The army generally and the commanding general specifically are determined that there be absolutely no discrimination based on race, creed, religion, or country of origin."

"Yes, sir."

"I am here, Mr. Franklin, to determine whether you are guilty as charged or whether this is an incident where you are being discriminated against because of the pigmentation of your skin."

"Yes, sir."

"Well?"

"Sir, I am guilty as charged. It had nothing to do with me being colored."

" 'Colored'?" Captain Parker asked, in an incredulous tone. "I was under the impression that the descriptions now in vogue to describe those of the Negro race were 'black' and 'Afro-American.' I haven't heard the term 'colored' used in some time."

Franklin, visibly uncomfortable, took a moment before replying.

"Sir," he said, "it had nothing to do with my race."

"As I just informed you, Mr. Franklin," Parker said, "I am the post equal opportunity and antidiscrimination officer. It is my function, not yours, to determine whether or not the charges that you 'recklessly endangered an aircraft' are based on fact, or are one more manifestation of racial prejudice against those whom you quaintly chose to refer to as 'colored.' "

"Yes, sir," WOC Franklin said.

"To that end, Mr. Franklin, I am about to subject you to an unscheduled check ride."

"Yes, sir," Franklin said, visibly surprised.

"Get your helmet and your flight suit, Mr. Franklin," Captain Parker said. "I will wait for you in a sedan parked in front of this building." He turned on his heel and walked out of the room.

WOC Franklin jerked open his locker and took out his gray flight coveralls and his helmet. He debated for a moment whether to put the flight suit on now, or wait until they got where they were going. He decided it would be best not to keep this Captain Parker waiting. He folded his flight suit over his arm, put the helmet on his head, and ran down the corridor toward the stairs.

Parker was sitting in the back of a Chevrolet sedan. Franklin saw the Collins antenna on the roof, and thought: Jesus Christ, this is the general's staff car!

He got in the front seat beside the driver.

"You know where we're going," Captain Parker said to the driver. The driver was a sergeant first class. Sergeants first class normally do not drive staff cars, unless they happen to be the general's personal driver.

What the fuck is going on? thought Franklin.

"Yes, sir," the general's driver said.

He drove them to post headquarters.

The general's white-painted H-13H sat on the helipad before post headquarters. The general's staff car pulled into the reserved parking place, and the driver jumped out to open the door for Captain Parker.

"Thank you, Sergeant," Captain Parker said. He beckoned with his finger to WOC Franklin to follow him and walked across the road to the general's H-13H.

Franklin trotted after him.

"The general," Captain Parker said, "as an indication of his deep concern that the colored should not be discriminated against, has graciously made his personal helicopter available for your check ride."

Franklin was now wholly baffled.

"The general," Captain Parker went on, "was taught to ride a horse by a colored soldier when he was a very young officer. That colored, so to speak, the general's thinking about the colored. He finds it difficult to accept the fact that some coloreds, from time to time, really do really stupid things." Parker paused. "I have been led to believe, Mr. Franklin, that you have been instructed in the techniques of preflight inspection of aerial vehicles such as the one before you. If so, please conduct the inspection."

Franklin conducted the preflight. Captain Parker strapped himself in the passenger seat.

"Fire it up, Mr. Franklin," he said, and Franklin started the engine.

Parker depressed the mike button on his stick.

"Laird local control, Chopper One on the pad in front of the CP for a local flight to Hanchey. The Six is not aboard."

"Laird local control clears Chopper One for a local flight to Hanchey."

"Were you aware, Mr. Franklin," Captain Parker politely commented over the intercom, "that Major General Angus Laird took off from this very helipad and, the application of carburetor heat having slipped his mind, flew a machine just like this one into the trees?"

Franklin looked at Parker. Parker put both hands out in front of his body and made a lifting motion, and then pointed in the general direction of Hanchey Field.

Franklin saw that the needles were in the green, and inched back on the cyclic.

"Laird local, Chopper One light on the skids," Parker's voice came over the helmet earphones.

Ten minutes later, his voice came again.

"Now that you've demonstrated you can get it up," he said, "let's see if you remember how to put it down." He pointed to a clearing in the pine forest in the center of which was a whitewashed circle with a fifteen-foot-tall "H" in the center.

Franklin made what he thought was one of his better landings.

Parker made a cutting motion across his throat with his hand. Franklin killed the engine, and the fluckata-fluckata-fluckata sound of the rotor changed pitch as it slowed.

"Tell me true, Franklin," Parker said, "out here where no one can hear us, as one Afro-American warrior to another, just how much bootleg chopper time do you have?"

"About 600 hours, sir."

"My, you really must have worked at it, getting that much time."

Franklin didn't reply.

"The safety-of-flight allegations made against you, which may yet see your black ass thrown out of WOC school, accuse you of flying one of these things hands-off, in order that you might take snapshots."

"Yes, sir," Franklin said.

" 'Yes, sir, that's what they say I did,' or 'Yes, sir, that's what I did'?"

"I was taking pictures, sir. I used to be a photographer."

"So I understand," Parker said, dryly. "Purely to satisfy my personal curiosity, will you show me how you performed this aerial feat of legerdemain?"

Franklin looked at him for a moment, as if making up his mind.

"What you have to do, Captain," he said, "is lock the cyclic under your knee. Like this."

He demonstrated how to fold the left leg over the cyclic control, the sticklike control to the left of the pilot's seat which controls both the angle of attack of the rotor blades and the amount of fuel fed to the engine.

"All you really can do is hold your attitude," Franklin explained. "You control the stick with your left foot and your right knee."

"Jesus Christ!" Parker said. "And somebody saw you doing this?"

"Yes, sir."

"The only reason they haven't thrown your ass out is probably because nobody believes it can be done."

"Am I to be thrown out, Captain? Is that what this is all about?"

"No, you're going to graduate. The 'incident' report has been lost."

"Jesus Christ, I'm glad to hear that," Franklin said.

"You really want to fly, huh?"

"Yes, sir, I do."

"You were doubtless inspired by some aviator with whom you had contact?"

"Yes, sir."

"Who taught you how to fly, despite regulations to the contrary?"

"Yes, sir."

"Who probably came up with this 'no-hands' technique of flying?"

"After he taught me how to fly," Franklin said, "we used to practice at 3,500 feet. He'd try to do it, and I grabbed the controls when something went wrong."

"In other words, one hell of a pilot, huh?"

"Yes, sir."

"Handsome devil, who when he is not doing something terribly John Wayneish, spends his time deciding which of the attractive ladies who gather around as moths to a candle he is going to honor with a screw?" Parker said. "A great big honky named Major Craig W. Lowell?"

"Do you know the major, sir?" Franklin asked.

"I wouldn't admit this to just anybody, Mr. Franklin," Captain Parker said, "but not only do I know the bastard, he's my best friend."

They grinned at each other for a moment.

"What happens now, sir?"

"I take you home for supper, what else?" Parker said. He made a wind-it-up signal with his index finger. Franklin reached out and held down the Engine Start switch.

"The colored guy I told you taught the general to ride?" Parker's voice came over the earphones.

"Yes, sir?"

"My father," Parker said. Then there was a click as he depressed the microphone switch on the stick to the second detent, activating the transmitter. "Laird local, Chopper One in the Hanchey area. Request low level clearance to Pad One."

He looked at Franklin, and made the pick-it-up gesture with his hands.

"Both hands, Bill," he said. "Use both hands."

XV

[ONE]
Quarters No. 3
Fort Meyers, Virginia
11 December 1958

Every week or so, the Chief of Staff of the U.S. Army "got together" with the Vice Chief of Staff of the U.S. Army. The meetings were social and unofficial. In the hourly logs of their activities carefully maintained by their respective aides-de-camp the time blocks contained the abbreviation "AIQ." Alone In Quarters.

Very rarely were they alone, and only from time to time were they actually in their quarters. They were never, of course, completely alone. There was always a master sergeant or a warrant officer hovering around someplace with a .45 pistol in the small of his back or an M2 carbine in the golf club bag. There were generally, too, a junior aide around to grab the phone and a driver; and more remotely officers with the duty of being instantly available should they be needed (physicians and military policemen; cryptographers and public relations officers; ad infinitum) kept themselves aware of the locations of *the* Five and *the* Six and of the shortest, fastest way to get from where they were to where *they* were.

Alone meant that *the* Five and *the* Six were not officially or semiofficially entertaining anyone, including each other. Alone meant that what was said in the room where they happened to be would stay within that room. Not because the room had been swept to make sure it contained no clever little listening devices (although that of course had been done) but because the people at their little get-togethers were absolutely trustworthy.

At 1840 hours, twenty minutes to seven, the Chief of Staff of the U.S. Army said to his wife and his senior aide, "I'm going to walk over to E. Z. Black's. I'll be back after a while."

As soon as *the* six had gone out the door, the senior aide made a couple of telephone calls to pass the word where *the* Six would be and where he himself would be, and then he went home. Unless he was grossly mistaken, *the* Six would stay in place for the next five or six hours.

At 1843 hours, *the* Six entered Quarters No. 3, General E. Z. Black's quarters, through the kitchen door. There he found Master Sergeant Wesley, who had been with Black since they wore riding breeches (they spent a lot of time on the backs of horses), Senator Fulton J. Oswald of South Carolina and the Military Affairs Committee, Carson W. Newburgh, chairman and chief executive officer of the Newburgh Corporation, and, of course, *the* Five, General Black.

"What can I get you to drink, General?" Master Sergeant Wesley asked. The men nodded at each other, but none spoke or offered a hand to be shaken.

"Has he got any of that good scotch left, Wes?" the Chief of Staff asked.

"Yes, suh, twenty-four years old an' as mellow as it's gonna git," Sergeant Wesley said, turning and taking a bottle from a kitchen cupboard.

"Carson brought the chow," the Vice Chief of Staff said. "You have your choice between steak or pheasant. The pheasant'll take Wes about an hour to fix."

"I'll have the steak, then," the Chief of Staff said.

"Does the general want it cooked like a steak?" Sergeant Wesley inquired. "Or are you gonna eat it raw like Colonel Newburgh and the senator?"

"Steak tartar?" the Chief of Staff asked, chuckling. "Why not?"

"It's guaranteed to put lead in your pencil, General," the senator said.

"It'll take a hell of a lot more than some chopped beef and an egg yolk to put lead in my pencil, Senator," the Chief of Staff said.

Sergeant Wesley handed him a glass, dark with barely diluted scotch.

"If you gentlemen would like to go into the study, I'll start seeing about supper," Master Sergeant Wesley said.

"Give us half an hour, Wes," General Black said. "Time for another drink."

"Anybody else coming?" the Chief of Staff asked as they walked into the study. A table covered with an army blanket had been set up in case they decided to play poker.

"This is it," E. Z. Black said. "I was about to ask you the same thing."

"Tell E.Z. what you told me, Senator," the Chief of Staff said.

"The air force knows about your rocket-armed helicopters," the senator said. "I got that straight from the horse's ass, the distinguished senior senator from Rhode Island."

"Helicopter," General Black said. "Singular. One."

"One is one more than I knew about, E.Z.," the Chief of Staff said.

"Does the air force *think* we have them, or do they *know* we have them?" He corrected himself: "That we have *one* of them?"

"They have still and motion pictures," the senator said.

"Dirty bastards must have planted a spy," General Black said, angrily.

"Maybe that's what I should have done," the Chief of Staff said. "Instead of relying on you to keep me up with the interesting minutiae of the field army."

"I try to spare you the minutiae, General," E. Z. Black said. "To save you for politics."

"If this isn't politics, then what the hell is it?"

"I spent an hour this afternoon, for example," E. Z. Black went on, "trying to decide what to do about an ordnance light colonel in Japan who's also been in the movies. He happens to have the key to the tactical nukes."

"What kind of movies?"

"Stag movies. Queer stag movies. He's the star," E. Z. Black said. "I was going to bring that minutia to the general's attention for a decision."

"Jesus!" the senator said.

"There are several options," E. Z. Black went on. "The CIC and the G-2 want him removed and court-martialed, or at least cashiered. Some other people want the game to go on, to see who's dealing."

"What other people?" the Chief of Staff asked.

"CIA," E. Z. Black said. "And Felter."

"And you want to go with Felter, right?" the Chief of Staff asked.

"That is my recommendation. Yes, sir."

"Let's get back to your armed helicopters," the Chief of Staff said. "We both know that Felter will call the tune in the end anyway. The President thinks he's a goddamned genius."

"Isn't he?" the senator asked.

"He's a goddamned major in the U.S. Army," the Chief of Staff said. "That's all he is."

The senator laughed. "Bull*shit!*" he said. "All he is is a major in the army who gets to whisper in the President's ear once a day."

"I'd be a lot happier if he'd resign and just . . ." the Chief of Staff began. Black interrupted him.

"Get a hard-on for the army?" he said. "Felter thinks of himself as an army officer, and I think that's just fine."

"The question is, does he? I mean, does he really?"

"Yes, he does," Black said, firmly.

The Chief of Staff looked at the Vice Chief of Staff for a moment. They didn't like each other. The Chief of Staff was West Point and infantry/airborne. The Vice Chief of Staff was Norwich and armor. The chemistry was bad between them. They had known and casually disliked each other for a quarter of a century. A mutual respect between them had slowly blossomed as their parallel careers had brought them to the top. They now deeply respected each other, but they were not friends.

Master Sergeant Wesley brought in a fresh tray of drinks and some cheddar cheese on toothpicks. The Chief of Staff put a cheddar chunk in his mouth.

"Tell me about your armed helicopters," he said.

"The idea's a natural," Black said. "I've been playing with it since before I went to Korea. When I commanded Fort Polk, Mac MacMillan strapped a 3.5 rocket launcher onto the skid of an old H-23 and showed me what he could do to M3 and M4 hulks on the known distance range."

"So Mac's involved in this?" the Chief of Staff asked. As an 82nd Airborne Division regimental commander, the Chief of Staff had recommended that Technical Sergeant Rudolph G. MacMillan of the Regimental Pathfinder Platoon be directly commissioned as a second lieutenant. Before MacMillan could be sworn in, he had been captured (at the time, it was thought he had been killed) under such circumstances that he had been recommended for the Medal of Honor.

"Mac and Bob Bellmon," E. Z. Black said.

"You realize this is liable to cost Bellmon his star?" the Chief of Staff asked.

"I am sure Colonel Bellmon recognized the inherent risk to his career," Black said.

"Anybody else?" the Chief of Staff asked. "E.Z., I'm getting a little annoyed pulling these details out of you like twelve-year molars."

"The chain of responsibility is me to Bellmon to MacMillan. There are two other officers involved. There's a young lieutenant named Greer, who served with the French Foreign Legion—who, as you know, regularly arm their choppers—in Algeria. He's at Fort Hood with the helicopter, and a couple of mechanics and an Ordnance Corps warrant officer I borrowed from Ted Davis."

"In other words, General Davis is also involved?"

"No, sir. General Davis could honestly testify that he had no inkling whatever of what was going on. I asked him for a competent ground rocket man who knew his way around ordnance depots. He didn't ask any questions, and I didn't volunteer any information."

"OK," the Chief of Staff said.

"And there's one more man, an officer in DCSLOG, here."

"What's his function?"

"This has cost a lot of money," E. Z. Black said. "This guy's good at getting it from other appropriations. He was also in North Africa and knows what's going on."

"Has he got a name?"

"Lowell. Major C. W. Lowell."

"What was that name, E.Z.?" the senator asked.

"Lowell. Major Craig Lowell," Black said.

"Oh, shit," the senator chuckled. "Well, that brings us to Item Two on the agenda," he said.

"I beg your pardon?" General Black asked, genuinely confused.

"E.Z.," the senator said, "I really hate to ask you if you know what else your Major Lowell has been up to."

"I don't understand," E. Z. Black said. He was a little worried that the senator was going to tell him Lowell's parties were getting to be too much the talk of the town.

"He's gotten himself involved with a senator's wife," the Chief of Staff exploded.

"It's probably really not his fault," the senator said. "But it could be awkward."

"What do mean, it's 'probably not his fault'?" the Chief of Staff snapped.

"The senator is old and rich. The senator's wife is young and healthy. The major is young—and a bachelor."

"Actually a widower," Carson Newburgh said.

"You know him, Carson?" the Chief of Staff asked.

"Yes, I know him. Fairly well, as a matter of fact," Newburgh said. "I didn't know about this, however. Who's the lady?"

"Constance," the senator told him.

"And who else knows about it?" Newburgh asked.

"Everybody, probably, but the husband. And I'm not too sure about that."

"Jesus H. Christ!" the Chief of Staff said. "E.Z., you really know how to pick them!"

"I didn't know about this," E. Z. Black said.

"You don't live in Georgetown," Carson Newburgh said. "All sorts of interesting things go on there."

"Lowell lives in Georgetown?" the Chief of Staff asked.

"Right next door to the senator whose wife we're talking about," the senator said.

"How the hell does he afford that?" the Chief of Staff asked.

"He's comfortable, General," Carson Newburgh said. "Very comfortable."

"What the hell does that mean?" the Chief of Staff asked.

"Are you familiar with Craig, Powell, Kenyon and Dawes?"

"Stockbrokers?" the Chief of Staff asked.

"That, too, but primarily investment bankers. There are two major stockholders. Porter Craig, chairman of the board and chief executive officer, who owns half. And his cousin, Major Lowell, who owns the other half."

"What the hell is a rich man like that doing in the army?"

"I wasn't aware that being poor was a soldierly virtue," Carson Newburgh said, icily.

"Georgie Patton was rich," E. Z. Black said. "He was a good soldier. So was Carson. So is Lowell, for that matter. He ran the breakout, Task Force Lowell, from Pusan."

"Oh, yeah," the Chief of Staff said. "I know about him. He's the wise-ass who then got up and testified in a court-martial that he could see nothing wrong with shooting officers who were running in the wrong direction. I knew he had a big mouth, but I didn't know he was rich." He stopped, then went on: "Nothing personal, Carson, goddamnit, you know that."

"You gennlemen just say when you want to eat," Master Sergeant Wesley said, from the door to the study.

"In fifteen minutes, Wes," General Black said.

"George Patton didn't go around fucking senator's wives," the Chief of Staff said. Black saw that he was working himself into a rage and wondered why.

"It can be controlled," the senator said. "I just thought it was worth mentioning."

"You bet your sweet ass it will be controlled," the Chief of Staff said. "We'll send the sonofabitch to Greenland and let him screw a polar bear."

"Hey, come on," the senator said. "The major is not the first soldier to get his ashes hauled outside the nuptial couch. MacArthur had a Eurasian mistress stashed in an apartment when he was Chief of Staff. Even the chastity part of Eisenhower's wartime sainthood had been questioned."

"You don't believe that cheap gossip, do you?" the Chief of Staff snapped. "I'll remind you, you're talking about the President."

"Of course, *I* don't believe it," the senator said, angrily, thickly sarcastic. "And *I was there*. I believe he commissioned that big-teated Limey as an American officer *solely* because she did such a splendid job driving his jeep. I also believe in the tooth fairy."

The Chief of Staff glowered at him.

"I just remembered something else about your man Lowell, General," he said to Black.

"What's that, sir?"

"Remember the flap when *Life* ran the story with the pictures of the M48 with 'Blueballs' painted on the turret? And that actress that doesn't wear any underwear with her arms around the crew? Georgia Paige? I remember that some damned fool of a young officer took her up to the front, and subsequently screwed her on every available horizontal surface, and I just remembered his name. That was your man Lowell, wasn't it, General?"

"I believe it was," Black said. "So what?"

"He gets around, doesn't he?" the senator chuckled.

"What do you mean, so what?" the Chief of Staff demanded, angrily.

"You remember, I'm sure," Black said, "what Phil Sheridan said about soldiers that don't fuck."

"He was speaking of soldiers, not officers of the General Staff Corps," the Chief of Staff said, so furiously that spittle flew.

"I don't give a good goddamn if he screws orangutangs," Black said. "So long as he does his duty and does it as well as this particular, young, unmarried officer does his."

"Hey! Hey!" the senator said. "Tempers, gentlemen!"

The Chief of Staff glowered at him and then at E. Z. Black. In a moment he got control of his voice.

"To sum up," the Chief of Staff said icily, "what we have here is a clear and blatant violation of the Key West Agreement of 1948, which says the army will not, repeat not, under any circumstances arm its aircraft. We have been caught with our ass hanging out. And for the cherry on top of the cake, one of the *officers* and *gentlemen* involved in this breach of good faith is involved with a senator's lady."

"I am the officer primarily involved, General," Black said. "And so far as the senator's lady is concerned, you can make that 'was involved.' I'll see that it's stopped."

"That still leaves us with your goddamned armed helicopters, which I'm sure the air force is sure to bring to the attention of the *Washington Post* just as soon as they can," the Chief of Staff said.

"I've been thinking about this helicopter thing," the senator said. "What I think you should do is go public with it. Call a press conference. Show the goddamned thing off. If it works, the air force would look pretty goddamned silly bitching about it."

"It works," E. Z. Black said. "And the bottom line is that we can afford to swap helicopters for tanks all day long."

The Chief of Staff looked at him for a long moment.

"I don't see where we have any other alternative to this mess in which the Vice Chief of Staff has enmeshed us," he said.

"You're going to have to get off the dime, General," the senator said, "before the air force lowers the boom."

"Wesley!" the Chief of Staff called out.

Master Sergeant Wesley appeared.

"Yes, suh?"

"Get somebody on the horn, please, Wes. See if you can find the Chief of Information. Ask him if he's free to join us for a drink. If you can't find the Chief of Information, get his deputy."

"Yes, sir," Sergeant Wesley said.

[TWO]
Ozark, Alabama
12 December 1958

"Mr. Dutton's office," Howard Dutton's private secretary purred into the telephone.

"I have a collect call for anyone from Mrs. Greer in San Antonio," the operator's somewhat twangy voice announced.

"This is Mr. Howard Dutton's office," Howard Dutton's secretary repeated."

"I have a collect call for anyone from Mrs. Greer in San Antonio," the operator repeated.

"Just a minute, Operator," Howard Dutton's secretary said. She laid the phone down and walked to Howard Dutton's office.

"Mistuh Dutton, we got a collect call for anybody from some Mrs. Greer," she said. "What do I tell her?"

"Good Christ!" Howard Dutton said, spinning around in his high-backed leather chair to face the credenza with the telephones on it. There were two telephones, each equipped with buttons that lit when the line was in use. There were four buttons on each telephone. Of the eight buttons, four were lit.

Howard Dutton got the San Antonio operator on the third try.

"Put it through, put it through," he had twice announced to somewhat startled users of the telephone.

"Go 'head, please," the operator finally said.

"Daddy?"

"How's my baby?" Howard Dutton asked. "Nothing wrong, honey, is there?"

"Daddy, could I come home a little early for Christmas?"

"Honey, you can come anytime you want to come home," Howard Dutton said. "What's wrong, honey?"

The baby began to cry.

Goddamn that bastard! What has he done to my Melody?

"He's throwing up again, damn him," Melody said. "All over my dress."

"Now, you just calm down, honey," Howard Dutton said. "Everything's going to be all right."

"Could I come home this afternoon? Or tonight, really? On the eight thirty-two flight from Atlanta?"

"Eight thirty-two," Howard Dutton repeated. He turned to his desk for a pencil, and saw his secretary. "Write this down," he snapped. "Eight thirty-two from Atlanta." He took his hand off the telephone mouthpiece.

"I'll be there, honey," he said. "I'll be waiting for you when you get off the plane."

He remembered that the call had been collect. Did that mean she didn't have any money?

Why doesn't she have any money?

"Now, you just tell me what's wrong," Howard Dutton said, "and your daddy'll take care of it."

"Nothing's wrong, Daddy," Melody said.

"Where's your husband?" he demanded.

" *'My husband,'* " Melody mocked him, "is halfway to Rucker in the Big Bad Bird. He got orders this morning to bring the Big Bad Bird to Rucker ASAP."

"I don't know what that means," Howard Dutton confessed, unhappily.

"He's flying the gunship up there. ASAP: As Soon As Possible. The orders said for a minimum period of thirty days. So I'm on my way, too."

"You sure you got enough money? I could call the bank down there, and see that you had some money right away."

"Eight thirty-two, Daddy," Melody said, and hung up.

Howard Dutton put the telephone back in its cradle and spun the chair around. His secretary was standing there with her pencil poised over her steno book. Stupid damned female! He sometimes almost wished that Prissy was back.

"I'll be at my house," he said to her and walked out of the office.

Prissy was sitting at the kitchen table having a cup of coffee with the maid when he walked in.

"What are you doing home?" she asked.

"Melody and the baby are coming on the eight thirty-two from Atlanta," he said. For some inexplicable reason, making the announcement made him feel like crying.

"Where's Ed? Is he coming?" Prissy asked.

"He's flying up by himself," Howard Dutton said.

"Why aren't they flying together?" Prissy asked.

Stupid damned female.

"I think they have a rule against flying infants in army helicopters," he said, sarcastically.

"You could have explained that he was flying with the army," Prissy said. "Well, we'll just have to get ready for them."

"She said they'll be here for at least thirty days," Howard said.

"Eight thirty-two? That's plenty of time. You didn't have to come home. You could have called from the office."

He went to his office and opened a drawer and took a long pull at the neck of a quart bottle of Jack Daniels.

Between a stupid female at home and a stupid female in the office, it was a miracle he hadn't lost his mind. He sat down at his desk and reached out and adjusted a double photo frame so that he could look at it better.

The left was Melody's graduation picture. The right was of Melody and the baby. She looked like a madonna, Howard Dutton thought. There was no other word to describe the way Melody looked holding her baby.

He took another pull at the bottle of Jack Daniels and then looked at his watch. It was nine forty. Melody would be home in less than twelve hours.

[THREE]
U.S. Army Aviation Combat Developments Agency
Fort Rucker, Alabama
12 December 1958

"You understand, Colonel, I'm sure, that I've had only the briefest of briefings. About the only orders I got from the general were to get my show on the road."

The speaker was Colonel Tim F. Brandon, Chief, Special Operations Branch, Media Relations Division, Office of the Chief of Information, Department of the Army.

"What general is that?" Colonel Robert F. Bellmon asked, innocently.

"The Chief of Information," Colonel Brandon said.

"Of course," Colonel Bellmon said. He had just noticed that if one was to judge from the display of ribbons on Colonel Brandon's tunic, he had managed to rise to colonel of infantry without ever once having heard a shot fired in anger.

"Now, this little operation of ours enjoys a very high priority," Colonel Brandon said.

"So I understand," Colonel Bellmon replied. He had received a telephone call at 11:30 the night before from the Vice Chief of the Staff of the U.S. Army, informing him that a couple of PIO assholes would be coming to see him; the decision had been to go public with the rocket-armed gunship.

The Big Bad Bird itself had already been ordered from Hood to Rucker and Hood had been ordered to fly the technicians and their equipment to Rucker as soon as that could be arranged.

"Go along as far as you can with these guys, Bob. Lean over backward. But if you need me, get on the horn."

"Yes, sir," Bellmon had said to the Vice Chief of Staff.

There was a knock on the door. Bellmon looked up and motioned for MacMillan to come in. MacMillan was in a flight suit. He had just returned, successfully, to judge from the OK sign he made, from arranging for a portable hangar to be erected to house the gunship out near Hanchey—and far from prying eyes.

"Colonel Brandon," Colonel Bellmon said, "this is Major MacMillan. Major MacMillan is the man you'll be working with."

"I had hoped that we would be working directly, so to speak, together on this," Colonel Brandon said.

"Major MacMillan knows as much, more, about the Big Bad Bird than I do," Colonel Bellmon said.

"I see," Colonel Brandon said.

"You got an ETA on the Bird, Mac?" Bellmon asked.

"Greer called from Dallas," MacMillan said. "About thirty minutes ago. Said he'd be on the ground about an hour. Unless he's called since, he's at Love Field."

"That's an unfortunate term," Colonel Brandon said.

"I beg your pardon?"

" 'Big Bad Bird,' " Colonel Brandon said. "We need something stronger. Like 'Tiger.' "

" 'Tiger' is a German tank," MacMillan said.

"We'll work on that later," Colonel Brandon said. " 'Big Bad Bird' is just not going to cut the mustard. Now, what about this guy with the Medal? What's he look like?"

MacMillan looked at Colonel Brandon in disbelief. Colonel Bellmon smiled broadly.

"I was told one of your officers has the Congressional," Colonel Brandon said. "I'm hoping two things: first, that he has been connected with the gunship and second, that he's photogenic and can talk."

"Say something for the colonel, Mac," Bellmon said.

"I beg your pardon, Major," Colonel Brandon said. "Certainly, no offense was intended. What I was saying was that I hoped you would turn out to be someone we can put on camera. Obviously, you're more than I hoped for."

Bellmon pushed his intercom button. "Darlene, would you have someone bring some coffee in here, please? And if Mrs. Hyde is in the building, would you run her down and ask her to come in here, please?"

"Now that we have the problem of the talking head solved," Colonel Brandon said, "we can think about a new name for the gunship. I don't even know what it looks like. There must be a photograph of it around somewhere?"

"They're classified Secret, Sensitive," Colonel Bellmon said. "I haven't been informed that you're so cleared, Colonel."

Rhonda Wilson Hyde knocked at the door and came in without waiting to be invited.

"Colonel," Colonel Bellmon said, "this is Mrs. Hyde, our administrative officer. Rhonda, this is Colonel Brandon, of the Office of the Chief of Information."

Colonel Brandon and Mrs. Hyde smiled at one another. Major MacMillan looked at Colonel Bellmon and mouthed the word "Geronimo."

"Mrs. Hyde will take care of getting you cleared, Colonel," Bellmon said. "And otherwise take care of your needs. And now, if you'll excuse us, I have some other matters to discuss with the Talking Head."

[**FOUR**]
McLean, Virginia
15 December 1958

The morning briefing, as it sometimes did, had become the afternoon briefing, and the blinds had been drawn against the afternoon sun in Conference Room III.

Sanford T. Felter stayed behind, as he sometimes did, when the briefing officers and the analysts were dismissed.

"Are you going to be in town over the holidays?" Felter asked, when everyone else had left the room.

"Yes," the Director said. "Special reason for asking?"

"If it can be worked in, I'd like to take a little leave. Say, ten days from the twenty-first?"

"You don't have to ask me, Felter."

"I hoped you'd take over briefing the boss," Felter said.

"Sure," the Director said. "Where you going?"

"To Fort Rucker," Felter said.

"What the hell is going on down there?" the Director asked. Felter looked at him curiously. The Director went on: "I noticed a memo that E. Z. Black is going to be at Rucker over the holidays."

"I'm not going with him," Felter said. "I'm just going to visit some friends."

"Well, at least the communications will be in. We can get the army to pay for them. Just have them get you a couple of secure lines."

Felter's curiosity got the best of him. He walked to one of the telephones on the conference table and dialed a two-digit number.

"Army liaison," a voice said. "Colonel Ford."

"Sanford Felter, Colonel," Felter said. "Why is General Black going to be at Fort Rucker over the holidays?"

"Sir, the army is going to go public about its helicopter gunship. There's going to be a press junket. The general's going to make the announcement himself."

"Thank you," Felter said and hung up.

The Director looked at him curiously.

"It would seem the air force has caught the army arming its helicopters," Felter said. "And have decided the best defense is a good offense. Black is going to make the announcement himself."

"Christ!" the Director said. "Well, at least we're not involved."

"No," Felter said.

"Who do you think is right, Sandy?" the Director said.

"The army," Felter said. "Was that the response you expected of me?"

"I'm sure it's based on your analysis of the problem," the Director said, "and not because you march in the rear rank of the Long Gray Line."

"We furnished the air force with the material generated in Algeria," Felter said. "They didn't do anything with it. Arming helicopters is an idea whose time has come. The army just filled the vacuum."

"The air force is going to cry 'foul,' " the Director said.

"The air force still believes they won the war in Europe with bombers," Felter said.

The Director chuckled. "Now, *that* was a voice from the Long Gray Line," he said.

Felter looked uncomfortable.

"Just kidding, Sandy," the Director said. "Just kidding."

XVI

[ONE]
U.S. Army Aviation Combat Development Agency
Fort Rucker, Alabama
16 December 1958

Colonel Bellmon pushed the lever on his intercom.

"Darlene, I can't raise Mac. Is he in the building?"

"No, sir. He's out at Hanchey."

"What about Mrs. Hyde?"

"She's out there, too, with Colonel Brandon and the camera crew."

"Come in here a moment, will you please, Darlene?"

When she came into his office, he told her that he wanted her to take the staff car and driver and go out to Laird Field.

"You've met Major Lowell, haven't you?"

"Yes, sir, I have."

"Major Lowell is about to land at Laird in a civilian airplane. I want you to meet him. Tell him that I sent you to bring him directly here. There may be other people meeting him. But you are to make him understand that he is to come directly here to see me before he does anything else. Can you handle that?"

"Yes, sir, I'm sure I can," Darlene Heatter said.

Darlene was waiting at the Base Operations building at Laird Army Airfield when the glistening, sleek Aero Commander taxied up to the transient parking area and was shown where to park.

When she started to go out the glass door, she almost bumped into a nigger woman. When she looked more closely, she recognized her as that nigger woman *doctor* they had over at the hospital, an object of some curiosity and a good deal of discussion.

"After you," Darlene said, priding herself on this demonstration of lack of prejudice.

"Thank you," the nigger woman doctor said and went through the glass door and started for the Aero Commander. The door in the back of the airplane opened and Major Lowell got out and stretched his arms and legs. Then he leaned back inside the airplane and took out a tunic. He put it on, and then he saw the nigger woman doctor.

"Well, as I live and breathe," he said, "my favorite lady chancre mechanic!"

He kissed her, as if it was the most natural thing in the world.

Well, that wasn't the only thing she'd seen at Rucker that she would never have believed in a thousand years.

"Phil's out stamping out racial prejudice," the nigger lady doctor said. "So here I am."

"Major Lowell," Darlene said, "do you remember me?"

He looked at her.

"I'm afraid not," he said, after a moment.

"I'm Colonel Bellmon's secretary," Darlene said. "He sent me to fetch you."

"I've already been 'fetched,' " he said.

"Colonel Bellmon said I was to bring you back to him before you did anything else," Darlene said. "I got the staff car."

"That sounds like an order," the nigger woman doctor said. "As opposed to a friendly invitation."

"Doesn't it?" Lowell said. "Well, let me see what he wants, and then I'll come over to the hospital."

"I'm on duty until half past four," the nigger woman doctor said. "But the maid knows you're coming; and Phil, I'm sure, will get loose as soon as he can."

"Sorry about the wild goose chase," Lowell said.

"Don't be silly," the nigger woman doctor said and kissed him on the cheek.

Lowell went back inside the Aero Commander and came out with several pieces of luggage, two limp garment bags, two suitcases, and a rigid oblong case that Darlene recognized after a moment as a gun case. The driver saw them and ran over to help with the luggage.

As they rode from Laird Field through Daleville onto the post, Darlene Heatter wondered what it would be like to do it with Major Lowell. Even if he did let himself get kissed by a nigger woman. Maybe it *was* true, what they said, about niggers really being good at it. Maybe nigger women were as good as it as the men were supposed to be.

Lowell knocked at Colonel Robert F. Bellmon's door.

"Come," Bellmon said.

Lowell marched in, saluted, and stood at attention.

"Sir, Major Lowell reporting as ordered, sir."

"Not quite as ordered, I'm afraid," Bellmon said. He walked over and closed his office door, and that was all that Darlene could hear.

"Oh, sit down, Craig," Bob Bellmon said. "You want a cup of coffee, or something?"

"No, thank you. I drank coffee all the way down."

"As I understand your orders, you were to proceed here by the first available commercial air transportation," Bellmon said. "And I further understand that you were taken to Washington National by an officer, to encourage you to carry out your orders."

Lowell said nothing.

"Well?"

"It didn't make a hell of a lot of sense to me to leave my airplane there at National," Lowell said. "What's the difference?"

"That's always been your trouble, Craig," Bellmon said. "You ask yourself what's the difference, and you answer yourself, 'none,' and then you do what suits you. In this case, to be honest, the answer is that it makes no difference whatever."

"If I've somehow embarrassed you, Bob, I'm truly sorry."

"Hell, yes, you've embarrassed me."

"I'm sorry," Lowell said.

"You don't really have any idea the trouble you're in, do you?"

"I have the feeling that I have someone *on high* a bit annoyed," Lowell said. "I'm not exactly sure who."

"I might as well get right to the point, Craig," Bellmon said. "I hope the senator's wife was a good lay."

"Oh. So that's it."

"Because that piece of ass has wiped you out," Bellmon said. "You're finished, Craig. I've got the unpleasant duty of making that clear to you."

"Define finished," Lowell said.

"You are on thirty days' temporary duty here," Bellmon said. "If you do not resign in that period, and it is hoped that you will resign today, you will be reassigned to U.S. Army, Caribbean. It will not be a flying assignment. Until they can think of some clever way of speeding up the process of separating you from the service as unfit, you'll probably be assigned as dependent housing officer, or special assistant to the garbage collection officer."

"Come on, Bob," Lowell said. "I'm not about to be, I'm not about *to let myself be* thrown out of the army over some horny woman."

"The horny woman was the straw that broke the camel's back, I'm afraid," Bellmon said.

"What else am I alleged to have done?"

"The air force knows about the Big Bad Bird."

"I'll bet I knew that before you did," Lowell said.

"We need a sacrifice," Bellmon said. "You're it."

"That needs an explanation."

"Here's the new scenario, which I don't think you've heard, because I got it on the telephone less than two hours ago."

"From whom?"

"Do you know Dan Brackmayer?"

"Dog robber to the Chief of Staff?"

"Colonel Brackmayer is Special Assistant to the Chief of Staff."

"I know who he is."

"This is the way it goes, Craig," Bellmon said. "We plead guilty."

"What's that mean?"

"The Chief of Staff admits that we have violated the Key West Agreement of 1948 by arming a helicopter. An overzealous officer, you, is responsible."

"And?"

"Most important, now that we have it, of course, it would be foolish to give it up. But since orders must be obeyed, the officer responsible must be punished. He will resign to spare the army embarrassment and himself the possibility of a court-martial."

"In other words, I take the rap for everybody? The West Point Protective Association forms a circle to fight off the Indians?"

"I offered to take full responsibility," Bellmon said.

"Oddly enough," Lowell said, "I believe that."

"Thank you," Bellmon said. "Oddly enough, it's very important to me that you do believe that."

"Where does E. Z. Black fit into all this?"

"The Vice Chief of Staff has given his word to the Chief of Staff that you'll resign."

"He seems pretty goddamned sure of himself," Lowell said.

"There was a last straw with him, too, Craig," Bellmon said.

"Which was?"

"He told you to stay away from Felter. I heard him, as a matter of fact. He told you to stay away from Felter, and why, and you haven't."

"I had Sharon and the kids over to that whorehouse I set up at Black's request a couple of times, so the kids could use the pool."

"You were ordered to stay away from Felter, and you didn't, period."

"Well, fuck him!"

Bellmon didn't respond to that.

"Everybody seems to think that I'll just take this lying down," Lowell said. "It must have occurred to somebody that I just might open the closet and show all the skeletons to the air force."

"I was asked that question," Bellmon said. "And I said there was absolutely no risk of that at all. I'm not sure the Chief of Staff believed me, but all your friends did."

"Why am I flattered by that?"

"Because you're a soldier," Bellmon said.

" 'You're a soldier,' says the vice president of the WPPA, 'now get your ass out of the army.' "

"The Big Bad Bird is what's important, Craig," Bellmon said.

"Oh, shit," Lowell said. "Don't wave the flag at me, Bob."

"I wasn't," Bellmon said. And then he corrected himself. "OK, I was. What's wrong with that?"

"You want to hear about this dame?" Lowell said. He went on without waiting for a reply. "She climbed over the wall into my backyard. Actually climbed over the fucking wall. And groped me. And when I suggested that might be a little risky, she said what was risky was her going to the senator and telling him I had made lewd advances."

"Oddly enough," Bellmon said, "I believe that, too."

"So what the hell do I do with my life, now?" Lowell asked. "The army's all I know."

"Well, you won't wind up on welfare," Bellmon said. "I'm sure that was a factor in the equation."

"I could go to Germany, I suppose," Lowell said. "God knows, I don't want to work for the fucking firm."

"Buy yourself an airline," Bellmon said.

"What am I going to tell my father-in-law?" Lowell said.

"The truth," Bellmon said. "He'll understand."

"In his army, they handed an officer a Luger with one round and let him do the honorable thing," Lowell said. "I've still got my Luger someplace, come to think of it."

"Don't be melodramatic," Bellmon said. "You don't mean that."

"I wouldn't have the courage," Lowell said. "When I was in Greece with Felter, the day we got there, the guy in the next room to us stuck a .45 in his mouth and pulled the trigger. That sort of thing is very messy."

He looked at Bellmon and smiled.

"Don't look so stricken, Colonel," he said. "I'm really not all that fucked up by this involuntary sacrifice I'm making."

"If there's ever anything I can do for—" Bellmon began. Lowell interupted him by holding up his hand.

"Resigning today is out of the question," Lowell said.

Bellmon's eyebrows went up.

"Why?" he asked.

"Well, there are several reasons. For one thing, I'll have to . . . you'll have to . . . find someone trustworthy to whom I can turn over the secrets of where I stole the money for the Big Bad Bird. If that doesn't get blown up, you can get money there again."

"And the other reason?"

"It's the holiday season," Lowell said. "Old Home Week. Sandy Felter is bringing Sharon down here. The little bastard has her on the edge of a nervous breakdown with his spy business. She wants to be an officer's lady on New Year's Eve, and I want her to have that."

"You're in no position to announce what you want," Bellmon said.

"Get on the phone, Bob," Lowell said. "Call Brackmayer and tell him I will silently steal away as of 1 January 1959. Not one day before. At least not quietly."

"OK," Bellmon said, after thinking it over. "I'll call Brackmayer. I'll tell him that you understand the situation and will do what is expected of you. I'll tell him that I need you to tie up the loose ends for the Big Bad Bird. I'll reassure him that his concerns about skeletons are groundless."

"Fuck him, tell him the opposite. Let him lose a little sleep."

"Until a decision is made, Major Lowell," Colonel Bellmon said, formally, "You will find yourself a BOQ, and you will stay in that BOQ, or the club, and you will not leave the post."

"I'm staying with Phil and Antoinette Parker," Lowell said.

Bellmon nodded. "All right, Lowell," he said. "So long as you understand me about keeping yourself under wraps."

"I understand," Lowell said. "Is that all, Bob?"

Bellmon nodded.

Lowell stood up, saluted, and walked out of the room.

[TWO]
Auxiliary Field Three
Hanchey Army Airfield
Fort Rucker, Alabama
22 December 1958

The hangar was constructed of plasticized cloth in the manner of an inflatable life raft. It had been erected in fifteen minutes. First four stakes were pounded into the ground at precise distances from each other. Then what looked like a pile of camouflaged tenting was spread out. Each corner was attached to one of the stakes.

A five-horsepower gasoline generator was started. The engine drove an electric motor, and the electric motor powered an air compressor. The pile of camouflaged tenting seemed to sit, then to grow and subside, grow and subside, until it rather suddenly assumed its ultimate shape, ninety feet long, forty feet wide, and fifteen feet high at the center. An enormous empty toilet tissue center half buried in the ground.

Whenever the pressure of the air in its hollow walls dropped below 7.5 psi, the generator started up automatically. There were doors of the same construction. There was another generator—larger, diesel, jeep-trailer mounted—which provided electricity, heat, and compressed air for the aircraft mechanic's tools.

The Kit, Hangar, Service, Field, Inflatable, Self-Contained, also included poles and ropes and camouflage netting. When the whole thing was in place, properly inflated, and covered by the netting, it was very hard to see from the air or the ground, even if you knew it was there.

The Big Bad Bird sat in the balloon, as the hangar inevitably came to be called, its fifty-six-foot-diameter rotor blades parallel with the fuselage.

The Big Bad Bird had been one of the very first Sikorsky H-19s the army had purchased. It had seen service in the Korean War, and had later been assigned to a transportation helicopter company at Fort Lewis, Washington. It had suffered three minor and two major accidents. After the second major accident, it had become a hangar queen at Fort Lewis, losing most of its remaining functioning parts as replacements to keep newer, better H-19s flying.

Just over a year before, it had left Fort Lewis on a truck, and had been dropped from Fort Lewis's property books. It had been acquired by Plans and Requirements Division (Fiscal), Aviation Maintenance Section, DCSLOG. It was thereafter logically assumed by those who knew Tail Number 50–3003 that the old wreck would be sold for junk, or maybe used as a target on a tank range, or something. It would never fly again, that was for goddamn sure.

The Army Aviation Base at Anchorage, Alaska, was that year scheduled to receive two new fire engines and three ground power generators. It got one of each. The Army Airfield at Fort Sill, Oklahoma, which was supposed to get two fire trucks got none, and neither did Kitzigen, Germany, or Headquarters, U.S. Army, Panama.

The Walla Walla (Washington) Flying Service, which operated civilian models of the Sikorsky H-19 in timber applications, received a purchase order from the Plans and Requirements Division (Fiscal) of the Aviation Maintenance Section, DCSLOG, to make such repairs as were necessary to restore H-19 50–3003 to minimum standards of flight safety. The funds expended had been intended for fire engines and ground power generators.

Double Ought Three, the Big Bad Bird, was not what someone coming across its listing in the inventory of Aircraft, Non-Serviceable, Awaiting Evaluation, would have envisioned. It had been restored to flyable condition and modified.

It had a new (actually rebuilt) engine, a new power train and rotor head, and new rotors. At Fort Hood, the fuselage had been modified.

The standard H-19 has one cargo compartment door, on the right. The Big Bad Bird had another cut through the left fuselage wall. The interior of the passenger compartment had been strengthened, the seats were removed, and "stores racks" installed.

The landing wheel struts had been reinforced, and on each strut was a circular canister, holding three 3.5 inch rockets with explosive heads. The canister functioned very much like the cylinder of a revolver. As the canister revolved, the rocket was fired, just as a cartridge is fired in a revolver when its cylinder is aligned with the barrel. (There was, of course, no barrel on the Bird's rocket canisters.) A feed chute ran from each canister into the Bird's fuselage. The chute was connected to a bin. The bin and the feed chute were filled with 3.5 inch rockets.

When the rocket launching device was activated (by a switch mounted on the pilot's control stick), an electric motor turned and an electric firing circuit was activated. The canister revolved 120 degrees, moving a 3.5 rocket into firing position, where it was fired. Then the canister revolved 120 degrees again, the empty cylinder picking up a 3.5 from the chute, and the chute picking up a 3.5 from the bin. There were a total of fifty-four 3.5s in the bins, the chutes, and the canisters, twenty-seven on each strut. They could all be fired in fifteen seconds.

There was no tank known to military intelligence with armor strong enough to resist a direct hit from a 3.5 inch rocket during the "most efficient" phase of the rocket's flight. That is to say, when the target was from 50 to 350 yards from the point where the rocket had been launched. It took the rocket about 50 yards to get up to speed, and after 350 yards it began to lose speed. But within the "most efficient" phase of its flight envelope, the rocket would pass through the armor of any known tank like a drop of molten steel through a stick of butter. And then it would explode.

The testing that the Big Bad Bird was going through now had little to do with the practical military application for which it was intended. It was now preparing for what the Big Bad Bird People, as they called themselves, had chosen to call its "screen test."

Colonel Tim F. Brandon was not particularly amused by this attitude, but he had been around long enough to understand that troops in the field seldom (if ever) understood how important public relations was to the army as a whole. And he also understood that it was unlikely that no explanation would ever change the attitude of the troops. It was something he just had to live with, meanwhile doing the best job he was capable of.

And he was correctly convinced that he could do one hell of a good job.

The debut of "the Viper" (which is what Colonel Brandon had decided to call the Big Bad Bird) would take place early in the morning of 27 December 1958. All three television networks were sending camera crews, and there would be the army crew to make film available to other outlets. A special camera platform had been erected. Additionally, three remote-controlled cameras had been set up in sandbag-protected emplacements along the route of the tank, so that the actual strike of the rockets on the tank could be filmed closeup.

Colonel Tim F. Brandon, again correctly, considered the tanks proof positive that he knew just what the hell he was about.

Eleven Russian T34 tanks had come into American possession from various sources. They had been studied in great detail by armor and ordnance tactical and technical experts and then turned over to Fort Riley, Kansas (less one tank which went to the Ordnance Museum at Aberdeen Proving Ground and another which went to the George S. Patton Museum at Fort Knox, Kentucky). Fort Riley had a unit trained in Soviet Army tactics, which was used in maneuvers. The availability of genuine Red Army T34s lent an aura of authenticity to the maneuvers that could be accomplished in no other manner.

They had bellowed in outrage when the TWX came.

```
HQ DEPT OF THE ARMY WASH DC 17 DEC 59
COMMANDING GENERAL FT RILEY KANSAS

TWX CONFIRMS TELECON CG FT RILEY AND VICE DSCOPS 0900 HRS 17
DEC 59:
CG FT RILEY WILL IMMEDIATELY TAKE STEPS TO MOVE THREE (3)
OPERATING T34 TANKS PRESENTLY ASSIGNED USA MANEUVER GROUP FT
RILEY TO USA AVIATION COMBAT DEVELOPMENTS AGENCY FT RUCKER
ALA. PRIORITY OF FT RUCKER OPERATION REQUIRES TANKS ARRIVE IN
OPERATING CONDITION NOT LATER THAN 2400 HOURS 20 DEC 59. CG FT
RILEY WILL ASSURE THAT SUFFICIENT REDUNDANT PERSONNEL,
EQUIPMENT, AND TRANSPORT EQUIPMENT ARE INVOLVED TO ACCOMPLISH
THE FOREGOING. DSCOPS DIRECTS THAT THE MOST REPEAT MOST
SERVICEABLE OF AVAILABLE T34S BE SENT TO FT RUCKER.

                              BY COMMAND OF DCSOPS:
                              WALTER HAGEMEN, BRIG GEN, USA
```

When the convoy arrived from Riley, the crews of the T34s were somewhat ambivalent about what Colonel Tim F. Brandon was going to do with their T34s. On the one hand, they had nursed them along for several years now, a difficult task in which they took justifiable pride, and it seemed like a goddamned shame to just blow the bastards away.

On the other hand, the T34s had been a real bitch to drive and maintain, and if the sonsofbitches were blown away, the army would have to come up with M46s or M48s for them. Their jobs would be a hell of a lot easier. If you needed a track for an M48, you called up Chrysler. You didn't have to make the sonofabitch yourself.

It looked like it was going to be one hell of a show, too.

More than one of the crew sergeants, after seeing what was going on, rethought his decision that the WOC program was so much bullshit.

They were particularly impressed with Warrant Officer Junior Grade William B. Franklin. Mr. Franklin told them he had just graduated from the WOC program and had been assigned to Aviation Combat Developments because of his service as an EM in Algeria.

Flying something like the Bird seemed to be a far more pleasant occupation than nursing a T34 or for that matter an M48 through the mud. Lieutenant Greer, the Big Bad Bird pilot, was also an ex-EM who had gone to WOC school earlier on. They'd just laid a commission on him.

And in the back of all their minds was the thought that if the Bird did what it was alleged it could do—blow away tanks—then it followed that the Russians would figure out how to do it, sooner or later, and they might one day find themselves sitting in an M48 with a Russian chopper ready to shoot a 3.5 up their ass.

And one of their number, a guy who had been in Korea in the early days, reported that he had run into his CO.

"I seen that 73rd Heavy Tank patch on his shoulder, and officer or not, I slapped his back, and it was an officer, all right. It was the goddamned post commander. But he remembered me, so it was all right. Even remembered my name, and told me if I wanted to apply for the WOC program, he'd do what he could to help me.

"And I tell you who else I saw here. I'm sure it was him. 'The Duke.' They called him that. Would you believe he was twenty-four years old when he made major? No shit. Twenty fucking four years old. He ran Task Force Lowell, forty-eight M48s and flock of half-tracks with multiple .50s on them, and just forget the flanks, fellas, through the gooks like shit through a goose. You see people like that around and you got to admit that everybody in aviation isn't a candy-ass who can't piss standing up. I'm getting a little sick of running around making like a fucking Russian anyhow. I'm thinking very seriously of giving this aviation a try. What have I got to lose?"

Colonel Tim F. Brandon believed in "practice makes perfect" nearly as devoutly as he believed in Murphy's Law.

In order that absolutely nothing could go wrong with the events scheduled for 27 December 1958, he not only ran dry runs, but dry runs of the dry runs.

He acquired control of two adjacent ranges, built as 105 cannon ranges in the 1940s. One of the ranges would house the actual demonstration for the media. The other was the dry run range.

There was only one "Viper," and the colonel had no intention of running any risk of damaging the Viper that wasn't absolutely necessary. After it did its thing (destroyed a *moving*, absolutely legitimate, Red Army T34 with rocket fire), it would immediately land in Area "A," where it would serve as a backdrop for the announcement by General E. Z. Black of the army's latest accomplishment to guarantee the peace. Major MacMillan would be there, wearing the Medal. Behind them, to show that the army was a youthful outfit which offered black youth an opportunity limited only by their ability, would be that colored warrant officer and Lieutenant Greer. Greer would actually fly the Viper during the demonstration, but it would be implied that MacMillan, the old soldier/hero figure had done so. Greer didn't look old enough to be the chief test pilot. It would look as if the army didn't have the sense to put someone mature in charge of something as important as the Viper.

The Viper had been painted. The Viper now had fangs. Colonel Brandon had gotten the idea from the P40s flown by the American Volunteer Group in China before War II. Colonel Brandon knew what the Big Bad Bird People thought about the Viper and the painted fangs. But he didn't even try to bring them around to his way of thinking. He had more important things to do with his time.

On Demonstration Day there would be no one in the moving, bona fide Russian T34, of course. The controls would be locked in place. The tank would be started across the range by one of the troops from Riley, who would then jump off to be picked up by a waiting jeep. He would then have ninety seconds—plenty of time—to get out of the way before the first rocket could possibly be fired.

In the dry run for the dry run, conducted on Alternate Range B, a regular unarmed H-19B from the post fleet was used. The dry run for the dry run was primarily to come up with times for the scenario. Once they had the rough times, they would move to the Demonstration Range for several levels of dry runs, starting out with the regular H-19B from the post fleet. On 26 December came the dress rehearsal, which would be identical to the actual demonstration, except that there would be no one there but the participants. The Viper would be flown, and the T34 would be moving with its controls locked in place, and the Viper would fly by the camera platform close enough to permit the army cameramen to get a good shot of the fangs and the canisters, and then the Viper would destroy one of the T34s.

The film of that event would be processed overnight in Atlanta (an L-23 with a backup had been laid on for that purpose), and copies would be available to the networks the next day immediately after the demonstration, in case something went wrong when they were filming the real thing.

There would be only one practice use of the Viper. Colonel Tim F. Brandon felt that was a risk he was just going to have to take.

Col. Brandon was not all surprised when he saw the whitepainted H-13H of the post commander making an approach to the inflatable hangar. The Chief of Information had told him on the telephone that morning that he was personally going to call General Jiggs to make him aware of how important it was that everything go smoothly on 27 December, and thus insure General Jiggs's wholehearted cooperation.

When he saw that the general was alone in the H-13H, Colonel Brandon had another thought: *flying generals*! That ought to be worth ninety seconds on the six o'clock news. Maybe he could even get some mileage out of it during the demonstration. He decided he would put that on the back burner for a while, give himself some time to think about it. His next-to-first thought now was that he should save it for a later day.

Colonel Brandon walked out to the H-13H. Some of the Big Bad Bird People had started to do the same thing, but when they saw him, they stopped.

General Jiggs put his cap on before he pushed open the plexiglass door in the H-13H's bubble. That would make a good shot, Colonel Brandon thought. That would be the first time the viewer would realize he wasn't looking at some ordinary captain or major. He'd see instead the two stars on the general's overseas hat.

Colonel Brandon saluted.

"Good afternoon, General," he said. "I'm Colonel Brandon."

"I was just talking about you," General Jiggs said.

"You were, sir?"

"Your boss just called me up," General Jiggs said, "to inquire if you were causing me any trouble. I told him that so far as I knew, you were behaving yourself and staying out of the way as much as possible."

Colonel Brandon didn't know how to take that. He said nothing.

"I understand Major Lowell is out here," General Jiggs said.

"Yes, sir," Colonel Brandon said. "He's working on the Viper ordnance."

"The *what* ordnance?"

"I have tentative approval for 'Viper' as semiofficial, that is to say, popular nomenclature for the gunship, sir."

"Fascinating," General Jiggs said. "Is Lowell in that tent?"

"I'll get him, sir," Colonel Brandon said.

"I'll find him," General Jiggs said. When Colonel Brandon fell in step with him, he added: "I want to see him alone, Colonel."

Major Lowell and Lieutenant Greer and Warrant Officers Franklin and Cramer (fifty-five, gray-haired, and leather-skinned, the old-model warrant officer) were doing something to the rocket launcher feed mechanism.

Mr. Cramer was the first to see the general approaching. He nodded his head, calling attention to him, but did not call attention. The others kept working. Mr. Franklin looked a little nervous, as if he was wondering if it was his function as the junior officer to call attention.

"That's all right, gentlemen," General Jiggs said, dryly sarcastic, "stand at ease."

They stood up from bending over the rocket launcher feed mechanism.

"Hello, Dutch," he said to CWO (W4) Cramer. "Long time, no see."

"Nice to see you again, General," Cramer said.

"If you had come by the office, Dutch," the general said, "my aides have orders to throw rocks only at certain people. You're not on their list." He looked at Franklin, and then put out his hand to him.

"You're the one that went right from WOC to experienced expert, right?"

Franklin looked very uncomfortable.

"You think this thing is going to work, Mr. Franklin?" the general pursued.

"Yes, sir. The problem the French had was aiming. Unless you're lucky, it takes three, four rounds to get on target . . ."

"You walk the rockets?" the general interrupted.

"Yes, sir," Franklin said, visibly less nervous now that he was talking about something he knew. "And if you only have six in the canister . . ."

"What have we got here?" the general asked.

"Twenty-seven," Franklin said. "With luck, that gives you up to five good runs."

General Jiggs nodded his comprehension.

"Where's MacMillan?" General Jiggs asked. "Also known as 'the Talking Head.' "

"I thought you knew, sir," Lowell said. The general shook his head. "He and Phil Parker took my plane to get the Felters," Lowell said.

"The way Captain Parker phrased his request was to ask if I minded if he 'picked up a little dual time.' In my innocence, I had pictured him as shooting touch-and-go's at Laird."

"They should be back in a couple of hours, General," Lowell said.

"You got a minute, Lowell?" the general asked.

"Yes, sir, of course."

The general took Lowell's arm and led him across the inflatable hangar, where they were alone.

"There's no good news and bad news," General Jiggs said. "It's all bad. I just made my pitch for you to Black. I got about as far as your name."

"I didn't expect you to do that much, sir," Lowell said. "But thank you."

"A senator's wife! What the hell were you thinking about?"

Lowell chuckled.

"I don't think it's funny," Jiggs said. "It's not funny at all, goddamnit."

"There's more to it than that," Lowell said. "And I don't think even Black could get me out of this one if he wanted to, and I have it on good authority that he doesn't."

"There aren't many majors," Jiggs said, "who managed to get the Chief of Staff of the U.S. Army personally pissed at them."

"Can it be kept quiet until after New Year's?" Lowell said. "Or is it getting to be pretty common knowledge?"

"I don't know," Jiggs said. "Bellmon won't talk about it."

"Bellmon's all right," Lowell said. "He'll make a good general."

"What are you going to do?"

"I think I'll go to Germany for a while. For six months or a year, anyway. It'll give me a chance to spend some time with my son."

"I'm sorry, Craig," General Jiggs said. "I really am."

"I appreciate that," Lowell said.

"I don't want you to sneak off this post," Jiggs said, visibly emotional. "You understand what I'm saying?"

Lowell smiled at him.

"You can come out to Laird on New Year's Day," Lowell said. "And wave so long. But between now and then, I don't want anybody, particularly the women, to know. I want the last party to be a good one."

"I'll do what I can," Jiggs said. "But I think that's wishful thinking. Men do the gossiping, not the women."

Lowell nodded and shrugged.

"I'll see you around before you go," General Jiggs said.

"I'll be around," Lowell said.

General Jiggs nodded and suddenly turned and walked out of the inflatable hangar to his H-13H.

Lowell walked back to the feed chute for the rocket launcher.

"Made his pitch to Black about what?" Greer demanded. Lowell looked at him in surprise.

"Interesting characteristic of these curved ceilings," Greer said, "is that when somebody talks close to one side, somebody on the other side can hear everything."

"You just keep your goddamned mouth shut about what you think you heard," Lowell said.

"What I heard," Greer said, "is that you're getting thrown out as of 1 January."

"Where did you get that?"

"My wife got it from her mother," Greer said.

"I don't know your wife or your mother-in-law," Lowell said.

"You don't know any of the lieutenants or the warrants in Annex 1, either," Franklin said, joining the conversation. "But they know all about the major who was run out of Washington on a rail."

"Honest to God, Bill?" Lowell asked.

"I'm afraid so," Franklin said.

"Well, you guys just keep your mouths shut. It's done. It came down from the Chief of Staff himself. I just don't want it to ruin the holidays."

"MacMillan knows," Lieutenant Ed Greer said. "He knows why you asked him to pick up Major Felter. By the time they get to Washington, you can bet Parker will have heard."

"Let's hope they have enough sense to keep their mouths shut," Lowell said.

"Ah, hell, yes," Greer said.

[THREE]
Washington National Airport
District of Columbia
22 December 1958

The first thing Sanford Felter did when MacMillan crawled out of the Aero Commander at Butler Aviation at Washington National Airport was take him aside to confide what he somewhat bitterly described as the "final chapter in the Lowell sexual saga."

"I went to Black," Felter said.

"And?"

"He told me this was the one time I should remember that I was a major in the army," Felter said.

"Shit," MacMillan said.

"Well, we shall all pretend that nobody knows," Felter said. "We can at least do that much."

"Dumb sonofabitch," MacMillan said. "That pecker of his has had him on the edge of something like this as long as I've known him. And I've known him a long goddamned time."

Sharon walked over.

"I guess Sandy told you?" she asked.

"I knew," MacMillan said.

"So that means Roxy knows," Sharon said.

"Roxy's mad at Craig," MacMillan said. "Barbara's mad at Bellmon for not trying hard enough to get him out of it."

"Bellmon couldn't do anything," Felter said. "Nobody could. The Chief of Staff is after Craig's scalp, and Black has apparently made up his mind to let him have it."

"Well, the best thing we can do is pretend we don't know," Sharon said.

"Yeah," MacMillan said.

"I hate that damned woman!" Sharon said, and flushed.

MacMillan leaned over and kissed her.

XVII

[ONE]
Auxiliary Field Three
Hanchey Army Airfield
Fort Rucker, Alabama
26 December 1958.

They had to roll the Big Bad Bird (a/k/a the Viper) out of the hangar twice. When they rolled it out the first time, it occurred to Colonel Tim F. Brandon that a crew consisting entirely of enlisted men pushing it out would make a better shot than what he had, one sergeant, three warrants, and two field-grade officers.

So it was pushed out again with the motion picture cameras rolling, and Colonel Brandon set up another shot: Major MacMillan and Lieutenant Greer first looking at a map, then walking around the helicopter to check the rocket canisters.

"You got about enough of your fucking pictures, Colonel?" MacMillan snapped finally. "Can we get the goddamned Bird in the air now?"

It was clearly disrespectful and insubordinate, but Colonel Brandon swallowed his resentment.

"Give me five minutes to check things on the other field," he said and climbed into his jeep and drove off.

"Pissant," Macmillan said, watching him drive away.

CWO (W4) Dutch Cramer checked the bins and the chute and the canisters a final time, and nodded his approval.

Lieutenant Greer climbed up the side of the fuselage, and through the pilot's window, and strapped himself in the seat.

"Off we go into the wild blue yonder," he crooned and reached for the Engine Start switch.

His eyes fell on Major Lowell, and for a moment their eyes met. Lowell gave him a wink. Greer gave Lowell a mocking, but friendly salute, and lowered his eyes to the instrument panel as the engine began to run.

He told himself the worst part was over. They'd all gotten through Christmas without anybody bringing up what was to happen to Lowell as of 1 Jan 1959. It had been decided among the women that they would spend Christmas eve and Christmas morning with their families (which meant that Lowell was with the Parkers) and then get together for Christmas dinner. At first, Barbara Bellmon insisted on having it at the Bellmon quarters, but she lost out to Dr. Parker, who pointed out that her quarters in the hospital (*hers*, as Contract surgeon, with the assimilated rate of colonel, not Captain Parker's), were much larger and better able to hold everybody.

There had been an enormous turkey, a standing rib of beef, a ham, and lots of booze. All Greer had been able to drink, however, was a glass of champagne when they got there and a glass of wine with dinner. He would be flying the Big Bad Bird today.

Everybody else had gotten pretty well sauced up, and even General Jiggs had appeared uninvited, with his wife.

"Can any old cavalryman come in here?" he had asked, when he walked in. "Or does being able to read and write disqualify me?"

Nobody mentioned what was about to happen to Lowell, but Jiggs came pretty close when he handed Lowell a Christmas-wrapped package.

"What the hell is this?" Lowell asked, embarrassed. It had been decided among them that there would be no exchange of gifts.

"One could reasonably presume it's your Christmas present," General Jiggs said. "Open it up."

Inside the silver foil imprinted with scenes of a White Christmas in Old England was a battalion guidon, a small flag bearing a unit's number. Guidons had come into use on battlefields before the telephone and radio as a unit identifier the troops could "guide on." The only place they were still used for that purpose in the modern army was flying from a tank radio antenna to identify the tank of the unit commander.

The guidon General Jiggs gave Major Lowell was frayed and stained. It was for a tank battalion, the 73rd, and someone had lettered on it, crudely, with a grease pencil: T/F LOWELL.

"I thought you should have that," General Jiggs said.

Major Craig W. Lowell looked very much as if he was going to cry.

"Paul," Mrs. Jiggs said, quickly, "tell them what Wonder Boy said to the colonel from X Corps. That's a marvelous story."

"Yeah," General Jiggs said. "Yeah. Well, I got the story from his operations sergeant. Let me set the stage. Lowell and forty M46s had just gone up the Korean peninsula to link up with X Corps, which had landed eleven days before at Inchon. With his well-known modesty and reticence, he'd modified the guidon he had flying from his tank. That one. I mean, what the hell, if you're going to be in the history books, make sure they spell your name right, right?

"Well, he went a little further and a little faster than the OPSORDER called for. I'd just found them myself, in an old L-4. He was a hundred miles further than he was supposed to be and about thirty-six hours ahead of the time he was supposed to be a hundred miles back, if you follow me. X Corps is nosing around just south of Suwon, when all of a sudden, balls to the leather, around the bend come a half dozen tracks, with multiple .50s and 20 mm Bofors, chased by the first of the M46s.

"The tracks were shooting at anything that moved or looked like it could move, and that included the people from X Corps. So they waved some flags, and Task Force Lowell stopped shooting at them. Lowell drives through the tracks, and rolls up to the people from X Corps. At the time he was a major with about two hours' time in grade.

"Well, the colonel from X Corps consults his OPSORDER and announces, 'You're not expected here, Major, and you're not expected for another thirty-six hours.' So you know what the Duke says? 'What would you have me do, Colonel? Go back?' "

They had all heard the story before, but they all laughed, and it took some of the tension away. Then Mrs. Jiggs handed Lowell a Christmas-wrapped tube. Lowell unwrapped it, glanced at it, and then started to roll it up again.

"Pass it around, Duke," Mrs. Jiggs said. "Some people haven't seen it."

"Hell," he said, but he handed it to Melody, and Greer read it over Melody's shoulder. It was a photograph of the front page of the *Chicago Tribune*, and it had been sealed in plastic. It was obviously a product of the post photo lab, and Greer suspected that it had just been made.

KOREAN REPORT: The Soldiers

by John E. Moran
United Press War Correspondent

SEOUL, SOUTH KOREA University Press September twenty-six—(Delayed) The world has already learned that Lt. General Walton Walker's Eighth Army, so long confined to the Pusan perimeter, has linked up with Lt. General Ned Almond's X United States Corps, following the brilliant amphibious invasion at Inchon.

But it wasn't an army that made the link-up, just south of a Korean town called Osan fifty-odd miles south of Seoul, it was soldiers, and this correspondent was there when it happened.

I was with the 31st Infantry Regiment, moving south from Seoul down a two-lane macadam road, when we first heard the peculiar, familiar sound of American 90 mm tank cannon. We were surprised. There were supposed to be no Americans closer than fifty miles south of our position.

It was possible, our regimental commander believed, that what we were hearing was the firing of captured American tank cannon. In the early days of this war we lost a lot of equipment to the enemy. It was prudent to assume what the army calls a defensive posture, and we did.

And then some strange-looking vehicles appeared a thousand yards down the road. They were trucks, nearly covered with sandbags. Our men had orders not to fire without orders. They were good soldiers, and they held their fire.

The strange-looking trucks came up the road at a goodly clip, and we

realized with horror that they were firing. They were firing at practically anything and everything.

"They're Americans," our colonel said, and ordered that an American flag be taken to our front lines and waved.

Now there were tanks visible behind the trucks—M46 "Patton" tanks. That should have put everyone's mind at rest, but on our right flank, one excited soldier let fly at the trucks and tanks coming up the road with a rocket launcher. He missed. Moments later, there came the crack of a high-velocity 90 mm tank cannon. He was a better shot than the man who had fired the rocket launcher. There was a soldier in front of our lines now, holding the American flag high above his head, waving it frantically back and forth. Our colonel's radio operator was frantically repeating the "Hold Fire! Hold Fire!" order into his microphone.

His message got through, for there was no more fire from our lines and no more from the column approaching us.

The first vehicles to pass through our lines were Dodge three-quarter-ton trucks. These mounted two .50 caliber machine guns, one where it's supposed to be, on a pedestal between the seats, and a second on an improvised mount in the truck bed. They were, for all practical purposes, rolling machine-gun nests.

Next came three M46 tanks, the lead tank flying a pennant on which was lettered Task Force Lowell. The name "Ilse" had been painted on the side of its turret. There was a dirty young man in "Ilse's" turret. He skidded his tank into a right turn and stopped. He stayed in the turret until the rest of his column had passed through the lines.

It was quite a column. There were more M46s and some M24 light tanks, fuel trucks, self-propelled 105 mm howitzers, and regular army trucks. We could tell that the dirty young man in the turret was an officer because some of the tank commanders and some of the truck drivers saluted him as they rolled past. Most of them didn't salute, however. Most of them gave the dirty young man a thumbs-up gesture, and many of them smiled, and called out, "Atta Boy, Duke!"

When the trucks passed us, we could see that "the Duke" had brought his wounded, and yes, his dead, with him. When those trucks passed, "the Duke" saluted.

When the last vehicle had passed, the dirty young man hoisted himself out of his turret, reached down and pulled a Garand from somewhere inside, and climbed down off the tank named "Ilse."

He had two days' growth of beard and nine days' road filth on him. He searched out our colonel and walked to him. When he got close, we could see a major's gold leaf on his fatigue jacket collar.

He saluted, a casual, almost in-

solent wave of his right hand in the vicinity of his eyes, not the snappy parade ground salute he'd given as the trucks with the wounded and dead had rolled past him.

"Major Lowell, sir," he said to our colonel. "With elements of the 73rd Heavy Tank."

We'd all heard about Lowell and his task force, how they had been ranging between the lines, raising havoc with the retreating North Korean army for nine days. I think we all expected someone older, someone more grizzled and battered than the dirty young man who stood before us.

At that moment our colonel got the word that the young soldier who had ignored his orders to hold fire and two others near him had been killed when one of Lowell's tanks had returned his fire. The death of any soldier upsets an officer, and it upset our colonel.

"If you had been where you were supposed to be, Major," our colonel said, "that wouldn't have happened!"

Young Major "Duke" Lowell looked at the colonel for a moment, and then he said, "What would you have us do, Colonel, go back?"

There shortly came a radio message for Major Duke Lowell, and he left his task force in Osan. He had been ordered to Tokyo, where General of the Army Douglas MacArthur was to personally pin the Distinguished Service Cross to his breast.

Greer wondered what Lowell would do with his guidon. Put it away probably and never look at it—even if he'd gotten more than a little shaken up when Jiggs gave it to him.

The needles were in the green. Greer depressed the stickmounted mike switch as he picked it up.

"Light on the skids with the Bird," he said. He dropped the nose to pick up speed and then picked the Big Bad Bird up to get over the tops of the pine trees.

"Viper," Colonel Brandon's voice came over the FM radio. "This is Viper Base. How do you read?"

"Loud and clear," Greer said.

"All right, Viper, I have you in sight," Colonel Brandon said.

Giving in to a perverse impulse, Greer dropped the Bird below the treeline so that PIO asshole couldn't see him. Then, when he was sure Brandon was searching for him, he pulled the cyclic and picked up a quick 500 feet.

"Viper," Colonel Brandon said, "what I want you to do is make one low level, low speed pass past the camera platform."

Greer complied.

"All right, Viper, very nice, thank you. What we're going to do now is do it. Take your position."

Greer flew a half mile away. Downrange he could see the T34.

"Start the T34," Brandon ordered.

"T34 ready to roll," a voice came back immediately.

"Move the T34," Colonel Brandon ordered. Greer couldn't detect any movement of the tank at first, but he saw a man hoist himself out of the driver's seat and leap off the T34 over the left track. Then he could see that the tank was moving. He saw the man run toward the jeep which would carry him off the range.

"Viper," Colonel Brandon ordered, "hold your position!"

Greer amused himself by doing precisely that, holding his position, a motionless hover 500 feet off the ground, the most difficult of all rotary wing flight maneuvers.

"Stand by, Viper!" Colonel Brandon ordered.

Greer did not bother to reply.

Thirty seconds later, Colonel Brandon gave the order.

"OK, Viper, kill it!"

"Jesus Christ!" Greer said, to himself. He dropped the nose, gave it the juice, and felt the forces of acceleration against his back.

When he was 300 yards from the tank, he depressed the trigger of the rocket firing mechanism for the right-side canister.

The fifty-four rockets had been manufactured at the Red River Arsenal in Texas. For facility of manufacture, the stabilizing fins at the rear of the rocket were about the last step of the manufacturing process. It had been determined that it was easier and, more important, safer, to save this step for last. All it involved was the positioning of three wedge-shaped pieces of aluminum—like the feathers of an arrow—into slots already in position at the rear of the rocket's cylindrical body.

Each stabilizing fin was held in place with three rivets. The fins, the slots for them, and the rivets were aluminum, which does not spark. The automatic riveting machine was powered by compressed air. There was no danger of a spark there, either.

The worker who installed the stabilizing fins was required by her job description to inspect each rivet on each fin. The automatic riveting machine was a fine machine and seldom failed to do what it was designed to do. Inevitably, the riveters found the three rivets in place where they were supposed to be. Inevitably, particularly at the end of a long day, the machine operators didn't look quite as closely as they should.

The fourth 3.5 rocket in the right-hand system on Greer's Bird had only one rivet, the most rearward one. The near perfect machine had run out of rivets.

The single rivet had been sufficient to hold the stabilizing fin rigidly in place during shipment and while passing through the bin into the chute when CWO (W4) Dutch Cramer had loaded the ordnance.

But the blast of firing the first three rockets in Greer's first firing run had been sufficient to loosen the stabilizing fin. When it was fired, the fin's nose came loose. The strength of the rivet fastening the fin to the cylinder was strong enough to keep the fin from separating from the cylinder, however. What it did was hold the fin sideward against what had now become the rocket's slipstream. Obeying the laws of aerodynamics, Ed Greer's fourth rocket, instead of moving horizontally toward the T34, raised its nose almost vertically.

The odds were that in such an event the rocket would pass harmlessly through the rotor arc. There were only three rotor blades, each only sixteen inches wide.

The odds went against Ed Greer and the Bird.

One of the rotor blades struck the impact fuse of the rocket 0.75 second later, and the firing mechanism detonated the explosive charge. The force blew off three-quarters of the blade and a half second later shattered the windshield of the Bird.

The Bird lost its aerodynamic lift and was simultaneously subjected to enormous out-of-balance dynamic pressures, as the engine whirled two intact rotor blades and the stump of the third.

The Bird crashed to the ground nose-first, striking it at 105 miles per hour and with sufficient force to detonate the explosive heads of the forty-seven, forty-eight, or forty-nine rockets still in the system. The precise number remaining at ground impact was never determined. There was not much left of the Big Bad Bird, nor of First Lieutenant Edward C. Greer.

[TWO]
Quarters No. 1
Fort Rucker, Alabama
26 December 1958

Master Sergeant Wesley, in his dress blues, knocked at the door of the guest room (actually two rooms and a bath) of Quarters No. 1.

"Come," General E. Z. Black said.

"That PIO colonel's out here, General," Master Sergeant Wesley said.

"Get the sonofabitch in here, Wes," General Black said. The general was bending over the bed, fixing his ribbons to his tunic.

"Zeke!" Mrs. Black said. "That's not going to change anything." Mrs. Black was adjusting her hat before a mirror.

Sergeant Wesley stepped out in the hall.

"The general'll see you now, Colonel," he said. He held the door open for him, and then followed him into the room.

When General Black straightened up, Master Sergeant Wesley busied himself with the ribbons of the general's tunic.

"I sent for you an hour ago," General Black began. "I am not in the custom of being made to wait."

"I was on the horn to Washington, sir," Colonel Brandon said.

"Talking to the Chief of Staff, were you?" General Black inquired.

"No, sir. To the Chief of Information, trying to salvage as much as we can from this."

"The next time I send for you," General Black said, "you put everybody but the Chief of Staff in second place."

"Yes, sir," Colonel Brandon said.

"For your general information, Colonel," Black went on, "I have spoken with the Chief of Staff. Two items on our agenda affect you."

"Yes, sir."

"One, I have been charged by the Chief of Staff with handling this situation,"

General Black said. "Two, the Chief of Staff has approval for the immediate posthumous award of the Distinguished Flying Cross to Lieutenant Greer."

"That's very nice, sir," Colonel Brandon said. "It fits right in with what I've discussed with the Chief of Information."

General Black looked as if he were going to say something, but then he was distracted by Master Sergeant Wesley, who was holding out the general's tunic. He slipped his arms into it.

"Mrs. Black, Sergeant Wesley, and myself are about to pay our respects to Mrs. Greer," General Black said. "You can ride with us and tell me what you have discussed with the Chief of Information."

There were four Chevrolet sedans sitting half on the grass along the driveway, an MP patrol car in front. With his hand on her arm, General Black led his wife to the car immediately behind the MP car.

"I'll drive," Master Sergeant Wesley said to the sergeant first class who held the door open. He got behind the wheel. General and Mrs. Black got in the back seat. Colonel Brandon got in front with Wesley.

Three of General Black's four aides-de-camp got in the car behind his, and four burly young men in civilian clothes got in the last car. The MP car started moving.

"Who are the guys in civvies?" General Black asked.

"CIC, sir," Colonel Brandon said. "Just in case."

"Don't do that again, Brandon," Black said. "Is there a radio in this thing, Wes?"

"The CIC is gone, General," Sergeant Wesley replied, picking up the microphone.

"I am paying a personal visit to the widow of a friend of mine, Colonel," General Black said. "Can you get that straight in your mind?"

"I was thinking of the press, sir," Brandon said. "They're sure to be at the house."

"Fuck the goddamn press!" Black said.

"Zeke, for God's sake, get control of yourself," Mrs. Black said.

He exhaled audibly.

"Let me have the benefit of your thinking, Colonel," General Black said. "Your's and the Chief of Information's."

"Yes, sir."

Colonel Brandon spoke reasonably, assuredly, and almost steadily during the fifteen minute ride off the post down Rucker Boulevard to Ozark and then up Broad Street to the plantation style residence of Mayor and Mrs. Howard F. Dutton.

The major points he made were these:

(1) The networks were in town, and they were going to come up with some sort of a story, and the only option the army had was to make that story as little embarrassing under the circumstances as possible.

(2) The air force had already begun to "take shots" at them in Washington, the gist of their argument being that the "tragedy" would not have occurred if (a) the army had only asked for air force expertise in aerial rocket fire and (b) by implication, if the army had lived up to the 1948 Key West Agreement not to arm their helicopters.

(3) The national television media was going to want visuals. It was Colonel Brandon's judgment that they had no choice but to turn over the film the army film crew

had shot of what was to have been the dress rehearsal. In response to General Black's inquiry, "how gory is it?" Colonel Brandon replied that it wasn't "really gory." It was "heart stopping." The explosion had been "spectacular" rather than "gory."

(4) Since the network TV crews *were* here, they could probably be talked into taking additional material. Colonel Brandon suggested that a full military funeral, with an aircraft flyover, would probably receive "good coverage." Greer's posthumous award of the DFC would "tie in nicely" there, particularly if Mrs. Greer could receive it from the hands of General Black.

(5) There was nothing the army could really do about getting caught in violation of the Key West Agreement of 1948 but plead excessive enthusiasm, as had been previously decided. A short announcement by General Black (Colonel Brandon handed him "Proposed Remarks *vis à vis* The Viper") could, if properly handled, take care of that nicely. In essence, what he would say was that the idea of rocket-armed helicopters was a good one, and one which, after joint air force-army development, was surely going to become an important weapon in the arsenal which guaranteed the peace. The implication, Colonel Brandon explained, was that all the army had done was investigate the feasibility of the idea. Now that they were convinced the idea had merit, they would of course, in keeping with the spirit of the Key West Agreement of 1948, turn responsibility for technical development over to the air force.

General Black grunted once or twice during Colonel Brandon's presentation. It was his only reaction to it.

There was a large crowd of people gathered on the sidewalk in front of Howard and Prissy Dutton's plantation-style mansion. There were half a dozen Ozark city policemen, as many Dale County deputy sheriffs, and even two Alabama state troopers. Only known personal friends of the Duttons were permitted to walk up the sidewalk to the porch of the house.

The state troopers waved the little convoy to the curb.

"Stay in the car, please, Colonel," General Black said. "I will give you my decision shortly."

Colonel Brandon was surprised to see that Sergeant Wesley marched into the house with the general.

They were greeted by Prissy Dutton, who looked as if she were dazed on tranquilizers. She announced that "the mayor's taken to his bed."

The sliding doors between the parlor and the dining room of the Dutton house had been opened. A buffet had been set up on the dining room table. There were thirty people munching in the dining room, as many standing around the parlor, and about as many filling folding chairs which lined the walls of both rooms.

Mrs. Edward C. Greer, in a black dress, a single strand of pearls around her neck, sat on a red plush couch resisting attempts from a black woman standing behind her to take the baby, who was sleeping on his mother's shoulders.

"Wes," General Black said, "close that door and get these people out of here."

Master Sergeant Wesley first closed the sliding doors, and then started easing people out of the room. The room emptied with surprising speed, until only three couples remained: Colonel and Mrs. Robert F. Bellmon; Major and Mrs. Rudolph G. MacMillan, and Major and Mrs. Sanford T. Felter.

"I said everybody, and I meant everybody," General Black said. "That includes you and Wes," he added to his wife. He looked at Melody Dutton Greer. "You want to give the baby to one of the women?" he asked.

"Is that a command, General?" Melody asked.

He took her meaning. He waited until the black woman, very reluctantly, had allowed herself to be ushered out of the room by a firmly gentle Master Sergeant Wesley, and then he closed the door after her.

He walked to where Melody sat and sat beside her.

"Let me hold him," he said. "Your shoulder will go to sleep."

"Why not?" Melody said, bitterly, and passed the sleeping infant to him. The child stirred, but did not wake.

"You been drinking?"

"Sure," Melody said.

"You want another drink?"

"No," she said.

"I just learned that Ed's being given the DFC," General Black said.

"You know what you can do with your goddamned medal," Melody said. "Is that what you're doing here? To tell me they're coming up with a medal?"

"No," he said. "I came to tell you I'm sorry."

"Thank you," she said. "Now, can my friends come back in?"

"Not just yet," he said.

"Why not?"

"Because I'm the one you want to see," he said.

"Is that so?"

"Yeah, I'm the one you want," he said.

"I don't know what the hell you're talking about," Melody said. "And forgive me, General, but I really don't much give a damn, either."

"Aside from the expected, ritual expressions of sympathy, let me tell you why the others feel bad," General Black said.

"Be my guest," Melody said, sarcastically.

"Felter feels guilty because Ed kept him alive when they walked out of the jungle at Dien Bien Phu," General Black said. "And because if Felter had not arranged for Ed to go to Algiers, he would not have ultimately wound up flying the Bird."

"Fascinating," Melody said.

"MacMillan feels guilty because it was Ed flying the Bird and not him. The Indo-China business, too, to a lesser degree. But primarily because he knew how to fly the Bird and wasn't flying it when it crashed."

"I'm getting just a little bored with this conversation," Melody said. She got up and walked to the door, and for a moment it looked as if she was going to open it. Instead, she went to a table with bottles on it and splashed whiskey in two glasses.

She walked back to General Black and handed him one. Then she sat down, drained hers at a gulp, and leaned back against the couch so far that her face was looking up at the ceiling. She sighed audibly.

"Shitshitshitshit," she said.

"Bob Bellmon," General Black went on and then stopped himself. "As of today, by the way, Brigadier General Bellmon. He doesn't know yet."

"Whoopee!" Melody Dutton Greer cried, raising her empty glass gaily.

"General Bellmon's feelings of guilt are somewhat more intellectual. He was the one who came to me and asked for permission to build the Bird. And he was the one who had to order your husband to fly it."

"He didn't have to order Ed," Melody objected. "My late husband was just as crazy as the rest of you. The ultimate volunteer: 'Look, Ma, no hands!' "

"But they're all wrong," Black said. "I'm the sonofabitch responsible."

"What are you on, General, some kind of a guilt trip? What the hell did you have to do with it?"

"I'm the one who sent him to helicopter school," Black said. "That's at the low end, the personal end. I didn't want him to go. But I fixed it so that he could go. At the other end of the guilt spectrum, I'm the one who made the decision to go ahead with the Bird. Statistically, there was no question that someone would be killed during the testing. All I could do was hope it would be somebody I never heard of. Not Ed. It didn't work out that way. So if you're looking for somebody to blame, Melody, here I am."

She looked at him for a moment, shook her head, and then leaned back again so that she was looking at the ceiling.

"Which leaves us where?" she asked.

"Has Major Lowell been to see you?" General Black asked.

"No, he hasn't. Every other uniformed sonofabitch and his brother has, but now that you mention it, I have *not* been honored with the condolences of the *legendary* Major Lowell."

"Lowell is the only practical one of us," General Black said. "He understands that when you really have nothing to say, the thing to do is to say nothing."

Melody looked at him again.

"Hey," she said, "I appreciate your coming here. I really do." She rested a hand momentarily on his arm. "It took, as Ed would say, 'balls.' "

He didn't reply.

"But, at the risk of repeating myself, where does all of this leave all of us."

"With him," General Black said, indicating the child.

"Don't worry about him," Melody said. "Not only is my father—who at the moment, by the way, is drunk out of his mind—rich, but that baby is now eligible for all sorts of benefits from a grateful government. There was a guy here already just bubbling over with facts and figures."

"He will not have his father," Black said.

"No fooling? Jesus!"

"You're a young and attractive woman," Black said. "You'll probably remarry, and the boy will have a man around. And I'm sure that Mac and Felter and Bellmon and his other friends will maintain their interest. But the boy will never know his father."

"What the hell are you up to now? Are you trying to make me cry? To make me start screaming and pulling my hair out? Is this some new kind of new console-the-widow therapy?"

"He'll never know what kind of a man his father was," Black said.

"He'll have that goddamned medal you talk about," Melody said. "He can look at that and say, 'My daddy was a hero; here's ten bucks worth of silver-plated metal to prove it.' "

"He can have more than that, if you're up to it," Black said.

"I don't have the faintest idea what you're talking about," Melody said.

"There are circumstances which make a very elaborate military funeral possible for Ed," General Black said.

"You can stick your elaborate military funeral up where you put the medal," Melody said.

"Bands, flags flying, troops marching, a . . . whatever they call it when they fly airplanes overhead . . . and a four-star general, the Vice Chief of Staff of the U.S. Army, pinning his medal on his widow."

"Maybe I am getting a little drunk," Melody said. "Because you sound just about as impressed with that bullshit as I am."

"It doesn't mean a thing to you, but to a kid in his impressionable years and older, looking at a movie of how the army buried his father, that just might make him think his father was something special."

She looked at him.

"Ed *was* something *special*," General Black said, barely audibly. After a moment, Melody Dutton Greer said: "Hey! Come on. For Christ's sake, what if somebody saw you? You're supposed to be a general. Stop crying."

XVIII

[ONE]
Fort Rucker, Alabama
28 December 1958

The main post chapel was a temporary building, thrown up as quickly as possible with the other temporary buildings in 1941, designed to last six years. But when Rucker reopened, it had been painted and there had been a "rehabilitation allocation" from the Office of the Chief of Chaplains which had provided for interior refurbishment, for a red carpet for the aisles, an electric organ, and the other accoutrements of a church.

It was full now. Admission had been by invitation only, and more invitations had been issued than there were seats.

The remains of Lieutenant Edward C. Greer in a government-issue gray steel casket, covered with an American flag, rested on a black cloth-covered stand in the center of the aisle.

There were three clergymen. The Dutton family clergyman was a Presbyterian. He was there. The post chaplain was a Baptist. He was there. And so was the Third Army chaplain. Ed and Melody had been married by an Anglican priest, and Melody had requested—the only thing she had asked for—an Episcopal funeral ceremony. An L-23 had been dispatched to Third Army headquarters in Atlanta to get the ranking Episcopal chaplain.

Sitting in the first pew on the left was the widow, holding Howard Dutton Greer on her lap, her parents (General Paul Jiggs wondered (a) how they had managed to sober up Howard Dutton and (b) if he was going to make it through the ceremony), and the black woman who had raised Melody and was now seeing her baby through this.

Across the aisle were the pallbearers. The pallbearers were the Bird People, plus Brigadier General Robert F. Bellmon, less Major Craig W. Lowell and CWO (W4) Dutch Cramer. Major Lowell and Dutch Cramer had declined the honor of serving as pallbearers. Jiggs knew where they were. They were either in Annex 1 of the officer's open mess or in Dutch Cramer's BOQ paying their last respects to a lost buddy by drinking themselves into oblivion. Dutch Cramer was taking Greer's accident personally and hard. It was his ordnance that had gone off at the wrong time.

The service was being filmed. Unobstrusive windows had been cut in the wall between the chaplain's and the choir's vesting rooms in the front of the church (permitting the camera to shoot the audience from that angle) and in the wall of the chaplain's office by the vestibule. These cameras, and the accompanying sound equipment, were manned by the army photo team. General Black had personally denied the television crews access to the chapel; the film the army shot would be made available to them.

The TV crews were outside the chapel. An army six-by-six truck would carry one crew during the procession from the chapel to Parade Ground No. 2 so that it could film the procession in process, and other crews were in place along the route the funeral procession would follow and at the parade ground itself.

An enormous amount of preparation had gone into Lieutenant Greer's final rites. The "Plan for the Memorial Services for Major General Angus Laird" had been taken from the file and used as the starting point. General Jiggs had been somewhat surprised at how far General Black had gone along with Colonel Tim F. Brandon. He had accepted most (but by no means all) of Brandon's suggestions. General Jiggs had been even more surprised at General Black's willingness to make himself available to keep the TV networks happy.

A tour of the WOC battalion, Colonel Brandon had pointed out, was not really news. A tour of the WOC battalion by the Vice Chief of Staff of the United States Army was news, worth forty-five seconds on the six o'clock news. The general had permitted himself to be trailed all over the post, out to Laird Field to the Aviation Board, anywhere Colonel Brandon had suggested. He had even (and this really had surprised General Jiggs) permitted himself to be taken for a ride in the white H-13H by General Jiggs. All they had done was take off and fly out of sight and then return to Pad No. 1, but it had given the network TV people a "shot" of general officers in flight, and Black had gone along.

And there had been, as there inevitably are when large numbers of people are involved in something solemn, elements of high comedy.

It had been decided and accepted without question that Lieutenant Greer's casket would be carried on a tank from the main post chapel to Parade Ground No. 2, where Mrs. Greer would receive her husband's Distinguished Flying Cross. There were no tanks at Rucker, so two M48s had been ordered down from Fort Benning. Someone had then realized (1) that not having been ordered to provide tank crews, Benning had not sent any and (2) there was no place on a tank where a casket could be carried.

Both of those problems had been solved by the Red Army maneuver troops from Fort Riley, the ones who had brought the Russian T34s down. They, of course, were qualified tank crewmen who could drive the M48s, and they quickly welded a platform to support the casket over the engine compartment.

Platforms. Both tanks had been so modified, in case something should go wrong with one of them. As the Red Army tank crews had brought six T34s from Riley to make sure three would be available, there were two M48s where one was going to be needed. There were two public address systems in place where one would be needed. There were four extra jeeps standing by in case something should go wrong with the four jeeps which would be used as flower cars. The term was redundancy.

There would be, of course, a riderless horse with reversed boots in the stirrups to be led in the procession behind the tank with Greer's casket. In the dry run, the first time the horse heard the tank engine start, he voided his bowels and then jerked loose from his handler and galloped wildly away with half a dozen field-grade officers in hot pursuit.

A second horse had been acquired, who was not terrified at the sound of a tank engine.

In the middle of all this, there had been grand theft, helicopter.

More than a little chagrined, the commanding officer of Rotary Wing Training had sought audience with General Jiggs. An H-19C was missing, and the colonel was absolutely convinced that it had been stolen. He wanted the FBI notified and a bulletin sent to all airfields within 350 miles of Rucker asking that they report any H-19C that had landed at their field.

General Jiggs had not been willing to go along with that. He didn't doubt that an H-19C was missing, but the idea that anyone would steal one was absurd. If someone had reported an H-34B was missing or an H-37 or one of the new YH-40s,

Jiggs would have been concerned. An H-34B could be flown somewhere and stripped for parts, for the Sikorsky was now in wide civilian use. It was conceivable, though unlikely, that the Russians might want to grab a YH-40, so they could study it. But a worn-out, ancient H-19C? Absurd!

What would you do with it? To whom could it be sold? He concluded, and so informed the commanding officer of Rotary Wing Training, that one of two things had happened to the "stolen" H-19C:

(1) It had simply been misplaced; that is, someone had taken the wrong H-19C when making an authorized flight. The thing to do, General Jiggs told him, was to conduct an inventory and see if anybody had an *extra* H-19C, which would be the case if someone had taken the wrong one off someplace.

(2) A practical joker was at work, someone who thought more of a good belly laugh than of his career and had taken the machine and hidden it somewhere on the reservation in the sure and certain knowledge that a lot of people would be running around like headless chickens when it was discovered missing. If this scenario were valid, the thing to do was look for the missing H-19C in places where someone so inclined would be likely to hide it.

None of this, however, affected the people or the proceedings in the chapel. On the right side of the chapel immediately behind the pallbearers, sat the brass: General and Mrs. E. Z. Black; Lieutenant General and Mrs. Richard D. Hoit (General Hoit commanded Third Army, in whose area Rucker was located. He had not known Lieutenant Greer, but if the Vice Chief of Staff was going to his funeral, so was he); Major General and Mrs. Paul Jiggs, and Mrs. Robert F. Bellmon.

Behind the family (on the left) and the brass (on the right) were the other distinguished guests and friends. An area of the lawn outside had been set aside for distinguished guests and friends who had invitations, but for whom there was no room inside. Loudspeakers would carry the ceremony to them.

The Third Army chaplain raised his hand in blessing.

"The peace of God, which passeth all understanding, be with you and yours," he said.

The pallbearers (Brigadier General Robert F. Bellmon; Major Rudolph G. MacMillan; WOJG William B. Franklin; Master Sergeant Wallace Horn; Staff Sergeant Jerry P. Davis and Corporal Sampson P. Killian) rose and took their places around the casket. The organ began to play "Nearer My God to Thee." On the fourth bar, the organ was joined by the 77th U.S. Army Band outside.

The casket was carried down the aisle.

The widow and her family followed it out and then the brass. By the time they were outside, the casket had been installed on the rack on the back of the M48. A line of soldiers moving quickly, but *not* running, carried the floral tributes from the chapel to waiting jeeps. The floral tributes included one from the French government, who had also ordered their consul general from New Orleans to pay final respects to a holder of the Croix de Guerre. The decision to send the consul may have been based more on the fact that network TV crews were going to be on hand than on Greer's service to France, but the point was that he was there, and his Citroen with the CD tags and his purple ribbon of office worn diagonally across his chest gave Colonel Brandon another good shot.

As soon as the widow and her baby and the black lady had gotten into the first of two limousines, the driver of the M48 started his engine. A cloud of acrid diesel smoke was blown down the line of cars and the people waiting to get in them.

There was a second Cadillac limousine carrying Mayor and Mrs. Dutton, and then General Black's staff car, and then (as protocol demanded, since a consul general of a friendly power ranks a three-star general) the Citroen with the CD tags, then General Hoit's and General Jiggs's staff cars. Mrs. Bellmon rode with General and Mrs. Jiggs.

Preceding the M48 were a company of the WOC battalion; the color guard; the staff car carrying the three clergy; and the four jeeps carrying the floral tributes.

Following General Jiggs's staff car were the 77th U.S. Army Band; a company of troops from the Aviation Center; the officers and men of the U.S. Army Aviation Combat Developments Agency; the officers and men of the U.S. Army Aviation Board; and then the other distinguished guests and friends.

The funeral parade moved slowly away from the main post chapel, down the winding street past the officer's open mess golf course, down Third Avenue, and finally to Parade Ground No. 2.

There were permanent bleachers erected on Parade Ground No. 2, and they were filled with people. Military personnel, except for essential operating personnel, had been ordered to be present. Civilian employees had been encouraged to be present.

The Cadillac hearse and a matching flower car which would take the casket from the post to Memory Gardens in Ozark following the award of the DFC were waiting behind the bleachers. Interment would be private.

When General Jiggs got out of his staff car, he saw, circling a mile or so away, the aircraft which would make the flyover, the final item on the agenda. When he got to the VIP stand, he saw something that was not on the schedule of events.

Drawn up at the end of the parade ground, just at the crest of the hill beyond which were the old artillery range impact areas, were the Russian T34s. They were parked in a line, twenty yards apart. Five of them. There had been, he recalled, six, but Greer had blown one of them away just before he went in.

He wondered if that was another of Colonel Tim F. Brandon's bullshit ideas or whether it had been the idea of the T34 tank crews, a tribute on their part. Well, no matter. It was too late to do anything about them now. There they sat, red stars and all.

The troops and the band had formed on the parade ground. The band was playing what the schedule of events called "appropriate music" (at the moment, "For in Her Hair, She Wore a Yellow Ribbon" in a mournful tempo) while people found their seats.

The M48 with Greer's casket was parked directly in front of the bleachers, equidistant between the troops and the bleachers. The color guard was standing next to it, facing the bleachers. They would serve as a background for the shot in which General Black would award the DFC to the widow.

When all but a few stragglers had found their seats, the band began to play "The Washington Post March." The troop units marched past the bleachers and then back where they had been.

General Black and party marched out onto the field. The post adjutant would read the orders awarding the DFC posthumously to First Lieutenant Edward C. Greer. General Black would then walk to where the widow sat in the bleachers and pin the decoration to her dress. He would then turn and make his "final remarks," during which he would apologize to the air force for violating the Key West Agreement of 1948. Then the flyover would take place, an empty slot in the final "V" formation representing the lost pilot.

When that was over, the pallbearers would carry the casket from the M48 to the hearse, and that would be the end of it.

It had been arranged for whatever was said over the microphones to be transmitted to the aircraft circling a mile or so away, so their flight over the parade ground would be when it was required sequentially, rather than at a specific time. It had been realized by the planners that it would be next to impossible to run the operation by the clock.

And, as always, there was one sonofabitch who hadn't gotten the word. In addition to the steady drone of the aircraft engines orbiting a mile or so away at 3,500 feet, there came the sound of one chopper, much lower and much closer. Heads turned to locate it.

The ground control officer behind the bleachers went on the air, repeating over and over, changing frequencies to make sure the dumb sonofabitch finally heard him, "Chopper operating in vicinity of Parade Ground No. 2, immediately leave this area. Chopper operating in vicinity of Parade Ground No. 2, immediately leave this area."

The pilot apparently wasn't listening to his radio, or more likely, the ground control officer decided, he was listening to the adjutant reading the general order awarding Greer his DFC. Whatever the reason, the sound of his engine didn't go away, and when they finished reading the order, it even grew louder.

And then as General Black walked across the field to present the DFC to Melody Dutton Greer, the machine came in view. It popped up behind a row of barracks behind the massed troops, and then a moment later dropped out of sight again. They could hear the engine, but they couldn't see it. The next time they saw it, it was behind them, and people just had time to turn their heads and spot it and identify it as an H-19C before it dropped out of sight again.

The ground controller ran from his portable radio to the VIP section of the bleachers and to the microphone General Black would use for his remarks. He grabbed it.

"Helicopter operating in vicinity of Parade Ground No. 2, leave the area immediately. Leave the area immediately."

If the dumb bastard was listening to the speeches, he would hear the order.

The chopper appeared a third time, this time to the left of Parade Ground No. 2. It popped up, but this time it did not immediately drop back down again. This time, the cyclic obviously in full up position, the engine obviously being called upon to deliver full emergency military power, it rose nearly straight up to maybe

2,500 feet. Then the nose dropped, and the sound of the rotors changed pitch. The chopper pilot made a full-bore, high-speed run down the center of the parade ground, coming so low that he actually had to pick the chopper up to get over the M48 with the flagged-draped casket on it.

One of the network TV cameramen, spinning rapidly to keep the chopper in his viewfinder, fell off the camera platform. In desperation, he grabbed for the camera and pulled it off the platform with him.

That meant, Colonel Brandon thought, that only two networks would be able to telecast the antics of this idiot. Then he realized that this was wishful thinking. The media stuck together. One of the two who had got the shot would make it available to the moron who fell off the platform. This whole thing would be on the six o'clock news, although not exactly in the way Colonel Brandon had intended.

When the pilot got to the tanks, he pulled the chopper up again and stood it on its side, then passed over the troops in ranks. Still banking, he turned back over the parade ground, slowing up, straightening out, until he was in an "out of ground effect hover" directly over the M48.

The downblast from the rotors blew dust thirty feet in the air. Hats flew. Major MacMillan and WOJG Franklin jumped up on the M48 to lie on the casket, to keep the flapping flag from being blown off.

The helicopter could be clearly seen now. The fuselage had been painted black. On the fuselage, between the trailing end of the door and the tail boom, was a white outline sketch of Woody Woodpecker. Woody was pictured leering with joy as he threw beer bottles.

Above him, in clear, legible letters was the legend: Big Bad Bird II.

There were strange-looking objects, which very few people had ever seen before, mounted on the landing wheel struts. Exactly fifteen seconds after Big Bad Bird II had come to a hover over the M48 carrying Ed Greer's casket, there was a dull rumbling noise from the helicopter. A stream of 3.5 inch rockets came from the left canister, twenty-seven in all in 7.5 seconds. Then in another 7.5 seconds, twenty-seven more from the right canister.

In fifteen seconds, fifty-four rockets. In fifteen seconds, five perfectly functioning T34 tanks were turned into so many tons of twisted, useless metal.

Big Bad Bird II dropped its nose and flew slowly down the parade ground through the clouds of dense black diesel smoke rising from the blown-away T34s and disappeared.

The TV cameras made an arty shot. They followed the dense cloud of smoke from the burning T34s as it rose up into the sky.

Melody Dutton Greer looked up at General E. Z. Black.

"Is that what Ed was working on?" she asked.

"That's it," General Black said.

"You really put on a show for me, didn't you?" Melody asked.

"I had nothing to do with it, honey," General Black said. "That was the 'legendary Major Lowell' paying his condolences."

General Black then delivered his final remarks. He departed from his prepared text. He made no reference whatever to the air force—or to the Key West Agreement of 1948.

Major General Paul Jiggs had concluded who was responsible long before General Black had. He had suspected who was responsible when he'd seen the spectacular climb the pilot had made before he made the high-speed run. When he'd returned to hover over the casket, there had been no doubt. Jiggs couldn't see the pilot, but the right-side window had had something taped to it: the soiled and somewhat frayed guidon that was once the property of the 73rd Heavy Battalion. General Jiggs had even been able to read the grease-pencil lettering which spelled out "T/F LOWELL."

He called over the provost marshal.

"Get me Major Craig W. Lowell," he said. "He's probably going to try to take off from Laird in the next couple of minutes in a civilian Aero Commander. But I don't care where he is. You get him for me."

[TWO]
Laird Army Airfield
Fort Rucker, Alabama
28 December 1958

General E. Z. Black walked into the VIP lounge where Major Lowell was being detained. An MP captain and the airfield commander called "atten-hut" almost in unison.

"Thank you, gentlemen," General Black said. "That will be all." He waited until they had left before speaking.

"Fascinating demonstration, Major," he said, finally.

"L'audace, l'audace, toujours l'audace, mon Général," Lowell replied.

"What I really would like to know, Lowell," General Black said, "is whether that was audacity or stupidity, and more importantly, whether you know the difference."

"I didn't want the Big Bad Bird going down the toilet, General," Lowell said.

"That's it. That's the bottom line?"

"Yes, sir."

"Where did you get the other firing mechanisms?" Black asked.

"Redundancy, General," Lowell said. "I learned all about redundancy when I was a young officer."

"And you got Cramer to help you?"

"I assume full responsibility, General."

"And besides, 'what the hell, they won't court-martial me anyhow; I'm being thrown out of the army anyway, and a court-martial would be embarrassing'?"

"That did occur to me, General," Major Lowell said.

General Black went to the window and pushed the curtain aside. An air force Grumman, a VIP transport, was waiting for him. He had been down here too long as it was.

"You have an interesting ally, Major," General Black said. "Actually, it's ironic."

"I'm afraid I don't quite understand you, sir," Lowell said.

"Brandon," General Black said. "That horse's ass actually tried to save your ass, Major. He lost no time in pointing out to me that socking it to you would not be in the best interests of the army."

"He's a horse ass," Lowell said. "But you need people like that."

"The army needs all kinds of strange people, Lowell. Horse's asses like Brandon, and even people like you."

"Sir?"

"Let me tell you what happened, Lowell," Black said. "I was so goddamned mad when that asshole came and said we should handle your case with what he called 'delicacy,' I almost kicked his ass. Literally, not figuratively. I had a nearly uncontrollable impulse to open the car door and kick his fat ass out."

He looked at Lowell to make sure Lowell understood he was telling the truth. "A long time ago, I learned something about myself," he went on. "It might be useful to you. Whenever you *really* lose your temper, there is a very good possibility that you're wrong about whatever pissed you off."

He paused again. "Phrased very simply, when you break a shoelace, that's your fault for not noticing the shoelace was worn and should have been replaced. You understand?"

"I don't get your point," Lowell said, simply.

"What really pissed me off about you, Lowell, had nothing to do with your screwing the senator's wife. What enraged me was that I had personally given you an order, and you had disobeyed me."

"You mean about staying away from Felter?"

"That's right. Here you are, a miserable major, with a well-deserved reputation for being, on occasion, a colossal fuck-up, and you get an order from the Vice Chief of Staff and you disobey it."

"I'm guilty of that, sir."

"And I'm guilty of violating a principle of command that I learned when I was a second lieutenant," General Black said. "Never give an order you know will not be obeyed."

"You had the right to expect me to obey your order, sir," Lowell said.

"The right, sure; but considering the personality, no reasonable expectation that you would."

Lowell looked at him and said nothing.

"I didn't think it through," Black said. "There was no way, no way, that you were going to sever your relationship with a man who had saved your ass in Greece, who had buried your wife when you were off at war, simply because some old fart who can't pour piss out of a boot tells you to."

"I don't think of you that way, General," Lowell said.

"OK. Put it this way. You decided the order made no sense, so fuck it."

"Yes, sir. That's pretty close."

"OK. Now I'll explain point two of this little lecture. Once I got pissed off at you, it was easy to keep pouring gas on the flames. Whatsername, the senator's horny wife, for example. And then I found the real excuse to get mad at you."

"What was that?"

" 'How dare that young sonofabitch, with a brain like his, with a proven capability of combat command, fuck up his own career the way he has? I'll fix his ass: I'll throw his ass out of the army.' "

He stopped and lit a cigarette, and then looked into Lowell's eyes.

"Am I getting through to you, Major?"

"I understand what you're saying, General Black, and I'm grateful for the explanation," Lowell replied. "But I don't understand the point of it."

"I dared entertain the hope," Black said, sarcastically, "that a few words of a philosophical nature might be of value to you in your later career, when you might lose your temper and make a bad decision."

"They make decisions by committee in the banking business, General," Lowell said.

"You missed my most important point, Lowell. Perhaps I should have spelled it out."

"Sir?"

"When you know you've made a mistake, you bust your ass to correct it. Even if it means you are going to have one hell of an argument with the Chief of Staff."

"I don't want to sound stupid," Lowell said, "but the only interpretation I can put on that is that you have changed your mind about throwing me out of the army. And I'm afraid to hope for that."

"As of 1 January 1959, you are relieved from DCSLOG and assigned here for duty with the Army Aviation Board as project officer for the rocket-armed helicopter."

"Thank you, sir," Lowell said.

"Don't make me regret it, Major," Black said. He met Lowell's eyes for a moment, and then he pushed open the glass door from the VIP lounge and walked out to the Grumman VIP transport.

They had not, Lowell realized, exchanged salutes. He pushed open the glass door and went out on the taxiway. The door to the Grumman was already closed, and the pilot was in the process of starting the port engine. The Grumman started to taxi.

Major Lowell raised his hand in salute and held it, even when there was no response from inside the airplane, until the Grumman had turned onto the runway and started the takeoff roll.